The Complete Tales
of Uncle Remus

Uncle Remus and the little boy

The Complete Tales of

Uncle Remus

JOEL CHANDLER HARRIS

Compiled by **RICHARD CHASE**
With illustrations by **ARTHUR BURDETTE FROST,
FREDERICK STUART CHURCH, J. M. CONDÉ, EDWARD
WINDSOR KEMBLE, AND WILLIAM HOLBROOK BEARD**

HOUGHTON MIFFLIN COMPANY BOSTON

GRATEFUL ACKNOWLEDGMENT is made to the following:

Appleton-Century-Crofts, Inc., for permission to reprint the tales from UNCLE REMUS, copyright, 1895, by D. Appleton and Company, New York.

Dodd, Mead & Company for permission to reprint six stories from UNCLE REMUS AND THE LITTLE BOY by Joel Chandler Harris, copyright, 1910, by Dodd, Mead & Company, Inc., New York.

Dr. Thomas H. English and Emory University for permission to reprint his Introduction to THE SEVEN TALES OF UNCLE REMUS, copyright, 1948, by Emory University, Atlanta.

22 2021
    4500826150

LIBRARY OF CONGRESS CATALOGUE CARD NUMBER: 54–12233

ISBN 0-618-15429-9
ISBN 978-0-618-15429-6

Printed in the United States of America

Contents

Foreword *by Richard Chase*

Acknowledgment

A Note on the Text

Introduction *by Joel Chandler Harris from* Uncle Remus: His Songs and His Sayings

Preface and Dedication *by Joel Chandler Harris to Arthur Burdette Frost—from* Uncle Remus: His Songs and His Sayings

The tales from

I UNCLE REMUS: *His Songs and His Sayings*
New and revised edition with illustrations by Arthur Burdette Frost, New York, D. Appleton-Century Company, 1896. (The first edition of this book was published in 1880 with illustrations by Frederick S. Church and J. H. Moser, New York, D. Appleton & Company)

The tales from

II NIGHTS WITH UNCLE REMUS: Myths and Legends of the Old Plantation

With illustrations by Frederick Stuart Church and William Holbrook Beard, Boston, James R. Osgood & Company, 1883

The tales from

III DADDY JAKE, THE RUNAWAY: And Short Stories Told After Dark
*With illustrations by Edward Windsor Kemble, New York, The Century
Company, 1889*

The tales from

IV UNCLE REMUS AND HIS FRIENDS: Old Plantation Stories,
Songs, and Ballads with Sketches of Negro Character
*With illustrations by Arthur Burdette Frost, Boston, Houghton Mifflin &
Company, 1892*

The tales from

V TOLD BY UNCLE REMUS: New Stories of the Old Plantation
*With illustrations by Arthur Burdette Frost and J. M. Condé, and line
drawings after half-tones by Frank Verbeck, New York, McClure, Phillips
& Company, 1905*

The tales from

VI UNCLE REMUS AND BRER RABBIT
*With illustrations by J. M. Condé, New York, Frederick A. Stokes
Company, 1907*

The tales from

VII UNCLE REMUS AND THE LITTLE BOY

With illustrations by J. M. Condé, Boston, Small, Maynard & Company, 1910

The tales from

VIII UNCLE REMUS RETURNS

With illustrations by Arthur Burdette Frost and J. M. Condé, Boston, Houghton Mifflin Company, 1918

The tales from

IX SEVEN TALES OF UNCLE REMUS

Edited by Thomas H. English, Atlanta, Emory University, 1948

Introduction by Thomas H. English

Glossary

Foreword

OFTEN, it seems, great and enduring books happen almost by accident. It is strange that certain wry half-apologetic explanations had to be offered by Mr. Harris in his Introductions. Yet, for seventy-five years now, Uncle Remus has held us by his charm. Great books are "great" because they embody a serenity and a simplicity that keep us close to the Earth. These tales grew up in the soil of our nation. They came from the soul of a people. They endure, in spite of any difficulties of dialect, for new generations by simply being what they are: the recording of one man's joy in the spirited genuineness of "the old tales."

In these confusing times, it is good to renew an acquaintance with things that endure. It is important to ask what, in the field of art, creates these lasting qualities. Perhaps one answer is an inherent understatement. This is what makes the Frost pictures as perfect as the tales. Yes, it might be a good thing nowadays to consider lasting elements in the cultural heritage of our nation. We have grown too self-conscious and our sense of values has gone astray.

This is an age of cultural confusion. Identity of race and race tradition is a treasure that all Americans, white or black or red, can keep in spite of the bewildering cross currents of lore and learning in our modern age. This identity, this integrity is important. Not that we can ever shut ourselves in water-tight cultural compartments. Traditions and separate cultures overlap always and everywhere in the ways of all races and nations.

My own feelings have sought out the Anglo-Saxon, the English-American elements of my own long past. Ever since I was a child my own gods have hovered over me: Woden, Vingthor, Baldur, Vidar, and the Earth-Mother. But I have known Israel and Hellas and sought my passage to India.

And I have been moved by the sundown voices of the Negroes in the country of my birth, singing their sacred songs into my childhood. This, too, has become a part of me, a strong sustenance that I have absorbed out of this "Land of lands."

When I was a child in Alabama my first love was for the music of the Negro. There were two old people in the circle of my family who made lasting impressions on me: "Aunt Julie" who cooked for us for thirty years, and "Aunt Lou" who nursed my younger brother. Their songs, their philosophy, their great human care for us children are treasures that, for me, have never diminished.

And *Uncle Remus* became part of my life when I was surrounded with these voices, this music. My debt to Joel Chandler Harris is untellable. I could not have written the tales of my own people without this background. The sound of the speaking voice of Uncle Remus is much the same as that of Mr. Ward or Tom Hunt.[1] Mr. Harris got it down on the printed page. His example, his accomplishment, encouraged me and helped me learn how to write with the Southern mountain idiom in my ears.

The American Negro, in his spirituals, finally roused others to wonder and to a depth of religious feeling unmatched elsewhere in the history of our nation. And in these tales, when we know them in the genuineness of their original form, are unsullied treasures of quiet and inimitable laughter.

All fineness, all true art, all our highest genius can hone for, rise in the living word of children who are close to the sanity and simplicity of the Earth.

Volumes might be written dealing with the origins of these tales. Did they come from Africa? Were they known by the American Indians? Folklorists tell us that many of these tales have parallels all over Europe, where Brer Rabbit's exploits are told on Renard the Fox, or the Bear.

In "old times" when our nation was being settled, Indians, Negroes, and Europeans must have enjoyed each other's company on all levels of life; and tales must have been swapped about freely.[2]

Tracing the origin of these tales seems almost impossible. Some are known widely in the Old World. For example, the sham sickness of Brer Rabbit when he pursuaded Brer Fox to carry him is known in the folktale traditions of Germany, Esthonia, Finland, Lapland, Denmark, Sweden, and Russia. In Europe it was the fox, not the rabbit, who was the trickster

[1] *The Jack Tales* (1943) and *Grandfather Tales* (1948), compiled by Richard Chase. Boston: Houghton Mifflin Company.

[2] The *Nineteenth Annual Report of the Bureau of Ethnology*, 1897–98, by J. W. Powell, Director. Washington: Government Printing Office, 1900. (See Part I, pp. 232–233): Reference is made to a statement by James Mooney on the interrelation of Cherokee Indian myths and Negro tales.

hero. The Tar-Baby tale, however, seems to be of African origin: Kaffir, Rhodesia, Hottentot.[3]

The tales in this edition have been left as Mr. Harris wrote them. Our concern has been with the folktales only, and not with the songs, rhymed versions of the tales, proverbs, and character sketches like "Uncle Remus and the Telephone." Nothing has been added except a few notes on word meanings. These, along with Mr. Harris's own word definitions, have been arranged alphabetically in a glossary at the back of the book. The tales are given in order of publication, from the first edition in 1880 through the small collection of seven tales edited by Dr. Thomas H. English and published by Emory University in 1948. One good tale has been included which Mr. Harris did not give as told by Uncle Remus—"Mr. Coon and the Frogs," told by Crazy Sue in *Daddy Jake, the Runaway: And Short Stories Told After Dark.*

The setting—the characters of the little boy, 'Tildy, Daddy Jack, Aunt Tempy—and all the matter leading to and from each tale have been left intact. These present the historical background of the tales: how they were told, how the "old-time" Negro felt about "the old tales," what life was like there in Georgia, before, during, and after the War Between the States.

Practically all of the illustrations which originally accompanied these tales have been included in this edition—the beloved drawings by A. B. Frost, Frederick Church, J. M. Condé, E. W. Kemble, and W. H. Beard.

1955   *Richard Chase*

---

[3] "The Types of the Folk Tale," A. Aarne and Stith Thompson. Folklore Fellows Communications: Helsinki, 1928.

Acknowledgment

IN PREPARING the manuscript for *The Complete Tales of Uncle Remus* I am indebted to Dr. Foye Gibson of Emory and Henry College for letting me have a place to work; to Diane Fox, Elaine Lee, Ellen Murray, Ralph Long, Dorothy Nace, and Charles William Montgomery for helping cut and paste one weekend at Pine Mountain, Kentucky; to Jerry and Fern Brewster at Emory and Henry College for help in typing. Thanks are also due Lucien Harris for taking me to visit "Wren's Nest," Mr. Harris's home in Atlanta; and to Dr. Thomas H. English for showing me the Joel Chandler Harris Collection at Emory University, and for help on certain footnotes.

RICHARD CHASE

A Note on the Text

It was our intention to present these stories in the most readable form possible. We discovered as we studied each of the books in the order of publication considerable variation in the spelling of even the simplest words, and it was our perhaps naïve hope that we could find that form of a word which Mr. Harris himself used most often and follow it consistently. This proved to be an extremely difficult task, and its outcome questionable in view of the fact that it ultimately would mean we must deny Mr. Harris the right to change his mind. He was an inspired storyteller, diligent and faithful, with an extraordinarily sensitive ear and an accurate memory. From the beginning it was his intention to tell these tales in written form as nearly like their spoken versions as he possibly could, and he took great pains to spell the language as it sounded—with all the inflections and rhythms, word combinations, and expressions characteristic of the dialect. Compare the way Uncle Remus speaks with the dialogue of Daddy Jack in *Nights with Uncle Remus*. It was only natural that over the period of nearly forty years during which he wrote his stories Mr. Harris would experiment, searching for better ways of expressing this elusive and fluid dialect. If it is possible to generalize, it would seem that he made more of an effort to spell phonetically in his early books, such words as bawn and mawnin' later on becoming born and mornin'. However, some words vary throughout the nine books: toofs, toofies and tushes, are all interchangeable for teeth. Indeed Mr. Harris was so careful to preserve the subtlest variations in speech that our changes began to appear heavy-handed and arbitrary, and our aim toward consistency more restrictive than helpful.

The fact that these books were originally published by a number of different publishers—some with more care than others—further complicated our considerations. There seemed no reason for us to perpetuate obvious typographical errors.

Our final decisions with regard to changes in spelling or punctuation were made sparingly. We listed all the variations of a single word as they appeared in any one book, and then we chose that word form for each book which Mr. Harris had used predominantly. We did not carry this form over to the next book unless Mr. Harris himself had done so. There seemed no more justification for following an early and perhaps awkward or difficult form of a word (which he abandoned in his later books) than there was for imposing a much later form on his earlier work.

It is our hope that we have stepped lightly, simplifying the spelling only in directions indicated by Mr. Harris, and preserving those variations which are characteristic of each book, and significant of his own thoughtful and careful development.

THE PUBLISHERS

Introduction

by JOEL CHANDLER HARRIS

From UNCLE REMUS: HIS SONGS AND HIS SAYINGS

Introduction

I AM ADVISED by my publishers that this book is to be included in their catalogue of humorous publications, and this friendly warning gives me an opportunity to say that however humorous it may be in effect, its intention is perfectly serious; and, even if it were otherwise, it seems to me that a volume written wholly in dialect must have its solemn, not to say melancholy features. With respect to the Folk-Lore series, my purpose has been to preserve the legends in their original simplicity, and to wed them permanently to the quaint dialect—if, indeed, it can be called a dialect—through the medium of which they have become a part of the domestic history of every Southern family; and I have endeavored to give to the whole a genuine flavor of the old plantation.

Each legend has its variants, but in every instance I have retained that particular version which seemed to me to be the most characteristic, and have given it without embellishment and without exaggeration. The dialect, it will be observed, is wholly different from that of the Hon. Pompey Smash and his literary descendants, and different also from the intolerable misrepresentations of the minstrel stage, but it is at least phonetically genuine. Nevertheless, if the language of Uncle Remus fails to give vivid hints of the really poetic imagination of the Negro; if it fails to embody the quaint and homely humor which was his most prominent characteristic; if it does not suggest a certain picturesque sensitiveness—a curious exaltation of mind and temperament not to be defined by words—then I have reproduced the form of the dialect merely, and not the essence, and my attempt may be accounted a failure. At any rate, I trust I have been successful in presenting what may be, at least to a large portion of Americ n readers, a new and by no means unattractive phase of Negro character—a phase which may be considered a curiously sympathetic supplement to Mrs. Stowe's wonderful defense of slavery as it existed in the South. Mrs. Stowe, let me hasten to say, attacked the possibilities of slavery with all the eloquence of genius; but the same genius painted the portrait of the Southern slaveowner, and defended him.

A number of the plantation legends originally appeared in the columns of a daily newspaper—*The Atlanta Constitution*—and in that shape they attracted the attention of various gentlemen who were kind enough to suggest that they would prove to be valuable contributions to myth-literature.

It is but fair to say that ethnological considerations formed no part of the undertaking which has resulted in the publication of this volume. Professor J. W. Powell, of the Smithsonian Institution, who is engaged in an investigation of the mythology of the North American Indians, informs me that some of Uncle Remus's stories appear in a number of different languages, and in various modified forms, among the Indians; and he is of the opinion that they are borrowed by the Negroes from the red men. But this, to say the least, is extremely doubtful, since another investigator (Mr. Herbert H. Smith, author of *Brazil and the Amazons*), has met with some of these stories among tribes of South American Indians, and one in particular he has traced to India, and as far east as Siam. Mr. Smith has been kind enough to send me the proof sheets of his chapter on "The Myths and Folk-Lore of the Amazonian Indians," in which he reproduces some of the stories which he gathered while exploring the Amazons.

In the first of his series, a tortoise falls from a tree upon the head of a jaguar and kills him; in one of Uncle Remus's stories, the terrapin falls from a shelf in Miss Meadows's house and stuns the fox, so that the latter fails to catch the rabbit. In the next, a jaguar catches a tortoise by the hind leg as he is disappearing in his hole; but the tortoise convinces him he is holding a root, and so escapes; Uncle Remus tells how the fox endeavored to drown the terrapin, but turned him loose because the terrapin declared his tail to be only a stump root. Mr. Smith also gives the story of how the tortoise outran the deer, which is identical as to incident with Uncle Remus's story of how Brer Tarrypin outran Brer Rabbit. Then there is the story of how the tortoise pretended that he was stronger than the tapir. He tells the latter he can drag him into the sea, but the tapir retorts that he will pull the tortoise into the forest and kill him besides. The tortoise thereupon gets a vine stem, ties one end around the body of the tapir, and goes to the sea, where he ties the other end to the tail of a whale. He then goes into the wood, midway between them both, and gives the vine a shake as a signal for the pulling to begin. The struggle between the whale and tapir goes on until each thinks the tortoise is the strongest of animals. Compare this with the story of the terrapin's contest with the bear, in which Miss Meadows's bed cord is used instead of a vine stem. One of the most characteristic of Uncle Remus's stories is that in which the rabbit proves to Miss Meadows and the girls that the fox is his riding horse. This is almost identical with a story quoted by Mr. Smith, where the jaguar is about to marry the deer's daughter. The cotia—a species of rodent—is also in love with her, and he tells the deer that he can make a riding horse of the jaguar. "Well," says the deer, "if you can make the jaguar carry you, you shall have my daughter." Thereupon the story proceeds pretty much as Uncle Remus tells it of the fox and the rabbit. The cotia finally jumps from the jaguar and takes refuge in a hole, where an owl is set to watch him, but he flings sand in the owl's eyes and escapes. In another story given by Mr. Smith, the cotia is very thirsty, and, seeing a man coming with a jar on his head, lies down in the road in front of him, and repeats this until the man puts down his jar to go back after all the dead cotias he has seen. This is almost identical with Uncle Remus's story of how the rabbit robbed the fox of his game. In a story from Upper Egypt, a fox lies down in the road in front of a man who is carrying fowls to market, and finally succeeds in securing them.

This similarity extends to almost every story quoted by Mr. Smith, and some are so nearly identical as to point unmistakably to a common origin; but when and where? When did the Negro or the North American Indian ever come in contact with the tribes of South America? Upon this point the author of *Brazil and the Amazons,* who is engaged in making a critical and comparative study of these myth-stories, writes:

> I am not prepared to form a theory about these stories. There can be no doubt that some of them, found among the Negroes and the Indians, had a common origin. The most natural solution would be to suppose that they originated in Africa, and were carried to South America by the Negro slaves. They are certainly found among the Red Negroes; but, unfortunately for the African theory, it is equally certain that they are told by savage Indians of the Amazon Valley (away up on the Tapajos, Red Negro, and Tapurá). These Indians hardly ever see a Negro, and their languages are very distinct from the broken Portuguese spoken by the slaves. The form of the stories, as recounted in the Tupi and Mundurucu languages, seems to show that they were originally formed in those languages or have long been adopted in them.

> It is interesting to find a story from Upper Egypt (that of the fox who pretended to be dead) identical with an Amazonian story, and strongly resembling one found by you among the Negroes. Varnhagen, the Brazilian historian (now Visconde de Rio Branco), tried to prove a relationship between the ancient

Egyptians, or other Turanian stock, and the Tupi Indians. His theory rested on rather a slender basis, yet it must be confessed that he had one or two strong points. Do the resemblances between Old and New World stories point to a similar conclusion? It would be hard to say with the material that we now have.

One thing is certain. The animal stories told by the Negroes in our Southern States and in Brazil were brought by them from Africa. Whether they originated there, or with the Arabs, or Egyptians, or with yet more ancient nations, must still be an open question. Whether the Indians got them from the Negroes or from some earlier source is equally uncertain. We have seen enough to know that a very interesting line of investigation has been opened.

Professor Hartt, in his *Amazonian Tortoise Myths,* quotes a story from the *Riverside Magazine* of November, 1868, which will be recognized as a variant of one given by Uncle Remus. I venture to append it here, with some necessary verbal and phonetic alterations, in order to give the reader an idea of the difference between the dialect of the cotton plantations as used by Uncle Remus, and the lingo in vogue on the rice plantations and Sea Islands of the South Atlantic States:

One time B'er Deer an' B'er Cooter [Terrapin] was courtin', and de lady did bin lub B'er Deer mo' so dan B'er Cooter. She did bin lub B'er Cooter, but she lub B'er Deer de morest. So de noung lady say to B'er Deer and B'er Cooter bofe day dey mus' hab a ten-mile race, an' de one dat beats, she will go marry him.

So B'er Cooter say to B'er Deer: "You has got mo' longer legs dan I has, but I will run you. You run ten mile on land, and I will run ten mile on de water!"

So B'er Cooter went an' git nine er his fam'ly, an' put one at ebery mile-pos', and he hisse'f, what was to run wid B'er Deer, he was right in front of de young lady's do', in de broom-grass.

Dat mornin' at nine o'clock, B'er Deer he did met B'er Cooter at de fus mile-pos', wey dey was to start fum. So he call: "Well, B'er Cooter, is you ready? Go long!" As he git on to de nex' mile-pos', he say: "B'er Cooter!" B'er Cooter say: "Hullo!" B'er Deer say: "You dere?" B'er Cooter say: "Yes, B'er Deer, I dere too."

Nex' mile-pos' he jump, B'er Deer say: "Hullo, B'er Cooter!"
B'er Cooter say: "Hullo, B'er Deer! you dere too?" B'er Deer say:
"Ki! it look like you gwine fer tie me; it look like we gwine fer
de gal tie!"

W'en he git to de nine-mile pos' he tought he git dere fus, 'cause
he mek two jump; so he holler: "B'er Cooter!" B'er Cooter answer: "You dere too?" B'er Deer say: "It look like you gwine tie
me." B'er Cooter say: "Go long, B'er Deer. I gil dere in due season time," which he does, and wins de race.

The story of the Rabbit and the Fox, as told by the Southern Negroes,
is artistically dramatic in this: it progresses in an orderly way from a beginning to a well-defined conclusion, and is full of striking episodes that
suggest the culmination. It seems to me to be to a certain extent allegori-
cal, albeit such an interpretation may be unreasonable. At least it is a fable thoroughly characteristic of the Negro; and it needs no scientific
investigation to show why he selects as his hero the weakest and most
harmless of all animals, and brings him out victorious in contests with the
bear, the wolf, and the fox. It is not virtue that triumphs, but helplessness;
it is not malice, but mischievousness. It would be presumptuous in me to
offer an opinion as to the origin of these curious myth-stories; but, if ethnologists should discover that they did not originate with the African, the
proof to that effect should be accompanied with a good deal of persuasive
eloquence.

Curiously enough, I have found few Negroes who will acknowledge to
a stranger that they know anything of these legends; and yet to relate one
of the stories is the surest road to their confidence and esteem. In this
way, and in this way only, I have been enabled to collect and verify the
folklore included in this volume. There is an anecdote about the Irishman
and the rabbit which a number of Negroes have told to me with great unction, and which is both funny and characteristic, though I will not undertake to say that it has its origin with the blacks. One day an Irishman who
had heard people talking about "mares' nests" was going along the big
road—it is always the big road in contradistinction to neighborhood paths
and by-paths, called in the vernacular "nigh-cuts"—when he came to a
pumpkin-patch. The Irishman had never seen any of this fruit before, and
he at once concluded that he had discovered a veritable mare's nest.
Making the most of his opportunity, he gathered one of the pumpkins in

his arms and went on his way. A pumpkin is an exceedingly awkward thing to carry, and the Irishman had not gone far before he made a mis-step, and stumbled. The pumpkin fell to the ground, rolled down the hill into a "brush-heap," and, striking against a stump, was broken. The story continues in the dialect: "W'en de punkin roll in de bresh-heap, out jump a rabbit; en soon's de I'shmuns see dat, he take atter de rabbit en holler: 'Kworp, colty! kworp, colty!' but de rabbit, he des flew." The point of this is obvious.

As to the songs,[4] the reader is warned that it will be found difficult to make them conform to the ordinary rules of versification, nor is it intended that they should so conform. They are written, and are intended to be read, solely with reference to the regular and invariable recurrence of the caesura, as, for instance, the first stanza of the Revival Hymn:

Oh, whar | shill we go | w'en de great | day comes |
Wid de blow | in' er de trumpits | en de bang | in' er de drums |
How man | y po' sin | ners'll be kotch'd | out late |
En fine | no latch | ter de gold | in gate |

In other words, the songs depend for their melody and rhythm upon the musical quality of *time*, and not upon long or short, accented or unac-cented syllables. I am persuaded that this fact led Mr. Sidney Lanier, who is thoroughly familiar with the metrical peculiarities of Negro songs, into the exhaustive investigation which has resulted in the publication of his scholarly treatise, *The Science of English Verse.*

The difference between the dialect of the legends and that of the char-acter sketches, slight as it is, marks the modifications which the speech of the Negro has undergone even where education has played no part in reforming it. Indeed, save in the remote country districts, the dialect of the legends has nearly disappeared. I am perfectly well aware that the character sketches are without permanent interest, but they are embod-ied here for the purpose of presenting a phase of Negro character wholly distinct from that which I have endeavored to preserve in the legends. Only in this shape, and with all the local allusions, would it be possible to adequately represent the shrewd observations, the curious retorts, the

---

[4] The songs, character sketches, and "A Story of the War" have not been included in *The Complete Tales of Uncle Remus.* See Foreword by Richard Chase, p. xiii—R. C.

homely thrusts, the quaint comments, and the humorous philosophy of the race of which Uncle Remus is the type.

If the reader not familiar with plantation life will imagine that the myth-stories of Uncle Remus are told night after night to a little boy by an old Negro who appears to be venerable enough to have lived during the period which he describes—who has nothing but pleasant memories of the discipline of slavery—and who has all the prejudices of caste and pride of family that were the natural results of the system; if the reader can imagine all this, he will find little difficulty in appreciating and sympathizing with the air of affectionate superiority which Uncle Remus assumes as he proceeds to unfold the mysteries of plantation lore to a little child who is the product of that practical reconstruction which has been going on to some extent since the war in spite of the politicians. Uncle Remus describes that reconstruction in his "A Story of the War," and I may as well add here for the benefit of the curious that that story is almost literally true.

J. C. H. [1880]

Preface and Dedication
To the New Edition

by
JOEL CHANDLER HARRIS
From UNCLE REMUS: HIS SONGS AND HIS SAYINGS

Preface *and* Dedication *to the New Edition*

TO ARTHUR BURDETTE FROST

MY DEAR FROST: I am expected to supply a preface for this new edition of my first book—to advance from behind the curtain, as it were, and make a fresh bow to the public that has dealt with Uncle Remus in so gentle and generous a fashion. For this event the lights are to be rekindled, and I am expected to respond in some formal way to an encore that marks the fifteenth anniversary of the book. There have been other editions—how many I do not remember—but this is to be an entirely new one, except as to the matter: new type, new pictures, and new binding.

But, as frequently happens on such occasions, I am at a loss for a word. I seem to see before me the smiling faces of thousands of children—some young and fresh, and some wearing the friendly marks of age, but all children at heart—and not an unfriendly face among them. And out of the confusion, and while I am trying hard to speak the right word, I seem to hear a voice lifted above the rest, saying: "You have made some of us happy." And so I feel my heart fluttering and my lips trembling, and I have to bow silently and turn away, and hurry back into the obscurity that fits me best.

Phantoms! Children of dreams! True, my dear Frost; but if you could see the thousands of letters that have come to me from far and near, and all fresh from the hearts and hands of children, and from men and women who have not forgotten how to be children, you would not wonder at the dream. And such a dream can do no harm. Insubstantial though it may be, I would not at this hour exchange it for all the fame won by my mightier brethren of the pen—whom I most humbly salute.

Measured by the material developments that have compressed years of experience into the space of a day, thus increasing the possibilities of life, if not its beauty, fifteen years constitute the old age of a book. Such a survival might almost be said to be due to a tiny sluice of green sap under the gray bark. Where it lies in the matter of this book, or what its source—if, indeed, it be really there—is more of a mystery to my middle age than it was to my prime.

But it would be no mystery at all if this new edition were to be more popular than the old one. Do you know why? Because you have taken it under your hand and made it yours. Because you have breathed the breath of life into these amiable brethren of wood and field. Because, by a stroke here and a touch there, you have conveyed into their quaint antics the illumination of your own inimitable humor, which is as true to our sun and soil as it is to the spirit and essence of the matter set forth.

The book was mine, but now you have made it yours, both sap and pith. Take it, therefore, my dear Frost, and believe me, faithfully yours,

JOEL CHANDLER HARRIS [1896]

. . ."*Manys en manys de time, deze long nights en deze rainy spells, dat I sets down dar in my house over ag'in de chimbley-jam—I sets dar en I dozes, en it seem lak dat ole Brer Rabbit, he'll stick he head in de crack er de do' en see my eye periently shot, en den he'll beckon back at de yuther creeturs, en den dey'll all come slippin' in on der tip-toes, en dey'll set dar en run over de ole times wid one er n'er, en crack der jokes . . . en den dey'll tu'n in en git up a reg'lar juberlee. Brer Rabbit, he'll retch up en take down de trivet, en Brer Fox, he'll snatch up de griddle, en Brer B'ar, he'll lay holt er de pot-hooks, en old Brer Tarrypin, he'll grab up de fryin' pan, en dar dey'll have it, up en down, en 'roun' en 'roun' . . . en dey plays dem kinder chunes w'at moves you fum 'way back yander; en manys de time w'en I gits lonesome kaze dey aint nobody year um 'ceppin' it's me . . .*

"*Do they play on them just like a band, Uncle Remus?*" . . .

"*Dey comes des lak I tell you, honey. W'en I shets my eyes en dozes, dey comes en dey plays, but w'en I opens my eyes dey ain't dar. Now, den, w'en dat's de shape er marters, w'at duz I do? I des shets my eyes en hol' um shot, en let um come en play dem ole time chunes twel long atter bed-time done come en gone . . .*"

From NIGHTS WITH UNCLE REMUS. "*A Dream and a Story.*"

I

The tales from

Uncle Remus

His Songs and His Sayings

With illustrations by
ARTHUR BURDETTE FROST

1
Uncle Remus Initiates the Little Boy

ONE EVENING recently, the lady whom Uncle Remus calls "Miss Sally" missed her little seven-year-old boy. Making search for him through the house and through the yard, she heard the sound of voices in the old man's cabin, and, looking through the window, saw the child sitting by Uncle Remus. His head rested against the old man's arm, and he was gazing with an expression of the most intense interest into the rough, weather-beaten face, that beamed so kindly upon him. This is what "Miss Sally" heard:

"Bimeby, one day, after Brer Fox bin doin' all dat he could fer ter ketch Brer Rabbit, en Brer Rabbit bin doin' all he could fer to keep 'im fum it, Brer Fox say to hisse'f dat he'd put up a game on Brer Rabbit, en he ain't mo'n got de wuds out'n his mouf twel Brer Rabbit come a lopin' up de big road, lookin' des ez plump, en ez fat, en ez sassy ez a Moggin hoss in a barley-patch.

"'Hol' on dar, Brer Rabbit,' sez Brer Fox, sezee.

"'I ain't got time, Brer Fox,' sez Brer Rabbit, sezee, sorter mendin' his licks.

"'I wanter have some confab wid you, Brer Rabbit,' sez Brer Fox, sezee.

"'All right, Brer Fox, but you better holler fum whar you stan'. I'm monstus full er fleas dis mawnin',' sez Brer Rabbit, sezee.

"'I seed Brer B'ar yistiddy,' sez Brer Fox, sezee, 'en he sorter rake me over de coals kaze you en me ain't make fr'en's en live neighborly, en I tole 'im dat I'd see you.'

"Den Brer Rabbit scratch one year wid his off hinefoot sorter jubously, en den he ups en sez, sezee:

"'All a settin', Brer Fox. Spose'n you drap roun' termorrer en take dinner wid me. We ain't got no great doin's at our house, but I speck de old 'oman en de chilluns kin sorter scramble roun' en git up sump'n fer ter stay yo' stummick.'

"'I'm 'gree'ble, Brer Rabbit,' sez Brer Fox, sezee.

"'Den I'll 'pen' on you,' sez Brer Rabbit, sezee.

"Nex' day, Mr. Rabbit en Miss Rabbit got up soon, 'fo' day, en raided

on a gyarden like Miss Sally's out dar, en got some cabbiges en some roas'n-years, en some sparrer-grass, en dey fix up a smashin' dinner. Bimeby one er de little Rabbits, playin' out in de backyard, come runnin' in hollerin', 'Oh, ma! oh, ma! I seed Mr. Fox a comin'!' En den Brer Rabbit he tuck de chilluns by der years en make um set down, en den him and Miss Rabbit sorter dally roun' waitin' for Brer Fox. En dey keep on waitin', but no Brer Fox ain't come. Atter 'while Brer Rabbit goes to de do', easy like, en peep out, en dar, stickin' fum behime de cornder, wuz de tip-een' er Brer Fox tail. Den Brer Rabbit shot de do' en sot down, en put his paws behime his years en begin fer ter sing:

> "'De place wharbouts you spill de grease,
>   Right dar you er boun' ter slide,
>   An' whar you fin' a bunch er ha'r,
>   You'll sholy fine de hide.'

"Nex' day. Brer Fox sont word by Mr. Mink, en skuze hisse'f kaze he wuz too sick fer ter come, en he ax Brer Rabbit fer to come en take dinner wid him, en Brer Rabbit say he wuz 'gree'ble.

"Bimeby, w'en de shadders wuz at der shortes', Brer Rabbit he sorter brush up en sa'nter down ter Brer Fox's house, en w'en he got dar, he hear somebody groanin', en he look in de do' an dar he see Brer Fox settin' up in a rockin'-cheer all wrop up wid flannil, en he look mighty weak. Brer Rabbit look all 'roun', he did, but he ain't see no dinner. De dishpan wuz settin' on de table, en close by wuz a kyarvin' knife.

"'Look like you gwine ter have chicken fer dinner, Brer Fox,' sez Brer Rabbit, sezee.

"'Yes, Brer Rabbit, dey er nice, en fresh, en tender,' sez Brer Fox, sezee.

"Den Brer Rabbit sorter pull his mustash, en say: 'You ain't got no calamus root, is you, Brer Fox? I done got so now dat I can't eat no chicken ceppin' she's seasoned up wid calamus root.' En wid dat Brer Rabbit lipt out er de do' and dodge 'mong de bushes, en sot dar watchin' fer Brer Fox; en he ain't watch long, nudder, kaze Brer Fox flung off de flannil en crope out er de house en got whar he could cloze in on Brer Rabbit, en bimeby Brer Rabbit holler out: 'Oh, Brer Fox! I'll des put yo' calamus root out yer on dish yer stump. Better come git it while hit's fresh,' and wid dat Brer Rabbit gallop off home. En Brer Fox ain't never cotch 'im yit, en w'at's mo', honey, he ain't gwine' ter."

2
The Wonderful Tar-Baby Story

"DIDN'T THE FOX *never* catch the rabbit, Uncle Remus?" asked the little boy the next evening.

"He come mighty nigh it, honey, sho's you born — Brer Fox did. One day atter Brer Rabbit fool 'im wid dat calamus root Brer Fox went ter wuk en got 'im some tar, en mix it wid some turkentime, en fix up a contrapshun w'at he call a Tar-Baby, en he tuck dish yer Tar-Baby en he sot 'er in de big road, en den he lay off in de bushes fer to see what de news wuz gwine ter be. En he didn't hatter wait long, nudder, kaze bimeby here come Brer Rabbit pacin' down de road — lippity-clippity, clippity-

lippity — dez ez sassy ez a jay-bird. Brer Fox, he lay low. Brer Rabbit come prancin' 'long twel he spy de Tar-Baby, en den he fotch up on his behime legs like he wuz 'stonished. De Tar-Baby, she sot dar, she did, en Brer Fox, he lay low.

"'Mawnin'!' sez Brer Rabbit, sezee — 'nice wedder dis mawnin',' sezee.

"Tar-Baby ain't sayin' nothin', en Brer Fox, he lay low.

"'How duz yo' sym'tums seem ter segashuate?' sez Brer Rabbit, sezee.

"Brer Fox, he wink his eye slow, en lay low, en de Tar-Baby, she ain't sayin' nothin'.

"'How you come on, den? Is you deaf?' sez Brer Rabbit, sezee. 'Kaze if you is, I kin holler louder,' sezee.

"Tar-Baby stay still, en Brer Fox, he lay low.

"'You er stuck up, dat's w'at you is,' says Brer Rabbit, sezee, 'en I'm gwine ter kyore you, dat's w'at I'm a gwine ter do,' sezee.

"Brer Fox, he sorter chuckle in his stummick, he did, but Tar-Baby ain't sayin' nothin'.

"'I'm gwine ter larn you how ter talk ter 'spectubble folks ef hit's de las' ack,' sez Brer Rabbit, sezee. 'Ef you don't take off dat hat en tell me howdy, I'm gwine ter bus' you wide open,' sezee.

"Tar-Baby stay still, en Brer Fox, he lay low.

"Brer Rabbit keep on axin' 'im, en de Tar-Baby, she keep on sayin' nothin', twel present'y Brer Rabbit draw back wid his fis', he did, en blip he tuck 'er side er de head. Right dar's whar he broke his merlasses jug. His fis' stuck, en he can't pull loose. De tar hilt 'im. But Tar-Baby, she stay still, en Brer Fox, he lay low.

"'Ef you don't lemme loose, I'll knock you agin,' sez Brer Rabbit, sezee, en wid dat he fotch 'er a wipe wid de udder han', en dat stuck. Tar-Baby, she ain't sayin' nothin', en Brer Fox, he lay low.

"'Tu'n me loose, fo' I kick de natchul stuffin' out'n you,' sez Brer Rabbit, sezee, but de Tar-Baby, she ain't sayin' nothin'. She des hilt on, en den Brer Rabbit lose de use er his feet in de same way. Brer Fox, he lay low. Den Brer Rabbit squall out dat ef de Tar-Baby don't tu'n 'im loose he butt 'er cranksided. En den he butted, en his head got stuck. Den Brer Fox, he sa'ntered fort', lookin' des ez innercent ez one er yo' mammy's mockin'-birds.

"'Howdy, Brer Rabbit,' sez Brer Fox, sezee. 'You look sorter stuck up dis mawnin',' sezee, en den he rolled on de groun', en laughed en laughed twel he couldn't laugh no mo'. 'I speck you'll take dinner wid me dis time, Brer Rabbit. I done laid in some calamus root, en I ain't gwine ter take no skuse,' sez Brer Fox, sezee."

Here Uncle Remus paused, and drew a two-pound yam out of the ashes.

"Did the Fox eat the Rabbit?" asked the little boy to whom the story had been told.

"Dat's all de fur de tale goes," replied the old man. "He mought, en den again he moughtent. Some say Jedge B'ar come long en loosed 'im — some say he didn't. I hear Miss Sally callin'. You better run 'long."

3
Why Mr. Possum Loves Peace

"ONE NIGHT," said Uncle Remus — taking Miss Sally's little boy on his knee, and stroking the child's hair thoughtfully and caressingly — "one night Brer Possum call by fer Brer Coon, 'cordin' ter 'greement, en atter gobblin' up a dish er fried greens en smokin' a seegyar, dey rambled fort' fer ter see how de balance er de settlement wuz gittin' 'long. Brer Coon, he wuz one er deze yer natchul pacers, en he racked 'long same ez Mars John's bay pony, en Brer Possum he went in a han'-gallup; en dey got over heap er groun', mon. Brer Possum, he got his belly full er 'simmons, en Brer Coon, he scoop up a 'bunnunce er frogs en tadpoles. Dey amble 'long, dey did, des ez sociable ez a basket er kittens, twel bimeby dey hear Mr. Dog talkin' ter hisse'f way off in de woods.

"'Sposen he runs up on us, Brer Possum, w'at you gwine ter do?' sez Brer Coon, sezee. Brer Possum sorter laugh 'round de cornders un his mouf.

"'Oh, ef he come, Brer Coon, I'm gwine ter stan' by you,' sez Brer Possum. 'W'at you gwine ter do?' sezee."

"'Who? me?' sez Brer Coon. 'Ef he run up onter me, I lay I give 'im one twis',' sezee."

"Did the dog come?" asked the little boy.

"Go 'way, honey!" responded the old man, in an impressive tone. "Go way! Mr. Dog, he come en he come a zoonin'. En he ain't wait fer ter say howdy, nudder. He des sail inter de two un um. De ve'y fus pass he make Brer Possum fetch a grin fum year ter year, en keel over like he wuz dead. Den Mr. Dog, he sail inter Brer Coon, en right dar's whar he drap his money purse, kaze Brer Coon wuz cut out fer dat kinder bizness, en he fa'rly wipe up de face er de yeth wid 'im. You better b'lieve dat w'en Mr. Dog got a chance to make hisse'f skace he tuck it, en w'at der wuz lef' un him went skaddlin' thoo de woods like hit wuz shot out'n a muskit. En Brer Coon, he sorter lick his cloze inter shape en rack off, en Brer Possum, he lay dar like he wuz dead, twel bimeby he raise up sorter keerful like, en w'en he fin' de coas' cle'r he scramble up en scamper off like sumpin' was atter 'im."

Here Uncle Remus paused long enough to pick up a live coal of fire in his fingers, transfer it to the palm of his hand, and thence to his clay pipe, which he had been filling — a proceeding that was viewed by the little boy with undisguised admiration. The old man then proceeded:

"Nex' time Brer Possum met Brer Coon, Brer Coon 'fuse ter 'spon' ter his howdy, en dis make Brer Possum feel mighty bad, seein' ez how dey useter make so many 'scurshuns tergedder.

"'W'at make you hol' yo head so high, Brer Coon?' sez Brer Possum, sezee.

"'I ain't runnin' wid cowerds deze days,' sez Brer Coon. 'W'en I wants you I'll sen' fer you,' sezee.

"Den Brer Possum git mighty mad.

"'Who's enny cowerd?' sezee.

"'You is,' sez Brer Coon, 'dat's who. I ain't soshatin' wid dem w'at lays down on de groun' en plays dead w'en dar's a free fight gwine on,' sezee.

"Den Brer Possum grin en laugh fit to kill hisse'f.

"'Lor', Brer Coon, you don't speck I done dat kaze I wuz feard, duz you?' sezee. 'W'y I want no mo' feard dan you is dis minnit. W'at wuz dey fer ter be skeered un?' sezee. 'I know'd you'd git away wid Mr. Dog ef I didn't, en I des lay dar watchin' you shake him, waitin' fer ter put in w'en de time come,' sezee.

"Brer Coon tu'n up his nose.

"'Dat's a mighty likely tale,' sezee, 'w'en Mr. Dog ain't mo'n tech you 'fo' you keel over, en lay dar stiff,' sezee.

"'Dat's des w'at I wuz gwine ter tell you 'bout,' sez Brer Possum, sezee. 'I want no mo' skeer'd dan you is right now, en' I wuz fixin' ter give Mr. Dog a sample er my jaw,' sezee, 'but I'm de most ticklish chap w'at you ever laid eyes on, en no sooner did Mr. Dog put his nose down yer 'mong my ribs dan I got ter laughin', en I laughed twel I ain't had no use er my lim's,' sezee, 'en it's a mussy unto Mr. Dog dat I wuz ticklish, kaze a little mo' en I'd e't 'im up,' sezee. 'I don't min' fightin', Brer Coon, no mo' dan you duz,' sezee, 'but I declar' ter gracious ef I kin stan' ticklin'. Git me in a row whar dey ain't no ticklin' 'lowed, en I'm your man,' sezee.

"En down ter dis day" — continued Uncle Remus, watching the smoke from his pipe curl upward over the little boy's head — "down ter

dis day, Brer Possum's bound ter s'render w'en you tech him in de short ribs, en he'll laugh ef he knows he's gwine ter be smashed fer it."

4

How Mr. Rabbit Was Too Sharp for Mr. Fox

"UNCLE REMUS," said the little boy one evening, when he had found the old man with little or nothing to do, "did the Fox kill and eat the Rabbit when he caught him with the Tar-Baby?"

"Law, honey, ain't I tell you 'bout dat?" replied the old darkey, chuckling slyly. "I 'clar ter gracious I ought er tole you dat, but old man Nod wuz ridin' on my eyeleds twel a leetle mo'n I'd a dis'member'd my own name, en den on to dat here come yo' mammy hollerin' atter you.

"W'at I tell you w'en I fus' begin? I tole you Brer Rabbit wuz a monstus soon creetur; leas'ways dat's w'at I laid out fer ter tell you. Well, den, honey, don't you go en make no udder calkalashuns, kaze in dem days Brer Rabbit en his fambly wuz at de head er de gang w'en enny racket wuz on han', en dar dey stayed. 'Fo' you begins fer ter wipe yo' eyes 'bout Brer Rabbit, you wait en see whar'bouts Brer Rabbit gwine ter fetch up at. But dat's needer yer ner dar.

"W'en Brer Fox fin' Brer Rabbit mixt up wid de Tar-Baby, he feel mighty good, en he roll on de groun' en laugh. Bimeby he up'n say, sezee:

"'Well, I speck I got you dis time, Brer Rabbit, sezee; 'maybe I ain't, but I speck I is. You bin runnin' roun' here sassin' atter me a mighty long time, but I speck you done come ter de een' er de row. You bin cuttin' up yo' capers en bouncin' 'roun' in dis neighborhood ontwel you come ter b'lieve yo'se'f de boss er de whole gang. En den you er allers somers whar you got no bizness,' sez Brer Fox, sezee. 'Who ax you fer ter come en strike up a 'quaintance wid dish yer Tar-Baby? En who stuck you up dar whar you iz? Nobody in de roun' worl'. You des tuck en jam yo'se'f on dat Tar-Baby widout waitin' fer enny invite,' sez Brer Fox, sezee, 'en dar you is, en dar you'll stay twel I fixes up a bresh-pile and fiers her up, kaze I'm gwine ter bobbycue you dis day, sho,' sez Brer Fox, sezee.

"Den Brer Rabbit talk mighty 'umble.

"'I don't keer w'at you do wid me, Brer Fox,' sezee, 'so you don't fling me in dat brier-patch. Roas' me, Brer Fox,' sezee, 'but don't fling me in dat brier-patch,' sezee.

"'Hit's so much trouble fer ter kindle a fier,' sez Brer Fox, sezee, 'dat I speck I'll hatter hang you,' sezee.

"'Hang me des ez high as you please, Brer Fox,' sez Brer Rabbit, sezee, 'but do fer de Lord's sake don't fling me in dat brier-patch,' sezee.

"'I ain't got no string,' sez Brer Fox, sezee, 'en now I speck I'll hatter drown you,' sezee.

"'Drown me des ez deep ez you please, Brer Fox,' sez Brer Rabbit, sezee, 'but don't fling me in dat brier-patch,' sezee.

"'Dey ain't no water nigh,' sez Brer Fox, sezee, 'en now I speck I'll hatter skin you,' sezee.

"'Skin me, Brer Fox,' sez Brer Rabbit, sezee, 'snatch out my eye-balls, t'ar out my years by de roots, en cut off my legs,' sezee, 'but do please, Brer Fox, don't fling me in dat brier-patch,' sezee.

"Co'se Brer Fox wanter hurt Brer Rabbit bad ez he kin, so he cotch 'im by de behime legs en slung 'im right in de middle er de brier-patch. Dar wuz a considerabul flutter whar Brer Rabbit struck de bushes, en Brer Fox sorter hang 'roun' fer ter see w'at wuz gwine ter happen. Bimeby he hear somebody call 'im, en way up de hill he see Brer Rabbit settin' cross-legged on a chinkapin log koamin' de pitch out'n his ha'r wid a chip. Den Brer Fox know dat he bin swop off mighty bad. Brer Rabbit wuz bleedzd fer ter fling back some er his sass, en he holler out:

"'Bred en bawn in a brier-patch, Brer Fox — bred en bawn in a brier-patch!' en wid dat he skip out des ez lively ez a cricket in de embers."

5

The Story of the Deluge, and How It Came About

"ONE TIME," said Uncle Remus — adjusting his spectacles so as to be able to see how to thread a large darning-needle with which he was patching his coat — "one time, way back yander, 'fo you wuz bawn, honey, en 'fo' Mars John er Miss Sally wuz borned — way back yander 'fo' enny un us wuz borned, de animils en de creeturs sorter 'lecshuneer roun' 'mong deyselves, twel at las' dey 'greed fer ter have a 'sembly. In dem days," continued the old man, observing a look of incredulity on the little boy's face, "in dem days creeturs had lots mo' sense dan dey got now; let 'lone dat, dey had sense same like folks. Hit was tech en go wid um, too, mon, en w'en dey make up der min's w'at hatter be done, 'twa'n't mo'n menshun'd 'fo' hit wuz done. Well, dey 'lected dat dey hatter hol' er 'sembly fer ter sorter straighten out marters en hear de complaints, en w'en de day come dey wuz on han'. De Lion, he wuz dar, kaze he wuz de king, en he hatter be der. De Rhynossyhoss, he wuz dar, en de Elephant, he wuz dar, en de Cammils, en de Cows, en plum' down ter de Crawfishes, dey wuz dar. Dey wuz all dar. En w'en de Lion shuck his mane, en tuck his seat in de big cheer, den de sesshun begun fer ter commence."

"What did they do, Uncle Remus?" asked the little boy.

"I can't skacely call to mine 'zackly w'at dey did do, but dey spoke speeches, en hollered, en cusst, en flung der langwidge 'roun' des like w'en yo' daddy wuz gwine ter run fer de legislater en got lef'. Howsomever, dey 'ranged der 'fairs, en splained der bizness. Bimeby, w'ile dey wuz 'sputin' 'longer one er nudder, de Elephant trompled on one er de Crawfishes. Co'se w'en dat creetur put his foot down, w'atsumever's under dar wuz boun' fer ter be squshed, en dey wa'n't nuff er dat Crawfish lef' fer ter tell dat he'd bin dar.

"Dis make de udder Crawfishes mighty mad, en dey sorter swarmed tergedder en draw'd up a kinder peramble wid some wharfo'es in it, en read her out in de 'sembly. But, bless gracious! sech a racket wuz a gwine

on dat nobody ain't hear it, ceppin' maybe de Mud Turkle en de Spring Lizzud, en dere enfloons wuz pow'ful lackin'.

"Bimeby, w'iles de Nunicorn wuz 'sputin' wid de Lion, en w'ile de Hyener wuz a laughin' ter hisse'f, de Elephant squshed anudder one er de Crawfishes, en a little mo'n he'd er ruint de Mud Turkle. Den de Crawfishes, w'at dey wuz lef' un um, swarmed tergedder en draw'd up anudder peramble wid sum mo' wharfo'es; but dey mought ez well er sung Ole Dan Tucker ter a harrycane. De udder creeturs wuz too busy wid der fussin' fer ter 'spon' unto de Crawfishes. So dar dey wuz, de Crawfishes, en dey didn't know w'at minnit wuz gwine ter be de nex'; en dey kep' on gittin madder en madder en skeer'der en skeer'der, twel bimeby dey gun de wink ter de Mud Turkle en de Spring Lizzud, en den dey bo'd little holes in de groun' en went down outer sight."

"Who did, Uncle Remus?" asked the little boy.

"De Crawfishes, honey. Dey bo'd inter de groun' en kep' on bo'in' twel dey onloost de fountains er de yeth; en de waters squirt out, en riz higher en higher twel de hills wuz kivvered, en de creeturs wuz all drowned; en all bekaze dey let on 'mong deyselves dat dey wuz bigger dan de Crawfishes."

Then the old man blew the ashes from a smoking yam, and proceeded to remove the peeling.

"Where was the ark, Uncle Remus?" the little boy inquired, presently.

"W'ich ark's dat?" asked the old man, in a tone of well-feigned curiosity.

"Noah's ark," replied the child.

"Don't you pester wid ole man Noah, honey. I boun' he tuck keer er dat ark. Dat's w'at he wuz dar fer, en dat's w'at he done. Leas'ways, dat's w'at dey tells me. But don't you bodder longer dat ark, ceppin' your mammy fetches it up. Dey mought er bin two deloojes, en den agin dey moughtent. Ef dey wuz enny ark in dish yer w'at de Crawfishes brung on, I ain't heern tell un it, en w'en dey ain't no arks 'roun', I ain't got no time fer ter make um en put em in dar. Hit's gittin' yo' bedtime, honey."

6
Mr. Rabbit Grossly Deceives Mr. Fox

ONE EVENING when the little boy, whose nights with Uncle Remus were as entertaining as those Arabian ones of blessed memory, had finished supper and hurried out to sit with his venerable patron, he found the old man in great glee. Indeed, Uncle Remus was talking and laughing to himself at such a rate that the little boy was afraid he had company. The truth is, Uncle Remus had heard the child coming, and when the rosy-cheeked chap put his head in at the door, was engaged in a monologue, the burden of which seemed to be —

> "Ole Molly Har',
> W'at you doin' dar,
> Settin' in de cornder
> Smokin' yo' seegyar?"

As a matter of course this vague allusion reminded the little boy of the fact that the wicked Fox was still in pursuit of the Rabbit, and he immediately put his curiosity in the shape of a question.

"Uncle Remus, did the Rabbit have to go clean away when he got loose from the Tar-Baby?"

"Bless gracious, honey, dat he didn't. Who? Him? You dunno nothin' 'tall 'bout Brer Rabbit ef dat's de way you puttin' 'im down. W'at he gwine 'way fer? He moughter stayed sorter close twel de pitch rub off'n his ha'r, but twern't menny days 'fo' he wuz lopin' up en down de neighborhood same ez ever, en I dunno ef he weren't mo' sassier dan befo'.

"Seem like dat de tale 'bout how he got mixt up wid de Tar-Baby got 'roun' 'mongst de neighbors. Leas'ways, Miss Meadows en de gals got win' un it, en de nex' time Brer Rabbit paid um a visit Miss Meadows tackled 'im 'bout it, en de gals sot up a monstus gigglement. Brer Rabbit, he sot up des ez cool ez a cowcumber, he did, en let 'em run on."

"Who was Miss Meadows, Uncle Remus?" inquired the little boy.

"Don't ax me, honey. She wuz in de tale, Miss Meadows en de gals wuz, en de tale I give you like hit wer' gun ter me. Brer Rabbit, he sot dar, he did, sorter lam' like, en den bimeby he cross his legs, he did, and wink his eye slow, en up and say, sezee:

" 'Ladies, Brer Fox wuz my daddy's ridin'-hoss fer thirty year; maybe mo', but thirty year dat I knows un,' sezee; en den he paid um his 'specks, en tip his beaver, en march off, he did, des ez stiff en ez stuck up ez a fier-stick.

"Nex' day, Brer Fox cum a callin', and w'en he 'gun fer ter laugh 'bout Brer Rabbit, Miss Meadows en de gals, dey ups en tells 'im 'bout w'at Brer Rabbit say. Den Brer Fox grit his tushes sho nuff, he did, en he look mighty dumpy, but w'en he riz fer ter go he up en say, sezee:

" 'Ladies, I ain't 'sputin' w'at you say, but I'll make Brer Rabbit chaw up his words en spit um out right yer whar you kin see 'im,' sezee, en wid dat off Brer Fox put.

"En w'en he got in de big road, he shuck de dew off'n his tail, en made a straight shoot fer Brer Rabbit's house. W'en he got dar, Brer Rabbit wuz spectin' un 'im, en de do' wuz shet fas'. Brer Fox knock. Nobody ain't ans'er. Brer Fox knock. Nobody ans'er. Den he knock agin — blam! blam! Den Brer Rabbit holler out mighty weak:

" 'Is dat you, Brer Fox? I want you ter run en fetch de doctor. Dat bait er pusly w'at I e't dis mawnin' is gittin' 'way wid me. Do, please, Brer Fox, run quick,' sez Brer Rabbit, sezee.

" 'I come atter you, Brer Rabbit,' sez Brer Fox, sezee. 'Dar's gwine ter be a party up at Miss Meadows's,' sezee. 'All de gals'll be dere, en I promus' dat I'd fetch you. De gals, dey 'lowed dat hit wouldn't be no party ceppin' I fotch you,' sez Brer Fox, sezee.

"Den Brer Rabbit say he wuz too sick, en Brer Fox say he wuzzent, en dar dey had it up and down, 'sputin' en contendin'. Brer Rabbit say he can't walk. Brer Fox say he tote 'im. Brer Rabbit say how? Brer Fox say in his arms. Brer Rabbit say he drap 'im. Brer Fox 'low he won't. Bimeby Brer Rabbit say he go ef Brer Fox tote 'im on his back. Brer Fox say he would. Brer Rabbit say he can't ride widout a saddle. Brer Fox say he git de saddle. Brer Rabbit say he can't set in saddles less he have bridle fer ter hol' by. Brer Fox say he git de bridle. Brer Rabbit say he can't ride widout blin' bridle, kaze Brer Fox be shyin' at stumps 'long de road, en fling 'im off. Brer Fox say he git blin' bridle. Den Brer Rabbit say he go. Den Brer Fox say he ride Brer Rabbit mos' up ter Miss Meadows's, en den he could git down en walk de balance er de way. Brer Rabbit 'greed, en den Brer Fox lipt out atter de saddle en de bridle.

"Co'se Brer Rabbit know de game dat Brer Fox wuz fixin' fer ter play, en he 'termin' fer ter outdo 'im, en by de time he koam his ha'r en twis' his mustash, en sorter rig up, yer come Brer Fox, saddle en bridle on, en lookin' ez peart ez a circus pony. He trot up ter de do' en stan' dar pawin' de ground en chompin' de bit same like sho nuff hoss, en Brer Rabbit he mount, he did, en dey amble off. Brer Fox can't see behime wid de blin' bridle on, but bimeby he feel Brer Rabbit raise one er his foots.

"'W'at you doin' now, Brer Rabbit?' sezee.

"'Short'nin' de lef' stir'p, Brer Fox,' sezee.

"Bimeby Brer Rabbit raise up de udder foot.

"'W'at you doin' now, Brer Rabbit?' sezee.

"'Pullin' down my pants, Brer Fox,' sezee.

"All de time, bless gracious, honey, Brer Rabbit wer' puttin' on his spurrers, en w'en dey got close to Miss Meadows's, whar Brer Rabbit wuz to git off, en Brer Fox made a motion fer ter stan' still, Brer Rabbit slap de spurrers into Brer Fox flanks, en you better b'lieve he got over groun'. W'en dey got ter de house, Miss Meadows en all de gals wuz settin' on de peazzer, en stidder stoppin' at de gate, Brer Rabbit rid on by, he did, en den come gallopin' down de road en up ter de hoss-rack, w'ich he hitch Brer Fox at, en den he sa'nter inter de house, he did, en shake han's wid de gals, en set dar, smokin' his seegyar same ez a town man. Bimeby he draw in a long puff, en den let hit out in a cloud, en squar hisse'f back en holler out, he did:

"'Ladies, ain't I done tell you Brer Fox wuz de ridin'-hoss fer our fambly? He sorter losin' his gait now, but I speck I kin fetch 'im all right in a mont' er so,' sezee.

"En den Brer Rabbit sorter grin, he did, en de gals giggle, en Miss Meadows, she praise up de pony, en dar wuz Brer Fox hitch fas' ter de rack, en couldn't he'p hisse'f."

"Is that all, Uncle Remus?" asked the little boy as the old man paused.

"Dat ain't all, honey, but 'twon't do fer ter give out too much doff fer ter cut one pa'r pants," replied the old man sententiously.

7

Mr. Fox Is Again Victimized

WHEN MISS SALLY'S little boy went to Uncle Remus the next night to hear the conclusion of the adventure in which the Rabbit made a riding-horse of the Fox to the great enjoyment and gratification of Miss Meadows and the girls, he found the old man in a bad humor.

"I ain't tellin' no tales ter bad chilluns," said Uncle Remus curtly.

"But, Uncle Remus, I ain't bad," said the little boy plaintively.

"Who dat chunkin' dem chickens dis mawnin'? Who dat knockin' out folks eyes wid dat Yallerbammer sling des 'fo' dinner? Who dat sickin' dat pinter puppy atter my pig? Who dat scatterin' my ingun sets? Who dat flingin' rocks on top er my house, w'ich a little mo' en one un em would er drap spang on my head?"

"Well, now, Uncle Remus, I didn't go to do it. I won't do so any more. Please. Uncle Remus, if you will tell me, I'll run to the house and bring you some tea-cakes."

"Seein' um's better'n hearin' tell un um," replied the old man, the severity of his countenance relaxing somewhat; but the little boy darted out, and in a few minutes came running back with his pockets full and his hands full.

"I lay yo' mammy 'll 'spishun dat de rats' stummicks is widenin' in dis neighborhood w'en she come fer ter count up 'er cakes," said Uncle Remus, with a chuckle. "Deze," he continued, dividing the cakes into two equal parts — "dese I'll tackle now, en dese I'll lay by fer Sunday.

"Lemme see. I mos' dis'member whar'bouts Brer Fox en Brer Rabbit wuz."

"The Rabbit rode the Fox to Miss Meadows's, and hitched him to the horse-rack," said the little boy.

"W'y co'se he did," said Uncle Remus. "Co'se he did. Well, Brer Rabbit rid Brer Fox up, he did, en tied 'im to de rack, en den sot out in de peazzer wid de gals a smokin' er his seegyar wid mo' proudness dan w'at you mos' ever see. Dey talk, en dey sing, en dey play on de peanner, de gals did, twel bimeby hit come time fer Brer Rabbit fer to be gwine, en he tell um all good-by, en strut out to de hoss-rack same's ef he wuz de king er de patter-rollers, en den he mount Brer Fox en ride off.

"Brer Fox ain't sayin' nothin' 'tall. He des rack off, he did, en keep his mouf shet, en Brer Rabbit know'd der wuz bizness cookin' up fer

him, en he feel monstus skittish. Brer Fox amble on twel he git in de long lane, outer sight er Miss Meadows's house, en den he tu'n loose, he did. He rip en he ra'r, en he cuss, en he swa'r; he snort en he cavort."

"What was he doing that for, Uncle Remus?" the little boy inquired.

"He wuz tryin' fer ter fling Brer Rabbit off'n his back, bless yo' soul! But he des mought ez well er rastle wid his own shadder. Every time he hump hisse'f Brer Rabbit slap de spurrers in 'im, en dar dey had it, up en down.

Brer Fox fa'rly to' up de groun' he did, en he jump so high en he jump so quick dat he mighty nigh snatch his own tail off. Dey kep' on gwine on dis way twel bimeby Brer Fox lay down en roll over, he did, en dis sorter onsettle Brer Rabbit, but by de time Brer Fox got back on his footses agin, Brer Rabbit wuz gwine thoo de underbresh mo' samer dan a race-hoss. Brer Fox he lit out atter 'im, he did, en he push Brer Rabbit so close dat it wuz 'bout all he could do fer ter git in a holler tree. Hole too little fer Brer Fox fer ter git in, en he hatter lay down en res' en gedder his min' tergedder.

"While he wuz layin' dar, Mr. Buzzard come floppin' 'long, en seein' Brer Fox stretch out on de groun', he lit en view de premusses. Den Mr.

Buzzard sorter shake his wing, en put his head on one side, en say to hisse'f like, sezee:

"'Brer Fox dead, en I so sorry,' sezee.

"'No I ain't dead, nudder,' sez Brer Fox, sezee. 'I got ole man Rabbit pent up in yer,' sezee, 'en I'm a gwine ter git 'im, dis time ef it take twel Chris'mus,' sezee.

"Den, atter some mo' palaver, Brer Fox make a bargain dat Mr. Buzzard wuz ter watch de hole, en keep Brer Rabbit dar wiles Brer Fox went atter his axe. Den Brer Fox, he lope off, he did, en Mr. Buzzard, he tuck up his stan' at de hole. Bimeby, w'en all git still, Brer Rabbit sorter scramble down close ter de hole, he did, en holler out:

"'Brer Fox! Oh! Brer Fox!'"

"Brer Fox done gone, en nobody say nothin'. Den Brer Rabbit squall out like he wuz mad; sezee:

"'You needn't talk less you wanter,' sezee; 'I knows you er dar, en I ain't keerin',' sezee. 'I des wanter tell you dat I wish mighty bad Brer Tukkey Buzzard wuz here,' sezee.

"Den Mr. Buzzard try ter talk like Brer Fox:

"'W'at you want wid Mr. Buzzard?' sezee.

"'Oh, nothin' in 'tickler, 'cep' dere's de fattes' gray squir'l in yer dat ever I see,' sezee, 'en ef Brer Tukkey Buzzard wuz 'roun' he'd be mighty glad fer ter git 'im,' sezee.

"'How Mr. Buzzard gwine ter git 'im?' sez de Buzzard, sezee.

"'Well, dar's a little hole 'roun' on de udder side er de tree,' sez Brer Rabbit, sezee, 'en ef Brer Tukkey Buzzard wuz here so he could take up his stan' dar,' sezee, 'I'd drive dat squir'l out,' sezee.

"'Drive 'im out, den,' sez Mr. Buzzard, sezee, 'en I'll see dat Brer Tukkey Buzzard gits 'im,' sezee.

"Den Brer Rabbit kick up a racket, like he wer' drivin' sump'n' out, en Mr. Buzzard he rush 'roun' fer ter ketch de squir'l, en Brer Rabbit, he dash out, he did, en he des fly fer home."

At this point Uncle Remus took one of the tea-cakes, held his head back, opened his mouth, dropped the cake in with a sudden motion, looked at the little boy with an expression of astonishment, and then

closed his eyes, and began to chew, mumbling as an accompaniment the plaintive tune of "Don't you Grieve atter Me."

The *séance* was over; but, before the little boy went into the "big house," Uncle Remus laid his rough hand tenderly on the child's shoulder, and remarked, in a confidential tone:

"Honey, you mus' git up soon Chris'mus mawnin' en open de do'; kase I'm gwine ter bounce in on Mars John en Miss Sally, en holler 'Chris'mus gif' ' des like I useter endurin' de farmin' days fo' de war, w'en ole Miss wuz 'live. I bound' dey don't fergit de ole nigger, nudder. W'en you hear me callin' de pigs, honey, you des hop up en onfassen de do'. I lay I'll give Mars John one er dese yer 'sprize parties."

8
Mr. Fox Is "Outdone" by Mr. Buzzard

"EF I DON'T run inter no mistakes," remarked Uncle Remus, as the little boy came tripping in to see him after supper, "Mr. Tukkey Buzzard wuz gyardin' de holler whar Brer Rabbit went in at, en w'ich he come out un."

The silence of the little boy verified the old man's recollection.

"Well, Mr. Buzzard, he feel mighty lonesome, he did, but he done prommust Brer Fox dat he'd stay, en he 'termin' fer ter sorter hang 'roun' en jine in de joke. En he ain't hatter wait long, nudder, kaze bimeby yer come Brer Fox gallopin' thoo de woods wid his axe on his shoulder.

" 'How you speck Brer Rabbit gittin' on, Brer Buzzard?' sez Brer Fox, sezee.

" 'Oh, he in dar,' sez Brer Buzzard, sezee. 'He mighty still, dough. I speck he takin' a nap,' sezee.

" 'Den I'm des in time fer ter wake 'im up,' sez Brer Fox, sezee. En wid dat he fling off his coat, en spit in his han's, en grab de axe. Den he draw back en come down on de tree — pow! En eve'y time he come down wid de axe — pow! — Mr. Buzzard, he step high, he did, en holler out:

" 'Oh, he in dar, Brer Fox. He in dar, sho.'

"En eve'y time a chip ud fly off, Mr. Buzzard, he'd jump, en dodge, en hol' his head sideways, he would, en holler:

" 'He in dar, Brer Fox. I done heer'd 'im. He in dar, sho.'

"En Brer Fox, he lammed away at dat holler tree, he did, like a man maulin' rails, twel bimeby, atter he done got de tree mos' cut thoo, he stop fer ter ketch his breff, en he seed Mr. Buzzard laughin' behime his

back, he did, en right den en dar, widout gwine enny fudder, Brer Fox, he smelt a rat. But Mr. Buzzard, he keep on holler'n:

"'He in dar, Brer Fox. He in dar, sho. I done seed 'im.'

"Den Brer Fox, he make like he peepin' up de holler, en he say, sezee:

"'Run yer, Brer Buzzard, en look ef dis ain't Brer Rabbit's foot hanging down yer.'

"En Mr. Buzzard, he come steppin' up, he did, same ez ef he wer' treddin' on kurkle-burs, en he stick his head in de hole: en no sooner did he done dat dan Brer Fox grab 'im. Mr. Buzzard flap his wings, en scramble 'roun' right smartually, he did, but 'twa'n't no use. Brer Fox had de 'vantage er de grip, he did, en he hilt 'im right down ter de groun'. Den Mr. Buzzard squall out, sezee:

"'Lemme 'lone, Brer Fox. Tu'n me loose,' sezee; 'Brer Rabbit'll git out. You er gittin' close at 'im,' sezee, 'en 'lev'm mo' licks'll fetch 'im,' sezee.

"'I'm nigher ter you, Brer Buzzard,' sez Brer Fox, sezee, 'dan I'll be ter Brer Rabbit dis day,' sezee. 'W'at you fool me fer?' sezee.

"'Lemme 'lone, Brer Fox,' sez Mr. Buzzard, sezee; 'my ole 'oman waitin' fer me. Brer Rabbit in dar,' sezee.

"'Dar's a bunch er his fur on dat black-be'y bush,' sez Brer Fox, sezee, 'en dat ain't de way he come,' sezee.

"Den Mr. Buzzard up'n tell Brer Fox how 'twuz, en he low'd, Mr. Buzzard did, dat Brer Rabbit wuz de lowdownest w'atsiz-name w'at he ever run up wid. Den Brer Fox say, sezee:

"'Dat's needer here ner dar, Brer Buzzard,' sezee. 'I lef' you yer fer ter watch dish yere hole, en I lef' Brer Rabbit in dar. I comes back en I fin's you at de hole en Brer Rabbit ain't in dar,' sezee. 'I'm gwine ter make you pay fer't. I done bin tampered wid twel plum' down ter de sap-sucker'll set on a log en sassy me. I'm gwine ter fling you in a bresh-heap en burn you up,' sezee.

"'Ef you fling me on der fier, Brer Fox, I'll fly 'way,' sez Mr. Buzzard, sezee.

"'Well, den, I'll settle yo' hash right now,' sez Brer Fox, sezee, en wid dat he grab Mr. Buzzard by de tail, he did, en make fer ter dash 'im 'gin de groun', but des 'bout dat time de tail fedders come out, en Mr. Buzzard sail off like one er dese yer berloons; en ez he riz, he holler back:

"'You gimme good start, Brer Fox,' sezee, en Brer Fox sot dar en watch 'im fly outer sight."

"But what became of the Rabbit, Uncle Remus?" asked the little boy.

"Don't you pester 'longer Brer Rabbit, honey, en don't you fret 'bout 'im. You'll year whar he went en how he come out. Dish yer col' snap rastles wid my bones, now," continued the old man, putting on his hat and picking up his walking-stick. "Hit rastles wid me monstus, en I gotter rack 'roun' en see if I kin run up agin some Chris'mus leavin's."

9
Miss Cow Falls a Victim to Mr. Rabbit

"UNCLE REMUS," said the little boy, "what became of the Rabbit after he fooled the Buzzard, and got out of the hollow tree?"

"Who? Brer Rabbit? Bless yo' soul, honey, Brer Rabbit went skippin' 'long home, he did, des ez sassy ez a jay-bird at a sparrer's nes'. He went gallopin' 'long, he did, but he feel mighty tired out, en stiff in his j'ints, en he wuz mighty nigh dead for sump'n' fer ter drink, en bimeby, w'en he got mos' home, he spied ole Miss Cow feedin' 'roun' in a fiel', he did, en he 'termin' fer ter try his han' wid 'er. Brer Rabbit know mighty well dat Miss Cow won't give 'im no milk, kaze she done 'fuse 'im mo'n once, en w'en his ole 'oman wuz sick, at dat. But never min' dat. Brer Rabbit sorter dance up 'long side er de fence, he did, en holler out:

"'Howdy, Sis Cow,' sez Brer Rabbit, sezee.

"'W'y howdy, Brer Rabbit,' sez Miss Cow, sez she.

"'How you fin' yo'se'f deze days, Sis Cow?' sez Brer Rabbit, sezee.

"'I'm sorter toler'ble, Brer Rabbit; how you come on?' sez Miss Cow, sez she.

"'Oh, I'm des toler'ble myse'f, Sis Cow; sorter linger'n' twix' a bauk en a break-down,' sez Brer Rabbit, sezee.

"'How yo' folks, Brer Rabbit?' sez Miss Cow, sez she.

"'Dey er des middlin', Sis Cow; how Brer Bull gittin' on?' sez Brer Rabbit, sezee.

"'Sorter so-so,' sez Miss Cow, sez she.

"'Dey er some mighty nice 'simmons up dis tree, Sis Cow,' sez Brer Rabbit, sezee, 'en I'd like mighty well fer ter have some un um,' sezee.

"'How you gwine ter git um, Brer Rabbit?' sez she.

"'I 'lowed maybe dat I mought ax you fer ter butt 'gin de tree, en shake some down, Sis Cow,' sez Brer Rabbit, sezee.

"Co'se Miss Cow don't wanter diskommerdate Brer Rabbit, en she march up ter de 'simmon tree, she did, en hit it a rap wid 'er horns — blam! Now, den," continued Uncle Remus, tearing off the corner of a plug of tobacco and cramming it into his mouth — "now, den, dem 'simmons wuz green ez grass, en na'er one never drap. Den Miss Cow butt de tree — blim! Na'er 'simmon drap. Den Miss Cow sorter back off little, en run agin de tree — blip! No 'simmons never drap. Den Miss Cow back off little fudder, she did, en hi'st her tail on 'er back, en come agin de tree, kerblam! en she come so fas', en she come so hard, twel one 'er her horns went spang thoo de tree, en dar she wuz. She can't go forerds, en she can't go backerds. Dis zackly w'at Brer Rabbit waitin' fer, en he no sooner seed ole Miss Cow all fas'en'd up dan he jump up, he did, en cut de pidjin-wing.

"'Come he'p me out, Brer Rabbit,' sez Miss Cow, sez she.

"'I can't clim', Sis Cow,' sez Brer Rabbit, sezee, 'but I'll run'n tell Brer Bull,' sezee; en wid dat Brer Rabbit put out fer home, en 'twa'n't long 'fo' here he come wid his ole 'oman en all his chilluns, en de las' one er de fambly wuz totin' a pail. De big uns had big pails, en de little uns had little pails. En dey all s'roundid ole Miss Cow, dey did, en you hear me, honey, dey milk't 'er dry. De ole uns milk't en de young uns milk't en den w'en dey done got nuff, Brer Rabbit, he up'n say, sezee:

"'I wish you mighty well, Sis Cow. I 'low'd bein's how dat you'd hatter sorter camp out all night dat I'd better come en swaje yo' bag,' sezee."

"Do which, Uncle Remus?" asked the little boy.

"Go 'long, honey! Swaje 'er bag. W'en cows don't git milk't, der bag swells, en you k'n hear um a moanin' en a beller'n des like dey wuz gittin' hurtid. Dat's w'at Brer Rabbit done. He 'sembled his fambly, he did, en he swaje ole Miss Cow's bag.

"Miss Cow, she stood dar, she did, en she study en study, en strive fer ter break loose, but de horn done bin jam in de tree so tight dat 'twuz way 'fo' day in de mawnin' 'fo' she loose it. Anyhow hit wuz endurin' er de night, en atter she git loose she sorter graze 'roun', she did, fer ter jestify 'er stummick she 'low'd, ole Miss Cow did, dat Brer Rabbit be hoppin' 'long dat way fer ter see how she gittin' on, en she tuck'n lay er trap fer 'im; en des 'bout sunrise w'at'd ole Miss Cow do but march up ter de 'simmon tree en stick er horn back in de hole? But, bless yo' soul, honey, w'ile she wuz croppin' de grass she tuck one mou'ful too menny, kaze w'en she hitch on ter de 'simmon tree agin, Brer Rabbit wuz settin' in de fence cornder a watchin' un 'er. Den Brer Rabbit he say ter hisse'f:

"'Heyo,' sezee, 'w'at dis yer gwine on now? Hol' yo' hosses, Sis Cow, twel you hear me comin',' sezee.

"En den he crope off down de fence, Brer Rabbit did, en bimeby here he come — lippity-clippity, clippity-lippity — des a sailin' down de big road.

"'Mawnin', Sis Cow,' sez Brer Rabbit, sezee, 'how you come on dis mornin'?' sezee.

"'Po'ly, Brer Rabbit, po'ly,' sez Miss Cow, sez she. 'I ain't had no res' all night,' sez she. 'I can't pull loose,' sez she, 'but ef you'll come en ketch holt er my tail, Brer Rabbit,' sez she, 'I reckin may be I kin fetch my horn out,' sez she. Den Brer Rabbit, he come up little closer, but he ain't gittin' too close.

"'I speck I'm nigh nuff, Sis Cow,' sez Brer Rabbit, sezee. 'I'm a mighty puny man, en I mought git trompled,' sezee. 'You do de pullin', Sis Cow,' sezee, 'en I'll do de gruntin',' sezee.

"Den Miss Cow, she pull out 'er horn, she did, en tuck atter Brer Rabbit, en down de big road dey had it. Brer Rabbit wid his years laid back, en Miss Cow wid 'er head down en 'er tail curl. Brer Rabbit kep' on gainin', en bimeby he dart in a brier-patch, en by de time Miss Cow come 'long he had his head stickin' out, en his eyes look big ez Miss Sally's chany sassers.

"'Heyo, Sis Cow! Whar you gwine?' sez Brer Rabbit, sezee.

"'Howdy, Brer Big-Eyes,' sez Miss Cow, sez she. 'Is you seed Brer Rabbit go by?'

"'He des dis minnit pass,' sez Brer Rabbit, sezee, 'en he look mighty sick,' sezee.

"En wid dat, Miss Cow tuck down de road like de dogs wuz atter 'er, en Brer Rabbit, he des lay down dar in de brier-patch en roll en laugh twel his sides hurtid 'im. He bleedzd ter laugh. Fox atter 'im. Buzzard atter 'im, en Cow atter 'im, en dey ain't cotch 'im yit."

10

Mr. Terrapin Appears upon the Scene

MISS SALLY'S little boy again occupying the anxious position of auditor, Uncle Remus took the shovel and "put de noses er de chunks tergedder," as he expressed it, and then began:

"One day, atter Sis Cow done run pas' 'er own shadder tryin' fer ter ketch 'im, Brer Rabbit tuck'n 'low dat he wuz gwine ter drap in en see Miss Meadows en de gals, en he got out his piece er lookin'-glass en primp up, he did, en sot out. Gwine canterin' 'long de road, who should Brer Rabbit run up wid but ole Brer Tarrypin — de same ole one-en-sixpunce. Brer Rabbit stop, he did, en rap on de roof er Brer Tarrypin house."

"On the roof of his house, Uncle Remus?" interrupted the little boy.

"Co'se honey, Brer Tarrypin kyar' his house wid 'im. Rain er shine, hot er col', strike up wid ole Brer Tarrypin w'en you will en w'ilst you may, en whar you fin' 'im, dar you'll fin' his shanty. Hit's des like I tell you. So den! Brer Rabbit he rap on de roof er Brer Tarrypin's house, he did, en ax wuz he in, en Brer Tarrypin 'low dat he wuz, en den Brer Rabbit, he ax 'im howdy, en den Brer Tarrypin he likewise 'spon' howdy, en den Brer Rabbit he say whar wuz Brer Tarrypin gwine, en Brer Tarrypin, he say w'ich he wern't gwine nowhar skacely. Den Brer Rabbit 'low he wuz on his way fer ter see Miss Meadows en de gals, en he ax Brer Tarrypin ef he won't jine in en go long, en Brer Tarrypin 'spon' he don't keer ef he do, en den dey sot out. Dey had plenty er time fer confabbin' 'long de way, but bimeby dey got dar, en Miss Meadows en de gals dey come ter de do', dey did, en ax um in, en in dey went.

"W'en dey got in, Brer Tarrypin wuz so flat-footed dat he wuz too low on de flo', en he wern't high nuff in a cheer, but while dey wuz all scramblin' 'roun' tryin' fer ter git Brer Tarrypin a cheer, Brer Rabbit, he pick 'im up en put 'im on de shelf whar de waterbucket sot, en ole Brer Tarrypin, he lay back up dar, he did, des es proud ez a nigger wid a cook 'possum.

"Co'se de talk fell on Brer Fox, en Miss Meadows en de gals make a great 'miration 'bout w'at a gaily ridin'-hoss Brer Fox wuz, en dey make lots er fun, en laugh en giggle same like gals duz deze days. Brer Rabbit, he sot dar in de cheer smokin' his seegyar, en he sorter cle'r up his th'oat, en say, sezee:

"'I'd er rid 'im over dis mawnin', ladies,' sezee 'but I rid 'im so hard yistiddy dat he went lame in de off fo' leg, en I speck I'll hatter swop 'im off yit,' sezee.

"Den Brer Tarrypin, he up'n say, sezee:

"'Well, ef you gwine ter sell 'im, Brer Rabbit,' sezee, 'sell him somers out'n dis neighborhood, kaze he done bin yer too long now,' sezee. 'No longer'n day 'fo' yistiddy,' sezee, 'Brer Fox pass me on de road, en whatter you reckin he say?' sezee:

"'Law, Brer Tarrypin,' sez Miss Meadows, sez she, 'you don't mean ter say he cusst?' sez she, en den de gals hilt der fans up 'fo' der faces.

"'Oh, no, ma'am,' sez Brer Tarrypin, sezee, 'he didn't cusst, but he holler out — "Heyo, Stinkin' Jim!"' sezee.

"'Oh, my! You hear dat, gals?' sez Miss Meadows, sez she; 'Brer Fox call Brer Tarrypin Stinkin' Jim,' sez she, en den Miss Meadows en de gals make great wonderment how Brer Fox kin talk dat away 'bout nice man like Brer Tarrypin.

"But bless gracious, honey! w'ilst all dis gwine on, Brer Fox wuz stannin' at de back do' wid one year at de cat-hole lissenin'. Eave-drappers don't hear no good er deyse'f, en de way Brer Fox wuz 'bused dat day wuz a caution.

"Bimeby Brer Fox stick his head in de do', en holler out:

"'Good evenin', folks, I wish you mighty well,' sezee, en wid dat he make a dash for Brer Rabbit, but Miss Meadows en de gals dey holler en squall, dey did, en Brer Tarrypin he got ter scramblin' 'roun' up dar on de shelf, en off he come, en blip he tuck Brer Fox on de back er de head. Dis sorter stunted Brer Fox, en w'en he gedder his 'membunce de mos' he seed wuz a pot er greens turnt over in de fierplace, en a broke cheer. Brer Rabbit wuz gone, en Brer Tarrypin wuz gone, en Miss Meadows en de gals wuz gone."

"Where did the Rabbit go, Uncle Remus?" the little boy asked, after a pause.

"Bless yo' soul, honey! Brer Rabbit he skint up de chimbley — dat's w'at turnt de pot er greens over. Brer Tarrypin, he crope under de bed, he did, en got behime de cloze-chist, en Miss Meadows en de gals, dey run out in de yard.

"Brer Fox, he sorter look roun' en feel er de back er his head, whar Brer Tarrypin lit, but he don't see no sine er Brer Rabbit. But de smoke en de ashes gwine up de chimbley got de best er Brer Rabbit, en bimeby he sneeze — *huckychow!*

"'Aha!' sez Brer Fox, sezee; 'you er dar, is you?' sezee. 'Well, I'm gwine ter smoke you out, ef it takes a mont'. You er mine dis time,' sezee. Brer Rabbit ain't sayin' nothin'.

"'Ain't you comin' down?' sez Brer Fox, sezee. Brer Rabbit ain't sayin' nothin'. Den Brer Fox, he went out atter some wood, he did, en w'en he come back he hear Brer Rabbit laughin'.

"'W'at you laughin' at, Brer Rabbit?' sez Brer Fox, sezee.

"'Can't tell you, Brer Fox,' sez Brer Rabbit, sezee.

"'Better tell, Brer Rabbit,' sez Brer Fox, sezee.

"''Tain't nothin' but a box er money somebody done gone en lef' up yer in de chink er de chimbley,' sez Brer Rabbit, sezee.

"'Don't b'lieve you,' sez Brer Fox, sezee.

"'Look up en see,' sez Brer Rabbit, sezee, en w'en Brer Fox look up, Brer Rabbit spit his eyes full er terbacker joose, he did, en Brer Fox, he make a break fer de branch, en Brer Rabbit he come down en tole de ladies good-by.

"'How you git 'im off, Brer Rabbit?' sez Miss Meadows, sez she.

"'Who? me?' sez Brer Rabbit, sezee; 'w'y I des tuck en tole 'im dat ef he didn't go 'long home en stop playin' his pranks on 'spectubble folks, dat I'd take 'im out and th'ash 'im,' sezee."

"And what became of the Terrapin?" asked the little boy.

"Oh, well den!" exclaimed the old man, "chilluns can't speck ter know all 'bout eve'ything 'fo' dey git some res'. Dem eyelids er yone wanter be propped wid straws dis minnit."

11
Mr. Wolf Makes a Failure

"I LAY YO' ma got company," said Uncle Remus, as the little boy entered the old man's door with a huge piece of mince-pie in his hand, "en ef she ain't got comp'ny, den she done gone en drap de cubberd key somers whar you done run up wid it."

"Well, I saw the pie lying there, Uncle Remus, and I just thought I'd fetch it out to you."

"Tooby sho, honey," replied the old man, regarding the child with admiration. "Tooby sho, honey; dat changes marters. Chris'mus doin's is outer date, en dey ain't got no bizness layin' roun' loose. Dish yer pie," Uncle Remus continued, holding it up and measuring it with an experienced eye, "will gimme strenk fer ter persoo on atter Brer Fox en Brer Rabbit en de udder creeturs w'at dey roped in 'long wid um."

Here the old man paused, and proceeded to demolish the pie — a feat accomplished in a very short time. Then he wiped the crumbs from his beard and began:

"Brer Fox feel so bad, en he git so mad 'bout Brer Rabbit, dat he dunner w'at ter do, en he look mighty down-hearted. Bimeby, one day w'iles he wuz gwine 'long de road, ole Brer Wolf come up wid 'im. W'en dey done howdyin' en axin' atter one nudder's fambly connexshun, Brer Wolf, he 'low, he did, dat der wuz sump'n' wrong wid Brer Fox, en Brer Fox, he 'low'd der wern't, en he went on en laugh en make great terdo kaze Brer Wolf look like he 'spishun sump'n'. But Brer Wolf, he got mighty long head, en he sorter broach 'bout Brer Rabbit's kyar'ns on, kaze de way dat Brer Rabbit 'ceive Brer Fox done got ter be de talk er de neighbors. Den Brer Fox en Brer Wolf dey sorter palavered on, dey did, twel bimeby Brer Wolf he up'n say dat he done got plan fix fer ter trap Brer Rabbit. Den Brer Fox say how. Den Brer Wolf up'n tell 'im dat de way fer ter git de drap on Brer Rabbit wuz ter git 'im in Brer Fox house. Brer Fox dun know Brer Rabbit uv ole, en he know dat sorter game done wo' ter a frazzle, but Brer Wolf, he talk mighty 'swadin'.

"'How you gwine git 'im dar?' sez Brer Fox, sezee.

"'Fool 'im dar,' sez Brer Wolf, sezee.

"'Who gwine do de foolin'?' sez Brer Fox, sezee.

"'I'll do de foolin',' sez Brer Wolf, sezee, 'ef you'll do de gamin',' sezee.

"'How you gwine do it?' sez Brer Fox, sezee.

"'You run 'long home, en git on de bed, en make like you dead, en don't you say nothin' twel Brer Rabbit come en put his han's onter you,' sez Brer Wolf, sezee, 'en ef we don't git 'im fer supper, Joe's dead en Sal's a widder,' sezee.

"Dis look like mighty nice game, en Brer Fox 'greed. So den he amble off home, en Brer Wolf, he march ter Brer Rabbit house. W'en he got dar, hit look like nobody home, but Brer Wolf he walk up en knock on de do' — blam! blam! Nobody come. Den he lam aloose en knock 'gin — blim! blim!

"'Who dar?' sez Brer Rabbit, sezee.

"'Fr'en',' sez Brer Wolf.

"'Too menny fr'en's spiles de dinner,' sez Brer Rabbit, sezee; 'w'ich un's dis?' sezee.

"'I fetch bad news, Brer Rabbit,' sez Brer Wolf, sezee.

"'Bad news is soon tole,' sez Brer Rabbit, sezee.

"By dis time Brer Rabbit done come ter de do', wid his head tied up in a red hankcher.

"'Brer Fox died dis mawnin',' sez Brer Wolf, sezee.

"'Whar yo' mo'nin' gown, Brer Wolf?' sez Brer Rabbit, sezee.

"'Gwine atter it now,' sez Brer Wolf, sezee. 'I des call by fer ter bring de news. I went down ter Brer Fox house little bit 'go, en dar I foun' 'im stiff,' sezee.

"Den Brer Wolf lope off. Brer Rabbit sot down en scratch his head, he did, en bimeby he say ter hisse'f dat he b'lieve he sorter drap 'roun' by Brer Fox house fer ter see how de lan' lay. No sooner said'n done. Up he jump, en out he went. W'en Brer Rabbit got close ter Brer Fox house, all look lonesome. Den he went up nigher. Nobody stirrin'. Den he look in, en dar lay Brer Fox stretch out on de bed des ez big ez life. Den Brer Rabbit make like he talkin' to hisse'f.

"'Nobody 'roun' fer ter look atter Brer Fox — not even Brer Tukkey Buzzard ain't come ter de funer'l,' sezee. 'I hope Brer Fox ain't dead, but I speck he is,' sezee. 'Even down ter Brer Wolf done gone en lef' 'im. Hit's de busy season wid me, but I'll set up wid 'im. He seem like he

dead, yit he mayn't be,' sez Brer Rabbit, sezee. 'W'en a man go ter see dead folks, dead folks allers raises up der behime leg en hollers, *wahoo!*' sezee.

"Brer Fox he stay still. Den Brer Rabbit he talk little louder:

"'Mighty funny. Brer Fox look like he dead, yit he don't do like he dead. Dead folks h'ists der behime leg en hollers *wahoo!* w'en a man come ter see um,' sez Brer Rabbit, sezee.

"Sho nuff, Brer Fox lif' up his foot en holler *wahoo!* en Brer Rabbit he tear out de house like de dogs wuz atter 'im. Brer Wolf mighty smart, but nex' time you hear fum 'im, honey, he'll be in trouble. You des hol' yo' breff'n wait."

12
Mr. Fox Tackles Old Man Tarrypin

"ONE DAY," said Uncle Remus, sharpening his knife on the palm of his hand — "one day Brer Fox strike up wid Brer Tarrypin right in de middle er de big road. Brer Tarrypin done heer'd 'im comin', en he 'low ter hisse'f dat he'd sorter keep one eye open; but Brer Fox wuz monstus perlite, en he open up de confab, he did, like he ain't see Brer Tarrypin sence de las' freshit.

"'Heyo, Brer Tarrypin, whar you bin dis long-come-short?' sez Brer Fox, sezee.

"'Lounjun 'roun', Brer Fox, lounjun 'roun',' sez Brer Tarrypin.

"'You don't look sprucy like you did, Brer Tarrypin,' sez Brer Fox, sezee.

"'Lounjun 'roun' en suffer'n',' sez Brer Tarrypin, sezee.

"Den de talk sorter run on like dis:

"'W'at ail you, Brer Tarrypin? Yo' eye look mighty red,' sez Brer Fox, sezee.

"'Lor', Brer Fox, you dunner w'at trouble is. You ain't bin lounjun 'roun' en suffer'n',' sez Brer Tarrypin, sezee.

"'Bofe eyes red, en you look like you mighty weak, Brer Tarrypin,' sez Brer Fox, sezee.

"'Lor', Brer Fox, you dunner w'at trouble is,' sez Brer Tarrypin, sezee.

"'W'at ail you now, Brer Tarrypin?' sez Brer Fox, sezee.

"'Tuck a walk de udder day, en man come 'long en sot de fiel' a-fier. Lor', Brer Fox, you dunner w'at trouble is,' sez Brer Tarrypin, sezee.

"'How you git out de fier, Brer Tarrypin?' sez Brer Fox, sezee.

"'Sot en tuck it, Brer Fox,' Brer Tarrypin, sezee. 'Sot en tuck it, en de smoke sif' in my eye, en de fier scorch my back,' sez Brer Tarrypin, sezee.

"'Likewise hit bu'n yo' tail off,' sez Brer Fox, sezee.

"'Oh, no, dar's de tail, Brer Fox,' sez Brer Tarrypin, sezee, en wid dat he oncurl his tail fum under de shell, en no sooner did he do dat dan Brer Fox grab it, en holler out:

"'Oh, yes, Brer Tarrypin! Oh, yes! En so you er de man w'at lam me on de head at Miss Meadows's is you? You er in wid Brer Rabbit, is you? Well, I'm gwine ter out you.'

"Brer Tarrypin beg en beg, but 'twa'n't no use. Brer Fox done been fool so much dat he look like he 'termin' fer ter have Brer Tarrypin haslett. Den Brer Tarrypin beg Brer Fox not fer ter drown 'im, but Brer Fox ain't makin' no prommus, en den he beg Brer Fox fer ter bu'n' 'im, kaze he done useter fier, but Brer Fox don't say nothin'. Bimeby Brer Fox drag Brer Tarrypin off little ways b'low de spring'ouse, en souze him under de water. Den Brer Tarrypin begin fer ter holler:

"'Tu'n loose dat stump root en ketch holt er me — tu'n loose dat stump root en ketch holt er me.'

"Brer Fox he holler back:

"'I ain't got holt er no stump root, en I is got holt er you.'

"Brer Tarrypin he keep on holler'n:

"'Ketch holt er me — I'm a drownin' — I'm a drownin' — tu'n loose de stump root en ketch holt er me.'

"Sho nuff, Brer Fox tu'n loose de tail, en Brer Tarrypin, he went down ter de bottom — kerblunkity-blink!"

No typographical combination or description could do justice to the guttural sonorousness — the peculiar intonation — which Uncle Remus imparted to this combination. It was so peculiar, indeed, that the little boy asked:

"How did he go to the bottom, Uncle Remus?"

"Kerblunkity-blink!"

"Was he drowned, Uncle Remus?"

"Who? Ole man Tarrypin? Is you drowndid w'en yo' ma tucks you in de bed?"

"Well, no," replied the little boy, dubiously.

"Ole man Tarrypin wuz at home I tell you, honey. Kerblinkity-blunk!"

13
The Awful Fate of Mr. Wolf

UNCLE REMUS was half-soling one of his shoes, and his Miss Sally's little boy had been handling his awls, his hammers, and his knives to such an extent that the old man was compelled to assume a threatening attitude; but peace reigned again, and the little boy perched himself on a chair, watching Uncle Remus driving in pegs.

"Folks w'at's allers pesterin' people, en bodderin' 'longer dat w'at ain't der'n, don't never come ter no good een'. Dar wuz Brer Wolf; stidder mindin' un his own bizness, he hatter take en go in pardnerships wid Brer Fox, en dey want skacely a minnit in de day dat he want atter Brer Rabbit, en he kep' on en kep' on twel fus' news you knowed he got cotch up wid — en he got cotch up wid monstus bad."

"Goodness, Uncle Remus! I thought the Wolf let the Rabbit alone, after he tried to fool him about the Fox being dead."

"Better lemme tell dish yer my way. Bimeby hit'll be yo' bed-time, en Miss Sally'll be a hollerin' atter you, en you'll be a whimplin' roun', en den Mars John'll fetch up de re'r wid dat ar strop w'at I made fer 'im."

The child laughed, and playfully shook his fist in the simple, serious face of the venerable old darkey, but said no more. Uncle Remus waited awhile to be sure there was to be no other demonstration, and then proceeded:

"Brer Rabbit ain't see no peace w'atsumever. He can't leave home 'cep' Brer Wolf 'ud make a raid en tote off some er de fambly. Brer Rabbit built 'im a straw house, en hit wuz tored down; den he made a house out'n pine-tops, en dat went de same way; den he made 'im a bark house, en dat wuz raided on, en eve'y time he los' a house he los' one er his chilluns. Las' Brer Rabbit got mad, he did, en cusst, en den he went off, he did, en got some kyarpinters, en dey built 'im a plank house wid rock foundashuns. Atter dat he could have some peace en quietness. He could go out en pass de time er day wid his neighbors, en come back en set by de fier, en smoke his pipe, en read de newspapers same like enny man w'at got a fambly. He made a hole, he did, in de cellar whar de little Rabbits could hide out w'en dar wuz much uv a racket in de neighborhood, en de latch er de front do' cotch on de inside. Brer Wolf, he see how de lan' lay, he did, en he lay low. De little Rabbits was mighty skittish, but hit got so dat col' chills ain't run up Brer Rabbit's back no mo' w'en he heerd Brer Wolf go gallopin' by.

"Bimeby, one day w'en Brer Rabbit wuz fixin' fer ter call on Miss Coon, he heerd a monstus fuss en clatter up de big road, en 'mos' 'fo' he could fix his years fer ter lissen, Brer Wolf run in de do'. De little Rabbits dey went inter der hole in de cellar, dey did, like blowin' out a cannle. Brer Wolf wuz far'ly kivver'd wid mud, en mighty nigh outer win'.

"'Oh, do pray save me, Brer Rabbit!' sez Brer Wolf, sezee. 'Do please, Brer Rabbit! de dogs is atter me, en dey'll t'ar me up. Don't you year um comin'? Oh, do please save me, Brer Rabbit! Hide me somers whar de dogs won't git me.'

"No quicker sed dan done.

"'Jump in dat chist dar, Brer Wolf,' sez Brer Rabbit, sezee, 'Jump in dar en make yo'se'f at home.'

"In jump Brer Wolf, down come the lid, en inter de hasp went de hook, en dar Mr. Wolf wuz. Den Brer Rabbit went ter de lookin'-glass, he did, en wink at hisse'f, en den he draw'd de rockin'-cheer in front er de fier, he did, en tuck a big chaw terbacker."

"Tobacco, Uncle Remus?" asked the little boy, incredulously.

"Rabbit terbacker, honey. You know dis yer life ev'lastin' w'at Miss Sally puts 'mong de cloze in de trunk; well, dat's rabbit terbacker. Den Brer Rabbit sot dar long time, he did, turnin' his min' over en wukken his thinkin' masheen. Bimeby he got up, en sorter stir 'roun'. Den Brer Wolf open up:

"'Is de dogs all gone, Brer Rabbit?'

"'Seem like I hear one un um smellin' roun' de chimbley-cornder des now.'

"Den Brer Rabbit git de kittle en fill it full er water, en put it on de fier.

"'W'at you doin' now, Brer Rabbit?'

"'I'm fixin fer ter make you a nice cup er tea, Brer Wolf.'

"Den Brer Rabbit went ter de cubberd en git de gimlet, en commence for ter bo' little holes in de chist-led.

"'W'at you doin' now, Brer Rabbit?'

"'I'm bo'in' little holes so you kin get breff, Brer Wolf.'

"Den Brer Rabbit went out en git some mo' wood, en fling it on de fier.

"'W'at you doin' now, Brer Rabbit?'

"'I'm a chunkin' up de fier so you won't git col', Brer Wolf.'

"Den Brer Rabbit went down inter de cellar en fotch out all his chilluns.

"'W'at you doin' now, Brer Rabbit?'

"'I'm a tellin' my chilluns w'at a nice man you is, Brer Wolf.'

"En de chilluns, dey had ter put der han's on der moufs fer ter keep fum laughin'. Den Brer Rabbit he got de kittle en commenced fer to po' de hot water on de chist-lid.

"'W'at dat I hear, Brer Rabbit?'

"'You hear de win' a blowin', Brer Wolf.'

"Den de water begin fer ter sif' thoo.

"'W'at dat I feel, Brer Rabbit?'

"'You feels de fleas a bitin', Brer Wolf.'

"'Dey er bitin' mighty hard, Brer Rabbit.'

"'Tu'n over on de udder side, Brer Wolf.'

"'W'at dat I feel now, Brer Rabbit?'

"'Still you feels de fleas, Brer Wolf.'

"'Dey er eatin' me up, Brer Rabbit,' en dem wuz de las' words er Brer Wolf, kaze de scaldin' water done de bizness.

"Den Brer Rabbit call in his neighbors, he did, en dey hilt a reg'lar juberlee; en ef you go ter Brer Rabbit's house right now, I dunno but w'at you'll fin' Brer Wolf's hide hangin' in de back-po'ch, en all bekaze he wuz so bizzy wid udder folks's doin's."

14
Mr. Fox and the Deceitful Frogs

WHEN THE LITTLE BOY ran in to see Uncle Remus the night after he had told him of the awful fate of Brer Wolf, the only response to his greeting was:

"I-doom-er-ker-kum-mer-ker!"

No explanation could convey an adequate idea of the intonation and pronunciation which Uncle Remus brought to bear upon this wonderful word. Those who can recall to mind the peculiar gurgling, jerking, liquid sound made by pouring water from a large jug, or the sound produced by throwing several stones in rapid succession into a pond of deep water, may be able to form a very faint idea of the sound, but it can not be reproduced in print. The little boy was astonished.

"What did you say, Uncle Remus?"

"I-doom-er-ker-kum-mer-ker! I-doom-er-ker-kum-mer-ker!"

"What is that?"

"Dat's Tarrypin talk, dat is. Bless yo' soul, honey," continued the old man, brightening up, "w'en you git ole ez me — w'en you see w'at I sees, en year w'at I years — de creeturs dat you can't talk wid'll be mighty skace — dey will dat. W'y, der's er ole gray rat w'at uses 'bout yer, en time atter time he comes out w'en you all done gone ter bed en sets up dar in de cornder en dozes, en me en him talks by de hour; en w'at dat ole rat dunno ain't down in de spellin' book. Des now, w'en you run in and broke me up, I wuz fetchin' into my min' w'at Brer Tarrypin say ter Brer Fox w'en he turn 'im loose in de branch."

"What did he say, Uncle Remus?"

"Dat w'at he said — I-doom-er-ker-kum-mer-ker! Brer Tarrypin wuz at de bottom er de pon', en he talk back, he did, in bubbles — I-doom-er-ker-kum-mer-ker! Brer Fox, he ain't sayin' nothin', but Brer Bull-Frog, settin' on de bank, he hear Brer Tarrypin, he did, en he holler back:

"'Jug-er-rum-kum-dum! Jug-er-rum-kum-dum!'

"Den n'er Frog holler out:

"'Knee-deep! Knee-deep!'

"Den ole Brer Bull-Frog, he holler back:

"'Don'-you-berlieve-'im! Don't-you-berlieve-'im!'"

"Den de bubbles come up fum Brer Tarrypin:

"'I-doom-er-ker-kum-mer-ker!'"

"Den n'er Frog sing out:

"'Wade in! Wade in!'"

"Den ole Brer Bull-Frog talk thoo his ho'seness:

"'Dar-you'll-fin'-yo'-brudder! Dar-you'll-fin'-yo'-brudder!'"

"Sho nuff, Brer Fox look over de bank, he did, en dar wuz n'er Fox lookin' at 'im outer de water. Den he retch out fer ter shake han's, en in he went, heels over head, en Brer Tarrypin bubble out:

"'I-doom-er-ker-kum-mer-ker!'"

"Was the Fox drowned, Uncle Remus?" asked the little boy.

"He wern't zackly drowndid, honey," replied the old man, with an air of cautious reserve. "He did manage fer ter scramble out, but a little mo' en de Mud Turkle would er got 'im, en den he'd er bin made hash un worl' widout een'.""

15

Mr. Fox Goes a-Hunting,
but Mr. Rabbit Bags the Game

"ATTER BRER FOX hear 'bout how Brer Rabbit done Brer Wolf," said Uncle Remus, scratching his head with the point of his awl, "he 'low, he did, dat he better not be so brash, en he sorter let Brer Rabbit 'lone. Dey wuz all time seein' one nudder, en 'bunnunce er times Brer Fox could er

nab Brer Rabbit, but eve'y time he got de chance, his min' 'ud sorter rezume 'bout Brer Wolf, en he let Brer Rabbit 'lone. Bimeby dey 'gun ter git kinder familious wid wunner nudder like dey useter, en it go so Brer Fox'd call on Brer Rabbit, en dey'd set up en smoke der pipes, dey would, like no ha'sh feelin's 'd ever rested 'twix' um.

"Las', one day Brer Fox come 'long all rig out, en ax Brer Rabbit fer ter go huntin' wid 'im, but Brer Rabbit, he sorter feel lazy, en he tell Brer Fox dat he got some udder fish fer ter fry. Brer Fox feel mighty sorry, he did, but he say he b'lieve he try his han' enny how, en off he put. He wuz gone all day, en he had a monstus streak er luck, Brer Fox did, en he

bagged a sight er game. Bimeby, to'rds de shank er de evenin', Brer Rabbit sorter stretch hisse'f, he did, en 'low hit's mos' time fer Brer Fox fer
ter git 'long home. Den Brer Rabbit, he went'n mounted a stump fer ter
see ef he could year Brer Fox comin'. He ain't bin dar long, twel sho nuff,
yer come Brer Fox thoo de woods, singing like a nigger at a frolic. Brer
Rabbit, he lipt down off'n de stump, he did, en lay down in de road en
make like he dead. Brer Fox he come 'long, he did, en see Brer Rabbit
layin' dar. He tu'n 'im over, he did, en 'zamine 'im, en say, sezee:

"'Dish yer rabbit dead. He look like he bin dead long time. He dead,
but he mighty fat. He de fattes' rabbit w'at I ever see, but he bin dead too
long. I feard ter take 'im home,' sezee.

"Brer Rabbit ain't sayin' nothin'. Brer Fox, he sorter lick his chops,
but he went on en lef' Brer Rabbit layin' in de road. Dreckly he wuz
outer sight, Brer Rabbit, he jump up, he did, en run 'roun' thoo de woods
en git befo' Brer Fox agin. Brer Fox, he come up, en dar lay Brer Rabbit,
periently col' en stiff. Brer Fox, he look at Brer Rabbit, en he sorter
study. Atter while he onslung his game-bag, en say ter hisse'f, sezee:

"'Deze yer rabbits gwine ter was'e. I'll des 'bout leave my game yer,
en I'll go back'n git dat udder rabbit, en I'll make folks b'lieve dat I'm
ole man Hunter fum Huntsville,' sezee.

"En wid dat he drapt his game en loped back up de road atter de udder rabbit, en w'en he got outer sight, ole Brer Rabbit, he snatch up Brer Fox game en put out fer home. Nex' time he see Brer Fox he holler out:

"'What you kill de udder day, Brer Fox?' sezee.

"Den Brer Fox, he sorter koam his flank wid his tongue, en holler back:

"'I cotch a han'ful er hard sense, Brer Rabbit,' sezee.

"Den ole Brer Rabbit, he laugh, he did, en up en 'spon', sezee:

"'Ef I'd a know'd you wuz atter dat, Brer Fox, I'd a loant you some er mine,' sezee."

16
Old Mr. Rabbit, He's a Good Fisherman

"BRER RABBIT en Brer Fox wuz like some chilluns w'at I knows un," said Uncle Remus, regarding the little boy, who had come to hear another story, with an affectation of great solemnity. "Bofe un um wuz allers atter wunner nudder, a prankin' en a pester'n 'roun', but Brer Rabbit did have some peace, kaze Brer Fox got skittish 'bout puttin' de clamps on Brer Rabbit.

"One day, w'en Brer Rabbit, en Brer Fox, en Brer Coon, en Brer B'ar, en a whole lot un um wuz clearin' up a new groun' fer ter plant a roas'n'-year patch, de sun 'gun ter git sorter hot, en Brer Rabbit he got tired; but he didn't let on, kaze he feard de balance un um'd call 'im lazy, en he keep on totin' off trash en pilin' up bresh, twel bimeby he holler out dat he gotter brier in his han', en den he take'n slip off, en hunt fer cool place fer ter res'. Atter w'ile he come 'crosst a well wid a bucket hangin' in it.

"'Dat look cool,' sez Brer Rabbit, sezee, 'en cool I speck she is. I'll des 'bout git in dar en take a nap,' en wid dat in he jump, he did, en he ain't no sooner fix hisse'f dan de bucket 'gun ter go down."

"Wasn't the Rabbit scared, Uncle Remus?" asked the boy.

"Honey, dey ain't been no wusser skeer'd beas' sence de worl' begin dan dish yer same Brer Rabbit. He fa'rly had a agur. He know whar he cum fum, but he dunner whar he gwine. Dreckly he feel de bucket hit de water, en dar she sot, but Brer Rabbit he keep mighty still, kaze he dunner w'at minnit gwine ter be de nex'. He des lay dar en shuck en shiver.

"Brer Fox allers got one eye on Brer Rabbit, en w'en he slip off fum de new groun', Brer Fox he sneak atter 'im. He know Brer Rabbit wuz atter some projick er nudder, en he tuck'n crope off, he did, en watch 'im. Brer Fox see Brer Rabbit come to de well en stop, en den he see 'im jump in de bucket, en den, lo en beholes, he see 'im go down outer sight. Brer Fox wuz de mos' 'stonish' Fox dat you ever laid eyes on. He sot off dar in de bushes en study en study, but he don't make no head ner tails ter dis kinder bizness. Den he say ter hisse'f, sezee:

"'Well, ef dis don't bang my times,' sezee, 'den Joe's dead en Sal's a widder. Right down dar in dat well Brer Rabbit keep his money hid, en ef 'tain't dat den he done gone en 'skiver'd a gol-mine, en ef 'tain't dat, den I'm a gwine ter see w'at's in dar,' sezee.

"Brer Fox crope up little nigher, he did, en lissen, but he don't year no fuss, en he keep on gittin' nigher, en yit he don't year nothin'. Bimeby he git up close en peep down, but he don't see nothin' en he don't year nothin'. All dis time Brer Rabbit mighty nigh skeer'd outen his skin, en he feard fer ter move kaze de bucket might keel over en spill him out in de water. W'ile he sayin' his pra'rs over like a train er kyars runnin', ole Brer Fox holler out:

"'Heyo, Brer Rabbit! Who you wizzitin' down dar?' sezee.

"'Who? Me? Oh, I'm des a fishin', Brer Fox,' sez Brer Rabbit, sezee. 'I des say ter myse'f dat I'd sorter sprize you all wid a mess er fishes fer dinner, en so here I is, en dar's de fishes. I'm a-fishin' fer suckers, Brer Fox,' sez Brer Rabbit, sezee.

"'Is dey many un um down dar, Brer Rabbit?' sez Brer Fox, sezee.

"'Lots un um, Brer Fox; scoze en scoze un um. De water is natchully 'live wid um. Come down en he'p me haul um in, Brer Fox,' sez Brer Rabbit, sezee.

"'How I gwine ter git down, Brer Rabbit?'

"'Jump inter de bucket, Brer Fox. Hit'll fetch you down all safe en soun'.'

"Brer Rabbit talk so happy en talk so sweet dat Brer Fox he jump in de bucket, he did, en, ez he went down, co'se his weight pull Brer Rabbit up. W'en dey pass one nudder on de half-way groun', Brer Rabbit he sing out:

"'Good-by, Brer Fox, take keer yo' cloze,
    Fer dis is de way de worl' goes;
    Some goes up en some goes down,
    You'll git ter de bottom all safe en soun'.'[1]

"W'en Brer Rabbit got out, he gallop off en tole de folks w'at de well b'long ter dat Brer Fox wuz down in dar muddyin' up de drinkin' water, en den he gallop back ter de well, en holler down ter Brer Fox:

"'Yer come a man wid a great big gun —
    W'en he haul you up, you jump en run.'"

"What then, Uncle Remus?" asked the little boy, as the old man paused.

"In des 'bout half 'n hour, honey, bofe un um wuz back in de new groun' wukkin des like dey never heer'd er no well, ceppin' dat eve'y now'n den Brer Rabbit'd bust out in er laugh, en ole Brer Fox, he'd git a spell er de dry grins."

[1] As a Northern friend suggests that this story may be somewhat obscure, it may be as well to state that the well is supposed to be supplied with a rope over a wheel, or pulley, with a bucket at each end. — J. C. H.

17
Mr. Rabbit Nibbles Up the Butter

"DE ANIMILS en de creeturs," said Uncle Remus, shaking his coffee around in the bottom of his tin cup, in order to gather up all the sugar, "dey kep' on gittin' mo' en mo' familious wid wunner nudder, twel bimeby, 'twa'n't long 'fo' Brer Rabbit, en Brer Fox, en Brer Possum got ter sorter bunchin' der perwishuns tergedder in de same shanty. After w'ile de roof sorter 'gun ter leak, en one day Brer Rabbit, en Brer Fox, en Brer Possum, 'semble fer ter see ef dey can't kinder patch her up. Dey had a big day's work in front un um, en dey fotch der dinner wid um. Dey lump de vittles up in one pile, en de butter w'at Brer Fox brung, dey goes en puts in de spring-'ouse fer ter keep cool, en den dey went ter wuk, en 'twa'n't long 'fo' Brer Rabbit stummick 'gun ter sorter growl en pester 'im. Dat butter er Brer Fox sot heavy on his min', en his mouf water eve'y time he 'member 'bout it. Present'y he say ter hisse'f dat he bleedzd ter have a nip at dat butter, en den he lay his plans, he did. Fus' news you know, w'ile dey wuz all wukkin' 'long, Brer Rabbit raise his head quick en fling his years forerd en holler out:

"'Here I is. W'at you want wid me?' en off he put like sump'n' wuz atter 'im.

"He sallied 'roun', ole Brer Rabbit did, en atter he make sho dat nobody ain't foller'n un 'im, inter de spring-'ouse he bounces, en dar he stays twel he git a bait er butter. Den he sa'nter on back en go to wuk.

"'Whar you bin?' sez Brer Fox, sezee.

"'I hear my chilluns callin' me,' sez Brer Rabbit, sezee, 'en I hatter go see w'at dey want. My ole 'oman done gone en tuck mighty sick,' sezee.

"Dey wuk on twel bimeby de butter tas'e so good dat ole Brer Rabbit want some mo'. Den he raise up his head, he did, en holler out:

"'Heyo! Hol' on! I'm a comin'!' en off he put.

"Dis time he stay right smart w'ile, en w'en he git back Brer Fox ax him whar he bin.

"'I been ter see my ole 'oman, en she's a sinkin',' sezee.

"Dreckly Brer Rabbit hear um callin' 'im agin en off he goes, en dis time, bless yo' soul, he gits de butter out so clean dat he kin see hisse'f in de bottom er de bucket. He scrape it clean en lick it dry, en den he go back ter wuk lookin' mo' samer dan a nigger w'at de patter-rollers bin had holt un.

"'How's yo' ole 'oman dis time?' sez Brer Fox, sezee.

"'I'm oblije ter you, Brer Fox,' sez Brer Rabbit, sezee, 'but I'm fear'd she's done gone by now,' en dat sorter make Brer Fox en Brer Possum feel in mo'nin' wid Brer Rabbit.

"Bimeby, w'en dinner-time come, dey all got out der vittles, but Brer Rabbit keep on lookin' lonesome, en Brer Fox en Brer Possum dey sorter rustle 'roun' fer ter see ef dey can't make Brer Rabbit feel sorter splimmy."

"What is that, Uncle Remus?" asked the little boy.

"Sorter splimmy-splammy, honey — sorter like he in a crowd — sorter like his ole 'oman ain't dead ez she mought be. You know how folks duz w'en dey gits whar people's a mo'nin'.'"

The little boy didn't know, fortunately for him, and Uncle Remus went on:

"Brer Fox en Brer Possum rustle 'roun', dey did, gittin out de vittles, en bimeby Brer Fox, he say, sezee:

"'Brer Possum, you run down ter de spring en fetch de butter, en I'll sail 'roun' yer en set de table,' sezee.

"Brer Possum, he lope off atter de butter, en dreckly here he come lopin' back wid his years a trimblin' en his tongue a hangin' out. 'Brer Fox,' he holler out.

"'W'at de matter now, Brer Possum?' sezee.

"'You all better run yer, folks,' sez Brer Possum, sezee. 'De las' drap er dat butter done gone!'

"'Whar she gone?' sez Brer Fox, sezee.

"'Look like she dry up,' sez Brer Possum, sezee.

"Den Brer Rabbit, he look sorter sollum, he did, en he up'n say, sezee:

"'I speck dat butter melt in somebody mouf,' sezee.

"Den dey went down ter de spring wid Brer Possum, en sho nuff de butter done gone. W'iles dey wuz sputin' over de wunderment, Brer Rabbit say he see tracks all 'roun' dar, en he p'int out dat ef dey'll all go ter sleep, he kin ketch de chap w'at stole de butter. Den dey all lie down en Brer Fox en Brer Possum dey soon drapt off ter sleep, but Brer Rabbit he stay 'wake, en w'en de time come he raise up easy en smear Brer Possum

mouf wid de butter on his paws, en den he run off en nibble up de bes' er
de dinner w'at dey lef' layin' out, en den he come back en wake up Brer Fox,
en show 'im de butter on Brer Possum mouf. Den dey wake up Brer Possum, en tell 'im 'bout it, but co'se Brer Possum 'ny it ter de las'. Brer Fox,
dough, he's a kinder lawyer, en he argafy dis way — dat Brer Possum wuz
de fus' one at de butter, en de fus' one fer ter miss it, en mo'n dat, dar hang
de signs on his mouf. Brer Possum see dat dey got 'im jammed up in a
cornder, en den he up en say dat de way fer ter ketch de man w'at stole de
butter is ter buil' a big bresh-heap en set her afier, en all han's try ter jump
over, en de one w'at fall in, den he de chap w'at stole de butter. Brer Rabbit en Brer Fox dey bofe 'gree dey did, en dey whirl in en buil' de bresh-
heap, en dey buil' her high en dey buil' her wide, en den dey totch her off.
W'en she got ter blazin' up good, Brer Rabbit, he tuck de fus' turn. He
sorter step back, en look 'roun' en giggle, en over he went mo' samer dan

a bird flyin'. Den come Brer Fox. He got back little fudder, en spit on his
han's, en lit out en made de jump, en he come so nigh gittin' in dat de een'
er his tail cotch afier. Ain't you never see no fox, honey?" inquired Uncle
Remus, in a tone that implied both conciliation and information.

The little boy thought probably he had, but he wouldn't commit himself.

"Well, den," continued the old man, "nex' time you see one un um,
you look right close en see ef de een' er his tail ain't w'ite. Hit's des like

I tell you. Dey b'ars de skyar er dat bresh-heap down ter dis day. Dey er marked — dat's w'at dey is — dey er marked."

"And what about Brother Possum?" asked the little boy.

"Ole Brer Possum, he tuck a runnin' start, he did, en he come lumberin' 'long, en he lit — kerblam! — right in de middle er de fier, en dat wuz de las' er ole Brer Possum."

"But, Uncle Remus, Brother Possum didn't steal the butter after all," said the little boy, who was not at all satisfied with such summary injustice.

"Dat w'at make I say w'at I duz, honey. In dis worl', lots er folks is gotter suffer fer udder folks sins. Look like hit's mighty onwrong; but hit's des dat away. Tribbalashun seem like she's a waitin' roun' de cornder fer ter ketch one en all un us, honey."

18
Mr. Rabbit Finds His Match at Last

"Hit look like ter me dat I let on de udder night dat in dem days w'en de creeturs wuz sa'nter'n 'roun' same like folks, none un um wuz brash nuff fer ter ketch up wid Brer Rabbit," remarked Uncle Remus, reflectively.

"Yes," replied the little boy, "that's what you said."

"Well, den," continued the old man with unction, "dar's whar my 'membunce gin out, kaze Brer Rabbit did git cotched up wid, en hit cool 'im off like po'in' spring water on one er deze yer biggity fices."

"How was that, Uncle Remus?" asked the little boy.

"One day w'en Brer Rabbit wuz gwine lippity-clippitin' down de road, he meet up wid ole Brer Tarrypin, en atter dey pass de time er day wid wunner nudder, Brer Rabbit, he 'low dat he wuz much 'blije ter Brer Tarrypin fer de han' he tuck in de rumpus dat day down at Miss Meadows's."

"When he dropped off of the water-shelf on the Fox's head," suggested the little boy.

"Dat's de same time, honey. Den Brer Tarrypin 'low dat Brer Fox run mighty fas' dat day, but dat ef he'd er bin atter 'im stidder Brer Rabbit, he'd er cotch 'im. Brer Rabbit say he could er cotch 'im hisse'f but he didn't keer 'bout leavin' de ladies. Dey keep on talkin', dey did, twel bimeby dey got ter 'sputin' 'bout w'ich wuz de swif'es'. Brer Rabbit, he say he kin outrun Brer Tarrypin, en Brer Tarrypin, he des vow dat he kin outrun Brer Rabbit. Up en down dey had it, twel fus' news you know Brer Tarrypin say he got a fifty-dollar bill in de chink er de chimbley at home, en dat bill done tole 'im dat he could beat Brer Rabbit in a fa'r race. Den Brer Rabbit say he got a fifty-dollar bill w'at say dat he kin leave Brer Tarrypin so fur behime, dat he could sow barley ez he went 'long en hit 'ud be ripe nuff fer ter cut by de time Brer Tarrypin pass dat way.

"Enny how dey make de bet en put up de money, en ole Brer Tukkey Buzzard, he wuz summonzd fer ter be de jedge, en de stakeholder; en 'twa'n't long 'fo' all de 'rangements wuz made. De race wuz a five-mile heat, en de groun' wuz medjud off, en at de een' er ev'ey mile a pos' wuz stuck up. Brer Rabbit wuz ter run down de big road, en Brer Tarrypin, he say he'd gallup thoo de woods. Folks tole 'im he could git long faster in de road, but ole Brer Tarrypin, he know w'at he doin'. Miss Meadows en de gals en mos' all de neighbors got win' er de fun, en w'en de day wuz sot dey 'termin' fer ter be on han'. Brer Rabbit he train hisse'f ev'ey day, en he skip over de groun' des ez gaily ez a June cricket. Ole Brer Tarrypin, he lay low in de swamp. He had a wife en th'ee chilluns, old Brer Tarrypin did, en dey wuz all de ve'y spit en image er de ole man. Ennybody w'at know one fum de udder gotter take a spyglass, en den dey er li'ble fer ter git fooled.

"Dat's de way marters stan' twel de day er de race, en on dat day, ole Brer Tarrypin, en his ole 'oman, en his th'ee chilluns, dey got up 'fo' sunup, en went ter de place. De ole 'oman, she tuck 'er stan' nigh de fus' mile-pos', she did, en de chilluns nigh de udders, up ter de las', en dar old Brer Tarrypin, he tuck his stan'. Bimeby, here come de folks: Jedge Buzzard, he come, en Miss Meadows en de gals, dey come, en den yer come Brer Rabbit wid ribbons tied 'roun' his neck en streamin' fum his years. De folks all went ter de udder een' er de track fer ter see how dey come out. W'en de time come Jedge Buzzard strut 'roun' en pull out his watch, en holler out:

"'Gents, is you ready?'

"Brer Rabbit, he say 'yes,' en old Miss Tarrypin holler 'go' fum de aidge er de woods. Brer Rabbit, he lit out on de race, en ole Miss Tarrypin, she put out for home. Jedge Buzzard, he riz en skimmed 'long fer ter see dat de race wuz runned fa'r.

W'en Brer Rabbit got ter de fus' mile-pos' wunner de Tarrypin chilluns crawl out de woods, he did, en make fer de place. Brer Rabbit, he holler out:

"'Whar is you, Brer Tarrypin?'

"'Yer I come a bulgin',' sez de Tarrypin, sezee.

"Brer Rabbit so glad he's ahead dat he put out harder dan ever, en de Tarrypin, he make fer home. W'en he come ter de nex' pos', nudder Tarrypin crawl out er de woods.

"'Whar is you, Brer Tarrypin?' sez Brer Rabbit, sezee.

"'Yer I come a bilin',' sez de Tarrypin, sezee.

"Brer Rabbit, he lit out, he did, en come ter nex' pos', en dar wuz de Tarrypin. Den he come ter nex', en dar wuz de Tarrypin. Den he had one mo' mile fer ter run, en he feel like he gittin' bellust. Bimeby, ole Brer Tarrypin look way off down de road en he see Jedge Buzzard sailin' 'long en he know hit's time fer 'im fer ter be up. So he scramble outen de woods, en roll 'cross de ditch, en shuffle thoo de crowd er folks en git ter de mile-pos' en crawl behime it. Bimeby, fus' news you know, yer come Brer Rabbit. He look 'roun' en he don't see Brer Tarrypin, en den he squall out:

"'Gimme de money, Brer Buzzard, Gimme de money!'

"Den Miss Meadows en de gals, dey holler and laugh fit ter kill dey-se'f, en ole Brer Tarrypin, he raise up fum behime de pos' en sez, sezee:

"'Ef you'll gimme time fer ter ketch my breff, gents en ladies, one en all, I speck I'll finger dat money myse'f,' sezee, en sho nuff, Brer Tarrypin tie de pu's 'roun' his neck en skaddle off home."

"But, Uncle Remus," said the little boy, dolefully, "that was cheating."

"Co'se, honey. De creeturs 'gun ter cheat, en den folks tuck it up, en hit keep on spreadin'. Hit mighty ketchin', en you min' yo' eye, honey, dat somebody don't cheat you 'fo' yo' ha'r git gray ez de ole nigger's."

19
The Fate of Mr. Jack Sparrow

"You'll tromple on dat bark twel hit won't be fitten fer ter fling 'way, let 'lone make hoss-collars out'n," said Uncle Remus, as the little boy came running into his cabin out of the rain. All over the floor long strips of "wahoo" bark were spread, and these the old man was weaving into horse-collars.

"I'll sit down, Uncle Remus," said the little boy.

"Well, den, you better, honey," responded the old man, "kaze I 'spizes fer ter have my wahoo trompled on. Ef 'twuz shucks, now, hit mought be diffunt, but I'm a gittin' too ole fer ter be projickin' longer shuck collars."

For a few minutes the old man went on with his work, but with a solemn air altogether unusual. Once or twice he sighed deeply, and the sighs ended in a prolonged groan, that seemed to the little boy to be the result of the most unspeakable mental agony. He knew by experience that he had done something which failed to meet the approval of Uncle Remus, and he tried to remember what it was, so as to frame an excuse; but his memory failed him. He could think of nothing he had done calculated to stir Uncle Remus's grief. He was not exactly seized with remorse, but he was very uneasy. Presently Uncle Remus looked at him in a sad and hopeless way, and asked:

"W'at dat long rigmarole you bin tellin' Miss Sally 'bout yo' little brer dis mawnin?"

"Which, Uncle Remus?" asked the little boy, blushing guiltily.

"Dat des w'at I'm axin' un you now. I hear Miss Sally say she's a gwine ter stripe his jacket, en den I knowed you bin tellin' on 'im."

"Well, Uncle Remus, he was pulling up your onions, and then he went and flung a rock at me," said the child plaintively.

"Lemme tell you dis," said the old man, laying down the section of horse-collar he had been plaiting, and looking hard at the little boy — "lemme tell you dis — der ain't no way fer ter make tattlers en tale-b'ar-ers turn out good. No, dey ain't. I bin mixin' up wid folks now gwine on eighty year, en I ain't seed no tattler come ter no good een'. Dat I ain't. En ef ole man M'thoozlum wuz livin' clean twel yit, he'd up'n tell you de same. Sho ez you er settin' dar. You 'member w'at 'come er de bird w'at went tattlin' 'roun' 'bout Brer Rabbit?"

The little boy didn't remember, but he was very anxious to know, and he also wanted to know what kind of a bird it was that so disgraced itself.

"Hit wuz wunner dese yer uppity little Jack Sparrers, I speck," said the old man; "dey wuz allers bodder'n' longer udder folks's bizness, en dey keeps at it down ter dis day — peckin' yer, en pickin' dar, en scratchin' out yander. One day, atter he bin fool by ole Brer Tarrypin, Brer Rabbit wuz settin' down in de woods studyin' how he wuz gwine ter git even. He feel mighty lonesome, en he feel mighty mad, Brer Rabbit did. 'Tain't put down in de tale, but I speck he cusst en r'ar'd 'roun' considerbul. Leas'ways, he wuz settin' out dar by hisse'f, en dar he sot, en study en study, twel bimeby he jump up en holler out:

"'Well, dog-gone my cats ef I can't gallop 'roun' ole Brer Fox, en I'm gwine ter do it. I'll show Miss Meadows en de gals dat I'm de boss er Brer Fox,' sezee.

"Jack Sparrer up in de tree, he hear Brer Rabbit, he did, en he sing out:

"'I'm gwine tell Brer Fox! I'm gwine tell Brer Fox! Chick-a-biddy-win'-a-blowin'-acuns-fallin'! I'm gwine tell Brer Fox!'"

Uncle Remus accompanied the speech of the bird with a peculiar whistling sound in his throat, that was a marvelous imitation of a sparrow's chirp, and the little boy clapped his hands with delight, and insisted on a repetition.

"Dis kinder tarrify Brer Rabbit, en he skacely know w'at he gwine do; but bimeby he study ter hisse'f dat de man w'at see Brer Fox fus' wuz boun' ter have de inturn, en den he go hoppin' off to'rds home. He didn't go fur w'en who should he meet but Brer Fox, en den Brer Rabbit, he open up:

"'W'at dis twix' you en me, Brer Fox?' sez Brer Rabbit, sezee. 'I hear tell you gwine ter sen' me ter 'struckshun, en nab my fambly, en 'stroy my shanty,' sezee.

"Den Brer Fox he git mighty mad.

"'Who bin tellin' you all dis?' sezee.

"Brer Rabbit make like he didn't want ter tell, but Brer Fox he 'sist en 'sist, twel at las' Brer Rabbit he up en tell Brer Fox dat he hear Jack Sparrer say all dis.

"'Co'se,' sez Brer Rabbit, sezee, 'w'en Brer Jack Sparrer tell me dat I flew up, I did, en I use some langwidge w'ich I'm mighty glad dey weren't no ladies 'roun' nowhars so dey could hear me go on,' sezee.

"Brer Fox he sorter gap, he did, en say he speck he better be sa'nter'n on. But, bless yo' soul, honey, Brer Fox ain't sa'nter fur, 'fo' Jack Sparrer flipp down on a 'simmon-bush by de side er de road, en holler out:

"'Brer Fox! Oh, Brer Fox! — Brer Fox!'

"Brer Fox he des sorter canter 'long, he did, en make like he don't hear 'im. Den Jack Sparrer up'n sing out agin:

"'Brer Fox! Oh, Brer Fox! Hol' on, Brer Fox! I got some news fer you. Wait Brer Fox! Hit'll 'stonish you.'

"Brer Fox he make like he don't see Jack Sparrer, ner needer do he hear 'im, but bimeby he lay down by de road, en sorter stretch hisse'f like he fixin' fer ter nap. De tattlin' Jack Sparrer he flew'd 'long, en keep on callin' Brer Fox, but Brer Fox, he ain't sayin' nothin'. Den little Jack Sparrer, he hop down on de groun' en flutter 'roun' 'mongst de trash. Dis sorter 'track Brer Fox 'tenshun, en he look at de tattlin' bird, en de bird he keep on callin':

"'I got sump'n' fer ter tell you, Brer Fox.'

"'Git on my tail, little Jack Sparrer,' sez Brer Fox, sezee, 'kaze I'm deaf in one year, en I can't hear out'n de udder. Git on my tail,' sezee.

"Den de little bird he up'n hop on Brer Fox's tail.

"'Git on my back, little Jack Sparrer, kaze I'm deaf in one year en I can't hear out'n de udder.'

"Den de little bird hop on his back.

"'Hop on my head, little Jack Sparrer, kaze I'm deaf in bofe years.'

"Up hop de little bird.

"'Hop on my toof, little Jack Sparrer, kaze I'm deaf in one year en I can't hear out'n de udder.'

"De tattlin' little bird hop on Brer Fox's toof, en den — "

Here Uncle Remus paused, opened wide his mouth and closed it again in a way that told the whole story.[1]

"Did the Fox eat the bird all — all — up?" asked the little boy.

"Jedge B'ar come 'long nex' day," replied Uncle Remus, "en he fin' some fedders, en fum dat word went roun' dat ole man Squinch Owl done cotch nudder whatsisname."

20
How Mr. Rabbit Saved His Meat

"ONE TIME," said Uncle Remus, whetting his knife slowly and thoughtfully on the palm of his hand, and gazing reflectively in the fire — "one time Brer Wolf — "

---

[1] An Atlanta friend heard this story in Florida, but an alligator was substituted for the fox, and a little boy for the rabbit. There is another version in which the impertinent gosling goes to tell the fox something her mother has said, and is caught; and there may be other versions. I have adhered to the middle Georgia version, which is characteristic enough. It may be well to state that there are different versions of all the stories — the shrewd narrators of the mythology of the old plantation adapting themselves with ready tact to the years, tastes, and expectations of their juvenile audiences. — J. C. H.

"Why, Uncle Remus!" the little boy broke in, "I thought you said the Rabbit scalded the Wolf to death a long time ago."

The old man was fairly caught and he knew it; but this made little difference to him. A frown gathered on his usually serene brow as he turned his gaze upon the child — a frown in which both scorn and indignation were visible. Then all at once he seemed to regain control of himself. The frown was chased away by a look of Christian resignation.

"Dar now! W'at I tell you?" he exclaimed as if addressing a witness concealed under the bed. "Ain't I done tole you so? Bless gracious! ef chilluns ain't gittin' so dey knows mo'n ole folks, en dey'll 'spute longer you en 'spute longer you, ceppin' der ma call um, w'ich I speck 'twon't be long 'fo' she will, en den I'll set yere by de chimbley-cornder en git some peace er min'. W'en ole Miss wuz livin'," continued the old man, still addressing some imaginary person, "hit 'uz mo'n enny her chilluns 'ud dast ter do ter come 'sputin' longer me, en Mars John"ll tell you de same enny day you ax 'im."

"Well, Uncle Remus, you know you said the Rabbit poured hot water on the Wolf and killed him," said the little boy.

The old man pretended not to hear. He was engaged in searching among some scraps of leather under his chair, and kept on talking to the imaginary person. Finally, he found and drew forth a nicely plaited whip-thong with a red snapper all waxed and knotted.

"I wuz fixin' up a whip fer a little chap," he continued, with a sigh, "but, bless gracious! 'fo' I kin git 'er done, de little chap done grow'd up twel he know mo'n I duz."

The child's eyes filled with tears and his lips began to quiver, but he said nothing; whereupon Uncle Remus immediately melted.

"I 'clar' to goodness," he said, reaching out and taking the little boy tenderly by the hand, "ef you ain't de ve'y spit en image er ole Miss w'en I brung 'er de las' news er de war. Hit's des like skeerin' up a ghos' w'at you ain't feard un."

Then there was a pause, the old man patting the little child's hand caressingly.

"You ain't mad, is you, honey?" Uncle Remus asked finally, "kaze ef you is, I'm gwine out yere en butt my head 'gin de do' jam'."

But the little boy wasn't mad. Uncle Remus had conquered him and he had conquered Uncle Remus in pretty much the same way before. But it was some time before Uncle Remus would go on with the story. He had to be coaxed. At last, however, he settled himself back in the chair and began:

"Co'se, honey, hit mought er bin ole Brer Wolf, er hit mought er bin er n'er Brer Wolf; it mought er bin 'fo' he got cotch up wid, er it mought er bin atterwards. Ez de tale wuz gun to me des dat away I gin it unter you. One time Brer Wolf wuz comin' 'long home fum a fishin' frolic. He sa'nter 'long de road, he did, wid his string er fish 'cross his shoulder, w'en fus' news you know ole Miss Pa'tridge, she hop outer de bushes en flutter 'long right at Brer Wolf nose. Brer Wolf he say ter hisse'f dat ole Miss Pa'tridge tryin' fer ter toll 'im 'way fum her nes', en wid dat he lay his fish down en put out inter de bushes whar ole Miss Pa'tridge come fum, en 'bout dat time Brer Rabbit, he happen 'long. Dar wuz de fishes, en dar wuz Brer Rabbit, en w'en dat de case w'at you speck a sorter innerpen'ent man like Brer Rabbit gwine do? I kin tell you dis, dat dem fishes ain't stay what Brer Wolf put um at, en w'en Brer Wolf come back dey wuz gone.

"Brer Wolf, he sot down en scratch his head, he did, en study en study, en den hit sorter rush inter his min' dat Brer Rabbit bin 'long dar, en den Brer Wolf, he put out fer Brer Rabbit house, en w'en he git dar he hail 'im. Brer Rabbit, he dunno nothin' tall 'bout no fishes. Brer Wolf he up'n say he bleedzd ter b'lieve Brer Rabbit got dem fishes. Brer Rabbit 'ny it up en down, but Brer Wolf stan' to it dat Brer Rabbit got dem fishes. Brer Rabbit, he say dat if Brer Wolf b'lieve he got de fishes, den he give Brer Wolf lief fer ter kill de bes' cow he got. Brer Wolf, he tuck Brer Rabbit at his word, en go off ter de pastur' en drive up de cattle en kill Brer Rabbit bes' cow.

"Brer Rabbit, he hate mighty bad fer ter lose his cow, but he lay his plans, en he tell his chilluns dat he gwine ter have dat beef yit. Brer Wolf, he bin tuck up by de patter-rollers 'fo' now, en he mighty skeer'd un um, en fus' news you know, yer come Brer Rabbit hollerin' en tellin' Brer Wolf dat de patter-rollers comin'.

"'You run en hide, Brer Wolf,' sez Brer Rabbit, sezee, 'en I'll stay yer en take keer er de cow twel you gits back,' sezee.

"Soon's Brer Wolf hear talk er de patter-rollers, he scramble off inter de underbrush like he bin shot out'n a gun. En he wa'n't mo'n gone 'fo' Brer Rabbit, he whirl in en skunt de cow en salt de hide down, en den he

tuck'n cut up de kyarkiss en stow it 'way in de smoke-'ouse, en den he tuck'n stick de een' er de cow-tail in de groun'. Atter he gone en done all dis, den Brer Rabbit he squall out fer Brer Wolf:

"'Run yer, Brer Wolf! Run yer! yo' cow gwine in de groun'! Run yer!'

"W'en ole Brer Wolf got dar, w'ich he come er scootin', dar wuz Brer Rabbit hol'in' on ter de cow-tail, fer ter keep it fum gwine in de groun'. Brer Wolf, he cotch holt, en dey 'gin a pull er two en up come de tail. Den Brer Rabbit, he wink his off eye en say, sezee:

"'Dar! de tail done pull out en de cow gone,' sezee.

"But Brer Wolf he wern't de man fer ter give it up dat away, en he got 'im a spade, en a pick-axe, en a shovel, en he dig en dig fer dat cow twel diggin' wuz pas' all endu'unce, en ole Brer Rabbit he sot up dar in his front po'ch en smoke his seegyar. Eve'y time ole Brer Wolf stuck de pick-axe in de clay, Brer Rabbit, he giggle ter his chilluns:

"'He diggy, diggy, diggy, but no meat dar! He diggy, diggy, diggy, but no meat dar!'

"Kaze all de time de cow wuz layin' pile up in his smoke-'ouse, en him en his chilluns wuz eatin' fried beef an inguns eve'y time dey mouf water.

"Now den, honey, you take dis yer whip," continued the old man, twining the leather thong around the little boy's neck, "en scamper up ter

de big 'ouse en tell Miss Sally fer ter gin you some un it de nex' time she
fin' yo' tracks in de sugar bar'l."

21
Mr. Rabbit Meets His Match Again

"DERE WUZ nudder man dat sorter play it sharp on Brer Rabbit," said
Uncle Remus, as, by some mysterious process, he twisted a hog's bristle
into the end of a piece of thread — an operation which the little boy
watched with great interest. "In dem days," continued the old man, "de
creeturs kyar'd on marters same ez folks. Dey went inter fahmin', en I
speck ef de troof wuz ter come out, dey kep' sto', en had der camp-
meetin' times en der bobbycues w'en de wedder wuz 'gree'ble."

Uncle Remus evidently thought that the little boy wouldn't like to
hear of any further discomfiture of Brer Rabbit, who had come to be a
sort of hero, and he was not mistaken.

"I thought the Terrapin was the only one that fooled the Rabbit," said
the little boy, dismally.

"Hit's des like I tell you, honey. Dey ain't no smart man, 'cep' w'at
dey's a smarter. Ef ole Brer Rabbit hadn't er got cotch up wid, de neighbors 'ud er took 'im for a ha'nt, en in dem times dey bu'nt witches 'fo' you
could squinch yo' eye-balls. Dey did dat."

"Who fooled the Rabbit this time?" the little boy asked.

When Uncle Remus had the bristle "sot" in the thread, he proceeded
with the story.

"One time Brer Rabbit en ole Brer Buzzard 'cluded dey'd sorter go
snacks, en crap tergedder. Hit wuz a mighty good year, en de truck tu'n
out monstus well, but bimeby, w'en de time come fer dividjun, hit come
ter light dat ole Brer Buzzard ain't got nothin'. De crap wuz all gone, en
dey wa'n't nothin' dar fer ter show fer it. Brer Rabbit, he make like he in
a wuss fix'n Brer Buzzard, en he mope 'roun', he did, like he feard dey
gwine ter sell 'im out.

"Brer Buzzard, he ain't sayin' nothin', but he keep up a monstus
thinkin', en one day he come 'long en holler en tell Brer Rabbit dat he
done fin' rich gol'-mine des 'cross de river.

"'You come en go 'longer me, Brer Rabbit,' sez Brer Tukkey Buzzard, sezee. 'I'll scratch en you kin grabble, en 'tween de two un us we'll make short wuk er dat gol'-mine,' sezee.

"Brer Rabbit, he wuz high up fer de job, but he study en study, he did, how he gwine ter git 'cross de water, kaze ev'y time he git his foot wet all de fambly cotch col'. Den he up'n ax Brer Buzzard how he gwine do, en Brer Buzzard he up'n say dat he kyar Brer Rabbit 'cross, en wid dat ole Brer Buzzard, he squot down, he did, en spread his wings, en Brer Rabbit, he mounted, en up dey riz." There was a pause.

"What did the Buzzard do then?" asked the little boy.

"Dey riz," continued Uncle Remus, "en w'en dey lit, dey lit in de top er de highest sorter pine, en de pine w'at dey lit in wuz growin' on er ilun, en de ilun wuz in de middle er de river, wid de deep water runnin' all 'roun'. Dey ain't mo'n lit 'fo' Brer Rabbit, he know w'ich way de win' 'uz blowin', en by de time ole Brer Buzzard got hisse'f balance on a lim', Brer Rabbit, he up'n say, sezee:

"'W'iles we er res'n here, Brer Buzzard, en bein's you bin so good, I got sump'n' fer ter tell you,' sezee. 'I got a gol'-mine er my own, one w'at I make myse'f, en I speck we better go back ter mine 'fo' we bodder 'longer yone,' sezee.

"Den ole Brer Buzzard, he laugh, he did, twel he shake, en Brer Rabbit, he sing out:

"'Hol' on, Brer Buzzard! Don't flop yo' wings w'en you laugh, kaze

den if you duz, sump'n' 'ill drap fum up yer, en my gol'-mine don't do you
no good, en needer will yone do me no good.'

"But 'fo' dey got down fum dar, Brer Rabbit done tole all 'bout de crap,
en he hatter prommus fer ter 'vide fa'r en squar. So Brer Buzzard, he kyar
'im back, en Brer Rabbit he walk weak in de knees a mont' atterwuds."

22
A Story About the Little Rabbits

"FIN' UM whar you will en w'en you may," remarked Uncle Remus with
emphasis, "good chilluns allers gits tuck keer on. Dar wuz Brer Rabbit's
chilluns; dey minded der daddy en mammy fum day's een' ter day's een'.
W'en ole man Rabbit say 'scoot,' dey scooted, en w'en ole Miss Rabbit
say 'scat,' dey scatted. Dey did dat. En dey kep' der cloze clean, en dey
ain't had no smut on der nose nudder."

Involuntarily the hand of the little boy went up to his face, and he
scrubbed the end of his nose with his coat-sleeve.

"Dey wuz good chilluns," continued the old man, heartily, 'en ef dey
hadn't er bin, der wuz one time w'en dey wouldn't er bin no little Rabbits — na'er one. Dat's w'at."

"What time was that, Uncle Remus?" the little boy asked.

"De time w'en Brer Fox drapt in at Brer Rabbit house, en didn't foun'
nobody dar ceppin' de little Rabbits. Ole Brer Rabbit, he wuz off somers
raiding on a collard patch, en ole Miss Rabbit she wuz tendin' on a
quiltin' in de neighborhood, en w'iles de little Rabbits wuz playin'
hidin'-switch, in drapt Brer Fox. De little Rabbits wuz so fat dey fa'rly
make his mouf water, but he 'member 'bout Brer Wolf, en he skeer'd fer
ter gobble um up ceppin' he got some skuse. De little Rabbits, dey
mighty skittish, en dey sorter huddle deyse'f up tergedder en watch Brer
Fox motions. Brer Fox, he sot dar en study w'at sorter skuse he gwine ter
make up. Bimeby he see a great big stalk er sugar-cane stan'in' up in de
cornder, en he cle'r up his th'oat en talk biggity:

"'Yer! you young Rabs dar, sail 'roun' yer en broke me a piece er dat
sweetnin'-tree,' sezee, en den he cough.

"De little Rabbits, dey got out de sugar-cane, dey did, en dey rastle wid it, en sweat over it, but 'twa'n't no use. Dey couldn't broke it. Brer Fox, he make like he ain't watchin', but he keep on holler'n':

"'Hurry up dar, Rabs! I'm a waitin' on you.'

"En de little Rabbits, dey hustle 'roun' en rastle wid it, but they couldn't broke it. Bimeby dey hear little bird singin' on top er de house, en de song w'at de little bird sing wuz dish yer:

> "'Take yo' toofies en gnyaw it,
> Take yo' toofies en saw it,
> Saw it en yoke it,
> En den you kin broke it.'

"Den de little Rabbits, dey git mighty glad, en dey gnyawed de cane mos' 'fo' ole Brer Fox could git his legs oncrosst, en w'en dey kyard 'im de cane, Brer Fox, he sot dar en study how he gwine ter make some mo' skuse fer nabbin' un um, en bimeby he git up en git down de sifter w'at wuz hangin' on de wall, en holler out:

"'Come yer, Rabs! Take dish yer sifter, en run down't de spring en fetch me some fresh water.'

"De little Rabbits, dey run down't de spring, en try ter dip up de water wid de sifter, but co'se hit all run out, en hit keep on runnin' out, twel bimeby de little Rabbits sot down en 'gun ter cry. Den de little bird settin' up in de tree he begin fer ter sing, en dish yer's de song w'at he sing:

" 'Sifter hol' water same ez a tray,
   Ef you fill it wid moss en dob it wid clay;
   De Fox git madder de longer you stay —
   Fill it wid moss en dob it wid clay.'

"Up dey jump, de little Rabbits did, en dey fix de sifter so 'twon't leak, en den dey kyar' de water ter ole Brer Fox. Den Brer Fox he git mighty mad, en p'int out a great big stick er wood, en tell de little Rabbits fer ter put dat on de fier. De little chaps dey got 'roun' de wood, dey did, en dey lif' at it so hard twel dey could see der own sins, but de wood ain't budge. Den dey hear de little bird singin', en dish yer's de song w'at he sing:

" 'Spit in yo' han's en tug it en toll it,
   En git behime it, en push it, en pole it;
   Spit in yo' han's en r'ar back en roll it.'

"En des 'bout de time dey got de wood on de fier, der daddy, he come skippin' in, en de little bird, he flew'd away. Brer Fox, he seed his game wuz up, en 'twa'n't long 'fo' he make his skuse en start fer ter go.

" 'You better stay en take a snack wid me, Brer Fox,' sez Brer Rabbit, sezee. 'Sence Brer Wolf done quit comin' en settin' up wid me, I gittin' so I feels right lonesome dese long nights,' sezee.

"But Brer Fox, he button up his coat-collar tight en des put out fer home. En dat w'at you better do, honey, kaze I see Miss Sally's shadder sailin' backerds en forerds 'fo' de winder, en de fus' news you know she'll be 'spectin' un you."

Mr. Rabbit and Mr. Bear

"DAR WUZ one season," said Uncle Remus, pulling thoughtfully at his whiskers, "w'en Brer Fox say to hisse'f dat he speck he better whirl in en plant a goober-patch, en in dem days, mon, hit wuz tech en go. De wud weren't mo'n out'n his mouf 'fo' de groun' 'uz brok'd up en de goobers 'uz planted. Ole Brer Rabbit, he sot off en watch de motions, he did, en he sorter shet one eye en sing to his chilluns:

> "'Ti-yi! Tungalee!
> I eat um pea, I pick um pea.
> Hit grow in de groun', hit grow so free;
> Ti-yi! dem goober pea.'

"Sho nuff w'en de goobers 'gun ter ripen up, eve'y time Brer Fox go down ter his patch, he fin' whar somebody bin grabblin' 'mongst de vines, en he git mighty mad. He sorter speck who de somebody is, but ole Brer Rabbit he cover his tracks so cute dat Brer Fox dunner how ter ketch 'im. Bimeby, one day Brer Fox take a walk all 'roun' de groun'-pea patch, en 'twa'n't long 'fo' he fin' a crack in de fence whar de rail done bin rub right smoove, en right dar he sot 'im a trap. He tuck'n ben' down a hick'ry saplin', growin' in de fence-cornder, en tie one een' un a plow-line on de top, en in de udder een' he fix a loop-knot, en dat he fasten wid a trigger right in de crack. Nex' mawnin' w'en ole Brer Rabbit come slippin' 'long en crope thoo de crack, de loop-knot cotch 'im behime de fo'legs, en de saplin' flew'd up, en dar he wuz 'twix' de heavens en de yeth. Dar he swung, en he fear'd he gwine ter fall, en he fear'd he weren't gwine ter fall. W'ile he wuz a fixin' up a tale fer Brer Fox, he hear a lumberin' down de road, en present'y yer cum ole Brer B'ar amblin' 'long fum whar he bin takin' a bee-tree. Brer Rabbit, he hail 'im:

"'Howdy, Brer B'ar!'

"Brer B'ar, he look 'roun' en bimeby he see Brer Rabbit swingin' fum de saplin', en he holler out:

"'Heyo, Brer Rabbit! How you come on dis mawnin'?'

"'Much oblije, I'm middlin', Brer B'ar,' sez Brer Rabbit, sezee.

"Den Brer B'ar, he ax Brer Rabbit w'at he doin' up dar in de elements, en Brer Rabbit, he up'n say he makin' dollar minnit. Brer B'ar, he say how. Brer Rabbit say he keepin' crows out'n Brer Fox's groun'-pea patch, en den he ax Brer B'ar ef he don't wanter make dollar minnit, kaze he got big fambly er chilluns fer to take keer un, en den he make sech nice skeercrow. Brer B'ar 'low dat he take de job, en den Brer Rabbit show 'im how ter ben' down de saplin', en 'twa'n't long 'fo' Brer B'ar wuz swingin' up dar in Brer Rabbit place. Den Brer Rabbit, he put out fer Brer Fox house, en w'en he got dar he sing out:

"'Brer Fox! Oh, Brer Fox! Come out yer, Brer Fox, en I'll show you de man w'at bin stealin' yo' goobers.'

"Brer Fox, he grab up his walkin'-stick, en bofe un um went runnin' back down ter der goober-patch, en w'en dey got dar, sho nuff, dar wuz ole Brer B'ar.

"'Oh, yes! you er cotch, is you?' sez Brer Fox, en 'fo' Brer B'ar could 'splain, Brer Rabbit he jump up en down, en holler out:

"'Hit 'im in de mouf, Brer Fox; hit 'im on de mouf;' en Brer Fox, he draw back wid de walkin'-cane, en blip he tuck 'im, en eve'y time Brer B'ar'd try ter 'splain, Brer Fox'd shower down on him.

"W'iles all dis 'uz gwine on, Brer Rabbit, he slip off en git in a mud-

hole en des lef' his eyes stickin' out, kaze he know'd dat Brer B'ar'd be a comin' atter 'im. Sho nuff, bimeby here come Brer B'ar down de road, en w'en he git ter de mud-hole, he say:

"'Howdy, Brer Frog; is you seed Brer Rabbit go by yer?'

"'He des gone by,' sez Brer Rabbit, en ole man B'ar tuck off down de road like a skeer'd mule, en Brer Rabbit, he come out en dry hisse'f in de sun, en go home ter his fambly same ez enny udder man."

"The Bear didn't catch the Rabbit, then?" inquired the little boy, sleepily.

"Jump up fum dar, honey!" exclaimed Uncle Remus, by way of reply. "I ain't got no time fer ter be settin' yer proppin' yo' eyelids open."

24
Mr. Bear Catches Old Mr. Bull-Frog

"WELL, UNCLE REMUS," said the little boy, counting to see if he hadn't lost a marble somewhere, "the Bear didn't catch the Rabbit after all, did he?"

"Now you talkin', honey," replied the old man, his earnest face breaking up into little eddies of smiles — "now you talkin' sho. 'Tain't bin proned inter no Brer B'ar fer ter cotch Brer Rabbit. Hit sorter like settin' a mule fer ter trap a hummin'bird. But Brer B'ar, he tuck'n got hisse'f inter some mo' trouble, w'ich it look like it mighty easy. Ef folks could make der livin' longer gittin' inter trouble," continued the old man, looking curiously at the little boy, "ole Miss Favers wouldn't be bodder'n yo' ma fer ter borry a cup full er sugar eve'y now en den; en it look like ter me dat I knows a nigger dat wouldn't be squattin' 'roun' yer makin' dese yer fish-baskits."

"How did the Bear get into more trouble, Uncle Remus?" asked the little boy.

"Natchul, honey. Brer B'ar, he tuck a notion dat ole Brer Bull-frog wuz de man w'at fool 'im en he say dat he'd come up wid 'im ef 'twuz a year atterwuds. But 'twa'n't no year, an 'twa'n't no mont', en mo'n dat, hit wa'n't skacely a week, w'en bimeby one day Brer B'ar wuz gwine home fum de takin' un a bee-tree, en lo en beholes, who should he see but ole Brer Bull-frog settin' out on de aidge er de mud-muddle fas' 'sleep! Brer B'ar drap his axe, he did, en crope up, en retch out wid his paw, en scoop ole Brer Bull-frog in des dis away." Here the old man used his hand ladle-fashion, by way of illustration. "He scoop 'im in, en dar he wuz. W'en Brer B'ar got his clampers on 'im good, he sot down en talk at 'im.

"'Howdy, Brer Bull-frog, howdy! En how yo' fambly? I hope dey er well, Brer Bull-frog, kaze dis day you got some bizness wid me w'at'll las' you a mighty long time.'

"Brer Bull-frog, he dunner w'at ter say. He dunner w'at's up, en he don't say nothin'. Ole Brer B'ar he keep runnin' on:

"'You er de man w'at tuck en fool me 'bout Brer Rabbit t'er day. You had yo' fun, Brer Bull-frog, en now I'll git mine.'

"Den Brer Bull-frog, he gin ter git skeer'd, he did, en he up'n say:

"'W'at I bin doin', Brer B'ar? How I bin foolin' you?'"

"Den Brer B'ar laugh, en make like he dunno, but he keep on talkin'.

"'Oh, no, Brer Bull-frog! You ain't de man w'at stick yo' head up out'n de water en tell me Brer Rabbit done gone on by. Oh, no! you ain't de man. I boun' you ain't. 'Bout dat time, you wuz at home with yo' fambly, whar you allers is. I dunner whar you wuz, but I knows whar you is, Brer Bull-frog, en hit's you en me fer it. Atter de sun goes down dis day you don't fool no mo' folks gwine 'long dis road.'

"Co'se, Brer Bull-frog dunner w'at Brer B'ar drivin' at, but he know sump'n' hatter be done, en dat mighty soon, kaze Brer B'ar 'gun to snap his jaws tergedder en foam at de mouf, en Brer Bull-frog holler out:

"'Oh, pray, Brer B'ar! Lemme off dis time, en I won't never do so no mo'. Oh, pray, Brer B'ar! do lemme off dis time, en I'll show you de fattes' bee-tree in de woods.'

"Ole Brer B'ar, he chomp his toofies en foam at de mouf. Brer Bull-frog he des up'n squall:

"'Oh, pray, Brer B'ar! I won't never do so no mo'! Oh, pray, Brer B'ar! Lemme off dis time!'

"But ole Brer B'ar say he gwine ter make way wid 'im, en den he sot en study, ole Brer B'ar did, how he gwine ter squench Brer Bull-frog. He know he can't drown 'im, en he ain't got no fier fer ter bu'n 'im, en he git

mighty pester'd. Bimeby ole Brer Bull-frog, he sorter stop his cryin' en
his boo-hooin', en he up'n say:

"'Ef you gwine ter kill me, Brer B'ar, kyar' me ter dat big flat rock out
dar on de aidge er de mill-pon', whar I kin see my fambly, en atter I see
um, den you kin take you axe en sqush me.'

"Dis look so fa'r and squar' dat Brer B'ar he 'gree, en he take ole Brer
Bull-frog by wunner his behime legs, en sling his axe on his shoulder, en
off he put fer de big flat rock. When he git dar he lay Brer Bull-frog down
on de rock, en Brer Bull-frog make like he lookin' 'roun' fer his folks.
Den Brer B'ar, he draw long breff en pick up his axe. Den he spit in his
han's en draw back en come down on de rock — pow!"

"Did he kill the Frog, Uncle Remus?" asked the little boy, as the old
man paused to scoop up a thimbleful of glowing embers in his pipe.

"'Deed, en dat he didn't, honey. 'Twix' de time w'en Brer B'ar raise
up wid his axe en w'en he come down wid it, ole Brer Bull-frog he lipt up

en dove down in de mill-pon', kerblink-kerblunk! En w'en he riz way out
in de pon' he riz a singin', en dish yer's de song w'at he sing:

"'Ingle-go-jang, my joy, my joy —
          Ingle-go-jang, my joy!
     I'm right at home, my joy, my joy —
          Ingle-go-jang, my joy!'"

"That's a mighty funny song," said the little boy.

"Funny now, I speck," said the old man, "but 'tweren't funny in dem
days, en 'twouldn't be funny now ef folks know'd much 'bout de Bull-frog
langwidge ez dey useter. Dat's what."

25
How Mr. Rabbit Lost His Fine Bushy Tail

"ONE TIME," said Uncle Remus, sighing heavily and settling himself back in his seat with an air of melancholy resignation — "one time Brer Rabbit wuz gwine 'long down de road shakin' his big bushy tail, en feelin' des ez scrumpshus ez a bee-martin wid a fresh bug." Here the old man paused and glanced at the little boy, but it was evident that the youngster had become so accustomed to the marvelous developments of Uncle Remus's stories, that the extraordinary statement made no unusual impression upon him. Therefore the old man began again, and this time in a louder and more insinuating tone:

"One time ole man Rabbit, he wuz gwine 'long down de road shakin' his long, bushy tail, en feelin' mighty biggity."

This was effective.

"Great goodness, Uncle Remus!" exclaimed the little boy in open-eyed wonder, "everybody knows that rabbits haven't got long, bushy tails."

The old man shifted his position in his chair and allowed his venerable head to drop forward until his whole appearance was suggestive of the deepest dejection; and this was intensified by a groan that seemed to be the result of great mental agony. Finally he spoke, but not as addressing himself to the little boy.

"I notices dat dem folks w'at makes a great 'miration 'bout w'at dey knows is de folks w'ich you can't put no 'pennunce in w'en de 'cashun come up. Yer one un um now, en he done come en excuse me er 'lowin dat rabbits is got long bushy tails, w'ich goodness knows ef I'd a dremp' it, I'd a whirl in en ondremp it."

"Well, but Uncle Remus, you said rabbits had long, bushy tails," replied the little boy. "Now you know you did."

"Ef I ain't fergit it off'n my min', I say dat ole Brer Rabbit wuz gwine down de big road shakin' his long, bushy tail. Dat w'at I say, en dat I stan's by."

The little boy looked puzzled, but he didn't say anything. After a while the old man continued:

"Now, den, ef dat's 'greed ter, I'm gwine on, en ef 'tain't 'greed ter,

den I'm gwine ter pick up my cane en look atter my own intrust. I got wuk lyin' 'roun' yer dat's des natchully gittin' moldy."

The little boy remained quiet, and Uncle Remus proceeded:

"One day Brer Rabbit wuz gwine down de road shakin' his long, bushy tail, w'en who should he strike up wid but ole Brer Fox gwine amblin' long wid a big string er fish! W'en dey pass de time er day wid wunner nudder, Brer Rabbit, he open up de confab, he did, en he ax Brer Fox whar he git dat nice string er fish, en Brer Fox, he up'n 'spon' dat he catch um, en Brer Rabbit, he say whar'bouts, en Brer Fox, he say down at de babtizin' creek, en Brer Rabbit he ax how, kaze in dem days dey wuz monstus fon' er minners, en Brer Fox, he sot down on a log, he did, en he up'n tell Brer Rabbit dat all he gotter do fer ter git er big mess er minners is ter go ter de creek atter sundown, en drap his tail in de water en set dar twel day-light, en den draw up a whole armful er fishes, en dem w'at he don't want, he kin fling back. Right dar's whar Brer Rabbit drap his watermillion, kaze he tuck'n sot out dat night en went a fishin'. De wedder wuz sorter col', en Brer Rabbit, he got 'im a bottle er dram en put out fer de creek, en w'en he git dar he pick out a good place, en he sorter squat down, he did, en let his tail hang in de water. He sot dar, en he sot dar, en he drunk his dram, en he think he gwine ter freeze, but bimeby day come, en dar he wuz. He make a pull, en he feel like he comin' in two, en he fetch nudder jerk, en lo en beholes, whar wuz his tail?"

There was a long pause.

"Did it come off, Uncle Remus?" asked the little boy, presently.

"She did dat!" replied the old man with unction. "She did dat, and dat w'at make all deze yer bob-tail rabbits w'at you see hoppin' en skaddlin' thoo de woods."

"Are they all that way just because the old Rabbit lost his tail in the creek?" asked the little boy.

"Dat's it, honey," replied the old man. "Dat's w'at dey tells me. Look like dey er bleedzd ter take atter der pa."

26
Mr. Terrapin Shows His Strength

"BRER TARRYPIN wuz de out'nes' man," said Uncle Remus, rubbing his hands together contemplatively, and chuckling to himself in a very significant manner; "he wuz de out'nes' man er de whole gang. He wuz dat."

The little boy sat perfectly quiet, betraying no impatience when Uncle Remus paused to hunt, first in one pocket and then in another, for enough crumbs of tobacco to replenish his pipe. Presently the old man proceeded:

"One night Miss Meadows en de gals dey gun a candy-pullin', en so many er de neighbors come in 'sponse ter de invite dat dey hatter put de 'lasses in de wash pot en buil' de fier in de yard. Brer B'ar, he holp Miss Meadows bring de wood, Brer Fox, he men' de fier, Brer Wolf, he kep' de dogs off, Brer Rabbit, he grease de bottom er de plates fer ter keep de candy fum stickin', en Brer Tarrypin, he klum up in a cheer, en say he'd watch en see dat de 'lasses didn't bile over. Dey wuz all dere, en dey weren't cuttin' up no didoes, nudder, kaze Miss Meadows, she done put her foot down, she did, en say dat w'en dey come ter her place dey hatter hang up a flag er truce at de front gate en 'bide by it.

"Well, den, w'iles dey wuz all a settin' dar en de 'lasses wuz a bilin' en a blubberin', dey got ter runnin' on talkin' mighty biggity. Brer Rabbit, he say he de swiffes'; but Brer Tarrypin, he rock 'long in de cheer en watch de 'lasses. Brer Fox, he say he de sharpes', but Brer Tarrypin he rock 'long. Brer Wolf, he say he de mos' suvvigus, but Brer Tarrypin, he rock en he rock 'long. Brer B'ar, he say he de mos' stronges', but Brer Tarrypin he rock, en he keep on rockin'. Bimeby he sorter shet one eye, en say, sezee:

"'Hit look like 'periently dat de ole hardshell ain't nowhars 'longside er dis crowd, yit yer I is, en I'm de same man w'at show Brer Rabbit dat he ain't de swiffes'; en I'm de same man w'at kin show Brer B'ar dat he ain't de stronges',' sezee.

"Den dey all laugh en holler, kaze it look like Brer B'ar mo' stronger dan a steer. Bimeby, Miss Meadows, she up'n ax, she did, how he gwine do it.

"'Gimme a good strong rope,' sez Brer Tarrypin, sezee, 'en lemme git in er puddle er water, en den let Brer B'ar see ef he kin pull me out,' sezee.

"Den dey all laugh 'gin, en Brer B'ar, he ups en sez, sezee: 'We ain't got no rope,' sezee.

"'No,' sez Brer Tarrypin, sezee, 'en needer is you got de strenk,' sezee, en den Brer Tarrypin, he rock en rock 'long, en watch de 'lasses a bilin' en a blubberin'.

"Atter w'ile Miss Meadows, she up en say, she did, dat she'd take'n loan de young men her bed-cord, en w'iles de candy wuz a coolin' in de plates, dey could all go ter de branch en see Brer Tarrypin kyar out his projick. Brer Tarrypin," continued Uncle Remus, in a tone at once confidential and argumentative, "weren't much bigger'n de pa'm er my han', en it look mighty funny fer ter year 'im braggin' 'bout how he kin outpull Brer B'ar. But dey got de bed-cord atter w'ile, en den dey all put out ter de branch. W'en Brer Tarrypin fin' de place he wanter, he tuck one een' er de bed-cord, en gun de yuther een' to Brer B'ar.

"'Now den, ladies en gents,' sez Brer Tarrypin, sezee, 'you all go wid Brer B'ar up dar in de woods en I'll stay yer, en w'en you year me holler, den's de time fer Brer B'ar fer ter see ef he kin haul in de slack er de rope. You all take keer er dat ar een',' sezee, 'en I'll take keer er dish yer een',' sezee.

"Den dey all put out en lef' Brer Tarrypin at de branch, en w'en dey got good en gone, he dove down inter de water, he did, en tie de bed-cord hard en fas' ter wunner deze yer big clay-roots, en den he riz up en gin a whoop.

"Brer B'ar he wrop de bed-cord roun' his han', en wink at de gals, en wid dat he gin a big juk, but Brer Tarrypin ain't budge. Den he take bof han's en gin a big pull, but, all de same, Brer Tarrypin ain't budge. Den he tu'n 'roun', he did, en put de rope cross his shoulders en try ter walk off wid Brer Tarrypin, but Brer Tarrypin look like he don't feel like walkin'. Den Brer Wolf he put in en hope Brer B'ar pull, but des like he didn't, en den dey all hope 'im, en, bless gracious! w'iles dey wuz all a pullin', Brer Tarrypin, he holler, en ax um w'y dey don't take up de slack. Den w'en Brer Tarrypin feel um quit pullin', he dove down, he did, en ontie de rope, en by de time dey got ter de branch, Brer Tarrypin, he wuz settin' in de aidge er de water des ez natchul ez de nex' un, en he up'n say, sezee:

"'Dat las' pull er yone wuz a mighty stiff un, en a leetle mo'n you'd er had me,' sezee. 'You er monstus stout, Brer B'ar,' sezee, 'en you pulls like a yoke er steers, but I sorter had de purchis on you,' sezee.

"Den Brer B'ar, bein's his mouf 'gun ter water atter de sweet'nin', he up'n say he speck de candy's ripe, en off dey put atter it!"

"It's a wonder," said the little boy, after a while, "that the rope didn't break."

"Break who?" exclaimed Uncle Remus, with a touch of indignation in his tone — "break who? In dem days, Miss Meadows's bed-cord would a hilt a mule."

This put an end to whatever doubts the child might have entertained.

27
Why Mr. Possum Has No Hair on His Tail

"HIT LOOK LIKE ter me," said Uncle Remus, frowning, as the little boy came hopping and skipping into the old man's cabin, "dat I see a young un 'bout yo' size playin' en makin' free wid dem ar chilluns er ole Miss Favers's yistiddy, en w'en I seed dat, I drap my axe, en I come in yer en sot flat down right whar you er settin' now, en I say ter myse'f dat it's 'bout time fer ole Remus fer ter hang up en quit. Dat's des zackly what I say."

"Well, Uncle Remus, they called me," said the little boy, in a penitent tone. "They come and called me, and said they had a pistol and some powder over there."

"Dar now!" exclaimed the old man, indignantly. "Dar now! w'at I bin sayin'? Hit's des a born blessin' dat you wa'n't brung home on a litter wid bofe eye-balls hangin' out en one year clean gone; dat's w'at 'tis. Hit's des a born blessin'. Hit hope me up might'ly de udder day w'en I haer Miss Sally layin' down de law 'bout you en dem Favers chillun, yit, lo en beholes, de fus' news I knows yer you is han'-in-glove wid um. Hit's nuff fer ter fetch ole Miss right up out'n dat berryin'-groun' fum down dar in Putmon County, en w'at yo' gran'ma wouldn't er stood me en yo' ma ain't gwine ter stan' nudder, en de nex' time I hear 'bout sech a come-off ez dis, right den en dar I'm boun' ter lay de case 'fo' Miss Sally. Dem

Favers's wa'n't no 'count 'fo' de war, en dey wa'n't no 'count endurin' er de war, en dey ain't no 'count atterwards 'en w'iles my head's hot you ain't gwine ter go mixin' up yo'se'f wid de riff-raff er creashun."

The little boy made no further attempt to justify his conduct. He was a very wise little boy, and he knew that, in Uncle Remus's eyes, he had been guilty of a flagrant violation of the family code. Therefore, instead of attempting to justify himself, he pleaded guilty, and promised that he would never do so any more. After this there was a long period of silence, broken only by the vigorous style in which Uncle Remus puffed away at his pipe. This was the invariable result. Whenever the old man had occasion to reprimand the little boy — and the occasions were frequent — he would relapse into a dignified but stubborn silence. Presently the youngster drew forth from his pocket a long piece of candle. The sharp eyes of the old man saw it at once.

"Don't you come a tellin' me dat Miss Sally gun you dat," he exclaimed, "kaze she didn't. En I lay you hatter be monstus sly 'fo' you gotter chance fer ter snatch up dat piece er cannle."

"Well, Uncle Remus," the little boy explained, "it was lying there all by itself, and I just thought I'd fetch it out to you."

"Dat's so, honey," said Uncle Remus, greatly mollified; "dat's so, kaze by now some er dem yuther niggers 'ud done had her lit up. Dey er mighty biggity, dem house niggers is, but I notices dat dey don't let nothin' pass. Dey goes 'long wid der han's en der mouf open, en w'at one don't ketch de tother one do."

There was another pause, and finally the little boy said:

"Uncle Remus, you know you promised to-day to tell me why the 'Possum has no hair on his tail."

"Law, honey! ain't you done gone en fergot dat off'n yo' min' yit? Hit look like ter me," continued the old man, leisurely refilling his pipe, "dat she sorter run like dis: One time ole Brer Possum, he git so hungry, he did, dat he bleedzd fer ter have a mess er 'simmons. He monstus lazy man, ole Brer Possum wuz, but bimeby his stummick 'gun ter growl en holler at 'im so dat he des hatter rack 'roun' en hunt up sump'n'; en w'iles he wuz rackin' 'roun', who sh'd he run up wid but Brer Rabbit, en dey wuz hail-fellers, kaze Brer Possum, he ain't bin bodder'n Brer Rabbit like dem yuther creeturs. Dey sot down by de side er de big road, en dar

dey jabber en confab 'mong wunner nudder, twel bimeby old Brer Possum, he take 'n tell Brer Rabbit dat he mos' pe'sh out, en Brer Rabbit, he
lip up in de a'r, he did, en smack his han's tergedder, en say dat he know
right whar Brer Possum kin git a bait er 'simmons. Den Brer Possum, he
say whar, en Brer Rabbit, he say which 'twuz over at Brer B'ar's 'simmon
orchard."

"Did the Bear have a 'simmon orchard, Uncle Remus?" the little boy
asked.

"Co'se, honey, kaze in dem days Brer B'ar wuz a bee-hunter. He make
his livin' findin' bee trees, en de way he fin' um he plant 'im some 'sim-
mon-trees, w'ich de bees dey'd come ter suck de 'simmons en den ole
Brer B'ar he'd watch um whar dey'd go, en den he'd be mighty ap' fer ter
come up wid um. No matter 'bout dat, de 'simmon patch 'uz dar des like
I tell you, en ole Brer Possum mouf 'gun ter water soon's he year talk un
um, en mos' 'fo' Brer Rabbit done tellin' 'im de news, Brer Possum, he
put out, he did, en 'twa'n't long 'fo' he wuz perch up in de highes' tree in
Brer B'ar 'simmon patch. But Brer Rabbit, he done 'termin' fer ter see
some fun, en w'iles all dis 'uz gwine on, he run 'roun' ter Brer B'ar house,
en holler en tell 'im w'ich dey wuz somebody 'stroyin' un his 'simmons,
en Brer B'ar, he hustle off ter ketch 'im.

"Eve'y now en den Brer Possum think he year Brer B'ar comin', but
he keep on sayin', sezee:

"'I'll des git one 'simmon mo' en den I'll go; one 'simmon mo' en den
I'll go.'

"Las' he year Brer B'ar comin' sho nuff, but 'twuz de same ole chune —
'One 'simmon mo' en den I'll go' — en des 'bout dat time Brer B'ar busted
inter de patch, en gin de tree a shake, en Brer Possum, he drapt out
longer de yuther ripe 'simmons, but time he totch de groun' he got his
foots tergedder, en he lit out fer de fence same ez a race-hoss, en 'cross
dat patch him en Brer B'ar had it, en Brer B'ar gain' eve'y jump, twel
time Brer Possum make de fence Brer B'ar grab 'im by de tail, en Brer
Possum, he went out 'tween de rails en gin a powerful juk en pull his tail
out 'twix Brer B'ar tushes; en, lo en beholes, Brer B'ar hol' so tight en
Brer Possum pull so hard dat all de ha'r come off in Brer B'ar's mouf,
w'ich, ef Brer Rabbit hadn't er happen up wid a go'd er water, Brer B'ar
'der got strankle.

"Fum dat day ter dis," said Uncle Remus, knocking the ashes carefully out of his pipe, "Brer Possum ain't had no ha'r on his tail, en needer do his chilluns."

28

The End of Mr. Bear

THE NEXT TIME the little boy sought Uncle Remus out, he found the old man unusually cheerful and good-humored. His rheumatism had ceased to trouble him, and he was even disposed to be boisterous. He was singing when the little boy got near the cabin, and the child paused on the outside to listen to the vigorous but mellow voice of the old man, as it rose and fell with the burden of the curiously plaintive song — a senseless affair so far as the words were concerned, but sung to a melody almost thrilling in its sweetness:

> "Han' me down my walkin'-cane
>   (Hey my Lily! go down de road!),
> Yo' true lover gone down de lane
>   (Hey my Lily! go down de road!)."

The quick ear of Uncle Remus, however, had detected the presence of the little boy, and he allowed his song to run into a recitation of nonsense, of which the following, if it be rapidly spoken, will give a faint idea:

"Ole M'er Jackson, fines' confraction, fell down sta'rs fer to git satisfaction; big Bill Fray, he rule de day, eve'ything he call fer come one, two by three. Gwine 'long one day, met Johnny Huby, ax him grin' nine yards er steel fer me, tole me w'ich he couldn't: den I hist 'im over Hickerson Dickerson's barndoors; knock 'im ninety-nine miles under water, w'en he rise, he rise in Pike straddle un a hanspike, en I lef' 'im dar smokin' er de hornpipe, Juba reda seda breda. Aunt Kate at de gate; I want to eat, she fry de meat en gimme skin, w'ich I fling it back agin. Juba!"[1]

All this, rattled off at a rapid rate and with apparent seriousness, was calculated to puzzle the little boy, and he slipped into his accustomed seat with an expression of awed bewilderment upon his face.

"Hit's all des dat away, honey," continued the old man, with the air of one who had just given an important piece of information. "En w'en you bin cas'n shadders long ez de ole nigger, den you'll fin' out who's w'ich, en w'ich's who."

The little boy made no response. He was in thorough sympathy with all the whims and humors of the old man, and his capacity for enjoying them was large enough to include even those he could not understand. Uncle Remus was finishing an axe-handle, and upon these occasions it was his custom to allow the child to hold one end while he applied sandpaper to the other. These relations were pretty soon established, to the mutual satisfaction of the parties most interested, and the old man continued his remarks, but this time not at random:

"W'en I see deze yer swell-head folks like dat 'oman w'at come en tell yo' ma 'bout you chunkin' at her chilluns, w'ich yo' ma make Mars

---

[1] This same kind of nonsense rigmarole is found in the Doctor's speeches in The Mummers' Play. See E. K. Chamber's *The English Folk Play.* Oxford, the Clarendon Press, 1933. — R. C.

John strop you, hit make my min' run back to ole Brer B'ar. Ole Brer
B'ar, he got de swell-headedness hisse'f, en ef der wuz enny swinkin', hit
swunk too late fer ter he'p ole Brer B'ar. Leas'ways dat's w'at dey tells
me, en I ain't never yearn it 'sputed."

"Was the Bear's head sure enough swelled, Uncle Remus?"

"Now you talkin', honey!" exclaimed the old man.

"Goodness! what made it swell?"

This was Uncle Remus's cue. Applying the sand-paper to the axe-
helve with gentle vigor, he began:

"One time when Brer Rabbit wuz gwine lopin' home fum a frolic w'at
dey bin havin' up at Miss Meadows's, who should he happin up wid but
ole Brer B'ar. Co'se, atter w'at done pass 'twix um dey wa'n't no good
feelin's 'tween Brer Rabbit en ole Brer B'ar, but Brer Rabbit, he wanter
save his manners, en so he holler out:

"'Heyo, Brer B'ar! how you come on? I ain't seed you in a coon's age.
How all down at yo' house? How Miss Brune en Miss Brindle?'"

"Who was that, Uncle Remus?" the little boy interrupted.

"Miss Brune en Miss Brindle? Miss Brune wuz Brer B'ar's ole 'oman,
en Miss Brindle wuz his gal. Dat w'at dey call um in dem days. So den
Brer Rabbit, he ax him howdy, he did, en Brer B'ar, he 'spon' dat he wuz

mighty po'ly, en dey amble 'long, dey did, sorter familious like, but Brer Rabbit, he keep one eye on Brer B'ar, en Brer B'ar, he study how he gwine nab Brer Rabbit. Las' Brer Rabbit, he up'n say, sezee:

"'Brer B'ar, I speck I got some bizness cut out fer you,' sezee.

"'What dat, Brer Rabbit?' sez Brer B'ar, sezee.

"'W'iles I wuz cleanin' up my new-groun' day 'fo' yistiddy,' sez Brer Rabbit, sezee, 'I come 'cross wunner deze yer ole time bee-trees. Hit start holler at de bottom, en stay holler plum' ter de top, en de honey's des natchully oozin' out, en ef you'll drap yo' 'gagements en go 'longer me,' sez Brer Rabbit, sezee, 'you'll git a bait dat'll las' you en yo' fambly twel de middle er nex' mon',' sezee.

"Brer B'ar say he much oblije en he b'lieve he'll go 'long, en wid dat dey put out fer Brer Rabbit's new-groun', w'ich 'twa'n't so mighty fur. Leas'ways, dey got dar atter w'ile. Ole Brer B'ar, he 'low dat he kin smell de honey. Brer Rabbit, he 'low dat he kin see de honey-koam. Brer B'ar, he 'low dat he can hear de bees a zoonin'. Dey stan' 'roun' en talk biggity, dey did, twel bimeby Brer Rabbit, he up'n say, sezee:

"'You do de clim'in', Brer B'ar, en I'll do de rushin' 'roun'; you clim' up ter de hole, en I'll take dis yer pine pole en shove de honey up whar you kin git 'er,' sezee.

"Ole Brer B'ar, he spit on his han's en skint up de tree, en jam his head in de hole, en sho nuff, Brer Rabbit, he grab de pine pole, en de way he stir up dem bees wuz sinful — dat's w'at it wuz.

Hit wuz sinful! En de bees dey swawm'd on Brer B'ar's head, twel 'fo' he could take it out'n de hole hit wuz done swell up bigger dan dat dinner-pot, en dar he swung, en ole Brer Rabbit, he dance 'roun' en sing:

> " 'Tree stan' high, but
>   honey mighty sweet —
>   Watch dem bees wid
>   stingers on der feet.'

"But dar ole Brer B'ar hung, en ef his head ain't swunk, I speck he hangin' dar yit — dat w'at I speck."

29
Mr. Fox Gets into Serious Business

"Hɪᴛ ᴛᴜʀɴ ᴏᴜᴛ one time," said Uncle Remus, grinding some crumbs of tobacco between the palms of his hands, preparatory to enjoying his usual smoke after supper — "hit turn out one time dat Brer Rabbit make so free wid de man's collard-patch dat de man he tuck'n sot a trap fer ole Brer Rabbit."

"Which man was that, Uncle Remus?" asked the little boy.

"Des a man, honey. Dat's all. Dat's all I knows — des wunner dese yer mans w'at you see trollopin' 'roun' eve'y day. Nobody ain't never year w'at his name is, en ef dey did dey kep' de news mighty close fum me. Ef dish yer man is bleedzd fer ter have a name, den I'm done, kaze you'll hatter go fudder dan me. Ef you bleedzd ter know mo' dan w'at I duz, den you'll hatter hunt up some er deze yer niggers w'at's sprung up sence I commence fer ter shed my ha'r."

"Well, I just thought, Uncle Remus," said the little boy, in a tone remarkable for self-depreciation, "that the man had a name."

"Tooby sho," replied the old man, with unction, puffing away at his pipe. "Co'se. Dat w'at make I say w'at I duz. Dish yer man mought a had a name, en den agin he moughtent. He mought er bin name Slip-Shot Sam, en he mought bin name ole One-eye Riley, w'ich ef 'twuz hit ain't bin handed 'roun' ter me. But dish yer man, he in de tale, en w'at we gwine do wid 'im? Dat's de p'int, kaze w'en I git ter huntin' 'roun' 'mong my 'membunce atter dish yer Mister W'atyoumaycollum's name, she ain't dar. Now den, le's des call 'im Mr. Man en let 'im go at dat."

The silence of the little boy gave consent.

"One time," said Uncle Remus, carefully taking up the thread of the story where it had been dropped, "hit turn out dat Brer Rabbit bin makin' so free wid Mr. Man's greens en truck dat Mr. Man, he tuck'n sot a trap for Brer Rabbit, en Brer Rabbit he so greedy dat he tuck'n walk right spang in it, 'fo' he know hisse'f. Well, 'twa'n't long 'fo' yer come Mr. Man, broozin' 'roun', en he ain't no sooner see ole Brer Rabbit dan he smack his han's tergedder en holler out:

"'You er nice feller, you is! Yer you bin gobblin' up my green truck, en now you tryin' ter tote off my trap. You er mighty nice chap — dat's w'at you is! But now dat I got you, I'll des 'bout settle wid you fer de ole en de new.'

"En wid dat, Mr. Man, he go off, he did, down in de bushes atter han'-ful er switches. Ole Brer Rabbit, he ain't sayin' nothin', but he feelin' mighty lonesome, en he sot dar lookin' like eve'y minnit wuz gwine ter be de nex'. En w'iles Mr. Man wuz off prepa'r'n his bresh-broom, who should come p'radin' 'long but Brer Fox. Brer Fox make a great 'miration, he did, 'bout de fix w'at he fin' Brer Rabbit in, but Brer Rabbit he make like he fit ter kill hisse'f laughin, en he up'n tell Brer Fox, he did, dat Miss Mead-ows's folks want 'im ter go down ter der house in 'tennunce on a weddin', en he 'low w'ich he couldn't, en dey 'low how he could, en den bimeby dey take'n tie 'im dar w'iles dey go atter de preacher, so he be dar w'en dey come back. En mo'n dat, Brer Rabbit up'n tell Brer Fox dat his chillun's mighty low wid de fever, en he bleedzd ter go atter some pills fer'm, en he ax Brer Fox fer ter take his place en go down ter Miss Meadows's en have nice time wid de gals. Brer Fox, he in fer dem kinder pranks, en 'twa'n't no time 'fo' Brer Rabbit had ole Brer Fox harness up dar in his place, en den he make like he got ter make 'as'e en git de pills fer dem sick chilluns. Brer Rabbit wa'n't mo'n out er sight 'fo' yer come Mr. Man wid a han'ful er hick'ries, but w'en he see Brer Fox tied up dar, he look like he 'stonish'.

"'Heyo!' sez Mr. Man, sezee, 'you done change color, en you done got bigger, en yo' tail done grow out. What kin'er watzyname is you, enny-how?' sezee.

"Brer Fox, he stay still, en Mr. Man, he talk on:

"'Hit's mighty big luck,' sezee, 'ef w'en I ketch de chap w'at nibble

my greens, likewise I ketch de feller w'at gnyaw my goose,' sezee, en wid
dat he let inter Brer Fox wid de hick'ries, en de way he play rap-jacket
wuz a caution ter de neighborhood. Brer Fox, he juk en he jump, en he
squeal en he squall, but Mr. Man, he shower down on 'im, he did, like
fightin' a red was'nes'."

The little boy laughed, and Uncle Remus supplemented this indorse-
ment of his descriptive powers with a most infectious chuckle.

"Bimeby," continued the old man, "de switches, dey got frazzle out,
en Mr. Man, he put out atter mo', en w'en he done got fa'rly outer yearin',
Brer Rabbit, he show'd up, he did, kaze he des bin hidin' out in de
bushes lis'nin' at de racket, en he 'low hit mighty funny dat Miss Meadows ain't come 'long, kaze he done bin down ter de doctor house, en dat's
fudder dan de preacher, yit. Brer Rabbit make like he hurr'in' on home,
but Brer Fox, he open up, he did, en he say:

"'I thank you fer ter tu'n me loose, Brer Rabbit, en I'll be 'blije,'
sezee, 'kaze you done tie me up so tight dat it make my head swim, en I
don't speck I'd las' fer ter git ter Miss Meadows's,' sezee.

"Brer Rabbit, he sot down sorter keerless like, en begin fer ter
scratch one year like a man studyin' 'bout sump'n'.

"'Dat's so, Brer Fox,' sezee, 'you duz look sorter stove up. Look like
sump'n' bin onkoamin' yo' ha'rs,' sezee.

"Brer Fox ain't sayin' nothin', but Brer Rabbit, he keep on talkin':

"'Dey ain't no bad feelin's 'twix' us, is dey, Brer Fox? Kaze ef dey is, I ain't got no time fer ter be tarryin' 'roun' yer.'

"Brer Fox say w'ich he don't have no onfrennelness, en wid dat Brer Rabbit cut Brer Fox loose des in time fer ter hear Mr. Man w'isserlin' up his dogs, en one went one way en de udder went nudder."

30
How Mr. Rabbit Succeeded in Raising a Dust

"IN DEM TIMES," said Uncle Remus, gazing admiringly at himself in a fragment of looking-glass, "Brer Rabbit, en Brer Fox, en Brer Coon, en dem yuther creeturs go co'tin' en sparklin' 'roun' de neighborhood mo' samer dan folks. 'Twa'n't no 'Lemme a hoss,' ner 'Fetch me my buggy,' but dey des up 'n lit out en tote deyse'f. Dar's ole Brer Fox, he des wheel 'roun' en fetch his flank one swipe wid 'is tongue en he'd be koam up; en Brer Rabbit, he des spit on his han' en twis' it 'roun' 'mongst de roots er his years en his ha'r'd be roach. Dey wuz dat flirtashus," continued the old man, closing one eye at his image in the glass, "dat Miss Meadows en de gals don't see no peace fum one week een' ter de udder. Chuseday wuz same as Sunday, en Friday wuz same as Chuseday, en hit come down ter dat pass dat w'en Miss Meadows 'ud have chicken-fixin's fer dinner, in 'ud drap Brer Fox en Brer Possum, en w'en she'd have fried greens in 'ud pop ole Brer Rabbit, twel 'las' Miss Meadows, she tuck'n tell de gals dat she be dad-blame if she gwine ter keep no tavvum. So dey fix it up 'mong deyse'f, Miss Meadows en de gals did, dat de nex' time de gents call dey'd gin um a game. De gents, dey wuz a co'tin', but Miss Meadows, she don't wanter marry none un um, en needer duz de gals, en likewise dey don't wanter have um pester'n 'roun.' Las', one Chuseday, Miss Meadows, she tole um dat ef dey come down ter her house de nex' Sat'-day evenin', de whole caboodle un um 'ud go down de road a piece, whar der wuz a big flint rock, en de man w'at could take a sludge-hammer en knock de dus' out'n dat rock, he wuz de man w'at 'ud git de pick er de gals. Dey all say dey gwine do it, but ole Brer Rabbit, he crope off whar der wuz a cool place under some jimson weeds, en dar he sot wukkin' his

min' how he gwine ter git dus' out'n dat rock. Bimeby, w'ile he wuz a settin' dar, up he jump en crack his heels tergedder en sing out:

> "'Make a bow ter de Buzzard en
>   den ter de Crow,
>   Takes a limber-toe gemmun fer
>   ter jump Jim Crow,'

en wid dat he put out for Brer Coon house en borrer his slippers. W'en
Sat'day evenin' come, dey wuz all dere. Miss Meadows en de gals, dey
wuz dere; en Brer Coon, en Brer Fox, en Brer Possum, en Brer Tarrypin,
dey wuz dere."

"Where was the Rabbit?" the little boy asked.

"You kin put yo' 'pennunce in ole Brer Rabbit," the old man replied,
with a chuckle. "He wuz dere, but he shuffle up kinder late, kaze w'en
Miss Meadows en de balance un um done gone down ter de place, Brer
Rabbit, he crope 'roun' ter de ash-hopper, en fill Brer Coon slippers full
er ashes, en den he tuck'n put um on en march off. He got dar atter w'ile,
en soon's Miss Meadows en de gals seed 'im, dey up'n giggle, en make a

great 'miration kaze Brer Rabbit got on slippers. Brer Fox, he so smart, he holler out, he did, en say he lay Brer Rabbit got de groun'-eatch, but Brer Rabbit, he sorter shet one eye, he did, en say, sezee:

"'I bin so useter ridin' hoss-back, ez deze ladies knows, dat I'm gittin' sorter tender-footed'; en dey don't hear much mo' fum Brer Fox dat day, kaze he 'member how Brer Rabbit done bin en rid him; en hit 'uz des 'bout much ez Miss Meadows en de gals could do fer ter keep der snickers fum gittin' up a 'sturbance 'mong de congregashun. But, never min' dat, ole Brer Rabbit, he wuz dar, en he so brash dat leetle mo' en he'd er grab up de sludge-hammer en er open up de racket 'fo' ennybody gun de word; but Brer Fox, he shove Brer Rabbit out'n de way en pick up de sludge hisse'f. Now den," continued the old man, with pretty much the air of one who had been the master of similar ceremonies, "de progance wuz dish yer: Eve'y gent were ter have th'ee licks at de rock, en de gent w'at fetch de dus' he were de one w'at gwine ter take de pick er de gals. Ole Brer Fox, he grab de sludge-hammer, he did, en he come down on de rock — *blim!* No dus' ain't come. Den he draw back en down he come agin — *blam!* No dus' ain't come. Den he spit in his han's, en give 'er a big swing en down she come — *kerblap!* En yit no dus' ain't flew'd. Den Brer Possum he make triul, en Brer Coon, en all de balance un um 'cep' Brer Tarrypin, en he 'low dat he got a crick in his neck. Den Brer Rabbit, he grab holt er de sludge, en he lipt up in de a'r en come down on de rock all at de same time — *pow!* — en de ashes, dey flew'd up so, dey did, dat Brer Fox, he tuck'n had a sneezin' spell, en Miss Meadows en de gals dey up'n cough. Th'ee times Brer Rabbit jump up en crack his heels tergedder en come down wid de sludge-hammer — *ker-blam!* — en eve'y time he jump up, he holler out:

"'Stan' fudder, ladies! Yer come de dus'!' en sho nuff, de dus' come.

"Leas'ways," continued Uncle Remus, "Brer Rabbit got one er de gals, en dey had a weddin' en a big infa'r."

"Which of the girls did the Rabbit marry?" asked the little boy, dubiously.

"I did year tell un 'er name," replied the old man, with a great affectation of interest, "but look like I done gone en fergit it off'n my min'. Ef I don't disremember," he continued, "hit wuz Miss Molly Cottontail, en I speck we better let it go at dat."

31
A Plantation Witch

THE NEXT TIME the little boy got permission to call upon Uncle Remus, the old man was sitting in his door, with his elbows on his knees and his face buried in his hands, and he appeared to be in great trouble.

"What's the matter, Uncle Remus?" the youngster asked.

"Nuff de matter, honey — mo' dan dey's enny kyo' fer. Ef dey ain't some quare gwines on 'roun' dis place I ain't name Remus."

The serious tone of the old man caused the little boy to open his eyes. The moon, just at its full, cast long, vague, wavering shadows in front of the cabin. A colony of tree-frogs somewhere in the distance were treating their neighbors to a serenade, but to the little boy it sounded like a chorus of lost and long-forgotten whistlers. The sound was wherever the imagination chose to locate it — to the right, to the left, in the air, on the ground, far away or near at hand, but always dim and always indistinct. Something in Uncle Remus's tone exactly fitted all these surroundings, and the child nestled closer to the old man.

"Yasser," continued Uncle Remus, with an ominous sigh and myste-rious shake of the head, "ef dey ain't some quare gwines on in dish yer neighborhood, den I'm de ball-headest creetur 'twix' dis en nex' Jinaw-erry wuz a year 'go, w'ich I knows I ain't. Dat's w'at."

"What is it, Uncle Remus?"

"I know Mars John bin drivin' Cholly sorter hard terday, en I say ter myse'f dat I'd drap 'round 'bout dus' en fling nudder year er corn in de troff en kinder gin 'im a techin' up wid de kurrier-koam; en bless gra-cious! I ain't bin in de lot mo'n a minnit 'fo' I seed sump'n' wuz wrong wid de hoss, and sho nuff dar wuz his mane full er witch-stirrups."

"Full of what, Uncle Remus?"

"Full er witch-stirrups, honey. Ain't you seed no witch-stirrups? Well, w'en you see two stran' er ha'r tied tergedder in a hoss's mane, dar you see a witch-stirrup, en, mo'n dat, dat hoss done bin rid by um."

"Do you reckon they have been riding Charley?" inquired the little boy.

"Co'se' honey, Tooby sho dey is. W'at else dey bin doin'?"

"Did you ever see a witch, Uncle Remus?"

"Dat ain't needer yer ner dar. W'en I see coon track in de branch, I know de coon bin 'long dar."

The argument seemed unanswerable, and the little boy asked, in a confidential tone:

"Uncle Remus, what are witches like?"

"Dey comes diffunt," responded the cautious old darkey. "Dey comes en dey cunjus folks. Squinch-owl holler eve'y time he see a witch, en w'en you hear de dog howlin' in de middle er de night, one un um's mighty ap' ter be prowlin' 'roun'. Cunjun folks kin tell a witch de minnit dey lays der eyes on it, but dem w'at ain't cunjun, hit's mighty hard ter tell w'en dey see one, kaze dey might come in de 'pearunce un a cow en all kinder creeturs. I ain't bin useter no cunjun myse'f, but I bin livin' long nuff fer ter know w'en you meets up wid a big black cat in de middle er de road, wid yaller eye-balls, dars yo' witch fresh fum de Ole Boy. En,

fuddermo', I know dat 'tain't proned inter no dogs fer ter ketch de rabbit w'at use in a berryin'-groun'. Dey er de mos' ongodlies' creeturs w'at you ever laid eyes on," continued Uncle Remus, with unction. "Down dar in Putmon County yo' Unk Jeems, he make like he gwine ter ketch wunner dem dar graveyard rabbits. Sho nuff, out he goes, en de dogs ain't no mo'n got ter de place 'fo' up jump de old rabbit right 'mong um, en atter runnin' 'roun' a time or two, she skip right up ter Mars Jeems, en Mars Jeems, he des put de gun-bar'l right on 'er en lammed aloose. Hit tored up de groun' all 'roun', en de dogs, dey rush up, but dey wa'n't no rabbit dar; but bimeby Mars Jeems, he seed de dogs tuckin' der tails 'tween der legs, en he look up, en dar wuz de rabbit caperin' 'roun' on a toom stone, en wid dat Mars Jeems say he sorter feel like de time done come w'en yo' gran'ma was 'spectin' un him home, en he call off de dogs en put out. But dem wuz ha'nts. Witches is deze yer kinder folks w'at kin drap der body en change inter a cat en a wolf en all kinder creeturs."

"Papa says there aren't any witches," the little boy interrupted.

"Mars John ain't live long ez I is," said Uncle Remus, by way of comment. "He ain't bin broozin' 'roun' all hours er de night en day. I know'd a nigger w'ich his brer wuz a witch, kaze he up'n tole me how he tuck'n kyo'd 'im; en he kyo'd 'im good, mon."

"How was that?" inquired the little boy.

"Hit seem like," continued Uncle Remus, "dat witch folks is got a slit in de back er de neck, en w'en dey wanter change derse'f, dey des pull de hide over der head same ez if 'twuz a shut, en dar dey is."

"Do they get out of their skins?" asked the little boy, in an awed tone.

"Tooby sho, honey. You see yo' pa pull his shut off? Well, dat des zackly de way dey duz. But dish yere nigger w'at I'm tellin' you 'bout, he kyo'd his brer de ve'y fus' pass he made at him. Hit got so dat folks in de settlement didn't have no peace. De chilluns 'ud wake up in de mawnins wid der ha'r tangle up, en wid scratches on um like dey bin thoo a brier-patch, twel bimeby one day de nigger he 'low dat he'd set up dat night en keep one eye on his brer; en sho' nuff dat night, des ez de chickens wuz crowin' fer twelve, up jump de brer and pull off his skin en sail out'n de house in de shape un a bat, en w'at duz de nigger do but grab up de hide, and turn it wrongsudout'ards en sprinkle it wid salt. Den he lay down en

watch fer ter see w'at de news wuz gwine ter be. Des 'fo' day yer come a big black cat in de do', en de nigger git up, he did, en druv her away. Bimeby, yer come a big black dog snuffin' roun', en de nigger up wid a chunk en lammed 'im side er de head. Den a squinch-owl lit on de koam er de house, en de nigger jam de shovel in de fier en make 'im flew away. Las', yer come a great big black wolf wid his eyes shinin' like fier coals, en he grab de hide and rush out. 'Twa'n't long 'fo' de nigger year his brer holler'n en squallin', en he tuck a light, he did, en went out, en dar wuz his brer des a waller'n on de groun' en squirmin' 'roun', kaze de salt on de skin wuz stingin' wuss'n ef he had his britches lineded wid yaller-jackets. By nex' mawnin' he got so he could sorter shuffle 'long, but he gun up cunjun, en ef dere wuz enny mo' witches in dat settlement dey kep' mighty close, en dat nigger he ain't skunt hisse'f no mo' not endurin' er my 'membunce."

The result of this was that Uncle Remus had to take the little boy by the hand and go with him to the "big house," which the old man was not loath to do; and, when the child went to bed, he lay awake a long time expecting an unseemly visitation from some mysterious source. It soothed him, however, to hear the strong, musical voice of his sable patron, not very far away, tenderly contending with a lusty tune; and to this accompaniment the little boy dropped asleep:

> "Hit's eighteen hunder'd, forty-en-eight,
> Christ done made dat crooked way straight —
>   En I don't wanter stay here no longer;
> Hit's eighteen hunder'd, forty-en-nine,
> Christ done turn dat water inter wine —
>   En I don't wanter stay here no longer."

32
"Jacky-My-Lantern"[1]

UPON HIS next visit to Uncle Remus, the little boy was exceedingly anxious to know more about witches, but the old man prudently refrained from exciting the youngster's imagination any further in that direction. Uncle Remus had a board across his lap, and, armed with a mallet and a shoe-knife, was engaged in making shoe-pegs.

"W'iles I wuz crossin' de branch des now," he said endeavoring to change the subject, "I come up wid a Jacky-my-lantern, en she wuz bu'nin' wuss'n a bunch er lightnin'-bugs, mon. I know'd she wuz a fixin' fer ter lead me inter dat quogmire down in de swamp, en I steer'd cle'r un er. Yasser. I did dat. You ain't never seed no Jacky-my-lanterns, is you, honey?"

---

[1] "Jacky-My-Lantern" — This story is popular on the coast and among the rice-plantations, and, since the publication of some of the animal-myths in the newspapers, I have received a version of it from a planter in southwest Georgia; but it seems to me to be an intruder among the genuine myth-stories of the Negroes. It is a trifle too elaborate. Nevertheless, it is told upon the plantations with great gusto, and there are several versions in circulation. — J. C. H.

The tale has been reported from Germany (Grimm, Nos. 81, 82), Estonia, Finland, Denmark, Norway, Sweden, Flanders, Russia, France, Costa Rica, and Florida.

See also appendix notes to "Wicked John" in *Grandfather Tales*, Houghton Mifflin Co., Boston, 1948. — R. C.

The little boy never had, but he had heard of them, and he wanted to know what they were, and thereupon Uncle Remus proceeded to tell him.

"One time," said the old darkey, transferring his spectacles from his nose to the top of his head and leaning his elbows upon his peg-board, "dere wuz a blacksmif man, en dish yer blacksmif man, he tuck'n stuck closer by his dram dan he did by his bellus. Monday mawnin' he'd git on a spree, en all dat week he'd be on a spree, en de nex' Monday mawnin' he'd take a fresh start. Bimeby, one day, atter de blacksmif bin spreein' 'roun' en cussin' might'ly, he hear a sorter rustlin' fuss at de do', en in walk de Bad Man."

"Who, Uncle Remus?" the little boy asked.

"De Bad Man, honey; de Ole Boy hisse'f right fresh from de ridjun w'at you year Miss Sally readin' 'bout. He done hide his hawns, en his tail, en his hoof, en he come dress up like w'ite folks. He tuck off his hat en he bow, en den he tell de blacksmif who he is, en dat he done come atter 'im. Den de blacksmif, he gun ter cry en beg, en he beg so hard en he cry so loud dat de Bad Man say he make a trade wid 'im. At de een' er one year de sperit er de blacksmif wuz to be his'n en endurin' er dat time de blacksmif mus' put in his hottes' licks in de intruss er de Bad Man, en den he put a spell on de cheer de blacksmif was settin' in, en on his sludge-hammer. De man w'at sot in de cheer couldn't git up less'n de blacksmif let 'im, en de man w'at pick up de sludge 'ud hatter keep on knockin' wid it twel de blacksmif say quit; en den he gun 'im money plenty, en off he put.

"De blacksmif, he sail in fer ter have his fun, en he have so much dat he done clean forgot 'bout his contrack, but bimeby, one day he look down de road, en dar he see de Bad Man comin', en den he know'd de year wuz out. W'en de Bad Man got in de do', de blacksmif wuz poundin' 'way at a hoss-shoe, but he wa'n't so bizzy dat he didn't ax 'im in. De Bad Man sorter do like he ain't got no time fer ter tarry, but de blacksmif say he got some little jobs dat he bleedzd ter finish up, en den he ax de Bad Man fer ter set down a minnit; en de Bad Man, he tuck'n sot down, en he sot in dat cheer w'at he done conju'd en co'se, dar he wuz. Den de blacksmif, he 'gun ter poke fun at de Bad Man, en he ax him don't he want a dram, en won't he hitch his cheer up little nigher de fier, en de Bad Man, he beg en he beg, but 'twa'n' doin' no good, kaze de blacksmif

'low dat he gwine ter keep 'im dar twel he prommus dat he let 'im off one
year mo', en, sho nuff, de Bad Man prommus dat ef de blacksmif let 'im
up he give 'im a n'er showin'. So den de blacksmif gun de wud, en de Bad
Man sa'nter off down de big road, settin' traps en layin' his progance fer
ter ketch mo' sinners.

"De nex' year hit pass same like t'er one. At de 'p'inted time yer come
de Ole Boy atter de blacksmif, but still de blacksmif had some jobs dat
he bleedzd ter finish up, en he ax de Bad Man fer ter take holt er de
sludge en he he'p 'im out; en de Bad Man, he 'low dat r'er'n be disperlite, he don't keer ef he do hit 'er a biff er two; en wid dat he grab up de
sludge, en dar he wuz 'gin, kaze he done cunju'd de sludge so dat who-
somedever tuck 'er up can't put 'er down less'n de blacksmif say de wud.
Dey perlaver'd dar, dey did, twel bimeby de Bad Man he up'n let 'im off
n'er year.

"Well, den, dat year pass same ez t'er one. Mont' in en mont' out dat
man wuz rollin' in dram, en bimeby yer come de Bad Man. De blacksmif

cry en he holler, en he rip 'roun' en t'ar his ha'r, but hit des like he didn't, kaze de Bad Man grab 'im up en cram 'im in a bag en tote 'im off. W'iles dey wuz gwine 'long dey come up wid a passel er folks w'at wuz havin' wunner deze yer Fote er July bobbycues, en de Ole Boy, he 'low dat maybe he kin git some mo' game, en w'at do he do but jine in wid um. He jines in en he talk politics same like t'er folks, twel bimeby dinnertime come 'roun', en day ax 'im up, w'ich 'greed wid his stummick, en he pozzit his bag underneed de table 'longside de udder bags w'at de hongry folks brung.

"No sooner did de blacksmif git back on de groun' dan he 'gun ter wuk his way outer de bag. He crope out, he did, en den he tuck'n change de bag. He tuck'n tuck a n'er bag en lay it down whar dish yer bag wuz, en den he crope outer de crowd en lay low in de underbresh.

"Las', w'en de time come fer ter go, de Ole Boy up wid his bag en slung her on his shoulder, en off he put fer de Bad Place. W'en he got dar he tuck'n drap de bag off'n his back en call up de imps, en dey des come a squallin' en a caperin', w'ich I speck dey mus' a bin hongry. Leas'ways dey des swawm'd 'roun', hollerin' out:

"'Daddy, w'at you brung — daddy, w'at you brung?'

"So den dey open de bag, en lo en beholes, out jump a big bull-dog, en de way he shuck dem little imps wuz a caution, en he kep' on gnyawin' un um twel de Ole Boy open de gate en t'un 'im out."

"And what became of the blacksmith?" the little boy asked, as Uncle Remus paused to snuff the candle with his fingers.

"I'm drivin' on 'roun', honey. Atter 'long time, de blacksmif he tuck'n die, en w'en he go ter de Good Place de man at de gate dunner who he is, en he can't squeeze in. Den he go down ter de Bad Place, en knock. De Ole Boy, he look out, he did, en he know'd de blacksmif de minnit he laid eyes on 'im; but he shake his head en say, sezee:

"'You'll hatter skuze me, Brer Blacksmif, kaze I dun had 'speunce 'longer you. You'll hatter go some'rs else ef you wanter raise enny racket,' sezee, en wid dat he shet de do'.

"En dey do say," continued Uncle Remus, with unction, "dat sence dat day de blacksmif bin sorter huv'rin' 'roun' 'twix' de heavens en de yeth, en dark nights he shine out so folks call 'im Jacky-my-lantern. Wat's w'at dey tells me. Hit may be wrong er't maybe right, but dat's w'at I years."

33
Why the Negro Is Black

ONE NIGHT, while the little boy was watching Uncle Remus twisting and waxing some shoe-thread, he made what appeared to him to be a very curious discovery. He discovered that the palms of the old man's hands were as white as his own, and the fact was such a source of wonder that he at last made it the subject of remark. The response of Uncle Remus led to the earnest recital of a piece of unwritten history that must prove interesting to ethnologists.

"Tooby sho de pa'm er my han's w'ite, honey," he quietly remarked, "en, w'en it come ter dat, dey wuz a time w'en all de w'ite folks 'uz black — blacker dan me, kaze I done bin yer so long dat I bin sorter bleach out."

The little boy laughed. He thought Uncle Remus was making him the victim of one of his jokes; but the youngster was never more mistaken. The old man was serious. Nevertheless, he failed to rebuke the ill-timed mirth of the child, appearing to be altogether engrossed in his work. After a while, he resumed:

"Yasser. Folks dunner w'at bin yit, let 'lone w'at gwine ter be. Niggers is niggers now, but de time wuz w'en we 'uz all niggers tergedder."

"When was that, Uncle Remus?"

"Way back yander. In dem times we 'uz all un us black; we 'uz all niggers tergedder, en 'cordin' ter all de 'counts w'at I years folks 'uz gittin' 'long 'bout ez well in dem days ez dey is now. But atter w'ile de news come dat dere wuz a pon' er water somers in de neighborhood, w'ich ef dey'd git inter dey'd be wash off nice en w'ite, en den one un um, he fin' de place en make er splunge inter de pon', en come out w'ite ez a town gal. En den, bless gracious! w'en de folks seed it, dey make a break fer de pon', en dem w'at wuz de soopless, dey got in fus' en dey come out w'ite; en dem w'at wuz de nex' soopless, dey got in nex', en dey come out merlatters; en dey wuz sech a crowd un um dat dey mighty nigh use de water up, w'ich w'en dem yuthers come 'long, de morest dey could do wuz ter paddle about wid der foots en dabble in it wid der han's. Dem

wuz de niggers, en down ter tis day dey ain't no w'ite 'bout a nigger ceppin' de pa'ms er der han's en de soles er der foot."

The little boy seemed to be very much interested in this new account
of the origin of races, and he made some further inquiries, which elicited
from Uncle Remus the following additional particulars:

"De Injun en de Chinee got ter be 'counted 'long er de merlatter. I
ain't seed no Chinee dat I knows un, but dey tells me dey er sorter 'twix'
a brown en a brindle. Dey er all merlatters."

"But mamma says the Chinese have straight hair," the little boy suggested.

"Co'se' honey," the old man unhesitatingly responded, "dem w'at git
ter de pon' time nuff fer ter git der head in de water, de water hit onkink
der ha'r. Hit bleedzd ter be dat away."

34
The Sad Fate of Mr. Fox

"NOW, DEN," said Uncle Remus, with unusual gravity, as soon as the little boy, by taking his seat, announced that he was ready for the evening's
entertainment to begin; "now, den, dish yer tale w'at I'm agwine ter gin
you is de las' row er stumps, sho. Dish yer's whar ole Brer Fox los' his
breff, en he ain't fin' it no mo' down ter dis day."

"Did he kill himself, Uncle Remus?" the little boy asked, with a curious air of concern.

"Hol' on dar, honey!" the old man exclaimed, with a great affectation
of alarm; "hol' on dar! Wait! Gimme room! I don't wanter tell you no
story, en ef you keep shovin' me forerd, I mought git some er de facks mix
up 'mong deyse'f. You gotter gimme room en you gotter gimme time."

The little boy had no other premature questions to ask, and after a
pause, Uncle Remus resumed:

"Well, den, one day Brer Rabbit go ter Brer Fox house, he did, en he
put up mighty po' mouf. He say his ole 'oman sick, en his chilluns col',
en de fier done gone out. Brer Fox, he feel bad 'bout dis, en he tuck'n s'ply
Brer Rabbit widder chunk er fier. Brer Rabbit see Brer Fox cookin' some

nice beef, en his mouf 'gun ter water, but he take de fier, he did, en he put out to'rds home; but present'y yer he come back, en he say de fier done gone out. Brer Fox 'low dat he want er invite to dinner, but he don't say nuthin', en bimeby Brer Rabbit he up'n say, sezee:

"'Brer Fox, whar you git so much nice beef?' sezee, en den Brer Fox he up'n 'spon', sezee:

"'You come ter my house termorrer ef yo' folks ain't too sick, en I kin show you whar you kin git plenty beef mo' nicer dan dish yer,' sezee.

"Well, sho nuff, de nex' day fotch Brer Rabbit, en Brer Fox say, sezee:

"'Der's a man down yander by Miss Meadows's w'at got heap er fine cattle, en he gotter cow name Bookay,' sezee, 'en you des go en say *Bookay*, en she'll open her mouf, en you kin jump in en git des as much meat ez you kin tote,' sez Brer Fox, sezee.

"'Well, I'll go 'long,' sez Brer Rabbit, sezee, 'en you kin jump fus' en den I'll come follerin' atter,' sezee.

"Wid dat dey put out, en dey went promernadin' 'roun' 'mong de cattle dey did, twel bimeby dey struck up wid de one dey wuz atter. Brer Fox,

he up, he did, en holler *Bookay*, en de cow flung 'er mouf wide open. Sho nuff, in dey jump, en w'en dey got dar, Brer Fox, he say, sezee:

"'You kin cut mos' ennywheres, Brer Rabbit, but don't cut 'roun' de haslett,' sezee.

"Den Brer Rabbit, he holler back, he did: 'I'm a gitten me out a roas'n'-piece,' sezee.

"'Roas'n,' er bakin', er fryin',' sez Brer Fox, sezee, 'don't git too nigh de haslett,' sezee.

"Dey cut en dey kyarved, en dey kyarv'd en dey cut, en w'iles dey wuz cuttin' en kyarvin', en slashin' 'way, Brer Rabbit, he tuck'n hacked inter de haslett, en wid dat down fell de cow dead.

"'Now, den,' sez Brer Fox, 'we er gone, sho,' sezee.

"'W'at we gwine do?' sez Brer Rabbit, sezee.

"'I'll git in de maul,' sez Brer Fox, 'en you'll jump in de gall,' sezee.

"Nex' mawnin' yer cum de man w'at de cow b'long ter, and he ax who kill Bookay. Nobody don't say nuthin'. Den de man say he'll cut 'er open en see, en den he whirl in, en 'twa'n't no time 'fo' he had 'er intruls spread out. Brer Rabbit, he crope out'n de gall, en say, sezee:

"'Mister Man! Oh, Mister Man! I'll tell you who kill yo' cow. You look in de maul, en dar you'll fin' 'im,' sezee.

"Wid dat de man tuck a stick and lam down on de maul so hard dat he kill Brer Fox stone-dead. W'en Brer Rabbit see Brer Fox wuz laid out fer good, he make like he mighty sorry, en he up'n ax de man fer Brer Fox head. Man say he ain't keerin', en den Brer Rabbit tuck'n brung it ter Brer Fox house. Dar he see ole Miss Fox, en he tell 'er dat he done fotch her some nice beef w'at 'er ole man sont 'er, but she ain't gotter look at it twel she go ter eat it.

"Brer Fox son wuz name Tobe, en Brer Rabbit tell Tobe fer ter keep still w'iles his mammy cook de nice beef w'at his daddy sont 'im. Tobe he wuz mighty hongry, en he look in de pot he did w'iles de cookin' wuz gwine on, en dar he see his daddy head, en wid dat he sot up a howl en tole his mammy. Miss Fox, she git mighty mad w'en she fin' she cookin' her ole man head, en she call up de dogs, she did, en sickt 'em on Brer Rabbit; en ole Miss Fox en Tobe en de dogs, dey push Brer Rabbit so close dat he hatter take a holler tree. Miss Fox, she tell Tobe fer ter stay dar en min' Brer Rabbit, w'ile she goes en git de ax, en w'en she gone, Brer Rabbit, he tole Tobe ef he go ter de branch en git 'im a drink er water dat he'll gin 'im a dollar. Tobe, he put out, he did, en bring some water in his hat, but by de time he got back Brer Rabbit done out en gone. Ole Miss Fox, she cut and cut twel down come de tree, but no Brer Rabbit dar. Den she lay de blame on Tobe, en she say she gwine ter lash 'im, en Tobe, he put out en run, de ole 'oman atter 'im. Bimeby, he come up wid Brer Rabbit, en sot down fer to tell 'im how 'twuz, en w'iles dey wuz a settin' dar, yer come ole Miss Fox a slippin' up en grab um bofe. Den she tell um w'at she gwine do. Brer Rabbit she gwine ter kill, en Tobe she gwine ter lam ef its de las' ack. Den Brer Rabbit sez, sezee:

"'Ef you please, ma'am, Miss Fox, lay me on de grinestone en groun' off my nose so I can't smell no mo' when I'm dead.'

"Miss Fox, she tuck dis ter be a good idee, en she fotch bofe un um ter de grinestone, en set um up on it so dat she could groun' off Brer Rabbit nose. Den Brer Rabbit, he up'n say, sezee:

"'Ef you please, ma'am, Miss Fox, Tobe he kin turn de handle w'iles you goes atter some water fer ter wet de grinestone,' sezee.

"Co'se, soon'z Brer Rabbit see Miss Fox go atter de water, he jump down en put out, en dis time he git clean away."

"And was that the last of the Rabbit, too, Uncle Remus?" the little boy asked, with something like a sigh.

"Don't push me too close, honey," responded the old man; "don't shove me up in no cornder. I don't wanter tell you no stories. Some say dat Brer Rabbit's ole 'oman died fum eatin' some pizen-weed, en dat Brer Rabbit married ole Miss Fox, en some say not. Some tells one tale en some tells nudder; some say dat fum dat time forerd de Rabbits en de Foxes make fr'en's en stay so; some say dey kep on quollin'. Hit look like it mixt. Let dem tell you what knows. Dat what I years you gits it straight like I yeard it."

There was a long pause, which was finally broken by the old man:

"Hit's 'gin de rules fer you ter be noddin' yer, honey. Bimeby you'll drap off en I'll hatter tote you up ter de big 'ouse. I hear dat baby cryin', en bimeby Miss Sally'll fly up en be a holler'n atter you."

"Oh, I wasn't asleep," the little boy replied. "I was just thinking."

"Well, dat's diffunt," said the old man. "Ef you'll clime up on my back," he continued, speaking softly, "I speck I ain't too ole fer ter be yo' hoss fum yer ter de house. Many en many's de time dat I toted yo' Unk Jeems dat away, en Mars Jeems wuz heavier sot dan what you is."

II

The tales from

Nights with Uncle Remus
Myths and Legends of the
Old Plantation

With illustrations by
FREDERICK STUART CHURCH
and **WILLIAM HOLBROOK BEARD**

1
Mr. Fox and Miss Goose

IT HAD BEEN raining all day so that Uncle Remus found it impossible to go out. The storm had begun, the old man declared, just as the chickens were crowing for day, and it had continued almost without intermission. The dark gray clouds had blotted out the sun, and the leafless limbs of the tall oaks surrendered themselves drearily to the fantastic gusts that drove the drizzle fitfully before them. The lady to whom Uncle Remus belonged had been thoughtful of the old man, and 'Tildy, the house-girl, had been commissioned to carry him his meals. This arrangement came to the knowledge of the little boy at supper time, and he lost no time in obtaining permission to accompany 'Tildy.

Uncle Remus made a great demonstration over the thoughtful kindness of his "Miss Sally."

"Ef she ain't one blessid white 'oman," he said, in his simple, fervent way, "den dey ain't none un um 'roun' in deze parts."

With that he addressed himself to the supper, while the little boy sat by and eyed him with that familiar curiosity common to children. Finally the youngster disturbed the old man with an inquiry:

"Uncle Remus, do geese stand on one leg all night, or do they sit down to sleep?"

"Tooby sho dey does, honey; dey sets down same ez you does. Co'se, dey don't cross der legs," he added, cautiously, "kaze dey sets down right flat-footed."

"Well, I saw one the other day, and he was standing on one foot, and I watched him and watched him, and he kept on standing there."

"Ez ter dat," responded Uncle Remus, "dey mought stan' on one foot an' drap off ter sleep en fergit deyse'f. Deze yer gooses," he continued, wiping the crumbs from his beard with his coat-tail, "is mighty kuse fowls; dey er mighty kuse. In ole times dey wuz 'mongs de big-bugs, en in dem days, w'en ole Miss Goose gun a-dinin', all de quality wuz dere. Likewise, en needer wuz dey stuck-up, kaze wid all der kyar'n's on, Miss Goose wer'n't too proud fer ter take in washin' fer de neighborhoods, en she make money, en get slick en fat lak Sis Tempy.

"Dis de way marters stan' w'en one day Brer Fox en Brer Rabbit, dey wuz settin' up at de cotton-patch, one on one side de fence, en t'er one on t'er side, gwine on wid one er n'er, w'en fus' news dey know, dey year sump'n' — *blim, blim, blim!*

"Brer Fox, he ax w'at dat fuss is, en Brer Rabbit, he up'n 'spon' dat it's ole Miss Goose down at de spring. Den Brer Fox, he up'n ax w'at she doin', en Brer Rabbit, he say, sezee, dat she battlin' cloze."

"Battling clothes, Uncle Remus?" said the little boy.

"Dat w'at dey call it dem days, honey. Deze times, dey rubs cloze on deze yer bodes w'at got furrers in um, but dem days dey des tuck'n tuck de cloze en lay um out on a bench, en ketch holt er de battlin'-stick en nat'ally paddle de fillin' out'n um.

"W'en Brer Fox year dat ole Miss Goose wuz down dar dabblin' in soapsuds en washin' cloze, he sorter lick he chops, en 'low dat some er dese odd-come-shorts he gwine ter call en pay he 'specks. De minnit he say dat, Brer Rabbit, he know sump'n' 'uz up, en he 'low ter hisse'f dat he speck he better whirl in en have some fun w'iles it gwine on. Bimeby Brer Fox up'n say ter Brer Rabbit dat he bleedzd ter be movin' 'long todes home, en wid dat dey bofe say good-bye.

"Brer Fox, he put out ter whar his fambly wuz, but Brer Rabbit, he slip 'roun', he did, en call on ole Miss Goose. Ole Miss Goose she wuz down at de spring, washin', en b'ilin', en battlin' cloze; but Brer Rabbit he march up en ax her howdy, en den she tuck'n ax Brer Rabbit howdy.

"'I'd shake han's 'long wid you, Brer Rabbit,' sez she, 'but dey er all full er suds,' sez she.

"'No marter 'bout dat, Miss Goose,' sez Brer Rabbit, sezee, 'so long ez yo' will's good,' sezee."

"A goose with hands, Uncle Remus!" the little boy exclaimed.

"How you know goose ain't got han's?" Uncle Remus inquired, with a frown. "Is you been sleepin' longer ole man Know-All? Little mo' en you'll up'n stan' me down dat snakes ain't got no foots and yit you take en lay a snake down yer 'fo' de fier, en his foots 'll come out right 'fo' yo' eyes."

Uncle Remus paused here, but presently continued:

"Atter ole Miss Goose en Brer Rabbit done pass de time er day wid one er n'er, Brer Rabbit, he ax 'er, he did, how she come on deze days, en Miss Goose say, mighty po'ly.

"'I'm gittin' stiff en I'm gittin' clumpsy,' sez she, 'en mo'n dat I'm gittin' bline,' sez she. 'Des 'fo' you happen 'long, Brer Rabbit, I drap my specks in de tub yer, en ef you'd a come 'long 'bout dat time,' sez ole Miss Goose, sez she, 'I lay I'd er tuck you for dat nasty, owdashus Brer Fox, en it ud er bin a born blessin' ef I hadn't er scald you wid er pan er b'ilin' suds,' sez she. 'I'm dat glad I foun' my specks I dunner w'at ter do,' sez ole Miss Goose, sez she.

"Den Brer Rabbit, he up'n say dat bein's how Sis Goose done fotch up Brer Fox name, he got sump'n' fer ter tell 'er, en den he let out 'bout Brer Fox gwine ter call on 'er.

"'He comin','' sez Brer Rabbit, sezee; 'he comin' sho, en w'en he come hit'll be des 'fo' day,' sezee.

"Wid dat, ole Miss Goose wipe 'er han's on 'er apun, en put 'er specks up on 'er forrerd, en look lak she done got trouble in 'er min'.

"'Laws-a-massy!' sez she, 'spozen he come, Brer Rabbit! W'at I gwine do? En dey ain't a man 'bout de house, n'er,' sez she.

"Den Brer Rabbit, he shot one eye, en he say, sezee:

"'Sis Goose, de time done come w'en you bleedzd ter roos' high. You look lak you got de dropsy,' sezee, 'but don't min' dat, kaze ef you don't roos' high, you er goner,' sezee.

"Den ole Miss Goose ax Brer Rabbit w'at she gwine do, en Brer Rabbit he up en tell Miss Goose dat she mus' go home en tie up a bundle er de white folks' cloze, en put um on de bed, en den she mus' fly up on a rafter, en let Brer Fox grab de cloze en run off wid um.

"Ole Miss Goose say she much 'blige, en she tuck'n tuck her things en waddle off home, en dat night she do lak Brer Rabbit say wid de bundle er cloze, en den she sont wud ter Mr. Dog, en Mr. Dog he come down, en say he'd sorter set up wid er.

"Des 'fo' day, yer come Brer Fox creepin' up, en he went en push on de do' easy, en de do' open, en he see sump'n' w'ite on de bed w'ich he took fer Miss Goose, en he grab it en run. 'Bout dat time Mr. Dog sail out fum und' de house, he did, en ef Brer Fox hadn't er drapt de cloze, he'd er got kotch. Fum dat, wud went 'roun' dat Brer Fox bin tryin' ter steal

Miss Goose cloze, en he come mighty nigh losin' his stan'in' at Miss
Meadows. Down ter dis day," Uncle Remus continued, preparing to fill
his pipe, "Brer Fox b'lieve dat Brer Rabbit wuz de 'casion er Mr. Dog
bein' in de neighborhoods at dat time er night, en Brer Rabbit ain't
'spute it. De bad feelin' 'twix' Brer Fox en Mr. Dog start right dar, en hit's
bin a-gwine on twel now dey ain't git in smellin' distuns er one er n'er
widout dey's a row."

2
Brother Fox Catches Mr. Horse

THERE WAS a pause after the story of old Miss Goose. The culmination was hardly sensational enough to win the hearty applause of the little boy, and this fact appeared to have a depressing influence upon Uncle Remus. As he leaned slightly forward, gazing into the depths of the great fireplace, his attitude was one of pensiveness.

"I 'speck I done wo' out my welcome up at de big house," he said, after a while. "I mos' knows I is," he continued, setting himself resignedly in his deep-bottomed chair. "Kaze de las' time I 'uz up dar, I had my eye on Miss Sally mighty nigh de whole blessid time, en w'en you see Miss Sally rustlin' 'roun' makin' lak she fixin' things up dar on de mantel-shelf, en bouncin' de cheers 'roun', en breshin' dus' whar dey ain't no dus', en flyin' 'roun' singin' sorter louder dan common, den I des knows sump'n' done gone en rile 'er."

"Why, Uncle Remus!" exclaimed the little boy; "Mamma was just glad because I was feeling so good."

"Mought er bin," the old man remarked, in a tone that was far from implying conviction. "Ef 'twa'n't dat, den she wuz gittin' tired er seein' me lounjun 'roun' up dar night atter night, en ef 'twa'n't dat, den she wuz watchin' a chance fer ter preach ter yo' pa. Oh, I done bin know Miss Sally long fo' yo' pa is!" exclaimed Uncle Remus, in response to the astonishment depicted upon the child's face. "I bin knowin' 'er sence she wuz so high, en endurin' er all dat time I ain't seed no mo' up'n-spoken w'ite 'oman dan w'at Miss Sally is.

"But dat ain't needer yer ner dar. You done got so you k'n rush down yer des like you useter, en we kin set yer en smoke, en tell tales, en study up' musements same like we wuz gwine on 'fo' you got dat splinter in yo' foot.

"I min's me er one time" — with an infectious laugh — "w'en ole Brer Rabbit got Brer Fox in de wuss trubble w'at a man wuz mos' ever got in yit, en dat 'uz w'en he fool 'im 'bout de Hoss. Ain't I never tell you 'bout dat? But no marter ef I is. Hoe-cake ain't cook done good twel hit's turnt over a couple er times.

"Well, atter Brer Fox done git rested fum keepin' out er de way er Mr.

Dog, en sorter ketch up wid his rations, he say ter hisse'f dat he be dog his cats ef he don't slorate ole Brer Rabbit ef it takes 'im a mont'; en dat, too, on top er all de 'speunce what he done bin had wid um. Brer Rabbit he sorter git win' er dis, en one day, w'iles he gwine 'long de road studyin' how he gwine ter hol' he hand wid Brer Fox, he see a great big Hoss layin' stretch out flat on he side in de pastur'; en he tuck'n crope up, he did, fer ter see ef dish yer Hoss done gone en die. He crope up en he crope 'roun', en bimeby he see de Hoss switch he tail, en den Brer Rabbit know he ain't dead. Wid dat, Brer Rabbit lope back ter de big road, en mos' de fus' man w'at he see gwine on by wuz Brer Fox, en Brer Rabbit he tuck atter 'im, en holler:

"'Brer Fox! O Brer Fox! Come back! I got some good news fer you. Come back, Brer Fox,' sezee.

"Brer Fox, he tu'n 'roun', he did, en w'en he see who callin' 'im, he come gallopin' back, kaze it seem like dat des ez good er time ez any fer ter nab Brer Rabbit; but 'fo' he git in nabbin' distance, Brer Rabbit he up'n say, sezee:

"'Come on, Brer Fox! I done fin' de place whar you kin lay in fresh meat nuff fer ter las' you plum twel de middle er nex' year,' sezee.

"Brer Fox, he ax whar'bouts, en Brer Rabbit, he say, right over dar in de pastur', en Brer Fox ax w'at is it, en Brer Rabbit, he say w'ich 'twuz a whole Hoss layin' down on de groun' whar dey kin ketch 'im en tie 'im. Wid dat, Brer Fox, he say come on, en off dey put.

"W'en dey got dar, sho nuff, dar lay de Hoss all stretch out in de sun, fas' 'sleep, en den Brer Fox en Brer Rabbit, dey had a 'spute 'bout how dey gwine ter fix de Hoss so he can't git loose. One say one way en de yuther say n'er way, en dar dey had it, twel atter w'ile Brer Rabbit, he say, sezee:

"'De onliest plan w'at I knows un, Brer Fox,' sezee, 'is fer you ter git down dar en lemme tie you ter de Hoss' tail, en den, w'en he try ter git up, you kin hol' 'im down,' sezee. 'Ef I wuz big man like w'at you is,' sez Brer Rabbit, sezee, 'you mought tie me ter dat Hoss' tail, en ef I ain't hol' 'im down, den Joe's dead en Sal's a widder. I des knows you kin hol' 'im down,' sez Brer Rabbit, sezee, 'but yit, ef you 'feard, we des better drap dat idee en study out some yuther plan,' sezee.

"Brer Fox sorter jubous 'bout dis, but he bleedzd ter play biggity 'fo' Brer Rabbit, en he tuck'n 'gree ter de progrance, en den Brer Rabbit, he tuck'n tie Brer Fox ter de Hoss' tail, en atter he git 'im tie dar hard en fas', he sorter step back, he did, en put he han's 'kimbo, en grin, en den he say, sezee:

"'Ef ever dey wuz a Hoss kotch, den we done kotch dis un. Look sorter lak we done put de bridle on de wrong een',' sezee, 'but I lay Brer Fox is got de strenk fer ter hol' 'im,' sezee.

"Wid dat, Brer Rabbit cut 'im a long switch en trim it up, en w'en he get it fix, up he step en hit de Hoss a rap — *pow!* De Hoss 'uz dat s'prise at dat kinder doin's dat he make one jump, en lan' on he foots. W'en he do dat, dar wuz Brer Fox danglin' in de a'r, en Brer Rabbit, he dart out de way en holler:

"'Hol' 'im down, Brer Fox! Hol' 'im down! I'll stan' out yer en see fa'r play. Hol' 'im down, Brer Fox! Hol' 'im down!'

"Co'se, w'en de Hoss feel Brer Fox hangin' dar onter he tail, he thunk sump'n' kuse wuz de marter, en dis make 'im jump en r'ar wusser en wusser, en he shake up Brer Fox same like he wuz a rag in de win', en Brer Rabbit, he jump en holler:

"'Hol' 'im down, Brer Fox! Hol' 'im down! You got 'im now, sho! Hol' yo' grip, en hol' 'im down,' sezee.

"De Hoss, he jump en he jump, en he rip en he r'ar, en he snort en he t'ar. But yit Brer Fox hang on, en still Brer Rabbit skip 'roun' en holler:

"'Hol' 'im down, Brer Fox! You got 'im whar he can't needer back ner squall. Hol' 'im down, Brer Fox!' sezee.

"Bimeby, w'en Brer Fox git chance, he holler back, he did:

"'How in de name er goodness I gwine ter hol' de Hoss down 'less I git my claw in de groun'?'

"Den Brer Rabbit, he stan' back little furder en holler little louder:

"'Hol' 'im down. Brer Fox! Hol' 'im down! You got 'im now, sho! Hol' 'im down!'

"Bimeby de Hoss 'gun ter kick wid he behime legs, en de fus' news you know, he fetch Brer Fox a lick in de stomach dat fa'rly make 'im squall, en den he kicks 'im ag'in, en dis time he break Brer Fox loose, en sont 'im a-whirlin'; en Brer Rabbit, he keep on a-jumpin' 'roun' en hollerin':

"'Hol' 'im down, Brer Fox!'"

"Did the fox get killed, Uncle Remus?" asked the little boy.

"He wa'n't zackly kil't, honey," replied the old man, "but he wuz de nex' do' ter't. He 'uz all broke up, en w'iles he 'uz gittin' well, hit sorter come 'cross he min' dat Brer Rabbit done play n'er game on 'im.'"

3
Brother Rabbit and the Little Girl

"WHAT DID Brother Rabbit do after that?" the little boy asked presently.

"Now, den, you don't wanter push ole Brer Rabbit too close," replied Uncle Remus significantly. "He mighty tender-footed creetur, en de mo' w'at you push 'im, de furder he lef' you."

There was prolonged silence in the old man's cabin, until, seeing that the little boy was growing restless enough to cast several curious glances in the direction of the tool-chest in the corner, Uncle Remus lifted one leg over the other, scratched his head reflectively, and began:

"One time, atter Brer Rabbit done bin trompin' 'roun' huntin' up some sallid fer ter make out he dinner wid, he fin' hisse'f in de neighborhoods er Mr. Man house, en he pass 'long twel he come ter de gyardin-gate, en nigh de gyardin-gate he see Little Gal playin' 'roun' in de san'. W'en Brer Rabbit look 'twix' de gyardin-palin's en see de colluds, en de sparrer-grass, en de yuther gyardin truck growin' dar, hit make he mouf water. Den he take en walk up ter de Little Gal, Brer Rabbit did, en pull he roach, en bow, en scrape he foot, en talk mighty nice en slick.

"'Howdy, Little Gal,' sez Brer Rabbit, sezee; 'how you come on?' sezee.

"Den de Little Gal, she 'spon' howdy, she did, en she ax Brer Rabbit how he come on, en Brer Rabbit, he 'low he mighty po'ly, en den he ax ef dis de Little Gal w'at 'er pa live up dar in de big w'ite house, w'ich de Little Gal, she up'n say 'twer'. Brer Rabbit, he say he mighty glad, kaze he des bin up dar fer to see 'er pa, en he say dat 'er pa, he sont 'im out dar fer ter tell de Little Gal dat she mus' open de gyardin-gate so Brer Rabbit kin go in en git some truck. Den de Little Gal, she jump 'roun', she did, en she open de gate, en wid dat, Brer Rabbit, he hop in, he did, en got 'im a mess er greens, en hop out ag'in, en w'en he gwine off he make a bow, he did, en tell de Little Gal dat he much 'blige, en den atter dat he put out fer home.

"Nex' day, Brer Rabbit, he hide out, he did, twel he see de Little Gal come out ter play, en den he put up de same tale, en walk off wid a n'er mess er truck, en hit keep on dis away, twel bimeby Mr. Man, he 'gun ter miss his greens, en he keep on a-missin' un um, twel he got ter excusin' eve'ybody on de place er 'stroyin' un um, en w'en dat come ter pass, de Little Gal, she up'n say:

"'My goodness, pa!' sez she, 'you don tole Mr. Rabbit fer ter come and make me let 'im in de gyardin atter some greens, en ain't he done come en ax me, en ain't I done gone en let 'im in?' sez she.

"Mr. Man ain't hatter study long 'fo' he see how de lan' lay, en den he laff, en tell de Little Gal dat he done gone en disremember all 'bout Mr. Rabbit, en den he up'n say, sezee:

"'Nex' time Mr. Rabbit come, you tak'n tu'n 'im in, en den you run des ez fas' ez you kin en come en tell me, kaze I got some bizness wid dat young chap dat's bleedzd ter be 'ten' ter,' sezee.

"Sho nuff, nex' mawnin' dar wuz de Little Gal playin' 'roun', en yer come Brer Rabbit atter he 'lowance er greens. He wuz ready wid de same tale, en den de Little Gal, she tu'n 'im in, she did, en den she run up ter de house en holler:

"'O pa! pa! O pa! Yer Brer Rabbit in de gyardin now! Yer he is, pa!'

"Den Mr. Man, he rush out, en grab up a fishin'-line w'at bin hangin' in de back po'ch, en make fer de gyardin, en w'en he git dar, dar wuz Brer Rabbit tromplin' 'roun' on de strawbe'y-bed en mashin' down de termartusses. W'en Brer Rabbit see Mr. Man, he squat behime a collud leaf, but 'twa'n't no use. Mr. Man done seed him, en 'fo' you kin count 'lev'm, he done got ole Brer Rabbit tie hard en fas' wid de fishin'-line. Atter he got him tie good, Mr. Man step back, he did, en say, sezee:

"'You done bin fool me lots er time, but dis time you er mine. I'm gwine ter take you en gin you a larrupin',' sezee, 'en din I'm gwine ter skin you en nail yo' hide on de stable do',' sezee; 'en den ter make sho dat you git de right kinder larrupin', I'll des step up ter de house,' sezee, 'en fetch de little red cowhide, en den I'll take en gin you brinjer,' sezee.

"Den Mr. Man call to der Little Gal ter watch Brer Rabbit w'iles he gone.

"Brer Rabbit ain't sayin' nothin', but Mr. Man ain't mo'n out de gate 'fo' he 'gun ter sing; en in dem days Brer Rabbit wuz a singer, mon," continued Uncle Remus, with unusual emphasis, "en w'en he chuned up fer ter sing he make dem yuther creeturs hol' der bref."

"What did he sing, Uncle Remus?" asked the little boy.

"Ef I ain't fergit dat song off'n my min'," said Uncle Remus, looking over his spectacles at the fire, with a curious air of attempting to remember something, "hit run sorter dish yer way:

> "'De jay-bird hunt de sparrer-nes',
> De bee-martin sail all 'roun';
> De squer'l, he holler from de top er de tree,
> Mr. Mole, he stay in de groun';
> He hide en he stay twel de dark drap down —
> Mr. Mole, he hide in de groun'.'

"W'en de Little Gal year dat, she laugh, she did, and she up'n ax Brer Rabbit fer ter sing some mo', but Brer Rabbit, he sorter cough, he did, en 'low dat he got a mighty bad ho'seness down inter he win'pipe some'rs. De Little Gal, she 'swade, en 'swade, en bimeby Brer Rabbit, he up'n 'low dat he kin dance mo' samer dan w'at he kin sing. Den de Little Gal, she ax 'im won't he dance, en Brer Rabbit, he 'spon' how in de name er goodness kin a man dance w'iles he all tie up dis a-way, en den de Little Gal, she say she kin ontie 'im, en Brer Rabbit, he say he ain't keerin'

ef she do. Wid dat de Little Gal, she retch down en onloose de fish-line, en Brer Rabbit, he sorter stretch hisse'f en look 'roun'."

Here Uncle Remus paused and sighed, as though he had relieved his mind of a great burden. The little boy waited a few minutes for the old man to resume, and finally he asked:

"Did the Rabbit dance, Uncle Remus?"

"Who? Him?" exclaimed the old man, with a queer affectation of elation. "Bless yo' soul, honey! Brer Rabbit gedder up his foots und' 'im, en he dance outer dat gyardin, en he dance home. He did dat! Sholy you don't speck dat a ole-timer w'at done had 'speunce like Brer Rabbit gwine ter stay dar en let dat ar Mr. Man sackyfice 'im? *Shoo!* Brer Rabbit dance, but he dance home. You year me!"

4

How Brother Fox Was Too Smart

UNCLE REMUS chuckled a moment over the escape of Brother Rabbit, and then turned his gaze upward toward the cobwebbed gloom that seemed to lie just beyond the rafters. He sat thus silent and serious a little while, but finally squared himself around in his chair and looked the little boy full in the face. The old man's countenance expressed a curious mixture of sorrow and bewilderment. Catching the child by the coat-sleeve, Uncle Remus pulled him gently to attract his attention.

"Hit look like ter me," he said presently, in the tone of one approaching an unpleasant subject, "dat no longer'n yistiddy I see one er dem ar Favers chillun clim'in' dat ar big red-oak out yan', en den it seem like dat a little chap 'bout yo' size, he tuck'n start up ter see ef he can't play smarty like de Favers's yearlin's. I dunner w'at in de name er goodness you wanter be a-copyin' atter dem ar Faverses fer. Ef you er gwine ter copy atter yuther folks, copy atter dem w'at's some 'count. Yo' pa, he got de idee dat some folks is good ez yuther folks; but Miss Sally, she know better. She know dat dey ain't no Favers 'pon de top side er de yeth w'at kin hol' der han' wid de Abercrombies in p'int er breedin' en raisin'. Dat w'at Miss Sally know. I bin keepin' track er dem Faverses sence way back yan' long 'fo' Miss Sally wuz born'd. Ole Cajy Favers, he went ter de po'house, en ez ter dat Jim Favers, I boun' you he know de inside er all de jails in dish yer State er Jawjy. Dey allers did hate niggers kaze dey ain't had none, en dey hates um down ter dis day.

"Year 'fo' las'," Uncle Remus continued, "I year yo Unk' Jeems Abercrombie tell dat same Jim Favers dat ef he lay de weight er he han' on one er his niggers, he'd slap a load er buck shot in 'im; en, bless yo' soul, honey, yo' Unk' Jeems wuz des de man ter do it. But dey er monstus perlite unter me, dem Faverses is," pursued the old man, allowing his indignation, which had risen to a white heat, to cool off, "en dey better be," he added spitefully, "kaze I knows der pedigree fum de fus' ter de las', en w'en I gits my Affikin up, dey ain't nobody, 'less it's Miss Sally 'erse'f, w'at kin keep me down.

"But dat ain't needer yer ner dar," said Uncle Remus, renewing his attack upon the little boy. "W'at you wanter go copyin' atter dem Favers chillun fer? You er settin' back dar, right dis minnit, bettin' longer yo'se'f dat I ain't gwine ter tell Miss Sally, en dar whar you er lettin' yo' foot slip, kaze I'm gwine ter let it pass dis time, but de ve'y nex' time w'at I ketches you in hollerin' distuns er dem Faverses, right den en dar I'm gwine ter take my foot in my han' en go en tell Miss Sally, en ef she don't nat'ally skin you 'live, den she ain't de same 'oman w'at she useter be.

"All dish yer copyin' atter deze yer Faverses put me in min' er de time w'en Brer Fox got ter copyin' atter Brer Rabbit. I done tole you 'bout de time w'en Brer Rabbit git de game fum Brer Fox by makin' like he dead?"[1]

The little boy remembered it very distinctly, and said as much.

"Well, den, ole Brer Fox, w'en he see how slick de trick wuk wid Brer Rabbit, he say ter hisse'f dat he b'lieve he'll up'n try de same kinder game on some yuther man, en he keep on watchin' fer he chance, twel bimeby, one day, he year Mr. Man comin' down de big road in a one-hoss waggin, kyar'n some chickens, en some eggs, en some butter, ter town. Brer Fox year 'im comin', he did, en w'at do he do but go en lay down in de road front er de waggin. Mr. Man, he druv 'long, he did, cluckin' ter

---

[1] See *Uncle Remus: His Songs and His Sayings*, "Mr. Fox Goes A-Hunting, but Mr. Rabbit Bags the Game," p. 45. — J. C. H.

de hoss en hummin' ter hisse'f, en w'en dey git mos' up ter Brer Fox, de hoss, he shy, he did, en Mr. Man, he tuck'n holler Wo! en de hoss, he tuck'n wo'd. Den Mr. Man, he look down, en he see Brer Fox layin' out dar on de groun' des like he col' en stiff, en w'en Mr. Man see dis, he holler out:

"'Heyo! Dar de chap w'at been nabbin' up my chickens, en some-body done gone en shot off a gun at 'im, w'ich I wish she'd er bin two guns — dat I does!'

"Wid dat, Mr. Man, he druv on en lef' Brer Fox layin' dar. Den Brer Fox, he git up en run 'roun' thoo de woods en lay down front er Mr. Man ag'in, en Mr. Man come drivin' 'long, en he see Brer Fox, en he say, sezee:

"'Heyo! Yer de ve'y chap w'at been 'stroyin' my pigs. Somebody done gone en kilt 'im, en I wish dey'd er kilt 'im long time ago.'

"Den Mr. Man, he druv on, en de waggin-w'eel come mighty nigh mashin' Brer Fox nose; yit, all de same, Brer Fox lipt up en run 'roun' 'head er Mr. Man, en lay down in de road, en w'en Mr. Man come 'long, dar he wuz all stretch out like he big nuff fer ter fill a two-bushel baskit, en he look like he dead nuff fer ter be skint. Mr. Man druv up, he did, en stop. He look down pun Brer Fox, en den he look all 'roun' fer ter see w'at de 'casion er all deze yer dead Fox is. Mr. Man look all 'roun', he did, but he ain't see nothin', en needer do he year nothin'. Den he set dar en study, en bimeby he 'low ter hisse'f, he did, dat he had better 'zamin' w'at kinder kuse 'zeeze done bin got inter Brer Fox fambly, en wid dat he lit down outer de waggin, en feel er Brer Fox year; Brer Fox year feel right wom. Den he feel Brer Fox neck; Brer Fox neck right wom. Den he feel er Brer Fox in de short ribs; Brer Fox all soun' in de short ribs. Den he feel er Brer Fox lim's; Brer Fox all soun' in de lim's. Den he tu'n Brer Fox over, en, lo en beholes, Brer Fox right limber. W'en Mr. Man see dis, he say ter hisse'f, sezee:

"'Heyo, yer! how come dis? Dish yer chicken-nabber look lak he dead, but dey ain't no bones broked, en I ain't see no blood, en needer does I feel no bruise; en mo'n dat he wom en he limber,' sezee. 'Sump'n' wrong yer, sho! Dish yer pig-grabber *mought* be dead, en den ag'in he moughtent,' sezee; 'but ter make sho dat he is, I'll des gin 'im a whack wid my w'ip-han'le,' sezee; en wid dat, Mr. Man draw back en fotch Brer Fox a clip behime de years — *pow!* — en de lick come so hard en it come so quick dat Brer Fox thunk sho he's a goner; but 'fo' Mr. Man kin draw back fer ter fetch 'im a n'er wipe, Brer Fox, he scramble ter his feet, he did, en des make tracks 'way fum dar."

Uncle Remus paused and shook the cold ashes from his pipe, and then applied the moral:

"Dat w'at Brer Fox git fer playin' Mr. Smarty en copyin' atter yuther folks, en dat des de way de whole Smarty fambly gwine ter come out."

5

Brother Rabbit's Astonishing Prank

"I 'SPECK dat 'uz de reas'n w'at make ole Brer Rabbit git 'long so well, kaze he ain't copy atter none er de yuther creeturs," Uncle Remus continued, after a while. "W'en he make his disappearance 'fo' um, hit 'uz allers in some bran' new place. Dey ain't know whar'bouts fer ter watch out fer 'im. He wuz de funniest creetur er de whole gang. Some folks mought er call him lucky, en yit, w'en he git in bad luck, hit look lak he mos' allers come out on top. Hit look mighty kuse now, but 'twa'n't kuse in dem days, kaze hit 'uz done gun up dat, strike 'im w'en you mought en whar you would, Brer Rabbit wuz de soopless creetur gwine.

"One time, he sorter tuck a notion, ole Brer Rabbit did, dat he'd pay Brer B'ar a call, en no sooner do de notion strike 'im dan he pick hisse'f up en put out fer Brer B'ar house."

"Why, I thought they were mad with each other," the little boy exclaimed.

"Brer Rabbit make he call w'en Brer B'ar en his fambly wuz off fum home," Uncle Remus explained, with a chuckle which was in the nature of a hearty tribute to the crafty judgment of Brother Rabbit.

"He sot down by de road, en he see um go by — ole Brer B'ar en ole Miss B'ar, en der two twin-chilluns, w'ich one un um wuz name Kubs en de t'er one wuz name Klibs."

The little boy laughed, but the severe seriousness of Uncle Remus would have served for a study, as he continued:

"Ole Brer B'ar en Miss B'ar, dey went 'long ahead, en Kubs en Klibs, dey come shufflin' en scramblin' 'long behime. W'en Brer Rabbit see

dis, he say ter hisse'f dat he 'speck he better go see how Brer B'ar gittin'
on; en off he put. En 'twa'n't long n'er 'fo' he 'uz ransackin' de prem-
muses same like he 'uz sho nuff patter-roller. W'iles he wuz gwine 'roun'
peepin' in yer en pokin' in dar, he got ter foolin' 'mong de shelfs, en a
bucket er honey w'at Brer B'ar got hid in de cubberd fall down en spill
on top er Brer Rabbit, en little mo'n he'd er bin drown. Fum head ter
heels dat creetur wuz kivver'd wid honey; he wa'n't des only bedobble
wid it, he wuz des kivver'd. He hatter set dar en let de nat'al sweetness
drip out'n he eye-balls 'fo' he kin see he han' befo' 'im, en den, atter he
look 'roun' little, he say to hisse'f, sezee:

"'Heyo, yer! W'at I gwine do now? Ef I go out in de sunshine, de bumly-
bees en de flies dey'll swom up'n take me, en if I stay yer, Brer B'ar'll come
back en ketch me, en I dunner w'at in de name er gracious I gwine do.'

"Ennyhow, bimeby a notion strike Brer Rabbit, en he tip 'long twel he
git in de woods, en w'en he git out dar, w'at do he do but roll in de leafs
en trash en try fer ter rub de honey off'n 'im dat a-way. He roll, he did,
en de leafs dey stick; Brer Rabbit roll, en de leafs dey stick, en he keep
on rollin' en de leafs keep on stickin', twel atter w'ile Brer Rabbit wuz de
mos' owdashus-lookin' creetur w'at you ever sot eyes on. En ef Miss
Meadows en de gals could er seed 'im den en dar, dey wouldn't er bin no
mo' Brer Rabbit call at der house; 'deed, en dat dey wouldn't.

"Brer Rabbit, he jump 'roun', he did, en try ter shake de leafs off'n
'im, but de leafs, dey ain't gwine ter be shuck off. Brer Rabbit, he shake
en he shiver, but de leafs dey stick; en de capers dat creetur cut up out
dar in de woods by he own-alone se'f wuz scan'lous — dey wuz dat; dey
wuz scan'lous.

"Brer Rabbit sees dis wa'n't gwine ter do, en he 'low ter hisse'f dat he
better be gittin' on todes home, en off he put. I 'speck you done year talk
ez deze yer booggers w'at gits atter bad chilluns," continued Uncle Remus, in a tone so seriously confidential as to be altogether depressing;
"well, den, des zackly dat a-way Brer Rabbit look, en ef you'd er seed
'im you'd er made sho he de gran'daddy er all de booggers. Brer Rabbit
pace 'long, he did, en eve'y motion he make, de leafs dey'd go *swishy-
swushy, splushy-splishy,* en, fum de fuss he make en de way he look,
you'd er tuck 'im ter be de mos' suvvigus varment w'at disappear fum de
face er de yeth sence ole man Noah let down de draw-bars er de ark en

tu'n de creeturs loose; en I boun' ef you'd er struck up long wid 'im, you'd er been mighty good en glad ef you'd er got off wid dat.

"De fus' man w'at Brer Rabbit come up wid wuz ole Sis Cow, en no sooner is she lay eyes on 'im dan she h'ist up 'er tail in de elements, en put out like a pack er dogs wuz atter 'er. Dis make Brer Rabbit laff, kaze he know dat w'en a ole settle' 'oman like Sis Cow run 'stracted in de broad open day-time, dat dey mus' be sump'n' mighty kuse 'bout dem leafs en dat honey, en he keep on a-rackin' down de road. De nex' man w'at he meet wuz a black gal tollin' a whole passel er plantation shotes, en w'en de gal see Brer Rabbit come prancin' 'long, she fling down 'er basket er corn en des fa'rly fly, en de shotes, dey tuck thoo de woods, en sech n'er racket ez dey kick up wid der runnin', en der snortin', en der squealin' ain't never bin year in dat settlement needer befo' ner since. Hit keep on dis a-way long ez Brer Rabbit meet anybody — dey des broke en run like de Ole Boy wuz atter um.

"Co'se, dis make Brer Rabbit feel monstus biggity, en he 'low ter hisse'f dat he 'speck he better drap 'roun' en skummish in de neighborhoods er Brer Fox house. En w'iles he wuz stan'in' dar runnin' dis 'roun' in he min', yer come old Brer B'ar en all er he fambly. Brer Rabbit he git crossways de road, he did, en he sorter sidle todes um. Old Brer B'ar, he stop en look, but Brer Rabbit, he keep on sidlin' todes um. Ole Miss B'ar, she stan' it long ez she kin, en den she fling down 'er parrysol en tuck a tree. Brer B'ar look lak he gwine ter stan' his groun', but Brer Rabbit he jump straight up in de a'r en gin hisse'f a shake, en, bless yo' soul, honey! ole Brer B'ar make a break, en dey tells me he to' down a whole panel er fence gittin' 'way fum dar. En ez ter Kubs en Klibs, dey tuck der hats in der han's, en dey went skaddlin' thoo de bushes des same ez a drove er hosses."

"And then what?" the little boy asked.

"Brer Rabbit p'raded on down de road," continued Uncle Remus, "en bimeby yer come Brer Fox en Brer Wolf, fixin' up a plan fer ter nab Brer Rabbit, en dey wuz so intents on der confab dat dey got right on Brer Rabbit 'fo' dey seed 'im; but gentermens! w'en dey is ketch a glimpse un 'im, dey gun 'im all de room he want. Brer Wolf, he try ter show off, he did, kaze he wanter play big 'fo' Brer Fox, en he stop en ax Brer Rabbit who is he. Brer Rabbit, he jump up en down in de middle er de road, en holler out:

"'I'm de Wull-er-de-Wust. I'm de Wull-er-de-Wust, en you er de man I'm atter!'

"Den Brer Rabbit jump up en down en make lak he gwine atter Brer Fox en Brer Wolf, en de way dem creeturs lit out fum dar wuz a caution.

"Long time atter dat," continued Uncle Remus, folding his hands placidly in his lap, with the air of one who has performed a pleasant duty — "long time atter dat, Brer Rabbit come up wid Brer Fox en Brer Wolf, en he git behime a stump, Brer Rabbit did, en holler out:

"'I'm de Wull-er-de-Wust, en you er de mens I'm atter!'

"Brer Fox en Brer Wolf, dey broke, but 'fo' dey got outer sight en outer year'n', Brer Rabbit show hisse'f, he did, en laugh fit ter kill hisse'f. Atterwuds, Miss Meadows she year 'bout it, en de nex' time Brer Fox call, de gals dey up en giggle, en ax 'im ef he ain't 'feard de Wull-er-de-Wust mought drap in."

6
Brother Rabbit Secures a Mansion

THE RAIN continued to fall the next day, but the little boy made arrangements to go with 'Tildy when she carried Uncle Remus his supper. This happened to be a waiter full of things left over from dinner. There was so much that the old man was moved to remark:

"I 'clar ter gracious, hit look lak Miss Sally done got my name in de pot dis time, sho. I des wish you look at dat pone er co'nbread, honey, en dem ar greens, en see ef dey ain't got Remus writ somers on um. Dat ar chick'n fixin's, dey look lak dey er good, yet 'tain't familious wid me lak dat ar bile ham. Dem ar sweet-taters, dey stan's fa'r fer dividjun, but dem ar puzzuv, I lay dey fit yo' palate mo' samer dan dey does mine. Dish yer hunk er beef, we kin talk 'bout dat w'en de time come, en dem ar biscuits, I des nat'ally knows Miss Sally put um in dar fer some little chap w'ich his name I ain't gwine ter call in comp'ny."

It was easy to perceive that the sight of the supper had put Uncle Remus in rare good-humor. He moved around briskly, taking the plates from the waiter and distributing them with exaggerated carefulness around upon his little pine table. Meanwhile he kept up a running fire of conversation.

"Folks w'at kin set down en have der vittles brung en put down right spang und' der nose — dem kinder folks ain't got no needs er no umbrell'. Night 'fo' las', w'iles I wuz settin' dar in de do', I year dem Willis-whistlers, en den I des know'd we 'uz gwine ter git a season."

"The Willis-whistlers, Uncle Remus," exclaimed the little boy. "What are they?"

"You er too hard fer me now, honey. Dat w'at I knows I don't min' tellin', but w'en you axes me 'bout dat w'at I dunno, den you er too hard fer me, sho. Deze yer Willis-whistlers, dey bangs my time, en I bin knockin' 'roun' in dish yer low-groun' now gwine on eighty year. Some folks wanter make out dey er frogs, yit I wish dey p'int out unter me how frogs kin holler so dat de nigher you come t'um, de furder you is off; I be mighty glad ef some un 'ud come 'long en tell me dat. Many en many's de time is I gone atter deze yer Willis-whistlers, en, no diffunce whar I goes, deyer allers off yander. You kin put de shovel in de fier en make de squinch-owl hush he fuss, en you kin go out en put yo' han' on de trees en make deze yere locus'-bugs quit der racket, but dem ar Willis-whistlers dey er allers 'way off yander."

Suddenly Uncle Remus paused over one of the dishes, and exclaimed:

"Gracious en de goodness! W'at kinder doin's is dis Miss Sally done gone sont us?"

"That," said the little boy, after making an investigation "is what mamma calls a floating island."

"Well, den," Uncle Remus remarked, in a relieved tone, "dat's diffunt. I wuz mos' 'feard it 'uz some er dat ar silly-bug, w'ich a whole jugful ain't skacely nuff fer ter make you seem like you dremp 'bout smellin' dram. Ef I'm gwine ter be fed on foam," continued the old man, by way of explaining his position on the subject of syllabub, "let it be foam, en ef I'm gwine ter git dram, lemme git in reach un it w'ile she got some strenk lef'. Dat's me up and down. W'en it come ter yo' floatin' ilun, des gimme a hunk er ginger cake en a mug er 'simmon-beer, en dey won't fin' no nigger w'ats got no slicker feelin's dan w'at I is.

"Miss Sally mighty kuse white 'oman," Uncle Remus went on. "She sendin' all deze doin's en fixin's down yer, en I 'speck dey er monstus nice, but no longer'n las' Chuseday she had all de niggers on de place, big en little, gwine squallin' 'roun' fer Remus. Hit 'uz Remus yer en Remus dar, en, lo en beholes, w'en I come ter fin' out, Miss Sally want Remus fer ter whirl in en cook 'er one er deze yer ole-time ashcakes. She bleedzd ter have it den en dar; en w'en I git it done, Miss Sally, she got a glass er buttermilk, en tuck'n sot right flat down on de flo', des like she useter w'en she wuz little gal." The old man paused, straightened up, looked at the child over his spectacles, and continued, with emphasis: "En I be bless ef she ain't eat a hunk er dat ashcake mighty nigh ez big ez yo' head, en den she tuck'n make out 'twa'n't cook right.

"Now, den, honey, all deze done fix. You set over dar, and I'll set over yer, en 'twix' en 'tween us we'll sample dish yer truck en see w'at is it Miss Sally done gone en sont us; en w'iles we er makin' 'way wid it, I'll sorter rustle 'roun' wid my 'membunce, en see if I kin call ter min' de tale 'bout how ole Brer Rabbit got 'im a two-story house widout layin' out much cash."

Uncle Remus stopped talking a little while and pretended to be trying to remember something — an effort that was accompanied by a curious humming sound in his throat. Finally, he brightened up and began:

"Hit tu'n out one time dat a whole lot er de creeturs tuck a notion dat dey'd go in cahoots wid buil'n' un um a house. Ole Brer B'ar, he was 'mongs' um, en Brer Fox, en Brer Wolf, en Brer 'Coon, en Brer Possum.

I won't make sho, but it seem like ter me dat plum' down ter ole Brer Mink 'uz 'mongs' um. Leas'ways, dey wuz a whole passel un um, en dey whirl in, dey did, en dey buil' de house in less'n no time. Brer Rabbit, he make lak it make he head swim fer ter climb up on de scaffle, en likewise he say it make 'im ketch de palsy fer ter wuk in de sun, but he got 'im a squar', en he stuck a pencil behime he year, en he went 'roun' medjun en markin' — medjun en markin' — en he wuz dat busy dat de yuther creeturs say ter deyse'f he doin' monstus sight er wuk, en folks gwine 'long de big road say Brer Rabbit doin' mo' hard wuk dan de whole kit en b'ilin' un um. Yet all de time Brer Rabbit ain't doin' nothin', en he des well bin layin' off in de shade scratchin' de fleas off'n 'im. De yuther creeturs, dey buil' de house, en, gentermens! she 'uz a fine un, too, mon. She'd a bin a fine un deze days, let 'lone dem days. She had er upsta'rs en downsta'rs, en chimbleys all 'roun', en she had rooms fer all de creeturs w'at went inter cahoots en hope make it.

"Brer Rabbit, he pick out one er de upsta'rs rooms, en he tuck'n' got 'im a gun, en one er deze yer brass cannons, en he tuck'n' put um in dar w'en de yuther creeturs ain't lookin', en den he tuck'n got 'im a tub er nasty slop-water, w'ich likewise he put in dar w'en dey ain't lookin'. So den, w'en dey git de house all fix, en w'iles dey wuz all a-settin' in de parlor atter supper, Brer Rabbit, he sorter gap en stretch hisse'f, en make his skuses en say he b'lieve he'll go ter he room. W'en he git dar, en w'iles all de yuther creeturs wuz a-laughin' en a-chattin' des ez sociable ez you please, Brer Rabbit, he stick he head out er de do' er he room en sing out:

"'W'en a big man like me wanter set down, whar'bouts he gwine ter set?' sezee.

"Den de yuther creeturs dey laugh, en holler back:

"'Ef big man like you can't set in a cheer, he better set down on de flo'.'

"'Watch out down dar, den,' sez ole Brer Rabbit, sezee. 'Kaze I'm a gwine ter set down,' sezee.

"Wid dat, *bang!* went Brer Rabbit gun. Co'se, dis sorter 'stonish de creeturs, en dey look 'roun' at one er n'er much ez ter say, W'at in de name er gracious is dat? Dey lissen en lissen, but dey don't year no mo' fuss, en 'twa'n't long 'fo' dey got ter chattin' en jabberin' some mo'. Bimeby, Brer Rabbit stick he head outer he room do', en sing out:

"'W'en a big man like me wanter sneeze, whar'bouts he gwine ter sneeze at?'

"Den de yuther creeturs, dey tuck'n holler back:

"'Ef big man like you ain't a-gone gump, he kin sneeze anywhar he please.'

"'Watch out down dar, den,' sez Brer Rabbit, sezee. 'Kaze I'm gwine ter tu'n loose en sneeze right yer,' sezee.

"Wid dat, Brer Rabbit let off his cannon — *bulderum-m-m!* De winder-glass dey shuck en rattle, en de house shuck like she gwine ter come down, en ole Brer B'ar, he fell out de rockin'-cheer — *kerblump!* W'en de creeturs git sorter settle, Brer 'Possum en Brer Mink, dey up'n' 'low dat Brer Rabbit got sech a monstus bad col', dey b'lieve dey'll step out and git some fresh a'r, but dem yuther creeturs, dey say dey gwine ter stick it out; en atter w'ile, w'en dey git der ha'r smoove down, dey 'gun ter jower 'mongs' deyse'f. 'Bout dat time, w'en dey get in a good way. Brer Rabbit, he sing out:

"'W'en a big man like me take a chaw terbacker, whar'bouts he gwine ter spit?'

"Den de yuther creeturs, dey holler back, dey did, sorter like dey er mad:

"'Big man er little man, spit whar you please.'

"Den Brer Rabbit, he squall out:

"'Dis de way a big man spit!' en wid dat he tilt over de tub er slop-water, en w'en de yuther creeturs year it come a-sloshin' down de sta'r-steps, gentermens! dey des histed deyse'f outer dar. Some un um went out de back do', en some un um went out de front do', en some un um fell out de winders; some went one way en some went n'er way; but dey all went sailin' out."

"But what became of Brother Rabbit?" the little boy asked.

"Brer Rabbit, he des tuck'n shot up de house en fassen de winders, en den he go ter bed, he did, en pull de coverled up 'roun' he years, en he sleep like a man w'at ain't owe nobody nothin'; en needer do he owe um, kaze ef dem yuther creeturs gwine git skeer'd en run off fum der own house, w'at bizness is dat er Brer Rabbit? Dat what I like ter know."

7
Mr. Lion Hunts for Mr. Man

UNCLE REMUS sighed heavily as he lifted the trivet on the head of his walking-cane, and hung it carefully by the side of the griddle in the cavernous fireplace.

"Folks kin come 'long wid der watchermaycollums," he said presently, turning to the little boy, who was supplementing his supper by biting off a chew of shoemaker's wax, "en likewise dey kin fetch 'roun' der watiznames. Dey kin walk biggity, en dey kin talk biggity, en, mo'n dat, dey kin feel biggity, but yit all de same deyer gwine ter git kotch up wid. Dey go 'long en dey go 'long, en den bimeby yer come trouble en snatch um slonchways, en de mo' bigger w'at dey is, de wusser does dey git snatched."

The little boy didn't understand this harangue at all, but he appreciated it because he recognized it as the prelude to a story.

"Dar wuz Mr. Lion," Uncle Remus went on: "he tuck'n' sot hisse'f up fer ter be de boss er all de yuther creeturs, en he feel so biggity dat he go ro'in' en rampin' roun' de neighborhoods wuss'n dat ar speckle bull w'at you see down at yo' Unk' Jeems Abercrombie place las' year. He went ro'in' 'roun', he did, en eve'ywhar he go he year talk er Mr. Man. Right in de middle er he braggin' some un 'ud up'n tell 'im 'bout w'at Mr. Man done done. Mr. Lion, he say he done dis, en den he year 'bout how Mr. Man done dat. Hit went on dis away twel bimeby Mr. Lion shake he mane, he did, en he up'n' say dat he gwine ter s'arch 'roun' en 'roun', en high en low, fer ter see ef he can't fin' Mr. Man, en he 'low, Mr. Lion did, dat w'en he do fin' 'im, he gwine ter tu'n in en 'gin Mr. Man sech n'er larrupin' w'at nobody ain't never had yit. Dem yuther creeturs, dey tuck'n' tell Mr. Lion dat he better let Mr. Man 'lone, but Mr. Lion say he gwine ter hunt 'im down spite er all dey kin do.

"Sho nuff, atter he done tuck some res', Mr. Lion, he put out down de big road. Sun, she rise up en shine hot, but Mr. Lion, he keep on; win', hit come up en blow, en fill de elements full er dust; rain, hit drif' up en drizzle down; but Mr. Lion, he keep on. Bimeby, w'iles he gwine on dis a-way, wid he tongue hangin' out, he come up wid Mr. Steer, grazin' 'long on de side er de road. Mr. Lion, he up'n ax 'im howdy, he did, monstus perlite, en Mr. Steer likewise he bow en scrape en show his manners. Den Mr. Lion, he do lak he wanter have some confab wid 'im, en he up'n say, sezee:

"'Is dey anybody 'roun' in deze parts name Mr. Man?' sezee.

"'Tooby sho dey is,' sez Mr. Steer; 'anybody kin tell you dat. I knows 'im mighty well,' sezee.

"'Well, den, he de ve'y chap I'm atter,' sezee.

"'What mought be yo' bizness wid Mr. Man?' sez Mr. Steer, sezee.

"'I done come dis long ways fer ter gin 'im a larrupin',' sez Mr. Lion, sezee. 'I'm gwine ter show 'im who de boss er deze neighborhoods,' sezee, en wid dat Mr. Lion, he shake he mane, en switch he tail, en strut up en down wuss'n one er deze yer town niggers.

"'Well, den, ef dat w'at you come atter,' sez Mr. Steer, sezee, 'you des better slew yo'se'f 'roun' en p'int yo' nose todes home, kaze you fixin' fer ter git in sho nuff trouble,' sezee.

"'I'm gwine ter larrup dat same Mr. Man,' sez Mr. Lion, sezee; 'I done come fer dat, en dat w'at I'm gwine ter do,' sezee.

"Mr. Steer, he draw long breff, he did, en chaw he cud slow, en atter w'ile he say, sezee:

"'You see me stan'in' yer front er yo' eyes, en you see how big I is, en w'at long, sharp hawns I got. Well, big ez my heft is, en sharp dough my hawns be, yit Mr. Man, he come out yer en he ketch me, en he put me und' a yoke, en he hitch me up in a kyart, en he make me haul he wood, en he drive me anywhar he min' ter. He do dat. Better let Mr. Man 'lone,' sezee. 'If you fool 'long wid 'im, watch out dat he don't hitch you up en have you prancin' 'roun' yer pullin' he kyart,' sezee.

"Mr. Lion, he fotch a roar, en put out down de road, en 'twa'n't so mighty long 'fo' he come up wid Mr. Hoss, w'ich he wuz a-nibblin' en a-croppin' de grass. Mr. Lion make hisse'f know'd, en den he tuck'n ax Mr. Hoss do he know Mr. Man.

"'Mighty well,' sez Mr. Hoss, sezee, 'en mo'n dat, I bin aknowin' 'im a long time. W'at you want wid Mr. Man?' sezee.

"'I'm a-huntin' 'im up fer ter larrup 'im,' sez Mr. Lion, sezee. 'Dey tels me he mighty stuck up,' sezee, 'en I gwine take 'im down a peg,' sezee.

"Mr. Hoss look at Mr. Lion like he sorry, en bimeby he up'n say:

"'I speck you better let Mr. Man 'lone,' sezee. 'You see how big I is, en how much strenk w'at I got, en how tough my foots is,' sezee; 'well, dish yer Mr. Man, he kin tak'n take me en hitch me up in he buggy, en make me haul 'im all 'roun', en den he kin tak'n fassen me ter de plow en make me break up all his new groun',' sezee. 'You better go 'long back home. Fus' news you know, Mr. Man'll have you breakin' up his new groun',' sezee.

"Spite er all dis, Mr. Lion, he shake he mane en say he gwine ter larrup Mr. Man anyhow. He went on down de big road, he did, en bimeby he come up wid Mr. Jack Sparrer, settin' up in de top er de tree. Mr. Jack Sparrer, he whirl 'roun' en chirp, en flutter 'bout up dar, en 'pariently make a great 'miration.

"'Heyo yer!' sezee; 'who'd er 'speckted fer ter see Mr. Lion 'way down yer in dis neighborhoods?' sezee. 'Whar you gwine, Mr. Lion?' sezee.

"Den Mr. Lion ax ef Mr. Jack Sparrer know Mr. Man, en Mr. Jack Sparrer say he know Mr. Man mighty well. Den Mr. Lion, he ax ef Mr. Jack Sparrer know whar he stay, w'ich Mr. Jack Sparrer say dat he do. Mr. Lion ax whar'bouts is Mr. Man, en Mr. Jack Sparrer say he right 'cross dar in de new groun', en he up'n ax Mr. Lion w'at he want wid 'im, w'ich Mr. Lion 'spon' dat he gwine larrup Mr. Man, en wid dat, Mr. Jack Sparrer, he up'n say, sezee:

"'You better let Mr. Man 'lone. You see how little I is, en likewise how high I kin fly; yit, 'spite er dat, Mr. Man, he kin fetch me down w'en he git good an' ready,' sezee. 'You better tuck yo tail en put out home,' sez Mr. Jack Sparrer, sezee, 'kaze bimeby Mr. Man'll fetch you down,' sezee.

"But Mr. Lion des vow he gwine atter Mr. Man, en go he would, en go he did. He ain't never see Mr. Man, Mr. Lion ain't, en he dunner w'at he look lak, but he go on todes de new groun'. Sho nuff, dar wuz Mr. Man, out dar maulin' rails fer ter make 'im a fence. He 'uz rippin' up de butt cut, Mr. Man wuz, en he druv in his wedge en den he stuck in de glut. He 'uz splittin' 'way, w'en bimeby he year rustlin' out dar in de bushes, en he look up, en dar wuz Mr. Lion. Mr. Lion ax 'im do he know Mr. Man, en Mr. Man 'low dat he know 'im mo' samer dan ef he wer' his twin brer. Den Mr. Lion 'low dat he wanter see 'im, en den Mr. Man say, sezee, dat ef Mr. Lion will come stick his paw in de split fer ter hol' de log open twel he git back, he go fetch Mr. Man. Mr. Lion he march up en slap his paw in de place, en den Mr. Man, he tuck'n knock de glut out, en de split close up, en dar Mr. Lion wuz. Mr. Man, he stan' off en say, sezee:

"'Ef you'd a bin a steer er hoss, you mought er run'd, en ef you'd a bin a sparrer, you mought er flew'd, but yer you is, en you kotch yo'se'f,' sezee.

"Wid dat, Mr. Man sa'nter out in de bushes en cut 'im a hick'ry, en he let in on Mr. Lion, en he frail en frail 'im twel frailin' un 'im wuz a sin. En down ter dis day," continued Uncle Remus, in a tone calculated to destroy all doubt, "you can't git no Lion ter come up whar dey's a Man a-maulin' rails en put he paw in de split. Dat you can't!"

8
The Story of the Pigs

UNCLE REMUS relapsed into silence again, and the little boy, with nothing better to do, turned his attention to the bench upon which the old man kept his shoemaker's tools. Prosecuting his investigations in this direction, the youngster finally suggested that the supply of bristles was about exhausted.

"I dunner w'at Miss Sally wanter be sendin' un you down yer fer, ef you gwine ter be stirr'n' en bodderin' 'longer dem ar doin's," exclaimed Uncle Remus, indignantly. "Now don't you scatter dem hog-bristle! De time wuz w'en folks had a mighty slim chance fer ter git bristle, en dey ain't no tellin' w'en dat time gwine come ag'in. Let 'lone dat, de time wuz w'en de breed er hogs wuz done run down ter one po' little pig, en it look lak mighty sorry chance fer dem w'at was bleedzd ter have bristle."

By this time Uncle Remus's indignation had vanished, disappearing as suddenly and unexpectedly as it came. The little boy was curious to know when and where and how the bristle famine occurred.

"I done tole you 'bout dat too long 'go ter talk 'bout," the old man declared; but the little boy insisted that he had never heard about it before, and he was so persistent that at last Uncle Remus, in self-defense, consented to tell the story of the Pigs.

"One time, 'way back yonder, de ole Sow en er chilluns wuz all livin' 'longer de yuther creeturs. Hit seem lak ter me dat de ole Sow wuz a widder 'oman, en ef I don't run inter no mistakes, hit look like ter me dat she got five chilluns. Lemme see," continued Uncle Remus, with the air of one determined to justify his memory by a reference to the record, and enumerating with great deliberation — "dar wuz Big Pig, en dar wuz Little Pig, en dar wuz Speckle Pig, en dar wuz Blunt, en las' en lonesomes' dar wuz Runt.

"One day, deze yer Pig ma she know she gwine kick de bucket, and she tuck'n call up all 'er chilluns en tell um dat de time done come w'en dey got ter look out fer deyse'f, en den she up'n tell um good ez she kin, dough 'er breff mighty scant, 'bout w'at a bad man is ole Brer Wolf. She say, sez she, dat if dey kin make der 'scape from ole Brer Wolf, dey'll be doin' monstus well. Big Pig 'low she ain't skeer'd, Speckle Pig 'low she ain't skeer'd, Blunt, he say he mos' big a man ez Brer Wolf hisse'f, en Runt, she des tuck'n root 'roun' in de straw en grunt. But ole Widder Sow, she lay dar, she did, en keep on tellin' um dat dey better keep der eye on Brer Wolf kaze he mighty mean en 'seetful man.

"Not long atter dat, sho nuff ole Miss Sow lay down en die, en all dem ar chilluns er hern wuz flung back on deyse'f, en dey whirl in, dey did, en dey buil' um all a house ter live in. Big Pig, she tuck'n buil' 'er a house outer bresh; Little Pig, she tuck'n buil' a stick house; Speckle Pig, she tuck'n buil' a mud house; Blunt, he tuck'n buil' a plank house; en Runt, she don't make no great ter-do, en no great brags, but she went ter wuk, she did, en buil' a rock house.

"Bimeby, w'en dey done got all fix, en marters wuz sorter settle, soon one mawnin' yer come ole Brer Wolf, a-lickin' un his chops en a-shakin' un his tail. Fus' house he come ter wuz Big Pig house. Brer Wolf walk ter de do', he did, en he knock sorter saf' — *blim! blim! blim!* Nobody ain't answer. Den he knock loud — *blam! blam! blam!* Dis wake up Big Pig, en she come ter de do', en she ax who dat. Brer Wolf 'low it's a fr'en', en den he sing out:

> "'Ef you'll open de do' en let me in,
> I'll wom my han's en go home ag'in.'

"Still Big Pig ax who dat, en den Brer Wolf, he up'n say, sezee:
"'How yo' ma?' sezee.
"'My ma done dead,' sez Big Pig, sezee, 'en 'fo' she die she tell me fer

ter keep my eye on Brer Wolf. I sees you thoo de crack er de do', en you look mighty like Brer Wolf,' sezee.

"Den ole Brer Wolf, he draw a long breff lak he feel mighty bad, en he up'n say, sezee:

"'I dunner what change yo' ma so bad, less'n she 'uz out'n 'er head. I year tell dat ole Miss Sow wuz sick, en I say ter myse'f dat I'd kinder drap 'roun' en see how de ole lady is, en fetch 'er dish yer bag er roas'n'-years. Mighty well does I know dat ef yo' ma wuz yer right now, en in 'er min', she'd take de roas'n'-years en be glad fer ter git um, en mo'n dat, she'd tak'n ax me in by de fier fer ter wom my han's,' sez ole Brer Wolf, sezee.

"De talk 'bout de roas'n'-years make Big Pig mouf water, en bimeby, atter some mo' palaver, she open de do' en let Brer Wolf in, en bless yo' soul, honey! dat uz de las' er Big Pig. She ain't had time fer ter squeal en needer fer ter grunt 'fo' Brer Wolf gobble 'er up.

"Next day, ole Brer Wolf put up de same game on Little Pig; he go en he sing he song, en Little Pig, she tuck'n let 'im in, en den Brer Wolf he tuck'n' 'turn de compelerments en let Little Pig in."

Here Uncle Remus laughed long and loud at his conceit, and he took occasion to repeat it several times.

"Little Pig, she let Brer Wolf in, en Brer Wolf, he let Little Pig in, en w'at mo' kin you ax dan dat? Nex' time Brer Wolf pay a call, he drop in on Speckle Pig, en rap at de do' en sing his song:

"'Ef you'll open de do' en let me in,
I'll wom my han's en go home ag'in.'

"But Speckle Pig, she kinder 'spicion sump'n', en she 'fuse ter open de do'. Yit Brer Wolf mighty 'seetful man, en he talk mighty saf' en he talk mighty sweet. Bimeby, he git he nose in de crack er de do' en he say ter Speckle Pig, sezee, fer ter des let 'im git one paw in, en den he won't go no furder. He git de paw in, en den he beg fer ter git de yuther paw in, en den w'en he git dat in he beg fer ter git he head in, en den w'en he git he head in, en he paws in, co'se all he got ter do is ter shove de do' open en walk right in; en w'en marters stan' dat way, 'twa'n't long 'fo' he done make fresh meat er Speckle Pig.

"Nex' day, he make way wid Blunt, en de day atter he 'low dat he make a pass at Runt. Now, den, right dar whar ole Brer Wolf slip up at. He lak some folks w'at I knows. He'd a bin mighty smart, ef he hadn't er bin too smart. Runt wuz de littles' one er de whole gang, yit all de same news done got out dat she 'uz pestered wid sense like grown folks.

"Brer Wolf, he crope up ter Runt house, en he got un'need de winder, he did, en he sing out:

> " 'Ef you'll open de do' en let me in,
>   I'll wom my han's en go home ag'in.'

"But all de same, Brer Wolf can't coax Runt fer ter open de do', en needer kin he break in, kaze de house done made outer rock. Bimeby Brer Wolf make out he done gone off, en den atter w'ile he come back en knock at de do' — *blam, blam, blam!*

"Runt she sot by de fier, she did, en sorter scratch 'er year, en holler out: " 'Who dat?' sez she.

" 'Hit's Speckle Pig,' sez ole Brer Wolf, sezee, 'twix' a snort en a grunt. 'I fotch yer some peas fer yo' dinner!'

"Runt, she tuck'n laugh, she did, en holler back:

" 'Sis Speckle Pig ain't never talk thoo dat many toofies.'

"Brer Wolf go off 'g'in, en bimeby he come back en knock. Runt she sot en rock, en holler out:

" 'Who dat?'

" 'Big Pig,' sez Brer Wolf. 'I fotch some sweet-co'n fer yo' supper.'

"Runt, she look thoo de crack un'need de do', en laugh en say, sez she:

" 'Sis Big Pig ain't had no ha'r on 'er huff.'

"Den ole Brer Wolf, he git mad, he did, en say he gwine come down de chimbley, en Runt, she say, sez she, dat de onliest way w'at he kin git in; en den, w'en she year Brer Wolf clim'in' up on de outside er de chimbley, she tuck'n pile up a whole lot er broom sage front er de h'a'th, en w'en she year 'im clim'in' down on de inside, she tuck de tongs en shove de straw on de fier, en de smoke make Brer Wolf head swim, en he drap down, en 'fo' he know it he 'uz done bu'nt ter a cracklin'; en dat wuz de las' er ole Brer Wolf. Leas'ways," added Uncle Remus, putting in a cautious proviso to fall back upon in case of an emergency, "leas'ways, hit 'uz de las' er dat Brer Wolf."

9
Mr. Benjamin Ram and His Wonderful Fiddle

"I 'SPECK you done year tell er ole man Benjermun Ram," said Uncle Remus, with a great affectation of indifference, after a pause.

"Old man who?" asked the little boy.

"Ole man Benjermun Ram. I 'speck you done year tell er him too long 'go ter talk 'bout."

"Why, no, I haven't, Uncle Remus!" exclaimed the little boy, protesting and laughing. "He must have been a mighty funny old man."

"Dat's ez may be," responded Uncle Remus, sententiously. "Fun deze days wouldn't er counted fer fun in dem days; en many's de time w'at I see folks laughin'," continued the old man, with such withering sarcasm that the little boy immediately became serious — "many's de time w'at I sees um laughin' en laughin', w'en I lay dey ain't kin tell w'at dey er laughin' at deyse'f. En 'tain't der laughin' w'at pesters me, nudder" — relenting a little — "hit's dish yer ev'lastin' snickle en giggle, giggle en snickle."

Having thus mapped out, in a dim and uncertain way, what older people than the little boy might have been excused for accepting as a sort of moral basis, Uncle Remus proceeded:

"Dish yer Mr. Benjermun Ram, w'ich he done come up inter my min', wuz one er deze yer ole-timers. Dey tells me dat he 'uz a fiddler fum a-way back yander — one er dem ar kinder fiddlers w'at can't git de chune down fine 'less dey pats der foot. He stay all by he own-alone se'f way out in de middle un a big new-groun', en he sech a handy man fer ter have at a frolic dat de yuther creeturs like 'im mighty well, en w'en dey tuck a notion fer ter shake der foot, w'ich de notion tuck'n struck um eve'y once in a w'ile, nothin' 'ud do but dey mus' sen' fer ole man Benjermun Ram en he fiddle; en dey do say," continued Uncle Remus, closing his eyes in a sort of ecstasy, "dat w'en he squar' hisse'f back in a cheer, en git in a weavin' way, he kin des snatch dem ole-time chunes him who lay de rail.[1] En den, w'en de frolic wuz done, dey'd all fling in, dem yuther

---

[1] That is, from the foundation, or beginning. — J. C. H.

creeturs would, en fill up a bag er peas fer ole Mr. Benjermun Ram fer
ter kyar' home wid 'im.

"One time, des 'bout Chris'mus, Miss Meadows en Miss Motts en de
gals, dey up'n say dat dey'd sorter gin a blowout, en dey got wud ter ole
man Benjermun Ram w'ich dey spected 'im fer ter be on han'. W'en de
time done come fer Mr. Benjermun Ram fer ter start, de win' blow col' en
de cloud 'gun ter spread out 'cross de elements — but no marter fer dat;
ole man Benjermun Ram tuck down he walkin'-cane, he did, en tie up he
fiddle in a bag, en sot out fer Miss Meadows. He thunk he know de way,
but hit keep on gittin' col'er en col'er, en mo' cloudy, twel bimeby, fus'
news you know, ole Mr. Benjermun Ram done lose de way. Ef he'd er kep'
on down de big road fum de start, it moughter bin diffunt, but he tuck a
nigh-cut, en he ain't git fur 'fo' he done los' sho' 'nuff. He do dis a-way, en
he go dat a-way, en he go de yuther way, yit all de same he wuz done los'.
Some folks would er sot right flat down whar dey wuz en study out de way,
but ole man Benjermun Ram ain't got wrinkle on he hawn fer nothin',
kaze he done got de name er ole Billy Hardhead long 'fo' dat. Den ag'in,
some folks would er stop right still in der tracks en holler en bawl fer ter
see ef dey can't roust up some er de neighbors, but ole Mr. Benjermun
Ram, he des stick he jowl in de win', he did, en he march right on des zackly like he know he ain't gwine de wrong way. He keep on, but 'twa'n't
long 'fo' he 'gun ter feel right lonesome, mo' speshually w'en hit come up
in he min' how Miss Meadows en de gals en all de comp'ny be bleedzd ter
do de bes' dey kin widout any fiddlin'; en hit kinder make he marrer git
col' w'en he study 'bout how he gotter sleep out dar in de woods by hisse'f.

"Yit, all de same, he keep on twel de dark 'gun ter drap down, en den
he keep on still, en bimeby he come ter a little rise whar dey wuz a clay-
gall. W'en he git dar he stop en look 'roun', he did, en 'way off down in
de holler, dar he see a light shinin', en w'en he see dis, old man Benjermun Ram tuck he foot in he han', en make he way todes it des lak it de
ve'y place w'at he bin huntin'. 'Twa'n't long 'fo' he come ter de house
whar de light is, en, bless you soul, he don't make no bones er knockin'.
Den somebody holler out:

"'Who dat?'

"'I'm Mr. Benjermun Ram, en I done lose de way, en I come fer ter ax
you ef you can't take me in fer de night,' sezee.

"In common," continued Uncle Remus, "ole Mr. Benjermun Ram wuz a mighty rough-en-spoken somebody, but you better b'lieve he talk monstus perlite dis time.

"Den some un on t'er side er de do' ax Mr. Benjermun Ram fer ter walk right in, en wid dat he open de do' en walk in, en make a bow like fiddlin' folks does w'en dey goes in comp'ny; but he ain't no sooner make he bow en look 'roun' twel he 'gun ter shake en shiver lak he done bin strucken wid de swamp-agur, kaze, settin' right dar 'fo' de fier wuz ole Brer Wolf, wid his toofies showin' up all w'ite en shiny like dey wuz bran' new. Ef ole Mr. Benjermun Ram ain't bin so ole en stiff I boun' you he'd er broke en run, but 'mos' 'fo' he had time fer ter study 'bout gittin' 'way, ole Brer Wolf done bin jump up en shet de do' en fassen 'er wid a great big chain. Ole Mr. Benjermun Ram he know he in fer't, en he tuck'n put on a bol' face ez he kin, but he des nat'ally hone fer ter be los' in de woods some mo'. Den he make n'er low bow, en he hope Brer Wolf and all his folks is well, en den he say, sezee, dat he des drap in fer ter wom hisse'f, en 'quire uv de way ter Miss Meadows', en ef Brer Wolf be so good ez ter set 'im in de road ag'in, he be off putty soon en be much 'blige in de bargains.

"'Tooby sho, Mr. Ram,' sez Brer Wolf, sezee, w'iles he lick he chops en grin; 'des put yo' walkin'-cane in de cornder over dar, en set yo' bag down on de flo', en make yo'se'f at home,' sezee. 'We ain't got much,' sezee, 'but w'at we is got is yone w'iles you stays, en I boun' we'll take good keer un you,' sezee; en wid dat Brer Wolf laugh en show his toofies so bad dat ole man Benjermun Ram come mighty nigh havin' n'er agur.

"Den Brer Wolf tuck'n flung n'er lighter'd-knot on de fier, en den he slip inter de back room, en present'y, w'iles ole Mr. Benjermun Ram wuz settin' dar shakin' in he shoes, he year Brer Wolf whispun ter he ole 'oman:

"'Ole 'oman! ole 'oman! Fling 'way yo' smoke meat — fresh meat fer supper! Fling 'way yo' smoke meat — fresh meat fer supper!'

"Den ole Miss Wolf, she talk out loud, so Mr. Benjermun Ram kin year:

"'Tooby sho I'll fix 'im some supper. We er 'way off yer in de woods, so fur fum comp'ny dat goodness knows I'm mighty glad ter see Mr. Benjermun Ram.'

"Den Mr. Benjermun Ram year ole Miss Wolf whettin' 'er knife on a rock — *shirrah! shirrah! shirrah!* — en eve'y time he year de knife say

shirrah! he know he dat much nigher de dinner-pot. He know he can't git 'way, en w'iles he settin' dar studyin', hit come 'cross he min' dat he des mought ez well play one mo' chune on he fiddle 'fo' de wuss come ter de wuss. Wid dat he ontie de bag en take out de fiddle, en 'gun ter chune 'er up — *plink, plank, plunk, plink! plunk, plank, plink, plunk!*"

Uncle Remus's imitation of the tuning of a fiddle was marvelous enough to produce a startling effect upon a much less enthusiastic listener than the little boy. It was given in perfect good faith, but the serious expression on the old man's face was so irresistibly comic that the child laughed until the tears ran down his face. Uncle Remus very properly accepted this as a tribute to his wonderful resources as a storyteller, and continued, in great good-humor:

"W'en ole Miss Wolf year dat kinder fuss, co'se she dunner w'at is it, en she drap 'er knife en lissen. Ole Mr. Benjermun Ram ain't know dis, en he keep on chunin' up — *plank, plink, plunk, plank!* Den ole Miss Wolf, she tuck'n hunch Brer Wolf wid 'er elbow, en she say, sez she:

"'Hey, ole man! w'at dat?'

"Den bofe un um cock up der years en lissen, en des 'bout dat time ole Mr. Benjermun Ram he sling de butt er de fiddle up und' he chin, en struck up one er dem ole-time chunes."

"Well, what tune was it, Uncle Remus?" the little boy asked, with some display of impatience.

"Ef I ain't done gone en fergit dat chune off'n my min'," continued

Uncle Remus; "hit sorter went like dat ar song 'bout 'Sheep shell co'n wid de rattle er his ho'n,' en yit hit mought er been dat ar yuther one 'bout 'Roll de key, ladies, roll dem keys.' Brer Wolf en ole Miss Wolf, dey lissen en lissen, en de mo' w'at dey lissen de skeerder dey git, twel bimeby dey tuck ter der heels en make a break fer de swamp at de back er de house des lak de patter-rollers wuz atter um.[2]

"W'en ole man Benjermun Ram sorter let up wid he fiddlin', he don't see no Brer Wolf, en he don't year no ole Miss Wolf. Den he look in de back room; no Wolf dar. Den he look in de back po'ch; no Wolf dar. Den he look in de closet en de cubberd; no Wolf ain't dar yit. Den ole Mr. Benjermun Ram, he tuck'n shot all de do's en lock um, en he s'arch 'roun' en he fin' some peas en fodder in de lof', w'ich he et um fer he supper, en den he lie down front er de fier en sleep soun' ez a log.

"Nex' mawnin' he 'uz up en stirrin' monstus soon, en he put out fum dar, en he fin' de way ter Miss Meadows' time nuff fer ter play at de frolic. W'en he git dar, Miss Meadows en de gals, dey run ter de gate fer ter meet 'im, en dis un tuck he hat, en dat un tuck he cane, en t'er'n tuck he fiddle, en den dey up'n say:

"'Law, Mr. Ram! whar de name er goodness is you bin? We so glad you come. Stir 'roun' yer, folks, en git Mr. Ram a cup er hot coffee.'

"Dey make a mighty big ter-do 'bout Mr. Benjermun Ram, Miss Meadows en Miss Molts en de gals did, but 'twix' you en me en de bedpos', honey, dey'd er had der frolic wh'er de ole chap 'uz dar er not, kaze de gals done make 'rangerments wid Brer Rabbit fer ter pat fer um, en in dem days Brer Rabbit wuz a patter, mon. He mos' sholy wuz."

10
Brother Rabbit's Riddle

"COULD BROTHER RABBIT pat a tune, sure enough, Uncle Remus?" asked the little boy, his thoughts apparently dwelling upon the new accomplishment of Brother Rabbit at which the old man had hinted in his story

---

2 There is a parallel tale in the southern mountains about the "fool Arshman" at a square dance, who "made a break for the door" when the fiddler started playing. — R. C.

of Mr. Benjamin Ram. Uncle Remus pretended to be greatly surprised
that any one could be so unfamiliar with the accomplishments of Brother
Rabbit as to venture to ask such a question. His response was in the nature of a comment:

"Name er goodness! w'at kinder pass dish yer we comin' ter w'en a
great big grow'd up young un axin' 'bout Brer Rabbit? Bless yo' soul,
honey! dey wa'n't no chune gwine dat Brer Rabbit can't pat. Let 'lone dat,
w'en dey wuz some un else fer ter do de pattin', Brer Rabbit kin jump out
inter de middle er de flo' en des nat'ally shake de eyeleds off'en dem
yuther creeturs. En 'twa'n't none er dish yer bowin' en scrapin', en slippin' en slidin', en han's all 'roun', w'at folks does deze days. Hit uz dish
yer up en down kinder dancin', whar dey des lips up in de a'r fer ter cut
de pidjin-wing, en lights on de flo' right in de middle er de double-shuffle.
Shoo! Dey ain't no dancin' deze days; folks' shoes too tight, en dey ain't
got dat limbersomeness in de hips w'at dey useter is. Dat dey ain't.

"En yit," Uncle Remus continued, in a tone which seemed to imply
that he deemed it necessary to apologize for the apparent frivolity of
Brother Rabbit — "en yit de time come w'en ole Brer Rabbit 'gun ter put
dis en dat tergedder, en de notion strak 'im dat he better be home lookin'
atter de intruss er he fambly, 'stidder trapesin' en trollopin' 'roun' ter all
de frolics in de settlement. He tuck'n study dis in he min' twel bimeby
he sot out 'termin' fer ter 'arn he own livelihoods, en den he up'n lay off
a piece er groun' en plant 'im a tater-patch.

"Brer Fox, he see all dis yer gwine on, he did, en he 'low ter hisse'f
dat he 'speck Brer Rabbit rashfulness done bin supjued kaze he skeer'd,
en den Brer Fox make up his min' dat he gwine ter pay Brer Rabbit back
fer all he 'seetfulness. He start in, Brer Fox did, en fum dat time forrerd
he aggervate Brer Rabbit 'bout he tater-patch. One night he leave de
draw-bars down, n'er night he fling off de top rails, en nex' night he t'ar
down a whole panel er fence, en he keep on dis away twel 'pariently Brer
Rabbit dunner w'at ter do. All dis time Brer Fox keep on foolin' wid de
tater-patch, en w'en he see w'ich Brer Rabbit ain't makin' no motion,
Brer Fox 'low dat he done skeer'd sho nuff, en dat de time done come fer
ter gobble him up widout lief er license. So he call on Brer Rabbit, Brer
Fox did, en he ax 'im will he take a walk. Brer Rabbit, he ax whar'bouts.
Brer Fox say, right out yander. Brer Rabbit, he ax w'at is dey right out

yander? Brer Fox say he know whar dey some mighty fine peaches, en he want Brer Rabbit fer ter go 'long en climb de tree en fling um down. Brer Rabbit say he don't keer ef he do, mo' speshually fer ter 'blige Brer Fox.

"Dey sot out, dey did, en atter w'ile, sho nuff, dey come ter de peach-orchud, en Brer Rabbit, w'at do he do but pick out a good tree, en up he clum. Brer Fox, he sot hisse'f at de root er de tree, kaze he 'low dat w'en Brer Rabbit come down he hatter come down backerds, en den dat 'ud be de time fer ter nab 'im. But, bless yo' soul, Brer Rabbit dun see w'at Brer Fox atter 'fo' he clum up. W'en he pull de peaches, Brer Fox say, sezee:

"'Fling um down yer, Brer Rabbit — fling um right down yer so I kin ketch um,' sezee.

"Brer Rabbit, he sorter wunk de furdest eye fum Brer Fox, en he holler back, he did:

"'Ef I fling um down dar whar you is, Brer Fox, en you misses um, dey'll git squshed,' sezee, 'so I'll des sorter pitch um out yander in de grass whar dey won't git bus',' sezee.

"Den he tuck'n flung de peaches out in de grass, en w'iles Brer Fox went atter um, Brer Rabbit, he skint down outer de tree, en hustle hisse'f twel he git elbow-room. W'en he get off little ways, he up'n holler back ter Brer Fox dat he got a riddle he want 'im ter read. Brer Fox, he ax w'at is it. Wid dat, Brer Rabbit, he gun it out ter Brer Fox lak a man sayin' a speech:

> "'Big bird rob en little bird sing,
>   De big bee zoon en little bee sting,
>   De little man lead en big hoss foller —
>   Kin you tell w'at's good fer a head in a holler?'

"Ole Brer Fox scratch he head en study, en study en scratch he head, but de mo' he study de wuss he git mix up wid de riddle, en atter w'ile he tuck'n tell Brer Rabbit dat he dunno how in de name er goodness ter on-riddle dat riddle.

"'Come en go 'longer me,' sez ole Brer Rabbit, sezee, 'en I boun' you I show you how ter read dat same riddle. Hit's one er dem ar kinder riddle,' sez ole man Rabbit, sezee, 'w'ich 'fo' you read 'er you got ter eat a bait er honey, en I done got my eye sot on de place whar we kin git de honey at,' sezee.

"Brer Fox, he ax whar'bouts is it, en Brer Rabbit, he say up dar in ole Brer B'ar cotton-patch, whar he got a whole passel er bee-gums. Brer Fox, he 'low, he did, dat he ain't got no sweet-toof much, yit he wanter git at de innerds er dat ar riddle, en he don't keer ef he do go 'long.

"Dey put out, dey did, en 'twa'n't long 'fo' dey come ter ole Brer B'ar bee-gums, en ole Brer Rabbit, he up'n gun um a rap wid he walkin'-cane, des lak folks thumps water-millions fer ter see ef dey er ripe. He tap en he rap, en bimeby he come ter one un um w'ich she soun' like she plum full, en den he go 'roun' behime it, ole Brer Rabbit did, en he up'n say, sezee:

"'I'll des sorter tilt 'er up, Brer Fox,' sezee, 'en you kin put yo' head und' dar en git some er de drippin's,' sezee.

"Brer Rabbit, he tilt her up, en, sho nuff, Brer Fox, he jam he head un'need de gum. Hit make me laugh," Uncle Remus continued, with a chuckle, "fer ter see w'at a fresh man is Brer Fox, kaze he ain't no sooner stuck he head un'need dat ar bee-gum, dan Brer Rabbit turnt 'er aloose, en down she come — *ker-swosh!* — right on Brer Fox neck, en dar he wuz. Brer Fox, he kick; he squeal; he jump; he squall; he dance; he prance; he beg; he pray; yit dar he wuz, en w'en Brer Rabbit git way off, en tu'n 'roun' fer ter look back, he see Brer Fox des a-wigglin' en a-squ'min', en right den en dar Brer Rabbit gun one ole-time whoop, en des put out fer home.

"W'en he git dar, de fus' man he see wuz Brer Fox gran'daddy, w'ich folks all call 'im Gran'sir' Gray Fox. When Brer Rabbit see 'im, he say, sezee:

"'How you come on, Gran'sir' Gray Fox?'

"'I still keeps po'ly, I'm 'blige ter you, Brer Rabbit,' sez Gran'sir' Gray Fox, sezee. 'Is you seed any sign er my gran'son dis mawnin'?' sezee.

"Wid dat Brer Rabbit laugh en say w'ich him en Brer Fox bin a-ramblin' 'roun' wid one er n'er havin' mo' fun dan w'at a man kin shake a stick at.

"'We bin a-riggin' up riddles en a-readin' un um,' sez Brer Rabbit, sezee. 'Brer Fox is settin' off somers in de bushes right now, aimin' fer ter read one w'at I gun 'im. I'll des drap you one,' sez ole Brer Rabbit, sezee, 'w'ich, ef you kin read it, hit'll take you right spang ter whar yo' gran'son is, en you can't git dar none too soon,' sez Brer Rabbit, sezee.

"Den ole Gran'sir' Gray Fox, he up'n ax w'at is it, en Brer Rabbit, he sing out, he did:

> "'De big bird rob en little bird sing;
> De big bee zoon en little bee sting,
> De little man lead en big hoss foller —
> Kin you tell w'at's good fer a head in a holler?'

"Gran'sir' Gray Fox, he tuck a pinch er snuff en cough easy ter hisse'f, en study en study, but he ain't make it out, en Brer Rabbit, he laugh en sing:

> "'Bee-gum mighty big fer ter make Fox collar,
> Kin you tell w'at's good fer a head in a holler?'

"Atter so long a time, Gran'sir' Gray Fox sorter ketch a glimpse er w'at Brer Rabbit tryin' ter gin 'im, en he tip Brer Rabbit good-day, en shuffle on fer ter hunt up he gran'son."

"And did he find him, Uncle Remus?" asked the little boy.

"Tooby sho, honey. Brer B'ar year de racket w'at Brer Fox kickin' up, en he go down dar fer ter see w'at de marter is. Soon ez he see how de lan' lay, co'se he tuck a notion dat Brer Fox bin robbin' de bee-gums, en he got 'im a han'ful er hick'ries, Brer B'ar did, en he let in on Brer Fox en he wom he jacket scannerlous, en den he tuck'n tu'n 'im loose; but 'twa'n't long 'fo' all de neighbors git wud dat Brer Fox bin robbin' Brer B'ar bee-gums."

11
How Mr. Rooster Lost His Dinner

IT SEEMED that the rainy season had set in in earnest, but the little boy went down to Uncle Remus's cabin before dark. In some mysterious way, it appeared to the child, the gloom of twilight fastened itself upon the dusky clouds, and the great trees without, and the dismal perspective beyond, gradually became one with the darkness. Uncle Remus had thought-fully placed a tin pan under a leak in the roof, and the *drip-drip-drip* of the water, as it fell in the resonant vessel, made a not unmusical accompaniment to the storm.

The old man fumbled around under his bed, and presently dragged forth a large bag filled with lightwood knots, which, with an instinctive economy in this particular direction, he had stored away for an emergency. A bright but flickering flame was the result of this timely discovery, and the effect it produced was quite in keeping with all the surroundings. The rain, and wind, and darkness held sway without, while within, the unsteady lightwood blaze seemed to rhyme with the *drip-drip-drip* in the pan. Sometimes the shadow of Uncle Remus, as he leaned over the hearth, would tower and fill the cabin, and again it would fade and disappear among the swaying and swinging cobwebs that curtained the rafters.

"W'en bed-time come, honey," said Uncle Remus, in a soothing tone, "I'll des snatch down vo' pa buggy umbrell' fum up dar in de cornder, des lak I bin a-doin', en I'll tak'n take you und' my arm en set you down on Miss Sally h'a'th des ez dry en ez wom ez a rat'-nes' inside a fodder-stack."

At this juncture 'Tildy, the house-girl, rushed in out of the rain and darkness with a water-proof cloak and an umbrella, and announced her mission to the little boy without taking time to catch her breath.

"Miss Sally say you got ter come right back," she exclaimed. "Kaze she skeer'd lightnin' gwine strak 'roun' in yer 'mongs' deze high trees somers."

Uncle Remus rose from his stooping posture in front of the hearth and assumed a threatening attitude.

"Well, is anybody year de beat er dat!" was his indignant exclamation. "Look yer, gal! don't you come foolin' 'longer me — now, don't you do it. Kaze ef yer does, I'll tak'n hit you a clip w'at'll put you ter bed 'fo' bedtime comes. Dat's w'at!"

"Lawdy! w'at I done gone en done ter Unk' Remus now?" asked 'Tildy, with a great affectation of innocent ignorance.

"I'm gwine ter put on my coat en take dat ar umbrell', en I'm gwine right straight up ter de big house en ax Miss Sally ef she sont dat kinder wud down yer, w'en she know dat chile sittin' yer 'longer me. I'm gwine ter ax her," continued Uncle Remus, "en if she ain't sont dat wud, den I'm gwine ter fetch myse'f back. Now, you des watch my motions."

"Well, I year Miss Sally say she feard lightnin' gwine ter strak somers on de place," said 'Tildy, in a tone which manifested her willingness to compromise all differences, "en den I axt 'er kin I come down yer, en den she say I better bring deze yer cloak en pairsol."

"Now you dun brung um," responded Uncle Remus, "you des better put um in dat cheer over dar, en take yo'se'f off. Thunder mighty ap' ter hit close ter whar deze here slick head niggers is."

But the little boy finally prevailed upon the old man to allow 'Tildy to remain, and after a while he put matters on a peace footing by inquiring if roosters crowed at night when it was raining.

"Dat dey duz," responded Uncle Remus. "Wet er dry, dey flops der wings en wakes up all de neighbors. Law, bless my soul!" he exclaimed suddenly, "w'at make I done gone en fergit 'bout Mr. Rooster?"

"What about him?" inquired the little boy.

"One time, 'way back yander," said Uncle Remus, knocking the ashes off his hands and knees, "dey wuz two plan'ations right 'longside one er ne'r, en on bofe er deze plan'ations wuz a whole passel of fowls. Dey wuz mighty sociable in dem days, en it tu'n out dat de fowls on one plan'ation gun a party, w'ich dey sont out der invites ter de fowls on de t'er plan'ation.

"W'en de day come, Mr. Rooster, he blow his hawn, he did, en 'semble um all tergedder, en atter dey 'semble dey got in line. Mr. Rooster, he tuck de head, en atter 'im come ole lady Hen en Miss Pullet, en den dar wuz Mr. Peafowl, en Mr. Tukkey Gobbler, en Miss Guinny Hen, en Miss Puddle Duck, en all de balance un um. Dey start off sorter raggedy, but 'twa'n't long 'fo' dey all kotch de step, en den day march down by de spring, up thoo de hoss-lot en 'cross by de gin-house, en 'twa'n't long 'fo' dey git ter whar de frolic wuz.

"Dey dance, en dey play, en dey sing. Mo' speshually did dey play en sing dat ar song w'ich it run on lak dis:

> " 'Come under, come under,
>   My honey, my love, my own true love;
>   My heart bin a-weepin'
>   Way down in Galilee.'

"Dey wuz gwine on dis a-way, havin' der 'musements, w'en, bimeby, ole Mr. Peafowl, he got on de comb er de barn en blow de dinner-hawn. Dey all wash der face en han's in de back po'ch, en den dey went in ter dinner. W'en dey git in dar, dey don't see nothin' on de table but a great big pile er co'n-bread. De pones was pile up on pones, en on de top wuz a great big ashcake. Mr. Rooster, he look at dis en he tu'n up he nose, en bimeby, atter aw'ile, out he strut. Ole Miss Guinny Hen, she watchin' Mr. Rooster motions, en w'en she see dis, she tak'n squall out, she did:

"'*Pot-rack! Pot-rack!* Mr. Rooster gone back! *Pot-rack! Pot-rack!* Mr. Rooster gone back!'

"Wid dat dey all make a great ter-do. Miss Hen en Miss Pullet, dey cackle en squall, Mr. Gobbler, he gobble, en Miss Puddle Duck, she shake 'er tail en say, *quickity-quack-quack.* But Mr. Rooster, he ruffle up he cape, en march on out.

"Dis sorter put a damper on de yuthers, but 'fo' Mr. Rooster git outer sight en year'n dey went ter wuk on de pile w'at wuz 'pariently co'n-bread, en, lo en beholes un'need dem pone er bread wuz a whole passel er meat en green, en bake' taters, en bile' turnips. Mr. Rooster, he year de ladies makin' great 'miration, en he stop en look thoo de crack, en dar he see all de doin's en fixin's. He feel mighty bad, Mr. Rooster did, w'en he see all dis, en de yuther fowls dey holler en ax 'im fer ter come back, en he craw, w'ich it mighty empty, likewise, it up'n ax 'im, but he mighty biggity en stuck up, en he strut off, crowin' ez he go; but he 'speunce er dat time done las' him en all er his fambly down ter dis day. En you nee'nter take my wud fer't, ne'r kaze ef you'll des keep yo' eye open en watch, you'll ketch a glimpse er ole Mr. Rooster folks scratchin' whar dey specks ter fin' der rations, en mo' dan dat, dey'll scratch wid der rations in plain sight. Since dat time, dey ain't none er de Mr. Roosters bin fool' by dat w'at dey see on top. Dey ain't res' twel dey see w'at und' dar. Dey'll scratch 'spite er all creation."

"Dat's de Lord's truth!" said 'Tildy, with unction. "I done seed um wid my own eyes. Dat I is."

This was 'Tildy's method of renewing peaceful relations with Uncle Remus, but the old man was disposed to resist the attempt.

"You better be up yander washin' up dishes, stidder hoppin' down yer wid er whole packet er stuff w'at Miss Sally ain't dreamp er sayin'."

12
Brother Rabbit Breaks Up a Party

As LONG as Uncle Remus allowed 'Tildy to remain in the cabin, the little boy was not particularly interested in preventing the perfunctory abuse which the old man might feel disposed to bestow upon the complacent girl. The truth is, the child's mind was occupied with the episode in the story of Mr. Benjamin Ram which treats of the style in which this romantic old wag put Mr. and Mrs. Wolf to flight by playing a tune upon his fiddle. The little boy was particularly struck with this remarkable feat, as many a youngster before him had been, and he made bold to recur to it again by asking Uncle Remus for all the details. It was plain to the latter that the child regarded Mr. Ram as the typical hero of all the animals, and this was by no means gratifying to the old man. He answered the little boy's questions as well as he could, and, when nothing more remained to be said about Mr. Ram, he settled himself back in his chair and resumed the curious history of Brother Rabbit:

"Co'se Mr. Ram mighty smart man. I ain't 'spute dat; but needer Mr. Ram ner yet Mr. Lam' is soon creeturs lak Brer Rabbit. Mr. Benjermum Ram, he tuck'n skeer off Brer Wolf en his ole 'oman wid his fiddle, but bless yo' soul, ole Brer Rabbit he gone en done wuss'n dat."

"What did Brother Rabbit do?" asked the little boy.

"One time," said Uncle Remus, "Brer Fox, he tuck'n ax some er de yuther creeturs ter he house. He ax Brer B'ar, en Brer Wolf, en Brer 'Coon, but he ain't ax Brer Rabbit. All de same, Brer Rabbit got win' un it, en he 'low dat ef he don't go, he 'speck he have much fun ez de nex' man.

"De creeturs w'at git de invite, dey tuck'n 'semble at Brer Fox house, en Brer Fox, he ax um in en got um cheers, en dey sot dar en laugh en talk, twel, bimeby, Brer Fox, he fotch out a bottle er dram en lay 'er out on de side-bode, en den he sorter step back en say, sezee:

"'Des step up, gentermens, en he'p yo'se'f,' en you better b'lieve dey he'p derse'f.

"W'iles dey wuz drinkin' en drammin' en gwine on, w'at you 'speck Brer Rabbit doin'? You des well make up yo' min' dat Brer Rabbit monstus busy, kaze he 'uz sailin' 'roun' fixin' up his tricks. Long time 'fo' dat,

Brer Rabbit had been at a bobbycue whar dey was a muster, en w'iles all de folks 'uz down at de spring eatin' dinner, Brer Rabbit he crope up en run off wid one er de drums. Dey wuz a big drum en a little drum, en Brer Rabbit he snatch up de littles' one en run home.

"Now, den, w'en he year 'bout de yuther creeturs gwine ter Brer Fox house, w'at do Brer Rabbit do but git out dis rattlin' drum en make de way down de road todes whar dey is. He tuk dat drum," continued Uncle Remus, with great elation of voice and manner, "en he went down de road todes Brer Fox house, en he make 'er talk like thunner mix up wid hail. Hit talk lak dis:

"'Diddybum, diddybum, diddybum-bum-bum — diddybum!'

"De creeturs, dey 'uz a-drinkin', en a-drammin', en a-gwine on at a terrible rate, en dey ain't year de racket, but all de same, yer come Brer Rabbit:

"'Diddybum, diddybum, diddybum-bum-bum — diddybum!'

"Bimeby Brer 'Coon, w'ich he allers got one year hung out fer de news, he up'n ax Brer Fox w'at dat, en by dat time all de creeturs stop en lissen; but all de same, yer come Brer Rabbit:

"'Diddybum, diddybum, diddybum-bum-bum — diddybum!'

"De creeturs dey keep on lis'nin', en Brer Rabbit keep on gittin' nigher, twel bimeby Brer 'Coon retch und' de cheer fer he hat, en say, sezee:

"'Well, gents, I 'speck I better be gwine. I tole my ole 'oman dat I won't be gone a minnit, en yer 'tis 'way 'long in de day.'

"Wid dat Brer 'Coon, he skip out, but he ain't git much furder dan de back gate, 'fo' yer come all de yuther creeturs like dey 'uz runnin' a foot-race, en ole Brer Fox wuz wukkin' in de lead."

"Dar, now!" exclaimed 'Tildy, with great fervor.

"Yasser! dar dey wuz, en dar dey went," continued Uncle Remus. "Dey tuck nigh cuts, en dey scramble over one er n'er, en dey ain't res' twel dey git in de bushes.

"Ole Brer Rabbit, he came on down de road — *diddybum, diddybum-bum-bum* — en bless gracious! w'en he git ter Brer Fox house dey ain't nobody dar. Brer Rabbit is dat owdacious, dat he hunt all 'roun' twel he fin' de a'r-hole er de drum, en he put his mouf ter dat en sing out, sezee:

"'Is dey anybody home?' en den he answer hisse'f, sezee, 'Law, no, honey — folks all gone.'

"Wid dat, ole Brer Rabbit break loose en laugh, he did, fit ter kill hisse'f, en den he slam Brer Fox front gate wide open, en march up ter de house. W'en he git dar, he kick de do' open en hail Brer Fox, but nobody ain't dar, en Brer Rabbit he walk in en take a cheer, en make hisse'f at home wid puttin' his foots on de sofy en spittin' on de flo'.

"Brer Rabbit ain't sot dar long 'fo' he ketch a whiff er de dram — "

"You year dat?" exclaimed 'Tildy, with convulsive admiration.

" — 'Fo' he ketch a whiff er de dram, en den he see it on de sidebode, en he step up en drap 'bout a tumbeler full somers down in de neighborhoods er de goozle. Brer Rabbit mighty lak some folks I knows. He tuck one tumbeler full, en 'twa'n't long 'fo' he tuck n'er'n, en w'en a man do dis a-way," continued Uncle Remus, somewhat apologetically, "he bleedzd ter git drammy."

"Truth, too!" said 'Tildy, by way of hearty confirmation.

"All des time de yuther creeturs wuz down in de bushes lissenin' fer de *diddybum*, en makin' ready fer ter light out fum dar at de drop uv a hat. But dey ain't year no mo' fuss, en bimeby Brer Fox, he say he gwine back en look atter he plunder, en de yuther creeturs say dey b'lieve dey'll go 'long wid 'im. Dey start out, dey did, en dey crope todes Brer Fox house, but dey crope mighty keerful, en I boun' ef somebody'd a shuck a bush, dem ar creeturs 'ud a nat'ally to' up de yeth gittin' 'way fum dar. Yit dey still ain't year no fuss, en dey keep on creepin' twel dey git in de house.

"W'en dey git in dar, de fus' sight dey see wuz ole Brer Rabbit stan'in' up by de dram-bottle mixin' up a toddy, en he wa'n't so stiff-kneed n'er kaze he sorter swage fum side ter side, en he look lak he mighty limbersome, w'ich, goodness knows, a man bleedzd ter be limbersome w'en he drink dat kinder licker w'at Brer Fox perwide fer dem creeturs.

"W'en Brer Fox see Brer Rabbit makin' free wid he doin's dat, a-way, w'at you 'speck he do?" inquired Uncle Remus, with the air of one seeking general information.

"I 'speck he cuss't," said 'Tildy, who was apt to take a vividly practical view of matters.

"He was glad," said the little boy, "because he had a good chance to catch Brother Rabbit."

"Tooby sho he wuz," continued Uncle Remus, heartily assenting to the child's interpretation of the situation: "tooby sho he wuz. He stan' dar, Brer Fox did, en he watch Brer Rabbit motions. Bimeby he holler out, sezee:

"'Ah-yi! Brer Rabbit!' sezee. 'Many a time is you made yo' 'scape, but now I got you!' En wid dat, Brer Fox en de yuther creeturs cloze in on Brer Rabbit.

"Seem like I done tole you dat Brer Rabbit done gone en tuck mo' dram dan w'at 'uz good fer he wholesome. Yit he head ain't swim so bad dat he dunner w'at he doin', en time he lay eyes on Brer Fox, he know he done got in close quarters. Soon ez he sees dis, Brer Rabbit make like he bin down in de cup mo' deeper dan w'at he is, en he stagger 'roun' like town gal stan'in' in a batteau, en he seem lak he des ez limber ez a wet rag. He stagger up ter Brer Fox, he did, en he roll he eyeballs 'roun', en slap 'im on he back en ax 'im how he ma. Den w'en he see de yuther creeturs," continued Uncle Remus, "he holler out, he did:

"'Vents yo' uppance, gentermens! Vents yo' uppance! Ef you'll des gimme han'-roomance en come one at a time, de tussle'll las' longer. How you all come on, nohow?' sezee.

"Ole Brer Rabbit talk so kuse dat de yuther creeturs have mo' fun dan w'at you k'n shake a stick at, but bimeby Brer Fox say dey better git down ter business, en den dey all cloze in on Brer Rabbit, en dar he wuz.

"In dem days, ole man B'ar wuz a jedge 'mongs' de creeturs, en day all ax 'im w'at dey gwine do 'long wid Brer Rabbit, en Jedge B'ar, he put on his specks, en cle'r up his th'oat, en say dat de bes' way ter do wid a man w'at kick up sech a racket, en run de neighbors outer der own house, en go in dar en level on de pantry, is ter take 'im out en drown 'im; en ole Brer Fox, w'ich he settin' on de jury, he up'n smack he hands togedder, en cry, en say, sezee, dat atter dis he bleedzd ter b'lieve dat Jedge B'ar done got all-under holt on de lawyer-books, kaze dat zackly w'at dey say w'en a man level on he neighbor pantry.

"Den Brer Rabbit, he make out he skeer'd, en he holler en cry, en beg um, in de name er goodness, don't fling 'im in de spring branch, kaze dey all know he dunner how ter swim; but ef dey bleedzd fer ter pitch 'im in, den for mussy sake gin' 'im a walkin'-cane, so he kin have sump'n' ter hol' ter w'iles he drownin'.

"Ole Brer B'ar scratch his head en say, sezee, dat, fur ez his 'membunce go back, he ain't come 'cross nothin' in de lawyer-book ter de contraries er dat, en den dey all 'gree dat Brer Rabbit kin have a walkin'-cane.

"Wid dat, dey ketch up Brer Rabbit en put 'im in a wheelborrow en kyar' 'im down ter de branch, en fling 'im in."

"Eh-eh!" exclaimed 'Tildy, with well-feigned astonishment.

"Dey fling 'im in," continued Uncle Remus, "en Brer Rabbit light on he foots, same ez a tomcat, en pick his way out by de helps er de walkin'-cane. De water wuz dat shaller dat it don't mo'n come over Brer Rabbit slipper, en w'en he git out on t'er side, he holler back, sezee:

"'So long, Brer Fox!'"

13
Brother Fox, Brother Rabbit, and King Deer's Daughter

NOTWITHSTANDING Brother Rabbit's success with the drum, the little boy was still inclined to refer to Mr. Benjamin Ram and his fiddle; but Uncle Remus was not by any means, willing that such an ancient vagabond as Mr. Ram should figure as a hero, and he said that, while it was possible that Brother Rabbit was no great hand with the fiddle, he was a drummer, and a capital singer to boot. Furthermore, Uncle Remus declared that Brother Rabbit could perform upon the quills, an accomplishment to which none of the other animals could lay claim. There was a time, too, the old man pointedly suggested, when the romantic rascal used his musical abilities to win the smiles of a nice young lady of quality — no less a personage, indeed, than King Deer's daughter. As a matter of course, the little boy was anxious to hear the particulars, and Uncle Remus was in nowise loath to give them.

"W'en you come ter ax me 'bout de year en day er de mont'," said the old man, cunningly arranging a defense against criticism, "den I'm done, kaze de almanick w'at dey got in dem times won't pass muster deze days, but, let 'lone dat, I 'speck dey ain't had none yit; en ef dey is, dey ain't none bin handed down ter Remus.

"Well, den, some time 'long in dar, ole Brer Fox en Brer Rabbit got ter flyin' 'roun' King Deer daughter. Dey tells me she 'uz a monstus likely gal, en I 'speck may be she wuz; leas'ways. Brer Fox, he hanker atter 'er, en likewise Brer Rabbit, he hanker atter 'er. Ole King Deer look lak he sorter lean todes Brer Fox, kaze ter a settle man like him, hit seem lak dat Brer Fox kin stir 'roun' en keep de pot a-b'ilin', mo' speshually bein's he de bigges'. Hit go on dis a-way twel hardly a day pass dat one er de yuther er dem creeturs don't go sparklin' 'roun' King Deer daughter, en it got so atter w'ile dat all day long Brer Rabbit en Brer Fox keep de front gate a-skreakin', en King Deer daughter ain't skacely had time fer ter eat a meal vittles in no peace er min'.

"In dem days," pursued Uncle Remus, in a tone of unmistakable historical fervor, "w'en a creetur go a-courtin' dey wa'n't none er dish yer bokay doin's mix' up 'longer der co'tship, en dey ain't cut up no capers like folks does now. Stidder scollopin' 'roun' en bowin' en scrapin', dey des go right straight atter de gal. Ole Brer Rabbit, he moughter had some bubby-blossoms wrop up in his hankcher, but mostly him en Brer Fox 'ud des drap in on King Deer daughter en 'gin ter cas' sheep-eyes at 'er time dey sot down en cross der legs."

"En I bet," said 'Tildy, by way of comment, and looking as though she wanted to blush, "dat dey wa'n't 'shame', nuther."

"Dey went 'long dis a-way," continued Uncle Remus, "twel it 'gun ter look sorter skittish wid Brer Rabbit, kaze ole King Deer done good ez say, sezee, dat he gwine ter take Brer Fox inter de fambly. Brer Rabbit, he 'low, he did, dat dis ain't gwine ter do, en he study en study how he gwine ter cut Brer Fox out.

"Las', one day, w'iles he gwine thoo King Deer pastur' lot, he up wid a rock en kil't two er King Deer goats. W'en he git ter de house, he ax King Deer daughter whar'bouts her pa, en she up'n say she go call 'im, en w'en Brer Rabbit see 'im, he ax w'en de weddin' tuck place, en King Deer ax w'ich weddin', en Brer Rabbit say de weddin' 'twix' Brer Fox en King Deer daughter. Wid dat, ole King Deer ax Brer Rabbit w'at make he go on so, en Brer Rabbit, he up'n 'spon' dat he see Brer Fox makin' monstus free wid de fambly, gwine 'roun' chunkin' de chickens en killin' up de goats.

"Ole King Deer strak he walkin'-cane down 'pon de flo', en 'low dat

he don't put no 'pennunce in no sech tale lak dat, en den Brer Rabbit tell
'im dat ef he'll des take a walk down in de pastur' lot, he kin see de
kyarkiss er de goats. Ole King Deer, he put out, en bimeby he come back,
en he 'low he gwine ter settle marters wid Brer Fox ef it take 'im a mont'.

"Brer Rabbit say he a good frien' ter Brer Fox, en he ain't got no room
ter talk 'bout 'im, but yit w'en he see 'im 'stroyin' King Deer goats en
chunkin' at his chickens, en rattlin' on de palin's fer ter make de dog
bark, he bleedzd ter come lay de case 'fo' de fambly.

"'En mo'n dat,' sez ole Brer Rabbit, sezee, 'I'm de man w'at kin make
Brer Fox come en stan' right at de front gate en tell you dat he is kill dem
goat; en ef you des wait twel ternight, I won't ax you ter take my wud,'
sezee.

"King Deer say ef Brer Rabbit man nuff ter do dat, den he kin git de
gal en thanky, too. Wid dat, Brer Rabbit jump up en crack he heels
tergedder, en put out fer ter fin' Brer Fox. He ain't git fur 'fo' he see Brer
Fox comin' down de road all primp up. Brer Rabbit, he sing out, he did:

"'Brer Foxy, whar you gwine?'

"En Brer Fox, he holler back:

"'Go 'way, Rab; don't bodder wid me. I'm gwine fer ter see my gal.'

"Brer Rabbit, he laugh 'way down in his stomach, but he don't let on,
en atter some mo' chat, he up'n say dat ole King Deer done tell 'im 'bout
how Brer Fox gwine ter marry he daughter, en den he tell Brer Fox dat
he done promise King Deer dat dey'd drap 'roun' ternight en gin 'im
some music.

"'En I up'n tole 'im,' sez Brer Rabbit, sezee, 'dat de music w'at we
can't make ain't wuth makin', — me wid my quills, en you wid yo' tr'angle. De nex' motion we makes,' sezee, 'we'll hatter go off somers en practise up on de song we'll sing, en I got one yer dat'll tickle um dat bad,'
sez Brer Rabbit, sezee, 'twel I lay dey'll fetch out a hunk er dat big
chicken-pie wa't I see um puttin' in de pot des now,' sezee.

"In a 'casion lak dis, Brer Fox say he de ve'y man w'at Brer Rabbit
huntin', en he 'low dat he'll des 'bout put off payin' he call ter King Deer
house en go wid Brer Rabbit fer ter practise on dat song.

"Den Brer Rabbit, he git he quills en Brer Fox he git he tr'angle, en
dey went down on de spring branch, en dar dey sing en play, twel dey git
it all by heart. Ole Brer Rabbit he make up de song he own se'f, en he fix

it so dat he sing de call, lak de captain er de co'n-pile, en ole Brer Fox, he hatter sing de answer."[1]

At this point Uncle Remus paused to indulge in one of his suggestive chuckles, and then proceeded:

"Don't talk 'bout no songs ter me. Gentermens! dat 'uz a funny song fum de wud go. Bimeby, w'en dey practise long time, dey gits up en goes 'roun' in de neighborhoods er King Deer house, en w'en night come dey tuck der stan' at de front gate, en atter all got still, Brer Rabbit, he gun de wink, en dey broke loose wid der music. Dey played a chune er two on de quills en tr'angle, en den dey got ter de song. Ole Brer Rabbit, he got de call, en he open up lak dis:

> "'Some folks pile up mo'n dey kin tote,
> En dat w'at de marter wid King Deer goat,'

en den Brer Fox, he make answer:

> "'Dat's so, dat's so, en I'm glad dat it's so!'

Den de quills en de tr'angle, dey come in, en den Brer Rabbit pursue on wid de call:

> "'Some kill sheep en some kill shote,
> But Brer Fox kill King Deer goat,'

en den Brer Fox, he jine in wid de answer:

> "'I did, dat I did, en I'm glad dat I did!'

En des 'bout dat time King Deer, he walk outer de gate en hit Brer Fox a clip wid his walkin'-cane, en he foller it up wid n'er'n, dat make Brer Fox fa'rly squall, en you des better b'lieve he make tracks 'way fum dar, en de gal she come out, en dey ax Brer Rabbit in."

"Did Brother Rabbit marry King Deer's daughter, Uncle Remus?" asked the little boy.

"Now, den, honey, you're crowdin' me," responded the old man. "Dey ax 'im in, en dey gun 'im a great big hunk er chicken-pie, but I won't make sho dat he tuck'n marry de gal. De p'int wid me is de way Brer Rabbit run Brer Fox off fum dar."

---

[1] That is to say, Brother Rabbit sang the air and Brother Fox the refrain. — J. C. H.

14
Brother Terrapin Deceives Brother Buzzard

THERE WAS a pause here, which was finally broken by 'Tildy, whose remark was in the shape of a very undignified yawn. Uncle Remus regarded her for a moment with an expression of undisguised scorn, which quickly expressed itself in words:

"Ef you'd er bin outer de house dat whack, you'd er tuck us all in. Pity dey ain't some place er n'er whar deze yer trollops kin go en l'arn manners."

'Tildy, however, ignored the old man, and, with a toss of her head, said to the little boy in a cool, exasperating tone, employing a pet name she had heard the child's mother use:

"Well, Pinx, I 'speck we better go. De rain done mos' hilt up now, en bimeby de stars 'll be a-shinin'. Miss Sally lookin' fer you right now."

"You better go whar you gwine, you triflin' huzzy, you!" exclaimed Uncle Remus. "You better go git yo' Jim Crow kyard en straighten out dem wrops in yo' ha'r. I allers year w'ite folks say you better keep yo' eye on niggers w'at got der ha'r wrop up in strings. Now I done gun you fa'r warnin's."

"Uncle Remus," said the little boy, when the old man's wrath had somewhat subsided, "why do they call them Jim Crow cards?"

"I be bless ef I know, honey, ceppin' it's kaze dey er de onliest machine w'at deze yer low-life niggers kin oncomb der kinks wid. Now, den," continued the old man, straightening up and speaking with considerable animation, "dat 'min's me 'bout a riddle w'at been runnin' 'roun' in my head. En dat riddle — it's de outdoin'es' riddle w'at I mos' ever year tell un. Hit go lak dis: Ef he come, he don't come; ef he don't come, he come. Now, I boun' you can't tell w'at is dat."

After some time spent in vain guessing, the little boy confessed that he didn't know.

"Hit's crow en co'n," said Uncle Remus sententiously.

"Crow and corn, Uncle Remus?"

"Co'se, honey. Crow come, de co'n don't come; crow don't come, den de co'n come."

"Dat's so," said 'Tildy. "I done see um pull up co'n, en I done see co'n grow w'at dey don't pull up."

If 'Tildy thought to propitiate Uncle Remus, she was mistaken. He scowled at her, and addressed himself to the little boy:

"De Crow, he mighty close kin ter de Buzzud, en dat puts me in min' dat we ain't bin a-keepin' up wid ole Brer Buzzud close ez we mought er done.

"W'at de case mought be deze days, I ain't a-sayin', but, in dem times, ole Brer Tarrypin love honey mo' samer dan Brer B'ar, but he wuz dat flat-footed dat, w'en he fin' a bee-tree, he can't clim' it, en he go so slow dat he can't hardly fin' um. Bimeby, one day, w'en he gwine 'long down de road des a-honin' atter honey, who should he meet but ole Brer Buzzud.

"Dey shuck han's mighty sociable en ax 'bout de news er de neighborhoods, en den, atter w'ile, Brer Tarrypin say ter ole Brer Buzzud, sezee, dat he wanter go inter cahoots wid 'im 'longer gittin' honey, en 'twa'n't long 'fo' dey struck a trade. Brer Buzzud wuz ter fly 'roun' en look fer de bee-tree, en Brer Tarrypin he wuz ter creep en crawl, en hunt on de groun'.

"Dey start out, dey did, ole Brer Buzzud sailin' 'roun' in de elements, en ole Brer Tarrypin shufflin' en shamblin' on de groun'. 'Mos' de ve'y fus' fiel' w'at he come ter, Brer Tarrypin strak up wid a great bumbly-bee nes' in de groun'. He look 'roun', ole Brer Tarrypin did, en bimeby he stick his head in en tas'e de honey, en den he pull it out en look all 'roun' fer ter see if he kin ketch a glimpse er Brer Buzzud; but Brer Buzzud don't seem lak he nowhar. Den Brer Tarrypin say to hisse'f, sezee, dat he 'speck dat bumbly-bee honey ain't de kinder honey w'at dey been talkin' 'bout, en dey ain't no great shakes er honey dar nohow. Wid dat, Brer Tarrypin crope inter de hole en gobble up de las' drop er de bumbly-bee honey by he own-alone se'f. Atter he done make 'way wid it, he come out, he did, en he whirl in en lick it all off'n his footses, so ole Brer Buzzud can't tell dat he done bin git a mess er honey.

"Den ole Brer Tarrypin stretch out he neck en try ter lick de honey off'n he back, but he neck too short; en he try ter scrape it off up 'gin' a tree, but it don't come off; en den he waller on de groun', but still it don't come off. Den ole Brer Tarrypin jump up, en say ter hisse'f dat he'll des 'bout rack off home, en when Brer Buzzud come he kin lie on he back en say he sick, so ole Brer Buzzud can't see de honey.

"Brer Tarrypin start off, he did, but he happen ter look up, en, lo en beholes, dar wuz Brer Buzzud huv'rin' right spang over de spot whar he is. Brer Tarrypin know Brer Buzzud bleedzd ter see 'im ef he start off home, en mo'n dat, he know he be fin' out ef he don't stir 'roun' en do sump'n mighty quick. Wid dat, Brer Tarrypin shuffle back ter de bumbly-bee nes' swif ez he kin, en buil' 'im a fier in dar, en den he crawl out en holler:

"'Brer Buzzud! O Brer Buzzud! Run yer, fer gracious sake, Brer Buzzud, en look how much honey I done fin'! I des crope in a little ways, en it des drip all down my back, same like water. Run yer, Brer Buzzud! Half yone en half mine, Brer Buzzud!'

"Brer Buzzud, he flop down, en he laugh en say he mighty glad, kaze he done git hongry up dar whar he bin. Den Brer Tarrypin tell Brer Buzzud fer ter creep in little ways en tas'e en see how he like um, w'iles he take his stan' on de outside en watch fer somebody. But no sooner is Brer Buzzud crope in de bumbly-bee nes' dan Brer Tarrypin tak'n roll a great big rock front er de hole. Terreckly, de fier 'gun ter bu'n Brer Buzzud, en he sing out like a man in trouble:

"'Sump'n' bitin' me, Brer Tarrypin — sump'n' bitin' me, Brer Tarrypin!'

"Den ole Brer Tarrypin, he holler back:

"'It's de bumbly-bees a-stingin' you, Brer Buzzud; stan' up en flop yo' wings, Brer Buzzud. Stan' up en flop yo' wings, Brer Buzzud, en you'll drive um off,' sezee.

"Brer Buzzud flop en flop he wings, but de mo' w'at he flop, de mo' he fan de fier, en 'twa'n't long 'fo' he done bodaciously bu'n up, all ceppin' de big een' er his wing-fedders, en dem ole Brer Tarrypin tuck en make inter some quills, w'ich he go 'roun' a-playin' un um, en de chune w'at he play was dish yer:

> "'I foolee, I foolee, I foolee po' Buzzud;
> Po' Buzzud I foolee, I foolee, I foolee.'"

15
Brother Fox Covets the Quills

"THAT MUST have been a mighty funny song," said the little boy.

"Fun one time ain't fun n'er time; some folks fin's fun whar yuther folks fin's trouble. Pig may laugh when he see de rock a-heatin', but dey ain't no fun dar fer de pig.[1]

"Yit, fun er no fun, dat de song w'at Brer Tarrypin play on de quills:

> "'I foolee, I foolee, I foolee po' Buzzud;
> Po' Buzzud I foolee, I foolee, I foolee.'

"Nobody dunner whar de quills cum fum, kaze Brer Tarrypin, he ain't makin' no brags how he git um; yit ev'ybody want um on account er der playin' sech a lonesome[2] chune, en ole Brer Fox, he want um wuss'n all. He beg en he beg Brer Tarrypin fer ter sell 'im dem quills; but Brer Tarrypin, he hol' on t'um tight, en say eh-eh! Den he ax Brer Tarrypin fer ter loan um t'um des a week, so he kin play fer he chilluns, but Brer Tarrypin, he shake he head en put he foot down, en keep on playin':

> "'I foolee, I foolee, I foolee po' Buzzud;
> Po' Buzzud I foolee, I foolee, I foolee.'

"But Brer Fox, he ain't got no peace er min' on account er dem quills, en one day he meet Brer Tarrypin en he ax 'im how he seem ter segashuate

---

[1] An allusion to the primitive mode of cleaning hogs by heating rocks, and placing them in a barrel or tank of water. — J. C. H.

[2] This word "lonesome," as used by the Negroes, is the equivalent of "thrilling," "romantic," etc., and in that sense is very expressive. — J. C. H.

en he fambly en all he chilluns; en den Brer Fox ax Brer Tarrypin ef he can't des look at de quills, kaze he got some goose-fedders at he house, en if he kin des get a glimpse er Brer Tarrypin quills, he 'speck he kin make some mighty like um.

"Brer Tarrypin, he study 'bout dis, but he hate ter 'ny small favors like dat, en bimeby he hol' out dem quills whar Brer Fox kin see um. Wid dat, Brer Fox, he tuck'n juk de quills out'n Brer Tarrypin han', he did, and dash off des ez hard ez he kin go. Brer Tarrypin, he holler en holler at 'im des loud ez he kin holler, but he know he can't ketch 'im, en he des sot dar, Brer Tarrypin did, en look lak he done los' all de kin-folks w'at he got in de roun' worl'.

"Atter dis, Brer Fox he strut 'roun' en play mighty biggity, en eve'y time he meet Brer Tarrypin in de road he walk all 'roun' 'im en play on de quills like dis:

> "'I foolee, I foolee, po' Buzzud;
> I foolee ole Tarrypin, too.'

"Brer Tarrypin, he feel mighty bad, but he ain't sayin' nothin'. Las', one day w'iles ole Brer Tarrypin was settin' on a log sunnin' hisse'f, yer come Brer Fox playin' dat same old chune on de quills, but Brer Tarrypin, he stay still. Brer Fox, he come up a little nigher en play, but Brer Tarrypin, he keep he eyes shot en he lay still. Brer Fox, he come nigher en git on de log; Brer Tarrypin ain't sayin' nothin'. Brer Fox still git up nigher en play on de quills; still Brer Tarrypin ain't sayin' nothin'.

"'Brer Tarrypin mighty sleepy dis mawnin',' sez Brer Fox, sezee.

"Still Brer Tarrypin keep he eyes shot en stay still. Brer Fox keep on gittin' nigher en nigher, twel bimeby Brer Tarrypin open he eyes en he mouf bofe, en he make a grab at Brer Fox en miss 'im.

"But hol' on!" exclaimed Uncle Remus, in response to an expression of intense disappointment in the child's face. "You des wait a minnit. Nex' mawnin', Brer Tarrypin take hisse'f off en waller in a mud-hole, en smear hisse'f wid mud twel he look des zackly lak a clod er dirt. Den he crawl off en lay down un'need a log whar he know Brer Fox come eve'y mawnin' fer ter freshen hisse'f.

"Brer Tarrypin lay dar, he did, en terreckly yer come Brer Fox. Time he git dar, Brer Fox 'gun ter lip backerds en forerds 'cross de log, and

Brer Tarrypin he crope nigher en nigher, twel bimeby he make a grab at Brer Fox en kotch him by de foot. Dey tells me," continued Uncle Remus, rubbing his hands together in token of great satisfaction, — "dey tells me dat w'en Brer Tarrypin ketch holt, hit got ter thunder 'fo' he let go. All I know, Brer Tarrypin git Brer Fox by de foot, en he hilt 'im dar. Brer Fox he jump en he r'ar, but Brer Tarrypin done got 'im. Brer Fox, he holler out:

"'Brer Tarrypin, please lemme go!'

"Brer Tarrypin talk way down in his th'oat:

"'Gim' my quills!'

"'Lemme go en fetch um.'

"'Gim' my quills!'

"'Do pray lemme go git um.'

"'Gim' my quills!'

"En, bless gracious! dis all Brer Fox kin git outer Brer Tarrypin. Las', Brer Fox foot hu't 'im so bad dat he bleedzd ter do sump'n', en he sing out fer his ole 'oman fer ter fetch de quills, but he ole 'oman, she busy 'bout de house, en she don't year 'im. Den he call he son, which he named Tobe. He holler en bawl, en Tobe make answer:

"'Tobe! O Tobe! You Tobe!'

"'W'at you want, daddy?'

"'Fetch Brer Tarrypin quills.'

"'W'at you say, daddy? Fetch de big tray ter git de honey in?'

"'No you crazy-head! Fetch Brer Tarrypin quills!'

"'W'at you say, daddy? Fetch de dipper ter ketch de minners in?'

"'No, you fool! Fetch Brer Tarrypin quills!'

"'W'at you say, daddy? Water done been spill?'

"Hit went on dis a-way twel atter w'ile ole Miss Fox year de racket, en den she lissen, en she know dat 'er ole man holler'n' fer de quills, en she fotch um out en gun um ter Brer Tarrypin, en Brer Tarrypin, he let go he holt. He let go he holt," Uncle Remus went on, "but long time atter dat, w'en Brer Fox go ter pay he calls, he hatter go *hoppity-fetchity, hoppity-fetchity.*"

The old man folded his hands in his lap, and sat quietly gazing into the lightwood fire. Presently he said:

"I 'speck Miss Sally blessin' us all right now, en fus' news you know

she'll h'ist up en have Mars John a-trapesin' down yer; en ef she do dat, den termorrer mawnin' my brekkuss 'll be col', en lakwise my dinner, en ef dey's sump'n' w'at I 'spizes hit's col' vittles."

Thereupon Uncle Remus arose, shook himself, peered out into the night to discover that the rain had nearly ceased, and then made ready to carry the little boy to his mother. Long before the chickens had crowed for midnight, the child, as well as the old man, had been transported to the land where myths and fables cease to be wonderful, — the land of pleasant dreams.

16
How Brother Fox Failed to Get His Grapes

ONE NIGHT the little boy failed to make his appearance at the accustomed hour, and the next morning the intelligence that the child was sick went forth from the "big house." Uncle Remus was told that it had been necessary during the night to call in two physicians. When this information was imparted to the old man, there was an expression upon his countenance of awe not unmixed with indignation. He gave vent to the latter:

"Dar now! Two un um! W'en dat chile rize up, ef rize up he do, he'll des nat'ally be a shadder. Yer I is, gwine on eighty year, en I ain't tuck none er dat ar doctor truck yit, 'ceppin' it's dish yer flas' er poke-root w'at ole Miss Favers fix up fer de stiffness in my j'ints. Dey'll come en dey'll go, en dey'll po' in der jollup yer en slap on der fly-plarster dar, en sprinkle der calomy yander, twel bimeby dat chile won't look like hisse'f. Dat's w'at! En mo'n dat, hit's mighty kuse unter me dat ole folks kin go 'long en stan' up ter de rack en gobble up der 'lowance, en yit chilluns is got ter be strucken down. Ef Miss Sally'll des tu'n dem docter mens loose onter me, I lay I lick up der physic twel dey go off 'stonish'.'"

But no appeal of this nature was made to Uncle Remus. The illness of the little boy was severe, but not fatal. He took his medicine and improved, until finally even the doctors pronounced him convalescent. But he was very weak, and it was a fortnight before he was permitted to leave his bed. He was restless, and yet his term of imprisonment was full of pleasure. Every night after supper Uncle Remus would creep softly into the back piazza, place his hat carefully on the floor, rap gently on the door by way of announcement, and so pass into the nursery. How patient his vigils, how tender his ministrations, only the mother of the little boy knew; how comfortable and refreshing the change from the bed to the strong arms of Uncle Remus, only the little boy could say.

Almost the first manifestation of the child's convalescence was the renewal of his interest in the wonderful adventures of Brother Rabbit, Brother Fox, and the other brethren who flourished in that strange past over which this modern Æsop had thrown the veil of fable. "Miss Sally," as Uncle Remus called the boy's mother, sitting in an adjoining room, heard the youngster pleading for a story, and after a while she heard the old man clear up his throat with a great affectation of formality and begin.

"Dey ain't skacely no p'int whar ole Brer Rabbit en ole Brer Fox made der 'greements side wid one er n'er; let 'lone dat, dey wuz one p'int 'twix 'um w'ich it wuz same ez fier en tow, en dat wuz Miss Meadows en de gals. Little ez you might 'speck, dem same creeturs wuz bofe un um flyin' 'roun' Miss Meadows en de gals. Ole Brer Rabbit, he'd go dar, en dar he'd fin' ole Brer Fox settin' up gigglin' wid de gals, en den he'd skuze hisse'f, he would, en gallop down de big road a piece, en paw up de san' same lak dat ar ball-face steer w'at tuck'n tuck off yo' pa' coattail las' Feberwary. En lakwise ole Brer Fox, he'd sa'nter in, en fin' ole man Rab settin' 'longside er de gals, en den he'd go down de road en grab a 'simmon-bush in he mouf, en nat'ally gnyaw de bark off'n it. In dem days, honey," continued Uncle Remus, responding to a look of perplexity on the child's face, "creeturs wuz wuss dan w'at dey is now. Dey wuz dat — lots wuss.

"Dey went on dis a-way twel, bimeby, Brer Rabbit gun ter cas' 'roun', he did, fer ter see ef he can't bus' inter some er Brer Fox 'rangerments, en, atter w'ile, one day w'en he wer' settin' down by de side er de road wukkin up de diffunt oggyment w'at strak pun he min', en fixin' up he tricks, des 'bout dat time he year a clatter up de long green lane, en yer come ole Brer Fox — *too-bookity* — *bookity* — *bookity-book* — lopin' 'long mo' samer dan a bay colt in de bolly-patch. En he wuz all primp up, too, mon, en he look slick en shiny lak he des come out'n de sto'. Ole man Rab, he sot dar, he did, en w'en ole Brer Fox come gallopin' 'long, Brer Rabbit, he up'n hail 'im. Brer Fox, he fotch up, en dey pass de time er day wid one er nudder monstus perlite; en den, bimeby atter w'ile, Brer Rabbit, he up'n say, sezee, dat he got some mighty good news fer Brer Fox; en Brer Fox, he up'n ax 'im w'at is it. Den Brer Rabbit, he sorter scratch he year wid his behime foot en say, sezee:

"'I wuz takin' a walk day 'fo' yistiddy,' sezee, w'en de fus' news I know'd I run up 'g'in' de bigges' en de fattes' bunch er grapes dat I ever lay eyes on. Dey wuz dat fat en dat big,' sezee, 'dat de nat'al juice wuz des drappin' fum um, en de bees wuz a-swarmin' atter de honey, en little ole Jack Sparrer en all er his fambly conneckshun wuz skeetin' 'roun' dar dippin' in der bills,' sezee.

"Right den en dar," Uncle Remus went on, "Brer Fox mouf 'gun ter water, en he look outer he eye like he de bes' frien' w'at Brer Rabbit got in de roun' worl'. He done fergit all 'bout de gals, en he sorter sidle up ter Brer Rabbit, he did, en he say, sezee:

"'Come on, Brer Rabbit,' sezee, 'en less you'n me go git dem ar grapes 'fo' dey er all gone,' sezee. En den ole Brer Rabbit, he laff, he did, en up'n 'spon', sezee:

"'I hungry myse'f, Brer Fox,' sezee, 'but I ain't hankerin' atter grapes, en I'll be in monstus big luck ef I kin rush 'roun' yer somers en scrape up a bait er pusley time nuff fer ter keep de breff in my body. En yit,' sezee, 'ef you tak'n rack off atter deze yer grapes, w'at Miss Meadows en de gals gwine do? I lay dey got yo' name in de pot,' sezee.

"'Ez ter dat,' sez ole Brer Fox, sezee, 'I kin drap 'roun' en see de ladies atterwards,' sezee.

"'Well, den, ef dat's yo' game,' sez ole man Rab, sezee, 'I kin squot right flat down yer on de groun' en p'int out de way de same ez leadin' you dar by de han',' sezee; en den Brer Rabbit sorter chaw on he cud lak he gedder'n up his 'membrunce, en he up'n say, sezee:

"'You know dat ar place whar you went atter sweetgum fer Miss Meadow en de gals t'er day?' sezee.

"Brer Fox 'low dat he know dat ar place same ez he do he own tater-patch.

"'Well, den,' sez Brer Rabbit, sezee, 'de grapes ain't dar. You git ter de sweetgum,' sezee, 'en den you go up de branch twel you come ter a lit-tle patch er bamboo-briar — but de grapes ain't dar. Den you follow yo' lef' han' strike 'cross de hill twel you come ter dat big red-oak root — but de grapes ain't dar. On you goes down de hill twel you come ter n'er branch, en on dat branch dars a dogwood-tree leanin' 'way over, en nigh dat dogwood dars a vine, en in dat vine, dar you'll fin' yo' grapes. Dey er dat ripe,' sez ole Brer Rabbit, sezee, 'dat dey look like dey er done melt tergedder, en I speck you'll fin' um full er bugs, but you kin take dat fine bushy tail er yone, Brer Fox,' sezee, 'en bresh dem bugs away.'

"Brer Fox 'low he much 'blige, en den he put out atter de grapes in a han'-gallop, en w'en he done got outer sight, en likewise outer year'n, Brer Rabbit, he tak'n git a blade er grass, he did, en tickle hisse'f in de

year, en den he holler en laff, en laff en holler, twel he hatter lay down
fer ter git he breff back 'g'in.

"Den, atter so long time, Brer Rabbit he jump up, he do, en take atter Brer Fox, but Brer Fox, he ain't look ter de right ner de lef', en needer
do he look behime; he des keep a-rackin' 'long twel he come ter de
sweetgum-tree, en den he tu'n up de branch twel he come ter de bamboo-briar, en den he tu'n squar' ter de lef' twel he come ter de big red-
oak root, en den he keep on down de hill twel he come ter de yuther
branch, en dar he see de dogwood; en mo'n dat, dar nigh de dogwood he
see de vine, en in dat vine dar wuz de big bunch er grapes. Sho nuff, dey
wuz all kivver'd wid bugs.

"Ole Brer Rabbit, he'd bin a-pushin 'long atter Brer Fox, but de des
hatter scratch gravel fer ter keep up. Las' he hove in sight, en he lay off
in de weeds, he did, fer ter watch Brer Fox motions. Present'y Brer Fox
crope up de leanin' dogwood-tree twel he come nigh de grapes, en den
he sorter balance hisse'f on a lim' en gun um a swipe wid his big bushy
tail, fer ter bresh off de bugs. But, bless yo' soul, honey! no sooner is he
done dat dan he fetch a squall w'ich Miss Meadows vow atterwards she
year plum' ter her house, en down he come — *ker-blim!*"

"W'at was the matter, Uncle Remus?" the little boy asked.

"Law, honey! dat 'seetful Brer Rabbit done fool ole Brer Fox. Dem ar
grapes all so fine wuz needer mo' ner less dan a great big was'-nes', en
dem bugs wuz deze yer red wassies — deze yer speeshy w'at's rank
pizen fum een' ter een'. W'en Brer Fox drap fum de tree de wassies dey
drap wid 'im, en de way dey wom ole Brer Fox up wuz sinful. Dey ain't
mo'n tetch 'im 'fo' dey had 'im het up ter de b'ilin' p'int. Brer Fox, he run,
en he kick, en he scratch, en he bite, en he scramble, en he holler, en he
howl, but look lak dey git wuss en wuss. One time, hit seem lak Brer Fox
en his new 'quaintance wuz makin' todes Brer Rabbit, but dey ain't no
sooner p'int dat way, dan ole Brer Rabbit, he up'n make a break, en he
went sailin' thoo de woods wuss'n wunner dese whully-win's, an he ain't
stop twel he fetch up at Miss Meadows.

"Miss Meadows en de gals, dey ax 'im dey did, wharbouts wuz Brer
Fox, en Brer Rabbit, he up'n 'spon' dat he done gone a-grape-huntin', en
den Miss Meadows, she 'low she did:

"'Law, gals! is you ever year de beat er dat? En dat, too, w'en Brer Fox done say he comin' ter dinner,' sez she. 'I lay I done wid Brer Fox, kaze you can't put no 'pennunce in deze yer men-folks,' sez she. 'Yer de dinner bin done dis long time, en we bin a-waitin' lak de quality. But now I'm done wid Brer Fox,' sez she.

"Wid dat, Miss Meadows en de gals dey ax Brer Rabbit fer ter stay ter dinner, en Brer Rabbit, he sorter make lak he wanter be skuze, but bimeby he tuck a cheer en sot um out. He tuck a cheer," continued Uncle Remus, "en he ain't bin dar long twel he look out en spy ole Brer Fox gwine 'long by, en w'at do Brer Rabbit do but call Miss Meadows en de gals en p'int 'im out? Soon's dey seed 'im dey sot up a monstus giggle-ment, kaze Brer Fox wuz dat swell up twel little mo'n he'd a bus'. He head wuz swell up, en down ter he legs, dey wuz swell up. Miss Meadows, she up'n say dat Brer Fox look lak he done gone en got all de grapes dey wuz in de neighborhoods, en one er de yuther gals, she squeal, she did, en say:

"'Law, ain't you 'shame', en right yer 'fo' Brer Rabbit!'

"En den dey hilt der han's 'fo' der face en giggle des like gals duz deze days."

17
Mr. Fox Figures As an Incendiary

THE NEXT NIGHT the little boy had been thoughtful enough to save some of his supper for Uncle Remus, and to this Miss Sally had added, on her own account, a large piece of fruitcake. The old man appeared to be highly pleased.

"Ef ders enny kinder cake w'at I likes de mos', hit's dish yer kin' w'at's got reezins strowed 'mongs' it. Wid sick folks, now," he continued, holding up the cake and subjecting it to a critical examination, "dish yer hunk 'ud mighty nigh las' a mont', but wid a well man lak I is, hit won't las' a minnit."

And it didn't. It disappeared so suddenly that the little boy laughed aloud, and wanted Uncle Remus to have some more cake; but the latter protested that he didn't come there "fer ter git founder'd," but merely to see "ef somebody's strenk uz strong nuff fer ter stan' n'er tale." The little boy said if Uncle Remus meant him, he was sure his health was good enough to listen to any number of stories. Whereupon, the old man, without any tantalizing preliminaries, began:

"Brer Fox done bin fool so much by Brer Rabbit dat he sorter look 'roun' fer ter see ef he can't ketch up wid some er de yuther creeturs, en so, one day, w'iles he gwine long down de big road, who should he strak up wid but ole Brer Tarrypin. Brer Fox sorter lick his chops, en 'low dat ef he kin fling ennybody en gin um all-under holt, Brer Tarrypin de man, en he march up, mighty biggity, like he gwine ter make spote un 'im. W'en he git up nigh 'nuff, Brer Fox hail 'im:

"'How you 'speck you fin' yo'se'f dis mawnin', Brer Tarrypin?' sezee.

"'Slow, Brer Fox — mighty slow,' sez Brer Tarrypin, sezee. 'Day in en day out I'm mighty slow, en it look lak I'm a-gittin' slower; I'm slow en po'ly, Brer Fox — how you come on?' sezee.

"'Oh, I'm slanchindickler, same ez I allers is,' sez Brer Fox, sezee. 'W'at make yo' eye so red, Brer Tarrypin?' sezee.

"'Hit's all 'longer de trouble I see, Brer Fox,' sez Brer Tarrypin, sezee. 'I see trouble en you see none; trouble come en pile up on trouble,' sezee.

"'Law, Brer Tarrypin!' sez Brer Fox, sezee, 'you ain't see no trouble yit. Ef you wanter see sho nuff trouble, you des oughter go 'longer me; I'm de man w'at kin show you trouble,' sezee.

"'Well, den,' sez ole Brer Tarrypin, sezee, 'ef you er de man w'at kin show me trouble, den I'm de man w'at want a glimpse un it,' sezee.

"Den Brer Fox, he ax Brer Tarrypin is he seed de Ole Boy, en den Brer Tarrypin, he make answer dat he ain't seed 'im yit, but he year tell un 'im. Wid dat, Brer Fox 'low de Ole Boy de kinder trouble he bin talkin' 'bout, en den Brer Tarrypin, he up'n ax how he gwine see 'im. Brer Fox, he tak'n lay out de pogrance, en he up'n tell Brer Tarrypin dat ef he'll step up dar in de middle er dat ole broom-sage fiel', en squot dar a spell, 'twon't be no time 'fo' he'll ketch a glimpse er de Ole Boy.

"Brer Tarrypin know'd ders sump'n' wrong somers, yit he mos' too flat-footed fer ter have enny scuffle wid Brer Fox, en he say ter hisse'f dat he'll go 'long en des trus' ter luck; en den he 'low dat ef Brer Fox he'p 'im 'cross de fence, he b'lieve he'll go up en resk one eye on de Ole Boy.

Co'se Brer Fox hope 'im 'cross, en no sooner is he good en gone, dan Brer Fox, he fix up fer ter make 'im see trouble. He lipt out ter Miss Meadows house, Brer Fox did, en he make like he wanter borry a chunk er fier fer ter light he pipe, en he tuck dat chunk, en he run 'roun' de fiel', en he sot de grass a-fier, en 'twa'n't long 'fo' it look lak de whole face er de yeth wuz a-blazin' up."

"Did it burn the Terrapin up?" interrupted the little boy.

"Don't push me, honey; don't make me git de kyart 'fo' de hoss. W'en ole Brer Tarrypin 'gun ter wade thoo de stray, de ve'y fus' man w'at he strak up wid wuz ole man Rabbit layin' dar sleepin' on de shady side uv a tussock. Brer Rabbit, he er deze yer kinder mens w'at sleep wid der eye wide open, en he wuz 'wake d'reckly he year Brer Tarrypin scufflin' en scramblin' 'long thoo de grass. Atter dey shuck han's en ax 'bout one er n'er fambly, hit ain't take long fer Brer Tarrypin fer ter tell Brer Rabbit w'at fotch 'im dar, en Brer Rabbit, he up'n say, sezee.

"'Hit's des nat'ally a born blessin' dat you struck up wid me w'en you did,' sezee, 'kaze little mo' en bofe un us would a bin bobbycu'd,' sezee.

"Dis kinder tarrify Brer Tarrypin, en he say he wanter git out fum dar; but Brer Rabbit he 'low he'd take keer un 'im, en he tuck'n tuck Brer Tarrypin in de middle er de fiel' whar dey wuz a big holler stump. Onter dis stump Brer Rabbit lif' Brer Tarrypin, en den he lip up hisse'f en crope in de holler, en, bless yo' soul, honey, w'en de fier come a-snippin' en a-snappin', dar dey sot des ez safe en ez snug ez you iz in yo' bed dis minnit.

"W'en de blaze blow over, Brer Tarrypin look 'roun', en he see Brer Fox runnin' up'n down de fence lak he huntin' sump'n'. Den Brer Rabbit, he stick he head up out'n de hole, en likewise he seed 'im, and den he holler like Brer Tarrypin" (Here Uncle Remus puckered his voice, so to say, in a most amusing squeak):

"'Brer Fox! Brer Fox! O Brer Fox! Run yer — we done kotch Brer Rabbit!'

"En den Brer Fox, he jump up on de top rail er de fence en fetch a spring dat lan' 'im 'way out in de bu'nin' grass, en it hurted 'im en sting 'im in de footses dat bad, dat he squeal en he roll, en de mo' he roll de wuss it bu'n him, en Brer Rabbit en Brer Tarrypin dey des holler en laff. Bimeby Brer Fox git out, en off he put down de road, limpin' fus' on one foot en den on de yuther."

The little boy laughed, and then there was a long silence — so long, indeed, that Uncle Remus's Miss Sally, sewing in the next room, concluded to investigate it. An exceedingly interesting tableau met her sight. The little child had wandered into the land of dreams with a smile on his face. He lay with one of his little hands buried in both of Uncle Remus's, while the old man himself was fast asleep, with his head thrown back and his mouth wide open. Miss Sally shook him by the shoulder and held up her finger to prevent him from speaking. He was quiet until she held the lamp for him to get down the back steps, and then she heard him say, in an indignantly mortified tone:

"Now den, Miss Sally'll be a-riggin' me 'bout noddin', but stidder dat she better be glad dat I ain't bus' loose en sno' en 'larm de house — let 'lone dat sick baby. Dat's w'at!"

18

A Dream and a Story

"I DREAMED all about Brother Fox and Brother Rabbit last night, Uncle Remus," exclaimed the little boy when the old man came in after supper and took his seat by the side of the trundle-bed; "I dreamed that Brother Fox had wings and tried to catch Brother Rabbit by flying after him."

"I don't 'spute it, honey, dat I don't!" replied the old man, in a tone which implied that he was quite prepared to believe the dream itself was true. "Many's en many's de time, deze long nights en deze rainy spells, dat I sets down dar in my house over ag'in' de chimbley-jam' — I sets dar en I dozes, en it seem lak dat ole Brer Rabbit, he'll stick he head in de crack er de do' en see my eye 'periently shot, en den he'll beckon back at de yuther creeturs, en den dey'll all come slippin' in on der tiptoes, en dey'll set dar en run over de ole times wid one er n'er, en crack der jokes same ez dey useter. En den ag'in," continued the old man, shutting his eyes and giving to his voice a gruesome intonation quite impossible to describe, — "en den ag'in hit look lak dat Brer Rabbit'll gin de wink all 'roun', en den dey'll tu'n in en git up a reg'lar juberlee. Brer Rabbit, he'll retch up en take down de trivet, en Brer Fox, he'll snatch up de griddle, en Brer B'ar, he'll lay holt er de pot-hooks, en ole Brer

Tarrypin, he'll grab up de fryin' pan, en dar dey'll have it, up en down, en 'roun' en 'roun'. Hit seem lak ter me dat ef I kin git my min' smoove down en ketch up some er dem ar chunes w'at dey sets dar en plays, den I'd lean back yer in dish yer cheer en I'd intrance you wid um, twel, by dis time termorrer night, you'd be settin' up dar at de supper-table 'sputin' 'longer yo' little brer 'bout de 'lasses pitcher. Dem creeturs dey sets dar," Uncle Remus went on, "en dey plays dem kinder chunes w'at moves you fum 'way back yander; en many's de time w'en I gits lonesome kaze dey ain't nobody year um ceppin' it's me. Dey ain't no tellin' de chunes dey is in dat trivet, en in dat griddle, en in dat fryin'-pan er mine; dat dey ain't. W'en dem creeturs walks in en snatches um down, dey lays Miss Sally's pianner in de shade, en Mars John's flute, hit ain't nowhars."

"Do they play on them just like a band, Uncle Remus?" inquired the little boy, who was secretly in hopes that the illusion would not be destroyed.

"Dey comes des lak I tell you, honey. W'en I shets my eyes en dozes, dey comes en dey plays, but w'en I opens my eyes dey ain't dar. Now, den, w'en dat's de shape er matters, w'at duz I do? I des shets my eyes en hol' um shot, en let um come en play dem ole time chunes twel long atter bedtime done come en gone."

Uncle Remus paused, as though he expected the little boy to ask some question or make some comment, but the child said nothing, and presently the old man resumed, in a matter-of fact tone:

"Dat dream er yone, honey, 'bout Brer Fox wid wings, fetches up de time w'en Brer Fox en Brer Wolf had der fallin' out wid one er n'er — but I 'speck I done tole you 'bout dat."

"Oh, no, you haven't, Uncle Remus! You know you haven't!" the little boy exclaimed.

"Well, den, one day, atter so long a time, Brer Wolf en Brer Fox dey got ter 'sputin' 'longer one er n'er. Brer Wolf, he tuck'n 'buse Brer Fox kaze Brer Fox let Brer Rabbit fool 'im, en den Brer Fox, he tuck'n quoll back at Brer Wolf, kaze Brer Wolf let ole man Rabbit lakwise fool 'im. Dey keep on 'sputin' en 'sputin', twel bimeby dey clinch, en Brer Wolf bein' de bigges' man, 'twouldn't a bin long 'fo' he'd a wool Brer Fox, but Brer Fox, he watch he chance, he did, en he gin 'im leg bail."

"Gave him what, Uncle Remus?"

"Gin 'im leg bail, honey. He juk loose fum Brer Wolf, Brer Fox did, en, gentermens, he des mosey thoo de woods. Brer Wolf, he tuck atter'm, he did, en dar dey had it, en Brer Wolf push Brer Fox so close, dat de onliest way Brer Fox kin save he hide is ter fin' a hole somers, en de fus' holler tree dat he come 'cross, inter it he dove. Brer Wolf fetch a grab at 'im, but he wuz des in time fer ter be too late.

"Den Brer Wolf, he sot dar, he did, en he study en study how he gwine git Brer Fox out, en Brer Fox, he lay in dar, he did, en he study en study w'at Brer Wolf gwine do. Bimeby, Brer Wolf, he tuck'n gedder up a whole lot er chunks, en rocks, en sticks, en den he tuck'n fill up de hole whar Brer Fox went in so Brer Fox can't git out. W'iles dis wuz gwine on, ole Brer Tukkey Buzzud, he wuz sailin' 'roun' way up in de elements, wid he eye peel fer bizness, en 'twa'n't long 'fo' he glance lit on Brer Wolf, en he 'low ter hisse'f, sezee:

"'I'll des sorter flop down,' sezee, 'en look inter dis, kaze ef Brer Wolf hidin' he dinner dar wid de expec'shun er findin' it dar w'en he come back, den he done gone en put it in de wrong place,' sezee.

"Wid dat ole Brer Tukkey Buzzud, he flop down en sail 'roun' nigher, en he soon see dat Brer Wolf ain't hidin' no dinner. Den he flop down furder, ole Brer Buzzud did, twel he lit on de top er de holler tree. Brer Wolf, he done kotch a glimpse er ole Brer Buzzud shadder, but he keep on puttin' chunks en rocks in de holler. Den, present'y, Brer Buzzud, he open up:

"'W'at you doin' dar, Brer Wolf?'

"'Makin' a toom-stone, Brer Buzzud.'

"Co'se Brer Buzzud sorter feel like he got intruss in marters like dis, en he holler back:

"'Who dead now, Brer Wolf?'

"'Wunner yo' 'quaintance, w'ich he name Brer Fox, Brer Buzzud.'

"'W'en he die, Brer Wolf?'

"'He ain't dead yit, but he won't las' long in yer, Brer Buzzud.'

"Brer Wolf, he keep on, he did, twel he done stop up de hole good, en den he bresh de trash off'n his cloze, en put out fer home. Brer Tukkey Buzzud, he sot up dar, he did, en ontankle his tail fedders, en lissen en lissen, but Brer Fox, he keep dark, en Brer Buzzud ain't year nothin'. Den Brer Buzzud, he flop he wings en sail away.

"Bimeby, nex' day, bright en early, yer he come back, en he sail all 'roun' en 'roun' de tree, but Brer Fox he lay low an keep dark, en Brer Buzzud ain't year nothin'. Atter w'ile, Brer Buzzud he sail 'roun' ag'in, en dis time he sing, en de song w'at he sing is dish yer:

> "'Boo, boo, boo, my filler-mer-loo,
> Man out yer wid news fer you!'

Den he sail all 'roun' en 'roun' n'er time en lissen, en bimeby he year Brer Fox sing back:

> "'Go 'way, go 'way my little jug er beer,
> De news you bring, I yeard las' year.'"

"Beer, Uncle Remus? What kind of beer did they have then?" the little boy inquired.

"Now, den, honey, you er gittin' me up in a close cornder," responded the old man, in an unusually serious tone. "Beer is de way de tale runs, but w'at kinder beer it moughter bin ain't come down ter me — en yit hit seem lak I year talk somers dat dish yer beer wuz mos' prins'ply 'simmon beer."

This seemed to satisfy the small but exacting audience, and Uncle Remus continued:

"So, den, w'en Brer Buzzud year Brer Fox sing back, he 'low he ain't dead, en wid dat, Brer Buzzud, he sail off en 'ten' ter he yuther business. Nex' day back he come, en Brer Fox, he sing back, he did, des ez lively ez a cricket in de ashes, en it keep on dis way twel Brer Fox stomach 'gun ter pinch him, en den he know dat he gotter study up some kinder plans fer ter git out fum dar. N'er day pass, en Brer Fox, he tuck'n lay low, en it keep on dat a-way twel hit look lak ter Brer Fox, pent up in dar, dat he mus' sholy pe'sh. Las', one day Brer Buzzud come sailin' all 'roun' en 'roun' wid dat

> "'Boo, boo, boo, my filler-mer-loo,'

but Brer Fox, he keep dark, en Brer Buzzud, he tuck'n spishun dat Brer Fox wuz done dead. Brer Buzzud, he keep on singin', en Brer Fox he keep on layin' low, twel bimeby Brer Buzzud lit en 'gun ter cle'r way de trash en truck fum de holler. He hop up, he did, en tuck out one chunk, en den he hop back en lissen, but Brer Fox stay still. Den Brer Buzzud hop up en tuck out n'er chunk, en den hop back en lissen, en all dis time Brer Fox mouf 'uz waterin' w'iles he lay back in dar en des nat'ally honed atter Brer Buzzud. Hit went on dis a-way, twel des 'fo' he got de hole un-kivver'd, Brer Fox, he break out he did, en grab Brer Buzzud by de back er de neck. Dey wuz a kinder scuffle 'mungs um, but 'twa'n't fer long, en dat wuz de las' er ole Brer Tukkey Buzzud.''

19
The Moon in the Mill-Pond

ONE NIGHT when the little boy made his usual visit to Uncle Remus, he found the old man sitting up in his chair fast asleep. The child said nothing. He was prepared to exercise a good deal of patience upon occasion, and the occasion was when he wanted to hear a story. But, in making himself comfortable, he aroused Uncle Remus from his nap.

"I let you know, honey," said the old man, adjusting his spectacles, and laughing rather sheepishly — "I let you know, honey, w'en I gits my head r'ar'd back dat a-way, en my eyeleds shot, en my mouf open, en my chin p'intin' at de rafters, den dey's some mighty quare gwines on in my min'. Dey is dat, des ez sho ez you er settin' dar. W'en I fus' year you comin' down de paf," Uncle Remus continued, rubbing his beard thoughtfully, "I 'uz sorter 'feard you mought 'spicion dat I done gone off on my journeys fer ter see ole man Nod."

This was accompanied by a glance of inquiry, to which the little boy thought it best to respond.

"Well, Uncle Remus," he said, "I did think I heard you snoring when I came in."

"Now you see dat!" exclaimed Uncle Remus, in a tone of grieved astonishment; "you see dat! Man can't lean hisse'f 'pun his 'membunce, ceppin' dey's some un fer ter come high-primin' 'roun' en 'lowin' dat he done gone ter sleep. *Shoo!* W'en you slept in dat do' dar I 'uz right in 'mungs some mighty quare notions — mighty quare notions. Dey ain't no two ways; ef I 'uz ter up en let on 'bout all de notions w'at I gits in 'mungs, folks 'ud hatter come en kyar me off ter de place whar dey puts 'stracted people.

"Atter I sop up my supper," Uncle Remus went on, "I tuck'n year some flutterments up dar 'mungs de rafters, en I look up, en dar wuz a Bat sailin' 'roun'. 'Roun' en 'roun', en 'roun' she go — und' de rafters, 'bove de rafters — en ez she sail she make noise lak she grittin' 'er toofies. Now, w'at dat Bat atter, I be bless ef I kin tell you, but dar she wuz; 'roun' en 'roun', over en under. I ax 'er w'at do she want up dar, but she ain't got no time fer ter tell; 'roun' en 'roun', en over en under. En bimeby, out she flip, en I boun' she grittin' 'er toofies en gwine 'roun' en 'roun' out dar, en dodgin' en flippin' des lak de elements wuz full er rafters en cobwebs.

"W'en she flip out I le'nt my head back, I did, en 'twa'n't no time 'fo' I git mix up wid my notions. Dat Bat wings so limber en 'er will so good dat she done done 'er day's work dar 'fo' you could 'er run ter de big house en back. De Bat put me in min' er folks," continued Uncle Remus, settling himself back in his chair, "en folks put me in min' er de creeturs."

Immediately the little boy was all attention.

"Dey wuz times," said the old man, with something like a sigh, "w'en de creeturs 'ud segashuate tergedder des like dey ain't had no fallin' out. Dem wuz de times w'en ole Brer Rabbit 'ud 'ten' lak he gwine quit he 'havishness, en dey'd all go 'roun' des lak dey b'long ter de same fambly connexion.

"One time atter dey bin gwine in cahoots dis a-way. Brer Rabbit 'gun ter feel his fat, he did, en dis make 'im git projecky terreckly. De mo' peace w'at dey had, de mo' wuss Brer Rabbit feel, twel bimeby he git restless in de min'. W'en de sun shine he'd go en lay off in de grass en kick at de gnats, en nibble at de mullen stalk en waller in de san'. One night atter supper, w'iles he 'uz romancin' 'roun', he run up wid ole Brer Tarrypin, en atter dey shuck han's dey sot down on de side er de road en run on 'bout ole times. Dey talk en dey talk, dey did, en bimeby Brer Rabbit say it done come ter dat pass whar he bleedzd ter have some fun, en Brer Tarrypin 'low dat Brer Rabbit des de ve'y man he bin lookin' fer.

"'Well den,' sez Brer Rabbit, sezee, 'we'll des put Brer Fox, en Brer Wolf, en Brer B'ar on notice, en termorrer night we'll meet down by de mill-pon' en have a little fishin' frolic. I'll do de talkin',' sez Brer Rabbit, sezee, 'en you kin set back en say *yea*,' sezee.

"Brer Tarrypin laugh.

"'Ef I ain't dar,' sezee, 'den you may know de grasshopper done fly 'way wid me,' sezee.

"'En you nee'nter bring no fiddle, n'er,' sez Brer Rabbit, sezee, 'kaze dey ain't gwine ter be no dancin' dar,' sezee.

"Wid dat," continued Uncle Remus, "Brer Rabbit put out fer home, en went ter bed, en Brer Tarrypin bruise 'roun' en make his way todes de place so he kin be dar 'gin de p'inted time.

"Nex' day Brer Rabbit sont wud ter de yuther creeturs, en dey all make great 'miration, kaze dey ain't think 'bout dis deyse'f. Brer Fox, he 'low, he did, dat he gwine atter Miss Meadows en Miss Motts, en de yuther gals.

"Sho nuff, w'en de time come dey wuz all dar. Brer B'ar, he fotch a hook en line; Brer Wolf, he fotch a hook en line; Brer Fox, he fotch a dip-net, en Brer Tarrypin, not ter be outdone, he fotch de bait."

"What did Miss Meadows and Miss Motts bring?" the little boy asked.

Uncle Remus dropped his head slightly to one side, and looked over his spectacles at the little boy.

"Miss Meadows en Miss Motts," he continued, "dey tuck'n stan' way back fum de aidge er de pon' en squeal eve'y time Brer Tarrypin shuck de box er bait at um. Brer B'ar 'low he gwine ter fish fer mud-cats; Brer Wolf 'low he gwine ter fish fer horneyheads; Brer Fox 'low he gwine ter fish fer peerch fer de ladies; Brer Tarrypin 'low he gwine ter fish fer min-ners, en Brer Rabbit wink at Brer Tarrypin en 'low he gwine ter fish fer suckers.

"Dey all git ready, dey did, en Brer Rabbit march up ter de pon' en make fer ter th'ow he hook in de water, but des 'bout dat time hit seem lak he see sump'n. De t'er creeturs, dey stop en watch his motions. Brer Rabbit, he drap he pole, he did, en he stan' dar scratchin' he head en lookin' down in de water.

"De gals dey 'gun ter git oneasy w'en dey see dis, en Miss Meadows, she up en holler out, she did:

"'Law, Brer Rabbit, w'at de name er goodness de marter in dar?'

"Brer Rabbit scratch he head en look in de water. Miss Motts, she hilt up 'er petticoats, she did, en 'low she monstus 'fear'd er snakes. Brer Rabbit keep on scratchin' en lookin'.

"Bimeby he fetch a long breff, he did, en he 'low:

"'Ladies en gentermens all, we des might ez well make tracks fum dish yer place, kaze dey ain't no fishin' in dat pon' fer none er dish yer crowd.'

"Wid dat, Brer Tarrypin, he scramble up ter de aidge en look over, en he shake he head, en 'low:

"'Tooby sho — tooby sho! Tut-tut-tut!' en den he crawl back, he did, en do lak he wukkin' he min'.

"'Don't be skeert, ladies, kaze we er boun' ter take keer un you, let come w'at will, let go w'at mus',' sez Brer Rabbit, sezee. 'Accidents got ter happen unter we all, des same ez dey is unter yuther folks; en dey ain't nuthin' much de marter, ceppin' dat de Moon done drap in de water. Ef you don't b'lieve me you kin look fer yo'se'f,' sezee.

"Wid dat dey all went ter de bank en lookt in; en, sho nuff, dar lay de Moon, a-swingin' an' a-swayin' at de bottom er de pon'.'"

The little boy laughed. He had often seen the reflection of the sky in shallow pools of water, and the startling depths that seemed to lie at his feet had caused him to draw back with a shudder.

"Brer Fox, he look in, he did, en he 'low, 'Well, well, well!' Brer Wolf, he look in, en he 'low, 'Mighty bad, mighty bad!' Brer B'ar, he look in, en he 'low, 'Tum, tum, tum!' De ladies dey look in, en Miss Meadows she squall out, 'Ain't dat too much?' Brer Rabbit, he look in ag'in, en he up en 'low, he did:

"'Ladies en gentermens, you all kin hum en haw, but less'n we gits dat Moon out er de pon', dey ain't no fish kin be ketch 'roun' yer dis night; en ef you'll ax Brer Tarrypin, he'll tell you de same.'

"Den dey ax how kin dey git de Moon out er dar, en Brer Tarrypin 'low dey better lef' dat wid Brer Rabbit. Brer Rabbit he shot he eyes, he did, en make lak he wukkin' he min'. Bimeby, he up'n 'low:

"'De nighes' way out'n dish yer diffikil is fer ter sen' 'roun' yer to ole Mr. Mud Turkle en borry his seine, en drag dat Moon up fum dar,' sezee.

"'I 'clar' ter gracious I mighty glad you mention dat,' says Brer Tarrypin, sezee. 'Mr. Mud Turkle is setch clos't kin ter me dat I calls 'im Unk' Muck, en I lay ef you sen' dar atter dat seine you won't fin' Unk' Muck so mighty disaccomerdatin'.'

"Well," continued Uncle Remus, after one of his tantalizing pauses, "dey sont atter de seine, en w'iles Brer Rabbit wuz gone, Brer Tarrypin, he 'low dat he done year tell time en time ag'in dat dem w'at fin' de Moon in de water en fetch 'im out, lakwise dey ull fetch out a pot er money. Dis make Brer Fox, en Brer Wolf, en Brer B'ar feel mighty good, en dey 'low, dey did, dat long ez Brer Rabbit been so good ez ter run atter de seine, dey ull do de seinin'.

"Time Brer Rabbit git back, he see how de lan' lay, en he make lak he wanter go in atter de Moon. He pull off he coat, en he 'uz fixin' fer ter shuck he wescut, but de yuther creeturs dey 'low dey wa'n't gwine ter let dry-foot man lak Brer Rabbit go in de water. So Brer Fox, he tuck holt er one staff er de seine, Brer Wolf he tuck holt er de yuther staff, en Brer B'ar he wade 'long behime fer ter lif' de seine cross logs en snags.

"Dey make one haul — no Moon; n'er haul — no Moon; n'er haul — no Moon. Den bimeby dey git out furder fum de bank. Water run in Brer Fox year, he shake he head; water run in Brer Wolf year, he shake he head; water run in Brer B'ar year, he shake he head. En de fus' news you know, w'iles dey wuz a-shakin', dey come to whar de bottom shelf'd off. Brer Fox he step off en duck hisse'f; den Brer Wolf duck hisse'f; en Brer B'ar he make a splunge en duck hisse'f; en, bless gracious, dey kick en splatter twel it look lak dey 'uz gwine ter slosh all de water outer de mill-pon'.

"W'en dey come out, de gals 'uz all a-snickerin' en a-gigglin', en dey well mought, kaze go whar you would, dey wa'n't no wuss lookin' creeturs dan dem; en Brer Rabbit, he holler, sezee:

"'I 'speck you all, gents, better go home en git some dry duds, en n'er time we'll be in better luck,' sezee. 'I hear talk dat de Moon'll bite at a hook ef you take fools fer baits, en I lay dat's de onliest way fer ter ketch 'er,' sezee.

"Brer Fox en Brer Wolf en Brer B'ar went drippin' off, en Brer Rabbit en Brer Tarrypin, dey went home wid de gals."

20
Brother Rabbit Takes Some Exercise

ONE NIGHT while the little boy was sitting in Uncle Remus's cabin, waiting for the old man to finish his hoe-cake, and refresh his memory as to the further adventures of Brother Rabbit, his friends and his enemies, something dropped upon the top of the house with a noise like the crack

of a pistol. The little boy jumped, but Uncle Remus looked up and exclaimed, "Ah-yi!" in a tone of triumph.

"What was that, Uncle Remus?" the child asked, after waiting a moment to see what else would happen.

"New fum Jack Fros', honey. W'en dat hick'y-nut tree out dar year
'im comin' she 'gins ter drap w'at she got. I mighty glad," he continued,
scraping the burnt crust from his hoe-cake with an old case-knife, "I
mighty glad hick'y-nuts ain't big en heavy ez grinestones."

He waited a moment to see what effect this queer statement would
have on the child.

"Yasser, I mighty glad — dat I is. Kaze ef hick'y-nuts 'uz big ez
grinestones dish yer ole callyboose 'ud be a-leakin' long 'fo' Chris'mus."

Just then another hickory-nut dropped upon the roof, and the little
boy jumped again. This seemed to amuse Uncle Remus, and he laughed
until he was near to choking himself with his smoking hoe-cake.

"You does des zackly lak ole Brer Rabbit done, I 'clar' to gracious ef
you don't!" the old man cried, as soon as he could git his breath; "dez zackly fer de worl'."

The child was immensely flattered, and at once he wanted to know
how Brother Rabbit did. Uncle Remus was in such good humor that he
needed no coaxing. He pushed his spectacles back on his forehead,
wiped his mouth on his sleeve, and began:

"Hit come 'bout dat soon one mawnin' todes de fall er de year, Brer
Rabbit wuz stirrin' 'roun' in de woods atter some bergamot fer ter make
'im some ha'r-grease. De win' blow so col' dat it make 'im feel right
frisky, en eve'y time he year de bushes rattle he make lak he skeer'd. He
'uz gwine on dis away, hoppity-skippity, w'en bimeby he year Mr. Man
cuttin' on a tree way off in de woods. He fotch up, Brer Rabbit did, en lissen fus' wid one year en den wid de yuther.

"Man, he cut en cut, en Brer Rabbit, he lissen en lissen. Bimeby,
w'iles all dis was gwine on, down come de tree — *kubber-lang-bang-
blam!* Brer Rabbit, he tuck'n jump des lak you jump, en let 'lone dat, he
make a break, he did, en he lipt out fum dar lak de dogs wuz atter 'im."

"Was he scared, Uncle Remus?" asked the little boy.

"Skeer'd! Who? *Him?* Shoo! don't you fret yo'se'f 'bout Brer Rabbit,
honey. In dem days dey wa'n't nothin' gwine dat kin skeer Brer Rabbit.

Tooby sho, he tuck keer hisse'f, en ef you know de man w'at 'fuse ter take keer hisse'f, I lak mighty well ef you p'int 'im out. Deed'n dat I would!"

Uncle Remus seemed to boil over with argumentative indignation.

"Well, den," he continued, "Brer Rabbit run twel he git sorter het up like, en des 'bout de time he makin' ready fer ter squot en ketch he win', who should he meet but Brer Coon gwine home atter settin' up wid ole Brer Bull-Frog. Brer Coon see 'im runnin', en he hail 'im.

"'W'at yo' hurry, Brer Rabbit?'

"'Ain't got time ter tarry.'

"'Folks sick?'

"'No, my Lord! Ain't got time ter tarry!'

"'Tryin' yo' soopleness?'

"'No, my Lord! Ain't got time ter tarry!'

"'Do pray, Brer Rabbit, tell me de news!'

"'Mighty big fuss back dar in de woods. Ain't got time ter tarry!'

"Dis make Brer Coon feel mighty skittish, kaze he fur ways fum home, en he des lipt out, he did, en went a-b'ilin' thoo de woods. Brer Coon ain't gone fur twel he meet Brer Fox.

"'Hey, Brer Coon, whar you gwine?'

"'Ain't got time ter tarry!'

"'Gwine at' de doctor?'

"'No, my Lord! Ain't got time ter tarry.'

"'Do pray, Brer Coon, tell me de news.'

"'Mighty quare racket back dar in de woods! Ain't got time ter tarry!'

"Wid dat, Brer Fox lipt out, he did, en fa'rly split de win'. He ain't gone fur twel he meet Brer Wolf.

"'Hey, Brer Fox! Stop en res' you'se'f!'

"'Ain't got time ter tarry!'

"'Who bin want de doctor?'

"'No'ne, my Lord! Ain't got time ter tarry!'

"'Do pray, Brer Fox, good er bad, tell me de news.'

"'Mighty kuse fuss back dar in de woods! Ain't got time ter tarry!'

"Wid dat, Brer Wolf shuck hisse'f loose fum de face er de yeth, en he ain't git fur twel he meet Brer B'ar. Brer B'ar he ax, en Brer Wolf make ans'er, en bimeby Brer B'ar he fotch a snort en run'd off; en, bless gracious! 'twa'n't long 'fo' de las' one er de creeturs wuz a-skaddlin' thoo de

woods lak de Ole Boy was atter um — en all kaze Brer Rabbit year Mr.
Man cut tree down.

"Dey run'd en dey run'd," Uncle Remus went on, "twel dey come ter
Brer Tarrypin house, en dey sorter slack up kaze dey done mighty nigh
los' der win'. Brer Tarrypin, he up'n ax um whar'bouts dey gwine, en dey
'low dey wuz a monstus tarryfyin' racket back dar in de woods. Brer Tarrypin, he ax w'at she soun' lak. One say he dunno, n'er he say he dunno,
den dey all say dey dunno. Den Brer Tarrypin, he up'n ax who year dis
monstus racket. One say he dunno, n'er say he dunno, den dey all say
dey dunno. Dis make ole Brer Tarrypin laff 'way down in he insides, en
he up'n say, sezee:

"'You all kin run 'long ef you feel skittish,' sezee. 'Atter I cook my
brekkus en wash up de dishes, ef I gits win' er any 'spicious racket
maybe I mought take down my pairsol en foller long atter you,' sezee.

"W'en de creeturs come ter make inquirements 'mungs one er n'er
'bout who start de news, hit went right spang back ter Brer Rabbit, but,
lo en beholes! Brer Rabbit ain't dar, en it tu'n out dat Brer Coon is de man
w'at seed 'im las'. Den dey got ter layin' de blame un it on one er n'er, en
little mo' en dey'd er fit dar scan'lous, but ole Brer Tarrypin, he up'n 'low
dat ef dey want ter git de straight un it, dey better go see Brer Rabbit.

"All de creeturs wuz 'gree'ble, en dey put out ter Brer Rabbit house.
W'en dey git dar, Brer Rabbit wuz a-settin' crosslegged in de front po'ch
winkin' he eye at de sun. Brer B'ar, he speak up:

"'W'at make you fool me, Brer Rabbit?'

"'Fool who, Brer B'ar?'

"'Me, Brer Rabbit, dat's who.'

"'Dish yer de fus' time I seed you dis day, Brer B'ar, en you er mo'
dan welcome ter dat.'

"Dey all ax 'im en git de same ans'er, en den Brer Coon put in:

"'What make you fool me, Brer Rabbit?'

"'How I fool you, Brer Coon?'

"'You make lak dey wuz a big racket, Brer Rabbit.'

"'Dey sholy wuz a big racket, Brer Coon.'

"'W'at kinder racket, Brer Rabbit?'

"'*Ah-yi!* You oughter ax me dat fus', Brer Coon.'

"'I axes you now, Brer Rabbit.'

"'Mr. Man cut tree down, Brer Coon.'

"Co'se dis make Brer Coon feel lak a nat'al-born Slink, en 'twa'n't long 'fo' all de creeturs make der bow ter Brer Rabbit en mosey off home."

"Brother Rabbit had the best of it all along," said the little boy, after waiting to see whether there was a sequel to the story.

"Oh, he did dat a-way!" exclaimed Uncle Remus. "Brer Rabbit was a mighty man in dem days."

21
Why Brother Bear Has No Tail

"I 'CLAR' ter gracious, honey," Uncle Remus exclaimed one night, as the little boy ran in, "you sholy ain't chaw'd yo' vittles. Hit ain't bin no time, skacely, sence de supper-bell rung, en ef you go on dis a-way, you'll des nat'ally pe'sh yo'se'f out."

"Oh, I wasn't hungry," said the little boy. "I had something before supper, and I wasn't hungry anyway."

The old man looked keenly at the child, and presently he said:

"De ins en de outs er dat kinder talk all come ter de same p'int in my min'. You er bin a-cuttin' up at de table, en Mars John, he tuck'n sont you 'way fum dar, en w'iles he think you er off somers a-snifflm' en a-feelin' bad, yer you is a-high-primin' 'roun' des lak you done had mo' supper dan de King er Philanders."

Before the little boy could inquire about the King of Philanders he heard his father calling him. He started to go out, but Uncle Remus motioned him back.

"Des set right whar you is, honey — des set right still."

Then Uncle Remus went to the door and answered for the child; and a very queer answer it was — one that could be heard over half the plantation:

"Mars John, I wish you en Miss Sally be so good ez ter let dat chile 'lone. He down yer cryin' he eyes out, en he ain't bodderin' 'long er nobody in de roun' worl'."

Uncle Remus stood in the door a moment to see what the reply would be, but he heard none. Thereupon he continued, in the same loud tone:

"I ain't bin use ter no sich gwines on in ole Miss time, en I ain't gwine git use ter it now. Dat I ain't."

Presently 'Tildy, the house-girl, brought the little boy his supper, and the girl was no sooner out of hearing than the child swapped it with Uncle Remus for a roasted yam, and the enjoyment of both seemed to be complete.

"Uncle Remus," said the little boy, after a while, "you know I wasn't crying just now."

"Dat's so, honey," the old man replied, "but 'twouldn't er bin long 'fo' you would er bin, kaze Mars John bawl out lak a man w'at got a strop in he han', so w'at de diffunce?"

When they had finished eating. Uncle Remus busied himself in cutting and trimming some sole-leather for future use. His knife was so keen, and the leather fell away from it so smoothly and easily, that the little boy wanted to trim some himself. But to this Uncle Remus would not listen.

"'Tain't on'y chilluns w'at got de consate er doin' eve'ything dey see yuther folks do. Hit's grown folks w'at oughter know better," said the old man. "Dat's des de way Brer B'ar git his tail broke off smick smack smoove, en down ter dis day he de funnies'-lookin' creetur w'at wobble on top er dry groun'.'"

Instantly the little boy forgot all about Uncle Remus's sharp knife.

"Hit seem lak dat in dem days Brer Rabbit en Brer Tarrypin done gone in cahoots fer ter outdo de t'er creeturs. One time Brer Rabbit tuck'n made a call on Brer Tarrypin, but w'en he git ter Brer Tarrypin house, he year talk fum Miss Tarrypin dat her ole man done gone fer ter spen' de day wid Mr. Mud Turkle, w'ich dey wuz blood kin. Brer Rabbit he put out atter Brer Tarrypin, en w'en he got ter Mr. Mud Turkle house, dey all sot up, dey did, en tole tales, en den w'en twelf er'clock come dey had crawfish fer dinner, en dey 'joy deyse'f right erlong. Atter dinner dey went down ter Mr. Mud Turkle mill-pon', en w'en dey git dar Mr. Mud Turkle en Brer Tarrypin dey 'muse deyse'f, dey did, wid slidin' fum de top uv a big slantin' rock down inter de water.

"I 'speck you moughter seen rocks in de water 'fo' now, whar dey git green en slipp'y," said Uncle Remus.

The little boy had not only seen them, but had found them to be very dangerous to walk upon, and the old man continued:

"Well, den, dish yer rock wuz mighty slick en mighty slantin'. Mr. Mud Turkle, he'd crawl ter de top, en tu'n loose, en go a-sailin' down inter de water — *kersplash!* Ole Brer Tarrypin, he'd foller atter, en slide down inter de water — *kersplash!* Ole Brer Rabbit, he sot off, he did, en praise um up.

"W'iles dey wuz a-gwine on dis a-way, a-havin' der fun, en 'joyin' deyse'f, yer come ole Brer B'ar. He year um laughin' en holl'in', en he hail um.

"'Heyo, folks! W'at all dis? Ef my eye ain't 'ceive me, dish yer's Brer Rabbit, en Brer Tarrypin, en ole Unk' Tommy Mud Turkle,' sez Brer B'ar, sezee.

"'De same,' sez Brer Rabbit, sezee, 'en yer we is 'joyin' de day dat passes lak dey wa'n't no hard times.'

"'Well, well, well!' sez ole Brer B'ar, sezee, 'a-slippin' en a-slidin' en makin' free! En w'at de matter wid Brer Rabbit dat he ain't j'inin' in?' sezee.

"Ole Brer Rabbit he wink at Brer Tarrypin, en Brer Tarrypin he hunch Mr. Mud Turkle, en den Brer Rabbit he up'n 'low, he did:

"'My goodness, Brer B'ar! you can't 'speck a man fer ter slip en slide de whole blessid day, kin you? I done had my fun, en now I'm a settin' out yer lettin' my cloze dry. Hit's tu'n en tu'n about wid me en deze gents w'en dey's any fun gwine on,' sezee.

"'Maybe Brer B'ar might jine in wid us,' sez Brer Tarrypin, sezee.

"Brer Rabbit he des holler en laff.

"'Shoo!' sezee, 'Brer B'ar foot too big en he tail too long fer ter slide down dat rock,' sezee.

"Dis kinder put Brer B'ar on the mettle, en he up'n 'spon', he did:

"'Maybe dey is, en maybe dey ain't, yit I ain't afear'd ter try.'

"Wid dat de yuthers tuck'n made way fer 'im, en ole Brer B'ar he git up on de rock, he did, en squot down on he hunkers, en quile he tail und' 'im, en start down. Fus' he go sorter slow, en he grin lak he feel good; den he go sorter peart, en he grin lak he feel bad; den he go mo' pearter, en he grin lak he skeer'd; den he strack de slick part, en, gentermens! he swaller de grin en fetch a howl dat moughter bin yeard a mile, en he hit de water lak a chimbley a-fallin'.

"You kin gimme denial," Uncle Remus continued after a little pause, "but des ez sho ez you er settin' dar, w'en Brer B'ar slick'd up en flew down dat rock, he break off he tail right smick smack smoove, en mo'n dat, w'en he make his disappear'nce up de big road, Brer Rabbit holler out:

"'Brer B'ar! — O Brer B'ar! I year tell dat flaxseed poultices is mighty good fer so' places!'"

"Yit Brer B'ar ain't lookin' back."

22
How Brother Rabbit Frightened His Neighbors

WHEN UNCLE REMUS was in a good humor he turned the most trifling incidents into excuses for amusing the little boy with his stories. One night while he was hunting for a piece of candle on the shelf that took the place of a mantel over the fireplace, he knocked down a tin plate. It fell upon the hearth with a tremendous clatter.

"Dar now!" exclaimed Uncle Remus. "Hit's a blessin' dat dat ar platter is got mo' backbone dan de common run er crockery, kaze 'twould er bin bust all ter flinderations long time ago. Dat ar platter is got dents on it w'at Miss Sally put dar w'en she 'uz a little bit er gal. Yet dar 'tis, en right dis minnit hit'll hol' mo' vittles dan w'at I got ter put up in it.

"I lay," the old man continued, leaning his head against the chimney and gazing at the little boy reflectively — "I lay ef de creeturs had a bin yer w'iles all dat clatterment gwine on dey'd a lef' widout tellin' anybody good-bye. All ceppin' Brer Rabbit. Bless yo' soul, he'd er stayed fer ter see de fun, des lak he did dat t'er time w'en he skeer um all so. I speck I done tole you 'bout dat."

"When he got the honey on him and rolled in the leaves?"

Uncle Remus thought a moment.

"Ef I make no mistakes in my 'membunce, dat wuz de time w'en he call hisse'f de Wull-er-de-Wust."

The little boy corroborated Uncle Remus's memory.

"Well, den, dish yer wuz n'er time, en he lak ter skeer um plum out'n de settlement. En it all come 'bout kaze dey wanter play smarty."

"Who wanted to play smarty, Uncle Remus?" asked the child.

"Oh, des dem t'er creeturs. Dey wuz allers a-layin' traps fer Brer Rabbit en gittin' kotch in um deyse'f, en dey wuz allers a-pursooin' atter 'im day in en day out. I ain't 'nyin' but w'at some er Brer Rabbit pranks wuz mighty ha'sh, but w'y'n't dey let 'im 'lone deyse'f?"

Naturally, the little boy was not prepared to meet these arguments, even had their gravity been less impressive, so he said nothing.

"In dem days," Uncle Remus went on, "de creeturs wuz same lak folks. Dey had der ups en dey had der downs; dey had der hard times, and dey had der saf' times. Some seasons der craps 'ud be good, en some seasons dey'd be bad. Brer Rabbit, he fa'r'd lak de res' un um. W'at he'd make, dat he'd spen'. One season he tuck'n made a fine chance er goobers, en he 'low, he did, dat ef dey fetch 'im anywhars nigh de money w'at he speck dey would, he go ter town en buy de truck w'at needcessity call fer.

"He ain't no sooner say dat dan ole Miss Rabbit, she vow, she did, dat it be a scannul en a shame ef he don't whirl in en git sev'm tin cups fer de chilluns fer ter drink out'n, en sev'm tin plates fer'm ter sop out'n, en a coffee-pot fer de fambly. Brer Rabbit say dat des zackly w'at he gwine do, en he 'low, he did, dat he gwine ter town de comin' We'n'sday."

Uncle Remus paused, and indulged in a hearty laugh before he resumed:

"Brer Rabbit wa'n't mo'n out'n de gate 'fo' Miss Rabbit, she slap on 'er bonnet, she did, en rush 'cross ter Miss Mink house, en she ain't bin dar a minnit 'fo' she up'n tell Miss Mink dat Brer Rabbit done promise ter go ter town We'n'sday comin' en git de chilluns sump'n'. Co'se, w'en Mr. Mink come home, Miss Mink she up'n 'low she want ter know w'at de reason he can't buy sump'n' fer his chilluns same ez Brer Rabbit do fer his'n, en dey quoll en quoll des lak folks. Atter dat Miss Mink she kyar' de news ter Miss Fox, en den Brer Fox he tuck'n got a rakin' over de coals. Miss Fox she tell Miss Wolf, en Miss Wolf she tell Miss B'ar, en 'twa'n't long 'fo' eve'ybody in dem diggin's know dat Brer Rabbit gwine ter town de comin' We'n'sday fer ter git his chilluns sump'n'; en all de yuther creeturs' chilluns ax der ma w'at de reason der pa can't git *dem* sump'n'. So dar it went.

"Brer Fox, en Brer Wolf, en Brer B'ar, dey make up der min's, dey did, dat ef dey gwine ter ketch up wid Brer Rabbit, dat wuz de time, en dey fix up a plan dat dey'd lay fer Brer Rabbit en nab 'im w'en he come back fum town. Dey tuck'n make all der 'rangements, en wait fer de day.

"Sho nuff, w'en We'n'sday come, Brer Rabbit e't he brekkus 'fo' sunup, en put out fer town. He tuck'n got hisse'f a dram, en a plug er terbacker, en a pocket-hankcher, en he got de ole 'oman a coffee-pot, en he got de chillun sev'm tin cups en sev'm tin plates, en den todes sundown he start back home. He walk 'long, he did, feelin' mighty biggity, but bimeby w'en he git sorter tired, he sot down und' a blackjack tree, en 'gun to fan hisse'f wid one er der platters.

"W'iles he doin' dis a little bit er teenchy sap-sucker run up'n down de tree en keep on makin' mighty quare fuss. Atter w'ile Brer Rabbit tuck'n shoo at 'im wid de platter. Seem lak dis make de teenchy little sap-sucker mighty mad, en he rush out on a lim' right over Brer Rabbit, en he sing out:

> "'Pilly-pee, pilly-wee!
> I see w'at he no see!
> I see, pilly-pee,
> I see, w'at he no see!'

"He keep on singin' dis, he did, twel Brer Rabbit 'gun ter look 'roun', en he ain't no sooner do dis dan he see marks in de san' whar sum un done bin dar 'fo' 'im, en he look little closer en den he see w'at de sap-sucker drivin' at. He scratch his head, Brer Rabbit did, en he 'low ter hisse'f:

"'Ah-yi! Yer whar Brer Fox bin settin', en dar de print er he nice bushy tail. Yer whar Brer Wolf bin settin', en dar de print er he fine long tail. Yer whar Brer B'ar bin squattin' on he hunkers, en dar de print w'ich he ain't got no tail. Dey er all bin yer, en I lay dey er hidin' out in de big gully down dar in de holler.'

"Wid dat, ole man Rab tuck'n put he truck in de bushes, en den he run 'way 'roun' fer ter see w'at he kin see. Sho nuff," continued Uncle Remus, with a curious air of elation — "sho nuff, w'en Brer Rabbit git over ag'in' de big gully down in de holler, dar dey wuz. Brer Fox, he 'uz on one side er de road, en Brer Wolf 'uz on de t'er side; en ole Brer B'ar he 'uz quiled up in de gully takin' a nap.

"Brer Rabbit, he tuck'n peep at um, he did, en he lick he foot en roach back he ha'r, en den hol' his han's cross he mouf en laff lak some chilluns does w'en dey t'ink dey er foolin' der ma."

"Not me, Uncle Remus — not me!" exclaimed the little boy promptly.

"Heyo dar! don't kick 'fo' you er spurred, honey! Brer Rabbit, he seed um all dar, en he tuck'n grin, he did, en den he lit out ter whar he done lef' he truck, en w'en he git dar he dance 'roun' en slap hisse'f on de leg, en make all sorts er kuse motions. Den he go ter wuk en tu'n de coffee-pot upside down en stick it on he head; den he run he gallus thoo de han'les er de cups, en sling um crosst he shoulder; den he 'vide de platters, some in one han' en some in de yuther. Atter he git good en ready, he crope ter de top er de hill, he did, en tuck a runnin' start, en flew down like a harrycane — *rickety, rackety, slambang!*"

The little boy clapped his hands enthusiastically.

"Bless yo' soul, dem creeturs ain't year no fuss lak dat, en dey ain't seed no man w'at look lak Brer Rabbit do, wid de coffee-pot on he head, en de cups a-rattlin' on he gallus, en de platters a-wavin' en a-shinin' in de a'r.

"Now, min' you, ole Brer B'ar wuz layin' off up de gully takin' a nap, en de fuss skeer 'im so bad dat he make a break en run over Brer Fox. He rush out in de road, he did, en w'en he see de sight, he whirl 'roun' en run over Brer Wolf. Wid der scramblin' en der scufflin', Brer Rabbit got right on um 'fo' dey kin git away. He holler out, he did:

"'Gimme room! Tu'n me loose! I'm ole man Spewter-Splutter wid long claws, en scales on my back! I'm snaggle-toofed en double-j'inted! Gimme room!'

"Eve'y time he'd fetch a whoop, he'd rattle de cups en slap de platters tergedder — *rickety, rackety, slambang!* En I let you know w'en dem creeturs got dey lim's tergedder dey split de win', dey did dat. Ole Brer B'ar, he struck a stump w'at stan' in de way, en I ain't gwine tell you how he to' it up kaze you won't b'lieve me, but de nex' mawnin' Brer Rabbit en his chilluns went back dar, dey did, en dey got nuff splinters fer ter make um kin'lin' wood all de winter. Yasser! Des ez sho ez I'm a-settin' by dish yer h'a'th."

23
Mr. Man Has Some Meat

THE LITTLE BOY sat watching Uncle Remus sharpen his shoe-knife. The old man's head moved in sympathy with his hands, and he mumbled fragments of a song. Occasionally he would feel of the edge of the blade with his thumb, and then begin to sharpen it again. The comical appearance of the venerable darkey finally had its effect upon the child, for suddenly he broke into a hearty peal of laughter; whereupon Uncle Remus stopped shaking his head and singing his mumbly-song, and assumed a very dignified attitude. Then he drew a long, deep breath, and said:

"When folks git ole en strucken wid de palsy, dey mus' 'speck ter be laff'd at. Goodness knows, I bin useter dat sence de day my whiskers 'gun to bleach."

"Why, I wasn't laughing at you, Uncle Remus; I declare I wasn't," cried the little boy. "I thought maybe you might be doing your head like Brother Rabbit did when he was fixing to cut his meat."

Uncle Remus's seriousness was immediately driven away by a broad and appreciative grin.

"Now, dat de way ter talk, honey, en I boun' you wa'n't fur wrong, n'er, kaze fer all dey'll tell you dat Brer Rabbit make he livin' er nibblin' at grass en greens, hit wa'n't dat a-way in dem days, kaze I got in my 'membunce right now de 'casion whar Brer Rabbit is tuck'n e't meat."

The little boy had learned that it was not best to make any display of impatience, and so he waited quietly while Uncle Remus busied himself with arranging the tools on his shoe-bench. Presently the old man began:

"Hit so happen dat one day Brer Rabbit meet up wid Brer Fox, en w'en dey 'quire atter der corporosity, dey fin' out dat bofe un um mighty po'ly. Brer Fox, he 'low, he do, dat he monstus hongry, en Brer Rabbit he 'spon' dat he got a mighty hankerin' atter vittles hisse'f. Bimeby dey look up de big road, en dey see Mr. Man comin' 'long wid a great big hunk er beef und' he arm. Brer Fox he up'n 'low, he did, dat he lak mighty well fer ter git a tas'e er dat, en Brer Rabbit he 'low dat de sight er dat nice meat all lineded wid taller is nuff fer ter run a body 'stracted.

"Mr. Man he come en he come 'long. Brer Rabbit en Brer Fox dey look en dey look at 'im. Dey wink der eye en der mouf water. Brer Rabbit he 'low he bleedzd ter git some er dat meat. Brer Fox he 'spon', he did, dat it look mighty fur off ter him. Den Brer Rabbit tell Brer Fox fer ter foller atter 'im in hailin' distuns, en wid dat he put out, he did, en 'twa'n't long 'fo' he kotch up wid Mr. Man.

"Dey pass de time er day, en den dey went joggin' 'long de road same lak dey 'uz gwine 'pun a journey. Brer Rabbit he keep on snuffin' de a'r. Mr. Man up'n ax 'im is he got a bad col', en Brer Rabbit 'spon' dat he smell sump'n' w'ich it don't smell like ripe peaches. Bimeby, Brer Rabbit 'gun to hol' he nose, he did, en atter w'ile he sing out:

"'Gracious en de goodness, Mr. Man! hit's dat meat er yone. *Phew!* Whar'bouts is you pick up dat meat at?'

"Dis make Mr. Man feel sorter 'shame' hisse'f, en ter make marters wuss, yer come a great big green fly a-zoonin' 'roun'. Brer Rabbit he git way off on t'er side er de road, en he keep on hol'in' he nose. Mr. Man, he look sorter sheepish, he did, en dey ain't gone fur 'fo' he put de meat down on de side er de road, en he tuck'n ax Brer Rabbit w'at dey gwine do 'bout it. Brer Rabbit he 'low, he did:

"'I year tell in my time dat ef you tak'n drag a piece er meat thoo' de dus' hit'll fetch back hits freshness. I ain't no superspicious man myse'f,' sezee, 'en I ain't got no 'speunce wid no sech doin's, but dem w'at tell me say dey done try it. Yit I knows dis,' says Brer Rabbit, sezee — 'I knows dat 'tain't gwine do no harm, kaze de grit w'at gits on de meat kin be wash off,' sez Brer Rabbit, sezee.

"'I ain't got no string,' sez Mr. Man, sezee.

"Brer Rabbit laugh hearty, but still he hol' he nose.

"'Time you bin in de bushes long ez I is, you won't miss strings,' sez Brer Rabbit, sezee.

"Wid dat Brer Rabbit lipt out, en he ain't gone long 'fo' he come hoppin' back wid a whole passel er bamboo vines all tied tergedder. Mr. Man, he 'low:

"'Dat line mighty long.'

"Brer Rabbit he 'low:

"'Tooby sho, you want de win' fer ter git 'twix' you en dat meat.'

"Den Mr. Man tuck'n tied de bamboo line ter de meat. Brer Rabbit he broke off a 'simmon bush, he did, en 'low dat he'd stay behime en keep de flies off. Mr. Man he go on befo' en drag de meat, en Brer Rabbit he stay behime, he did, en take keer un it."

Here Uncle Remus was compelled to pause and laugh before he could proceed with the story.

"En he is take keer un it, mon — dat he is. He tuck'n git 'im a rock, en whiles Mr. Man gwine 'long widout lookin' back he ondo de meat en tie de rock ter de bamboo line, en w'en Brer Fox foller on, sho nuff, dar lay de meat. Mr. Man, he drug de rock, he did, en Brer Rabbit he keep de flies off, twel atter dey gone on right smart piece, en den w'en Mr. Man look 'roun', whar wuz ole man Rabbit?

"Bless yo' soul, Brer Rabbit done gone back en jine Brer Fox, en he wuz des in time, at dat, kaze little mo' en Brer Fox would a done bin outer sight en yearin'. En so dat de way Brer Rabbit git Mr. Man meat."

The little boy reflected a little, and then said:

"Uncle Remus, wasn't that stealing?"

"Well, I tell you 'bout dat, honey," responded the old man, with the air of one who is willing to compromise. "In dem days de creeturs bleedzd ter look out fer deyse'f, mo' speshually dem w'at ain't got hawn en huff. Brer Rabbit ain't got no hawn en huff, en he bleedzd ter be he own lawyer."

Just then the little boy heard his father's buggy rattling down the avenue, and he ran out into the darkness to meet it. After he was gone, Uncle Remus sat a long time rubbing his hands and looking serious. Finally he leaned back in his chair, and exclaimed:

"Dat little chap gittin' too much fer ole Remus — dat he is!"

24
How Brother Rabbit Got the Meat

WHEN THE LITTLE BOY next visited Uncle Remus the cabin was dark and empty and the door shut. The old man was gone. He was absent for several nights, but at last one night the little boy saw a welcome light in the cabin, and he made haste to pay Uncle Remus a visit. He was full of questions:

"Goodness, Uncle Remus! Where in the world have you been? I thought you were gone for good. Mamma said she reckoned the treatment here didn't suit you, and you had gone off to get some of your town friends to hire you."

"Is Miss Sally tell you dat, honey? Well, ef she ain't de beatenes' white 'oman dis side er kingdom come, you kin des shoot me. Miss Sally tuck'n writ me a pass wid her own han's fer ter go see some er my kin down dar in de Ashbank settlement. Yo' mammy quare 'oman, honey, sho!

"En yit, w'at de good er my stayin' yer? T'er night, I ain't mo'n git good en started 'fo' you er up en gone, en I ain't seed ha'r ner hide un you sence. W'en I see you do dat, I 'low ter myse'f dat hit's des 'bout time fer ole man Remus fer ter pack up he duds en go hunt comp'ny somers else."

"Well, Uncle Remus," exclaimed the little boy, in a tone of expostulation, "didn't Brother Fox get the meat, and wasn't that the end of the story?"

Uncle Remus started to laugh, but he changed his mind so suddenly that the little boy was convulsed. The old man groaned and looked at the rafters with a curious air of disinterestedness. After a while he went on with great seriousness:

"I dunner w'at kinder idee folks got 'bout Brer Rabbit no-how, dat I don't. S'pozen you lays de plans so some yuther chap kin git a big hunk er goody, is you gwine ter set off somers en see 'im make way wid it?"

"What kind of goody, Uncle Remus?"

"Dish yer kinder goody w'at town folks keeps. Mint draps and reezins, en sweet doin's lak Miss Sally keep und' lock en key. Well, den, if you gits some er dat, er may be some yuther kinder goody, w'ich I wish 'twuz yer right dis blessid minnit, is you gwine ter set quile up in dat cheer en let n'er chap run off wid it? Dat you ain't — dat you ain't!"

"Oh, I know!" exclaimed the little boy. "Brother Rabbit went back and made Brother Fox give him his part of the meat."

"Des lak I tell you, honey; dey wa'n't no man 'mungs de creeturs w'at kin stan' right flat-footed en wuk he min' quick lak Brer Rabbit. He tuck'n tie de rock on de string, stidder de meat, en he pursue long after it, he did, twel Mr. Man tu'n a ben' in de road, en den Brer Rabbit, he des lit out fum dar — *terbuckity-buckity, buck-buck-buckity!* en 'twa'n't long 'fo' he tuck'n kotch up wid Brer Fox. Dey tuck de meat, dey did, en kyar'd it way off in de woods, en laid it down on a clean place on de groun'.

"Dey laid it down, dey did," continued Uncle Remus, drawing his chair up closer to the little boy, "en den Brer Fox 'low dey better sample it, en Brer Rabbit he 'gree. Wid dat, Brer Fox he tuck'n gnyaw off a hunk, en he shut bofe eyes, he did, en he chaw en chaw, en tas'e en tas'e, en chaw en tas'e. Brer Rabbit, he watch 'im, but Brer Fox, he keep bofe eyes shot, en he chaw en tas'e, en tas'e en chaw."

Uncle Remus not only furnished a pantomime accompaniment to this recital by shutting his eyes and pretending to taste, but he lowered his voice to a pitch of tragical significance in reporting the dialogue that ensued:

"Den Brer Fox smack he mouf en look at de meat mo' closeter, en up'n 'low:

"'Brer Rabbit, *hit's lam'!*'

"'*No*, Brer Fox! *sholy not!*'

"'Brer Rabbit, *hit's lam'!*'

"'Brer Fox, *tooby sholy not!*'

"Den Brer Rabbit, he tuck'n gnyaw off a hunk, en he shot bofe eyes, en chaw en tas'e, en tas'e en chaw. Den he smack he mouf, en up'n 'low:

"'Brer Fox, *hit's shote!*'

"'Brer Rabbit, you foolin' me!'

"'Brer Fox, *I vow hit's shote!*'

"'Brer Rabbit, hit des *can't be!*'

"'Brer Fox, *hit sholy is!*'

"Dey tas'e en dey 'spute, en dey 'spute en dey tas'e. Atter w'ile, Brer Rabbit make lak he want some water, en he rush off in de bushes, en d'reckly yer he come back wipin' he mouf en cle'rin' up he th'oat. Den Brer Fox he want some water sho nuff:

"'Brer Rabbit, whar you fin' de spring?'

"''Cross de road, en down de hill en up de big gully.'

"Brer Fox, he lope off, he did, en atter he gone Brer Rabbit totch he year wid he behime foot lak he flippin' 'im good-bye. Brer Fox, he cross de road en rush down de hill, he did, yit he ain't fin' no big gully. He keep on gwine twel he fin' de big gully, yit he ain't fin' no spring.

"W'iles all dish yer gwine on, Brer Rabbit he tuck'n grabble a hole in de groun', he did, en in dat hole he hid de meat. Atter he git it good en hid, he tuck'n cut 'im a long keen hick'ry, en atter so long a time, w'en he year Brer Fox comin' back, he got in a clump er bushes, en tuck dat hick'ry en let in on a saplin', en eve'y time he hit de saplin', he 'ud squall out, Brer Rabbit would, des lak de patter-rollers had 'im:

"*Pow, pow!* 'Oh, pray, Mr. Man!' — *Pow, pow!* 'Oh, pray. Mr. Man!' — *Chippy-row-pow!* 'Oh, Lordy, Mr. Man! Brer Fox tuck yo' meat!' — *Pow!* 'Oh, pray, Mr. Man! Brer Fox tuck yo' meat!'"

Every time Uncle Remus said *"Pow!"* he struck himself in the palm of his hand with a shoe-sole by way of illustration.

"Co'se," he went on, "w'en Brer Fox year dis kinder doin's, he fotch

up, he did, en lissen, en eve'y time he year de hick'ry come down *pow!*
he tuck'n grin en 'low ter hisse'f, 'Ah-yi! you fool me 'bout de water!'

"Atter so long a time, de racket sorter die out, en seem lak Mr. Man
wuz draggin' Brer Rabbit off. Dis make Brer Fox feel mighty skittish.
Bimeby Brer Rabbit come a-cally-hootin' back des a-hollerin':

"'Run, Brer Fox, run! Mr. Man say he gwine to kyar' dat meat up de
road ter whar he son is, en den he's a-comin' back atter you. Run, Brer
Fox, run!'

"En I let you know," said Uncle Remus, leaning back and laughing
to see the little boy laugh, "I let you know Brer Fox got mighty skace in
dat neighborhood!"

Introduction to the Tales of Daddy Jack

THE DISCRIMINATING READER does not need to be told that it would be impossible to separate these stories from the idiom in which they have been
recited for generations. The dialect is a part of the legends themselves,
and to present them in any other way would be to rob them of everything
that gives them vitality. The dialect of Daddy Jack, which is that of the
Negroes on the Sea Islands and the rice plantations, though it may seem
at first glance to be more difficult than that of Uncle Remus, is, in reality, simpler and more direct. It is the Negro dialect in its most primitive
state — the "Gullah" talk of some of the Negroes on the Sea Islands, being merely a confused and untranslatable mixture of English and African
words. A key to the dialect may be given very briefly. The vocabulary is
not an extensive one — more depending upon the manner, the form of
expression, and the inflection, than upon the words employed. It is thus
an admirable vehicle for story-telling. It recognizes no gender, and scorns
the use of the plural number except accidentally. "'E" stands for "he"
"she" or "it," and "dem" may allude to one thing, or may include a thousand. The dialect is laconic and yet rambling, full of repetitions, and
abounding in curious elisions, that give an unexpected quaintness to the
simplest statements. A glance at the following vocabulary will enable the
reader to understand Daddy Jack's dialect perfectly, though allowance
must be made for inversions and elisions.

B'er, brother

Beer, bear

Bittle, victuals

Bre't', breath

Buckra, white man, overseer, boss

Churrah, churray, spill, splash

Da, the, that

Dey, there

Dey-dey, here, down there, right here

Enty, ain't he? an exclamation of astonishment or assent

Gwan, going

Leaf, leave

Lif, live

Lil, lil-a, or *lilly*, little

Lun, learn

Mek, make

Neat' or *nead*, underneath, beneath

Oona, you, all of you

Sem, same

Shum, see them, saw them

Tam, time

'Tan', stand

Tankee, thanks, thank you

Tark, or *tahlk*, talk

Teer, tear

Tek, take

Tink, or *t'ought*, think, thought

Trow, throw

Titty, or *titter*, sissy, sister

Trute, truth

Turrer, or *tarrah*, the other

Tusty, thirsty

Urrer, other

Wey, where

Wun, when

Wut, what

Y'et, or *ut*, earth

Yeddy, or *yerry*, heard, hear

Yent, ain't, isn't

The trick of adding a vowel to sound words is not unpleasing to the ear. Thus: "I bin-a wait fer you; come-a ring-a dem bell. Wut mek-a (or mekky) you stay so?" "Yeddy," "yerry," and probably "churry" are the result of this — heard-a, yeard-a, yeddy; hear-a, year-a, yerry; chur-a; churray. When "eye" is written "y-eye," it is to be pronounced "yi." In such words as "back," "ax," a has the sound of ah. They are written "bahk," "ahx." J. C. H.

25

African Jack

USUALLY, THE LITTLE BOY, who regarded himself as Uncle Remus's partner, was not at all pleased when he found the old man entertaining, in his

simple way, any of his colored friends; but he was secretly delighted
when he called one night and found Daddy Jack sitting by Uncle Remus's hearth. Daddy Jack was an object of curiosity to older people than
the little boy. He was a genuine African, and for that reason he was
known as African Jack, though the child had been taught to call him
Daddy Jack. He was brought to Georgia in a slave-ship when he was
about twenty years old, and remained upon one of the sea-islands for
several years. Finally, he fell into the hands of the family of which Uncle
Remus's little partner was the youngest representative, and became the
trusted foreman of a plantation, in the southern part of Georgia, known
as the Walthall Place. Once every year he was in the habit of visiting the
Home Place in Middle Georgia, and it was during one of these annual
visits that the little boy found him in Uncle Remus's cabin.

Daddy Jack appeared to be quite a hundred years old, but he was
probably not more than eighty. He was a little, dried-up old man, whose
weazened, dwarfish appearance, while it was calculated to inspire awe in
the minds of the superstitious, was not without its pathetic suggestions. The
child had been told that the old African was a wizard, a conjurer, and a
snake-charmer; but he was not afraid, for, in any event, — conjuration,
witchcraft, or what not — he was assured of the protection of Uncle Remus.

As the little boy entered the cabin Uncle Remus smiled and nodded
pleasantly, and made a place for him on a little stool upon which had
been piled the odds and ends of work. Daddy Jack paid no attention to
the child; his thoughts seemed to be elsewhere.

"Go en shake han's, honey, en tell Daddy Jack howdy. He laks good
chilluns." Then to Daddy Jack: "Brer Jack, dish yer de chap w'at I bin
tellin' you 'bout."

The little boy did as he was bid, but Daddy Jack grunted ungra-
ciously and made no response to the salutation. He was evidently not
fond of children. Uncle Remus glanced curiously at the dwarfed and
withered figure, and spoke a little more emphatically:

"Brer Jack, ef you take good look at dis chap, I lay yo'll see mo'n you
speck ter see. You'll see sump'n' dat'll make you grunt wusser dan you
grunted deze many long year. Go up dar, honey, whar Daddy Jack kin see
you."

The child went shyly up to the old African and stood at his knee. The sorrows and perplexities of nearly a hundred years lay between them; and now, as always, the baffled eyes of age gazed into the Sphinx-like face of youth, as if by this means to unravel the mysteries of the past and solve the problems of the future.

Daddy Jack took the plump, rosy hands of the little boy in his black, withered ones, and gazed into his face so long and steadily, and with such curious earnestness, that the child didn't know whether to laugh or

cry. Presently the old African flung his hands to his head, and rocked his body from side to side, moaning and mumbling, and talking to himself, while the tears ran down his face like rain.

'Ole Missy! Ole Missy! 'E come back! I bin shum dey-dey, I bin shum de night! I bin yeddy 'e v'ice, I bin yeddy de sign!"

"Ah-yi!" exclaimed Uncle Remus, into whose arms the little boy had fled; "I des know'd dat 'ud fetch 'im. Hit's bin many's de long days since Brer Jack seed ole Miss, yit ef he ain't seed 'er dat whack, den I ain't set-tin' yer."

After a while Daddy Jack ceased his rocking, and his moaning, and his crying, and sat gazing wistfully into the fireplace. Whatever he saw there fixed his attention, for Uncle Remus spoke to him several times without receiving a response. Presently, however, Daddy Jack exclaimed with characteristic but laughable irrelevance:

"I no lakky dem gal wut is bin-a-stan' pidjin-toe. Wun 'e fetch pail er water on 'e head, water churray, churray. I no lakky dem gal wut tie 'e wool up wit' string; mekky him stan' ugly fer true. I bin ahx da' 'Tildy gal fer marry me, un 'e no crack 'im bre't' fer mek answer 'cep' 'e bre'k out un lahff by me werry face. Da' gal do holler un lahff un stomp 'e fut dey-dey, un dun I shum done gone pidjin-toe. Oona bin know da' 'Tildy gal?"

"I bin a-knowin' dat gal," said Uncle Remus, grimly regarding the old African; "I bin a-knowin' dat gal now gwine on sence she 'uz knee-high ter one er deze yer puddle-ducks; en I bin noticin' lately dat she mighty likely nigger."

"Enty!" exclaimed Daddy Jack, enthusiastically, "I did bin mek up ter da' lilly gal troo t'ick un t'in. I bin fetch 'im one fine 'possum, un mo' ez one, two, t'ree pecka taty, un bumbye I bin fetch 'im one bag pop-co'n. Wun I bin do dat, I is fley 'roun' da' lilly gal so long tam, un I yeddy 'im talk wit' turrer gal. 'E do say: 'Daddy Jack fine ole man fer true.' Dun I is bin talk: 'Oona no call-a me Daddy Jack wun dem preacher man come fer marry we.' Dun da' lilly gal t'row 'e head back; 'e squeal lak filly in canebrake."

The little boy understood this rapidly spoken lingo perfectly well, but he would have laughed anyhow, for there was more than a suggestion of the comic in the shrewd seriousness that seemed to focus itself in Daddy Jack's pinched and wrinkled face.

"She tuck de truck w'at you tuck'n fotch 'er," said Uncle Remus, with the air of one carefully and deliberately laying the basis of a judicial opinion, "en den w'en you sail in en talk bizness, den she up en gun you de flat un 'er foot en de back un 'er han', en den, atter dat, she tuck'n laff en make spote un you."

"Enty!" assented Daddy Jack, admiringly.

"Well, den, Brer Jack, you er mighty ole, en yit hit seem lak you er mighty young; kaze a man w'at ain't got no mo' speunce wid wimmen folks dan w'at you is nee'nter creep 'roun' yer callin' deyse'f ole. Dem kinder folks ain't ole nuff, let 'lone bein' too ole. W'en de gal tuck'n laff, Brer Jack, w'at 'uz yo' nex' move?" demanded Uncle Remus, looking down upon the shrivelled old man with an air of superiority.

Daddy Jack shut his shrewd little eyes tightly and held them so, as if by that means to recall all the details of the flirtation. Then he said:

"Da' lilly gal is bin tek dem t'ing. 'E is bin say 'T'anky, t'anky' Him eaty da' 'possum, him eaty da' pop-co'n, him roas'n da' taty. 'E do say, 'T'anky, t'anky!' Wun I talk marry, 'e is bin ris 'e v'ice un squeal lak lilly pig stuck in 'e t'roat. 'E do holler: 'Hi, Daddy Jack! wut is noung gal gwan do wit' so ole man lak dis?' Un I is bin say: 'Wut noung gal do wit' ole Chris'mus 'cep' 'e do joy 'ese'f?' Un da' lil gal 'e do lahff un flut 'ese'f way fum dey-dey."

"I know'd a nigger one time," said Uncle Remus, after pondering a moment, "w'at tuck a notion dat he want a bait er 'simmons, en de mo' w'at de notion tuck 'im de mo' w'at he want um, en bimeby, hit look lak he des nat'ally erbleedzd ter have um. He want de 'simmons, en dar dey is in de tree. He mouf water, en dar hang de 'simmons. Now, den, w'at do dat nigger do? W'en you en me en dish yer chile yer wants 'simmons, we goes out en shakes de tree, en ef dey er good en ripe, down dey comes, en ef dey er good en green, dar dey stays. But dish yer yuther nigger, he too smart fer dat. He des tuck'n tuck he stan' und' de tree, en he open he mouf, he did, en wait fer de 'simmons fer ter drap in dar. Dey ain't none drap in yit," continued Uncle Remus, gently knocking the cold ashes out of his pipe; "en w'at's mo', dey ain't none gwine ter drap in dar. Dat des zackly de way wid Brer Jack yer, 'bout marryin'; he stan' dar, he do, en he hol' bofe han's wide open he 'speck de gal gwine ter drap right spang in um. Man want gal, he des got ter grab 'er — dat's w'at. Dey may squall en dey may flutter, but flutter'n' en squallin' ain't done no damage yit ez I knows un, en 'tain't gwine ter. Young chaps kin make great 'miration 'bout gals, but w'en dey gits ole ez I is, dey ull know dat folks is folks, en w'en it come ter bein' folks, de wimmen ain't gut none de 'vantage er de men. Now dat's des de plain up en down tale I'm a-tellin' un you."

This deliverance from so respectable an authority seemed to please Daddy Jack immensely. He rubbed his withered hands together, smacked his lips and chuckled. After a few restless movements he got up and went shuffling to the door, his quick, short steps causing Uncle Remus to remark:

"De gal w'at git ole Brer Jack 'ull git a nat'al pacer, sho. He move mo' one-sideder dan ole Zip Coon, w'ich he rack up de branch all night long wid he nose p'int lak he gwine 'cross."

While the little boy was endeavoring to get Uncle Remus to explain the nature of Daddy Jack's grievances, muffled laughter was heard outside, and almost immediately 'Tildy rushed in the door. 'Tildy flung herself upon the floor and rolled and laughed until, apparently, she could laugh no more. Then she seemed to grow severely angry. She arose from the floor and flopped herself down in a chair, and glared at Uncle Remus with indignation in her eyes. As soon as she could control her inflamed feelings, she cried:

"W'at is I done ter you, Unk' Remus? 'Fo' de Lord, ef anybody wuz ter come en tole me dat you gwine ter put de Ole Boy in dat ole Affikin nigger head, I wouldn't er b'lieved um — dat I wouldn't. Unk' Remus, w'at is I done ter you?"

Uncle Remus made no direct response; but he leaned over, reached out his hand, and picked up an unfinished axe-helve that stood in the corner. Then he took the little boy by the arm, and pushed him out of the way, saying in his gentlest and most persuasive tone:

"Stan' sorter 'roun' dar, honey, kaze w'en de splinters 'gin ter fly, I want you ter be out'n de way. Miss Sally never gimme 'er fergivance in de roun' worl' ef you 'uz ter git hurted on account er de frazzlin' er dish yer piece er timber."

Uncle Remus's movements and remarks had a wonderful effect on 'Tildy. Her anger disappeared, her eyes lost their malignant expression, and her voice fell to a conversational tone.

"Now, Unk' Remus, you oughtn't ter do me dat a-way, kaze I ain't done nothin' ter you. I 'uz settin' up yon' in Aunt Tempy house, des now, runn'n on wid Riah, en yer come dat ole Affikin Jack en say you say he kin marry me ef he ketch me, en he try ter put he arm 'roun' me en kiss me."

'Tildy tossed her head and puckered her mouth at the bare remembrance of it.

"W'at wud did you gin Brer Jack?" inquired Uncle Remus, not without asperity.

"W'at I gwine tell him?" exclaimed 'Tildy disdainfully. "I des tuck'n up en tole 'im he foolin' wid de wrong nigger."

'Tildy would have continued her narration, but just at that moment the shuffling of feet was heard outside, and Daddy Jack came in, puffing and blowing and smiling. Evidently he had been hunting for 'Tildy in every house in the Negro quarter.

"Hi!" he exclaimed, "lil gal, 'e bin skeet sem lak ma'sh hen. 'E no run no mo'."

"Pick 'er up, Brer Jack," exclaimed Uncle Remus; "she's yone."

'Tildy was angry as well as frightened. She would have fled, but Daddy Jack stood near the door.

"Look yer, nigger man!" she exclaimed, "ef you come slobbun 'roun' me, I'll take one er deze yer dog-iüns en brain you wid it. I ain't gwine ter have no web-foot nigger follerin' atter me. Now you des come! — I ain't feard er yo' cunjun. Unk' Remus, ef you got any intruss in dat ole Affikin ape, you better make 'im lemme 'lone. G'way fum yer now!"

All this time Daddy Jack was slowly approaching 'Tildy, bowing and smiling, and looking quite dandified, as Uncle Remus afterward said. Just as the old African was about to lay hands upon 'Tildy, she made a rush for the door. The movement was so unexpected that Daddy Jack was upset. He fell upon Uncle Remus's shoe-bench, and then rolled off on the floor, where he lay clutching at the air, and talking so rapidly that nobody could understand a word he said. Uncle Remus lifted him to his feet, with much dignity, and it soon became apparent that he was neither hurt nor angry. The little boy laughed immoderately, and he was still laughing when 'Tildy put her head in the door and exclaimed:

"Unk' Remus, I ain't kil't dat ole nigger, is I? Kaze ef I got ter go ter de gallus, I want to go dar fer sump'n' n'er bigger'n dat."

Uncle Remus disdained to make any reply, but Daddy Jack chuckled and patted himself on the knee as he cried:

"Come 'long, lilly gal! come 'long! I no mad. I fall down dey fer lahff. Come 'long, lilly gal, come 'long."

'Tildy went on laughing loudly and talking to herself. After a while Uncle Remus said:

"Honey, I speck Miss Sally lookin' und' de bed en axin' whar you is. You better leak out fum yer now, en by dis time termorrer night I'll git Brer Jack all primed up, en he'll whirl in en tell you a tale."

Daddy Jack nodded assent, and the little boy ran laughing to the "big house."

26
Why the Alligator's Back Is Rough

THE NIGHT AFTER the violent flirtation between Daddy Jack and 'Tildy, the latter coaxed and bribed the little boy to wait until she had finished her work about the house. After she had set things to rights in the dining-room and elsewhere, she took the child by the hand, and together they went to Uncle Remus's cabin. The old man was making a door-mat of shucks and grass and white-oak splits, and Daddy Jack was dozing in the corner.

"W'at I tell you, Brer Jack?" said Uncle Remus, as 'Tildy came in. "Dat gal atter you, mon!"

"Fer de Lord sake, Unk' Remus, don't start dat ole nigger. I done promise Miss Sally dat I won't kill 'im, en I like ter be good ez my word; but ef he come foolin' longer me I'm des nat'ally gwine ter onj'int 'im. Now you year me say de word."

But Daddy Jack made no demonstration. He sat with his eyes closed, and paid no attention to 'Tildy. After a while the little boy grew restless, and presently he said:

"Daddy Jack, you know you promised to tell me a story tonight."

"He wukkin' wid it now, honey," said Uncle Remus, soothingly. "Brer Jack," he continued, "wa'n't dey sump'n' n'er 'bout ole man Yalligater?"

"Hi!" exclaimed Daddy Jack, arousing himself, "'e 'bout B'er 'Gater fer true. Oona no bin see da' B'er 'Gater?"

The child had seen one, but it was such a very little one he hardly knew whether to claim an acquaintance with Daddy Jack's 'Gater.

"Dem all sem," continued Daddy Jack. "Big mout', pop-eye, walk on 'e belly; 'e is bin got bump, bump, bump 'pon 'e bahk, bump, bump, bump 'pon 'e tail. 'E dife 'neat' de water, 'e do lif 'pon de lan'."

"One tam Dog is bin run B'er Rabbit, tel 'e do git tire; da' Dog is bin run 'im tel him ent mos' hab no bre't' in 'e body; 'e hide 'ese'f by de crik side. 'E come close 'pon B'er 'Gater, en B'er 'Gater, 'e do say:

"'Ki, B'er Rabbit! wut dis is mek you blow so? Wut mekky you' bre't' come so?'

"'Eh-eh! B'er 'Gater, I hab bin come 'pon trouble. Dog, 'e do run un-a run me.'

"'Wey you no fetch 'im 'long, B'er Rabbit? I is bin git fat on all da' trouble lak dem. I proud fer yeddy Dog bark, ef 'e is bin fetch-a me trouble lak dem.'

"'Wait, B'er 'Gater! Trouble come bisitin' wey you lif; 'e mekky you' side puff; 'e mekky you' bre't' come so.'

"'Gater, he do flup 'e tail un 'tretch 'ese'f, un lahff. 'E say:

"'I lak fer see dem trouble. Nuddin' no bodder me. I ketch-a dem swimp, I ketch-a dem crahb, I mekky my bed wey de sun shiün hot, un I do 'joy mese'f. I proud fer see dem trouble.'

"''E come 'pon you, B'er 'Gator, wun you bin hab you' eye shed; 'e come 'pon you fum de turrer side. Ef 'e no come 'pon you in da' crik, dun 'e come 'pon you in da' broom-grass.'

"'Dun I shekky um by de han', B'er Rabbit; I ahx um howdy.'

"'Eh-eh, B'er 'Gater! you bin-a lahff at me; you no lahff wun dem trouble come. Dem trouble bin ketch-a you yit.'"

Daddy Jack paused to wipe his face. He had reported the dialogue between Brother Rabbit and Brother Alligator with considerable animation, and had illustrated it as he went along with many curious inflections of the voice, and many queer gestures of head and hands impossible to describe here, but which added picturesqueness to the story. After a while he went on:

"B'er Rabbit, 'e do blow un 'e do ketch um bre't'. 'E pit one year wey Dog is bin-a bark; 'e pit one eye 'pon B'er 'Gater. 'E lissen, 'e look; 'e look, 'e lissen. 'E no yeddy Dog, un 'e comforts come back. Bumbye B'er 'Gater, 'e come drowsy; 'e do nod, nod, un 'e head sway down, tel ma'sh-grass tickle 'e nose, un 'e do cough sem lak 'e teer up da' crik by da' root. 'E no lak dis place fer sleep at, un 'e is crawl troo da' ma'sh 'pon dry lan'; 'e is mek fer da' broom-grass fiel'. 'E mek 'e bed wid 'e long tail, un 'e is 'tretch 'ese'f out at 'e lenk. 'E is shed 'e y-eye, un opun 'e mout', un tek 'e nap.

"B'er Rabbit, 'e do hol' 'e y-eye 'pon B'er 'Gater. Him talk no wud; him wallup e cud; him stan' still. B'er 'Gater, 'e do tek 'e nap; B'er Rabbit 'e do watch. Bumbye, B'er 'Gater bre't', 'e do come *loud;* 'e is bin sno' *hard!* 'E dream lilly dream; 'e wuk 'e fut un shek 'e tail in 'e dream. B'er Rabbit wink 'e y-eye, un 'e do watch. B'er 'Gater, he do leaf 'e dream bahine, un 'e sleep soun'. B'er Rabbit watch lil, wait lil. Bumbye, 'e do go wey fier bu'n in da' stump, un 'e is fetch some. 'E say 'Dis day I is mek you know dem trouble; I is mek you know dem well.' 'E hop 'roun' dey-dey, un 'e do light da' broom-grass; 'e bu'n, bu'n — bu'n, bu'n; 'e do bu'n smaht.

"B'er 'Gater, 'e is dream some mo' lilly dream. 'E do wuk 'e fut, 'e do shek 'e tail. Broom-grass bu'n, bu'n; B'er 'Gater dream. 'E dream da' sun is shiün' hot; 'e wom 'e back, 'e wom 'e belly; 'e wuk 'e fut, 'e shek 'e tail. Broom-grass bu'n high, 'e bu'n low; 'e bu'n smaht, 'e bu'n hot. Bumbye, B'er 'Gater is wek fum 'e dream; 'e smell-a da' smoke, 'e feel-a da' fier. 'E run dis way, 'e run turrer way; no diffran' wey 'e is run, dey da' smoke, dey da' fier. *Bu'n, bu'n, bu'n!* B'er 'Gater lash 'e tail, un grine 'e toof. Bumbye, 'e do roll un holler:

"'Trouble, trouble, trouble! *Trouble, trouble!*'

"B'er Rabbit, 'e is stan' pas' da' fier, un 'e do say:

"'Ki! B'er 'Gater! Wey you fer l'arn-a dis talk 'bout dem trouble?'

"B'er 'Gater, 'e lash 'e tail, 'e fair teer da' ye't, un 'e do holler:

"'Oh, ma Lord! Trouble! *Trouble, trouble, trouble!*'

"'Shekky um by de han', B'er 'Gater. Ahx um howdy!'

"'Ow, ma Lord! *Trouble, trouble, trouble!*'

"'Lahff wit' dem trouble, B'er 'Gater, lahff wit' dem! Ahx dem is dey he'lt' bin well! You bin-a cry fer dey 'quaintun', B'er 'Gater; now you mus' beer wit' dem trouble!'

"B'er 'Gater come so mad, 'e mek dash troo da' broom-grass; 'e fair teer um down. 'E bin scatter da' fier wide 'part, un 'e do run un dife in da' crik fer squinch da' fier 'pon 'e bahk. 'E bahk swivel, 'e tail swivel wit'

da' fier, un fum dat dey is bin stan' so. Bump, bump 'pon 'e tail; bump, bump 'pon 'e bahk, wey da' fier bu'n."

"Hit's des lak Brer Jack tell you, honey," said Uncle Remus, as Daddy Jack closed his eyes and relapsed into silence. "I done seed um wid my own eyes. En dey er mighty kuse creeturs, mon. Dey back is all ruffed up en down ter dis day en time, en mo'n dat, you ain't gwine ter ketch Brer Rabbit rackin' 'roun' whar de Yallergaters is. En de Yallergaters deyse'f, w'en dey years any crackin' en rattlin' gwine on in de bushes, dey des makes a break fer de creek en splunges in."

"Enty!" exclaimed Daddy Jack, with momentary enthusiasm. "'E do tu'n go da' bahnk, un dife 'neat' da' crik. 'E bin so wom wit' da' fier, 'e mek de crik go si-z-z-z!"

Here Daddy Jack looked around and smiled. His glance fell on 'Tildy, and he seemed suddenly to remember that he had failed to be as polite as circumstances demanded.

"Come-a set nex' me, lilly gal. I gwan tell you one tale."

"Come 'long, Pinx," said 'Tildy, tossing her head disdainfully, and taking the little boy by the hand. "Come 'long, Pinx; we better be gwine. I done say I won't kill dat ole nigger man. Yit ef he start atter me dis blessid night, I lay I roust de whole plantation. Come on, honey; less go."

The little boy was not anxious to go, but Uncle Remus seconded 'Tildy's suggestion.

"Better let dat gal mosey 'long, honey, kaze she mought start in fer ter cut up some 'er capers in yer, en I hate mighty bad ter bus' up dis yer axe-helve, w'ich I'm in needs un it eve'y hour er de day."

Whereupon the two old Negroes were left sitting by the hearth.

27

Brother Wolf Says Grace

'TILDY, THE HOUSE-GIRL, made such a terrible report of the carryings on of Daddy Jack that the little boy's mother thought it prudent not to allow him to visit Uncle Remus so often. The child amused himself as best he could for several nights, but his playthings and picture-books finally lost their interest. He cried so hard to be allowed to go to see Uncle Remus that his mother placed him under the care of Aunt Tempy — a woman of large authority on the place, and who stood next to Uncle Remus in the confidence of her mistress. Aunt Tempy was a fat, middle-aged woman, who always wore a head-handkerchief, and kept her sleeves rolled up, displaying her plump, black arms, winter and summer. She never hesitated to exercise her authority, and the younger Negroes on the place regarded her as a tyrant; but in spite of her loud voice and brusque manners she was thoroughly good-natured, usually good-humored, and always trustworthy. Aunt Tempy and Uncle Remus were secretly jealous of each other, but they were careful never to come in conflict, and, to all appearances, the most cordial relations existed between them.

"Well de goodness knows!" exclaimed Uncle Remus, as Aunt Tempy went in with the little boy. "How you come on, Sis Tempy? De rainy season ain't so mighty fur off w'en you come a-sojourneyin' in dis house. Ef I'd a know'd you'd a bin a-comin' I'd a sorter steered 'roun' en bresh'd de cobwebs out'n de cornders."

"Don't min' me, Brer Remus. Luck in de house whar de cobwebs hangs low. I 'uz des a-passin' — a-passin' 'long — en Miss Sally ax me ef I kin come fur ez de do' wid dat chile dar, but bless you, 'tain't in my manners ter tu'n back at de do'. How you come on, Brer Remus?"

"Po'ly, Sis Tempy; en yit I ain't complainin'. Pain yer, en a ketch yander, wid de cramps th'ow'd in, ain't no mo' dan ole folks kin 'speck. How you is, Sis Tempy?"

"I thank de Lord I'm able to crawl, Brer Remus, en dat's 'bout all. Ef I wa'n't so sot in my ways, deze yer niggers would er run me 'stracted d'reckly."

Daddy Jack was sitting in the corner laughing and talking to himself, and the little boy watched him not without a feeling of awe. After a while he said:

"Uncle Remus, won't Daddy Jack tell us a story tonight?"

"Now, den, honey," responded the old man, "we ain't got ter push Brer Jack too closte; we ull des hatter creep up on 'im en ketch 'im fer er tale w'ence he in de humors. Sometimes hoss pull, sometime he ain't pull. You ain't bin down yer so long, hit sorter look lak it my tu'n; kaze it done come 'cross my 'membunce dat dey wuz one time w'en Brer Wolf kotch Brer Rabbit, w'ich I ain't never gun it out ter you yit."

"Brother Wolf caught Brother Rabbit, Uncle Remus?" exclaimed the little boy, incredulously.

"Yasser! dat's de up en down un it, sho," responded the old man with emphasis, "en I be mighty glad ef Sis Tempy yer will 'scuze me w'iles I runs over de tale 'long wid you."

"Bless yo' soul, Brer Remus, don't pay no 'tention ter me," said Aunt Tempy, folding her fat arms upon her ample bosom, and assuming an attitude of rest and contentment. "I'm bad ez de chillun 'bout dem ole tales, kaze I kin des set up yer un lissen at um de whole blessid night, un a good part er de day. Yass, Lord!"

"Well, den," said Uncle Remus, "we ull des huddle up yer en see w'at 'come er Brer Rabbit w'en ole Brer Wolf kotch 'im. In dem days," he continued, looking at Daddy Jack and smiling broadly, "de creeturs wuz constant gwine a-courtin'. Ef 'twa'n't Miss Meadows en de gals dey wuz flyin' 'roun', hit 'uz Miss Motts. Dey wuz constant a-courtin'. En 'twa'n't none er dish yer 'Howdy-do-ma'am-I-speck-I-better-be-gwine,' n'er. Hit 'uz go atter brekkus en stay twel atter supper. Brer Rabbit, he got tuk wid a likin' fer Miss Motts, en soon one mawnin', he tuck'n slick hisse'f up, he did, en put out ter call on 'er. W'en Brer Rabbit git ter whar Miss Motts live, she done gone off some'rs.

"Some folks 'ud er sot down en wait twel Miss Motts come back, en den ag'in some folks 'ud er tuck der foot in der han' en went back; but ole Brer Rabbit, he ain't de man fer ter be outdone, en he des tuck'n go in de kitchen en light he seegyar, en den he put out fer ter pay a call on Miss Meadows en de gals.

"W'en he git dar, lo en beholes, he fin' Miss Motts dar, en he tipped in, ole Brer Rabbit did, en he galanted roun' 'mungs um, same lak one er dese yer town chaps, w'at you see come out ter Harmony Grove meetin'-house. Dey talk en dey laff; dey laff en dey giggle. Bimeby, 'long todes night, Brer Rabbit 'low he better be gwine. De wimmen folks dey all ax 'im fer ter stay twel atter supper, kaze he sech lively comp'ny, but Brer Rabbit 'fear'd some er de yuther creeturs be hidin' out fer 'im; so he tuck'n pay his 'specks, he did, en start fer home.

"He ain't git fur twel he come up wid a great big basket settin' down by de side er de big road. He look up de road; he ain't see nobody. He look down de road; he ain't see nobody. He look befo', he look behime, he look all 'roun'; he ain't see nobody. He lissen, en lissen; he ain't year nothin'. He wait, en he wait; nobody ain't come.

"Den, bimeby Brer Rabbit go en peep in de basket, en it seem lak it half full er green truck. He retch he han' in, he did, en git some en put it in he mouf. Den he shet he eye en do lak he studyin' 'bout sump'n'. Atter w'ile, he 'low ter hisse'f, 'Hit look lak sparrer-grass, hit feel like sparrer-grass, hit tas'e lak sparrer-grass, en I be bless ef 'tain't sparrer-grass.'

"Wid dat Brer Rabbit jump up, he did, en crack he heel tergedder, en he fetch one leap en lan' in de basket, right spang in 'mungs de sparrer-grass. Dar whar he miss he footin','" continued Uncle Remus, rubbing his beard meditatively, "kaze w'en he jump in 'mungs de sparrer-grass, right den en dar he jump in mungs ole Brer Wolf, w'ich he wer' quile up at de bottom."

"Dar now!" exclaimed Aunt Tempy, enthusiastically. "W'at I tell you? W'at make him pester t'er folks doin's? I boun' Brer Wolf nail't 'im."

"Time Brer Wolf grab 'im," continued Uncle Remus, "Brer Rabbit knowed he 'uz a gone case; yit he sing out he did:

"'I des tryin' ter skeer you, Brer Wolf; I des tryin' ter skeer you. I know'd you 'uz in dar, Brer Wolf. I know'd you by de smell!' sez Brer Rabbit, sezee.

"Ole Brer Wolf grin, he did, en lick he chops, en up'n say:

"'Mighty glad you know'd me, Brer Rabbit, kaze I know'd you des time you drapt in on me. I tuck'n tell Brer Fox yistiddy dat I 'uz gwine take a nap 'longside er de road, en I boun' you 'ud come 'long en wake me up, en sho nuff, yer you come en yer you is,' sez Brer Wolf sezee."

"Oh-ho, Mr. Rabbit! How you feel now?" exclaimed Aunt Tempy, her sympathies evidently with Brother Wolf.

"W'en Brer Rabbit year dis," said Uncle Remus, paying no attention to the interruption, "he 'gun ter git mighty skeer'd, en he whirl in en beg Brer Wolf fer ter please tu'n 'im loose; but dis make Brer Wolf grin wusser, en he toof look so long en shine so w'ite, en he gum look so red, dat Brer Rabbit hush up en stay still. He so skeer'd dat he bref come quick, en he heart go lak flutter-mill. He chune up lak he gwine cry:

"'Whar you gwine kyar' me, Brer Wolf?'

"'Down by de branch, Brer Rabbit.'

"'W'at you gwine down dar fer, Brer Wolf?'

"'So I kin git some water ter clean you wid atter I done skunt you, Brer Rabbit.'

"'Please, sir, lemme go. Brer Wolf.'

"'You talk so young you make me laff, Brer Rabbit.'

"'Dat sparrer-grass done make me sick, Brer Wolf.'

"'You ull be sicker'n dat 'fo' I git done wid you, Brer Rabbit.'

"'Whar I come fum nobody dast ter eat sick folks, Brer Wolf.'

"'Whar I come fum dey ain't dast ter eat no yuther kin', Brer Rabbit.'"

"Ole Mr. Rabbit wuz a-talkin', mon," said Aunt Tempy, with a chuckle that caused her to shake like a piece of jelly.

"Dey went on dis a-way," continued Uncle Remus, "plum twel dey git ter de branch. Brer Rabbit, he beg en cry, en cry en beg, en Brer Wolf, he 'fuse en grin, en grin en 'fuse. W'en dey come ter de branch, Brer Wolf lay Brer Rabbit down on de groun' en hilt 'im dar, en den he study how he gwine make way wid 'im. He study en he study, en w'iles he studyin' Brer Rabbit, he tuck'n study some on he own hook.

"Den w'en it seem lak Brer W'olf done fix all de 'rangerments, Brer Rabbit, he make lak he cryin' wusser en wusser; he des fa'rly blubber."

Uncle Remus gave a ludicrous imitation of Brother Rabbit's waitings.

"'Ber — ber — Brer Wooly — ooly — oolf! Is you gwine — is you gwine ter sakerfice-t me right now — ow — ow?'

"'Dat I is, Brer Rabbit; dat I is.'

"'Well, ef I blee-eedzd ter be kil't, Brer Wooly — ooly — oolf, I wants ter be kil't right, en ef I blee-eedzd ter be e't, I wants ter be e't ri — ight, too, now!'

"'How dat, Brer Rabbit?'

"'I want you ter show yo' p'liteness, Brer Wooly — ooly — oolf!'

"'How I gwine do dat, Brer Rabbit?'

"'I want you ter say grace, Brer Wolf, en say it quick, kaze I gittin' mighty weak.'

"'How I gwine say grace, Brer Rabbit?'

"'Fol' yo' han's und' yo' chin, Brer Wolf, en shet yo' eyes, en say: "Bless us en bine us, en put us in crack whar de Ole Boy can't fin' us." Say it quick, Brer Wolf, kaze I failin' mighty fas'.'"

"Now ain't dat des too much!" exclaimed Aunt Tempy, as delighted as the little boy. Uncle Remus laughed knowingly and went on:

"Brer Wolf, he put up he han's, he did, en shot he eyes, en 'low, 'Bless us en bine us'; but he ain't git no furder, kaze des time he take up he han's, Brer Rabbit fotch a wiggle, he did, en lit on he foots, en he des nat'ally lef' a blue streak behime 'im."

"Ah-yi-ee!" exclaimed Daddy Jack, while Aunt Tempy allowed her arms to drop helplessly from her lap as she cried "Dar now;" and the little boy clasped his hands in an ecstasy of admiration.

"Oh, I just knew Brother Rabbit would get away," the child declared.

"Dat's right, honey," said Uncle Remus. "You put yo' 'pennunce in Brer Rabbit en yo' won't be fur out er de way."

There was some further conversation among the Negroes, but it was mostly plantation gossip. When Aunt Tempy rose to go, she said:

"Goodness knows, Brer Remus, ef dis de way you all runs on, I'm gwine ter pester you some mo'. Hit come 'cross me like ole times, dat it do."

"Do so, Sis Tempy, do so," said Uncle Remus, with dignified hospitality. "You allers fin' a place at my h'a'th. Ole times is about all we got lef'."

"Trufe, too!" exclaimed Aunt Tempy; and with that she took the child by the hand and went out into the darkness.

28
Spirits, Seen and Unseen

IT WAS NOT many nights before the same company was gathered in Uncle Remus's cabin, — Daddy Jack, Aunt Tempy, and the little boy. The conversation took a turn that thrilled the child with mingled fear and curiosity. Uncle Remus had inquired as to the state of Aunt Tempy's health, when the latter came in, and her response was:

"I feelin' mighty creepy, Brer Remus, sho. Look like I bleedzd ter hunt comp'ny. W'en I come 'long down I felt dat skittish twel ef a leaf had blow'd 'crost de paff, I'd a des about drapt in my tracks."

"How come dat, Sis Tempy?" Uncle Remus inquired.

"You know dat little gal er Riah's? Well, I 'uz settin' up dar in my house 'w'ile ergo, w'en, bless gracious! fus' news I know, I year dat chile talkin' in de yuther room. I 'low ter myse'f, she ain't talkin' ter Riah, kaze Riah ain't come yit, un den I crope up, un dar wuz de chile settin' right flat in de middle er de flo', laffin' un talkin' un makin' motions like she see somebody in de cornder. I des stood dar un watch 'er, un I ain't a livin' human ef she don't do like dey 'uz somebody er n'er in dar wid 'er. She ax um fer ter stay on dey own side, un den, w'en it seem like dey come todes 'er, den she say she gwine git a switch un drive um back. Hit make me feel so col' un kuse dat I des tuck'n come 'way fum dar, un ef dey's sump'n' n'er dar, hit'll be dem un Riah fer't."

"'E do talk wid ghos'; 'e is bin lahff wit' harnt," exclaimed Daddy Jack.

"I 'speck dat's 'bout de upshot un it," said Uncle Remus. "Dey tells me dat w'ence you year chilluns talkin' en gwine on 'periently wid dey-se'f, der er bleedzd ter see ha'nts."

The little boy moved his stool closer to his venerable partner. Daddy Jack roused himself.

"Oona no bin-a see dem ghos'? Oona no bin-a see dem harnt? Hi! I is bin-a see plenty ghos'; I no 'fraid dem; I is bin-a punch dem 'way wit' me cane. I is bin-a shoo dem 'pon dey own sïed da' road. Dem is bin walk wun da' moon stan' low; den I is bin shum. Oona no walk wit' me dun. 'E berry bahd. Oona call, dey no answer. Wun dey call, hol' you' mout' shet. 'E berry bahd fer mek answer, wun da' harnt holler. Dem call-a you 'way fum dis lan'. I yeddy dem call; I shetty me y-eye, I shekkey me head.

"Wun I is bin noung mahn, me der go fer git water, un wun I dip der piggin 'neat' da' crik, I yeddy v'ice fer call me — *'Jahck! O Jahck!'* I stan', I lissen, I yeddy de v'ice — *'Jahck! Jahck! O Jahck!'* I t'ink 'e bin Titty Ann; I ahx um:

"'Wey you bin call-a me, Titty Ann?' Titty Ann 'tretch 'e y-eye big:

"'I no bin-a call. Dead ghos' is bin-a call. Dem harnt do call-a you.'

"Dun I rise me y-eye, un I is bin shum gwan by sundown; 'e is bin gwan bahckwud. I tell Titty Ann fer look at we nuncle, gwan bahckwud by sundown. Titty Ann pit 'e two han' 'pon me y-eyes, un 'e do bline me. 'E say I bin-a see one dead ghos'."

"What then, Daddy Jack?" asked the little boy, as the old African paused.

"Ki! nuff dun. Kaze bumbye, so long tam, folks come fetch-a we nuncle 'tretch out. 'E is bin-a tek wit' da' *he*cup; 'e t'row 'e head dis way; 'e t'row 'e head dat way." Daddy Jack comically suited the action to the word. "'E is bin tek-a da' *he*cup; da' *he*cup is bin tek um — da' cramp is bin fetch um. I is bin see mo' dead ghos', but me no spot um lak dis."

"I boun' you is," said Uncle Remus. "Dey tells me, Brer Jack," he continued, "dat w'en you meets up wid one er deze ha'nts, ef you'll tak'n tu'n yo' coat wrongsudouterds, dey won't use no time in makin' der disappearance."

"Hey!" exclaimed Daddy Jack, "tu'n coat no fer skeer dead ghos'. 'E skeer dem Jack-me-Lantun. One tam I is bin-a mek me way troo t'ick swamp. I do come hot, I do come cole. I feel-a me bahck quake; me bre't' come fahs'. I look; me ent see nuttin'; I lissen; me ent yeddy nuttin'. I look, dey de Jack-me-Lantun mekkin 'e way troo de bush; 'e comin' stret by me. 'E light bin-a flick-flicker; 'e git close un close. I yent kin stan' dis; one foot git heffy, da' heer 'pon me head lif' up. Da' Jack-me-Lantun, 'e git-a high, 'e git-a low, 'e come close. Dun I t'ink I bin-a yeddy ole folks talk *tu'n you' coat-sleef* wun da' Jack-me-Lantun is bin run you. I pull, I twis', I yerk at dem jacket; 'e yent come. 'E is bin grow on me bahck. Jack-me-Lantun fly close. I say me pray 'pon da' jacket; 'e is bin-a yerk loose; da' sleef 'e do tu'n. Jack-me-Lantun, 'e see dis, 'e lif' up, 'e say *'Phew!'* 'E done gone! Oona no walk in da swamp 'cep' you is keer you' coat 'cross da' arm. Enty!"

"Dat w'at make me say," remarked Aunt Tempy, with a little shiver, "dat 'oman like me, w'at ain't w'ar no jacket, ain't got no business traipsin' un trollopin' 'roun' thoo the woods atter dark."

"You mought tu'n yo' head-hankcher, Sis Tempy," said Uncle Remus, reassuringly, "en ef dat ain't do no good den you kin whirl in en gin um leg-bail."

"I year tell," continued Aunt Tempy, vouchsafing no reply to Uncle Remus, "dat dish yer Jacky-me-Lantun is a sho nuff sperit. Sperits ain't gwine to walk un walk less'n dey got sump'n' n'er on der min', un I year tell dat dish yer Jacky-ma-Lantun is 'casioned by a man w'at got kil't. Folks kil't 'im un tuck his money, un now his ha'nt done gone un got a light fer ter hunt up whar his money is. Mighty kuse ef folks kin hone at-ter money w'en dey done *gone*. I dunner w'at he wanter be ramblin' 'roun' wid a light w'en he done *dead*. Ef anybody got any hard feelin's 'gin me, I want um ter take it out w'ile dey er in de flesh; w'en dey come a-ha'ntin' me, den I'm done — I'm des *done*."

"Are witches spirits?" the little boy asked.

The inquiry was not especially directed at Daddy Jack, but Daddy Jack was proud of his reputation as a witch, and he undertook to reply.

"None 'tall. Witch, 'e no dead ghos' — 'e life folks, wey you shekky han' wit'. Oona witch mebbe; how you is kin tell?"

Here Daddy Jack turned his sharp little eyes upon the child. The lat-ter moved closer to Uncle Remus, and said he hoped to goodness he wasn't a witch.

"How you is kin tell diffran 'cep' you bin fer try um?" continued Daddy Jack. "'E good t'ing fer be witch; 'e mek-a dem folks fred. 'E mek-a dem fred; 'e mek-a dem hol' da' bre't, wun dey is bin-a come by you' place."

"In de name er de Lord, Daddy Jack, how kin folks tell wh'er dey er witches er no?" asked Aunt Tempy.

"Oo! 'e easy nuff. Wun da' moon is shiün low, wet-a you' han' wit' da' pot-licker grease; rub noung heifer 'pon 'e nose; git 'pon 'e bahck. Mus' hol' um by 'e year; mus' go gallop, gallop down da' lane, tel 'e do come 'cross one-a big gully. Mus' holler, '*Double, double, double up! double, double, double up!*' Heifer jump, oona witch; heifer no jump, oona no witch."

"Did you ever ride a heifer, Daddy Jack?" asked the little boy.

"Mo' tam es dem," replied the old Negro, holding up the crooked fingers of one withered hand.

"Did — did she jump across the big gully?"

The child's voice had dropped to an awed whisper, and there was a glint of malicious mischief in Daddy Jack's shrewd eyes as he looked up at Uncle Remus. He got his cue. Uncle Remus groaned heavily and shook his head.

"Hoo!" exclaimed Daddy Jack, "wun I is bin-a tell all, dey no mo' fer tell. Mus' kip some fer da' Sunday. Lilly b'y no fred dem witch; 'e no bodder lilly b'y. Witch, 'e no rassel wit' 'e ebry-day 'quaintan'; 'e do go pars 'e own place."

It was certainly reassuring for the child to be told that witches didn't trouble little boys, and that they committed their depredations outside of their own neighborhood.

"I is bin-a yeddy dem talk 'bout ole witch. 'E do leaf 'e skin wey 'e is sta't fum. Man bin-a come pars by; 'e is fine dem skin. 'E say:

"'Ki! 'E one green skin; I fix fer dry um.'

"Man hang um by da' fier. Skin, 'e do swink, 'e do swivel. Bumbye 'e do smell-a bahd; man, 'e hol' 'e nose. 'E do wait. Skin swink, skin stink, skin swivel. 'E do git so bahd, man pitch um in da' ya'd. 'E wait; 'e is wait, 'e is lissen. Bumbye, 'e yeddy da' witch come. Witch, 'e do sharp' 'e claw on-a da' fence; 'e is snap 'e jaw — *flick! flick! flick!* 'E come-a hunt fer him skin. 'E fine un. 'E trey um on dis way; 'e no fit. 'E trey um on dat way; 'e not fit. 'E trey um on turrer way; 'e no fit. 'E pit um 'pon 'e head; skin 'e no fit. 'E pit um 'pon 'e foot; skin 'e no fit. 'E cuss, 'e sweer; skin 'e no fit. 'E cut 'e caper; skin 'e no fit. Bumbye 'e holler:

"'Tiss-a me, Skin! wey you no know me? Skin, 'tiss-a me! wey you no know me?'

"Skin, 'e no talk nuttin' 'tall. Witch 'e do jump, 'e do holler; à mek no diffran. Skin 'e nuttin' 'tall. Man, 'e tekky to'ch, 'e look in ya'd. 'E see big blahck Woolf lay by da' skin. 'E toof show; 'e y-eye shiün. Man drife um 'way; 'e is come bahck. Man bu'n da' skin; 'e is bin-a come bahck no mo'.'"

The little boy asked no more questions. He sat silent while the others talked, and then went to the door and looked out. It was very dark, and he returned to his stool with a troubled countenance.

"Des wait a little minnit, honey," said Uncle Remus, dropping his hand caressingly on the child's shoulder. "I bleedzd ter go up dar ter de big house fer ter see Mars John, en I'll take you 'long fer comp'ny."

And so, after a while, the old man and the little boy went hand in hand up the path.

29

A Ghost Story

THE NEXT TIME the little boy visited Uncle Remus he persuaded 'Tildy to go with him. Daddy Jack was in his usual place, dozing and talking to himself, while Uncle Remus oiled the carriage-harness. After a while Aunt Tempy came in.

The conversation turned on Daddy Jack's story about "haunts" and spirits. Finally 'Tildy said:

"W'en it come ter tales 'bout ha'nts," said she, "I year tell er one dat'll des nat'ally make de kinks on yo' head onquile deyse'f."

"W'at tale dat, chile?" asked Aunt Tempy.

"Unk' Remus, mus' I tell it?"

"Let 'er come," said Uncle Remus.

"Well, den," said 'Tildy, rolling her eyes back and displaying her white teeth, "one time dey wuz a 'Oman en a Man. Seem like dey live close ter one er n'er, en de Man he sot his eyes on de 'Oman, en de

'Oman, she des went 'long en 'ten' ter her bizness. Man, he keep his eyes sot on 'er. Bimeby, de 'Oman, she 'ten' ter her bizness so much tel she tuck'n tuck sick en die. Man, he up'n tell de folks she dead, en de folks dey come en fix 'er. Dey lay 'er out, en dey light some candles, en dey sot up wid 'er, des like folks does now; en dey put two great big roun' shiny silver dollars on 'er eyes fer ter hol' 'er eyeleds down."

In describing the silver dollars 'Tildy joined the ends of her thumbs and fore-fingers together, and made a figure as large as a saucer.

"Dey wuz lots bigger dan dollars is deze days," she continued, "en dey look mighty purty. Seem like dey wuz all de money de 'Oman got, en de folks dey put um on 'er eyelids fer to hol' um down. Den w'en de folks do dat dey call up de Man en tak'n tell 'im dat he mus' dig a grave en bury de 'Oman, en den dey all went off 'bout der bizness.

"Well, den, de Man, he tuck'n dig de grave en make ready fer ter bury de 'Oman. He look at dat money on 'er eyeleds, en it shine mighty purty. Den he tuck it off en feel it. Hit feel mighty good, but des 'bout dat time de Man look at de 'Oman, en he see 'er eyeleds open. Look like she lookin' at 'im, en he tak'n put de money whar he git it fum.

"Well, den, de Man, he tak'n git a waggin en haul de 'Oman out ter de buryin'-groun', en w'en he git dar he fix eve'ything, en den he grab de money en kivver up de grave right quick. Den he go home, en put de money in a tin box en rattle it 'roun'. Hit rattle loud en hit rattle nice, but de Man, he ain't feel so good. Seem like he know de 'Oman eyeled stretch wide open lookin' fer 'im. Yit he rattle de money 'roun', en hit rattle loud en hit rattle nice.

"Well, den, de Man, he tak'n put de tin box w'at de money in on de mantel-shel-uf. De day go by, en de night come, en w'en night come de win' 'gun ter rise up en blow. Hit rise high, hit blow strong. Hit blow on top er de house, hit blow und' de house, hit blow 'roun' de house. Man, he feel quare. He set by de fier en lissen. Win' say *'Buzz-zoo-o-o-o-o!'* Man lissen. Win' holler en cry. Hit blow top er de house, hit blow und' de house, hit blow 'roun' de house, hit blow in de house. Man git closte up in de chimbley-jam'. Win' fin' de cracks en blow in um. *'Bizzy, bizzy, buzz-zoo-o-o-o-o!'*

"Well, den, Man, he lissen, lissen, but bimeby he git tired er dis, en he 'low ter hisse'f dat he gwine ter bed. He tuck'n fling a fresh light'd knot in de fier, en den he jump in de bed, en quile hisse'f up en put his head und' de kivver. Win' hunt fer de cracks — *bizzy-buzz, bizzy-buzz, buzz-zoo-o-o-o-o-o!* Man keep his head und' de kivver. Light'd knot flar' up en flicker. Man ain't dast ter move. Win' blow en w'issel *Phew-fee-e-e-e!* Light'd knot flicker en flar'. Man, he keep his head kivver'd.

"Well, den, Man lay dar, en git skeer'der en skeer'der. He ain't dast ter wink his eye skacely, en seem like he gwine ter have swamp agur. W'iles he layin' der shakin', en de win' a-blowin', en de fier flickin', he year some yuther kind er fuss. Hit mighty kuse kind er fuss. *Clinkity, clinkalinkle!* Man 'low:

"'Hey! who stealin' my money?'

"Yit he keep his head kivver'd w'iles he lay en lissen. He year de win' blow, en den he year dat yuther kinder fuss — *Clinkity, clink, clinkity, clinkalinkle!* Well, den, he fling off de kivver en sot right up in de bed. He look, he ain't see nothin'. De fier flicker en flar' en de win' blow. Man go en put chain en bar 'cross de do'. Den he go back to bed, en he ain't mo'n totch his head on de piller tel he year de yuther fuss — *clink, clink, clinkity, clinkalinkle!* Man rise up, he ain't see nothin' 'tall. Mighty quare!

"Des 'bout time he gwine ter lay down 'g'in, yer come de fuss — *clinkity, clinkalinkle.* Hit soun' like it on de mantel-shel-uf; let 'lone dat, hit soun' like it in de tin box on de mantel-shel-uf; let 'lone dat, hit soun' like it de money in de tin box on de mantel-shel-uf. Man say:

"'Hey! rat done got in box!'

"Man look; no rat dar. He shet up de box, en set it down on de shel-uf. Time he do dat yer come de fuss — *clinkity, clinkity, clinkalinkle!* Man open de box en look at de money. Dem two silver dollars layin' in dar des like he put um. W'iles de man dun dis, look like he kin year sump'n' say 'way off yander:

"'*Whar my money? Oh, gim me my money!*'

"Man, he sot de box back on de shel-uf, en time he put it down he year de money rattle — *clinkity, clinkalinkle, clink!* — en den fum 'way off yander sump'n' say:

"'*Oh, gim me my money! I want my money!*'

"Well, den, de Man git skeer'd sho nuff, en he got er flat-iün en put it

on de tin box, en den he tuck'n pile all de cheers 'g'in de do', en run en
jump in de bed. He des know dey's a booger comin'. Time he git in bed en
kivver his head, de money rattle louder, en sump'n' cry 'way off yander:

"*I want my money! Oh, gim me my money!*"

"Man, he shake en he shiver; money, hit clink en rattle; booger, hit
holler en cry. Booger came closter, money clink louder. Man shake
wusser en wusser. Money say: '*Clinkity, clinkalinkle!*' Booger cry, '*Oh,
gim me my money!*' Man holler, '*O Lordy, Lordy!*'

"Well, den, hit keep on dis a-way, tel d'reckly Man year de do' open.
He peep fum und' de kivver, en in walk de 'Oman w'at he done bury in
de buryin'-groun'. Man shiver en shiver, win' blow en blow, money rattle
en rattle, 'Oman cry en cry. '*Buzz-zoo-o-o-o-o!*' sez de win'; '*Clinkalink!*'
sez de box; '*Oh, gim me my money!*' sez de 'Oman; '*O Lordy!*' sez de Man.
'Oman year de money, but look like she ain't kin see, en she grope 'roun',
en grope 'roun', en grope 'roun' wid 'er han' h'ist in de a'r des dis a-way."

Here 'Tildy stood up, pushed her chair back with her foot, raised her
arms over her head, and leaned forward in the direction of Daddy Jack.

"Win' blow, fier flicker, money rattle, Man shake en shiver, 'Oman
grope 'roun' en say, '*Gim me my money! Oh, who got my money?*'"

'Tildy advanced a few steps.

"Money look like it gwine ter t'ar de tin box all ter flinders. 'Oman
grope en cry, grope en cry, tel bimeby she jump on de man en holler:

"'*You got my money!*'"

As she reached this climax, 'Tildy sprang at Daddy Jack and seized
him, and for a few moments there was considerable confusion in the corner. The little boy was frightened, but the collapsed appearance of
Daddy Jack convulsed him with laughter. The old African was very angry. His little eyes glistened with momentary malice, and he shook his
cane threateningly at 'Tildy. The latter coolly adjusted her ear-rings, as
she exclaimed:

"Dar, now! I know'd I'd git even wid de ole vilyun. Come a-callin' me
pidjin-toed!"

"Better keep yo' eye on 'im, chile," said Aunt Tempy. "He 'witch you,
sho."

"'Witch who? Ef he come witchin' 'roun' me, I lay I break his back. I
tell you dat right pine-blank."

30

Brother Rabbit and His Famous Foot

THE LITTLE BOY was very glad, one night shortly after he had heard about Daddy Jack's ghosts and witches and 'Tildy's "ha'nts," to find Uncle Remus alone in his cabin. The child liked to have his venerable partner all to himself. Uncle Remus was engaged in hunting for tobacco crumbs with which to fill his pipe, and in turning his pockets a rabbit foot dropped upon the hearth.

"Grab it, honey!" he exclaimed. "Snatch it up off'n de h'a'th. In de name er goodness, don't let it git in de embers; kaze ef dat ar rabbit foot git singe, I'm a goner, sho'!"

It was the hind foot of a rabbit, and a very large one at that, and the little boy examined it curiously. He was in thorough sympathy with all the superstitions of the Negroes, and to him the rabbit foot appeared to be an uncanny affair. He placed it carefully on Uncle Remus's knee, and after the pipe had been filled, he asked:

"What do you carry that for, Uncle Remus?"

"Well, honey," responded the old man, grimly, "ef you want me ter make shorts out'n a mighty long tale, dat rabbit foot is fer ter keep off boogers. W'en I hatter run er'n's fer myse'f all times er night, en take nigh cuts thoo de woods, en 'cross by de buryin'-groun', hits monstus handy fer ter have dat ar rabbit foot. Keep yo' head studdy, now; min' yo' eye; I ain't sayin' dey er any boogers anywhars. Brer Jack kin say what he min'-ter; I ain't sayin' nothin'. But yit, ef dey wuz any, en dey come slinkin' atter me, I let you know dey'd fin' out terreckly dat de ole nigger heel'd wid rabbit foot. I 'ud hol' it up des dis away, en I boun' you I'd shoo um off'n de face er de yeth. En I tell you w'at," continued Uncle Remus, seeing that the little boy was somewhat troubled, "w'en it come to dat pass dat you gotter be dodgin' 'roun' in de dark, ef you'll des holler fer me, I'll loan you dish yer rabbit foot, en you'll be des ez safe ez you is w'en Miss Sally stan'in' by yo' bed wid a lit can'le in 'er han'.

"Strip er red flannil tied 'roun' yo' arm'll keep off de rheumatis; stump-water'll kyo 'spepsy; some good fer one 'zeeze, en some good fer n'er, but de p'ints is dat dish yer rabbit foot'll gin you good luck. De man w'at tote it mighty ap' fer ter come out right een' up w'en dey's any racket gwine on in de neighborhoods, let 'er be whar she will en w'en she may; mo' espeshually ef de man w'at got it know zackly w'at he got ter do. Wite folks may laugh," Uncle Remus went on, "but w'en rabbit run 'cross de big road front er me, w'at does I do? Does I shoo at um? Does I make fer ter kill um? Dat I don't — *dat* I don't! I des squots right down in de middle er de road, en I makes a cross-mark in de san' des dis way, en den I spits in it."[1]

Uncle Remus made a practical illustration by drawing a cross-mark in the ashes on the hearth.

"Well, but, Uncle Remus, what good does all this do?" the little boy asked.

"Lots er good, honey; bless yo' soul, lots er good. W'en rabbit crosses yo' luck, w'at you gwine do, less'n you sets down en crosses it out, right den en dar? I year talk er folks shootin' rabbit in de big road, yit I notices dat dem w'at does de shootin' ain't come ter no good een' — dat w'at I notices."

"Uncle Remus," the little boy asked, after a while, "how did people happen to find out about the rabbit's foot?"

"Oh, you let folks 'lone fer dat, honey! You des let um 'lone. W'at de wimmen ain't up'n tell widout anybody axin' un um, folks mighty ap' fer ter fin' out fer deyse'f. De wimmen, dey does de talkin' en de flyin', en de mens, dey does de walkin' en de pryin', en betwixt en betweenst um, dey ain't much dat don't come out. Ef it don't come out one day it do de nex', en so she goes — Ant'ny over, Ant'ny under — up one row en down de udder, en clean acrosst de bolly-patch!"

It may be that the child didn't understand all this, but he had no doubt of its wisdom, and so he waited patiently for developments.

"Dey's a tale 'bout de rabbit foot," continued Uncle Remus, "but yo' eye look watery, like ole man Nod 'bout ter slip up behime you; en let 'lone dat, I speck Miss Sally clock clickin' fer you right now."

---

[1] If, as some ethnologists claim, the animal myths are relics of zoötheism, there can scarcely be a doubt that the practice here described by Uncle Remus is the survival of some sort of obeisance or genuflexion by which the Negroes recognized the presence of the Rabbit, the great central figure and wonder-worker of African mythology. — J. C. H.

"Oh, no, it isn't, Uncle Remus," said the child, laughing. "Mamma said she'd make 'Tildy call me."

"Dar, now!" exclaimed the old man, indignantly, "'Tildy dis en 'Tildy dat. I dunner w'at yo' mammy dreamin' 'bout fer ter let dat nigger gal be a-'holl'in' en a-bawlin' atter you all 'roun' dish yer plan'ation. She de mos' uppity nigger on de hill, en de fus' news you know dey ull all hatter make der bows en call 'er Mistiss. Ef ole Miss wuz 'live, dey wouldn't be no sech gwines on 'roun' yer. But nummin'. You des let 'er come a-cuttin' up front er my do', en I lay you'll year squallin'. Now, den," continued the old man, settling himself back in his chair, "whar'bouts wuz I?"

"You said there was a tale about the rabbit foot," the little boy replied.

"So dey is, honey! so dey is!" Uncle Remus exclaimed, "but she got so many crooks en tu'ns in 'er dat I dunner but w'at I ain't done gone en fergotted some un um off'n my min'; kaze ole folks lak me knows lots mo' dan w'at dey kin 'member.

"In de days w'ence Brer Rabbit wuz sorter keepin' de neighborhoods stirred up, de yuther creeturs wuz studyin' en studyin' de whole blessid time how dey gwine ter nab 'im. Dey ain't had no holiday yit, kaze w'en de holiday come, dey'd go ter wuk, dey would, en juggle wid one er n'er fer ter see how dey gwine ter ketch up wid Brer Rabbit. Bimeby, w'en all der plans, en der traps, en der jugglements ain't do no good, dey all 'gree, dey did, dat Brer Rabbit got some cunjerment w'at he trick um wid. Brer B'ar, he up'n 'low, he did, dat he boun' Brer Rabbit is a nat'al bawn witch; Brer Wolf say, sezee, dat he 'speck Brer Rabbit des in ca-hoots wid a witch; en Brer Fox, he vow dat Brer Rabbit got mo' luck dan smartness. Den Jedge B'ar, he drap he head one side, he did, en he ax how come Brer Rabbit got all de luck on he own side. De mo' dey ax, de mo' dey git pestered, en de mo' dey git pestered, de wuss dey worry. Day in en day out dey wuk wid dis puzzlement; let 'lone dat, dey sot up nights; en bimeby dey 'gree 'mungs deyse'f dat dey better make up wid Brer Rabbit, en see ef dey can't fin' out how come he so lucky.

"W'iles all dis gwine on, ole Brer Rabbit wuz a-gallopin' 'roun' fum Funtown ter Frolicville, a-kickin' up de devilment en terrifyin' de neighbor-hoods. Hit keep on dis a-way, twel one time, endurin' de odd-come-shorts, ole Jedge B'ar sont wud dat one er his chilluns done bin tooken wid a sickness, en he ax won't ole Miss Rabbit drap 'roun' en set up wid 'im. Ole Miss Rabbit, she say, co'se she go, en atter she fill 'er satchy full er yerbs en truck, off she put.

"I done fergit," said Uncle Remus, scratching his head gravely, "w'ich one er dem chilluns wuz ailin'. Hit mought er bin Kubs, en hit moughter bin Klibs; but no marter fer dat. W'en ole Miss Rabbit git dar, ole Miss B'ar wuz a-settin' up in de chimbley-cornder des a-dosin' en a-nussin' de young un; en all de wimmin er de neighborhoods wuz dar, a-whispun en a-talkin', des fer all de worl' lak wimmin does deze days. It 'uz:

"'Come right in, Sis Rabbit! I mighty proud to see you. I mighty glad you fotch yo' knittin', kaze I'm powful po' comp'ny w'en my chillun sick. Des fling yo' bonnet on de bed dar. I'm dat flustrated twel I dunner w'ich een's up, skacely. Sis Wolf, han' Sis Rabbit dat rockin'-cheer dar, kaze 'tain't no one step fum her house ter mine.'

"Dat de way ole Miss B'ar run on," continued Uncle Remus, "en dey set dar en dey chatter en dey clatter. Ole Brer Wolf, he 'uz settin' out on de back peazzer smokin' en noddin'. He 'ud take en draw a long whiff, he would, en den he 'ud drap off ter noddin' en let de smoke oozle out thoo he nose. Bimeby ole Sis Rabbit drap 'er knittin' in 'er lap, en sing out, sez she:

"'Law, Sis B'ar! I smells 'backer smoke,' sez she.

"Ole Sis B'ar, she jolt up de sick baby, en swap it fum one knee ter de yuther, en 'low:

"'My ole man bin smokin' 'roun' yer de whole blessid day, but soon'z dish yer chile tuck sick, I des tuck'n tole 'im, sez I, fer ter take hisse'f off in de woods whar he b'long at, sez I. Yessum! I did dat! I pities any 'oman w'at 'er ole man is fer'verlastin' stuck 'roun' de house w'en dey's any sickness gwine on,' sez she.

"Ole Brer Wolf sot out dar on de back peazzer, en he shot one eye, he did, en open um 'g'in, en let de smoke oozle out'n he nose. Sis B'ar, she jolt de sick baby en swap it fum one knee ter de yuther. Dey sot dar en talk twel bimeby der confab sorter slack up. Fus' news dey know Sis Rabbit drap 'er knittin' en fling up 'er han's en squall out:

"'De gracious en de goodness! Ef I ain't done come traipsin' off en lef' my ole man money-pus, en he got sump'n' in dar w'at he won't take a purty fer, needer! I'm dat fergitful,' sez she, 'twel hit keep me mizerbul mighty nigh de whole time,' sez she.

"Brer Wolf, he lif' up he year en open he eye, en let de smoke oozle out'n he nose. Sis B'ar, she jolt de sick baby wuss en wuss, en bimeby, she up'n say, sez she:

"'I mighty glad 'tain't me, dat I is,' sez she, 'bekaze ef I wuz ter lef' my ole man money-pus layin' 'roun' dat a-way, he'd des nat'ally rip up de planks in de flo', en t'ar all de bark off'n de trees,' sez she.

"Ole Miss Rabbit, she sot dar, she did, en she rock en study en study en rock, en she dunner w'at ter do. Ole Sis B'ar, she jolt en jolt de baby. Ole Brer Wolf, he let de 'backer smoke oozle thoo he nose, he did, en den he open bofe eyes en lay he pipe down. Wid dat, he crope down de back steps en lit out fer Brer Rabbit house. Brer Wolf got gait same lak race-hoss, en it ain't take 'im long fer ter git whar he gwine. W'en he git ter Brer Rabbit house, he pull de latch-string en open de do', en w'en he do dis, one er de little Rabs wake up, en he holler out:

"'Dat you, mammy?'

"Den Brer Wolf wish he kin sing 'Bye-O-Baby,' but 'fo' he kin make answer, de little Rab holler out 'g'in:

"'Dat you, mammy?'

"Ole Brer Wolf know he got ter do sump'n', so he tuck'n whisper, he did:

"'Sh-sh-sh! Go ter sleep, honey. De boogers'll git you!' en wid dat de little Rab 'gun ter whimple, en he whimple hisse'f off ter sleep.

"Den w'en it seem lak de little Rabs, w'ich dey wuz mighty nigh forty-eleven un ums, is all gone ter sleep, Brer Wolf he crop 'roun', he did, en feel on de mantel-shelf, en feel, en feel, twel he come ter ole Brer Rabbit money-pus. Ef he wa'n't so light wid he han'," Uncle Remus went on, glancing quizzically at the child, "he'd a knock off de pollygollic vial w'at ole Miss Rabbit put up dar. But nummin'! Brer Wolf, he feel, en feel, twel he come ter de money-pus, en he grab dat, he did, en he des flew'd away fum dar.

"W'en he git out er sight en year'n', Brer Wolf look at de money-pus, en see w'at in it. Hit 'uz one er deze yer kinder money-pus wid tossle on de een' en shiny rings in de middle. Brer Wolf look in dar fer ter see w'at he kin see. In one een' dey wuz a piece er calamus-root en some collard-seeds, en in de t'er een' dey wuz a great big rabbit foot. Dis make Brer Wolf feel mighty good, en he gallop off home wid de shorance un a man w'at done foun' a gol' mine."

Here Uncle Remus paused and betrayed a disposition to drop off to sleep. The little boy, however, touched him upon the knee, and asked him what Brother Rabbit did when he found his foot was gone. Uncle Remus laughed and rubbed his eyes.

"Hit's mighty kuse 'bout Brer Rabbit, honey. He ain't miss dat money-pus fer mighty long time, yet w'en he do miss it, he miss it mighty bad. He miss it so bad dat he git right-down sick, kaze he know he bleedzd ter fin' dat ar foot let go w'at may, let come w'at will. He study en he study, yit 'tain't do no good, en he go all 'roun' 'lowin' ter hisse'f:

"'I know whar I put dat foot, yit I dunner whar I lef' um; I know whar I put dat foot, yit I dunner whar I lef' um.'

"He mope en he mope 'roun'. Look lak Brer Wolf got all de luck en Brer Rabbit ain't got none. Brer Wolf git fat, Brer Rabbit git lean; Brer Wolf run fas', Brer Rabbit lope heavy lak ole Sis Cow; Brer Wolf feel funny, Brer Rabbit feel po'ly. Hit keep on dis a-way, twel bimeby Brer Rabbit know sump'n' n'er bleedzd ter be done. Las' he make up he min' fer ter take a journey, en he fix up he tricks, he do, en he go en see ole Aunt Mammy-Bammy Big-Money."

"And who was old Aunt Mammy-Bammy Big-Money, Uncle Remus?" the little boy inquired.

"Ah-yi!" exclaimed Uncle Remus, in a tone of triumph, "I know'd w'en I fotch dat ole creetur name up, dey wa'n't gwine ter be no noddin' 'roun' dish yer h'a'th. In dem days," he continued, "dey wuz a Witch-Rabbit, en dat wuz her entitlements — ole Aunt Mammy-Bammy Big-Money. She live way off in a deep, dark swamp, en ef you go dar you hatter ride some, slide some; jump some, hump some; hop some, flop some; walk some, balk some; creep some, sleep some; fly some, cry some; foller some, holler some; wade some, spade some; en ef you ain't monstus keerful you ain't git dar den. Yit Brer Rabbit he git dar atter so long a time, en he mighty nigh wo' out.

"He sot down, he did, fer ter res' hisse'f, en bimeby he see black smoke comin' outer de hole in de groun' whar de ole Witch-Rabbit stay.

Smoke git blacker en blacker, en atter w'ile Brer Rabbit know de time done come fer 'im ter open up en tell w'at he want."

As Uncle Remus interpreted the dialogue, Brother Rabbit spoke in a shrill, frightened tone, while the voice of the Rabbit-Witch was hoarse and oracular:

"'Mammy-Bammy Big-Money, I needs yo' he'p.'

"'Son Riley Rabbit, why so? Son Riley Rabbit, why so?'

"'Mammy-Bammy Big-Money, I los' de foot you gim me.'

"'O Riley Rabbit, why so? Son Riley Rabbit, why so?'

"'Mammy-Bammy Big-Money, my luck done gone. I put dat foot down 'pon de groun'. I lef' um dar I know not whar.'

"'De Wolf done tuck en stole yo' luck, Son Riley Rabbit, Riley. Go fin' de track, go git hit back, Son Riley Rabbit, Riley.'

"Wid dat," continued Uncle Remus, "ole Aunt Mammy-Bammy Big-Money sucked all de black smoke back in de hole in de groun', and Brer Rabbit des put out fer home. W'en he git dar, w'at do he do? Do he go off in a cornder by hisse'f, en wipe he weepin' eye? Dat he don't — dat he don't. He des tuck'n wait he chance. He wait en he wait; he wait all day, he wait all night; he wait mighty nigh a mont'. He hang 'roun' Brer Wolf house; he watch en he wait.

"Bimeby, one day, Brer Rabbit git de news dat Brer Wolf des come back fum a big frolic. Brer Rabbit know he time comin', en he keep bofe eye open en bofe years h'ist up. Nex' mawnin' atter Brer Wolf git back fum de big frolic, Brer Rabbit see 'im come outer de house en go down de spring atter bucket water. Brer Rabbit, he slip up, he did, en he look in. Ole Miss Wolf, she 'uz sailin' 'roun' fryin' meat en gittin' brekkus, en dar hangin' 'cross er cheer wuz Brer Wolf wes'cut where he keep he money-pus. Brer Rabbit rush up ter do' en pant lak he mighty nigh fag out. He rush up, he did, en he sing out:

"'Mawnin', Sis Wolf, mawnin'! Brer Wolf sont me atter de shavin'-brush, w'ich he keep it in dat ar money-pus w'at I loant 'im.'

"Sis Wolf, she fling up 'er han's en let um drap, en she laugh en say, sez she:

"'I 'clar' ter gracious, Brer Rabbit! You gimme sech a tu'n, dat I ain't got room ter be perlite skacely.'

"But mos' 'fo' she git de wuds out'n 'er mouf, Brer Rabbit done grab de money-pus en gone!"

"Which way did he go, Uncle Remus?" the little boy asked, after a while.

"Well, I tell you dis," Uncle Remus responded emphatically, "Brer Rabbit road ain't lay by de spring; I boun' you dat!"

Presently 'Tildy put her head in the door to say that it was bedtime, and shortly afterward the child was dreaming that Daddy Jack was Mammy-Bammy Big-Money in disguise.

31
"In Some Lady's Garden"

WHEN THE LITTLE BOY next visited Uncle Remus the old man was engaged in the somewhat tedious operation of making shoe-pegs. Daddy Jack was assorting a bundle of sassafras roots, and Aunt Tempy was transforming a meal-sack into shirts for some of the little Negroes — a piece of economy of her own devising. Uncle Remus pretended not to see the child.

"Hit's des lak I tell you," he remarked, as if renewing a conversation; "I monstus glad dey ain't no bad chilluns on dis place fer ter be wadin' in de spring-branch en flingin' mud on de yuther little chilluns, w'ich de goodness knows dey er nasty nuff widout dat. I monstus glad dey ain't none er dat kinder young uns 'roun' yer — I is dat."

"Now, Uncle Remus," exclaimed the little boy, in an injured tone, "somebody's been telling you something on me."

The old man appeared to be very much astonished.

"Heyo! whar you bin hidin', honey? Yer 'tis mos' way atter supper en you ain't in de bed yit. Well — well — well! Sit over ag'in de chimbley jam dar whar you kin dry dem hoes. En de ve'y nex' time w'at I see you wadin' in dat branch, wid de sickly season comin' on, I'm a-gwine ter take you 'cross my shoulder en kyar' you ter Miss Sally, en ef dat ain't do no good, den I'll kyar' you ter Mars John, en ef dat ain't do no good, den I'm done wid you, so dar now!"

The little boy sat silent a long time, listening to the casual talk of Uncle Remus and his guests, and watching the vapor rise from his wet shoes. Presently there was a pause in the talk, and the child said:

"Uncle Remus, have I been too bad to hear a story?"

The old man straightened himself up and pushed his spectacles back on his forehead.

"Now, den, folks, you year w'at he say. Shill we pursue on atter de creeturs? Shill er shan't?"

"Bless yo' soul, Brer Remus, I mos' 'shame' myse'f, yit I tell you de Lord's trufe, I'm des ez bad atter dem ar tales ez dat chile dar."

"Well, den," said Uncle Remus, "a tale hit is. One time dey wuz a man, en dish yer man he had a gyardin. He had a gyardin, en he had a little gal fer ter min' it. I don't 'speck dish yer gyardin wuz wide lak Miss Sally gyardin, but hit 'uz lots longer. Hit 'uz so long dat it run down side er de big road, 'cross by de plum thicket, en back up de lane. Dish yer gyardin wuz so nice en long dat it tuck'n 'track de 'tention er Brer Rabbit; but de fence wuz built so close en so high, dat he can't git in nohow he kin fix it."

"Oh, I know about that!" exclaimed the little boy. "The man catches Brother Rabbit and ties him, and the girl lets him loose to see him dance."

Uncle Remus dropped his chin upon his bosom. He seemed to be humbled.

"Sis Tempy," he said, with a sigh, "you'll hatter come in some time w'en we ain't so crowded, en I'll up en tell 'bout Billy Malone en Miss Janey."

"*That* wasn't the story I heard, Uncle Remus," said the little boy. "*Please* tell me about Billy Malone and Miss Janey."

"Ah-yi!" exclaimed Uncle Remus, with a triumphant smile; "I 'low'd maybe I wa'n't losin' de use er my 'membunce, en sho nuff I ain't. Now, den, we'll des wuk our way back en start fa'r en squar'. One time dey wuz a man, en dish yer man he had a gyardin en a little gal. De gyardin wuz chock full er truck, en in de mawnin's, w'en de man hatter go off, he call up de little gal, he did, en tell 'er dat she mus' be sho en keep ole Brer Rabbit outer de gyardin. He tell 'er dis eve'y mawnin'; but one mawnin' he tuck en forgit it twel he git ter de front gate, en den he stop en holler back:

"'O Janey! You Janey! Min' w'at I tell you 'bout ole Brer Rabbit. Don't you let 'im get my nice green peas.'

"Little gal, she holler back: 'Yes, daddy.'

"All dis time, Brer Rabbit he 'uz settin' out dar in de bushes dozin'. Yit, w'en he year he name call out so loud, he cock up one year en lissen, en he 'low ter hisse'f dat he bleedzd ter outdo Mr. Man. Bimeby, Brer Rabbit, he went 'roun' en come down de big road des ez nat'al ez ef he bin trafflin' somers. He see de little gal settin' by de gate, en he up'n 'low:

"'Ain't dish yer Miss Janey?'

"Little gal say: 'My daddy call me Janey.'" Uncle Remus mimicked the voice and manner of a little girl. He hung his head, looked excessively modest, and spoke in a shrill tone. The effect was so comical that even Daddy Jack seemed to enjoy it.

"'My daddy call me Janey; w'at yo' daddy call you?'

"Brer Rabbit look on de groun', en sorter study lak folks does w'en dey feels bad. Den he look up en 'low:

"'I bin lose my daddy dis many long year, but w'en he 'live he call me Billy Malone.' Den he look at de little gal hard en 'low: 'Well, well, well! I ain't seed you sence you 'uz a little bit er baby, en now yer you is mighty nigh a grown 'oman. I pass yo' daddy in de road des now, en he say I mus' come en tell you fer ter gimme a mess er sparrer-grass.'

"Little gal, she fling de gate wide open, en let Mr. Billy Malone git de sparrer-grass.

"Man come back en see whar somebody done bin tromplin' on de gyardin truck, en den he call up de little gal, en up'n ax 'er who bin dar since he bin gone; en de little gal, she 'low, she did, dat Mr. Billy Malone bin dar. Man ax who in de name er goodness is Mr. Billy Malone. Little gal 'low hit's des a man w'at say 'er daddy sont 'im fer ter git some sparrer-grass on account er ole acquaintance. Man got his 'spicions, but he ain't say nothin'.

"Nex' day, w'en he start off, he holler en tell de little gal fer ter keep one eye on ole Brer Rabbit, en don't let nobody git no mo' sparrer-grass. Brer Rabbit, he settin' off dar in de bushes, en he year w'at de man say, en he see 'im w'en he go off. Bimeby, he sorter run 'roun', ole Brer Rabbit did, en come hoppin' down de road, twel he git close up by de little gal at de gyardin gate. Brer Rabbit drapt 'er his biggest bow, en ax 'er how she come on. Den, atter dat, he low', he did:

"'I see yo' daddy gwine 'long down de road des now, en he gimme a rakin' down kaze I make 'way wid de sparrer-grass, yit he say dat bein's how I sech a good fr'en' er de fambly I kin come en ax you fer ter gimme a mess er Inglish peas.'

"Little gal, she tuck'n fling de gate wide open, en ole Brer Rabbit, he march in, he did, en he git de peas in a hurry. Man come back atter w'ile, en he 'low:

"'Who bin tromplin' down my pea-vines?'

"'Mr. Billy Malone, daddy.'

"'Man slap he han' on he forrud; he dunner w'at ter make er all dis. Bimeby, he 'low:

"'W'at kinder lookin' man dish yer Mr. Billy Malone?'

"'Split lip, pop eye, big year, en bob-tail, daddy.'

"Man say he be bless ef he ain't gwine ter make de acquaintance er Mr. Billy Malone; en he went ter wuk, he did, en fix 'im up a box-trap, en he put some goobers in dar, en he tell de little gal nex' time Mr. Billy Malone come fer 'vite 'im in. Nex' mawnin', Man git little ways fum de house en tuck'n holler back, he did:

"'Whatsumever you does, don't you dast ter let nobody git no mo' sparrer-grass, en don't you let um git no mo' Inglish peas.'

"Little gal holler back: 'No, daddy.'

"Den, atter dat, 'twa'n't long 'fo' yer come Mr. Billy Malone, hoppin' 'long down de big road. He drapt a bow, he did, en 'low:

"'Mawnin', Miss Janey, mawnin'! Met yo' daddy down de big road, en he say dat I can't git no mo' sparrer-grass en green peas, but you kin gimme some goobers.'

"Little gal, she lead de way, en tell Mr. Billy Malone dar dey is in de box. Mr. Billy Malone, he lick he chops, he did, en 'low:

"'You oughter be monstus glad, honey, dat you got sech a good daddy lak dat.'

"Wid dat, Mr. Billy Malone wunk he off eye, en jump in de box."

"W'at I done tell you!" exclaimed Aunt Tempy.

"He jump in de box," continued Uncle Remus, "en dar he wuz, en ef de little gal hadder bin a minnit bigger, I lay she'd a tuck'n done some mighty tall winkin'.

"Man ain't gone fur, en 'twa'n't long 'fo' yer he come back. W'en Brer

Rabbit year 'im comin' he bounce 'roun' in dar same ez a flea in a piller-case, but 'tain't do no good. Trap done fall, en Brer Rabbit in dar. Man look thoo de slats, en 'low:

"'Dar you is — same old hoppum-skippum run en jumpum. You er de ve'y chap I'm atter. I want yo' foot fer ter kyar in my pocket, I want yo' meat fer ter put in de pot, en I want yo' hide fer ter w'ar on my head.'

"Dis make col' chill rush up en down Brer Rabbit backbone, en he git more 'umble dan a town nigger w'at been kotch out atter nine er clock.[1] He holler en cry, en cry en holler:

"'Do pray, Mr. Man, tu'n me go! I done 'ceive you dis time, but I ain't gwine ter 'ceive you no mo'. Do pray, Mr. Man, tu'n me go, des dis little bit er time.'

"Man he ain't sayin' nothin'. He look lak he studyin' 'bout somp'n' n'er way off yan', en den he take de little gal by de han' en go off todes de house."

"Sholy Brer Rabbit time done come now!" exclaimed Aunt Tempy, in a tone of mingled awe and expectation.

Uncle Remus paid no attention to the interruption, but went right on:

"Hit seem lak dat Brer Rabbit got mo' luck dan w'at you kin shake a stick at, kaze de men en de little gal ain't good en gone skacely twel yer come Brer Fox a-pirootin' 'roun'. Brer Fox year Brer Rabbit holl'in' en he up'n ax w'at de 'casion er sech gwines on right dar in de broad open daylight. Brer Rabbit squall out:

"'Lordy, Brer Fox! you better make 'as'e 'way fum yer, kaze Mr. Man ull ketch you en slap you in dish yer box en make you eat mutton twel you ull des nat'ally bus' right wide open. Run, Brer Fox, run! He bin feedin' me on mutton the whole blessid mawnin' en now he done gone atter mo'. Run, Brer Fox, run!'

"Yit, Brer Fox ain't run. He up'n ax Brer Rabbit how de mutton tas'e.

"'He tas'e mighty good 'long at fus', but nuff's a nuff, en too much is a plenty. Run, Brer Fox, run! He ull ketch you, sho!'

"Yit, Brer Fox ain't run. He up'n 'low dat he b'lieve he want some

---

[1] During slavery, the ringing of the nine-o'clock bell in the towns and villages at night was the signal for all Negroes to retire to their quarters. — J. C. H.

mutton hisse'f, en wid dat he onloose de trap en let Brer Rabbit out, en den tuck'n git in dar. Brer Rabbit ain't wait fer ter see what de upshot gwine ter be, needer — I boun' you he ain't. He des tuck'n gallop off in de woods, en he laff en laff twel he hatter hug a tree fer ter keep fum drappin' on de groun'."

"Well, but what became of Brother Fox?" the little boy asked, after waiting some time for Uncle Remus to proceed.

"Now, den, honey," said the old man, falling back upon his dignity, "hit e'en about takes all my spar' time fer ter keep up wid you en Brer Rabbit, let 'lone keepin' up wid Brer Fox. Ole Brer Rabbit tuck'n tuck keer hisse'f, en now let Brer Fox take keer hisse'f."

"I say de word!" exclaimed Aunt Tempy.

32
Brother 'Possum Gets in Trouble

WHEN UNCLE REMUS began his story of Billy Malone and Miss Janey, Daddy Jack sat perfectly quiet. His eyes were shut, and he seemed to be dozing; but, as the story proceeded, he grew more and more restless. Several times he was upon the point of interrupting Uncle Remus, but he restrained himself. He raised his hands to a level with his chin, and beat the ends of his fingers gently together, apparently keeping time to his own thoughts. But his impatience exhausted itself, and when Uncle Remus had concluded, the old African was as quiet as ever. When Brother Fox was left so unceremoniously to his fate, Daddy Jack straightened himself temporarily and said:

"Me yent bin-a yerry de tale so. 'E nice, fer true, 'e mek lahf come; oona no bin-a yerry um lak me."

"No," said Uncle Remus, with grave affability, "I 'speck not. One man, one tale; n'er man, n'er tale. Folks tell um diffunt. I boun' yo' way de bes', Brer Jack. Out wid it — en we ull set up yer, en hark at you en laff wid you plum' twel de chick'ns crow."

Daddy Jack needed no other invitation. He clasped his knee in his hands and began:

"Dey is bin lif one Màn wut plan' some pea in 'e geerden. 'E plan'
some pea, but 'e mek no pea; B'er Rabbit, 'e is fine um. 'E fine um un 'e
eat um. Màn mek no pea, B'er Rabbit 'e 'stroy um so. 'E plan' dem pea;
dey do grow, un 'e go off. 'E come bahk; pea no dere. B'er Rabbit teer um
up un mek 'e cud wit' dem. So long tam, Màn say 'e gwan ketch um, un
'e no ketch um. Màn go, B'er Rabbit come; Màn come, B'er Rabbit go.
Bumbye, Màn, 'e is git so mad, 'e y-eye bin-a come red; 'e crack 'e toof,
'e do cuss. 'E oby 'e gwan ketch B'er Rabbit nohow. Dun 'e is bin-a call
'e lilly gal. 'E talk, 'e tell 'im fer let B'er Rabbit go troo da geerden gett
Lil gal say yasser. 'E talk, 'e tell 'im wun B'er Rabbit go troo da gett, dun
'e mus' shed da gett, un no le'm come pas' no mo'. Lil gal say yasser.

"Ole Màn is bin-a gone 'bout 'e wuk; lil gal, 'e do lissun. B'er Rabbit,
'e come tippy-toe, tippy-toe; gone in da geerden; eat dem pea tel 'e full
up; eat tel he mos' git seeck wit' dem pea. Dun 'e start fer go out; 'e fine
da gett shed. 'E shek um, 'e no open; 'e push um, 'e no open; 'e fair grunt,
'e push hard 'e no open. 'E bin-a call da lil gal; 'e say:

"'Lil gal, lil gal! cum y-open da gett. 'T is hu't me feelin' fer fine da
gett shed lak dis.'

"Lil gal no talk nuttin'. B'er Rabbit say:

"'Tis-a bin hu't me feelin', lil gal! Come y-open da gett, lil gal, less
I teer um loose from da hinch.'

"Lil gal v'ice come bahk. 'E talk:

"'Daddy say mus'n'.'

"B'er Rabbit open 'e mout'. 'E say:

"'See me long sha'p toof? 'E bite you troo un troo!'

"Lil gal skeer; 'e tu'n loose de gett un fly. B'er Rabbit *gone!* Ole Màn
come bahk; 'e ahx 'bout B'er Rabbit. Lil gal say:

"''E done gone, daddy. I shed da gett, I hol' um fas'. B'er Rabbit bin
show 'e toof; 'e gwan fer bite-a me troo un troo. I git skeer, daddy.' Màn ahx:

"'How 'e gwin fer bite you troo un troo, wun 'e toof fix bite grass? B'er
Rabbit tell one big tale. 'E no kin bite-a you. Wun 'e come 'g'in, you shed
dem gett, you hol' um tight, you no le'm go pas' no mo'.' Lil gal say yasser.

"Nex' day mawnin', Màn go 'long 'bout 'e wuk. Lil gal, 'e play 'roun',
un 'e play 'roun'. B'er Rabbit, 'e is come tippy-tippy. 'E fine gett open; 'e
slip in da geerden. 'E chew dem pea, 'e gnyaw dem pea; 'e eat tel dem

pea tas'e bad. Dun 'e try fer go out; gett shed fas'. 'E no kin git troo. 'E push, gett no open; 'e keeck wit' um fut, gett no open; 'e butt wit' um head, gett no open. Dun 'e holler:

"'Lil gal, lil gal! come y-open da gett. 'E berry bad fer fool wit' ole màn lak me. I no kin hol' me feelin' down wun you is do lak dis. 'E berry bad.'

"Lil gal hol' 'e head down; 'e no say nuttin'. B'er Rabbit say:

"'Be shame, lil gal, fer do ole man lak dis. Me feelin' git wusser. Come y-open de gett 'fo' I is teer um down.'

"Lil gal say: 'Daddy say mus'n'.'

"B'er Rabbit open 'e y-eye wide; 'e is look berry mad. 'E say:

"'See me big y-eye? I pop dis y-eye stret at you, me kill-a you dead. Come y-open da gett 'fo' me y-eye pop.'

"Lil gal skeer fer true. 'E loose de gett, 'e fair fly. B'er Rabbit done *gone!* Lil gal daddy bahk. 'E ahx wey is B'er Rabbit. Lil gal say:

"''E done gone, daddy. I hol' gett fas'; 'e is bin-a 'come berry mad. 'E say he gwan pop 'e y-eye at me, shoot-a me dead.' Màn say:

"'B'er Rabbit tell-a too big tale. How 'e gwan shoot-a you wit' 'e y-eye? 'E y-eye sem lak turrer folks y-eye. Wun 'e come some mo', you shed dem gett, you hol' um fas'.' Lil gal say yasser.

"Nex' day mawnin', Màn go, B'er Rabbit come. 'E is ma'ch in de gett un eat-a dem pea tel 'e kin eat-a no mo'. 'E sta't out; gett shed. 'E no kin come pas'. 'E shek, 'e push, 'e pull; gett shed. Dun 'e holler:

"'Lil gal, lil gal! come y-open da gett. 'Tis berry bad fer treat you' kin lak dis. Come y-open da gett, lil gal. 'Tis full me up wit' sorry wun you do lak dis.'

"Lil gal, 'e no say nuttin'. B'er Rabbit say:

"''E berry bad fer treat you' kin lak dis. Tu'n go da gett, lil gal.' Lil gal say:

"''How you is kin wit' me, B'er Rabbit?'

"''You' gran'daddy foller at' me nuncle wit' 'e dog. Da mek we is kin. Come y-open da gett, lil gal.'"

"Dat ole Rabbit wuz a-talkin', mon!" exclaimed Aunt Tempy, enthusiastically.

"Lil gal no say nuttin' 'tall!" Daddy Jack went on with renewed animation. "Dun B'er Rabbit say:

"'See me long, sha'p toof, lil gal? Me bite-a you troo un troo.' Lil gal say:

"'Me no skeer da toof. 'E bite nuttin' 'tall 'cep' 'e bite grass.' B'er Rabbit say:

"'See me big y-eye? I pop um at you, shoot-a you dead.' Lil gal say:

"'Me no skeer da y-eye. 'E sem lak turrer folks y-eye.' B'er Rabbit say:

"'Lil gal, you mek me 'come mad. I no lak fer hu't-a me kin. Look at me ho'n! I run you troo un troo.'

"B'er Rabbit lif' 'e two year up; 'e p'int um stret at da lil gal. Lil gal 'come skeer da ho'n; e' do tu'n go da gett; 'e fly fum dey-dey."

"Well, ef dat don't beat!" exclaimed Aunt Tempy, laughing as heartily as the little boy. "Look at um one way, en Rabbit year does look lak sho nuff ho'ns."

"Lil gal tu'n go da gett," Daddy Jack continued: "B'er Rabbit *gone!* Màn come bahk; 'e ahx wey is B'er Rabbit. Lil gal cry; 'e say 'e skeer Brer Rabbit ho'n. Màn say 'e is hab no ho'n. Lil gal is stan' um down 'e see ho'n. Màn say da ho'n is nuttin' 'tall but B'er Rabbit year wut 'e yeddy wit'. 'E tell lil gal nex' tam B'er Rabbit come, 'e must' shed da gett; 'e mus' run fum dey-dey un leaf um shed. Lil gal say yasser.

"Màn gone, B'er Rabbit come. 'E is go in da gett; 'e eat-a dem pea tel 'e tire'. 'E try fer go pas' da gett, gett shed. 'E call lil gal; lil gal *gone!* 'E call, call, call; lil gal no yeddy. 'E try fer fine crack in da palin'; no crack dey. 'E try fer jump over; de palin' too high. 'E 'come skeer; 'e is 'come so skeer 'e squot 'pun da groun'; 'e shek, 'e shiver.

"Màn come bahk. 'E ahx wey B'er Rabbit. Lil gal say 'e in da geerden. Màn hug lil gal, 'e is lub um so. 'E go in da geerden; 'e fine B'er Rabbit. 'E ketch um — 'e ca' um off fer kill um; 'e mad fer true. Lil gal come holler:

"'Daddy, daddy! missus say run dere! 'E wan' you come stret dere!'

"Màn tie B'er Rabbit in da bag; 'e hang um on tree lim'. 'E say:

"'I gwan come bahk. I l'arn you fer mek cud wit' me green pea.'

"Màn gone fer see 'e missus. Bumbye, B'er 'Possum is bin-a come pas'. 'E look up, 'e ketch glimp' da bag 'pun da lim'. 'E say:

"'Ki! Wut dis is bin-a hang in da bag 'pun da tree-lim'?' B'er Rabbit say:

"'Hush, B'er 'Possum! 'Tis-a me. I bin-a lissen at dem sing in da cloud.'

"B'er 'Possum lissen. 'E say:

"'I no yed dem sing, B'er Rabbit.'

"'Hush, B'er 'Possum! How is I kin yeddy dem sing wun you is mek-a da fuss dey-dey?'

"B'er 'Possum, 'e hol' 'e mout' still, 'cep' 'e do grin. B'er Rabbit say:

"'I yed dem now! I yed dem now! B'er 'Possum, I wish you is yeddy dem sing!'

"B'er 'Possum say 'e mout' water fer yeddy dem sing in da cloud. B'er Rabbit, 'e say 'e is bin-a hab so long tam 'quaintun wit' B'er 'Possum, 'e le'm yeddy dem sing. 'E say:

"'I git fum da bag, I tu'n-a you in tel you is yeddy dem sing. Dun you is git fum da bag, tel I do come bahk un 'joy mese'f.'

"B'er 'Possum, 'e do clam up da tree; 'e git dem bag, 'e bring um down. 'E tak off da string; 'e tu'n B'er Rabbit go. 'E crawl in un 'e quile up. 'E say:

"'I no yeddy dem sing, B'er Rabbit!'

"'Hi! wait tel da bag it tie, B'er 'Possum. You yed dem soon nuff!' 'E wait.

"'I no yeddy dem sing, B'er Rabbit!'

"'Hi! wait tel I clam da tree, B'er 'Possum. You yed dem soon nuff!' 'E wait.

"'I no yeddy dem sing, B'er Rabbit!'

"'Wait tel I fix um 'pun da lim', B'er 'Possum. You yed dem soon nuff!' 'E wait.

"B'er Rabbit clam down; 'e run 'way fum dey-dey; 'e hide in da bush side. Màn come bahk. 'E see de bag moof. B'er 'Possum say:

"'I no yeddy dem sing. I wait fer yed um sing!'

"Màn t'ink 'e B'er Rabbit in da bag. 'E say:

"'Ah-yi-ee! I mekky you yed dem sing!'

"Màn tek-a da bag fum da tree-lim'; 'e do slam da bag 'g'in' da face da ye't'. 'E tek-a 'e walkin'-cane, un 'e beat B'er 'Possum wut is do um no ha'm tel 'e mos' kill um. Màn t'ink B'er Rabbit mus' bin dead by dis. 'E look in da bag; 'e 'tretch 'e y-eye big; 'e 'stonish'. B'er Rabbit, 'e do come fum da bush side; 'e do holler, 'e do laff. 'E say:

"'You no is ketch-a me! I t'ief you' green pea — I t'ief um some mo' — I t'ief um tel I dead!'

"Màn, 'e 'come so mad, 'e is fling hatchet at B'er Rabbit un chop off 'e tail."

At this moment Daddy Jack subsided. His head drooped forward, and he was soon in the land of Nod. Uncle Remus sat gazing into the fireplace, as though lost in reflection. Presently, he laughed softly to himself, and said:

"Dat's des 'bout de long en de short un it. Mr. Man clip off Brer Rabbit tail wid de hatchet, en it bleed so free dat Brer Rabbit rush off ter de cotton-patch en put some lint on it, en down ter dis day dat lint mos' de fus' t'ing you see w'en Brer Rabbit jump out'n he bed en tell you good-bye."

"But, Uncle Remus, what became of Brother 'Possum?"

Uncle Remus smacked his lips and looked wise.

"Don't talk 'bout Brer 'Possum, honey, ef dat ar Mr. Man wuz nice folks lak we all is, en I ain't 'spute it, he tuck'n tuck Brer 'Possum en bobbycue 'im, en I wish I had a great big piece right now. Dat I does."

33
Why the Guinea-Fowls Are Speckled

ONE NIGHT, while the little boy was watching Uncle Remus broil a piece of bacon on the coals, he heard a great commotion among the guinea-fowls. The squawking and *pot-racking* went on at such a rate that the geese awoke and began to scream, and finally the dogs added their various voices to the uproar. Uncle Remus leaned back in his chair and listened.

"I 'speck may be dat's de patter-rollers gwine by," he said, after a while. "But you can't put no 'pennunce in dem ar Guinny-hins, kaze dey'll wake up en holler ef dey year deyse'f sno'. Dey'll fool you, sho."

"They are mighty funny, anyhow," said the little boy.

"Dat's it!" exclaimed Uncle Remus. "Dey looks quare, en dey does quare. Dey ain't do lak no yuther kinder chick'n, en dey ain't look lak no yuther kinder chick'n. Yit folks tell me," the old man went on, reflectively, "dat dey er heap mo' kuse lookin' now dan w'at dey useter be. I year tell dat dey wuz one time w'en dey wuz all blue, stidder havin' all dem ar teenchy little spots on um."

"Well, how did they get to be speckled, Uncle Remus?" asked the little boy, seeing that the old man was disposed to leave the subject and devote his attention to his broiling bacon.

Uncle Remus did not respond at once. He turned his meat over carefully, watched it a little while, and then adroitly transferred it to the cover of a tin bucket, which was made to answer the purpose of a plate. Then he searched about in the embers until he found his ashcake and in a little while his supper was ready to be eaten.

"I ain't begrudgin' nobody nothin'," said Uncle Remus, measuring the victuals with his eye; "yit I'm monstus glad Brer Jack ain't nowhar's 'roun', kaze dey ain't no tellin' de gawm dat ole nigger kin eat. He look shaky, en he look dry up, en he ain't got no toof, yit w'ence he set hisse'f down whar dey any vittles, he des nat'ally laps hit up. En let 'lone dat, he ull wipe he mouf en look 'roun' des lak he want mo'. Time Miss Sally see dat ole nigger eat one meal er vittles, I boun' you he hatter go back down de country. I ain't begrudgin' Brer Jack de vittles," Uncle Remus went on, adopting a more conciliatory tone, "dat I ain't, kaze folks is got ter eat; but, gentermens! you be 'stonish' w'en you see Brer Jack 'pesterin' 'long er he dinner."

The little boy sat quiet awhile, and then reminded Uncle Remus of the guinea-fowls.

"Tooby sho, honey, tooby sho! W'at I doin' runnin' on dis away 'bout ole Brer Jack? W'at he done ter me? Yer I is gwine on 'bout ole Brer Jack, en dem ar Guinny-hins out dar waitin'. Well, den, one day Sis Cow wuz a-grazin' 'bout in de ole fiel' en lookin' atter her calf. De wedder wuz kinder hot, en de calf, he tuck'n stan', he did, in he mammy shadder, so he kin keep cool, en so dat one flip un he mammy tail kin keep the flies off'n bofe un um. Atter w'ile, 'long come a drove er Guinnies. De Guinnies, dey howdied, en Sis Cow, she howdied, en de Guinnies, dey sorter picked 'roun' en sun deyse'f; en Sis Cow, she crap de grass en ax um de news er de neighborhoods. Dey went on dis a-way twel 'twa'n't long 'fo' dey year mighty kuse noise out dar t'er side er de ole fiel'. De Guinnies, dey make great 'miration, des lak dey does deze days, en ole Sis Cow fling up 'er head en look all 'roun'. She ain't see nothin'.

"Atter w'ile dey year de kuse fuss 'g'in, en dey look 'roun', en bless gracious! stan'in' right dar, 'twix' dem en sundown, wuz a great big Lion!"

"A Lion, Uncle Remus?" asked the little boy, in amazement.

"Des ez sho' ez you er settin' dar, honey — a great big Lion. You bet-ter b'lieve dey wuz a monstus flutterment 'mungs de Guinnies, en ole Sis Cow, she looked mighty skeer'd. De Lion love cow meat mos' better dan he do any yuther kinder meat, en he shake he head en 'low ter hisse'f dat he'll des about ketch ole Sis Cow en eat 'er up, en take en kyar' de calf ter he fambly.

"Den he tuck 'n shuck he head, de Lion did, en make straight at Sis Cow. De Guinnies dey run dis away, en dey run t'er way, en dey run all 'roun' en 'roun'; but ole Sis Cow, she des know she got ter stan' 'er groun', en w'en she see de Lion makin' todes 'er, she des tuck'n drapt 'er head down en pawed de dirt. De Lion, he crope up, he did, en crope 'roun', watchin' fer good chance fer ter make a jump. He crope 'roun', he did, but no diffunce w'ich away he creep, dar wuz ole Sis Cow hawns p'intin' right straight at 'im. Ole Sis Cow, she paw de dirt, she did, en show de white er her eyes, en beller way down in 'er stomach.

"Dey went on dis away, dey did, twel bimeby de Guinnies, dey see dat Sis Cow ain't so mighty skeer'd, en den dey 'gun ter take heart. Fus' news you know, one un um sorter drap he wings en fuzzle up de fedders en run out 'twix' Sis Cow en de Lion. W'en he get dar, he sorter dip down, he did, en fling up dirt des lak you see um do in de ash-pile. Den he tuck'n run back, he did, en time he git back, n'er one run out en raise de dus' 'twix' Sis Cow en de Lion. Den n'er one, he run out en dip down en shoo up de dus'; den n'er one run out en dip down, en n'er one en yit n'er one, twel, bless gracious! time dey all run out en dip down en raise de dus', de Lion wuz dat blin' twel he ain't kin see he han' befo' 'im. Dis make 'im so mad dat he make a plunge at Sis Cow, en de ole lady, she kotch 'im on her hawns en got 'im down, en des nat'ally to' intruls out."

"Did she kill the Lion, Uncle Remus?" asked the little boy, incredu-lously.

"Dat she did — dat she did! Yit 'tain't make 'er proud, kaze atter de Lion done gone en dead, she tuck en call up de Guinnies, she did, en she 'low, dey bin so quick fer ter he'p 'er out, dat she wanter pay um back. De Guinnies, dey say, sezee:

"'Don't bodder 'long er we all, Sis Cow,' sezee. 'You had yo' fun en we all had ourn, en 'ceppin' dat ar blood en ha'r on yo' hawn,' sezee, 'dey ain't none un us any de wuss off,' sezee.

"But ole Sis Cow, she stan' um down, she did, dat she got ter pay um back, en den atter w'ile she ax um w'at dey lak bes'.

"One un um up en make answer dat w'at dey lak bes', Sis Cow, she can't gi' um. Sis Cow, she up en 'low dat she dunno 'bout dat, en she ax um w'at is it.

"Den de Guinnies, dey tuck'n huddle up, dey did, en hol' er confab wid one er n'er, en w'iles dey er doin' dis, ole Sis Cow, she tuck'n fetch a long breff, en den she call up 'er cud, en stood dar chawin' on it des lak she ain't had no tribalation dat day.

"Bimeby one er de Guinnies step out fum de huddlement en make a bow en 'low dat dey all 'ud be mighty proud ef Sis Cow kin fix it some way so dey can't be seed so fur thoo de woods, kaze dey look blue in de sun, en dey look blue in de shade, en dey can't hide deyse'f nohow. Sis Cow, she chaw en 'er cud, en shet 'er eyes, en study. She chaw en chaw, en study en study. Bimeby she 'low:

"'Go fetch me a pail!' Guinny-hin laff!

"'Law, Sis Cow! w'at de name er goodness you gwine do wid a pail?'

"'Go fetch me a pail!'

"Guinny-hin, she run'd off, she did, en atter w'ile yer she come trottin' back wid a pail. She sot dat pail down," continued Uncle Remus, in the tone of an eye-witness to the occurrence, "en Sis Cow, she tuck 'er stan' over it, en she let down 'er milk in dar twel she mighty nigh fill de pail full. Den she tuck'n make dem Guinny-hins git in a row, en she dip 'er tail in dat ar pail, en she switch it at de fust un en sprinkle 'er all over wid de milk; en eve'y time she switch 'er tail at um she 'low:

"'I loves dis un!' Den she 'ud sing:

> "'Oh, Blue, go 'way! you shill not stay!
>   Oh, Guinny, be Gray, be Gray!'

"She tuck'n sprinkle de las' one un um, en de Guinnies, dey sot in de sun twel dey git dry, en fum dat time out dey got dem little speckles un um."

34
Brother Rabbit's Love-Charm

"DEY WUZ ONE TIME," said Uncle Remus one night, as they all sat around the wide hearth — Daddy Jack, Aunt Tempy, and the little boy in their accustomed places — "dey wuz one time w'en de t'er creeturs push Brer Rabbit so close dat he tuck up a kinder idee dat may be he wa'n't ez smart ez he mought be, en he study 'bout dis plum' twel he git humble ez de nex' man. 'Las' he 'low ter hisse'f dat he better make inquirements — "

"Ki!" exclaimed Daddy Jack, raising both hands and grinning excitedly, "wut tale dis? I bin yerry de tale wun I is bin wean't fum me mammy."

"Well, den, Brer Jack," said Uncle Remus, with instinctive deference to the rules of hospitality, "I 'speck you des better whirl in yer en spin 'er out. Ef you git 'er mix up anywhars I ull des slip in front er you en ketch holt whar you lef' off."

With that, Daddy Jack proceeded:

"One tam, B'er Rabbit is bin lub one noung leddy."

"Miss Meadows, I 'speck," suggested Uncle Remus, as the old African paused to rub his chin.

"'E no lub Miss Meadows nuttin' 't all!" exclaimed Daddy Jack, emphatically. "'E bin lub turrer noung leddy fum dat. 'E is bin lub werry nice noung leddy. 'E lub 'um hard, 'e lub 'um long, un 'e is gwan try fer mek dem noung leddy marry wit' 'im. Noung leddy seem lak 'e no look 'pon B'er Rabbit, un dis is bin-a mek B'er Rabbit feel werry bad all da day long. 'E moof 'way off by 'ese'f; 'e lose 'e fat, un 'e heer is bin-a come out. Bumbye, 'e see one ole Affiky màns wut is bin-a hunt in da fiel' fer root en yerrub fer mek 'e met'cine truck. 'E see um, un he go toze um. Affiky màns open 'e y-eye big; 'e 'stonish'. 'E say:

" 'Ki, B'er Rabbit! you' he'lt' is bin-a gone; 'e bin-a gone un lef' you. Wut mekky you is look so puny lak dis? Who is bin hu't-a you' feelin'?'

"B'er Rabbit lahf wit' dry grins. 'E say:

" 'Shoo! I bin got well. Ef you is see me wun I sick fer true, 't will mekky you heer stan' up, I skeer you so.'

"Affiky màns, 'e mek B'er Rabbit stick out 'e tongue; 'e is count B'er Rabbit pulse. 'E shekky 'e head; 'e do say:

" 'Hi, B'er Rabbit! Wut all dis? You is bin ketch-a da gal-fever, un 'e strak in 'pon you' gizzud.'

"Den B'er Rabbit, 'e is tell-a da Affiky màns 'bout dem noung leddy wut no look toze 'im, un da Affiky màns, 'e do say 'e bin know gal sem lak dat, 'e is bin shum befo'. 'E say 'e kin fix all dem noung leddy lak dat. B'er Rabbit, 'e is feel so good, 'e jump up high; 'e is bin crack 'e heel; 'e shekky da Affiky màns by de han'.

"Affiky màns, 'e say B'er Rabbit no kin git da gal 'cep' 'e is mek 'im one cha'm-bag. 'E say 'e mus' git one el'phan' tush, un 'e mus' git one 'gater toof, un 'e mus' git one rice-bud bill. B'er Rabbit werry glad 'bout dis, un 'e hop way fum dey-dey.

" 'E hop, 'e run, 'e jump all nex' day night, un bumbye 'e see one great big el'phan' come breakin' 'e way troo da woots. B'er Rabbit, 'e say:

" 'Ki! Oona big fer true! I bin-a yeddy talk 'bout dis in me y-own countree. Oona big fer true; too big fer be strong.'

"El'phan' say: 'See dis!'

" 'E tek pine tree in 'e snout; 'e pull um by da roots; 'e toss um way off. B'er Rabbit say:

" 'Hi! dem tree come 'cause you bin high; 'e no come 'cause you bin strong.'

"El'phan' say: 'See dis!'

"'E rush troo da woods; 'e fair teer um down. B'er Rabbit say:

"'Hoo! dem is bin-a saplin' wey you 'stroy. See da big pine? Oona no kin 'stroy dem.'

"El'phan' say: 'See dis!'

"'E run 'pon da big pine; da big pine is bin too tough. El'phan' tush stick in deer fer true; da big pine hol' um fas'. B'er Rabbit git-a dem tush; 'e fetch um wey da Affiky màns lif. Affiky màns say el'phan' is bin too big fer be sma't. 'E say 'e mus' haf one 'gater toof fer go wit el'phan' tush.

"B'er Rabbit, 'e do crack 'e heel; 'e do far fly fum dey-dey. 'E go 'long, 'e go 'long. Bumbye 'e come 'pon 'gater. Da sun shiün hot; da 'gater do joy 'ese'f. B'er Rabbit say:

"'Dis road, 'e werry bad; less we mek good one by da crickside.'

"'Gater lak dat. 'E wek 'ese'f up fum 'e head to 'e tail. Dey sta't fer clean da road. 'Gater, 'e do teer da bush wit' 'e toof; 'e sweep-a da trash way wit' 'e tail. B'er Rabbit, 'e do beat-a da bush down wit' 'e cane. 'E hit lef, 'e hit right; 'e hit up, 'e hit down; 'e hit all 'roun'. 'E hit un 'e hit, tel bumbye 'e hit 'gater in 'e mout' un knock-a da toof out. 'E grab um up; 'e gone fum dey-dey. 'E fetch-a da 'gater toof wey da Affiky màns lif. Affiky màns say:

"'"Gater is bin-a got sha'p toof fer true. Go fetch-a me one rice-bud bill.'

"B'er Rabbit gone! 'E go 'long, 'e go 'long, tel 'e see rice-bud swingin' on bush. 'E ahx um kin 'e fly.

"Rice-bud say: 'See dis!'

"'E wissle, 'e sing, 'e shek 'e wing; 'e fly all 'roun' un 'roun'.

"B'er Rabbit say rice-bud kin fly wey da win' is bin blow, but 'e no kin fly wey no win' blow.

"Rice-bud say, 'Enty!'

"'E wait fer win' stop blowin'; 'e wait, un 'e fly all 'roun' un 'roun'.

"B'er Rabbit say rice-bud yent kin fly in house wey dey no win'.

"Rice-bud say, 'Enty!'

"'E fly in house, 'e fly all 'roun' un 'roun'. B'er Rabbit pull de do' shed; 'e look at dem rice-bud; 'e say, 'Enty!'

"'E ketch dem rice-bud; 'e do git um bill, 'e fetch um wey da Affiky màns lif. Affiky màns says dem rice-bud bill slick fer true. 'E tekky da el'phan' tush, 'e tekky da 'gater toof, 'e tekky da rice-bud bill, he pit um in lil bag; 'e swing dem bag 'pon B'er Rabbit neck. Den B'er Rabbit kin marry dem noung gal. Enty!"

Here Daddy Jack paused and flung a glance of feeble tenderness upon 'Tildy. Uncle Remus smiled contemptuously, seeing which 'Tildy straightened herself, tossed her head, and closed her eyes with an air of indescribable scorn.

"I dunner w'at Brer Rabbit moughter done," she exclaimed; "but I lay ef dey's any ole nigger man totin' a cunjer-bag in dis neighborhood, he'll git mighty tired un it 'fo' it do 'im any good — I lay dat!"

Daddy Jack chuckled heartily at this, and dropped off to sleep so suddenly that the little boy thought he was playing 'possum.

35
Brother Rabbit Submits to a Test

"UNCLE REMUS," SAID the child, "do you reckon Brother Rabbit really married the young lady?"

"Bless yo' soul, honey," responded the old man, with a sigh, "hit b'long ter Brer Jack fer ter tell you dat. 'Tain't none er my tale."

"Wasn't that the tale you started to tell?"

"Who? Me? *Shoo!* I ain't 'sputin' but w'at Brer Jack tale des ez purty ez dey er any needs fer, yit 'tain't none er my tale."

At this, the little boy laid his head upon Uncle Remus's knee and waited.

"Now, den," said the old man, with an air of considerable importance, "we er got ter go 'way back behime dish yer yalligater doin's w'at Brer Jack bin mixin' us up wid. Ef I makes no mistakes wid my 'membunce, de place whar'bouts I lef' off wuz whar Brer Rabbit had so many 'p'int-ments fer ter keep out de way er de t'er creeturs dat he 'gun ter feel mon-stus humblyfied. Let um be who dey will, you git folks in a close place ef you wanter see um shed der proudness. Dey beg mo' samer dan a nigger w'en de patter-rollers ketch 'im. Brer Rabbit ain't do no beggin', kaze dey ain't kotch; yit dey come so nigh it, he 'gun ter feel he weakness.

"W'en Brer Rabbit feel dis a-way, do he set down flat er de groun' en let de t'er creeturs rush up en grab 'im? He mought do it deze days, kaze times done change; but in dem days he des tuck'n sot up wid hisse'f en study 'bout w'at he gwine do. He study en study, en las' he up'n tell he ole 'oman, he did, dat he gwine on a journey. Wid dat, ole Miss Rabbit, she tuck'n fry 'im up a rasher er bacon, en bake 'im a pone er bread. Brer Rabbit tied dis up in a bag en tuck down he walkin' cane en put out."

"Where was he going, Uncle Remus?" asked the little boy.

"Lemme 'lone, honey! Lemme sorter git hit up, lak. De trail mighty col' 'long yer, sho; kaze dish yer tale ain't come 'cross my min' not sence yo' gran'pa fotch us all out er Ferginny, en dat's a monstus long time ago.

"He put out, Brer Rabbit did, fer ter see ole Mammy-Bammy Big-Money."

"Dat 'uz dat ole Witch-Rabbit," remarked Aunt Tempy, complacently.

"Yasser," continued Uncle Remus, "de ve'y same ole creetur w'at I done tell you 'bout w'en Brer Rabbit los' he foot. He put out, he did, en atter so long a time he git dar. He take time fer ter ketch he win', en den he sorter shake hisse'f up en rustle 'roun' in de grass. Bimeby he holler:

"'Mammy-Bammy Big-Money! O Mammy-Bammy Big-Money! I journeyed fur, I journeyed fas'; I glad I foun' de place at las'.'

"Great big black smoke rise up out er de groun', en ole Mammy-Bammy Big-Money 'low:

"'Wharfo', Son Riley Rabbit, Riley? Son Riley Rabbit, wharfo'?'

"Wid dat," continued Uncle Remus, dropping the sing-song tone by means of which he managed to impart a curious dignity and stateliness to the dialogue between Brother Rabbit and Mammy-Bammy Big-Money — "wid dat Brer Rabbit up'n tell 'er, he did, 'bout how he 'fear'd he losin' de use er he min', kaze he done come ter dat pass dat he ain't kin fool de yuther creeturs no mo', en dey push 'im so closte twel 'twon't be long 'fo' dey'll git 'im. De ole Witch-Rabbit she sot dar, she did, en suck in black smoke en puff it out 'g'in, twel you can't see nothin' 'tall but 'er great big eye-balls en 'er great big years. Atter w'ile she 'low:

"'Dar sets a squer'l in dat tree, Son Riley; go fetch dat squer'l straight ter me, Son Riley Rabbit, Riley.'

"Brer Rabbit sorter study, en den he 'low, he did:

"'I ain't got much sense lef', yit ef I can't coax dat chap down from dar, den hit's kaze I done got some 'zeeze w'ich it make me fibble in de min',' sezee.

"Wid dat, Brer Rabbit tuck'n empty de provender out'n he bag en got 'im two rocks, en put de bag over he head en sot down und' de tree whar he squer'l is. He wait little w'ile, en den he hit de rocks tergedder — *blip!*

"Squer'l he holler, 'Hey!'

"Brer Rabbit wait little, en den he tuck'n slap de rocks tergedder —
blap!

"Squer'l he run down de tree little bit en holler, 'Heyo!'

"Brer Rabbit ain't sayin' nothin'. He des pop de rocks togedder —
blop!

"Squer'l, he come down little furder, he did, en holler, 'Who dat?'

"'Biggidy Dicky Big-Bag!'

"'W'at you doin' in dar?'

"'Crackin' hick'y nuts.'

"'Kin I crack some?'

"'Tooby sho, Miss Bunny Bushtail; come git in de bag.'

"Miss Bunny Bushtail hang back," continued Uncle Remus, chuck-
ling; "but de long en de short un it wuz dat she got in de bag, en Brer
Rabbit he tuck'n kyar'd 'er ter ole Mammy-Bammy Big-Money. De ole
Witch-Rabbit, she tuck'n tu'n de squer'l a-loose, en 'low:

"'Dar lies a snake in 'mungs de grass. Son Riley; go fetch 'im yer, en
be right fas', Son Riley Rabbit, Riley.'

"Brer Rabbit look 'roun', en sho nuff dar lay de bigges' kinder rattlesnake, all quile up ready fer business. Brer Rabbit scratch he year
wid he behime leg, en study. Look lak he gwine git in trouble. Yit atter
w'ile he go off in de bushes, he did, en cut 'im a young grape-vine, en he
fix 'im a slip-knot. Den he come back. Snake 'periently look lak he sleep.
Brer Rabbit ax 'im how he come on. Snake ain't say nothin', but he quile
up a little tighter, en he tongue run out lak it bin had grease on it. Mouf
shot, yit de tongue slick out en slick back 'fo' a sheep kin shake he tail.
Brer Rabbit, he 'low, he did:

"'Law, Mr. Snake, I mighty glad I come 'cross you,' sezee. 'Me en ole
Jedge B'ar bin havin' a tumble 'spute 'bout how long you is. We bofe 'gree
dat you look mighty purty w'en you er layin' stretch out full lenk in de
sun; but Jedge B'ar, he 'low you ain't but th'ee foot long, en I stood 'im
down dat you 'uz four foot long ef not mo',' sezee. 'En de talk got so hot
dat I come mighty nigh hittin' 'im a clip wid my walkin'-cane, en ef I had
I boun' dey'd er bin some bellerin' done 'roun' dar,' sezee.

"Snake ain't say nothin', but he look mo' complassy dan w'at he bin
lookin'.

"'I up'n tole ole Jedge B'ar,' sez Brer Rabbit, sezee, 'dat de nex' time I run 'cross you I gwine take'n medjur you; en goodness knows I mighty glad I struck up wid you, kaze now dey won't be no mo' 'casion fer any 'sputin' 'twix' me en Jedge B'ar,' sezee.

"Den Brer Rabbit ax Mr. Snake ef he won't be so good ez ter onquile hisse'f. Snake he feel mighty proud, he did, en he stretch out fer all he wuff. Brer Rabbit he medjur, he did, en 'low:

"'Dar one foot fer Jedge B'ar; dar th'ee foot fer Jedge B'ar; en, bless goodness, dar four foot fer Jedge B'ar, des lak I say!'

"By dat time Brer Rabbit done got ter snake head, en des ez de las' wud drop out'n he mouf, he slip de loop 'roun' snake neck, en den he had 'im good en fas'. He tuck'n drag 'im, he did, up ter whar de ole Witch-Rabbit settin' at; but w'en he git dar, Mammy-Bammy Big-Money done make 'er disappearance, but he year sump'n' way off yander, en seem lak it say:

"'Ef you git any mo' sense, Son Riley, you'll be de ruination ev de whole settlement, Son Riley Rabbit, Riley.'

"Den Brer Rabbit drag de snake 'long home, en stew 'im down en rub wid de grease fer ter make 'im mo' soopler in de lim's. Bless yo' soul, honey, Brer Rabbit mought er bin kinder fibble in de legs, but he wa'n't no ways cripple und' de hat."[1]

36
Brother Wolf Falls a Victim

"UNCLE REMUS," SAID the little boy, one night, when he found the old man sitting alone in his cabin, "did you ever see Mammy-Bammy Big-Money?"

Uncle Remus placed his elbows on his knees, rested his chin in the palms of his hands, and gazed steadily in the fire. Presently he said:

---

[1] A version of this story makes Brother Rabbit capture a swarm of bees. Mr. W. O. Tuggle, of Georgia, who has made an exhaustive study of the Creek Indians, has discovered a variant of the legend. The Rabbit (Chufee) becomes alarmed because he has nothing but the nimbleness of his feet to take him out of harm's way. He goes to his Creator and begs that greater intelligence be bestowed upon him. Thereupon the snake test is applied, as in the Negro story, and the Rabbit also catches a swarm of gnats. He is then told that he has as much intelligence as there is any need for, and he goes away satisfied. — J. C. H.

"W'en folks 'gin ter git ole en no 'count, hit look lak der 'membunce git slack. Some time hit seem lak I done seed sump'n' n'er mighty nigh de make en color er ole Mammy-Bammy Big-Money, en den ag'in seem lak I ain't. W'en dat de case, w'at does I do? Does I stan' tip-toe en tetch de rafters en make lak I done seed dat ole Witch-Rabbit, w'en, goodness knows, I ain't seed 'er? Dat I don't. No, bless you! I'd say de same in comp'ny, much less settin' in yer 'long side er you. De long en de short un it," exclaimed Uncle Remus, with emphasis, "is des dis. Ef I bin run 'crost ole Mammy-Bammy Big-Money in my day en time, den she tuck'n make 'er disappearance dat quick twel I ain't kotch a glimp' un 'er."

The result of this good-humored explanation was that the child didn't know whether Uncle Remus had seen the Witch-Rabbit or not, but his sympathies led him to suspect that the old man was thoroughly familiar with all her movements.

"Uncle Remus," the little boy said, after a while, "if there is another story about Mammy-Bammy Big-Money, I wish you would tell it to me all by my own-alone self."

The idea seemed to please the old man wonderfully, and he chuckled over it for several minutes.

"Now, den, honey," he said, after a while, "you hit me whar I'm weak — you mos' sholy does. Comp'ny mighty good fer some folks en I kin put up wid it long ez de nex' un, but you kin des tak'n pile comp'ny 'pun top er comp'ny, en dey won't kyore de liver complaint. W'en you talk dat away you fetches me, sho, en I'll tell you a tale 'bout de ole Witch-Rabbit ef I hatter git down yer on my all-fours en grabble it out'n de ashes. Yit dey ain't no needs er dat, kaze de tale done come in my min' des ez fresh ez ef 'twas day 'fo' yistiddy.

"Hit seem lak dat one time atter Brer Wolf tuck'n steal Brer Rabbit foot, dey wuz a mighty long fallin'-out 'twix' um. Brer Rabbit, he tuck'n got ashy kaze Brer Wolf tuck'n tuck he foot; en Brer Wolf, he tuck'n got hot kaze Brer Rabbit wuk en wuk 'roun' en git he foot ag'in. Hit keep on dis a-way twel bimeby de ole Witch-Rabbit sorter git tired er Brer Wolf, en one day she tuck'n sont wud ter Brer Rabbit dat she lak mighty well fer ter see 'im.

"Dey fix up der plans, dey did, en 'twa'n't so mighty long 'fo' Brer Rabbit run inter Brer Wolf house in a mighty big hurry, en he 'low, he did:

"'Brer Wolf! O Brer Wolf! I des now come fum de river, en des ez sho ez you er settin' in dat cheer, ole Big-Money layin' dar stone dead. Less we go eat 'er up.'

"'Brer Rabbit, sho'ly you er jokin'!'

"'Brer Wolf, I'm a-ginin' un you de fatal fack. Come on, less go!'

"'Brer Rabbit, is you sho she dead?'

"'Brer Wolf, she done dead; come on, less go!'

"En go dey did. Dey went 'roun' en dey got all de yuther creeturs, en Brer Wolf, livin' so nigh, he let all he chilluns go, en 'twa'n't so mighty long 'fo' dey had a crowd dar des lak camp-meetin' times.

"W'en dey git dar, sho nuff, dar lay ole Big-Money all stretch out on de river bank. Dis make Brer Wolf feel mighty good, en he tuck'n stick he han's in he pocket en strut 'roun' dar en look monstus biggity. Atter he done tuck'n 'zamine ole Big-Money much ez he wanter, he up'n 'low, he did, dat dey better sorter rustle 'roun' en make a fa'r dividjun. He ax Brer Mink, he ax Brer Coon, he ax Brer 'Possum, he ax Brer Tarrypin, he ax Brer Rabbit, w'ich part dey take, en dey all up'n 'low, dey did, dat bein' ez Brer Wolf de biggest en de heartiest in de neighborhoods er de appetite, dey 'speck he better take de fus' choosement.

"Wid dat Brer Wolf, he sot down on a log, en hang he head ter one side, sorter lak he 'shame' er hisse'f. Bimeby, he up'n 'low:

"'Now, den, folks en fr'en's, sence you shove it on me, de shortes' way is de bes' way. Brer Coon, we bin good fr'en's a mighty long time; how much er dish yer meat ought a fibble ole man lak me ter take?' sezee.

"Brer Wolf talk mighty lovin'. Brer Coon snuff de a'r, en 'low:

"'I 'speck you better take one er de fo'-quarters, Brer Wolf,' sezee.

"Brer Wolf look lak he 'stonish'. He lif' up he han's en 'low:

"'Law, Brer Coon, I tuck you ter be my fr'en', dat I did. Man w'at talk lak dat ain't go no feelin' fer me. Hit make me feel mighty lonesome,' sezee.

"Den Brer Wolf tu'n 'roun' en talk mighty lovin' ter Brer Mink:

"'Brer Mink, many's de day you bin a-knowin' me; how much er dish yer meat you 'speck oughter fall ter my sheer?' sezee.

"Brer Mink sorter study, en den he 'low:

"'Bein' ez you er sech a nice man, Brer Wolf, I 'speck you oughter take one er de fo'-quarters, en a right smart hunk off'n de bulge er de neck,' sezee.

"Brer Wolf holler out, he did:

"'Go 'way, Brer Mink! Go 'way! You ain't no 'quaintance er mine!'

"Den ole Brer Wolf tu'n 'roun' ter Brer 'Possum en talk lovin':

"'Brer 'Possum, I done bin tuck wid a likin' fer you long time 'fo' dis. Look at me, en den look at my fambly, en den tell me, ef you be so good, how much er dish yer meat gwine ter fall ter my sheer.'

"Brer 'Possum, he look 'roun', he did, en grin, en he up'n low:

"'Take half, Brer Wolf, take half!'

"Den ole Brer Wolf holler out:

"'Shoo, Brer 'Possum! I like you no mo'.'

"Den Brer Wolf tu'n to Brer Tarrypin, en Brer Tarrypin say Brer Wolf oughter take all 'cep' one er de behime quarters, en den Brer Wolf 'low dat Brer Tarrypin ain't no fr'en' ter him. Den he up'n ax Brer Rabbit, en Brer Rabbit, he tuck'n 'spon', he did:

"'Gentermens all! you see Brer Wolf chillun? Well, dey er all monstus hongry, en Brer Wolf hongry hisse'f. Now I puts dis plan straight at you: less we all let Brer Wolf have de fus' pass at Big-Money; less tie 'im on dar, en le'm eat much ez he wanter, en den we kin pick de bones,' sezee.

"'You er my pardner, Brer Rabbit!' sez Brer Wolf, sezee; 'you er my honey-pardner!'

"Dey all 'gree ter dis plan, mo' 'spechually ole Brer Wolf, so den dey tuck'n tie 'im onter Big-Money. Dey tie 'im on dar, dey did, en den ole Brer Wolf look all 'roun' en wunk at de yuthers. Brer Rabbit, he tuck'n wunk back, en den Brer Wolf retch down en bite Big-Money on de back er de neck. Co'se, w'en he do dis, Big-Money bleedzd ter flinch; let 'lone dat, she bleedzd ter jump. Brer Wolf holler out:

"'Ow! Run yer somebody! Take me off! She ain't dead. O Lordy! I feel 'er move!'

Brer Rabbit holler back:

"'Nummin' de flinchin', Brer Wolf. She done dead; I done year 'er sesso 'erse'f. She dead, sho. Bite er ag'in, Brer Wolf, bite 'er ag'in!'

"Brer Rabbit talk so stiff, hit sorter tuck de chill off'n Brer Wolf, en he dipt down en bit ole Big-Money ag'in. Wid dat, she 'gun ter move off, en Brer Wolf he holler des lak de woods done kotch a-fier:

"'Ow! O Lordy! Ontie me, Brer Rabbit, ontie me! She ain't dead! Ow! Run yer, Brer Rabbit, en ontie me!'

"Brer Rabbit, he holler back:

"'She er sholy dead, Brer Wolf! Nail 'er, Brer Wolf. Bite 'er! gnyaw 'er!'

"Brer Wolf keep on bitin', en Big-Money keep on movin' off. Bimeby, she git ter de bank er de river, en she fall in — *cumber-joom!* — en dat 'uz de las' er Brer Wolf."

"What did Brother Rabbit do?" the little boy asked, after a while.

"Well," responded Uncle Remus, in the tone of one anxious to dispose of a disagreeable matter as pleasantly as possible, "you know w'at kinder man Brer Rabbit is. He des went off somers by he own-alone se'f en tuck a big laugh."

37
Brother Rabbit and the Mosquitoes

THE NEXT NIGHT Daddy Jack was still away when the little boy went to see Uncle Remus, and the child asked about him.

"Bless yo' soul, honey! don't ax me 'bout Brer Jack. He look lak he mighty ole en trimbly, but he mighty peart nigger, mon. He look lak he shufflin' 'long, but dat ole nigger gits over groun', sho. Forty year ergo, maybe I mought er kep' up wid 'im, but I let you know Brer Jack is away 'head er me. He mos' sholy is."

"Why, he's older than you are, Uncle Remus!" the child exclaimed.

"Dat w'at I year tell. Seem lak hit mighty kuse, but sho ez you er bawn Brer Jack is a heap mo' pearter nigger dan w'at ole Remus is. He little, yit he mighty hard. Dat's Brer Jack, up en down."

Uncle Remus paused and reflected a moment. Then he went on:

"Talkin' 'bout Brer Jack put me in min' 'bout a tale w'ich she sholy mus' er happen down dar in dat ar country whar Brer Jack come fum, en it sorter ketch me in de neighborhoods er de 'stonishment kaze he ain't done up'n tell it. I 'speck it done wuk loose fum Brer Jack 'membunce."

"What tale was that, Uncle Remus?"

"Seem lak dat one time w'en eve'ything en eve'ybody was runnin' 'long des lak dey bin had waggin grease 'un um, ole Brer Wolf — "

The little boy laughed incredulously and Uncle Remus paused and frowned heavily.

"Why, Uncle Remus! how did Brother Wolf get away from Mammy-Bammy Big-Money?"

The old man's frown deepened and his voice was full of anger as he replied:

"Now, den, is I'm de tale, er is de tale me? Tell me dat! Is I'm de tale, er is de tale me? Well, den, ef I ain't de tale en de tale ain't me, den how come you wanter tak'n rake me over de coals fer?"

"Well, Uncle Remus, you know what you said. You said that was the end of Brother Wolf."

"I bleedzd ter 'spute dat," exclaimed Uncle Remus, with the air of one performing a painful duty; "I bleedzd ter s'pute it. Dat w'at de tale say. Ole Remus is one nigger en de tale, hit's a n'er nigger. Yit I ain't got no time fer ter set back yer en fetch out de oggyments."

Here the old man paused, closed his eyes, leaned back in his chair, and sighed. After a while he said, in a gentle tone:

"So den, Brer Wolf done dead, en yer I wuz runnin' on des same lak he wuz done 'live. Well! well! well!"

Uncle Remus stole a glance at the little boy, and immediately relented.

"Yit," he went on, "ef I ain't de tale en de tale ain't me, hit ain't skacely make no diffunce whe'er Brer Wolf dead er whe'er he's a high-primin' 'roun' bodder'n 'longer de yuther creeturs. Dead er no dead, dey wuz one time w'en Brer Wolf live in de swamp down dar in dat ar country whar Brer Jack come fum, en, mo'n dat, he had a mighty likely gal. Look lak all de yuther creeturs wuz atter 'er. Dey 'ud go down dar ter Brer Wolf house, dey would, en dey 'ud set up en court de gal, en 'joy deyse'f.

"Hit went on dis away twel atter w'ile de skeeters 'gun ter git monstus bad. Brer Fox, he went flyin' 'roun' Miss Wolf, en he sot dar, he did, en run on wid 'er en fight skeeters des es big ez life en twice-t ez nat'al. Las' Brer Wolf, he tuck'n kotch Brer Fox slappin' en fightin' at de skeeters. Wid dat he tuck'n tuck Brer Fox by de off year en led 'im out ter de front gate, en w'en he git dar, he 'low, he did, dat no man w'at can't put up wid skeeters ain't gwine ter come a-courtin' his gal.

"Den Brer Coon, he come flyin' 'roun' de gal, but he ain't bin dar no time skacely 'fo' he 'gun ter knock at de skeeters; en no sooner is he done dis dan Brer Wolf show 'im de do'. Brer Mink, he come en try he han', yit he bleedzd ter fight de skeeters, en Brer Wolf ax 'im out.

"Hit went on dis a-way twel bimeby all de creeturs bin flyin' 'roun' Brer Wolf's gal ceppin' it's ole Brer Rabbit, en w'en he year w'at kinder treatments de yuther creeturs bin ketchin' he 'low ter hisse'f dat he b'lieve in he soul he mus' go down ter Brer Wolf house en set de gal out one whet ef it's de las' ack.

"No sooner say, no sooner do. Off he put, en 'twa'n't long 'fo' he fin' hisse'f knockin' at Brer Wolf front do'. Ole Sis Wolf, she tuck'n put down 'er knittin' en she up'n 'low, she did:

"'Who dat?'

"De gal, she 'uz stan'in' up 'fo' de lookin'-glass sorter primpin', en she choke back a giggle, she did, en 'low:

"'Sh-h-h! My goodness, mammy! dat's Mr. Rabbit. I year de gals say he's a mighty prop-en-tickler gentermun, en I des hope you ain't gwine ter set dar en run on lak you mos' allers does w'en I got comp'ny 'bout how much soap-grease you done save up en how many kittens de ole cat got. I gits right 'shame' sometimes, dat I does!'"

The little boy looked astonished.

"Did she talk that way to her mamma?" he asked.

"*Shoo*, chile! 'Mungs all de creeturs dey ain't no mo' kuse creeturs dan de gals. Ole ez I is, ef I wuz ter start in dis minnit fer ter tell you how kuse de gals is, en de Lord wuz ter spar' me plum' twel I git done, yo' head 'ud be gray, en Remus 'ud be des twice-t ez ole ez w'at he is right now."

"Well, what did her mamma say, Uncle Remus?"

"Ole Sis Wolf, she sot dar, she did, en settle 'er cap on 'er head, en snicker, en look at de gal lak she monstus proud. De gal, she tuck'n shuck 'erse'f 'fo' de lookin'-glass a time er two, en den she tipt ter de do' en open' it little ways en peep out des lak she skeer'd some un gwine ter hit 'er a clip side de head. Dar stood ole Brer Rabbit lookin' des ez slick ez a race-hoss. De gal, she tuck'n laff, she did, en holler:

"'W'y law, maw! hit's Mr. Rabbit, en yer we bin 'fraid it 'uz some 'un w'at ain't got no business 'roun' yer!'

Ole Sis Wolf she look over 'er specks, en snicker, en den she up'n 'low:

"'Well, don't keep 'im stan'in' out dar all night. Ax 'im in, fer goodness sake.'

"Den de gal, she tuck'n drap 'er hankcher, en Brer Rabbit, he dipt down en grab it en pass it ter 'er wid a bow, en de gal say she much 'blige, kaze dat 'uz mo' den Mr. Fox 'ud done, en den she ax Brer Rabbit how he come on, en Brer Rabbit 'low he right peart, en den he ax 'er whar'bouts 'er daddy, en ole Sis Wolf 'low she go fin' 'im.

"'Twa'n't long 'fo' Brer Rabbit year Brer Wolf stompin' de mud off'n he foots in de back po'ch, en den bimeby in he come. Dey shuck han's, dey did, en Brer Rabbit say dat w'en he go callin' on he 'quaintunce, hit ain't feel nat'al 'ceppin' de man er de house settin' 'roun' some'rs.

"'Ef he don't talk none,' sez Brer Rabbit, sezee, 'he kin des set up ag'in de chimbley-jam' en keep time by noddin'.'

"But ole Brer Wolf, he one er deze yer kinder mens w'at got de whimzies, en he up'n 'low dat he don't let hisse'f git ter noddin' front er comp'ny. Dey run on dis a-way twel bimeby Brer Rabbit year de skeeters come zoonin' roun', en claimin' kin wid 'um."

The little boy laughed; but Uncle Remus was very serious.

"Co'se dey claim kin wid 'um. Dey claims kin wid folks yit, let 'lone Brer Rabbit. Many's en many's de time w'en I year um sailin' 'roun' en singin' out *'Cousin! Cousin!'* en I let you know, honey, de skeeters is mighty close kin w'en dey gits ter be yo' cousin.

"Brer Rabbit, he year um zoonin'," the old man continued, "en he know he got ter do some mighty nice talkin', so he up'n ax fer drink er water. De gal, she tuck'n fotch it.

"'Mighty nice water, Brer Wolf.' *(De skeeters dey zoon.)*[1]

"'Some say it too full er wiggletails, Brer Rabbit.' *(De skeeters, dey zoon en dey zoon.)*

"'Mighty nice place you got, Brer Wolf.' *(Skeeters dey zoon.)*

"'Some say it too low in de swamp, Brer Rabbit.' *(Skeeters dey zoon en dey zoon.)*

"Dey zoon so bad," said Uncle Remus, drawing a long breath, "dat Brer Rabbit 'gun ter git skeer'd, en w'en dat creetur git skeer'd, he min' wuk lak one er deze yer flutter-mills. Bimeby, he 'low:

---

[1] The information in parentheses is imparted in a low, impressive, confidential tone. — J. C. H.

"'Went ter town t'er day, en dar I seed a sight w'at I never 'spected ter see.'

"'W'at dat, Brer Rabbit?'

"'Spotted hoss, Brer Wolf.'

"'*No,* Brer Rabbit!'

"'I mos' sholy seed 'im, Brer Wolf.'

"Brer Wolf, he scratch he head, en de gal she hilt up 'er han's en make great 'miration 'bout de spotted hoss *(De skeeters dey zoon, en dey keep on zoonin'.)* Brer Rabbit, he talk on, he did:

"'Twa'n't des one spotted hoss, Brer Wolf, 'twuz a whole team er spotted hosses, en dey went gallin'-up des lak de yuther hosses,' sezee. 'Let 'lone dat, Brer Wolf, my grandaddy wuz spotted,' sez Brer Rabbit, sezee.

"Gal, she squeal en holler out:

"'W'y, Brer Rabbit! ain't you 'shame' yo'se'f fer ter be talkin' dat away, en 'bout yo' own-lone blood kin too?'

"'Hit's de naked trufe I'm a-ginin' un you,' sez Brer Rabbit, sezee. *(Skeeter zoon en come closeter.)*

"Brer Wolf 'low 'Well — well — well!' Ole Sis Wolf, she 'low 'Tooby sholy, tooby sholy!' *(Skeeter zoon en come nigher en nigher.)* Brer Rabbit 'low:

"'Yasser! Des ez sho ez you er settin' dar, my grandaddy wuz spotted.

Spotted all over. *(Skeeter come zoonin' up en light on Brer Rabbit jaw.)* He wuz dat. He had er great big spot right yer!'"

Here Uncle Remus raised his hand and struck himself a resounding slap on the side of the face where the mosquito was supposed to be, and continued:

"No sooner is he do dis dan n'er skeeter come zoonin' 'roun' en light on Brer Rabbit leg. Brer Rabbit, he talk, en he talk:

"'Po' ole grandaddy! I boun' he make you laff, he look so funny wid all dem spots en speckles. He had spot on de side er de head, whar I done show you, en den he had n'er big spot right yer on de leg,' sezee."

Uncle Remus slapped himself on the leg below the knee, and was apparently so serious about it that the little boy laughed loudly. The old man went on:

"Skeeter zoon en light 'twix' Brer Rabbit shoulder-blades. Den he talk:

"'B'lieve me er not b'lieve me ef you min' to, but my grandaddy had a big black spot up yer on he back w'ich look lak saddle-mark.'

"Blip Brer Rabbit tuck hisse'f on de back!

"Skeeter sail 'roun' en zoon en light down yer beyan de hipbone. He say he grandaddy got spot down dar.

"Blip he tuck hisse'f beyan de hip-bone.

"Hit keep on dis a-way," continued Uncle Remus, who had given vigorous illustrations of Brer Rabbit's method of killing mosquitoes while pretending to tell a story, "twel bimeby ole Brer Wolf en ole Sis Wolf dey lissen at Brer Rabbit twel dey 'gun ter nod, en den ole Brer Rabbit en de gal dey sot up dar en kill skeeters right erlong."

"Did he marry Brother Wolf's daughter?" asked the little boy.

"I year talk," replied Uncle Remus, "dat Brer Wolf sont Brer Rabbit wud nex' day he kin git de gal by gwine atter 'er, but I ain't never year talk 'bout Brer Rabbit gwine. De day atterwuds wuz mighty long time, en by den Brer Rabbit moughter had some yuther projik on han'."[2]

---

2 This story, the funniest and most characteristic of all the Negro legends, cannot be satisfactorily told on paper. It is full of action, and all the interest centers in the gestures and grimaces that must accompany an explanation of Brother Rabbit's method of disposing of the mosquitoes. The story was first called to my attention by Mr. Marion Erwin, of Savannah, and it is properly a coast legend, but I have heard it told by three Middle Georgia Negroes. — J. C. H.

38
The Pimmerly Plum

ONE NIGHT when the little boy had grown tired of waiting for a story, he looked at Uncle Remus and said: "I wonder what ever became of old Brother Tarrypin." Uncle Remus gave a sudden start, glanced all around the cabin, and then broke into a laugh that ended in a yell like a view-halloo.

"Well, well, well! How de name er goodness come you ter know w'at runnin' on in my min', honey? Mon, you skeer'd me; you sholy did; en w'en I git skeer'd I bleedzd ter holler. Let 'lone dat, ef I keep on gittin' skeer'der en skeer'der, you better gimme room, kaze ef I can't git 'way fum dar somebody gwine ter git hurted, en dey er gwine ter git hurted bad. I tell you dat right pine-blank.

"Ole Brer Tarrypin!" continued Uncle Remus in a tone of exultation. "Ole Brer Tarrypin! Now, who bin year tell er de beat er dat? Dar you sets studyin' 'bout ole Brer Tarrypin, en yer I sets studyin' 'bout ole Brer Tarrypin. Hit make me feel so kuse dat little mo'n en I'd a draw'd my Rabbit-foot en shuck it at you."

The little boy was delighted when Uncle Remus went off into these rhapsodies. However nonsensical they might seem to others, to the child they were positively thrilling, and he listened with rapt attention, scarcely daring to stir. "Ole Brer Tarrypin? Well, well, well! —

> "W'en in he prime
> He tuck he time!

"Dat w'at make he hol' he age so good. Dey tells me dat somebody 'cross dar in Jasper county tuck'n kotch a Tarrypin w'ich he got marks cut in he back 'uz put dar 'fo' our folks went fer ter git revengeance in de Moccasin war. Dar whar yo' Unk' Jeems bin," Uncle Remus explained, noticing the little boy's look of astonishment.

"Oh!" exclaimed the child, "that was the Mexican war."

"Well," responded Uncle Remus, closing his eyes with a sigh, "I ain't one er deze yer kinder folks w'at choke deyse'f wid names. One name ain't got none de 'vantage er no yuther name. En ef de Tarrypin got de

marks on 'im, hit don't make no diffunce whe'er yo' Unk' Jeems Abercrombie git his revengeance out'n de Moccasin folks, er whe'er he got it
out'n de Mackersons."

"Mexicans, Uncle Remus."

"Tooby sho, honey; let it go at dat. But don't less pester ole Brer Tarrypin wid it, kaze he done b'long ter a tribe all by he own-lone se'f. — I
'clar' ter gracious," exclaimed the old man after a pause, "ef hit don't
seem 'periently lak 'twuz yistiddy!"

"What, Uncle Remus?"

"Oh, des ole Brer Tarrypin, honey; des ole Brer Tarrypin en a tale
w'at I year 'bout 'im, how he done tuck'n do Brer Fox."

"Did he scare him, Uncle Remus?" the little boy asked, as the old
man paused.

"No, my goodness! Wuss'n dat!"

"Did he hurt him?"

"No, my goodness! Wuss'n dat!"

"Did he kill him?"

"No, my goodness! Lots wuss'n dat!"

"Now, Uncle Remus, what *did* he do to Brother Fox?"

"Honey!" — here the old man lowered his voice as if about to describe a great outrage — "Honey! he tuck'n make a fool out'n 'im!"

The child laughed, but it was plain that he failed to appreciate the
situation, and this fact caused Uncle Remus to brighten up and go on
with the story.

"One time w'en de sun shine down mighty hot, ole Brer Tarrypin wuz
gwine 'long down de road. He 'uz gwine 'long down, en he feel mighty
tired; he puff, en he blow, en he pant. He breff come lak he got de azmy
'way down in he win'-pipe; but, nummin'! he de same ole Creep-um-
crawl-um Have-some-fun-um. He 'uz gwine 'long down de big road, ole
Brer Tarrypin wuz, en bimeby he come ter de branch. He tuck'n crawl in,
he did, en got 'im a drink er water, en den he crawl out on t'er side en set
down und' de shade un a tree. Atter he sorter ketch he win', he look up
at de sun fer ter see w'at time er day is it, en, lo en beholes; he tuck'n
'skivver dat he settin' in de shade er de sycamo' tree. No sooner is he
'skivver dis dan he sing de ole song:

"'Good luck ter dem w'at come and go.
W'at set in de shade er de sycamo'.'

"Brer Tarrypin he feel so good en de shade so cool, dat 'twa'n't long 'fo' he got ter noddin', en bimeby he drapt off en went soun' asleep. Co'se, Brer Tarrypin kyar' he house wid 'im eve'ywhar he go, en w'en he fix fer ter go ter sleep, he des shet de do' en pull to de winder-shetters, en dar he is des ez snug ez de ole black cat und' de barn.

"Brer Tarrypin lay dar, he did, en sleep, en sleep. He dunner how long he sleep, but bimeby he feel somebody foolin' 'long wid 'im. He keep de do' shet, en he lay dar en lissen. He feel somebody tu'nin' he house 'roun' en 'roun'. Dis sorter skeer Brer Tarrypin, 'kaze he know dat ef dey tu'n he house upside down he ull have all sorts er times gittin' back. Wid dat, he open de do' little ways, en he see Brer Fox projickin' wid 'im. He open de do' little furder, he did, en he break out in a great big hoss-laff, en holler:

"'Well! well, well! Who'd a thunk it! Ole Brer Fox, cuter dan de common run, is done come en kotch me. En he come at sech a time, too! I feels dat full twel I can't see straight skacely. Ef dey wuz any jealousness proned inter me, I'd des lay yer en pout kaze Brer Fox done fin' out whar I gits my Pimmerly Plum.'

"In dem days," continued Uncle Remus, speaking to the child's look of inquiry, "de Pimmerly Plum wuz monstus skace. Leavin' out Brer Rabbit en Brer Tarrypin dey wa'n't none er de yuther creeturs dat yuvver got a glimp' un it, let 'lone a tas'e. So den w'en Brer Fox year talk er de Pimmerly Plum, bless gracious! he h'ist up he head en let Brer Tarrypin 'lone. Brer Tarrypin keep on laffin' en Brer Fox 'low:

"'Hush, Brer Tarrypin! you makes my mouf water! Whar'bouts de Pimmerly Plum?'

"Brer Tarrypin, he sorter cle'r up de ho'seness in he th'oat, en sing:

"'Poun' er sugar, en a pint er rum,
Ain't nigh so sweet ez de Pimmerly Plum!'

"Brer Fox, he lif' up he han's, he did, en holler:

"'Oh, hush, Brer Tarrypin! you makes me dribble! Whar'bouts dat Pimmerly Plum?'

"'You stan'in' right und' de tree, Brer Fox!'

"'Brer Tarrypin, sholy not!'

"'Yit dar you stan's, Brer Fox!'

"Brer Fox look up in de tree dar, en he wuz 'stonish'.'"

"What did he see in the sycamore tree, Uncle Remus?" inquired the little boy.

There was a look of genuine disappointment on the old man's face, as he replied:

"De gracious en de goodness, honey! Ain't you nev' is see dem ar little bit er balls w'at grow on de sycamo' tree?"[1]

The little boy laughed. There was a huge sycamore tree in the center of the circle made by the carriage way in front of the "big house," and there were sycamore trees of various sizes all over the place. The little balls alluded to by Uncle Remus are very hard at certain stages of their growth, and cling to the tree with wonderful tenacity. Uncle Remus continued:

"Well, den, w'en ole Brer Tarrypin vouch dat dem ar sycamo' balls wuz de ginnywine Pimmerly Plum, ole Brer Fox, he feel mighty good, yit he dunner how he gwine git at um. Push 'im closte, en maybe he mought beat Brer Tarrypin clim'in' a tree, but dish yer sycamo' tree wuz too big fer Brer Fox fer ter git he arms 'roun'. Den he up'n 'low:

"'I sees um hangin' dar, Brer Tarrypin, but how I gwine git um?'

"Brer Tarrypin open he do' little ways en holler out:

"'Ah-yi! Dar whar ole Slickum Slow-come got de 'vantage! You er mighty peart, Brer Fox, yit somehow er nudder you ain't bin a-keepin' up wid ole Slickum Slow-come.'

"'Brer Tarrypin, how de name er goodness does you git um?'

"'Don't do no good fer ter tell you, Brer Fox. Nimble heel make restless min'. You ain't got time fer ter wait en git um, Brer Fox.'

"'Brer Tarrypin, I got all de week befo' me.'

"'Ef I tells you, you'll go en tell all de t'er creeturs, en den dat'll be de las' er de Pimmerly Plum, Brer Fox.'

"'Brer Tarrypin, dat I won't. Des try me one time en see.'

"Brer Tarrypin shet he eye lak he studyin', en den he 'low:

---

[1] In another version of this story current among the Negroes the sweet gum tree takes the place of the sycamore. — J. C. H.

"'I tell you how I does, Brer Fox. W'en I wants a bait er de Pimmerly Plum right bad, I des takes my foot in my han' en comes down yer ter dish yer tree. I comes en I takes my stan'. I gits right und' de tree, en I r'ars my head back en opens my mouf. I opens my mouf, en w'en de Pimmerly

Plum draps, I boun' you she draps right spang in dar. All you got ter do is ter set en wait, Brer Fox.'

"Brer Fox ain't sayin' nothin'. He des sot down und' de tree, he did,

en r'ar'd he head back, en open he mouf, en I wish ter goodness you mought er bin had er chance fer ter see 'im settin' dar. He look scan'lous, dat's de long en de short un it; he des looks scan'lous."

"Did he get the Pimmerly Plum, Uncle Remus?" asked the little boy.

"*Shoo!* How he gwine git plum whar dey ain't no plum?"

"Well, what did he do?"

"He sot dar wid he mouf wide open, en eve'y time Brer Tarrypin look at 'im, much ez he kin do fer ter keep from bustin' aloose en laffin'. But bimeby he make he way todes home, Brer Tarrypin did, chucklin' en laffin', en 'twa'n't long 'fo' he met Brer Rabbit tippin' 'long down de road. Brer Rabbit, he hail 'im.

"'W'at 'muse you so mighty well, Brer Tarrypin?'

"Brer Tarrypin kotch he breff atter so long a time, en he 'low:

"'Brer Rabbit, I'm dat tickle' twel I can't shuffle 'long, skacely, en I'm feard ef I up'n tell you de 'casion un it, I'll be tooken wid one er my spells whar folks hatter set up wid me kaze I laff so loud en laff so long.'

"Yit atter so long a time, Brer Tarrypin up'n tell Brer Rabbit, en dey sot dar en chaw'd terbacker en kyar'd on des lak sho nuff folks. Dat dey did!"

Uncle Remus paused; but the little boy wanted to know what became of Brer Fox.

"Hit's mighty kuse," said the old man, stirring around in the ashes as if in search of a potato, "but endurin' er all my days I ain't nev' year nobody tell 'bout how long Brer Fox sot dar waitin' fer de Pimmerly Plum."

39

Brother Rabbit Gets the Provisions

THE NEXT TIME the little boy called on Uncle Remus a bright fire was blazing on the hearth. He could see the light shining under the door before he went into the cabin, and he knew by that sign that the old man had company. In fact, Daddy Jack had returned, and was dozing in his accustomed corner, Aunt Tempy was sitting bolt upright, nursing her contempt, and Uncle Remus was making a curious-looking box. None of the Negroes paid any attention to the little boy when he entered, but somehow he felt that they were waiting for him. After a while Uncle Re-

mus finished his curious-looking box and laid it upon the floor. Then he
lifted his spectacles from his nose to the top of his head, and remarked:

"Now, den, folks, dar she is, en hit's bin so long sence I uv made one
un um dat she make me sweat. Yasser! She did dat. Howsumev', hit ain't
make no diffunce wid me. Promise is a promise, dough you make it in de
dark er de moon. Long time ago, I tuck'n promise one er my passin'
'quaintance dat some er deze lonesome days de ole nigger'd whirl in en
make 'im a rabbit-trap ef he'd des be so good ez to quit he devilment, en
l'arn he behavishness."

"Is that my rabbit-trap, Uncle Remus?" exclaimed the child. He
would have picked it up for the purpose of examining it, but Uncle Remus waved him off with a dignified gesture.

"Don't you dast ter tetch dat ar trap, honey, kaze ef you does, dat
spiles all. I'll des hatter go ter wuk en make it bran'-new, en de Lord
knows I ain't got no time fer ter do dat."

"Well, Uncle Remus, you've had your hands on it."

"Tooby sho I is — tooby sho I is! En w'at's mo' dan dat, I bin had my
han's in tar-water."

"I year talk er dat," remarked Aunt Tempy, with an approving nod.

"Yasser! in de nat'al tar-water," continued Uncle Remus. "You put
yo' han' in a pa'tridge nes', en he'll quit dem premises dough he done got
'lev'm dozen aigs in dar. Same wid Rabbit. Dey ain't got sense lak de ole-
time Rabbit, but I let you know dey ain't gwine in no trap whar dey smell
folks' han's — dat dey ain't. Dat w'at make I say w'at I does. Don't put
yo' han' on it; don't tetch it; don't look at it skacely."

The little boy subsided, but he continued to cast longing looks at the
trap, seeing which Uncle Remus sought to change the current of his
thoughts.

"She bin er mighty heap er trouble, mon, yet I mighty glad I tuck'n
make dat ar trap. She's a solid un, sho, en ef dey wuz ter be any skace-
ness er vittles, I lay dat ar trap 'ud help us all out."

"De Lord knows," exclaimed Aunt Tempy, rubbing her fat hands together, "I hope dey ain't gwine ter be no famishin' 'roun' yer 'mungs we all."

"Likely not," said Uncle Remus, "yet de time mought come w'en a
big swamp rabbit kotch in dat ar trap would go a mighty long ways in a
fambly no bigger dan w'at mine is."

"Mo' speshually," remarked Aunt Tempy, "ef you put dat wid w'at de neighbors mought sen' in."

"Eh-eh!" Uncle Remus exclaimed, "don't you put no 'pennunce in dem neighbors — don't you do it. W'en famine time come one man ain't no better dan no yuther man ceppin' he be soopless; en he got ter be mighty soople at dat."

The old man paused and glanced at the little boy. The child was still looking longingly at the trap, and Uncle Remus leaned forward and touched him lightly on the shoulder. It was a familiar gesture, gentle and yet rough, a token of affection, and yet a command to attention; for the venerable darkey could be imperious enough when surrendering to the whims of his little partner.

"All dish yer talk 'bout folks pe'shin' out," Uncle Remus went on with an indifferent air, "put me in min' er de times w'en de creeturs tuck'n got up a famine 'mungs deyse'f. Hit come 'bout dat one time vittles wuz monstus skace en high, en money mighty slack. Long ez dey wuz any vittles gwine 'roun', Brer Rabbit, he 'uz boun' ter git he sheer un um, but bimeby hit come ter dat pass dat Brer Rabbit stomach 'gun ter pinch 'im; en w'iles he gittin' hongry de yuther creeturs, dey 'uz gettin' hongry deyse'f. Hit went on dis a-way twel one day Brer Rabbit en Brer Wolf meet up wid one er n'er in de big road, en atter dey holler howdy dey sat down, dey did, en make a bargain.

"Dey tuck'n 'gree one er n'er dat dey sell der mammy en take de money en git sump'n' n'er ter eat. Brer Wolf, he 'low, he did, dat bein's hit seem lak he de hongriest creetur on de face er de yeth, dat he sell his mammy fus', en den, atter de vittles gin out, Brer Rabbit kin sell he own mammy en git some mo' grub.

"Ole Brer Rabbit, he chipt in en 'greed, he did, en Brer Wolf, he tuck'n hitch up he team, en put he mammy in de waggin, en den him en Brer Rabbit druv off. Man come 'long:

"'Whar you gwine?'

"'Gwine 'long down ter town,
    Wid a bag er co'n fer ter sell;
We ain't got time fer ter stop en talk,
    Yit we wish you mighty well!'

"Did they talk poetry that way, Uncle Remus?" the little boy inquired.

"Shoo! lot's wuss dan dat, honey. Dey wuz constant a-gwine on dat away, en ef I wa'n't gittin' so mighty weak-kneed in de 'membunce I'd bust aloose yer en I'd fair wake you up wid de gwines on er dem ar creeturs.

"Now, den, dey tuck'n kyar' Brer Wolf mammy ter town en sell 'er, en dey start back wid a waggin-load er vittles. De day wuz a-wanin' en de sun wuz a-settin'. De win' tuck'n blow up sorter stiff, en de sun look red when she settin'. Dey druv on, en druv on. De win' blow, en de sun shine red. Bimeby, Brer Wolf scrooch up en shiver, en 'low:

"'Brer Rabbit, I'm a-gittin' mighty col'.'

"Brer Rabbit, he laugh en 'low:

"'I'm gittin' sorter creepy myself, Brer Wolf.'

"Dey druv on en druv on. Win' blow keen, sun shine red. Brer Wolf scrooch up in little knot. Bimeby he sing out:

"'Brer Rabbit, I'm freezin'! I'm dat col' I dunner w'at ter do!'

"Brer Rabbit, he p'int ter de settin' sun en say:

"'You see dat great big fier 'cross dar in de woods, Brer Wolf? Well, dey ain't nothin' ter hender you fum gwine dar en wommin' yo'se'f en I'll wait yer fer you. Gimme de lines, Brer Wolf, en you go wom yo'se'f all over.'

"Wid dat Brer Wolf, he put out des ez hard ez he kin, fer ter see of he can't fin' de fier; en w'ile he wuz gone, bless goodness, w'at should Brer Rabbit do but cut off de hosses' tails en stick um down deep in de mud — "

"Le' 'im 'lone, now! Des le' 'im lone!" exclaimed Aunt Tempy in an ecstasy of admiration.

"He stick de hosses' tails down in de mud," continued Uncle Remus, "en den he tuck'n druv de waggin 'way off in de swamp en hide it. Den he tuck'n come back, ole Brer Rabbit did, fer ter wait fer Brer Wolf.

"Atter so long a time, sho nuff, yer come Brer Wolf des a-gallin'-up back. Brer Rabbit he hail 'im.

"'Is you wom yo'se'f, Brer Wolf?'

"'Brer Rabbit, don't talk! Dat de mos' 'seetful fier w'at I had any 'speunce un. I run, en I run, en I run, en de mo' w'at I run de furder de fier git. De nigher you come ter dat fier de furder hit's off.'

"Brer Rabbit, he sorter scratch hisse'f behime de shoulderblade, en 'low:

"'Nummin' 'bout de fier, Brer Wolf. I got sump'n' yer dat'll wom you up. Ef you ain't nev' bin wom befo', I lay you'll get wom dis time.'

"Dis make Brer Wolf sorter look 'roun', en w'en he see Brer Rabbit hol'in' on ter de two hoss-tails, he up'n squall out, he did:

"'Lawdy mussy, Brer Rabbit! Whar my vittles? Whar my waggin? Whar my hosses?'

"'Dey er all right yer, Brer Wolf; dey er all right yer. I stayed dar whar you lef' me twel de hosses 'gun ter git restless. Den I cluck at um, en, bless gracious, dey start off en lan' in a quicksan'. W'en dey 'gun ter mire, I des tuck'n tu'n eve'y thing a-loose en grab de hosses by de tail, en I bin stan'in' yer wishin' fer you, Brer Wolf, twel I done gone gray in de min'. I 'low ter myse'f dat I'd hang on ter deze yer hoss-tails ef it kil't eve'y cow in de islan'. Come he'p me, Brer Wolf, en I lay we'll des nat'ally pull de groun' out but w'at we'll git deze creeturs out.'

"Wid dat, Brer Wolf, he kotch holt er one hoss-tail, en Brer Rabbit, he kotch holt er de yuther, en w'en dey pull, co'se de tails come out'n de mud. Dey stood dar, dey did, en dey look at de tails en den dey look at one n'er. Bimeby Brer Rabbit 'low:

"'Well, sir, Brer Wolf; we pull so hard twel we pull de tails plum' out!'

"Ole Brer Wolf, he dunner w'at ter do, but it 'gun ter git dark, en 'twa'n't long 'fo' he tell Brer Rabbit good-bye, en off he put fer home. Dat

ar Brer Rabbit," Uncle Remus went on, "he des tuck'n wait twel Brer
Wolf git out'n yearin', en den he went into de swamp en druv de hosses
home en git all de vittles, en he ain't hatter sell he ole mammy n'er. Dat
he ain't."

40

"Cutta Cord-La!"

TO ALL APPEARANCES Daddy Jack had taken no interest in Uncle Remus's
story of the horses' tails, and yet, as soon as the little boy and Aunt
Tempy were through laughing at a somewhat familiar climax, the old
African began to twist and fidget in his chair, and mumble to himself in
a lingo which might have been understood on the Guinea coast, but which
sounded out of place in Uncle Remus's Middle Georgia cabin. Presently,
however, his uneasiness took tangible shape. He turned around and exclaimed impatiently:

"Shuh-shuh! w'en you sta't fer tell-a dem tale, wey you no tell um lak
dey stan'? 'E bery bad fer twis' dem tale 'roun' un 'roun'. Wey you no talk
um stret?"

"Well, Brer Jack," said Uncle Remus, smiling good-humoredly upon
the queer little old man, "ef we done gone en got dat ar tale all twis' up,
de way fer you ter do is ter whirl in en ontwis' it, en we-all folks'll set up
yer en he'p you out plum' twel Mars John comes a-hollerin' en a-bawlin'
atter dish yer baby; en atter he done gone ter bed, den me en Sis Tempy
yer we ull set up wid you plum' twel de chickens crow fer day. Dem's de
kinder folk we all is up yer. We ain't got many swimps en crabs up yer in
Putmon county, but w'en it come ter settin' up wid comp'ny en hangin'
'roun' atter dark fer ter make de time pass away, we er mighty rank. Now
den, Brer Jack, I done call de roll wid my eye, en we er all yer ceppin'
dat ar 'Tildy gal, en 'twon't be long 'fo' she'll be a-drappin' in. Run over
in yo' min', en whar my tale 'uz wrong, des whirl in en put 'er ter rights."

"Shuh-shuh!" exclaimed the old African, "Oona no git dem tale stret.
I yed dem wey me lif; 'e soun' lak dis: One tam dem bittle bin git bery
skace. Da rice crop mek nuttin; da fish swim low; da bud fly high. Hard
times bin come dey-dey. 'E so hard, dem creeturs do git honkry fer true.

B'er Rabbit un B'er Wolf dey come pit bote 'e head tergerrer; dey is mek talk how honkry dey is 'way down in da belly.

"Bumbye, B'er Rabbit, 'e shed 'e y-eye, 'e say dey mus' kill dey gran-mammy. B'er Wolf say 'e mek 'e y-eye come wat'ry fer yeddy da talk lak dat. B'er Rabbit say:

"'Ki, B'er Wolf! da water come in you' y-eye wun you is bin honkry. Me y-eye done bin-a come wat'ry so long tam befo' I bin talky wit' you 'bout we gran'mammy.'

"B'er Wolf, 'e des keep on cryin'; 'e wipe 'e y-eye 'pon 'e coat-sleef. B'er Rabbit, 'e bin say:

"'Ef you is bin tek it so ha'd lak dis, B'er Wolf, 'e bery good fer kill-a you' gran-mammy fus', so you is kin come glad ag'in.'

"B'er Wolf, 'e go dry 'e y-eye un kill 'e gran'mammy, un dey is bin tek 'im gran'mammy off un sell um fer bittle. Dun dey is bin eat dis bittle day un night tel 'e all done gone. Wun-a tam come fer B'er Rabbit fer kill 'e gran'mammy, B'er Wolf, 'e go bisitin' 'im. 'E say:

"'B'er Rabbit, I is bin-a feel honkry troo un troo. Less we kill-a you' gran'mammy.'

"B'er Rabbit lif' up 'e head high; 'e lahff. 'E shekky one year, 'e shed-a one eye. 'E say:

"'Eh-eh, B'er Wolf, you t'ink I gwan kill-a me gran'mammy? Oh, no, B'er Wolf! Me no kin do dat.'

"Dis mek B'er Wolf wuss mad den 'e is bin befo'. 'E fair teer de yet' wit' 'e claw; 'e yowl sem lak Injun màns. 'E say 'e gwan mek B'er Rabbit kill 'e gran'mammy nohow.

"B'er Rabbit say 'e gwan see 'im 'bout dis. 'E tek 'e gran-mammy by da han'; 'e lead um way off in da woods; 'e hide um in da top one big co-coanut tree; 'e tell um fer stay deer."

The mention of a cocoanut tree caused the little boy to glance in-credulously at Uncle Remus, who made prompt and characteristic reply:

"Dat's it, honey; dat's it, sho. In dem days en in dem countries dey wuz plenty er cocoanut trees. Less we all set back yer en give Brer Jack a livin' chance."

"''E hide 'e gran'mammy in top cocoanut tree," continued Daddy Jack, "un 'e gi' um lilly bahskit wit' cord tie on um. In de day-mawnin', B'er Rabbit, 'e is bin go at da foot da tree. 'E make 'e v'ice fine; 'e holler:

" '*Granny! — Granny! — O Granny! Jutta cord-la!*'

"Wun 'e granny yeddy dis, 'e let bahskit down wit' da cord, un B'er Rabbit 'e fill um wit' bittle un somet'ing t'eat. Ebry day dey is bin-a do dis t'ing; ebry day B'er Rabbit is come fer feed 'e granny.

"B'er Wolf 'e watch, 'e lissun; 'e sneak up, 'e creep up, 'e do lissun. Bumbye, 'e do yeddy B'er Rabbit call; 'e see da bahskit swing down, 'e see um go back. Wun B'er Rabbit bin-a go 'way fum dey-dey, B'er Wolf, 'e come by da root da tree. 'E holler; 'e do say:

" '*Granny! — Granny! — O Granny! Shoot-a cord-la!*'

"Da ole Granny Rabbit lissun; 'e bin lissun well. 'E say:

" 'Ki! how come dis? Me son is no talky lak dis. 'E no shoot-a da cord lak dat.'

"Wun B'er Rabbit come back da granny is bin-a tell um 'bout somet'ing come-a holler shoot-a da cord-la, un B'er Rabbit, 'e lahff tel 'e is kin lahff no mo'. B'er Wolf, 'e hidin' close; 'e yed B'er Rabbit crackin' 'e joke; 'e is git bery mad.

"Wun B'er Rabbit is gone 'way, B'er Wolf bin-a come back. 'E stan' by da tree root; 'e holler:

" '*Granny! — Granny! — O Granny! Jutta cord-la!*'

"Granny Rabbit hoi 'e head 'pon one side; 'e lissun good. 'E say:

" 'I bery sorry, me son, you bin hab so bad col'. You' v'ice bin-a soun' rough, me son.'

"Dun Granny Rabbit is bin peep down; 'e bin say:

" 'Hi! B'er Wolf! Go 'way fum dey-dey. You no is bin fool-a me lak dis. Go 'way, B'er Wolf!'

"B'er Wolf, 'e come bery mad; 'e grin tel 'e tush bin shiün. 'E go in da swamp; 'e scratch 'e head; 'e t'ink. Bumbye, 'e go bisitin' one Blacksmit', un 'e ahx 'im how kin 'e do fer mek 'e v'ice come fine lak B'er Rabbit v'ice. Da Blacksmit', 'e say:

" 'Come, B'er Wolf; I run dis red-hot poker in you' t'roat, 'e mekky you talk easy.'

"B'er Wolf say, 'Well, I lak you for mekky me v'ice fine.'

"Dun da Blacksmit' run da red-hot poker in B'er Wolf t'roat, un 'e hu't um so bad, 'tiss-a bin long tam befo' B'er Wolf kin tekky de long walk by da cocoanut tree. Bumbye 'e git so 'e kin come by, un wun 'e git dey-dey, 'e holler:

" '*Granny! — Granny! — O Granny! Jutta cord-la!*'

"Da v'ice soun' so nice un fine da' Granny Rabbit is bin t'ink 'e B'er Rabbit v'ice, un 'e is bin-a let da bahskit down. B'er Wolf, 'e shekky da cord lak 'e is put some bittle in da bahskit, un dun 'e is bin-a git in 'ese'f. B'er Wolf, 'e keep still. Da Granny Rabbit pull on da cord; 'e do say:

" '*Ki!* 'e come he'ffy; 'e he'ffy fer true. Me son, 'e love 'e Granny heap.'

"B'er Wolf, 'e do grin; 'e grin, un 'e keep still. Da Granny Rabbit pull; 'e pull ha'd. 'E pull tel 'e is git B'er Wolf mos' by da top, un dun 'e stop fer res'. B'er Wolf look-a down, 'e head swim; 'e look up, 'e mout' water; 'e look-a down 'g'in, 'e see B'er Rabbit. 'E git skeer, 'e juk on da rope. B'er Rabbit, 'e holler:

" '*Granny! — Granny! — O Granny! Cutta cord-la!*'

"Da Granny Rabbit cut da cord, un B'er Wolf is fall down un broke 'e neck."

41
Aunt Tempy's Story

THE LITTLE BOY observed that Aunt Tempy was very much interested in Daddy Jack's story. She made no remarks while the old African was telling it, but she was busily engaged in measuring imaginary quilt patterns on her apron with her thumb and forefinger — a sure sign that her interest had been aroused. When Daddy Jack had concluded — when, with a swift, sweeping gesture of his wrinkled hand, he cut the cord and allowed Brother Wolf to perish ignominiously — Aunt Tempy drew a long breath, and said:

"Dat ar tale come 'cross me des like a dream. Hit put me in min' er one w'at I year w'en I wuz little bit er gal. Look like I kin see myse'f right now, settin' flat down on de h'a'th lis'nin' at ole Unk' Monk. You know'd ole Unk' Monk, Brer Remus. You bleedzd ter know'd 'im. Up dar in Ferginny. I 'clar' ter goodness, it makes me feel right foolish. Brer Remus, I des know you know'd Unk' Monk."

For the first time in many a day the little boy saw Uncle Remus in a serious mood. He leaned forward in his chair, shook his head sadly, as he gazed into the fire.

"Ah, Lord, Sis Tempy!" he exclaimed sorrowfully, "don't less we all go foolin' 'roun' 'mungs dem ole times. De bes' kinder bread gits sours. W'at's yistiddy wid us wuz 'fo' de worl' begun wid dish yer chile. Dat's de way I looks at it."

"Dat's de Lord's trufe, Brer Remus," exclaimed Aunt Tempy with unction, "un I mighty glad you call me ter myse'f. Little mo' un I'd er sot right yer un a gone 'way back to Ferginny, un all on 'count er dat ar tale w'at I year long time ago."

"What tale was that, Aunt Tempy?" asked the little boy.

"Eh-eh, honey!" replied Aunt Tempy, with a display of genuine bashfulness; "eh-eh, honey! I 'fraid you all'll set up dar un laugh me outer de house. I ain't dast ter tell no tale 'longside er Brer Remus un Daddy Jack yer I 'fraid I git it all mix up."

The child manifested such genuine disappointment that Aunt Tempy relented a little.

"Ef you all laugh, now," she said, with a threatening air, "I'm des gwine ter pick up en git right out er dish yer place. Dey ain't ter be no laughin', kaze de tale w'at I year in Ferginny ain't no laughin' tale."

With this understanding Aunt Tempy adjusted her head-handkerchief, looked around rather sheepishly, as Uncle Remus declared afterwards in confidence to the little boy, and began:

"Well, den, in de times w'en Brer Rabbit un Brer Fox live in de same settlement wid one n'er, de season's tuck'n come wrong. De wedder got hot un den a long dry drouth sot in, un it seem like dat de nat'al leaf on de tree wuz gwine ter tu'n ter powder."

Aunt Tempy emphasized her statements by little backward and forward movements of her head, and the little boy would have laughed, but a warning glance from Uncle Remus prevented him.

"De leaf on de trees look like dey gwine ter tu'n ter powder, un de groun' look like it done bin cookt. All de truck w'at de creeturs plant wuz all parched up, un dey wa'n't no crops made nowhars. Dey dunner w'at ter do. Dey run dis a-way, dey run dat a-way; yit w'en dey quit runnin' dey dunner whar dey bread comin' frun. Dis de way it look ter Brer Fox, un so one day when he got mighty hankerin' atter sumpin' sorter joosy, he meet Brer Rabbit in de lane, un he ax um, sezee:

"'Brer Rabbit, whar'bouts our bread comin' frun?'

"Brer Rabbit, he bow, he did, un answer, sezee:

"'Look like it mought be comin' frun nowhar,' sezee."

"You see dat, honey!" exclaimed Uncle Remus, condescending to give the story the benefit of his patronage; "You see dat! Brer Rabbit wuz allus a-waitin' a chance fer ter crack he jokes."

"Yas, Lord!" Aunt Tempy continued, with considerable more animation; "he joke, un joke, but bimeby, he ain't feel like no mo' jokin', un den he up'n say, sezee, dat him un Brer Fox better start out'n take der fammerlies wid um ter town un swap off for some fresh-groun' meal; un Brer Fox say, sezee, dat dat look mighty fa'r un squar', un den dey tuck'n make dey 'greements.

"Brer Fox wuz ter s'ply de waggin un team, un he promise dat he gwine ter ketch he fammerly un tie um hard un fast wid a red twine string. Brer Rabbit he say, sezee, dat he gwine ter ketch he fammerly un tie um all, un meet Brer Fox at de fork er de road.

"Sho nuff, soon in de mawnin', w'en Brer Fox draw up wid he waggin, he holler 'Wo!' un Brer Rabbit he tuck'n holler back, 'Wo yo'se'f!' un den Brer Fox know dey 'uz all dar. Brer Fox, he tuck'n sot up on de seat, un all er he fammerly, dey wuz a-layin' under de seat. Brer Rabbit, he tuck'n put all he fammerly in de behime een' er de waggin, un he say, sezee, dat he 'speck he better set back dar twel dey git sorter usen ter dey surrounderlings, un den Brer Fox crack he whip, un off dey wen' toze town. Brer Fox, he holler ev'y once in a while, sezee:

"'No noddin' back dar, Brer Rabbit!'

"Brer Rabbit he holler back, sezee:

"'Brer Fox, you miss de ruts en de rocks, un I'll miss de noddin'.'

"But all dat time, bless yo' soul! Brer Rabbit wuz settin' dar ontyin' he ole 'oman un he childun, w'ich dey wuz sev'm uv um. W'en he git him all ontie, Brer Rabbit, he tuck'n h'ist hisse'f on de seat 'long er Brer Fox, un dey sot dar un talk un laugh 'bout de all-sorts er times dey gwine ter have w'en dey git de co'n meal. Brer Fox sez, sezee, he gwine ter bake hoe-cake; Brer Rabbit sez, sezee, he gwine ter make ashcake.

"Des 'bout dis time one er Brer Rabbit's childun raise hisse'f up easy un hop out de waggin. Miss Fox, she sing out:

"'One frun sev'm
Don't leave 'lev'm.'

"Brer Fox hunch he ole 'oman wid he foot fer ter make 'er keep still. Bimeby 'n'er little Rabbit pop up un hop out. Miss Fox say, se' she:

> "'One frun six
>   Leaves me less kicks.'

"Brer Fox go on talkin' ter Brer Rabbit, un Brer Rabbit go on talkin' ter Brer Fox, un 'twa'n't so mighty long 'fo' all Brer Rabbit fammerly done pop up un dive out de waggin', un eve'y time one 'ud go Miss Fox she 'ud fit it like she did de yuthers."

"What did she say, Aunt Tempy?" asked the little boy, who was interested in the rhymes.

"Des lemme see:

> "'One frun five
>   Leaves four alive;
> "'One frun four
>   Leaves th'ee un no mo';
> "'One frun th'ee
>   Leaves two ter go free;
> "'One frun one,
>   Un all done gone.'"

"What did Brother Rabbit do then?" inquired the little boy.

"Better ax w'at Brer Fox do," replied Aunt Tempy, pleased with the effect of her rhymes. "Brer Fox look 'roun' atter while, un w'en he see dat all Brer Rabbit fammerly done gone, he lean back un holler 'Wo!' un den he say sezee:

"'In de name er goodness, Brer Rabbit! whar all yo' folks?'

"Brer Rabbit look 'roun', un den he make like he cryin'. He des fa'rly boo-hoo'd, un he say, sezee:

"'Dar now, Brer Fox! I des know'd dat ef I put my po' little childun's in dar wid yo' folks dey'd git e't up. I des know'd it!'

"Ole Miss Fox, she des vow she ain't totch Brer Rabbit fammerly. But Brer Fox, he bin wantin' a piece un um all de way, un he begrudge um so dat he mighty mad wid he ole 'oman un de childuns, un he say, sezee:

"'You kin des make de most er dat, kaze I'm a-gwine ter bid you good riddance dis ve'y day;' un sho nuff, Brer Fox tuck'n tuck he whole fammerly ter town un trade um off fer co'n.

"Brer Rabbit wuz wid 'em, des ez big ez life un twice ez nat'al. Dey start back, dey did, un w'en dey git four er five mile out er town, hit come 'cross Brer Fox min' dat he done come away un lef' a plug er terbacker in de sto', en he say he bleedzd ter go back atter it.

"Brer Rabbit, he say, sezee, dat he'll stay en take keer er de waggin, w'ile Brer Fox kin run back un git terbacker. Soon ez Brer Fox git out er sight, Brer Rabbit laid de hosses under line un lash un drove de waggin home, un put de hosses in he own stable, un de co'n in de smoke-house, un de waggin in de barn, un den he put some co'n in he pocket, un cut de hosses' tails off, un went back up de road twel he come ter a quog-mire, un in dat he stick de tails un wait fer Brer Fox.

"Atter w'ile yer he come, un den Brer Rabbit gun ter holler un pull at de tails. He say, sezee:

"'Run yer, Brer Fox! run yer! You er des in time ef you ain't too late. Run yer, Brer Fox! run yer!'

"Brer Fox, he run'd en juk Brer Rabbit away, un say, sezee:

"'Git out de way, Brer Rabbit! You too little! Git out de way, un let a man ketch holt.'

"Brer Fox tuck holt," continued Aunt Tempy, endeavoring to keep from laughing, "un he fetch'd one big pull, un I let you know dat 'uz de onliest pull he make, kaze de tails come out un he tu'n a back summerset. He jump up, he did, en 'gun ter grabble in de quog-mire des ez hard ez he kin.

"Brer Rabbit, he stan' by, un drop some co'n in onbeknowns' ter Brer Fox, un dis make 'im grabble wuss un wuss, un he grabble so hard un he grabble so long dat 'twa'n't long 'fo' he fall down dead, un so dat 'uz de las' er ole Brer Fox in dat day un time."

As Aunt Tempy paused, Uncle Remus adjusted his spectacles and looked at her admiringly. Then he laughed heartily.

"I declar', Sis Tempy," he said, after a while, "you gives tongue same ez a lawyer. You'll hatter jine in wid us some mo'."

Aunt Tempy closed her eyes and dropped her head on one side.

"Don't git me started, Brer Remus," she said, after a long pause; "kaze ef you does you'll hatter set up yer long pas' yo' bed-time."

"I b'lieve you, Sis Tempy, dat I does!" exclaimed the old man, with the air of one who has made a pleasing discovery.

42
The Fire-Test

"WE ER SORTER bin a-waitin' fer Sis Tempy," Uncle Remus remarked when the little boy made his appearance the next night; "but somehow er n'er look lak she fear'd she hatter up en tell some mo' tales. En yit maybe she bin strucken down wid some kinder ailment. Dey ain't no countin' on deze yer fat folks. Dey er up one minnit en down de nex'; en w'at make it dat a-way I be bless ef I know, kaze w'en folks is big en fat look lak dey oughter be weller dan deze yer long hongry kinder folks.

"Yit all de same, Brer Jack done come," continued Uncle Remus, "en we ull des slam de do' shet, en ef Sis Tempy come she'll des hatter hol' 'er han's 'fo' 'er face en holler out:

"'Lucky de Linktum, chunky de chin,
      Open de do' en let me in!'

"Oh you kin laugh ef you wanter, but I boun' you ef Sis Tempy wuz ter come dar en say de wuds w'at I say, de button on dat ar do' 'ud des nat'ally twis' hitse'f off but w'at 'twould let 'er in. Now, I boun' you dat!"

Whatever doubts the child may have had he kept to himself, for experience had taught him that it was useless to irritate the old man by disputing with him. What effect the child's silence may have had in this instance it is impossible to say, for just then Aunt Tempy came in laughing.

"You all kin des say w'at you please," she exclaimed, as she took her seat, "but dat ar *Shucky Cordy* in de tale w'at Daddy Jack done tole bin runnin' 'roun' in my min' en zoonin' in my years all de time."

"Yer too!" exclaimed Uncle Remus, with emphasis. "Dat's me up en down. Look lak dat ar cricket over dar in de cornder done tuck it up, en now he gwine, '*Shucky-cordy! Shucky-cordy!*'"

"Shuh-shuh!" exclaimed Daddy Jack, with vehement contempt, "'e *jutta cord-la!* 'E no 'shucky-cordy' no'n 't all."

"Well, well, Brer Jack," said Uncle Remus, soothingly, "in deze low groun's er sorrer, you des got ter lean back en make 'lowances fer all sorts er folks. You got ter 'low fer dem dat knows too much same ez dem w'at knows too little. A heap er sayin' en a heap er doin's in dis roun' worl' got ter be tuck on trus'. You got yo' sayin's, I got mine; you got yo' knowin's, en I got mine. Man come 'long en ax me how does de wum git in de scaly-bark. I tell 'im right up en down, I dunno, sir. N'er man come 'long en ax me who raise de row 'twix' de buzzud en de bee-martin. I tell 'im I dunno, sir. Yit kaze I dunno," continued Uncle Remus, "dat don't hender um. Dar dey is, spite er dat — wum in de scaly-bark, bee-martin atter de buzzud."

"Dat's so," exclaimed Aunt Tempy, "dat's de Lord's trufe!"

"Dat ar pullin' at de string," Uncle Remus went on, "en dat ar hollerin' 'bout shucky-cordy — "

"*Jutta cord-la!*" said Daddy Jack, fiercely.

"'Bout de watsizname," said Uncle Remus, with a lenient and forgiving smile, — "all dish yer hollerin' en gwine on 'bout de watsizname put me in min' er one time w'en Brer Rabbit wuz gwine off fum home fer ter git a mess er green truck.

"W'en Brer Rabbit git ready fer ter go, he call all he chilluns up, en he tell um dat w'en he go out dey mus' fas'n de do' on de inside, en dey mus'n' tu'n nobody in, nohow, kaze Brer Fox en Brer Wolf bin layin' 'roun' waitin' chance fer ter nab um. En he tuck'n tole um dat w'en he come back, he'd rap at de do' en sing:

> "'I'll stay w'en you away,
> 'Kaze no gol' will pay toll!'

"De little Rabs, dey hilt up der han's en promise dat dey won't open de do' fer nobody ceppin' dey daddy, en wid dat, Brer Rabbit he tuck'n put out, he did, at a han'-gallop, huntin' sump'n' n'er ter eat. But all dis time, Brer Wolf bin hidin' out behime de house, en he year eve'y wud dat pass, en ole Brer Rabbit wa'n't mo'n out'n sight 'fo' Brer Wolf went ter de do', en he knock, he did — *blip, blip, blip!*

"Little Rab holler out, 'Who dat?'

"Brer Wolf he sing:

> " 'I'll stay w'en you away,
>   'Kaze no gol' will pay toll!'

"De little Rabs dey laugh fit ter kill deyse'f, en dey up'n 'low:

" 'Go 'way, Mr. Wolf, go 'way! You ain't none er we-all daddy!'

"Ole Brer Wolf he slunk off, he did, but eve'y time he thunk er dem plump little Rabs, he des git mo' hongry dan befo', en 'twa'n't long 'fo' he 'uz back at de do' — *blap, blap, blap!*

"Little Rab holler: 'Who dat?'

"Brer Wolf, he up'n sing:

> " 'I'll stay w'en you away,
>   Kaze no gol' will pay toll!'

"De little Rabs dey laugh en roll on de flo', en dey up'n 'low:

" 'Go 'way, Mr. Wolf! We-all daddy ain't got no bad col' lak dat.'

"Brer Wolf slunk off, but bimeby he come back, en dis time he try mighty hard fer ter talk fine. He knock at de do' — *blam, blam, blam!*

"Little Rab holler: 'Who dat?'

"Brer Wolf tu'n loose en sing:

> " 'I'll stay w'en you away,
>   Kaze no gol' will pay toll!'

"Little Rab holler back, he did:

" 'Go 'way, Mr. Wolf! go 'way! We-all daddy kin sing lots puttier dan dat. Go 'way, Mr. Wolf! go 'way!'

"Brer Wolf he slunk off, he did, en he go 'way out in de woods, en he sing, en sing, twel he kin sing fine ez de nex' man. Den he go back en knock at de do', en w'en de little Rabs ax who dat, he sing dem de song; en he sing so nice, en he sing so fine, dat dey ondo de do', en ole Brer Wolf walk in en gobble um all up, fum de fus' ter de las'.

"W'en ole Brer Rabbit git back home, he fin' de do' stan'in' wide open en all de chilluns gone. Dey wa'n't no sign er no tussle; de h'a'th 'uz all swep' clean, en eve'ything wuz all ter rights, but right over in de corder he see a pile er bones, en den he know in reason dat some er de yuther creeturs done bin dar en make hash out'n he chilluns.

"Den he go 'roun' en ax um 'bout it, but dey all 'ny it; dey all 'ny it ter de las', en Brer Wolf, he 'ny it wuss'n all un um. Den Brer Rabbit tuck'n lay de case 'fo' Brer Tarrypin. Ole Brer Tarrypin wuz a mighty man in dem days," continued Uncle Remus, with something like a sigh — "a mighty man, en no sooner is he year de state er de condition dan he up'n call all de creeturs tergedder. He call um tergedder, he did, en den he up'n tell um 'bout how somebody done tuck'n 'stroy all er Brer Rabbit chillun, en he 'low dat de man w'at do dat bleedzd ter be kotch, kaze ef he ain't dey ain't no tellin' how long it'll be 'fo' de same somebody 'ill come 'long en 'stroy all de chillun in de settlement.

"Brer B'ar, he up'n ax how dey gwine fin' 'im, en Brer Tarrypin say dey er allers a way. Den he 'low:

"'Less dig a deep pit.'

"'I'll dig de pit,' sez Brer Wolf, sezee.

"Atter de pit done dug, Brer Tarrypin say:

"'Less fill de pit full er lighter'd knots en bresh.'

"'I'll fill de pit,' sez Brer Wolf, sezee.

"Atter de pit done fill up, Brer Tarrypin say:

"'Now, den, less set it a-fier.'

"'I'll kindle de fier,' sez Brer Wolf, sezee.

"W'en de fier 'gun ter blaze up, Brer Tarrypin 'low dat de creeturs mus' jump 'cross dat, en de man w'at 'stroy Brer Rabbit chilluns will drap in en git bu'nt up. Brer Wolf bin so uppity 'bout diggin', en fillin', en kindlin', dat dey all 'spected 'im fer ter make de fus' trial; but bless yo' soul en body! Brer Wolf look lak he got some yuther business fer ter 'ten' ter.

"De pit look so deep, en de fier bu'n so high, dat dey mos' all 'fear'd fer ter make de trial, but atter w'ile, Brer Mink 'low dat he ain't hunted none er Brer Rabbit chilluns, en wid dat, he tuck runnin' start, en lipt across. Den Brer Coon say he ain't hunted um, en over he sailed. Brer B'ar say he feel mo' heavy dan he ever is befo' in all he born days, but he ain't hurted none er Brer Rabbit po' little chillun, en wid dat away he went 'cross de fier. Dey all jump, twel bimeby hit come Brer Wolf time. Den he 'gun ter git skeer'd, en he mighty sorry kaze he dig dat pit so deep en wide, en kindle dat fier so high. He tuck sech a long runnin' start, dat time he git ter de jumpin' place, he 'uz done wo' teetotally out, en he lipt up, he did, en fetch'd a squall en drapt right spang in de middle er de fier."

"Uncle Remus," said the little boy, after a while, "did Brother Terrapin jump over the fier?"

"W'at Brer Tarrypin gwine jump fer?" responded Uncle Remus, "w'en eve'ybody know Tarrypins ain't eat Rabbits."

"Well, you know you said everything was different then," said the child.

"Look yer, Brer Jack," exclaimed Uncle Remus, "ef you got any tale on yo' min', des let 'er come. Dish yer youngster gittin' too long-headed fer me; dat he is."

43
The Cunning Snake

DADDY JACK, thus appealed to, turned half round in his seat, winked his bright little eyes very rapidly, and said, with great animation:

"Hoo! me bin yeddy one sing-tale; me yeddy um so long tam 'go. One tam dere bin one ole Affiky ooman, 'e call 'im name Coomba. 'E go walky troo da woots, 'e walky troo da fiel'. Bumbye 'e is bin come 'pon one snake-nes' fill wit' aig. Snake big snake, aig big aig. Affiky oomans is bin want-a dem aig so bahd; 'e 'fraid fer tek um. 'E gone home; 'e is see dem aig in 'e dream, 'e want um so bahd. Wun da nex' day mornin' come, da Affiky oomans say 'e bleeze fer hab dem aig. 'E go 'way, 'e bin-a see da snake-nes', 'e is git-a da aig; 'e fetch um at 'e own house; 'e cook um fer 'e brekwuss.

"Bumbye da snake bin-a come by 'e nes'. Aig done gone. 'E pit 'e nose 'pon da groun', 'e is track da Affiky oomans by 'e own house. Snake come by da Affiky oomans house; 'e ahx 'bout 'e aig. Affiky oomans say 'e no hab bin see no aig. Snake see da skin wut bin 'pon 'e aig; 'e ahx wut is dis. Affiky oomans no say nuttin' 't all. Snake 'e say:

"'Wey fer you come brek up me nes' un tekky me aig?'

"Affiky oomans 'e no say nuttin' 't all. 'E toss 'e head, 'e mek lak 'e no yeddy da snake v'ice, 'e go 'bout 'e wuk. Snake, 'e say:

"'Ooman! you is bin yed me v'ice wun me cry out. You bin tekky me aig; you is bin 'stroy me chillun. Tek keer you' own; tek keer you' own.'

"Snake gone 'way; 'e slick out 'e tongue, 'e slide 'way. Bumbye de Affiky oomans, 'e hab one putty lil pickaninny; 'e lub um ha'd all over. 'E is mine wut da snake say; 'e tote da pickaninny 'roun' 'pon 'e bahck. 'E call um Noncy, 'e tote um fur, 'e lub um ha'd.

"Snake, 'e bin-a stay in da bush-side; 'e watch all day, 'e wait all night; 'e git honkry fer da pickaninny, 'e want um so bahd. 'E bin slick out 'e tongue, 'e bin slide troo da grass, 'e bin hanker fer da pickaninny.

"Bumbye da Affiky oomans tote-a da Noncy til 'e git tire; 'e puff, 'e blow, 'e wuk 'e gill sem lak cat-fish."

Aunt Tempy burst into loud laughter at this remarkable statement.

"Whoever is year de beat er dat!" she exclaimed. "Daddy Jack, you goes on owdashus 'bout de wimmen, dat you does!"

"'E puff, 'e blow, 'e pant; 'e say:

"'Da pickaninny, 'e der git-a big lak one bag rice. 'E der git-a so heffy, me yent mos' know wut fer do. Me yent kin tote um no mo'.'

"Da Affiky oomans is bin-a pit da pickaninny down 'pon da groun'. 'E mek up one sing[1] in 'e head, un 'e l'arn da lilly gal fer answer da sing. 'E do show um how fer pull out da peg in da do'. Snake, 'e is bin lay quile up in da bush; 'e say nuttin' 't all.

"Affiky oomans is l'arn-a da pickaninny fer answer da sing, un wun he sta't fer go off, 'e say:

"'Pit da peg in da do' un you no y-open um fer nobody 'cep' you is yeddy me sing.'

"Lil gal, 'e say yassum, un da Affiky oomans gone off. Snake stay still. 'E quile up in 'e quile; 'e yent moof 'e tail. Bumbye, toze night-time, da Affiky oomans come bahck wey 'e lif. 'E stan' by da do'; 'e talk dis sing:

> "'Walla walla witto, me Noncy,
> Walla walla witto, me Noncy,
> Walla walla witto, me Noncy!'

"'E v'ice 'come finer toze da las' tel 'e do git loud fer true. Da lilly gal, 'e do mek answer lak dis:

[1] "'E mek up one sing." She composed a song and taught the child the refrain. — J. C. H.

"'Andolee! Andoli! Andolo!'

"'E know 'e mammy v'ice, en 'e bin pull out da peg queek. 'E run to 'e mammy; 'e mammy der hug um up. Nex' day, 'e da sem t'ing; two, t'ree, sev'm day, 'e da sem t'ing. Affiky oomans holler da sing; da lilly gal mek answer 'pon turrer side da do'. Snake, 'e lay quile up in da bush. 'E watch da night, 'e lissun da day; 'e try fer l'arn-a da sing; 'e no say nuttin' 't all. Bumbye, one tam wun Affiky oomans bin gone 'way, snake, 'e wait 'til 'e mos' tam fer oomans fer come bahck. 'E gone by da do'; 'e y-open 'e mout'; 'e say:

> "'Wullo wullo widdo, me Noncy,
> Wullo wullo widdo, me Noncy,
> Wullo wullo widdo, me Noncy!'

"'E try fer mekky 'e v'ice come fine lak da lil gal mammy; 'e der hab one rough place in 'e t'roat, un 'e v'ice come big. Lilly gal no mek answer. 'E no y-open da do'. 'E say:

"'Go 'way fum dey-dey! Me mammy no holler da sing lak dat!'

"Snake, 'e try one, two, t'ree time; 'e yent no use; Lilly gal no y-open da do', 'e no mek answer. Snake 'e slick out 'e tongue un slide 'way; 'e say 'e mus' l'arn-a da sing sho' 'nuff.

"Bumbye, da Affiky oomans come bahck. 'E holler da sing:

> "'Walla walla witto, me Noncy,
> Walla walla witto, me Noncy,
> Walla walla witto, me Noncy!'

"Lilly gal say: 'Da' me mammy!' 'E answer da sing:

"'Andolee! Andoli! Andolo!'

"Snake, 'e quile up in da chimmerly-cornder; 'e hol' 'e bre't' fer lissun; 'e der l'arn-a da sing. Nex' day mornin' da Affiky oomans bin-agone 'way un lef' da lilly gal all by 'ese'f. All de day long da snake 'e t'ink about da song; 'e say um in 'e min', 'e say um forwud, 'e say um bahckwud. Bumbye, mos' toze sundown, 'e come at da do'; 'e come, 'e holler da sing:

> "'Walla walla witto, me Noncy,
> Walla walla witto, me Noncy,
> Walla walla witto, me Noncy!'

"Da lil gal, 'e t'ink-a da snake bin 'e mammy; 'e is answer da sing:

"'Andolee! Andoli! Andolo!'

"'E mek answer lak dat, un 'e y-open da do' queek. 'E run 'pon da snake 'fo' 'e is *shum*. Snake, 'e bin-a hug da lilly gal mo' sem dun 'e mammy; 'e is twis' 'e tail 'roun' um; 'e is ketch um in 'e quile. Lilly gal 'e holler, 'e squall, 'e holler. Nobody bin-a come by fer yeddy um. Snake 'e 'quees' um tight, 'e no l'em go; 'e 'quees' um tight, 'e swaller um whole; 'e bre'k-a no bone; 'e tekky da lilly gal lak 'e stan'.

"Bumbye da lil mammy come home at 'e house. 'E holler da sing, 'e git-a no answer. 'E come skeer'; 'e v'ice shek, 'e body trimple. 'E lissun, 'e no yeddy no fuss. 'E push de do' y-open, 'e no see nuttin' 't all; da lilly gal gone! Da ooman 'e holler, 'e cry; 'e ahx way 'e lilly gal bin gone; 'e no git no answer. 'E look all 'roun', 'e see way da snake bin-a 'cross da road. 'E holler:

"'Ow, me Lard! da snake bin come swaller me lil Noncy gal. I gwan hunt 'im up; I gwan foller da snake pas' da een' da yet'.'

"'E go in da swamp, 'e cut 'im one cane; 'e come bahck, 'e fine da snake track, un 'e do foller 'long wey 'e lead. Snake 'e so full wit de lilly gal 'e no walk fas'; lil gal mammy, 'e bin mad, 'e go stret 'long. Snake 'e so full wit' da lilly gal, 'e come sleepy. 'E lay down, 'e shed-a 'e y-eye. 'E y-open um no mo'," continued Daddy Jack, moving his head slowly from side to side, and looking as solemn as he could. "Da ooman come 'pon de snake wun 'e bin lay dar 'sleep; 'e come 'pon 'im, un 'e tekky da cane un bre'k 'e head, 'e mash um flat. 'E cut da snake open, 'e fine da lilly gal sem lak 'e bin 'sleep. 'E tek um home, 'e wash um off. Bumbye da lilly gal y-open 'e y-eye, un soon 'e see 'e mammy, 'e answer da sing. 'E say:

"'Andolee! Andoli! Andolo!'"

"Well, well, well!" exclaimed Aunt Tempy, sympathetically.

"Un de po' little creetur wuz 'live?"

"Enty!" exclaimed Daddy Jack. No reply could possibly have been more prompt, more emphatic, or more convincing.

44
How Brother Fox Was Too Smart

"UNCLE REMUS," said the little boy, one night when he found the old man alone, "I don't like these stories where somebody has to stand at the door and sing, do you? They don't sound funny to me."

Uncle Remus crossed his legs, took off his spectacles and laid them carefully on the floor under his chair, and made a great pretense of arguing the matter with the child.

"Now, den, honey, w'ich tale is it w'at you ain't lak de mos'?"

The little boy reflected a moment and then replied:

"About the snake swallowing the little girl. I don't see any fun in that. Papa says they have snakes in Africa as big around as his body; and, goodness knows, I hope they won't get after me."

"How dey gwine git atter you, honey, w'en you settin' up yer 'long side er me en de snakes 'way 'cross dar in Affiky?"

"Well, Daddy Jack, he came, and the snakes might come too."

Uncle Remus laughed, more to reassure the child than to ridicule his argument.

"Dem ar snakes ain't no water-moccasin, not ez I knows un. Brer Jack bin yer mighty long time, en dey ain't no snake foller atter 'im yit."

"Now, Uncle Remus; papa says they have them in shows."

"I 'speck dey is, honey, but who's afear'd er snake stufft wid meal-bran? Not none er ole Miss gran'chillun, sho!"

"Well, the stories don't sound funny to me."

"Dat mought be, yit dey er funny ter Brer Jack, en dey do mighty well fer ter pass de time. Atter w'ile you'll be a-gwine 'roun' runnin' down ole Brer Rabbit en de t'er creeturs, en somehow er n'er you'll tak'n git ole Remus mix up wid um twel you won't know w'ich one un um you er runnin' down, en let 'lone dat, you won't keer needer. Shoo, honey! you ain't de fus' chap w'at I done tole deze yer tales ter."

"Why, Uncle Remus," exclaimed the little boy, in a horrified tone, "I *wouldn't;* you *know* I wouldn't!"

"Don't tell me!" insisted the old man, "you er outgrowin' me, en you er outgrowin' de tales. Des lak Miss Sally change de lenk er yo' britches, des dat a-way I got ter do w'ence I whirl in en persoo atter de creeturs. Time wuz w'en you 'ud set down yer by dish yer h'a'th, en you'd tak'n holler en laugh en clap yo' han's w'en ole Brer Rabbit 'ud kick out'n all er he tanglements; but deze times you sets dar wid yo' eyes wide open, en you don't crack a smile. I say it!" Uncle Remus exclaimed, changing his tone and attitude, as if addressing some third person concealed in the room. "I say it! Stidder j'inin' in wid de fun, he'll tak'n lean back dar en 'spute 'long wid you des lak grow'd-up folks. I'll stick it out dis season, but w'en Chris'mus come, I be bless ef I ain't gwine ter ax Miss Sally fer my remoovance papers, en I'm gwine ter hang my bundle on my walkin'-cane, en see w'at kinder dirt dey is at de fur een' er de big road."

"Yes!" exclaimed the little boy, triumphantly, "and, if you do, the patter-rollers will get you."

"Well," replied the old man, with a curious air of resignation, "ef dey does, I ain't gwine ter do lak Brer Fox did w'en Brer Rabbit showed him de tracks in de big road."

"How did Brother Fox do, Uncle Remus?"

"Watch out, now! Dish yer one er de tales w'at ain't got no fun in it."

"Uncle Remus, please tell it."

"Hol' on dar! Dey mought be a snake somers in it — one er deze yer meal-bran snakes."

"*Please*, Uncle Remus, tell it."

The old man never allowed himself to resist the artful pleadings of the little boy. So he recovered his specks from under the chair, looked up the chimney for luck, as he explained to his little partner, and proceeded:

"One day w'en Brer Fox went callin' on Miss Meadows en Miss Motts en de t'er gals, who should he fin' settin' up dar but ole Brer Rabbit? Yasser! Dar he wuz, des ez sociable ez you please. He 'uz gwine on wid de gals, en w'en Brer Fox drapt in dey look lak dey wuz mighty tickled 'bout sump'n' n'er Brer Rabbit bin sayin'. Brer Fox, he look sorter jubous, he did, des lak folks does w'en dey walks up in a crowd whar de yuthers all a-gigglin'. He tuck'n kotch de dry grins terreckerly. But dey all howdied, en Miss Meadows, she up'n say:

"'You'll des hatter skuse us, Brer Fox, on de 'count er dish yer gigglement. Tooby sho, hit monstus disperlite fer we-all fer to be gwine on dat a-way; but I mighty glad you come, en I sez ter de gals, s'I, "'Fo' de Lord, gals! dar come Brer Fox, en yer we is a-gigglin' en a-gwine on scan'lous; yit hit done come ter mighty funny pass," s'I, "ef you can't run on en laugh 'fo' home folks," s'I. Dat des zackly w'at I say, en I leave it ter ole Brer Rabbit en de gals yer ef 'tain't.'

"De gals, dey tuck'n jine in, dey did, en dey make ole Brer Fox feel right slimmy-slammy, en dey all sot dar en run on 'bout dey neighbors des lak folks does deze days. Dey sot dar, dey did, twel atter w'ile Brer Rabbit look out todes sundown, en 'low:

"'Now, den, folks and fr'en's, I bleedzd ter say goo'-bye. Cloud comin' up out yan, en mos' 'fo' we know it de rain'll be a-po'in' en de grass 'll be a-growin'.'"

"Why, that's poetry, Uncle Remus!" interrupted the little boy.

"Tooby she 't is, honey! tooby sho 't is. I des let you know Brer Rabbit 'uz a mighty man in dem days. Brer Fox, he see de cloud comin' up, en he up'n 'low he 'speck he better be gittin' 'long hisse'f, kaze he ain't wanter git he Sunday-go-ter-meetin' cloze wet. Miss Meadows en Miss Motts, en de gals, dey want um ter stay, but bofe er dem ar creeturs 'uz mighty feard er gittin' der foots wet, en atter w'ile dey put out.

"W'iles dey 'uz gwine down de big road, jawin' at one er n'er, Brer Fox, he tuck'n stop right quick, en 'low:

"'Run yer, Brer Rabbit! run yer! Ef my eye ain't 'ceive me yer de signs whar Mr. Dog bin 'long, en mo'n dat dey er right fresh.'

"Brer Rabbit, he sidle up en look. Den he 'low:

"'Dat ar track ain't never fit Mr. Dog foot in de roun' worl'. W'at make it mo' bindin',' sezee, 'I done gone en bin 'quainted wid de man w'at make dat track, too long 'go ter talk 'bout,' sezee.

"'Brer Rabbit, please, sir, tell me he name.'

"Brer Rabbit, he laugh lak he makin' light er sump'n' n'er.

"'Ef I ain't make no mistakes, Brer Fox, de po' creetur w'at make dat track is Cousin Wildcat; no mo' en no less.'

"'How big is he, Brer Rabbit?'

"'He des 'bout yo' heft, Brer Fox.' Den Brer Rabbit make lak he talkin' wid hisse'f. 'Tut, tut, tut! Hit mighty funny dat I should run up on Cousin Wildcat in dis part er de worl'. Tooby sho, tooby sho! Many en many's de time I see my ole Granddaddy kick en cuff Cousin Wildcat, twel I git sorry 'bout 'im. Ef you want any fun, Brer Fox, right now de time ter git it.'

"Brer Fox up'n ax, he did, how he gwine have any fun. Brer Rabbit, he 'low:

"'Easy nuff; des go en tackle ole Cousin Wildcat, en lam 'im 'roun'.'

"Brer Fox, he sorter scratch he year, en 'low:

"'Eh-eh, Brer Rabbit, I feard. He track too much lak Mr. Dog.'

Brer Rabbit des set right flat down in de road, en holler en laugh. He 'low, sezee:

"'Shoo, Brer Fox! Who'd a thunk you 'uz so skeery? Des come look at dish yer track right close. Is dey any sign er claw anywhar's?'

"Brer Fox bleedzd ter 'gree dat dey wa'n't no sign er no claw. Brer Rabbit say: —

"'Well, den, ef he ain't got no claw, how he gwine ter hu't you, Brer Fox?'

"'W'at gone wid he toofs, Brer Rabbit?'

"'Shoo, Brer Fox! Creeturs w'at barks de trees ain't gwine bite.'

"Brer Fox tuck'n 'n'er good look at de tracks, en den him en Brer Rabbit put out fer ter foller um up. Dey went up de road, en down de lane, en 'cross de turnip patch, en down a dreen, en up a big gully. Brer Rabbit, he done de trackin', en eve'y time he fin' one, he up'n holler:

"'Yer n'er track, en no claw dar. Yer n'er track, en no claw dar!'

"Dey kep' on en kep' on, twel bimeby dey run up wid de creetur. Brer Rabbit, he holler out mighty biggity:

"'Heyo dar! W'at you doin'?'

"De creetur look 'roun', but he ain't sayin' nothin'. Brer Rabbit 'low:

"'Oh, you nee'nter look so sullen! We ull make you talk 'fo' we er done 'long wid you! Come, now! W'at you doin' out dar?'

"De creetur rub hisse'f 'g'in' a tree des lak you see deze yer house cats rub 'g'in' a cheer, but he ain't sayin' nothin'. Brer Rabbit holler:

"'W'at you come pesterin' 'long wid us fer, w'en we ain't bin a-pesterin' you? You got de consate dat I dunner who you is, but I does. You er de same ole Cousin Wildcat w'at my gran'daddy use ter kick en cuff w'en you 'fuse ter 'spon'. I let you know I got a better man yer dan w'at my gran'daddy ever is bin, en I boun' you he ull make you talk. Dat w'at I boun' you.'

"De creetur lean mo' harder 'g'in' de tree, en sorter ruffle up he bristle, but he ain't sayin' nothin'. Brer Rabbit, he 'low:

"'Go up dar, Brer Fox, en ef he 'fuse ter 'spon' slap 'im down! Dat de way my gran'daddy done. You go up dar, Brer Fox, en ef he dast ter try ter run, I'll des whirl in en ketch 'im.'

"Brer Fox, he sorter jubous, but he start todes de creetur. Ole Cousin Wildcat walk all 'roun' de tree, rubbin' hisse'f, but he ain't sayin' nothin'. Brer Rabbit, he holler:

"'Des walk right up en slap 'im down, Brer Fox — de owdashus vilyun! Des hit 'im a surbinder, en ef he dast ter run, I boun' you I'll ketch 'im.'

"Brer Fox, he went up a little nigher. Cousin Wildcat stop rubbin' on de tree, en sot up on he behime legs wid he front paws in de a'r, en he balance hisse'f by leanin' 'g'in' de tree, but he ain't sayin' nothin'. Brer Rabbit, he squall out, he did:

"'Oh, you nee'nter put up yo' han's en try ter beg off. Dat de way you fool my ole gran'daddy; but you can't fool we-all. All yo' settin' up en beggin' ain't gwine ter he'p you. Ef you er so humble ez all dat, w'at make you come pesterin' longer we-all? Hit 'im a clip, Brer Fox! Ef he run, I'll ketch 'im!'

"Brer Fox see de creetur look so mighty humble, settin' up dar lak he beggin' off, en he sorter take heart. He sidle up todes 'im, he did, en des ez he 'uz makin' ready fer ter slap 'im ole Cousin Wildcat draw'd back en fotch Brer Fox a wipe 'cross de stomach."

Uncle Remus paused here a moment, as if to discover some term strong enough to do complete justice to the catastrophe. Presently he went on:

"Dat ar Cousin Wildcat creetur fetch Brer Fox a wipe 'cross de stomach, en you mought a yeard 'im squall fum yer ter Harmony Grove. Little mo' en de creetur would er to' Brer Fox in two. W'ence de creetur made a pass at 'im Brer Rabbit knew w'at gwine ter happen, yit all de same he tuck'n holler:

"'Hit 'im ag'in, Brer Fox! Hit 'im ag'in! I'b a-backin' you, Brer Fox! Ef he dast ter run, I'll inabout cripple 'im — dat I will. Hit 'im ag'in!'

"All dis time, w'iles Brer Rabbit gwine on dis a-way, Brer Fox, he 'uz a-squattin' down, hol'in' he stomach wid bofe han's en des a-moanin':

"'I'm ruint, Brer Rabbit! I'm ruint! Run fetch de doctor! I'm teetotally ruint!'

"'Bout dat time, Cousin Wildcat, he tuck'n tuck a walk. Brer Rabbit, he make lak he 'stonish' dat Brer Fox is hurted. He tuck'n 'zamin' de place, he did, en he up'n 'low:

"'Hit look lak ter me, Brer Fox, dat dat owdashus vilyun tuck'n struck you wid a reapin'-hook.'

"Wid dat Brer Rabbit lit out fer home, en w'en he git out er sight, he tuck'n shuck he han's des lak cat does w'en she git water on 'er foots, en he tuck'n laugh en laugh twel it make 'im sick fer ter laugh."

45
Brother Wolf Gets in a Warm Place

THE LITTLE BOY thought that the story of how the wildcat scratched Brother Fox was one of the best stories he had ever heard, and he didn't hesitate to say so. His hearty endorsement increased Uncle Remus's good-humor; and the old man, with a broad grin upon his features and something of enthusiasm in his tone, continued to narrate the adventures of Brother Rabbit.

"Atter Brer Fox git hurted so bad," said Uncle Remus, putting an edge upon his axe with a whetstone held in his hand, "hit wuz a mighty long time 'fo' he could ramble 'roun' en worry ole Brer Rabbit. Der time Cousin Wildcat fetch'd 'im dat wipe 'cross de stomach, he tuck'n lay de blame on Brer Rabbit, en w'en he git well, he des tuck'n juggle wid de yuther creeturs, en dey all 'gree dat dem en Brer Rabbit can't drink out er de same branch, ner walk de same road, ner live in de same settlement, ner go in washin' in de same wash-hole.

"Tooby sho Brer Rabbit bleedzd ter take notice er all dish yer kinder jugglements en gwines on, en he des tuck'n strenken he house, in de neighborhoods er de winders, en den he put 'im up a steeple on top er dat. Yasser! A sho nuff steeple, en he rise 'er up so high dat folks gwine 'long de big road stop en say, 'Hey! W'at kinder meetin'-house dat?'"

The little boy laughed loudly at Uncle Remus's graphic delineation of the astonishment and admiration of the passers-by. The old man raised

his head, stretched his eyes, and seemed to be looking over his spectacles right at Brother Rabbit's steeple.

"Folk 'ud stop en ax, but Brer Rabbit ain't got time fer ter make no
answer. *He* hammer'd, *he* nailed, *he* knock'd, *he* lamm'd! Folks go by, he
ain't look up; creeturs come stan' en watch 'im, he ain't look 'roun'; wuk,
wuk, wuk, from sunup ter sundown, twel dat ar steeple git done. Den ole
Brer Rabbit tuck'n draw long breff, en wipe he forrerd, en 'low dat ef
dem t'er creeturs w'at bin atter 'im so long is got any de 'vantage er him,
de time done come fer um fer ter show it.

"Wid dat he went en got 'im a snack er sump'n' t'eat, en a long piece
er plough-line, en tole he ole 'oman fer ter put a kittle er water on de fier,
en stan' 'roun' close by, en eve'yt'ing he tell 'er not ter do, dat de ve'y
t'ing she sholy mus' do. Den ole Brer Rabbit sot down in he rockin'-
cheer en lookt out fum de steeple fer ter see how de lan' lay.

"'Twa'n't long 'fo' all de creeturs year talk dat Brer Rabbit done stop
wuk, en dey 'gun ter come 'roun' fer ter see w'at he gwine do nex'. But
Brer Rabbit, he got up dar, he did, en smoke he seegyar, en chaw he
'backer, en let he min' run on. Brer Wolf, he stan' en look up at de
steeple, Brer Fox, he stan' en look up at it, en all de t'er creeturs dey
done de same. Nex' time you see a crowd er folks lookin' at sump'n' right
hard, you des watch um, honey. Dey'll walk 'roun' one er n'er en swap
places, en dey'll be constant on de move. Dat des de way de creeturs
done. Dey walk 'roun' en punch one er n'er en swap places, en look en
look. Ole Brer Rabbit, he sot up dar, he did, en chaw he 'backer, en
smoke he seegyar, er let he min' run on.

"Bimeby ole Brer Tarrypin come 'long, en ole Brer Tarrypin bin in
cahoots wid Brer Rabbit so long dat he des nat'ally know dey wuz gwine
ter be fun er plenty 'roun' in dem neighborhoods 'fo' de sun go down. He
laugh 'way down und' de roof er he house, ole Brer Tarrypin did, en den
he hail Brer Rabbit:

"'Heyo, Brer Rabbit! W'at you doin' 'way up in de elements lak dat?'

"'I'm a-sojourneyin' up yer fer ter res' myse'f, Brer Tarrypin. Drap up
en see me.'

"''Twix' you en me, Brer Rabbit, de drappin' 's all one way. S'posin'
you tu'n loose en come. Man live dat high up bleedzd ter have wings. I

ain't no high-flyer myse'f. I fear'd ter shake han's wid you so fur off, Brer Rabbit.'

"'Not so, Brer Tarrypin, not so. My sta'rcase is a mighty limbersome one, en I'll des let it down ter you.'

"Wid dat, Brer Rabbit let down de plough-line.

"'Des ketch holt er dat, Brer Tarrypin,' sez Brer Rabbit, sezee, 'en up you comes, *linktum sinktum binktum boo!*' sezee."

"What was that, Uncle Remus?" said the little boy, taking a serious view of the statement.

"Creetur talk, honey — des creetur talk. Bless yo' soul, chile!" the old man went on, with a laughable assumption of dignity, "ef you think I got time fer ter stop right short off en 'stribbit out all I knows, you er mighty much mistaken — mighty much mistaken.

"Ole Brer Tarrypin know mighty well dat Brer Rabbit ain't got nothin' 'g'in' 'im, yet he got sech a habit er lookin out fer hisse'f dat he tuck'n ketch de plough-line in he mouf, he did, en try de strenk un it. Ole Brer Rabbit, he holler 'Swing on, Brer Tarrypin!' en Brer Tarrypin, he tuck'n swung on, en 'twa'n't long 'fo' he 'uz settin' up dar side er Brer Rabbit.

"But I wish ter goodness you'd a bin dar," continued Uncle Remus, very gracefully leaving it to be inferred that *he* was there; "I wish ter goodness you'd a bin dar so you could er seed ole Brer Tarrypin w'iles Brer Rabbit 'uz haulin' 'im up, wid he tail a-wigglin' en he legs all spraddled out, en him a-whirlin' 'roun' en 'roun' en lookin' skeer'd.

"De t'er creeturs dey see Brer Tarrypin go up safe en soun', en dey see de vittles passin' 'roun', en dey 'gun ter feel lak dey wanter see de inside er Brer Rabbit steeple. Den Brer Wolf, he hail 'im:

"'Heyo dar, Brer Rabbit! You er lookin' mighty scrumptious 'way up dar! How you come on?'

"Brer Rabbit, he look down, he did, en he see who 'tis hollerin', en he 'spon':

"'Po'ly, mighty po'ly, but I thank de Lord I'm able to eat my 'lowance. Won't you drap up, Brer Wolf?'

"'Hit's a mighty clumsy journey fer ter make, Brer Rabbit, yit I don't keer ef I does.'

"Wid dat, Brer Rabbit let down de plough-line, en Brer Wolf kotch holt, en dey 'gun ter haul 'im up. Dey haul en dey haul, en w'en Brer Wolf git mos' ter de top he year Brer Rabbit holler out:

"'Stir 'roun', ole 'oman, en set de table; but 'fo' you do dat, fetch de kittle fer ter make de coffee.'

"Dey haul en dey haul on de plough-line, en Brer Wolf year Brer Rabbit squall out:

"'Watch out dar, ole 'oman! You'll spill dat b'ilin' water on Brer Wolf!'

"En, bless yo' soul!" continued Uncle Remus, turning half around in his chair to face his enthusiastic audience of one, "dat 'uz 'bout all Brer Wolf did year, kaze de nex' minnit down come de scaldin' water, en Brer Wolf des fetch one squall en turn't hisse'f aloose, en w'en he strak de groun' he bounce des same ez one er deze yer injun-rubber balls w'at you use ter play wid 'long in dem times 'fo' you tuck'n broke yo' mammy lookin'-glass. Ole Brer Rabbit, he lean fum out de steeple en 'pollygize de bes' he kin, but no 'pollygy ain't gwine ter make ha'r come back whar de b'ilin' water hit."

"Did they spill the hot water on purpose, Uncle Remus?" the little boy inquired.

"Now, den, honey, you er crowdin' me. Dem ar creeturs wuz mighty kuse — mo' speshually Brer Rabbit. W'en it come down ter dat," said Uncle Remus, lowering his voice and looking very grave, "I 'speck ef you'd er s'arch de country fum hen-roost to river-bank,[1] you won't fin' a no mo' kuser man dan Brer Rabbit. All I knows is dat Brer Rabbit en Brer Tarrypin had a mighty laughin' spell des 'bout de time Brer Wolf hit de groun'."

46
Brother Wolf Still in Trouble

"EN STILL we er by ourse'fs," exclaimed Uncle Remus, as the little boy ran into his cabin, the night after he had heard the story of how Brother Rabbit scalded Brother Wolf. "We er by ourse'fs en time's a-passin'.

---

[1] Based on a characteristic Negro saying. For instance: "Where's Jim?" "You can't keep up wid dat nigger. Des let night come, en he's runnin' fum hen-roost to river-bank." In other words, stealing chickens and robbing fish baskets. — J. C. H.

Dem ar folks dunner w'at dey er missin'. We er des gittin' ter dat p'int whar we kin keep de run er creeturs, en it keeps us dat busy we ain't got time fer ter bolt our vittles skacely.

"I done tell you 'bout Brer Rabbit makin' 'im a steeple; but I ain't tell you 'bout how Brer Rabbit got ole Brer Wolf out'n er mighty bad fix."

"No," said the little boy, "you haven't, and that's just what I have come for now."

Uncle Remus looked at the rafters, then at the little boy, and finally broke into a loud laugh.

"I 'clar' ter goodness," he exclaimed, addressing the imaginary third person to whom he related the most of his grievances, "I 'clar' ter goodness ef dat ar chile ain't gittin' so dat he's eve'y whit ez up-en-spoken ez w'at ole Miss ever bin. Dat he is!"

The old man paused long enough to give the little boy some uneasiness, and then continued:

"Atter ole Brer Wolf git de nat'al hide tuck off'n 'im on de 'count er Brer Rabbit kittle, co'se he hatter go 'way off by hisse'f fer ter let de ha'r grow out. He 'uz gone so long dat Brer Rabbit sorter 'low ter hisse'f dat he 'speck he kin come down out'n he steeple, en sorter rack 'roun' 'mungs de t'er creeturs.

"He sorter primp up, Brer Rabbit did, en den he start out 'pun he journeys hether en yan. He tuck'n went ter de crossroads, en dar he stop en choose 'im a road. He choose 'im a road, he did, en den he put out des lak he bin sent fer in a hurry.

"Brer Rabbit gallop on, he did, talkin' en laughin' wid hisse'f, en eve'y time he pass folks, he'd tu'n it off en make lak he singin'. He 'uz gwine on dis a-way, w'en fus' news you know he tuck'n year sump'n'. He stop talkin' en 'gun ter hum a chune, but he ain't meet nobody. Den he stop en lissen en he year sump'n' holler:

"'O Lordy! Lordy! Won't somebody come he'p me?'"

The accent of grief and despair and suffering that Uncle Remus managed to throw into this supplication was really harrowing.

"Brer Rabbit year dis, en he stop en lissen. 'Twa'n't long 'fo' sump'n' n'er holler out:

"'O Lordy, Lordy! Please, somebody, come en he'p me.'

"Brer Rabbit, he h'ist up he years, he did, en make answer back:

"'Who is you, nohow, en w'at de name er goodness de marter?'

"'Please, somebody, do run yer!'

"Brer Rabbit, he tuck'n stan' on th'ee legs fer ter make sho er gittin' a good start ef dey wuz any needs un it, en he holler back:

"'Whar'bouts is you, en how come you dar?'

"'Do please, somebody, run yer en h'ep a po' mizerbul creetur. I'm down yer in de big gully und' dish yer great big rock.'

"Ole Brer Rabbit bleedzd ter be mighty 'tickler in dem days, en he crope down ter de big gully en look in, en who de name er goodness you 'speck he seed down dar?"

Uncle Remus paused and gave the little boy a look of triumph, and then proceeded without waiting for a reply:

"Nobody in de roun' worl' but dat ar ole Brer Wolf w'at Brer Rabbit done bin scalt'd de week 'fo' dat. He 'uz layin' down dar in de big gully, en, bless gracious! 'pon top un 'im wuz a great big rock, en ef you want ter know de reason dat ar great big rock ain't teetotally kil't Brer Wolf, den you'll hatter ax some un w'at know mo' 'bout it dan w'at I does, kaze hit look lak ter me dat it des oughter mash 'im flat.

"Yit dar he wuz, en let 'lone bein kil't, he got strenk nuff lef' fer ter make folks year 'im holler a mile off, en he holler so lonesome dat it make Brer Rabbit feel mighty sorry, en no sooner is he feel sorry dan he hol' he coat-tails out de way en slid down de bank fer ter see w'at he kin do.

"W'en he git down dar Brer Wolf ax 'im please, sir, kin he he'p 'im wid de removance er dat ar rock, en Brer Rabbit 'low he 'speck he kin; en wid dat Brer Wolf holler en tell 'im fer mussy sake won't he whirl in en do it, w'ich Brer Rabbit tuck'n ketch holt er de rock en hump hisse'f, en 'twa'n't long 'fo' he git a purchis on it, en, bless yo' soul, he lif' 'er up des lak nigger at de log-rollin'.

"Hit tu'n out dat Brer Wolf ain't hurted much, en w'en he fin' dis out, he tuck'n tuck a notion dat ef he ev' gwine git he revengeance out'n Brer Rabbit, right den wuz de time, en no sooner does dat come 'cross he min' dan he tuck'n grab Brer Rabbit by de nap er de neck en de small er de back.

"Brer Rabbit he kick en squeal, but 'tain't do no manner er good, kaze de mo' w'at he kick de mo' tighter Brer Wolf clamp 'im, w'ich he squoze 'im so hard dat Brer Rabbit wuz fear'd he 'uz gwine ter cut off he breff. Brer Rabbit, he 'low:

"'Well, den, Brer Wolf! Is dish yer de way you thanks folks fer savin' yo' life?'

"Brer Wolf grin big, en den he up'n 'low:

"'I'll thank you, Brer Rabbit, en den I'll make fresh meat out'n you.'

"Brer Rabbit 'low, he did:

"'Ef you talk dat a-way, Brer Wolf, I never is to do yer n'er good turn w'iles I live.'

"Brer Wolf, he grin some mo' en 'low:

"'Dat you won't, Brer Rabbit, dat you won't! You won't do me no mo' good turn twel you er done dead.'

"Brer Rabbit, he sorter study ter hisse'f, he did, en den he 'low:

"'Whar I come fum, Brer Wolf, hit's ag'in' de law fer folks fer to kill dem w'at done done um a good turn, en I 'speck hit's de law right 'roun' yer.'

"Brer Wolf say he ain't so mighty sho 'bout dat. Brer Rabbit say he willin' fer ter lef' de whole case wid Brer Tarrypin, en Brer Wolf say he 'gree'ble.

"Wid dat, dey put out, dey did, en make der way ter whar ole Brer Tarrypin stay; en w'en dey git dar, Brer Wolf he tuck'n tell he side, en den Brer Rabbit he tuck'n tell he side. Ole Brer Tarrypin put on he specks en cle'r up he th'oat, en den he 'low:

"'Dey's a mighty heap er mixness in dish yer 'spute, en 'fo' I kin take any sides you'll des hatter kyar' me fer ter see de place whar-bouts Brer Wolf wuz w'en Brer Rabbit foun' 'im,' sezee.

"Sho nuff, dey tuck'n kyar'd ole Brer Tarrypin down de big road twel dey come ter de big gully, en den dey tuck 'im ter whar Brer Wolf got kotch und' de big rock. Ole Brer Tarrypin, he walk 'roun', he did, en poke at de place wid de een' er he cane. Bimeby he shuck he head, he did, en 'low:

"'I hates might'ly fer ter put you all gents ter so much trouble; yit, dey ain't no two ways, I'll hatter see des how Brer Wolf was kotch, en des how de rock wuz layin' 'pun top un 'im,' sezee. 'De older folks gits, de mo' trouble dey is,' sezee, 'en I ain't 'nyin' but w'at I'm a-ripenin' mo' samer dan a 'simmon w'at's bin strucken wid de fros',' sezee.

"Den Brer Wolf, he tuck'n lay down whar he wuz w'en Brer Rabbit foun' im, en de yuthers dey up'n roll de rock 'pun top un 'im. Dey roll de rock 'pun 'im," continued Uncle Remus, looking over his spectacles to see what effect the statement had on the little boy, "en dar he wuz. Brer Tarrypin, he walk all 'roun', en look at 'im. Den he sot down, he did, en make marks in de san' wid he cane lak he studyin' 'bout sump'n' n'er. Bimeby, Brer Wolf, he open up:

"'Ow, Brer Tarrypin! Dish yer rock gittin' mighty heavy!'

"Brer Tarrypin, he mark in de san', en study, en study. Brer Wolf holler:

"'Ow Brer Tarrypin! Dish yer rock mashin' de breff out'n me.'

"Brer Tarrypin, he r'ar back, he did, en he 'low, sezee:

"'Brer Rabbit, you wuz in de wrong. You ain't had no business fer ter come bodderin' 'longer Brer Wolf w'en he ain't bodderin' 'longer you. He 'uz 'ten'in' ter he own business en you oughter bin 'ten'in' ter y'own.'

"Dis make Brer Rabbit look 'shame' er hisse'f, but Brer Tarrypin talk right erlong:

"'W'en you 'uz gwine down dish yer road dis mawnin', you sholy mus' bin a-gwine somers. Ef you *wuz* gwine somers you better be gwine on. Brer Wolf, he wa'n't gwine nowhars den, en he ain't gwine nowhars now. You foun' 'im und' dat ar rock, en und' dat ar rock you lef' 'im.'

"En, bless gracious!" exclaimed Uncle Remus, "dem ar creeturs racked off fum dar en lef' ole Brer Wolf und' dat ar rock."

47
Brother Rabbit Lays In His Beef Supply

"I WONDER where Daddy Jack is," said the little boy, one night after he had been waiting for some time for Uncle Remus to get leisure to tell him a story.

Uncle Remus, who was delightfully human in his hypocrisy, as well as in other directions, leaned back in his chair, looked at the little boy with an air of grieved resignation, and said:

"I boun' you does, honey, I boun' you does. Ole Brer Jack look mighty weazly ter de naked eye, but I lay he's a lots mo' likelier nigger dan w'at ole Remus is. De time done gone by w'en a po' ole no-'count nigger lak me kin hol' he han' wid a bran-new nigger man lak Brer Jack."

The child stared at Uncle Remus with open-eyed astonishment.

"Now, Uncle Remus! I didn't mean that; you know I didn't," he exclaimed.

"Bless yo' heart, honey! hit don't pester me. I done got de 'speunce un it. Dat I is. Plough-hoss don't squeal en kick when dey puts 'n'er hoss in he place. Brer Jack got de age on 'im but he new ter you. Ole er young, folks is folks, en no longer 'n day 'fo' yistiddy, I year you braggin' 'bout how de vittles w'at dey feeds you on up at de big house ain't good ez de vittles w'at yuther childun gits. Nummin' ole Remus, honey; you en Brer Jack des go right erlong en I'll be much 'blige ef you'll des lemme set in de cornder yer en chunk de fier. Sholy I ain't pas' doin' dat."

The child was troubled to think that Uncle Remus should find it necessary to depreciate himself, and he made haste to explain his position.

"I thought that if Daddy Jack was here he could tell me a story while you are working, so you wouldn't be bothered."

A broad grin of appreciation spread over Uncle Remus's face. He adjusted his spectacles, looked around and behind him, and then, seeing no one but the child, addressed himself to the rafters and cobwebs:

"Well! well! well! ef dish yer don't beat all! Gentermens! dish yer little chap yer, he puny in de legs, yit he mighty strong in de head."

He paused, as if reflecting over the whole matter, and then turned to the child:

"Is *dat* w'at make you hone atter Daddy Jack, honey — des kaze you

wanter set back dar en lissen at a tale? Now, den, ef you hadn't a got me
off'n de track, you'd a bin settin' yer lis'nen at one un um dis blessid
minnit, kaze des time I year talk dat Mars John gwine ter have dat ar
long-hornd'd steer kil't fer beef, hit come 'cross my min' 'bout de time
w'en Brer Rabbit en Brer Fox j'ined in wid one er n'er en kil't a cow."

"Killed a cow, Uncle Remus?"

"Des ez sho ez you er settin' dar," replied the old man with emphasis.
"Look lak dey wa'n't no kinder doin's w'at dem ar creeturs wa'n't up ter,
mo' speshually ole Brer Rabbit. Day in en day out, fum mawnin' twel
night en fum night twel mawnin', he 'uz constant a-studyin' up some
bran' new kinder contrapshun fer ter let de yuther creeturs know he 'uz
somers in de neighborhoods.

"Come down ter dat, you kin b'lieve me er not b'lieve me, des ez you
er min' ter; you kin take yo' choosement; but ole Brer Rabbit en ole Brer
Fox, spite er dey fallin' out, dey tuck'n go into cahoots en kil't a cow.
Seem lak I disremember who de cow b'long ter," continued the old man,
frowning thoughtfully, and thus, by a single stroke, imparting an air of
reality to the story; "but she sholy b'long'd ter some er de neighbors,
kaze you kin des put it down, right pine-blank, dat Brer Rabbit ain't
gwine ter kill he own cow, en needer is Brer Fox.

"Well, den, dey tuck'n kil't a cow, en 'twa'n't dey own cow, en atter
dey done skunt 'er, Brer Rabbit, he up'n 'low, he did, dat ef Brer Fox
wanter git de good er de game, he better run home en fetch a tray er
sump'n' fer put de jiblets in."

"Jiblets, Uncle Remus?"

"Tooby sho, honey. Dats w'at we-all calls de liver, de lights, de heart,
en de melt. Some calls um jiblets en some calls um hasletts, but ef you'll
lemme take um en kyar' um home, you kin des up en call um mos' by any
name w'at creep inter yo' min'. You do de namin'," the old man went on,
smacking his lips suggestively, "en I'll do de eatin', en ef I'm de loser, I
boun' you won't hear no complaints fum me.

"But, law bless me! w'at is I'm a-doin? De time's a-passin', en I'm
ain't skacely got start on de tale. Dey kil't de cow, dey did, en Brer Rabbit tell Brer Fox 'bout de jiblets, en w'iles Brer Fox gwine on home atter
de bucket fer ter put um in, he say ter hisse'f dat Brer Rabbit ain't bad ez
he crackt up ter be. But no sooner is Brer Fox outer sight dan Brer Rab-

bit cut out de jiblets, he did, en kyar'd um off en hide um. Den he come back en tuck a piece er de meat en drap blood 'way off de udder way.

"Bimeby yer come Brer Fox wid he bucket, en w'en he git dar Brer Rabbit wuz settin' down cryin'. Mon, he 'uz des a-boo-hooin'. Brer Fox, he 'low:

"'Name er goodness, Brer Rabbit! w'at de marter?'

"'Nuff de marter — nuff de marter. I wish you'd a stayed yer w'iles you wuz yer — dat I does, Brer Fox!'

"'How come, Brer Rabbit — how come?'

"'Man come, Brer Fox, en stole all yo' nice jiblets. I bin a-runnin' atter im, Brer Fox, but he outrun me.'

"'W'ich a-way he go, Brer Rabbit?'

"'Yer de way he went, Brer Fox; yer whar he drap de blood. Ef you be right peart, Brer Fox, you'll ketch 'im.'

"Brer Fox he drapt de bucket, he did, en put out atter de man w'at tuck de jiblets, en he wa'n't out'n sight good, 'fo' ole Brer Rabbit sail in en cut out all de fat en taller, en kyar' it off en hide it. Atter w'ile, yer come Brer Fox back des a-puffin' en a-pantin'. He ain't see no man. Brer Rabbit, he hail 'im:

"'You ain't come a minnit too soon, Brer Fox, dat you ain't. W'iles you bin gone n'er man come 'long en kyar'd off all de taller en fat. He went right off dat a-way, Brer Fox, en ef you'll be right peart, you'll ketch 'im.'

"Brer Fox, he tuck'n put out, he did, en run, yit he ain't see no man. W'iles he done gone Brer Rabbit kyar' off one er de behime quarters. Brer Fox come back; he ain't see no man. Brer Rabbit holler en tell 'im dat n'er man done come en got a behime quarter en run'd off wid it.

"Brer Fox sorter study 'bout dis, kaze it look lak nobody yever see de like er mens folks passin' by dat one lonesome cow. He make out he gwine ter run atter de man w'at steal de behime quarters, but he ain't git fur 'fo' he tuck'n tu'n 'roun' en crope back, en he 'uz des in time fer ter see Brer Rabbit makin' off wid de yuther behime quarter. Brer Fox mighty tired wid runnin' hether en yan, en backards en forrerds, but he git so mad w'en he see Brer Rabbit gwine off dat a-way, dat he dash up en ax 'im whar is he gwine wid dat ar beef.

"Brer Rabbit lay de beef down, he did, en look lak he feelin's hurted. He look at Brer Fox lak he feel mighty sorry fer folks w'at kin ax foolish questions lak dat. He shake he head, he did, en 'low:

"'Well, well, well! Who'd a thunk dat Brer Fox would a come axin' me 'bout dish yer beef, w'ich anybody would er know'd I 'uz a-kyar'n off fer ter save fer 'im, so nobody couldn't git it?'

"But dish yer kinder talk don't suit Brer Fox, en he tuck'n make a motion 'zef ter ketch Brer Rabbit, but Brer Rabbit he 'gun 'im leg bail, en dar dey had it thoo de woods twel Brer Rabbit come 'pon a holler tree, en inter dat he went, des lak one er deze streaked lizzuds goes inter a hole in de san'.""

"And then," said the little boy, as Uncle Remus paused, "along came Brother Buzzard, and Brother Fox set him to watch the hole, and Brother Rabbit said he had found a fat squirrel which he would run out on the other side; and then he came out and ran home."

This was the climax of a story that Uncle Remus had told a long time before, and he looked at his little partner with astonishment not unmixed with admiration.

"I 'clar' ter gracious, honey!" he exclaimed, "ef you hol's on ter yo' pra'rs lak you does ter deze yer tales you er doin' mighty well. But don't you try der hol' Brer Rabbit down ter one trick, you won't never keep up wid 'im in de 'roun' worl' — dat you won't.

"Ole Brer Buzzard wuz dar, en Brer Fox ax 'im fer ter watch de hole, but he ain't bin dar long 'fo' Brer Rabbit sing out:

"'I got de 'vantage un you, dis whet, Brer Buzzard, I sholy is.'

"'How dat, Brer Rabbit?'

"'Kaze I kin see you, en you can't see me.'

"Wid dat Brer Buzzard stuck he head in de hole, en look up; en no sooner is he do dis dan Brer Rabbit fill he eyes full er san', en w'iles he gone ter de branch fer ter wash it out, Brer Rabbit he come down outer de holler, en went back ter whar de cow wuz; en mo' dan dat, Brer Rabbit got de balance un de beef."

48
Brother Rabbit and Mr. Wildcat

"Uncle Remus," said the little boy, after a pause, "where did Brother Rabbit go when he got out of the hollow tree?"

"Well, sir," exclaimed Uncle Remus, "you ain't gwine ter b'lieve me, skacely, but dat owdashus creetur ain't no sooner git out er dat ar tree dan he go en git hisse'f mix up wid some mo' trouble, w'ich he git mighty nigh skeer'd out'n he skin.

"W'en Brer Rabbit git out'n de holler tree, he tuck'n fling some sass back at ole Brer Buzzard, he did, en den he put out down de big road, stidder gwine 'long back home en see 'bout he fambly. He 'uz gwine 'long — *lickety-clickety, clickety-lickety* — w'en fus' news you know he feel sump'n' n'er drap down 'pun 'im, en dar he wuz. Bless yo' soul, w'en Brer Rabbit kin git he 'membunce terge'er, he feel ole Mr. Wildcat a-huggin' 'im fum behime, en w'ispun in he year."

"What did he whisper, Uncle Remus?" asked the little boy.

"Dis, dat, en de udder, one thing en a nudder."

"But what did he say?"

"De way un it wuz dis," said Uncle Remus, ignoring the child's question, "Brer Rabbit, he 'uz gallin-up down de road, en ole Mr. Wildcat, he 'uz layin' stretch' out takin' a nap on a tree-lim' hangin' 'crosst de road. He year Brer Rabbit come a-lickity-clickitin' down de road, en he des sorter fix hisse'f, en w'en Brer Rabbit come a-dancin' und' de lim', all Mr. Wildcat got ter do is ter drap right down on 'im, en dar he wuz. Mr. Wildcat hug 'im right up at 'im, en laugh en w'isper in he year."

"Well, Uncle Remus, what did he *say?*" persisted the little boy.

The old man made a sweeping gesture with his left hand that might mean everything or nothing, and proceeded to tell the story in his own way.

"Ole Mr. Wildcat hug Brer Rabbit up close en w'isper in he year. Brer Rabbit, he kick, he squall, Bimeby he ketch he breff en 'low:

"'Ow! O Lordy-lordy. W'at I done gone en done now?'

"Mr. Wildcat, he rub he wet nose on Brer Rabbit year, en make col' chill run up he back. Bimeby he say:

"'O Brer Rabbit, I des nat'ally loves you! You bin a-foolin' all er my cousins en all er my kinfolks, en 'tain't bin so mighty long sence you set Cousin Fox on me, en little mo' en I'd a-to' 'im in two. O Brer Rabbit! I des nat'ally loves you,' sezee.

"Den he laugh, en he toofs strak terge'er right close ter Brer Rabbit year. Brer Rabbit, he 'low, he did:

"'Law, Mr. Wildcat, I thunk maybe you mought lak ter have Brer Fox fer supper, en dat de reason I sent 'im up ter whar you is. Hit done come

ter mighty purty pass w'en folks can't be fr'en's ceppin' sump'n' n'er step
in 'twix' en 'tween um, en ef dat de case I ain't gwine ter be fre'n's no
mo' — dat I ain't.'

"Mr. Wildcat wipe he nose on Brer Rabbit year, en he do sorter lak he
studyin'. Brer Rabbit he keep on talkin'. He' low:

"'Endurin' er all dis time, is I ever pester 'long wid you, Mr. Wildcat?'

"'No, Brer Rabbit, I can't say ez you is.'

"'No, Mr. Wildcat, dat I ain't. Let 'lone dat, I done my level bes' fer
ter he'p you out. En dough you done jump on me en skeer me scan'lous,
yit I'm willin' ter do you n'er good tu'n. I year some wil' tukkeys yelpin'
out yan, en ef you'll des lem me off dis time, I'll go out dar en call um up,
en you kin make lak you dead, en dey'll come up en stretch dey neck
over you, en you kin jump up en kill a whole passel un um 'fo' dey kin
git out de way.'

"Mr. Wildcat stop en study, kaze ef dey er one kinder meat w'at he lak
dat meat is tukkey meat. Den he tuck'n ax Brer Rabbit is he jokin'. Brer
Rabbit say ef he wuz settin' off somers by he own-lone se'f he mought be
jokin', but how de name er goodness is he kin joke w'en Mr. Wildcat got
'im hug up so tight? Dis look so pleezy-plozzy dat 'twa'n't long 'fo' Mr.
Wildcat 'low dat he 'uz mighty willin' ef Brer Rabbit mean w'at he say,
en atter w'ile, bless yo' soul, ef you'd a come 'long dar, you'd er seed ole
Mr. Wildcat layin' stretch out on de groun' lookin' fer all de worl' des lak
he done bin dead a mont', en you'd er year'd ole Brer Rabbit a-yelpin'
out in de bushes des lak a sho nuff tukkey-hen."

The little boy was always anxious for a practical demonstration, and
he asked Uncle Remus how Brother Rabbit could yelp like a turkey-hen.
For reply, Uncle Remus searched upon his rude mantel-piece until he
found a reed, which he intended to use as a pipe-stem. One end of this
he placed in his mouth, enclosing the other in his hands. By sucking the
air through the reed with his mouth, and regulating the tone and volume
by opening or closing his hands, the old man was able to produce a mar-
vellous imitation of the call of the turkey-hen, much to the delight and
astonishment of the little boy.

"Ah, Lord!" exclaimed Uncle Remus, after he had repeated the call
until the child was satisfied, "many's en many's de time is I gone out in

de woods wid old marster 'fo' de crack er day en call de wil' tukkeys right spang up ter whar we could er kil't um wid a stick. W'en we fus' move yer fum Ferginny, dey use ter come right up ter whar de barn sets, en mo'n dat I done seed ole marster kill um right out dar by de front gate. But folks fum town been comin' 'roun' yer wid der p'inter dogs twel hit done got so dat ef you wanter see tukkey track you gotter go down dar ter de Oconee, en dat's two mile off."

"Did the Wildcat catch the turkeys?" the little boy inquired, when it seemed that Uncle Remus was about to give his entire attention to his own reminiscences.

"De gracious en de goodness!" exclaimed the old man. "Yer I is runnin' on en dar lays Mr. Wildcat waitin' fer Brer Rabbit fer ter yelp dem tukkeys up. En ain't take 'im long nudder, kaze, bless yo' soul, ole Brer Rabbit wuz a yelper, mon.

"Sho nuff, atter w'ile yer dey come, ole Brer Gibley Gobbler wukkin' in de lead. Brer Rabbit, he run'd en meet um en gun um de wink 'bout ole Mr. Wildcat, en by de time dey git up ter whar he layin', Brer Gibley Gobbler en all his folks wuz 'jined in a big 'spute. One 'low he dead, n'er one 'low he ain't, n'er one 'low he stiff, udder one 'low he ain't, en t'udder 'low he is. So dar dey had it. Dey stretch out dey neck en step high wid dey foot, yit dey ain't git too close ter Mr. Wildcat.

"He lay dar, he did, en he ain't move. Win' ruffle up he ha'r, yit he ain't move; sun shine down 'pun 'im, yit he ain't move. De tukkeys dey gobble en dey yelp, but dey ain't go no nigher; dey holler en dey 'spute, but dey ain't go no nigher; dey stretch dey neck en dey lif' dey foot high, yit dey ain't go no nigher.

"Hit keep on dis a-way, twel bimeby Mr. Wildcat git tired er waitin', en he jump up, he did, en make a dash at de nighest tukkey; but dat tukkey done fix, en w'en Mr. Wildcat come at 'im, he des riz in de a'r, en Mr. Wildcat run und' 'im. Den he tuck'n run at n'er one, en dat un fly up; en dey keep on dat a-way twel 'twa'n't long 'fo' Mr. Wildcat wuz so stiff in de j'ints en so short in de win' dat he des hatter lay down on de groun' en res', en w'en he do dis, ole Brer Gibley Gobbler en all er he folks went on 'bout dey own business; but sence dat day dey er constant a-'sputin' 'long wid deyse'f en eve'ybody w'at come by. Ef you don't b'lieve me,"

with an air of disposing of the whole matter judicially, "you kin des holler at de fus' Gobbler w'at you meets, en ef he 'fuse ter holler back atter you, you kin des use my head fer a hole in de wall; en w'at mo' kin you ax dan dat?"

"What became of Brother Rabbit, Uncle Remus?"

"Well, sir, Brer Rabbit tuck'n lef' dem low-groun's. W'iles de 'sputin' wuz gwine on, he tuck'n bowed his good-byes, en den he des put out fum dar. Nex' day ole Brer Gibley Gobbler tuck'n sent 'im a tukkey wing fer ter make a fan out'n, en Brer Rabbit, he tuck'n sent it ter Miss Meadows en de gals. En I let you know," continued the old man, chuckling heartily to himself, "dey make great 'miration 'bout it."

49
Mr. Benjamin Ram Defends Himself

"I 'SPECK we all dun gone en fergot ole Mr. Benjermun Ram offn our min'," said Uncle Remus, one night, as the little boy went into the cabin with a large ram's horn hanging on his arm.

"About his playing the fiddle and getting lost in the woods!" exclaimed the child. "Oh, no, I haven't forgotten him, Uncle Remus. I remember just how he tuned his fiddle in Brother Wolf's house."

"Dat's me!" said Uncle Remus with enthusiasm; "dat's me up en down. Mr. Ram des ez fresh in my min' now ez he wuz de day I year de tale. Dat ole creetur wuz a sight, mon. He mos' sholy wuz. He wrinkly ole hawn en de shaggy ha'r on he neck make 'im look mighty servigous, en w'ence he shake he head en snort, hit seem lak he gwine ter fair paw de yeth fum und' 'im.

"Ole Brer Fox bin pickin' up ole Mr. Benjermun Ram chilluns w'en dey git too fur fum home, but look lak he ain't never bin close ter de ole creetur.

"So one time w'en he 'uz comin' on down de road, talkin' 'long wid Brer Wolf, he up'n 'low, ole Brer Fox did, dat he mighty hongry in de neighborhoods er de stomach. Dis make Brer Wolf look lak he 'stonish'd, en he ax Brer Fox how de name er goodness come he hongry w'en ole Mr. Benjermun Ram layin' up dar in de house des a-rollin' in fat.

"Den Brer Fox tuck'n 'low, he did, dat he done bin in de habits er eatin' Mr. Benjermun Ram chillun, but he sorter feard er de ole creetur kaze he look so bad on de 'count er he red eye en he wrinkly hawn.

"Brer Wolf des holler en laugh, en den he 'low:

"'Lordy, Brer Fox! I dunner w'at kinder man is you, nohow! W'y, dat ar ole creetur ain't never hurted a flea in all he born days — dat he ain't,' sezee.

"Brer Fox, he look at Brer Wolf right hard, he did, en den he up'n 'low:

"'Heyo, Brer Wolf! many's de time dat you bin hongry 'roun' in deze diggin's en I ain't year talk er you makin' a meal off'n Mr. Benjermun Ram,' sezee.

"Brer Fox talk so close ter de fatal trufe, dat Brer Wolf got tooken wit de dry grins, yit he up'n 'spon', sezee:

"'I des lak ter know who in de name er goodness wanter eat tough creetur lak dat ole Mr. Benjermun Ram — dat w'at I lak ter know,' sezee.

"Brer Fox, he holler en laugh, he did, en den he up'n say:

"'Ah-yi, Brer Wolf! You ax me w'at I goes hongry fer w'en ole Mr. Benjermun Ram up dar in he house, yit you done bin hongry many's en many's de time, en still ole Mr. Benjermun Ram up dar in he house. Now, den, how you gwine do in a case lak dat?' sez Brer Fox, sezee.

"Brer Wolf, he strak de een' er he cane down 'pun de groun', en he say, sezee:

"'I done say all I got ter say, en w'at I say, dat I'll stick ter. Dat ole creetur lots too tough.'

"Hongry ez he is, Brer Fox laugh way down in he stomach. Atter w'ile he low:

"'Well, den, Brer Wolf, stidder 'sputin' 'longer you, I'm gwine do w'at you say; I'm gwine ter go up dar en git a bait er ole Mr. Benjermun Ram, en I wish you be so good ez ter go 'long wid me fer comp'ny,' sezee.

"Brer Wolf jaw sorter fall w'en he year dis, en he 'low:

"'Eh-eh, Brer Fox! I druther go by my own 'lone se'f,' sezee.

"'Well, den,' sez Brer Fox, sezee, 'you better make 'as'e,' sezee, 'kaze 't ain't gwine ter take me so mighty long fer to go up dar en make hash out'n ole Mr. Benjermun Ram,' sezee.

"Brer Wolf know mighty well," said Uncle Remus, snapping his huge tongs in order to silence a persistent cricket in the chimney, "dat ef he dast ter back out fum a banter lak dat he never is ter year de las' un it fum Miss Meadows en Miss Motts en de gals, en he march off todes Mr. Benjermun Ram house.

"Little puff er win' come en blow'd up some leafs, en Brer Wolf jump lak somebody shootin' at 'im, en he fly mighty mad w'en he year Brer Fox laugh. He men' he gait, he did, en 'twa'n't 'long 'fo' he 'uz knockin' at Mr. Benjermun Ram do'.

"He knock at de do', he did, en co'se he 'speck somebody fer ter come open de do'; but stidder dat, lo en beholes yer come Mr. Benjermun Ram 'roun' de house. Dar he wuz — red eye, wrinkly hawn en shaggy head. Now, den, in case lak dat, w'at a slim-legged man lak Brer Wolf gwine do? Dey ain't no two ways, he gwine ter git 'way fum dar, en he went back ter whar Brer Fox is mo' samer dan ef de patter-rollers wuz atter 'im.

"Brer Fox, he laugh en he laugh, en ole Brer Wolf, he look mighty glum. Brer Fox ax 'im is he done kil't en e't Mr. Benjermun Ram, en ef so be, is he lef' any fer him. Brer Wolf say he ain't feelin' well, en he don't lak mutton nohow. Brer Fox 'low:

"'You may be puny in de min', Brer Wolf, but you ain't feelin' bad in de leg, kaze I done seed you wuk um.'

"Brer Wolf 'low he des a-runnin' fer ter see ef 'twon't make 'im feel better. Brer Fox, he say, sezee, dat w'en he feelin' puny, he ain't ax no mo' dan fer somebody fer ter git out de way en let 'im lay down.

"Dey went on in dis a-way, dey did, twel bimeby Brer Fox ax Brer Wolf ef he'll go wid 'im fer ter ketch Mr. Benjermun Ram. Brer Wolf, he 'low, he did:

"'Eh-eh, Brer Fox! I fear'd you'll run en lef' me dar fer ter do all de fightin'.'

"Brer Fox, he 'low dat he'll fix dat, en he tuck'n got 'im a plough-line, en tied one een' ter Brer Wolf en t'er een' ter he own se'f. Wid dat dey put out fer Mr. Benjermun Ram house. Brer Wolf, he sorter hang back, but he 'shame' fer ter say he skeer'd, en dey went on en went on plum' twel dey git right spang up ter Mr. Benjermun Ram house.

"W'en dey git dar, de ole creetur wuz settin' out in de front po'ch sorter sunnin' hisse'f. He see um comin', en w'en dey git up in hailin' distance, he sorter cle'r up he th'oat, he did, en holler out:

"'I much 'blige to you, Brer Fox, fer ketchin' dat owdashus vilyun en fetchin' 'im back. My smoke-'ouse runnin' short, en I'll des chop 'im up en pickle 'im. Fetch 'im in, Brer Fox! fetch 'im in!'

"Des 'bout dat time ole Miss Ram see dem creeturs a-comin', en gentermens! you mought er year'd 'er blate plum' ter town. Mr. Benjermun Ram, he sorter skeer'd hisse'f, but he keep on talkin':

"'Fetch 'im in, Brer Fox! fetch 'im in! Don't you year my ole 'oman cryin' fer 'im? She ain't had no wolf meat now in gwine on mighty nigh a mont'. Fetch 'im in, Brer Fox! fetch 'im in!'

"Fus' Brer Wolf try ter ontie hisse'f, den he tuck'n broke en run'd, en he drag ole Brer Fox atter 'im des lak he ain't weigh mo'n a poun', en I let you know hit 'uz many a long day 'fo' Brer Fox git well er de thumpin' he got."

"Uncle Remus," said the little boy after a while, "I thought wolves always caught sheep when they had the chance."

"Dey ketches lam's, honey, but bless yo' soul! dey ain't ketch deze yer ole-time Rams wid red eye en wrinkly hawn."

"Where was Brother Rabbit all this time?"

"Now, den, honey, don't less pester wid ole Brer Rabbit right now. Des less gin 'im one night rest, mo' speshually w'en I year de seven stares say yo' bedtime done come. Des take yo' foot in yo' han' en put right out 'fo' Miss Sally come a-callin' you, kaze den she'll say I'm a-settin' yer a-noddin' en not takin' keer un you."

The child laughed and ran up the path to the big-house, stopping a moment on the way to mimic a bull-frog that was bellowing at a tremendous rate near the spring.

50
Brother Rabbit Pretends to Be Poisoned

NOT MANY NIGHTS after the story of how Mr. Benjamin Ram frightened Brother Wolf and Brother Fox, the little boy found himself in Uncle Remus's cabin. It had occurred to him that Mr. Ram should have played on his fiddle somewhere in the tale, and Uncle Remus was called on to explain. He looked at the little boy with an air of grieved astonishment, and exclaimed:

"Well, I be bless if I ever year der beat er dat. Yer you bin a-persooin' on atter deze yer creeturs en makin' der 'quaintunce, en yit look lak ef you 'uz ter meet um right up dar in der paff you'd fergit all 'bout who dey is."

"Oh, no, I wouldn't, Uncle Remus!" protested the child, glancing at the door and getting a little closer to the old man.

"Yasser! you'd des nat'ally whirl in en forgit 'bout who dey is. 'Tain't so mighty long sence I done tole you 'bout ole Mr. Benjermun Ram playin' he fiddle at Brer Wolf house, en yer you come en ax me how come he don't take en play it at 'im 'g'in. W'at kinder lookin' sight 'ud dat ole creetur a-bin ef he'd jump up en grab he fiddle en go ter playin' on it eve'y time he year a fuss down de big road?"

The little boy said nothing, but he thought the story would have been a great deal nicer if Mr. Benjamin Ram could have played one of the old-time tunes on his fiddle and while he was thinking about it, the door opened and Aunt Tempy made her appearance. Her good-humor was infectious.

"Name er goodness!" she exclaimed, "I lef' you all settin' yer way las' week; I goes off un I does my wuk, un I comes back, un I fin's you settin' right whar I lef' you. Goodness knows, I dunner whar you gits yo' vittles. I dunner whar I ain't bin sence I lef' you all settin' yer. I let you know I bin a-usin' my feet un I been a-usin' my han's. Dat's me. No use ter ax how you all is, kaze you looks lots better'n me."

"Yas, Sis Tempy, we er settin' yer whar you lef' us, en der Lord, he bin a-pervidin'. W'en de vittles don't come in at de do' hit come down de chimbley, en so w'at de odds? We er sorter po'ly, Sis Tempy, I'm 'blige ter you. You know w'at de jay-bird say ter der squinch owl! 'I'm sickly but sassy.'"

Aunt Tempy laughed as she replied: "I 'speck you all bin a-havin' lot er fun. Goodness knows I wish many a time sence I bin gone dat I 'uz settin' down yer runnin' on wid you all. I ain't bin gone fur — dat's so, yit Mistiss put me ter cuttin'-out, un I tell you now dem w'at cuts out de duds fer all de niggers on dis place is got ter wuk fum soon in de mawnin' plum' twel bedtime, dey ain't no two ways. 'Tain't no wuk you k'n kyar' 'bout wid you needer, kaze you got ter spread it right out on de flo' un git down on yo' knees. I mighty glad I done wid it kaze my back feel like it done broke in a thous'n pieces. Honey, is Brer Remus bin a-tellin' you some mo' er dem ole-time tales?"

Aunt Tempy's question gave the little boy an excuse for giving her brief outlines of some of the stories. One that he seemed to remember particularly well was the story of how Brother Rabbit and Brother Fox killed a cow, and how Brother Rabbit got the most and the best of the beef.

"I done year talk uv a tale like dat," exclaimed Aunt Tempy, laughing heartily, "but 'tain't de same tale. I mos' 'shame' ter tell it."

"You gittin' too ole ter be blushin', Sis Tempy," said Uncle Remus with dignity.

"Well den," said Aunt Tempy, wiping her fat face with her apron: "One time Brer Rabbit un Brer Wolf tuck'n gone off somers un kil't a cow, un w'en dey come fer ter 'vide out de kyarkiss, Brer Wolf 'low dat bein's he de biggest he oughter have de mos', un he light in, he did, un do like he gwine ter take it all. Brer Rabbit do like he don't keer much, but he keer so bad hit make 'im right sick. He tuck'n walk all 'roun' de kyarkiss, he did, un snuff de air, un terreckly he say:

"'Brer Wolf! — O Brer Wolf! — is dis meat smell zackly right ter you?'

"Brer Wolf, he cuttin' un he kyarvin' un he ain't sayin' nothin'. Brer Rabbit, he walk all 'roun' un 'roun' de kyarkiss. He feel it un he kick it. Terreckly he say:

"'Brer Wolf! — O Brer Wolf! — Dis meat feel mighty flabby ter me; how it feel ter you?'

"Brer Wolf, he year all dat's said, but he keep on a-cuttin' un a-kyarvin'. Brer Rabbit say:

"'You kin talk er not talk, Brer Wolf, des ez you er min' ter, yit ef I ain't mistooken in de sign, you'll do some tall talkin' 'fo' you er done wid dis beef. Now you mark w'at I tell you!'

"Brer Rabbit put out fum dar, en 'twa'n't long 'fo' yer he come back wid a chunk er fier, un a dish er salt. W'en Brer Wolf see dis, he say:

"'W'at you gwine do wid all dat, Brer Rabbit?'

"Brer Rabbit laugh like he know mo' dan he gwine tell, un he say:

"'Bless yo' soul, Brer Wolf! I ain't gwine ter kyar' er poun' er dis meat home twel I fin' out w'at de matter wid it. No I ain't — so dar now!'

"Den Brer Rabbit built 'im a fier un cut 'im off a slishe er steak un br'ilte it good un done, un den he e't little uv it. Fus' he'd tas'e un den he'd nibble; den he'd nibble un den he'd tas'e. He keep on twel he e't right smart piece. Den he went'n sot off little ways like he waitin' fer sump'n'.

"Brer Wolf, he kyarve un he cut, but he keep one eye on Brer Rabbit. Brer Rabbit sot up dar same ez Jedge on de bench. Brer Wolf, he watch his motions. Terreckly Brer Rabbit fling bofe han's up ter he head un fetch a groan. Brer Wolf cut un kyarve un watch Brer Rabbit motions. Brer Rabbit sorter sway backerds un forrerds un fetch n'er groan. Den he sway fum side to side un holler 'O Lordy!' Brer Wolf, he sorter 'gun ter git skeer'd un he ax Brer Rabbit w'at de matter. Brer Rabbit, he roll on de groun' un holler:

"'O Lordy, Lordy! I'm pizen'd, I'm pizen'd! O Lordy! I'm pizen'd; Run yer, somebody, run yer! De meat done got pizen on it. Oh, do run yer!'

"Brer Wolf git so skeer'd dat he put out fum dar, un he wa'n't out er sight skacely 'fo' Brer Rabbit jump up fum dar un cut de pidjin-wing, un 'twa'n't so mighty long atter dat 'fo' Brer Rabbit done put all er dat beef in his smoke-house."

"What became of Brother Wolf?" the little boy inquired.

"Brer Wolf went atter de doctor," continued Aunt Tempy, making little tucks in her apron, "un w'en he come back Brer Rabbit un de beef done gone; un, bless goodness, ef it hadn't er bin fer de sign whar Brer Rabbit built de fier, Brer Wolf would er bin might'ly pester'd fer ter fin' der place whar de cow bin kil't."

At this juncture, 'Tildy, the house-girl, came in to tell Aunt Tempy that one of the little Negroes had been taken suddenly sick.

"I bin huntin' for you over de whole blessid place," said 'Tildy.

"No, you ain't — no, you ain't. You ain't bin huntin' nowhar. You know'd mighty well whar I wuz."

"Law, Mam' Tempy, I can't keep up wid you. How I know you down yer courtin' wid Unk' Remus?"

"Yo' head mighty full er courtin', you nas' stinkin' huzzy!" exclaimed Aunt Tempy.

Uncle Remus, strange to say, was unmoved. He simply said:

"W'en you see dat ar 'Tildy gal pirootin' 'roun' I boun' you ole Brer Affikin Jack ain't fur off. 'Twon't be so mighty long 'fo' de ole creetur'll show up."

"How you know dat, Unk' Remus?" exclaimed 'Tildy, showing her white teeth and stretching her eyes. "Hit's de Lord's trufe; Mass Jeems done writ a letter ter Miss Sally, an' he say in dat letter dat Daddy Jack ax 'im fer ter tell Miss Sally ter tell me dat he'll be up yer dis week. Dat ole Affikin ape got de impidence er de Ole Boy. He dunner who he foolin' 'longer!"

51
More Trouble for Brother Wolf

THE NEXT NIGHT the little boy hardly waited to eat his supper before going to Uncle Remus's house; and when Aunt Tempy failed to put in an appearance as early as he thought necessary, he did not hesitate to go after her. He had an idea that there was a sequel to the story she had told the night before, and he was right. After protesting against being dragged around from post to pillar by children, Aunt Tempy said:

"Atter Brer Rabbit tuck'n make out he 'uz pizen'd un git all de beef, 'twa'n't long 'fo' he chance to meet ole Brer Wolf right spang in de middle uv de road. Brer Rabbit, he sorter shied off ter one side, but Brer Wolf hail 'im:

"'W'oa dar, my colty! don't be so gayly. You better be 'shame' you'se'f 'bout de way you do me w'en we go inter cahoots wid dat beef.'

"Brer Rabbit, he up'n ax Brer Wolf how all his folks. Brer Wolf say:

"'You'll fin' out how dey all is 'fo' dis day gone by. You took'n took de beef, un now I'm a-gwine ter tak'n take you.'

"Wid dis Brer Wolf make a dash at Brer Rabbit, but he des lack a little bit uv bein' quick nuff, un Brer Rabbit he des went a-sailin' thoo de woods. Brer Wolf, he tuck atter 'im, un yer dey had it — fus' Brer Rabbit un den Brer Wolf. Brer Rabbit mo' soopler dan Brer Wolf, but Brer Wolf got de 'vantage er de win', un terreckly he push Brer Rabbit so close dat he run in a holler log.

"Brer Rabbit bin in dat log befo' un he know dey's a hole at de t'er een', un he des keep on a-gwine. He dart in one een' un he slip out de udder. He ain't stop ter say goo'-bye; bless you! he des keep on gwine.

"Brer Wolf, he see Brer Rabbit run in de holler log, un he say ter hisse'f:

"'Heyo, dey bin callin' you so mighty cunnin' all dis time, un yer you done gone un shot yo'se'f up in my trap.'

"Den Brer Wolf laugh un lay down by de een' whar Brer Rabbit went in, un pant un res' hisse'f. He see whar Brer B'ar burnin' off a new groun', un he holler un ax 'im fer ter fetch 'im a chunk er fier, un Brer B'ar he fotch it, en dey sot fier ter de holler log, un dey sot dar un watch it till it burn plum' up. Den dey took'n shuck han's, un Brer Wolf say he hope dat atter dat dey'll have some peace in de neighborhoods."

Uncle Remus smiled a knowing smile as he filled his pipe, but Aunt Tempy continued with great seriousness:

"One time atter dat, Brer Wolf, he took'n pay a call down ter Miss Meadows, un w'en he git dar un see Brer Rabbit settin' up side uv one er de gals, he like to 'a' fainted, dat he did. He 'uz dat 'stonish'd dat he look right down-hearted all endurin' uv de party.

"Brer Rabbit, he bow'd his howdies ter Brer Wolf un shuck han's 'long wid 'im, des like nothin' ain't never happen 'twixt um, un he up'n say:

"'Ah-law, Brer Wolf! You er much mo' my fr'en' dan you ever 'spected ter be, un you kin des count on me right straight 'long.'

"Brer Wolf say he feel sorter dat away hisse'f, un he ax Brer Rabbit w'at make 'im change his min' so quick.

"'Bless you, Brer Wolf, I had needs ter change it,' sez Brer Rabbit, sezee.

"Brer Wolf, he ax 'im how come.

"'All about bein' burnt up in a holler log, Brer Wolf, un w'en you gits time I wish you be so good ez ter bu'n me up some mo',' sez Brer Rabbit, sezee.

"Brer Wolf, he ax 'im how so. Brer Rabbit say:

"'I'm feard ter tell you, Brer Wolf, kaze I don't want de news ter git out.'

"Brer Wolf vow he won't tell nobody on de top side er de worl'. Brer Rabbit say:

"'I done fin' out, Brer Wolf, dat w'en you git in a holler tree un somebody sets it a-fier, dat de nat'al honey des oozles out uv it, un mor'n dat, atter you git de honey all over you, 'tain't no use ter try ter burn you up, kaze de honey will puzzuv you. Don't 'ny me dis favor, Brer Wolf, kaze I done pick me out a n'er holler tree,' sez Brer Rabbit, sezee.

"Brer Wolf, he wanter put right out den un dar, un Brer Rabbit say dat des de kinder man w'at he bin huntin' fer. Dey took deyse'f off un 'twa'n't long 'fo' dey came ter de tree w'at Brer Rabbit say he done pick out. W'en dey git dar, Brer Wolf, he so greedy fer ter git a tas'e er de honey dat he beg un beg Brer Rabbit fer ter let 'im git in de holler. Brer Rabbit, he hol' back, but Brer Wolf beg so hard dat Brer Rabbit 'gree ter let 'im git in de holler.

"Brer Wolf, he got in, he did, un Brer Rabbit stuff de hole full er dry leaves un trash, un den he got 'im a chunk er fier un totch 'er off. She smoked un smoked, un den she bust out in a blaze. Brer Rabbit, he pile up rocks, un brush, un sticks, so Brer Wolf can't git out. Terreckly Brer Wolf holler:

"'Gittin' mighty hot, Brer Rabbit! I ain't see no honey yit.'

"Brer Rabbit he pile on mo' trash, un holler back:

"'Don't be in no hurry, Brer Wolf; you'll see it un tas'e it too.'

"Fier burn un burn, wood pop like pistol. Brer Wolf, he holler:

"'Gittin' hotter un hotter, Brer Rabbit. No honey come yit.'

"'Hol' still, Brer Wolf, hit'll come.'

"'Gimme a'r, Brer Rabbit; I'm a-chokin'.'

"'Fresh a'r make honey sour. Des hol' still, Brer Wolf!'

"'*Ow!* she gittin' hotter en hotter, Brer Rabbit!'

"'Des hol' right still, Brer Wolf; mos' time fer de honey!'

"'*Ow-ow!* I'm a-burnin', Brer Rabbit!'

"'Wait fer de honey, Brer Wolf.'

"'I can't stan' it, Brer Rabbit.'

"'Stan' it like I did, Brer Wolf.'

"Brer Rabbit he pile on de trash un de leaves. He say:

"'I'll gin you honey, Brer Wolf; de same kinder honey you wanted ter gimme.'

"Un it seem like ter me," said Aunt Tempy, pleased at the interest the little boy had shown, "dat it done Brer Wolf des right."

52
Brother Rabbit Outdoes Mr. Man

THE LITTLE BOY had heard Uncle Remus lamenting that his candle was getting rather short, and he made it his business to go around the house and gather all the pieces he could find. He carried these to the old man, who received them with the liveliest satisfaction.

"Now dish yer sorter look lak sump'n', honey. W'en ole Brer Jack come back, en Sis Tempy git in de habits er hangin' 'roun', we'll des light some er dese yer, en folks'll come by en see de shine, en dey'll go off en 'low dat hit's de night des 'fo' camp-meetin' at ole Remus house.

"I got little piece dar in my chist w'at you brung me long time ergo, en I 'low ter myse'f dat ef shove ever git ter be push,[1] I'd des draw 'er out en light 'er up."

"Mamma says Daddy Jack is coming back Sunday," said the little boy.

"Dat w'at I year talk," replied the old man.

"What did he go off for, Uncle Remus?"

"Bless yo' soul, honey! Brer Jack bleedzd ter go en see yo' Unk' Jeems. He b'lieve de worl go wrong ef he ain't do dat. Dat ole nigger b'lieve he white mon. He come up yer fum down de country whar de Lord done fersook um too long 'go ter talk 'bout, — he come up yer en he put on mo' a'rs dan w'at I dast ter do. Not dat I'm keerin', kaze goodness knows I ain't, yit I notices dat w'en I has ter go somers, dey's allers a

---

[1] A plantation saying. It means if hard times get harder. A briefer form is "when shove 'come push" — when the worst comes to the worst. — J. C. H.

great ter-do 'bout w'at is I'm a-gwine fer, en how long is I'm gwine ter stay; en ef I ain't back at de ve'y minnit, dars Mars John a-growlin', en Miss Sally a-vowin' dat she gwine ter put me on de block."

Perhaps Uncle Remus's jealousy was more substantial than he was willing to admit; but he was talking merely to see what the little boy would say. The child, however, failed to appreciate the situation, seeing which the old man quickly changed the subject.

"Times is mighty diffunt fum w'at dey use ter wuz, kaze de time has bin dat ef ole Brer Rabbit had er run'd up wid Brer Jack w'iles he comin' fum yo' Unk' Jeems place, he'd outdone 'im des ez sho ez de worl' stan's. Deze days de Rabbits has ter keep out de way er folks, but in dem days folks had ter keep out der way er ole Brer Rabbit. Ain't I never tell you 'bout how Brer Rabbit whirl in en outdo Mr. Man?"

"About the meat tied to the string, Uncle Remus?"

"*Shoo!* Dat ain't a drap in de bucket, honey. Dish yer wuz de time w'en ole Brer Rabbit wuz gwine 'long de big road, en he meet Mr. Man drivin' 'long wid a waggin chock full er money."

"Where did he get so much money, Uncle Remus?"

"Bruisin' 'round en peddlin' 'bout. Mr. Man got w'at lots er folks ain't got, — good luck, long head, quick eye, en slick fingers. But no marter 'bout dat, he got de money; en w'en you sorter grow up so you kin knock 'roun', 'twon't be long 'fo' some un'll take en take you off 'roun' de corner en tell you dat 'tain't make no diffunce whar de money come fum so de man got it. Dey won't tell you dat in de meeting-house, but dey'll come mighty nigh it.

"But dat ain't needer yer ner dar. Mr. Man, he come a-drivin' 'long de big road, en he got a waggin full er money. Brer Rabbit, he come a-lippity-clippitin' 'long de big road, en he ain't got no waggin full er money. Ole Brer Rabbit, he up'n tuck a notion dat dey's sump'n' wrong somers, kaze ef dey wa'n't, he 'ud have des ez much waggin en money ez Mr. Man. He study, en study, en he can't make out how dat is. Bimeby he up'n holler out:

"'Mr. Man, please, sir, lemme ride.'

"Mr. Man, he tuck'n stop he waggin, en 'low:

"'Heyo, Brer Rabbit! how come dis? You comin' one way en I gwine nudder; how come you wanter ride?'

"Brer Rabbit, he up'n scratch hisse'f on de back er de neck wid he behime foot, en holler out:

"'Mr. Man, yo' sholy can't be 'quainted 'long wid me. I'm one er dem ar ole-time kinder folks w'at aint a-keerin' w'ich way dey er gwine long ez dey er ridin'.'"

The little boy laughed a sympathetic laugh, showing that he heartily endorsed this feature of Brother Rabbit's program.

"Atter so long a time," Uncle Remus went on, "Mr. Man 'gree ter let Brer Rabbit ride a little piece. He try ter git Brer Rabbit fer ter ride up on de seat wid 'im so dey kin get ter 'sputin' 'bout sump'n' n'er, but Brer Rabbit say he feard he fall off, en he des tuck'n sot right flat down in dey bottom er de waggin, en make lak he fear'd ter move.

"Bimeby, w'iles dey goin' down hill, en Mr. Man hatter keep he eye on de hosses, Brer Rabbit he tuck'n fling out a great big hunk er de money. Dez ez de money hit de groun' Brer Rabbit holler out:

"'*Ow!*'

"Mr. Man look 'roun' en ax w'at de marter. Brer Rabbit 'low:

"'Nothin' 'tall, Mr. Man, ceppin' you 'bout ter jolt my jawbone a-loose.'

"Dey go on little furder, en Brer Rabbit fling out n'er hunk er de money. W'en she hit the groun', Brer Rabbit holler:

"'*Blam!*'

"Mr. Man look 'roun' an ax w'at de marter. Brer Rabbit 'low:

"'Nothin' 'tall, Mr. Man, ceppin' I seed a jaybird flyin' 'long, en I make lak I had a gun.'

"Hit keep on dis a-way twel fus' news you know Mr. Man ain't got a sign er money in dat waggin. Seem lak Mr. Man ain't notice dis twel he git a mighty fur ways fum de place whar Brer Rabbit drap out de las' hunk; but, gentermens! w'en he do fin' it out, you better b'lieve he sot up a howl.

"'Whar my money? Whar my nice money? Whar my waggin full er purty money? O you long-year'd rascal! Whar my money? Oh, gimme my money!'

"Brer Rabbit sot dar en lissen at 'im lak he 'stonish'd. Den he up'n 'low:

"'Look out, Mr. Man! Folks'll come 'long en year you gwine on dat a-way, en dey'll go off en say you done gone ravin' 'stracted.'

"Yit Mr. Man keep on holler'n en beggin' Brer Rabbit fer ter gin 'im de money, en bimeby Brer Rabbit, he git sorter skeer'd en he up'n 'low:

"'Sun gittin' low, Mr. Man, en I better be gittin' 'way fum yer. De sooner

I goes de better, kaze ef you keep on lak you gwine, 't won't be long 'fo' you'll be excusin' me er takin' dat ar money. I'm 'blige fer de ride, Mr. Man, en I wish you mighty well.'

"Brer Rabbit got de money," continued Uncle Remus, gazing placidly into the fire, "en hit's mighty kuse ter me dat he ain't git de waggin en hosses. Dat 'tis!"

53
Brother Rabbit Takes a Walk

"EVE'Y TIME I run over in my min' 'bout the pranks er Brer Rabbit," Uncle Remus continued, without giving the little boy time to ask any more embarrassing questions about Mr. Man and his wagon full of money, "hit make me laugh mo' en mo'. He mos' allers come out on top, yit dey wuz times w'en he hatter be mighty spry."

"When was that, Uncle Remus?" inquired the little boy.

"I min' me er one time w'en de t'er creeturs all git de laugh on 'im," responded the old man, "en dey make 'im feel sorter 'shame'. Hit seem lak dat dey 'uz some kinder bodderment 'mungs de creeturs en wud went out dat dey all got ter meet terge'er somers en ontangle de tanglements.

"W'en de time come, dey wuz all un um dar, en dey hilt der confab right 'long. All un um got sump'n' ter say en dey talk dar, dey did, des lak dey 'uz paid fer talkin'. Dey all had der plans, en dey jabbered des lak folks does w'en dey call deyse'f terge'er. Hit come 'bout dat Mr. Dog git a seat right close by Brer Rabbit, en w'en he open he mouf fer ter say sump'n', he toofs look so long en so strong, en dey shine so w'ite, dat it feel mighty kuse.

"Mr. Dog, he'd say sump'n', Brer Rabbit, he'd jump en dodge. Mr. Dog, he'd laugh, Brer Rabbit, he'd dodge en jump. Hit keep on dis away, twel eve'y time Brer Rabbit'd dodge en jump, de t'er creeturs dey'd slap der han's terge'er en break out in a laugh. Mr. Dog, he tuck'n tuck a notion dat dey 'uz laughin' at him, en dis make 'im so mad dat he 'gun ter growl en snap right smartually, en it come ter dat pass dat w'en Brer Rabbit'd see Mr. Dog make a motion fer ter say a speech, he'd des drap down en git und' de cheer.

"Co'se dis make um laugh wuss en wuss, en de mo' dey laugh de madder it make Mr. Dog, twel bimeby he git so mad he fa'rly howl, en Brer Rabbit he sot dar, he did, en shuck lak he got er agur.

"Atter w'ile Brer Rabbit git sorter on t'er side, en he make a speech en say dey oughter be a law fer ter make all de creeturs w'at got tushes ketch en eat der vittles wid der claws. All un um 'gree ter dis 'cep' hit's Mr. Dog, Brer Wolf, en Brer Fox.

"In dem days," continued Uncle Remus, "ef all de creeturs ain't 'gree, dey put it off twel de nex' meetin' en talk it over some mo', en dat's de way dey done wid Brer Rabbit projick. Dey put it off twel de nex' time.

"Brer Rabbit got a kinder sneakin' notion dat de creeturs ain't gwine do lak he want um ter do, en he 'low ter Brer Wolf dat he 'speck de bes' way fer ter do is ter git all de creeturs ter 'gree fer ter have Mr. Dog mouf sew'd up, kaze he toofs look so venomous; en Brer Wolf say dey ull all go in fer dat.

"Sho nuff, w'en de day done come, Brer Rabbit he git up en say dat de bes' way ter do is have Mr. Dog mouf sew'd up so he toofs won't look so venomous. Dey all 'gree, en den Mr. Lion, settin' up in de arm-cheer, he ax who gwine do de sewin'.

"Den dey all up'n 'low dat de man w'at want de sewin' done, he de man fer ter do it, kaze den he ull know it done bin done right. Brer Rabbit, he sorter study, en den he 'low:

"'I ain't got no needle.'

"Brer B'ar, he sorter feel in de flap er he coat collar, en he 'low:

"'Yer, Brer Rabbit; yer a great big one!'

"Brer Rabbit, he sorter study 'g'in, en den he 'low:

"'I ain't got no th'ead.'

"Brer B'ar, he tuck'n pull a rav'lin' fum de bottom er he wescut, en he 'low:

"'Yer, Brer Rabbit; yer a great long one!'

"Ef it had er bin anybody in de roun' worl' he'd er 'gun ter feel sorter ticklish," Uncle Remus went on. "But ole Brer Rabbit, he des tuck'n lay he finger 'cross he nose, en 'low:

"'Des hol' um dar fer me, Brer B'ar, en I'll be much 'blige ter you. *Hit's des 'bout my time er day fer ter take a walk!*'"

Uncle Remus laughed as heartily as the child, and added, "Some folks say de creeturs had de grins on Brer Rabbit 'bout dat time; but I tell you right pine-blank dey ain't grin much w'en dey year Brer Rabbit say dat."

54
Old Grinny Granny Wolf

AT LAST Daddy Jack returned, and the fact that the little boy had missed him and inquired about him, seemed to give the old African particular pleasure. It was probably a new experience to Daddy Jack, and it vaguely stirred some dim instinct in his bosom that impelled him to greet the child with more genuine heartiness than he had ever displayed in all his life. He drew the little boy up to him, patted him gently on the cheek, and exclaimed:

"Ki! I bin want fer see you bery bahd. I bin-a tell you' nunk Jeem' how fine noung màn you is. 'E ahx wey you no come fer shum. Fine b'y — fine b'y!"

"Well, ef dat's de way you er gwine on, Brer Jack, you'll spile dat chap sho. A whole sack er salt won't save 'im."

"I dunno 'bout dat, Brer Remus," said Aunt Tempy, who had come in. "Don't seem like he bad like some yuther childun w'at I seen. Bless you, I know childun w'at'd keep dish yer whole place tarryfied — dat dey would!"

"Well, sir," said Uncle Remus, shaking his head and groaning, "you all ain't wid dat young un dar much ez I is. Some days w'en dey ain't nobody lookin' en dey ain't nobody nowhar fer ter take keer un me, dat ar little chap dar'll come down yer en chunk me wid rocks, en 'buze me en holler at me scan'lous."

The little boy looked so shocked that Uncle Remus broke into a laugh that shook the cobwebs in the corners; then, suddenly relapsing into seriousness, he drew himself up with dignity and remarked:

"Good er bad, you can't git 'long wid 'im less'n you sets in ter tellin' tales, en, Brer Jack, I hope you got some 'long wid you."

Daddy Jack rubbed his hands together, and said:

"Me bin yeddy one tale; 'e mekky me lahff tel I is 'come tire'."

"Fer de Lord sake less have it den!" exclaimed Aunt Tempy, with unction. Whereupon, the small but appreciative audience disposed itself comfortably, and Daddy Jack, peering at each one in turn, his eyes shining between his half-closed lids as brightly as those of some wild animal, began:

"One tam B'er Rabbit is bin traffel 'roun' fer see 'e neighbor folks. 'E bin mahd wit' B'er Wolf fer so long tam; 'e mek no diffran, 'e come pas' 'e house 'e no see nuttin', 'e no yeddy nuttin'. 'E holler:

"'Hi, B'er Wolf! wey you no fer mek answer wun me ahx you howdy? Wey fer you is do dis 'fo' me werry face? Wut mekky you do dis?'

"'E wait, 'e lissen; nuttin' no mek answer. B'er Rabbit, 'e holler:

"'Come-a show you'se'f, B'er Wolf! Come-a show you'se'f. Be 'shame fer not show you'se'f wun you' 'quaintun' come bisitin' wey you lif!'

"Nuttin' 'tall no mek answer, un B'er Rabbit 'come berry mahd. 'E 'come so mahd 'e stomp 'e fut un bump 'e head 'pon da fence-side. Bumbye 'e tek heart, 'e y-opun da do', 'e is look inside da house. Fier bu'n in da chimbley, pot set 'pon da fier, ole ooman sed by da pot. Fier bu'n, pot, 'e bile, ole ooman, 'e tek 'e nap.

"Da ole ooman, 'e ole Granny Wolf; 'e cripple in 'e leg, 'e bline in 'e y-eye, 'e mos' deaf in 'e year. 'E deaf, but 'e bin yeddy B'er Rabbit mek fuss at da do', un 'e is cry out:

"'Come-a see you' ole Granny, me gran'son — come-a see you' Granny! Da fier is bin bu'n, da pot is bin b'ile; come-a fix you' Granny some bittle, me gran'son.'"

Daddy Jack's representation of the speech and action of an old woman was worth seeing and hearing. The little boy laughed, and Uncle Remus smiled good-humoredly; but Aunt Tempy looked at the old African with open-mouthed astonishment. Daddy Jack, however, cared nothing for any effect he might produce. He told the story for the story's sake, and he made no pause for the purpose of gauging the appreciation of his audience.

"B'er Rabbit, 'e is bin mek 'ese'f comfuts by da fier. Bumbye, 'e holler:

"'Hi, Granny! I bin cripple mese'f; me y-eye bin-a come bline. You mus' b'ile-a me in da water, Granny, so me leg is kin come well, un so me y-eye kin come see.'

"B'er Rabbit, 'e mighty ha'd fer fool. 'E bin tek 'im one chunk woot, 'e drap da woot in da pot. 'E bin say:

"'I is bin feelin' well, me Granny. Me leg, 'e comin' strong, me y-eye 'e fix fer see.'

"Granny Wolf, 'e shek 'e head; 'e cry:

"'Me one leg cripple, me turrer leg cripple; me one eye bline, me turrer y-eye bline. Wey you no fer pit me in da pot fer mek me well?'

"B'er Rabbit lahff in 'e belly: 'e say:

"'Hol' you'se'f still, me Granny; I fix you one place in da pot wey you is kin fetch-a back da strenk in you' leg un da sight in you' eye. Hol' still, me Granny!'

"B'er Rabbit, 'e is bin tekky da chunk y-out da pot; 'e tekky da chunk, un 'e is bin pit Granny Wolf in dey place. 'E tetch da water, 'e holler:

"'Ow! tekky me way fum dis!'

"B'er Rabbit say 'tiss not da soon 'nuff tam. Granny Wolf, 'e holler:

"'Ow! tekky me way fum dis! 'E bin too hot!'

"B'er Rabbit, 'e no tekky da Mammy Wolf fum da pot, un bumbye 'e die in dey. B'er Rabbit 'e tek 'e bone un t'row um 'way; 'e leaf da meat. 'E tek Granny Wolf frock, 'e tu'n um 'roun', 'e pit um on; 'e tek Granny Wolf cap, 'e tu'n 'roun', 'e pit um on. 'E sed deer by da fier, 'e hol' 'e'se'f in 'e cheer sem lak Granny Wolf.

"Bumbye B'er Wolf is bin-a come back. 'E walk in 'e house, 'e say:

"'Me honkry, Grinny-Granny! Me honkry, fer true!'

"'You' dinner ready, Grin'son-Gran'son!'

"B'er Wolf, 'e look in da pot, 'e smell in da pot, 'e stir in da pot. 'E eat 'e dinner, 'e smack 'e mout'.""

The little boy shuddered, and Aunt Tempy exclaimed, "In de name er de Lord!" The old African paid no attention to either.

"B'er Wolf eat 'e dinner; 'e call 'e chilluns, 'e ahx um is dey no want nuttin' 'tall fer eat. 'E holler back:

"'We no kin eat we Grinny-Granny!'

"B'er Rabbit, 'e run 'way fum dey-dey; 'e holler back:

"'B'er Wolf, you is bin eat you' Grinny-Granny.'

"B'er Wolf bin-a git so mad 'e yent mos' kin see. 'E yeddy B'er Rabbit holler, un 'e try fer ketch um. 'E feer teer up da grass wey 'e run 'long. Bumbye 'e come 'pon B'er Rabbit. 'E is bin push um ha'd. B'er Rabbit run un-a run tel 'e yent kin run no mo'; 'e hide 'neat' leanin' tree. B'er Wolf, 'e fine um; B'er Rabbit 'e holler:

"'Hi! B'er Wolf! mek 'as'e come hol' up da tree, 'fo' 'e is fall dey-dey; come-a hol' um, B'er Wolf, so I is kin prop um up.'

"B'er Wolf, 'e hol' up da tree fer B'er Rabbit; 'e hol' um till 'e do come tire'. B'er Rabbit gone!"

Daddy Jack paused. His story was ended. The little boy drew a long breath and said:

"I didn't think Brother Rabbit would burn anybody to death in a pot of boiling water."

"Dat," said Uncle Remus, reassuringly, "wuz endurin' er de dog days. Dey er mighty wom times, mon, dem ar dog days is."

This was intended to satisfy such scruples as the child might have, and it was no doubt successful, for the youngster said no more, but watched Uncle Remus as the latter leisurely proceeded to fill his pipe.

55
How Wattle Weasel Was Caught

UNCLE REMUS chipped the tobacco from the end of a plug, rubbed it between the palms of his hands, placed it in his pipe, dipped the pipe in the glowing embers, and leaned back in his chair, and seemed to be completely happy.

"Hit mought not er bin endurin' er de dog days," said the old man, recurring to Daddy Jack's story, "kaze dey wuz times dat w'en dey push ole Brer Rabbit so close he 'uz des bleedzd ter git he revengeance out'n um. Dat mought er bin de marter 'twix' him en ole Grinny-Granny Wolf, kaze w'en ole Brer Rabbit git he dander up, he 'uz a monstus bad man fer ter fool wid.

"Dey tuck atter 'im," continued Uncle Remus, "en dey 'buzed 'im, en dey tried ter 'stroy 'im, but dey wuz times w'en de t'er creeturs bleedzd ter call on 'im fer ter he'p 'em out dey trouble. I ain't nev' tell you 'bout little Wattle Weasel, is I?" asked the old man, suddenly turning to the little boy.

The child laughed. The dogs on the plantation had killed a weasel a few nights before, — a very cunning-looking little animal — and some of the Negroes had sent it to the big house as a curiosity. He connected this fact with Uncle Remus's allusions to the weasel. Before he could make any reply, however, the old man went on:

"No, I boun' I ain't, en it come 'cross me right fresh en hot time I year talk er Brer Wolf eatin' he granny. Dey wuz one time w'en all de creeturs wuz livin' in de same settlement en usin' out'n de same spring, en it got so dat dey put all dey butter in de same piggin'. Dey put it in dar, dey did, en dey put it in de spring-house, en dey'd go off en 'ten' ter dey business. Den w'en dey come back dey'd fin' whar some un been nibblin' at dey butter. Dey tuck'n hide dat butter all 'roun' in de spring-house; dey sot it on de rafters, en dey bury it in de san'; yit all de same de butter 'ud come up missin'.

"Bimeby it got so dey dunner w'at ter do; dey 'zamin' de tracks, en dey fin' out dat de man w'at nibble dey butter is little Wattle Weasel. He come in de night, he come in de day; dey can't ketch 'im. Las' de creeturs tuck'n helt er confab, en dey 'gree dat dey hatter set some un fer ter watch en ketch Wattle Weasel.

"Brer Mink wuz de fus' man 'p'inted, kaze he wa'n't mo'n a half a han'[1] no way you kin fix it. De t'er creeturs dey tuck'n went off ter dey wuk, en Brer Mink he tuck'n sot up wid de butter. He watch en he lissen, he lissen en he watch; he ain't see nothin', he ain't year nothin'. Yit he watch, kaze der t'er creeturs done fix up a law dat ef Wattle Weasel come w'iles somebody watchin' en git off widout gittin' kotch, de man w'at watchin' ain't kin eat no mo' butter endurin' er dat year.

"Brer Mink, he watch en he wait. He set so still dat bimeby he gits de cramps in de legs, en des 'bout dat time little Wattle Weasel pop he head und' de do'. He see Brer Mink, en he hail 'im:

"'Heyo, Brer Mink! you look sorter lonesome in dar. Come out yer en less take a game er hidin'-switch.'

"Brer Mink, he wanter have some fun, he did, en he tuck'n jine Wattle Weasel in de game. Dey play en dey play twel, bimeby, Brer Mink git so wo' out dat he ain't kin run, skacely, en des soon ez dey sets down ter

---

[1] That is, could do no more than half the work of a man. — J. C. H.

res', Brer Mink, he draps off ter sleep. Little Wattle Weasel, so mighty big en fine, he goes en nibbles up de butter, en pops out de way he come in.

"De creeturs, dey come back, dey did, en dey fin' de butter nibbled, en Wattle Weasel gone. Wid dat, dey marks Brer Mink down, en he ain't kin eat no mo' butter dat year. Den dey fix up n'er choosement en 'p'int Brer Possum fer ter watch de butter.

"Brer Possum, he grin en watch, and bimeby, sho nuff, in pop little Wattle Weasel. He come in, he did, en he sorter hunch Brer Possum in de short ribs, en ax 'im how he come on. Brer Possum mighty ticklish, en time Wattle Weasel totch 'im in de short ribs, he 'gun ter laugh. Wattle Weasel totch 'im ag'in en he laugh wusser, en he keep on hunchin' 'im dat a-way twel bimeby Brer Possum laugh hisse'f plum' outer win', en Wattle Weasel lef' 'im dar en nibble up de butter.

"De creeturs, dey tuck'n mark Brer Possum down, en 'p'int Brer Coon. Brer Coon, he tuck'n start in all so mighty fine; but w'iles he settin' dar, little Wattle Weasel banter 'im fer a race up de branch. No sooner say dan yer dey went! Brer Coon, he foller de tu'ns er de branch, en little Wattle Weasel he take'n take nigh cuts, en 'twa'n't no time 'fo' he done run Brer Coon plum' down. Den dey run down de branch, an 'fo' Brer Coon kin ketch up wid 'im, dat little Wattle Weasel done got back ter de noggin er butter, en nibble it up.

"Den de creeturs tuck'n mark Brer Coon down, dey did, en 'p'int Brer Fox fer ter watch de butter. Wattle Weasel sorter fear'd er Brer Fox. He study long time, en den he wait twel night. Den he tuck'n went 'roun' in de ole fiel' en woke up de Killdees en druv um 'roun' todes de springhouse. Brer Fox year um holler, en it make he mouf water. Bimeby, he 'low ter hisse'f dat 'tain't no harm ef he go out en slip up on one."

"Dar now!" said Aunt Tempy.

"Brer Fox tuck'n slip out, en Wattle Weasel he slicked in, en bless yo' soul! dar goes de butter!"

"Enty!" exclaimed Daddy Jack.

"Brer Fox he git marked down," continued Uncle Remus, "en den de creeturs tuck'n 'p'int Brer Wolf fer ter be dey watcher. Brer Wolf, he sot up dar, he did, en sorter nod, but bimeby he year some un talkin' outside de spring-house. He h'ist up he years en lissen. Look lak some er de creeturs wuz gwine by, en talkin' 'mungs deysef'; but all Brer Wolf kin year is dish yer:

"'I wonder who put dat ar young sheep down dar by de chinkapin tree, en I like ter know whar'bouts Brer Wolf is.'

"Den it seem lak dey pas on, en ole Brer Wolf, he fergotted w'at he in dar fer, en he dash down ter de chinkapin tree, fer ter git de young sheep. But no sheep dar, en w'en he git back, he see signs whar Wattle Weasel done bin in dar en nibble de butter.

"Den de creeturs tuck'n mark Brer Wolf down, en 'p'int Brer B'ar fer ter keep he eye 'pun de noggin er butter. Brer B'ar he tuck'n sot up dar, he did, en lick he paw, en feel good. Bimeby Wattle Weasel come dancin' in. He 'low:

"'Heyo, Brer B'ar, how you come on? I 'low I year'd you snortin' in yer, en I des drapt in fer ter see.'

"Brer B'ar tell him howdy, but he sorter keep one eye on 'im. Little Wattle Weasel 'low:

"'En you got ticks on yo' back, Brer B'ar?'

"Wid dat Wattle Weasel 'gun ter rub Brer B'ar on de back en scratch 'im on de sides, en 'twa'n't long 'fo' he 'uz stretch out fast asleep en sno'in' lak a saw-mill. Co'se Wattle Weasel git de butter. Brer B'ar he got marked down, and den de creeturs ain't know w'at dey gwine do skacely.

"Some say sen' fer Brer Rabbit, some say sen' fer Brer Tarrypin; but las' dey sent fer Brer Rabbit. Brer Rabbit he tuck a notion dat dey 'uz fixin' up some kinder trick on 'im, en dey hatter beg mightily, mon, 'fo' he 'ud come en set up 'longside er dey butter.

"But bimeby he 'greed, en he went down ter de spring-house en look 'roun'. Den he tuck'n got 'im a twine string, en hide hisse'f whar he kin keep he eye on de noggin er butter. He ain't wait long 'fo' yer come Wattle Weasel. Des ez he 'bout ter nibble at de butter, Brer Rabbit holler out:

"'Let dat butter 'lone!'

"Wattle Weasel jump back lak de butter bu'nt 'im. He jump back, he did, en say:

"'Sholy dat mus' be Brer Rabbit!'

"'De same. I 'lowed you'd know me. Des let dat butter 'lone.'

"'Des lemme git one little bit er tas'e, Brer Rabbit.'

" 'Des let dat butter 'lone.'

"Den Wattle Weasel say he want er run a race. Brer Rabbit 'low he tired. Wattle Weasel 'low he want er play hidin'. Brer Rabbit 'low dat all he hidin' days is pas' en gone. Wattle Weasel banter'd en banter'd 'im, en bimeby Brer Rabbit come up wid a banter er he own.

" 'I'll tak'n tie yo' tail,' sezee, 'en you'll tak'n tie mine, en den we'll see w'ich tail de strongest.' Little Wattle Weasel know how weakly Brer Rabbit tail is, but he ain't know how strong Brer Rabbit bin wid he tricks. So dey tuck'n tie der tails wid Brer Rabbit twine string.

"Wattle Weasel wuz ter stan' inside en Brer Rabbit wuz ter stan' out-side, en dey wuz ter pull 'g'in' one er n'er wid dey tails. Brer Rabbit, he tuck'n slip out'n de string, en tie de een' 'roun' a tree root, en den he went en peep at Wattle Weasel tuggin' en pullin'. Bimeby Wattle Weasel 'low:

" 'Come en ontie me, Brer Rabbit, 'kaze you done outpull me.'

"Brer Rabbit sot dar, he did, en chaw he cud, en look lak he feel sorry 'bout sump'n'. Bimeby all de creeturs come fer ter see 'bout dey butter, kaze dey fear'd Brer Rabbit done make way wid it. Yit w'en dey see lit-tle Wattle Weasel tie by de tail, dey make great 'miration 'bout Brer Rab-bit, en dey 'low he de smartest one er de whole gang."

56
Brother Rabbit Ties Mr. Lion

THERE WAS some comment and some questions were asked by the little boy in regard to Wattle Weasel and the other animals; to all of which Uncle Re-mus made characteristic response. Aunt Tempy sat with one elbow on her knee, her head resting in the palm of her fat hand. She gazed intently into the fire, and seemed to be lost in thought. Presently she exclaimed: —

"Well, de Lord he'p my soul!"

"Dat's de promise, Sis Tempy," said Uncle Remus, solemnly.

Aunt Tempy laughed, as she straightened herself in her chair, and said:

"I des knowed dey wuz sump'n' n'er gwine 'cross my min' w'en I year talk 'bout dat ar sheep by de chinkapin tree."

"Out wid it, Sis Tempy," said Uncle Remus, by way of encourage-ment; "out wid it; free yo' min', en des make yo'se'f welcome."

"No longer'n Sunday 'fo' las', I 'uz 'cross dar at de Spivey place un I tuck'n year'd a nigger man tellin' de same tale, un I 'low ter myse'f dat I'd tak'n take it un kyar' it home un gin it out w'en I come ter pass de time wid Brer Remus un all uv um. I 'low ter myse'f I'll take it un kyar' it dar, un I'll des tell it my own way."

"Well, den," said Uncle Remus, approvingly, "me en dish yer chap, we er willin' en a-waitin', en ez fer Brer Jack over dar, we kin say de same fer him, kaze I up en year 'im draw mighty long breff des now lak he fixin' fer ter snort. But you nee'nter min' dat ole creetur, Sis Tempy. Des push right ahead."

"Ah-h-h-e-e!" exclaimed Daddy Jack, snapping his bright little eyes at Uncle Remus with some display of irritation; "you tek-a me fer be sleep ebry tam I shed-a my y-eye, you is mek fool-a you'se'f. *Warrah yarrah garrah tarrah!*"[1]

"Brer Remus!" said Aunt Tempy, in an awed whisper, "maybe he's a-cunju'n un you."

"No-no!" exclaimed Daddy Jack, snappishly, "me no cuncher no'n' 't all. Wun me cuncher you all you yeddy bone crack. Enty!"

"Well, in de name er de Lord, don't come a-cunju'n wid me, kaze I'm des as peaceable ez de day's long," said Aunt Tempy.

Uncle Remus smiled and closed his eyes with an air of disdain, caught from his old Mistress, the little boy's grandmother, long since dead.

"Tell yo' tale, Sis Tempy," he said pleasantly, "en leave de talk er cunju'n ter de little nigger childun. We er done got too ole fer dat kinder foolishness."

This was for the ear of the little boy. In his heart Uncle Remus was convinced that Daddy Jack was capable of changing himself into the blackest of black cats, with swollen tail, arched back, fiery eyes, and protruding fangs. But the old man's attitude reassured Aunt Tempy, as well as the child, and forthwith she proceeded with her story:

"Hit seem like dat one time w'en Brer Rabbit fin' hisse'f way off in de middle er de woods, de win' strike up un 'gun ter blow. Hit blow down on de groun' un it blow up in de top er de timber, un it blow so hard twel ter-

---

[1] This is simply "gullah" Negro talk intended to be unintelligible, and therefore impressive. It means "One or the other is as good as t'other." — J. C. H.

reckerly Brer Rabbit tuck a notion dat he better git out fum dar 'fo' de timber 'gun ter fall.

"Brer Rabbit, he broke en run, un, Man — Sir! w'en dat creetur run'd he run'd, now you year w'at I tell yer! He broke un run, he did, un he fa'rly flew 'way fum dar. W'iles he gwine 'long full tilt, he run'd ag'in' ole Mr. Lion. Mr. Lion, he hail 'im:

" 'Heyo, Brer Rabbit! W'at yo' hurry?'

" 'Run, Mr. Lion, run! Dey's a harrycane comin' back dar in de timbers. You better run!'

"Dis make Mr. Lion sorter skeer'd. He 'low:

" 'I mos' too heavy fer ter run fur, Brer Rabbit. W'at I gwine do?'

" 'Lay down, Mr. Lion, lay down! Git close ter de groun'!'

"Mr. Lion shake his head. He 'low:

" 'Ef win' lierbul fer ter pick up little man like you is, Brer Rabbit, w'at it gwine do wid big man like me?'

" 'Hug a tree, Mr. Lion, hug a tree!'

"Mr. Lion lash hisse'f wid his tail. He 'low:

" 'W'at I gwine do ef de win' blow all day un a good part er de night, Brer Rabbit?'

" 'Lemme tie you ter de tree, Mr. Lion! lemme tie you ter de tree!'

"Mr. Lion, he tuk'n 'gree ter dis, un Brer Rabbit, he got 'im a hick'ry split un tie 'im hard un fas' ter de tree. Den he tuck'n sot down, ole Brer Rabbit did, un wash his face un han's des same ez you see de cats doin'. Terreckerly Mr. Lion git tired er stan'in' dar huggin' de tree, un he ax Brer Rabbit w'at de reason he ain't keep on runnin', un Brer Rabbit, he up'n 'low dat he gwine ter stay der un take keer Mr. Lion.

"Terreckerly Mr. Lion say he ain't year no harrycane. Brer Rabbit say he ain't needer. Mr. Lion say he ain't year no win' a-blowin'. Brer Rabbit say he ain't needer. Mr. Lion say he ain't so much ez year a leaf a-stirrin'. Brer Rabbit say he ain't needer. Mr. Lion sorter study, un Brer Rabbit sot dar, he did, un wash his face un lick his paws.

"Terreckerly Mr. Lion ax Brer Rabbit fer ter onloose 'im. Brer Rabbit say he fear'd. Den Mr. Lion git mighty mad, un he 'gun ter beller wuss'n one er deze yer bull-yearlin's. He beller so long un he beller so loud twel present'y de t'er creeturs dey 'gun ter come up fer ter see w'at de matter.

"Des soon ez dey come up, Brer Rabbit, he tuck'n 'gun ter talk biggity un strut 'roun', un, Man — Sir! w'en dem yuthers see dat Brer Rabbit done got Mr. Lion tied up, I let you know dey tuck'n walked way
'roun' 'im, un 'twuz many a long day 'fo' dey tuck'n pestered ole Brer
Rabbit."

Here Aunt Tempy paused. The little boy asked what Brother Rabbit
tied Mr. Lion for; but she didn't know; Uncle Remus, however, came to
the rescue.

"One time long 'fo' dat, honey, Brer Rabbit went ter de branch fer ter
git a drink er water, en ole Mr. Lion tuck'n druv 'im off, en fum dat time
out Brer Rabbit bin huntin' a chance fer ter ketch up wid 'im."

"Dat's so," said Aunt Tempy, and then she added:

"I 'clare I ain't gwine tell you all not na'er n'er tale, dat I ain't. Kaze
you des set dar en you ain't crack a smile fum de time I begin. Ef dat'd a
bin Brer Remus, now, dey'd a bin mo' gigglin' gwine on dan you kin
shake a stick at. I'm right down mad, dat I is."

"Well, I tell you dis, Sis Tempy," said Uncle Remus, with unusual
emphasis, "ef deze yer tales wuz des fun, fun, fun, en giggle, giggle, giggle, I let you know I'd a-done drapt um long ago. Yasser, w'en it come
down ter gigglin' you kin des count ole Remus out."

57

Mr. Lion's Sad Predicament

THE DISCUSSION over Aunt Tempy's fragmentary story having exhausted itself, Daddy Jack turned up his coat collar until it was as high as the top of his head, and then tried to button it under his chin. If this attempt had been successful, the old African would have presented a diabolical appearance; but the coat refused to be buttoned in that style. After several attempts, which created no end of amusement for the little boy, Daddy Jack said:

"Da Lion, 'e no hab bin sma't lak B'er Rabbit. 'E strong wit' 'e fut, 'e strong wit' 'e tush, but 'e no strong wit' 'e head. 'E bery foolish, 'cep' 'e is bin hab chance ter jump 'pon dem creetur.

"One tam 'e bin come by B'er Rabbit in da road; 'e ahx um howdy; 'e ahx um wey 'e gwan. B'er Rabbit say 'e gwan git fum front de Buckra Màn wut bin comin' 'long da road. B'er Rabbit say:

"'Hide you'se'f, B'er Lion; da Buckra ketch-a you fer true; 'e is bin ketch-a you tam he pit 'e y-eye 'pon you; 'e mekky you sick wit' sorry. Hide fum da Buckra, B'er Lion!'

"Da Lion, 'e shekky 'e head; 'e say:

"'Ki! Me no skeer da Buckra Màn. I glad fer shum. I ketch um un I kyar um wey I lif; me hab da Buckra Màn fer me bittle. How come you bein' skeer da Buckra Màn, B'er Rabbit?'

"B'er Rabbit look all 'bout fer see ef da Buckra bin comin'. 'E say:

"'Me hab plenty reason, B'er Lion. Da Buckra Màn shoot-a wit' one gun. 'E r'ise um to 'e y-eye, 'e p'int um stret toze you; 'e say *bang!* one tam, 'e say *bang!* two tam; dun you is bin git hu't troo da head un cripple in da leg.'

"Lion, 'e shek 'e head; 'e say:

"'Me no skeer da Buckra Màn. I grab-a da gun. I ketch um fer me brekwus.'

"B'er Rabbit, 'e lahff; 'e say:

"'Him quare fer true. Me skeer da Buckra, me no skeer you; but you no skeer da Buckra. How come dis?'

"Da Lion lash 'e tail; 'e say:

"'Me no skeer da Buckra, but me skeer da Pa'tridge; me berry skeer da Pa'tridge.'

"B'er Rabbit, 'e lahff tel 'e lahff no mo'. 'E say:

"'How come you skeer da Pa'tridge? 'E fly wun you wink-a you' eye; 'e run un 'e fly. Hoo! me no skeer 'bout dem Pa'tridge. Me skeer da Buckra.'

"Da Lion, 'e look all 'bout fer see ef da Pa'tridge bin comin'. 'E say:

"'I skeer da Pa'tridge. Wun me bin walk in da bushside, da Pa'tridge 'e hol' right still 'pon da groun' tel me come dey-dey, un dun 'e fly up — *fud-d-d-d-d-d-e-c!* Wun 'e is bin do dat me is git-a skeer berry bahd.'"

No typographical device could adequately describe Daddy Jack's imitation of the flushing of a covey of partridges, or quail; but it is needless to say that it made its impression upon the little boy. The old African went on:

"B'er Rabbit, 'e holler un lahff; 'e say:

"'Me no skeer da Pa'tridge. I bin run dem up ebry day. Da no hu't-a you, B'er Lion. You hol' you' eye 'pon da Buckra Màn. Da Pa'tridge, 'e no hab no gun fer shoot-a you wit'; da Buckra, 'e is bin hab one gun two tam.[1] Let da Pa'tridge fly, B'er Lion; but wun da Buckra Màn come you bes' keep in de shady side. I tell you dis, B'er Lion.'

"Da Lion, 'e stan' um down, 'e no skeer da Buckra Màn, un bumbye 'e say goo'-bye; 'e say 'e gwan look fer da Buckra Màn fer true.

"So long tam, B'er Rabbit is bin yeddy one big fuss in da timber; 'e yeddy da Lion v'ice. B'er Rabbit foller da fuss tel 'e is bin come 'pon da Lion wey 'e layin' 'pon da groun'. Da Lion, 'e is moan; 'e is groan; 'e is cry. 'E hab hole in 'e head, one, two, t'ree hole in 'e side; 'e holler, 'e groan. B'er Rabbit, 'e ahx um howdy. 'E say:

"'Ki, B'er Lion, wey you hab fine so much trouble?'

"Da Lion, 'e moan, 'e groan, 'e cry; 'e say:

"'Ow, ma Lord! I hab one hole in me head, one, two, t'ree hole in me side, me leg bin bruk!'

"B'er Rabbit bin hol' 'e head 'pon one side; 'e look skeer. 'E say:

"'Ki, B'er Lion! I no know da Pa'tridge is so bahd lak dat. I t'ink 'e fly

---

[1] One gun two times is a double-barrelled gun. — J. C. H.

'way un no hu't-a you. Shuh-shuh! wun I see dem Pa'tridge I mus' git
'pon turrer side fer keep me hide whole.'

"Da Lion, 'e groan, 'e moan, 'e cry. B'er Rabbit, 'e say:

"'Da Pa'tridge, 'e berry bahd; 'e mus' bin borry da Buckra Màn gun.'

"Da Lion, 'e groan, 'e cry:

"''E no da Pa'tridge no'n 'tall. Da Buckra Màn is bin stan' way off un
shoot-a me wit' 'e gun. Ow, ma Lord!'

"B'er Rabbit, 'e h'ist 'e han'; 'e say:

"'Wut I bin tell-a you, B'er Lion? Wut I bin tell you 'bout da Buckra
Màn? Da Pa'tridge no hu't-a you lak dis. 'E mek-a da big fuss, but 'e no
hu't-a you lak dis. Da Buckra Màn, e' no mek no fuss 'cep 'e p'int 'e gun
at you — *bang!*'"

"And what then?" the little boy asked, as Daddy Jack collapsed in
his seat, seemingly forgetful of all his surroundings.

"No'n 'tall," replied the old African, somewhat curtly.

"De p'ints er dat tale, honey," said Uncle Remus, covering the
brusqueness of Daddy Jack with his own amiability, "is des 'bout lak dis,
dat dey ain't no use er dodgin' w'iles dey's a big fuss gwine on, but you
better tak'n hide out w'en dey ain't no racket; mo' speshually w'en you
see Miss Sally lookin' behime de lookin'-glass fer dat ar peach-lim' w'at
she tuck'n make me kyar' up dar day 'fo' yistiddy; yit w'en she fin' it don't
you git too skeer'd, kaze I tuck'n make some weak places in dat ar switch,
en Miss Sally won't mo'n strak you wid it 'fo' hit'll all come onj'inted."

Parts of this moral the little boy understood thoroughly, for he laughed,
and ran to the big house, and not long afterwards the light went out in Uncle Remus's cabin; but the two old Negroes sat and nodded by the glowing
embers for hours afterwards, dreaming dreams they never told of.

58
The Origin of the Ocean

"UNCLE REMUS," said the little boy, one night shortly after Daddy Jack's
story of the lion's sad predicament, "mamma says there are no lions in
Georgia, nor anywhere in the whole country."

"Tooby sholy not, honey; tooby sholy not!" exclaimed Uncle Remus.

"I dunner who de name er goodness bin a-puttin' dat kinder idee in yo' head, en dey better not lemme fin' um out, needer, kaze I'll take en put Mars John atter um right raw en rank, dat I will."

"Well, you know Daddy Jack said that Brother Rabbit met the Lion coming down the road."

"Bless yo' soul, honey! dat's 'way 'cross de water whar ole man Jack tuck'n come fum, en a mighty long time ergo at dat. Hit's away off yan, lots furder dan Ferginny yit. We-all er on one side de water, en de lions en mos' all de yuther servigous creeturs, dey er on t'er side. Ain't I never tell you how come dat?"

The little boy shook his head.

"Well, *sir!* I dunner w'at I bin doin' all dis time dat I ain't tell you dat, kaze dat's whar de wussest kinder doin's tuck'n happen. Yasser! de wussest kinder doin's; en I'll des whirl in en gin it out right now 'fo' ole man Jack come wobblin' in.

"One time way back yander, 'fo' dey wuz any folks a-foolin' 'roun', Mr. Lion, he tuck'n tuck a notion dat he'd go huntin', en nothin' 'ud do 'im but Brer Rabbit must go wid 'im. Brer Rabbit, he 'low dat he up fer any kinder fun on top side er de groun'. Wid dat dey put out, dey did, en dey hunt en hunt clean 'cross de country.

"Mr. Lion, he'd lam a-loose en miss de game, en den Brer Rabbit, he'd lam a-loose en fetch it down. No sooner is he do dis dan Mr. Lion, he'd squall out:

"'Hit's mine! hit's mine! I kil't it!'

"Mr. Lion sech a big man dat Brer Rabbit skeer'd ter 'spute 'long wid 'im, but he lay it up in he min' fer to git even wid 'im. Dey went on en dey went on. Mr. Lion, he'd lam a-loose en miss de game, en ole Brer Rabbit, he'd lam a-loose en hit it, en Mr. Lion, he'd tak'n whirl in en claim it.

"Dey hunt all day long, en w'en night come, dey 'uz sech a fur ways fum home dat dey hatter camp out. Dey went on, dey did, twel dey come ter a creek, en w'en dey come ter dat, dey tuck'n scrape away de trash en built um a fier on de bank, en cook dey supper.

"Atter supper dey sot up dar en tole tales, dey did, en Brer Rabbit, he tuck'n brag 'bout w'at a good hunter Mr. Lion is, en Mr. Lion, he leant back on he yelbow, en feel mighty biggity. Bimeby, w'en dey eyeleds git sorter heavy, Brer Rabbit, he up'n 'low:

"'I'm a monstus heavy sleeper, Mr. Lion, w'en I gits ter nappin', en I hope en trus' I ain't gwine 'sturb you dis night, yit I got my doubts.'

"Mr. Lion, he roach he ha'r back outen he eyes, en 'low:

"'I'm a monstus heavy sleeper myse'f, Brer Rabbit, en I'll feel mighty glad ef I don't roust you up in the co'se er de night.'

"Brer Rabbit, he tuck'n change his terbacker fum one side he mouf ter de yuther, he did, en he up'n 'low:

"'Mr. Lion, I wish you be so good ez ter show me how you sno' des 'fo' you git soun' asleep.'

"Mr. Lion, he tuck'n draw in he breff sorter hard, en show Brer Rabbit; den Brer Rabbit 'low:

"'Mr. Lion, I wish you be so good ez ter show me how you sno' atter you done git soun' asleep.'

"Mr. Lion, he tuck'n suck in he breff, en eve'y time he suck in he breff it soun' des lak a whole passel er mules w'en dey whinney atter fodder. Brer Rabbit look 'stonish'. He roll he eye en 'low:

"'I year tell you er mighty big man, Mr. Lion, en you sholy is.'

"Mr. Lion, he hol' he head one side en try ter look 'shame', but all de same he ain't feel 'shame'. Bimeby, he shot he eye en 'gun ter nod, den he lay down en stretch hisse'f out, en 'twa'n't long 'fo' he 'gun ter sno' lak he sno' w'en he ain't sleepin' soun'.

"Brer Rabbit, he lay dar. He ain't sayin' nothin'. He lay dar wid one year h'ist up en one eye open. He lay dar, he did, en bimeby Mr. Lion 'gun ter sno' lak he sno' w'en he done gone fas' ter sleep.

"W'en ole Brer Rabbit year dis, he git up fum dar, en sprinkle hisse'f wid de col' ashes 'roun' de fier, en den he tuck'n fling er whole passel der hot embers on Mr. Lion. Mr. Lion, he jump up, he did, en ax who done dat, en Brer Rabbit, he lay dar en kick at he year wid he behime foot, en holler *'Ow!'*

"Mr. Lion see de ashes on Brer Rabbit, en he dunner w'at ter t'ink. He look all 'roun', but he ain't see nothin'. He drap he head en lissen, but he ain't year nothin'. Den he lay down 'g'in en drap off ter sleep. Atter w'ile, w'en he 'gun ter sno' lak he done befo', Brer Rabbit, he jump up en sprinkle some mo' col' ashes on hisse'f, en fling de hot embers on Mr. Lion. Mr. Lion jump up, he did, en holler:

"'Dar you is 'g'in!'

"Brer Rabbit, he kick en squall, en 'low:

"'You oughter be 'shame' yo'se'f, Mr. Lion, fer ter be tryin' ter bu'n me up.'

"Mr. Lion hol' up he han's en des vows 'tain't him. Brer Rabbit, he look sorter jubous, but he ain't say nothin'. Bimeby he holler out:

"'Phewee! I smell rags a-bu'nin'!'

"Mr. Lion, he sorter flinch, he did, en 'low:

"''Tain't no rags, Brer Rabbit; hit's my ha'r a-sinjin'.

"Dey look all 'roun', dey did, but dey ain't see nothin ner nobody. Brer Rabbit, he say he gwine do some tall watchin' nex' time, kaze he boun' ter ketch de somebody w'at bin playin' dem kinder pranks on um. Wid dat, Mr. Lion lay down 'g'in, en 'twa'n't long 'fo' he drap ter sleep.

"Well, den," continued Uncle Remus, taking a long breath, "de ve'y same kinder doin's tuck'n happen. De col' ashes fall on Brer Rabbit, en de hot embers fall on Mr. Lion. But by de time Mr. Lion jump up, Brer Rabbit, he holler out:

"'I seed um, Mr. Lion! I seed um! I seed de way dey come fum 'cross de creek! Dey mos' sholy did!'

"Wid dat Mr. Lion, he fetch'd a beller en he jumped 'cross de creek. No sooner is he do dis," Uncle Remus went on in a tone at once impressive and confidential, "no sooner is he do dis dan Brer Rabbit cut de string w'at hol' de banks togedder, en, lo en beholes, dar dey wuz!"

"What was, Uncle Remus?" the little boy asked, more amazed than he had been in many a day.

"Bless yo' soul, honey, de banks! Co'se w'en Brer Rabbit tuck'n cut de string, de banks er de creek, de banks, dey fall back, dey did, en Mr. Lion can't jump back. De banks dey keep on fallin' back, en de creek keep on gittin' wider en wider, twel bimeby Brer Rabbit en Mr. Lion ain't in sight er one er n'er, en fum dat day to dis de big waters bin rollin' 'twix' um."

"But, Uncle Remus, how could the banks of a creek be tied with a string?"

"I ain't ax um dat, honey, en darfo' you'll hatter take um ez you git um. Nex' time de tale-teller come 'roun' I'll up'n ax 'im, en ef you ain't too fur off, I'll whirl in en sen' you wud, en den you kin go en see fer yo'se'f. But 'tain't skacely wuth yo' w'ile fer ter blame me, honey, 'bout de creek banks bein' tied wid a string. Who put um dar, I be bless ef *I* knows, but I knows who onloose um, dat w'at I knows!"

It is very doubtful if this copious explanation was satisfactory to the child, but just as Uncle Remus concluded, Daddy Jack came shuffling in, and shortly afterwards both Aunt Tempy and 'Tildy put in an appearance, and the mind of the youngster was diverted to other matters.

59
Brother Rabbit Gets Brother Fox's Dinner

AFTER THE NEW-COMERS had settled themselves in their accustomed places, and 'Tildy had cast an unusual number of scornful glances at Daddy Jack, who made quite a pantomime of his courtship, Uncle Remus startled them all somewhat by breaking into a loud laugh.

"I boun' you," exclaimed Aunt Tempy, grinning with enthusiastic sympathy, "I boun' you Brer Remus done fin' out some mo' er Brer Rabbit funny doin's; now I boun' you dat."

"You hit it de fus' clip, Sis Tempy, I 'clar' ter gracious ef you ain't. You nailed it! You nailed it," Uncle Remus went on, laughing as boisterously as before, "des lak ole Brer Rabbit done."

The little boy was very prompt with what Uncle Remus called his "inquirements," and the old man, after the usual "hems" and "haws," began.

"Hit run'd 'cross my min' des lak a rat 'long a rafter, de way ole Brer Rabbit tuk'n done Brer Fox. 'Periently, atter Brer Rabbit done went en put a steeple on top er he house, all de yuther creeturs wanter fix up dey house. Some put new cellars und' um, some slapped on new winderblines, some one thing and some er n'er, but ole Brer Fox, he tuck a notion dat he'd put some new shingles on de roof.

"Brer Rabbit, he tuck'n year tell er dis, en nothin'd do but he mus' rack 'roun' en see how ole Brer Fox gittin' on. W'en he git whar Brer Fox house is, he year a mighty lammin' en a blammin', en lo en beholes, dar 'uz Brer Fox settin' straddle er de comb er de roof nailin' on shingles des hard ez he kin.

"Brer Rabbit cut he eye 'roun' en he see Brer Fox dinner settin' in de fence-cornder. Hit 'uz kivvered up in a bran' new tin pail, en it look so nice dat Brer Rabbit mouf 'gun ter water time he see it, en he 'low ter hisse'f dat he bleedzd ter eat dat dinner 'fo' he go 'way fum dar.

"Den Brer Rabbit tuck'n hail Brer Fox, en ax 'im how he come on. Brer Fox 'low he too busy to hol' any confab. Brer Rabbit up en ax 'im w'at is he doin' up dar. Brer Fox 'low dat he puttin' roof on he house 'g'in' de rainy season sot in. Den Brer Rabbit up en ax Brer Fox w'at time is it, en Brer Fox, he 'low dat hit's wukkin time wid him. Brer Rabbit, he up en ax Brer Fox ef he ain't stan' in needs er some he'p. Brer Fox, he 'low he did, dat ef he does stan' in needs er any he'p, he dunner whar in de name er goodness he gwine to git it at.

"Wid dat, Brer Rabbit sorter pull he mustash, en 'low dat de time wuz w'en he 'uz a mighty handy man wid a hammer, en he ain't too proud fer to whirl in en he'p Brer Fox out'n de ruts.

"Brer Fox 'low he be mighty much erblige, en no sooner is he say dat dan Brer Rabbit snatched off he coat en lipt up de ladder, en sot in dar en put on mo' shingles in one hour dan Brer Fox kin put on in two.

"Oh, he 'uz a rattler — ole Brer Rabbit wuz," Uncle Remus exclaimed, noticing a questioning look in the child's face. "He 'uz a rattler, mon, des ez sho' ez you er settin' dar. Dey wa'n't no kinder wuk dat Brer Rabbit can't put he han' at, en do it better dan de nex' man.

"He nailed on shingles plum' twel he git tired, Brer Rabbit did, en all de time he nailin', he study how he gwine git dat dinner. He nailed en he nailed. He 'ud nail one row, en Brer Fox 'ud nail n'er row. He nailed en he nailed. He kotch Brer Fox en pass 'im — kotch 'im en pass 'im, twel bimeby w'iles he nailin' 'long, Brer Fox tail git in he way.

"Brer Rabbit 'low ter hisse'f, he did, dat he dunner w'at de name er goodness make folks have such long tails fer en he push it out de way. He ain't no mo'n push it out'n de way, 'fo' yer it come back in de way. Co'se," continued Uncle Remus, beginning to look serious, "w'en dat's de case dat a soon man lak Brer Rabbit git pester'd in he min', he bleedzd ter make some kinder accidents some'rs.

"Dey nailed en dey nailed, en, bless yo' soul! 'twa'n't long 'fo' Brer Fox drap eve'yt'ing en squall out:

"'Laws-a-massy, Brer Rabbit! You done nail my tail. He'p me, Brer Rabbit, he'p me! You done nail my tail!'"

Uncle Remus waved his arms, clasped and unclasped his hands, stamped first one foot and then the other, and made various other demonstrations of grief and suffering.

"Brer Rabbit, he shot fus' one eye en den de yuther en rub hisse'f on de forrerd, en 'low:

"'Sholy I ain't nail yo' tail, Brer Fox; sholy not. Look right close, Brer Fox, be keerful. Fer goodness sake don't fool me, Brer Fox!'

"Brer Fox, *he* holler, *he* squall, *he* kick, *he* squeal.

"'Laws-a-massy, Brer Rabbit! You done nailed my tail. Onnail me, Brer Rabbit, onnail me!'

"Brer Rabbit, he make fer de ladder, en w'en he start down, he look at Brer Fox lak he right down sorry, en he up'n 'low, he did:

"'Well, well, well! Des ter t'ink dat I should er lamm'd a-loose en nail Brer Fox tail. I dunner w'en I year tell er anyt'ing dat make me feel so mighty bad; en ef I hadn't er seed it wid my own eyes I wouldn't er 'bliev'd it skacely — dat I wouldn't!'

"Brer Fox holler, Brer Fox howl, yit 'tain't do no good. Dar he wuz wid he tail nail hard en fas'. Brer Rabbit, he keep on talkin' w'iles he gwine down de ladder.

"'Hit make me feel so mighty bad,' sezee, 'dat I dunner w'at ter do. Time I year tell un it, hit make a empty place come in my stomach,' sez Brer Rabbit, sezee.

"By dis time Brer Rabbit done git down on de groun', en w'iles Brer Fox holler'n, he des keep on a-talkin'.

"'Dey's a mighty empty place in my stomach,' sezee, 'en ef I ain't run'd inter no mistakes dey's a tin-pail full er vittles in dish yer fence-cornder dat'll des 'bout fit it,' sez ole Brer Rabbit, sezee.

"He open de pail, he did, en he eat de greens, en sop up de 'lasses, en drink de pot-liquor, en w'en he wipe he mouf 'pun he coat-tail, he up'n 'low:

"'I dunner w'en I bin so sorry 'bout anything, ez I is 'bout Brer Fox nice long tail. Sholy, sholy my head mus' er bin wool-getherin' w'en I tuck'n nail Brer Fox fine long tail,' sez ole Brer Rabbit, sezee.

"Wid dat, he tuck'n skip out, Brer Rabbit did, en 'twa'n't long 'fo' he 'uz playin' he pranks in some yuther parts er de settlement."

"How did Brother Fox get loose?" the little boy asked.

"Oh, you let Brer Fox 'lone fer dat," responded Uncle Remus. "Nex' ter Brer Rabbit, ole Brer Fox wuz mos' de shiftiest creetur gwine. I boun' you he tuck'n tuck keer hisse'f soon ez Brer Rabbit git outer sight en year'n."

60
How the Bear Nursed the Little Alligator

WHILE THE NEGROES were talking of matters which the little boy took little or no interest in, he climbed into Uncle Remus's lap, as he had done a thousand times before. Presently the old man groaned, and said:

"I be bless ef I know w'at de marter, honey. I dunner whe'er I'm a-gittin' fibble in de lim's, er whe'er you er outgrowin' me. I lay I'll hatter sen' out en git you a nuss w'at got mo' strenk in dey lim's dan w'at I is."

The child protested that he wasn't very heavy, and that he wouldn't have any nurse, and the old man was about to forget that he had said anything about nurses, when Daddy Jack, who seemed to be desirous of appearing good-humored in the presence of 'Tildy, suddenly exclaimed:

"Me bin yeddy one tale 'bout da tam w'en da lil Bear is bin nuss da 'Gator chilluns. 'E bin mek fine nuss fer true. 'E stan' by dem lilly 'Gator tel dey no mo' fer stan' by."

Seeing that Daddy Jack manifested symptoms of going to sleep, the little boy asked if he wouldn't tell the story, and, thus appealed to, the old African began:

"One tam dey is bin one ole Bear; 'e big un 'e strong. 'E lif way in da swamp; 'e hab nes' in da holler tree. 'E hab one, two lilly Bear in da nes'; 'e bin lub dem chillun berry ha'd. One day, 'e git honkry; 'e tell 'e chillun 'e gwan 'way off fer git-a some bittle fer eat; 'e tell dem dey mus' be good chillun un stay wey dey lif. 'E say 'e gwan fer fetch dem one fish fer dey brekwus. Dun 'e gone off.

"Da lil Bear chillun hab bin 'sleep till dey kin sleep no mo'. Da sun, 'e der shine wom, 'e mekky lilly Bear feel wom. Da lil boy Bear, 'e rub 'e y-eye, 'e say 'e gwan off fer hab some fun. Da lil gal Bear, 'e say:

"'Wut will we mammy say?'

"Lil boy Bear, 'e der lahff. 'E say:

"'Me gwan down by da crik side fer ketch some fish 'fo' we mammy come.'

"Lil gal Bear, 'e look skeer; 'e say:

"'We mammy say somet'ing gwan git-a you. Min' wut 'e tell you.'

"Lil boy Bear, 'e keep on lahff. 'E say:

"'Shuh-shuh! 'E yent nebber know less you tell um. You no tell um, me fetch-a you one big fish.'

"Lil boy Bear, 'e gone! 'E gone by da crik side, 'e tek 'e hook, 'e tek 'e line, 'e is go by da crik side fer ketch one fish. Wun 'e come dey-dey, 'e see somet'ing lay dey in de mud. 'E t'ink it bin one big log. 'E lahff by 'ese'f; 'e say:

"''E one fine log fer true. Me 'tan' 'pon da log fer ketch-a da fish fer me lil titty.'

"Lil boy Bear, 'e der jump down; 'e git 'pon da log; 'e fix fer fish; 'e fix 'e hook, 'e fix 'e line. Bumbye da log moof. Da lil boy Bear holler:

"'Ow ma Lordy!'

"''E look down; 'e skeer mos' dead. Da log bin one big 'Gator. Da 'Gator 'e swim 'way wit' da lil boy Bear 'pon 'e bahck. 'E flut 'e tail, 'e knock da lil boy Bear spang in 'e two han'. 'E grin *wide*, 'e feel da lil boy Bear wit' 'e nose; 'e say:

"'I tekky you wey me lif; me chillun is hab you fer dey brekwus.'

"Da 'Gator, 'e bin swim toze da hole in da bank wey 'e lif. 'E come by da hole, 'e ca' da lil boy Bear in dey. 'E is call up 'e chillun; 'e say:

"'Come see how fine brekwus me bin brung you.'

"Da ole 'Gator, 'e hab seben chillun in 'e bed. Da lil boy Bear git skeer; 'e holler, 'e cry, 'e beg. 'E say:

"'*Please,* Missy 'Gator, gib me chance fer show you how fine nuss me is — *please,* Missy 'Gator. Wun you gone 'way, me min' dem chillun, me min' um well.'

"Da 'Gator flut 'e tail; 'e say:

"'I try you dis one day; you min' dem lil one well, me luf you be.'

"Da ole 'Gator gone 'way; 'e luf da lil boy Bear fer min' 'e chillun. 'E gone git somet'ing fer dey brekwus. Da lil boy Bear, 'e set down dey-dey; 'e min' dem chillun; 'e wait un 'e wait. Bumbye, 'e is git honkry. 'E wait

un 'e wait. 'E min' dem chillun. 'E wait un 'e wait. 'E 'come so honkry 'e
yent mos' kin hol' up 'e head. 'E suck 'e paw. 'E wait un 'e wait. Da 'Gator
no come. 'E wait un 'e wait. Da 'Gator no come some mo'. 'E say:

"'Ow! me no gwan starf mese'f wun da planty bittle by side er me!'

"Da lil boy Bear grab one da lil 'Gator by 'e neck; 'e tek um off in da
bush side; 'e der eat um up. 'E no leaf 'e head, 'e no leaf 'e tail; 'e yent
leaf nuttin' 't all. 'E go bahck wey da turrer lil 'Gator bin huddle up in da
bed. 'E rub 'ese'f 'pon da 'tomach; 'e say:

"'Hoo! me feel-a too good fer tahlk 'bout. I no know wut me gawn fer
tell da ole 'Gator wun 'e is come bahck. Ki! me no keer. Me feel too good
fer t'ink 'bout dem t'ing. Me t'ink 'bout dem wun da 'Gator is bin come;
me t'ink 'bout dem bumbye wun da time come fer t'ink.'

"Da lil boy Bear lay down; 'e quile up in da 'Gator bed; 'e shed 'e y-eye;
'e sleep ha'd lak bear do wun ef full up. Bumbye, mos' toze night, da
'Gator come; 'e holler:

"'Hey! lil boy Bear! How you is kin min' me chillun wun you is gone
fer sleep by um?'

"Da lil boy Bear, 'e set up 'pon 'e ha'nch; 'e say:

"'Me y-eye gone fer sleep, but me year wide 'wake.'

"Da 'Gator flut 'e tail; 'e say:

"'Wey me chillun wut me leaf you wit'?'

"Da lil boy Bear 'come skeer; 'e say:

"'Dey all dey-dey, Missy 'Gator. Wait! lemme count dem, Missy 'Gator.

"'Yarrah one, yarrah narrah,
Yarrah two, 'pon top er tarrah,
Yarrah t'ree pile up tergarrah!'[1]

"Da 'Gator y-open 'e mout', 'e grin wide; 'e say:

"''Oona nuss dem well, lil boy Bear; come, fetch-a me one fer wash un git 'e supper.'

"Da lil boy Bear, 'e ca' one, 'e ca nurrer, 'e ca' turrer 'e ca' um all tel 'e ca' six, den 'e come skeer. 'E t'ink da 'Gator gwan fine um out fer true. 'E stop, 'e yent know wut fer do. Da 'Gator holler:

"''Fetch-a me turrer!'

"Da lil boy Bear, 'e grab da fus' one, 'e wullup um in da mud, 'e ca' um bahck. Da 'Gator bin wash un feed um fresh; 'e yent know da diffran.

"Bumbye, nex' day mornin', da 'Gator gone 'way. Da lil boy Bear stay fer nuss dem lil 'Gator. 'E come honkry; 'e wait, but 'e come mo' honkry. 'E grab nurrer lil 'Gator, 'e eat um fer 'e dinner. Mos' toze night, da 'Gator come. It sem t'ing:

"''Wey me chillun wut me leaf you fer nuss?'

"Dey all dey-dey, Missy 'Gator. Me count um out:

"'Yarrah one, yarrah narrah,
Yarrah two 'pon top er tarrah,
Yarrah t'ree pile up tergarrah!'

"''E ca' um one by one fer wash un git dey supper. 'E ca' two bahck two tam. Ebry day 'e do dis way tel 'e come at de las'. 'E eat dis one, un 'e gone luf da place wey da 'Gator lif. 'E gone down da crik side tel 'e is come by da foot-log, un 'e is run 'cross *queek*. 'E git in da bush, 'e fair fly tel 'e is come by da place wey 'e lil titty bin lif. 'E come dey-dey, un 'e yent go 'way no mo'.''"

---

[1] Here is one, here's another; here are two on top of t'other; here are three piled up to-gether. — J. C. H.

61

Why Mr. Dog Runs Brother Rabbit

THE LITTLE BOY was not particularly pleased at the summary manner in which the young Alligators were disposed of; but he was very much amused at the somewhat novel method employed by the Bear to deceive the old Alligator. The Negroes, however, enjoyed Daddy Jack's story immensely, and even 'Tildy condescended to give it her approval; but she qualified this by saying, as soon as she had ceased laughing:

"I 'clar' ter goodness you all got mighty little ter do fer ter be settin' down yer night atter night lis'nin' at dat nigger man."

Daddy Jack nodded, smiled, and rubbed his withered hands together apparently in a perfect ecstacy of good-humor, and finally said:

"Oona come set-a by me, lil gal; E berry nice tale wut me tell-a you. Come sit-a by me, lil gal; 'e berry nice tale. Ef you want me fer tell-a you one tale, dun you is kin tell-a me one tale."

"Humph!" exclaimed 'Tildy, contemptuously, "you'll set over dar in dat cornder an dribble many's de long day 'fo' I tell you any tale."

"Look yer, gal!" said Uncle Remus, pretending to ignore the queer courtship that seemed to be progressing between Daddy Jack and 'Tildy, "you gittin' too ole fer ter be sawin' de a'r wid yo' head en squealin' lak a filly. Ef you gwine ter set wid folks, you better do lak folks does. Sis Tempy dar ain't gwine on dat a-way, en she ain't think 'erse'f too big fer ter set up dar en jine in wid us en tell a tale, needer."

This was the first time that Uncle Remus had ever condescended to accord 'Tildy a place at his hearth on an equality with the rest of his company, and she seemed to be immensely tickled. A broad grin spread over her comely face as she exclaimed:

"*Oh!* I 'clar' ter goodness, Unk Remus, I thought dat ole nigger man wuz des a-projickin' 'long wid me. Ef it come down ter settin' up yer 'long wid you all an' tellin' a tale, I ain't 'nyin' but w'at I got one dat you all ain't never year tell un, kaze dat ar Slim Jim w'at Mars Ellick Akin got out'n de speckerlater waggin, he up'n tell it dar at Riah's des 'fo' de patter-rollers tuck'n slipt up on um."

"Dar now!" remarked Aunt Tempy. 'Tildy laughed boisterously.

"W'at de patter-rollers do wid dat ar Slim Jim?" Uncle Remus inquired.

"Done nothin'!" exclaimed 'Tildy, with an air of humorous scorn. "Time dey got in dar Slim Jim 'uz up de chimbley, an' Riah 'uz noddin' in one cornder an' me in de udder. Nobody never is ter know how dat ar long-leg-nigger slick'd up dat chimbley — dat dey ain't. He put one foot on de pot-rack, an' whar he put de t'er foot *I* can't tell you."

"What was the story?" asked the little boy.

"I boun' fer you, honey!" exclaimed Uncle Remus.

"Well, den," said 'Tildy, setting herself comfortably, and bridling a little as Daddy Jack manifested a desire to give her his undivided attention, — "well, den, dey wuz one time w'en ole Brer Rabbit 'uz bleedzd ter go ter town atter sump'n n'er fer his fambly, an' he mos' 'shame' ter go kaze his shoes done wo' teetotally out. Yit he bleedzd ter go, an' he put des ez good face on it ez he kin, an' he take down he walkin'-cane an' sot out des ez big ez de next un.

"Well, den, ole Brer Rabbit go on down de big road twel he come ter de place whar some folks bin camp out de night befo', an' he sot down by de fier, he did, fer ter wom his foots, kaze dem mawnin's 'uz sorter col', like deze yer mawnin's. He sot dar an' look at his toes, an' he feel mighty sorry fer hisse'f.

"Well, den, he sot dar, he did, en 'twa'n't long 'fo' he year sump'n n'er trottin' down de road, an' he tuck'n look up an' yer come Mr. Dog a-smellin' an' a-snuffin' 'roun' fer ter see ef de folks lef' any scraps by der camp-fier. Mr. Dog 'uz all dress up in his Sunday-go-ter-meetin' cloze, an' mo'n dat, he had on a pa'r er bran' new shoes.

"Well, den, w'en Brer Rabbit see dem ar shoes he feel mighty bad, but he ain't let on. He bow ter Mr. Dog mighty perlite, an' Mr. Dog he bow back, he did, an' dey pass de time er day, kaze dey 'uz ole 'quaintance. Brer Rabbit, he say:

"'Mr. Dog, whar you gwine all fix up like dis?'

"'I gwine ter town, Brer Rabbit; whar you gwine?'

"'I thought I go ter town myse'f fer ter git me new pa'r shoes, kaze my ole uns done wo' out en dey hu'ts my foots so bad I can't w'ar um. Dem mighty nice shoes w'at you got on, Mr. Dog; whar you git um?'

"'Down in town, Brer Rabbit, down in town.'

"'Dey fits you mighty slick, Mr. Dog, an' I wish you be so good ez ter lemme try one un um on.'

"Brer Rabbit talk so mighty sweet dat Mr. Dog sot right flat on de groun' an' tuck off one er de behime shoes, an' loan't it ter Brer Rabbit. Brer Rabbit, he lope off down de road en den he come back. He tell Mr. Dog dat de shoe fit mighty nice, but wid des one un um on, hit make 'im trot crank-sided.

"Well, den, Mr. Dog, he pull off de yuther behime shoe, an' Brer Rabbit trot off an' try it. He come back, he did, an' he say:

"'Dey mighty nice, Mr. Dog, but dey sorter r'ars me up behime, an' I dunner zackly how dey feels.'

"Dis make Mr. Dog feel like he wanter be perlite, an' he take off de befo' shoes, an' Brer Rabbit put um on an' stomp his foots, an' 'low:

"'Now dat sorter feel like shoes;' an' he rack off down de road, an' w'en he git whar he oughter tu'n 'roun', he des lay back he years an' keep on gwine; an' 'twa'n't long 'fo' he git outer sight.

"Mr. Dog, he holler, an' tell 'im fer ter come back, but Brer Rabbit keep on gwine; Mr. Dog, he holler, Mr. Rabbit, he keep on gwine. An' down ter dis day," continued 'Tildy, smacking her lips, and showing her white teeth, "Mr. Dog bin a-runnin' Brer Rabbit, an' ef you'll des go out in de woods wid any Dog on dis place, des time he smell de Rabbit track he'll holler an' tell 'im fer ter come back."

"Dat's de Lord's trufe!" said Aunt Tempy.

62

Brother Wolf and the Horned Cattle

DADDY JACK appeared to enjoy 'Tildy's story as thoroughly as the little boy.

"'E one fine tale. 'E mekky me lahff tel tear is come in me y-eye," the old African said. And somehow or other 'Tildy seemed to forget her pretended animosity to Daddy Jack, and smiled on him as pleasantly as she did on the others. Uncle Remus himself beamed upon each and every one, especially upon Aunt Tempy; and the little boy thought he had never seen everybody in such good-humor.

"Sis Tempy," said Uncle Remus, "I 'speck it's yo' time fer ter put in."

"I des bin rackin' my min'," said Aunt Tempy, thoughtfully. "I see you fixin' dat ar hawn, un terreckerly hit make me think 'bout a tale w'at I ain't year none un you tell yit."

Uncle Remus was polishing a long cow's-horn, for the purpose of making a hunting-horn for his master.

"Hit come 'bout one time dat all de creeturs w'at got hawns tuck a notion dat dey got ter meet terge'er un have a confab fer ter see how dey gwine take keer deyse'f, kaze dem t'er creeturs w'at got tush un claw, dey 'uz des a-snatchin' um fum 'roun' eve'y cornder."

"Tooby sho!" said Uncle Remus, approvingly.

"Dey sont out wud, de hawn creeturs did, un dey tuck'n meet terge'er 'way off in de woods. Man — Sir! — dey wuz a big bang un um, un de muster dey had out dar 'twa'n't b'ar tellin' skacely. Mr. Bull, he 'uz dar, un Mr. Steer, un Miss Cow" —

"And Mr. Benjamin Ram, with his fiddle," suggested the little boy.

— "Yes, 'n Mr. Billy Goat, un Mr. Unicorn" —

"En ole man Rhinossyhoss," said Uncle Remus.

— "Yes, 'n lots mo' w'at I ain't know de names un. Man — Sir! — dey had a mighty muster out dar. Ole Brer Wolf, he tuck'n year 'bout de muster, un he sech a smarty dat nothin' ain't gwine do but he mus' go un see w'at dey doin'.

"He study 'bout it long time, un den he went out in de timber un cut 'im two crooked sticks, un tie um on his head, un start off ter whar de hawn creeturs meet at. W'en he git dar Mr. Bull ax 'im who is he, w'at he want, whar he come fum, un whar he gwine. Brer Wolf, he 'low:

"'Ba-a-a! I'm name little Sook Calf!'"

"Eh-eh! Look out, now!" exclaimed 'Tildy, enthusiastically.

"Mr. Bull look at Brer Wolf mighty hard over his specks, but atter a w'ile he go off somers else, un Brer Wolf take his place in de muster.

"Well, den, bimeby, terreckerly, dey got ter talkin' un tellin' der 'spe-unce des lak de w'ite folks does at class-meetin'. W'iles dey 'uz gwine on dis a-way, a great big hoss-fly come sailin' 'roun', un Brer Wolf tuck'n fergit hisse'f, un snap at 'im.

"All dis time Brer Rabbit bin hidin' out in de bushes watchin' Brer Wolf, un w'en he see dis he tuck'n break out in a laugh. Brer Bull, he tuck'n holler out, he did:

"'Who dat laughin' un showin' der manners?'

"Nobody ain't make no answer, un terreckerly Brer Rabbit holler out:

"'O kittle-cattle, kittle-cattle, whar yo' eyes?
Who ever see a Sook Calf snappin' at flies?'

"De hawn creeturs dey all look 'roun' un wonder w'at dat mean, but bimeby dey go on wid dey confab. 'Twa'n't long 'fo' a flea tuck'n bite Brer Wolf 'way up on de back er de neck, un 'fo' he know w'at he doin', he tuck'n squat right down un scratch hisse'f wid his behime foot."

"Enty!" exclaimed Daddy Jack. "Dar you is!" said 'Tildy.

"Brer Rabbit, he tuck'n broke out in n'er big laugh un 'sturb um all, un den he holler out:

"'Scritchum-scratchum, lawsy, my laws!
Look at dat Sook Calf scratchin' wid claws.'

"Brer Wolf git mighty skeer'd, but none er de hawn creeturs ain't take no notice un 'im, un 'twa'n't long 'fo' Brer Rabbit holler out ag'in:

"'Rinktum-tinktum, ride 'im on a rail!
Dat Sook Calf got a long bushy tail!'

"De hawn creeturs, dey go on wid der confab, but Brer Wolf git skeer'der un skeer'der, kaze he notice dat Mr. Bull got his eye on 'im. Brer Rabbit, he ain't gin 'im no rest. He holler out:

"'One un one never kin make six,
Sticks ain't hawns, un hawns ain't sticks!'

"Wid dat Brer Wolf make ez ef he gwine 'way fum dar, un he wa'n't none too soon, needer, kaze ole Mr. Bull splunge at 'im, en little mo' un he'd er nat'ally to' 'im in two."

"Did Brother Wolf get away?" the little boy asked.

"Yas, Lord!" said Aunt Tempy, with unction; "he des scooted 'way fum dar, un he got so mad wid Brer Rabbit, dat he tuck'n play dead, un wud went 'roun' dat dey want all de creeturs fer ter go set up wid 'im. Brer Rabbit, he went down dar fer ter look at 'im, un time he see 'im, he ax:

"'Is he grin yit?'

"All de creeturs dey up'n say he ain't grin, not ez dey knows un. Den Brer Rabbit, he 'low, he did:

"'Well, den gentermens all, ef he ain't grin, den he ain't dead good. In all my 'speunce folks ain't git dead good twel dey grins.'[1]

"W'en Brer Wolf year Brer Rabbit talk dat a-way, he tuck'n grin fum year ter year, un Brer Rabbit, he picked up his hat un walkin'-cane un put out fer home, un w'en he got 'way off in de woods he sot down un laugh fit ter kill hisse'f."

Uncle Remus had paid Aunt Tempy the extraordinary tribute of pausing in his work to listen to her story, and when she had concluded it, he looked at her in undisguised admiration, and exclaimed:

"I be bless, Sis Tempy, ef you ain't wuss'n w'at I is, en I'm bad nuff, de Lord knows I is!"

63
Brother Fox and the White Muscadines

AUNT TEMPY did not attempt to conceal the pleasure which Uncle Remus's praise gave her. She laughed somewhat shyly, and said:

"Bless you, Brer Remus! I des bin a-settin' yer l'arnin. 'Sides dat, Chris'mus ain't fur off un I 'speck we er all a-feelin' a sight mo' humorsome dan common."

"Dat's so, Sis Tempy. I 'uz comin' thoo de lot des 'fo' supper, en I seed de pigs runnin' en playin' in de win', en I 'low ter myse'f, sez I, 'Sholy dey's a-gwine ter be a harrycane,' en den all at once hit come in my min' dat Chris'mus mighty close at han', en den on ter dat yer come de chickens a-crowin' des now en 'tain't nine er' clock. I dunner how de creeturs know Chris'mus comin', but dat des de way it stan's."

The little boy thought it was time enough to think about Christmas when the night came for hanging up his stockings, and he asked Uncle Remus if it wasn't his turn to tell a story. The old man laid down the piece of glass with which he had been scraping the cow's horn, and

---

[1] See *Uncle Remus: His Songs and His Sayings*, p. 36. — J. C. H.

hunted around among his tools for a piece of sandpaper before he replied. But his reply was sufficient. He said:

"One time w'iles Brer Rabbit wuz gwine thoo de woods he tuck'n strak up wid ole Brer Fox, en Brer Fox 'low, he did, dat he mighty hongry. Brer Rabbit 'low dat he ain't feelin' dat a-way hisse'f, kaze he des bin en had er bait er w'ite muscadimes, en den he tuck'n smack he mouf en lick he chops right front er Brer Fox. Brer Fox, he ax, sezee:

"'Brer Rabbit, whar de name er goodness is deze yer w'ite muscadimes, en how come I'm ain't never run 'crosst um?' sezee.

"'I dunner w'at de reason you ain't never come up wid um,' sez Brer Rabbit sezee; 'some folks sees straight, some sees crooked, some sees one thing, some sees n'er. I done seed dem ar w'ite muscadimes, en let 'lone dat, I done wipe um up. I done e't all dey wuz on one tree, but I lay dey's lots mo' un um 'roun' in dem neighborhoods,' sezee.

"Ole Brer Fox mouf 'gun to water, en he git mighty restless.

"'Come on, Brer Rabbit; come on! Come show me whar dem ar w'ite muscadimes grows at,' sezee.

"Brer Rabbit, he sorter hang back. Brer Fox, he 'low:

"'Come on, Brer Rabbit, come on!'

"Brer Rabbit, he hang back, en bimeby he 'low:

"'Uh-uh, Brer Fox! You wanter git me out dar in de timber by myse'f en do sump'n ter me. You wanter git me out dar en skeer me.'

"Ole Brer Fox, he hol' up he han's, he do, en he 'low:

"'I des 'clar' 'fo' gracious, Brer Rabbit, I ain't gwine do no sech uv a thing. I dunner w'at kinder 'pinion you got 'bout me fer ter have sech idee in yo' head. Come on, Brer Rabbit, en less we go git dem ar w'it muscadimes. Come on, Brer Rabbit.'

"'Uh-uh, Brer Fox! I done year talk er you playin' so many prank wid folks dat I feard fer ter go 'way off dar wid you.'

"Dey went on dat a-way," continued Uncle Remus, endeavoring to look at the little boy through the crooked cow's horn, "twel bimeby Brer Fox promise he ain't gwine ter bodder 'long er Brer Rabbit, en den dey tuck'n put out. En whar you 'speck dat ar muscheevous Brer Rabbit tuck'n kyar' Brer Fox?"

Uncle Remus paused and gazed around upon his audience with uplifted eyebrows, as if to warn them to be properly astonished. Nobody made any reply, but all looked expectant, and Uncle Remus went on:

"He ain't kyar 'im nowhars in de roun' worl' but ter one er deze yer great big scaly-bark trees. De tree wuz des loaded down wid scaly-barks, but dey wa'n't ripe, en de green hulls shined in de sun des lak dey ben whitewash'. Brer Fox look 'stonish'. Atter w'ile he up'n 'low:

"'Is dem ar de white muscadimes? Mighty funny I ain't fin' it out 'fo' dis.'

"Ole Brer Rabbit, he scratch hisse'f en 'low:

"'Dems um. Dey mayn't be ripe ez dem w'at I had fer my brekkus, but dems de w'ite muscadimes sho ez you er bawn. Dey er red bullaces en dey er black bullaces, but deze yer, dey er de white bullaces.'

"Brer Fox, sezee, 'How I gwine git um?'

"Brer Rabbit, sezee, 'You'll des hatter do lak I done.'

"Brer Fox, sezee, 'How wuz dat?'

"Brer Rabbit, sezee, 'You'll hatter clim' fer 'm.'

"Brer Fox, sezee, 'How I gwine clim'?'

"Brer Rabbit, sezee, 'Grab wid yo' han's, dim' wid yo' legs, en I'll push behime!'"

"Man — Sir! — he's a-talkin' now!" exclaimed Aunt Tempy, enthusiastically.

"Brer Fox, he clom', en Brer Rabbit, he push, twel, sho nuff, Brer Fox got whar he kin grab de lowmos' lim's, en dar he wuz! He crope on up, he did, twel he come ter whar he kin retch de green scaly-bark, en den he tuck'n pull one en bite it, en, gentermens! hit uz dat rough en dat bitter twel little mo' en he'd a drapt spang out'n de tree.

"He holler *'Ow!'* en spit it out'n he mouf des same ez ef 'twuz rank pizen, en he make sech a face dat you wouldn't b'lieve it skacely less'n you seed it. Brer Rabbit, he hatter cough fer ter keep fum laughin', but he make out ter holler, sezee:

"'Come down, Brer Fox! Dey ain't ripe. Come down en less go some'rs else.'

"Brer Fox start down, en he git 'long mighty well twel he come ter de lowmos' lim's, en den when he git dar he can't come down no further, kaze he ain't got no claw fer cling by, en not much leg fer clamp.

"Brer Rabbit keep on hollerin', 'Come down!' en Brer Fox keep on studyin' how he gwine ter come down. Brer Rabbit, he 'low, sezee:

"'Come on, Brer Fox! I tuck'n push you up, en ef I 'uz dar whar you is, I'd tak'n push you down.'

"Brer Fox sat dar on de lowmos' lim's en look lak he skeer'd. Bimeby Brer Rabbit tuck he stan' 'way off fum de tree, en he holler, sezee:

"'Ef you'll tak'n jump out dis way, Brer Fox, I'll ketch you.'

"Brer Fox look up, he look down, he look all 'roun'. Brer Rabbit come little closer, en 'low, sezee:

"'Hop right down yer, Brer Fox, en I'll ketch you.'

"Hit keep on dis away, twel, bimeby, Brer Fox tuck a notion to jump, en des ez he jump Brer Rabbit hop out de way en holler, sezee:

"'*Ow!* Scuze me, Brer Fox! I stuck a brier in my foot! Scuze me, Brer Fox! I stuck a brier in my foot!'

"En dat ole Brer Fox," continued Uncle Remus, dropping his voice a little, "dat ole Brer Fox, gentermens! you oughter bin dar! He hit de groun' like a sack er taters, en it des nat'ally knock de breff out'n im. W'en he git up en count hisse'f fer ter see ef he all dar, he ain't kin walk skacely, en he sat dar en lick de so' places a mighty long time 'fo' he feel lak he kin make he way todes home."

When the little boy wanted to know what became of Brother Rabbit Uncle Remus said:

"Shoo! don't you pester 'bout Brer Rabbit. He kick up he heels en put out fum dar." Then he added: "Dem ar chick'ns crowin' 'gin, honey. Done gone by nine er'clock. Scoot out fum dis. Miss Sally 'll be a-rakin' me over de coals."

64
Mr. Hawk and Brother Buzzard

ONE NIGHT the little boy ran into Uncle Remus's cabin singing:

> "T-u Turkey, t-u Ti,
> T-u Turkey Buzzard's eye!"

Uncle Remus, Daddy Jack, Aunt Tempy, and 'Tildy were all sitting around the fire, for the Christmas weather was beginning to make itself rather severely felt. As they made room for the child, Daddy Jack flung his head back, and took up the song, beating time with his foot:

> "T-u Tukry, t-u Ti,
> T-u Tukry-Buzzud y-eye!
> T-u Tukry, t-u Ting,
> T-u Tukry-Buzzud wing!"

"Dey er mighty kuse creeturs," said 'Tildy, who was sitting rather nearer to Daddy Jack than had been her custom — a fact to which Aunt Tempy had already called the attention of Uncle Remus by a motion of her head, causing the old man to smile a smile as broad as it was wise. "Dey er mighty kuse, an' I'm feard un um," 'Tildy went on. "Dey looks so lonesome hit makes me have de creeps fer ter look at um."

"Dey no hu't-a you," said Daddy Jack, soothingly. "You flut you' han' toze um dey fly 'way fum dey-dey."

"I dunno 'bout dat," said 'Tildy. "Dey er bal'-headed, an' dat w'at make me 'spize um."

Daddy Jack rubbed the bald place on his head with such a comical air that even 'Tildy laughed. The old African retained his good-humor.

"You watch dem Buzzud," he said after awhile, addressing himself particularly to the little boy. "'E fly high, 'e fly low, 'e fly 'way 'roun'. Rain come, 'e flup 'e wings, 'e light 'pon dead pine. Rain fall, 'e hug 'ese'f wit' 'e wing, 'e scrooge 'e neck up. Rain come, win' blow, da Buzzud bin-a look ragged. Da Buzzud bin-a wink 'e y-eye, 'e say:

"'Wun da win' fer stop blow un da rain fer stop drip, me go mek me one house. Me mek um tight fer keep da rain out; me pit top on strong fer keep da win' out.'

"Dun da rain dry up un da win' stop. Da Buzzud, 'e stan' 'pon top da dead pine. Wun da sun bin-a shine, 'e no mek um no house no'n 'tall. 'E stay 'pon da dead pine; 'e 'tretch 'e wing wide open; 'e bin dry hisse'f in da sun. 'E hab mek no house sence 'e bin born. 'E one fool bud."

"En yit," said Uncle Remus, with a grave, judicial air, "I year tell er one time w'en ole Brer Buzzard wa'n't so mighty fur outer de way wid he notions."

"Me yent yeddy tahlk 'bout dis," Daddy Jack explained.

"I 'speck not," responded Uncle Remus. "Hit seem lak dat dey wuz one time w'en Mr. Hawk come sailin' 'roun' huntin' fer sump'n' n'er t'eat, en he see Brer Buzzard settin' on a dead lim', lookin' mighty lazy en lonesome.

"Mr. Hawk, sezee, 'How you come on, Brer Buzzard?'

"Brer Buzzard, sezee, 'I'm mighty po'ly, Brer Hawk; po'ly en hongry.'

"Mr. Hawk, sezee, 'W'at you waitin' yer fer ef you hongry, Brer Buzzard?'

"Brer Buzzard, sezee, 'I'm a-waitin' on de Lord.'

"Mr. Hawk, sezee, 'Better run en git yo' brekkus, Brer Buzzard, en den come back en wait.'

"Brer Buzzard, sezee, 'No, Brer Hawk, I'll go widout my brekkus druther den be biggity 'bout it.'

"Mr. Hawk, he 'low, sezee, 'Well, den, Brer Buzzard, you got yo' way en I got mine. You see dem ar chick'ns, down dar in Mr. Man hoss-lot? I'm a-gwine down dar en git one un um, en den I'll come back yer en wait 'long wid you.'

"Wid dat, Mr. Hawk tuck'n sail off, en Brer Buzzard drop he wings down on de lim' en look mighty lonesome. He sot dar en look mighty lonesome, he did, but he keep one eye on Mr. Hawk.

"Mr. Hawk, he sail 'roun' en 'roun', en he look mighty purty. He sail 'roun' en 'roun' 'bove de hoss-lot — 'roun' en 'roun' — en bimeby he dart down at chick'ns. He shot up he wings en dart down, he did, des same ef he 'uz fired out'n a gun."

"Watch out, pullets!" exclaimed 'Tildy, in a tone of warning.

"He dart down, he did," continued Uncle Remus, rubbing his hand thoughtfully across the top of his head, "but stidder he hittin' de chick'ns, he tuck'n hit 'pon de sharp een' un a fencerail. He hit dar, he did, en dar he stuck."

"Ah-yi-ee!" exclaimed Daddy Jack.

"Dar he stuck. Brer Buzzard sot en watch 'im. Mr. Hawk ain't move. Brer Buzzard sot en watch 'im some mo'. Mr. Hawk ain't move. He done stone dead. De mo' Brer Buzzard watch 'im de mo' hongrier he git, en bimeby he gedder up he wings, en sorter clean out he year wid he claw, en 'low, sezee:

"'I know'd de Lord 'uz gwine ter pervide.'"

"Trufe too!" exclaimed Aunt Tempy. "'Tain't bin in my min' dat Buzzard got sense lak dat!"

"Dar's whar you missed it, Sis Tempy," said Uncle Remus gravely. "Brer Buzzard, he tuck'n drap down fum de dead lim', en he lit on Mr. Hawk, en had 'im fer brekkus. Hit's a mighty 'roun' about way fer ter git chick'n-pie, yit hit's lots better dan no way."

"I 'speck Hawk do tas'e like chicken," remarked 'Tildy.

"Dey mos' sholy does," said Uncle Remus, with emphasis.

65
Mr. Hawk and Brother Rabbit

"I YEAR tell er one time," said 'Tildy, 'w'en ole Mr. Hawk tuck'n kotch Brer Rabbit, but 'tain't no tale like dem you all bin tellin'.''

"Tell it, anyhow, 'Tildy," said the little boy.

"Well, 'tain't no tale, I tell you dat now. One time Brer Rabbit wuz gwine 'long thoo de bushes singin' ter hisse'f, an' he see a shadder pass befo' 'im. He look up, an' dar 'uz Mr. Hawk sailin' 'roun' an 'roun'. Time he see 'im, Brer Rabbit 'gun ter kick up an' sassy 'im.

"Mr. Hawk ain't pay no 'tention ter dis. He des sail all 'roun' an' 'roun'. Eve'y time he sail 'roun', he git little closer, but Brer Rabbit ain't notice dis. He too busy wid his devilment. He shuck his fis' at Mr. Hawk, an' chunk'd at 'im wid sticks; an' atter w'ile he tuck'n make out he got a gun, an' he tuck aim at Mr. Hawk, an' 'low'd, 'Pow!' an' den he holler an' laugh.

"All dis time Mr. Hawk keep on sailin' 'roun' an' 'roun' an' gittin' nigher an' nigher, an' bimeby down he drapt right slambang on Brer Rabbit, an' dar he had 'im. Brer Rabbit fix ter say his pra'rs, but 'fo' he do dat, he talk to Mr. Hawk, an' he talk mighty fergivin'. He 'low he did:

"'I 'uz des playin', Mr. Hawk; I 'uz dez a-playin'. You oughtn' ter fly up an' git mad wid a little bit er man like me.'

"Mr. Hawk ruffle up de fedders on his neck an' say:

"'I ain't flyin' up, I'm a-flyin' down, an' w'en I fly up, I'm a-gwine ter fly 'way wid you. You bin a-playin' de imp 'roun' in dis settlement long nuff, an' now ef you got any will ter make, you better make it quick, kaze you ain't got much time.'

"Brer Rabbit cry. He say:

"'I mighty sorry, Mr. Hawk, dat I is. I got some gol' buried right over dar in fence cornder, an' I wish in my soul my po' little childuns know whar 'twuz, kaze den dey could git long widout me fer a mont' er two.'

"Mr. Hawk 'low, 'Whar'bouts is all dis gol'?'

"Brer Rabbit 'low, 'Right over dar in de fence-cornder.'

"Mr. Hawk say show it ter 'im. Brer Rabbit say he don't keer ef he do, an' he say:

"'I'd a done show'd it ter you long 'fo' dis, but you hol' me so tight, I can't wink my eye skacely, much less walk ter whar de gol' is.'

"Mr. Hawk say he fear'd he gwine ter try ter git 'way. Brer Rabbit say dey ain't no danger er dat, kaze he one er deze yer kinder mens w'en dey er kotch once dey er kotch fer good.

"Mr. Hawk sorter let Brer Rabbit loose, an' dey went todes de fence-cornder. Brer Rabbit, he went 'long so good dat dis sorter ease Mr. Hawk min' 'bout he gittin' 'way. Dey got ter de place an' Brer Rabbit look all 'roun', an' den he frown up like he got some mighty bad disap'intment, an' he say:

"'You may b'lieve me er not, Mr. Hawk, but we er on de wrong side er de fence. I hid dat gol' some'rs right in dat cornder dar. You fly over an' I'll go thoo.'

"Tooby sho dis look fa'r, an' Brer Rabbit, he crope thoo' de fence, an' Mr. Hawk flew'd 'cross. Time he lit on t'er side, Mr. Hawk year Brer Rabbit laugh."

The little boy asked what Brother Rabbit laughed for, as 'Tildy paused to adjust a flaming red ribbon-bow pinned in her hair.

"'Kaze dey wuz a brier-patch on t'er side de fence," said 'Tildy, "an' Brer Rabbit wuz in dar."

"I boun' you!" Aunt Tempy exclaimed. "He 'uz in dar, an' dar he stayed twel Mr. Hawk got tired er hangin' 'roun' dar."

"Ah, Lord, chile!" said Uncle Remus, with the candor of an expert, "some er dat tale you got right, en some you got wrong."

"Oh, I know'd 'twan't no tale like you all bin tellin'," replied 'Tildy modestly.

"Tooby sho 'tis" continued Uncle Remus, by way of encouragement; "but w'iles we gwine 'long we better straighten out all de kinks dat'll b'ar straightenin'."

"Goodness knows I ain't fittin' 'ter tell no tale," persisted 'Tildy.

"Don't run yo'se'f down, gal," said Uncle Remus, encouragingly; "ef dey's to be any runnin' down let yuther folks do it; en, bless yo' soul, dey'll do nuff un it widout waitin' fer yo' lettin'.

"Now, den, old man Hawk, — w'ich dey call 'im Billy Bluetail in my day en time — ole man Hawk, he tuck'n kotch Brer Rabbit des lak you done said. He kotch 'im en he hilt 'im in a mighty tight grip, let 'lone dat he hilt 'im so tight dat it make Brer Rabbit breff come short lak he des come off'n a long journey.

"He holler en he beg, but dat ain't do no good; he squall en he cry, but dat ain't do no good; he kick en he groan, but dat ain't do no good. Den Brer Rabbit lay still en study 'bout w'at de name er goodness he gwine do. Bimeby he up'n 'low:

"'I dunner w'at you want wid me, Mr. Hawk, w'en I ain't a mouf full fer you, skacely!'

"Mr. Hawk, sezee, 'I'll make way wid you, en den I'll go ketch me a couple er Jaybirds.'

"Dis make Brer Rabbit shake wid de allovers, kaze ef dey's any kinder creetur w'at he nat'ally 'spize on de topside er de yeth, hit's a Jaybird.

"Brer Rabbit, sezee, 'Do, pray, Mr. Hawk, go ketch dem Jaybirds fus', kaze I can't stan' um bein' on top er me. I'll stay right yer, plum' twel you come back,' sezee.

"Mr. Hawk, sezee, 'Oh-oh, Brer Rabbit, you done bin fool too many folks. You ain't fool me,' sezee.

"Brer Rabbit, sezee. 'Ef you can't do dat, Mr. Hawk, den de bes' way fer you ter do is ter wait en lemme git tame, kaze I'm dat wil' now dat I don't tas'e good.'

"Mr. Hawk, sezee, 'Oh-oh!'

"Brer Rabbit, sezee, 'Well, den, ef dat won't do, you better wait en lemme grow big so I'll be a full meal er vittles.'

"Mr. Hawk, sezee, 'Now you er talkin' sense!'

"Brer Rabbit, sezee, 'En I'll rush 'roun' 'mungs de bushes, en drive out Pa'tridges fer you, en we'll have mo' fun dan w'at you kin shake a stick at.'

"Mr. Hawk sorter study 'bout dis, en Brer Rabbit, he beg en he 'splain, en de long en de short un it wuz," said Uncle Remus, embracing his knee with his hands, "dat Brer Rabbit tuck'n git loose, en he ain't git no bigger, en needer is he druv no Pa'tridges fer Mr. Hawk."

"De Lord he'p my soul!" exclaimed 'Tildy, and this was the only comment made upon this extraordinary story.

66
The Wise Bird and the Foolish Bird

ALL THIS TALK about Hawks and Buzzards evidently reminded Daddy Jack of another story. He began to shake his head and mumble to himself; and, finally, when he looked around and found that he had attracted the attention of the little company, he rubbed his chin and grinned until his yellow teeth shone in the firelight like those of some wild animal, while his small eyes glistened under their heavy lids with a suggestion of cunning not unmixed with ferocity.

"Talk it out, Brer Jack," said Uncle Remus; "talk it out. All nex' week we'll be a-fixin' up 'bout Chris'mus. Mars Jeems, he's a-comin' up, en Miss Sally'll have lots er yuther comp'ny. 'Tildy yer, she'll be busy, en dish yer little chap, he won't have no time fer ter be settin' up wid de ole niggers, en Sis Tempy, she'll have 'er han's full, en ole Remus, he'll be a-pirootin' 'roun' huntin' fer dat w'at he kin pick up. Time's a-passin', Brer Jack, en we all er passin' wid it. Des whirl in en gin us de upshot er w'at you got in yo' min'."

"Enty!" exclaimed Daddy Jack, by way of approval. "One tam dey bin two bud. One bin sma't bud; da turrer, 'e bin fool bud. Dey bin lif in de sem country; dey bin usin' da sem swamp. Da sma't bud, 'e is bin come 'pon da fool bud; 'e bin tahlk. 'E bin say:

"'Ki! you long in da leg, you deep in da craw. You bin 'tan' well; you bin las' long tam.'

"Fool bud, 'e look proud, 'e toss 'e head; 'e say:

"'Me no mekky no brag.'

"Smat'd bud, 'e say:

"'Less we try see fer how long tam we kin go 'dout bittle un drink.'

"Fool bud, 'e 'tretch 'e neck, 'e toss 'e head; 'e say:

"'All-a right; me beat-a you all day ebry day. Me beat-a you all da tam.'

"Sma't bud, 'e say:

"'Ef you bin 'gree wit' dis, less we tek we place. You git 'pon da crik-side un tekky one ho'n, I git 'pon da tree y-up dey, un tekky nurrer ho'n. Less we 'tan' dey-dey tel we see how long tam we is kin do 'dout bittle un drink. Wun I blow 'pon me ho'n dun you blow 'pon you' ho'n fer answer me; me blow, you blow, dun we bote blow.'

"Fool bud walk 'bout big; 'e say:

"'Me will do um!'

"Nex' day mornin' come. Da sma't bud bin tekky one ho'n un fly 'pon da tree. De fool bud bin tekky one nurrer ho'n un set by da crick-side. Dey bin sta't in fer starf deyse'f. Da fool bud, 'e stay by da crik-side wey dey bin no'n 't all fer eat; 'e no kin fin' no bittle dey-dey. Sma't bud git in da tree da y-ant un da bug swa'm in da bark plenty. 'E pick dem ant, 'e y-eat dem ant; 'e pick dem bug, 'e y-eat dem bug. 'E pick tel 'e craw come full; he feel berry good.

"Fool bud, 'e down by da crik-side. 'E set down, 'e come tire'; 'e 'tan' up, 'e come tire'; 'e walk 'bout', 'e come tire'. 'E 'tan' 'pon one leg, he 'tan' 'pon turrer; 'e pit 'e head need 'e wing; still he come tire'. Sma't bud shed 'e y-eye; 'e feel berry good. Wun 'e come honkry, 'e pick ant, 'e pick bug, 'e hab plenty, toze dinner-time 'e pick up 'e ho'n, 'e toot um strong:

"'Tay-tay, tenando wanzando waneanzo!'

"Fool bud craw bin empty, but 'e hab win'. 'E tekky da ho'n, 'e blow berry well; he mek um say:

"'Tay-tay tenando wanzando olando!'

"Sma't bud pick ant plenty; 'e git full up. 'E wait tel mos' toze sun-down; 'e blow 'pon da ho'n:

"'Tay-tay tenando wanzando waneanzo!'

"Fool bud mek answer, but 'e come weak; 'e yent hab eat nuttin' 't all. Soon nex' day mornin' sma't bud tek 'e ho'n un toot um. 'E done bin eat, 'e done bin drink dew on da leaf. Fool bud, 'e toot um ho'n, 'e toot um slow.

"Dinner-time, sma't bud bin tek 'e ho'n un blow; 'e yent bin honkry no'n 't all; 'e hab good feelin'. Fool bud toot um ho'n; 'e toot um slow.

Night tam come, 'e no toot um no mo'. Sma't bud come down, 'e fin' im done gone dead.

"Watch dem 'ceitful folks; 'e bin do you bad."[1]

67
Old Brother Terrapin Gets Some Fish

"DAT TALE," SAID Uncle Remus, "puts me in min' er de time w'en ole Brer Tarrypin had a tussle wid Brer Mink. Hit seem lak," he went on, in response to inquiries from the little boy, "dat dey bofe live 'roun' de water so much en so long dey git kinder stuck up long wid it. Leasways dat 'uz de trouble wid Brer Mink. He jump in de water en swim en dive twel he 'gun ter b'lieve dey wa'n't nobody kin hol' der han' long wid 'im.

"One day Brer Mink 'uz gwine long de creek wid a nice string er fish swingin' on he walkin'-cane, w'en who should he meet up wid but ole Brer Tarrypin. De creeturs 'uz all hail feller wid ole Brer Tarrypin, en no sooner is he seed Brer Mink dan he bow 'im howdy. Ole Brer Tarrypin talk 'way down in he th'oat lak he got bad col'. He 'low:

"'Heyo, Brer Mink! Whar you git all dem nice string er fish?'

"Brer Mink 'uz mighty up-en-spoken in dem days. He 'low, he did:

"'Down dar in de creek, Brer Tarrypin.'

"'Well, well, well! In de creek! Who'd er b'lieved it?'

"Brer Mink, sezee: 'Whar I gwine ketch um, Brer Tarrypin, ef I ain't ketch um in de creek?'

"Ole Brer Tarrypin, sezee: 'Dat's so, Brer Mink; but a highlan' man lak you gwine in de creek atter fish! Hit looks turrible, Brer Mink — dat w'at it do; hit des looks turrible!'

"Brer Mink, sezee: 'Look er no looks, dar whar I got um.'

"Brer Tarrypin sorter sway he head fum side ter side en 'low:

"'Ef dat de case, Brer Mink, den sholy you mus' be one er dem ar kinder creeturs w'at usen ter de water.'

"'Dat's me,' sez Brer Mink, sezee.

---

1 Mrs. H. S. Barclay, of Darien, who sends this story, says it was told by a native African woman, of good intelligence, who claimed to be a princess. She had an eagle tattooed on her bosom — a sign of royalty. — J. C. H.

"'Well, den,' sez Brer Tarrypin, sezee, 'I'm a highlan' man myse'f, en it's bin a mighty long time sence I got my foots wet, but I don't min' goin' in washin' 'long wid you. Ef you er de man you sez you is, you kin outdo me,' sezee.

"Brer Mink, sezee: 'How we gwine do, Brer Tarrypin?'

"Ole Brer Tarrypin, sezee: 'We ull go down dar ter de creek, en de man w'at kin stay und' de water de longest, let dat man walk off wid dat string er fish.'

"Brer Mink, sezee: 'I'm de ve'y man you bin lookin' fer.'

"Brer Mink say he don't wanter put it off a minnit. Go he would, en go he did. Dey went down ter creek en make der 'rangements. Brer Mink lay he fish down on der bank, en 'im en ole Brer Tarrypin wade in. Brer Tarrypin he make great 'miration 'bout how col' he water is. He flinch, he did, en 'low:

"'Ow, Brer Mink! Dish yer water feel mighty col' and 'tain't no mo'n up ter my wais'. Goodness knows how she gwine feel w'en she git up und' my chin.'

"Dey wade in, dey did, en Brer Tarrypin say, sezee:

"'Now, den, Brer Mink, we'll make a dive, en de man w'at stay und' de water de longest dat man gits de fish.'

"Brer Mink 'low dat's de way he look at it, en den Brer Tarrypin gun de wud, en und' dey went. Co'se," said Uncle Remus, after a little pause, "Brer Tarrypin kin stay down in de water longer'n Brer Mink, en Brer Mink mought er know'd it. Dey stay en dey stay, twel bimeby Brer Mink bleedzd ter come up, en he tuck'n kotch he breff, he did, lak he mighty glad fer ter git back ag'in. Den atter w'ile Brer Tarrypin stuck he nose out er de water, en den Brer Mink say Brer Tarrypin kin beat 'im. Brer Tarrypin 'low:

"'No, Brer Mink; hit's de bes' two out er th'ee. Ef I beats you dis time den de fish, dey er mine; ef I gits beated, den we kin take n'er trial.'

"Wid dat, down dey went, but Brer Tarrypin ain't mo'n dove 'fo' up he come, en w'ile Brer Mink 'uz down dar honin' fer fresh a'r, he tuck'n gobble up de las' one er de fish, ole Brer Tarrypin did. He gobble up de fish, en he 'uz fixin' fer ter pick he toof, but by dis time Brer Mink bleedzd ter come up, en ole Brer Tarrypin, he tuck'n slid down in de water. He slid so slick," said Uncle Remus, with a chuckle, "dat he ain't lef' a bubble.

He ain't stay down long, n'er, 'fo' he come up en make lak he teetotally out er win'.

"Ole Brer Tarrypin come up, he did, en look 'roun', en 'fo' Brer Mink kin say a wud, he holler out:

"'You er nice man, Brer Mink! You er a mighty nice man!'

"'W'at I done now, Brer Tarrypin?'

"Don't ax me. Look up dar whar you bin eatin' dem fish en den ax yo'se'f. You er mighty nice man!'

"Brer Mink look 'roun' en, sho nuff, de fish done gone. Ole Brer Tarrypin keep on talkin':

"'You tuck'n come up fust, en w'iles I bin down dar in de water, nat'ally achin' fer lack er win', yer you settin' up chawin' on de fish w'ich dey oughter bin mine!'

"Brer Mink stan' 'im down dat he ain't eat dem fish; he 'ny it ter de las', but ole Brer Tarrypin make out he don't b'lieve 'im. He say, sezee:

"'You'll keep gwine on dis a-way, twel atter w'ile you'll be wuss'n Brer Rabbit. Don't tell me you ain't git dem fish, Brer Mink, kaze you know you is.'

"Hit sorter make Brer Mink feel proud kaze ole Brer Tarrypin mix 'im up wid Brer Rabbit, kaze Brer Rabbit wuz a mighty man in dem days, en he sorter laugh, Brer Mink did lak he know mo' dan he gwine tell. Ole Brer Tarrypin keep on grumblin'.

"'I ain't gwine ter git mad long wid you, Brer Mink, kaze hit's mighty keen trick, but you oughter be 'shame' yo'se'f fer ter be playin' tricks on a ole man lak me — dat you ought!'

"Wid dat ole Brer Tarrypin went shufflin' off, en atter he git outer sight he draw'd back in he house en shot de do' en laugh en laugh twel dey wa'n't no fun in laughin'.'"

68
Brother Fox Makes a Narrow Escape

THE NEXT TIME the little boy had an opportunity to visit Uncle Remus the old man was alone, but he appeared to be in good spirits. He was cob-

bling away upon what the youngster recognized as 'Tildy's Sunday shoes,
and singing snatches of a song something like this:

> "O Mr. Rabbit! yo' eye mighty big —
>   Yes, my Lord! dey er made fer ter see;
> O Mr. Rabbit! yo' tail mighty short —
>   Yes, my Lord! hit des fits me!"

The child waited to hear more, but the song was the same thing over
and over again — always about Brother Rabbit's big eyes and his short
tail. After a while Uncle Remus acknowledged the presence of his little
partner by remarking:

"Well, sir, we er all yer. Brer Jack and Sis Tempy en dat ar 'Tildy nigger may be a-pacin' 'roun' lookin' in de fence-cornders fer Chris'mus,
but me en you en ole Brer Rabbit, we er all yer, en ef we ain't right on de
spot, we er mighty close erroun'. Yasser, we is dat; mo' speshually ole
Brer Rabbit, wid he big eye and he short tail. Don't tell me 'bout Brer
Rabbit!" exclaimed Uncle Remus, with a great apparent enthusiasm,
"kaze dey ain't no use er talkin' 'bout dat creetur."

The little boy was very anxious to know why.

"Well, I tell you," said the old man. "One time dey wuz a monstus dry
season in de settlement whar all de creeturs live at, en drinkin'-water got
mighty skace. De creeks got low, en de branches went dry, en all de
springs make der disappearance ceppin' one great big un whar all de
creeturs drunk at. Dey'd all meet dar, dey would, en de bigges' 'ud drink
fus', en by de time de big uns all done 'swaje de thuss dey wa'n't a drap
lef' fer de little uns skacely.

"Co'se Brer Rabbit wuz on de happy side. Ef anybody gwine git water
Brer Rabbit de man. De creeturs 'ud see he track 'roun' de spring, but
dey ain't nev' ketch 'im. Hit got so atter w'ile dat de big creeturs 'ud
crowd Brer Fox out, en den 'twa'n't long 'fo' he hunt up Brer Rabbit en
ax 'im w'at he gwine do.

"Brer Rabbit, he sorter study, en den he up'n tell Brer Fox fer ter go
home en rub some 'lasses all on hisse'f en den get out en waller in de
leafs. Brer Fox ax w'at he mus' do den, en Brer Rabbit say he mus' go
down by de spring, en w'en de creeturs come ter de spring fer ter git dey

water, he mus' jump out at um, en den atter dat he mus' waller lak he one
er dem ar kinder varmint w'at gots bugs on um.

"Brer Fox, he put out fer home, he did, en w'en he git dar he run ter
de cubberd en des gawm hisse'f wid 'lasses, en den he went out en de
bushes, he did, en waller in de leafs en trash twel he look mos' bad ez
Brer Rabbit look when he play Wuller-de-Wust on de creeturs.

"W'en Brer Fox git hisse'f all fix up, he went down ter de spring en
hide hisse'f. Bimeby all de creeturs come atter der water, en w'iles dey
'uz a-scuffin' en a-hunchin', en a-pushin' en a-scrougin', Brer Fox he
jump out'n de bushes en sorter switch hisse'f 'roun', en, bless yo' soul,
he look lak de Ole Boy.

"Brer Wolf tuck'n see 'im fus', en he jump spang over Brer B'ar head.
Brer B'ar, he lip back, en ax who dat, en des time he do dis t'er creeturs
dey tuck'n make a break, dey did, lak punkins rollin' down hill, en mos'
'fo' you k'n wink yo' eye-ball, Brer Fox had de range er de spring all by
hisse'f.

"Yit 'twa'n't fur long, 'kaze 'fo' de creeturs mov'd fur, dey tuck'n tu'n
'roun', dey did, en crope back fer ter see w'at dat ar skeery-lookin'
varmint doin'. W'en dey git back in seein' distuns dar wuz Brer Fox
walkin' up en down switchin' hisse'f.

"De creeturs dunner w'at ter make un 'im. Dey watch, en he march.
Hit keep on dis a-way twel bimeby Brer Fox 'gun ter waller in de water,
en right dar," continued Uncle Remus, leaning back to laugh, "right dar
wuz whar Brer Rabbit had 'im. Time he 'gun ter waller in de water de
'lasses 'gun ter melt, en 'twa'n't no time skacely 'fo' de 'lasses en de leafs
done all wash off, en dar wuz ole Brer Fox des ez natchul ez life.

"De fus' Brer Fox know 'bout de leafs comin' off, he year Brer B'ar
holler on top er de hill:

"'You head 'im off down dar, Brer Wolf, en I'll head 'im off 'roun' yer!'

"Brer Fox look 'roun' 'en he see all de leafs done come off, en wid dat
he make a break, en he wa'n't none too soon, n'er, kaze little mo' en de
creeturs 'ud a kotch 'im."

Without giving the little boy time to ask any questions, Uncle Remus
added another verse to his Rabbit song, and harped on it for several
minutes:

"O Mr. Rabbit! yo' year mighty long —
   Yes, my Lord! dey made fer ter las';
O Mr. Rabbit! yo' toof mighty sharp —
   Yes, my Lord! dey cuts down grass!"

69
Brother Fox's Fish-Trap

THE LITTLE BOY wanted Uncle Remus to sing some more; but before the old man could either consent or refuse, the notes of a horn were heard in the distance. Uncle Remus lifted his hand to command silence, and bent his head in an attitude of attention.

"Des listen at dat!" he exclaimed, with some show of indignation. "Dat ain't nothin' in de roun' worl' but ole man Plato wid dat tin hawn er his'n, en I boun' you he's a-drivin' de six mule waggin, en de waggin full er niggers fum de River place, en let 'lone dat, I boun' you dey er niggers strung out behime de waggin fer mo'n a mile, en dey er all er comin' yer ter eat us all out'n house en home, des kaze dey year folks say Chris'mus mos' yer. Hit's mighty kuse unter me dat ole man Plato ain't done toot dat hawn full er holes long 'fo' dis.

"Yit I ain't blamin' um," Uncle Remus went on, with a sigh, after a little pause. "Dem ar niggers bin livin' 'way off dar on de River place whar dey ain't no white folks twel dey er done in about run'd wil'. I ain't a-blamin' um, dat I ain't."

Plato's horn — a long tin bugle — was by no means unmusical. Its range was limited, but in Plato's hands its few notes were both powerful and sweet. Presently the wagon arrived, and for a few minutes all was confusion, the Negroes on the Home place running to greet the new-comers, who were mostly their relatives. A stranger hearing the shouts and outcries of these people would have been at a loss to account for the commotion.

Even Uncle Remus went to his cabin door, and, with the little boy by his side, looked out upon the scene — a tumult lit up by torches of resinous pine. The old man and the child were recognized, and for a few moments the air was filled with cries of:

"Howdy, Unk' Remus! Howdy, little Marster!"

After a while Uncle Remus closed his door, laid away his tools, and drew his chair in front of the wide hearth. The child went and stood beside him, leaning his head against the old Negro's shoulder, and the two — old age and youth, one living in the past and the other looking forward only to the future — gazed into the bed of glowing embers illuminated by a thin, flickering flame. Probably they saw nothing there, each being busy with his own simple thoughts; but their shadows, enlarged out of all proportion, and looking over their shoulders from the wall behind them, must have seen something, for, clinging together, they kept up a most incessant pantomime; and Plato's horn, which sounded again, to call the Negroes to supper after their journey, though it aroused Uncle Remus and the child from the contemplation of the fire, had no perceptible effect upon the Shadows.

"Dar go de vittles!" said Uncle Remus, straightening himself. "Dey tells me dat dem ar niggers on de River place got appetite same ez a mule. Let 'lone de vittles w'at dey gits from Mars John, dey eats oodles en oodles er fish. Ole man Plato say dat de nigger on de River place w'at ain't got a fish-baskit in de river er some intruss in a fish-trap ain't no 'count w'atsomever."

Here Uncle Remus suddenly slapped himself upon the leg, and laughed uproariously; and when the little boy asked him what the matter was, he cried out:

"Well, sir! Ef I ain't de fergittenest ole nigger 'twix' dis en Phillimerdelphy! Yer 'tis mos' Chris'mus en I ain't tell you 'bout how Brer Rabbit do Brer Fox whence dey bofe un um live on de river. I dunner w'at de name er sense gittin' de marter 'long wid me."

Of course the little boy wanted to know all about it, and Uncle Remus proceeded:

"One time Brer Fox en Brer Rabbit live on de river. Atter dey bin livin' dar so long a time, Brer Fox 'low dat he got a mighty hankerin' atter sump'n 'sides fresh meat, en he say he b'lieve he make 'im a fish-trap. Brer Rabbit say he wish Brer Fox mighty well, but he ain't honin' atter fish hisse'f, en ef he is he ain't got no time fer ter make no fish-trap.

"No marter fer dat, Brer Fox, he tuck'n got 'im out some timber, he did, en he wuk nights fer ter make dat trap. Den w'en he git it done, he tuck'n hunt 'im a good place fer ter set it, en de way he sweat over dat ar trap wuz a sin — dat 'twuz.

"Yit atter so long a time, he got 'er sot, en den he tuck'n wash he face en han's en go home. All de time he 'uz fixin' un it up, Brer Rabbit 'uz settin' on de bank watchin' 'im. He sot dar, he did, en play in de water, en cut switches fer ter whip at de snake-doctors, en all dat time Brer Fox, he pull en haul en tote rocks fer ter hol' dat trap endurin' a freshet.

"Brer Fox went home en res' hisse'f, en bimeby he go down fer ter see ef dey any fish in he trap. He sorter feard er snakes, but he feel 'roun' an he feel 'roun', yit he ain't feel no fish. Den he go off.

"Bimeby, 'long todes de las' er de week, he go down en feel 'roun' 'gin, yit he ain't feel no fish. Hit keep on dis a-way twel Brer Fox git sorter fag out. He go en he feel, but dey ain't no fish dar. Atter w'ile, one day, he see de signs whar somebody bin robbin' he trap, en he 'low ter hisse'f dat he'll des e'en 'bout watch en fin' out who de somebody is.

"Den he tuck'n got in he boat en paddle und' de bushes on de bank en watch he fish-trap. He watch all de mornin'; nobody ain't come. He watch all endurin' er atter dinner; nobody ain't come. 'Long todes night, w'en he des 'bout makin' ready fer ter paddle off home, he year fuss on t'er side de river, en lo en beholes, yer come Brer Rabbit polin' a boat right todes Brer Fox fish-trap.

"Look lak he dunner how to use a paddle, en he des had 'im a long pole, en he'd stan' up in de behime part er he boat, en put de een' er de pole 'g'in' de bottom, en shove 'er right ahead.

"Brer Fox git mighty mad w'en he see dis, but he watch en wait. He 'low ter hisse'f, he did, dat he kin paddle a boat pearter dan anybody kin pole um, en he say he sholy gwine ketch Brer Rabbit dis time.

"Brer Rabbit pole up ter de fish-trap, en feel 'roun' en pull out a great big mud-cat; den he retch in en pull out n'er big mud-cat; den he pull out a big blue cat, en it keep on dis a-way twel he git de finest mess er fish you mos' ever laid yo' eyes on.

"Des 'bout dat time, Brer Fox paddle out fum und' de bushes, en make todes Brer Rabbit, en he holler out:

"'Ah-yi! You er de man w'at bin robbin' my fish-trap dis long time! I got you dis time! Oh, you nee'nter try ter run! I got you dis time sho!'

"No sooner said dan no sooner done. Brer Rabbit fling he fish in he boat en grab up de pole en push off, en he had mo' fun gittin' 'way fum dar dan he y-ever had befo' in all he born days put terge'er."

"Why didn't Brother Fox catch him, Uncle Remus?" asked the little boy.

"*Shoo!* Honey, you sho'ly done lose yo' min' 'bout Brer Rabbit."

"Well, I don't see how he could get away."

"Ef you'd er bin dar you'd er seed it, dat you would. Brer Fox, he wuz dar, en he seed it, en Brer Rabbit, he seed it, en e'en down ter ole Brer Bull-frog, a-settin' on de bank, he seed it. Now, den," continued Uncle Remus, spreading out the palm of his left hand like a map and pointing at it with the forefinger of his right, "w'en Brer Rabbit pole he boat, he bleedzd ter set in de behime een', en w'en Brer Fox paddle he boat, *he* bleedzd ter set in de behime een'. Dat bein' de state er de condition, how Brer Fox gwine ketch 'im? I ain't 'sputin' but w'at he kin paddle pearter dan Brer Rabbit, but de long en de shorts un it is, de pearter Brer Fox paddle de pearter Brer Rabbit go."

The little boy looked puzzled. "Well, I don't see how," he exclaimed.

"Well, sir!" continued Uncle Remus, "w'en de nose er Brer Fox boat git close ter Brer Rabbit boat all Brer Rabbit got ter do in de roun' worl' is ter take he pole en put in 'g'in' Brer Fox boat en push hisse'f out de way. De harder he push Brer Fox boat back, de pearter he push he own boat forrerd. Hit look mighty easy ter ole Brer Bull-frog settin' on de bank, en all Brer Fox kin do is ter shake he fist en grit he toof, w'iles Brer Rabbit sail off wid de fish."

70
Brother Rabbit Rescues Brother Terrapin

THE ARRIVAL of the Negroes from the River place added greatly to the enthusiasm with which the Christmas holidays were anticipated on the Home place, and the air was filled with laughter day and night. Uncle Remus appeared to be very busy, though there was really nothing to be done except to walk around and scold at everybody and everything, in a good-humored way, and this the old man could do to perfection.

The night before Christmas Eve, however, the little boy saw a light in

Uncle Remus's cabin, and he interpreted it as in some sort a signal of invitation. He found the old man sitting by the fire and talking to himself:

"Ef Mars John and Miss Sally 'specks me fer ter keep all deze yer niggers straight dey er gwine ter be diserp'inted, — dat dey is. Ef dey wuz 'lev'm Remuses 'twouldn't make no diffunce, let 'lone one po' ole cripple creetur lak me. Dey ain't done no damage yit, but I boun' you by termorrer night dey'll tu'n loose en tu'n de whole place upside down, en t'ar it up by de roots, en den atter hit's all done gone en done, yer'll come Miss Sally a-layin' it all at ole Remus do'. Nigger ain't got much chance in deze yer low-groun's, mo' speshually w'en dey gits ole en cripple lak I is."

"What are they going to do tomorrow night, Uncle Remus?" the little boy inquired.

"Now w'at make you ax dat, honey?" exclaimed the old man in a grieved tone. "You knows mighty well how dey done las' year en de year 'fo' dat. Dey tuck'n cut up 'roun' yer wuss'n ef dey 'uz wil' creeturs, en termorrer night dey'll be a-hollin' en whoopin' en singin' en dancin' 'fo' it git dark good. I wish w'en you go up ter de big house you be so good ez ter tell Miss Sally dat ef she want any peace er min' she better git off'n de place en stay off twel atter deze yer niggers git dey fill er Chris'mus. Goodness knows, she can't 'speck a ole cripple nigger lak me fer ter ketch holt en keep all deze yer niggers straight."

Uncle Remus would have kept up his vague complaints, but right in the midst of them Daddy Jack stuck his head in at the door, and said:

"Oona bin fix da' 'Tildy gal shoe. Me come fer git dem shoe; me come fer pay you fer fix dem shoe."

Uncle Remus looked at the grinning old African in astonishment. Then suddenly the truth dawned upon him and he broke into a loud laugh. Finally he said:

"Come in, Brer Jack! Come right 'long in. I'm sorter po'ly myse'f, yit I'll make out ter make you welcome. Dey wuz a quarter dollar gwine inter my britches-pocket on de 'count er dem ar shoes, but ef you er gwine ter pay fer um 'twon't be but a sev'mpunce."

Somehow or other Daddy Jack failed to relish Uncle Remus's tone and manner, and he replied, with some display of irritation:

"Shuh-shuh! Me no come in no'n 'tall. Me no pay you se'mpunce. Me come fer pay you fer dem shoe; me come fer tek um 'way fum dey-dey."

"I dunno 'bout dat, Brer Jack, I dunno 'bout dat. De las' time I year you en 'Tildy gwine on, she wuz 'pun de p'ints er knockin' yo' brains out. Now den, s'pozen I whirls in en gins you de shoes, en den 'Tildy come 'long an ax me 'bout um, w'at I gwine say ter 'Tildy?"

"Me pay you fer dem shoe," said Daddy Jack, seeing the necessity of argument, "un me tek um wey da lil 'Tildy gal bin stay. She tell me fer come git-a dem shoe."

"Well, den, yer dey is," said Uncle Remus, sighing deeply as he handed Daddy Jack the shoes. "Yer dey is, en you er mo' dan welcome, dat you is. But spite er dat, dis yer quarter you flingin' 'way on um would er done you a sight mo' good dan w'at dem shoes is."

This philosophy was altogether lost upon Daddy Jack, who took the shoes and shuffled out with a grunt of satisfaction. He had scarcely got out of hearing before 'Tildy pushed the door open and came in. She hesitated a moment, and then, seeing that Uncle Remus paid no attention to her, she sat down and picked at her fingers with an air quite in contrast to her usual "uppishness," as Uncle Remus called it.

"Unk' Remus," she said, after awhile, in a subdued tone, "is dat old Affikin nigger bin yer atter dem ar shoes?"

"Yas, chile," replied Uncle Remus, with a long-drawn sigh, "he done bin yer en got um en gone. Yas, honey, he done got um en gone; done come en pay fer 'm, en got um en gone. I sez, sez I, dat I wish you all mighty well, en he tuck'n tuck de shoes en put. Yas, chile, he done got um en gone."

Something in Uncle Remus's sympathetic and soothing tone seemed to exasperate 'Tildy. She dropped her hands in her lap, straightened herself up and exclaimed:

"Yas, I'm is gwine ter marry dat ole nigger an' I don't keer who knows it. Miss Sally say she don't keer, an' t'er folks may keer ef dey wanter, an' much good der keerin' 'll do um."

'Tildy evidently expected Uncle Remus to make some characteristic comment, for she sat and watched him with her lips firmly pressed together and her eyelids half-closed — an attitude of defiance significant enough when seen, but difficult to describe. But the old man made no response to the challenge. He seemed to be very busy. Presently 'Tildy went on:

"Somebody bleedzd to take keer er dat ole nigger, an' I dunner who gwine ter do it ef I don't. Somebody bleedzd ter look atter 'im. Good win' come 'long hit 'ud in about blow 'im 'way ef dey wa'n't somebody close 'roun' fer ter take keer un 'im. Let 'lone dat, I ain't gwine ter have dat ole nigger man f'ever 'n' 'ternally trottin' atter me. I tell you de Lord's trufe, Unk' Remus," continued 'Tildy, growing confidential, "I ain't had no peace er min' sence dat ole nigger man come on dis place. He des bin a-pacin' at my heels de whole blessed time, an' I bleedzd ter marry 'im fer git rid un 'im."

"Well," said Uncle Remus, "hit don't s'prize me. You marry en den you er des lak Brer Fox wid he bag. You know w'at you put in it, but you dunner w'at you got in it."

'Tildy flounced out without waiting for an explanation, but the mention of Brother Fox attracted the attention of the little boy, and he wanted to know what was in the bag, how it came to be there, and all about it.

"Now, den," said Uncle Remus, "hit's a tale, en a mighty long tale at dat, but I'll des hatter cut it short, kaze termorrer night you'll wanter be a-settin' up lis'nen at de kyar'n's on er dem ar niggers, w'ich I b'lieve in my soul dey done los' all de sense dey ever bin bornded wid.

"One time Brer Fox wuz gwine on down de big road en he look ahead en he see ole Brer Tarrypin makin' he way on todes home. Brer Fox 'low dis a mighty good time fer ter nab ole Brer Tarrypin, en no sooner is he thunk it dan he put out back home, w'ich 'twa'n't but a little ways, en he git 'im a bag. He come back, he did, en he run up behime ole Brer Tarrypin en flip 'im in de bag en sling de bag 'cross he back en go gallin-up back home.

"Brer Tarrypin, he holler, but 'tain't do no good, he rip en he r'ar, but 'tain't do no good. Brer Fox des keep on a-gwine, en 'twa'n't long 'fo' he had ole Brer Tarrypin slung up in de cornder in de bag, en de bag tied un hard en fas'.

"But w'iles all dis gwine on," exclaimed Uncle Remus, employing the tone and manner of some country preacher he had heard, "whar wuz ole Brer Rabbit? Yasser — dats it, whar wuz he? En mo'n dat, w'at you 'speck he 'uz doin' en whar you reckon he wer' gwine? Dat's de way ter talk it; whar'bouts wuz he?"

The old man brought his right hand down upon his knee with a thump that jarred the tin-plate and cups on the mantel-shelf, and then looked around with a severe frown to see what the chairs and the work-bench, and the walls and the rafters, had to say in response to his remarkable argument. He sat thus in a waiting attitude a moment, and then, finding that no response came from anything or anybody, his brow gradually cleared, and a smile of mingled pride and satisfaction spread over his face, as he continued in a more natural tone:

"You k'n b'lieve me er not b'lieve des ez you er min' ter, but dat ar long-year creetur — dat ar hoppity-skippity — dat ar up-en-down-en-sailin'-'roun' Brer Rabbit, w'ich you bin year me call he name 'fo' dis, he wa'n't so mighty fur off w'iles Brer Fox gwine 'long wid dat ar bag slung 'cross he back. Let 'lone dat, Brer Rabbit 'uz settin' right dar in de bushes by de side er de road, en w'ence he see Brer Fox go trottin' by, he ax hisse'f w'at is it dat creetur got in dat ar bag.

"He ax hisse'f, he did, but he dunno. He wunder en he wunder, yit de mo' he wunder de mo' he dunno. Brer Fox, he go trottin' by, en Brer Rabbit, he sot in de bushes en wunder. Bimeby he 'low ter hisse'f, he did, dat Brer Fox ain't got no business fer ter be trottin' 'long down de road, totin' doin's w'ich yuther folks dunner w'at dey is, en he 'low dat dey won't be no great harm done ef he take atter Brer Fox en fin' out w'at he got in dat ar bag.

"Wid dat, Brer Rabbit, he put out. He ain't got no bag fer ter tote, en he pick up he foots mighty peart. Mo'n dat, he tuck'n tuck a nigh-cut, en by de time Brer Fox git home, Brer Rabbit done had time fer ter go 'roun' by de watermillion-patch en do some er he devilment, en den atter dat he tuck'n sot down in de bushes whar he kin see Brer Fox w'en he come home.

"Bimeby yer come Brer Fox wid de bag slung 'cross he back. He on-latch de do', he did, en he go in en sling Brer Tarrypin down in de corn-der, en set down front er de h'a'th fer ter res' hisse'f."

Here Uncle Remus paused to laugh in anticipation of what was to follow.

"Brer Fox ain't mo'n lit he pipe," the old man continued, after a tantalizing pause, "'fo' Brer Rabbit stick he head in de do' en holler:

"'Brer Fox! O Brer Fox! You better take yo' walkin'-cane en run down yan. Comin' 'long des now I year a mighty fuss, en I look 'roun' en dar wuz a whole passel er folks in yo' watermillion-patch des a-tromplin' 'roun' en a-t'arin' down. I holler'd at um, but dey ain't pay no 'tention ter little man lak I is. Make 'a'se, Brer Fox! make 'a'se! Git yo' cane en run down dar. I'd go wid you myse'f, but my ole 'oman ailin' en I bleedzd ter be makin' my way todes home. You better make 'a'se, Brer Fox, ef you wanter git de good er yo' watermillions. Run, Brer Fox! run!'

"Wid dat Brer Rabbit dart back in de bushes, en Brer Fox drap he pipe en grab he walkin'-cane en put out fer he watermillion-patch, w'ich 'twer' down on de branch; en no sooner is he gone dan ole Brer Rabbit come out de bushes en make he way in de house.

"He go so easy dat he ain't make no fuss; he look 'roun' en dar wuz de bag in de cornder. He kotch holt er de bag en sorter feel un it, en time he do dis, he year sump'n' holler:

"'Ow! Go 'way! Lem me 'lone! Tu'n me loose! Ow!'

"Brer Rabbit jump back 'stonish'd. Den 'fo' you kin wink yo' eye-ball, Brer Rabbit slap hisse'f on de leg en break out in a laugh. Den he up'n 'low:

"'Ef I ain't make no mistakes, dat ar kinder fuss kin come fum nobody in de roun' worl' but ole Brer Tarrypin.'

"Brer Tarrypin, he holler, sezee: 'Ain't dat Brer Rabbit?'

"'De same,' sezee.

"'Den whirl in en tu'n me out. Meal dus' in my th'oat, grit in my eye, en I ain't kin git my breff, skacely. Tu'n me out, Brer Rabbit.'

"Brer Tarrypin talk lak somebody down in a well. Brer Rabbit, he holler back:

"'You er lots smarter dan w'at I is, Brer Tarrypin — lots smarter. You er smarter en pearter. Peart ez I come yer, you is ahead er me. I know how you git in de bag, but I dunner how de name er goodness you tie yo'se'f up in dar, dat I don't.'

"Brer Tarrypin try ter 'splain, but Brer Rabbit keep on laughin', en he laugh twel he git he fill er laughin'; en den he tuck'n ontie de bag en take Brer Tarrypin out en tote 'im 'way off in de woods. Den, w'en he done dis, Brer Rabbit tuck'n run off en git a great big hornet-nes' w'at he see w'en he comin' long — "

"A hornet's nest, Uncle Remus?" exclaimed the little boy, in amazement.

"Tooby sho, honey. 'Tain't bin a mont' sence I brung you a great big hornet-nes', en yer you is axin' dat. Brer Rabbit tuck'n slap he han' 'cross de little hole whar de hornets goes in at, en dar he had um. Den he tuck'n tuck it ter Brer Fox house, en put it in de bag whar Brer Tarrypin bin.

"He put de hornet-nes' in dar," continued Uncle Remus, lowering his voice, and becoming very grave, "en den he tie up de bag des lak he fin' it. Yit 'fo' he put de bag back in de cornder, w'at do dat creetur do? I ain't settin' yer," said the ole man, seizing his chair with both hands, as if by that means to emphasize the illustration, "I ain't settin' yer ef dat ar creetur ain't grab dat bag en slam it down 'g'in' de flo', en hit it 'g'in' de side er de house twel he git dem ar hornets all stirred up, en den he put de bag back in de cornder, en go out in de bushes ter whar Brer Tarrypin waitin', en den bofe un um sot out dar en wait fer ter see w'at de upshot gwine ter be.

"Bimeby, yer come Brer Fox back fum he watermillion-patch en he look lak he mighty mad. He strak he cane down 'pun de groun', en do lak he gwine take he revengeance out'n po' ole Brer Tarrypin. He went in de do', Brer Fox did, en shot it atter 'im. Brer Rabbit en Brer Tarrypin lissen', but dey ain't year nothin'.

"But bimeby, fus' news you know, dey year de mos' owdashus racket, tooby sho. Seem lak, fum whar Brer Rabbit en Brer Tarrypin settin' dat dey 'uz a whole passel er cows runnin' 'roun' in Brer Fox house. Dey year de cheers a-fallin', en de table turnin' over, en de crock'ry breakin', en den de do' flew'd open, en out come Brer Fox, a-squallin' lak de Ole Boy wuz atter 'im. En sech a sight ez dem t'er creeturs seed den en dar ain't never bin seed befo' ner sence.

"Dem ar hornets des swarmed on top er Brer Fox. 'Lev'm dozen un um 'ud hit at one time, en look lak dat ar creetur bleedzd ter fin' out fer hisse'f w'at pain en suffin' is. Dey bit 'im en dey stung 'im, en fur ez Brer Rabbit en Brer Tarrypin kin year 'im, dem hornets 'uz des a-nailin' 'im. Gentermens! dey gun 'im binjer!

"Brer Rabbit en Brer Tarrypin, dey sot dar, dey did, en dey laugh en laugh, twel bimeby, Brer Rabbit roll over en grab he stomach, en holler:

"'Don't, Brer Tarrypin! don't! One giggle mo' en you'll hatter tote me.'

"En dat ain't all," said Uncle Remus, raising his voice. "I know a little chap w'ich ef he set up yer 'sputin' 'longer me en de t'er creeturs, he won't have much fun termorrer night."

The hint was sufficient, and the little boy ran out laughing.

71
The Night Before Christmas

THE DAY and the night before Christmas were full of pleasure for the little boy. There was pleasure in the big house, and pleasure in the humble cabins in the quarters. The peculiar manner in which the Negroes celebrated the beginning of the holidays was familiar to the child's experience, but strange to his appreciation, and he enjoyed everything he saw and heard with the ready delight of his years, — a delight, which, in this instance, had been trained and sharpened, if the expression may be used, in the small world over which Uncle Remus presided.

The little boy had a special invitation to be present at the marriage of Daddy Jack and 'Tildy, and he went, accompanied by Uncle Remus and Aunt Tempy. It seemed to be a very curious affair, but its incongruities made small impression upon the mind of the child.

'Tildy wore a white dress and had a wreath of artificial flowers in her hair. Daddy Jack wore a high hat, which he persisted in keeping on his head during the ceremony, and a coat the tails of which nearly dragged the floor. His bright little eyes glistened triumphantly, and he grinned and bowed to everybody again and again. After it was all over, the guests partook of cake baked by Aunt Tempy, and persimmon beer brewed by Uncle Remus.

It seemed, however, that 'Tildy was not perfectly happy; for, in response to a question asked by Aunt Tempy, she said:

"Yes'm, I'm gwine down de country 'long wid my ole man, an' I lay ef eve'ything don't go right, I'm gwine ter pick up an' come right back."

"No-no!" exclaimed Daddy Jack, "'e no come bahck no'n 't all. 'E bin stay dey-dey wit' 'e nice ole-a màn."

"You put yo' 'pennunce in dat!" said 'Tildy, scornfully. "Dey ain't nobody kin hol' me w'en I takes a notion, ceppin' hit's Miss Sally; en, goodness knows, Miss Sally ain't gwine ter be down dar."

"Who Miss Sally gwine put in de house?" Aunt Tempy asked.

"Humph!" exclaimed 'Tildy, scornfully, "Miss Sally say she gwine take dat ar Darkess[1] nigger an' put 'er in my place. An' a mighty nice

[1] Dorcas. — J. C. H.

mess Darkess gwine ter make un it! Much she know 'bout waitin' on w'ite folks! Many's an' many's de time Miss Sally'll set down in 'er rockin'-cheer an' wish fer 'Tildy — many's de time."

This was 'Tildy's grievance — the idea that someone could be found to fill her place; and it is a grievance with which people of greater importance than the humble Negro house-girl are more or less familiar.

But the preparations for the holidays went on in spite of 'Tildy's grievance. A large platform, used for sunning wheat and seed cotton, was arranged by the Negroes for their dance, and several wagon-loads of resinous pine — known as lightwood — were placed around about it in little heaps, so that the occasion might lack no element of brilliancy.

At nightfall the heaps of lightwood were set on fire, and the little boy, who was waiting impatiently for Uncle Remus to come for him, could hear the Negroes singing, dancing, and laughing. He was just ready to cry when he heard the voice of his venerable partner.

"Is dey a'er passenger anywhar's 'roun' yer fer Thumptown? De stage done ready en de hosses a-prancin'. Ef dey's a'er passenger 'roun' yer, I lay he des better be makin' ready fer ter go."

The old man walked up to the back piazza as he spoke, held out his strong arms, and the little boy jumped into them with an exclamation of delight. The child's mother gave Uncle Remus a shawl to wrap around the child, and this shawl was the cause of considerable trouble, for the youngster persisted in wrapping it around the old man's head, and so blinding him that there was danger of his falling. Finally, he put the little boy down, took off his hat, raised his right hand, and said:

"Now, den, I bin a-beggin' un you fer ter quit yo' 'havishness des long ez I'm a-gwine ter, en I ain't gwine beg you no mo', kaze I'm des teeto-tally wo' out wid beggin', en de mo' I begs de wuss you gits. Now I'm done! You des go yo' ways en I'll go mine, en my way lays right spang back ter de big house whar Miss Sally is. Dat's whar I'm a-gwine!"

Uncle Remus started to the house with an exaggerated vigor of movement comical to behold; but, however comical it may have been, it had its effect. The little boy ran after him, caught him by the hand, and made him stop.

"Now, Uncle Remus, *please* don't go back. I was just playing."

Uncle Remus's anger was all pretense, but he managed to make it very impressive.

"My playin' days done gone too long ter talk 'bout. W'en I plays, I plays wid wuk, dat w'at I plays wid."

"Well," said the child, who had tactics of his own, "if I can't play with you, I don't know who I am to play with."

This touched Uncle Remus in a very tender spot. He stopped in the path, took off his spectacles, wiped the glasses on his coat-tail, and said very emphatically:

"Now den, honey, des lissen at me. How de name er goodness kin you call dat playin', w'ich er little mo' en I'd er fell down on top er my head, en broke my neck en yone too?"

The child promised that he would be very good, and Uncle Remus picked him up, and the two made their way to where the Negroes had congregated. They were greeted with cries of "Dar's Unk' Remus." "Howdy, Unk' Remus!" "Yer dey is!" "Ole man Remus don't sing; but w'en he do sing — gentermens! des go 'way!"

All this and much more, so that when Uncle Remus had placed the little boy upon a corner of the platform, and made him comfortable, he straightened himself with a laugh and cried out:

"Howdy, boys! howdy all! I des come up fer ter jine in wid you fer one roun' fer de sakes er ole times, ef no mo'."

"I boun' fer Unk' Remus!" someone said. "Now des hush en let Unk' Remus 'lone!" exclaimed another.

The figure of the old man, as he stood smiling upon the crowd of Negroes, was picturesque in the extreme. He seemed to be taller than all the rest; and, notwithstanding his venerable appearance, he moved and spoke with all the vigor of youth. He had always exercised authority over his fellow-servants. He had been the captain of the corn-pile, the stoutest at the log-rolling, the swiftest with the hoe, the neatest with the plough, and the plantation hands still looked upon him as their leader.

Some Negro from the River place had brought a fiddle, and, though it was a very feeble one, its screeching seemed to annoy Uncle Remus.

"Put up dat ar fiddle!" he exclaimed, waving his hand. "Des put 'er up; she sets my toof on aidje. Put 'er up en less go back ter ole times. Dey ain't no room fer no fiddle 'roun' yer, kaze w'en you gits me started dat ar fiddle won't be nowhars."

"Dat's so," said the man with the fiddle, and the irritating instrument was laid aside.

"Now, den," Uncle Remus went on, "dey's a little chap yer dat you'll all come ter know mighty well one er deze odd-come-shorts, en dish yer little chap ain't got so mighty long fer ter set up 'long wid us. Dat bein' de case we oughter take'n put de bes' foot fo'mus' fer ter commence wid."

"You lead, Unk' Remus! You des lead en we'll foller."

Thereupon the old man called to the best singers among the Negroes and made them stand near him. Then he raised his right hand to his ear and stood perfectly still. The little boy thought he was listening for something, but presently Uncle Remus began to slap himself gently with his left hand, first upon the leg and then upon the breast. The other Negroes kept time to this by a gentle motion of their feet, and finally, when the thump — thump — thump of this movement had regulated itself to suit the old man's fancy, he broke out with what may be called a Christmas dance song.

His voice was strong, and powerful, and sweet, and its range was as astonishing as its volume. More than this, the melody to which he tuned it, and which was caught up by a hundred voices almost as sweet and as powerful as his own, was charged with a mysterious and pathetic tenderness.

The fine company of men and women at the big house — men and women who had made the tour of all the capitals of Europe — listened with swelling hearts and with tears in their eyes as the song rose and fell upon the air — at one moment a tempest of melody, at another a heartbreaking strain breathed softly and sweetly to the gentle winds. The song that the little boy and the fine company heard was something like this — ridiculous enough when put in cold type, but powerful and thrilling when joined to the melody with which the Negroes had invested it:

MY HONEY, MY LOVE

Hit's a mighty fur ways up de Far'well Lane,
 My honey, my love!
You may ax Mister Crow, you may ax Mr. Crane,
 My honey, my love!

Dey'll make you a bow, en dey'll tell you de same,
    My honey, my love!
Hit's a mighty fur ways fer to go in de night,
    My honey, my love!
My honey, my love, my heart's delight —
    My honey, my love!

Mister Mink, he creep twel he wake up de snipe,
    My honey, my love!
Mister Bull-Frog holler, "Come-a-light my pipe,"
    My honey, my love!
En de Pa'tridge ax, "Ain't yo' peas ripe?"
    My honey, my love!
Better not walk erlong dar much atter night,
    My honey, my love!
My honey, my love, my heart's delight —
    My honey, my love!

De Bully-Bat fly mighty close ter de groun',
    My honey, my love!
Mister Fox, he coax 'er, "Do come down!"
    My honey, my love!
Mister Coon, he rack all 'roun' en 'roun',
    My honey, my love!
In de darkes' night, oh, de nigger, he's a sight!
    My honey, my love!
My honey, my love, my heart's delight —
    My honey, my love!

Oh, flee, Miss Nancy, flee ter my knee,
    My honey, my love!
'Lev'm big fat coons lives in one tree,
    My honey, my love!
Oh, ladies all, won't you marry me?
    My honey, my love!

Tu'n lef', tu'n right, we 'ull dance all night,
   My honey, my love!
My honey, my love, my heart's delight —
   My honey, my love!

De big Owl holler en cry fer his mate,
   My honey, my love!
Oh, don't stay long! Oh, don't stay late!
   My honey, my love!
Hit ain't so mighty fur ter de Good-by Gate,
   My honey, my love!
Whar we all got ter go w'en we sing out de night,
   My honey, my love!
My honey, my love, my heart's delight —
   My honey, my love!

After a while the song was done, and other songs were sung; but it was not long before Uncle Remus discovered that the little boy was fast asleep. The old man took the child in his arms and carried him to the big house, singing softly in his ear all the way; and somehow or other the song seemed to melt and mingle in the youngster's dreams. He thought he was floating in the air, while somewhere near all the Negroes were singing, Uncle Remus's voice above all the rest; and then, after he had found a resting-place upon a soft warm bank of clouds, he thought he heard the songs renewed. They grew fainter and fainter in his dreams until at last (it seemed) Uncle Remus leaned over him and sang

Good Night.

III

The tales from

Daddy Jake,
the Runaway

And Short Stories Told After Dark

With illustrations by
EDWARD WINDSOR KEMBLE

1
Crazy Sue's Story[1]

THE CHILDREN had a good supper, and they would have gone to sleep directly afterward, but the thought of going home with Daddy Jake kept them awake. Randall managed to tell Daddy Jake, out of hearing of the children, that Dr. Gaston and some of his Negroes had been seen at Ross's mill that morning

"Well," said Daddy Jake, "I bleedzd ter beat Marster home. Ef he go back dar widout de chillun my mistiss'll drap right dead on de flo'." This was his only comment.

Around the fire the Negroes laughed and joked, and told their adventures. Lillian felt comfortable and happy, and as for Lucien, he himself felt a hero. He had found Daddy Jake, and now he was going to carry him back home.

Once, when there was a lull in the talk, Lillian asked why the frogs made so much fuss.

"I speck it's kaze dey er mad wid Mr. Rabbit," said Crazy Sue. "Dey er tryin' der best ter drive 'im out'n de swamp."

"What are they mad with the Rabbit for?" asked Lucien, thinking there might be a story in the explanation.

"Hit's one er dem ole-time fusses," said Crazy Sue. "Hit's most too ole ter talk about."

"Don't you know what the fuss was about?" asked Lucien.

"Well," said Crazy Sue, "one time Mr. Rabbit an' Mr. Coon live close ter one anudder in de same neighborhoods. How dey does now, I ain't a-tellin' you; but in dem times dey wa'n't no hard feelin's 'twix' um. Dey des went 'long like two ole cronies. Mr. Rabbit, he wuz a fisherman, and Mr. Coon, he wuz a fisherman — "

1 This story, which I have titled "Crazy Sue's Story," appears in the longer story entitled *Daddy Jake, the Runaway*. While it is not properly an Uncle Remus story, it is so closely related to these that I felt it should be included. The tale of Brer Coon and the frogs was told by Crazy Sue, a runaway slave in hiding, to Lucien and Lillian, two children from the Gaston plantation, who had come in search of their beloved Daddy Jake, also a runaway at the time. — R. C.

"And put um in pens," said Lillian, remembering an old rhyme she had heard.

"No, honey, dey ain't no William-Come-Trimbletoe in dis. Mr. Rabbit an' Mr. Coon wuz bofe fishermans, but Mr. Rabbit, he kotch fish, an' Mr. Coon, he fished fer frogs. Mr. Rabbit, he had mighty good luck, an' Mr. Coon, he had mighty bad luck. Mr. Rabbit, he got fat an' slick, an' Mr. Coon, he got po' an' sick.

"Hit went on dis a-way tell one day Mr. Coon meet Mr. Rabbit in de big road. Dey shook han's, dey did, an' den Mr. Coon, he 'low:

"'Brer Rabbit, whar you git sech a fine chance er fish?'

"Mr. Rabbit laugh an' say: 'I kotch um out'n de river, Brer Coon. All I got ter do is ter bait my hook,' sezee.

"Den Mr. Coon shake his head an' 'low: 'Den how come I ain't ketch no frogs?'

"Mr. Rabbit sat down in de road an' scratched fer fleas, an' den he 'low: 'Hit's kaze you done make um all mad, Brer Coon. One time in de dark er de moon, you slipped down ter de branch an' kotch de ole King Frog; an' ever sence dat time, w'enever you er passin' by, you kin year um sing out, fus' one an' den anudder — *Yer he come! Dar he goes! Hit 'im in de eye; hit 'im in de eye! Mash 'im an' smash 'im; mash 'im an' smash 'im!* Yasser, dat w'at dey say. I year um constant, Brer Coon, an' dat des w'at dey say.'

"Den Mr. Coon up an' say: 'Ef dat de way dey gwine on, how de name er goodness kin I ketch um, Brer Rabbit? I bleedzd ter have sump'n' ter eat fer me an' my fambly connection.'

"Mr. Rabbit sorter grin in de cornder er his mouf, an' den he say: 'Well, Brer Coon, bein' ez you bin so sociable 'long wid me, an' ain't never showed yo' toofies w'en I pull yo' tail, I'll des whirl in an' he'p you out.'

"Mr. Coon, he say: 'Thanky, thanky-do, Brer Rabbit.'

"Mr. Rabbit hung his fish on a tree lim', an' say: 'Now, Brer Coon, you bleedzd ter do des like I tell you.'

"Mr. Coon 'lowed dat he would ef de Lord spared 'im.

"Den Mr. Rabbit say: 'Now, Brer Coon, you des rack down yander, an' git on de big san'-bar 'twix' de river an' de branch. W'en you git dar you mus' stagger like you sick, and den you mus' whirl roun' an' roun' an drap down like you dead. Atter you drap down, you must sorter jerk yo' legs once er twice, an' den you mus' lay right still. Ef fly light on yo' nose, let 'im stay dar. Don't move; don't wink yo' eye; don't switch yo' tail. Des lay right dar, an' 'twon't be long 'fo' you year fum me. Yit don't you move till I give you word.'

"Mr. Coon, he paced off, he did, an' done des like Mr. Rabbit tol' 'im. He staggered roun' on de san'-bank, an' den he drapped down dead. At-ter so long a time, Mr. Rabbit come lopin' 'long, an' soon's he git dar, he squall out, 'Coon dead!' Dis roust'd de frogs, an' dey stuck dey heads up fer ter see what all de rippit wuz 'bout. One great green un up an' holler, *What de matter? What de matter?* He talk like he got a bad col'.

"Mr. Rabbit 'low: 'Coon dead!'

"Frog say: *Don't believe it! Don't believe it!*

"N'er frog say: *Yes, he is! Yes, he is!* Little bit er one say: *No, he ain't! No, he ain't!*

"Dey kep' on 'sputin' an' sputin', tell bimeby hit look like all de frogs in de neighborhoods wuz dar. Mr. Rabbit look like he ain't a-yearin' ner a-keerin' w'at dey do er say. He sot dar in de san' like he gwine in mournin' fer Mr. Coon. De Frogs kep' gittin' closer an' closer. Mr. Coon, he ain't move. W'en a fly'd git on 'im Mr. Rabbit he'd bresh 'im off.

"Bimeby he 'low: 'Ef you want ter git 'im outen de way, now's yo' time, Cousin Frogs. Des whirl in an' bury him deep in de san'.'

"Big ole Frog say: *How we gwine ter do it? How we gwine ter do it?*

"Mr. Rabbit 'low: 'Dig de san' out fum under 'im an' let 'im down in de hole.'

"Den de Frogs dey went ter work sho nuff. Dey mus' a' bin a hundred un um, an' dey make dat san' fly, mon. Mr. Coon, he ain't move. De Frogs,

dey dig an' scratch in de san' tell atter while dey had a right smart hole, an' Mr. Coon wuz down in dar.

"Bimeby big Frog holler: *Dis deep nuff? Dis deep nuff?*

"Mr. Rabbit 'low: 'Kin you jump out?'

"Big Frog say: *Yes, I kin! Yes, I kin!*

"Mr. Rabbit say: 'Den 'tain't deep nuff.'

"Den de Frogs dey dig an' dey dig, tell, bimeby, Big Frog say: *Dis deep nuff? Dis deep nuff?*

Mr. Rabbit 'low: 'Kin you jump out?'

"Big Frog say: *I dess kin! I dess kin!*

"Mr. Rabbit say: 'Dig it deeper.'

"De Frogs keep on diggin' twel bimeby, big Frog holler out: *Dis deep nuff? Dis deep nuff?*

"Mr. Rabbit 'low: 'Kin you jump out?

"Big Frog say: *No, I can't! No, I can't! Come he'p me! Come he'p me!*

"Mr. Rabbit bust out laughin', an' holler out:

"'RISE UP, SANDY, AN' GIT YO' MEAT!' an' Mr. Coon riz."

2
How a Witch Was Caught[2]

THE LITTLE BOY sat in a high chair and used his legs as drumsticks, much to the confusion of Uncle Remus, as it appeared. After a while the old man exclaimed

"Well, my goodness en de gracious! how you ever in de roun' worl' er anywheres else speck me fer ter make any headway in tellin' a tale w'iles all dish yer racket gwine on? I don't want ter call nobody's pa, kaze he mos' allers talks too loud, en if I call der ma 'twon't make so mighty much difference, kaze she done got so usen ter it dat she dunner w'en dey er makin' any fuss. I believe dat ef everything wuz ter git right good en still on deze premises des one time, you' ma would e'en about die wid de headache. Anyway, she'd be mighty sick, bekaze she ain't usen ter not havin' no fuss, en she des couldn't git 'long widout it.

"I tell you right now, I'd be afeard fer ter tell any tale 'roun' yer, kaze de fus' news I know'd I'd git my eyes put out, er my leg broke, er sump'n' n'er. I knows deze yer white chillun, mon! dat I does; I knows um. Dey'll git de upper hand er de niggers ef de Lord spar's um. En he mos' inginer'lly spar's um.

"Well, now, ef you want ter year dish yer tale w'at I bin tu'nin' over in my min' you des got ter come en set right yer in front er me, whar I kin keep my two eyes on you; kaze I ain't gwine ter take no resks er no foolishness. Now, den, you des better behave, bekaze hit don't cost me nothin' fer ter cut dis tale right short off.

"One time der wuz a miller man w'at live by a river en had a mill. He wuz a mighty smart man. He tuck so much toll dat he tuck'n buyed 'im a house, en he want ter rent dat ar house out ter folks, but de folks dey 'lowed dat de house wuz ha'nted. Dey'd come en rent de house, dey would, en move in dar, en den go upsta'rs en go ter bed. Dey'd go ter bed, dey would, but dey couldn't sleep, en time it got day dey'd git out er dat house.

"De miller man, he ax'd um w'at de matter wuz, but dey des shuck

---

2 See "Sop Doll!" in *The Jack Tales,* and notes on this tale. The tale is widespread. — R. C.

der head en 'low de house wuz ha'nted. Den he tuck'n try ter fin' out w'at kind er ha'nt she wuz dat skeer folks. He sleep in de house, but he ain't see nothin', en de mos' w'at he year wuz a big ole gray cat a-promenadin' roun' en hollerin'. Bimeby hit got so dat dey wa'n't no fun in havin' de ha'nted house, en w'en folks'd come 'long de miller man, he'd des up en tell um dat de house 'uz ha'nted. Some 'ud go up en some wouldn't, but dem w'at went up didn't stay, kaze des 'bout bedtime dey'd fetch a yell en des come a-rushin' down, en all de money in de Nunited States er Georgy wouldn't git um fer ter go back up dar.

"Hit went on dis a-way twel one time a preacher man com' 'long dar en say he wanted somers ter stay. He was a great big man, en he look like he wuz good accordin'. De miller man say he hate mighty bad for to dis-commerdate 'im, but he des p'intedly ain't got no place whar he kin put 'im 'cep' dat ar ha'nted house. De preacher man say he des soon stay dar ez anywhar's, kaze he bin livin' in deze low-groun's er sorrer too long fer ter be sot back by any one-hoss ha'nts. De miller man 'lowed dat he wuz afeard de ha'nts 'ud worry 'im might'ly, but de preacher man 'low, he did, dat he use ter bein' worried, en he up en tell de miller man dat he'd a heap rather stay in de house wid de ha'nt, no matter how big she is, dan ter stay outdoors in de rain.

"So de miller man, he 'low he ain't got no mo' 'pology fer ter make, bekaze ef de preacher man wuz ready fer ter face de ha'nts and set up dar en out blink um, dey wouldn't be nobody in de roun' worl' no glad-der dan 'im. Den de miller man showed de preacher man how ter git in de house en had 'im a great big fier built. En atter de miller man wuz done gone, de preacher man drawed a cheer up ter de fier en waited fer de ha'nts, but dey ain't no ha'nts come. Den w'en dey ain't no ha'nts come, de preacher man tuck 'n open up he satchel en got 'im out some spar' ribs en sot um by de fier fer ter cook, en den he got down en said he pra'rs, en den he got up en read he Bible. He wuz a mighty good man, mon, en he prayed en read a long time. Bimeby, w'en his spar' ribs git done, he got some bread out'n he satchel, en fixed fer ter eat his supper.

"By de time he got all de meat off'n one er de ribs, de preacher man listened, en he year'd a monstus scramblin' en scratchin' on de wall. He look 'roun', he did, en dar wuz a great big black cat a-sharpenin' 'er claws on de door facin'. Folks, don't talk! dat ar cat wuz er sight! Great

long w'ite toofs en great big yaller eye-balls a-shinin' like dey wuz lit up
way back in 'er head. She stood dar a minnit, dat ole black cat did, en
den she 'gun ter sidle up like she wuz gwine ter mount dat preacher man

right dar en den. But de preacher man, he des shoo'd at 'er, en it seem
like dis sorter skeer'd 'er, kaze she went off.

"But de preacher man, he kep' his eye open, en helt on ter his spar'
rib. Present'y he year de ole black cat comin' back, en dis time she fotch
wid 'er a great big gang er cats. Dey wuz all black des like she wuz, en
der eye-balls *shineded* en der lashes wuz long en w'ite. Hit look like de
preacher man wuz a-gwine ter git surroundered.

"Dey come a-sidlin' up, dey did, en de ole black cat made a pass at
de preacher man like she wuz a-gwine ter t'ar he eyes out. De preacher
man dodged, but de nex' pass she made de preacher man fotch 'er wipe
with his spar' rib en cut off one er 'er toes. Wid dat de ole black cat fotch

a yell dat you might a yeard a mile, en den she gin 'erself a sort er a twis' en made her disappearance up de chimbley, en w'en she do dat all de yuther cats made der disappearance up de chimbley. De preacher man he got up, he did, en looked und' de bed fer ter see ef he kin fin' any mo' cats, but dey wuz all done gone.

"Den he tuck'n pick up de cat toe w'at he done knock off wid de spar' rib, en wrop it up in a piece er paper en put it in he pocket. Den he say his pra'rs some mo', en went ter bed en slep' right straight along twel broad daylight, en nothin' ain't dast ter bodder 'im.

"Nex' mornin' de preacher man got up, he did, en say his pra'rs en eat his brekkus, en den he 'low ter hisse'f dat he'll go by en tell de miller man dat he mighty much erblige. 'Fo' he start, hit come 'cross he min' 'bout de cats w'at pester 'im de night befo', and he tuck'n feel in he pockets fer de big black cat toe he done cut off wid de spar' rib. But it seems like de toe done grow in de night, en bless goodness! when he unwrop it 'twa'n't nothin' less dan a great big finger wid a ring on it.

"So de preacher man tuck'n fix up all his contrapments, en den call on de miller man en tol' 'im he wuz mighty much erblige kaze he let 'im stay in de house. De miller man wuz 'stonish' fer ter see de preacher man, kaze he knew dat w'en folks stay all night in dat house dey ain't come down no mo'. He wuz 'stonish', but he didn't say much. He des stan' still en wunder.

"But de preacher man, he up 'n ax 'bout de miller man's wife, en say he wants ter see 'er en tell 'er good-by, bein' ez how dey'd all bin so good. So de miller man, he tuck'n kyar de preacher inter de room whar his wife wuz layin' in bed. De ole 'oman had de counterpin drawed up und' 'er chin, but she look mighty bad roun' de eyes. Yit, she tuck'n howdied de preacher man en tol' 'im he wuz mighty welcome.

"Dey talk en talk, dey did, en atter w'ile de preacher man hol' out his han' fer ter tell de 'oman good-by; but de 'oman, she helt out 'er lef han', she did, like she want dat fer ter git shucken. But de preacher man wouldn't shake dat un. He say dat ain't nigh gwine ter do, bekaze w'en folks got any perliteness lef dey don't never hol' out de lef han'. De 'oman she say her right wuz cripple, but her ole man 'low he ain't never hear 'bout dat befo', en den he tuck'n make 'er pull it out from und' de kivver, en den dey seed dat one er 'er fingers wuz done clean gone. De miller man he up'n 'low:

"'How come dis?'

"De 'oman she 'low, 'I cut it off.'

"De miller man he 'low, 'How you cut it off?'

"De 'oman she 'low, 'I knock it off.'

"De miller man he 'low, 'Whar'bouts you knock it off?'

"De 'oman she 'low, 'I broke it off.'

"De miller man he 'low, 'When you break it off?'

"Den de 'oman she ain't say nothin'. She des lay dar, she did, en pant en look skeered. De preacher man he study a little en den he say he speck he kin kyo' dat han', en he tuck de finger out'n he pocket en tried it on de 'oman's han', en it fit! Yasser! it fit in de place right smick smack smoove. Den de preacher man he up en tell de miller man dat de 'oman wuz a witch, en wid dat de 'oman fetched a yell en kivvered 'er head wid de counterpin.

"Yit dis ain't do 'er no good, kaze de preacher man say he done look in de books en de onliest way fer ter kyo' a witch is ter bu'n 'er; en it ain't look so bad, nuther, kaze w'en dey tied 'er she tuck'n tu'n ter be a great big black cat, en dat's de way she wuz w'en she wuz burnt."

3
The Little Boy and His Dogs

UNCLE REMUS'S little patron seemed to be so shocked at the burning of the woman that the old man plunged at once into a curious story about a little boy and his two dogs.

"One time," said Uncle Remus, scratching his head as if by that means to collect his scattered ideas, "dere wuz a 'oman livin' 'longside er de big road, en dish yer 'oman she had one little boy. Seem like ter me dat he mus' a' bin des 'bout yo' size. He mought a bin a little broader in de shoulder en a little longer in de leg, yit, take 'im up one side en down de udder, he wuz des 'bout yo' shape en size. He wuz a mighty smart lit- tle boy, en his mammy sot lots by 'im. Seem like she ain't never have no

luck 'ceppin' 'long wid dat boy, kaze dey wuz one time w'en she had a little gal, en, bless yo' soul! somebody come 'long en tote de little gal off,
en w'en dat happen de 'oman ain't have no mo' little gal, en de little boy
ain't have no mo' little sister. Dis make bofe er um mighty sorry, but look
like de little boy wuz de sorriest, kaze he show it de mos'est.

"Some days he'd take a notion fer ter go en hunt his little sister, en
den he'd go down de big road en clim' a big pine-tree, en git right spang
in de top, en look all 'roun' fer ter see ef he can't see his little sister
somers in de woods. He couldn't see 'er, but he'd stay up dar in de tree en
swing in de win' en 'low ter hisself dat maybe he mought see 'er bimeby.

"One day, w'iles he wuz a-settin' up dar, he see two mighty fine ladies
walkin' down de road. He clom' down out'n de tree, he did, en run en tol'
his mammy. Den she up en ax:

"'How is dey dress, honey?'

"'Mighty fine, mammy, mighty fine, puffy-out petticoats en long
green veils.'

"'How des dey look, honey?'

"'Spick span new, mammy.'

"'Dey ain't none er our kin, is dey, honey?'

"'Dat dey ain't, mammy — dey er mighty fine ladies.'

"De fine ladies, dey come on down de road, dey did, en stop by de
'oman's house, en beg 'er fer ter please en gi' um some water. De little
boy, he run en fetch 'em a gourd full, en dey put de gourd und' der veils,
en drunk, en drunk, en drunk des like dey wuz mighty nigh perish fer
water. De little boy watch um. 'Reckly he holler out:

"'Mammy, mammy! W'at you recken? Dey er lappin' de water.' De
woman hollered back:

"'I recken dat's de way de quality folks does, honey.'

"Den de ladies beg fer some bread, en de little boy tuck um a pone.
Dey eat it like dey wuz mighty nigh famish fer bread. Bimeby de little
boy holler out en say:

"Mammy, mammy! W'at you recken? Dey er got great long tushes."
De 'oman, she holler back:

"'I recken all de quality folks is got um, honey.'

"Den de ladies ax fer some water fer to wash der han's, en de little
boy brung um some. He watch um, en bimeby he holler out:

"'Mammy, mammy! W'at you recken? Dey got little bit er hairy han's en arms.' De 'oman, she holler back:

"'I recken all de quality folks is got um, honey.'

"Den de ladies beg de 'oman fer ter please en let de little boy show um whar de big road forks. But de little boy don't want ter go. He holler out:

"Mammy, folks don't hatter be showed whar de road forks;' but de 'oman she 'low:

"'I recken de quality folks does, honey.'

"De little boy, he 'gun ter whimple en cry kaze he don't want ter go wid de ladies, but de 'oman say he oughter be 'shame er hisse'f fer ter be gwine on dat a-way 'fo' de quality folks, en mo'n dat, he mought run upon his little sister en fetch 'er home.

"Now dish yer little boy had two mighty bad dogs. One er um wuz name Minnyminny Morack, en de t'er one wuz name Follerlinsko, en dey wuz so bad dey hatter be tied in de yard day er night, 'cep' w'en dey wuz a-huntin'. So de little boy, he went en got a pan er water en sot 'im down in de middle er de flo', en den he went en got 'im a willer lim', en he stuck it in de groun'. De he 'low:

"'Mammy, w'en de water in dish yer pan tu'ns ter blood, den you run out en tu'n loose Minnyminny Morack en Follerlinsko, en den w'en you see dat dar willer lim' a-shakin', you run en sick um on my track.'

"De 'oman, she up an' say she'd tu'n de dogs loose, en den de little boy he stuck his han's in he pockets en went on down de road a wisserlin' des same ez enny yuther little boy, 'cep' dat he wuz lots smarter. He went on down de road, he did, en de fine quality ladies dey come on behin'.

"De furder he went de faster he walk. Dis make de quality ladies walk fas', too, en 'twa'n't so mighty long 'fo' de little boy year um makin' a mighty kuse fuss, en w'en he tu'n 'roun', bless gracious! dey wuz a-pantin', kaze dey wuz so tired en hot. De little boy 'low ter hisse'f dat it mighty kuse how ladies kin pant same es a wil' varmint, but he say he speck dat de way de quality ladies does w'en dey gits hot en tired, en he make like he can't year um, kaze he want ter be nice en perlite.

"Atter a w'ile, w'en de quality ladies t'ink de little boy wa'n't lookin' at um, he seed one er um drap down on 'er all-fours en trot 'long des like a varmint, en 'twa'n't long 'fo' de yuther one drapt down on 'er all-fours. Den de little boy 'lowed:

"'*Shoo!* Ef dat de way quality ladies res' derse'f w'en dey git tired I reckon a little chap 'bout my size better be fixin' fer ter res' hisse'f.'

"So he look 'roun', he did, en he tuck'n pick 'im out a great big pine-tree by de side er de road, en 'gun to clim' it. Den w'en dey see dat, one er de quality ladies 'low:

"'My goodness! W'at in de worl' you up ter now?' Little boy he say, sezee:

"'I'm des a-climin' a tree fer ter res' my bones.' Ladies, dey 'low:

"'Whyn't you res' um on de groun'?' Little boy say, sezee:

"'Bekaze I like ter git up whar it cool en high.'

"De quality ladies, dey tuck'n walk 'roun' en 'roun' de tree like dey wuz medjun it fer ter see how big it is. Bimeby, atter w'ile dey say, sez dey:

"'Little boy, little boy! you better come down fum dar en show us de way ter de forks er de road.' Den de little boy 'low:

"'Des keep right on, ladies — you'll fin' de forks er de road; you can't miss um. I'm afeard fer ter come down, kaze I might fall en hurt some er you all.' De ladies dey say, sez dey:

"'You'd better come down yer 'fo' we run en tell yo' mammy how bad you is.' De little boy 'low:

"'W'iles you er tellin' 'er please'm tell 'er how skeer'd I is.'

"Den de quality ladies got mighty mad. Dey walked 'roun' dat tree en fairly snorted. Dey pulled off der bonnets, en der veils, en der dresses, en, lo en beholes! de little boy seen dey wuz two great big pant'ers. Dey had great big eyes, en big sharp tushes, en great long tails, en dey look up at de little boy en growl en grin at 'im twel he come mighty nigh havin' a chill. Dey tried ter clim' de tree, but dey had done trim der claws so dey could git on gloves, en dey couldn't clim' no mo'.

"Den one er um sot down in de road en made a kuse mark in de san', en der great long tails tu'n'd ter axes, en no sooner is der tails tu'n ter axes den dey 'gun ter cut de tree down. I ain't dast ter tell you how sharp dem axes wuz, kaze you wouldn't nigh b'lieve me. One er um stood on one side er de tree, en de yuther one stood on de yuther side, en dey whack at dat tree like dey wuz takin' a holiday. Dey whack out chips ez big ez yo' hat, en 'twa'n't so mighty long 'fo' de tree wuz ready fer ter fall.

"But w'iles de little boy wuz settin' up dar, skeer'd mighty nigh ter deff, hit come inter his min' dat he had some eggs in his pocket w'at he done brung wid 'im fer ter eat w'enever he git hongry. He tuck out one er de eggs en broke it, en say: 'Place, fill up!' en bless yo' soul! de place fill up sho nuff, en de tree look des zackly like nobody ain't bin a-cuttin' on it.

"But dem ar pant'ers dey wuz werry vig'rous. Dey des spit on der han's en cut away. W'en dey git de tree mighty nigh cut down de little boy he pull out 'n'er egg en broke it, en say, 'Place, fill up!' en by de time he say it de tree wuz done made soun' ag'in. Dey kep' on dis a-way twel de little boy 'gun ter git skeer'd ag'in. He done broke all he eggs, ceppin' one, en dem ar creeturs wuz des a-cuttin' away like dey wuz venomous, w'ich dey mos' sholy wuz.

"Des 'bout dat time de little boy mammy happen ter stumble over de pan er water w'at wuz settin' down on de flo', en dar it wuz all done tu'n ter blood. Den she tuck'n run en onloose Minnyminny Morack en Follerlinsko. Den w'en she do dat she see de willer lim' a'shakin', en den she put de dogs on de little boy track, en away dey went. De little boy year um a-comin', en he holler out:

"'Come on, my good dogs. Here, dogs, here.'

"De pant'ers dey stop choppin' en lissen. One ax de yuther one w'at she year. Little boy say:

"'You don' year nothin'. Go on wid yo' choppin'.'

"De pant'ers dey chop some mo', en den dey think dey year de dogs a-comin'. Den dey try der bes' fer ter git away, but 'twa'n't no use. Dey ain't got time fer ter change der axes back inter tails, en co'se dey can't run wid axes draggin' behin' um. So de dogs kotch um. De little boy, he 'low:

"'Shake um en bite um. Drag um 'roun' en 'roun' twel you drag um two mile.' So de dogs dey drag um 'roun' two mile. Den de little boy say, sezee:

"'Shake um en t'ar um. Drag um 'roun' en 'roun' twel you drag um ten mile.' So dey drag um ten mile, en by de time dey got back, de pant'ers wuz col' en stiff.

"Den de little boy clom' down out'n de tree, en sot down fer ter res' hisse'f. Bimeby atter w'ile, he 'low ter hisse'f dat bein' he have so much fun, he b'lieve he takes his dogs en go way off in de woods fer ter see ef he can't fin' his little sister. He call his dogs, he did, en went off in de woods, en dey ain't bin gone so mighty fur 'fo' he seed a house in de woods away off by itse'f.

"De dogs dey went up en smelt 'roun', dey did, en come wid der bristles

up, but de little boy 'low he'd go up dar anyhow en see w'at de dogs wuz
mad 'bout. So he call de dogs en went todes de house, en when he got
close up he saw a little gal totin' wood en water. She wuz a mighty purty
little gal, kaze she had a milk-white skin, en great long yaller hair; but
'er cloze wuz all in rags, en she wuz cryin' kaze she hatter work so hard.
Minnyminny Morack en Follerlinsko wagged der tails w'en dey seed de
little gal, en de little boy know'd by dat dat she wuz his sister.

"So he went up en ax 'er w'at 'er name is, en she say she dunner w'at
'er name is, kaze she so skeer'd she done fergit. Den he ax 'er w'at de
name er goodness she cryin' 'bout, en she say she cryin' kaze she hatter
work so hard. Den he ax 'er who de house belong ter, en she 'low it b'long
ter a great big ole black B'ar, en dis old B'ar make 'er tote wood en water all de time. She say de water is ter go in de big wash-pot, en de wood
is fer ter make de pot bile, en de pot wuz ter cook folks w'at de great big
ole B'ar brung home ter he chilluns.

"De little boy didn't tell de little gal dat he wuz 'er br'er, but he 'low
dat he was gwine ter stay en eat supper wid de big ole B'ar. De little girl
cried en 'low he better not, but de little boy say he ain't feared fer ter eat
supper wid a B'ar. So dey went in de house, en w'en de little boy got in
dar, he seed dat de B'ar had two great big chilluns, en one er um wuz
squattin' on de bed, en de yuther one wuz squattin' down in de h'a'th. De
chilluns, dey wuz bofe er um name Cubs, fer short, but de little boy
wa'n't skeer'd er um, kaze dar wuz his dogs fer ter make way wid um ef
dey so much ez roll der eye-ball.

"De ole B'ar wuz a mighty long time comin' back, so de little gal she
up'n fix supper, anyhow, en de little boy he tuck'n scrouge Cubs fus' on
one side en den on yuther, en him en de little gal got much ez dey want.
Atter supper de little boy tol' de little gal dat he'd take en comb 'er ha'r
des ter w'ile away de time; but de little gal ha'r ain't bin comb fer so long,
en it am got in such a tankle, dat it make de po' creetur cry fer ter year
anybody talkin' 'bout combin' un it. Den de little boy 'low he ain't gwine
ter hurt 'er, en he tuck 'n warm some water in a pan en put it on 'er ha'r,
en den he comb en curlt it des ez nice as you mos' ever see.

"W'en de ole B'ar git home he wuz mighty tuck'n back w'en he seed
he had com'ny, en w'en he see um all settin' down like dey come dar fer
ter stay. But he wuz mighty perlite, en he shuck han's all 'roun', en set

down by de fier en dry his boots, en ax 'bout de craps, en 'low dat de wedder would be monstus fine ef dey could git a little season er rain.

"Den he tuck'n make a great 'miration over de little gal's ha'r, en he
ax de little boy how in de 'roun' worl' kin he curl it en fix it so nice. De
little un 'low it's easy nuff. Den de ole B'ar say he b'lieve he like ter git
his ha'r curlt up dat way, en de little boy say:

"'Fill de big pot wid water.'

"De ole B'ar filled de pot wid water. Den de little boy say:

"'Buil' a fier und' de pot en heat de water hot.'

"W'en de water got scaldin' hot, de little boy say:

"'All ready, now. Stick yo' head in. Hit's de onliest way fer ter make
yo' ha'r curl.'

"Den de ole B'ar stuck he head in de water, en dat wuz de las' er him,
bless gracious! De scaldin' water curlt de h'ar twel it come off, en I speck
dat whar dey get de idee 'bout puttin' b'ar grease on folks' ha'r. De young
b'ars dey cry like eve'thing w'en dey see how der daddy bin treated, en

dey want bite and scratch de little boy en his sister, but dem dogs — dat Minnyminny Morack en dat Follerlinsko — dey des laid holt er dem dar b'ars, en dey wa'n't enough lef' er um ter feed a kitten."

"What did they do then?" asked the little boy who had been listening to the story. The old man took off his spectacles and cleaned the glasses on his coat-tail.

"Well, sir," he went on, "de little boy tuck'n kyar'd his sister home, an' his mammy says she ain't never gwine ter set no sto' by folks wid fine cloze, kaze dey so 'ceitful; no, never, so long as de Lord mought spar' 'er. En den, atter dat, dey tuck'n live terge'er right straight 'long, en ef it hadn't but a bin fer de war, dey'd a bin a-livin' dar now. Bekaze war is a mighty dangersome business."

4
How Black Snake Caught the Wolf

"ONE TIME," said Uncle Remus, putting the "noses" of the chunks together with his cane, so as to make a light in his cabin, "Brer Rabbit en ole Brer Wolf wuz gwine down de road terge'er, en Brer Wolf, he 'low dat times wus mighty hard en money skace. Brer Rabbit, he 'gree 'long wid 'im, he did, dat times wuz mighty tight, en he up en say dat 'twuz e'en about much ez he kin do fer ter make bofe en's meet. He 'low, he did:

"'Brer Wolf, you er gittin' mighty ga'nt, t'won't be so mighty long 'fo' we'll hatten be tuck up en put in de po'-house. W'at make dis?' says Brer Rabbit, sezee. 'I be bless ef I kin tell, kaze yer er all de creeturs gittin' ga'nt w'iles all de reptules is a-gittin' seal fat. No longer'n yistiddy, I wuz comin' along thoo de woods, w'en who should I meet but ole Brer Snake, en he wuz dat put dat he ain't kin skacely pull he tail 'long atter he head. I 'low ter mese'f, I did, dat dish yer country gittin' in a mighty bad way w'en de creeturs is got ter go 'roun' wid der ribs growin' terge'er w'iles de reptules layin' up in de sun des natchully fattenin' on der own laziness. Yessar, dat w'at I 'lowed.'

"Brer Wolf, he say, he did, dat if de reptules wuz gittin' de 'vantage er de creeturs dat a-way, dat hit wuz 'bout time fer ter clean out de reptules er leaf de country, en he 'low, fuddermo', dat he wuz ready fer ter jine in wid de patter-rollers en drive um out.

"But Brer Rabbit, he 'low, he did, dat de bes' way fer ter git 'long wuz ter fin' out whar'bouts de reptules hed der smokehouse en go in dar en git some er de vittles w'at by good rights b'long'd ter de creeturs. Brer Wolf say maybe dis de bes' way, kaze ef de reptules git word dat de patter-rollers is a-comin' dey'll take en hide de gingercakes, en der 'simmon beer, en der w'atzisnames, so dat de creeturs can't git um. By dis time dey come ter de forks er de road, en Brer Rabbit he went one way, en Brer Wolf he went de yuther.

"Whar Brer Wolf went," Uncle Remus went on, with increasing gravity, "de goodness knows, but Brer Rabbit, he went on down de road todes he own house, en w'iles he wuz lippitin' long, nibblin' a bite yer en a bite dar, he year a mighty kuse fuss in de woods. He lay low, Brer Rabbit did, en lissen. He look sharp, he did, en bimeby he ketch a glimp' er ole Mr. Black Snake gwine 'long thoo de grass. Brer Rabbit, he lay low en watch 'im. Mr. Black Snake crope 'long, he did, des like he wuz greased. Brer Rabbit say ter hisse'f:

"'Hi! dar goes one er de reptules, en ez she slips she slides 'long.'

"Yit, still he lay low en watch. Mr. Black Snake crope 'long, he did, en bimeby he come whar dey wuz a great big poplar-tree. Brer Rabbit, he crope on his belly en follow 'long atter. Mr. Black Snake tuck'n circle all 'roun' de tree, en den he stop en sing out:

"'Watsilla, watsilla,
    Consario wo!
Watsilla, watsilla,
    Consario wo!'

"En den, mos' 'fo' Brer Rabbit kin wink he eye, a do' w'at wuz in de tree flew'd open, en Mr. Black Snake tuck'n crawl in. Brer Rabbit 'low, he did:

"'Ah-yi! Dar whar you stay! Dar whar you keeps yo' 'simmon beer! Dar whar you hides yo' backbone en spar' ribs. Ah-yi!'

"W'en Mr. Black Snake went in de house, Brer Rabbit crope up, he did, en lissen fer ter see w'at he kin year gwine on in dar. But he ain't year nothin'. Bimeby, w'iles he settin' 'roun' dar, he year de same song:

"'Watsilla, watsilla,
      Consario wo!
   Watsilla, watsilla,
      Consario wo!'

"En mos' 'fo' Brer Rabbit kin hide in de weeds, de do' hit flew'd open, en out Mr. Black Snake slid. He slid out, he did, en slid off, en atter he git out er sight, Brer Rabbit, he tuck 'n went back ter de poplar-tree fer ter see ef he kin git in dar. He hunt 'roun' en he hunt 'roun', en yit ain't fin' no do'. Den he sat up on he behime legs, ole Brer Rabbit did, en 'low:

"'Hey! w'at kinder contrapshun dish yer? I seed a do' dar des now, but dey ain't no do' dar now.'

"Ole Brer Rabbit scratch he head, he did, en bimeby hit come inter he min' dat maybe de song got sump'n' n'er ter do wid it, en wid dat he chuned up, he did, en sing:

"*'Watsilla, watsilla,
      Bandario, wo-haw!'*

"Time he say fus' part, de do' sorter open, but w'en he say de las' part hit slammed shet ag'in. Den he chune up some mo':

"'Watsilla, watsilla,
      Bandario, wo-haw!'

"Time he say de fus' part de do' open little ways, but time he say de las' part hit slammed shet ag'in. Den Brer Rabbit 'low he'd hang 'roun' dar en fin' out w'at kind er hinges dat er do' wuz a-swingin' on. So he stays 'roun' dar, he did, twel bimeby Mr. Black Snake came 'long back. Brer Rabbit crope up, he did, en he year 'im sing de song:

"'Watsilla, watsilla,
      Consario wo!
   Watsilla, watsilla,
      Consario wo!'

"Den de do' open, en Mr. Black Snake, he slid in, en Brer Rabbit, he lipp'd off in de bushes en sung de song by hisse'f. Den he went home en tuck some res', en nex' day he went back; en w'en Mr. Black Snake come out en went off, Brer Rabbit, he tuck 'n sing de song, en de do' flew'd open, en in he went. He went in, he did, en w'en he got in dar, he fin' lots er goodies. He fin' cakes en sausages, en all sorts er nice doin's. Den he come out, en de nex' day he went he tol' ole Brer Wolf, en Brer Wolf, he 'low dat, bein' ez times is hard, he b'lieves he'll go 'long en sample some er Mr. Black Snake's doin's.

"Dey went, dey did, en soon ez dey fin' dat Mr. Black Snake is gone, Brer Rabbit he sing de song, en de do' open, en in he went. He went in dar, he did, en he gobbled up his bellyful, en w'iles he doin' dis Brer Wolf he gallop 'roun' en 'roun', tryin' fer ter git in. But de do' done slam shet, en Brer Wolf ain't know de song. Bimeby Brer Rabbit he come out, he did, lickin' he chops en wipin' he mustash, en Brer Fox ax 'im what de name er goodness is de reason he ain't let 'im go in 'long wid 'im.

"Brer Rabbit, he vow, he did, dat he 'spected any gump 'ud know dat somebody got ter stay outside en watch w'iles de yuther one wuz on de inside. Brer Wolf say he ain't thunk er dat, en den he ax Brer Rabbit fer ter let 'im in, en please be so good ez ter stay out dar en watch w'iles he git some er de goodies.

"Wid dat Brer Rabbit, he sung de song:

> "'Watsilla, watsilla,
> Consario wo!
> Watsilla, watsilla,
> Consario wo!'

"He sung de song, he did, en de do' flew'd open, en Brer Wolf he lipt in, en gun ter gobble up de goodies. Brer Rabbit, he stayed outside, en make like he gwine ter watch. Brer Wolf, he e't en e't, en he keep on a-eatin'. Brer Rabbit, he tuck'n stan' off in de bushes, en bimeby he year Mr. Black Snake a-slidin' thoo de grass. Brer Rabbit, he ain't say nothin'. He 'low ter hisse'f, he did, dat he was dar ter watch, en dat w'at he gwine ter do ef de good Lord spar' 'im. So he set dar en watch, en Mr. Black Snake, he come a-slidin' up ter de house en sing de song, en den de do' flew'd open en in he went.

"Brer Rabbit set dar en watch so hard, he did, dat it look like he eyes gwine to pop out. 'Twa'n't long 'fo' he year sump'n' n'er like a scuffle gwine on in de poplar-tree, en, fus' news you know, Brer Wolf come tumberlin' out. He come tumberlin' out, he did, en down he fell, kaze Mr. Black Snake got 'im tie hard en fas' so he ain't kin run.

"Den, atter so long a time, Mr. Black Snake tuck 'n tie Brer Wolf up ter a lim', en dar dat creetur swung 'twix' de hevin en de yeth. He swung

en swayed, en eve'y time he swung Mr. Black Snake tuck'n lash 'im wid he tail, en eve'y time he lash 'im Brer Rabbit holler out, he did:

"'Sarve 'im right! Sarve 'im right!'

"En I let you know," said the old man, refilling his pipe, "dat w'en Mr. Black Snake git thoo wid dat creetur, he ain't want no mo' goodies."

5

Why the Guineas Stay Awake

ONE NIGHT when the little boy was waiting patiently for Uncle Remus to tell him a story, the guineas began to scream at a great rate, and they kept it up for some time.

"Ah, Lord!" exclaimed Uncle Remus, blowing the ashes from a sweet potato that had been roasting in the embers. "Ah, Lord! dem ar creeturs is mighty kuse creeturs. I boun' you ef you go up dar whar dey is right now, you'll fin' some kind er varmint slippin' 'roun' und' de bushes. Hit mought be ole Brer Fox. I won't say p'intedly dat it's Brer Fox," the old man continued, with the air of one who is willing to assert only what he can prove, "yit it mought be. But ne'er min' 'bout dat; Brer Fox er no Brer Fox, dem guinea hens ain't gwine ter be kotch. De varmints kin creep up en slip up ez de case may be, but dey ain't gwine to slip up en ketch dem creeturs asleep."

"Don't the guineas ever sleep, Uncle Remus?" the little boy inquired. His curiosity was whetted.

"Oh, I speck dey does sleep," replied the old man. "Yasser, dey er bleedzd ter sleep, but dey ain't bin kotch at it — leastways, dey ain't bin kotch at it not sence Brer Fox crope up on um long time ago. He kotch um a-snorin' den, but he ain't kotch um sence, en he ain't gwine kotch um no mo'."

"You may go ter bed now," Uncle Remus went on, in a tone calculated to carry conviction with it, "you may go ter bed en go ter sleep right now, but wake up w'enst you will en you'll year dem guineas a-cacklin' en a confabbin' out dar des same ez ef 'twuz broad daylight. Seem like dey ain't gwine ter fergit de time w'en Brer Fox crope up on um, en kotch um 'sleep."

"When was that, Uncle Remus?" the little boy asked, as he settled himself in the split-bottom chair in anticipation of a story.

"Well," said the old man, noticing the movement, "you nee'nter primp yo'se'f fer no great long tale, honey, kaze dish yer tale ain't skacely long nuff fer ter tie a snapper on. Yit sech es 'tis you er mo' dan welcome.

"One time 'way long back yander dem guineas wuz des ez drowsy w'en night come ez any er de yuther folks. Dey'd go ter roos', dey would, en dey'd drap off ter sleep time der head totch de piller."

"The pillow, Uncle Remus!" exclaimed the little boy.

"Well," said the old man, rubbing his hand over his weather-beaten face to hide a smile, "hit's all de same. In dem days dey could a had pillers ef dey'd a-wanted um, en bolsters, too, fer dat matter, en likewise fedder-beds, kaze dey wouldn't a had ter go no fur ways fer de fedders.

"But ne'er mind 'bout dat; no sooner did dey git up on de roos' dan dey drap off ter sleep, en dey kep' on dat a-way twel bimeby one time Brer Fox made up he min' dat he better be kinder sociable en pay um a call atter dey done gone ter bed.

"Dar wuz times," continued Uncle Remus, as if endeavoring to be perfectly fair and square to all the parties concerned, "w'en Brer Fox tuck a notion fer ter walk 'bout in de daytime, but mos' allers inginer'lly he done he pomernadin' 'twix' sun-down en sun-up. I dunner w'at time er night hit wuz w'en Brer Fox call on de guineas, but I speck 'twuz long todes de shank er de evenin', ez you may say.

"Yit, soon er late, w'en he got ter whar de guineas live at, he foun' um all soun' asleep. Now, some folks w'en dey go anywhars fer ter make dey-se'f sociable, en fin' eve'ybody fas' asleep, would a tu'n 'roun' en made der way back home; but Brer Fox ain't dat kin' er man. Dem guineas roos' so low en dey look so fine en fat dat it make Brer Fox feel like dey wuz his fus' cousin.

"He sot down on his hunkers, Brer Fox did, en he look at um en grin. Den he 'low ter hisse'f:

"'I'll des shake han's wid one un um en den I'll go.'

"Well," continued Uncle Remus, "Brer Fox went up en shuck han's wid one un um, en he mus' a squoze mighty hard, kaze de guinea make a mighty flutterment; en he mus' a helt on wid a mighty tight grip, kaze w'en he tuck off his hat en bowed good-by de guinea went 'long wid 'im.

"Well, suh," said the old man solemnly, "you never is year tell er sech a racket ez dem guineas kicked up w'en dey 'skiver dat Brer Fox done make off wid one un um. Dey squall en dey squall twel dey roust'd up de whole neighborhoods. De dogs got ter barkin', de owls got ter hootin', de hosses got ter kickin', de cows got ter lowin', en de chickens got ter crowin'.

"En mo' dan dat," Uncle Remus continued, "de guineas wuz dat skeered dat dey tu'n right pale on de neck en on de gills, en ef you don't b'lieve me you kin go up dar in de gyarden en look at um fer yo'se'f."

But the little boy had no idea of going. He saw by Uncle Remus's air of preoccupation that the story was not yet concluded.

"En mo' dan dat," said the old man, after a short pause, "dey got skeer'd so bad dat from dat day ter dis dey don't sleep soun' at night. Dey may squat 'roun' in de shade en nod in de daytime, dough I ain't kotch um at it, en dey may sort er nod atter dey go ter roos' at night; but ef a betsey bug flies by um, er yit ef a sparrer flutters in de bushes, dey er wide awake; dey mos' sholy is.

"Hit seem like ter me," Uncle Remus continued, "dat dey mus' be ha'nted in der dreams by ole Brer Fox, kaze all times er night you kin year um gwine on:

"'L-o-o-o-o-k, look, look! Dar he is, dar he is! Go 'way, go 'way!'

"Some folks say dat dey holler, 'Pot-rack! pot-rack!' but dem w'at talk dat a-way is mostly white folks, en dey ain't know nothin' 'tall 'bout dem ole times. Mars John en Miss Sally mought know, but ef dey does I ain't year um sesso."

6

How the Terrapin Was Taught to Fly

UNCLE REMUS had the weakness of the genuine story-teller. When he was in the humor, the slightest hint would serve to remind him of a story, and one story would recall another. Thus, when the little boy chanced to manifest some curiosity in regard to the whippoorwill, which, according to an old song, had performed the remarkable feat of carrying the sheep's corn to mill, the old man took great pains to describe the bird, explaining, in his crude way, how it differed from the chuckwill's-widow, which is frequently mistaken for the whippoorwill, especially in the South. Among other things, he told the child how the bird could fly through the darkness and flap its wings without making the slightest noise.

The little boy had a number of questions to ask about this, and the talk about flying reminded Uncle Remus of a story. He stopped short in his explanations and began to chuckle. The little boy asked him what the matter was.

"Shoo, honey!" said the old man, "W'en you git ole ez I is, en yo' 'membunce cropes up en tickles you, you'll laugh too, dat you will. Talkin' all 'bout dish yer flyin' business fotch up in my min' de time w'en ole Brer Tarrypin boned ole Brer Buzzard fer 'ter l'arn him how ter fly. He got atter 'im, en he kep' atter 'im; he begged en 'suaded, en 'suaded en he begged. Brer Buzzard tol' 'im dat dey wuz mos' too much un 'im in one place, but Brer Tarrypin, he des kep' on atter 'im, en bimeby Brer Buzzard 'low dat ef nothin' else ain't gwine do 'im, he'll des whirl in en gin 'im some lessons in flyin' fer ole 'quaintance sakes.

"Dis make ole Brer Tarrypin feel mighty good, en he say he ready fer ter begin right now, but Brer Buzzard say he ain't got time des den, but he'll be sho en come 'roun' de nex' day en gin ole Brer Tarrypin de fus' lesson.

"Ole Brer Tarrypin, he sot dar en wait, he did, en dough he nodded year en dar thoo de night, hit look like ter 'im dat day ain't never gwine ter come. He wait en he wait, he did, but bimeby de sun riz, en 'twa'n't so mighty long atter dat 'fo' yer come Brer Buzzard sailin' 'long. He sailed 'roun' en 'roun', en eve'y time he sail 'roun' he come lower, en atter w'ile he lit.

"He lit, he did, en pass de time er day wid Brer Tarrypin en ax 'im is he ready. Brer Tarrypin 'low he been ready too long ter talk 'bout, en w'en Brer Buzzard year dis, he tuck'n squat in de grass en ax Brer Tarrypin fer ter crawl upon he back. But Brer Buzzard back mighty slick, en de mo' Brer Tarrypin try fer ter crawl up, de mo' 'ud he slip back. But he tuck'n crawl up atter w'ile, en w'en he git sorter settled down, he 'low, he did:

"'You kin start now, Brer Buzzard, but you'll hatter be mighty keerful not ter run over no rocks en stumps, kaze ef dish yer waggin gits ter joltin', I'm a goner,' sezee.

"Brer Buzzard, he tuck'n start off easy, en he move so slick en smoove en swif dat Brer Tarrypin laugh en 'low dat he ain't had no sech sweet ridin' sence he crossed de river in a flat. He sail 'roun' en 'roun', he did, en gun Brer Tarrypin a good ride, en den bimeby he sail down ter de groun' en let Brer Tarrypin slip off'n he back.

"Nex' day he come 'roun' ag'in, ole Brer Buzzard did, en gun Brer Tarrypin n'er good ride, en de nex' day he done de same, en he keep on doin' dis away, twel atter w'ile Brer Tarrypin got de consate dat he kin do some fly'n on he own hook. So he up en ax Brer Buzzard for call 'roun' one mo' time, en gin 'im a good start."

Here Uncle Remus paused to chuckle a moment, and then went on:

"Gentermens! It tickles me eve'y time it come in my min', dat it do! Well, sir, ole Brer Buzzard wuz dat full er rascality dat he ain't got no better sense dan ter come, en de nex' day he sail up, he did, bright en yearly.

He lit on de grass, en ole Brer Tarrypin, he crops up on he back, en den Brer Buzzard riz. He riz up in de elements, now, en w'en he git up dar he sorter fetched a flirt en a swoop en slid out from under Brer Tarrypin.

"Ole Brer Tarrypin, he flapped he foots en wagged he head en shuck he tail, but all dis ain't done no good. He start off right-side up, but he ain't drap fur, 'fo' he 'gun ter turn somersets up dar, en down he come on he back — *kerblam* — *m* — *m!* En ef it hadn't but er bin fer de strenk er he shell, he'd er got bust wide open. He lay dar, ole Brer Tarrypin did, en try ter ketch he breff, en he groan en he pant like eve'y minnit gwine ter be nex'.

"Ole Brer Buzzard, he sail 'roun', he did, en look at Brer Tarrypin, en bimeby he lit fer ter make inquirements.

" 'Brer Tarrypin, how you feel?' sezee.

" 'Brer Buzzard, I'm teetotally ruint,' sezee.

" 'Well, Brer Tarrypin, I tol' you not ter try ter fly,' sezee.

" 'Hush up, Brer Buzzard!' sezee; 'I flew'd good ez anybody, but you fergot ter l'arn me how ter light. Flyin' is easy as fallin', but I don't speck I kin l'arn how ter light, en dat's whar de trouble come in,' sezee."

Uncle Remus laughed as heartily at the result of Brother Terrapin's attempts to fly as if he had heard of them for the first time; but before the little boy could ask him any questions, he remarked:

"Well, de goodness en de gracious! dat put me in min' er de time w'en ole Brer Rabbit make a bet wid Brer Fox."

"How was that, Uncle Remus?" the child inquired.

"Ef I ain't make no mistakes," responded Uncle Remus, with the air of one who was willing to sacrifice everything to accuracy, "ole Brer Rabbit bet Brer Fox dat he kin go de highest up in de elements, en not clim' no holler tree nudder. Brer Fox, he tuck 'im up, en dey 'pinted de day fer de trial ter come off.

"W'iles dey wuz makin' all der 'rangerments, Brer Fox year talk dat Brer Rabbit have done gone en hire Brer Buzzard fer ter tote 'im 'way 'bove de tops er de trees. Soon's he year dis, Brer Fox went ter Brer Buzzard, he did, en tol' 'im dat he gin 'im a pot er gol' ef he'd whirl in en kyar Brer Rabbit clean out'n de county. Brer Buzzard 'low dat he wuz de ve'y man fer ter do dat kind er bizness.

"So den w'en de time come fer de trial, Brer Fox, he wuz dar, en Brer Rabbit he was dar, en Brer Buzzard, he was dar, en lots er de yuther creeturs. Dey flung cross en piles fer ter see w'ich gwine ter start fus', en it fell ter Brer Fox. He look 'roun', ole Brer Fox did, en wink at Brer Buzzard, an Brer Buzzard, he wink back good ez he kin. Wid dat, Brer Fox tuck a runnin' start en clom' a leanin' tree. Brer Rabbit say dat better dan he 'spected Brer Fox kin do, but he 'low he gwine ter beat dat. Den he tuck 'n jump on Brer Buzzard back, en Brer Buzzard riz en sail off wid 'im. Brer Fox laugh w'en he see dis, en 'low, sezee:

"'Folks, ef you all got any intruss in ole Brer Rabbit, you des better tell 'im good-by, kaze you won't see 'im no mo' in dese diggin's.'

"Dis make all de yuther creeturs feel mighty good, kaze in dem days ole Brer Rabbit wuz a tarrifier, dat he wuz. But dey all sot dar, dey did, en keep der eye on Brer Buzzard w'ich he keep on gittin' higher en higher, en littler en littler. Dey look en dey look, en bimeby dey sorter see Brer Buzzard flop fus' one wing, en den de yuther. He keep on floppin' dis away, en eve'y time he flop, he git nigher en nigher de groun'. He flop en fall, en flop en fall, en circle 'roun', en bimeby he come close ter de place whar he start fum, en him en Brer Rabbit come down *ker-flip!*

En Brer Rabbit ain't no sooner hit de groun' dan he rush off in de bushes, en sot dar fer ter see w'at gwine ter happen nex'."

"But, Uncle Remus," said the little boy, "why didn't Brother Buzzard carry Brother Rabbit off, and get the pot of gold?"

"Bless yo' soul, honey, dey wuz some mighty good reasons in de way! W'en ole Brer Buzzard got 'way up in de elements, he 'low, he did:

"'We er gwine on a mighty long journey, Brer Rabbit.'

"Brer Rabbit he laugh like a man w'at's a-drivin' a plow-hoss wid a badoon bit.

"'You may be a-gwine on a long journey, Brer Buzzard; I don't 'spute dat,' sezee, 'but it'll be atter you done kyar'd me back whar we start fum.'

"Den Brer Buzzard he up en tell Brer Rabbit 'bout de bargain he done make wid Brer Fox. Dis make Brer Rabbit laugh wuss'n befo'.

"'Law, Brer Buzzard,' sezee, 'W'en it come ter makin' dat kinder bargain, you oughter make it wid me, kaze I'm a long ways a better trader dan w'at Brer Fox is.'

"Brer Buzzard he don't 'spon' ter dat, but he keep on flyin' higher en higher, en furder en furder away. Bimeby Brer Rabbit 'gun ter git kinder oneasy, en he 'low:

"'Look like ter me we done got fur 'nuff, Brer Buzzard,' sezee, 'en I'll be mighty much erbleedzd ef you kyar me back.'

"Brer Buzzard keep on flyin' furder. Bimeby Brer Rabbit ax 'im ag'in, but Brer Buzzard keep on flyin' furder. Den ole Brer Rabbit he 'low, sezee:

"'Ef I got ter des natchully *make* you go back, I speck I better start in right now,' sezee.

"Wid dat Brer Rabbit retch down, he did, en bit Brer Buzzard und' de wing."

The little boy clapped his hands and laughed at this, and Uncle Remus laughed in sympathy.

"Yessir," the old man went on, "ole Brer Rabbit retch down en bit Brer Buzzard und' de wing, right spang in he most ticklish en tendersome spot. Co'se dis make Brer Buzzard shet he wing quick, en w'en he shet he wing, he bleedzd ter fall some. Den w'en he open de wing out en ketch hisse'f, Brer Rabbit holler out:

"'Is you gwine back, Brer Buzzard?'

"Brer Buzzard ain't say nothin', en den Brer Rabbit retch down en bit 'im und' de yuther wing. It keep on dis away twel it got so dat Brer Rabbit kin guide Brer Buzzard along des same ez ef he done bin broke ter harness, en dat's de way he made 'im kyar 'im back."

The little boy enjoyed these stories very much, and was very sorry to see that Uncle Remus was not in the humor for telling any more. Perhaps his store was exhausted. At any rate, the old man flatly refused to cudgel his memory for another legend.

7
The Creature with No Claws

"W'EN YOU GIT a leetle bit older dan w'at you is, honey," said Uncle Remus to the little boy, "you'll know lots mo' dan you does now."

The old man had a pile of white oak splits by his side, and these he was weaving into a chair-bottom. He was an expert in the art of "bottoming chairs," and he earned many a silver quarter in this way. The little boy seemed to be much interested in the process.

"Hit's des like I tell you," the old man went on; "I done had de speunce un it. I done got so now dat I don't b'lieve w'at I see, much less w'at I year. It got ter be whar I kin put my han' on it en fumble wid it. Folks kin fool deyse'f lots wuss dan yuther folks kin fool um, en ef you don't b'lieve w'at I'm a-tellin' un you, you kin des ax Brer Wolf de nex' time you meet 'im in de big road."

"What about Brother Wolf, Uncle Remus?" the little boy asked, as the old man paused to refill his pipe.

"Well, honey, 'tain't no great long rigmarole; hit's des one er deze yer tales w'at goes in a gallop twel hit gits ter de jumpin'-off place.

"One time Brer Wolf wuz gwine 'long de big road feelin' mighty proud en high-strung. He wuz a mighty high-up man in dem days, Brer Wolf wuz, en mos' all de yuther creeturs wuz feard un 'im. Well, he wuz gwine 'long lickin' his chops en walkin' sorter stiff-kneed, w'en he happen ter look down 'pon de groun' en dar he seed a track in de san'. Brer Wolf stop, he did, en look at it, en den he 'low:

"'Heyo! w'at kind er creetur dish yer? Brer Dog ain't make dat track, en needer is Brer Fox. Hit's one er deze yer kind er creeturs w'at ain't got no claws. I'll des 'bout foller 'im up, en ef I ketch 'im he'll sholy be my meat.'

"Dat de way Brer Wolf talk. He followed 'long atter de track, he did, en he look at it close, but he ain't see no print er no claw. Bimeby de track tuck'n tu'n out de road en go up a dreen whar de rain done wash out. De track wuz plain dar in de wet san', but Brer Wolf ain't see no sign er no claws.

"He foller en foller, Brer Wolf did, en de track git fresher en fresher, but still he ain't see no print er no claw. Bimeby he come in sight er de creetur, en Brer Wolf stop, he did, en look at 'im. He stop stock-still en look. De creetur wuz mighty quare lookin', en he wuz cuttin' up some mighty quare capers. He had a big head, sharp nose, an bob tail, en he wuz walkin' 'roun' en 'roun' a big dog-wood tree, rubbin' his sides ag'in' it. Brer Wolf watch 'im a right smart w'ile, en den he 'low:

"'Shoo! dat creetur done bin in a fight en los' de bes' part er he tail, en mo'n dat, he got de eatch, kaze ef he ain't got de eatch w'at make he scratch hisse'f dat away? I lay I'll let 'im know who he foolin' 'long wid.'

"Atter w'ile, Brer Wolf went up a leetle nigher de creetur, en holler out:

"'Heyo, dar! w'at you doin' scratchin' yo' scaly hide on my tree, en tryin' fer ter break hit down?'

"De creetur ain't make no answer. He des walk 'roun' en 'roun' de tree scratchin' he sides en back. Brer Wolf holler out:

"'I lay I'll make you year me ef I hatter come dar whar you is.'

"De creetur des walk 'roun' en 'roun' de tree, en ain't make no answer. Den Brer Wolf hail 'im ag'in, en talk like he mighty mad:

"'Ain't you gwine ter min' me, you imperdent scoundul? Ain't you gwine ter mosey outer my woods en let my tree 'lone?'

"Wid dat, Brer Wolf march todes dis creetur des like he gwine ter squ'sh 'im in de groun'. De creetur rub hisse'f ag'in' de tree en look like he feel mighty good. Brer Wolf keep on gwine todes 'im, en bimeby w'en he git sorter close de creetur tuck'n sot up on his behime legs des like you see squir'ls do. Den Brer Wolf, he 'low, he did:

"'Ah-yi! you beggin', is you? But 'tain't gwine ter do you no good. I mought er let you off ef you'd a-minded me w'en I fus' holler atter you, but I ain't gwine ter let you off now. I'm a-gwine ter l'arn you a lesson dat'll stick by you.'

"Den der creetur sorter wrinkle up his face en mouf, en Brer Wolf 'low:

" 'Oh, you nee'nter swell up en cry, you 'ceitful vilyun. I'm a-gwine ter gi' you a frailin' dat I boun' yer won't fergit.'

"Brer Wolf make like he gwine ter hit de creetur, en den — "

Here Uncle Remus paused and looked all around the room and up at the rafters. When he began again his voice was very solemn.

— "Well, suh, dat creetur des fotch one swipe dis away, en n'er swipe dat away, en mos' 'fo' you kin wink yo' eye-balls, Brer Wolf hide wuz mighty nigh teetotally tor'd off'n 'im. Atter dat de creetur sa'nter'd off in de woods, en 'gun ter rub hisse'f on 'n'er tree."

"What kind of a creature was it, Uncle Remus?" asked the little boy.

"Well, honey," replied the old man in a confidential whisper, "hit wa'n't nobody on de top-side er de yeth but ole Brer Wildcat."

8

Uncle Remus's Wonder Story

THERE WAS one story that the little boy whom Uncle Remus delighted to entertain asked for with great regularity, perhaps because it has in it an element of witchcraft, and was as marvelous as it was absurd. Sometimes Uncle Remus pretended to resent this continued demand for the story, although he himself, like all the Negroes, was very superstitious, and believed more or less in witches and witchcraft.

"Dat same ole tale," he would say. "Well! well! well! W'en is we gwine ter year de las' un it? I done tol' you dat tale so much dat it make my flesh crawl, kaze I des know dat some er deze yer lonesome nights I'll be a-settin' up yer by de fier atter you done gone. I'll be a-settin' up yer dreamin' 'bout gwine ter bed, en sump'n' n'er er'll come a-clawin' at de do', en I'll up en ax, 'Who dat?' En dey'll up en 'spon', 'Lemme in.' En I'll ondo de do', en dat ole creetur'll walk in, en dat'll be de las' er po' ole Remus. En den w'en dat come ter pass, who gwine take time fer ter tell you tales? Dat w'at I like ter know."

The little boy, although he well knew that there were no witches, would treat this statement with gravity, as the story to him was as fascinating as one of the "Thousand and One Nights."

"Well, Uncle Remus," he would say, "just tell it this time!" Whereupon the old Negro, with the usual preliminary flourishes, began:

"One time, 'way back yander, w'en de moon wuz lots bigger dan w'at
she is now, dar wuz er ole Witch-Wolf livin' 'way off in de swamp, en dish
yer ole Witch-Wolf wuz up ter all sorts er contrariness. Look like she wuz
cross-ways wid de whole er creation. W'en she wa'n't doin' devilment,
she wuz studyin' up devilment. She had a mighty way, de ole Witch-Wolf
did, dat w'en she git hungry she'd change 'erse'f ter be a 'oman. She
could des shet 'er eye en smack 'er mouf, en stidder bein' a big black
wolf, wid long claws en green eyeballs, she'd come ter be the likelies'
lookin' gal dat you mos' ever seed.

"It seem like she love ter eat folks, but 'fo' she kin eat um she hatter
marry um; en w'en she take a notion, she des change 'erse'f ter be a
likely lookin' gal, en sails in en git married. Den w'en she do dat, she des
take en change 'erse'f back ter be a wolf, en eat um up raw. Go whar you
kin, en whar you mought, en yit I don't speck you kin fin' any wuss creetur dan w'at dis ole Witch-Wolf wuz.

"Well, sir, at de same time w'en dis ole Witch-Wolf gwine on dis
away, dey wuz a man livin' in de neighborhood w'at she took a mighty notion fer ter marry. De man had lan', but she ain't want de lan'; de man
had hosses, but she ain't want de hosses; de man had cows, but she ain't
want de cows. She des natchully want de man hisse'f, kaze he mighty fat
en nice."

"Did she want to marry him, Uncle Remus?" the little boy asked, as
though the tale were true, as indeed it seemed to be while Uncle Remus
was telling it and acting it.

"Tooby sho, honey! Dat zackly w'at she want. She want ter marry 'im,
en eat 'im up. Well, den, w'en she git eve'ything good en ready, she des
tuck'n back 'er years, en bat 'er eyes, en smack 'er mouf, and dar she
wuz — a likely young gal! She up en got ter de lookin'-glass, she did, en
swinge 'er ha'r wid de curlin'-tongs, en tie ribbons on 'er cloze, en fix up
'er beau-ketchers. She look nice, fit ter kill, now. Den she tuck 'n pass by
de man house, en look back en snicker, en hol' 'er head on one side, en
sorter shake out 'er cloze, en put 'er han' up fer ter see ef de ha'rpins in
der place. She pass by dis away lots er times, en bimeby de man kotch a
glimp' un 'er; en no sooner is he do dis dan she wave her hankcher. De

man he watch 'er en watch er, en bimeby, atter she kep' on whippin' by, he come out en hail 'er. En den she tuck'n stop, en nibble at 'er fan en fumble wid 'er hankcher, en dey tuck 'n stan' dar, dey did, en pass de time er day. Atter dat de sun never riz en set widout she hol' some confab wid de man; en 'twan't long 'fo' de man took a notion dat she de very gal fer a wife, w'at he bin a-huntin' fer. Wid dat dey des got right down ter ole-fashion courtin'. Dey'd laugh, dey'd giggle, dey'd 'spute, dey'd pout. You ain't never seen folks a-courtin', is you, honey?"

The little boy never had, and he said so.

"Well, den," Uncle Remus would continue, "you ain't none de wuss off fer dat, kaze dey ain't nothin' in de roun' worl' dat'll turn you' stomach quicker. But dar dey wuz, en de ole Witch-Wolf make sho' she wuz gwine ter git de man; let lone dat, de man he make sho he wuz gwine ter git de gal. Yit de man he helt back, en ef de Witch-Wolf hadn't er bin afeard she'd drap de fat in de fier, she'd er des come right out en pop de question den en dar. But de man he helt back en helt back, en bimeby he say ter hisse'f, he did, dat he speck he better make some inquirements 'bout dis yer gal. Yit who sh'll he go ter?

"He study en study, en atter w'ile hit come 'cross he min' dat he better go en ax ole Jedge Rabbit 'bout 'er, bein' ez he bin livin' 'roun' dar a mighty long time.

"Ole Jedge Rabbit," Uncle Remus would explain, "done got ole in age en gray in de min'. He done sober up en settle down, en I let you know dey wa'n't many folks in dem diggin's but w'at went ter ole Jedge Rabbit w'en dey git in trouble. So de man he went ter Jedge Rabbit house en rap at de do'. Jedge Rabbit, he 'low, he did, 'Who dat?'

"Man he up en 'spon', 'Hit's me.'

"Den Jedge Rabbit 'gin ter talk like one er deze yer town lawyers. He 'low, he did, 'Mighty short name fer grown man. Gimme de full entitlements.'

"Man he gun um ter 'im, en den ole Jedge Rabbit open de do' en let 'im in. Dey sot dar by de fier, dey did, twel bimeby 'twa'n't long 'fo' de man 'gun ter tell 'im 'bout dish yer great gal w'at he bin courtin' 'long wid. Bimeby Jedge Rabbit ax 'im, sezee, 'W'at dish yer great gal name?'

"Man he 'low, 'Mizzle-Mazzle.'

"Jedge Rabbit look at de man sort er like he takin' pity on 'im, en den he tuck he cane en make a mark in de ashes. Den he ax de man how ole is dish yer great gal. Man tol' 'im. Jedge Rabbit make n'er mark in de ashes. Den he ax de man is she got cat eyes. Man sort er study 'bout dis, but he say he speck she is. Jedge Rabbit make n'er mark. Den he ax is 'er years peaked at de top. Man 'low he disremember, but he speck dey is. Jedge Rabbit make n'er mark in de ashes. Den he ax is she got yaller ha'r. Man say she is. Jedge Rabbit make n'er mark. Den he ax is 'er toofs sharp. Man say dey is. Jedge Rabbit make n'er mark. Atter he done ax all dis, Jedge Rabbit got up, he did, en went 'cross de room ter de lookin'-glass. W'en he see hisse'f in dar, he tuck'n shet one eye, *s-l-o-w*. Den he sot down en leant back in de cheer, en 'low, sezee:

"'I done had de idee in my head dat ole Mizzle-Mazzle done moove out'n de country, en yit yer she is gallopin' 'roun' des ez natchul ez a dead pig in de sunshine!'

"Man look 'stonish, but he ain't say nothin'. Jedge Rabbit keep on talkin'.

"'You ain't never bin trouble' wid no trouble yit, but ef you wan' ter be trouble' wid trouble dat's double en thribble trouble, you des go en marry ole Mizzle-Mazzle,' sezee. 'You nee'nter b'lieve me less'n you wan' ter,' sezee. 'Des go 'long en marry 'er,' sezee.

"Man he look skeer'd. He up en 'low, he did, 'W'at de name er goodness I gwine do?'

"Ole Jedge Rabbit look sollumcolly. 'You got any cows?' sezee.

"Man say he got plenty un um.

"'Well, den,' sez ole Jedge Rabbit, sezee, 'ax 'er ef she kin keep house. She'll say yasser. Ax 'er ef she kin cook. She'll say yasser. Ax 'er ef she kin scour. She'll say yasser. Ax 'er ef she kin wash cloze. She'll say yasser. Ax 'er ef she kin milk de red cow. Den see w'at she say.'

"Man, he 'low, he did, dat he mighty much erbleedzd ter ole Jedge Rabbit, en wid dat he make he bow en tuck he leaf. He went home, he did, en w'en he git dar, sho nuff dar wuz dish yer nice-lookin' gal a prommynadin' up en down de road, en shakin' 'er hankcher. Man, he hail 'er, he did, en ax 'er how she come on. She 'low she purty well, en how do he do. Man say he feelin' sort er po'ly. Den she up en ax 'im w'at de matter.

Man say he speck he feel po'ly kaze he so powerful lonesome. Den dish yer nice-lookin' gal, she ax 'im w'at make he so powerful lonesome. Man he say he speck he so powerful lonesome kaze he want ter marry.

"Time de man come out so flat-footed 'bout marryin', de gal, she 'gun ter work wid 'er fan, en chaw at 'er hankcher. Den, atter w'ile, she up en ax 'im who he wan' ter marry. Man 'low he ain't no ways 'tickler, kaze he des want somebody fer ter take keep er de house w'en he gone, en fer ter set down by de fier, en keep 'im comp'ny w'en he at home. Den he up en ax de gal kin she keep house. De gal she 'low, 'Yasser!' Den he ax 'er ef she kin cook. She 'low, 'Yasser!' Den he ax 'er ef she kin scour. She 'low, 'Yasser!' Den he ax 'er ef she kin wash cloze. She 'low, 'Yasser!' Den he ax 'er ef she kin milk de red cow. Wid dat she flung up 'er han's, en fetched a squall dat make de man jump.

"'Law!' sez she, 'does you speck I'm a-gwine ter let dat cow hook me?'

"Man, he say de cow des ez gentle ez a dog.

"'Does you speck I'm a-gwine ter let dat cow kick me crank-sided?' sez she.

"Man, he 'low, he did, dat de cow won't kick, but dat ar gal she tuck'n make mo' skuses dan dey is frogs in de spring branch, but bimeby she say she kin try. But she 'low dat fus' 'fo' she try dat she'll show 'im how she kin keep house. So the nex' mornin' yer she come, en I let you know she sailed in dar, en sot dat house ter rights 'fo' some wimmen folks kin tu'n 'roun'. Man, he say, he did, dat she do dat mighty nice.

"Nex' day, de gal sot in en got dinner. Man say, he did, dat dey ain't nobody w'at kin beat dat dinner. Nex' day, she sot in en scour'd, en she make that flo' shine same ez a lookin'-glass. Man, he say dey ain't nobody in dat neighborhoods kin beat dat scourin'. Nex' day, she come fer ter milk de red cow, en de man, he 'low ter hisse'f, he did, dat he gwine ter see w'at make she don't like ter milk dat cow.

"De gal come, she did, en git de milk-piggin, en scald it out, en den she start fer de cow-lot. Man, he crope 'long atter de gal fer ter watch 'er. Gal went on, en w'en she come ter de lot dar wuz de red cow stan'in' in de fence-cornder wallopin' 'er cud. Gal, she sorter shuck de gate, she did, en holler, 'Sook, cow! Sook, cow!' Cow, she pearten up at dat, kaze she know w'en folks call 'er dat away, she gwine ter come in fer a bucket er slops.

"She pearten up, de red cow did, en start todes de gate, but, genter-mens! time she smell dat gal, she 'gun a blate like she smell blood, en paw'd de groun' en shuck 'er head des like she fixin' fer ter make fight. Man, he 'low ter hisse'f dat dish yer kinder business mighty kuze, en he keep on watchin'. Gal, she open de gate, but stidder de cow makin' fight, she 'gun ter buck. Gal, she say, 'So, cow! so, cow, so!' but de cow she h'ist her tail in de elements, en run 'roun' dat lot like de dogs wuz atter 'er. Gal, she foller on, en hit sorter look like she gwine ter git de cow hemmed up in a cornder, but de cow ain't got no notion er dis, en bimeby she whirl en make a splunge at de gal, en ef de gal hadn't er lipt de fence quick es she did de cow would er got 'er. Ez she lipt de fence, de man seed 'er foots, en, lo en beholes, dey wuz wolf foots! Man, he holler out:

"'You oughter w'ar shoes w'en you come a-milkin' de red cow!' en wid dat, de ole Witch-Wolf gun a twist, en fetched a yell, en made 'er dis-appearance in de elements."

Here Uncle Remus paused awhile. Then he shook his head, and ex-claimed:

"'Tain't no use! Dey may fool folks, but cows knows wil' creeturs by der smell."

9

The Rattlesnake and the Polecat

"I LAY 'TWON'T BE LONG," said Uncle Remus, as the little boy drew his chair closer to the broad fireplace, "'fo' I'll hatter put on a backlog en pile up de chunks. Dem w'at gits up 'bout de crack er day like I does is mighty ap' fer ter fin' de a'r sorter fresh deze mornin's. Fus' news you know old Jack Frost'll be a-blowin' his horn out dar in de woods, en he'll blow it so hard dat he'll jar down de hick'ry nuts, de scalybarks, de chinkapins, en de bullaces, en den ole Brer 'Possum will begin fer ter take his prommynades, en ef I don't ketch 'im hit'll be kaze I'm too stiff in my j'ints fer ter foller 'long atter de dogs.

"Dish yer kinder freshness in de a'r w'at make yo' breff smoke w'en you blow it out'n yo' mouf," continued Uncle Remus, "puts me in de min' er de time w'en Brer Polecat was a-huntin' fer a new house. De wedder wuz gittin' kinder shivery, en Brer Polecat he sot out ter fin' a good warm place whar he kin stay w'en de freeze come on.

"He mosey 'long, Brer Polecat did, twel he come ter Brer Rattlesnake house, w'ich it wuz in a holler tree. Brer Polecat knock at de do'. Brer Rattlesnake 'low, 'Who dat?'

"Brer Polecat 'spon', 'Hit's me; open de do'.'

"Brer Rattlesnake say, 'W'at you want?'

"Brer Polecat say, 'Hit mighty cool out yer.'

"Brer Rattlesnake 'low, 'Dat w'at I year folks say.'

"Brer Polecat up en 'spon', sezee, 'Hit too col' fer ter stan' out yer.'

"'Dat w'at I year tell,' says Brer Rattlesnake, sezee.

"'I wanter come in dar whar hit's warm,' says Brer Polecat, sezee.

"Brer Rattlesnake 'low dat two in dat house would be a big crowd.

"Brer Polecat say he got de name er bein' a mighty good housekeeper.

"Brer Rattlesnake say hit mighty easy fer anybody fer ter keep tother folks' house.

"Brer Polecat say he gwine come in anyhow.

"Brer Rattlesnake 'low, 'Dey ain't no room in yer fer you.'

"Brer Polecat laugh en say: 'Shoo, Brer Rattlesnake! eve'ybody gives me room. I go 'long de road, I does, en meet Mr. Man. I walks right todes 'im, en he bleedzd ter gi' me room. I meet all de creeturs, en dey bleedzd ter gi' me room.'

"Brer Rattlesnake say, 'Dat w'at I year tell.'

"Brer Polecat 'low, 'Don't you pester yo'se'f 'bout room. You des lemme git in dar whar you is, en *I'll make room!*'

"Wid dat Brer Rattlesnake shot de do' er his house en sprung de latch, en atter so long a time Brer Polecat went pacin' off somers else."

10
How the Birds Talk

UNCLE REMUS was not a "field hand"; that is to say, he was not required to plow and hoe and engage in the rough work on the plantation.

It was his business to keep matters and things straight about the house, and to drive the carriage when necessary. He was the confidential family servant, his attitude and his actions showing that he considered himself a partner in the various interests of the plantation. He did no great amount of work, but he was never wholly idle. He tanned leather, he made shoes, he manufactured horse-collars, fish-baskets, foot-mats, scouring-mops, and ax-handles for sale; he had his own watermelon and cotton-patches; he fed the hogs, looked after the cows and sheep, and, in short, was the busiest person on the plantation.

He was reasonably vain of his importance, and the other Negroes treated him with great consideration. They found it to their advantage to do so, for Uncle Remus was not without influence with his master and mistress. It would be difficult to describe, to the satisfaction of those not familiar with some of the developments of slavery in the South, the peculiar relations existing between Uncle Remus and his mistress, whom he called "Miss Sally." He had taken care of her when she was a child, and he still regarded her as a child.

He was dictatorial, overbearing and quarrelsome. These words do not describe Uncle Remus's attitude, but no other words will do. Though he was dictatorial, overbearing and quarrelsome, he was not even grim. Beneath everything he said there was a current of respect and affection that was thoroughly understood and appreciated. All his quarrels with his mistress were about trifles, and his dictatorial bearing was inconsequential. The old man's disputes with his "Miss Sally" were thoroughly amusing to his master, and the latter, when appealed to, generally gave a decision favorable to Uncle Remus.

Perhaps an illustration of one of Uncle Remus's quarrels will give a better idea than any attempt at description. Sometimes, after tea, Uncle Remus's master would send the house-girl for him, under pretense of giving him orders for the next day, but really for the purpose of hearing him quarrel. The old man would usually enter the house by way of the dining-room, leaving his hat and his cane outside. He would then go to the sitting-room and announce his arrival, whereupon his master would tell him what particular work he wanted done, and then Uncle Remus would say, very humbly:

"Miss Sally, you ain't got no cold vittles, nor no piece er pie, nor nothin', layin' 'roun' yer, is you? Dat ar Tildy gal say you all have a mighty nice dinner terday."

"No, there's nothing left. I gave the last to Rachel."

"Well, I dunner w'at business dat ar nigger got comin' up yer eatin' Mars John out er house en home. I year tell she l'arnin' how to cook, en goodness knows, ef eatin' gwine ter make anybody cook good, she de bes' cook on dis hill."

"Well, she earns what she eats, and that's more than I can say for some of the others."

"I lay ef ole Miss' wuz 'live, she'd sen' dat ar nigger ter de cotton-patch. She would, mon; she'd sen' er dar a-whirlin'. Nigger w'at wrop up 'er ha'r wid a string ain't never seed de day w'en dey kin go on de inside er ole Miss's kitchen, let 'lone mommuck up de vittles. Now, I boun' you dat!"

"Well, there's nothing here for you, and if there was you wouldn't get it."

"No, 'm, dat's so, I done know dat long time ago. All day long, en half de night, hit's 'Remus, come yer,' en 'Remus, go dar,' ceppin' w'en it's eatin'-time, en w'en dat time come, dey ain't nobody dast ter name de name er Remus. Dat Rachel nigger new ter de business, yet she mighty quick fer ter l'arn how ter tote off de vittles, en how ter make all de chillun on de place do 'er er'ns."

"John," to her husband, "I put some cold potatoes for the children on the sideboard in the dining-room. Please see if they are still there."

"Nummine 'bout gettin' up, Mars John. All de taters is dar. Old Remus ain't never 'grudge w'at dem po' little chillun gits. Let 'lone dat; dey comes down ter my house, en dey looks so puny en lonesome dat I 'vides my own vittles wid um. Goodness knows, I don't 'grudge de po' creeturs de little dey gits. Good-night, Mars John! Good-night, Miss Sally!"

"Take the potatoes, Remus," said Mars John.

"I'm mighty much erbleedzd ter you," said Uncle Remus, putting the potatoes in his pocket, "en thanky too; but I ain't gwine ter have folks say in' dat ole Remus took 'n sneaked up yer en tuck de vittles out er deze yer chillun's mouf, dat I ain't."

The tone in which Uncle Remus would carry on his quarrels was inimitable, and he generally succeeded in having his way. He would sometimes quarrel with the little boy to whom he told the stories, but either by dint of coaxing, or by means of complete silence, the youngster usually managed to restore the old man's equanimity.

"Uncle Remus," said the boy, "it's mighty funny that the birds and the animals don't talk like they used to."

"Who say dey don't?" the old man cried, with some show of indignation. "Who say dey don't? Now, dat's des w'at I'd like ter know."

Uncle Remus's manner implied that he was only waiting for the name of the malicious person to go out and brain him on the spot.

"Well," replied the child, "I often listened at them, but I never hear them say a word."

"Ah-yi!" exclaimed Uncle Remus, in a tone of exultation; "dat's diffunt. Now, dat's diffunt. De creeturs talk des 'bout like dey allers did, but folks ain't smart ez dey used ter wuz. You kin year de creeturs talkin', but you dunner w'at dey say. Yit I boun' you ef I wuz ter pick you up, en set you down in de middle er de Two-Mile Swamp, you'd year talkin' all night long."

The little boy shivered at the suggestion.

"Uncle Remus, who talks out there in the swamp?"

"All de creeturs, honey, all de creeturs. Mo' speshually ole man Owl, en all he fambly connexion."

"Have you ever heard them, Uncle Remus?"

"Many's en many's de time, honey. W'en I gits lonesome wid folks, I des up en takes down my walkin'-cane, I does, en I goes off dar whar I kin year um, en I sets dar en feels dez es familious ez w'en I'm a-settin' yer jawin' 'long er you."

"What do they say, Uncle Remus?"

"It seems like ter me," said the old man, frowning, as if attempting to recall familiar names, "dat one er um name Billy Big-Eye, en t'er one name Tommy Long-Wing. One er um sets in a poplar-tree on one side er de swamp, en t'er one sets in a pine on t'er side," Uncle Remus went on, as the child went a little closer to him.

"W'en night come, good en dark, Billy Big-Eye sorter cle'r up he th'oat en 'low:

"'*Tom!* Tommy *Long*-Wing! *Tom!* Tommy *Long*-Wing!'"

Uncle Remus allowed his voice to rise and fall, giving it a far-away but portentous sound, the intonation being a weirdly exact imitation of the hooting of a large swamp-owl. The italicized words will give a faint idea of this intonation.

"Den," Uncle Remus went on, "ole Tommy Long-Wing he'd wake up en holler back:

"*'Who* — who dat a-*call*in'? *Who* — who dat a-*call*in'?'

"*'Bill* — Billy *Big*-Eye! *Bill* — Billy *Big*-Eye!'

"*'Whyn't* you come *down* — come *down* ter *my* house?'

"'I *coodn't* — I *coodn't* come down to *yo'* house!'

"*'Tom* — Tommy *Long*-Wing! Why *coodn't* you?'

"'Had *coom*penny, *Bill* — Billy *Big*-Eye! Had *coom*penny!'

"*'Who* — who wuz de *coom*penny?'

"*'Heel* Tap 'n *his* wife, *Deel* Tap 'n *his* wife, en I don't know *who*-all, *who*-all, *who*-all!'

"Ez ter Heel Tap en Deel Tap," Uncle Remus continued, noticing a puzzled expression on the child's face, "I dunno ez I ever bin know anybody zackly wid dat name. Some say dat's de name er de Peckerwoods en de Yallerhammers, but I speck w'en we git at de straight un it, dey er all in de Owl fambly."

"Who heard them talking that way, Uncle Remus?" asked the little boy.

"Goodness en de gracious, honey!" exclaimed Uncle Remus, "you don't speck er ole nigger like I is fer ter note all deze yer folks' name in he head, does you? S'pose'n de folks w'at year um done gone and move off, w'at good it gwine do you fer ter git der name? S'pose'n dey wuz settin' right yer 'long side er you, w'at good dat gwine do? De trufe's de trufe, en folks' name ain't gwine make it no trufer. Yit w'en it come ter dat, I kin go ter de do' dar, en fetch a whoop, en fin' you lots er niggers w'at done bin year dat Owl fambly gwine on in de swamp dar. En you ne'en ter go no fudder dan Becky's Bill, nudder. W'en dat nigger wuz growin' up, he went frolickin' 'roun', en one night he come thoo de Two-Mile Swamp.

"He come thoo dar," Uncle Remus went on, emphasizing the seriousness of the situation by a severe frown, "des ez soople in de min' ez w'at you is dis blessid minnit. He come 'long, he did, en de fus' news you know a great big ole owl flew'd up in a tree en snap he bill des like somebody crackin' a whip. Becky's Bill make like he ain't take no notice, but he sorter men' he gait. Present'y, ole Mr. Owl flew'd up in n'er tree little ways ahead, en smack he mouf. Den he holler out:

"'*Who* cooks — *who* cooks — *who* cooks fer *you*-all?'

"Becky's Bill move on — he make like he ain't year nothing. Ole Mr. Owl holler out:

"'*Who* cooks — *who* cooks — *who* cooks fer *you*-all?'

"By dat time Becky's Bill done git sorter skeer'd, en he stop en say:

"'Well, sir, endurin' er de week, mammy, she cooks, but on Sundays, en mo' speshually ef dey got comp'ny, den ole Aunt Dicey, she cooks.'

"Ole Mr. Owl, he ruffle up he fedders, he did, en smack he mouf, en look down at Becky's Bill, en 'low:

"'*Who* cooks — *who* cooks — *who* cooks fer *you*-all?'

"Becky's Bill, he take off he hat, he did, en 'low, sezee:

"'Well, sir, hit's des like I tell you. Mo' inginer'lly endurin' er de week, mammy, she cooks, but on Sundays, mo' speshually w'en dey got comp'ny, ole Aunt Dicey, she cooks.'

"Ole Mr. Owl, he keep axin', en Becky's Bill keep on tellin' twel, bimeby, Becky's Bill, he got skeer'd, en tired, en mad, en den he le'pt out

fum dar en he run home like a quarter-hoss; en now ef you git 'im in dat
swamp you got ter go 'long wid 'im."

The little boy sat and gazed into the fire after Uncle Remus had
paused. He evidently had no more questions to ask. After a while the old
man resumed:

"But 'tain't des de owls dat kin talk. I des want you ter git up in de
mornin' en lissen at de chickens. I kin set right yer en tell you des zackly
w'at you'll year um say."

The little boy laughed, and Uncle Remus looked up into the rafters to
hide a responsive smile.

"De old Dominicker Hen, she'll fly off'n 'er nes' in de hoss-trough, en
squall out:

"*'Aigs* I *lay* eve'y *day* en yer dey *come* en *take* um *'way!* I *lay,* I *lay,* I
lay, en yit I hatter go *bare*-footed, *bare*-footed, *bare*-footed! Ef I *lay,* en
lay twel *dooms*day, I know I'll hatter go *bare*-footed, *bare*-footed, *bare*-
footed!"

Uncle Remus managed to emphasize certain words so as to give a
laughably accurate imitation of a cackling hen. He went on:

"Now, den, w'en de rooster year de Dominicker Hen a-cacklin', I
boun' you he gwine ter jine in. He'll up en say, sezee:

"'Yo' foot so *big,* yo' foot so *wide,* yo' foot so *long.* I can't git a shoe
ter-fit-it, *ter*-fit-it, *ter*-fit-it!'

"En den dar dey'll have it, up en down, quollin' des like sho nuff folks."

The little boy waited for Uncle Remus to go on, but the old man was
done. He leaned back in his chair and began to hum a tune.

After a while the youngster said:

"Uncle Remus, you know you told me that you'd sing me a song every
time I brought you a piece of cake."

"I speck I did, honey — I speck I did. Ole ez I is, I got a mighty sweet
toof. Yit I ain't see no cake dis night."

"Here it is," said the child, taking a package from his pocket.

"Yasser!" exclaimed the old man, with a chuckle, "dar she is! En all
wrop up, in de bargain. I'm mighty glad you helt 'er back, honey, kaze
now I can take dat cake en chune up wid 'er en sing you one er dem ole-
time songs, en folks gwine by'll say we er kyar'n on a camp-meetin'.""

11
The Foolish Woman

"WHEN YOU SEE dese yer niggers w'at wrop de ha'r wid a string," said Uncle Remus to the little boy one day, apropos of nothing in particular except his own prejudices, "you des keep yo' eye on um. You des watch um, kaze ef you don't dey'll take en trip you up — dey will dat, dez ez sho ez de worl'. En ef you don't b'lieve me, you kin des ax yo' mammy. Many's en many's de time is Miss Sally driv niggers out'n de big house yard kaze dey got der ha'r wrop up wid a string. I bin lookin' en peepin', en lis'nin' en eavesdrappin' in dese low groun's a mighty long time, en I ain't ne'er sot eyes on no nigger w'at wrop der ha'r wid a string but w'at dey wuz de meanes' kind er nigger. En if you ax anybody w'at know 'bout niggers dey'll tell you de same."

"But, Uncle Remus," said the little boy protestingly, "doesn't Aunt Tempy wrap her hair with a string?"

"Who? Sis Tempy? Shoo!" exclaimed the old man scornfully. "Why, whar yo' eyes, honey? Nex' time you see Sis Tempy, you take en look at 'er right close, en ef 'er ha'r ain't platted den I'm a Chinee. Now, dat's w'at!"

"Well, they don't bother me," said the little boy.

"Dat dey don't!" exclaimed Uncle Remus enthusiastically. "Dey don't dast ter, kaze dey knows ef dey do, dey'll have ole Remus atter um, en mean ez dey is, dey know hit ain't gwine ter do ter git de ole nigger atter um.

"Hit seem like ter me dat one time I year a mighty funny tale 'bout one er deze yer niggers w'at wrop der ha'r wid a string, but I speck it mos' too late fer ter start in fer ter tell a tale — kaze present'y you'll be a-settin' up dar in dat cheer dar fas' 'sleep, en I'm a-gittin' too ole en stiff fer ter be totin' you roun' yer like you wuz a sack er bran."

"Oh, I'm not sleepy, Uncle Remus," the little boy exclaimed. "Please tell me the story."

The old man stirred the embers with the end of his cane, and seemed to be in a very solemn mood. Presently he said:

"'Tain't so mighty much of a tale, yit it'll do fer ter go ter bed on. One time dey wuz a nigger man w'at tuck'n married a nigger 'oman, en dish yer nigger 'oman kep' 'er h'ar wrop up wid a string night en day. Dey married, en dey went home ter housekeepin'. Dey got um some pots, en dey got um some kittles, en dey got um some pans, en dey got um some dishes, en dey start in, dey did, des like folks does w'en dey gwine ter stay at home.

"Dey rocked on, dey did," said Uncle Remus, scratching his head with some earnestness, "en it seem like dey wuz havin' a mighty good time; but one day w'en dish yer nigger man wuz gone ter town atter some vittles, the nigger 'oman she 'gun ter git fretted. Co'se, honey, you dunner how de wimmen folks goes on, but I boun' you'll know 'fo' you gits ez ole en ez crippled up in de j'ints ez w'at I is. Well, dish yer nigger 'oman, she 'gun ter fret en ter worry, en bimeby she got right down mad."

"But what did she get mad about, Uncle Remus?" the little boy asked.

"Well, suh," said the old man condescendingly, "I'll up en tell you. She wuz des like yuther wimmen folks, en she got fretted kaze de days wuz long en de wedder hot. She got mad en she stayed mad. Eve'y time she walked 'cross de flo' de dishes 'ud rattle in de cubberd, en de mo' she'd fix um de wuss dey'd rattle. Co'se, dis make 'er lots madder dan w'at she wuz at fus', en bimeby she tuck'n holler out:

"'W'at make you rattle?'

"Dishes dey keep on a-rattlin'.

"'W'at make you rattle so? I ain't gwine ter have no rattlin' 'roun' yer!'

"Dishes dey keep on a-rattlin' en a-rattlin'. De 'oman she holler out:

"'Who you rattlin' at? I'm de mistiss er dis house. I ain't gwine ter have none er yo' rattlin' 'roun' yer!'

"Dishes dey rattle en rattle. De 'oman, she holler out:

"'Stop dat rattlin'. I ain't gwine ter have you sassin' back at me dat way. I'm de mistiss er dis house!'

"Den she walked up en down, en eve'y time she do dat de dishes dey rattle wuss en wuss. Den she holler out:

"'Stop dat sassin' at me, I tell you! I'm de mistiss in dis house!'

"Yit de dishes keep on rattlin' en shakin', en bimeby de 'oman run ter de cubberd, she did, en grab de dishes en fling um out in de yard, en no sooner's she do dis dan dey wuz busted all ter flinders.

"I tell you w'at, mon," said Uncle Remus, after pausing a moment to see how this proceeding had affected the little boy. "I tell you w'at, mon, wimmen folks is mighty kuse. Dey is dat, des ez sho ez de worl'. Bimeby de nigger man come home, en w'en he see all de dishes broke up he wuz 'stonish', but he ain't say nothin'. He des look up at de sun fer ter see w'at time it is, en feel er hisse'f fer ter see ef he well. Den he up 'n holler:

"'Ole 'oman, yer some fish w'at I bring you. I speck you better clean um fer dinner.' De 'oman, she 'low:

"'Lay um down dar.' De man, he tuck en lay um down en draw'd a bucket er water out er de well.

"Den, bimeby, de 'oman, she come out en start ter clean de fish. She pick um up, she did, en start ter scrape de scales off, but she sees der eyes wide open, en she 'low:

"'Shet dem eyes! don't you be a-lookin' at me!'

"Fish, dey keep on a-lookin'. 'Oman, she squall out:

"'Shet dem eyes, you impident villyuns! I'm de mistiss in dish yer house!'

"Fish, dey helt der eyes wide open, en den de 'oman tuck en flung um in de well."

"And then what?" asked the little boy, as Uncle Remus paused.

"Ah, Lord, honey! You too hard fer me now. De 'oman tuck'n 'stroy de dishes, en den she flung de fishes in de well, en dey des natchully ruint de well. I dunner w'at de man say, but ef he wuz like de balance un um, he des sot down en lit his pipe, en tuck a smoke en den lit out fer bed. Dat's de way men folks does, en ef you don't b'lieve me you kin ax yo' pa, but fer de Lord's sake don't ax 'im whar Miss Sally kin year you, kaze den she'll light on me, en mo'n dat, she won't save me no mo' col' vittles."

12
The Adventures of Simon and Susanna[3][4]

"I GOT ONE TALE on my min'," said Uncle Remus to the little boy one night. "I got one tale on my min' dat I ain't ne'er tell you; I dunner how

---

[3] It may be of interest to those who approach Folk-Lore stories from the scientific side, to know that this story was told to one of my little boys three years ago by a Negro named John Holder. I have since found a variant (or perhaps the original) in Theal's *Kaffir Folk-Lore*. — J. C. H.

[4] See "Jack and King Marock" in *The Jack Tales*. The magic flight appears also in the old Irish tale of Deirdre. (Joseph Jacobs, *More Celtic Fairy Tales*.) — R. C.

come; I speck it des kaze I git mixt up in my idees. Deze is busy times, mon, en de mo' you does de mo' you hatter do, en w'en dat de case, it ain't ter be 'spected dat one ole broke-down nigger kin 'member 'bout eve'ything."

"What is the story, Uncle Remus?" the little boy asked.

"Well, honey," said the old man, wiping his spectacles, "hit sorter run dis away: One time dey wuz a man w'at had a mighty likely daughter."

"Was he a white man or a black man?" the little boy asked.

"I 'clar' ter gracious, honey!" exclaimed the old man, "you er pushin' me mos' too close. Fer all I kin tell you, de man mought er bin ez w'ite ez de driven snow, er he mought er bin de blackes' Affikin er de whole kit en b'ilin'. I'm des tellin' you de tale, en you kin take en take de man en w'itewash 'im, er you kin black 'im up des ez you please. Dat's de way I looks at it.

"Well, one time dey wuz a man, en dish yer man he had a mighty likely daughter. She wuz so purty dat she had mo' beaus dan w'at you got fingers en toes. But de gal daddy, he got his spishuns 'bout all un um, en he won't let um come 'roun' de house. But dey kep' on pesterin' 'im so, dat bimeby he give word out dat de man w'at kin cle'r up six acres er lan' en roll up de logs, en pile up de bresh in one day, dat man kin marry his daughter.

"In co'se, dis look like it unpossible, en all de beaus drap off ceppin' one, en he wuz a great big strappin' chap w'at look like he kin knock a steer down. Dis chap he wuz name Simon, en de gal, she wuz name Susanna. Simon, he love Susanna, en Susanna, she love Simon, en dar it went.

"Well, sir, Simon, he went ter de gal daddy, he did, en he say dat ef anybody kin cle'r up dat lan', he de one kin do it, leas'ways he say he gwine try mighty hard. De ole man, he grin en rub his han's terge'er, he did, en tol' Simon ter start in in de mornin'. Susanna, she makes out she wuz fixin' sump'n' in de cubberd, but she tuck 'n kiss 'er han' at Simon, en nod 'er head. Dis all Simon want, en he went out er dar des ez happy ez a jay-bird atter he done robbed a sparrer-nes'.

"Now, den," Uncle Remus continued, settling himself more comfortably in his chair, "dish yer man wuz a witch."

"Why, I thought a witch was a woman," said the little boy.

The old man frowned and looked into the fire.

"Well, sir," he remarked with some emphasis, "ef you er gwine ter

tu'n de man inter a 'oman, den dey won't be no tale, kaze dey's bleedzd
ter be a man right dar whar I put dis un. Hit's des like I tol' you 'bout de
color er de man. Black 'im er w'itewash 'im des ez you please, en ef you
want ter put a frock on 'im ter boot, hit ain't none er my business; but I'm
gwine ter 'low he wuz a man ef it's de las' ac'.'"

The little boy remained silent, and Uncle Remus went on:

"Now, den, dish yer man was a witch. He could cunjer folks, mo'
'speshually dem folks w'at ain't got no rabbit foot. He bin at his cunjerments so long, dat Susanna done learn mos' all his tricks. So de nex'
mornin' w'en Simon come by de house fer ter borry de axe, Susanna she
run en got it fer 'im. She got it, she did, en den she sprinkles some black
san' on it, en say, 'Axe, cut; cut, axe.' Den she rub 'er ha'r 'cross it, en
give it ter Simon. He tuck de axe, he did, en den Susanna say:

"'Go down by de branch, git sev'm white pebbles, put um in dis little
cloth bag, en w'enever you want the axe ter cut, shake um up.'

"Simon, he went off in de woods, en started in ter cle'rin' up de six
acres. Well, sir, dem pebbles en dat axe dey done de work — dey did dat.
Simon could a' bin done by de time de dinner-horn blow'd, but he hung
back kaze he ain't want de man fer ter know dat he doin' it by cunjerments.

"When he shuck de pebbles de axe 'ud cut, en de trees 'ud fall, en de
lim's 'ud drap off, en de logs 'ud roll up terge'er, en de bresh 'ud pile itself up. Hit went on dis away twel by de time it wuz two hours b' sun, de
whole six acres wuz done cleaned up.

"'Bout dat time de man come 'roun', he did, fer ter see how de work
gittin' on, en, mon! he wuz 'stonish'. He ain't know w'at ter do er say. He
ain't want ter give up his daughter, en yit he ain't know how ter git out'n
it. He walk 'roun' en 'roun', en study, en study, en study he gwine rue de
bargain. At las' he walk up ter Simon, he did, en he say:

"'Look like you sort er forehanded wid you work.'

"Simon, he 'low: 'Yasser, w'en I starts in on a job I'm mighty restless
twel I gits it done. Some er dis timber is rough en tough, but I bin had
wuss jobs dan dis in my time.'

"De man say ter hiss'f: 'W'at kind er folks is dis chap?' Den he say
out loud: 'Well, sence you er so spry, dey's two mo' acres 'cross de branch
dar. Ef you'll cle'r dem up 'fo' supper you kin come up ter de house en
git de gal.'

"Simon sorter scratch his head, kaze he dunner whedder de pebbles gwine ter hol' out, yit he put on a bol' front en he tell de man dat he'll go 'cross dar en clean up de two acres soon ez he res' a little.

"De man he went off home, en soon's he git out er sight, Simon went 'cross de branch en shook de pebbles at de two acres er woods, en t'wa'n't no time skacely 'fo' de trees wuz all cut down en pile up.

"De man, he went home, he did, en call up Susanna, en say:

"'Daughter, dat man look like he gwine git you, sho.'

"Susanna, she hang 'er head, en look like she fretted, en den she say she don't keer nothin' fer Simon, nohow."

"Why, I thought she wanted to marry him," said the little boy.

"Well, honey, w'en you git growed up, en git whiskers on yo' chin, en den atter de whiskers git gray like mine, you'll fin' out sump'n' n'er 'bout de wimmin folks. Dey ain't ne'er say zackly w'at dey mean, none er um, mo' 'speshually w'en dey er gwine on 'bout gittin' married.

"Now, dar wuz dat gal Susanna w'at I'm a-tellin' you 'bout. She mighty nigh 'stracted 'bout Simon, en yit she make 'er daddy b'lieve dat

she 'spize 'im. I ain't blamin' Suzanna," Uncle Remus went on with a judicial air, "'kaze she know dat 'er daddy wuz a witch en a mighty mean
one in de bargain.

"Well, atter Susanna done make 'er daddy b'lieve dat she ain't keerin'
nothin' 'tall 'bout Simon, he 'gun ter set his traps en fix his tricks. He up'n
tell Susanna dat atter 'er en Simon git married dey mus' go upsta'rs in de
front room, en den he tell 'er dat she mus' make Simon go ter bed fus'. Den
de man went upsta'rs en tuck'n tuck all de slats out'n de bedstid ceppin'
one at de head en one at de foot. Atter dat he tuck'n put some foot-valances
'round' de bottom er de bed — des like dem w'at you bin see on yo'
gran'ma bed. Den he tuck'n sawed out de floor und' de bed, en dar wuz de
trap all ready.

"Well, sir, Simon come up ter de house, en de man make like he
mighty glad fer ter see 'im, but Susanna, she look like she mighty shy. No
matter 'bout dat; atter supper Simon en Susanna got married. Hit ain't in
de tale wedder dey sont fer a preacher er wedder dey wuz a squire
browsin' 'roun' in de neighborhoods, but dey had cake wid reezins in it,
en some er dish yer silly-bug w'at got mo' foam in it dan dey is dram, en
dey had a mighty happy time.

"W'en bedtime come, Simon en Susanna went upsta'rs, en w'en dey
got in de room, Susanna kotch 'im by de han', en helt up her finger. Den
she whisper en tell 'im dat ef dey don't run away fum dar dey bofe gwine
ter be kil't. Simon ax 'er how come, en she say dat 'er daddy want ter kill
'im kaze he sech a nice man. Dis make Simon grin; yit he wuz sorter restless 'bout gittin' 'way fum dar. But Susanna, she say wait. She say:

"'Pick up yo' hat en button up yo' coat. Now, den, take dat stick er
wood dar en hol' it 'bove yo' head.'

"W'iles he stan'in' dar, Susanna got a hen egg out'n a basket, den she
got a meal-bag, en a skillet. She 'low:

"'Now, den, drap de wood on de bed.'

"Simon done des like she say, en time de wood struck de bed de tick
en de mattruss went a-tumblin' thoo de floor. Den Susanna tuck Simon
by de han' en dey run out de back way ez hard ez dey kin go.

"De man, he wuz down dar waitin' fer de bed ter drap. He had a big long
knife in he han', en time de bed drapped, he lit on it, he did, en stobbed

it scan'lous. He des natchully ripped de tick up, en w'en he look, bless gracious, dey ain't no Simon dar. I lay dat man wuz mad den. He snorted 'roun' dar twel blue smoke come out'n his nose, en his eye look red like varmint eye in de dark. Den he run upsta'rs en dey ain't no Simon dar, en nudder wuz dey any Susanna.

"Gentermens! den he git madder. He rush out, he did, en look 'roun', en 'way off yander he see Simon en Susanna des a-runnin', en a-holdin' one nudder's han'.'"

"Why, Uncle Remus," said the little boy, "I thought you said it was night?"

"Dat w'at I said, honey, en I'll stan' by it. Yit, how many times dis blessid night is I got ter tell you dat de man wuz a witch? En bein' a witch, co'se he kin see in de dark.

"Well, dish yer witch-man, he look off en he see Simon en Susanna runnin' ez hard ez dey kin. He put out atter um, he did, wid his knife in his han', an' he kep' on a gainin' on um. Bimeby, he got so close dat Susanna say ter Simon:

"'Fling down yo' coat.'

"Time de coat tech de groun', a big thick woods sprung up whar it fell. But de man, he cut his way thoo it wid de knife, en kep' on a-pursuin' atter um.

"Bimeby, he got so close dat Susanna drap de egg on de groun', en time it fell a big fog riz up fum de groun', en a little mo' en de man would a got los'. But atter so long a time fog got blowed away by de win', en de man kep' on a-pursuin' atter um.

"Bimeby, he got so close dat Susanna drap de meal-sack, en a great big pon' er water kivered de groun' whar it fell. De man wuz in sech a big hurry dat he tried ter drink it dry, but he ain't kin do dis, so he sot on de bank en blow'd on de water wid he hot breff, en atter so long a time de water made hit's disappearance, en den he kep' on atter um.

"Simon en Susanna wuz des a-runnin', but run ez dey would, de man kep' a-gainin' on um, en he got so close dat Susanna drapped de skillet. Den a big bank er darkness fell down, en de man ain't know w'ich away ter go. But atter so long a time de darkness lif up, en de man kep' on a-pursuin' atter um. Mon, he made up fer los' time, en he got so close dat Susanna say ter Simon:

" 'Drap a pebble.'

"Time Simon do dis a high hill riz up, but de man clom' it en kep' on atter um. Den Susanna say ter Simon:

" 'Drap nudder pebble.'

"Time Simon drap de pebble, a high mountain growed up, but de man crawled up it en kep' on atter um. Den Susanna say:

" 'Drap de bigges' pebble.'

"No sooner is he drap it dan a big rock wall riz up, en hit wuz so high dat de witch-man can't git over. He run up en down, but he can't find no end, en den, atter so long a time, he turn 'roun' en go home.

"On de yuther side er dis high wall, Susanna tuck Simon by de han', en say:

" 'Now we kin res'.'

"En I reckon," said the old man slyly, "dat we all better res'."

13
Brother Rabbit and the Gingercakes

"Now, I DES TELL YOU W'AT, honey," said Uncle Remus to the little boy, "if you wan' ter year dish yer tale right straight thoo, widout any balkin' er stallin', you'll des hatter quit makin' any fuss. Kaze w'en der's any fuss gwine on hit mos' allers inginer'lly gits me mixt up, en w'en I git mixt up I ain't wuth nothin' 'tall skacely fer tellin' a tale, en ef you don't b'lieve me, you may des ax some er my blood kin. Now, den, you des set right whar you is en stop you behavishness. Kaze de fus' time you wink loud, you got ter git right up on de bed-pos' dar en ride straddle.

"So, den! Well, one time Brer Mink en Brer Coon en Brer Polecat all live terge'er in de same settlement. Let 'lone dat, dey live in de same house, en de house w'at dey live in wuz made in de resemble uv a great holler log. In dem days, Brer Polecat wuz de king er de creeturs w'at run 'bout atter dark, en you better make up yo' min' dat he made um stan' 'roun' might'ly.

"Why, Uncle Remus," said the little boy, "I thought Brother Rabbit — "

"Well, de goodness en de gracious! ain't I ax you fer ter please ma'am don't make no fuss? Kaze I know mighty well Brer Rabbit use ter be de slickes' en de sooples', but dey bleedzd ter be a change, kaze 'tain't in natur' fer de t'er creeturs not ter kotch on ter his ins en his outs, en I speck dat de time w'en dey fin' 'im out is de time w'en ole Brer Polecat got ter be de king er de creeturs — dat's w'at I speck.

"But no matter 'bout dat — by hook er by crook, Brer Polecat come ter be de king er de creeturs, en w'en he come ter be dat dey'd all er um go a long ways out er de way fer ter take off der hats en bow der howdies, dey would, en some un um would tag atter 'im, en laugh eve'y time Brer Polecat laughed, en grin eve'y time he grinned.

"W'iles dish yer wuz gwine on Brer Rabbit wuz in de crowd, en he wuz des ez big ez any er um, en I dunner ef he wa'n't de bigges'. Well, Brer Rabbit he move en secondary dat bein' ez how Brer Polecat wuz sech a nice king dey oughter pass a law dat eve'y time de yuther creeturs meet um in de road dey mus' shet der eyes en hol' der nose. Some er um say dey don't min' holdin' der nose, but dey don't like dish yer way er shettin' der eyes, kaze dey mought run up ag'in' a tree, er stick a brier in der foot; but Brer Rabbit, he up en 'low, he did, dat 'twuz des 'bout ez lit-tle ez dey kin do ter shet der eye en hol' der nose w'en dey git whar sech a nice king is, en so dey all hatter come 'roun'.

"De nex' day atter all dis happen, Brer Rabbit he come by de house whar ole King Polecat live 'long wid Brer Coon en Brer Mink. Brer Coon he wuz a great han' fer ter bake gingercake. Fur en wide de folks knows 'bout Brer Coon gingercakes, en dey couldn't be no camp-meetin' 'roun' in dem diggin's, but w'at he wuz hangin' on de aidges sellin' his ginger-cakes en his 'simmon beer; en it seem like eve'ytime Brer Rabbit see Brer Coon dat he whirl right in en git hongry fer gingercakes.

"So de nex' day atter dey done fix it all up 'bout ole King Polecat, Brer Rabbit he come sailin' by Brer Coon's house, en he ax 'im ef he got any gingercakes fer ter sell. Brer Coon 'low, he did, dat he got um des ez fine ez fine kin be, en Brer Rabbit say he b'lieve he'll buy some, en wid dat he run his han' in his pocket, he did, en pull out de change en bought 'im a great big stack er gingercakes.

"Den he tuck'n ax Brer Coon ef he won't keep his eye on de ginger-cakes w'iles he go git some gyarlic fer to eat wid um. Brer Coon 'low he'll take keer un um de bes' w'at he kin. Brer Rabbit rush off, en des 'bout dat time ole King Polecat come in sight. In de accordance er de rules, soon ez Brer Coon see ole King Polecat he mus' shet he eye en hol' he nose; en w'iles Brer Coon doin' dis, ole King Polecat walk up, he did, en grab de gingercakes en make off wid um. Co'se, w'en Brer Rabbit come lippitin' back, he hunt fer he gingercakes, but he can't fin' um nowhar. Den he holler out:

"'My goodness, Brer Coon! Whar my gingercakes?'

"All Brer Coon kin say is dat he ain't see nobody take de gingercakes. Brer Rabbit 'low, he did, dat dis a mighty quare way fer ter do a man w'at done bought de gingercakes en pay fer um. Yit he say he bleedzd ter have some, en so he tuck 'n pitch in en buy n'er stack un um. Den he 'low:

"'Now, den, I done got de gyarlic fer ter go wid um, en I'll des 'bout squat right down yer en watch deze yer gingercakes my own se'f.'

"So he squat down en fix hisse'f, en des 'bout de time w'en he wuz ready fer ter 'stroy de gingercakes, yer come ole King Polecat. Brer Rabbit, he got up, he did, en made a bow, en den he helt he nose en make like he wuz a-shettin' he eyes. Ole King Polecat, he come 'long, he did, en start fer ter pick up de gingercakes, but Brer Rabbit holler out:

"'Drap dem gingercakes!'

"Ole King Polecat jump back en look like his feelin's bin hurted, en he squall out:

"'My goodness! How come yo' eye open? How come you break up de rules dat away?'

"Brer Rabbit pick up de gingercakes, en 'low:

"'I kin hol' my nose ez good ez de nex' man, but I can't shet my eyes ter save my life, kaze dey er so mighty big!'

"Dis make ole King Polecat mad nuff fer ter eat all de gingercakes w'at Brer Coon got in de chist, but he can't help hisse'f, kaze he know dat ef Brer Rabbit tu'n ag'in' 'im, he won't be much uv a king in dat ar country. Atter dat it got so dat Brer Rabbit kin put down his gingercakes anywheres he want ter; en folks 'low dat he wuz mighty nigh ez big a man ez ole King Polecat."

14
Brother Rabbit's Courtship

ONE NIGHT, as the little boy went tripping down the path to Uncle Remus's cabin, he thought he heard voices on the inside. With a gesture of vexation he paused at the door and listened. If the old man had company, the youngster knew, by experience, that he would get no story that night. He could hear Uncle Remus talking as if carrying on an animated conversation. Presently he crept up to the door, which was ajar, and peeped in. There was nobody in sight but the old darkey, and the little boy went in. Uncle Remus made a great pretense of being astonished.

"Were you just talking to yourself, Uncle Remus?" asked the little boy.

"Yasser," said the old man with a serious air, "dat des w'at I wuz a-doin'. I done clean fergit myse'f. I year tell dat dem w'at take en talk 'long wid deyse'f dat dey owe de Ole Boy a day's work. Ef dat de state er de case den he done got my name down on de books, en hit's all on account er deze yer uppity-biggity niggers w'at come 'long yer little w'ile ago en ax me ter go 'way off yan ter de Spivey place whar Nancy's Jim gwine ter git married.

"I wuz settin' yer runnin' on in my min'," Uncle Remus continued, "'bout de time w'en Brer Rabbit went a-courtin'. I boun' you dey ain't bin no sech courtin' sence dat day, en dey ain't gwine ter be no mo' sech."

Here Uncle Remus paused and leaned back in his chair, gazing thoughtfully at the rafters. He paused so long that the little boy finally asked him if he couldn't tell about Brother Rabbit's wonderful courtship.

"Well, honey," said the old man, "you haf ter gi' me time fer to shet my eye-balls en sorter feel 'roun' 'mongst my reckermembunce atter de wharfo'es en de whatsisnames. Kaze I'm like a broke-down plow-mule: I'll go 'long ef you lemme take my time, but ef you push me, I'll stop right in de middle er de row."

"I can wait until bedtime," the little boy remarked, "and then I'll have to go."

"Dat's so," Uncle Remus assented cheerfully, "en bein' ez dat's de case, we haf ter be sorter keerful. Lemme go 'roun' de stumps en over de roots, en git in meller groun', en den we kin des back right 'long.

"Now den! You done year talk er Miss Meadows en de gals, en 'bout how Brer Rabbit bin gwine dar so much. Well, hit done happen so dat Brer Rabbit wuz tuck wid a likin' er one er de gals. Dis make 'im sorter glad at de offstart, but bimeby he 'gun ter git droopy. He laid 'roun' en sot 'bout, he did, en look like he studyin' 'bout sump'n' n'er way off yander.

"Hit went on dis away twel bimeby Miss Meadows, she up en ax Brer Rabbit w'at de name er sense in de matter 'long wid 'im, en Brer Rabbit, he feel so bad dat he up en 'spon', he did, dat he dead in love wid one er de gals. Den Miss Meadows, she ax 'im w'at de reason he ain't tell de gal dat he want ter be 'er b'ide-g'oom. Brer Rabbit say he 'shame'. Miss Meadows, she toss 'er head, she did, en 'low:

"'Ya-a-a-s! You look like you 'shame', now don't you? You mought er bin 'shame' 'fo' hens had der toofies pulled out, but you ain't bin 'shame' sence. I done see you cut up too many capers; I know dey ain't no gal on de top side er de yeth w'at kin faze you,' sez Miss Meadows, sez she.

"Den Brer Rabbit 'low dat he skeer'd de gal won't have 'im, but Miss Meadows 'fuse ter hol' any mo' confab wid 'im; she des broke out singin' en washin' de dishes, en w'at wid de chune en de clatter er de dishes Brer Rabbit can't year his own years. Bimeby, he tuck'n sneak out, he did, en went en sot in de shade by de spring.

"He ain't set dar long 'fo' yer come de gal w'at he bin studyin' 'bout. She had a pail in 'er han' en she wuz comin' atter water. She come 'long down de paff swingin' de pail in her han' en singin'."

"What did she sing, Uncle Remus?" the little boy asked, becoming more and more interested.

The old darkey looked slyly at the youngster, and chuckled softly to himself. Presently he said:

"Hit wuz sorter like dis, ef I ain't make no mistakes in de chune:

> "'Oh, says de woodpecker, peckin' on de tree,
>   Once I courted Miss Kitty Killdee,
>   But she proved fickle en fum me fled,
>   En sence dat time my head bin red.'

"Brer Rabbit bin feelin' mighty droopy en low-spereted all de mornin', but time he year de gal singin', he h'ist up his years en look sassy, en w'en she stop singin' he broke out en 'gun ter sing hisse'f. He sung dish yer kinder chune:

>   "'Katy, Katy! won't you marry?
>   Katy, Katy! choose me den!
>   Mammy say ef you will marry
>   She will kill de turkey hen;
>   Den we'll have a new convention,
>   Den we'll know de rights er men.'"

"Why, I've heard grandma sing that song," exclaimed the little boy.

"Tooby sho you is — tooby sho you is, honey," said Uncle Remus, assuming an argumentative air that was irresistibly comic. "Ef Brer Rabbit kin sing dat chune, w'at gwine hender w'ite folks fum singin' it? Bless yo' soul, w'ite folks smart, mon, en I lay der ain't no chune w'at Brer Rabbit kin sing dat dey can't reel off.

"Well, suh, de gal year Brer Rabbit singin', en she sorter toss 'er head en giggle. Brer Rabbit he look at 'er sideways en sorter grin. Den Brer Rabbit 'low:

"'Mornin', ma'am; how you come on dis fine mornin'?'

"De gal say: 'I'm des toler'ble; how you do yo'se'f?'

"Brer Rabbit 'low, he did: 'I thank you, ma'am, I'm right po'ly. I ain't bin feelin' ter say really peart in mighty nigh a mont'.'

"De gal laugh en say: 'Dat w'at I year tell. I speck you in love, Brer Rabbit. You ought ter go off somers en git you a wife.'

"Dis make Brer Rabbit feel sorter 'shame', en he hung his head en make marks in de san' wid his foots. Bimeby he say: 'How come, ma'am dat you don't git married?'

"De gal laugh wuss'n wuss, en atter she kin ketch 'er breff she 'low: 'Lordy, Brer Rabbit! I got too much sense — *myse'f* — fer ter be gittin' married widout no sign er no dream.'

"Den Brer Rabbit say: 'W'at kinder sign does you want, ma'am?'

"De gal 'low: 'Des any kinder sign; don't make no diffunce w'at. I done try all de spells, en I ain't see no sign yit.'

"Brer Rabbit say: 'W'at kinder spells is you done tried, ma'am?'

"De gal 'low: 'Dey ain't no tellin', Brer Rabbit, dat dey ain't. I done try all dat I year talk 'bout. I tuck'n fling a ball er yarn out'n de window at midnight, en dey ain't nobody come en wind it. I tuck a lookin'-glass en look down in de well en I ain't see nothin' 't all. I tuck a hard-b'iled egg en scoop de yaller out, en fill it up wid salt en eat it widout drinkin' any water. Den I went ter bed, but I ain't dream 'bout a blessed soul. I went out 'twix' sunset and dark en fling hempseed over my lef shoulder, but I ain't see no beau yit.'

"Brer Rabbit, he 'low, he did: 'Ef you'd a-tol' me w'en you wuz a-gwine, ma'am, I lay you'd a seed a beau.'

"De gal, she giggle, en say: 'Oh, hush, Brer Rabbit! Ef you don't g'way fum yer I gwine hit you! You too funny fer anything. W'at beau you speck I'd a seed?'

"Brer Rabbit, he up en 'low, he did: 'You'd a seed me, ma'am, dat's who you'd a seed.'

"De gal, she look at Brer Rabbit des like 'er feelin's is bin hurted, en say: 'Ain't you 'shame' er yo'se'f ter be talkin' dat away en makin' fun? I'm a-gwine away fum dis spring, kaze 'tain't no place fer me.' Wid dat de gal fotch 'er frock a flirt, en went up de paff like de patter-roller wuz atter her.

"She went so quick en so fas' dat she lef 'er pail, en Brer Rabbit, he tuck'n fill it full er water, en kyar it on up ter de house whar Miss Meadows en de gals live at. Atter so long a time, he came on back ter de spring, en he sot dar, he did, en study en study. He pull his mustashes en scratch his head, en bimeby, atter he bin settin' dar a mighty long time, he jump up en crack his heels terge'er, en den he laugh fit ter kill hisse'f.

"He 'low: 'You want a sign, does you? Well, I'm a gwine ter gi' you one, ma'am, en ef dat don't do you, I'll gi' you mo' dan one.'

"De gal done gone, but Brer Rabbit, he hang 'roun' dar, he did, en lay his plans. He laid um so good dat w'en dark come he had um all fixt. De fus' thing w'at he done, he went down ter de canebrake en dar he cut 'im a long reed like dem w'at you see me bring Mars John fer fishin'-pole."

"How did he cut it?" the little boy asked.

"He gnyaw it, honey; he des natchully gnyaw it. Den w'en he do dat, he tuck'n make a hole in it fum een' to een', right thoo de j'ints. W'en dark come, Brer Rabbit tuck his cane en made his way ter de house whar Miss Meadows en de gals stay at. He crope up, he did, en lissen, en he year um talkin' en laughin' on de inside. Seem like dey wuz done eatin' supper en settin' 'roun' de fier-place.

"Bimeby de gal say: 'W'at you reckon? I seed Brer Rabbit down at de spring.'

"'T'er gal say: 'W'at de doin' down dar?'

"De gal say: 'I speck he wuz gwine a-gallantin'; he mos' sholy did look mighty slick.'

"'T'er gal say: 'I'm mighty glad ter year dat, kaze de las' time I seed 'im hit look like his britches wuz needin' patchin'.'

"Dis kinder talk make Brer Rabbit look kinder sollumcolly. But de gal, she up en 'low: 'Well, he ain't look dat away terday, bless you! He look like he des come out'n a ban'box.'

"Miss Meadows, she hove a sigh, she did, en say: 'Fine er no fine, I wish 'im er some yuther man er 'oman would come en wash up dese yer dishes, kaze my back is dat stiff twel I can't skacely stan' up straight.'

"Den dey all giggle, but de gal say: 'You all shan't talk 'bout Brer Rabbit behime his back. He done say he gwine ter be my beau.'

"Miss Meadows, she 'low: 'Well, you better take 'im en make sump'n' er somebody outer 'im.'

"De gal laugh en say: 'Oh, no! I done tol' 'im dat 'fo' I git married, I got ter have some sign, so I'll know p'intedly w'en de time done come.'

"W'en Brer Rabbit year dis, he got in a big hurry. He tuck one een' er de reed en stuck it in de crack er de chimbley, en den he run ter de yuther een', w'ich it wuz layin' out in de weeds en bushes. W'en he git dar, he held it up ter his head en lissen, en he kin year um des ez plain ez ef dey wuz right at 'im.

"Miss Meadows ax de gal w'at kinder sign she want, en de gal she say she don't keer w'at kinder one 'tis, des so hit's a sign. 'Bout dat time Brer Rabbit put his mouf ter de reed, en talk like he got a bad col'. He sing out, he did:

> "'Some likes cake, en some likes pie,
> Some loves ter laugh, en some loves ter cry,
> But de gal dat stays single will die, will die!

"Miss Meadows 'low: 'Who dat out dar?' Den dey got a light en hunted all 'roun' de place en und' de house, but dey ain't see nothin' ner nobody. Dey went back en sot down, dey did, but 'twa'n't long 'fo' Brer Rabbit sing out:

> " 'De drouth ain't wet en de rain ain't dry,
>   Whar you sow yo' wheat you can't cut rye.
>   But de gal dat stays single will die, will die.'

"Miss Meadows, en de gals wuz dat 'stonish' dat dey ain't know w'at ter do, en bimeby Brer Rabbit, he sing out ag'in:

> " 'I wants de gal dat's atter a sign,
>   I wants de gal en she mus' be mine —
>   She'll see 'er beau down by de big pine.'

"En sho nuff," Uncle Remus continued, "de nex' mornin' w'en de gal went down by de big pine, dar sot Brer Rabbit des ez natchul ez life. De gal, she make out, she did, dat she des come down dar atter a chaw er rozzum. Dey jawered 'roun' a right smart, en 'spute 'long wid one n'er. But Brer Rabbit, he got de gal."

IV

The tales from

Uncle Remus
and His Friends

Old Plantation Stories, Songs, and Ballads with Sketches of Negro Character

With illustrations by
ARTHUR BURDETTE FROST

1
Why the Hawk Catches Chickens

ONE DAY, Uncle Remus sat in the sun making a fish basket. The little boy watched him weave the white oak splits together a long time, waiting for a story. Finally a bantam rooster, wandering near, crowed shrilly three or four times. The noise broke the silence so unexpectedly that Uncle Remus jumped nervously, and then hurled the unfinished basket at the rooster, which ran away screaming and cackling. The rooster belonged to the little boy, and was a favorite pet, but the youngster laughed heartily at Uncle Remus's irritation, which was partly real and partly affected.

"Nummine!" exclaimed the old man, recovering his basket, "what fattens de chickens fattens de hawk."

"Now, Uncle Remus," the child protested, not catching the meaning of the homely proverb, "you know hawks don't eat corn and dough, and worms and bugs."

"No, dey don't," responded the old man emphatically. "Ef dey did, dat ar bantin chicken mought live ter git gray. Mos' eve'y mornin' der's a big hawk sailin' 'roun' here, en he'll sholy git dat ar uppity little rooster. You better have 'im put in de pot now. I bin noticin' deze many odd-come-shorts dat hawks is got a spite at roosters, speshually when dey ain't too big fer um ter tote off. Dey wuz a time when de hawks ain't had no mouf fer chicken, but dat time done gone by."

"Didn't the hawks always catch chickens, Uncle Remus?" asked the little boy.

"Sholy I done tell you 'bout dat," the old man remarked, looking at the child with a great affectation of astonishment. "Now den, — rack yo' brain, en tell me ef I ain't done tol' you how come de hawk fer ter be constant a-huntin' chickens en flyin' off wid um."

The little boy thought the matter over, and then shook his head. He didn't know whether to make a vigorous denial or to say nothing. So he compromised by shaking his head.

"Well!" exclaimed Uncle Remus, "ef dat don't bang my time, Joe's dead an' Sal's a widder. You'll wake up some er deze fine mornin's en hear yo' mammy laugh en say she got a mighty big load off'n her min' kaze dey done sont ole man Remus ter de 'sylum. En I ain't never been tell you dat? Hit's in about de fus' tale I hear my grandaddy tell. I mos' shame ter go back en pick it up now."

The little boy said nothing, but sat in an expectant attitude. The old man gathered together a dozen or more splits, placed them where they would be in reach, and then began:

"'Tain't no use ter tell you nothin' 'tall 'bout how hawks does now. Dey er done broke in ter ketchin' chickens — de goshawk, de swamp-hawk en de bluedarter, de forky tail en de fan tail, — all un um. But way back yonder dey ain't know nothin' 'tall 'bout no chicken, kaze dey ain't had de tas'e un um. I dunner what dey did eat, but I hear tell dat times got so hard wid ole Brer Hawk dat he had ter scuffle 'roun' right smartu-ally. Yit it seem like scufflin' ain't do no good. He fly dis away, en he fly dat, yet he ain't fin' nothin' fer ter eat, en it look like hit 'uz gwine ter be all-night-Isom wid 'im. Whiles he wuz flyin' roun', he seed de Sun shinin' up dar in de elements, so he bowed his head en say, 'Howdy.' En de Sun he howdied back, he did, en dey struck up a kinder speakin' 'quaintance.

"Bimeby, Brer Hawk made so bol' ez ter tell de Sun 'bout de trouble what he got, en so de Sun, he up'n 'low, he did, dat ef Brer Hawk kin ketch 'im in bed, he'll gi' 'im all de vittles he kin eat en show 'im whar ter git mo'.'"

"Catch the Sun in bed, Uncle Remus?" asked the little boy.

"Dat what I said, honey. Ef Brer Hawk kin ketch de Sun in bed, den de Sun say he willin' fer ter show Brer Hawk whar ter git his vittles. Dis make mo' trouble fer Brer Hawk. He got up sooner en sooner eve'y mornin', but eve'y time he lay eyes on de Sun, he wuz up en a-shinin'. Den he sot up all night, but dat ain't make no diffunce. He can't ketch de Sun in bed. Hit went on dis away twel Brer Hawk git so weak he kin skacely ruffle a fedder. He got dat poor en light dat he can't fly ag'in' de win' nohow, en den he des natchully gun out.

"He 'uz hoppin' 'bout in de top uv a great big pine when he hear Brer Rooster callin' 'im. He tuck a notion dat Brer Rooster wuz des makin' game un 'im, so he holler back, sezee:

"'Don't bodder 'long er me, Brer Rooster. Scratch up yo' little grub woims en cackle over um, en eat um, but don't pester 'long er me.'

"Brer Rooster holler back, sezee:

"'What de matter wid you? How come you look so pale? How come you look so lonesome?'"

Uncle Remus made each question as near as possible an imitation of the crowing of a rooster, which amused the little boy very much.

"Well," the old man continued, "atter while Brer Hawk drapped down en sot on de fence, whar he kin talk ter Brer Rooster, kaze he so hongry it make his tongue weak. He sot dar on de fence, he did, en up'n tol' Brer Rooster 'bout how he been tryin' fer ter ketch de Sun in bed. Dis make Brer Rooster laugh twel you mought er heerd 'im squall all over de hoss lot. He 'low, sezee:

"'Massy massy! Whyn't you tell me? Whyn't you tell me long ago?'

"Wid dat, Brer Rooster up'n say, sezee, dat dey ain't no mornin' but what he kin ketch de Sun in bed, en he tell Brer Hawk dat ef he'll des come en roos' somers close by, he kin ketch de Sun de ve'y nex' mornin'. Brer Rooster say, sezee, dat when he clap his wing en crow, den de time done come fer Brer Hawk ter start off fer ter ketch de Sun in bed.

"Well, den, ole Brer Hawk look like he mighty thankful. He bowed his head, he did, en look des ez nice ez a nigger does when you gi' 'im biscuit en gravy; en he say he gwine stay ez close ter Brer Rooster ez he kin scrouge. Brer Rooster, he sorter cluck down in his goozle, en 'low, sezee:

"'Git des ez close ez you please, Brer Hawk, but don't hunch me. I'm mighty nervous in my sleep, en ef you hunch me endurin' er de night, der's bleedzd ter be trouble.'

"Ole Brer Hawk, he say, sezee:

"'I ain't a tetchous man myse'f, Brer Rooster, yit I speck I got manners nuff not ter pester dem what is.'

"Dey sot dar on de roos', dey did, des like two bluebirds on a fence pos', en ef dey wuz any fuss made it wuz when ole Dominicker hen dremp 'bout little Billy Black Mink, en holler'd out in 'er sleep. Dey sot dar, dey did, en nodded right along. Bimeby, 'bout er nour 'fo' day, Brer Rooster woke up, en clap his wings en holler:

"'Now yo' time ter go!' Den he wait little, en holler n'er time: 'Now yo' time ter go!'

"Wid dat, Brer Hawk riz en flew, en he flew'd so fas' en he flew'd so fur dat he come ter de place whar de Sun live at, en he cotch de Sun in bed."

"The Sun in bed, Uncle Remus?" exclaimed the little boy.

"In bed!" responded the old man, with unusual emphasis, "right dar in bed. En 'twa'n't no trundle bed needer. It wuz one er deze yer big beds wid high posties. Yasser! De Sun wuz in dar, en he had de bed kivver all drawd up 'roun' his head, en he 'uz snorin' same ez somebody filin' a cowhorn. Brer Hawk rapped on de head-board, en holler out, sezee:

"'Mos' time fer day ter break! Git up fum dar! Brekkus 'll be mighty late ef you lay dar all day!'

"Sun 'low, 'Who dat?'

"Brer Hawk say, ''Tain't nobody but me.'

"Sun 'low, 'What you wanter come wakin' me up fer? I boun' I'll have de headache de whole blessid day.'

"Den Brer Hawk put de Sun in min' er de prommus what he made. Den de Sun got mad. He 'low, sezee:

"'How you speck I gwine fin' you in vittles? Who show you de way ter my bed?'

"Brer Hawk say it 'uz Brer Rooster. Den de Sun raise up in bed, he did, en wink one eye, en 'low, sezee:

"'Go back dar en tell yo' Brer Rooster dat he got to fin' you in vittles.'

"Brer Hawk ain't like dis much, en he sorter hung 'roun', like he waitin' fer sump'n'. Dis make de Sun mad, en he jump out er bed en run Brer Hawk out'n de house wid de poker. Brer Hawk ain't know what to do. He flew'd back ter whar Brer Rooster wuz scratchin' in de trash pile, en tol' 'im what de Sun say. Dis make Brer Rooster laugh. He 'low, sezee:

"'How I gwine ter fin' you in vittles? I got a mighty big fambly ter look atter, en I be bless ef dey don't git hongrier en hongrier eve'y day dat comes.'

"Brer Hawk 'low, 'I bleedzd ter eat, Brer Rooster, en I'm lots hongrier dan what yo' fambly is.'

"Brer Rooster 'low, sezee: 'Well, Brer Hawk, you 'er mo' dan welcome ter drap down here en scratch in de trash. I speck yo' claws des ez good ez what mine is. 'Sides dat, you ain't bleedzd ter holler en cackle eve'y time you fin' a woim.'

"But Brer Hawk shake his head. Dat kinder doin's don't nigh suit 'im. Hit look too much like work. So he sail up in de tree-top, en sot dar, en bimeby here come ole Miss Hen wid 'er chickens, which dey let in ter scratchin' 'longside Brer Rooster. Brer Hawk look at um, en he ax hisse'f, sezee: 'What make my mouf water?' Den he 'membered 'bout how de Sun wunk at 'im, en it come 'cross his min' dat chicken meat mought tas'e good. Wid dat he drapped down on one er Brer Rooster's chilluns, en kyar'd it off, en it fit his appetite so mighty well dat he been eatin' Brer Rooster's fambly eve'y chance he git."

Uncle Remus paused to trim and smooth the end of a split. Then he said:

"Brer Hawk hongry yit. You better watch out fer yo' bantin."

2
Brother Bear and the Honey Orchard

ONE DAY while Uncle Remus was oiling the harness in the carriage-house, he heard the little boy's baby brother crying, and went out to investigate the matter. He soon discovered that the baby was crying for a piece of cake which the little boy held in his hand, and refused to give up. The old man stood watching long enough for the little boy to see him, whereupon he exclaimed solemnly, "Laws a massy!" Then he shook his head solemnly from side to side, and returned to the carriage-house. It was not long before the little boy followed him there. Uncle Remus pretended not to notice the youngster's presence, and began to talk to himself.

"I done put it down in my min' long time ago dat stingy folks ain't gwine ter come ter no good een'. I done seed too much un it. Dar wuz ole man Dickerson — he save money en save money; he pinch here en he pinch dar, en he so stingy he won't buy him a dram skacely. En de gracious en de goodness! What good do it do 'im? He sot dar in de house too stingy to scratch hisse'f right hard, en swivel up en die, en now dem ar chillun er his'n is flingin' it fur en wide. Shoo! When it come ter stingy folks, take em 'way fum me! Don't lemme come nigh um! I done see too much un um."

"Well, Uncle Remus" — began the little boy, but the old man interrupted, —

"Heyo, dar! Dat you? Whyn't you stay out dar en feed dat ar baby some mo'?"

"Well, Uncle Remus, I had a piece of cake for you, and the baby saw it and cried for it, and I didn't want him to have it. He gets everything, anyhow."

"What dat in yo' pocket?" asked the old man.

"Well, that's my piece of cake."

"Den whyn't you gi' de baby my piece, en den fetch me yone?"

"Then I wouldn't have had any."

"I speck dat's so," said Uncle Remus, thoughtfully. "Maybe de cake mought er flung de baby in a spasm, en den I'd a had ter got on a hoss en gallop atter de doctor, en de hoss mought er stumbled en broke my neck, en den deze yer triflin' good-fer-nothin' niggers 'roun' de house would a had a big jollification.

"En yit," the old man went on, slowly eating the cake from the little boy's hand, "I 'spizes ter see stinginess. Hit put me in min' er ole Brer B'ar en de honey orchard. Ef I ain't done tol' you dat tale, I'd like ter know de reason why, kaze it all de time a poppin' in my head."

The little boy was very, very sure he had never heard of the honey orchard before.

"Well," said Uncle Remus, "dey wuz one time when mos' all de creeturs, horn, claw, en wing, live in de same settlement. Dey'd have some fusses, but dey ain't had no fallin' out, en dey wuz livin' des ez satisfactual ez what folks does. Times wuz mighty hard, en 'twuz e'en about all dey kin do fer ter scuffle 'long en make buckle en tongue meet. Rake en scrape ez dey would, some un um 'ud hatter go ter bed hongry. Yit dey took notice er one thing, dat whiles all un um wuz gittin' po' en po'er, ole Brer B'ar wuz gittin' fatter en fatter. Whiles de t'er creeturs' ribs wuz stan'in' out like bar'l hoops, Brer B'ar wuz slick en roun' ez a butter ball. He des waller'd in fat; he wuz too fat ter keep de flies off'n hisse'f.

"Dey all study en study how Brer B'ar kin keep so fat when times is so hard. Brer Rabbit made up his min' dat he gwine ter git at de bottom er de matter, an' so he keep his eye on Brer B'ar. He watch 'im, he did, en 'twan't long 'fo' he seed dat Brer B'ar wuz doin' mighty quare. Stidder settin' up late en talkin' politics, he'd go ter bed wid de chickens, en by good daylight he'd be up en gone. Dis bodder Brer Rabbit might'ly. He got so pester'd en fretted dat many's de time when he'd be gwine 'long de road he'd squat right flat on de groun' en scratch his head en study.

"Brer Rabbit had done got de knack er settin' up all night en sleepin' late in de day, but bimeby, one night he tuck'n pay Brer B'ar a visit fer to see what he kin fin' out. He got ter de do', he did, en scrape his foot on de step en sorter cle'r up his th'oat. Ole Miss B'ar, she come out on de porch fer ter see who 'tis, en she uz monstus perlite. She howdied wid Brer Rabbit, en ax 'im ef he won't come in en take off his things en set awhile wid um. Brer Rabbit say he don't keer ef he do, bein's how he ain't seed um all in so long, en ole Miss B'ar, she rustle 'roun' en fotch a cheer, en ax Brer Rabbit fer ter make hisse'f at home.

"Brer Rabbit cross his legs, he did, en 'low dat he ain't seed Brer B'ar in a coon's age; en Miss B'ar, she fan herse'f wid a turkey-tail fan, en 'low dat times so hard her ole man hatter work soon en late fer ter make bofe eens meet. Den she skusen herse'f, en say she got ter go right now en fix a bag er ashes fer 'im ter take ter work wid 'im in de mornin'.

"Brer Rabbit ax what in de name er goodness Brer B'ar do wid a bag er ashes, en ole Miss B'ar laugh en say she dunner what on top side er yeth he do wid um, but she speck hit's des one er his notions.

"Ole Miss B'ar work her fan twel it fair flutter, en she 'low, 'Goodness knows, dat ole bag er ashes is done 'casion me mo' trouble dan it wuth. But you know how men folks is, Brer Rabbit, dey'll have der way ef it's de las' ac'. What my ole man want wid a bag er ashes eve'y mornin' is mo'n I kin tell you, but have um he will, spite er all creation. Dey got ter be out dar by de chimbley cornder so he kin git um when he start ter work.'

"Brer Rabbit say, 'Whar Brer B'ar now? I ain't hear 'im in dar.'

"Ole Miss B'ar laugh twel she bent over. She 'low, 'You ain't gwine ter hear 'im nuther, Brer Rabbit, 'less you happen ter hear him sno'. Sleep! I ain't never is see nobody what kin sleep like my ole man. He ain't take time ter eat, skacely, 'fo' he's ready fer de bed, en he don't mo'n strike de bed 'fo' he's soun' er sleep. I laugh, en tell 'im it's mighty blessin' for 'im dat I ain't know what a sleepy-head he is 'fo' I marry 'im.'"

The little boy wanted to laugh, but the gravity with which Uncle Remus narrated the conversation warned him that his mirth would be ill-timed. The old man made no pause.

"Wid dat Brer Rabbit say he better be gwine, en he tip ole Miss B'ar a bow en wish 'er mighty well. He went off a little piece, he did, en sot down by de road, en twis' his mustashes, en study 'bout dat bag er ashes. He ax hisse'f wuz ole Miss Bar tryin' fer ter fool 'im, en he got so pestered dat he ain't know what ter do.

"Atter so long a time, he slipt back ter Brer B'ar's house, en, sho nuff, dar wuz de bag er ashes in de chimbley cornder, en inside de house he could hear Brer B'ar sno'in away like somebody sawin' gourds. Brer Rabbit make up his min' dat he'd sorter hang 'roun' en see whar Brer B'ar go ter so soon in de mornin'. So he capered 'roun' in de grass one half de night, en played wid de lightnin' bugs tudder half.

"Time de chickens 'gun to crow fer day, Brer B'ar wuz up en a-stirrin', en by de time it wuz light good, he'd done slung de bag er ashes 'cross his shoulder en wuz a-makin' for de woods. Brer Rabbit try ter keep up, but he skeered ter git too close, en fus' news he know Brer B'ar done make his disappearance. When dat happen, dey ain't nothin' mo' fer Brer Rabbit ter do but go home en dream 'bout what de name er goodness Brer B'ar gwine do wid dat bag er ashes.

"De nex' night Brer Rabbit played 'roun' en run atter lightnin' bugs twel everything got still at Brer B'ar's house, en den he went ter look fer de bag er ashes. Sho nuff, dar 'twuz — same bag in de same chimbley cornder. Brer Rabbit felt de heft un it, en it seem like ter him dat dey wuz 'bout a bushel er ashes in dar. Den he grab holt er one cornder er de bag en tored a hole in it. Some er de ashes got up Brer Rabbit's nose, en he fin' out he bleedzd ter sneeze. He hol' in ez long ez he kin, en make a break fer ter git ez fur fum de house ez he kin 'fo' de sneeze come. He helt his breff he did, long ez he kin, en when de sneeze did bus' a-loose, gentermens! he turned a fair somerset backerds, en dey wuz sech a splutterment dat de Guinny hens got ter hollerin' en de chickens ter cacklin', en ole Brer Rabbit tuck his foot in his han' en lit out fum dar.

"Well, suh, nex' mornin' he got up some sooner dan he in de habits er doin' en he went 'roun' by Brer B'ar's house. He went 'roun' de same way whar he see Brer B'ar go de mornin' 'fo' dat, en he ain't gone fur twel he see whar de ashes been spillin' out'n de bag. Dat what he make de hole in de bag fer. Eve'ytime Brer B'ar take a step, he'd jolt de ashes out. Brer Rabbit, he foller'd de track er de ashes. He foller'd long, he did, up hill en down, thoo bushes en thoo briers, twel bimeby he come 'pon Brer B'ar, en what you reckon dat creetur wuz a-doin'?"

Uncle Remus paused, as if he expected the youngster to give an answer. Receiving none he went on:

"Well, suh, he wa'n't doin' nothin' in de roun' word' but eatin' honey! Pyo honey! Eatin' honey en cleanin' de comb. Des de natchul start-naked bee-juice! When Brer Rabbit see dat, he like ter fainted. He flung bofe han's up en fell down on de groun' like he dead. De sight skeer 'im."

"Why, there wasn't anything to frighten him," said the little boy.

"He bleedzd ter be skeer'd. Ole Brer B'ar ain't look like hisse'f. He done empty de bag er ashes on de groun' en waller in um twel he look like he done turn gray endurin' de night. He put um on 'im, I speck, fer ter keep bees fum stingin' 'im. Dar he wuz, up a tree, eatin' honey by de han'ful, en all 'roun' dat place dey wuz a clump er big poplar trees. Eve'y one un um wuz holler, en eve'y one un um wuz full er honey, kaze Brer Rabbit seed de bees des a-swarmin' in en out constant. He sot dar, he did, en watch Brer B'ar eatin' honey twel he 'gun ter dribble at de mouf, en he got so hongry dat bimeby he went up closter, en ax Brer B'ar fer ter please, suh, gi' 'im a han'ful er honey.

"Brer B'ar 'low, 'G'way fum dar, you triflin', low-down vilyun! I gi' you nothin'! Go on 'bout yo' business, 'fo' I come down dar en w'ar you out ter a frazzle!'

"Brer Rabbit say, 'Please, suh, Brer B'ar, des gimme a little piece; des a teenchy bit er de comb, Brer B'ar.'

"Wid dat, Brer B'ar sorter scramble down de tree like he comin' atter Brer Rabbit, en I bet you Brer Rabbit got up en dusted 'way fum dar. He tuck a nigh cut home, en he sot down in de chimbley cornder en studied out a plan fer ter git even wid Brer B'ar. So de nex' day, whiles Brer B'ar done gone ter de honey orchard, Brer Rabbit 'semble all de creeturs, horn, claw, en wing, en tell um how de lan' lay, en how Brer B'ar been foolin' um. He say 'tain't no wonder dat Brer B'ar rollin' in fat when he go off dar eve'y day en gorge hisse'f on honey, en not let nobody get a smell un it, much less a tas'e.

"All de creeturs 'gree wid Brer Rabbit, en dey say dey'd do anything he tell um, ef dey kin l'arn Brer B'ar some manners. Den Brer Rabbit say he speck de bes' way ter do is ter git up a harrycane. De creeturs ax 'im how de name er goodness dey gwine do dat, en Brer Rabbit say he'll fix it. Den he tuck um all out dar close ter de honey orchard, en all de big creeturs he made stan' by big saplin's, en de little uns he put at de little saplin's.

"He 'low, 'Now den, when you hear me holler, you rub up 'g'in' deze saplin's en shake um ez hard ez you kin.'

"De wing creeturs what kin fly, he made git up in de top er de trees. He 'low, 'When you hear me holler, you flutter des ez hard ez you kin.'

"De wing creeturs what kin run, he made um git in de broom-sage, en he 'low, 'When you hear me holler, run thoo de grass ez hard ez you kin.'

"Brer Rabbit had a long rope, en he went off a little piece fer ter git a good start, en terreckly here he come, draggin' de rope en runnin' like a

yaller dog wid a tin pail tied ter his tail. Brer B'ar, up dar in de bee-tree, hear 'im runnin', en ax 'im what de matter.

"Wid dat Brer Rabbit fetch a whoop, en 'low, 'Dey's a harrycane comin', Brer B'ar, en I bleedzd ter run somers en tie myse'f ter a tree, fer ter keep fum bein' blow'd away. Don't you hear it comin'?'

"Co'se, when Brer Rabbit holler'd, de creeturs at de saplin's 'gun ter shake um, en de wing creeturs in de trees 'gun ter flutter, en de yuthers 'gun ter run in de grass, en dey make de bigges' kin' er noise. Brer B'ar, he scrambled 'bout half-way down de bee-tree, en den he turn eve'ything loose en hit de groun' *kerbiff!* Look like 'twuz nuff ter jolt de life out'n 'im.

"He say, 'Fer massy sake, Brer Rabbit, tie me 'long wid you. Dis des ez good a place ez you'll fin'. Tie me wid you, Brer Rabbit.'

"De creeturs keep on makin' der fuss, en Brer B'ar git skeer'der en skeer'der. Brer Rabbit tuck Brer B'ar at his word, en he tied 'im hard en fas' ter a tree. When he had 'im fastened so he can't git loose, he call ter all de creeturs, Brer Rabbit did, en tell um ter come look at Brer B'ar.

"Den he 'low, 'Whiles de harrycane gwine on, less us go git a bait er honey. Dey ain't no win' what kin blow Brer B'ar off whiles he fix dis away.'

"Wid dat dey raided de honey orchard, en gobble up all dey want, en tuck some home fer der wimmen folks en chilluns."

"Who unfastened Brother Bear?" the little boy asked.

"Eh-eh, honey!" exclaimed Uncle Remus. "You pushes yo' inquirements too fur. Dat what's in de tale I kin tell you; dat what ain't you'll hatter figger out fer yo'se'f."

3
Brother Rabbit Has Fun at the Ferry

ONE NIGHT when the little boy ran out to Uncle Remus's house, he heard the old man talking with some of the other Negroes about an accident at Armour's Ferry. The flat, as the ferry-boat was called, had broken the rope which was used to tow it across the Oconee, and had drifted down the river. Two mules, hitched to a wagon, jumped overboard and were drowned.

"Ah, Lord," exclaimed Uncle Remus, when the Negroes had gone.

"Ef ole Brer B'ar had been de fe'yman, I lay dey wouldn't er been none er dat kinder gwines on."

"Uncle Johnny Roach is the ferryman now," remarked the little boy, by way of saying something.

"Dat man is ole, mon," said Uncle Remus; "he ole en shaky. He bin dar I dunner how long. He gray en trimbly. 'Twa'n't dat away wid Brer B'ar. He wuz young, en he ain't had a gray ha'r in his head. Folks use ter come 'long dat away, en gi' 'im a sev'mpunce des ter see 'im r'ar back on his footses en snatch dat ar flat 'cross de river. I tell you, mon, dem wuz gay times."

Here Uncle Remus paused, and looked steadily into the fireplace, and sighed. The impression he left on the little boy was that he himself had crossed on the ferry while Brother Bear was in charge. But where was the story? The youngster looked at the old man intently, and waited patiently.

"Brer B'ar wuz a mighty fine fe'yman," said Uncle Remus, after a while, taking off his spectacles and rubbing them gently on his knee. "Dey ain't no two ways 'bout dat. But dey wuz one time when he got outdone. I dunner what time er de day, ner what day er de mont', but 'twas somers 'twixt two sun-ups. Brer B'ar wuz settin' in de shade, wishin' dat some un 'ud come long en drap a sev'mpunce in his pocket. He wuz des 'bout ter doze off when he hear somebody holler.

"Man 'cross de river say, 'Hello!'

"Brer B'ar raise up en 'low, 'How you like fer somebody ter call you Hello?'

"Man holler back, 'Come put me 'cross.'

"Brer B'ar 'spon', 'Ah-yi.'

"De man wuz ridin' a gray mar', en de gray mar' had a gray colt wid 'er. Brer B'ar swung de flat on t'er side, en whiles she wuz a-swingin' he 'uz countin' his money.

> "Oh, de rope is long, ketch a holt, ketch a holt.
>   Oh, de rope is long, ketch a holt —
> A dime fer de mar', a dime fer de man.
>   En a thrip fer de little gray colt."

"De flat she swung 'roun', en Brer B'ar he sung out, 'Ride in, mister, en make yo'se'f at home.'

"Right den en dar," continued Uncle Remus, leaning back in his chair and lifting his eyebrows, "right den en dar de trouble begun. Nobody wa'n't ter blame; nobody wa'n't de 'casion un it. Hit des come up dry so, des like de measles did when you had um."

"What trouble was it, Uncle Remus?" the little boy asked.

"Hit des broke out by hit's own 'lonese'f," responded the old man, solemnly. "De man, he cluck ter de mar', en try fer ter ride 'er in de flat, but de mar' she hilt er head down en sorter snort, en 'fuse ter budge. De man try ter coax 'er, but she won't be coaxed. Den he gi' 'er whip en spur, but she whirl 'roun' en 'fuse ter go in de flat. She'd go up, she'd go down, she'd go anywhar en eve'ywhar ceppin' in de flat. Den de man lit en tried ter lead 'er, but de mar' drug 'im 'bout over de san' like he ain't weigh mo'n two poun' en a half. Brer B'ar try ter he'p, but 'tain't do no good. De colt seed dat his mammy wuz skeer'd, en he 'gun ter whicker en squeal en run 'roun' like a pig wid hot dish-water on his back. Dis make a bad matter wuss.

"Dar dey stood. De man, he study, en Brer B'ar, he study, but 'tain't do no good. Bimeby Brer B'ar look 'roun', en who should he see settin' cross-legged on a stump a-watchin' un um, but ole Brer Rabbit? Dar he wuz, des ez natchul ez one er deze yer dagarrytypes. Fum whar he stood Brer B'ar couldn't tell whedder Brer Rabbit wuz laughin' er whedder he wuz cryin', but his face wuz mighty wrinkled up. Brer B'ar call 'im, but Brer Rabbit shuck his head. Brer B'ar ax 'im ter come he'p 'im git de mar' on de flat, but Brer Rabbit shuck his head. Brer B'ar wuz 'bout ter 'buze Brer Rabbit 'fo' comp'ny, but a n'er notion struck 'im, en he tuck en wobbled off ter whar Brer Rabbit wuz settin'. Time he got whar dey could hold er confab, Brer Rabbit 'low:

"'What de name er goodness is you all tryin' ter do down dar? What kinder capers is you cuttin' up? I bin settin' here watchin' you, en des dyin' er laughin' at de way you en de man en dem creeturs been gwine on.'

"Brer B'ar try ter 'splain, but Brer Rabbit keep a-talkin':

"'Go on back down dar, Brer B'ar, en fool 'roun' wid um some mo'. Fer gracious sake lemme have my fun out! Go on, Brer B'ar — go on!

Whiles I'm a-settin' here chawin' my ter-backer, lemme 'joy myse'f, en git de wuth er my holiday. Go joon 'roun' some mo'!'

"Den Brer B'ar up'n tell Brer Rabbit what de matter is, en Brer Rabbit laugh en holler fit ter kill hisse'f. He low: 'My goodness, Brer B'ar, I had de idee dat you all been cuttin' up dem capers a-purpose.'

"Brer B'ar 'low: 'No, bless gracious! Dat man yonder want ter be put 'cross. He des bleedzd ter be put 'cross, but how I gwine do it, I'll never tell you.'

"Brer Rabbit say, sezee: 'Well, Brer B'ar, ef you let dat bodder you mo'n a minnit, you'll make me b'lieve dat you got dropsy er de head. I hear tell dat lots er folks is gittin' down wid dat kinder sickness.'

"Den Brer B'ar say he speck he got it, kaze he can't make no 'rangement fer ter git dat ole mar' on de flat. Brer Rabbit look at 'im right hard, en sorter wrinkle up his face. He 'low, sezee:

"'Brer B'ar, hit des ez easy ez gwine ter sleep in a swing.'

"Brer B'ar say, sezee: 'Brer Rabbit, how I gwine do! Ef you'll tell me dat, I'll do anything you ax me; you can't ax me nothin' I won't do.'

"Brer Rabbit 'low, sezee: 'Well den, Brer B'ar, all you got ter do is ter shove de colt on de flat, en de mammy'll foller right atter.'

"Old Brer B'ar went a-wobblin' back ter de river, en when he got dar he driv de colt on de flat, en de mar' follered atter, same ez ef she'd a been born en raise on a flat. When Brer B'ar see dat, he 'low, *'Well!'*

"De man ax 'im who tol' 'im how ter do dat. Brer B'ar make answer dat 'twuz Brer Rabbit, en den he went on to tell de man 'bout what er soon creetur Brer Rabbit is, dat nobody can't fool 'im, en nobody can't outdo 'im. De man lissen, an den he 'low dat he comin' back dat away in a day er two, en he bet a pot er honey ag'in' a dish er cream dat he kin outdo Brer Rabbit. Brer B'ar tuck de bet, en den dey shuck han's ter make it mo' bindin'.

"Well, 'twa'n't long atter 'fo' her come de man back, en dis time he had two mar's. He wuz ridin one, en leadin' de udder, en dey wuz bofe des ez much alike ez two peas. Dey wuz de same color, de same size, en de same gait. Brer B'ar tuck de man 'cross on t'er side, en den he say dat now is de time fer ter settle de bet. He 'low, sezee:

"'One er deze mar's is de mammy, en de udder one is de colt. Now call up Brer Rabbit, en ax 'im ter tell me which is which, en which is de

udder. Ax 'im ter tell me which is de mammy, en which is de colt. En he
ain't got ter look in der mouf nudder.'

"Brer B'ar look at um mighty close, en den he shake his head.

"Man say, 'Go fetch me my dish er cream.'

"Brer B'ar look, en look, en still he shake his head.

"Man say, 'Go fetch my dish er cream.'

"Brer B'ar feel mighty bad, kaze he smell de pot er honey in de man's
saddle-bags, en it make his mouf water.

"Man keep on sayin', 'Go fetch my dish er cream.'

"But Brer B'ar ain't gwine ter give up dat away. He done made de
'rangement fer ter call Brer Rabbit when de man come back, en he went

'pon top er de hill en holler fer 'im. I tell you now, 'twa'n't long 'fo' Brer Rabbit hove in sight. He come a-hoppin' en a-jumpin', he come a-rippin' en a-rarin'.

"Brer B'ar 'low, sezee: 'Ef you know'd what you got ter do, I lay you wouldn't be in sech a hurry.'

"Den he up'n tell Brer Rabbit de whole circumstance er de case. Brer Rabbit laugh, but Brer B'ar he look sollumcolly. Brer Rabbit tuck'n tol' Brer B'ar fer ter git two bunches er grass en put um dar front er de mar's. Brer B'ar do des like Brer Rabbit tell 'im, en den de mar's sot in ter eatin'; but one un um eat 'er bunch fust, en start ter eatin' on t'er bunch. Den de mar' what wuz eatin' on dat bunch helt up 'er head.

"Brer Rabbit 'low, sezee: 'Dat un what holdin' up 'er head, she de mammy.'

"De man he give up. He say dat beat his time, en den he ax Brer Rabbit how kin he tell.

"Brer Rabbit 'low, sezee: 'De colt, bein' ez she is de youngest, is got de bes' toofies. De best toofies eat de grass fust. Den when de mammy see de colt ain't got none, she willin' ter 'vide wid 'er. Ef de mammy had made at de colt's bundle, de colt'd sholy a bit at 'er.'

"De man look 'stonish, but he ain't sati'fied. He gun Brer B'ar de pot er honey, but he say he got n'er pot, en he willin' ter bet dat he kin fool Brer Rabbit nex' time. Brer B'ar tuck de bet.

"Den de man lef' his hosses dar, en tuck a little basket en went off in de woods. He wuz gone a right smart little whet, but bimeby, here he come back. He hilt de basket high, so Brer Rabbit can't see de inside, en den he hung it on a tree lim'. Den he ax Brer Rabbit what de basket got in it.

"Brer Rabbit study, en den he 'low, sezee: *'De sparrer kin tell you.'*

"De man look at 'im hard, en den he say, sezee: 'What kinder creetur is you, nohow?'

"He tuck de basket down, he did, en sho nuff, dar wuz a sparrer in it. He gun Brer B'ar de t'er pot, en ez he wuz gwine, he holler back at Brer Rabbit, sezee:

"'You er one er deze yer graveyard rabbits, dat what you is.'

"Brer Rabbit laugh, but he ain't say nothin'. He des dip like it tas'e mighty good."

"Uncle Remus," said the little boy, as the old man paused, "how did Brother Rabbit know there was a sparrow in the basket?"

"Who say he know it, honey?"

"Didn't you say so?"

"Shoo, honey, freshun up yo' 'membunce. When de man ax Brer Rabbit, What in dar? he make answer dat a sparrer kin tell 'im, kaze a sparrer flyin' 'roun' kin see what in de basket."

"Well," said the little boy, with a sigh, "I thought Brother Rabbit knew."

"Luck tol' 'im, honey; Brer Rabbit wuz a mighty man fer luck."

4

Death and the Negro Man

ONE DAY Uncle Remus was grinding the axe with which he chopped kindling for the kitchen and the big house. The axe was very dull. It was full of "gaps," and the work of putting an edge on it was neither light nor agreeable. A Negro boy turned the grindstone, and the little boy poured on water when water was needed.

"Ef dis yer axe wuz a yard longer, it ud be a cross-cut saw, en den ef we had de lumber we could saw it up en build us a house," said the old man.

The Negro boy rolled his eyes and giggled, seeing which Uncle Remus bore so heavily on the axe that the grindstone could hardly be turned. The Negro boy ceased giggling, but he continued to roll his eyes.

"Turn it!" exclaimed the old man. "Turn it! Ef you don't turn it, I'll make you stan' dar plum' twel night gwine thoo de motions. I'll make you do like de nigger man done when he got tired er work."

The old man stopped talking, but the grinding went on. After a while, the little boy asked, —

"What did the man do when he got tired of work?"

"Dat's a tale, honey, en tellin' tales is playin'," replied Uncle Remus. He wiped the blade of the axe on the palm of his hand, and tried the edge with his thumb. "She won't shave," he said, by way of comment, "but I speck she'll do ter knock out kindlin'. Yit ef I had de time, I'd like ter stan' here en see how long dish yer triflin' vilyun would roll dem eyes at me."

In a little while the axe was supposed to be sharp enough, and then, dismissing the Negro boy, Uncle Remus seated himself on one end of the frame that supported the grindstone, wiped his forehead on his coat sleeve, and proceeded to enjoy what he called a breathing spell.

"Dat ar nigger man you hear me talk about," he remarked, "wuz a-gittin' sorter ole, en he got so he ain't want ter work nohow you kin fix it. When folks hangs back fum work what dey bin set ter do, hit natchully makes bad matters wuss, en dat de way 'twuz with dish yer nigger man. He helt back, en he hung back, en den de white folks got fretted wid 'im en sot 'im a task. Gentermens! dat nigger man wuz mad. He wuz one er deze yer Affiky niggers, en you know how dey is — bowlegged en bad-tempered. He quolled en he quolled when he 'uz by his own lone se'f, en he quolled when he 'uz wid tudder folks.

"He got so mad dat he say he hope ole Gran'sir Death 'll come take him off, en take his marster en de overseer 'long wid 'im. He talk so long en he talk so loud, dat de white folks hear what he say. Den de marster en de overseer make it up 'mongst deyse'f dat dey gwine ter play a prank on dat nigger man.

"So den, one night, a leetle atter midnight, de marster got'm a white counterpin, he did, en wrop hisse'f in it, en den he cut two eye-holes in a piller-case, en drawed it down over his head, en went down ter de house whar de nigger man stay. Nigger man ain't gone ter bed. He been fryin' meat en bakin' ashcake, en he sot dar in de cheer noddin', wid grease in his mouf en big hunk er ashcake in his han'. De do' wuz half-way open, en de fier burnin' low.

"De marster walk in, he did, en sorter cle'r up his th'oat. Nigger man ain't wake up. Ef he make any movement, it uz ter clinch de ashcake a leetle tighter. Den de marster knock on de do' — *blim-blim-blim!* Nigger man sorter fling his head back, but 'twa'n't long 'fo' hit drapt forrerd ag'in, en he went on wid his noddin' like nothin' ain't happen. De marster knock some mo' — *blam-blam-blam!* Dis time de nigger wake up en roll his eye-balls roun'. He see de big white thing, en he skeered ter move. His han' shake so he tu'n de ashcake loose.

"Nigger man 'low, 'Who dat?'

"De marster say: 'You call me, en I come.'

"Nigger man say: 'I ain't call you. What yo' name?'

"Marster 'low, 'Gran'sir Death.'

"Nigger man shake so he can't skacely set still. De col' sweat come out on 'im. He 'low, 'Marse Death, I ain't call you. Somebody been fool you.'

"De marster 'low, 'I been hear you call me p'intedly. I lissen at you terday, en yistiddy, en day 'fo' yistiddy. You say you want me ter take you en yo' marster en de overseer. Now I done come at yo' call.'

"Nigger man shake wuss. He say: 'Marse Death, go git de overseer fus'. He lots bigger en fatter dan what I is. You'll like him de bes'. Please, suh, don't take me dis time, en I won't bodder you no mo' long ez I live.'

"De marster 'low, 'I come fer de man dat call me! I'm in a hurry! Daylight mustn't ketch me here. Come on!'

"Well, suh, dat nigger man make a break for de winder, he did, en he went thoo it like a frog divin' in de mill pon'. He tuck ter de woods, en he 'uz gone mighty nigh a week. When he come back home he went ter work, en he work harder dan any er de res'. Somebody come 'long en try ter buy 'im, but his marster 'low he won't take lev'm hunder'd dollars for 'im, — cash money, paid down in his han'!'"

5

Where the Harrycane Comes From

WHILE UNCLE REMUS was telling the little boy how the Negro man had been frightened by his master, the clouds began to gather in the southwest, dark and threatening. They rose higher and higher, and presently they began to fly swiftly overhead. Uncle Remus studied them carefully a moment, and then remarked sententiously:

"Mo' win' dan water, I speck."

"How can you tell, Uncle Remus?" asked the little boy.

"Kaze when cloud got water in it you kin see de shadder er de rain; you can see where she starts ter break off fum de cloud. Dat cloud yonder look black, but she's all stirred up; you can't see no rain trailin' down. She look like she been tousled and tumbled."

Just then the old man and the little boy felt the cool wind strike their faces, and the leaves of the trees began to rustle. Straightway they heard a sighing sound in the distance, which gradually increased to a steady roar, accompanied by an occasional gleam of lightning and rumbling of thunder.

"I speck we better git in und' de shingles," said Uncle Remus. "It mought be a harrycane, an den agin it moughtn't."

They went into the old Negro's cabin, and sat there watching the approaching storm. It was not much of a storm after all. There was a very high wind, which seemed to blow through the tops of the trees (as Uncle Remus expressed it, "She rid high") without reaching the ground. While the gale in the upper air was at its height, there was a sudden downpour of hail, which rattled on the roof with startling effect for a few moments. In half an hour the clouds had been whisked away out of sight, and the sun was shining again. The little boy had a good many remarks to make about the wind and the hail, and a great many questions to ask. Uncle Remus himself was unusually talkative, and, finally, in response to some suggestion of the child's, said:

"Dem what done seed one harrycane ain't gwine hone atter no mo' — dat dey ain't. I use ter hear ole Miss talk 'bout a bed tick dat wuz blow'd fum Jones county mos' ter 'Gusty. Dat same harrycane blow'd de roof off'n a house whar de folks wuz eatin' supper, en didn't put de candle out. Dat what ole Miss say," said the old man, noting the little boy's look of astonishment, — "dat what ole Miss say, en she yo' gran-mammy. You kin 'spute it ef you wanter. It tuck a mule en landed 'im in de tree top, en tuck de mattress fum under a baby in de cradle en lef' de baby layin' dar. I wuz stannin' right by when ole Miss sesso."

"Where do the harrycanes start from, Uncle Remus?" asked the little boy.

The old man chuckled, as he took a chew of tobacco.

"What de use er me tellin' you, honey? You won't nigh believe me, en mo'n dat; you'll go up yander en tell Miss Sally dat de ole nigger done gone ravin' 'stracted."

"Now, Uncle Remus, you know I won't," protested the little boy.

"Well, folks lots older en bigger dan what you is 'ud go en do it, en not so much ez bat der eyes."

The old man paused, took off his spectacles, and rubbed his eyes with thumb and forefinger. Replacing the glasses, he looked carefully around, laid his hand confidentially on the little boy's shoulder, and said in a low whisper:

"I'll tell you whar de harrycane starts. Dey starts in de big swamp! In a hollow tree! Down dar whar de bullace vines grows! Dat's whar dey starts."

"I don't see how that can be," said the puzzled youngster.

"I speck not," remarked Uncle Remus, dryly. "You dunner how 'tis dat dat ar acorn in yo' han' is got a great big oak tree in it. Dey got ter be a startin' place. Ef trees wuz ter start out trees, you'd see a monstus up-settin' all 'roun' ev'ywheres. Dey'd be trouble, mon, en a heap un it."

"But how can a harrycane start in a hollow tree, Uncle Remus?" the child asked.

"Well, suh, one time when I wuz a little bigger dan what you is, dey wuz a ole Affiky man live on de place en he kep' a-tellin' me tales, and bimeby one day he 'low he wanter shew me some harrycane seed. I ain't had much sense, but I had nuff fer ter tell 'im I don't wanter look at um, kaze I feard dey'd sprout en come up right 'fo' my eyes. Den dat ole Affiky man, he squinch his eyes at me en tell me de tale how de harrycane start.

"Hit's all on account er ole Sis Swamp-Owl. All de birds er de a'r sot her ole man fer ter watch de vittles one time, en he tuck'n went ter sleep en let some un steal it. Dey kotch 'im 'sleep, en fum dat time out dey start in ter fight 'im eve'y time he show his head in daylight. Dis make Ole Sis Swamp-Owl mad, en so one day, when de hot wedder come, she make up her min' dat she gwine ter gi' de tudder birds some trouble. She come out de holler tree en sot up in de top lim's. She look to'rds sundown, rain-seeds floatin' 'roun'; she look up in de elements, dey look hazy. She tap on de tree.

"'Wake up, ole man; harrycane gittin' ripe.'

"She stretch out 'er wings, so — en flop um down — dis away — en right den an dar de harrycane seed sprouted."

Uncle Remus used his arms to illustrate the motion of the wings.

"When she flop 'er wings, de tree leafs 'gun ter rustle. She flop um some mo', en de lim's 'gun ter shake, en de win' kotch up mo' win, en git harder en harder, twel bimeby it look like it gwine ter claw de grass out de groun'. Den de thunder en de lightnin' dey jin'd it, en it des went a-whirlin'.

"Sence dat time, whenever ole Sis Owl gits tired er de crows en de jaybirds, en de bee-martins pickin' at her en her folks, she des comes out en flops her wings, en dar's yo' harrycane."

6
Why Brother Wolf Didn't Eat the Little Rabbits

"UNCLE REMUS," said the little boy one day, "why don't you come up to the big house sometimes, and tell me stories?"

"Shoo, honey, de spoon hatter go ter de bowl's house. Ef I wuz atter you ter tell me tales, I'd come up dar en set in de back porch en lissen at you eve'y day, en sometimes eve'y night. But when de spoon want anything, it hatter go ter de bowl. Hit bleedzd ter be dat away."

"Well, you used to come."

"Des so!" exclaimed Uncle Remus. "But whar wuz you 'bout dat time? Right flat er yo' back, dat's whar you wuz. You laid dar en swaller'd dat doctor truck twel I be blest ef you had mo' heft dan a pa'tridge egg wid de innerds blow'd out. En dar wuz Miss Sally a-cryin' en gwine on constant. Ef she wa'n't cryin' 'bout you, she wuz quollin' at me en Marse John. 'Oman tongue ain't got no Sunday. Co'se, when I git dar whar you wuz, I hatter set down en tell tales fer ter make you fergit 'bout de fuss dat wuz gwine on. I 'member one time," Uncle Remus went on, laughing, "I wuz settin' dar by yo' bed, tellin' some great tale er nudder, en de fus' news I know'd I woke up and foun' myse'f fast asleep, en you woke up en foun' yo'se'f in de land er Nod. Dar we wuz, — me in de cheer, en you in de bed; en I'd nod at you, en you'd sno' back at me, en dar wuz de ole torty-shell cat settin' by the h'a'th, runnin' dat ar buzz-wheel what cats has got somewhars in der innerds; en de clock wuz a-clockin' en de candle a-splutterin'; en des 'bout dat time Miss Sally come in en rap me 'pon topper de naked place on my head wid er thimble; en I kotch my breff like a cow a-coughin', en den Miss Sally start in ter quollin', en Marse John ax 'er what she doin', en she 'low she des whisperin' ter me; en Marse John say ef she call dat whisperin', he dunner what she call squallin'; en den I up en groanded one er deze yer meetin'-house groans.

"Dem wuz great times, mon," continued the old man, after pausing to recover his breath. "Dey mos' sholy wuz. Hit look like ter me 'bout dem days dat you wa'n't no bigger dan a young rabbit atter de hide been tuck off. You cert'nly wuz spare-made den. I sot dar by yo' bed, en I say ter myse'f dat ef I wuz de ole Brer Wolf en you wuz a young rabbit, I wouldn't git hongry nuff fer ter eat you, kaze you wuz too bony."

"When did Brother Wolf want to eat the young rabbit, Uncle Remus?" inquired the little boy, thinking that he saw the suggestion of a story here.

He was not mistaken. The old man regarded him with well-feigned astonishment.

"Ain't I done tol' you 'bout dat, honey? Des run over in yo' min', en see ef I ain't."

The youngster shook his head most emphatically.

"Well," said Uncle Remus, "ole Brer Wolf want ter eat de little Rabs all de time, but dey wuz one time in 'tickeler dat dey make his mouf water, en dat wuz de time when him en Brer Fox wuz visitin' at Brer Rabbit's house. De times wuz hard, but de little Rabs wuz slick en fat, en des ez frisky ez kittens. Ole Brer Rabbit wuz off somers, en Brer Wolf en Brer Fox wuz waitin' 'fer 'im. De little Rabs wuz playin' 'roun', en dough dey wuz little dey kep' der years open. Brer Wolf look at um out'n de cornder uv his eyes, en lick his chops en wink at Brer Fox, en Brer Fox wunk back at 'im. Brer Wolf cross his legs, en den Brer Fox cross his'n. De little Rabs, dey frisk en dey frolic.

"Brer Wolf ho'd his head to'rds um en 'low, 'Dey er mighty fat.'

"Brer Fox grin, en say, 'Man, hush yo' mouf!'

"De little Rabs frisk en frolic, en play furder off, but dey keep der years primed.

"Brer Wolf look at um en 'low, 'Ain't dey slick en purty?'

"Brer Fox chuckle, en say, 'Oh, I wish you'd hush!'

"De little Rabs play off furder en furder, but dey keep der years open.

"Brer Wolf smack his mouf; en 'low, 'Dey er joosy en tender.'

"Brer Fox roll his eye en say, 'Man, ain't you gwine ter hush up, 'fo' you gi' me de fidgets?'

"De little Rabs dey frisk en dey frolic, but dey hear eve'ything dat pass.

"Brer Wolf lick out his tongue quick, en 'low, 'Less us whirl in en eat um.'

"Brer Fox say, 'Man, you make me hongry! Please hush up!'

"De little Rabs play off furder en furder, but dey know zackly what gwine on. Dey frisk en dey frolic, but dey got der years wide open.

"Den Brer Wolf make a bargain wid Brer Fox dat when Brer Rabbit git home, one un um ud git 'im wropped up in a 'spute 'bout fus' one thing en den anudder, whiles tudder one ud go out en ketch de little Rabs.

"Brer Fox 'low, 'You better do de talkin', Brer Wolf, en lemme coax de little Rabs off. I got mo' winnin' ways wid chilluns dan what you is.'

"Brer Wolf say, 'You can't make gourd out'n punkin, Brer Fox. I ain't no talker. Yo' tongue lots slicker dan mine. I kin bite lots better'n I kin talk. Dem little Rabs don't want no coaxin'; dey wants ketchin' — dat what dey wants. You keep ole Brer Rabbit busy, en I'll ten' ter de little Rabs.'

"Bofe un um know'd dat whichever kotch de little Rabs, de tudder one ain't gwine smell hide ner ha'r un um, en dey flew up en got ter s'putin', en whiles dey wuz 'sputin' en gwine on dat away, de little Rabs put off down de road, — *blickety-blickety*, — fer ter meet der daddy. Kaze dey know'd ef dey stayed dar dey'd git in big trouble.

"Dey went off down de road, de little Rabs did, en dey ain't gone so mighty fur 'fo' dey meet der daddy comin 'long home. He had his walkin' cane in one han' en a jug in de udder, en he look ez big ez life, en twice ez natchul.

"De little Rabs run to'rds 'im en holler, 'What you got, daddy? What you got, daddy?'

"Brer Rabbit say, 'Nothin' but er jug er 'lasses.'

"De little Rabs holler, 'Lemme tas'e, daddy! Lemme tas'e, daddy!'

"Den ole Brer Rabbit sot de jug down in de road en let um lick de stopper a time er two, en atter dey done get der win' back, dey up'n tell 'im 'bout de 'greement dat Brer Wolf en Brer Fox done make, en 'bout de 'spute what dey had. Ole Brer Rabbit sorter laugh ter hisse'f, en den he pick up his jug en jog on to'rds home. When he git mos' dar he stop en tell de little Rabs ter stay back dar out er sight, en wait twel he call um 'fo' dey come. Dey wuz mighty glad ter do des like dis, kaze dey'd done seed Brer Wolf tushes, en Brer Fox red tongue, en dey huddle up in de broom-sage ez still ez a mouse in de flour bar'l.

"Brer Rabbit went on home, en sho nuff, he fin' Brer Wolf en Brer Fox waitin' fer 'im. Dey'd done settle der 'spute, en dey wuz settin' dar des ez smilin' ez a basket er chips. Dey pass de time er day wid Brer Rabbit, en

den dey ax 'im what he got in de jug. Brer Rabbit hummed en haw'd, en looked sorter sollum.

"Brer Wolf look like he wuz bleedzd ter fin' out what wuz in de jug, en he keep a-pesterin' Brer Rabbit 'bout it; but Brer Rabbit des shake his head en look sollum, en talk 'bout de wedder en de craps, en one thing en anudder. Bimeby Brer Fox make out he wuz gwine atter a drink er water, en he slip out, he did, fer ter ketch de little Rabs. Time he git out de house, Brer Rabbit look all 'roun' ter see ef he lis'nen, en den he went ter de jug en pull out de stopper.

"He han' it ter Brer Wolf en say, 'Tas'e dat.'

"Brer Wolf tas'e de 'lasses, en smack his mouf. He 'low, 'What kinder truck dat? Hit sho is good.'

"Brer Rabbit git up close ter Brer Wolf en say, 'Don't tell nobody. Hit's Fox-blood.'

"Brer Wolf look 'stonish'. He 'low, 'How you know?'

"Brer Rabbit say, 'I knows what I knows!'

"Brer Wolf say, 'Gimme some mo'!'

"Brer Rabbit say, 'You kin git some mo' fer yo'se'f easy nuff, en de fresher 'tis, de better.'

"Brer Wolf 'low, 'How you know?'

"Brer Rabbit say, 'I knows what I knows!'

"Wid dat Brer Wolf stepped out, en start to'rds Brer Fox. Brer Fox seed 'im comin', en he sorter back off. Brer Wolf got little closer, en bimeby he make a dash at Brer Fox. Brer Fox dodge, he did, en den he put out fer de woods wid Brer Wolf right at his heels.

"Den atter so long a time, atter Brer Rabbit get done laughin', he call up de little Rabs, gi' um some 'lasses fer supper, en spanked um en sont um ter bed."

"Well, what did he spank 'em for, Uncle Remus?" asked the little boy.

"Ter make um grow, honey — des ter make um grow! Young creeturs is got ter have der hide loosen'd dat away, same ez young chilluns."

"Did Brother Wolf catch Brother Fox?"

"How I know, honey? Much ez I kin do ter foller de tale when it keeps in de big road, let 'lone ter keep up wid dem creeturs whiles dey gone sailin' thoo de woods. De tale ain't persoo on atter um no furder dan de place whar dey make der disappear'nce. I tell you now, when I goes in de woods, I got ter know whar I'm gwine."

7
Mrs. Partridge Has a Fit

"I RECKON maybe you done got de idee dat Brer Rabbit is e'en about de smartes' creetur in de whole er creation," said Uncle Remus, after he had cleaned out his pipe, and refilled it. "Well, suh, ef you got dat idee, you er mighty much mistaken, kaze eve'y once in a while sump'n' er nudder 'ud happen fer ter take de starch out'n Brer Rabbit. Hit allers happen dat away. Go whar you will en when you may, en stay long ez you

choosen ter stay, en right dar en den you'll sholy fin' dat folks what git
full er consate en proudness is gwine ter git it tuck out'n um. You kin see
it gwine on right here 'fo' yo' eyes. Look at dat Yaller Jake. Miss Sally got
'im ter drive de carriage t'er Sunday, en 'fo' he got back home he done
fergot dat his mammy wuz a nigger 'oman. He 'uz high up one day, en
und' de strap de nex'.

"Dat de way wid Brer Rabbit. Des 'bout time he git it stuck in his
min' dat dey ain't nobody kin outdo 'im, up somebody'd jump en do 'im
scan'lous. Dem what he ain't got in de cornder er his min', dey de ve'y
ones what make 'im feel mighty 'umble-come-tumble.

"One time, when Brer Rabbit wuz feelin' like he 'uz high ez a poplar
tree en big aroun' ez a gin-house, he tuck a notion dat he want some
bird eggs. Creeturs gits notions in der heads same ez folks does, en dat
de kind er notion Brer Rabbit tuck up. Nothin'll do but he mus' have
some bird eggs. Dat de way he put it down. He bleedzd ter have bird
eggs.

"He got 'im a basket, he did, en hung it on his arm, en sot out ter hunt
um. He tuck a nigh cut thoo de woods, en whiles he gwine 'long struttin'
en hummin' one er deze yer sassy chunes, he come 'cross Miss Pa'tridge.
You done hear 'bout Miss Pa'tridge, ain't you?" Uncle Remus asked, noting the little boy's look of surprise. "Mos' any day in de week, en Sunday
flung in fer good medjur you kin hear um hollerin' en axin ole Bob White
ef his peas mos' ripe, en will 'is dogs bite, speshul at night.

"Well, suh, whiles Brer Rabbit gwine 'long huntin' bird eggs, he
struck up wid' Miss Pa'tridge. She'd done grabbled a hole in de hot san',
en she wuz settin' in it, flingin' up de dus' wid foot en wing.

"Atter dey'd howdied, Brer Rabbit 'low, 'What make you waller in
de dus'?'

"Miss Pa'tridge say, 'I'm tryin' ter git de freckles off. Where you
gwine wid dat baskit?'

"Brer Rabbit 'low he huntin' bird eggs. Miss Pa'tridge ask 'im ef
'tain't bad manners ter rob bird-nesses. Brer Rabbit 'low he done hear
talk 'bout it, but when a man git hongry, he can't stan' on manners. Dey
jower'd, dey did, twel bimeby Miss Pa'tridge say dat ef Brer Rabbit is
bent on robbin' bird-nesses, she'd take en show 'im whar some wuz; en
wid dat, off dey put, Miss Pa'tridge leadin' de way.

"Fus' dey come whar dey wuz a nes' wid two big eggs in it. Brer Rabbit 'low, 'Dat ain't no bird-nes'. Dat's a hen-nes'.'

"Miss Pa'tridge wuz 'stonished. She say, 'Lawsy, Brer Rabbit, I hear tell dat hens lays mo' dan two eggs.'

"Dey went on, en bimeby dey come ter a Guinny-nes'. Miss Pa'tridge 'low, 'Dis is sho nuff bird-nes'.'

"Brer Rabbit say, 'Ain't you got no sense, 'oman? Dis is Pot Rack nes'. Lemme go 'head. I'll fin' bird-nes'.'

"Brer Rabbit lead de way right spang ter Miss Pa'tridge nes'. Dis kinder flustrate de ole lady, but she say ter herse'f dat her nes' is so hid by de grass dat sholy Brer Rabbit won't be able ter fin' it. But Brer Rabbit got sharp eyes. He see whar de nes' is, but he sorter snuffle 'roun' en make like he huntin' it.

"He 'low, 'Look like I smell bird-egg.'

"Miss Pa'tridge laugh en fan 'erse'f wid a heart-leaf, en say, 'How de name er goodness kin anybody smell bird-egg?'

"Brer Rabbit 'low, 'I'll show you;' en wid dat he unkivered de nes', en dar 'twuz wid in 'bout a hatful er eggs piled up in it.

"Miss Pa'tridge make a great 'miration. She say, 'Lawsy, yes! you kin smell um, Brer Rabbit, en who'd a thunk it?'

"Brer Rabbit start ter put um in his basket, but Miss Pa'tridge sorter dance 'roun', she did, en say, 'Wait, Brer Rabbit, you better lemme see ef dey er good, kaze I done fergit mo' 'bout bird-eggs dan you ever know'd.'

"Wid dat Miss Pa'tridge break one uv um en tas'e it, en, man, suh! she ain't mo' 'n git it in 'er mouf 'fo' she fell over backerds, en had de wuss kinder fit. You done see chickens wid der head chop off. Well, Miss Pa'tridge done wuss'n dat. She flew'd up, en fell down en flutter, en scramble 'roun' in de leaves twel Brer Rabbit 'gun ter git skeer'd. When Miss Pa'tridge ud sorter flutter to'rds him, he'd jump back en shake his foots like a cat does when she git water on um, en he feel so funny he'd whirl 'roun' en shake hisse'f when a piece er grass tickle 'im on de leg.

"When Miss Pa'tridge kin ketch 'er breff, she squall out, 'Run, Brer Rabbit, run! Dey er snake eggs. Run, Brer Rabbit, run! Dey er rank pizen!'

"When Brer Rabbit hear dis, I let you know he put out fum dar like de dogs wuz atter 'im. Miss Pa'tridge went off in de bushes en made anudder nes', en tuck her eggs dar, en sot down on um en res' 'erse'f; en sometimes when she'd be noddin' she'd wake up en laugh at de way she fool ole Brer Rabbit.

"Maybe you'll be a-tellin' dis tale some er dese days," Uncle Remus went on, beaming down on the little boy, "en some un'll whirl in en 'spute it. When dat de case, you des ax um ter go whar Miss Pa'tridge got 'er nes' en see ef she don't do des like she done when she fool Brer Rabbit. She seed how it work den, en she done tell all 'er chilluns dat dat de bes' way ter do. En den, 'pon top er dat, you ax um ef dey ever hear er Brer Rabbit huntin' bird-eggs sence dat time. Des ax um dat, en I boun' dey won't 'spute yo' word no mo' atter dat."

"Well, Uncle Remus," said the little boy, "why doesn't Brother Rabbit hunt bird eggs?"

"Kaze he skeer'd he'll git pizened," responded the old man promptly.

8

Brother Fox "Smells Smoke"

ONE DAY the little boy was going through the Negro quarters yelling at the top of his voice, repeating the refrain of a nonsense song he had heard the plough-hands sing:

"High, my lady! Brinjer, ho."

When he came near Uncle Remus's house, the old man called out: —
"Heyo dar? Who dat?"

"Me! It's me-me! Brinjer, ho!"

"Well, I 'clar ter gracious I'm glad er dat. I low'd maybe it 'uz ole Brer Rabbit gwine by sellin' mustard poultices. You holler des like 'im."

This, of course, was a challenge to the little boy to ask for a story, and he accepted it at once.

"Shoo!" exclaimed Uncle Remus, after he had teased the youngster awhile. "I done tol' you dat tale too long ago ter fergit about."

But the little boy protested so seriously that the old man settled himself back in his chair and began.

"Well, one time dey wuz a man, en dish yer man had a farm. He had pigs, en he had chickens, en he had ducks. He wuz gwine on farmin', en raisin' pigs en ducks en chickens, twel bimeby, one day, he miss a pig. He ain't say nothin', en nex' day he miss a chicken. Still he ain't say nothin', en de nex' day atter he miss a duck.

"Den he 'low, 'Hi! what kinder doin's is dis?'

"He study 'bout it, en den he fix 'im up a trap, en put a pig in it, en set it out by de hoss lot. He ain't cotch nothin', but he see tracks 'roun' de trap.

"He 'low, 'Hey! Dish yer look like Brer Fox been foolin' 'roun' here. I know 'im, kaze de holler er his foot makes a hole in de groun'.'

"Den he tuck de pig out en put a chicken in de trap. Nex' mornin' he went out, he did, en, sho nuff, dar wuz Brer Fox settin' in dar' long wid some chicken fedders, en he look mighty 'umble-come-tumble.

"De man look at de fedders, en 'low, 'I glad you brung yo' bed wid you, kaze you'd a slep' hard ef you hadn't.'

"Brer Fox, he talk mighty polite. He 'low, 'I wish you please, suh, tu'n me out. I wuz passin' by las' night on my way home fum de dance, en I heard a chicken hollerin', en flutterin', en I come in fer ter see what de matter. When I got in, de chicken wuz done gone, en den de do' shot tight, en here I hatter stay.'

"Man say, 'Ef dat chicken wuz ter holler now, I boun' he'd skeer you.'

"Brer Fox 'low, 'How come?'

"Man say, 'Kaze he so close ter you.'

"Man got 'im a rope en tied Brer Fox hard en fas'. He tied all his foots tergedder, en den he tuck Brer Fox home en hung 'im up on a nail in de wall, en tol' his ole 'oman dat she mus' watch 'im twel he come home. Den de man went ter work in de fiel'.

"De man's wife, she watch en watch whiles she shelled peas. Den she'd go en stir de stew in de pot, en come back en watch, en shell mo' peas.

"Bimeby, Brer Fox say, 'Look like you got a mighty heap er peas dar.'

"De 'oman 'low, 'Laws a massy, yes! A heap here, en a heap mo' ter come! Han's in de fiel' got ter be fed. Lawsy, yes! A whole passel er peas, en mo' ter come!'

"Brer Fox say, 'Ef you'll take me down en ontie me, I'll shell dem peas fer you, whiles you er fixin' de rest er de dinner. Den you kin tie me up ag'in en hang me on de nail.'

"De 'oman, she shuck 'er head, but she keep on studyin' 'bout it. Brer

Fox, he keep on a-talkin', en he talk so saf' en he talk so smart dat de 'oman put it down in 'er min' dat he ain't bad ez dey say he is. Den she tuck Brer Fox down en ontied 'im, en he lit in ter shellin' peas des ez hard ez he kin. He kep' one eye on de 'oman, en de 'oman she kep' one eye on him. De 'oman stirred de stew in de pot, en Brer Fox, he fumble wid de peas. De 'oman, she sif' de meal, en Brer Fox, he fumble wid de peas.

"Hit went on dis away, twel bimeby Brer Fox make a break fer de door, but de 'oman 'uz too quick fer 'im. She slam de do', she did, en chase Brer Fox 'roun' de room wid a battlin-stick, en she push 'im so close dat he bleedzd ter run up de chimbley. Man, suh! dey wuz trouble den ef dey never wuz none befo'! When Brer Fox light up de chimbley he turned de pot er stew over, en put out de fier, en scald de 'oman. She gun a squall, she did, but Brer Fox done gone!

"'Twa'n't long 'fo' de man en de fiel' han's come home fer ter git der dinner, en when dey fin' dey ain't no dinner dar, den dey wuz a rippit. De man, he jower en jower, en de 'oman, she tuck'n cry, twel bimeby she flew mad, en den she sot in ter jowerin', en she outjowered de man. She ax 'im how come he ain't kill Brer Fox while he had 'im, stidder bringin' 'im dar whar he kin cut up his didos, en spile de dinner, en scald her all on de foots, en ruin her shoes, en put out de fier? De man can't say nothin'; he des hush up en go long 'bout his business, hongry dough he mought be."

"Well, Uncle Remus," said the little boy, as the old man closed his eyes and leaned back his head against his chair, "did the man catch Brother Fox?"

"De man ain't ketch 'im, but he got cotch. When de man lef' his ole 'oman a-jowerin' en a-jawin' at 'im, he went out in de pastur', en sot on de fence. He sot dar, he did, en he feel mighty bad. He done plum' out-done. He le'nt his head on his han', en do like somebody got de jaw-ache.

"On top er de hill, not so mighty fur fum dar, wuz de place whar Brer Rabbit live at. He see de man come out en set on de fence, en he watch 'im. De man still set dar, en Brer Rabbit crope little closer, en watch 'im. Bimeby Brer Rabbit come out de bushes en ax de man what de matter. De man up an tell 'im; en den ole Brer Rabbit laugh, en say he ain't know Brer Fox wuz so sassy en spry. He 'low, 'I speck I'll hatter take 'im down a peg or two. He been fightin' shy er me dis long time. I feard he bin studyin' up some bran' new tricks.'

"Den Brer Rabbit ax de man how much he'll gi' 'im ef he'll make Brer
Fox feel sorry en sore on account er his prank. De man say he'll let Brer
Rabbit grabble in his goober patch, en nibble de cabbige des ez much er
he want ter.

"Brer Rabbit 'low, 'En you won't sic de dog on me?'

"Man say, 'I won't sic de dog on you.'

"Brer Rabbit 'low, 'It's a bargain.'

"Den ole Brer Rabbit begin fer ter commence fer ter rope Brer Fox in.
He tell de man he mus' have some chicken gizzuds. Man went en got um.
Den Brer Rabbit wen' back on de hill whar he live at, en got his wallet
en his walkin' cane. In de wallet he put de chicken gizzuds, en on his
walkin' cane he hung de wallet. Den he went out fer ter take a walk.

"He ain't gone so mighty fur 'fo' he see Brer Fox gwine 'long sniffin' de
a'r en trottin' wid his head up like a blin' hoss. Brer Rabbit hail Brer Fox,
an ax 'im whar he gwine. Brer Fox 'spon' dat he ain't gwine nowhars in 'tickler, en he ax whar'bouts Brer Rabbit gwine wid his walkin' cane en wallet.
Brer Rabbit 'spon' dat he huntin' fer somebody fer ter he'p 'im move in
some hay. All dis time Brer Fox wuz walkin' 'roun' en 'roun' sniffin' de a'r.

"Bimeby, he up'n 'low, 'Brer Rabbit, I b'lieve in my soul I smell
chicken gizzuds.'

"Brer Rabbit say, 'I 'speck you does, Brer Fox, kaze I got um right
here in my wallet."

"Den Brer Fox jaw begun ter trimble, en he fair dribble at de mouf,
kaze ef dey is anything on de topper side er de yeth what he love mo' dan
anudder, 'tis chicken gizzuds.

"He 'low, 'How many is you got, Brer Rabbit?'

"Brer Rabbit say, 'Somers 'twixt sev'm en 'lev'm.'

"Brer Fox 'low, 'What you gwine do wid um, Brer Rabbit?'

"Brer Rabbit say, 'I gwine gi' um ter de man what he'ps me wid my hay.'

"Brer Fox jump up in de a'r, he did, en 'low, 'Show me de hay, Brer
Rabbit! Show me de hay! I'm de man what kin move it."

"So Brer Rabbit start back de way he come, en Brer Fox went 'long
wid 'im. Brer Fox trot 'long on de side whar de wallet wuz, en one time
he went ter look in it, but Brer Rabbit too smart fer dat.

"He 'low, 'You kin look at um when you done yearned um, en not a
blessed minnit sooner.'

"Well, 'twa'n't long 'fo' dey come ter whar de pile er hay wuz. Brer Fox ax Brer Rabbit what he gwine do wid all dat dry grass, en Brer Rabbit say he gwine ter feed his cow wid some, en some he gwine ter stuff in his bed tick. Dey sorter palaver'd, dey did, but bimeby Brer Fox he got a good big turn er de ruffage on his back, en start up de hill. Brer Rabbit tuck out his flint en steel en struck it on de hay.

"Brer Fox 'low, 'What dat?'

"Brer Rabbit say, 'Cricket hollerin'.'

"Den de gras 'gun ter crackle en blaze, en Brer Fox 'low, 'What dat?'

"Brer Rabbit say, 'Grasshopper singin'.'

"Brer Fox, he mosey 'long, he did, en bimeby he 'low, 'I smell smoke.'

"Brer Rabbit say, 'Somebody burnin' de new groun'.'

"Atter while, Brer Fox 'low, 'I feel mighty hot.'

"Brer Rabbit say, 'Wedder monstus warm.'

"'Twa'n't long 'fo' de hay burn down en Brer Fox, he fetched one squall en jump out fum und' it. He twis', he turn, he roll, he jump, but 'tain't do no good, en den he make a break fer de creek. De ha'r done burnt off'n his back, en de hide blistered. Dat what he git fer tryin' ter steal fum de man, en fer turnin' over de pot er stew, stidder waitin' twel he got a good chance ter go out de do'. Ef he'd 'a' done dat, he'd 'a' saved his manners en his hide too."

"I think," said the little boy, as Uncle Remus paused to fill his pipe, "that Brother Rabbit was very cruel."

"Shoo, honey," exclaimed the old man. "You might talk dat away 'bout folks, but creeturs — well, folks is folks en creeturs is creeturs, en you can't make um needer mo' ner less."

9

Brother Fox Still in Trouble

"UNCLE REMUS sat and smoked his pipe reflectively for some time after the little boy had criticized the heartlessness of the "creeturs." When he spoke, he showed that he had been thinking the matter over. He took the pipe from his mouth and blew a cloud of smoke in the air.

"Uh-uh!" he exclaimed, "'tain't no use er talkin'. Creeturs is creeturs.

You er what you is, en you can't be no is-er; I'm what I am en I can't be no am-er. It all done been fix, en I ain't see nobody yit what kin onfix it. Creeturs is natchully got ha'sh idees, en you may take notice: wharsomever you see ha'r en bristles, right dar you er mo' dan ap' ter fin' claws en tushes. Hit's des like I tell you, honey!

"You flung me off'n de track, but I ain't done wid dat fuss 'twix' Brer Rabbit en Brer Fox. You sorter flinch'd kaze Brer Rabbit tuck en burnt a blister on Brer Fox back, en it sot me ter studyin'; but we ain't come ter de wuss. Ef you er too tetchy fer ter set dar whiles I runs on, you kin des go up ter de big house en watch Sis Tempy fret over dat churn. I hear 'er quollin' now."

The only reply the little boy made was to settle himself more firmly on the split-bottom chair in which he was sitting. Seeing which, the old man continued:

"Now, den, what do Brer Rabbit do atter he scorch Brer Fox? Do he go off somers en set down en mope, kaze Brer Fox rushed out fum und' de burnin' straw? Ef you think he gwine do dat away, you mighty much mistaken. He des ez restless ez he yever is been. He move 'bout en he work his min', he jump 'roun' en study.

"He got 'im a string er red pepper, en he stewed it down wid some hog fat en mutton suet. Den he pick out de pepper, en when de fat en de suet git col' he tuck'n spread de salve on a long piece er rag. He tuck dis rag, he did, en put it in his wallet, en den he got down his walkin' cane, en went down de road to'rds de place whar Brer Fox live at. He ain't gone so mighty fur 'fo' he see Brer Fox settin' down nussin' hisse'f. Time he see 'im Brer Rabbit 'gun ter holler:

"'N'yam! n'yam! 'Intment fer swellin's! Salve fer burns en blisters! N'yam, n'yam!'

"He kep' a-hollerin' dis away des loud ez he kin. He hol' his head up like he ain't see Brer Fox, en he wuz gwine on by, but Brer Fox call 'im. Brer Rabbit look at 'im, but he ain't stop. Den Brer Fox call 'im ag'in. Den Brer Rabbit stop en look mighty hard.

"He holler back: 'What you want 'long er me? Ef 'twa'n't kaze you got de impidence er Ole Scratch hisse'f, you wouldn't dast ter have de face ter hail me whiles I gwine 'long 'tendin' ter my own business. Talk quick! I ain't got no time fer ter fool wid yo' sort!'

"Den Brer Fox ax 'im what he so mighty mad 'bout, en Brer Rabbit 'low, 'Look how you done me 'bout dat hay. Ain't you say you gwine ter fetch it on top er de hill fer me?'

"Brer Fox look 'stonish. He say, 'Name er goodness, Brer Rabbit! You see wid yo' own eyes what de reason I can't fetch it up dar. Look at my back, what got a blister on it fum de top er my head plum to de een' er my tail! I des like ter see de man what kin tote grass when she git dat hot.'

"Brer Rabbit look at Brer Fox back, en he make a great 'miration. He 'low, 'She sho wuz hot, Brer Fox, en you got de marks un it. I des tuck a notion you wuz playin' off one er yo' pranks on me, en my feelin's wuz hurted.'

"Brer Fox say, 'I hear you gwine on by hollerin' 'bout some kind er 'intment er nuther what'll pacify burns, en dat what make I holler at you.'

"Wid dat Brer Rabbit went down in his wallet en fotch out de red-pepper salve, en say ter Brer Fox dat he mus' git his ole 'oman fer ter spread de plarster on de place des soon ez he kin. Brer Fox tuck it en wobble off home des fas' ez he kin. Brer Rabbit, he foller 'long out er sight, en hide in de bushes whar he kin see en hear what gwine on.

"Well, suh, 'twa'n't long 'fo' Brer Rabbit hear Brer Fox fetch a squall, en he shot out'n de house, en in 'bout sev'm jumps he landed in de creek, dough de creek wuz mo'n a half mile off. Foxes is skeer'd er water, same ez cats, but dat ar fox, he des roll en waller in de water. Brer Rabbit still foller atter, en when he git whar he kin see Brer Fox, he des sot down en hol' his han's on his side fer ter keep fum bustin' de buttons off'n his wescut wid laughin'.

"Bimeby he holler out, 'Gracious goodness, Brer Fox! what de matter? Is dat de way you goes a-fishin'?'

"Brer Fox say: 'I'm ruint, Brer Rabbit! You done ruint me! Dat er stuff you gi' me is right rank pizen!'

"Brer Rabbit open his wallet, en look in it. Den he 'low: 'Sholy I ain't gun you de wrong physic! Lawsy! yes I is! Stidder de n'yam-n'yam 'intment, I done gone en gun you de n'yip-n'yip plarster. I b'lieve 'n my soul I'm a-losin' my sev'm senses!'

"Den he sorter fell back in de bushes en like ter kill hisse'f laughin'. Ef ole Brer Fox could er seed Brer Rabbit rollin' 'bout in de leaves en makin' de trash fly, he'd a made sho dat he done gone en got some er de n'yip-n'yip plarster on hisse'f."

"What do n'yam-n'yam and n'yip-n'yip mean, Uncle Remus?" inquired the youngster.

"Hit's des de name er de physic, I speck. You know yo'se'f what quare names doctors is got fer der truck. Dars ippygag, en jollup, en bone-set, en burdock, en one thing en ernudder. De names tas'e bitter, let 'lone de truck."

"Well, Uncle Remus, what became of Brother Fox?"

"Ef you er anyways tetchy, honey, you better put yo' finger in yo' years, kaze de tale gits wuss en wuss. 'Tain't nothin' but trouble 'pon top er trouble for Brer Fox. You done got yo' years plugged? Well, den, atter so long a time, Brer Fox got well er de burn en de blister, en he went on 'bout his business same ez any udder creetur. He wuz gwine 'long by de river bank one day, en he hear a mighty hammerin' not fur off, en he say ter hisse'f dat he b'lieve he'll go see what all de fuss wuz 'bout. He went 'long, he did, en, bless gracious! who should he see but Brer Rabbit wid his coat off en his sleeves rolled up, hammerin' en nailin'; en nailin' en hammerin'.

"Brer Fox 'low 'What you doin' dar, Brer Rabbit?'

"Brer Rabbit say: 'Des makin' a boat, Brer Fox.'

"Brer Fox 'low, What you want wid a boat, Brer Rabbit?'

"Brer Rabbit say, 'Ter go ter my fishtraps in.'

"Brer Fox look 'roun', en see planks en scantlin's a-lyin' 'roun', en he make up his min' dat he ain't gwine ter go ter all dat trouble des fer de sake er one little boat. So he set on de bank en fight san'flies en skeeters, en watch Brer Rabbit make his boat. En he ain't had ter wait long nudder, kaze Brer Rabbit, dough he wuz light in de body, wuz mighty handy, en he got his boat ready in a little er no time. Den he got in it en paddle up de river, en 'twa'n't long 'fo' here he come back wid a long string er fish.

"Dis make Brer Fox dribble at de mouf, kaze ef dey's any kinder vittles what he like mo' dan any udder kind, it's fish. So he make up his min' dat he bleedzd ter have a boat. Den he ax Brer Rabbit ef a mud boat won't do des good ez any yuther kind, en Brer Rabbit make answer dat while mud boats might suit some folks, dey don't suit him.

"Brer Fox ain't got de knack er makin' plank boats, en so he say ter hisse'f dat he gwine ter show Brer Rabbit dat some folks know a thing er two ez well ez yuther folks. Wid dat, he whirl in, en make 'im a boat out'n clay, en when it done got dry in de sun, he shove it out in de water en jump in wid his paddle.

"Brer Rabbit wuz dar wid his plank boat, fer ter see it well done, en when Brer Fox start, he start too. Well, suh, hit's des like I tell you! Brer Fox ain't hit many licks wid his paddle 'fo' de mud 'gun ter melt; de boat went down, en dar wuz ole Brer Fox a scufflin' in de water. Atter so long a time he got back ter de bank, but I let you know he ain't make no mo' boats, needer mud boats nor plank boats."

10
Why Brother Fox's Legs Are Black

"HONEY," said Uncle Remus, shaking the ashes from his pipe by tapping it gently on the hearthstone, "how long sence you seed a fox?"

"Why, don't you know papa brought two home not very long ago?"

"Dat wuz las' fall," suggested Uncle Remus. "One wuz a red en tudder one wuz a gray. Ain't you notice how der legs look?"

The child thought a moment. "Why, yes," he exclaimed. "Their legs were black."

"Now, den," said the old man, leaning back in his chair and looking wise, "how come dat? Dar dey wuz — one fox red en tudder fox gray, en yit der legs black. I wish you'd please, suh, be so good en so kind, ef you got der time ter spar', ter tell me how come dey bofe got black legs?" Uncle Remus's tone was that of a humble seeker after knowledge, and his earnestness was comic indeed, though it seemed to the child to be properly serious.

"I never thought of that," said the little boy. "I can ask papa."

Uncle Remus gave a derisive snort, and shut his mouth with a snap, and began to hum a tune through his nose. It was a sure sign of displeasure.

"Well, Uncle Remus," said the child in a penitent tone, "I thought you wanted to know sure enough. And, anyhow, if you don't, I do."

"Go ax yo' pa," exclaimed Uncle Remus. "Go ax 'im. Ole nigger man like me don't know nothin'. Go ax yo' pa."

"You tell me," said the child coaxingly. "If papa knows, he's too busy to tell me right now."

"He'll never tell you in de 'roun' worl'," remarked Uncle Remus emphatically. "He dunner no mo' 'bout it dan de man in de moon — ef dey's any man dar; en ef dey ain't no man dar, he dunno no mo' 'bout it dan de man what ain't dar."

Then the old Negro made a pretense of changing the conversation, but this the little boy wouldn't hear to.

"Well," Uncle Remus said, after a while, "ef I don't tell you, you'll pester me twel I does tell you, en so what de odds? 'Tain't no great tale nohow, en so I des might ez well out wid it, en git some peace er mind.

"One time Brer Rabbit en Brer Fox went out in de woods huntin', en atter so long a time, dey 'gun ter git hongry. Leas'ways Brer Fox did, kaze Brer Rabbit had brung a ashcake in his wallet, en eve'y time he got a chance he'd eat a mou'ful — eve'y time Brer Fox'd turn his back, Brer Rabbit'd nibble at it. Well, endurin' er de day, Brer Fox 'gun ter git mighty hongry. Dey had some game what dey done kill, but dey wuz a fur ways fum home, en dey ain't had no fier fer ter cook it.

"Dey ain't know what ter do. Brer Fox so hongry it make his head ache. Bimeby de sun 'gun ter git low, en it shine red thoo de trees.

"Brer Rabbit 'low, 'Yonder, whar you kin git some fier.'

"Brer Fox say, 'Whar'bouts?'

"Brer Rabbit 'low, 'Down whar de sun is. She'll go in her hole ter-reckly, en den you kin git a big chunk er fier. Des leave yo' game here wid me, en go git de fier. You er de biggest en de swiftest, en kin go quicker.

"Wid dat Brer Fox put out ter whar de sun is. He trot, he lope, en he gallup, en bimeby he git dar. But by dat time de sun done gone down in her hole en de groun', fer ter take a night's rest, en Brer Fox he can't git no fier. He holler en holler, but de sun ain't pay no 'tention. Den Brer Fox git mad en say he gwine ter stay dar twel he gits some fier. So he lay down topper de hole, en 'fo' he knowed it he drapt asleep. Dar he wuz, en dar whar he got cotch.

"Now you know mighty well de sun bleedzd ter rise. Yo' pa kin tell you dat. En when she start ter rise, dar wuz Brer Fox fas' asleep right 'pon topper de hole whar she got ter rise fum. When dat de case, sump'n' n'er bleedzd ter happen. De sun rise up, en when she fin' Brer Fox in de way, she het 'im up en scorch his legs twel dey got right black. Dey got black, en dey er black ter dis ve'y day."

"What became of Brother Rabbit?" the little boy asked.

Uncle Remus laughed, or pretended to laugh, until he bent double.

"Shoo, honey," he exclaimed, when he could catch his breath, "time Brer Fox got out'n sight, Brer Rabbit tuck all de game en put out fer home. En dar whar you better go yo'se'f."

11

Why Brother Bull Growls and Grumbles

ONE DAY as Uncle Remus, assisted by the little boy, was sorting out shucks and dampening them, for the purpose of making horse-collars, a big red bull went along the public road. He held his head down, and every few steps he gave forth a low, rumbling bellow. Uncle Remus looked at the bull, and then at the little boy, and then shook his head solemnly.

"You hear dat, don't you? You hear dat creetur, gwine 'long out dar, growlin' en grumblin' en complainin' ter hisse'f? Well, he got a mighty good reason fer gwine on dat away; but who'll tell you? You may spit on yo' thumb en turn over de leaves er all de books up dar in Mars John's liberry, yit you won't fin' out in um. You may ax Mars John, you may ax Miss Sally, you may ax a preacher, yit; but none un um'll ever tell you. Den who kin tell you? Me! Ole Man Remus, de nigger what smell cake en yit can't git none!"

The little boy laughed, and drew forth from his pocket a slice of cake. The old man's features lost something of their severity, as he took the cake and placed it on the plank that served as a mantel.

"I'll lay er up dar," he remarked, "twel I 'gin ter feel a cravin' in my gizzud. Now, den, lemme see: what p'int wuz we 'sputin' 'bout? We wa'n't 'sputin' 'bout deze shucks, en we wa'n't 'sputin' 'bout no plain corn-bread. I 'clar ter gracious! De sight er cake natchully drives eve'ything else out'n my head."

"Why, Uncle Remus! You were talking about the bull that went along the road just now," said the little boy.

"Tooby sho!" exclaimed the old man. "Look like a bull is too big fer ter be driv' out'n my min' by a little piece er cake like dat, but dat des de way it come 'bout. Well, dat ar bull wuz gwine on by, grumblin' en a-growlin'. You wuz settin' right whar you could hear 'im wid yo' own years. Dat zackly what he wuz doin'. Time I hear 'im, it put me in min' er de time when ole Brer Bull change hisse'f inter a man en went 'roun' courtin'. Whiles he wuz gwine on dis away, he come 'cross a 'oman which he like 'er looks mighty well, en seem like she like him.

"Well, suh, Brer Bull, he'd graze 'roun' in de pastur' all night, en in de daytime he'd turn ter be a man en call on de 'oman, en cas' sheep-eyes at 'er, en tell 'er right pine-blank how purty she is. Hit kep' on dis away twel bimeby de 'oman got so she can't do nothin' 'tall widout run-nin' over in 'er min' 'bout dish yer nice man what comin' courtin'. She can't skacely cook dinner. She'd lif' de ladle fer ter stir de pot, en hol' it in de a'r a minnit, en den — *belingy-bang-dang!* — it'd drap on de flo'. She can't keep 'way fum de lookin'-glass, a-breshin' 'er ha'r en plarsterin' down 'er beau-ketchers.

"Now, den, dey wuz a little boy livin' dar wid de 'oman. He mought 'er been some bigger dan what you is, but he wa'n't no older. He wuz sharp ez a bamboo brier, en his foot wuz light en quick ez ole Brer Rabbit hisse'f. He watch mighty close. He notice dat when de man wuz courtin', dey wa'n't no Brer Bull in de pastur', en when dey wa'n't no man er courtin', dar wuz Brer Bull grazin' 'roun'. He got behime a 'simmon tree, de little boy did, en watch how Brer Bull change hisse'f. He watch, en he see Brer Bull set down on his hunkers des like a dog. Den he'd shake his head en say, *'Ballybaloo-bill!'* Wid dat his horns 'ud swink, en his tail 'ud swivel, en mos' 'fo' you kin bat yo' eye dar he'd stan' change' inter a man. Den de little boy 'ud slip back ter de house, en pick up chips fer ter put on de oven-lid ter bake bread.

"Bimeby de little boy got so oneasy dat he don't eat much. He wuz skeer'd de 'oman gwine ter marry Brer Bull. En sho nuff, dat des zackly what de 'oman laid off ter do. When de boy see dat, he des up'n tell de 'oman all 'bout it, but stidder b'lievin' 'im, she got mad, en come mighty nigh snatchin' 'im bal'-headed. But de boy, he watch, en keep on watchin', en bimeby he hear what de man say when he change back inter Brer Bull.

"So, one day, whiles de man eatin' dinner at de 'oman house, de boy han' 'roun' de vittles, en when he come ter de man, he say, *'Billybaloo-bal!'* De man looked skeer'd en put his han's up ter his head, but 'tain't do no good; he horns done 'gun ter grow, en hoofs come out on his han's en foots, en de cloze drap off, en mos' 'fo' de man kin git out'n de do', he done change inter Brer Bull, en he curl his tail top er his back en rush out ter de pastur'.

"Well, de 'oman make 'umble 'polergy ter de boy, but he rub hisse'f in de neighborhoods er de coat-tails, whar she spank 'im." The old man paused a moment, and then went on: "I been livin' 'roun' here a mighty long time, but I ain't never see no 'polergy what wuz poultice er plarster nuff fer ter swaje a swellin' er kyo a bruise. Now you des keep dat in yo' min' en git sorry 'fo' you hurt anybody. I been takin' notice deze many long years dat *'Didn't-go-ter-do-it'* is de ve'y chap what do it all."

"But, Uncle Remus," said the little boy, "what became of Brother Bull and the boy that found him out?"

"Well, I tell you," responded the old man, "dat boy wuz name Simmy-Sam, en he wuz mo' sharper dan what folks tuck 'im ter be. His common sense done tell 'im dat atter he make dat explosure 'bout Brer Bull he'd

hatter keep his wedder eye open. So he slip off ter whar his mammy live
at, en she gun 'im a little bundle er flapjacks, en tol' 'im ter go back en
'ten' ter his business, en keep out'n Brer Bull's way.

"Ole Brer Bull wuz grazin' in de pastur' des like nothin' ain't happen,
but he keep on de watch. When he'd see Simmy-Sam anywhars out'n de
yard, Brer Bull 'ud sorter feed to'rds 'im, but Simmy-Sam wa'n't takin' no
chances, en he kep' close ter kivver. But creeturs is mo' patient-like dan
what folks is, en bimeby it got so dat Simmy-Sam 'ud go furder en furder
fum de house, en one day de 'oman sont 'im out in de woods atter some
pine kindlin', en he got ter playin' en foolin' 'roun'. You know how
chillun is, en how dey will do: well, dat des de way Simmy-Sam done. He
des frolicked 'roun' out dar in de brush, twel bimeby he hear ole Brer

Bull come a-rippin' en a-snortin' thoo de woods! Hit in about looked like his time wuz up."

"What did he do?" the little boy asked, as Uncle Remus paused to search in his pocket for some tobacco crumbs. The old man had a knack of holding the youngster in suspense at a critical point in a story.

"What he do? Well, suh, dar wuz Simmy-Sam, yonder wuz a tree, en here come Brer Bull. Now, in a case er dat kind, what Simmy-Sam gwine do? 'Fo' you kin ax de question, he des shinned up de tree like one er deze yer rusty-back lizzuds. Brer Bull come up en hit de tree wid 'is horns — *kerblip!* But 'tain't do no good. He walk 'roun' en switch his tail en shake his head, but Simmy-Sam des laugh at 'im. Brer Bull back, he did, en hit de tree wid his horns — *kerblam!* 'Tain't do no good.

"He kep' on dis away twel he got plum tired, en den he stop en res'. Atter he got his win' back, he sot down, he did, en change hisse'f inter a man, en de man had a axe. Den Simmy-Sam git skeer'd, kaze he know dat when de axe start ter talk, dat tree got ter come down. De man look up, en sorter grin.

"He 'low, 'I got you, is I?'

"Simmy-Sam say, 'Yasser, I speck you is.'

"Man 'low, 'You better come down en save me de trouble er cuttin' down de tree.'

"Simmy-Sam say, 'I skeer'd.'

"Man 'low, 'Skeer'd er no skeer'd, you better come down.'

"Simmy-Sam say, 'Cut some fus', en lemme see how it feel.'

"Wid dat, de man let in ter cuttin' hard ez he kin — *blap! blip! blip! blap!* 'Bout dat time, Simmy-Sam, whiles he wuz feelin' in his pocket fer his hankcher so he kin wipe de water out'n his eyes, come 'cross de little bundle er flapjacks what his mammy gi' 'im. He onroll de bundle, en dey wuz three un um in dar. He tuck one un um, he did, en drap it down on de man, en one er de man's arms fall off. De man ain't wait ter put de arm back on; he des tuck de ax in one han' en kep' on choppin' hard ez he kin.

"Simmy-Sam see dis, en he mak 'ase en drap anudder flapjack. It no sooner drap dan de man's tudder arm fall off. Dar he wuz — ain't got no arms, en can't do no cuttin'. Look like nobody can be skeer'd un 'im when he in dat kinder fix. But Simmy-Sam feard de man kin run at 'im en fall top er 'im. So den, ter make sho, he drapt de las' flapjack, en de man head fell off. Wid dat, Simmy-Sam clum down de tree, en tuck his foot in his han' en put out fer home."

"His foot in his hand, Uncle Remus?" The little boy was somewhat perplexed, and the familiar saying struck strangely on his ear.

"Shoo, honey! You done hear me say dat many en many's de time. When anybody run fas', dey say he done tuck his foot in his han'."

"Did the man die?" the little boy inquired.

The old man laughed softly to himself, and looked at the eager face of the child.

"Why tooby sho not! tooby sho not! 'Twa'n't no man. Ole Brer Bull had des change hisse'f inter a man, en how kin it be a sho nuff man? Atter Simmy-Sam done got out er sight, Brer Bull got his man parts tergidder des like a j'inted snake does, en den he change hisse'f back ter his own se'f, en he done stay dat away, kaze he feard dat some little chap er nudder will come 'long en fling a battercake at 'im.

"En mo' dan dat, he bin gwine 'long fum dat day ter dis, holdin' his head down en growlin' en grumblin' like sump'n' n'er done hurted his feelin's. En ef you'll notice right close, he don't like fer no youngsters fer ter come foolin' 'roun' whar he stay at."

"What became of Simmy-Sam?" asked the little boy.

"He des grow'd up, I speck, like yuther chaps. He grow'd up en got ter huntin' wil' cattle, kaze Brer Bull sot 'im ag'in' all de cattle kin'. What he done en how he done it, I'll tell you some er deze odd-come-shorts when I ain't got time fer ter be ez busy ez I'll hatter be fum dis on. I hear Miss Sally holler'n' atter you now. Ef she ax you whar you been en what you been doin', des tell 'er you been down here runnin' on wid de ole nigger."

12

The Man and the Wild Cattle

ONE DAY Uncle Remus saw the little boy going round the place with a bow and arrow, shooting at the chickens and everything that came in his way. The bow Uncle Remus had made himself, under protest, and he had also gathered a handful of reeds from the swamp and showed the enterprising youngster how to fashion them into arrows. The outfit was crude and clumsy enough, but it was used with such unexpected effect that the old man was compelled to interfere.

"I lay ef Miss Sally see you gwine on dis away, she'll put dat er bow behime de chimbley, en she'll take dem ar arrers en w'ar um out on you. I boun' I ain't gwine ter fix you up no mo' contraptions, ef dat de way you does — massycreein' de cats, en de chickens, en de Lord knows what!"

"Uncle Remus," said the little boy quite seriously, "don't you see I am a wild Indian?" He had a half-dozen feathers stuck in the band of his hat. The old man looked at the child and smiled, in spite of his efforts to assume an air of severity.

"What kinder Injuns is dem?" he asked, "what goes a-pursuin' atter chickens? Ef you er huntin' war, des go up yonder whar dat ar Dominicker hen got de young chickens; go up dar en 'sturb 'er, en ef she don't make you squall, de fus' letter er my name ain't ole man Remus. Dey wuz a man one time what had a bow en arrers dat done 'im some good, but dat time gone by."

"Tell me about it, Uncle Remus," said the little boy.

"Oh, you ain't got time for dat!" responded the old man. "You er lots too busy! Go on en pursue atter de chickens en den atter de cats. Go on! ef you don't make 'aste dey'll git away, en den de Injun man'll hatter go widout his dinner. Go on, Injun!"

But the little boy put down his bow and arrows, and remained, and after a while Uncle Remus told him the story.

"Well, suh, one time dey wuz a man, en he live close by a great big woods. Dey ain't no woods 'roun' here big ez what dat woods wuz. Git on a swif' hoss en gallop 'im sev'm days en sev'm nights, en you'd go ez fur ez de woods wuz wide. Git on de same hoss and gallop 'im under whip en spur 'lev'm days en 'lev'm nights, en you'd go ez fur ez de woods wuz long. De woods wuz full er horned creeturs, en in about all un um wuz cattle. Dey mought er been some deer 'mongst um, but de big run un um wuz horned cattle. Dey roamed 'roun' in de woods, crappin' de grass, en cuttin' up der capers. Dey ain't had no trouble 'bout nothin' ceppin' what de man brung um.

"Now, dish yer man, he hunt de cattle fer der hide en taller. He had a bow en arrer, en he had two big dogs, en de cattle what 'scape fum his bow en arrer he'd ketch wid his dogs. Dey wa'n't no common run er dogs — dey wuz big ez a good size calf — en dey wuz mo' servigrous dan a pant'er. Dey worried de horned creeturs constant. One on um wuz name — "

"Minny-Minny-Morack!" exclaimed the little boy, "and the other was named Follamalinska!"

"Lord-a-massy, honey!" exclaimed Uncle Remus, pretending to be astonished. "Who tol' you dat?"

"Don't you know you told me about the little boy in the tree that called his dogs to kill the leopard woman?"[1]

The old Negro threw his head back and laughed. After a while he went on.

"Well, suh, dat little boy what I been tell you 'bout, he grow'd up, en come ter be a hunter: en dem two dogs, dey grow'd 'long wid 'im, en dey got wuss dan dey wuz when dey kil't de 'oman — lots wuss. So he hunt de cattle, en de dogs kill um scan'lous.

"It went on dat away twel bimeby de wil' cattle helt a meetin' fer ter git up some kinder plan ter make way wid de man. De onliest way dey kin do is ter fix it so dey kin ketch de man by hisse'f. Dey study en study, but dey dunner how dey gwine ter fetch dat about. De dogs wuz in de way. Ef dey kin git de man by hisse'f, dey kin run in on 'im en hook 'im inter jiblets, but ef de dogs 'long wid 'im, den dey git kil't deyse'f. So dey study en study.

"Bimeby a nice young cow, white ez snow, say she gwine ter try a trick. She 'low she gwine ter change inter a young 'oman en make 'im marry 'er. Den she say she'll 'swade 'im ter stay home long ez she kin, en when she can't 'swade 'im no longer, den she'll take en tie de dogs so dey can't go 'long wid 'im when he go huntin', en den de horned creeturs kin cloze in on 'im en make way wid 'im. De Brindle Cow shuck 'er head en 'low, 'Oh-ho!' en de Dun Cow switch 'er tail en 'low, 'Ah-ha!' en dat de way dey settle it.

---

[1] He is referring to the story entitled "The Little Boy and His Dogs," from *Daddy Jake, the Runaway* (p. 393). I have followed the original versions of these two stories in which the spelling of the dogs' names varies slightly. — R. C.

"So den, de nex' time de man start fer ter go huntin', he come 'cross a young 'oman in de woods. She wuz a likely lookin' gal, mon! — des ez purty ez red shoes wid blue strings in um. De man he look at 'er, he did, en de gal, she look back at 'im, en den dey bofe look at one anudder."

"That was the white cow, wasn't it, Uncle Remus?" asked the little boy.

"Tooby sho 'twuz, honey!" exclaimed the old man, warming up to the story; "'twa'n't nobody else in de roun' worl'. She des went en change 'erse'f bodaciously fum a cow en come ter be a likely young 'oman. How she done it, I'll never tell you, but de creeturs in dem days wuz des ez mischievious ez dey could be; dey wan't no een' ter der tricks. Des ter set here en chat about it, don't seem like dat a cow kin change 'erse'f twel she come ter be a 'oman, but dar she wuz right 'fo' de man's two eyes, en how you gwine git 'roun' dat? Dat what I'd like ter know!

"Now, den, dar wuz de likely young 'oman, en dar wuz de man. De 'oman, she hilt 'er head down like she 'shame; en de man, he stood dar, he did, en make sheep-eyes at 'er. Well, you know how 'tis when folks do dat away. Atter 'while, de man, he sorter sidle up ter de young 'oman en ax 'er ef she'll have 'im, en de young 'oman, she tuck'n chaw on 'er bonnet string, en 'low dat she ain't know nothin' contrary ter de question. Dat de way wimmin folks say, 'Yasser, en thanky too!' Den dey went off en got married, en de man took de young 'oman home, en dey sot up housekeepin'.

"De man sorter drapt his huntin' atter dat. Look like he sorter los' de appetite fer killin' de wil' cattle fer der hide en taller. His bow en arrer wuz put up on de shelf, en he stayed 'roun' de house. De dogs ain't know what ter make er dis; dey wonder en wonder what de matter is, en some days dey'd stan' on de door-sill en look at de man en whine. All dis time de wil' cattle wuz roamin' in de woods, grazin', en cuttin' up der capers.

"Bimeby de man 'gun ter hone fer ter go huntin', en one night he tuck'n tol' de young 'oman dat he bleedzd ter go huntin' de nex' day. So, 'fo' day de nex' mornin', de 'oman went out en tied de dogs hard en fas', en den crope back ter bed. De man, he got up, he did, en fried him a rasher er meat, en drapt a pone er corn-bread in his wallet, en den he put out fer ter hunt de wil' cattle. He ain't pay no 'tention ter de dogs, kaze he been in de habits er gwine a-huntin' widout 'em, en when he need um right bad, he'd des holler en call um. No matter how fur off he mought be, he'd des put his han' ter his mouf en holler:

"'Minny-Minny-Morack! Follamalinska! Here, boys, here!'

"Some er de wil' cattle seed 'im a-comin', en dey went en tol' de yuthers, en den de whole drove tuck ter der heels en made off ez hard ez dey could. De man follow'd der tracks, en dis wuz zackly what dey want. Dey wanter toll de man des ez fur in de woods ez dey kin. Bimeby he come on um in one er deze yer big open places, like de clay galls you see in a pine thicket. Dar de wil' cattle tuck der stan', en dey wuz so many un um it look like dey fa'r swarmed all over de face er de yeth.

"Den de man draw'd his bow en let fly his arrers, en called his dogs ez loud ez he could. He lissen fer de dogs, but de mo' he lissen de mo' he ain't hear um, en he keep shootin' at de cattle en callin' de dogs, twel he ain't got but three arrers lef'. Den de wil' cattle put der heads down en histed der tails in de a'r, en come er rushin' at 'im same ez a harrycane. De big ole bulls 'low, *'Oo-hoo! Now we got you!'* en de cows dey holler, *'Ma-hah! Now we git yo' hide en taller!'*

"But des 'bout dat time de man tuck one er de arrers what he got lef' en stuck it in de groun', en 'fo' you kin say Jack Robinson wid yo' mouf open, de arrer grow'd to be a great big tree, wid de man straddlin' de top lim's. Dis make de wil' cattle feel 'stonish, en den dey got mad en run at de tree en hook it twel der horns got sore. Den dey pawed up de groun' en beller, des like de cows does when dey smell fresh beef blood. But 'tain't do no good — dar de tree wuz, en dar she stood.

"Den some er de wil' cattle put out en got some axes, en 'gun ter cut de tree down, en it look like mighty skeery times fer de man.

"Settin' in de top er de tree, he call his dogs, *'Minny-Minny-Morack! Follamalinska! Here, boys, here!'*

"Down at de bottom er de tree de wil' cattle dey chop en chop, *'Blam! blip-blip-blam! Blip-blip-blam! blam! Blam-blam-blam! Blip-blip-blam!'*

"Co'se no tree can't stan' dat kinder doin's, en dis un 'gun ter git shaky. De man call de dogs, en dey ain't come! De axes call de tree, en bimeby down she come! Time she struck de groun' de man stuck anudder arrer in de groun', en up it grow'd bigger dan tudder one.

"De man he call his dogs, *'Minny-Minny-Morack! Follamalinska! Here, boys, here!'*

"De axes dey call on de tree, *'Down! down! Dip-dip-down! Down-dip! Dip-down! Dippy-dip! Dippy-down!'*

"De dogs ain't come, but de tree come, en de man des had time fer ter stick his onliest arrer in de groun' 'fo' de wil' cattle swarmed in on 'im. De arrer grow'd up bigger en bigger dan de yuthers. In de top de man sot en call de dogs louder en louder, en at de butt de wil' cattle cut harder en harder.

"Now all dis time, de dogs hear de man callin', en dey pull at de ropes en tug at um hard ez dey kin, but de ropes big en strong. De man, he call, en de dogs, dey tug. Bimeby dey sot in ter gnyawin', en des 'fo' de las' tree fell dey gnyaw'd de ropes in two. Man, suh! When dey did git loose, dey des come a callyhootin'! De man hear um comin', en he call louder. De wil' cattle hear um comin', en dey cut harder.

"De man call, *'Minny-Minny-Morack! Follamalinska! Come, boys, come!'*

"De axes talk, *'Tree-down! Tree-down! Trip-trip-tree-down!'*

"Bimeby, des ez de tree come down *kerblashity-blam!* de dogs rush'd up. De man sik't um on, en dey wuz so mad dat dey 'stroy'd mighty nigh all de wil' cattle. Atter dey done kil't all dey could, de man seed a snow white cow layin' 'mongst de res'. De hide wuz so nice dat he save it fer hisse'f.

"He went back home, but his wife done gone, en he ain't never see 'er twel dis day. He ain't know nothin' 'tall 'bout de white cow."

13
Brother Rabbit Frightens Brother Tiger

"'TAIN'T DE BIGGEST en de strongest dat does de mostest in dis world," said Uncle Remus one day, when he and the little boy were talking over matters and things in general. The little boy had been talking about the elephant and the tiger which he had seen in a traveling menagerie, and he had asked the old man why the elephant was so strong and the tiger so fierce.

"No, honey, don't let nobody fool you 'bout dat. De cuckle-burr got needer life ner lim', yit when it git in de sheep wool it kin travel fast ez de sheep, you know dat yo'se'f. De elephen may be strong; I speck he is; en de tiger maybe servigrous ez dey say he is; but Brer Rabbit done out-done bofe un um."

"How was that, Uncle Remus?" the little boy asked.

"Well, he done it so easy, honey, dat 'tain't skacely no tale. 'Tain't nothin' dat'll 'stonish you, en 'tain't nothin' dat'll make you laugh. Hit's des some er Brer Rabbit's eve'y-day doin's, des like you'd set down ter eat a plain dinner er pot-liquor en dumplin's, wid no pie fer ter take de greasy tas'e out'n yo' mouf."

The youngster wanted to hear about it anyhow, and he said so. Whereupon Uncle Remus continued:

"One time, whiles Brer Rabbit wuz gwine 'long thoo de woods, he struck up wid Brer Tiger. 'Twa'n't nowhars 'bout here, honey," explained the old man, observing the child's look of astonishment. "'Twuz in some er de 'jinin' counties. Brer Rabbit struck up wid Brer Tiger, he did, en atter dey passed de time er day, dey went amblin' 'long tergedder. Brer Rabbit talk so big en walk so uppity dat Brer Tiger look at 'im sideways en grin. Bimeby dey come ter whar der wuz a creek, en dey want no foot-log in sight. Brer Tiger ain't want ter wet his feet no mo' dan a cat do, en needer do Brer Rabbit, en so dey went up de creek huntin' fer a foot-log. Dey go, en go, but dey ain't fin' none.

"Bimeby Brer Rabbit 'low he know how ter cross. Brer Tiger ax 'im how. Den Brer Rabbit grab a grape-vine hangin' fum de tree lim', en tuck a runnin' start en swung hisse'f on tudder side. When he tu'n de vine loose, it flew back ter whar Brer Tiger wuz, en Brer Tiger he cotch holt en made fer ter swing hisse'f 'cross. Time he done lef' de groun' good, de vine broke, en he come down on his back in de creek, *kersplash!*

"Co'se dis make 'im feel bad, en when he crawl'd out en shuck hisse'f, en see Brer Rabbit settin' up dar, dry en clean, a-laughin' fit ter kill, hit make 'im feel wuss. He fetched er growl er two, en popped his mouf tergedder, but Brer Rabbit kep' one eye on 'im.

"Brer Tiger 'low, 'How come you ain't skeer'd er me, Brer Rabbit? All de yuther creeturs run when dey hear me comin'.'

"Brer Rabbit say, 'How come de fleas on you ain't skeer'd un you? Dey er lots littler dan what I is.'

"Brer Tiger 'low, 'Hit's mighty good fer you dat I done had my dinner, kaze ef I'd a been hongry I'd a snapped you up back dar at de creek.'

"Brer Rabbit say, 'Ef you'd done dat, you'd er had mo' sense in yo' hide dan what you got now.'

"Brer Tiger 'low, 'I gwine ter let you off dis time, but nex' time I see you, watch out!'

"Brer Rabbit say, 'Bein's you so monstus perlite, I'll let you off too, but keep yo' eye open nex' time you see me, kaze I'll git you sho.'

"Brer Rabbit talk so biggity dat Brer Tiger put on his studyin' cap, en he make up his min' dat dey ain't room nuff in dat county fer bofe him en

Brer Rabbit. Brer Tiger turn 'roun', he did, en watch Brer Rabbit go tippin' off, en he look so little en so sassy dat it make Brer Tiger mad. Hit make 'im so mad dat he cotch holt uv a tree en clawed mos' all de bark off'n it. Bless gracious! de furder he git fum Brer Rabbit, de mo' madder he got. He des declar' dat de nex' time he strike up wid Brer Rabbit he gwine ter gobble 'im up widout sayin' grace.

"So, den, dar 'twuz, Brer Tiger 'g'inst Brer Rabbit, en Brer Rabbit 'g'inst Brer Tiger: one big, en tudder one little; one servigrous fum de word go, en tudder one got needer tush ner claw. Hit look mighty bad fer Brer Rabbit! Well, I wish ter goodness you could er seed 'im 'bout dat time. He went 'long thoo de woods ez gay ez a colt in a barley-patch. He wunk at de trees, he shuck his fisties at de stumps, he make like he wuz quollin' wid 'is shadder kaze it foller 'long atter 'im so close; en he went on scan'lous, mon!

"Brer Rabbit ain't gone so mighty fur 'fo' he hear a big noise in de bushes, en lo en beholes, dar wuz ole Brer Elephen trompin' 'roun' en th'ashin' out de tops er de saplin's. He look big ez a young house, but, bless yo' soul! dat ain't set Brer Rabbit back none. He des march up en ax ole Brer Elephen how he come on, en one word led to anudder, twel Brer Rabbit up'n tell ole Brer Elephen all 'bout de confab what he been had wid Brer Tiger. Den he 'low dat ef ole Brer Elephen will loan 'im a helpin' han' dey kin drive Brer Tiger bodaciously out'n de county. Ole Brer Elephen flop his years en shake his snout like he sorter jubous.

"He 'low, 'I ain't gwine ter git hurted, is I, Brer Rabbit?'

"Dis make Brer Rabbit roll his eyes en study.

"He ax, 'Who de name er goodness gwine hurt you, Brer Elephen?'

"Brer Elephen 'low, 'Brer Tiger got sharp claws en long tushes. I skeer'd he bite me en scratch me.'

"Brer Rabbit say, ''Cordin' ter dat I oughter be skeer'd uv a flea, kaze des ez I kin squ'sh a flea, des dat away you kin squ'sh Brer Tiger. Yit dey ain't gwine be no squ'shin' done. Ef you'll do what I tell you, we'll des take'n run Brer Tiger out'n de county. Goodness knows, ef my upper lip wuz long en limber like yone, I 'boun' I'd a done got rid er Brer Tiger long 'fo' now!'

"Brer Elephen, he 'gree ter do what Brer Rabbit say, but he flop his years en work his snout like he mighty restless in de min', en Brer Rabbit holp 'im up de best way he kin wid biggity talk.

"Soon nex' mornin' Brer Rabbit wuz up en a-movin'. He done had eve'ything fix, en he sot 'roun' in de bushes whar he kin see Brer Tiger long ways off. Bimeby he see Brer Tiger come sidlin' down de path, en no sooner is Brer Rabbit seed 'im dan he make a break en run ter whar

Brer Elephen stannin'. Den Brer Rabbit tuck en wrop a long vine 'roun' one er ole Brer Elephen's behime legs, en den 'roun' a tree. He fix it so dat anybody passin' 'long would make sho de leg tied hard en fas'. Den ole Brer Elephen kneel down, en Brer Rabbit tuck a runnin' start en light up on his back. Dey done had all de 'rangements made, en when Brer Tiger come 'long, he seed a sight dat make 'im open his eyes. Dar wuz Brer Rabbit on top er ole Brer Elephen back, en dar wuz ole Brer Elephen wid his behime leg tied ter de tree, a-swingin' backerds en for-rerds, en a-rockin' fum side ter side.

"Brer Tiger look at um a little while, en de notion strike 'im dat Brer Rabbit wuz cotch up dar en can't git down. Dis make Brer Tiger laugh twel he show all his tushes. He walk 'roun', he did, en feel so good he rub hisse'f 'g'inst de saplin's des like you seen cats rub up 'g'inst cheer-legs. Den he sot down flat er de groun' en grin at Brer Rabbit, en lick his chops. Ole Brer Elephen swing backerds en forrerds, en rock fum side to side.

"Brer Tiger 'low, 'I tol' you I'd git you, Brer Rabbit, en now I done come atter you.'

"Brer Elephen swing backerds en forrerds, en rock fum side ter side.

"Brer Rabbit say, 'You done come, is you? Well, des wait a minnit twel I git thoo skinnin' dis creetur what I des cotch. Stay dar twel I git good en ready fer you.'

"Den Brer Rabbit dip down his head by ole Brer Elephen's year en whisper, 'Squall when I put my nose on yo' neck. Don't be skeer'd. Des squall.'

"Den ole Brer Elephen squeal thoo dat snout er his'n; you mought er heerd 'im a mile er mo'.

"Brer Rabbit holler out, 'Des wait, Brer Tiger. Yo' turn'll come ter-reckly. It'll go mighty hard wid you ef I hatter run atter you.'

"Ole Brer Elephen swing backerds en forrerds, en rock fum side ter side. Eve'y time Brer Rabbit'd nibble behime his years, he'd squall out en tromple de groun'.

"When he fus' seed Brer Rabbit up dar on ole Brer Elephen's back, Brer Tiger sorter sot hisse'f on de groun' fer ter make a jump at 'im, but time he see how ole Brer Elephen hollerin' en prancin', Brer Tiger riz en 'gun ter back off. A hick'y nut fell off'n a tree en hit de groun', en Brer

Tiger jump like somebody shot at 'im. When Brer Rabbit see dis, it tickle 'im so dat he come mighty nigh laughin' out loud. But he dip his head down, en make like he gnyawin' ole Brer Elephen on de neck, an ole Brer Elephen, he squall loud ez he kin.

"Brer Rabbit prance up en down on Brer Elephen back like he huntin' fer a mo' tender place, en holler out:

"'Don't go 'way, Brer Tiger. Des wait; I'll be ready fer you terreckly.'

"Brer Tiger he back off, en Brer Elephen swing backerds en forrerds, en rock fum side ter side, en squall thoo his snout.

"Brer Rabbit holler out, 'No use ter git weak-kneed, Brer Tiger. Gi' me time. Dis Elephen blood tas'e salty. It make me dry. You won't have long ter wait.'

"Brer Tiger, he back off en back off. Brer Rabbit, he make out he bitin' ole Brer Elephen on de year. Ole Brer Elephen swing backerds en forrerds, en rock fum side ter side, en snort en tromple de grass.

"'Bout dat time Brer Rabbit make like he gwine ter come down. He make like he huntin' fer a saft place ter jump, en when Brer Tiger see dat, he made a break en des fell over hisse'f tryin' ter get out'n reach. Brer Rabbit holler at 'im, but he ain't stop; he des keep a-runnin', en 'twuz many a long day 'fo' de creeturs seed 'im back dar in dat settlement.

"Elephen skeer'd er tiger," Uncle Remus went on, by way of explanation. "En all de time dat Brer Rabbit wuz talkin' ter Brer Tiger, Brer Elephen wuz so skeer'd dat a little mo'n he'd a went t'arin' thoo de woods like a harrycane. Ez 'twuz, des ez soon ez Brer Tiger got out'n sight, old Brer Elephen retched up wid his snout en wrung de top off'n er saplin' en 'gun ter fan hisse'f wid it."

"Uncle Remus," said the little boy, when the old man had brought the story to a close, "did you ever see an elephant?"

"Well, suh," said Uncle Remus, after a long pause, "you tetch me in a tender place, you sholy does. I seed um, en I ain't seed um. Now, how kin you make dat out?"

"How could that be?" asked the child, laughing.

"I tell you now, dey ain't no fun in it," continued the old Negro, trying to frown. "I done hear talk dat dey wuz a show gwine ter come 'long de road, on de way ter town, but it drapt out'n my min', twel one day I wuz ridin' dat ar roan mule, takin' a letter over ter Mars Bill Little's. I went on, I did, en tuck de note en start back wid de answer. Mars Bill Little had done gi' me a dram fer ole 'quaintunce sake, en I wuz warm in my feelin's. Dat ar roan mule des paced 'long free en easy, en dey want no happier nigger dan what I wuz.

"Well, suh, I heard a little fuss in front er me, en I raise my head, en right dar at me, right spang 'pon topper me, wuz a great big elephen. I des got a glimpse un 'im, kaze de roan mule seed 'im time I did, en she des give a squat en a flutter, en de nex' thing I know'd my head wuz driv in de groun' in about up ter my neck. I dunner how long I laid dar, but time I got de mud en grit out'n my eyes de elephen wuz done gone. You may say I seed de elephen, er you may say I ain't seed 'im; I ain't gwine ter 'spute 'bout it. But dat ar roan mule seed 'im."

14
Brother Billy Goat Eats His Dinner

ONE SATURDAY afternoon, Uncle Remus was sitting in the door of his cabin enjoying the sunshine, while the little boy was mending, or trying to mend, a small wagon with which he had been playing. It was a half holiday on the plantation, and there were several groups of Negroes loitering about the quarters. Ordinarily the little boy would have been interested in their songs or in the drolleries that were passing from lip to lip, and from group to group; but now he was too busy with his broken wagon. The old man watched the child through half closed eyes, and with a smile that was grim only in appearance. Finally, seeing that the little chap was growing impatient, Uncle Remus cried out with some asperity:

"What you doin' longer dat waggin? Gi' me here! Fus' news you know, you won't have no waggin."

The little boy carried it to the old man very readily.

"Sump'n' the matter wid de runnin' gear," Uncle Remus remarked. "I dunner how come it got any runnin' gear. If you had a i'on waggin, it wouldn't las' you twel termorrer night."

Just at that moment, Big Sam happened to get into an angry dispute with Becky's Bill. Big Sam was almost a giant, but Becky's Bill had a free mind and a loud tongue, and he made a great deal more noise than Sam. This seemed to irritate Uncle Remus.

"Hush up, you triflin' vilyun!" he said. "You talk bigger dan de Billy Goat did."

The other Negroes laughed at this, and Becky's Bill soon dropped the quarrel, which was not hard to do, seeing that Big Sam was saying very little. The allusion to the Billy Goat attracted the attention of the little boy. He felt sure there was a story somewhere behind it, and when Uncle Remus had finished his wagon, he began to investigate it.

"What did the Billy Goat talk about?" he asked.

"Go en break yo' waggin; you gwine ter break it anyhow, en you des ez well go now."

"I won't break it any more, Uncle Remus," said the little boy. "I'm going to grease it and put it away. What did the Billy Goat talk about?"

"He talked 'bout deze yer little chaps what pesters folks constant, en he say dey better quit der 'havishness en l'arn how ter don't. Dat what he say."

"Now, Uncle Remus, you know that isn't what the Billy Goat said."

"Well, he ought ter say it if he ain't," remarked the old man.

The shrewd youngster placed himself in the attitude of a listener and patiently waited. Uncle Remus watched him a moment. Then he shook his head and said resignedly:

"You sho does bang my time. You er wuss'n Brer Rabbit."

The little boy flushed and smiled at this, for he regarded it as a high compliment.

"Yasser," Uncle Remus went on, "wuss'n Brer Rabbit — lots wuss. Hen can't cackle widout you wanter see what kinder egg she lay; ole Brer Billy Goat can't take a chaw terbacker in jue season widout you want ter know what he talkin' 'bout. En ef dey is any tale 'bout Brer Billy Goat, 'tain't no good tale fer chilluns, kaze dey might take a notion dat big talk is de right kinder talk, en when dey take dat notion, somebody got ter frail 'em out wid a bresh broom."

The little boy said nothing, but sat listening.

"I mighty fear'd you'll hatter skuzen me," Uncle Remus remarked, after a pause. "Look like my 'membunce wobblin' 'roun' like a hoss wid de blin' staggers. Yit, nigh ez I kin git at all de ins en outs er dish yer tale what we been talkin' 'bout, dey wuz one time when Brer Wolf wuz gwine lopin' 'roun' de settlement feelin' mighty hongry. He want some vittles fer hisse'f, en he want some fer his fambly, yit it seem like he can't fin' none nowhars. He talk wid Brer B'ar, en he hear tell dat shote meat mighty good, but he can't fin' no shote; he hear tell dat goat meat mighty good, but he can't fin' no goat.

"But bimeby, one day whiles he gwine 'long de road, he seed a big rock layin' in a fiel', en on top er dish yer rock wuz Brer Billy Goat. 'Twa'n't none er deze yer little bit er rocks; it 'uz mighty nigh ez big ez dish yer house, en ole Brer Billy Goat wuz a-standin' up dar kinder ru-minatin' 'bout ole times. Brer Wolf loped up, he did, en made ready fer ter see what kinder tas'e goat meat got. Yit he took notice dat Brer Billy Goat wuz chawin' away like he eatin' sump'n. Brer Wolf sorter wait awhile, but Brer Billy Goat wuz constant a-chawin' en a-chawin'. Brer Wolf look en he look, but Brer Billy Goat keep on a-chawin' en a-chawin'.

"Brer Wolf look close. He ain't see no green grass, he ain't see no shucks, he ain't see no straw, he ain't see no leaf. Brer Billy Goat keep on a-chawin' en a-chawin'. Brer Wolf study, but he dunner what de name er goodness Brer Billy Goat kin be eatin' up dar. So bimeby he hail 'im.

"He 'low, sezee, 'Howdy, Brer Billy Goat, howdy. I hope you er mid-dlin' peart deze hard times?'

"Brer Billy Goat shake his long beard en keep on a-chawin'.

"Brer Wolf 'low, sezee, 'What you eatin', Brer Billy Goat? Look like it tas'e mighty good.'

"Brer Billy Goat 'low, 'I'm a-eatin' dish yer rock; dat what I'm a-eatin'.'

"Brer Wolf make answer, 'I'm mighty hongry myself, — but I don't speck I kin go dat.'

"Brer Billy Goat 'low, 'Come up whar I is, en I'll break you off a hunk wid my horns.'

"Brer Wolf say, sezee, dat he mighty much erbleege, but he speck he hatter be gittin' 'long, en he 'low ter hisse'f, 'Ef Brer Billy Goat kin eat rock like dat, I speck I better go 'long en let 'im 'lone.'

"Brer Billy Goat holler at 'im en say, sezee, 'Ef you can't clim' up Brer Wolf, I kin come down dar en help you up. De rock whar I is is mo' fresher dan dat down dar. It's some harder, but it's lots mo' fresher.'

"But Brer Wolf ain't stop ter make answer. He des kep' a-gwine. He

tuck it in his head dat if Brer Billy Goat kin eat rock dat away, 't won't do
ter fool 'long wid 'im, kaze ef a creetur kin eat rock, he kin eat what-
somdever dey put 'fo' 'im."

"What was Brother Goat chewing?" asked the little boy.

"Nothin' 'tall, honey. He wuz des chawin' his cud en talkin' big, en I
done seed lots er folks do dat away — niggers well ez white folks."

15
The King That Talked Biggity

UNCLE REMUS paused, leaned his head sidewise on his hand, and regarded the little boy intently. After a while he closed his eyes slowly and
remarked:

"I speck maybe you done git de idee dat biggity talk goes a mighty
long ways. Well, den, you des well ter git dat idee out'n yo' head. De bluf-
fin' man is mos' sholy gwine ter git bluffed — dey ain't no two ways 'bout
dat. Brer Billy Goat tuck'n bluff Brer Wolf, but spozen Brer Wolf had de
sense what he oughter bin bo'n wid? Man, suh! he'd a made mincemeat
out'n Brer Billy Goat 'fo' you kin wink yo' fingers en wiggle yo' eye-lids.
You hear de fuss what dat ar Becky's Bill wuz a-makin' des now? Well, ef
Big Sam had a made at 'im, he'd a galloped off bellerin' like a calf.

"Dat put me in min' er de time when dey wuz a king somers. Hit
mought er bin 'roun' here, er it mought er bin back up dar in Ferginny;
no matter 'bout dat, hit 'uz somers. Dat ar king wuz one er deze yer ole-
timey kings. He bin settin' up dar kingin' over um so long dat his ha'r
done drap out, en his toofies got loose, en his han' shake wid de palsy.
When de folks see dat, dey say dat it's in about time for dat king ter stop
kingin', en let some yuther somebody do some kingin'. But de ole king
he nelt on, like tick on a cow. He des kep' on a-kingin'.

"Bimeby de folks git tired, en dey meet tergedder en choosen a n'er
king. De ole king ax who is he; but de folks 'fuse ter give his name out.
Dey feard de ole king gwine ter whirl in en make way wid 'im. De ole
king ax is he ole man. De people 'spon' dat he older dan some folks, en
lots younger dan some yuthers. Kaze he mighty mean man, en dey know
dat ef dey tell 'im dey done choosen a ole man, he'll sen' out en have all

de ole folks kil't; en ef dey tell 'im dey done gone en choosen a young man, dey know he'll never res' tell he done massycreed all de young people. Yasser! Dat zackly de kinder man what he wuz, en dem folks what he been kingin' over, dey know dat dey hatter step mighty thin ef dey want to keep der hides whole.

"Den you oughter hear dat ole king talk biggity. He des fa'rly poun' de groun'. He rip, he rave, he fume, he fret. Yit t'ain't do no good. Dar wuz de folks, en dey des stood der groun' en kep' der eye on 'im. Bimeby de ole king sorter cool down. He seed 'twa'n't no use fer ter be cuttin' up no didos, so he pick up his hat en his hankcher whar he done drap um, en got back on de whatzisname."

"On his throne?" the little boy suggested.

"I speck so, honey," responded Uncle Remus, with a laugh. "He got back on de place whar dey set when dey do der kingin', en he 'low, sezee:

"'You all got de idee dat kaze I'm ole en shaky dat I ain't got no sense, but I'm des a-gwine ter show you. Go en tell de man what you done choosen dat 'fo' he kin be king he got ter sen' me a beef. 'Tain't got ter be no bull, en 'tain't got ter be no cow. When he do dat, he kin be king; kaze den I'll know he got sense nuff fer ter do de kingin' fer you all des same ez I bin doin' it.'

"De folks look at one anudder en shake der heads, en den dey go off en hol' a confab. Dey dunner what dey gwine to do. De man what dey choosen fer ter be der new king wuz a young man, en dey skeer'd he can't do what de ole king say. Bimeby some un um went en broke de news, en de young man sorter raise his head en wink one eye. He 'low, sezee:

"'Go back en tell de ole king, dat I got a fine steer fattenin' in my pens, but he got ter come git 'im; but he ain't got to come in de day ner needer in de night.'

"When de folks hear dis, it make um feel sorter holp up, en dey went back en tol' de ole king what de young man say. He sot dar, he did, en sorter study, en scratch his head. Den he ax um ef dey be so good ez ter gi' 'im a chaw terbacker. He tuck a big chaw, en den he pick up his hat en his cane, en grab his kyarpet-bag, en tell 'um, 'So long.'

"Now, den," said Uncle Remus, after a pause, "what good is it do dat man fer ter talk his biggity talk? I wish somebody be so good ez ter tell me dat."

16
Brother Rabbit's Money Mint

ONE DAY the little boy was telling Uncle Remus about how much money one of his mother's brothers was going to make. Oh, it was ever so much — fifty, a hundred, maybe a thousand bales of cotton in one season. Uncle Remus groaned a little during this recital.

"Whar'bouts he gwine ter make it?" the old man inquired with some asperity.

"Oh, in Mississippi," said the little boy. "Uncle James told papa that the cotton out there grows so high that a man sitting on his horse could hide in it."

"Did Marse Jeems see dat cotton hisse'f?" asked Uncle Remus.

"Yes, he did. He's been out there, and he saw it with his own eyes. He says he can make ever so many hundred dollars in Mississippi where he makes one here."

"Marse John ain't gwine, is he?"

"No; I heard papa tell mamma that Uncle James was drawing his long bow, and then mamma said she reckoned that her kinfolks were as truthful as anybody else's."

Immediately Uncle Remus's features lost their severity, and he lay back in his chair to laugh.

"Dat Miss Sally, up en down. Hit her kinnery en you got ter hit her. But yo' pa know Marse Jeems, en I been knowin' 'im sence he wuz in his teens; en when he git ter talkin' he'll stretch his blanket spite er de worl'. He allers would do dat, en he allers will. Now, dat des de long en de short un it. I don't keer ef he is kin ter Miss Sally, he'll talk wil'.

"Bless yo' soul, honey. I done hear talk er Massasip long 'fo' you wuz bornded. I done seed um go dar, en I done seed um come back, en eve'y time I hear folks talk 'bout makin' mo' money off dar dan dey kin any-whars nigher home, it put me in min' er de time when Brer Fox went huntin' de place whar dey make money."

"Is it a story, Uncle Remus?" asked the little boy.

"Well, 'tain't ez you may say one er deze yer reg'lar up-en-down tales, what runs crossways. Dish yer tale goes right straight. Brer Fox meet up wid Brer Rabbit in de big road, en dey pass de time er day, en ax one er nudder how der fambly connection is. Brer Fox say he sorter middlin' peart, en Brer Rabbit say he sorter betwix *'My gracious!'* en *'Thank gracious!'* Whiles dey er runnin' on en confabbin', Brer Fox hear sump'n' rattlin' in Brer Rabbit's pocket.

"He 'low, 'Ef I ain't mighty much mistaken, Brer Rabbit, I hear money rattlin'.'

"Brer Rabbit sorter grin slow en hol' his head keerless.

"He say, ''Tain't nothin' much — des some small change what I bleedzd ter take wid me in de case er needcessity.'

"Wid dat he drawed out a big han'ful er speeshy-dollars, en quarters, en sev'mpunces, en thrips, en all right spang-bang new. Hit shined in de sun twel it fair blin' yo' eyes.

"Brer Fox 'low, 'Laws a massy, Brer Rabbit! I ain't seed so much money sence I sol' my watermilions las' year. Ain't you skeer'd some un'll fling you down en take it 'way fum you?'

"Brer Rabbit say, 'Dem what man nuff ter take it kin have it'; en he des strut 'long de road dar mo' samer dan one er deze yer milliumterry mens what got yaller stripes on der britches.

"Brer Fox 'low, 'Whar de name er goodness you git so much new speeshy, Brer Rabbit?'

"Brer Rabbit say, 'I git it whar dey make it at; dat whar I git it.'

"Brer Fox stop by de side er de road, en look 'stonish. He low, 'Whar'bouts does dey make dish yer speeshy at?'

"Brer Rabbit say, 'Fus' in one place en den in anudder. You got ter do like me, Brer Fox; you got ter keep yo' eye wide open.'

"Brer Fox 'low, 'Fer massy sake, Brer Rabbit, tell me how I gwine ter fin' de place.'

"He beg en he beg, Brer Fox did, en Brer Rabbit look at 'im hard, like he got some doubts on his min'. Den Brer Rabbit sot down by de side er de road en mark in de san' wid his walkin' cane.

"Bimeby he say, 'Well, spozen I tell you, you'll go blabbin' it 'roun' de whole neighborhoods, en den dey'll git it all, en we won't git none 't all.'

"But Brer Fox des vows en declar' ter gracious dat he won't tell a livin' soul, en den ole Brer Rabbit sorter bent hisse'f back en cle'r up his th'oat.

"He say, ''Tain't much atter you fin' it out, Brer Fox; all you got ter do

is ter watch de road twel you see a waggin come 'long. Ef you'll look right
close, you'll see dat de waggin, ef hit's de right kind er waggin, is got two
front wheels en two behime wheels; en you'll see fuddermo' dat de front
wheels is lots littler dan de behime wheels. Now, when you see dat, what
is you bleedzd ter b'lieve?'

"Brer Fox study little while, en den shuck his head. He 'low, 'You too
much fer me, Brer Rabbit.'

"Brer Rabbit look like he feel sorry kaze Brer Fox sech a numbskull.
He say, 'When you see dat, you bleedzd ter b'lieve dat atter so long a
time de big wheel gwine ter ketch de little one. Yo' common sense ought
ter tell you dat.'

"Brer Fox 'low, 'Hit sholy look so.'

"Brer Rabbit say, 'Ef you know dat de big wheel gwine ter ketch de little wheel, en dat bran' new money gwine ter drap turn betwixt um when dey grind up 'g'inst one anudder, what you gwine do den?'

"Still Brer Fox study, en shake his head. Brer Rabbit look like he gittin' sick.

"He say, 'You kin set down en let de waggin go on by, ef you don't want no bran' new money. Den ag'in, ef you want de money, you kin foller 'long en keep watch, en see when de behime wheels overtake de front uns en be on han' when de money starts ter drappin'.

"Brer Fox look like he got de idee. He sorter laugh.

"Brer Rabbit say, 'Nex' time you see a waggin gwine by, Brer Fox, des holler for me ef you don't want ter take no chances. Des bawl out! I ain't got nuff speeshy, en I ain't gwine ter have nuff.'

"Brer Fox, he broke off a broom straw en 'gun ter chaw on it, en des 'bout dat time dey hear a waggin comin' 'cross de hill.

"Brer Rabbit 'low, 'Des say de word, Brer Fox, en ef you ain't gwine 'long atter de waggin, I'll go myse'f!'

"Brer Fox say, 'Maybe de wheels done grinded tergedder back yonder a piece.'

"Brer Rabbit 'low, 'I ain't got time ter 'spute, Brer Fox. Ef you ain't gwine, des say de word!'

"Brer Fox sorter laugh like he shame. He say, 'I b'lieve I'll go a little piece er de way en see how de wheels run.'

"Wid dat," said Uncle Remus, looking up at the ceiling with a peculiar smile, "Brer Rabbit wish Brer Fox good luck, en went on 'bout his business. Yit he ain't go so fur dat he can't watch Brer Fox's motions. At de rise er de nex' hill he look back, en dar he see Brer Fox trottin' 'long atter de waggin. When he see dat, Brer Rabbit des lay down in de grass en kick up his heels en holler."

Uncle Remus laughed, and the little boy laughed. The old Negro's merriment was as keen as that of the youngster, for his humor swept over a wide field of human experience. The little boy laughed at the transparent trick; Uncle Remus no doubt beheld in his imagination a long procession of human Brer Foxes "polin' 'long," up hill and down hill, waiting for the hind wheels to overtake the front ones. After a while the little boy asked what became of Brother Fox.

"Well, honey," said Uncle Remus, "he des foller 'long, trottin' en gallopin', waitin' fer de wheels ter ketch up wid one anudder. Ef he ain't in Massasip by dis time, I'm mighty much mistaken. I boun' yo' Unk' Jeems'll see 'im when he go out dar! Brer Fox had ter take his foot in his han', en git dar de bes' way he kin; yo' Unk' Jeems gwine by conveyance."

17
Why the Moon's Face Is Smutty

"HIT'S MONEY, honey, de worl' over," remarked Uncle Remus, after a somewhat prolonged silence. "Go whar you will, en go when you may, en stay ez long ez mought be, en you'll fin' folks huntin' atter money — mornin' en evenin', day en night.

"Look at um! Why, dar's de Moon" — Something in the attitude or the countenance of the child caused Uncle Remus to stop suddenly and laugh.

"The Moon, Uncle Remus?" exclaimed the youngster, "What about the Moon?"

"Well, you know how folks talk 'bout de Moon. You'll hear um say she's on her fus' quarter, en den on 'er las' quarter; en dat des zackly de way dey talk 'bout money. I hear tell dat one time dey wuz a man gwine 'long en de woods, en he hear a mighty jinglin' en rattlin'. He look 'roun', en see it wuz de Moon er changin'. Seem like she lacked a quarter, en de man pulled out his money-purse en flung de quarter in, en den she change all right.

"But dat ain't no tale; hits des a rig," Uncle Remus continued, not waiting to see the effect of this venerable joke. "De tale dat I been hearin' 'bout de moon ain't got no money in it, en dat mighty funny, too, kaze it look like money is mix up wid mos' eve'ything.

"In dem days, way back yander, de Moon use ter come down en get behime a big poplar log when she wanter make a change. She ain't want nobody to see 'er. She'd rise later en later eve'y night, des like she do now, en den to'rds de las' she'd drap down on de fur een' er de lan', over dat away, en slip behime de poplar log en change all she want ter.

"But one time dey wuz a man gwine 'long thoo de woods totin' a bag er charcoal, what he been burnin'. He been watchin' de coal kil' sence midnight de night befo', en he 'uz so tired out en broke down dat stidder singin' er whistlin', like folks does when dey go thoo de woods, he 'uz des gwine 'bout his business widout making any fuss. He wuz axin hisse'f ef dey'd be any hot ashcake waitin' fer 'im, en whedder de ole 'oman'd save 'im any pot-liquor fum dinner.

"He wuz gwine 'long dis away, when de fus' news he know, he come right 'pon de Moon whiles she wuz changin'. Man, suh! Dey wuz de bigges' flutterment den en dar dat dey's ever been befo' er since. Folks 'way off thought dey could hear thunder, dough dey wan't nothin' in de roun' worl' but de Moon tryin' fer ter git out de way er de man.

"De man, he drapt de bag er charcoal en run like ole Scratch wuz atter 'im. He des tored thoo de woods like a harrycane wuz blowin' 'im 'long. He 'uz gwine one way en de Moon anudder, but de Moon she tripped en fell right top er de bag er charcoal, en you kin see de signs un it down ter dis day. Look at 'er when you will, en you'll see dat she look like she been hit 'cross de face wid a sut-bag. Don't take my word fer it. Des look fer yo'se'f! Dar 'tis! Ever sence dat day de Moon done got so she do 'er changin' up in de elements."

After a while the little boy asked what became of the man that had the bag of charcoal.

"What dat got ter do wid de tale?" said Uncle Remus, sharply. "Long ez de Moon is up dar all safe en soun', ceppin' de smut, it don't make no diffunce 'bout no man. You run 'long en tell yo' Unk' Jeems dat ef he gwine gi' you anything he better let you have it 'fo' he go out dar ter Massasip — kaze, I tell you right now, Massasip is des anudder name fer trouble. I done seed it work out dat away."

18

Brother Rabbit Conquers Brother Lion

"UNCLE REMUS," remarked the little boy, one day, "papa says that the animals haven't got sure enough sense."

"Did Marse John tell you dat?" asked the old man, letting his shoehammer drop from his hands, as though astonishment had rendered him helpless. "Did Marse John set up flat-footed in a cheer and tell you dat de creeturs ain't got sho nuff sense? Ain't he wink his eye when he tell you dat? Ain't you see his chin drap?"

The little boy had seen none of these manifestations, and he said so.

"Well," exclaimed Uncle Remus, with a groan, "I dunner how come Marse John fer ter take on dat away. He used to be a mighty joker when he wuz fus' married; but look like he too ole fer dat kinder doin's now. When you go back up dar, you tell Marse John, dat time he been wid de creeturs long ez I is, he won't set up dar wid a straight face en say dat dey ain't got sho nuff sense. Des ax 'im how dat ole blue sow up dar in de woods pastur' know when ter shake de plum tree. Ax 'im who tol' 'er how ter bump 'er head 'g'inst de floor er de crib en shatter de corn out. En den, when he git thoo tellin' you 'bout dat, ax 'im how dat brindle cow larn't how ter open all de plantation gates wid 'er horn.

"I be blest," continued Uncle Remus, laughing a little, "ef dat cow ain't a sight. Ef Marse John'll des let 'er come in de house, she'll go up sta'rs en onlock his trunk wid 'er horn, en chaw up dat ar claw-hammer coat what he got married in. She mos' sholy will. Co'se de creeturs can't talk none, so folks kin tell what dey say; but ef you gwine ter blame anybody fer dat, blame de folks, don't blame de creeturs.

"Take um up one side en down de yuther, en all 'roun' ez fur ez dey go, en dey got much sense ez folks. Dey ain't got law sense, en dey ain't got buyin' en sellin' sense, but what dey want wid it? What dey gwine do wid it ef dey had it? Tell me dat! De ole cow, she want ter git in de sallid patch, en she know how ter open de gate. De ole sow want ripe plums, en she shake de tree; she want corn, en she bump 'er head 'g'inst de planks en shatter it out. What mo' do dey want? Dey done got der eddycation.

"De littler de creeturs is, de mo' sense dey got, kaze dey bleedzd ter have it. You hear folks say dat Brer Rabbit is full er tricks. It's des de name dey give it. What folks calls tricks is creetur sense. Ef ole Brer Lion had much sense ez Brer Rabbit, what de name er goodness would de balance er de creeturs do? Dey wouldn't be none un um lef' by dis time."

"The Lion couldn't catch Brother Rabbit, could he, Uncle Remus?" said the little boy.

"Now you talkin', honey," exclaimed the old man, enthusiastically. "'long side er Brer Rabbit ole Brer Lion ain't knee high ter a duck. He mighty strong; he mighty servigrous; but when it come ter head-work he ain't nowhar.

"Dey wuz one time when Brer Lion wuz sorter playin' overseer wid de yuther creeturs. It seem like he got de idee dat all un um got ter pay 'im toll, kaze he de strongest en de mos' servigrous. He claim one out'n eve'y fambly: one sheep fum de sheeps, one goat fum de goats, en one fum all de kinds. Bimeby, atter so long a time, he sont word ter Brer Rabbit dat his turn done come, en Brer Rabbit he sont back word, 'All a-settin'.' Co'se dis make ole Miss Rabbit en all de chilluns feel mighty bad. De chilluns, dey sot 'roun' a-whimperin' en a-snufflin', en ole Miss Rabbit, she went 'bout cryin' en wipin' 'er eyes on 'er apern. But Brer Rabbit, he sot up en smoke his seegyar, en tell um for ter quit der 'havishness en l'arn how ter don't.

"He 'low, 'Ole 'oman, ef I ain't back by supper-time, des set my vittles down dar on de h'a'th, so it'll keep sorter warm.'

"Ole Miss Rabbit say, dat stidder wantin' vittles, he'll be vittles hisse'f, en den she snuffle wuss en wuss. But Brer Rabbit he des hoot at 'er, en den he tuck down his walkin' cane en put out fer ter see Brer Lion. De little Rabs, dey holler out, 'Good-by, daddy!' en Brer Rabbit, he holler back, 'So long!' Ole Miss Rabbit, she look atter 'im, she did, en den she flung 'er apern over 'er head, en des boo-hoo.

"But Brer Rabbit, he march down de road ez gay ez ef he gwine ter a frolic. He march on, he did, en des 'fo' he git ter de place whar ole Brer Lion stay at, he hid his walkin' cane in de fence cornder, en rumpled up his ha'r en draw'd hisse'f up twel he look like he ain't bigger'n a poun' er soap atter a hard day's washin'. Den he went whar dey wuz a big, deep spring, a little piece off fum de road, en look at hisse'f in de water. He sort er roach back his years, en make hisse'f look 'umble-come-tumble, en den he draw'd his mouf 'roun' en wunk one eye, en shuck his fist at his shadder in de water.

"He got back in de big road, he did, en crope 'long like he ailin', limpin' fus' on one foot en den on tudder, en bimeby he come ter de place whar ole Brer Lion stay at. Brer Rabbit sorter drag hisse'f 'long, en make a bow. Brer Lion look at 'im sideways, en ax 'im whar he gwine. Brer Rabbit say he come de mo' willin' kaze it's his turn ter come, en he been feelin' mighty po'ly dis long time. He talk mighty weak en trimbly.

"Brer Lion look at 'im right close, en 'low, 'You won't make a mou'ful. Time I eat you, I'll des be gettin' hongry good.'

"Brer Rabbit say, 'Yasser, I know I ain't fat, en I speck I got lots er fleas on me, but I'm mighty willin'. I got a bad cough, en I'm tired er fallin' off. I'm des about ez fat ez de mule de man had, which he hatter tie a knot in his tail fer ter keep 'im fum slippin' thoo de collar.'

"Brer Lion look at 'im, en study. Brer Rabbit 'uz so skeer'd he talk weaker en weaker.

"He say, 'Whiles I comin' 'long des now, I seed a creetur dat 'uz mos' big en fat ez what you is, en I 'low ter myse'f dat I wish ter goodness I 'uz fat ez he is; so Brer Lion kin make out his dinner.'

"Brer Lion 'low, 'Who is he?'

"Brer Rabbit say, 'I ain't ax 'im 'is name. He 'fuse ter 'spon' ter my howdy, en he look so servigrous dat I put out fum dar.'

"Brer Lion say, 'Come, show me whar he is.'

"Brer Rabbit say, I'd do it in a minnit, Brer Lion, but I skeer'd he'll hurt you.'

"Brer Lion sorter bristle up at dis. He 'low, 'Hurt who? Come on, en go wid me whar he is, en I'll show you who'll git hurted, en dat in short order!'

"Brer Rabbit shuck his head. He say, 'You better take me, Brer Lion. I ain't much, but I'm sump'n', en dat ar creetur what I seed will sholy hurt you. He got claws en he got tushes, kaze I done seed um. Don't go whar he is, Brer Lion, ef you got any friendly feelin' fer yo' fambly. Dat creetur will sholy cripple you!'

"Dis make Brer Lion mighty mad. He 'low, 'Git right in de road dar en show me whar he is!'

"Brer Rabbit say, 'Well, ef I bleedzd ter go, Brer Lion, I'll go. I done tol' you, en dat's all I kin do.'

"Dey went on, dey did, en Brer Rabbit tuck Brer Lion ter de spring. When dey got dar, Brer Rabbit look 'roun' en say, 'He 'uz right 'roun' here somers, en he ain't so mighty fur off now, kaze I feel it in my bones.'

"Den he crope up, Brer Rabbit did, en look in de spring. Time he do dis, he fetched a squall en jump back: 'Ouch, Brer Lion! he in dar! Less run! He'll git us, sho!'

"Brer Lion walk up ter de spring en look in. Sho nuff, dar wuz a big creetur lookin' back at 'im. Brer Lion holler at 'im. De creetur in de

spring ain't say nothin'. Brer Lion shuck his head; de creetur shuck his. Brer Lion showed his tushes; de creetur grin at 'im. Dey kep' on dis away, twel bimeby Brer Lion git so mad dat he jump in de spring head foremos'. When he in dar he can't git out no mo', en so dar he is, strangled wid de water en drownded fer de want er bofe sense en breff.

"Brer Rabbit, he caper 'roun' dar some little time, en den he put out fer home, en when he git dar, he tuck his chilluns on his knee en tol' um a mighty tale 'bout how he make way wid ole Brer Lion; en all de creeturs hear 'bout it, en dey go 'roun' en say dat Brer Rabbit sholy is got deze 'ere things up here."

Uncle Remus tapped his forehead significantly, and the little boy laughed.

19
"Heyo, House!"

"I DON'T think Brother Lion had much sense," remarked the little boy after awhile.

"Yit he had some," responded Uncle Remus. "He bleedzd ter had some, but he ain't got much ez Brer Rabbit. Dem what got strenk ain't got so mighty much sense. You take niggers — dey er lots stronger dan what white folks is. I ain't so strong myse'f," remarked the old man, with a sly touch of vanity that was lost on the little boy, "but de common run er niggers is lots stronger dan white folks. Yit I done tuck notice in my time dat what white folks calls sense don't turn out ter be sense eve'y day en Sunday too. I ain't never see de patter-roller what kin keep up wid me. He may go hoss-back, he may go foot-back, it don't make no diffunce ter me. Dey never is cotch me yit, en when dey does I'll let you know.

"Dat de way wid Brer Rabbit," Uncle Remus went on, after a pause. "De few times what he been outdone he mighty willin' fer ter let um talk 'bout it, ef it'll do um any good. Dem what outdo 'im got de right ter brag, en he ain't make no deniance un it.

"Atter he done make way wid ole Brer Lion, all de yuther creeturs say he sholy is a mighty man, en dey treat 'im good. Dis make 'im feel so proud dat he bleedzd ter show it, en so he strut 'roun' like a boy when he git his fus' pa'r er boots.

"'Bout dat time, Brer Wolf tuck a notion dat ef Brer Rabbit kin outdo ole Brer Lion, he can't outdo him. So he pick his chance one day whiles ole Miss Rabbit en de little Rabs is out pickin' sallid fer dinner. He went in de house, he did, en wait fer Brer Rabbit ter come home. Brer Rabbit had his hours, en dis wuz one un um, en 'twa'n't long 'fo' here he come. He got a mighty quick eye, mon, en he tuck notice dat ev'ything mighty still. When he got little nigher, he tuck notice dat de front do' wuz on de crack, en dis make 'im feel funny, kaze he know dat when his ole 'oman en de chillun out, dey allers pulls de door shet en ketch de latch. So he went up a little nigher, en he step thin ez a batter-cake. He peep here, en he peep dar, yit he ain't see nothin'. He lissen in de chimbley cornder, en he lissen und' de winder, yit he ain't hear nothin'.

"Den he sorter wipe his mustash en study. He 'low ter hisse'f, 'De pot rack know what gwine on up de chimbley, de rafters know who's in de loft, de bed-cord know who und' de bed. I ain't no pot-rack, I ain't no rafter, en I ain't no bed-cord, but, please gracious! I'm gwine ter fin' who's in dat house, en I ain't gwine in dar nudder. Dey mo' ways ter fin' out who fell in de mill-pond widout fallin' in yo'se'f.'

"Some folks," Uncle Remus went on, "would 'a' rushed in dar, en ef dey had, dey wouldn't 'a' rushed out no mo', kaze dey wouldn't 'a' been nothin' 't all lef' un um but a little scrap er hide en a han'ful er ha'r.

"Brer Rabbit got better sense dan dat. All he ax anybody is ter des gi' 'im han'-roomance, en dem what kin ketch 'im is mo' dan welly-come ter take 'im. Dat zackly de kinder man what Brer Rabbit is. He went off a little ways fum de house en clum a 'simmon stump en got up dar en 'gun ter holler.

"He 'low, 'Heyo, house!'

"De house ain't make no answer, en Brer Wolf, in dar behime de do', open his eyes wide. He ain't know what ter make er dat kinder doin's.

"Brer Rabbit holler, 'Heyo, house! Whyn't you heyo?'

"House ain't make no answer, en Brer Wolf in dar behime de do' sorter move roun' like he gittin' restless in de min'.

"Brer Rabbit out dar on de 'simmon stump holler mo' louder dan befo', 'Heyo, house! Heyo!'

"House stan' still, en Brer Wolf in dar behime de do' 'gun ter feel col' chills streakin' up and down his back. In all his born days he ain't never hear no gwines on like dat. He peep thoo de crack er de do', but he can't see nothin'.

"Brer Rabbit holler louder, 'Heyo, house! Ain't you gwine ter heyo? Is you done los' what little manners you had?'

"Brer Wolf move 'bout wuss'n befo'. He feel des like some un done hit 'im on de funny-bone.

"Brer Rabbit holler hard ez he kin, but still he ain't git no answer, en den he 'low, 'Sholy sump'n' nudder is de matter wid dat house, kaze all de times befo' dis, it been holler'n back at me, Heyo, yo'se'f!'

"Den Brer Rabbit wait little bit, en bimeby he holler one mo' time, 'Heyo, house!'

"Ole Brer Wolf try ter talk like he speck a house 'ud talk, en he holler back, 'Heyo, yo'se'f!'

"Brer Rabbit wunk at hisse'f. He low, 'Heyo, house! whyn't you talk hoarse like you got a bad col'?'"

"Den Brer Wolf holler back, hoarse ez he kin, 'Heyo, yo'se'f!'"

"Dis make Brer Rabbit laugh twel a little mo' en he'd a drapt off'n dat ar 'simmon stump en hurt hisse'f."

"He 'low, 'Eh-eh, Brer Wolf! dat ain't nigh gwine ter do. You'll hatter stan' out in de rain a mighty long time 'fo' you kin talk hoarse ez dat house!'"

"I let you know," continued Uncle Remus, laying his hand gently on the little boy's shoulder, "I let you know, Brer Wolf come a-slinkin' out, en made a break fer home. Atter dat, Brer Rabbit live a long time widout any er de yuther creeturs a-pesterin un 'im!'"

20
According to How the Drop Falls

"Is I GWINE tell you a tale right now?" said Uncle Remus, in response to a question by the little boy. "Well, I ain't right certain en sho' 'bout dat. It's 'cordin ter how de drap falls."

"Pshaw!" exclaimed the youngster, "I've heard you say that before. I don't know what you mean when you say it's according to how the drop falls."

"Ah-yi!" retorted Uncle Remus triumphantly, "Den I'm a punkin ahead er yo' 'simmon, is I?"

"It's according to how the drop falls," rejoined the little boy, laughing.

"De way dat sayin' come 'bout," said Uncle Remus, "may be funny, but 'tain't no tale. It des happen so. One time dey wuz a 'oman call on a neighbor 'oman des 'fo' dinner-time. I dunner whedder de neighbor 'oman like dis mighty well, but she 'uz monstus perlite all de same.

"She 'low, 'Come right in, en take off yo' things en make yo'se'f at home. You'll hatter skuzen my han's, kaze I'm makin' up dough. Fling yo' bonnet on de bed dar, en take a seat en be seated.'

"Well, de tudder' 'oman, she sot dar en talk, en watch de neighbor 'oman mix dough fer de bread, en dey run'd on des like wimmin folks does. It seem like de neighbor 'oman got a bad col', en her eyes run water twel some un it crope down ter de een' er her nose en hang dar. De tudder 'oman, she watch it, whiles dey er talkin'. De neighbor 'oman she work up de dough, en work it up, en talk. Sometimes she'd hol' her head fum over de tray en talk, en den ag'in she'd hol' it right spang over de dough, en shake 'er head en talk.

"Bimeby she 'low, 'Won't you stay ter dinner? I'll have dis bread done in two shakes uv a sheep's tail.'

"De tudder 'oman say, 'I can't tell you, ma'am; it's 'cordin' ter how de drap falls.'

"De tudder 'oman say, 'Dey ain't a cloud in de sky, so 'twa'n't gwine ter rain. You des ez well stay.'

"De tudder 'oman 'low, 'I done tol' you de trufe; hit's 'cordin' ter how de drap falls.'

"So, atter dat, when folks wan't right certain en sho 'bout what dey gwine do, dey'd up en say 'twuz 'cordin' ter how de drap fall."

"Well, how did it fall, Uncle Remus — in the bread-tray, or on the table, or on the floor?" the little boy inquired.

"Lawsy, honey!" responded the old man, "ef I 'uz er tell you, I'd hatter dream it, en dreamin' ain't gwine do you er me any mo' good dan it done de nigger man what had de possum."

"I never heard of that," said the little boy.

"Oh, yes you is!" Uncle Remus asserted with some emphasis. "You been hearin' 'bout it off'n on sence you 'uz knee-high ter a duck, en you ain't much mo'n dat right now. No suh! You des got de idee in yo' min' dat when I set down fer ter tell you sump'n' hit's bleedzd ter be a tale, en when yuther folks tells it 'tain't nothin' but talk. I ain't got no secret 'bout dish yer nigger man what had de possum, but I tell you right now, 'tain't no tale. Too many folks done been fool wid it.

"Well, den, one time dey wuz a nigger man, en dish yer nigger man had a big fat possum en a half er peck er sweet taters. He tuck de possum en de taters home, en he lay um down — de possum on one side de fierplace en de taters on tudder side. Den he get some wood and chips en make 'im a fier, en den he fotch out de skillet. He put de possum in dar, he did, en he put de taters in de ashes close by fer ter keep 'im comp'ny. Den he raked out some hot embers en sot de skillet on um, en he put on de skillet lid, en piled some embers 'pon top er dat.

"He sot dar, he did, en wait fer de possum fer ter git done, en whiles he wuz a-waitin' he struck up a song. Maybe you done hear it 'fo' now, but dat ain't make no diffunce ter me, kaze when I git started dis away, I'm like de bull yearlin' gwine down de lane; dem what gits in de way gwine ter git run'd over — dey mos' sholy is!"

Uncle Remus leaned back in his chair, closed his eyes, and began to pat his foot. Then, after a little pause, he sang this fragment of a song:

> "Virginny cut, chaw terbacker,
>   Nigger dance ter merlatter;
>   Hoe de corn, dig er tater.
>   Plant terbacker, 'tis no matter.
>
> Mix de meal, fry de batter.
>   Nigger dance ter merlatter,
>   Warm de cake in er platter,
>   Fry um in de cooney fat.
>
> Grab er later out de ash
>   Nigger dance ter merlatter;
>   Possum meat dar in der platter,
>   Shoo! he make de nigger fatter."

Uncle Remus's voice was full of melody, and he sang the song to a rollicking tune. The little boy was so much pleased that he asked the old man to sing it again.

"Bless yo' soul, honey. Ef I git in a fa'r way er singin', de niggers'll all quit der work en crowd 'roun' here en jine in wid me, en we'll have a reg'lar ole-timey camp-meetin' gwine on here 'fo' you know it. I ain't got no time fer dat.

"Now, den, dish yer nigger man, what I been tellin' you 'bout, he got his taters in de ashes en his possum in de skillet, he sot dar en sing de song, en watch um all cook. Atter so long a time dey got done, en he pull de taters out'n de embers, en push de skillet 'way fum de fier. He 'low ter hisse'f, he did, dat col' possum is better'n hot possum, dough bofe un um is good nuff fer anybody. So he say he'll des let it set dar en cool, en soak in de gravy. Den he say he b'lieve he'll do some noddin', kaze den he'll dream he eatin' de possum, en den he'll wake up en eat 'im sho nuff, en have de 'joyment er eatin' 'im two times.

"Well, suh, dat des de way he done. He sot back in his cheer, de nigger man did, en he nodded en nodded, en he work his mouf des like he eatin' possum, en he grunt in his sleep like he feelin' good. But whiles he settin' dar sleepin', anudder nigger man smell de possum, en he crope up ter de do' en peep in. He seed how de lan' lay, en he slipped off his shoes en stole in. He lif' up de lid er de skillet, en dar wuz de possum. He look on de side er de h'a'th, en dar wuz de taters. Now, den, when dat de case, what gwine ter happen? Possum, en later, en hongry nigger! Well, suh, de fus' news you know, de possum wuz all bones, de taters wuz all peelin's, en de nigger wuz mo' dan a nigger. He fix de bones in one little pile, en he fix de peelin's in anudder little pile, en den he tuck some er de possum gravy en rub it on de tudder nigger's mouf en han's, en den he went on 'bout his business.

"'Twa'n't so mighty long atter dat 'fo' de noddin' nigger wake up. He open his eyes, he did, en stretch hisse'f, en look at de skillet en laugh.

"He 'low, 'You er dar, is you? Well, I'll tell you howdy now, en ter-reckly I'll tell you good-by!'

"He tuck de lid off'n de skillet, en dey ain't no possum dar. He look 'roun' fer de taters, en dey ain't no taters dar. Dey ain't nothin' dar but a pile er bones en a pile er tater-peelin's. De nigger sot down in his cheer en went ter studyin'. He look at his han's, en he see possum grease on um. He lick out his tongue, en he tas'e possum gravy on his mouf. He shuck his head en study. He look at his han's: 'Possum been dar!' He lick his mouf: 'Possum been dar, too!' He rub his stomach: 'But I be bless ef any possum been here!'"

21
A Fool for Luck[2]

UNCLE REMUS did not pause to see whether the little boy liked the possum story or not. Perhaps he felt that it deserved no attention, being only a plantation joke — a remnant of a tale which had not sufficient interest to preserve it.

2 See *The Jack Tales*, Boston, Houghton Mifflin Co., 1943, and notes on "Jack's Hunting Trip" in appendix; also, in *Grandfather Tales*, Houghton Mifflin Co., 1948. "Only a Fair Day's Huntin'." — R. C.

"Dat nigger man," he remarked, "wuz big nuff fool fer ter have mo' luck dan dat. You heern what de ole sayin' sez, 'fool fer luck en po' man fer chillun.' Well, one time dey wuz a man what do so funny dat folks call 'im a fool. He 'uz a hard workin' man, too, en he raise good craps, but he do like he cripple und' de hat. He had a crib full er corn, en bimeby he 'gun ter miss it. He watch de crib at night en in de daytime, but he ain't see nobody takin' none, en de corn keep on gettin' lower en lower. De man live on de river, en on de yuther side de river dey wuz a big woods. Bimeby somebody tell de man dat de squir'ls wuz totin' off his corn. De man laugh en say dat ef squir'ls kin tote off his corn, sev'm bushels at a time, dey er mo' dan welcome. But he watch all de same.

"He got up 'fo' day, en went en sot by de crib, en 'twa'n't long 'fo' he seed a sight dat make 'im rub his eyes. He hear a racket on de fence en a clatter in de bushes, en de squir'ls 'gun ter swarm 'roun' de crib, en all un um come fum to'rds de river. De man sot en watch um. Dey clum up in de crib, dey did, en eve'y blessed one un um tuck a year er corn in dey mouf en start back 'cross de river. De man foller 'long atter um.

"When dey git ter de river, dey put de corn down, en hunt 'roun' twel dey git a piece er bark. Dey put de bark in de water en lay de corn in it, den dey shove out fum sho', en h'ist der tails fer sails en go on 'cross. Eve'y one had a piece er bark, en dey ferry dat corn 'cross like dey done been use ter dat kinder business.

"De man, he sot dar like he dazed. He go back de nex' mornin' en watch, en he see de same kind er doin's. Eve'y squir'l tuck a year er corn, en eve'y squir'l got 'im a piece er bark, en h'ist his tail 'pon his back en sail 'cross de river. De man ain't say a word. He ain't so much ez shoo at um. He des set dar en watch um en laugh. Mo' dan dat, he went en tol' yuther folks 'bout it en laugh some mo'. Dey ax 'im whyn't he make de squir'ls drap de corn, en he des wunk at um en grin. Den dey say he bleedzd ter be a fool, en he wunk en laugh some mo'.

"Bimeby, when de corn 'gun ter git low in de crib, de man tuck his gun en his ax, en went 'cross de river fer ter look atter it. He wuz gwine 'long, huntin' fer de corn, when up jump a rabbit. He raise his gun en shot, en des ez he shot de rabbit run inter a covey er pa'tridges. At de shot a turkey gobbler flopped up en flew'd in a big poplar, en de man lammed loose wid de yuther barrel, en de gobbler drapt over en lodged up dar. Den he look over de groun' en fin' one dead rabbit, en 'lev'm dead pa'tridges. One pa'tridge had 'er wing broke, en she scrambled off in de bushes. De man foller'd on atter, en terreckly he come ter whar dey wuz a turkey nes' wid a hatful er turkey eggs.

"Den he clum up de tree fer ter git de turkey. When he got up dar, he see dat de turkey done drap in a hole like, en he pull 'er out, en down in dar wuz all his corn. He clum down, he did, en got de axe an 'gun ter cut de tree down. He ain't mo'n chopped thoo de bark 'fo' he seed sump'n nudder runnin' out, en he look at it close, en it 'uz de pyo honey.

"He 'low, 'Hi! I'm gittin' de rent fer my corn!'

"Den he chopped him out a stob en plugged up de hole, en got his game en his turkey eggs, en put out fer home. Whiles he gwine back anudder rabbit jump up. De man ain't got no load in his gun, so he des flung de gun at 'im. De rabbit went on, but when de man start ter pick up de gun, he feel de groun' givin' way 'neat' his foots, en 'fo' he kin ketch hisse'f he done drapt down in a hole."

"Was it a big, deep hole?" the little boy inquired, with some show of eagerness.

"Well, suh, 'twuz over his head," responded Uncle Remus, vaguely. "It seem like some un had made de hole en kivvered it wid' a plank, en den put dirt on de plank. It been done so long dat de man come 'long des in time fer ter fall thoo. When he 'gun ter fall, he make up his min' dat 'twuz all-night-Isom dar wid him. But he struck bottom quicker'n he 'spected he would, en when he git over his skeer he 'gun ter feel 'roun' fer ter see if it's him er some yuther man what drapt in dar. Whiles he 'uz feelin' 'roun' fer ter see who he wuz, en whar he wuz, en what he doin' dar, he put his han' on sump'n' hard en col'.

"Yasser! right den en dar he put his han' on sump'n' hard en col' — en what you reckon it was? Nothin' in de roun' worl' but a keg er money! He scrambled out er dar, atter he lif' de keg out, en den he roll it down to his canoe, en tuck it home. He count it up, de man did, en he fin' he got forty-'lev'm hundr'd dollars in hard speeshy. When he git rested, he tuck his hoss en waggin en a empty bar'l, en went 'roun' by de bridge, en back ter de place whar he fin' de honey. He pull de plug out'n de tree en let de honey run in de bar'l twel it's full, en den he tuck it home en fetch back two mo' bar'ls, en got dem full. Hit went on dis away twel he got I dunner how many bar'ls er honey. En den, when he cut down de tree en haul de corn home, he fin' he got mo' dan he had at fus', kaze de squir'ls been stealin' somebody else corn 'long wid his'n!

"So den, dar he wuz, wid ez much money ez he want, en mo' honey dan a drove er mules kin pull, en mo' corn dan what he had befo', en all de game he want, en all bekaze he de biggest fool in sev'm Nunited States."

Seeing that the little boy was disposed to regard his story somewhat dubiously, Uncle Remus made this concluding remark:

"Tooby sho, dis ain't no creetur tale, but ef 'tain't so, how come folks talkin' 'bout it yit? I wish you be so good ez ter tell me dat."

But the little boy was not prepared to argue the matter.

22
The Man and His Boots

"YOU DONE HEAR me say dat de creeturs is got mos' ez much sense ez folks, ain't you, honey?" inquired Uncle Remus, one day, when he and the little boy were alone together. The youngster nodded assent. "Well, den," said the old man solemnly, "I'm bleedzd ter tell you dat sense don't stan' fer goodness. De creeturs dunno nothin' 'tall 'bout dat dat's good en dat dat ain't good. Dey dunno right fum wrong. Dey see what dey want, en dey git it ef dey kin, by hook er by crook. Dey don't ax who it b'longs ter, ner wharbouts it come fum. Dey dunno de diffunce 'twix' what's dern en what ain't dern.

"Miss Sally say no longer'n yistiddy, dat I'd keep on tellin' you deze creetur tales twel bimeby you'll git mix up in de min' en fergit all 'bout yo' Sunday-school lesson; but I laid down dis p'int ter Miss Sally, dat ef a chap 'bout yo' age en size dunno de diffunce 'twix' creetur doin's en folks' doin's, he better be turned out ter graze. I ain't tellin' you deze tales on account er what de creeturs does, I'm a tellin' um on account er de way de creeturs does. How de name er goodness kin folks go on en steal en tell fibs, like de creeturs done, en not git hurted? Dey des can't do it. Dead dog never dies, en cheatin' never th'ives — not when folks git at it.

"One time," Uncle Remus continued, after delivering this little ser-

mon, "dey wuz a man what hear talk er some er Brer Rabbit's doin's —
how he lay down in de road whiles a man wuz gwine 'long wid some
fishes in a waggin, en how he run 'roun' en lay down ag'in; en keep on
doin' dat twel bimeby de man went back atter de fus' rabbit he seed, en
den Brer Rabbit had a chance fer ter git de fishes — I done mos' fergit
dat ar tale off'n my min'. But howsomever hit wuz, de man done hear tell
'bout it, en he 'low ter hisse'f dat he des ez smart ez what Brer Rabbit is.

"So, one day, he got 'im a bran' new pa'r er boots wid red tops on um,
en whiles he settin' side er de road looking at um, he hear somebody
comin' 'long in a waggin. He know'd who de somebody wuz, kaze he seed
um on de rise er de hill.

"De man in de waggin had some calico fer ter make his wife a dress,
en some blue chany ware fer ter put in de cubberd. De man what had de
boots, he tuck'n flung one un um in de road, en hid hisse'f in de bushes
fer ter see what de tudder man gwine do.

"Well, suh, de man in de waggin, he come 'long, en he see de boot in
de road. He holler at his hoss fer ter 'w'o dar!' en he look at de boot right
hard, like he studyin'.

"He 'low, 'Ef dey wuz two un you, I'd take you, but one boot ain't
gwine do nobody no good, 'ceppin' hit's a wooden-legged man.'

"So he driv on, en de man what lay de boot dar, he put out en went on
ahead en flung de yuther boot in de road. De man in de waggin, he come
'long, he did, en he see de yuther boot.

"He 'low, 'Heyo! dish yer boot makes tudder boot good. W'o, dar,
hoss! I'll go back en git 'er.'

"Wid dat, he drapt de lines on de dashboard en went back atter de
odd boot. Whiles he gone, de man what had de boots tuck de calico en
de crockery en made off wid um.

"He hid um in de underbresh, en den he come back en lissen fer ter
see what de yuther man gwine do. Well, suh, de yuther man come back
wid de boot, en den he had two. Time he clum in de waggin he seed dat
somebody done steal his calico en his crockery, but he ain't say nothin'.
He des look at de boots en laugh.

"De man in de bushes ain't know what ter make er dis. He stood dar,
he did, en scratch his head en study. He watch de yuther man, en fur ez
he kin see him he wuz lookin' at de boots en laughin'. De man in de

bushes say he gwine ter see what de matter wid dem ar boots, when de yuther man in de waggin kin swap off calico en crockery fer um en still feel good nuff fer ter laugh. So de man in de bushes he run 'roun' en head de yuther man off, en met 'im in de road. He come drivin' 'long, still lookin' at de boots en laughin'. Look like when he see de man in de road it make 'im laugh wusser dan befo'.

"De man in de road 'low, 'You mus' be havin' a mighty heap er fun all by yo'se'f.'

"De man in de waggin laugh like he gwine ter bus' wide open. All he kin say is, 'Lawsy massy! deze boots! deze boots! deze boots!'

"De man in de road 'low, 'What de matter wid de boots, dat dey er so mighty funny? Dey ain't look funny ter me.'

"De man in de waggin look like he choke wid laughin. When he ketch his breff he holler, 'Oh, deze boots! deze boots!'

"Man in de road 'low, 'You ain't gwine crazy, is you?'

"Man in de waggin say, 'You'd be crazy too ef somebody had 'a' come 'long en drapt deze boots whar you could git um. Lawsy massy! deze boots!'

"Man in de road 'low, 'What kinder doin's is deze? You better lemme git up dar en take you home ter yo' fambly!'

"Man in de waggin say, 'My folks'll laugh too, when dey know what I knows; en you'd laugh yo'se'f ef you'd a been comin' 'long de road en fin' deze boots what got red in de top.'

"Man in de road say, 'I had a pair des like um, en day ain't make me laugh."

"Man in de waggin say, 'You'd laugh wusser dan me ef you'd er pick deze boots up in de road en foun' one ten-dollar bill in one un um, en anudder ten-dollar bill in tudder one.'

"Man in de road 'low, 'Lemme see dem boots! — Dey er mine! Han' um here! I tuck'n los' um yistiddy whiles I comin' fum town. Gi' me de money!'

"Man in de waggin shet his eye. He say, 'You right sho dey er yone?'

"Man in de road 'low, 'Yes dey is, en I got de proof un it!'

"Man in de waggin say, 'Well en good! Git up here en go along wid me, en show de proof.'

"Man in de road jump up on de wheel, but 'fo' he kin set down de man in de waggin flung 'im back in de waggin body en jump on 'im en tie 'im, en tuck 'im off ter de calaboose. Dar dey make 'im tell what he done wid de calico en de chany ware, en dey kep' 'im, I dunner how long; en 'fo' dey turn him loose dey tuck 'im out en hit 'im thirty-nine on de naked hide.

"Co'se," continued Uncle Remus, seeing a shade of perplexity on the little boy's face, "de man in de waggin ain't fin' no money in de boots. He des puttin' on, so he kin fin' de man what drap um, kaze he know dat right whar he fin' de man dat drap um, right dar he'll fin' de man what stoled his calico en crockery. Dat what make I say dat folks ain't got no business mockin' de way de creeturs does. Dey er bound ter git cotch up wid, en right den dey er in deep trouble. Creeturs kin take what ain't dern, en tell fibs, en dey don't no harm come fum it; but when folks tries it, dey er bleedzd ter come ter some bad een'. Now, you des watch um."

23

Brother Mud Turtle's Trickery

"I DON'T like deze yer tales 'bout folks, no how you kin fix um," said Uncle Remus, after an unusually long pause, during which he rubbed his left hand with the right, in order to run the rheumatism out. "No, suh, I don't like um, kaze folks can't play no tricks, ner git even wid der neighbors, widout hurtin' somebody's feelin's, er breakin' some law er nudder, er gwine 'g'inst what de preacher say.

"Look at dat man what I des been tellin' you 'bout. He let de udder man fool 'im en ketch 'im, en mo' dan dat, he let um tote 'im off ter de calaboose. He oughter been tuck dar; I ain't 'sputin' dat, yit ef dat had been some er de creeturs, dey'd er sholy got loose fum dar.

"When it comes ter talkin' 'bout gittin' loose," Uncle Remus continued, settling himself comfortably in his chair, "I git ter runnin' on in my min' 'bout ole Brer Fox en ole Brer Mud Turkle. Dey had some kinder fallin' out once 'pon a time. I dunner what. I speck hit's got a tale hung on it, but de tale done switch itself out'n my min'. Yit dey'd done had a fallin' out, en dey wa'n't no love los' betwixt um. Well, suh, one day Brer Fox wuz gwine down de creek fishin'. Little ez you may think un it, Brer Fox was monstus fon' er fishes, so eve'y chance he got he'd go fishin'."

"On Sunday, too?" inquired the little boy. He had been lectured on that subject not long before.

"Well, I tell you now," replied Uncle Remus, laughing, "Brer Fox is like 'oman's tongue, he ain't got no Sunday."

"What kind of bait did he have?" the youngster asked.

"What he want wid bait, honey? He ain't got no bait, en no pole, en no hook. He des went down de creek, en when he come ter a good place, he'd wade in en feel und' de rocks en und' de bank. Sometimes he'd ketch a horny-head, en den ag'in he'd ketch a peerch. Well, suh, he went on en went on, en he had bad luck. Look like de fishes wuz all gone fum home, but he kep' on, en kep' on. He 'low ter hisse'f dat he bleedzd ter have some fish fer dinner. One time he put his han' in a crawfish nes' en got nipt, en anudder time he tetched a eel, en it made de col' chills run 'cross 'im. Yit he kep' on.

"Bimeby Brer Fox come ter whar ole Brer Mud Turkle live at. I dunner what make ole Brer Mud Turkle live in such a damp place like dat. Look like him en his folks 'ud have a bad col' de whole blessid time. But dar he wuz in de water und' de bank, layin' dar fas' asleep, dreamin' 'bout de good times he'd have when de freshet come. He 'uz layin' dar wid his eyes shot, when de fus' news he know he feel sump'n' nudder fumblin' 'roun' his head. 'Twa'n't nobody but ole Brer Fox feelin' 'roun' und' de bank fer fishes.

"Brer Mud Turkle move his head, he did, but de fumblin' kep' on, en bimeby he open his mouf en Brer Fox fumble en fumble, twel bimeby he got 'is han' in dar, en time he do dat, ole Brer Mud Turkle shet down on it. En I let you know," continued Uncle Remus, shaking his head slowly from side to side as if to add emphasis to the statement, "I let you know when ole Brer Mud Turkle shet down on yo' han', you got ter cut off his head, en den wait twel it thunder 'fo' he turn loose.

"Well, suh, he shet down on ole Brer Fox en ef you'd a been anywhars in dat settlement you'd a heard squallin' den ef you ain't never hear none befo'.

"Brer Fox des hilt his head back en holler 'Ouch! Ouch! What dis got me? Ouch! Turn me aloose! Ouch! Somebody better run here quick! Laws a massy! Ouch!'

"But Brer Mud Turkle, he helt on, en he feel so much comfort dat he'd er in about went ter asleep ag'in ef Brer Fox hadn't er snatched en jerked so hard en a-holler'd so loud.

"Brer Fox holler, en Brer Mud Turkle hol' on — Brer Fox holler, en Brer Mud Turkle hol' on. Dar dey wuz — nip en tug, holler en hol' fas'! Bimeby it hurt so bad dat Brer Fox des fetched one loud squall en made one big pull, en out come ole Brer Mud Turkle, a-hangin' ter his han'.

"Well, suh, when dey got out on de bank en Brer Mud Turkle sorter woke up, he tuck'n turn Brer Fox loose widout waitin' fer de thunder. He ax Brer Fox pardon, but Brer Fox, he ain't got no pardon fer ter gi' 'im.

"Brer Mud Turkle make like he skeer'd. He 'low, 'I clar' ter gracious, Brer Fox! Ef I'd a know'd 'twuz you, I'd a never shet down on you in de roun' worl'; kaze I know what a dangersome man you is. I know'd yo' daddy befo' you, en he wuz a dangersome man.'

"But Brer Fox 'fuse ter lissen ter dat kinder talk. He say, 'I been wantin' you a long time, en now I got you. I got you right where I want you, en when I git thoo wid you, yo' own folks wouldn't know you, ef dey wuz ter meet you in de middle er de road.'

"Brer Mud Turkle cry on one side his face en laugh on tudder. He 'low, 'Please, suh, Brer Fox, des let me off dis time, en I'll be good fr'en' 'long wid you all de balance er de time. Please, suh, Brer Fox, let me off dis time!'

"Brer Fox say, 'Oh, yes! I'll let you off, I'm all de time a-lettin' off folks what bite me ter de bone! Oh, yes! I'll let you off, but I'll take en skin you fus'.'

"Brer Mud Turkle 'low, 'Spozen I ain't got no hide on me — den what you gwine ter do?'

"Brer Fox grit his tushes. He say, 'Ef you ain't got no hide, I'll fin' de place whar de hide oughter be — dat's what!'

"Wid dat, he make a grab at Brer Mud Turkle's neck, but Brer Mud Turkle draw his head en his foots und' his shell, en quile up his tail, en dar he wuz. He so ole and tough he got moss on his shell. Brer Fox fool wid 'im, en gnyaw en gouge at de shell, but he des mought ez well gnyaw en gouge at a flint rock. He work en he work, but 'tain't do no good; he can't git Brer Mud Turkle out er his house no way he kin fix it.

"Ole Brer Mud Turkle talk at 'im. He 'low, 'Hard ain't no name fer it, Brer Fox! You'll be jimber-jaw'd long 'fo' you gnyaw thoo my hide!'

"Brer Fox gnyaw en gouge, en gouge en gnyaw.

"Brer Mud Turkle 'low, 'Dey ain't but one way fer ter git dat shell off, Brer Fox!'

"Brer Fox 'fuse ter make answer. He gouge en gnyaw, en gnyaw en gouge.

"Brer Mud Turkle 'low, 'Tushes ain't gwine git it off! Claws ain't gwine git it off! Yit mud en water will do de work. Now I'm gwine ter sleep.'

"Brer Fox gnyaw en gouge, en gouge en gnyaw, en bimeby he git tired, mo' speshually when he hear ole Brer Mud Turkle layin' in dar snorin' des like somebody sawin' gourds. Den he sot down en watch Brer Mud Turkle, but he ain't move. He do des like he sleep.

"Den Brer Fox git de idee dat he'll play a trick on Brer Mud Turkle. He holler out, 'Good-by, Brer Mud Turkle! You er too much fer me dis time. My han' hurt me so bad, I got ter go home en git a poultice on it. But I'll pay you back ef hit's de las' ac'!'

"Brer Fox made like he gwine off, but he des run 'roun' en hid in de bushes. Yit does you speck he gwine fool Brer Mud Turkle? Shoo, honey! Dat creetur got moss on his back, en he got so much sense in his head his eyes look red. He des lay dar, ole Brer Mud Turkle did, en sun hisse'f same ez ef he wuz on a rock in de creek. He lay dar so still dat Brer Fox got his impatients stirred up, en he come out de bushes en went ter Brer Mud Turkle en shuck 'im up en ax'd 'im how he gwine git de shell off.

"Brer Mud Turkle 'low, 'Tushes ain't gwine git it off! Claws ain't gwine git it off! Yit mud en water will do de work!'

"Brer Fox say, 'Don't riddle me no riddles. Up en tell me like a man how I gwine ter git yo' shell off!'

"Brer Mud Turkle 'low, 'Put me in de mud en rub my back hard ez you kin. Den de shell bleedzd ter come off. Dat de reason dey calls me Brer Mud Turkle.'

"Well, suh," said Uncle Remus, laughing heartily, "Brer Fox ain't got no better sense dan ter b'lieve all dat truck, so he tuck en shove Brer Mud Turkle 'long twel he got 'im in de mud, en den he 'gun ter rub on his back like somebody curryin' a hoss. What happen den? Well, dey ain't nothin' 'tall happen, 'ceppin' what bleedzd ter happen. De mo' he rub on de back, de deeper Brer Mud Turkle go in de mud. Bimeby, whiles Brer Fox wuz rubbin' right hard, Brer Mud Turkle sorter gun hisse'f a flirt en went down out er reach. Co'se dis make Brer Fox splunge in de water, en a little mo' en he'd a drownded right den en dar. He went out on de bank, he did, en whiles he settin' dar dryin' hisse'f he know'd dat Brer Mud Turkle wuz laughin' at 'im, kaze he kin see de signs un it."

The little boy laughed, but he shook his head incredulously.

"Well," said Uncle Remus, "ef you gwine ter 'spute dat, you des ez well ter stan' up en face me down 'bout de whole tale. Kaze when Brer Fox see bubbles risin' on de water en follerin' atter one anudder he bleedzd ter know dat Brer Mud Turkle down under dar laughin' fit ter kill hisse'f."

This settled the matter. The child was convinced.

24
How the King Recruited His Army

ONE DAY Uncle Remus had occasion several times to go to his "Miss Sally" with information about some incident, accident, or happening on the plantation. Each time his mistress would say, "Didn't I tell you so?" She had, in fact, said to him the night before, when the little boy's father was preparing to take a short journey away from home, that she was certain everything would go to ruin on the place. Uncle Remus, on the other hand, had assured her that everything would go along all right. It happened, however, that everything seemed to go wrong. A mule ran over a calf and hurt it. A cow trying to get out of the way of the mule had her horn knocked off, and the mule, a little later, snagged itself on the end of a fence rail. Consequently, when Uncle Remus went to tell his mistress of these things, making three separate visits, the lady exclaimed, with increasing emphasis each time, "Didn't I tell you so?"

Finally Uncle Remus remarked, as he was going away: "Nex' time I come, Miss Sally, I'm gwine ter tell you de cow done swaller'd de grinestone."

Whereat his mistress laughed and told him not to worry her any more. The little boy happened to hear the remark about the cow swallowing the grindstone, and so he followed the old man to find out something about it.

"Dat what you taggin' atter me 'bout?" said Uncle Remus. "Well, goodness knows! it done got so now dat folks can't open der mouf but what dey got ter be tagged at, en nagged at, kaze udder folks git de idee dat dey's a tale somers behime it. I thank my stars dey ain't no tale in dat grinestone, kaze dey ain't no livin' man kin set flat down en tell tales while dish yer plantation gwine ter rack en ruin. Marse John'll row me up de river when he come back here en fin' de whole blessid place turned wrongsudouterds. I'm dat pestered I dunner whedder I'm eend uperds er eend downerds!"

"Well, Uncle Remus," persisted the little boy, "how can a cow swallow a grindstone?"

"Dar now!" exclaimed the old man, stopping suddenly and staring at the child; "des lissen at dat! No wonder I'm gittin' bal'-headed en wob-

bly in de legs. Mules en cows gwine ter rack. Miss Sally hollerin' 'I tol'
you so!' en chilluns gwine 'roun' axin' 'bout cows swall'in' grinestones.
Ef dat ain't nuff fer ter run anybody ravin' 'stracted, I wish you'd tell me
what is!'"

"Well, you said something to mamma about a cow swallowing a grindstone," remarked the boy, confidently.

"Oh!" said Uncle Remus, "dat's diffunt! Now I know what you talkin'
'bout! Man, suh! you had me skeer'd. My min' wuz up yander at de corn-
crib wid dat fool mule what snag hisse'f, en when I hear you talk 'bout
cow eatin' grinestone, I 'lowed dat I had mo' trouble on my han's. Dat
what I tol' Miss Sally ain't got no tale behime it. Hit's des a sayin'.

"It seem like dey wuz a man which had a wife, en eve'y time sump'n'd
happen, she up en 'low, 'I tol' you so!' Hit kep' on dis away, twel one day
dish yer man seed de cow run thoo de yard en turn over de grinestone.
So de man, he run en tell his wife dat de cow done swaller'd de grinestone, en she up'n say, 'I tol' you so!' "

But, after all, the saying reminded Uncle Remus of a story, and he
told it by fits and starts, while he was looking after the welfare of the
wounded mule, and the crippled calf, and the cow with the broken horn.

"One time, dey wuz a boy, en dish yer boy wuz mighty smart. He wuz
like a slick thrip — little but ole. I dunner what dey call 'im in dem
times, but in deze days we'd call 'im a runt, en laugh at 'im. Well, dish
yer boy had a head on 'im. He look like he dried up, but nummine dat.
Dem what got ahead er 'im had ter git up long 'fo' day, en ef dey ain't take
keer dey'd fin' 'im up befo' um.

"One season, when de blackberries wuz ripe, he went 'roun' en tol' de
folks dat ef dey'd take der baskets en der buckets en go out en git de
blackberries, he'd gi' um half dey pick. Hit been so seldom dat de folks
git a chance fer ter make any extry money dat dey mighty glad ter have
de chance ter pick blackberries. So dey all went out en pick en pick,
twel dey pick two waggin loads un um. Well, dis yer swunk-up boy,
which he look like he ain't got no sense skacely, he 'vide fa'r, dey ain't
no two ways 'bout dat. He tuck half en gi' um der half back."

"What was his name, Uncle Remus?" asked the little boy, somewhat
interested in this remarkable transaction.

"Linktum Lidy Lody," the old man answered promptly. "I had de idee

I done tol' you dat. But nummine! Dat what dey call 'im, en dat what he call hisse'f — Linktum Tidlum Tidy. Hit run 'long so funny dat I dunner wharbouts de fergiven name stops at en wharbouts de fambly name begins at. Fer short en sweet dey call 'im Tinktum Tidy.

"Well, dish yer Tinktum Tidlum, he 'vide out f'ar wid de folks. He tuck his half er de blackberries en gi' um der half. Dey wa'n't no 'sputin' 'bout it. But den when de folks git der half, dey ax deyse'f what dey gwine do wid it. Dey want ter sell it ter Tinktum Tidy, but he 'low he got des ez much blackberries ez he know what ter do wid. Atter a while de folks say dat ef dey can't sell der share er de blackberries, dey des ez well put um in Tinktum Tidy's pile, en dat what dey done; en den he tuck de two waggin loads to town en sold um fer de cash money.

"Bimeby some er de mo' longer-headed folks sot down en got ter studyin' 'bout it, en dey ax deyse'f how come dey got ter go out en pick blackberries fer dat little bit er swunk-up chap. Dey study en study, but de mo' dey study de mo' foolish dey feel.

"Well, suh, de tale got out, en it travel 'roun' en 'roun' twel de King got wind un it, en he tuck en sont fer Tinktum Tidy. Dis make de folks what pick de blackberries mighty glad, kaze dey got de idee dat de King gwine ter put de little swunk-up chap in de calaboose fer foolin' um. But Tinktum Tidy ain't skeer'd. He wrop up a change er cloze in his hankcher, en put out ter whar de King stay at. Some er de folks went 'long fer ter see what gwine ter come er de little swunk-up chap what fool um.

"Bimeby dey got ter whar de King live, en Tinktum Tidy des march right 'long in, en tol' um dat de King done sont fer 'im. Dey tuck 'im in a big room whar dey wuz a whole passel er yuther folks, en tol' 'im ter wait dar twel de King come. Eve'ybody look at 'im hard, he wuz so swunk-up en puny, en he look right back at um, des like he wuz one er de quality. Atter while, here come de King. Time he got settled on de flatform, his eye drapt on Tinktum Tidy, en he ax what dat ar runt doin' dar.

"Dey up'n tell de King dat dat's de chap what make de folks pick so much blackberries. When de King hear dis, he lay back en laugh fit ter kill hisse'f. He call Tinktum Tidy up en ax 'im all 'bout how he been doin', en den he 'low, de King did, dat Tinktum Tidy mus' be mighty smart. But Tinktum Tidy, he say dat 'tain't him dat's smart, hit's de folks what pick de blackberries, kaze folks what kin pick dat much in so little time is bleedzd ter be smart.

"Den de King run his han' in his pocket en pull out lev'm grains er corn. He 'low, 'Take dish yer corn en do what you please wid it, but de crap I want fum it is 'lev'm strong men fer ter put in my army.'

"Tinktum Tidy tuck de corn en tie it up in one cornder er his hankcher. He 'low, 'Not countin' harrycanes en high water, I'll be back in a fortnight. Ef 'lev'm strong men wuz ez easy ter pick ez blackberries, I'd sen' some yuther folks, but I'll hatter go atter de men myse'f.'

"Wid dat he make his bow, he did, en tuck his foot in his han' en put out. He travel all dat day, en 'bout night he come ter a tavern, en dar he stop. De man ax 'im whar he come fum, what his name, en whar he gwine. He say he come fum Chuckerluckertown, en he name Tinktum Tidy, en he gwine on a long journey. When bedtime come, he call de man in de room en show 'im de corn.

"He 'low, 'Here de 'lev'm grains er corn de King gi' me. I'll lay it on de table. I'm feard de Big Gander gwine ter eat it.'

"De man say he'll shet de do' so de Big Gander can't git it. Den dey all went ter bed. Tinktum Tidy wait twel eve'ybody got still, en den he got up en drapt de corn thoo de crack er de floor. Den he went ter sleep.

"Nex' mornin' he wake up soon en 'larm de neighborhood. He holler out: 'I tol' you so! I tol' you so! De Big Gander done eat de 'lev'm grains er corn what de King gi' me! De Big Gander done eat de 'lev'm grains er corn de King gi' me!'

"Tinktum Tidy holler so loud en so long dat he skeer de man. Den de man's ole 'oman, she stuck 'er head out de winder en sot up a squall.

"She say, 'Take de Big Gander en go on off fum here! Take 'im en go!'

"Tinktum Tidy tuck de Big Gander und' his arm en went polin' down de big road. He travel all dat day twel night, en he come ter anudder town, en he went en put up at de tavern. When bedtime come, he tied de gander by de leg ter de bedstid, en den he call de man.

"Here de Big Gander dat eat de 'lev'm grains er corn dat de King gi' me. I'll tie 'im here, kaze I'm feared de Boo-Boo Black Sheep'll kill 'im.'

"Man say, 'Black Sheep can't git 'im here.'

"In de middle er de night Tinktum Tidy got up en broke de Big Gander's neck en flung 'im out in de barn-yard. Nex' mornin' he got up soon, en 'gun ter holler.

"He 'low, 'I tol you so! I tol' you so! Boo-Boo Black Sheep done kill de Big Gander dat eat de 'lev'm grains er corn de King gi' me!'

"When de man hear talk er de King, he got skeer'd. Hit make 'im shake in his shoes. He say, 'Take Boo-Boo Black Sheep en go 'long! You done fetch me bad luck!'

"Den Tinktum Tidy fastened Boo-Boo Black Sheep wid a rope, en led 'im off down de big road. Bimeby he come ter whar dey wuz anudder town, en he went en put up at de tavern. When bedtime come he call de man.

"He 'low, 'Here Boo-Boo Black Sheep dat kill de Big Gander, dat eat de 'lev'm grains er corn de King gi' me. I'll tie 'im here ter de bedstid kaze I'm feard de Brindle Cow'll hook 'im.'

"Man say, 'Brindle Cow can't git 'im in here.'

"'Twix' midnight en day, Tinktum Tidy got up en kill de Black Sheep en put 'im in de lot wid de Brindle Cow. Den he got up soon in de mornin', en 'gun ter holler.

"He 'low, 'I tol' you so! I tol' you so! De Brindle Cow done kill Boo-Boo Black Sheep dat kill de Big Gander dat eat de 'lev'm grains er corn de King gi' me!'

"Dis make de man feel skeer'd. He say, 'Take de Brindle Cow en go!'

"Tinktum Tidy led de Brindle Cow off down de road en make his way ter de nex' town. He got dar by de time night come, en put up at de tavern. When bedtime come, he tuck en call de man.

"He 'low, 'Here de Brindle Cow dat kill de Boo-Boo Black Sheep dat kill de Big Gander dat eat de 'lev'm grains er corn de King gi' me. I'll tie 'er here by de chimbley, whar de Roan Hoss can't git 'er.'

"De man say, 'I know mighty well de Roan Hoss can't git 'er here.'

"Des 'fo' day Tinktum Tidy tuck de Brindle Cow in de stable en made way wid 'er. Den when daylight come he 'gun ter holler.

"He 'low, 'I tol' you so! I tol' you so! De Roan Hoss done kill de Brindle Cow dat kill de Boo-Boo Black Sheep dat kill de Big Gander dat eat de 'lev'm grains er corn de King gi' me.'

"De man git skeer'd when he hear de name er de King, en he say, 'Take de Roan Hoss en go on whar you gwine!'

"Tinktum Tidy got on de Roan Hoss en went trottin' down de big road. He went on en went on, he did, twel he come ter a place whar he had ter cross a creek. Close by de road he seed a ole man settin'. He look at de ole man en de ole man look at 'im.

"Bimeby de ole man say, 'Howdy, son!' Tinktum Tidy say, 'Howdy, Gran'sir!'

"De ole man 'low, 'Son, come wipe my eyes!'

"Tinktum Tidy say, 'I'll wipe um, Gran'sir, ef so be it'll do you any good.' Den he got down off'n de Roan Hoss en wipe de ole man's eyes.

"De ole man say, 'Thanky-do, son! thanky-do!' Tinktum Tidy say, 'You er mo' dan welcome, Gran'sir!' Den he got on de Roan Hoss en wuz 'bout ter ride off.

"De ole man 'low, 'Son, come scratch my head!'

"Tinktum Tidy say, 'I'll scratch yo' head, Gran'sir, ef so be it'll do you any good.' Den he got down off'n de Roan Hoss en scratch de ole man's head.

"De ole man say, 'Thanky-do, son! thanky-do!' Tinktum Tidy say, 'You er mo' dan welcome, Gran'sir!'

"Den he start fer ter ride off ag'in, but de ole man 'low, 'Son, come he'p me up!'

"Tinktum Tidy say, 'I'll he'p you up, Gran'sir, ef so be it'll do you any good!'

"So he went en he'ped 'im up, en it seem like dat when de ole man got on his foots his strenk come back. He straighten up, he did, en look lots younger dan what he did.

"He 'low, 'Son, I been settin' here gwine on ten year, en you er de onliest one dat ever do what I ax um. Some laugh at me, en some cuss at me, but all went on der way, en eve'yone dat pass fell in wid 'lev'm robbers what live down de road a piece en got robbed. Now bein's ez you done what I ax you, I'm mo' dan willin' fer ter do what you ax me.'

"Wid dat, Tinktum Tidy up en tol' de ole man how come he ter be gwine 'long dar, en 'bout how de King want 'im ter fetch back 'lev'm strong men fer ter go in de army.

"De ole man 'low, 'Son, dey er waitin' fer you right down de road. Keep right on twel you come ter whar dey's a big white house. Ride 'roun' dat house sev'm times one way en sev'm times de udder way, en say de words dat come in yo' head. Don't git skeer'd, kase I won't be so mighty fur off.'

"Tinktum Tidy rid off down de road, he did, en went on twel he come ter de big white house. Den he rid 'roun' it sev'm time one way en sev'm times de udder way.

"He 'low, 'Dis is de Roan Hoss dat kill de Brindle Cow dat kill de Boo-Boo Black Sheep dat kill de Big Gander dat eat 'lev'm grains er corn de King gi' me. I want 'lev'm strong men fer de King's army.'

"En bless yo' soul, honey!" exclaimed Uncle Remus, by way of emphasis, "de do' er de big white house flew'd open, en 'lev'm strong men come marchin' out. By dat time de ole man had come up, en dey ax 'im what dey mus' do.

"He 'low, 'Mount yo' hosses, sons, en go jine de King's army!'"

"So dey went, en de King wuz mighty proud. He look 'roun' at eve'y-body en say, 'I tol' you so!' en he fix it up so dat Tinktum Tidy hed des ez much ez he kin eat en w'ar, en mighty little work fer ter do all de balance er his days."

V

The tales from

Told By Uncle Remus
New Stories of the Old Plantation

With Illustrations by
ARTHUR BURDETTE FROST *and* **J. M. CONDÉ**
and line drawings after half-tones by **FRANK VERBECK**

1
The Reason Why

THE MAIN REASON why Uncle Remus retired from business as a story-teller was because the little boy to whom he had told his tales grew to be a very big boy. He grew and grew till he couldn't grow any bigger. Meanwhile, his father and mother moved to Atlanta, and lived there for several years. Uncle Remus moved with them, but he soon grew tired of the dubious ways of city life, and one day he told his Miss Sally that if she didn't mind he was going back to the plantation where he could get a breath of fresh air.

He was overjoyed when the lady told him that they were all going back as soon as the son married. As this event was to occur in the course of a few weeks, Uncle Remus decided to wait for the rest of the family. The wedding came off, and then the father and mother returned to the plantation, and made their home there, much to the delight of the old Negro.

In course of time, the man who had been the little boy for ever so long came to have a little boy of his own. And then it happened in the most natural way in the world that the little boy's little boy fell under the spell of Uncle Remus, who was still hale and hearty in spite of his age.

This latest little boy was frailer and quieter than his father had been; indeed, he was fragile, and had hardly any color in his face. But he was a beautiful child, too beautiful for a boy. He had large, dreamy eyes, and the quaintest little ways that ever were seen; and he was polite and thoughtful of others. He was very choice in the use of words, and talked as if he had picked his language out of a book. He was a source of perpetual wonder to Uncle Remus. Indeed, he was the wonder of wonders, and the old Negro had a way of watching him curiously. Sometimes, as the result of this investigation, which was continuous, Uncle Remus would shake his head and chuckle. At other times, he would shake his head and sigh.

This little boy was not like the other little boy. He was more like a girl in his refinement. All the boyishness had been taken out of him by that mysterious course of discipline that some mothers know how to apply. He seemed to belong to a different age — to a different time; just how or why, it would be impossible to say. Still, the fact was so plain that any one old enough and wise enough to compare the two little boys — one the father of the other — could not fail to see the difference; and it was a difference not wholly on the surface. Miss Sally, the grandmother, could see it, and Uncle Remus could see it; but for all the rest the tendencies and characteristics of this later little boy were a matter of course.

"Miss Sally," said Uncle Remus, a few days after the arrival of the little boy and his mother, "what dey gwine ter do wid dat chile? What dey gwine ter make out'n 'im?"

"I'm sure I don't know," she replied. "A grandmother doesn't count for much these days unless there is illness. She is everything for a few hours, and then she is nothing." There was no bitterness in the lady's tone, but there was plenty of feeling — feeling that only a grandmother can appreciate and understand.

"I speck dat's so," Uncle Remus remarked, "an' a ol' nigger dat oughter been dead long ago, by good rights, don't count no time an' nowhar. But it's a pity — a mighty pity."

"What is a pity?" the lady inquired, though she knew full well what was in the old Negro's mind.

"I can't tell you, ma'am, an' 'twouldn't be my place ter tell you ef I could; but dar 'tis, an' you can't rub it out. I see it, but I can't say it. I knows it, but I can't show you how ter put yo' finger on it; yit it's dar ef I'm name Remus."

The grandmother sat silent so long, and gazed at the old Negro so seriously, that he became restive. He placed the weight of his body first on one foot and then on the other, and finally struck blindly at some imaginary object with the end of his walking-cane.

"I hope you ain't mad wid me, Miss Sally," he said.

"With you?" she cried. "Why — " She was sitting in an easy-chair on the back porch, where the warmth of the sun could reach her, but she rose suddenly and went into the house. She made a noise with her throat as she went, so that Uncle Remus thought she was laughing, and chuckled in response, though he felt little like chuckling. As a matter of fact, if his Miss Sally had remained on the porch one moment longer she would have burst into tears.

She went in the house, however, and was able to restrain herself. The little boy caught at the skirt of her dress, saying: "Grandmother, you have been sitting in the sun, and your face is red. Mother never allows me to sit in the sun for fear I will freckle. Father says a few freckles would help me, but mother says they would be shocking."

Uncle Remus received his dinner from the big house that day, and by that token he knew that his Miss Sally was very well pleased with him. The dinner was brought on a tray by a strapping black girl, with a saucy smile and ivory-white teeth. She was a favorite with Uncle Remus, because she was full of fun. "I dunner how come de white folks treat you better dan dey does de balance un us," she declared, as she sat the tray on the small pine table, and removed the snowy napkin with which it was covered. "I know it ain't on 'count er yo' beauty, kaze yo' ain't no purtier dan what I is," she went on, tossing her head and showing her white teeth.

Uncle Remus looked all around on the floor, pretending to be looking for some weapon that would be immediately available. Finding none, he turned with a terrible make-believe frown, and pointed his forefinger at the girl, who was now as far as the door, her white teeth gleaming as she laughed.

"Mark my words," he said solemnly, "ef I don't brain you befo' de week's out it'll be bekaze you done been gobbled up by de Unkollop-sanall." The girl stopped laughing instantly, and became serious. The threats of age have a meaning that all the gaiety of youth cannot overcome. The gray hair of Uncle Remus, his impersonation of wrath, his forefinger held up in warning, made his threat so uncanny that the girl shivered in spite of the fact that she thought he was joking. Let age shake a finger at you, and you feel that there is something serious behind the gesture.

Now, Miss Sally had taken advantage of the opportunity to send the grandchild with the girl. She was anxious that he should make the acquaintance of Uncle Remus, and have instilled into his mind the quaint humor that she knew would remain with him all his life, and become a fragrant memory when he grew old. But the later little boy was very shy, and when he saw the terrible frown and the threatening gesture with which Uncle Remus had greeted the girl, he shrank back in a corner, seeing which the old Negro began to laugh. It was not a genuine laugh, but it was so well done that it answered every purpose.

"I don't see nothin' ter laugh at," remarked the girl, and with that she flirted out.

Uncle Remus turned to the little boy. "Honey, you look so much like Brer Rabbit dat I bleeze ter laugh. 'Long at fust, I had a notion dat you mought be Mr. Cricket. But you er too big fer dat, an' den you ain't got no elbows in yo' legs. An' den I know'd 'twuz Brer Rabbit I had in min'. Yasser, dey ain't no two ways 'bout dat — you look like Brer Rabbit when he tryin' fer ter make up his min' whedder ter run er no."

Then, without waiting to see the effect of this remark, Uncle Remus turned his attention to the tray and its contents. "Well, suh!" he exclaimed, with apparent surprise, "ef dar ain't a slishe er tater custard! An' ef I ain't done gone stone blin', dar's a dish er hom'ny wid ham gravy on it! Yes, an' bless gracious, dar's a piece er ham! Dey all look like ol' 'quaintances which dey been gone a long time an' des come back; an' dey look like dey er laughin' kaze dey er glad ter see me. I wish you'd come here, honey, an' see ef dey ain't laughin'; you got better eyes dan what I is."

The lure was entirely successful. The little boy came forward timidly, and when he was within reach, Uncle Remus placed him gently on his knee. The child glanced curiously at the dishes. He had heard so much of Uncle Remus from his father and his grandmother that he was inclined to believe everything the old man said. "Why, they are not laughing," he exclaimed. "How could they?"

"I speck my eyes is bad," replied Uncle Remus. "When anybody gits ter be a himbly an' hombly-hombly year ol', dey er liable fer ter see double."

The child was a very serious child, but he laughed in spite of himself. "Oh, pshaw!" he exclaimed.

"I'm mighty glad you said dat," remarked Uncle Remus, smacking his lips, "kaze ef you hadn't a said it, I'd a been a bleeze ter say it myse'f."

"Say what?" inquired the little boy, who was unused to the quips of the old man.

"'Bout dat tater custard. It's de funniest tater custard dat I ever laid eyes on, dey ain't no two ways 'bout dat."

"Grandmother wanted to give me some," said the little boy longingly, "but mother said it wasn't good for me."

"Aha!" exclaimed Uncle Remus in a tone of triumph. "What I tell you? Miss Sally writ on here wid dese dishes dat she want you ter eat dat tater custard. Mo' dan dat she sont two pieces. Dar's one, an' dar de yuther." There wasn't anything wrong about this counting, except that Uncle Remus pointed twice at the same piece.

The little boy was sitting on Uncle Remus's knee, and he turned suddenly and looked into the weather-beaten face that had harbored so many smiles. The child seemed to be searching for something in that venerable countenance, and he must have found it, for he allowed his head to fall against the old Negro's shoulder and held it there. The movement was as familiar to Uncle Remus as the walls of his cabin, for among all the children that he had known well, not one had failed to lay his head where that of the little boy now rested.

"Miss Sally is de onliest somebody in de roun' worl' dat know what you an' me like ter eat," remarked Uncle Remus, making a great pretense of chewing. "I dunner how she fin' out, but fin' out she did, an' we oughter be mighty much beholden ter 'er. I done et my piece er tater custard," he went on, "an' you kin eat yone when you git good an' ready."

"I saw only one piece," remarked the child, without raising his head, "and if you have eaten that there is none left for me." Uncle Remus closed his eyes, and allowed his head to fall back. This was his favorite attitude when confronted by something that he could not comprehend. This was his predicament now, for there was something in this child that was quite beyond him. Small as the lad was, he was old-fashioned. He thought and spoke like a grown person; and this the old Negro knew was not according to nature. The trouble with the boy was that he had had no childhood; he had been subdued and weakened by the abnormal training he had received.

"Tooby sho you ain't seed um," Uncle Remus declared, returning to the matter of the potato custard. "Ef yo' pa had a been in yo' place he'd a seed um, kaze when he wuz long 'bout yo' age, he had mo' eyes in his stomach dan what he had in his head. But de ol' nigger wuz a little too quick fer you. I seed de two pieces time de gal snatch de towel off, an' I 'low ter myse'f dat ef I didn't snatch one, I'd not git none. Yasser! I wuz a little too quick fer you."

The child turned his head, and saw that the slice of potato custard was still on the plate. "I'm so sorry that mother thinks it will hurt me," he said with a sigh.

"Well, whatsomever she say 'bout de yuther piece er custard, I boun' she ain't say dat dat piece 'ud hurt you, kaze she ain't never lay eyes on it. An' mo' dan dat," Uncle Remus went on with a very serious face, "Miss Sally writ wid de dishes dat one er de pieces er tater custard wuz fer you."

"I don't see any writing," the child declared, with a longing look at the potato custard.

"Miss Sally ain't aim fer you ter see it, kaze ef you could see it, eve'y-body could see it. An' dat ain't all de reason why you can't see it. You been hemmed up dar in a big town, an' yo' eyes ain't good. But dar's de writin' des ez plain ez pig-tracks." Uncle Remus made believe to spell out the writing, pointing at a separate dish every time he pronounced a word. "Le' me see: she put dis dish fust — 'One piece is fer de chil'.'"

The little boy reflected a moment. "There are only five dishes," he said very gravely, "and you pointed at one of them twice."

"Tooby sho I did," Uncle Remus replied, with well-affected solem-nity. "Ain't dat de way you does in books?"

The little lad was too young to be well-grounded in books, but he had his ideas, nevertheless. "I don't see how it can be done," he suggested. "A is always A."

"Ah-yi!" exclaimed Uncle Remus triumphantly. "It's allers big A er little a. But I wa'n't callin' out no letters; I wuz callin' out de words what yo' granmammy writ wid de dishes." The little boy still looked doubtful, and Uncle Remus went on. "Now, spozin' yo' pa wuz ter come 'long an' say, 'Unk Remus, I wanter gi' you a cuff.' An' den, spozin' I wuz ter 'low, 'Yasser, an' thanky, too, but you better gi' me a pa'r un um while you 'bout it.' An' spozin' he'd be talkin' 'bout maulin' me, whiles I wuz talkin' 'bout dem contraptions what you got on yo' shirt-sleeves, an' you ain't got no mo' business wid um dan a rooster is wid britches. Spozin' all dat wuz ter happen, how you speck I'd feel?"

Something in the argument, or the way Uncle Remus held his head, appealed to the little boy's sense of humor, and he laughed heartily for the first time since Uncle Remus had known him. It was real laughter, too, so real that the old Negro joined in with gusto, and the two laughed and laughed until it seemed unreasonable to laugh any more. To make matters worse, Uncle Remus pretended to become very solemn all of a sudden, and then just as suddenly went back to laughter again. This was more than the little chap could stand. He laughed until he writhed in the old man's arms; in fact, till laughter became painful.

"Ef we go on dis away," Uncle Remus remarked, "you'll never eat yo' tater custard in de worl'." With that, he seized a biscuit and pretended to place the whole of it in his mouth at once, closing his eyes with a smile of ecstasy on his face. "Don't, Uncle Remus! please don't!" cried the little boy, who had laughed until he was sore.

At this the old man became serious again. "I hear um say," he remarked with some gravity, "dat ef you laugh too much you'll sprain yo' goozle-um, er maybe git yo' th'oat-latch outer j'int. Dat de reason you see me lookin' so sollumcolly all de time. You watch me right close, an' you'll see fer yo'se'f."

The little boy ceased laughing, and regarded Uncle Remus closely. The old Negro's face was as solemn as the countenance of one of the early Puritans. "You were laughing just now," said the child. "You were laughing when I laughed."

The old man looked off into space as though he were considering a serious problem. Then he said with a sigh, "I speck I did, honey, but how I gwine ter he'p myse'f when I see you winkin' at dat tater custard? I mought not a laughed des at dat, but when I see you bek'nin' at it wid yo' tongue, I wuz bleeze ter turn loose my hyuh-hyuh-hyuhs!"

This was the beginning of the little boy's acquaintance with Uncle Remus, of whom he had heard so much. Some of the results of that acquaintance are to be set forth in the pages that follow.

2

Why Mr. Cricket Has Elbows on His Legs

IT WAS NOT OFTEN that Uncle Remus had to search for the boys who had, in the course of a very long life, fallen under his influence. On the contrary, he had sometimes to plan to get rid of them when he had work of importance to do. But now, here he was in his old age searching all about for a little chap who wasn't as big as a pound of soap after a hard day's washing, as the old man had said more than once.

The child had promised to go with Uncle Remus to fetch a wagon-load of corn that had been placed under shelter in a distant part of the plantation, and though the appointed hour had arrived, and the carriage-horses had been hitched to the wagon, he had failed to put in an appearance.

Uncle Remus had asked the nurse, a mulatto woman from the city, where the child was, and the only reply she deigned to make was that he was all right. This nurse had been offended by Uncle Remus, who, on more than one occasion, had sent her about her business when he wanted the little boy to himself. She resented this and lost no opportunity to show her contempt.

All his other resources failing, Uncle Remus went to the big house and asked his Miss Sally. She, being the child's grandmother, was presumed to know his whereabouts; but Miss Sally was not in a very good humor. She sent word that she was very busy, and didn't want to be bothered; but before Uncle Remus could retire, after the message had been delivered, she relented. "What is it now?" she inquired, coming to the door.

"I wuz des huntin' fer de little chap," Uncle Remus replied, "an' I 'lowed maybe you'd know whar he wuz at. We wuz gwine fer ter haul a load er corn, but he ain't showed up."

"Well, I made him some molasses candy — something I shouldn't have done — and he has been put in jail because he wiped his mouth on his coat-sleeve."

"In jail, ma'am?" Uncle Remus asked, astonishment written on his face.

"He might as well be in jail; he's in the parlor."

"Wid de winders all down? He'll stifle in dar."

The grandmother went into the house too indignant to inform Uncle Remus that she had sent the house-girl to open the windows under the pretense of dusting and cleaning. The old man was somewhat doubtful as to how he should proceed. He knew that in a case of this kind, Miss Sally could not help him. She had set herself to win over the young wife of her son, and she knew that she would cease to be the child's grandmother and become the mother-in-law the moment her views clashed with those of the lad's mother — and we all know from the newspapers what a terrible thing a mother-in-law is.

Knowing that he would have to act alone, Uncle Remus proceeded very cautiously. He went around into the front yard, and saw that all the parlor windows were up and the curtains looped back, something that had never happened before in his experience. To his mind the parlor was a dungeon, and a very dark one at that, and he chuckled when he saw the sunshine freely admitted, with no fear that it would injure the carpet. If one little bit of a boy could cause such a change in immemorial custom, what would two little boys be able to do? With these and similar homely thoughts in his mind, Uncle Remus cut short his chuckle and began to sing about little Crickety Cricket, who lives in the thicket.

Naturally, this song attracted the attention of the little lad, who had exhausted whatever interest there had been in an album, and was now beginning to realize that he was a prisoner. He stuck his head out of the window, and regarded the old man rather ruefully. "I couldn't go with you after the corn, Uncle Remus. Mother said I was too naughty."

"I ain't been atter no corn, honey. I hear tell er yo' gwines on, an' I felt too bad fer ter go atter de corn; but de waggin's all ready an' a-waitin'. Dey ain't no hurry 'bout dat corn. Ef you can't go ter-day, maybe you kin go termorrer, er ef not, den some yuther day. Dey ain't nobody hankerin' atter corn but de ol' gray mule, an' he'd hanker an' whicker fer it ef you wuz ter feed 'im a waggin-load three times a day. How come you ter be so bad dat yo' ma hatter shet you up in dat dungeon? What you been doin'?"

"Mother said I was very naughty and made me come in here," the little lad replied.

"I bet you ef dey had a put yo' pa in der, dey wouldn't a been no pennaner lef', an' de kyarpit would a looked like it been thoo a harrycane. Dey shet 'im up in a room once, an' dey wuz a clock in it, an' he tuck'n tuck dat clock ter pieces fer ter see what make it run. 'Twa'n't no big clock, needer, but yo' pa got nuff wheels out er dat clock fer ter fill a peck medjur, an' when dey sont it ter town fer ter have it mended, de clock man say he know mighty well dat all dem wheels ain't come outer dat clock. He mended it all right, but he had nuff wheels an' whirligigs left over fer ter make a n'er clock."

"There's a clock in here," said the little boy, "but it's in a glass case."

"Don't pester it, honey, kaze it's yo' granma's, an' 'twa'n't yo' granma dat had you shot up in dar. No, suh, not her — never in de roun' worl'."

The little prisoner sighed, but said nothing. He was not a talkative chap. He had been taught that it is impolite to ask questions, and as a child's conversation must necessarily be made up of questions, he had little to say. Uncle Remus found a rake leaning against the chimney. This he took and examined critically, and found that one of the teeth was broken out. "Now, I wonder who could a done dat!" he exclaimed. "Sholy nobody wouldn't a come 'long an' knock de toof out des fer fun. Ef de times wuz diffunt, I'd say dat a cricket hauled off an' kicked it out wid one er his behime legs. But times done change; dey done change so dat when I turn my head an' look backerds, I hatter ketch my breff I gits so skeer'd. Dey done been sech a change dat de crickets ain't dast ter kick sence ol' Grandaddy Cricket had his great kickin' match. I laid off ter tell you 'bout it when we wuz gwine atter dat load er corn dat's waitin' fer us; but stidder gwine atter corn, here you is settin' in de parlor countin' out yo' money." Uncle Remus came close to the window and looked in. 'Ol' Miss useter keep de Bible on de table dar — yasser! Dar 'tis, de same ol' Bible dat's been in de fambly sence de year one. You better git it down, honey, an' read dat ar piece 'bout de projickin' son, kaze ef dey shet you up in de parlor now, dey'll hatter put you in jail time you er ten year ol'."

This remark was intended for the ear of the young mother, who had come into the front yard searching for roses. Uncle Remus had seen her from the corner of his eye, and he determined to talk so she could hear and understand.

"But what will they put me in jail for?" the child asked.

"What dey put you in dar fer? Kaze you wipe yo' mouf on yo' sleeve. Well, when you git a little bigger, you'll say ter yo'se'f, 'Dey shet me in de parlor fer nothin', an' now I'll see ef dey'll put me in jail fer sump'n'; an' den you'll make a mouf at de gov'ner up dar in Atlanty — I know right whar his house is — an' dey'll slap you in jail an' never ax yo' name ner whar you come fum. Dat's de way dey does in dat town, kaze I done been dar an' see der carryin's on."

"I believe I'll try it when I go back home," said the little lad.

"Co'se you will," Uncle Remus assented, "an' you'll be glad fer ter git in jail atter bein' in a parlor what de sun ain't shine in sence de war. You come down here fer ter git strong an' well, an' here you is in de dampest room in de house. You'll git well — oh, yes! I see you well right now, speshually atter you done had de croup an' de pneumony, an' de brown-creeturs."

"There's Mother," said the little boy under his breath.

"I wish 'twuz yo' daddy!" Uncle Remus replied. "I'd gi' 'im a piece er my min' ez long ez a waggin tongue."

But the young mother never heard this remark. She had felt she was doing wrong when she banished the child to the parlor for a trivial fault, and now she made haste to undo it. She ran into the house and released the little boy, and told him to run to play. "Thank you, Mother," he said courteously, and then when he disappeared, what should the young mother do but cry?

The child, however, was very far from crying. He ran around to the front yard just in time to meet Uncle Remus as he came out. He seized the old darky's hand and went skipping along by his side. "You put me in min' er ol' Grandaddy Cricket 'bout de time he had his big kickin' match. He sho wuz lively."

"That was just what I was going to ask you about," said the child enthusiastically, for his instinct told him that Uncle Remus's remarks about Grandaddy Cricket were intended to lead up to a story. When they had both climbed into the wagon, and were well on their way to the Wood Lot, where the surplus corn had been temporarily stored, the old man, after some preliminaries, such as looking in his hat to see if he had lost his hankcher, as he called it, and inquiring of the horses if they knew where they were going and what they were going after, suddenly turned to the child with a question: "Ain't I hear you ax me 'bout sump'n' n'er, honey? I'm gittin' so ol' an' wobbly dat it seem like I'm deaf, yit ef anybody wuz ter call me ter dinner, I speck I could hear um a mile off ef dey so much ez whispered it."

"Yes," the child replied. "It was about old Grandaddy Cricket. I thought maybe you knew something about him."

"Who? Me, honey? Why, my great-grandaddy's great-grandaddy live nex' door ter whar ol' Grandaddy Cricket live at. Folks is lots littler now

dan what dey wuz in dem days, an' likewise de creeturs, an' de creepin'
an' crawlin' things. My grandaddy say dat his great-grandaddy would
make two men like him, an' my grandaddy wuz a monstus big man, dey
ain't no two ways 'bout dat. It seems like dat folks is swunk up. My
grandaddy's great-grandaddy say it's kaze dey done quit eatin' raw meat.

"I can't tell you 'bout dat myself, but my great-grandaddy's great-
great-grandaddy could eat a whole steer in two days, horn an' huff, an'
dem what tol' me ain't make no brags 'bout it; dey done like dey'd seen
it happen nine times a mont' off an' on fer forty years er mo'. Well den,"
Uncle Remus went on, looking at the little chap to see if he was swallowing the story with a good digestion — "well, den, dat bein' de case, it
stan's ter reason dat de creeturs an' de crawlin' an' creepin' things wuz
lots bigger dan what dey is now. Dey had bigger houses, ef dey had any
'tall, an' ef dey had bigger houses dey must a had bigger chimbleys.

"So den, all dat bein' settle', I'm gwine tell yo' 'bout ol' Grandaddy
Cricket. He must a been a grandaddy long 'bout de time dat my great-
grandaddy's great-grandaddy wuz workin' for his great grandaddy. Howsomever dat mought be, o' Grandaddy Cricket wuz on han', an' fum all I
hear he wuz bigger dan a middlin'-size goat. All endurin' er de hot wedder, he'd stay out in de woods wid his fife an' his fiddle, an' I speck he
had great times. One day he'd fiddle fer de fishes fer ter dance, an' de
nex' he'd l'arn de young birds how ter whistle wid his fife. Day in an' day
out he frolicked an' had his fun, but bimeby de wedder 'gun ter git cool
an' de days 'gun ter git shorter, an' ol' Grandaddy Cricket hatter keep his
han's in his pockets fum soon in de mornin' twel ten o'clock. An' 'long
'bout de time when de sun start down hill, he'd hatter put his fiddle under his arm an' his fife in his side-pocket.

"Dis wuz bad nuff, but wuss come. It got so col' dat Grandaddy
Cricket can't skacely walk twel de sun wuz shinin' right over 'im. Mo'
dan dat, he 'gun ter git hongry and stay hongry. Ef you'd a seed 'im in de
hot wedder, fiddlin' an' dancin', an' fifin' an' prancin', you'd a thunk dat
he had a stack er vittles put by ez big ez de barn back yander; but
bimeby it got so cold dat he know sump'n' got ter be done. He know
sump'n' got ter be done, but how er when he couldn't a tol' you ef it had
a been de las' ac'. He went 'long, creepin' an' crawlin' fum post ter pil-

lar, an' he 'membered de days when he went wid a hop, skip an' a jump, but he wuz too col' fer ter cry.

"He crope along, tryin' ter keep on de sunny side er de worl', twel bimeby, one day he seed smoke a-risin' way off yander, an' he know'd mighty well dat whar der's smoke dey bleeze ter be fier. He crope an' he crawled, an' bimeby he come close nuff ter de smoke fer ter see dat it wuz comin' out'n a chimbley dat'd been built on one een' uv a house. 'Twa'n't like de houses what you see up yander in Atlanty, kaze 'twuz made out er logs, an' de chink 'twix' de logs wuz stopped up wid red clay. De chimbley wuz made out'n sticks an' stones an' mud.

"Grandaddy Cricket wuz forty-'lev'm times bigger dan what his fambly is deze days, but he wa'n't so big dat he couldn't crawl und' de house, kaze 'twuz propped up on pillars. So und' de house he went an' scrouge close ter de chimbley fer ter see ef he can't got some er de warmf, but, bless you, it 'uz stone col'. Ef it had a been like de chimbleys is deze days, ol' Grandaddy Cricket would a friz stiff, but 'twuz plain, eve'yday mud plastered on some sticks laid crossways. 'Twuz hard fer ol' Grandaddy Cricket fer ter work his way inter de chimbley, but harder fer ter stay out'n de col' — so he sot in ter work. He gnyawed an' he sawed, he scratched an' he clawed, he pushed an' he gouged, an' he shoved an' he scrouged, twel, bimeby, he got whar he could feel some er de warmf er de fier, an' 'twa'n't long 'fo' he wuz feelin' fine. He snickered ter hisse'f when he hear de win' whistlin' 'roun' de cornders, an' blowin' des like it come right fresh fum de place whar de ice-bugs live at."

The little boy laughed and placed his hand caressingly on Uncle Remus's knee. "You mean ice-bergs, Uncle Remus," he said.

"Nigh ez I kin 'member," replied the old darky, with affected dignity, "ice-bugs is what I meant. I tell you dat p'intedly. What I know 'bout ice-berrigs?"

The little lad eyed the old darky curiously, but said nothing more for some time. Uncle Remus regarded him from the corner of his eye and smiled, for this was a little chap whose ways he was yet to understand. Finally, he took up the thread of his story. "It's des like I tell you, honey; he ain't no sooner git thawed out dan he 'gun ter feel good. Dey wuz some cracks an' crannies in de h'a'th er de fierplace, an' when de chillun eat der mush an' milk, some er de crum's 'ud sift thoo de h'a'th. Ol' Grandaddy Cricket smelt um, an' felt um, an' helt um, an' atter dat you couldn't make 'im b'lieve dat he wa'n't in hog-heav'm.

"De place whar he wuz at wa'n't roomy nuff fer fiddlin', but he tuck out his fife an' 'gun ter play on it, an' eve'y time he hear a noise he'd cut de chune short. He'd blow a little an' den break off, but take de day ez it come, he put in a right smart lot er fifin'. When night come, an' eve'ything wuz dark down dar whar he wuz at, he des turned hisse'f loose. De chillun in de house, dey des lis'n an' laugh, but dey daddy shake his head an' look sour. Dey wa'n't no crickets in de country whar he come fum, an' he wa'n't usen ter um. But de mammy er de chillun ain't pay no 'tention ter de fifin'; she des went on 'bout her business like dey ain't no cricket in de roun' worl'. Ol' Grandaddy Cricket he fifed an' fifed like he wuz doin' it fer pay. He played de chillun off ter bed an' played um ter sleep; he played twel de ol' man got ter nid-nid-noddin' by de fier; he played twel dey all went ter bed 'cept de mammy, an' he played whiles she sot by de

h'a'th, an' dremp 'bout de times when she wuz a gal — de ol' times dat make de gran'chillun feel so funny when dey hear tell 'bout um.

"Night atter night de fifin' went on, an' bimeby de man 'gun ter git tired. De 'oman, she say dat de crickets brung good luck, but de man, he say he'd ruther have mo' luck an' less fifin'. So he holler down thoo de crack in de h'a'th, an' tell ol' Grandaddy Cricket fer ter hush his fuss er change his chune. But de fifin' went on. De man holler down an' say dat ef de fifin' don't stop, he gwine ter pour 'b'ilin' water on de fifer. Ol' Grandaddy Cricket holler back:

"'Hot water will turn me brown.
    An' den I'll kick yo' chimbley down.'

"De man, he grin, he did, an' den he put de kittle on de fier an' kep' it dar twel de water 'gun ter bile, an' den, whiles de fifin' wuz at de loudest, he tuck de kittle an' tilted it so de scaldin' water will run down thoo de cracks, an' den de fust thing he know'd he ain't know nothin, kaze de water weakened de clay an de h'a'th fell in an' ol' Grandaddy Cricket sot in ter kickin' an' de chimbley come down, it did, an' bury de man, an' when dey got 'im out, he wuz one-eyed an' splayfooted.

"De 'oman an' de chillun ain't skacely known 'im. Dey hatter ax 'im his name, an' whar he come fum, an' how ol' he wuz; an' atter he satchified um dat he wuz de same man what been livin' dar all de time, de 'oman say, 'Ain't I tell you dat crickets fetch good luck?' An' de man, he 'low, 'Does you call dis good luck?'"

"What became of the cricket?" asked the little boy, after a long pause, during which Uncle Remus appeared to be thinking about other things.

"Oh!" exclaimed the old darky. "Dat's so! I ain't tol' you, is I? Well, ole Grandaddy Cricket kicked so hard, an' kicked so high, dat he onj'inted bofe his legs, an', when he crawled out fum de chimbley, his elbows wuz whar his knees oughter be at."

"But it was cold weather," suggested the little boy. "Where did he go when he kicked the chimney down?"

Uncle Remus smiled as he took another chew of tobacco. "Dey wa'n't but one thing he could do," he replied; "he went on ter nex' house an' got in de chimbley an' he been livin' in chimbleys off an' on down ter dis day an' time."

3

How Wiley Wolf Rode in the Bag

UNCLE REMUS soon had the wagon loaded with corn, and he and the little boy started back home. The plantation road was not a good one to begin with, and the spring rains had not improved it. Consequently there were times when Uncle Remus deemed it prudent to get out of the wagon and walk. The horses were fat and strong, to be sure, but some of the small hills were very steep, so much so that the old darky had to guide the team first to the right and then to the left in order to overcome the sheer grade. In other words, he had to see-saw as he explained to the little boy. "Drive um straight up, an' dey fall back," he explained, "but on de see-saw dey fergits dat dey er gwine uphill."

All this was Dutch to the little boy, who knew nothing about driving horses, but he had been well trained, and so he said, "Yes, that is so." The last time that Uncle Remus had to vacate the driver's seat in order to relieve the horses of his weight, he stumbled into a ditch that had been dug on the side of the road to prevent the rains from washing it into gullies. He recovered himself immediately, but not before he had startled a little rabbit, which ran on ahead of the horses for a considerable distance. Instinct came to its aid after a while, and it darted into the underbrush which grew profusely on both sides of the road.

Before the little rabbit disappeared, however, Uncle Remus had time to give utterance to a hunting halloo that aroused the echoes all around and made the little boy jump, for he was not used to this sort of thing. "I declar' ter gracious ef it don't put me in min' er ol' times — de times dey tell 'bout in de tales dat been handed down. Ef dat little rab had a bin five times ez big ez he is, an' twice ez young, I'd a thunk we'd done got back ter de days when my great-grandaddy's great-grandaddy lived. You mayn't b'lieve me, but ef you'll count fum de time when my great-grandaddy's great-grandaddy wuz born'd down ter dis minnit, you'll fin' dat you er lookin' back on many a long year, an' a mighty heap er Chris'mus-come-an'-gone.

"You may think dat deze times is de bes'; well, den, you kin have um ef you'll des gi' me de ol' times when de nights wuz long an' de days short, wid plenty er wood on de fier an' taters an' ashcake in de embers. Han' um here!" Uncle Remus held out his hand as if he thought the little chap had the old times and the ashcakes and the roasted potatoes in his pocket. "Den you ain't got um," he went on, as the child drew away and pretended to hold his pocket tight; "you ain't got um, an' you can't git um. I done been had um, but I got ter nippy-nappin' one night, an' some un come 'long an' tuck um — some nigger man, I speck, kaze dey wuz a big fat 'possum mixed up wid um, an' a heap er yuther things liable ter make a nigger's mouf water. Yasser! dey tuck um right away fum me, an' I ain't seed um sence; an' maybe ef I wuz ter see um I wouldn't know um."

"Were the rabbits very large in old times?" inquired the little boy.

"Dey mought er been runts in de fambly," replied Uncle Remus cautiously, "but fum all I kin hear fum dem what know'd, ol' Brer Rabbit wuz a sight bigger dan any er de rabbits you see deze days."

Uncle Remus paused to give the little boy an opportunity to make some comment, or ask such questions as occurred to him, as the other little boy had been so ready to do; but he said nothing. It seemed that his curiosity had been satisfied, and yet he wanted very much to hear a story such as Uncle Remus had been in the habit of telling his father when he was the little boy. But he had been so rigidly trained to silence in the presence of his elders that he hesitated about making his desires known.

The old Negro, however, was so accustomed to anticipating the wants of children, especially those in whom he took an interest, that he knew perfectly well what the little boy wanted. The child's attitude was expectant, even if his lips refused to give form to his thoughts. This sort of thing — the old Negro could give it no name — was so new to Uncle Remus that he chuckled, and presently the chuckle developed into a hearty laugh.

The little boy regarded him with surprise. "Are you laughing at me, Uncle Remus?" he inquired, after some hesitation.

"Why, honey, what put dat idee in yo' head? What I gwine ter laugh at you fer? Ef you wuz a little bigger, I might laugh at you, des ter see how you'd take it. Ef you want me ter laugh at you, you'll hatter do some growin'."

"Grandmother says I'm a big boy," said the child.

"Fer yo' age an' size, you er right smart chunk uv a boy," assented Uncle Remus, "but you'll hatter be lots bigger dan what you is 'fo' I laugh at you. No, suh; I wuz gigglin' at de way Brer Rabbit got away wid ol' Brer Wolf endurin' er de time when der chillun played tergedder; an' dat little rabbit dat run 'cross de road put me in min' un it. I bet ef I'd a been dar, I'd a done mo' dan laugh — I'd a holler'd. Yasser, dey ain't no two ways 'bout it — I'd a des flung back my head an' a fetched a whoop dat you could a hearn fum here ter de big house. Dat's what I'd a done."

"It must have been very funny, then," remarked the little boy.

Uncle Remus looked at the child with a serious face. Surely something must be wrong with him. And yet he was still expectant — expectant and patient. The old Negro had never had dealings with such a youngster as this, and he was not in the habit of telling stories "des dry so," as he put it; so he went at it in a new, but still a characteristic, way. "Ef yo' pa had a been settin' wha you settin' he wouldn't gi' me no peace twel I tol' im zackly what I wuz laughin' 'bout; an' he'd a pestered me wid his inquirements twel he foun' out all about it. Does he pester you dat away, honey? Kaze ef he does, I'll tell you de way ter fetch 'im up wid a roun' turn; des tell 'im you gwine ter tell his mammy on him, an' I bet you he won't pester you much atter dat."

This tickled the little boy very much. The idea of asking his grand-mother to make his father stop bothering him was so new and so ridicu-lous that he laughed unrestrainedly.

"De minnit dat little rab jumped out'n de bushes," Uncle Remus went on, apparently paying no attention to the child's laughter, "it put me in min' er de time when ol' Brer Rabbit had a lot er chillun an' gran'chillun pirootin' roun' de neighborhoods whar he live at. Dey mought a not been any granchillun in de bunch, but dey wuz plenty er chillun, bofe young an' ol'.

"Brer Rabbit 'ud move sometimes des like de folks does deze days, speshually up dar in 'Lantamatantarum, whar you come fum." The little boy smiled at this new name for Atlanta, and snuggled a little closer to Uncle Remus, for the old man had, with this one word, entered the fields that belong to childhood. "He'd move, but mos' allers he'd take a notion fer ter come back ter his ol' home. Sometimes he hatter move, de yuther creeturs pursued atter 'im so close, but dey allers got de ragged een' er de pursuin', an' dey wuz times when dey'd be right neighborly wid 'im.

"'Twuz 'bout de time dat Brer Wolf had kinder made up his min' dat he can't outdo Brer Rabbit, no way he kin fix it, an' he say ter hisse'f dat he better let 'im 'lone twel he kin git 'im in a corner whar he can't git out. So Brer Wolf, he live wid his fambly on one side de road, an' Brer Rab-bit live wid his fambly on de yuther side, not close nuff fer ter quoll 'bout de fence line, an' yit close nuff fer der youngest chillun ter play terged-der whiles de ol' folks wuz payin' der Sunday calls.

"It went on an' went on dis way twel it look like Brer Rabbit done fer-git how ter play tricks on his neighbors an' Brer Wolf done disremem-ber'd dat he yever is try fer ter ketch Brer Rabbit fer meat fer his fambly. One Sunday is speshual, dey wuz mighty frien'ly. It wuz Brer Rabbit's time fer ter call on Brer Wolf, an' bofe un um wuz settin' up in de porch des ez natchal ez life. Brer Rabbit wuz chawin' his terbacker an' spittin' over de railin' an' Brer Wolf wuz grinnin' 'bout ol' times, an' pickin' his toofies, which dey look mighty white an' sharp. Dey wuz settin' up dar, dey wuz, des ez thick ez fleas on a dog's back, an' lookin' like butter won't melt in der mouf.

"An' whiles dey wuz settin' dar, little Wiley Wolf an' Riley Rabbit wuz playin' in de yard des like chillun will. Dey run an' dey romped, dey frisk an' dey frolic, dey jump an' dey hump, dey hide an' dey slide, an' it look like dey had mo' fun dan a mule kin pull in a waggin. Little Wiley Wolf, he'd run atter Riley Rabbit, an' den Riley Rabbit 'ud run atter Wiley Wolf, an' here dey had it up an' down an' roun' an' 'roun', twel it look like dey'd run deyse'f ter death. 'Bout de time you'd think dey bleeze ter drap, one un um would holler out, 'King's Excuse!' an' in dem days, when you say dat, nobody can't ketch you, it ain't make no diffunce who, kaze ef dey dast ter lay han's on you atter you say dat, dey could be tuck ter de place whar dey done der judgin', and ef dey wa'n't mighty sharp dey'd git put in jail.

"Now, whiles Wiley Wolf an' Riley Rabbit wuz havin' der fun, der daddies wuz bleeze ter hear de racket what dey make, an' see de dus' dey raise. Dey squealed an' dey squalled, an' ripped aroun' twel you'd a thunk dey wuz a good size whirly-win' blowin' in de yard. Brer Rabbit chaw'd his terbacker right slow an' shot one eye, an' ol' Brer Wolf lick his chops an' grin. Brer Rabbit 'low, 'De youngsters is gittin' mighty familious,' an' ol' Brer Wolf say, 'Dey is indeedy, an' I hope dey'll keep it up. You know how we useter be, Brer Rabbit; we wuz constant a-playin tricks on one an'er, an' it lookt like we wuz allers at outs. I hope de young uns'll have better manners!'

"Dey sot dar, dey did, talkin' 'bout ol' times, twel de sun got low, an' de visitin' had ter be cut short. Brer Rabbit say dat he had ter cut some kindlin' so his ole 'oman kin git supper, an' Brer Wolf 'low dat he allers cut his kindlin' on Sat'day so he kin have all Sunday ter hisse'f, an' smoke his pipe in peace. He went a piece er de way wid Brer Rabbit, an' Wiley Wolf, he come, too, an' him an' Riley Rabbit had all sorts uv a time atter dey got in de big road. Dey wuz bushes on bofe sides, an' dey kep' up der game er hide an' seek des ez fur ez Brer Wolf went, but bimeby, he say he gone fur nuff, an' he say he hope Brer Rabbit'll come ag'in right soon, an' let Riley come an' play wid Wiley endurin' er de week.

"Not ter be outdone, Brer Rabbit invite Brer Wolf fer ter come an' see him, an' likewise ter let Wiley come an' play wid Riley. 'Dey ain't nothin' but chillun,' sezee, 'an' look like dey done tuck a likin' ter one an'er.'

"On de way back home, Brer Wolf make a mighty strong talk ter Wiley. He say, 'It's mo' dan likely dat de little Rab will come ter play wid you some day when dey ain't nobody here, an' when he do, I want you ter

play de game er ridin' in de bag.' Wiley Wolf say he ain't never hear tell er dat game, an' ol' Brer Wolf say it's easy ez fallin' off a log. 'You git in de bag,' sezee, 'an' let 'im haul you 'roun' de yard, an' den he'll git in de bag fer you ter haul him 'roun'. What you wanter do is ter git 'im use ter de bag; you hear dat, don't you? Git 'im use ter de bag.'

"So when little Riley come, de two un um had a great time er ridin' in de bag; 'twuz des like ridin' in a waggin, ceppin' dat Riley Rabbit look like he ain't got no mo' sense dan ter haul little Wiley Wolf over de rough-est groun' he kin fin', an' when Wiley holler'd dat he hurt 'im, Riley 'ud say he won't do it no mo', but de nex' chance he got, he'd do it ag'in.

"Well, dey had all sorts uv a time, an' when Riley Rabbit went home, he up an' tol' um all what dey'd been a-playin'. Brer Rabbit ain't say nothin'; he des sot dar, he did, an' chaw his terbacker, an' shot one eye. An' when ol' Brer Wolf come home dat night, Wiley tol' 'im 'bout de good time dey'd had. Brer Wolf grin, he did, an' lick his chops. He say, sezee,

'Dey's two parts ter dat game. When you git tired er ridin' in de bag, you tie de bag.' He went on, he did, an' tol' Wiley dat what he want 'im ter do is ter play ridin' in de bag twel bofe got tired, an' den play tyin' de bag, an' at de las' he wuz ter tie de bag so little Riley Rabbit can't git out, an' den ter go ter bed an' kiver up his head.

"So said, so done. Little Riley Rabbit come an' played ridin' in de bag, an' den when dey got tired, dey played tyin' de bag. 'Twuz mighty funny fer ter tie one an'er in de bag, an' not know ef twuz gwine ter be ontied. I dunner what would a happen ter little Riley Rab ef ol' Brer Rabbit ain't come along wid a big load er 'spicions. He call de little Rabbit ter de fence. He talk loud an' he say dat he want 'im fer ter fetch a turn er kindlin' when he start home, an' den he say ter Riley, 'Be tied in de bag once mo', an' den when Wiley gits in tie 'im in dar hard an' fas'. Wet de string in yo' mouf, an' pull it des ez tight ez you kin. Den you come on home; yo' mammy want you.'

"De las' time Wiley Wolf got in de bag, little Riley tied it so tight dat he couldn't a got it loose ef he'd a tried. He tied it tight, he did, an' den he 'low, 'I got ter go home fer ter git some kindlin', an' when I do dat, I'll come back an' play twel supper-time.' But ef he yever is went back dar, I ain't never hear talk un it."

Uncle Remus closed his eyes apparently, but not so tight that he couldn't watch the little boy. The youngster had been listening to the story too intently to ask questions, and now he sat silent waiting for Uncle Remus to finish. He waited and waited until he grew impatient, and then he raised his head. He still waited a few moments longer, but Uncle Remus to all appearances was nodding. "Uncle Remus," he cried, "what became of Wiley Wolf?"

The old Negro pretended to wake with a start. "Ain't I hear some un talkin'?" He looked all around, and then his eye fell on the little boy. "Dar you is!" he exclaimed with a laugh. "I done been ter sleep an' drempt dat I wuz eatin' a slishe er tater custard ez big ez de waggin body." The little boy repeated his question, whereupon Uncle Remus held up his hands with a gesture of astonishment. "Ain't I tol' you dat? Den I mus' be gittin' ol' an' wobbly. De fus' thing when I get ter de house I'm gwineter be weighed fer ter see how ol' I is. Now, whar wuz I at?"

"Wiley Wolf was in the bag," the little boy answered.

"Ah-h-h! Right whar Riley Rab lef' 'im. He wuz in de bag an' dar he stayed twel o' Brer Wolf come fum whar he been workin' in de fiel' — de creeturs wuz mos'ly farmers in dem days. He come back, he did, an' he see de bag, an' he know by de bulk un it dat dey wuz sump'n' in it, an' he 'uz so greedy dat his mouf fa'r dribbled. Now, den, when Wiley Wolf got in de bag, he wuz mighty tired. He'd been a-scufflin' an' a-rastlin' twel he wuz plum' wo' out. He hear Riley Rab say he wuz comin' back, an' while he wuz waitin', he drapt off ter sleep, an' dar he wuz when his daddy come home — soun' asleep.

"Ol' Brer Wolf ain't got but one idee, an' dat wuz dat Riley Rab wuz

in de bag, so he went ter de winder, an' ax ef de pot wuz b'ilin', an' his ol'
'oman say 'twuz. Wid dat, he pick up de bag, an' fo' you could bat yo'
eye, he had it soused in de pot."

"In the boiling water!" exclaimed the child.

"Dat's de way de tale runs," replied Uncle Remus. "Ez dey gun it ter
me, so I gin it to you."

4
Brother Rabbit's Laughing-Place

THIS NEW LITTLE BOY was intensely practical. He had imagination, but it
was unaccompanied by any of the ancient illusions that make the memory of childhood so delightful. Young as he was he had a contempt for
those who believed in Santa Claus. He believed only in things that his
mother considered valid and vital, and his training had been of such a
character as to leave out all the beautiful romances of childhood.

Thus when Uncle Remus mentioned something about Brother Rabbit's laughing-place, he pictured it forth in his mind as a sure-enough
place that the four-footed creatures had found necessary for their comfort and convenience. This way of looking at things was, in some measure, a great help; it cut off long explanations, and stopped many an
embarrassing question.

On one occasion when the two were together, the little boy referred to
Brother Rabbit's laughing-place and talked about it in much the same
way that he would have talked about Atlanta. If Uncle Remus was un-
prepared for such literalness he displayed no astonishment, and for all
the child knew, he had talked the matter over with hundreds of other little boys.

"Uncle Remus," said the lad, "when was the last time you went to
Brother Rabbit's laughing-place?"

"To tell you de trufe, honey, I dunno ez I ever been dar," the old man
responded.

"Now, I think that is very queer," remarked the little boy.

Uncle Remus reflected a moment before committing himself. "I
dunno ez I yever went right spang ter de place an' put my han' on it. I

speck I could a gone dar wid mighty little trouble, but I wuz so use ter hearin' 'bout it dat de idee er gwine dar ain't never got in my head. It's sorter like ol' Mr. Grissom's house. Dey say he lives in a quare little shanty not fur fum de mill. I know right whar de shanty is, yit I ain't never been dar, an' I ain't never seed it.

"It's de same way wid Brer Rabbit's laughin'-place. Dem what tol' me 'bout it had likely been dar, but I ain't never had no 'casion fer ter go dar myse'f. Yit ef I could walk fifteen er sixty mile a day, like I use ter, I boun' you I could go right now an' put my han' on de place. Dey wuz one time — but dat's a tale, an', goodness knows, you done hear nuff tales er one kin' an' anudder fer ter make a hoss sick — dey ain't no two ways 'bout dat."

Uncle Remus paused and sighed, and then closed his eyes with a groan, as though he were sadly exercised in spirit; but his eyes were not shut so tight that he could not observe the face of the child. It was a prematurely grave little face that the old man saw and whether this was the result of the youngster's environment, or his training, or his temperament, it would have been difficult to say. But there it was, the gravity that was only infrequently disturbed by laughter. Uncle Remus perhaps had seen more laughter in that little face than any one else. Occasionally the things that the child laughed at were those that would have convulsed other children, but more frequently, as it seemed, his smiles were the result of his own reflections and mental comparisons.

"I tell you what, honey," said Uncle Remus, opening wide his eyes, "dat's de ve'y thing you oughter have."

"What is it?" the child inquired, though apparently he had no interest in the matter.

"What you want is a laughin'-place, whar you kin go an' tickle yo'se'f an' laugh whedder you wanter laugh er no. I boun' ef you had a laughin'-place, you'd gain flesh, an' when yo' pa comes down fum 'Lantamatanta-rum, he wouldn't skacely know you."

"But I don't want father not to know me," the child answered. "If he didn't know me, I should feel as if I were some one else."

"Oh, he'd know you bimeby," said Uncle Remus, "an' he'd be all de gladder fer ter see you lookin' like somebody."

"Do I look like nobody?" asked the little boy.

"When you fust come down here," Uncle Remus answered, "you look like nothin' 'tall, but sence you been ramblin' 'roun' wid me, you done 'gun ter look like somebody — mos' like um."

"I reckon that's because I have a laughing-place," said the child. "You didn't know I had one, did you? I have one, but you are the first person in the world that I have told about it."

"Well, suh!" Uncle Remus exclaimed with his well-feigned astonishment; "an' you been settin' here lis'nin' at me, an' all de time you got a laughin'-place er yo' own! I never would a b'lieved it uv you. Wharbouts is dish yer place?"

"It is right here where you are," said the little boy with a winning smile.

"Honey, you don't tell me!" exclaimed the old man, looking all around. "Ef you kin see it, you see mo' dan I does — dey ain't no two ways 'bout dat."

"Why, you are my laughing-place," cried the little lad with an extraordinary burst of enthusiasm.

"Well, I thank my stars!" said Uncle Remus with emotion. "You sho does need ter laugh lots mo' dan what you does. But what make you laugh at me, honey? Is my britches too big, er is I too big fer my britches? You neen'ter laugh at dis coat, kaze it's one dat yo' grandaddy use ter have. It's mighty nigh new, kaze I ain't wo'd it mo' dan 'lev'm year. It may look shiny in places, but when you see a coat look shiny, it's a sign dat it's des ez good ez new. You can't laugh at my shoes, kaze I made um myse'f, an' ef dey lack shape dat's kaze I made um fer ter fit my rheumatism an' my foots bofe."

"Why, I never laughed at you!" exclaimed the child, blushing at the very idea. "I laugh at what you say, and at the stories you tell."

"La, honey! You sho dunno nothin'; you oughter hearn me tell tales when I could tell um. I boun' you'd a busted de buttons off'n yo' whatchermacollums. Yo' pa use ter set right whar you er settin' an' laugh twel he can't laugh no mo'. But dem wuz laughin' times, an' it look like dey ain't never comin' back. Dat 'uz 'fo' eve'ybody wuz rushin' 'roun' trying fer ter git money what don't b'long ter um by good rights."

"I was thinking to myself," remarked the child, "that if Brother Rabbit had a laughing-place I had a better one."

"Honey, hush!" exclaimed Uncle Remus with a laugh. "You'll have me gwine 'roun' here wid my head in de a'r, an' feelin' so biggity dat I won't look at my own se'f in de lookin'-glass. I ain't too ol' fer dat kinder talk ter spile me."

"Didn't you say there was a tale about Brother Rabbit's laughing-place?" inquired the little boy, when Uncle Remus ceased to admire himself.

"I dunner whedder you kin call it a tale," replied the old man. "It's mighty funny 'bout tales," he went on. "Tell um ez you may an' whence you may, some'll say 'tain't no tale, an' den ag'in some'll say dat it's a fine tale. Dey ain't no tellin'. Dat de reason I don't like ter tell no tale ter grown folks, speshually ef dey er white folks. Dey'll take it an' put it by de side er some yuther tale what dey got in der min' an' dey 'll take on dat slonchidickler grin what allers say, 'Go way, nigger man! You dunner what a tale is!' An' I don't — I'll say dat much fer ter keep some un else fum sayin' it.

"Now, 'bout dat laughin'-place — it seem like dat one time de creeturs got ter 'sputin' 'mongs' deyselves ez ter which un kin laugh de loudest. One word fotch on an'er twel it look like dey wuz gwine ter be a free fight, a rumpus an' a riot. Dey show'd der claws an' tushes, an' shuck der horns, an' rattle der hoof. Dey had der bristles up, an' it look like der eyes wuz runnin' blood, dey got so red.

"Des 'bout de time when it look like you can't keep um 'part, little Miss Squinch Owl flew'd up a tree an' 'low, 'You all dunner what laughin' is — ha-ha-ha-ha! You can't laugh when you try ter laugh — ha-ha-ha-haha!' De creeturs wuz 'stonisht. Here wuz a little fowl not much bigger dan a jay-bird laughin' herse'f blin' when dey wa'n't a thing in de roun' worl' fer ter laugh at. Dey stop der quollin' atter dat an' look at one an'er. Brer Bull say, 'Is anybody ever hear de beat er dat? Who mought de lady be?' Dey all say dey dunno, an' dey got a mighty good reason fer der sesso, kaze Miss Squinch Owl, she flies at night wid de bats an' de Betsy Bugs.

"Well, dey quit der quollin', de creeturs did, but dey still had der 'spute; de comin' er Miss Squinch Owl ain't settle dat. So dey 'gree dat dey'd meet som'ers when de wedder got better, an' try der han' at laughin' fer ter see which un kin outdo de yuther." Observing that the little boy was laughing very heartily, Uncle Remus paused long enough to inquire what had hit him on his funny-bone.

"I was laughing because you said the animals were going to meet an' try their hand at laughing," replied the lad when he could get breath enough to talk.

Uncle Remus regarded the child with a benevolent smile of admiration. "You er long ways ahead er me — you sho is. Dey ain't na'er an'er chap in de worl' what'd a cotch on so quick. You put me in min' er de peerch, what grab de bait 'fo' it hit de water. Well, dat's what de creeturs done. Dey say dey wuz gwine ter make trial fer ter see which un is de out-laughin'est er de whole caboodle, an' dey name de day, an' all prommus fer ter be dar, ceppin' Brer Rabbit, an' he 'low dat he kin laugh well nuff fer ter suit hise'f an' his fambly, 'sides dat, he don't keer 'bout laughin' less'n dey's sump'n' fer ter laugh at. De yuther creeturs dey beg 'm fer ter come, but he shake his head an' wiggle his mustash, an' say dat when he wanter laugh, he got a laughin'-place fer ter go ter, whar he won't be pestered by de balance er creation. He say he kin go dar an' laugh his fill, an' den go on 'bout his business, ef he got any business, an' ef he ain't got none, he kin go ter play.

"De yuther creeturs ain't know what ter make er all dis, an' dey wonder an' wonder how Brer Rabbit kin have a laughin'-place an' dey ain't got none. When dey ax 'im 'bout it, he 'spon', he did, dat he speck 'twuz des de diffunce 'twix' one creetur an' an'er. He ax um fer ter look at folks, how diffunt dey wuz, let 'lone de creeturs. One man'd be rich an' an'er man po', an' he ax how come dat.

"Well, suh, dey des natchally can't tell 'im what make de diffunce 'twix' folks no mo' dan dey kin tell 'im de diffunce 'twix' de creeturs. Dey wuz stumped; dey done fergit all 'bout de trial what wuz ter come off, but Brer Rabbit fotch um back ter it. He say dey ain't no needs fer ter see which kin outdo all de balance un um in de laughin' business, kaze anybody what got any sense know dat de monkey is a natchal laugher, same as Brer Coon is a natchal pacer.

"Brer B'ar look at Brer Wolf, an' Brer Wolf look at Brer Fox, an' den dey all look at one an'er. Brer Bull, he say, 'Well, well, well!' an' den he groan; Brer B'ar say, 'Who'd a thunk it?' an' den he growl; an' Brer Wolf say 'Gracious me!' an' den he howl. Atter dat, dey ain't say much, kaze dey ain't much fer ter say. Dey des stan' 'roun' an' look kinder sheepish. Dey ain't 'spute wid Brer Rabbit, dough dey'd a like ter a done it, but dey sot about an' make marks in de san' des like you see folks do when dey er tryin' fer ter git der thinkin' machine ter work.

"Well, suh, dar dey sot an' dar dey stood. Dey ax Brer Rabbit how he know how ter fin' his laughin'-place, an' how he know it wuz a laughin'-place atter he got dar. He tap hisse'f on de head, he did, an' 'low dat dey wuz a heap mo' und' his hat dan what you could git out wid a fine-toof comb. Den dey ax ef dey kin see his laughin'-place, an' he say he'd take de idee ter bed wid 'im, an' study 'pon it, but he kin say dis much right den, dat if he did let um see it, dey'd hatter go dar one at a time, an' dey'd hatter do des like he say; ef dey don't dey'll git de notion dat it's a cryin'-place.

"Dey 'gree ter dis, de creeturs did, an' den Brer Rabbit say dat while dey er all der tergedder, dey better choosen 'mongs' deyse'f which un uv um wuz gwine fus', an' he'd choosen de res' when de time come. Dey jower'd an' jower'd, an' bimeby, dey hatter leave it all ter Brer Rabbit. Brer Rabbit, he put his han' ter his head, an' shot his eye-balls an' do like he studyin'. He say 'De mo' I think 'bout who shill be de fus' one, de mo' I git de idee dat it oughter be Brer Fox. He been here long ez any-body, an' he's purty well thunk uv by de neighbors — I ain't never hear nobody breave a breff ag'in 'im.'

"Dey all say dat dey had Brer Fox in min' all de time, but somehow dey can't come right out with his name, an' dey vow dat ef dey had 'greed on somebody, dat somebody would sho a been Brer Fox. Den, atter dat, 'twuz all plain sailin'. Brer Rabbit say he'd meet Brer Fox at sech an' sech a place, at sech an' sech a time, an' atter dat dey wa'n't no mo' ter be said. De creeturs all went ter de place whar dey live at, an' done des like dey allers done.

"Brer Rabbit make a soon start fer ter go ter de p'int whar he prommus ter meet Brer Fox, but soon ez he wuz, Brer Fox wuz dar befo' 'im. It seem like he wuz so much in de habits er bein' outdone by Brer Rabbit dat he can't do widout it. Brer Rabbit bow, he did, an' pass de time er day wid Brer Fox, an' ax 'im how his fambly wuz. Brer Fox say dey wuz peart ez kin be, an' den he 'low dat he ready an' a-waitin' fer ter go an' see dat great laughin'-place what Brer Rabbit been talkin' 'bout.

"Brer Rabbit say dat suit him ter a gnat's heel, an' off dey put. Bimeby dey come ter one er deze here cle'r places dat you sometimes see in de middle uv a pine thicket. You may ax yo'se'f how come dey don't no trees grow dar when dey's trees all round, but you ain't gwine ter git no answer, an' needer is dey anybody what kin tell you. Dey got dar, dey did, an' den Brer Rabbit make a halt. Brer Fox 'low, 'Is dis de place? I don't feel no mo' like laughin' now dan I did 'fo' I come.'

"Brer Rabbit, he say, 'Des keep yo' jacket on, Brer Fox; ef you git in too big a hurry it might come off. We done come mighty nigh ter de place, an' ef you wanter do some ol' time laughin', you'll hatter do des like I tell you; ef you don't wanter laugh, I'll des show you de place, an' we'll go on back whar we come fum, kaze dis is one er de days dat I ain't got much time ter was'e laughin' er cryin'.' Brer Fox 'low dat he ain't so mighty greedy ter laugh, an' wid dat, Brer Rabbit whirl 'roun', he did, an' make out he gwine on back whar he live at. Brer Fox holler at 'im; he say, 'Come on back, Brer Rabbit; I'm des a-projickin' wid you.'

"'Ef you wanter projick, Brer Fox, you'll hatter go home an' projick wid dem what wanter be projicked wid. I ain't here kaze I wanter be here. You ax me fer ter show you my laughin'-place, an' I 'greed. I speck we better be gwine on back.' Brer Fox say he come fer ter see Brer Rabbit's laughin'-place, an' he ain't gwine ter be satchify twel he see it. Brer Rabbit 'low dat ef dat de case, den he mus' ac' de gentermun all de way thoo, an' quit his behavishness. Brer Fox say he'll do de best he kin, an' den Brer Rabbit show 'im a place whar de bamboo briars, an' de blackberry bushes, an' de honeysuckles done start ter come in de pine thicket, an' can't come no furder. 'Twa'n't no thick place; 'twuz des whar de swamp at de foot er de hill peter'd out in tryin' ter come ter dry lan'. De bushes an' vines wuz thin an' scanty, an' ef dey could a talked dey'd a hollered loud fer water.

"Brer Rabbit show Brer Fox de place, an' den tell 'im dat de game is fer ter run full tilt thoo de vines an' bushes, an' den run back, an' thoo um ag'in an' back, an' he say he'd bet a plug er terbacker 'g'in' a ginger cake dat by de time Brer Fox done dis he'd be dat tickled dat he can't stan' up fer laughin'. Brer Fox shuck his head; he ain't nigh b'lieve it, but fer all dat, he make up his min' fer ter do what Brer Rabbit say, spite er de fac' dat his ol' 'oman done tell 'im 'fo' he lef' home dat he better keep his eye open, kaze Brer Rabbit gwine ter run a rig on 'im.

"He tuck a runnin' start, he did, an' he went thoo de bushes an' de vines like he wuz runnin' a race. He run an' he come back a-runnin', an' he run back, an' dat time he struck sump'n' wid his head. He try ter dodge it, but he seed it too late, an' he wuz gwine too fas'. He struck it, he did, an' time he do dat, he fetched a howl dat you might a hearn a mile, an' atter dat, he holler'd yap, yap, yap, an' ouch, ouch, ouch, an' yow, yow, yow, an' whiles dis wuz gwine on Brer Rabbit wuz thumpin' de

ground wid his behime foot, an' laughin' fit ter kill. Brer Fox run 'roun'
an' 'roun', an' kep' on snappin' at hisse'f an' doin' like he wuz tryin' fer
ter t'ar his hide off. He run, an' he roll, an' wallow, an' holler, an' fall, an'
squall twel it look like he wuz havin' forty'-lev'm duck fits.

"He got still atter while, but de mo' stiller he got, de wuss he looked.
His head wuz all swell up, an' he look like he been run over in de road
by a fo'-mule waggin. Brer Rabbit 'low, 'I'm glad you had sech a good
time, Brer Fox; I'll hatter fetch you out ag'in. You sho done like you wuz
havin' fun.' Brer Fox ain't say a word; he wuz too mad fer ter talk. He des
sot aroun' an' lick hisse'f an' try ter git his ha'r straight. Brer Rabbit 'low,
'You ripped aroun' in dar twel I wuz skeer'd you wuz gwine ter hurt
yo'se'f, an' I b'lieve in my soul you done gone an' bump yo' head ag'in' a
tree, kaze it's all swell up. You better go home, Brer Fox, an' let yo' ol'
'oman poultice you up.'

"Brer Fox show his tushes, an' say, 'You said dis wuz a laughin'-
place.' Brer Rabbit 'low, 'I said 'twuz my laughin'-place, an' I'll say it
ag'in. What you reckon I been doin' all dis time? Ain't you hear me
laughin'? An' what you been doin'? I hear you makin' a mighty fuss in
dar, an' I say ter myse'f dat Brer Fox is havin' a mighty big time.'

"'I let you know dat I ain't been laughin',' sez Brer Fox, sezee."

Uncle Remus paused, and waited to be questioned. "What was the matter with the Fox, if he wasn't laughing?" the child asked after a thoughtful moment.

Uncle Remus flung his head back, and cried out in a sing-song tone,

> "He run ter de Eas', an' he run ter de Wes'
> An' jammed his head in a hornets' nes'!"

5

Brother Rabbit and the Chickens

UNCLE REMUS was sorely puzzled as to the best method of pleasing this youngster. He wasn't sure the little boy enjoyed such tales as the one in which Riley Rabbit turned the tables on Wiley Wolf. So he ventured a question. "Honey, what kinder tales does you like?"

"Oh, I like them all," replied the little boy, "only some are nicer than the others"; and then, without waiting for an invitation, he told Uncle Remus the story of Cinderella. He told it very well for a small chap, and Uncle Remus pretended to enjoy it, although he had heard it hundreds of times.

"It's a mighty purty tale," he said. "It's so purty dat you dunner whedder ter b'lieve it er not. Yit I speck it's so, kaze one time in forty'-lev'm hundred matters will turn out right een' upperds. Now, de creeturs never had no god-m'ers; dey des hatter scuffle an' scramble an' git 'long de bes' way dey kin."

"But they were very cruel," remarked the little boy, "and they told stories."

"When it come ter dat," Uncle Remus replied, "de creeturs ain't much ahead er folks, an' yit folks is got preachers fer ter tell um when dey er gwine wrong. Mo' dan dat, dey got de Bible; an' yit when you git a little older, you'll wake up some fine day an' say ter yo'se'f dat de creeturs is got de 'vantage er folks, spite er de fac' dat dey ain't know de diffunce 'twix' right an' wrong. Dey got ter live 'cordin' ter der natur', kaze dey ain't know no better. I had in min' a tale 'bout Brer Rabbit an' de chickens, but I speck it'd hurt you' feelin's."

The little boy said nothing for some time; he was evidently expecting Uncle Remus to go ahead with his story. But he was mistaken about this, for when the old man broke the silence, it was to speak of something trivial or commonplace. The child, in spite of the training to which he had been subjected, retained his boy's nature. "Uncle Remus," he said, "what about Brother Rabbit and the chickens?"

"Which Brer Rabbit wuz dat, honey?" he asked with apparent surprise.

"You said something about Brother Rabbit and the chickens."

"Who? Me? I mought er said sump'n' 'bout um day 'fo' yistiddy, but it done gone off'n my min'. I done got so ol' dat my min' flutters like a bird in de bush."

"Why, you said that there was a tale about Brother Rabbit and the chickens, but if you told it, my feelings would be hurt. You must think I am a girl."

Uncle Remus laughed. "Not ez bad ez dat, honey; but I'm feard you er monstus tetchous. I'll tell you de tale, an' den you kin tell it ter yo' pa, kaze it's one he ain't never hear tell 'bout.

"Well, den, one time, 'way back yander dey wuz a man what live neighbor ter de creeturs. Dey wa'n't nothin' quare 'bout dis Mr. Man; he wuz des a plain, eve'yday kinder man, an' he try ter git 'long de best he kin. He ain't had no easy time, needer, kaze 'twa'n't den like 'tis now, when you kin take yo' cotton er yo' corn ter town an' have de money planked down fer you.

"In dem times dey wa'n't no town, an' not much money. What folks dey wuz hatter git 'long by swappin' an' traffickin'. How dey done it, I'll never tell you, but do it dey did, an' it seem like dey wuz in about ez happy ez folks is deze days.

"Well, dish yer Mr. Man what I'm a-tellin' you 'bout, he had a truck patch, an' a roas'n'-year patch, an' a goober patch. He grow'd wheat an' barley, an' likewise rye, an' kiss de gals an' make um cry. An' on top er dat, he had a whole yard full er chickens, an' dar's whar de trouble come in. In dem times, all er de creeturs wuz meat-eaters, an' 'twuz in about ez much ez dey kin do, an' sometimes a little mo', fer ter git 'long so dey won't go ter bed hongry. Dey got in de habit er bein' hongry, an' dey ain't never git over it. Look at Brer Wolf — gaunt; look at Brer Fox — gaunt! Dey ain't never been able fer ter make deyse'f fat.

"So den, ez you see um now, dat de way dey wuz in dem days, an' a little mo' so. Mr. Man, he had chickens, des like I tell you. Hens ez plump ez a pa'tridge; pullets so slick dey'd make yo' mouf water, an' fryin'-size chickens dat look like dey want ter git right in de pan. Now, when dat's de case, what you reckon gwine ter happen? Brer Wolf want chicken, Brer Fox want chicken, an' Brer Rabbit want chicken. An' dey ain't got nothin' what dey kin swap fer um. In deze days dey'd be called po', but I take notice dat po' folks gits des ez hongry ez de rich uns — an' hongrier, when it comes ter dat; yes, Lord! Lots hongrier.

"Well, de creeturs got mighty frien'ly wid Mr. Man. Dey'd call on 'im, speshually on Sundays, an' he ain't had no better sense dan ter cluck up his chickens des ter show um what a nice passel he had. When dis happen, Brer Wolf under-jaw would trimble, an' Brer Fox would dribble at de mouf same ez a baby what cuttin' his toofies. Ez fer Brer Rabbit, he'd des laugh, an' nobody ain't know what he laughin' at. It went on dis way twel it look like natur' can't stan' it, an' den, bimeby, one night when de moon ain't shinin', Brer Rabbit take a notion dat he'd call on Mr. Man; but when he got ter de place, Mr. Man done gone ter bed. De lights wuz all out, an' de dog wuz quiled up und' de house soun' asleep.

"Brer Rabbit shake his head. He 'low, 'Sholy dey's sump'n' wrong, kaze allers, when I come Mr. Man call up his chickens whar I kin look at um. I dunner what de matter wid 'im. An' I don't see no chickens, needer. I boun' you sump'n' done happen, an' nobody ain't tell me de news, kaze dey know how sorry I'd be. Ef I could git in de house, I'd go in dar an' see ef ever'thing is all right; but I can't git in.'

"He walk all 'roun', he did, but he ain't see nobody. He wuz so skeer'd he'd wake um up dat he walk on his tippy-toes. He 'low, 'Ef Mr. Man know'd I wuz yer, he'd come out an' show me his chickens, an' I des might ez well look in an' see ef dey er all right.' Wid dat he went ter de chicken-house an' peep in, but he can't see nothin'. He went ter de do', an' foun' it onlocked. Brer Rabbit grin, he did, an' 'low, 'Mr. Man mos' know'd dat I'd be 'long some time terday, an' done gone an' lef' his chicken-house open so I kin see his pullets — an' he know'd dat ef I can't see um, I'd wanter feel um fer ter see how slick an' purty dey is.'

"Brer Rabbit slap hisse'f on de leg an' laugh fit ter kill. He ain't make fuss nuff fer ter wake Mr. Man, but he woke de fat hens an' de slick pullets, an' dey ax one an'er what de name er goodness is de matter. Brer Rabbit laugh an' say ter hisse'f dat ef he'd a brung a bag, it'd make a good overcoat fer four er five er de fat hens, an' six er sev'm er de slick pullets. Den he 'low, 'Why, what is I thinkin' 'bout? I got a bag in my han', an' I fergit dat I had it. It's mighty lucky fer de chickens dat I fotch it, kaze a little mo' — an' dey'd a been friz stiff!' So he scoop in de bag ez many ez he kin tote. He 'low, 'I'll take um home an' kinder git um warm, an' termorrer Mr. Man kin have um back — ef he want um.' An' wid dat he mighty nigh choke hisse'f tryin' fer ter keep fum laughin'. De chickens kinder flutter, but dey ain't make much fuss, an' Brer Rabbit flung de sack 'cross his shoulders an' went off home des ez gaily ez a colt in a barley patch."

"Wouldn't you call that stealing, Uncle Remus?" inquired the little boy very seriously.

"Ef Brer Rabbit had a been folks, it'd be called stealin', but you know mighty well dat de creeturs dunno de diffunce 'twix' takin' an' stealin'. When it comes ter dat, dey's a-plenty folks dat ain't know de diffunce, an' how you gwine ter blame de creeturs?" Uncle Remus paused to see what comment the little boy would make, but he was silent, though it is doubtful if he was satisfied.

"Brer Rabbit tuck de chickens on home, he did, an' made way wid um. Now, dat wuz de las' er de chickens, but des de beginnin's er de fedders. Ol' Miss Rabbit, she wanter burn um in de fier, but Brer Rabbit say de whole neighborhood would smell um, an' he 'low dat he got a better way dan dat. So, nex' mornin' atter brekkus, he borried a bag fum ol' Brer Wolf, an' inter dis he stuff de fedders, an' start off down de road.

"Well, suh, ez luck would have it, Brer Rabbit hatter pass by Brer Fox house, an' who should be stan'in' at de gate wid his walkin'-cane in han', but Brer Fox? Brer Fox, he fetched a bow, wid, 'Brer Rabbit, whar you gwine?' Brer Rabbit 'low, 'Ef I had de win', Brer Fox, I'd be gwine to mill. Dish yer's a turrible load I got, an' I dunner how soon I'll gi' out. I ain't strong in de back an' limber in de knees like I useter be, Brer Fox. You may be holdin' yo' own, an' I hope you is, but I'm on de down grade, dey ain't no two ways 'bout dat.' Wid dat, he sot de bag down by de side er de road, an' wipe his face wid his hankcher.

"Brer Fox, he come on whar Brer Rabbit wuz a-settin' at, an' ax ef it's corn er wheat. Brer Rabbit 'low dat 'tain't na'er one; it's des some stuff dat he gwine ter sell ter de miller. Brer Fox, he want ter know what 'tis so bad he ain't know what ter do, an' he up an' ax Brer Rabbit p'intedly. Brer Rabbit say he feard ter tell 'im kaze de truck what he got in de bag is de onliest way he kin make big money. Brer Fox vow he won't tell nobody, an' den Brer Rabbit say dat bein' ez him an' Brer Fox is sech good frien's — neighbors, ez you might say — he don't min' tellin' 'im, kaze he know dat atter Brer Fox done prommus, he won't breave a word 'bout it. Den he say dat de truck what he got in de bag is roots er de Winniannimus grass, an' when dey er groun' up at de mill, dey er wuff nine dollars a poun'.

"Dis make Brer Fox open his eyes. He felt de heft er de bag, he did, an' he say dat it's mighty light, an' he dunner what make Brer Rabbit pant an' grunt when 'tain't no heftier dan what it is.

"Brer Rabbit 'low dat de bag wouldn't a felt heavy ter him ef he wuz big an' strong like Brer Fox. Dat kinder talk make Brer Fox feel biggity, an' he 'low dat he'll tote de bag ter mill ef Brer Rabbit feel like it's too heavy. Brer Rabbit say he'll be mighty much erbleeged, an' be glad fer ter pay Brer Fox sump'n ter boot. An' so, off dey put down de road, Brer Fox a-trottin' an' Brer Rabbit gwine in a canter.

"Brer Fox ax what dey does wid de Winniannimus grass atter dey gits it groun' up at de mill. Brer Rabbit 'low dat rich folks buys it fer ter make Whipmewhopme puddin'. Brer Fox say he'll take some home when de miller git it groun' an' see how it tas'es, an' Brer Rabbit say he's mo' dan welcome. Atter dey been gwine on some little time, Brer Rabbit look back an' see Mr. Man a-comin', an' he say ter Brer Fox, sezee, 'Brer Fox, you is de outdoinist man I ever is see. You done got me plum' wo' out, an' I'm bleeze ter take a res'. You go on an' I'll ketch up wid you ef I kin; ef not, des wait fer me at de mill.' Brer Fox 'low, 'Shucks, Brer Rabbit! you ain't 'quainted wid me; you dunner nothin' 'tall 'bout me. I kin go on dis way all day long an' half de night.' Brer Rabbit roll his big eyes, an' say, 'Well, suh!'

"An' den he sot down by de side er de road, an' 'twuz all he kin do fer ter keep fum bustin' out in a big laugh.

"Bimeby, Mr. Man come 'long an' say, 'Who dat wid de big bag on his back?' Brer Rabbit make answer dat it's Brer Fox. Mr. Man say, 'What he got in his bag?' Brer Rabbit 'low, 'I ax 'im, an' he say it's some kinder grass what he takin' ter de mill fer ter git groun', but I seed mo' dan one chicken fedder stickin' ter de bag.' Mr. Man say, 'Den he's de chap what tuck an' tuck my fat hens an' my slick pullets, an' I'll make 'im sorry dat he yever is see a chicken.'

"Wid dat he put out atter Brer Fox, an' Brer Rabbit, he put out too, but he stay in de bushes, so dat nobody can't see 'im. Mr. Man he cotch up wid Brer Fox, an' ax 'im what he got in de bag. Brer Fox say he got Winniannimus grass what he gwine ter have groun' at de mill. Mr. Man say he wanter see what Winniannimus grass look like. Brer Fox sot de bag down an' say dat when it's groun' up de rich folks buys it fer ter make Whipmewhopme puddin'. Mr. Man open de bag, an' dey wa'n't nothin' in it but chicken fedders. He 'low, 'Whipmewhopme puddin'! I'll whip you an' whop you,' an' wid dat he grab Brer Fox in de collar, an' mighty nigh frailed de life out'n 'im.

"Brer Rabbit seed it well done, an' he des fell down in de bushes an' roll an' laugh twel he can't laugh no mo'.'"

"Well, I don't see why he should think it was funny," the little boy remarked.

Uncle Remus looked hard at this modern little boy before he answered: "Maybe you dunno Brer Fox, honey; I don't speck you hear talk er de way he try ter git de inturn on Brer Rabbit. But on top er dat, Brer Rabbit wuz so ticklish dat mos' anything would make 'im laugh. It sholy wuz scan'lous de way Brer Rabbit kin laugh."

6

Little Mister Cricket and the Other Creatures

UNCLE REMUS was very anxious to know what the child thought about the story of Brother Rabbit and the chicken feathers, but he made no inquiries; he was willing to let the youngster's preferences show themselves without any urging on his part.

When the little boy did speak, he made no reference to Brother Rabbit and the chicken feathers; his thoughts were elsewhere. "Uncle Remus," he said, "I never saw a cricket. What do they look like?"

"You ain't never see no cricket!" exclaimed Uncle Remus, with a great display of amazement. "Well, dat bangs my time! What yo' ma an' pa — speshually yo' pa — what dey been doin' all deze lonesome years dat they ain't never show'd you no cricket? How dey speck you ter git 'long in de worl' ef dey ain't gwine ter tell you 'bout de things you oughter know, an' show you de things dat you oughter see? You ain't never see no cricket, an' here you is mos' ready ter shave off de down on your face!"

The child blushed. "Why, I have no down on my face, Uncle Remus," he protested.

"Well, you will have some er deze days, an' den what will folks think uv a great big man what ain't never seed no cricket?"

"Mother has never seen one," replied the little boy, somewhat triumphantly.

"She's a lady," Uncle Remus explained, "an' dat's diffunt. She been brung up in 'Lantamatantarum, an' I speck she'd fall down an' faint ef she wuz ter see one. Folks ain't like dey use ter be; in my day an' time, ef man er boy wuz ter say dat he ain't never seed no cricket, dem what he tol' de news ter would git up an' go 'way fum 'im; but deze days I boun' you dey'd huddle up close 'roun' 'im, an' jine in wid 'im, an' say dey ain't never is seed one nudder."

"If you had never seen one, you wouldn't talk that way, Uncle Remus," remarked the little boy quite seriously. "How can I help myself, if I have never seen one? It isn't my fault, is it?"

"Tooby sho it ain't, honey. Nobody ain't blamin' you. Yit when I see a great big boy what ain't never seed no cricket, I bleeze ter ax myse'f whar he come fum an' what he been doin'. I boun' ef you'd a been wid yo' gran'mammy an' me you'd a seed crickets twel you got tired er seein' um. Dat's de kinder folks we-all is. 'Tain't no trouble ter we-all ter show chillun what dey oughter see. I bet you, you' pa know'd what a cricket wuz long 'fo' he wuz ol' ez you is. Dey wa'n't nothin' fer ter hender 'im. Miss Sally des turned 'im over ter me, an' say, 'Don't let 'im git hurted,' an' dar he wuz. Ef he ain't seed all dey wuz ter be seed, it 'uz kaze it 'uz in a show, an' de show in town whar he can't git at it. Dat's de way we done wid him, an' dat's de way I'd like ter do wid you. It's a mighty pity you wa'n't brung up here at home, stidder up dar in 'Lantamatantarum, whar dey ain't nothin' 'tall but dust, an' mud, an' money. De folks up dar ain't want de mud an' dust, an' de mo' dey wash it off de mo' dey gits on um; but dey does want de money, an' de mo' dey scuffles fer it, de mo' dey has ter scuffle."

"Is a cricket like a grasshopper, Uncle Remus?" inquired the little boy, who took no interest in the old man's prejudice against Atlanta.

"Dey mos'ly is, an' den ag'in dey mos'ly ain't. Befo' de time dat ol' Grandaddy Cricket kick down de chimbley, dey wa'n't no mo' like grasshoppers dan I'm like a steer, but atter dat, when he git his knees on wrongsudouterds, dey sorter look like grasshoppers ceppin' when you look at um right close, an' den dey don't look like um.

"Dey got lots mo' sense dan de yuther crawlin' an' hoppin' creeturs. Dey ought not ter be put wid de hoppin' creeturs, kaze dey don't b'long wid um, an' dey wouldn't be a-hoppin' in deze days ef ol' Grandaddy Cricket hadn't a got cripple' when he kick de chimbley down. In de times when ol' Boss Elephant, an' Brer Lion, an' Brer Tiger wuz meanderin' 'roun' in deze parts, little Mr. Cricket wuz on mighty good terms wid um. Ez dey say er folks, he stood mighty well whar dey know'd 'im — mighty well — an' he wuz 'bout de sharpes' er de whole caboodle, ef you'll leave out de name er Brer Rabbit.

"It come 'bout one time dat de creeturs wuz all sunnin' deyse'f — it mought er been Sunday fer all I know — an' dey des stretch out an' sot an' sot 'roun' lickin' der chops, an' blinkin' der eyes, an' combin' der ha'r. Mr. Elephant wuz swingin' hisse'f backerds an' forerds, an' flingin' de san' on his back fer ter keep off de flies, an' all de res' wuz gwine on 'cordin' ter der breed an' need.

"Ef you'll watch right close, honey, you'll fin' out fer yo'se'f dat when folks ain't got much ter do, an' little er nothin' fer ter talk 'bout, dey'll soon git ter braggin', an' dat's des de way wid de creeturs. Brer Fox start it up; he say, 'Gents, 'fo' I fergit it off'n my min', I wanter tell you dat I'm de swiffes' one in dis bunch.' Mr. Elephant wink one er his little eye-balls, an' fling his snout in de a'r an' whispered — an' you mought a hearn dat whisper a mile — 'I'm de strenkiest; I wanter call yo' 'tention ter dat.' Mr. Lion shuck his mane an' showed his tushes. He say, 'Don't fergit dat I'm de King er all de creetur tribe.' Mr. Tiger stretched hisse'f an' gap'd. He say, 'I'm de purtiest an' de mos' servigrous.'

"Fum one ter de yuther de braggin' went 'roun'. Ef 'twa'n't dis it 'uz dat, an' ef 'twa'n't dat, 'twuz de yuther. Dey went on so twel bimeby little Mr. Cricket chirped up an' say he kin make all un um run dey heads off, fum ol' Mr. Elephant down ter de las' one. Dey all laugh like it's a good joke, an' Brer Fox he 'low dat he had de idee dat dey wuz all doin' some monstus tall braggin', but Mr. Cricket wuz away ahead er de whole gang, an' den he say, 'How you gwine ter begin fer ter commence fer ter do all deze great deeds an' didoes?' Mr. Cricket say, 'Des gi' me time; gi' me time, an' you'll all hear fum me — you'll hear, but you won't stop fer ter lissen an' den he work his jaws fer all de worl' like Brer Rabbit does when he's chawin' terbacker.

"Now, ol' Brer Rabbit know'd dat Mr. Cricket wuz up ter some sharp trick er n'er, an' so he wait twel he kin have a confab wid 'im. He ain't had long ter wait, kaze Mr. Crickley Cricket make up his min' dat Brer Rabbit wuz de one what kin he'p him out. Dey bofe wanter see one an'er, an' when dat's de case, dey ain't much trouble 'bout it. Dey soon got off by deyse'f, an' Brer Rabbit 'low dat Mr. Cricket got a mighty big job on his han's, an' Mr. Cricket, he say it's sech a big job dat he can't git thoo

wid it less'n Brer Rabbit will he'p 'im out. Mr. Cricket say 'tain't much
he gwine ter ax er Brer Rabbit, but little ez 'tis, he bleeze ter ax it. Brer
Rabbit look at 'im right hard an' twis' his mustash. 'Out wid it, Mr.
Cricket; out wid it, an' I'll see ef I kin he'p you out. But I want you ter
take notice dat all de yuthers is got a crow fer ter pick wid me, on account er de way I been doin'.'

"Mr. Cricket chirp up, 'So I hear, Brer Rabbit — so I hear,' an' den
he went on fer ter tell Brer Rabbit what he want 'im ter do. Brer Rabbit
laugh, he did, an' say, 'Ef dat's all you want, Mr. Cricket, you kin count
me in, kaze I laid off fer ter he'p you lot's mo' dan dat — lots mo'.' Mr.
Cricket say dat'll be de greates' plenty, an' wid dat dey went off home fer
ter kinder res' deyse'f, but not 'fo' dey fix on a day when dey'll have time
fer ter work der trick on de yuther creeturs.

"Dey 'greed on de day, an' dat day dey met, an' atter colloguin'
tergedder, off dey put ter de place whar dey 'spected ter fin' de yuther
creeturs. De fust one dey meet wuz ol' Mr. Elephant. Dey pass de time er
day, dey did, an' Brer Rabbit say he got bad news. Mr. Elephant flung up
his snout like he 'stonish'd, an' swung backerd an' forerds like he 'bout
ter cry. Brer Rabbit 'low dat de win' blow'd a hick'y-nut down right 'pon
top er Mr. Cricket an' cripple 'im so he can't go home, an' he ax ef Mr.
Elephant won't tote 'im ez fur ez he kin. Mr. Elephant say tooby sho he
will an' be glad in de bargain, an' so he kneel down, he did, an' let Mr.
Cricket crawl on his back.

"But Mr. Cricket crawl furder dan de back; he crawl on Mr. Elephant
neck, an' den inter his year. Dis whar he wanter git, an' soon ez he got
settle', he flutter his wings right fas' an' Mr. Elephant think de win' is
blowin' thoo de trees. Mr. Cricket flutter his wings harder, an' Mr. Elephant think dey's a storm comin' up. He splunge thoo de bushes, he did,
an' ef Mr. Cricket hadn't a been inside his year, he'd a been knocked off
by de lim's er de trees. Ez 'twuz, he sot back an' laugh, an' say ter hisse'f
dat Mr. Elephant ain't hear nothin' 'tall ter what he will hear.

"Wid dat, he chune up his whistle, an' started fer ter blow on it. He
blow'd kinder low ter begin wid, an' den he 'gun ter git louder. An' de
louder he got de mo' he skeer'd Mr. Elephant, an' he went splungin' thoo
de woods same ez a harrycane. He went so fas' dat he come mighty nigh
runnin' over King Lion whiles he wuz talkin' ter ol' Brer Tiger. He ain't

hear 'um say, 'Mr. Elephant, whar you gwine?' but he stop right whar dey wuz an' 'gun ter turn 'roun' an' 'roun'. King Lion ax 'im what de matter, an' Mr. Elephant say he b'lieve he gwine ravin' 'stracted. He 'low, 'I got a singin' an' a whistlin' in one er my years, an' I dunner which un it's in. Don't you-all hear it?'

"Dey lissen, dey did, an' bless gracious, dey kin hear it. Ol' King Lion look like he 'stonished. He say, 'It soun's fer all de worl', Mr. Elephant, like you des 'bout ter bile over, an' ef dat's what yer gwine ter do, I wanter be out'n de way — clean out'n de way.'

"Mr. Elephant turn 'roun' an' 'roun', he did, an' ef he'd a been light-headed like some folks I knows, he'd a drapt right dar. Mr. Cricket watch his chance, an' when Mr. Elephant got nigh ter King Lion, he tuck a flyin' jump an' lit right in King Lion's mane, an' 'twa'n't long 'fo' he made his way ter de year. But while he wuz makin' his way dar Mr. Elephant stopped whirlin' 'roun'; he stop an' lis'n, he did, an' he ain't hear nothin'; he lis'n some mo' an' still he ain't hear nothin'. He say, 'I b'lieve in my soul dat I'm kyo'd! I'm mighty glad I met you-all, kaze I know one un you is a doctor, an' ever which un it is, he sho has done de work.'

"By dis time, Mr. Cricket had got in King Lion year, an' t'wa'n't long 'fo' he start up his whistlin'. He whistle low fer ter start wid, an' King Lion hol' his head sideways an' lis'n. He say, 'I still hears it, Mr. Elephant, an' ef you er kyo'd I done cotch de thing you had.' Mr. Cricket went a little louder, an' King Lion 'gun ter back off like he had business ter ten' ter. Mr. Tiger say, 'Whar you gwine? I hope you ain't skeer'd er Brer Elephant, kaze he ain't gwine ter hurt you. Ef you gwine any whar, you better turn 'roun' an' go right.'

"But King Lion ain't pay no 'tention ter Mr. Tiger; he des back off, he did, an' wave his tail an' shake his mane. Mr. Cricket 'gun ter whistle louder an' flutter his wings, an' make um zoon like a locus'. King Lion say, 'I hear de win' a-blowin' an' I better git home ter my wife an' chillun,' an' off he put, runnin' like he wuz gwine atter de doctor. Mr. Tiger laugh, an' say dat some folks is so funny he dunner what ter make un um. Dey stayed dar confabbin', an' bimeby dey hear a fuss, an' here come King Lion gwine ez hard ez he kin. Tryin' fer ter git away fum de fuss in his year, he had run all 'roun' twel he come back ag'in ter whar he start fum. He had his tongue out, an' his tail wuz droopin'; he wuz mighty nigh wo' out.

"He say, 'Heyo! what you-all doin' here? I had de idee dat I lef' you back yander whar I come fum.' Mr. Elephant 'low, 'We ain't skacely move out'n our tracks. You run away an' lef' us, an' here you is back; what de name er goodness is de matter wid you?' King Lion say, 'I done got a whistlin' in my head, an' look like I can't 'scape fum it. It's in dar yit, an' I dunner what I'm gwine ter do 'bout it.' Mr. Elephant say, 'Do like I done — stan' it de bes' you kin.' Brer Tiger 'low, 'I hear it, an' it soun' zactly like you wuz 'bout ter bile over, an' when you does I wanter be out'n de way.'

"By dat time little Mr. Cricket had done made a flyin' jump an' lit on Mr. Tiger, an' 'twa'n't long 'fo' he wuz snug in Mr. Tiger year. Mr. Tiger lis'n, he did, an' den he 'gun ter back off an' wave his tail. Mr. Elephant swing his snout, an' say, 'What de matter, Mr. Tiger? I hope you ain't thinkin' 'bout leavin' us.' But Mr. Tiger wuz done gone. He des flit away. Long 'bout dat time, Mr. Rabbit come lopin' up, laughin' fit ter kill. He 'low, 'Brer Cricket say he gwine ter make you-all run an' dat's des what he done. Bofe un you been runnin' kaze I see you pantin', an' ef you'll des wait here, Mr. Cricket will fetch Mr. Tiger back safe an' soun',' an' dey ain't had ter wait long, nudder, kaze bimeby, here come Mr. Tiger, tongue out an' tail a-droopin'. He say, 'Hello! how come you-all ter out-run me? I got de idee dat you wuz back yander in de woods whar I come fum,' an' den dey got ter laughin' at 'im, an' dey laugh twel dey can't laugh no mo'. Mr. Cricket jump outer Mr. Tiger's year, an' git in de grass, an' bimeby he show hisse'f.

"He come close up wid a 'Howdy do, gents?' an' dey pass de time er day wid 'im. Bimeby Mr. Elephant 'low, 'Mr. Cricket, ain't you say de yuther day dat you wuz gwine ter make we-all run?' an' Mr. Cricket, he make answer, 'Why, I wouldn't talk 'bout runnin' ef I'd been runnin' same ez what you been doin'.' Mr. Elephant swing his snout kinder slow an' say, 'How you know I been runnin'?' Mr. Cricket 'low, 'I know bekaze ef I hadn't er helt on monstus tight, I'd 'a' fell off; mo' dan dat, ef I hadn't er stopped singin' an' whistlin' you'd a been runnin' yit.' Mr. Elephant shot his two little eyes, an' say, 'Well, suh!'"

"What did the others do?" the little boy inquired, when he was sure that the story was ended.

"Dey mos'ly got 'way fum dem parts, kaze dey wuz skeer'd Mr. Cricket would git on um ag'in. King Lion say he got ter look atter some fresh meat what he got, Mr. Elephant say he bleeze ter go an' cut some grass, an' Mr. Tiger 'low dat he got ter hunt up some vittles fer his fambly. An' ez fer Mr. Cricket, he clomb on Brer Rabbit's back, an' dey mosey'd off somers, I dunner whar. All I know is dat dey giggle 'ez dey went."

7

When Brother Rabbit Was King

ONE AFTERNOON, while Uncle Remus was sitting in the sun, he felt so comfortable and thankful for all the blessings that he enjoyed, and for those that he had seen others enjoy, that he suddenly closed his eyes; and he had no sooner done so than he drifted across the dim and pleasant borderland that lies somewhere between sleeping and waking. He must have drifted back again immediately, for it seemed that he was not so fast asleep that he was unable to hear the sound of stealthy footsteps somewhere near him. Instantly he was on the alert, but still kept his eyes closed. He knew at once that the little boy was trying to surprise him. The lad had improved much in health since coming to the plantation, and with the growth of his strength had come a certain degree of boisterousness that his mother thought was somewhat unusual, but which his grandmother and Uncle Remus knew was the natural result of good health.

By opening one eye a trifle, Uncle Remus could watch the youngster, who was creeping, Indian-like, upon him, and this gave the old Negro an immense advantage, for just as the little boy was about to jump at him, Uncle Remus straightened himself in his chair and uttered a bloodcurdling yell that would have alarmed a much larger and older person than the lad. As a matter of fact, the little fellow was almost paralyzed with fright, and for a moment or two could hardly get his breath.

"Why, what in the world is the matter with you, Uncle Remus?" he asked as soon as he could speak.

"Wuz dat you comin' 'long dar, honey?" said Uncle Remus, by way of response. "Well, ef 'twuz, you kin des go up dar ter de big house an' tell um all dat you saved my life, kaze dat what you done. Dey ain't no tellin' what would a happen' ef you hadn't a come creepin' 'long an' woke me up, kaze whiles I wuz dozin' dar I wuz on a train, an' de bullgine look like it wuz runnin' away. 'Twa'n't one er deze yer 'commydatin' trains, kaze de man what tuck up de tickets say he wa'n't in no hurry fer ter see how fur anybody gwine; dey wuz all boun' fer de same place, an' when dey got dar dey'd know it. De kyars wuz lined wid caliker, an' de brakeman wuz made out'n straw. It went on, it did, an' de bullgine run faster an' faster twel it run so fast you couldn't hear it toot fer brakes, an' des 'bout de time dat eve'ything wuz a gittin' smashed up, here you come an' wokened me — an' a mighty good thing, kaze ef I'd a stayed on dat train dey wouldn't a been nuff er me left fer de congergation ter sing a song over. I'm mighty thankful dat dey's somebody got sense nuff fer ter come 'long an' skeer me out er my troubles."

This statement was intended to change the course of the little boy's thoughts — to cause him to forget that he had been frightened — and it was quite successful, for he began to talk about dreams in general, telling some peculiar ones of his own, such as children have.

"Talkin' 'bout dreams," remarked Uncle Remus, "it put me in min' er de man what been sick off an' on, he hatter be mighty keerful er his eatin'. One night he had a dream. It seemed like dat somebody come 'long an' gi' him a great big hunk er ol'-time ginger cake, an' it smell so sweet an' taste so good dat he e't 'bout a poun'. He wuz eatin' it in his sleep, but de dream wuz so natchal dat de nex' mornin' dey hatter sen' fer de doctor, an' 'twuz e'en 'bout all dey could do fer ter pull 'im thoo. De doctor gun 'im all de truck what he had in his saddle-bags, an' 'low dat he b'lieve in his soul he'd hatter sen' fer mo', an' den atter dat he tuck an' lay down de law ter de man. He say dat whatsomever else he mought do, he better not eat no ginger cakes in his dreams, kaze de next un 'ud be sho fer ter take 'im off spite er all de doctor truck in de roun' worl'."

Then the little boy told of a dream he had had. It seems that he had slipped into the pantry, when no one was looking, and had taken a piece of apple-pie. It wasn't stealing, he said, for he knew that if he asked his grandmother for a piece she would have given it to him; but he didn't want to bother her while she was talking to the sewing-woman, and so he just went in the pantry and got it for himself. Perhaps he took a larger piece than his grandmother would have given him, but he had nothing to measure it by, and so he was compelled to guess how much she would have given him.

"I boun' you stretched yo' guesser, honey," said Uncle Remus dryly.

The child admitted with a laugh that perhaps he had, and he was very sorry for it afterwards, for when he went to bed he dreamed that something scratched at his door and made such a fuss that he was obliged to get up and let it in. He didn't wait to see what it was, but just flung the door open, and ran and jumped back in bed, pulling the cover over his head. In the dream he lay right still and listened. Everything was so quiet that he became curious, and finally ventured to look out from under the cover. Well, sir, the sight that he saw was enough, for between the door and the bed a big black dog was lying. He seemed to be very tired, for his tongue hung out long and red, and he was panting as though he had come a long way in a very short time.

Uncle Remus groaned in sympathy. The black dog that gallops through a dream with his tongue hanging out was one of his familiars. "I know dat dog," he said. "He got a bunch er white on de een' er his tail, an' his eye-balls look like dey green in de dark. You call him an' he'll growl, call him ag'in, an' he'll howl. I'd know dat dog ef I wuz ter see him in de daytime — I'd know him so well dat I'd run an' ax somebody fer ter please, suh, wake me up, an' do it mighty quick."

The little boy didn't know anything about that; what he did know was that the dog in his dream, when he had rested himself, jumped up on the bed, and began to nose at the cover, and he seemed to get mad when he failed to pull it off the little boy. He tried and tried, and then he seized a corner of the counterpane, or the spread, or whatever you call it, and shook it with his teeth. When he grew tired of this, the little boy could hear him smelling all about over the bed, and then he knew the creature was hunting for the piece of apple-pie.

Uncle Remus agreed with the child about this. "'Cordin' ter my notion," he said, "when folks slip 'roun' an' take dat what don't b'long ter um er dat what dey oughtn't ter have by good rights, de big black dog is sho ter come 'roun' growlin' an' smellin' atter dey goes ter bed. Dey ain't no two ways 'bout dat. Dey may not know it, dey may be too sleepy fer ter see 'im in der dreams, but de dog's dar. Mo' dan dat, dogs will growl an' smell 'roun' ef dey er in dreams er outer dreams. Dey got in de habits er smellin' 'way back yander in de days when ol' Brer Rabbit had tooken de place er de King one time when de King wanter go off down de country fishin'.'"

The little boy seemed to be very much interested in this information, but while they were speaking of this curious habit that is common to dogs, a hound that had been raised on the place came into view. He was going at a gallop, as if he had important business to attend to, but when he had galloped past a large tree, he paused suddenly, and turned back to investigate it with his nose; and though he was entirely familiar with the tree, it seemed to be new to him now, for he smelled all around the trunk of it and was apparently much perplexed. Whatever information he received was sufficient to cause him to forget all about the business that had caused him to come galloping past the tree, for when his investigation had ended, he turned about and went back the way he had come.

"Now, you see dat, don't you?" exclaimed Uncle Remus, with some show of indignation. "Ain't it des a little mo' dan you wanter stan? Here he come, gwine, I dunner whar, des a-gallin'-up like he done been sent fer. He come ter dat ar tree, he did, an' went on by — spang by! — an'

den 'fo' you kin bat yo' eye-ball, whiff, he turn 'roun' an' go ter smellin'
at de tree, des like he ain't never seed it befo'; an' he must a got some
kind er news whar he smellin' at, kaze atter he smell twel it look like he
gwine ter smell de bark clean off, he fergit all 'bout whar he gwine, an'
tuck his tail an' go on back whar he come fum. Maybe you know sump'n'
'bout it, honey — you an' de balance er de white folks, but me — I'm
bofe blin' an' deaf when it come ter tellin' you what de dog foun' out. I
may know what make 'im smell at de tree, but what news he got I never
is ter tell you."

"Well, you know you said that dogs got in the habit of smelling away
back yonder when old Brother Rabbit took the place of the King, who
had gone fishing. I was wondering if that was a story."

"Wuz you, honey?" Uncle Remus asked with a pleased smile. "Well,
you sho is got a dumplin' eye fer de kinder tales what I tells. I b'lieve
ef I wuz ter take one er dem ol'-time tales an' skin it an' drag de hide
thoo de house an' 'roun' de lot — ef I wuz ter do dat, I b'lieve you'd open
up on de trail same ez ol' Louder follerin' on atter Brer Possum; I sho
does!"

The child seemed to appreciate the compliment, and he laughed in a
way that did the old Negro a world of good. "I have found out one thing,"
said the little boy with emphasis. "Whenever you are hinting at a story,
you always look at me out of the corner of your eye, and there's always a
funny little wrinkle at the corner of your mouth."

"Well, suh!" exclaimed Uncle Remus, gleefully; "well, suh! an' me a-
settin' right here an' doin' dat away 'fo' yo' face an' eyes! I never would a
speckted it. Peepin' out de cornder er my eye-ball, an' a-wrinklin' at de
mouf! It look like I mus' be gettin' ol' an' fibble in de min'.'" He chuckled as proudly as if some one had given him a piece of pound cake of
which he was very fond. But presently his chuckling ceased, and he
leaned back in his chair with a serious air.

"I dunno so mighty well 'bout all de yuther times you talkin' 'bout,
honey, but when I say what I did 'bout ol' Brer Rabbit takin' de place er
der King, I sho had a tale in my min'. I say tale, but I dunner what you'll
say 'bout it; you kin name it atter you git it. Well, 'way back yander, mos'
'fo' de time when folks got in de habits er dreamin' dreams, dey wuz a

King an' dish yer King king'd it over all un um what wuz dar, mo'
speshually de creeturs, kaze what folks dey wuz ain't know nothin' 'tall
'bout whedder dey need any kingin' er not; look like dey didn't count.

"Well, dish yer King what I'm a-tellin' you 'bout had purty well
grow'd up at de business, and de time come when he got mighty tired er
settin' in one place an' hol'in' a crown on his head fer ter keep it fum
fallin' on de flo'. He say ter hisse'f dat he wanter git out an' git de fresh
a'r, an' have some fun 'long wid dem what he been kingin' over. He 'low
dat he wanter fix it so dat he ain't a-keerin' whedder school keep er no,
an' he ax um all what de best thing he kin do. Well, one say one thing an'
de yuther say tother, but bimeby some un um chipped in an' say dat de
best way ter have fun is ter go fishin', an' dis kinder hit de King right in
de middle er his notions.

"He jump up an' crack his heels tergedder, he did, an' he say dat
dat's what he been thinkin' 'bout all de time. A-fishin' it wuz an' a-fishin'
he'd go, ef his life wuz spar'd twel he kin git ter de creek. An', wid dat,
dey wuz a mighty stirrin' 'roun' 'mongs' dem what he wuz a-kingin' over;
some un um run off ter git fishin'-poles, an' some run fer ter dig bait, an'
some run fer ter git de bottle, an' dar dey had it — you'd a thunk dat all
creation wuz gwine fishin'."

"Uncle Remus," said the little boy, interrupting the old man, "what
did they want with a bottle?"

The old man looked at the child with a puzzled expression on his
face. "De bottle?" he asked with a sigh. "I b'lieve I did say sump'n' 'bout
de bottle. I dunner whedder it 'uz a long white bottle er a chunky black
un. Dem what handed de tale down ter me ain't say what kinder one it
wuz, an' I'm feard ter say right short off dat it 'uz one er de yuther. We'll
des call it a plain, eve'y-day bottle an' let it go at dat."

"But what did they want with a bottle, Uncle Remus?" persisted the
little boy.

"You ain't never been fishin', is you honey? An' you ain't never see
yo' daddy go fishin'. All I know is dat whar dey's any fishin' gwine on,
you'll fin' a bottle somers in de neighborhoods ef you'll scratch about in
de bushes. Well, de creeturs done like folks long 'fo' folks got ter doin'
dat away, an' when dish yer King went a-fishin', he had ter have a bottle
fer ter put de bait in.

"When eve'ything got good an' ready, an' de King wuz 'bout ter start off, ol' Brer Rabbit kinder hung his head on one side an' set up a snigger. De King, he look 'stonish' an' den he 'low, 'What's de joke, ol' frien'?' 'Well,' sez ol' Brer Rabbit, sezee, 'it look like ter me dat you 'bout ter go off an' fergit sump'n'. 'Tain't none er my business, but I couldn't he'p fum gigglin'.' De King, he say, 'Up an' out wid it, ol' frien'; le's hear de wust dey is ter hear.' Ol' Brer Rabbit, he say, sezee, 'I dunner ef it makes any diffunce, but who gwine ter do de kingin' whiles you gone a-fishin'?'

"Well, de King look like he wuz might'ly tuck back; he flung up bofe han's an' sot right flat in a cheer, an' den he 'low, 'I done got so dat I'm de fergittines' creetur what live on top er de groun'; you may hunt high an' low an' you won't never fin' dem what kin beat me a-fergittin'. Here I wuz 'bout fer ter go off an' leave de whole business at sixes an' sev'ms.' Ol' Brer Rabbit, he say, sezee, 'Oh, I speck dat would a been all right; dey ain't likely ter be no harrycane, ner no fresh' whiles you gone.' De King, he 'low, 'Dat ain't de thing; here I wuz 'bout ter go off on a frolic an' leave eve'ything fer ter look atter itse'f. What yo' reckon folks would a said? I tell you now, dey ain't no fun in bein' a King, kaze yo' time ain't yo' own, an' you can't turn 'roun' widout skinnin' yo' shins on some by-law er 'nother. 'Fo' I go, ef go I does, I got ter 'p'int somebody fer ter take my place an' be King whiles I'm gone; an' ef 'twa'n't dat, it'd be sump'n'

else, an' so dar you go year in an' year out.' He sot dar, he did, an' study an' study, an' bimeby he say, sezee, 'Brer Rabbit, s'posin' you take my place whiles I'm gone? I'll pay you well; all you got to do is ter set right flat in a cheer an' make a dollar a day.' Ol' Brer Rabbit say dat would suit him mighty well, kaze he bleeze fer ter have some money so he kin buy his ol' 'oman a caliker dress. Well, it ain't take um long fer ter fix it all up, an' so Brer Rabbit, he done de kingin' whiles de King gone a-fishin'. He made de job a mighty easy one, kaze stidder settin' up an' hol'in' de crown on his head, he tied some strings on it an' fix it so it'd stay on his head widout hol'in'.

"Well, when de King went a-fishin', he went de back way, an' he ain't

mo' dan got out de gate twel ol' Brer Rabbit hear a big rumpus in de front yard. He hears sump'n' growlin' an' howlin' an' whinin', an' he ax what it

wuz. Some er dem what wait on de King shuck der heads an' say dat ef
de King wuz dar he wouldn't pay no 'tention ter de racket fer der longest;

dey say dat de biggest kind er fuss ain't 'sturb de King, kaze he'd des set
right flat an' wait fer some un ter come tell somebody what de rumpus is
'bout, an' den dat yuther somebody would tell some un else, an' maybe
'bout dinner-time de King would fin' out what gwine on, when all he hatter do wuz ter look out de winder an' see fer hisse'f.

"When ol' Brer Rabbit hear dat, he lay back ez well ez he kin wid dat
ar crown on top er his head, an' make out he takin' a nap. Atter so long
a time, word come dat Mr. Dog wuz out dar in de entry whar dey all hatter wait at, an' he sont word dat he bleeze ter see de King. Ol' Brer Rabbit, he sot dar, he did, an' do like he studyin', an' atter so long a time, he
tell um fer ter fetch Mr. Dog in an' let him say what he got ter say. Well,
Mr. Dog come creepin' in, he did, an' he look mighty 'umble-come-tumble.
He wuz so po' dat it look like you kin see eve'y bone in his body an' he wuz
mangy lookin'. His head hung down, an' he wuz kinder shiverin' like he
wuz col'. Brer Rabbit make out he tryin' fer ter fix de crown on his head
so it'll set up straight, but all de time he wuz lookin' at Mr. Dog fer ter see
ef he know'd 'im — an' sho nuff, he did, kaze it 'uz de same Mr. Dog
what done give him many a long chase.

"Well, Mr. Dog, he stood dar wid his head hangin' down an' his tail
'tween his legs. Eve'ything wuz so still an' sollum dat he 'gun ter git
oneasy, an' he look 'roun' fer ter see ef dey's any way fer ter git out wid-

out runnin' over somebody. Dey ain't no way, an' so Mr. Dog sorter wiggle de een' er his tail fer ter show dat he ain't mad, an' he stood dar 'spectin' dat eve'y minnit would be de nex'.

"Bimeby, somebody say, 'Who dat wanter see de King an' what business is he got wid 'im?' When Mr. Dog hear dat de howl dat he sot up mought a been hearn a mile er mo'. He up an' 'low, he did, dat him an' all his tribe, an' mo' speshually his kinnery, is been havin' de wuss times dat anybody ever is hear tell un. He say dat whar dey use ter git meat, dey now gits bones, an' mighty few er dem, an' whar dey use ter be fat, dey now has ter lean up ag'in' de fence, an' lean mighty hard, ef dey wanter make a shadder. Mr. Dog had lots mo' ter say, but de long an' de short un it wuz dat him an' his kinnery wa'n't treated right.

"Ol' Brer Rabbit, which he playin' King fer de day, he kinder study, an' den he cle'r up his th'oat an' look sollum. He ax ef dey's any turkentime out dar in de back yard er in de cellar whar dey keep de harness grease, an' when dey say dey speck dey's a drap er two lef', ol' Brer Rabbit tell um fer ter fetch it in, an' den he tell um ter git a poun' er red pepper an' mix it wid de turkentime. So said, so done. Dey grab Mr. Dog, an' rub de turkentime an' red pepper fum head ter heel, an' when he holler dey run 'im out'n de place whar de kingin' wuz done at.

"Well, time went on, an' one day follered an'er des like dey does now, an' Mr. Dog ain't never gone back home, whar his tribe an' his kinnery wuz waitin' fer 'im. Dey wait, an' dey wait, an' bimeby dey 'gun ter git oneasy. Den dey wait some mo' but it git so dey can't stan' it no longer, an' den a whole passel un um went ter de house whar dey do de kingin' at, an' make some inquirements 'bout Mr. Dog. Dem dat live at de King's house up an' tell um dat Mr. Dog done come an' gone. Dey say he got what he come atter, an' ef he ain't gone back home dey dunner whar he is. Dey tol' 'bout de po' mouf he put up, an' dey say dat dey gun 'im purty well all dat a gentermun dog could ax fer.

"De yuther dogs say dat Mr. Dog ain't never come back home, an' dem what live at de King's house say dey mighty sorry fer ter hear sech bad news, an' dey tell de dogs dat dey better hunt 'im up an' fin' out what he done wid dat what de king gi' 'im. De dogs ax how dey gwine ter know

'im when dey fin' him, an' dem at de King's house say dey kin tell 'im by de smell, kaze dey put some turkentime an' red pepper on 'im fer ter kill de fleas an' kyo de bites. Well, sence dat day de yuther dogs been huntin' fer de dog what went ter de King's house; an' how does dey hunt? 'Tain't no needs fer ter tell you, honey, kaze you know pine-blank ez good ez I kin tell you. Sence dat day an' hour dey been smellin' fer 'im. Dey smells on de groun' fer ter see ef he been 'long dar; dey smells de trees, de stumps, an' de bushes, an' when dey comes up wid an'er dog dey ain't never seed befo' dey smells him good fer ter see ef he got any red pepper an' turkentime on 'im; an' ef you'll take notice dey sometimes smells at a bush er a stump, an' der bristles will rise, an' dey'll paw de groun' wid der fo' feet, an' likewise wid der behime feet, an' growl like dey er mad. When dey do dat, dey er tellin' you what dey gwine ter do when dey git holt er dat dog what went to de King's house an' ain't never come back. I may be wrong, but I'll bet you a white ally ag'in' a big long piece er mince-pie dat dey'll be gwine on dat away when you git ter be ol' ez I is."

8
How Old Craney-Crow Lost His Head

ONE DAY, while Uncle Remus was preparing some wild cherry bark for a decoction which he took for his rheumatism, the little boy, who was an interested spectator of the proceedings, chanced to hear a noise overhead. Looking up, he saw a very large bird flying over. He immediately called the attention of Uncle Remus to the bird, which was indeed a singular-looking creature. Its long neck stretched out in front, and its long legs streamed out behind. Its wings were not very large, and it had no tail to speak of, but it flew well and rapidly, apparently anxious to reach its destination in the shortest possible time.

Uncle Remus shaded his eyes with his right hand as he gazed upward at the bird. "Laws-a-mussy!" he exclaimed; "is dey anybody yever see de beat er dat!" He knew well that the bird was a blue heron going to join its kindred in Florida, but he affected great surprise at sight of the bird, and continued to gaze at it as long as it remained in sight. He drew a long breath when it could no longer be seen, and shook his head sadly. "Ef she ain't got no mo' sense dan what her great-grandaddy had, I'm mighty sorry fer her," he declared.

"What kind of a bird is it, Uncle Remus?" the child inquired.

"Folks use ter call um Craney-Crows, honey, but now dey ain't got no name but des plain blue crane — an' I dunner whedder dey er wuff sech a big name. Yit I ain't got nothin' ag'in um dat I knows un. Mo' dan dat, when I ermembers 'bout de ol' grandaddy crane what drifted inter deze parts, many's de long time ago, 'twouldn't take much fer ter make me feel right sorry fer de whole kit an' bilin' un um — dey er sech start natchul fools."

"But what is there to be sorry about, Uncle Remus?" the little boy asked. He was rapidly learning to ask questions at the proper time.

"'Bout dey havin' sech a little grain er sense, honey. Ef you know'd what I does, I dunner ef you'd be tickled, er ef you'd feel sorry, an' it's de same way wid me. When I think er dat ol' Great-Grandaddy Crane, I dunner whedder ter laugh er cry."

This was small satisfaction to the little boy, and he was compelled to inquire about it. As this was precisely what the old Negro wanted him to do, he lost nothing by being inquisitive. "Dey wuz one time — I dunno de day, an' I dunno de year, but 'twuz one time — dey come a big storm. De win' blow'd a harrycane, an' de rain rained like all de sky an' de clouds in it done been turn ter water. De win' blow'd so hard dat it lifted ol' Craney-Crow fum his root in de lagoons way down yan' whar dey live at, an' fotch 'im up in deze parts, an' when he come, he come a -whirlin'. De win' tuck 'im up, it did, an' turn 'im 'roun' an' 'roun', an' when he lit whar he did, he stagger des like he wuz drunk — you know how you feel when you been turnin' 'roun' an' 'roun'. Well, dat wuz de way wid him; he wuz so drunk dat he hatter lean up ag'in' a tree.

"But 'twa'n't long 'fo' he 'gun ter feel all right, an' he look 'roun' fer ter see whar he at. He look an' he look, but he ain't fin' out, kaze he wuz a mighty fur ways fum home. Yit he feel de water half-way up his legs, an' ef ol' Craney-Crow is in a place whar he kin do a little wadin', he kinder has de home-feelin' — you know how dat is yo'se'f. Well, dar he wuz, a mighty fur ways fum home, an' yit up ter his knees in water, an' he des stood dar, he did, an' tuck his ease, hopin' fer better times bimeby. Now, de place whar he wuz blow'd ter wuz Long Cane Swamp, an' I wish I had

time fer ter take you over dar an' show you right whar he wuz at when he
lit, an' I wish I had time fer ter take you all thoo de Swamp an' let you
see fer yo'se'f what kinder Thing it is. 'Tain't only des a Swamp; it's
sump'n' wuss'n dat. You kin stan' in de middle un it, an' mos' hear it
ketch its breff, an' dat what make I say dat 'tain't no Swamp, fer all it
look like one.

"Well, dar wuz ol' Craney-Crow, an' der wuz de Thing you call de
Swamp, an' bimeby de sun riz an' let his lamp shine in dar in places; an'
den ol' Craney-Crow had time fer ter look 'roun' an' see whar he wuz at.
But when he fin' out, he ain't know no mo' dan what he know at fus'. Now,
you kin say what you please, an' you kin laugh ef you wanter, but I'm a-
gwine ter tell you dat de Swamp know'd dat dey wuz somebody dar what
ain't b'long dar. Ef you ax me how de Swamp know'd, I'll shake my head
an' shet my eyes; an' ef you ax me how I know it know'd, I'll des laugh at
you. You'll hatter take my word er leave it, I don't keer which. But dar
'twuz. De Swamp know'd dat somebody wuz dar what ain't b'long dar, an'
it went ter sleep an' had bad dreams, an' it keep on havin' dem dreams
all day long."

The little boy had accepted Uncle Remus's statements up to this
point, but when he said that the Swamp went to sleep and had bad
dreams, the child fairly gasped with doubtful astonishment. "Why, Uncle Remus, how could a swamp go to sleep?"

"It's des like I tell you, honey; you kin take my word er you kin leave it.
One way er de yuther, you won't be no better off dan what you is right now.
All I know is dis, dat you can't tell no tale ter dem what don't b'lieve it."

"Do you believe it, Uncle Remus? My mother says the stories are fables." Thus the little boy was imbued, without knowing it, with the modern spirit of scientific doubt.

"Does you speck I'd tell you a tale dat I don't b'lieve? Why, I dunner
how I'd put de words one atter de yuther. Whensomever you ain't
b'lievin' what I'm a-tellin', honey, des le' me know, an' I won't take de
time an' trouble fer ter tell it."

"Well, tell me about the Swamp and old Craney-Crow," said the little
boy, placing his small hand on Uncle Remus's knee coaxingly.

"Well, suh, ef so be I must, den I shill. Whar wuz I? Yasser! de
Swamp, bein' wide a-wake all night long, is bleeze ter sleep endurin' er

de day, an' so, wid ol' Craney-Crow stan'in' in de water, when de sun rise up, de Swamp know dat sump'n' wuz wrong, an' it went ter sleep an' had mighty bad dreams. De sun riz an' riz; it come up on one side er de Swamp, an' atter so long a time stood over it an' look down fer ter see what de matter. But bright ez de lamp er de sun wuz, it can't light up de Swamp, an' so it went on over an' went down on t'er side.

"De day wuz e'en about like deze days is, an' whiles de sun wuz s'archin' roun' tryin' fer ter fin' out what de trouble is in de Swamp, ol' Craney-Crow wuz wadin' 'bout in de water tryin' ter fin' some frog steak fer his dinner, er maybe a fish fer ter whet his appetite on. But dey wa'n't nary frog ner nary fish, kaze de Swamp done gone ter sleep. De mo' ol' Craney-Crow waded de mo' shallerer de water got, twel bimeby dey wa'n't nuff fer ter mo' dan wet his foots. He say, 'Hey! how come dis?' But he ain't got no answer, kaze de Swamp, wid all its bad dreams, wuz soun' asleep. Dey wuz pools er water 'roun' an' about, an' ol' ol' Craney-Crow went fum one ter de yuther, an' fum yuther ter t'other, but 'tain't do him no good. He went an' stood by um, he did, but whiles he stan'in' dar, dey wa'n't a riffle on top un um. Bimeby he got tired er walkin' about, an' he stood on one leg fer ter res' hisse'f — dough ef anybody'll tell me how you gwine ter res' yo'se'f wid stan'in' on one leg, I'll set up an' tell um tales fum now tell Chris'mus, kaze ef I git tired I kin stan' on one leg an' do my restin' dat a-way.

"Well, den, dar wuz ol' Craney-Crow, an' dar wuz de Swamp. Ol' Craney-Crow wuz wide awake, but de Swamp wuz fast asleep an' dreamin' bad dreams like a wil' hoss an' waggin gwine down hill. But de Swamp wa'n't no stiller dan ol' Craney-Crow, stan'in' on one leg wid one eye lookin' in de tops er de trees, an' de yuther one lookin' down in de grass. But in de Swamp er out'n de Swamp, time goes on an' night draps down, an' dat's de way it done dis time. An' when night drapped down, de Swamp kinder stretch itse'f an' 'gun ter wake up. Ol' Brer Mud Turkle opened his eyes an' sneeze so hard dat he roll off de bank inter de water — kersplash — an' he so close ter ol' Craney-Crow dat he fetched a hop sideways, an' come mighty nigh steppin' on Mr. Billy Black Snake. Dis skeer'd 'im so dat he fetched an'er hop, an' mighty nigh lit on de frog what he been huntin' fer. De frog he say 'hey!' an' dove in de mud-puddle.

"Atter dat, when ol' Craney-Crow move 'bout, he lif' his foots high, an'

he done like de ladies does when dey walk in a wet place. De whole caboodle wuz bran' new ter ol' Craney-Crow, an' he look wid all his eyes, an'
lissen wid all his years. Dey wuz sump'n' n'er gwine on, but he can't make
out what 'twuz. He ain't never is been in no swamp befo', mo' speshually
a Swamp what got life in it. He been use ter ma'shy places, whar dey ain't
nothin' but water an' high grass, but dar whar he fin' hisse'f atter de harrycane, dey wa'n't no big sight er water, an' what grass dey wuz, wa'n't
longer'n yo' finger. Stidder grass an' water, dey wuz vines, an' reeds, an'
trees wid moss on um dat made um look like Gran-suh Graybeard, an' de
vines an' creepers look like dey wuz reachin' out fer 'im.

"He walked about, he did, like de groun' wuz hot, an' when he walk
he look like he wuz on stilts, his legs wuz so long. He hunt 'roun' fer a
place fer ter sleep, an' whiles he wuz doin' dat he tuck notice dat dey wuz
sump'n' n'er gwine on dat he ain't never is see de like un. De jacky-
malantuns, dey lit up en' went sailin' 'roun' des like dey wuz huntin' fer
'im an' de frogs, dey holler at 'im wid, 'What you doin' here? What you
doin' here?' Mr. Coon rack by an' laugh at 'im; Mr. Billy Gray Fox peep
out'n de bushes an' bark at 'im; Mr. Mink show 'im de green eyes, an' Mr.
Whipperwill scol' 'im.

"He move 'bout, he did, an' atter so long a time dey let 'im 'lone, an'
den when dey wa'n't nobody ner nothin' pesterin' 'im, he 'gun ter look
'roun' fer hisse'f. Peepin' fust in one bush an' den in an'er, he tuck notice dat all de birds what fly by day had done gone ter bed widout der
heads. Look whar he mought, ol' Craney-Crow ain't see na'er bird but
what had done tuck his head off 'fo' he went ter bed. Look close ez he
kin, he ain't see no bird wid a head on. Dis make 'im wonder, an' he ax
hisse'f how come dis, an' de onliest answer what he kin think un is dat
gwine ter bed wid der heads on wuz done gone out er fashion in dat part
er de country.

"Now, you kin say what you please 'bout de creeturs an' der kin' —
'bout de fowls dat fly, an' de feathery creeturs what run on de groun' —
you kin say what you please 'bout um, but dey got pride; dey don't wanter
be out'n de fashion. When it comes ter dat, dey er purty much like folks,
an' dat 'uz de way wid ol' Craney-Crow; he don't wanter be out er fashion.
He 'shame' fer ter go ter bed like he allers been doin', kaze he ain't want
de yuthers fer ter laugh an' say he 'uz fum de country deestrick, whar dey

dunno much. Yit, study ez he mought, he dunner which a-way ter do fer ter git his head off. De yuthers had der heads und' der wing. But he ain't know dat.

"He look 'roun', he did, fer ter see ef dey ain't some un he kin ax 'bout it, an' he ain't hatter look long nudder, fer dar, settin' right at 'im, wuz ol' Brer Pop-Eye."

"But, Uncle Remus, who was old Brother Pop-Eye?" inquired the little boy.

"Nobody in all de roun' worl', honey, but Brer Rabbit. He had one name fer de uplan' an' an'er name fer de bottom lan' — de swamps an' de dreens. Wharsomever dar wuz any mischieviousness gwine on, right dar wuz Brer Rabbit ez big ez life an' twice ez natchul. He wuz so close ter ol' Craney-Crow dat he hatter jump when he seed 'im. Brer Pop-Eye say: 'No needs fer ter be skeer'd, frien' Craney-Crow. You may be mo' dan sho dat I'm a well-wisher.' Ol' Craney-Crow 'low: 'It do me good fer ter hear you sesso, Mr. Pop-Eye, an' seein' dat it's you an' not some un else, I don't min' axin' you how all de flyin' birds takes der heads off when dey go ter bed. It sho stumps me.' Brer Pop-Eye say, 'An' no wonder, frien' Craney-Crow, kaze you er stranger in deze parts. Dey ain't nothin' ter hide 'bout it. De skeeters is been so bad in dis swamp sence de year one, an' endurin' er de time what's gone by, dat dem what live here done got in de habits er takin' off der heads an' puttin' um in a safe place.'

"De Craney-Crow 'low: 'But how in de name er goodness does dey do it, Brer Pop-Eye?' Mr. Pop-Eye laugh ter hisse'f 'way down in his gizzard. He say: 'Dey don't do it by deyse'f, kaze dat 'ud be axin' too much. Oh, no! dey got some un hired fer ter do dat kin' er work.' 'An' whar kin I fin' 'im, Brer Pop-Eye?' sez ol' Craney-Crow, sezee. Brer Pop-Eye 'low: 'He'll be 'roun' terreckly; he allers hatter go 'roun' fer ter see dat he ain't miss none un um.' Ol' Craney-Crow sorter study, he did, an' den he 'low: 'How does dey git der heads back on, Brer Pop-Eye?' Brer Pop-Eye shuck his head. He say: 'I'd tell you ef I know'd, but I hatter stay up so much at night, dat 'long 'bout de time when dey gits der heads put on, I'm soun' asleep an' sno'in' right along. Ef you sesso, I'll hunt up de doctor what does de business, an' I speck he'll commerdate you — I kin prommus you dat much, sence you been so perlite.' Ol' Craney-Crow laugh an' say: 'I done fin' out in my time dat dey don't nothin' pay like perliteness, speshually ef she's ginnywine.'

"Wid dat, Brer Pop-Eye put out, he did, fer ter fin' Brer Wolf. Knowin' purty well whar he wuz, 'twa'n't long 'fo' here dey come gallopin' back. Brer Pop-Eye say: 'Mr. Craney-Crow, dis is Mr. Dock Wolf; Mr. Dock Wolf, dis is Mr. Craney-Crow; glad fer ter make you 'quainted, gents.'" At this point, Uncle Remus paused and glanced at the little boy, who was listening to the story with almost breathless interest. "You ain't got yo' hankcher wid you, is you?" the old man inquired gently.

"Mother always makes me carry a handkerchief," the child replied, "and it makes the pocket of my jacket stick out. Why did you ask, Uncle Remus?"

"Kaze we er comin' ter de place whar you'll need it," said the old man. "You better take it out an' hol' it in yo' han'. Ef you got any tears inside er you, dey'll come ter de top now."

The child took out his handkerchief, and held it in his hand obediently. "Well, suh," Uncle Remus went on, "atter dey been made 'quainted, ol' Craney-Crow tell Dock Wolf 'bout his troubles, an' how he wanter do like de rest er de flyin' creeturs, an' Dock Wolf rub his chin an' put his thumb in his wescut pocket fer all de worl' like a sho nuff doctor. He say ter ol' Craney-Crow dat he ain't so mighty certain an' sho dat he kin he'p 'im much. He say dat in all his born days he ain't never see no flyin' creetur wid sech a long neck, an' dat he'll hatter be mighty intickler how he fool wid it. He went close, he did, an' feel un it an' fumble wid it, an' all de time his mouf wuz waterin' des like yone do when you see a piece er lemon-pie.

"He say: 'You'll hatter hol' yo' head lower, Mr. Craney-Crow,' an' wid dat he snap down on it, an' dat wuz de last er dat Craney-Crow. He ain't never see his home no mo', an' mo' dan dat, ol' Dock Wolf slung 'im cross his back an' cantered off home. An' dat's de reason dat de Craney-Crows all fly so fas' when dey come thoo dis part er de country."

"But why did you ask me to take out my handkerchief, Uncle Remus?"

"Kaze I wanter be on de safe side," remarked the old man with much solemnity. "Ef you got a hankcher when you cry, you kin wipe off de weeps, an' you kin hide de puckers in yo' face."

9
Brother Fox Follows the Fashion

THE LITTLE BOY was not sure whether Uncle Remus had finished the story; it would have been hard for a grown man to keep up with the whimsical notions of the venerable old darkey, and surely you couldn't expect a little bit of a boy, who had had no experience to speak of, to do as well. The little lad waited a while, and, seeing that Uncle Remus showed no sign of resuming the narrative, he spoke up. "I didn't see anything to cry about," he remarked.

"Well, some folks cries, an' yuther folks laugh. Dey got der reasons, too. Now, I dunno dat ol' Brer Rabbit wuz hard-hearted er col'-blooded any mo' dan de common run er de creeturs, but it look like he kin see mo' ter tickle 'im dan de yuthers, an' he wuz constant a-laughin'. Mos' er de time he'd laugh in his innerds, but den ag'in, when sump'n' tetch his funny-bone, he'd open up wid a big ha-ha-ha dat 'ud make de yuther creeturs take ter de bushes.

"An' dat 'uz de way he done when ol' Craney-Crow had his head tooken off fer ter be in de fashion. He laugh an' laugh twel it hurt 'im ter laugh, an' den he laugh some mo' fer good medjur. He laughed plum twel mornin', an' den he laugh whiles he wuz rackin' on todes home. He'd lope a little ways, an' den he'd set down by de side er de road an' laugh some mo'. Whiles he gwine on dis away, he come ter de place whar Brer Fox live at, an' den it look like he can't git no furder. Ef a leaf shook on de tree, it 'ud put 'im in min' er de hoppin' an' jumpin' an' scufflin' dat ol' Craney-Crow done when Dock Wolf tuck an' tuck off his head fer 'im.

"Ez luck would have it, Brer Fox wuz out in his pea-patch fer ter see how his crap wuz gittin' on, an' huntin' 'roun' fer ter see ef dey wuz any stray tracks whar somebody had bin atter his truck. Whiles he wuz lookin' 'roun' he hear some un laughin' fit ter kill, an' he looked over de fence fer ter see who 'tis. Dar wuz Brer Rabbit des a-rollin' in de grass an' laughin' hard ez he kin. Brer Fox 'low: 'Heyo, Brer Rabbit! what de name er goodness de matter wid you?' Brer Rabbit, in de middle er his laughin' can't do nothin' but shake his head an' kick in de grass.

"'Bout dat time, ol' Miss Fox stuck 'er head out'n de winder fer ter see what gwine on. She say, 'Sandy, what all dat fuss out dar? Ain't you know dat de baby's des gone ter sleep?' Brer Fox, he say, ''Tain't nobody in de roun' worl' but Brer Rabbit, an' ef I ain't mighty much mistooken, he done gone an' got a case er de highstericks.' Ol' Miss Fox say, 'I don't keer what he got, I wish he'd go on 'way fum dar, er hush up his racket. He'll wake de chillun, an' dem what ain't 'sleep he'll skeer de wits out'n 'um.'

"Wid dat, ol' Brer Rabbit cotch his breff, an' pass de time er day wid Brer Fox an' his ol' 'oman. Den he say, 'You see me an' you hear me, Brer Fox; well, des ez you see me now, dat de way I been gwine on all night long. I speck maybe it ain't right fer ter laugh at dem what ain't got de sense dey oughter been born wid, but I can't he'p it fer ter save my life; I try, but de mo' what I try de wusser I gits. I oughter be at home right now, an' I would be ef it hadn't a been fer sump'n' I seed las' night,' an' den he went ter laughin' ag'in. Ol' Miss Fox, she fix de bonnet on her head, an' den she say, 'What you see, Brer Rabbit? It mus' be mighty funny; tell us 'bout it, an' maybe we'll laugh wid you.' Brer Rabbit 'low, 'I don't min' tellin' you, ma'am, ef I kin keep fum laughin', but ef I hatter stop fer ter ketch my breff, I know mighty well dat you'll skuzen me.' Ol' Miss Fox say, 'Dat we will, Brer Rabbit.'

"Wid dat Brer Rabbit up an' tol' all 'bout ol' Craney-Crow comin' in de Swamp, an' not knowin' how ter go ter bed. He say dat de funny part un it wuz dat ol' Craney-Crow ain't know dat when anybody went ter bed dey oughter take der head off, an' den he start ter laughin' ag'in. Ol' Miss Fox look at her ol' man an' he look at her; dey dunner what ter say er how ter say it.

"Brer Rabbit see how dey er doin', but he ain't pay no 'tention. He 'low, 'Dat ol' Craney-Crow look like he had travel fur an' wide; he look like he know what all de fashions is, but when he got in de Swamp an' see all de creeturs — dem what run an' dem what fly — sleepin' wid der heads off, he sho wuz tuck back; he say he ain't never her er sech doin's ez dat. You done seed how country folks do — well, des dat away he done. I been tryin' hard fer ter git home, an' tell my ol' 'oman 'bout it, but eve'y time I gits a good start it pop up in my min' 'bout how ol' Craney-Crow done when he fin' out what de fashion wuz in dis part er de country.' An' den Brer Rabbit sot inter laughin', and Brer Fox an' ol' Miss Fox

dey j'ined in wid 'im, kaze dey ain't want nobody fer ter git de idee dat
dey don't know what de fashion is, speshually de fashion in de part er de
country whar dey er livin' at.

"Ol' Miss Fox, she say dat ol' Craney-Crow must be a funny sort er
somebody not ter know what de fashions is, an' Brer Fox he 'gree twel he
grin an' show his tushes. He say he ain't keerin' much 'bout fashions
hisse'f, but he wouldn't like fer ter be laughed at on de 'count er plain ig-
nunce. Brer Rabbit, he say he ain't makin' no pertence er doin' eye'y-
thing dat's done, kaze he ain't dat finnicky, but when fashions is
comfertubble an' coolin' he don't min' follerin' um fer der own sake ez
well ez his'n. He say now dat he done got in de habits er sleepin' wid his
head off, he wouldn't no mo' sleep wid it on dan he'd fly.

"Ol' Miss Fox, she up'n' spon', 'I b'lieve you, Brer Rabbit — dat I
does!' Brer Rabbit, he make a bow, he did, an' 'low, 'I know mighty well
dat I'm ol'-fashion', an' dey ain't no 'nyin' it, Miss Fox, but when de new
gineration hit on ter sump'n' dat's cool an' comfertubble, I ain't de man
ter laugh at it des kaze it's tollerbul new. No, ma'am! I'll try it, an' ef it
work all right I'll foller it; ef it don't, I won't. De fus' time I try ter sleep
wid my head off I wuz kinder nervous, but I soon got over dat, an' now

ef it wuz ter go out er de fashion, I'd des keep right on wid it, I don't keer what de yuthers'd think. Dat's me; dat's me all over.'

"Bimeby, Brer Rabbit look at de sun, an' des vow he bleeze ter git home. He wish ol' Miss Fox mighty well, an' made his bow, an' put out down de road at a two-forty gait. Brer Fox look kinder sheepish when his ol' 'oman look at 'im. He say dat de idee er sleepin' wid yo' head off is bran' new ter him. Ol' Miss Fox 'low dat dey's a heap er things in dis worl' what he dunno, an' what he won't never fin' out. She say, 'Here I is a-scrimpin' an' a-workin' my eye-balls out fer ter be ez good ez de bes', an' dar you is a projickin' 'roun' an' not a-keerin' whedder yo' fambly is in de fashion er not.' Brer Fox 'low dat ef sleepin' wid yo' head off is one er de fashions, he fer one ain't keerin' 'bout tryin'. Ol' Miss Fox say, 'No, an' you ain't a-keerin' what folks say 'bout yo' wife an' fambly. No won- der Brer Rabbit had ter laugh whiles he wuz tellin' you 'bout Craney- Crow, kaze you stood dar wid yo' mouf open like you ain't got no sense. It'll be a purty tale he'll tell his fambly 'bout de tacky Fox fambly.'

"Wid dat ol' Miss Fox switch away fum de winder an' went ter cleanin' up de house, an' bimeby Brer Fox went in de house hopin' dat brekfus wuz ready; but dey wa'n't no sign er nothin' ter eat. Atter so long a time, Brer Fox ax when he wuz gwine ter git brekfus. His ol' 'oman 'low dat eatin' brekfus, an' gittin' it, too, wuz one er de fashions. Ef he ain't follerin' fashions, she ain't needer. He ain't say no mo' but went off be- hin' de house an' had a mighty time er thinkin' an' scratchin' fer fleas.

"When bedtime come, ol' Miss Fox wuz mighty tired, an' she ain't a- keerin' much 'bout fashions right den. Des ez she wuz fixin' fer ter roll 'erse'f in de kivver, Brer Fox come in fum a hunt he'd been havin'. He fotch a weasel an' a mink wid 'im, an' he put um in de cubberd whar dey'd keep cool. Den he wash his face an' han's, an' 'low dat he's ready fer ter have his head tooken off fer de night, ef his ol' 'oman'll be so good ez ter he'p 'im.

"By dat time ol' Miss Fox had done got over de pouts, but she ain't got over de idee er follerin' atter de fashions, an' so she say she'll be glad fer ter he'p 'im do what's right, seein' dat he's so hard-headed in gin'ul. Den come de knotty part. Na'er one un um know'd what dey wuz 'bout, an' dar dey sot an' jowered 'bout de bes' way fer ter git de head off. Brer Fox say dey ain't but one way, less'n you twis' de head off, an' goodness knows he ain't want nobody fer ter be twis'in' his neck, kaze he ticklish anyhow. Dat one way wuz ter take de ax an' cut de head off. Ol' Miss Fox, she squall, she did, an' hol' up her han's like she skeer'd.

"Brer Fox sot dar lookin' up de chimbley. Bimeby his ol' 'oman 'low, 'De ax look mighty skeery, but one thing I know, an' dat ain't two, it ain't gwine ter hurt you ef it's de fashion.' Brer Fox kinder work his under jaw, but he ain't sayin' nothin'. So his ol' 'oman went out ter de woodpile an' got de ax, an' den she say, I'm ready, honey, whenever you is,' an' Brer Fox, he 'spon', I'm des ez ready now ez I ever is ter be,' an' wid dat she up wid de ax an' *blip!* she tuck 'im right on de neck. De head come right off wid little er no trouble, an' ol' Miss Fox laugh an' say ter herse'f dat she glad dey follerin' de fashion at las'.

"Brer Fox sorter kick an' squirm when de head fus' come off, but his ol' 'oman 'low dat dat wuz de sign he wuz dreamin', an' atter he lay right still she say he wuz havin' a better night's res' dan what he'd had in a mighty long time. An' den she happen fer ter think dat whiles her ol' man done gone an' got in de fashion, dar she wuz ready fer ter go ter bed wid 'er head on. She dunner how ter git 'er head off, an' she try ter wake up her ol' man, but it look like he wuz one er dem stubborn kinder sleepers what won't be woken'd atter dey once drap off. She shake 'im an' holler at 'im, but 'tain't do no good. She can't make 'im stir, spite er all de racket she make, an' she hatter go ter bed wid her head on.

"She went ter bed, she did, but she ain't sleep good, kaze she had trouble in de min'. She'd wake up an' turn over, an' roll an' toss, an' wonder what de yuther creeturs'd say ef dey know'd she wuz so fur outer de fashion ez ter sleep wid 'er head on. An' she had bad dreams; she dremp dat Brer Rabbit wuz laughin' at 'er, an' she start fer ter run at 'im, an' de fust news she know'd de dogs wuz on her trail an' gwine in full cry. 'Twuz dat away all night long, an' she wuz mo' dan thankful when mornin' come.

"She try ter wake up her ol' man, but still he won't be woke. He lay dar, he did, an' won't budge, an' bimeby ol' Miss Fox git mad an' go off an' leave 'im. Atter so long a time she went back ter whar he wuz layin', an' he wuz des like she lef' 'im. She try ter roust 'im up, but he won't be rousted. She holler so loud dat Brer Rabbit which he wuz gwine by, got de idee dat she wuz callin' him, an' he stick his head in de do' an' 'low, 'Is you callin' me, ma'am?'

"She say, 'La! Brer Rabbit? I ain't know you wuz anywheres aroun'. I been tryin' fer ter wake up my ol' man; he mo' lazier dis mornin' dan I ever is know 'im ter be. Ef my house wa'n't all to' up, I'd ax you in an' git you ter drag 'im out an' git 'im up.'

"Brer Rabbit say, 'Ef dey ain't nothin' de matter wid Brer Fox he'll git up in good time.' Ol' Miss Fox 'low, 'La! I dunner what you call good time. Look at de sun — it's way up yander, an' dar he is sleepin' like a log. 'Fo' he went ter bed he made me take his head off, an' he ain't woke up sence.' 'An' how did you git it off, mum?' sez ol' Brer Rabbit, sezee. 'I tuck an' tuck de ax an' cut it off,' se'she. Wid dat Brer Rabbit flung bofe han's over his face, an' mosey'd off like he wuz cryin'. Fum de way he look you'd a thunk his heart wuz broke; yit he wa'n't cryin'."

"Then what was he doing, Uncle Remus?" the little boy asked.

"Des a-laughin' — laughin' fit ter kill. When ol' Miss Fox see 'im gwine long like he wuz cryin', she spicion'd dat sump'n' wuz wrong, an' sho nuff 'twuz, kaze Brer Fox ain't wake up no mo'. She 'low, 'Ol' honey look like he dead, but he better be dead dan out er de fashion!'

"I take notice, honey, dat you ain't use yo' hankcher yit. What de matter wid you? Is yo' weeps all dry up?"

The child laughed and stuffed his handkerchief back in his pocket.

10

Why the Turkey Buzzard Is Bald-Headed

"MOTHER," said the little boy one day, "do you know why the turkey buzzards are bald?"

"Why, no," replied the young mother, very much surprised. "I didn't even know they were bald. But why do you ask such a silly question?"

"Because Uncle Remus said you knew why they are bald."

"You tell Uncle Remus," said the grandmother, laughing heartily, "that I say he is an old rascal, and he had better behave himself."

The way of it was this: The little boy had been walking out in the fields with Uncle Remus, and had seen, away up in the sky, two or three turkey buzzards floating lazily along on motionless wings. From the fields they had gone into the woods, and in these woods they had found what Uncle Remus had said was a buzzard's nest. It was in a hollow tree, flat on the ground, and when they came near, the mother buzzard issued forth from the hollow, with such a hissing and flapping of wings that the little boy was frightened for a moment.

"Go on 'way fum here, you bal'-headed ol' rapscallion; ef you don't I'll do you wuss dan Brer Rabbit done you. Honey," he went on, turning to the child, "you better put yo' hankcher ter yo' nose ef you gwine ter look in dat nes', kaze ol' Miss Turkey Buzzard is a scandalious housekeeper."

The child did as he was bid, and, peeping in the nest, he saw two young ones, as white as goslings. While he was peeping in he got a whiff of the odor of the buzzards, and turned and ran away from the place as hard as he could. Uncle Remus followed suit, and hobbled away as fast as his legs could carry him. When they were both out of range of the buzzard's nest, they stopped and laughed at each other.

"You nee'nter be skeer'd dat anything'll ketch you, honey. Dey ain't nothin' but a race-hoss got yo' gait. Why, ef I hadn't a been wid you, you'd a been home by now, kaze you'd a started when ol' Miss Buzzard fus' flew out er dat hole."

The little boy made no denial, for he knew that what Uncle Remus said had much more than a grain of truth in it. Besides, he was thinking of other things just then. He soon made known what it was. "Why did you call the buzzard bald-headed, Uncle Remus?"

"A mighty good reason," responded the old man. "Dey ain't no mo' got fedders on de top er der head dan you got ha'r in de pa'm er yo' han'. You ketch one un um, an' ef you kin hol' yo' breff long nuff ter look, you'll see dat I'm tellin' you de trufe. I ain't blamin' um fer dat, kaze dey got a mighty good reason fer bein' bal'-headed. Dey's mighty few folks dat know what de reason is, an' one un um is yo' ma. Ef you'll kinder coax 'er, I speck she'll tell you."

This was what led up to the question the child had asked his mother, and was the occasion of the grandmother's laughing remark that Uncle Remus was an old rascal.

The little boy gave Uncle Remus the full particulars the next time he saw him. The old man laughed merrily when he heard that his Miss Sally had called him an old rascal. "Talk 'bout yo' smart wimmen folks!" he exclaimed. "Dey ain't na'er man in de worl' what kin hol' a candle ter yo' gran'ma; an' des ez you see 'er now, dat des de way she been sence she wuz a gal. She know what you gwine ter say long 'fo' you kin git de words out'n yo' mouf; she kin look right thoo you an' tell you what you thinkin' 'bout. You may laugh all you wanter, but ef you er feelin' bad she'll know it. When Miss Sally goes an' dies, dey won't be na'er nudder somebody fer ter take her place. Dey ain't no two ways 'bout dat."

"I think she is getting used to mother," the little boy remarked in his old-fashioned way — a way that was a source of constant amazement to Uncle Remus, who could hardly understand how a child could act and talk like a grown person. He regarded the child with a puzzled look, and closed his eyes with a sigh. The child had no idea that Uncle Remus was either puzzled or amazed, and so he harked back to the original problem. "Why is the buzzard bald-headed?" he asked.

"Ef yo' ma an' yo' gran'ma dunno," replied Uncle Remus, "I speck I'll hatter tell you, an' de bes' way ter do dat is ter tell de tale dat de ol' folks tol' der chillun. What make it mo' easy, is dat dey ain't nothin' er Brer Turkey Buzzard in it but his name. Ef he wuz in it hisse'f, I don't speck you'd stay long nuff fer ter hear me tell it." The child laughed, for he remembered how he wanted to run away from the tree when old Mrs.

Buzzard came flopping out. He laughed, but said nothing, and Uncle Remus resumed:

"Dey wuz a time when Brer Rabbit live in one side uv a holler tree. One day whiles he wuz gwine pirootin' 'roun', ol' Miss Turkey Buzzard come knockin' at de do', an' when she don't hear nothin' she stuck 'er head in an' look 'roun'. Ter see 'er den an' see 'er now you wouldn't know she wuz de same creetur. She had a fine top-knot on 'er head, bigger dan de one on de freezlin' hen, which de win' done blow all her fedders de wrong way. Yasser, she had a fine top-knot, an' she 'uz purty good-lookin'.

"Well, suh, she peeped in, she did, an' den she seed dat dey wa'n't nobody in dar, needer Grandaddy Owl, ner Brer Polecat, ner Brer Rattlesnake. She take an 'er look, an' den in she walked, an' made 'erself mighty much at home. It ain't take ol' Miss Buzzard long fer ter fix her nes', kaze she ain't want nothin' but five sticks an' a han'ful er leaves. She went out an' fotch um in an' dar she wuz. She went right straight ter house-keepin', kaze she ain't had ter put down no kyarpits, ner straighten out no rugs, ner move de cheers roun', ner wash no dishes.

"Well, long todes night, er maybe a little later, Brer Rabbit come home, an' like he mos' allers done, he come a-laughin'. He been projickin' wid some er de yuther creeturs, an he wuz mighty pleased wid hisse'f. When he fus' come he ain't take no notice er ol' Miss Buzzard. He come in a-laughin', an' he laugh twel he don't wanter laugh no mo'. But bimeby he 'gun ter take notice dat ever'thing wa'n't des like it useter be. He 'low, 'Somebody done been here while I'm gone, an' whoever 'twuz, is got a mighty bad breff.' He keep still, kaze 'twuz mighty dark in de holler, but he keep on wigglin' his nose an' tryin' ter sneeze. Bimeby, he say, 'I dunner who 'twuz; all I know, is dat he better go see de doctor.'

"Dis 'uz too much fer ol' Miss Buzzard, an' she say, 'I thank you kin'ly, Brer Rabbit! You er in de way er makin' frien's wharsomever you go!' Brer Rabbit, he jump mos' out'n his skin, he wuz so skeer'd. He cotch his breff an' sneeze, an' den he 'low, 'Heyo, Sis Buzzard! Is dat you? I thought you stayed in de trees. What win' blow you here, an' how is ol' Brer Buzzard?' She say, 'Oh, he's doin' ez well ez you kin speck a man ter do; he's 'way fum home when he oughter be dar, an' when he's dar, he's in de way. Men folks is monstus tryin', Brer Rabbit; you know dat yo'se'f.' Brer Rabbit 'low, 'I ain't 'sputin' what you say, but when wimmen gits out er sorts, an' has de all-overs, ez you may say, de men folks has ter b'ar de brunt er der ailments. You kin put dat down fer a fac'.'

"Dey went on dat away, 'sputin' 'bout de seck twel ol' Miss Buzzard 'gun ter git sleepy. She say, 'Brer Rabbit, ef you took mo' time for sleep, you'd be lots better off.' Brer Rabbit 'low, 'Maybe so — maybe so, Sis Buzzard, but I can't he'p my habits. I'm a light sleeper, but I wuz born so, an' if you so much ez move endurin' er de night I'll have one eye open.' Ol' Miss Buzzard say, 'Ef dat's de case, Brer Rabbit, I'll thank you fer ter wake me ef you hear a snake crawlin'. Dey ain't many things I'm afeard un, an' one uv um is a snake.' Brer Rabbit laugh hearty, an' low, 'Ef snakes wuz all dat trouble me, Sis Buzzard, I'd be mo' dan happy. Many an' many's de time when I uv woke up an' foun' um quiled up in my britches laig.' Miss Buzzard, she sorter flutter her wings, an' say, 'Oh, hush, Brer Rabbit! you gi' me de creeps; you sho do.'

"Dat 'uz de fust night," said Uncle Remus, flinging away a quid of tobacco and taking a fresh one. "By de nex' day ol' Miss Buzzard had done took up her 'bode an' lodgin' whar Brer Rabbit wuz livin' at. He ain't say nothin', kaze he des waitin' de time when he kin play some kinder prank on her an' her fambly. All dat he need fer ter brace 'im up wuz ter have a mighty strong stomach, an' he thank de Lord dat he got dat. Time went on, an' ez any kinder soun' egg will hatch ef you gi' it time, so ol' Miss Buzzard egg hatch, an' mos' 'fo' you know it, ef you ain't hatter live dar like Brer Rabbit, she hatch out her eggs an' have a pa'r er mighty likely chillun, ef you kin call Buzzards likely.

"Ol' Miss Buzzard wuz monstus proud er deze young uns, an' time come when she wuz hard put ter git um vittels. She'd fly off an' dey'd holler fer sump'n' ter eat when dey hear 'er come back, an' it got so atter while dat dey'd hatter go hongry, dey wuz so ravenous. An' den she 'gun ter look sideways at Brer Rabbit. He knew mighty well what she thinkin' 'bout, but he ain't say nothin'. He'd come an' go des like ol' Miss Buzzard want in de back part er her head, but all de time, he know'd what she plannin' ter do, an' he ack accordin'. He low ter ol' Miss Buzzard dat he know she wanter be kinder private when she raisin' a fambly, an' ez dey wuz two hollers in de tree, he say he gwine ter make his home in de

yuther one. Miss Buzzard, she say, she did, dat Brer Rabbit wuz mighty
good fer ter be thinkin' 'bout yuther people, but Brer Rabbit make a bow
an' say he been raise' dat a-way.

"But 'fo' Brer Rabbit went in de yuther holler he made sho dat dey
wuz mo' dan one way er gittin' out. He went in dar, he did, an' scratch
about an' make a new bed, an' den he git in it fer ter git it warm. He sat
dar wid one eye open an' t'er one shot. He sot so still dat ol' Miss Buzzard got de idee dat he gone abroad, an' so when her chillun cry fer dey
dinner, she say, 'Don't cry, honey babies; mammy gwine ter git you a
good warm dinner 'fo' long, an' it'll be fresh meat, too, you kin 'pen' on
dat.' De chillun, dey cry wuss at dis, kaze dey so hongry dey don't wanter wait a minnit. Dey say, 'Git it now, mammy! git it now!' Ol' Brer Rabbit wuz settin' in dar lis'nin', an' he 'low ter hisse'f, 'It'll tas'e mighty
good when you does git it, honey babies!' Wid dat, he skip out fum dar,
an' went off ter his laughin'-place.

"Atter so long a time, ol' Miss Buzzard went 'roun' ter de yuther
holler, an' peep in. Ef Brer Rabbit had a been in dar, she wuz gwine ter
ax 'im how he like his new house, but he wa'n't dar, an' she hove a long
breff, kaze when you gwine ter do mischief, it seem like eve'ybody know
what you gwine ter do. Anyhow, she 'uz mighty glad dat Brer Rabbit
wa'n't dar fer ter look at 'er wid his pop-eyes. Den she tell her chillun dat
she gwine off atter some vittles, an' she flop 'er wings a time er two, an'
off she flew'd.

"Dey got 'long tollable well dat day an' de nex' but 'twa'n't long 'fo' der craw 'gun ter feel like a win'-bag, an' den dey set up a cry fer mo' vittles, an' der mammy ain't got no vittles fer ter gi' um. Brer Rabbit went abroad mighty soon dat day, an' atter he had his fill er fun an' turnip greens he

come home an' went ter bed. He went ter bed, he did, an' went ter sleep, but he ain't sleep long, kaze he hear some kinder noise. He wake up, an' open an' shet his pop-eyes kinder slow, an' wiggle his mouf an' nose. He kin hear ol' Miss Buzzard trompin' 'roun' at his front do', kinder hummin' a chune ter herself. He say, 'Heyo, dar! who dat projickin' at my front do'?' Ol' Miss Buzzard, she say, 'Take yo' res', Brer Rabbit; 'tain't nobody but me. I got de idee dat some un wuz pirootin' 'roun' de place, an' I des got up fer ter see dat eve'ything wuz all right.'

"Brer Rabbit say, 'It's mighty dark in here,' an' 'A mighty good reason,' sez ol' Miss Buzzard, sez she, 'kaze it's black night out here,' sez she; 'you can't see yo' han' befo' you,' sez she. Dis make Brer Rabbit laugh, kaze de mornin' sun wuz shinin' thoo a knot-hole right in Brer Rabbit's face. He laugh an' 'low ter hisse'f, 'Shoot yo' shekels, ol' 'oman, an' shoot um hard, kaze you er gwine ter git de rough een' er dis business. You hear my horn!' He hear ol' Miss Buzzard walkin' 'roun' out dar,

an' he holler out, 'I can't git out! I b'lieve it's daytime out dar, an' I can't git out! Somebody better run here an' he'p me ter git out. Some un done lock me in my own house, an' I can't git out! Ain't somebody gwine ter run here an' turn me out! I can't git a breff er fresh a'r.'

"Well, ol' Miss Buzzard ain't got no mo' sense dan ter b'lieve Brer Rabbit, an' she wuz des certain an' sho dat he wuz her meat. She say, 'I'm de one what shet you up in dar, an' I'm gwine ter keep you in dar twel you er done dead, an' den I'll pull de meat off'n yo' bones, bofe fat an' lean, an' feed my chillun. I done got you shot up wid red clay an' white, an' I'm gwine ter keep you in dar bofe day an' night, twel you ain't got no breff in you.' Wid dat she went in her own house an' sot down wid 'er chillun fer ter wait an' see what gwine ter happen. Brer Rabbit he stay still fer de longes', kaze he one er de mos' fidgetty creeturs you yever is lay yo' eyes on. He stay right still, he did, twel ol' Miss Turkey Buzzard git tired

er waitin' an' come out fer ter promenade up an' down 'fo' Brer Rabbit front do'.

"He hear de ol' huzzy, an' he say, 'I know you des jokin' wid me, Sis Buzzard; please, ma'am, le' me out. My breff gittin' shorter, an' dish yer an' what in here smell mos' ez bad ez what yo' breff do. Please, ma'am, make 'as'e an' let me out.' Den she got mad. 'My breff, I hear you say! Well, 'fo' I git thoo wid you, you won't have no breff — I prommus you dat.' Atter ol' Miss Buzzard went back in her part er de house, Brer Rabbit tuck a notion dat he'd git out er dar, an' pay 'er back fer de ol' an' de new. An' out er his back do' he went. He ain't take time fer ter go ter de laughin'-place — no, suh! not him. Stidder dat he put off ter whar he know'd Mr. Man had been cle'rin' up a new groun'. Dey wuz a tin bucket what Mr. Man had done gone off an' forgot, an' Brer Rabbit tuck dat an' fill it full er red-hot embers, an' went sailin' back home wid it.

"When he git dar, he stuck his head in Miss Buzzard do', an' 'low

'Peep-eye, Sis Buzzard! I hope you done had yo' dinner ter day, an' ef you ain't I got it right here fer you an' you mo' dan welcome ter all dat's in it.' He ain't mo' dan got de words out'n his mouf, 'fo' ol' Miss Buzzard flew'd out at 'im des like she flew'd out at you, de yuther day. She flew'd out, she did, but she ain't flew'd fur 'fo' she got de hot ashes over her head an' neck, an' de way she hopp'd 'roun' wuz so scandalious dat folks calls dat kinder doin's de buzzard-dance ter dis day an' time.

"Some er de ashes got on de little buzzards, an' fum dat time on none er de buzzard tribe is had any ha'r er fedders on der head, an' not much on der neck. An' ef you look at um right close, you'll fin' dat I'm 'a' tellin' you de plain trufe. Dey look so b'ar on der head an' neck dat you wanter gi' um a piece er rag fer to tie roun' it ter keep um fum ketchin' col'.''

11
Brother Deer and King Sun's Daughter

It is only fair to say that the little boy came to the plantation somewhat prejudiced. His mother had never known the advantages of association with the old-time Negroes, and was a great stickler for accuracy of speech. She was very precise in the use of English and could not abide the simple dialect in which the stories had been related to the little boy's father. She was so insistent in this matter that the child's father, when asked for a story such as Uncle Remus had told him, thought it best to avoid the dialect that he knew so well. In consequence, the essence of the stories was dissipated for the child, and he lacked the enthusiasm which Uncle Remus had hoped to find.

But this enthusiasm came by degrees as Uncle Remus wandered from one tale to another. The child never told his mother how he enjoyed the stories, and yet he came to play the part that had been played by his father long before he was born, and matters came to such a pass, that, if he was long with Uncle Remus without hearing a story, he straightway imagined that the old man was angry or out of sorts. The lad was gaining in health and strength every day he remained on the plantation, and in consideration of this fact — and as the result of wise diplomacy of Uncle Remus — the child's mother relaxed the discipline that she had thought necessary for his welfare, so that not many weeks elapsed before his cheeks became ruddy with health. Uncle Remus hailed him as a town rowdy, and declared that the plantation would soon be too small to hold him.

"I pity yo' gran'ma," said Uncle Remus, "kaze ef you stay 'roun' here, she'll hatter buy all de 'j'inin' plantations ef she gwine ter keep you on her lan'."

There was no more corn to be hauled, but there was harness to be mended, and the little boy, sitting on a high stool in the workshop, or leaning against Uncle Remus, watched the operation with great interest. He observed one day that the old man was frowning darkly. His forehead was puckered into knots and seamed with wrinkles that did not belong there, and his eyebrows were drawn together over his nose.

"What is the matter with you, Uncle Remus? Are you angry, or are you going to cry?"

"I'll tell you de trufe, honey. I'm mighty nigh on de p'int er cryin'. You see my face puckered up, don't you? Well, ef you had ez much on yo' min' ez what I got on mine, you'd be boo-hooin' same ez a baby. I tell you dat. An' des ter show you dat I'm in deep trouble, I'll ax you ter tell me how many times dey is."

"How many times? How many times what?" the child inquired.

Uncle Remus regarded him sorrowfully, and then returned to his work with a heavy sigh. "Did I ax you 'bout what? No, I ain't; I ax'd you 'bout times. I say ez plain ez writin': 'How many times is dey?' an' you 'spon', 'How many times what?' It look mighty funny ter me. Dar's day-time an' night-time, bed-time an' meal-time, an' some time an' no time, an' high time an' fly time, an' long time an' wrong time, 'simmon time an' plum time. Dey ain't no use er talkin'; it's nuff fer ter make yo' head swim. I been tryin' fer ter count um up, but de mo' I count um up de mo' dey is."

The little boy looked at the old man with a half-smile on his face. He was plainly puzzled, but he didn't like to admit it even to himself. "Why do you want to know how many times there are?" he asked.

"Kaze I wanter live an' l'arn," replied Uncle Remus. "Le' me see," he went on, puckering his face again. "Dars de ol' time an' de new time, de col' time an' de due time — bless yo' soul, honey, I can't count um up. No, suh; you'll hatter skusen me!"

He paused and looked at the little boy to see what the child could make out of all he had said.

He saw nothing in the small countenance but curiosity. "What made you think of it?" was the question the child asked.

"Mos' eve'ything I see make me think 'bout it, an' you'll think 'bout it you'se'f, when you come ter be ol' ez what I is. But de reason it wuz runnin' in my head dis time wuz kaze I start ter tell a tale widout knowin' when de time wuz. I know it wuz 'way back yander, but de mont' er de year I can't tell, an' when I try ter fix on de time eve'ything look dim an' smoky, an' I say ter myse'f dat dey mus' be a fog in my mind."

"Can't you tell the story unless you can find out about the time?" inquired the little boy.

"Tooby sho I kin, honey; but you'd b'lieve it lots quicker ef you know'd what time it happen. 'Fo' yo' great-gran'ma died she had a trunk full er ollymenacks, an' I boun' you ef I had 'em here whar you could look at um, we wouldn't have no trouble. I speck dey done got strow'd about endurin' er de war time.

"Well, anyhow, once 'pon a time, when dey wuz mighty few folks in de worl', ef any, Brer Deer fell in love wid ol' King Sun's daughter." Having made this preliminary statement, Uncle Remus paused to see what effect it had on the child. Amazement and incredulity were written on the little boy's face, observing which the old man smiled. "You nee'nter git de idee in yo' head dat ol' King Sun is like he wuz in dem days. No, bless you! He was des es diffunt ez dem times wuz fum deze times, an' when you git ter readin' in de books you'll fin' out what de diffunce wuz. He wuz closer by, an' he ain't hide out at night like he does now. He wuz up in de sky, but he ain't live ez high up; he wuz mo' neighborly, ez you may say.

"He live so close by dat he useter sen' de house-gal down ter de spring fer drinkin'-water. Three times a day she'd come ter fetch it; she'd clim' down wid de bucket in her han' an' she'd clim' back wid de bucket on her head, an' she'd sing bofe ways, comin' an' gwine. In dem times day all know'd dat ol' King Sun had a daughter, but dey ain't know what 'er name is; an' dey know she wuz purty. Well, Brer Deer he hear talk un 'er, an' he tuck a notion dat he gwine ter marry 'er, but he dunner how he gwine ter git up dar whar she live at. He study an' study, but he can't fin' no way.

"He was settin' down by de road studyin' out a plan fer ter git word ter de gal, when ol' Brer Rabbit come lopin' down de lane. He mus' a been playin' hoss, kaze when he see Brer Deer, he shied an' sneezed, he did, an' make like he gwine ter run away. But he ain't run. He pass de time er day wid Brer Deer an' ax 'im how his copperosity seem to segashuate. Brer Deer 'low dat his copperosity is segashuatin' all right, but he got trouble in his min' an' he can't git it out. He looked mighty sollumcolly when he say dis, an' Brer Rabbit say he sorry.

"He sot down, Brer Rabbit did, an' cross his legs, an' rub his chin same like de doctor do when he gwine ter slap a dose er bitter truck on yo' insides. He rub his chin, he did, an' look like he know all dey is fer ter be know'd. He say, 'Brer Deer, when I wuz growin' up I useter hear de ol' folks say dat a light heart made a long life, an' I b'lieve um. I sho' does. Dey know'd what dey wuz talkin' bout, kaze I done had de 'speunce un it.

"Brer Deer shuck his head an' grieve. Ef he'd a had a hankcher, he a had need un it right den an' dar, but he wink his eye fas' fer ter git de tears out'n um. He 'low, 'I speck you er tellin' me de trufe, Brer Rabbit, but I can't he'p it ef you is. I am what I am, an' I can't be no ammer. I feels mo' like cryin' dan I does like eatin', an' I'm dat fractious dat I can't skacely see straight. Ol' Mr. Ram tol' me howdy a while ago, an' I ain't done a thing but run at 'im and butt him slonchways. You nee'nter tell me dat I ain't got no business fer ter do dat a-way; I des can't he'p it.'

"Brer Rabbit kinder edge hisse'f away fum Brer Deer. He say, 'Dat bein' de case, Brer Deer, I speck I better gi' you mo' room. When I lef' home dis mornin' my ol' 'oman 'low, "You better take keer er yo'se'f, honey," an' I'm gwine ter do dat identual thing. I dunno dat I'm skeered er gittin' hurted, but I'm monstus ticklish when de horned creeturs is 'roun'.' Brer Deer say, 'You nee'nter be fear'd er me, Brer Rabbit. I been knowin' you a long time, an' many's de night we bofe graze in de same pastur', you a-nibblin' on de green grass an' me a-crappin' it. I'm monstus glad I run 'cross you, kaze ef I can't tell my troubles ter some un, I b'lieve in my soul I'll bust wide open.'

"Wid dat Brer Deer went on fer ter tell Brer Rabbit dat he done fell

dead in love wid ol' King Sun's daughter. He dunner how come it ter be so, but anyhow so it is. He ain't had no talk wid 'er; he ain't mo' dan cotch a glimp' er de gal, yet dar he wuz dead in love wid 'er. Brer Rabbit mought laugh at 'im ef he wanter; he'll des set dar an' take it. He talk an' talk, he did, twel Brer Rabbit got right sorry fer 'im. He sot dar, he did, an' study, an' he tell Brer Deer dat he'll he'p 'im ef he kin, an' he mos' know he kin.

"Brer Deer raise his head, an' open his eyes. He say, 'Brer Rabbit, you 'stonish me — you sho does. Ef you'll he'p me out in dis, I'll stan' by you thoo thick an' thin.' But Brer Rabbit say he ain't doin' it fer no pay; he done lay by his crap, an' he ain't got nothin' much ter do, an' he say he'll he'p Brer Deer des fer ter keep his han' in. Brer Deer look like he wuz might'ly holp up. Fust he smole a smile, an' den he broke out in a laugh. He say, 'You er de man fer my money!'

"Brer Rabbit kinder wiggle his nose. He say, 'Ef you keep yo' money twel you think you got too much, you'll have it by you fer many a long year ter come.' Wid dat, he got up an' bresh de dus' off'n his britches, an' shuck han's wid Brer Deer. He say, 'I hope fer ter have some good news fer you de nex' time we meet in de big road.' He bowed, he did, an' den off he put, lippity-clip. He look back fer ter see ef Brer Deer wuz follerin' 'im, but Brer Deer had sense nuff fer ter hunt 'im a cool place in de woods, whar he kin take de fust nap what he had in many a night an' day.

"Brer Rabbit lope off todes de spring, kaze he know'd dat de spring wuz de place whar King Sun's house-gal come atter water — an' she hatter tote a mighty heap un it. It look like de mo' water what King Sun drunk de mo' he want, an' dat bein' de case, de gal had 'bout ez much totin' ez she kin do. Brer Rabbit went down ter de spring, but dey wa'n't nobody dar, an' he look in it an' see hisse'f in de water. Dar he wuz, his ha'r all comb, his face clean, an' he look slicker dan sin. He laugh, he did, an' say ter de Rabbit what he see in de water, 'You sho is mighty good-lookin', whoever you is, an' ef you blame anybody, don't blame me, kaze I can't he'p it.'

"Now, down at de bottom er de spring wuz ol' man Spring Lizzard. He wuz takin' his mornin' nap, when he hear some un talkin'. He raise up, he did, an' lissen; den he look an' see Brer Rabbit lookin' at hisse'f in de water, an' he holler out, 'Maybe you ain't ez good-lookin' ez you think you is.' Brer Rabbit holler back, 'Hello, dar! dis is de fus' time I know'd dat yo' shadder in de water kin talk back at you.'

"Wid dat, Mr. Spring Lizzard come fum under de green moss, an' float ter de top er de water. He pass de time er day wid Brer Rabbit, an' ax 'im whar he gwine, an' what he gwine ter do when he git dar. Brer Rabbit 'low dat he tryin' fer to do a good turn ter a frien' what's in trouble an' den he went on an' tol' de ol' Spring Lizzard 'bout Brer Deer an' King Sun's daughter. De Spring Lizzard say she's a mighty likely gal, kaze he seed her one

time when she slip off an' come wid de house-gal atter water. He say she
got long ha'r dat look like spun silk, an' eyes dat shine like de mornin' star.

"Brer Rabbit say he don't 'spute it, but what he wanter know is how
he kin git word ter King Sun 'bout Brer Deer. De Spring Lizzard say dat's
easy. He say dat when de house-gal come atter water, she hatter let down
de step-ladder, an' Brer Rabbit kin slip by 'er an' go up, er he hisse'f kin
git in de bucket an' go up. Brer Rabbit say he kinder jub'us 'bout gwine,
kaze he's a kinder home body, an' den de Spring Lizzard 'low dat ef Brer
Deer will write a note, he'll take it.

"Well, Brer Deer can't write an' Brer Rabbit kin; so dey fix it up 'twix'
um, an' 'twa'n't long 'fo' dey had de note writ, an' Brer Rabbit tuck it an'
gi' it ter de Spring Lizzard. He say, 'Don't let it git wet, whatever you does,'
and de Spring Lizzard ax how it gwine ter git wet when he put it in his
pocket? He say dat eve'ybody but him, de fishes an' de frogs got a wrong
idee 'bout water, kaze 'tain't wet ez it mought be, 'ceppin' on a rainy day.

"Time went on des like it do now; night swung by an' day swung in,
an' here come King Sun's house-gal atter a bucket er water. She let down
de step-ladder an' come singin' ter de spring. She drapped her bucket in,
an' de Spring Lizzard stepped in, an' crope 'roun' ter whar de shadder wuz
de heaviest. De gal clomb up de step-ladder, an' pulled it atter her, an'
went 'long de path ter King Sun's house. She took de water in de settin'-
room fer ter gi' King Sun a fresh drink, an' he grabbed up de gourd an'
drunk an' drunk twel it look like he gwine ter bust. Atter dat he went in
de liberry an' de Spring Lizzard crope out an lef' Brer Deer note on de
table, an' den he crope back in de bucket.

"Atter while, King Sun's daughter come bouncin' in de room atter a
drink er water, an' she see de note. She grab it up an' read it, an' den she
holler: 'Pa, oh, pa! here's a letter fer you, an' I mos' know dey's sump'n'
in it 'bout me! La! I dunner who 't is dat's got de impidence fer ter put my
name in a letter.' Ol' King Sun run his fingers thoo his beard, des like he
coinbin' it, an' den he cle'r up his throat. He take de letter an' hol' it off
fum 'im, an' den put on his specks. He 'low, 'Well, well, well! who'd a
thunk it?' an' den he look at his daughter. She look at de flo' an' pat 'er
foot. He say, 'I ain't never hear er sech impidence.' De gal 'low, 'What do
he say, pa?' Wid dat, he han' 'er de letter, an' when she read it, she got
red in de face, an' den she got white. She think one way, an' den she

think an'er. She got mad an' she got glad, an' den she had de allovers, des like gals does deze days when some un ax um fer ter have um.

"So den, dar 'twuz; Brer Deer want ter marry de gal, an' de gal dunner whedder she wanter marry er not. Den ol' King Sun got his pen, an' put a little water in de ink, kaze it wuz mighty nigh dried up, an' den he writ a letter back ter Brer Deer. He say dat ef de one what writ de letter will sen' 'im a bag er gold, he kin have de gal. He fol' de letter up an' han' it ter de gal, an' she not knowin' what else ter do, tuck an' put it on de table whar she fin' de yuther one.

"De Spring Lizzard had his eye on 'er, an' when she went out'n de room, he clomb up on de table an' got de letter, an' went back in de bucket ag'in. Dat evenin' de house-gal hatter fetch water fer de night, an' she let down de step-ladder an' went ter de spring. When she dip de bucket in, de Spring Lizzard, he slide out, an' went ter his bed un' de long green moss. 'Twa'n't long 'fo' Brer Rabbit had de letter, an' atter dat, 'twa'n't no time 'fo' Brer Deer know'd what de intents wuz. 'Twix' an' 'twen um dey got up a bag er gold, an' Brer Rabbit tuck it ter de spring whar de house-gal got water.

"De nex' mornin' de daughter come 'erse'f, kaze she wanter see what kinder man Brer Deer is. At de spring she fin' a bag er gold. She clap 'er han's an' holler out: 'Look what I fin' — fin', fin', fin'y! It's min' — min', min', min'y!' Brer Rabbit wuz settin' in de bushes, an' Brer Deer wa'n't fur off, an' dey bofe watch de gal a-prancin' an' dancin'; an' den, bimeby Brer Deer went out whar she kin see 'im, an' he des walk up ter 'er an' say, 'Look what I fin'; honey, you er mine!' An' dat 'uz de way Brer Deer got ol' King Sun's daughter."

12

Brother Rabbit's Cradle

"I WISH you'd tell me what you tote a hankcher fer," remarked Uncle Remus, after he had reflected over the matter a little while. "Why, to keep my mouth clean," answered the little boy.

Uncle Remus looked at the lad, and shook his head doubtfully. "Uh-uh!" he exclaimed. "You can't fool folks when dey git ez ol' what I is. I been watchin' you now mo' days dan I kin count, an' I ain't never see yo' mouf dirty nuff fer ter be wiped wid a hankcher. It's allers clean — too clean ter suit me. Dar's yo' pa now; when he wuz a little chap like you, his mouf useter git dirty in de mornin' an' stay dirty plum twel night. Dey wuz skacely a day dat he didn't look like he been playin' wid de pigs in de stable lot. Ef he yever is tote a hankcher, he ain't never show it ter me."

"He carries one now," remarked the little boy with something like a triumphant look on his face.

"Tooby sho," said Uncle Remus; "tooby sho he do. He start ter totin' one when he tuck an' tuck a notion fer ter go a-courtin'. It had his name in one cornder, an' he useter sprinkle it wid stuff out'n a pepper-sauce bottle. It sho wuz rank, dat stuff wuz; it smell so sweet it make you fergit whar you live at. I take notice dat you ain't got none on yone."

"No; mother says that cologne or any kind of perfumery on your hand-kerchief makes you common."

Uncle Remus leaned his head back, closed his eyes, and permitted a heart-rending groan to issue from his lips. The little boy showed enough anxiety to ask him what the matter was. "Nothin' much, honey; I wuz des tryin' fer ter count how many diffunt kinder people dey is in dis big worl', an' 'fo' I got mo' dan half done wid my countin', a pain struck me in my mizry, an' I had ter break off."

"I know what you mean," said the child. "You think mother is queer; grandmother thinks so too."

"How come you ter be so wise, honey?" Uncle Remus inquired, opening his eyes wide with astonishment.

"I know by the way you talk, and by the way grandmother looks some-times," answered the little boy.

Uncle Remus said nothing for some time. When he did speak, it was to lead the little boy to believe that he had been all the time engaged in thinking about something else. "Talkin' er dirty folks," he said, "you oughter seed yo' pa when he wuz a little bit er chap. Dey wuz long days when you couldn't tell ef he wuz black er white, he wuz dat dirty. He'd come out'n de big house in de mornin' ez clean ez a new pin, an' fo' ten er-clock you couldn't tell what kinder clof his cloze wuz made out'n. Many's de day when I've seed ol' Miss — dat's yo' great-gran'mammy — comb nuff trash out'n his head fer ter fill a basket."

The little boy laughed at the picture that Uncle Remus drew of his father. "He's very clean now," said the lad loyally.

"Maybe he is an' maybe he ain't," remarked Uncle Remus, suggesting a doubt. "Dat's needer here ner dar. Is he any better off clean dan what he wuz when you couldn't put yo' han's on 'im widout havin' ter go an' wash um? Yo' gran'-mammy useter call 'im a pig, an' clean ez he may be now, I take notice dat he makes mo' complaint er headache an' de heartburn dan what he done when he wuz runnin' roun' here half-naked an' full er mud. I hear tell dat some nights he can't git no sleep, but when he wuz little like you — no, suh, I'll not say dat, bekaze he wuz bigger dan what you is fum de time he kin toddle 'roun' widout nobody he'pin' him; but when he wuz ol' ez you an' twice ez big, dey ain't narry night dat he can't sleep — an' not only all night, but half de day ef dey'd a let 'im. Dey ought ter let you run 'roun' here like he done, an' git dirty. Dey ain't nothin' mo' wholesomer dan a peck er two er clean dirt on a little chap like you."

There is no telling what comment the child would have made on this sincere tribute to clean dirt, for his attention was suddenly attracted to something that was gradually taking shape in the hands of Uncle Remus. At first it seemed to be hardly worthy of notice, for it had been only a thin piece of board. But now the one piece had become four pieces, two long and two short, and under the deft manipulations of Uncle Remus it soon assumed a boxlike shape.

The old man had reached the point of his work where silence was necessary to enable him to do it full justice. As he fitted the thin boards together, a whistling sound issued from his lips, as though he were letting off steam; but the singular noise was due to the fact that he was completely absorbed in his work. He continued to fit and trim, and trim and fit, until finally the little boy could no longer restrain his curiosity. "Uncle Remus, what are you making?" he asked plaintively.

"Larroes fer ter ketch meddlers," was the prompt and blunt reply.

"Well, what are larroes to catch meddlers?" the child insisted.

"Nothin' much an' sump'n' mo'. Dicky, Dicky, kil't a chicky, an' fried it quicky, in de oven, like a sloven. Den ter his daddy's Sunday hat, he tuck'n hitched de ol' black cat. Now what you reckon make him do dat? Ef you can't tell me word fer word an' spellin' we'll go out an' come in an' take a walk."

He rose, grunting as he did so, thus paying an unintentional tribute to the efficacy of age as the partner of rheumatic aches and stiff joints. "You hear me gruntin'," he remarked — "well, dat's bekaze I ain't de chicky fried by Dicky, which he e't nuff fer ter make 'im sicky." As he went out the child took his hand, and went trotting along by his side, thus affording an interesting study for those who concern themselves with the extremes of life. Hand in hand the two went out into the fields, and thence into the great woods, where Uncle Remus, after searching about for some time, carefully deposited his oblong box, remarking: "Ef I don't make no mistakes, dis ain't so mighty fur fum de place whar de creeturs has der play-groun', an dey ain't no tellin' but what one un um 'll creep in dar when dey er playin' hidin', an' ef he do, he'll sho be our meat."

"Oh, it's a trap!" exclaimed the little boy, his face lighting up with enthusiasm.

"An' dey wa'n't nobody here fer ter tell you!" Uncle Remus declared, astonishment in his tone. "Well, ef dat don't bang my time, I ain't no free nigger. Now, ef dat had a been yo' pa at de same age, I'd a had ter tell 'im forty-'lev'm times, an' den he wouldn't a b'lieved me twel he see sump'n' in dar tryin' fer ter git out. Den he'd say it wuz a trap, but not befo'. I ain't blamin' 'im," Uncle Remus went on, "kaze 'tain't eve'y chap dat kin tell a trap time he see it, an' mo' dan dat, traps don' allers ketch what dey er sot fer."

He paused, looked all around, and up in the sky, where fleecy clouds were floating lazily along, and in the tops of the trees, where the foliage was swaying gently in the breeze. Then he looked at the little boy. "Ef I ain't gone an' got los'," he said, "ain't so mighty fur fum de place whar Mr. Man, once 'pon a time — not yo' time ner yit my time, but some time — tuck 'n' sot a trap fer Brer Rabbit. In dem days, dey hadn't l'arnt how to be kyarpenters, an' dish yer trap what I'm tellin' you 'bout wuz a great big contraption. Big ez Brer Rabbit wuz, it wuz lots too big fer him.

"Now, whiles Mr. Man wuz fixin' up dis trap, Mr. Rabbit wa'n't so mighty fur off. He hear de saw — er-rash! er-rash! — an' he hear de hammer — bang, bang, bang! — an' he ax hisse'f what all dis racket wuz 'bout. He see Mr. Man come out'n his yard totin' sump'n', an' he got furder off; he see Mr. Man comin' todes de bushes, an' he tuck ter de woods; he see 'im comin' todes de woods, an' he tuck ter de bushes. Mr.

Man tote de trap so fur an' no furder. He put it down, he did, an' Brer Rabbit watch 'im; he put in de bait, an' Brer Rabbit watch 'im; he fix de trigger, an' still Brer Rabbit watch 'im. Mr. Man look at de trap an' it satchify him. He look at it an' laugh, an' when he do dat, Brer Rabbit wunk one eye, an' wiggle his mustash, an' chaw his cud.

"An' dat ain't all he do, needer. He sot out in de bushes, he did, an' study how ter git some game in de trap. He study so hard, an' he got so errytated, dat he thumped his behime foot on de groun' twel it soun' like a cow dancin' out dar in de bushes, but 'twa'n't no cow, ner yit no calf — 'twuz des Brer Rabbit studyin'. Atter so long a time, he put out down de road todes dat part er de country whar mos' er de creeturs live at. Eve'y time he hear a fuss, he'd dodge in de bushes, kaze he wanter see who comin'. He keep on an' he keep on, an' bimeby he hear ol' Brer Wolf trottin' down de road.

"It so happen dat Brer Wolf wuz de ve'y one what Brer Rabbit wanter see. Dey was perlite ter one an'er, but dey wa'n't no frien'ly feelin' twix'

um. Well, here come ol' Brer Wolf, hongrier dan a chicken-hawk on a
frosty mornin', an' ez he come up he see Brer Rabbit settin' by de side er
de road lookin' like he done los' all his fambly an' his frien's ter boot.

"Dey pass de time er day, an' den Brer Wolf kinder grin an' say,
'Laws-a-massy, Brer Rabbit, what ail you? You look like you done had a
spell er fever an' ague; what de trouble?' 'Trouble, Brer Wolf? You ain't
never see no trouble twel you git whar I'm at. Maybe you wouldn't min'
it like I does, kaze I ain't usen ter it. But I boun' you done seed me light-
minded fer de las' time. I'm done — I'm plum wo' out,' sez Brer Rabbit,
sezee. Dis make Brer Wolf open his eyes wide. He say, 'Dis de fus' time
I ever is hear you talk dat a-way, Brer Rabbit; take yo' time an' tell me
'bout it. I ain't had my brekkus yit, but dat don't make no diffunce, long
ez you er in trouble. I'll he'p you out ef I kin, an' mo' dan dat, I'll put
some heart in de work.' When he say dis, he grin an' show his tushes, an'
Brer Rabbit kinder edge 'way fum 'im. He say, 'Tell me de trouble, Brer
Rabbit, an' I'll do my level bes' fer ter he'p you out.'

"Wid dat, Brer Rabbit 'low dat Mr. Man done been hire him fer ter
take keer er his truck patch, an' keep out de minks, de mush-rats, an' de
weasels. He say dat he done so well settin' up night atter night, when he
des mought ez well been in bed, dat Mr. Man prommus 'im sump'n' extry 'sides de mess er greens what he gun 'im eve'y day. Atter so long a
time, he say, Mr. Man 'low dat he gwine ter make 'im a present uv a cradle so he kin rock de little Rabs ter sleep when dey cry. So said, so done,
he say. Mr. Man make de cradle an' tell Brer Rabbit he kin take it home
wid 'im. He start out wid it, he say, but it got so heavy he hatter set it
down in de woods, an' dat's de reason why Brer Wolf seed 'im settin'
down by de side er de road, lookin' like he in deep trouble. Brer Wolf sot
down, he did, an' study, an' bimeby he say he'd like mighty well fer ter
have a cradle fer his chillun, long ez cradles wuz de style. Brer Rabbit
say dey been de style fer de longest, an' ez fer Brer Wolf wantin' one, he
say he kin have de one what Mr. Man make fer him, kaze it's lots too big
fer his chillun. 'You know how folks is,' sez Brer Rabbit, sezee. 'Dey try
ter do what dey dunner how ter do, an' dar's der house bigger dan a barn,
an' dar's de fence wid mo' holes in it dan what dey is in a seine, an' kaze
dey have great big chillun dey got de idee dat eve'y cradle what dey

make mus' fit der own chillun. An' dat's how come I can't tote de cradle what Mr. Man make fer me mo' dan ten steps at a time.'

"Brer Wolf ax Brer Rabbit what he gwine ter do fer a cradle, an' Brer Rabbit 'low he kin manage fer ter git long wid de ol' one twel he kin 'suade Mr. Man ter make 'im an'er one, an' he don't speck dat'll be so mighty hard ter do. Brer Wolf can't he'p but b'lieve dey's some trick in it, an' he say he ain't see de ol' cradle when las' he wuz at Brer Rabbit house. Wid dat, Brer Rabbit bust out laughin'. He say, 'Dat's been so long back, Brer Wolf, dat I done fergit all 'bout it; 'sides dat, ef dey wuz a cradle dar, I boun' you my ol' 'oman got better sense dan ter set it in de parler, whar comp'ny comes;' an' he laugh so loud an' so long dat he make Brer Wolf right shame er himse'f.

"He 'low, ol' Brer Wolf did, 'Come on, Brer Rabbit, an' show me whar de cradle is. Ef it's too big fer yo' chillun, it'll des 'bout fit mine.' An' so off dey put ter whar Mr. Man done sot his trap. 'Twa'n't so mighty long 'fo' dey got whar dey wuz gwine, an' Brer Rabbit say, 'Brer Wolf, dar yo' cradle, an' may it do you mo' good dan it's yever done me!' Brer Wolf walk all 'roun' de trap an' look at it like 'twuz 'live. Brer Rabbit thump one er his behime foots on de groun' an' Brer Wolf jump like some un done shot a gun right at 'im. Dis make Brer Rabbit laugh twel he can't laugh no mo'. Brer Wolf, he say he kinder nervous 'bout dat time er de year, an' de leas' little bit er noise'll make 'im jump. He ax how he gwine ter git any purchis on de cradle, an' Brer Rabbit say he'll hatter git inside an' walk wid it on his back, kaze dat de way he done done.

"Brer Wolf ax what all dem contraptions on de inside is, an' Brer Rabbit 'spon' dat dey er de rockers, an' dey ain't no needs fer ter be skeer'd un um, kaze dey ain't nothin' but plain wood. Brer Wolf say he ain't zackly skeer'd, but he done got ter de p'int whar he know dat you better look 'fo' you jump. Brer Rabbit 'low dat ef dey's any jumpin' fer ter be done, he de one ter do it, an' he talk like he done fergit what dey come fer. Brer Wolf, he fool an' fumble 'roun', but bimeby he walk in de cradle, sprung de trigger, an' dar he wuz! Brer Rabbit, he holler out, 'Come on, Brer Wolf; des hump yo'se'f, an' I'll be wid you.' But try ez he will an' grunt ez he may, Brer Wolf can't budge dat trap. Bimeby Brer Rabbit git tired er waitin' an' he say dat ef Brer Wolf ain't gwine ter come on he's gwine home. He 'low dat a frien' what say he gwine ter he'p you, an' den go in a cradle an' drap off ter sleep, dat's all he wanter know 'bout um; an' wid dat he made fer de bushes, an' he wa'n't a minnit too soon, kaze here come Mr. Man fer ter see ef his trap had been sprung. He look, he did, an' sho nuff, it 'uz sprung, an' dey wuz sump'n' in dar, too, kaze he kin hear it rustlin' 'roun' an' kickin' fer ter git out.

"Mr. Man look thoo de crack, an' he see Brer Wolf, which he wuz so skeer'd twel his eye look right green. Mr. Man say, 'Aha! I got you, is I?' Brer Wolf say, 'Who?' Mr. Man laugh twel he can't skacely talk, an' still Brer Wolf say, 'Who? Who you think you got?' Mr. Man 'low, 'I don't think, I knows. You er ol' Brer Rabbit, dat's who you is.' Brer Wolf say, 'Turn me outer here, an' I'll show you who I is.' Mr. Man laugh fit ter kill. He 'low, 'You nee'nter change yo' voice; I'd know you ef I met you in de dark. You er Brer Rabbit, dat's who you is.' Brer Wolf say, 'I ain't not; dat's what I'm not!'

"Mr. Man look thoo de crack ag'in, an' he see de short years. He 'low, 'You done cut off yo' long years, but still I knows you. Oh, yes! an' you done sharpen yo' mouf an' put smut on it — but you can't fool me.' Brer Wolf say, 'Nobody ain't tryin' fer ter fool you. Look at my fine long bushy tail.' Mr. Man 'low, 'You done tied an'er tail on behime you, but you can't fool me. Oh, no, Brer Rabbit! You can't fool me.' Brer Wolf say, 'Look at de ha'r on my back; do dat look like Brer Rabbit?' Mr. Man 'low, 'You done wallered in de red san', but you can't fool me.'

"Brer Wolf say, 'Look at my long black legs; do dey look like Brer Rabbit?' Mr. Man 'low, 'You kin put an'er j'int in yo' legs, an' you kin smut um, but you can't fool me.' Brer Wolf say, 'Look at my tushes; does dey look like Brer Rabbit?' Mr. Man 'low, 'You done got new toofies, but you can't fool me.' Brer Wolf say, 'Look at my little eyes; does dey look like Brer Rabbit?' Mr. Man 'low, 'You kin squinch yo' eyeballs, but you can't fool me, Brer Rabbit.' Brer Wolf squall out, 'I ain't not Brer Rabbit, an' you better turn me out er dis place so I kin take hide an ha'r off'n Brer Rabbit.' Mr. Man say, "Ef bofe hide an' ha'r wuz off, I'd know you, kaze 'tain't in you fer ter fool me.' An' it hurt Brer Wolf feelin's so bad fer Mr. Man ter 'spute his word, dat he bust out inter a big boo-hoo, an' dat's 'bout all I know."

"Did the man really and truly think that Brother Wolf was Brother Rabbit?" asked the little boy.

"When you pin me down dat away," responded Uncle Remus, "I'm bleeze ter tell you dat I ain't too certain an' sho' 'bout dat. De tale come down fum my great-grandaddy's great-grandaddy; it come on down ter my daddy, an' des ez he gun it ter me, des dat away I done gun it ter you."

13
Brother Rabbit and Brother Bull-Frog

THE DAY that the little boy got permission to go to mill with Uncle Remus was to be long remembered. It was a brand-new experience to the city-bred child, and he enjoyed it to the utmost. It is true that Uncle Remus didn't go to mill in the old-fashioned way, but even if the little chap had known of the old-fashioned way, his enjoyment would not have been less. Instead of throwing a bag of corn on the back of a horse, and perching himself on top in an uneasy and a precarious position, Uncle Remus placed the corn in a spring wagon, helped the little boy to climb into the seat, clucked to the horse, and went along as smoothly and as rapidly as though they were going to town.

Everything was new to the lad — the road, the scenery, the mill, and the big mill-pond, and, best of all, Uncle Remus allowed him to enjoy himself in his own way when they came to the end of their journey. He was such a cautious and timid child, having little or none of the spirit of adventure that is supposed to dominate the young, that the old Negro was sure he would come to no harm. Instead of wandering about, and going to places where he had no business to go, the little boy sat where he could see the water flowing over the big dam. He had never seen such a sight before, and the water seemed to him to have a personality of its own — a personality with both purpose and feeling.

The river was not a very large one, but it was large enough to be impressive when its waters fell and tumbled over the big dam. The little boy watched the tumbling water as it fell over the dam and tossed itself into foam on the rocks below; he watched it so long, and he sat so still that he was able to see things that a noisier youngster would have missed altogether. He saw a big bull-frog creep warily from the water, and wipe his mouth and eyes with one of his fore legs and he saw the same frog edge himself softly toward a white butterfly that was flitting about near the edge of the stream. He saw the frog lean forward, and then the butterfly vanished. It seemed like a piece of magic. The child knew that the frog had caught the butterfly, but how? The fluttering insect was more than a foot from the frog when it disappeared, and he was sure that the frog had neither jumped nor snapped at the butterfly. What he saw, he saw as plainly as you can see your hand in the light of day.

And he saw another sight too that is not given to every one to see. While he was watching the tumbling water, and wondering where it all came from and where it was going, he thought he saw swift-moving shadows flitting from the water below up and into the mill-pond above. He never would have been able to discover just what the shadows were if one of them had not paused a moment while half-way to the top of the falling water. It poised itself for one brief instant, as a humming-bird poises over a flower, but during that fraction of time the little boy was able to see that what he thought was a shadow was really a fish going from the water below to the mill-pond above. The child could hardly believe his eyes, and for a little while it seemed that the whole world was turned topsy-turvy, especially as the shadows continued to flit from the water below to the mill-pond above.

And he was still more puzzled when he reported the strange fact to Uncle Remus, for the old Negro took the information as a matter of course. With him the phenomenon was almost as old as his experience. The only explanation that he could give of it was that the fish — or some kinds of fish, and he didn't know rightly what kind it was — had a habit of falling from the bottom of the falls to the top. The most that he knew was that it was a fact, and that it was occurring every day in the year when the fish were running. It was certainly wonderful, as in fact everything would be wonderful if it were not so familiar.

"We ain't got but one way er lookin' at things," remarked Uncle Remus, "an' ef you'll b'lieve me, honey, it's a mighty one-sided way. Ef you could git on a perch somers an' see things like dey reely is, an' not like dey seem ter us, I be boun' you'd hol' yo' breff an' shet yo' eyes."

The old man, without intending it, was going too deep into a deep subject for the child to follow him, and so the latter told him about the bull-frog and the butterfly. The statement seemed to call up pleasing reminiscences, for Uncle Remus laughed in a very hearty way. And when his laughing had subsided, he continued to chuckle until the little boy wondered what the source of his amusement could be. Finally he asked the old Negro point-blank what had caused him to laugh at such a rate.

"Yo' pa would a know'd," Uncle Remus replied, and then he grew solemn again and sighed heavily. For a little while he seemed to be listening to the clatter of the mill, but, finally, he turned to the little boy. "An' so you done made de 'quaintance er ol' Brer Bull-Frog? Is you take notice whedder he had a tail er no?"

"Why, of course he didn't have a tail!" exclaimed the child. "Neither toad-frogs nor bull-frogs have tails. I thought everybody knew that."

"Oh, well, ef dat de way you feel 'bout um, 'tain't no use fer ter pester wid um. It done got so now dat folks don't b'lieve nothin' but what dey kin see, an' mo' dan half un um won't b'lieve what dey see less'n dey kin feel un it too. But dat ain't de way wid dem what's ol' nuff fer ter know. Ef I'd a tol' you 'bout de fishes swimmin' ag'in' fallin' water, you wouldn't a b'lieved me, would you? No, you wouldn't — an' yit, dar 'twuz right 'fo' yo' face an' eyes. Dar dey wuz a-skeetin' fum de bottom er de dam right up in de mill-pon', an' you settin' dar lookin' at um. S'pos'n' you wuz ter say dat you won't b'lieve um less'n you kin feel um; does you speck de fish gwine ter hang dar in de fallin' water an' wait twel you kin wade 'cross de slipp'y rocks an' put yo' han' on um? Did you look right close fer ter see ef de bull-frog what you seed is got a tail er no?"

The little boy admitted that he had not. He knew as well as anybody that no kind of a frog has a tail, unless it is the Texas frog, which is only a horned lizard, for he saw one once in Atlanta and it was nothing but a rusty-back lizard with a horn on his head.

"I ain't 'sputin' what you say, honey," said Uncle Remus, "but de creetur what you seed mought a been a frog an' you not know it. One thing I does know is dat in times gone by de bull-frog had a tail, kaze I hear de ol' folks sesso, an' mo' dan dat, dey know'd des how he los' it — de whar, an' de when, an' de which-away. Fer all I know it wuz right here at dish yer identual mill-pon'. I ain't gwine inter court an' make no affle-dave on it, but ef anybody wuz ter walk up an' p'int der finger at me, an' say dat dis is de place whar ol' Brer Bull-Frog lose his tail, I'd up an' 'low, 'Yasser, it mus' be de place, kaze it look might'ly like de place what I been hear tell 'bout.' An' den I'd shet my eyes an' see ef I can't git it straight in my dream."

Uncle Remus paused, and pretended to be counting a handful of red grains of corn that he had found somewhere in the mill. Seeing that he showed no disposition to tell how Brother Bull-Frog had lost his tail, the little boy reminded him of it. But the old man laughed. "Ef Brer Bull-Frog ain't never had no tail," he said, "how de name er goodness he gwine ter lose um? Ef he yever is had a tail, why den dat's a gray hoss uv an'er color. Dey's a tale 'bout 'im havin' a tail an' losin' it, but how kin dey be a tale when dey ain't no tail?"

Well, the little boy didn't know at all, and he looked so disconsolate and so confused that the old Negro relented. "Now, den," he remarked, "ef ol' Brer Bull-Frog had a tail an' he ain't got none now, dey must a been sump'n' happen. In dem times — de times what all deze tales tells you 'bout — Brer Bull-Frog stayed in an' aroun' still water des like he do now. De bad col' dat he had in dem days, he's got it yit — de same pop-eyes, an' de same bal' head. Den, ez now, dey wa'n't a bunch er ha'r on it dat you could pull out wid a pa'r er tweezers. Ez he bellers now, des dat a-way he bellered den, mo' speshually at night. An' talk 'bout settin' up late — why, ol' Brer Bull-Frog could beat dem what fust got in de habits er settin' up late.

"Dey's one thing dat you'll hatter gi' 'im credit fer, an' dat wuz keepin' his face an' han's clean, an' in takin' keer er his cloze. Nobody, not even his mammy, had ter patch his britches er tack buttons on his coat. See 'im whar you may an' when you mought, he wuz allers lookin' spick an' span des like he done come right out'n a ban'-box. You know what de riddle say 'bout 'im; When he stan' up he sets down, an' when he walks he hops. He'd a been mighty well thunk un, ef it hadn't but a been fer his habits. He holler so much at night dat de yuther creeturs can't git no sleep. He'd holler an' holler, an' 'bout de time you think he bleeze ter be 'shame' er hollerin' so much, he'd up an' holler ag'in. It got so dat de creeturs hatter go 'way off somers ef dey wanter git any sleep, an' it seem like dey can't git so fur off but what Brer Bull-Frog would wake um up time dey git ter dozin' good.

"He'd raise up an' 'low, *'Here I is! Here I is! Whar'bouts is you? Whar'bouts is you? Come along! Come along!'* It 'uz des dat a-way de

whole blessed night, an' de yuther creeturs, dey say dat it sholy was a shame dat anybody would set right flat-footed an' ruin der good name.

Look like he pestered eve'ybody but ol' Brer Rabbit, an' de reason dat he liked it wuz kaze it worried de yuther creeturs. He'd set an' lissen, ol' Brer Rabbit would, an' den he'd laugh fit ter kill kaze he ain't a-keerin' whedder er no he git any sleep er not. Ef dey's anybody what kin set up twel de las' day in de mornin' an' not git red-eyed an' heavy-headed, it's ol' Brer Rabbit. When he wanter sleep, he'd des shet one eye an' sleep, an' when he wanter stay 'wake, he'd des open bofe eyes, an' dar he wuz wid all his foots under 'im, an' a-chawin' his terbacker same ez ef dey wa'n't no Brer Bull-Frog in de whole Nunited State er Georgy.

"It went on dis way fer I dunner how long — ol' Brer Bull-Frog a-bellerin' all night long an' keepin' de yuther creeturs 'wake, an' Brer Rabbit a-laughin'. But, bimeby, de time come when Brer Rabbit hatter lay in some mo' calamus root, ag'in' de time when 'twould be too col' fer ter dig it, an' when he went fer ter hunt fer it, his way led 'im down todes de mill-pon' whar Brer Bull-Frog live at. Dey wuz calamus root a-plenty down dar, an' Brer Rabbit, atter lookin' de groun' over, prommus hisse'f dat he'd fetch a basket de nex' time he come, an' make one trip do fer two. He ain't been down dar long 'fo' he had a good chance fer ter hear Brer Bull-Frog at close range. He hear him, he did, an' he shake his head an' say dat a mighty little bit er dat music would go a long ways, kaze dey ain't nobody what kin stan' flat-footed an' say dat Brer Bull-Frog is a better singer dan de mockin'-bird.

"Well, whiles Brer Rabbit wuz pirootin' 'roun' fer ter see what mought be seed, he git de idee dat he kin hear thunder way off yander. He lissen ag'in, an' he hear Brer Bull-Frog mumblin' an' grumblin' ter hisse'f, an' he must a had a mighty bad col', kaze his talk soun' des like a bummil-eye bee been kotch' in a sugar-barrel an' can't git out. An' dat creetur must a know'd dat Brer Rabbit wuz down in dem neighborhoods, kaze, atter while, he 'gun to talk louder, an' yit mo' louder. He say, *'Whar you gwine? Whar you gwine?'* an' den, *'Don't go too fur — don't go too fur!'* an', atter so long a time, *'Come back — come back! Come back soon!'* Brer Rabbit, he sot dar, he did, an' work his nose an' wiggle his mouf, an' wait fer ter see what gwine ter happen nex'.

"Whiles Brer Rabbit settin' dar, Brer Bull-Frog fall ter mumblin' ag'in an' it look like he 'bout ter drap off ter sleep, but bimeby he talk

louder, *'Be my frien' — be my frien'! Oh, be my frien'!'* Brer Rabbit wunk one eye an' smole a smile, kaze he done hear a heap er talk like dat. He wipe his face an' eyes wid his pocket-hankcher, an' sot so still dat you'd a thunk he wa'n't nothin' but a chunk er wood. But Brer Bull-Frog, he know'd how ter stay still hisse'f, an' he ain't so much ez bubble a bubble. But atter whiles, when Brer Rabbit can't stay still no mo', he got up fum whar he wuz settin' at an' moseyed out by de mill-race whar de grass is fresh an' de trees is green.

"Brer Bull-Frog holler, *'Jug-er-rum — jug-er-rum! Wade in here — I'll gi' you some!'* Now dey ain't nothin' dat ol' Brer Rabbit like better dan a little bit er dram fer de stomach-ache, an' his mouf 'gun ter water right den an' dar. He went a little closer ter de mill-pon', an' Brer Bull-Frog keep on a-talk-in' 'bout de jug er rum, an' what he gwine do ef Brer

Rabbit will wade in dar. He look at de water, an' it look mighty col'; he
look ag'in an' it look mighty deep. It say, 'Lap-lap!' an' it look like it's a-
creepin' higher. Brer Rabbit drawed back wid a shiver, an' he wish
mighty much dat he'd a fotch his overcoat.

   "Brer Bull-Frog say, *'Knee deep — knee deep! Wade in — wade in!'*
an' he make de water bubble des like he takin' a dram. Den an' dar,
sump'n' n'er happen, an' how it come ter happen Brer Rabbit never kin
tell; but he peeped in de pon' fer ter see ef he kin ketch a glimp er de jug,
an' in he went — *kerchug!* He ain't never know whedder he fall in, er
slip in, er ef he was pushed in, but dar he wuz! He come mighty nigh not
gittin' out; but he scramble an' he scuffle twel he git back ter de bank

whar he kin clim' out, an' he stood dar, he did, an' kinder shuck hisse'f, kaze he mighty glad fer ter fin' dat he's in de worl' once mo'. He know'd dat a leetle mo' an' he'd a been gone fer good, kaze when he drapped in, er jumped in, er fell in, he wuz over his head an' years, an' he hatter do a sight er kickin' an' scufflin' an' swallerin' water 'fo' he kin git whar he kin grab de grass on de bank.

"He sneeze an' snoze, an' wheeze an' whoze, twel it look like he'd drown right whar he wuz stan'in' any way you kin fix it. He say ter hisse'f dat he ain't never gwine ter git de tas'e er river water outer his mouf an' nose, an' he wonder how in de worl' dat plain water kin be so watery. Ol' Brer Bull-Frog, he laugh like a bull in de pastur', an' Brer Rabbit gi' a sidelong look dat oughter tol' 'im ez much ez a map kin tell one er deze yer school scholars. Brer Rabbit look at 'im, but he ain't say narry a word. He des shuck hisse'f once mo', an' put out fer home whar he kin set in front er de fier an' git dry.

"Atter dat day, Brer Rabbit riz mighty soon an' went ter bed late, an' he watch Brer Bull-Frog so close dat dey wa'n't nothin' he kin do but what Brer Rabbit know 'bout it time it 'uz done; an' one thing he know'd better dan all — he know'd dat when de winter time come Brer Bull-Frog would have ter pack up his duds an' move over in de bog whar de water don't git friz up. Dat much he know'd, an' when dat time come, he laid off fer ter make Brer Bull-Frog's journey, short ez it wuz, ez full er hap'nin's ez de day when de ol' cow went dry. He tuck an' move his bed an' board ter de big holler poplar, not fur fum de mill-pon', an' dar he stayed an' keep one eye on Brer Bull-Frog bofe night an' day. He ain't lose no flesh whiles he waitin', kaze he ain't one er deze yer kin' what mopes an' gits sollumcolly; he wuz all de time betwixt a grin an' a giggle.

"He know'd mighty well — none better — dat time goes by turns in deze low groun's, an' he wait fer de day when Brer Bull-Frog gwine ter move his belongin's fum pon' ter bog. An' bimeby dat time come, an' when it come, Brer Bull-Frog is done fergit off'n his mind all 'bout Brer Rabbit an' his splashification. He rig hisse'f out in his Sunday best, an' he look kerscrumptious ter dem what like dat kinder doin's. He had on a little sojer hat wid green an' white speckles all over it, an' a long green coat, an' satin britches, an' a white silk wescut, an' shoes wid silver buckles. Mo' dan dat, he had a green umbrell', fer ter keep fum havin' freckles, an' his long spotted tail wuz done up in de umbrell' kivver so dat it won't drag on de groun'."

Uncle Remus paused to see what the little boy would say to this last statement, but the child's training prevented the asking of many questions, and so he only laughed at the idea of a frog with a tail, and the tail done up in the cover of a green umbrella. The laughter of the youngster was hearty enough to satisfy the old Negro, and he went on with the story.

"Whiles all dis gwine on, honey, you better b'lieve dat Brer Rabbit wa'n't so mighty fur fum dar. When Brer Bull-Frog come out an' start fer ter promenade ter de bog, Brer Rabbit show hisse'f an' make like he skeered. He broke an' run, an' den he stop fer ter see what 'tis — an' den he run a leetle ways an' stop ag'in, an' he keep on dodgin' an' runnin' twel he fool Brer Bull-Frog inter b'lievin' dat he wuz skeer'd mighty nigh ter death.

"You know how folks does when dey git de idee dat some-body's 'fear'd un um — ef you don't you'll fin' out long 'fo' yo' whiskers gits ter hangin' to yo' knees. When folks take up dis idee, dey gits biggity, an' dey ain't no stayin' in de same country wid um.

"Well, Brer Bull-Frog, he git de idee dat Brer Rabbit wuz 'fear'd un 'im, an' he shuck his umbrell' like he mad, an' he beller: 'Whar my gun?' Brer Rabbit flung up bofe han's like he wuz skeer'd er gittin' a load er

shot in his vitals, an' den he broke an' run ez hard ez he kin. Brer Bull-Frog holler out, 'Come yer, you vilyun, an' le' me gi' you de frailin' what I done prommus you!' but ol' Brer Rabbit, he keep on a-gwine. Brer Bull-Frog went hoppin' atter, but he ain't make much headway, kaze all de time he wuz hoppin' he wuz tryin' to strut.

"'Twuz e'en about ez much ez Brer Rabbit kin do fer ter keep fum laughin', but he led Brer Bull-Frog ter de holler poplar, whar he had his hatchet hid. Ez he went in, he 'low, 'You can't git me!' He went in, he did, an' out he popped on t'er side. By dat time Brer Bull-Frog wuz mighty

certain an' sho dat Brer Rabbit wuz skeer'd ez he kin be, an' inter de
holler he went, widout so much ez takin' de trouble ter shet up his umbrell'. When he got in de holler, in co'se he ain't see hide ner ha'r er Brer
Rabbit, an' he beller out, 'Whar is you? You may hide, but I'll fin' you,
an' when I does — when I does!' He ain't say all he wanter say, kaze by
dat time Brer Rabbit wuz lammin' on de tree wid his hatchet. He hit it
some mighty heavy whacks, an' Brer Bull-Frog git de idee dat somebody
wuz cuttin' it down.

"Dis kinder skeer'd 'im, kaze he know dat ef de tree fell while he in
de holler, it'd be all-night-Isom wid him. But when he make a move fer

ter turn 'roun' in dar fer ter come out, Brer Rabbit run 'roun' ter whar he wuz, an' chop his tail off right smick-smack-smoove."

The veteran story-teller paused, and looked at the clouds that were gathering in the sky. "'Twouldn't 'stonish me none," he remarked dryly, "ef we wuz ter have some fallin' wedder."

"But, Uncle Remus, what happened when Brother Rabbit cut off the Bull-Frog's tail?" inquired the little boy.

The old man sighed heavily, and looked around, as if he were hunting for some way of escape. "Why, honey, when de Frog tail wuz cut off, it stayed off, but dey tells me dat it kep' on a wigglin' plum twel de sun went down. Dis much I does know, dat sence dat day, none er de Frog fambly has been troubled wid tails. Ef you don't believe me you kin ketch um an' see."

14

Why Mr. Dog Is Tame

THERE WERE quite a number of dogs on the plantation — foxhounds, harriers, a sheep dog, and two black-and-tan hounds that had been trained to tree coons and 'possums. In these, the little boy took an abiding interest, and he soon came to know the name and history of each individual dog. There was Jonah, son of Hodo, leader of the foxhounds, Jewel, leader of the harriers, and Walter, the sheep dog, who drove up the cows and hogs every evening. Indeed, it was not long before the little boy knew as much about the dogs as Uncle Remus did.

He imagined he knew more, for one day he informed the old man that once upon a time all dogs were wild, and roamed about the woods and fields just as the wild animals do now.

"You see me settin' here," Uncle Remus remarked; "well, suh, ol' ez I is, I'd like mighty well ter fin' out how you come ter know 'bout deze happ'nin's 'way back yander."

The little boy made no secret of the matter; he answered with pride that his mother had been reading to him out of a great big book with pictures in it. Uncle Remus stretched his arms above his head, and opened wide his eyes. Astonishment took possession of his countenance. The child laughed with delight when he saw the amazement of Uncle Remus. "Yes," he went on, "mother read about all the wild animals. The book said that when the dogs were wild they used to go in droves, just as the wolves do now."

"Yasser, dat's so!" exclaimed Uncle Remus with admiration, "an' ef you keep on like you gwine, 'twon't be long 'fo' you'll know lot's mo' 'bout de creeturs dan what I does — lot's mo'." Then he became confidential — "Wuz dey anything in de big book, honey, 'bout de time dat de Dog start in fer ter live wid Mr. Man?" The little boy shook his head. If there was anything about it in the big book from which his mother had been reading, she had kept it to herself.

"Well, I'm mighty glad dey ain't nothin' in dar 'bout it, kaze ef dey had a been, I'd a been bleeze ter gi' up my job, kaze when dey gits ter puttin' tales in a book, dat's a sign."

"A sign of what, Uncle Remus?"

"Des a sign, honey — a plain sign. Ef you dunner what a sign is, I'll never tell you."

"When did the Dog begin to live with Mr. Man?" the little boy inquired. "Once he was wild, and now he's tame. How did he become tame?"

"Ah-yi! den you got de idee dat ol' man Remus know sump'n' n'er what ain't down in de books?"

"Why, you asked me if there was anything in the big book that told about the time when the Dog went to live with Mr. Man," the little boy replied.

"Dat's what I done," exclaimed Uncle Remus with a laugh.

"An' I done it kaze I laid off ter tell you 'bout it one er deze odd-come-shorts when de moon ridin' high, an' de win' playin' a chune in de big pine."

"Why not tell it now?" the little boy asked.

"Le' me see, is I well er is I sick? Is I full er is I hongry? Ef I done fergot what I had fer dinner day 'fo' yistiddy, den 'tain't no use fer ter tell a tale 'bout ol' times. Wuz it cake? No, 'twa'n't cake. Wuz it chicken-pie? No, 'twa'n't chicken-pie. What, den? Ah-h-h! Now I knows: 'Twuz tater custard, an' it seem like I kin tas'e it yit. Yasser! Day 'fo' yistiddy wuz so long ago dat it look like a dream."

"It wasn't any dream," the little boy declared. "Mother wouldn't let me have any at the house, and when grandmother sent your dinner, she put two pieces of potato custard on a plate, and you said that one of them was for me."

"An' you e't it," Uncle Remus declared; "you e't it, an' you liked it so well dat you sot yo' eye on my piece, an' ef I hadn't a grabbed it, I boun' I wouldn't a had no tater custard."

The little boy laughed and blushed. "How did you know I wanted the other piece?" he asked.

"I know it by my nose an' my two big toes," Uncle Remus replied. "Put a boy in smellin' distance uv a piece er tater custard, an' it seem like de custard will fly up an' hit him in de mouf, no matter how much he try ter dodge."

Uncle Remus paused and pulled a raveling from his shirtsleeve, looking at the little boy meanwhile.

"I know very well you haven't forgotten the story," remarked the child, "for grandmother says you never forgot anything, especially the old-time tales."

"Well, suh, I speck she knows. She been knowin' me ev'ey sence she wuz a baby gal, an' mo' dan dat, she know right p'int-blank what I'm a-thinkin' 'bout when she kin git her eye on me."

"And she says she never caught you tellin' a fib."

"Is she say dat?" Uncle Remus inquired with a broad grin. "Ef she did, I'm lots sharper dan I looks ter be, kaze many and many's de time when I been skeer'd white, thinkin' she done cotch me. Tooby sho, tooby sho!"

"But what about the Dog, Uncle Remus?"

"What dog, honey? Oh, you'll hatter scuzen me — I'm lots older dan what I looks ter be. You mean de Dog what tuck up at Mr. Man's house. Well, ol' Brer Dog wuz e'en about like he is deze days, scratchin' fer fleas, an' growlin' over his vittles stidder sayin' grace, an' berryin' de bones when he had one too many. He wuz des like he is now, 'ceppin' dat he wuz wil'. He galloped wid Brer Fox, an' loped wid Brer Wolf, an' cantered wid Brer Coon. He went all de gaits, an' he had des ez good a time ez any un um, an' des ez bad a time.

"Now, one day, somers 'twix' Monday mornin' an' Saddy night, he wuz settin' in de shade scratchin' hisse'f, an' he wuz tooken wid a spell er

thinkin'. He'd des come thoo a mighty hard winter wid de yuther creeturs, an' he up an' say ter hisse'f dat ef he had ter do like dat one mo' season, it'd be de een' er him an' his fambly. You could count his ribs, an'
his hip-bones stuck out like de horns on a hat-rack.

"Whiles he wuz settin' dar, scratchin' an' studyin', an' studyin' an'
scratchin', who should come meanderin' down de big road but ol' Brer
Wolf; an' it 'uz 'Hello, Brer Dog! you look like you ain't seed de inside uv
a smokehouse fer quite a whet. I ain't sayin' dat I got much fer ter brag
on, kaze I ain't in no better fix dan what you is. De colder it gits, de
skacer de vittles grows.' An' den he ax Brer Dog whar he gwine an' how
soon he gwine ter git dar. Brer Dog make answer dat it don't make no diffunce whar he go ef he don't fin' dinner ready.

"Brer Wolf 'low dat de way ter git dinner is ter make a fier, kaze 'tain't
no use fer ter try ter eat ef dey don't do dat. Ef dey don't git nothin' fer
ter cook, dey'll have a place whar dey kin keep warm. Brer Dog say he
see whar Brer Wolf is dead right, but whar dey gwine git a fier? Brer Wolf
say de quickest way is ter borry a chunk fum Mr. Man er his ol' 'oman.
But when it come ter sayin' who gwine atter it, dey bofe kinder hung
back, kaze dey know'd dat Mr. Man had a walkin'-cane what he kin p'int
at anybody an' snap a cap on it an' blow de light right out.

"But bimeby, Brer Dog say'll go atter de chunk er fier, an' he ain't no
mo' dan say dat, 'fo' off he put, an' he travel so peart, dat 'twa'n't long 'fo'
he come ter Mr. Man's house. When he got ter de gate he sot down an'
done some mo' studyin', an' ef de gate had a been shot, he'd a turned
right roun' an' went back like he come; but some er de chillun had been
playin' out in de yard, an' dey lef' de gate open, an so dar 'twuz. Study ez
he mought, he can't fin' no skuse fer gwine back widout de chunk er fier.
An' in he went.

"Well, talk 'bout folks bein' 'umble; you ain't seed no 'umble-come-
tumble twel you see Brer Dog when he went in dat gate. He ain't take
time fer ter look 'roun', he so skeer'd. He hear hogs a-gruntin' an' pigs a-
squealin', he hear hens a-cacklin' an' roosters crowin', but he ain't turn
his head. He had sense nuff not ter go in de house by de front way. He
went 'roun' de back way whar de kitchen wuz, an' when he got dar he
'fraid ter go any furder. He went ter de do', he did, an' he 'fraid ter knock.

He hear chillun laughin' an' playin' in dar, an' fer de fust time in all his born days, he 'gun ter feel lonesome.

"Bimeby, some un open de do' an' den shot it right quick. But Brer

Dog ain't see nobody; he 'uz too 'umble-come-tumble fer dat. He wuz lookin' at de groun', an' wonderin' what 'uz gwine ter happen nex'. It must a been one er de chillun what open de do', kaze 'twa'n't long 'fo' here come Mr. Man wid de walkin'-cane what had fier in it. He come ter de do', he did, an' he say, 'What you want here?' Brer Dog wuz too skeer'd fer ter talk; all he kin do is ter des wag his tail. Mr. Man, he 'low, 'You in de wrong house, an' you better go on whar you got some business.'

"Brer Dog, he crouch down close ter de groun', an' wag his tail. Mr. Man, he look at 'im, an' he ain't know whedder fer ter turn loose his gun er not, but his ol' 'oman, she hear him talkin', an' she come ter de do', an' see Brer Dog crouchin' dar, 'umbler dan de 'umblest, an' she say, 'Po' feller! you ain't gwine ter hurt nobody, is you?' an' Brer Dog 'low, 'No, ma'am, I ain't; I des come fer ter borry a chunk er fier.' An' she say,

'What in de name er goodness does you want wid fier? Is you gwine ter burn us out'n house an' home?' Brer Dog 'low, 'No, ma'am! dat I ain't; I des wanter git warm.' Den de 'oman say, 'I clean fergot 'bout de col' wedder — come in de kitchen here an' warm yo'se'f much ez you wanter.'

"Dat wuz mighty good news fer Brer Dog, an' in he went. Dey wuz a nice big fier on de h'a'th, an' de chillun wuz settin' all roun' eatin' der dinner. Dey make room fer Brer Dog, an' down he sot in a warm cornder, an' 'twa'n't long 'fo' he wuz feelin' right splimmy-splammy. But he wuz mighty hongry. He sot dar, he did, an' watch de chillun' eatin' der ashcake an' buttermilk, an' his eye-balls 'ud foller eve'y mou'ful dey e't. De 'oman, she notice dis, an' she went ter de cubberd an' got a piece er warm ashcake, an' put it down on de h'a'th.

"Brer Dog ain't need no secon' invite — he des gobble up de ashcake 'fo' you kin say Jack Robberson wid yo' mouf shot. He ain't had nigh nuff, but he know'd better dan ter show what his appetites wuz. He 'gun ter feel good, an' den he got down on his hunkers, an' lay his head down on his fo'paws, an' make like he gwine ter sleep. Atter 'while, he smell Brer Wolf, an' he raise his head an' look todes de do'. Mr. Man he tuck notice, an' he say he b'lieve dey's some un sneakin' 'roun'. Brer Dog raise his head, an' snuff todes de do', an' growl ter hisse'f. So Mr. Man tuck down his gun fum over de fierplace, an' went out. De fust thing he see when he git out in de yard wuz Brer Wolf runnin' out de gate, an' he up wid his gun — bang! — an' he hear Brer Wolf holler. All he got wuz a han'ful er ha'r, but he come mighty nigh gittin' de whole hide.

"Well, atter dat, Mr. Man fin' out dat Brer Dog could do 'im a heap er good, fus' one way an' den an'er. He could head de cows off when dey make a break thoo de woods, he could take keer er de sheep, an' he could warn Mr. Man when some er de yuther creeturs wuz prowlin' 'roun'. An' den he wuz some comp'ny when Mr. Man went huntin'. He could trail de game, an' he could fin' his way home fum anywheres; an' he could play wid de chillun des like he wuz one un um.

"'Twa'n't long 'fo' he got fat, an' one day when he wuz amblin' in de woods, he meet up wid Brer Wolf. He howdied at 'im, he did, but Brer Wolf won't skacely look at 'im. Atter while he say, 'Brer Dog, why'n't you come back dat day when you went atter fier?' Brer Dog p'int ter de collar on his neck. He 'low, 'You see dis? Well, it'll tell you lots better dan what I kin.' Brer Wolf say, 'You mighty fat. Why can't I come dar an' do like you does?' Brer Dog 'low, 'Dey ain't nothin' fer ter hinder you.'

"So de next mornin', bright an' early, Brer Wolf knock at Mr. Man's do'. Mr. Man peep out an' see who 'tis, an' tuck down his gun an' went out. Brer Wolf try ter be perlite, an' he smile. But when he smile he show'd all his tushes, an' dis kinder skeer Mr. Man. He say, 'What you doin' sneakin' 'roun' here?' Brer Wolf try ter be mo' perliter dan ever, an' he grin fum year ter year. Dis show all his tushes, an' Mr. Man lammed aloose at 'im. An' dat 'uz de las' time dat Brer Wolf ever try ter live wid Mr. Man, an fum dat time on down ter dis day, it 'uz war 'twix' Brer Wolf an' Brer Dog."

15
Brother Rabbit and the Gizzard-Eater

"IT SEEM like ter me dat I hear somebody say, not longer dan day 'fo' yistiddy, dat dey'd be mighty glad ef dey could fin' some un fer ter bet wid um," said Uncle Remus, staring hard at the little boy, and then suddenly shutting his eyes tight, so that he might keep from laughing at the expression he saw on the child's face. Receiving no immediate response to his remark, the old man opened his eyes again, and found the little boy regarding him with a puzzled air.

"My mother says it is wrong to bet," said the child after a while. He was quite serious, and it was just this aspect of seriousness that made him a little different from another little boy that had been raised at Uncle Remus's knee. "Mother says that no Christian would want to bet."

The old man closed his eyes again, as though trying to remember something. He frowned and smacked his mouth before he spoke. "It look like dat I never is ter git de tas'e er dat chicken-pie what yo' gran'ma sont me out'n my mouf. I dunner when I been had any chicken-pie what stayed wid me like dat chicken-pie. But 'bout dat bettin'," he remarked, straightening himself in his chair, "I speck I mus' a been a-dreamin'. I know mighty well it couldn't a been you; so we'll des up an' say it wuz little Dreamus, an' let it go at dat. All I know is dat dey wuz a little chap loungin' 'roun' here tryin' fer ter l'arn how ter play mumbly-peg wid one er de case-knives what he tuck fum de white folks' dinner-table, an' whiles he wuz in de middle er his l'arnin', de ol' speckled hen run fum under de house here, an' sot up a mighty cacklin', kaze she fear'd some un wuz gwine ter interrupt de eggs what she been nussin' an' warmin' up. She cackle, an' she cackle, an' den she cackle some mo' fer ter keep fum fergittin' how; an' 'long 'bout dat time, dish yer little boy what I been tellin' you 'bout — I speck we'll be bleeze ter call him Dreamus — he up wid a rock an' flung it right at 'er, an' ef she'd a been in de way er de rock, he'd a come mighty nigh hittin' her. Dis make de ol' hen bofe skeer'd an' feard an' likewise mad, an' she hitched a squall on ter her cackle, an' flop her wings. Seein' dat de hen wuz mad, dis little chap, which he name Dreamus, he got mad, too, an' he 'lowed, 'I bet you I make you hush!' an' dar dey had it, de ol' hen runnin' an' squallin', an' de little chap zoonin' rocks at her. I speck de hen would a bet ef she'd a know'd how — an' she sho would a won de bet, kaze de las' news I hear fum 'er she wuz runnin' an' squallin'.''

The little boy squirmed uneasily in his chair. He remembered the incident very well, so well that he hardly knew what to say. But after a while, thinking that it was both necessary and polite to say something, he declared that when he made that remark to the hen he knew she wouldn't understand him, and that what he said about betting was just a saying.

"Dat mought be, honey," said Uncle Remus, "but don't you fool yo'se'f 'bout dat hen not knowin' how ter talk, kaze dey has been times an' places when de creeturs kin do lots mo' talkin' dan folks. When you git ter be ol' ez what I is, you'll know dat talkin' ain't got nothin' in de roun' worl' ter do wid fedders, an' needer wid fur. I hear you say you want ter bet wid de ol' hen, an' ef you still wantin' you got a mighty good chance dis day ef de sun is mighty nigh down. I'll bet you a thrip ag'in' a gingercake dat when you had yo' dinner you ain't fin' no chicken gizzard in yo' part er de pie."

"No," replied the child, "I didn't, and when I asked grandmother about it, she said she was going to raise some chickens next year with double gizzards."

"Did she say dat? Did Miss Sally say dat?" inquired Uncle Remus, laughing delightedly. "Well, suh, dat sho do bang my time! How come she ter know dat some er de creeturs got double gizzards? She sho is de outdoin'est white 'oman what's yever been bornded inter de worl'. She done sont me de chicken gizzard des so I kin tell you 'bout de double gizzards an' de what-nots. Double gizzards! De ve'y name flings me 'way back yander ter ol' folks an' ol' times. Laws-a-massy! I wonder what Miss Sally gwine do nex'; anybody what guess it oughter be president by good rights." Uncle Remus paused, and lowered his voice to a confidential tone — "She ain't tell you 'bout de time when de Yalligater wuz honin' fer ol' Brer Rabbit's double gizzards, is she, honey?"

"No, she didn't tell me that, but she laughed, and when I asked her what she was laughing at, she said I'd find out by the time I was seven feet tall."

"You hear dat, don't you?" Uncle Remus spoke as though there were a third person in the room. "What I been tellin' you all dis time?" and then he laughed as though this third person were laughing with him. "You may try, an' you may fly, but you never is ter see de beat er Miss Sally."

"Was grandmother talking about a tale, Uncle Remus? It must have been a very funny one, for she laughed until she had to take off her spectacles and wipe them dry," said the little boy.

"Dat's her! dat's Miss Sally up an' down, an' dey can't nobody git ahead er her. She know'd mighty well dat time you say sump'n' 'bout double gizzards my min' would fly right back ter de time when de Yalligater wuz dribblin' at de mouf, an' ole Brer Rabbit wuz shaking in his shoes."

"If it's a long story, I'm afraid you haven't time to tell it now," suggested the little boy.

The child was so polite that the old Negro stood somewhat in awe of him, and he was afraid, too, that it was ominous of some misfortune — there was something uncanny about it from Uncle Remus's point of view. "Bless you, honey! I got des ez much time ez what dey is — it all b'longs ter me an' you. Maybe you wanter go somers else; maybe you'll wait twel some yuther day fer de platted whip dat I hear you talkin' 'bout."

"No; I'll wait and get the story and the whip together — if you are not too tired."

The old Negro looked at the little boy from the corner of his eye to see if he was really in earnest. Satisfying himself on that score, he promptly began to plait the whip while he unraveled the story. He seemed to be more serious than usual, but one of the peculiarities of Uncle Remus, as many a child had discovered, was that he was not to be judged by any outward aspect. This is the way he began:

"Ever since I been pirootin' 'roun' in deze lowgroun's, it's been de talk er dem what know'd dat Brer Rabbit wuz a mighty man at a frolic. I don't speck he'd show up much in deze days, but in de times when de creeturs wuz bossin' dey own jobs, Brer Rabbit wuz up fer perty nigh ev'ything dat wuz gwine on ef dey wa'n't too much work in it. Dey couldn't be a dance er a quiltin' nowhar's aroun' but what he'd be dar; he wuz fust ter come an' last ter go.

"Well, dey wuz one time when he went too fur an' stayed too late, bekaze a big rain come endurin' de time when dey wuz playin' an' dancin', an' when Brer Rabbit put out fer home, he foun' dat a big freshet done come an' gone. De dreens had got ter be creeks, de creeks had got ter be rivers, an' de rivers — well, I ain't gwine ter tell you what de rivers wuz kaze you'd think dat I done tol' de trufe good-by. By makin' big jumps an' gwine out er his way, Brer Rabbit manage fer ter git ez close ter home ez de creek, but when he git dar, de creek wuz so wide dat it make him feel like he been los' so long dat his fambly done fergot him. Many an' many a time had he cross' dat creek on a log, but de log done gone, an' de water wuz spread out all over creation. De water wuz wide, but dat wa'n't mo' dan half — it look like it wuz de wettest water dat Brer Rabbit ever lay eyes on.

"Dey wuz a ferry dar fer times like dis, but it look like it wuz a bigger fresh' dan what dey had counted on. Brer Rabbit, he sot on de bank an' wipe de damp out'n his face an' eyes, an' den he holler'd fer de man what run de ferry. He holler'd an' holler'd, an' bimeby, he hear some un answer him, an' he looked a little closer, an' dar wuz de man, which his name wuz Jerry, way up in de top lim's uv a tree; an' he looked still closer, an' he seed dat Jerry had company, kaze dar wuz ol' Brer B'ar settin' at de foot er de tree, waitin' fer Jerry fer ter come down so he kin tell 'im howdy." Uncle Remus paused to see what effect this statement would have on the little boy. The youngster said nothing, but his shrewd smile showed the old man that he fully appreciated the reason why Jerry was in no hurry to shake hands with Brother Bear.

"Well, suh, Brer Rabbit took notice dat dey wuz sump'n' mo' dan dampness 'twix' um, an' he start in ter holler again, an' he holler'd so loud, an' he holler'd so long, dat he woke up ol' Brer Yalligater. Now, it ain't make ole Brer Yalligater feel good fer ter be wokened up at dat hour, kaze he'd des had a nice supper er pine-knots an' sweet taters, an' he wuz layin' out at full lenk on his mud bed. He 'low ter hisse'f, he did, 'Who in de nation is dis tryin' fer ter holler de bottom out er de creek?' He lissen, an' den he turn over an' lissen ag'in. He shot one eye, an' den he shot de yuther one, but dey ain't no sleepin' in dat neighborhood. Jerry in de tree, he holler back, 'Can't come — got comp'ny!'

"Brer Yalligater, he hear dis, an' he say ter hisse'f dat ef nobody can't come, he kin, an' he riz ter de top wid no mo' fuss dan a fedder-bed makes when you let it 'lone. He riz, he did, an' his two eyes look des perzackly like two bullets floatin' on de water. He riz an' wunk his eye, an' ax Brer Rabbit howdy, an' mo' speshually how is his daughter. Brer

Rabbit, he say dat dey ain't no tellin' how his daughter is, kaze when he lef' home her head wuz a-swellin'. He say dat some er de neighbors' chillun come by an' flung rocks at her an' one un um hit her on top er de head right whar de cow-lick is, an' he hatter run atter de doctor.

"Brer Yalligater 'low, 'You don't tell me, Brer Rabbit, dat it's come ter dis! Yo' chillun gittin' chunked by yo' neighbors' chillun! Well, well, well! I wish you'd tell me whar'bouts it's all a-gwine ter een' at. Why, it'll git so atter while dat dey ain't no peace anywhars 'ceppin' at my house in de bed er de creek.'

"Brer Rabbit say, 'Ain't it de trufe? An' not only does Brer Fox's chillun chunk my chillun on dey cow-licks, but no sooner is I gone atter de doctor dan here come de creek a-risin'. I may be wrong, but I ain't

skeer'd ter say dat it beats anything I yever is lay eyes on. Over yander
in de fur woods is whar my daughter is layin' wid de headache, an' here's
her pa, an' 'twix' us is de b'ilin' creek. Ef I wuz ter try ter wade, ten ter
one de water would be over my head, an' ef not dat bad, all de pills what
de doctor gi' me would melt in my pocket. An' dey might pizen me, kaze
de doctor ain't say dey wuz ter be tuck outside.'

   "Ol' Brer Yalligater float on de water like he ain't weigh no mo' dan
one er deze yer postitch stomps, an' he try ter drop a tear. He groan, he
did, an' float backerds an' forrerds like a tired canoe. He say, 'Brer Rab-

bit, ef dey yever wuz a rover you is one. Up you come an' off you go, an'
dey ain't no mo' keepin' up wid you dan ef you had wings. Ef you think
you kin stay in one place long nuff, I'll try ter put you 'cross de creek.'
Brer Rabbit kinder rub his chin whiles he wiggle his nose. He 'low,
sezee, 'Brer 'Gater, how deep is dat water what you floatin' in?' Brer Yalligater say, sezee, 'Brer Rabbit, ef me an' my ol' 'oman wuz ter jine
heads, an' I wuz ter stan' on de tip-een' my tail, dey'll still be room nuff
fer all er my chillun 'fo' we totch bottom.'

   "Brer Rabbit, he fell back like he gwine ter faint. He 'low, 'Brer
'Gater, you don't tell me! You sholy don't mean dem last words! Why, you
make me feel like I'm furder fum home dan dem what's done lost fer
good! How de name er goodness you gwine ter put me 'cross dis slippery
water?' Brer Yalligater, he blow a bubble or two out'n his nose, an' den
he say, sezee, 'Ef you kin stay still in one place long nuff, I'm gwine ter
take you 'cross on my back. You nee'nter say thanky, yit I want you ter
know dat I ain't eve'ybody's water-hoss.' Brer Rabbit he 'low, sezee, 'I

kin well b'lieve dat, Brer 'Gater, but somehow, I kinder got a notion dat
yo' tail mighty limber. I hear ol' folks say dat you kin knock a chip fum
de back er yo' head wid de tip-een' er yo' tail an' never ha'f try.' Brer Yalligater smack his mouf, an' say, sezee, 'Limber my tail may be, Brer Rabbit, an' fur-reachin', but don't blame me. It wuz dat a-way when it wuz
'gun ter me. It's all j'inted up 'cordin' ter natur'.'

"Brer Rabbit, he study an' study, an' de mo' he study, de wuss he like
it. But he bleeze ter go home — dey wa'n't no two ways 'bout dat — an'
he 'low, sezee, 'I speck what you say is somers in de neighborhoods er de
trufe, Brer 'Gater, an' mo' dan dat, I b'lieve I'll go 'long wid you. Ef you'll
ride up a leetle closer, I'll make up my mind so I won't keep you waitin'.'
Brer Yalligater, he float by de side er de bank same ez a cork out'n a
pickle bottle. He ain't do like he in a hurry, kaze he drapt a word er two
about de wedder, an' he say dat de water wuz mighty col' down dar in de
slushes. But Brer Rabbit tuck notice dat when he smole one er his
smiles, he show'd up a double row er tushes, dat look like dey'd do
mighty good work in a saw-mill. Brer Rabbit, he 'gun ter shake like he
havin' a chill; he 'low, 'I feel dat damp, Brer 'Gater, dat I mought des ez
well be in water up ter my chin!' Brer Yalligater ain't say nothin', but he
can't hide his tushes. Brer Rabbit look up, he look down, an' he look all
aroun'. He ain't skacely know what ter do. He 'low, 'Brer 'Gater, yo' back
mighty roughnin'; how I gwine ter ride on it?' Brer Yalligater say, sezee,
'De roughnin' will he'p you ter hol' on, kaze you'll hatter ride straddle.
You kin des fit yo' foots on de bumps an' kinder brace yo'se'f when you
think you see a log floatin' at us. You kin des set up dar same ez ef you
wuz settin' at home in yo' rockin'-cheer.'

"Brer Rabbit shuck his head, but he got on, he did, an' he ain't no
sooner git on dan he wish mighty hard he wuz off. Brer Yalligater say,
sezee, 'You kin pant ef you wanter, Brer Rabbit, but I'll do de paddlin','
an' den he slip thoo de water des like he greased. Brer Rabbit sho wuz
skeer'd but he keep his eye open, an' bimeby he tuck notice dat Brer
Yalligater wa'n't makin' fer de place whar de lan'in's at, an' he up an'
sesso. He 'low, 'Brer 'Gater, ef I ain't mighty much mistooken, you ain't
headin' fer de lan'in'.' Brer Yalligater say, sezee, 'You sho is got mighty
good eyes, Brer Rabbit. I been waitin' fer you a long time, an' I'm de wust

kinder waiter. I most know you ain't ferget dat day in de stubble, when you say you gwine ter show me ol' man Trouble. Well, you ain't only show 'im ter me, but you made me shake han's wid 'im. You sot de dry grass afier, an' burn me scandalious. Dat de reason my back so rough, an' dat de reason my hide so tough. Well, I been a-waitin' sence dat time, an' now here you is. You burn me twel I hatter squench de burnin' in de big quagmire.'

"Brer Yalligater laugh, but he had de laugh all on his side, kaze dat wuz one er de times when Brer Rabbit ain't feel like gigglin'. He sot dar a-shakin' an' a-shiverin'. Bimeby he 'low, sezee, 'What you gwine do, Brer 'Gater?' Brer Yalligater, say, sezee, 'It look like ter me dat sence you sot de dry grass afier, I been havin' symptoms. Dat what de doctor say. He look at my tongue, an' feel er my pulsh, an' shake his head. He say dat bein's he's my frien', he don't min' tellin' me dat my symptoms is git-tin' mo' wusser dan what dey been, an' ef I don't take sump'n' I'll be fallin' inter one deze yer inclines what make folks flabby an' weak.'

"Brer Rabbit, he shuck an' he shiver'd. He 'low, sezee, 'What else de doctor say, Brer 'Gater?' Brer Yalligater keep on a-slippin' along; he say, sezee, 'De doctor ain't only look at my tongue — he medjur'd my breff, an' he hit me on my bosom — tip-tap-tap! — an' he say dey ain't but one thing dat'll kyo me. I ax 'im what dat is, an' he say it's Rabbit gizzard.' Brer Yalligater slip an' slide along, an' wait fer ter see what Brer Rabbit gwine ter say ter dat. He ain't had ter wait long, kaze Brer Rabbit done his thinkin' like one er deze yer machines what got lightnin' in it. He 'low, sezee, 'It's a mighty good thing you struck up wid me dis day, Brer 'Gater, kaze I got des perzackly de kinder physic what you lookin' fer. All de neighbors say I'm mighty quare an' I speck I is, but quare er not quare, I'm long been lookin' fer de gizzard-eater.'

"Brer Yalligater ain't say nothin'; he des slide thoo de water, an' lis-sen ter what Brer Rabbit sayin'. Brer Rabbit 'low, sezee, 'De las' time I wuz tooken sick, de doctor come in a hurry, an' he sot up wid me all night — not a wink er sleep did dat man git. He say he kin tell by de way I wuz gwine on, rollin' an' tossin', an' moanin' an' groanin', dat dey wa'n't no physic gwine ter do me no good. I ain't never see no doctor scratch his head like dat doctor did; he done like he wuz stumped, he sho' did. He say he ain't never see nobody wid my kind er trouble, an' he went off an' call in one er his brer doctors, an' de two knock dey heads tergedder, an' say my trouble all come fum havin' a double gizzard. When my ol' 'oman hear dat, she des flung her apron over her head, an' fell back in a dead faint, an' a little mo' an' I'd a had ter pay a doctor bill on her accounts. When she squalled, some er my chillun got skeer'd an' tuck ter de woods, an' dey ain't all got back when I lef' home las' night.'

"Brer Yalligater, he des went a-slippin' 'long thoo de water; he lissen, but he ain't sayin' nothin'. Brer Rabbit, he 'low, sezee, 'It's de fatal trufe, all dis dat I'm a-tellin' you. De doctor, he flew'd 'roun' twel he fotch my ol' 'oman to, an' den he say dey ain't no needs ter be skittish on accounts er my havin' a double gizzard, kaze all I had ter do wuz ter be kinder keerful wid my chawin's an' gnyawin's, an' my comin's an' gwines. He say dat I'd hatter suffer wid it twel I fin' de gizzard-eater. I ax 'im whar'bouts is he, an' he say dat I'd know him when I seed him, an' ef I fail ter know 'im, he'll make hisse'f beknown ter me. Dis kinder errytate me, kaze when a man's a doctor, an' is got de idee er kyoin' anybody, dey ain't no needs ter deal in no riddles. But he say dat 'tain't no use fer ter tell all you know, speshually 'fo' dinner.'

"Brer Yalligater went a-slidin' 'long thoo de water; he lissen an' smack his mouf, but he ain't sayin' nothin'. Brer Rabbit, he talk on; he 'low, sezee, 'An' dey wuz one thing he tol' me mo' plainer dan all de rest. He say dat when anybody wuz 'flicted wid de double gizzard, dey dassen't cross water wid it, kaze ef dey's anything dat a double gizzard won't stan' it's de smell er water. '

"Brer Yalligater went slippin' 'long thoo de water, but he feel like de time done come when he bleeze ter say sump'n'. He say, sezee, 'How come you er crossin' water now, ef de doctor tell you dat?' Dis make Brer Rabbit laugh; he 'low, 'Maybe I oughtn't ter tell you, but 'fo' I kin cross water dat double gizzard got ter come out. De doctor done tol' me dat ef she ever smell water, dey'll be sech a swellin up dat my skin won't hol' me; an' no longer dan las' night, 'fo' I come ter dis creek — 'twuz a creek den, whatsomever you may call it now — I tuck out my double gizzard an' hid it in a hick'ry holler. An' ef you er de gizzard-eater, now is yo' chance, kaze ef you put it off, you may rue de day. Ef you er in de notion I'll take you right dar an' show you de stump whar I hid it at — er ef you wanter be lonesome 'bout it, I'll let you go by yo'se'f an' I'll stay right here.'

"Brer Yalligater, he slip an' slide thoo de water. He say, sezee, 'Whar'd you say you'd stay?' Brer Rabbit 'low, sezee, 'I'll stay right here, Brer 'Gater, er anywhar's else you may choosen; I don't keer much whar I stays er what I does, so long ez I get rid er' dat double gizzard what's been a-tarrifyin' me. You better go by yo'se'f, kaze bad ez dat double gizzard is done me, I got a kinder tendersome feelin' fer it, an' I'm fear'd ef I wuz ter go 'long wid you, an' see you grab it, dey'd be some boo-hooin' done. Ef you go by yo'se'f, des rap on de stump an' say — *Ef you er ready, I'm ready an' a little mo' so,* an' you won't have no trouble wid her. She's hid right in dem woods yander, an' de holler hick'ry stump ain't so mighty fur fum whar de bank er de creek oughter be.'

"Brer 'Gater ain't got much mo' sense dan what it 'ud take fer ter clim' a fence atter somebody done pulled it down, an' so he kinder slew'd hisse'f aroun', an' steered fer de woods — de same woods whar dey's so many trees, an' whar ol' Sis Owl starts all de whirl-win's by fannin' her wings. Brer Yalligater swum an' steered, twel he come close ter lan', an' when he done dat Brer Rabbit make a big jump an' lan' on solid ground. He mought er got his feet wet, but ef he did 'twuz ez much. He 'low, sezee:

> "'You po' ol' 'Gater, ef you know'd A fum Izzard,
>   You'd know mighty well dat I'd keep my Gizzard.'

An' wid dat, he wuz done gone — done clean gone!"

16
Brother Rabbit and Miss Nancy

ONE DAY, when Uncle Remus had told one of the stories that have already been set forth, the little boy was unusually thoughtful. He had asked his mother whether there was ever a time when the animals acted and talked like people, and she, without reflecting, being a young and an impulsive woman, had answered most emphatically in the negative. Now, this little boy was shrewder than he was given credit for being, and he knew that neither his grandmother nor Uncle Remus would set great store by what his mother said. How he knew this would be difficult to explain, but he knew it all the same. Therefore, when he interjected a doubt as to the truth of the tales, he kept the name of his authority to himself.

"Uncle Remus," said the little boy, "how do you know that the tales you tell are true? Couldn't somebody make them up?"

The old man looked at the little child, and knew who had sown the seeds of doubt in his mind, and the knowledge made him groan and shake his head. "Maybe you think I done it, honey, but ef you does, de sooner you fergit it off'n yo' min', de better fer you, kaze I'd set here an' dry up an' blow way 'fo' I kin tell a tale er my own make-up; an' ef dey's anybody deze days what kin make um up, I'd like fer ter snuggle up ter 'im, an' ax 'im ter l'arn me how."

"Do you really believe the animals could talk?" asked the child.

"What diffunce do it make what I b'lieve, honey? Ef dey kin talk in dem days, er ef dey can't, b'lievin' er not b'lievin' ain't gwine ter he'p matters. Ol' folks what live in dem times dey say de creeturs kin talk, kaze dey done talk wid um, an' dey tell it ter der chillun an' der chillun tell it ter der chillun right on down ter deze days. So den what you gwine ter do 'bout it — b'lieve dem what had it fum de ol' folks dat know'd, er dem what ain't never hear nothin' 'tall about it twel dey git it second han' fum a ol' nigger man?"

The child perceived that Uncle Remus was hitting pretty close to home, as the saying is, and he said nothing for a while. "I haven't said that I don't believe them," he remarked presently.

"Ef you said it, honey, you ain't say it whar I kin hear you, but I take notice dat you hol' yo' head on one side an' kinder wrinkle yo' face up when I tell deze tales. Ef you don't b'lieve um, 'tain't no mo' use fer me ter tell um dan 'tis fer me ter fly."

"My face always wrinkles when I laugh, Uncle Remus."

"An' when you cry," responded the old man so promptly that the child laughed, though he hardly knew what he was laughing at.

"I'm gwine ter tell you one now," remarked Uncle Remus, wiping a smile from his face with the back of his hand, "an' you kin take it er leave it, des ez you please. Ef you see anything wrong in it anywhar, you kin p'int it out ez we go 'long. I been tellin' you dat Brer Rabbit wuz a heap bigger in dem days dan what he is now. It looks like de fambly done run ter seed, an' I bet you dat ninety-nine thousan' year fum dis ve'y day, de Rabbit-tum-a-hash crowd won' be bigger dan fiel'-mice — I bet you dat. He wa'n't only bigger, but he wuz mighty handy 'bout a farm, when he tuck a notion, speshually ef Mr. Man had any greens in his truck-patch. Well, one time, times wuz so hard dat he hatter hire out fer his vittles an' cloze. He had de idee dat he wuz gittin' a mighty heap fer de work he done, an' Mr. Man tell his daughter dat he gittin' Brer Rabbit mighty cheap. Dey wuz bofe satchified, an' when dat's de case, eve'ybody else oughter be satchified. Brer Rabbit kin hoe taters, an' chop cotton, an' fetch up breshwood, an' split de kindlin', an' do right smart.

"He say ter hisse'f, Brer Rabbit did, dat ef he ain't gittin' no money an' mighty few cloze, he boun' he'd have a plenty vittles. De fust week er two, he ain't cut up no shines; he wuz gittin' usen ter de place. He stuck ter his work right straight along twel Mr. Man say he one er de bes' han's on de whole place, an' he tell his daughter dat she better set 'er cap fer Brer Rabbit. De gal she toss her head an' make a mouf, but all de samey she 'gun ter cas' sheep eyes at 'im.

"One fine day, when de sun shinin' mighty hot, Brer Rabbit 'gun ter git mighty hongry. He say he want some water. Mr. Man say, 'Dar de bucket, an' yan' de spring. Eve'ything fix so you kin git water monstus easy.' Brer Rabbit git de water, but still dey wuz a gnyawin' in his stomach, an' bimeby he say he want some bread. Mr. Man say, "Tain't been so mighty long sence you had brekkus, but no matter 'bout dat. Yan's de house, in de house you'll fin' my daughter, an' she'll gi' you what bread you want.'

"Wid dat Brer Rabbit put out fer de house, an' dar he fin' de gal. She say, 'La, Brer Rabbit, you oughter be at work, but stidder dat here you is at de house. I hear pap say dat you er mighty good worker, but ef dis de way you does yo' work, I dunner what make 'im sesso.' Brer Rabbit say, 'I'm here, Miss Nancy, kaze yo' daddy sont me.' Miss Nancy 'low, 'Ain't you 'shame er yo'se'f fer ter talk dat away? You know pap ain't sont you.' Brer Rabbit say, 'Yassum, he did,' an' den he smole one er deze yer lop-sided smiles. Miss Nancy kinder hang 'er head an' 'low, 'Stop lookin' at me so brazen.' Brer Rabbit stood dar wid his eyes shot, an' he ain't say nothin'. Miss Nancy say, 'Is you gone ter sleep? You oughter be 'shame fer ter drap off dat away whar dey's ladies.'

"Brer Rabbit make a bow, he did, an' 'low, 'You tol' me not ter look at you, an' ef I ain't ter look at you, I des ez well ter keep my eyes shot.' De gal she giggle an' say Brer Rabbit oughtn't ter make fun er her right befo' her face an' eyes. She ax what her pap sont 'im fer, an' he 'low dat Mr. Man sont 'im for a dollar an' a half, an' some bread an' butter. Miss Nancy say she don't b'lieve 'im, an' wid dat she run down todes de fiel' whar her pa wuz workin' an' holler at 'im — 'Pap! Oh, pap!' Mr. Man make answer, 'Hey?' an' de gal say, 'Is you say what Brer Rabbit say you say?' Mr. Man he holler back dat dat's des what he say, an' Miss Nancy she run back ter der house, an' gi' Brer Rabbit a dollar an' a half an' some bread an' butter.[1]

"Time passed, an' eve'y once in a while Brer Rabbit'd go ter de house endurin' de day, an' tell Miss Nancy dat her daddy say fer ter gi' 'im money an' some bread an' butter. An' de gal, she'd go part er de way ter whar Mr. Man is workin', an' holler an' ax ef he sesso, an' Mr. Man'd holler back, 'Yes, honey, dat what I say.' It got so atter while dat dey ain't so mighty much money in de house, an' 'bout dat time, Miss Nancy, she had a beau, which he useter come ter see her eve'y Sunday, an' sometimes Sat'day, an' it got so, atter while, dat she won't skacely look at Brer Rabbit.

"Dis make 'im laugh, an' he kinder studied how he gwine ter git even wid um, kaze de beau got ter flingin' his sass 'roun' Brer Rabbit, an' de gal, she'd giggle, ez gals will. But Brer Rabbit des sot dar, he did, an'

---

[1] See "Big Jack and Little Jack" in *The Jack Tales*, Boston, Houghton Mifflin Co., 1943. — R. C.

chaw his terbacker, an' spit in de fier. But one day Mr. Man hear 'im
talkin' ter hisse'f whiles dey er workin' in de same fiel', and he ax Brer
Rabbit what he say. Brer Rabbit 'low dat he des tryin' fer ter l'arn a
speech what he hear a little bird say, an' wid dat he went on diggin' in de
groun' des like he don't keer whedder anything happen er not. But dis
don't satchify Mr. Man, an' he ax Brer Rabbit what de speech is. Brer
Rabbit 'low dat de way de little bird say it dey ain't no sense ter it fur ez
he kin see. But Mr. Man keep on axin' 'im what 'tis, an' bimeby he up an'
'low, 'De beau kiss de gal an' call her honey; den he kiss her ag'in, an'
she gi' 'im de money.'

"Mr. Man say, 'Which money?' Brer Rabbit 'low, 'You er too much fer
me. Dey tells me dat money's money, no matter whar you git it, er how
you git it. Ef de little bird wa'n't singin' a song, den I'm mighty much
mistooken.' But dis don' make Mr. Man feel no better dan what he bin
feelin'. He went on workin', but all de time de speech dat de little bird
made wuz runnin' in his min':

> 'De beau kiss de gal, an' call her honey;
> Den he kiss her agin, an' she gi' 'im de money.'

"He keep on sayin' it over in his min', an' de mo' he say it de mo' it
worry him. Dat night when he went home, de beau wuz dar, an' he wuz

mo' gaily dan ever. He flung sass at Brer Rabbit, an' Brer Rabbit does sot dar an' chaw his terbacker, an' spit in de fier. Den Mr. Man went ter de place whar he keep his money, an' he fin' it mos' all gone. He come back, he did, an' he say, 'Whar my money?' De gal, she ain't wanter have no words 'fo' her beau, an' 'spon', 'You know whar 'tis des ez well ez I does,' an' de man say, 'I speck you er right 'bout dat, an' sence I does, I want you ter pack up an' git right out er dis house an' take yo' beau wid you.' An' so dar 'twuz.

"De gal, she cry some, but de beau muched her up, an' dey went off an' got married, an' Mr. Man tuck all his things an' move off somers, I dunner whar, an' dey wa'n't nobody lef' in dem neighberhoods but me an' Brer Rabbit."

"You and Brother Rabbit?" cried the little boy.

"Dat's what I said," replied Uncle Remus. "Me an' Brer Rabbit. De gal, she tol' her chillun 'bout how Brer Rabbit had done her an' her pa, an' fum dat time on, dey er been persooin' on atter him."

17
The Hard-Headed Woman

UNCLE REMUS had observed a disposition on the part of the little boy to experiment somewhat with his elders. The child had come down to the plantation from the city such a model youngster that those who took an interest in his behavior, and who were themselves living the free and easy life possible only in the country places, were inclined to believe that he had been unduly repressed. This was particularly the case with the little fellow's grandmother, who was aided and abetted by Uncle Remus himself, with the result that the youngster was allowed liberties he had never had before. The child, as might be supposed, was quick to take advantage of such a situation, and was all the time trying to see how far he could go before the limits of his privileges — new and inviting so far as he was concerned — would be reached. They stretched very much farther on the plantation than they would have done in the city, as was natural and proper, but the child, with that adventurous spirit common to boys, was inclined to push them still farther than they had ever yet gone; and he soon lost the most obvious characteristics of a model lad.

Little by little he had pushed his liberties, the mother hesitating to bring him to task for fear of offending the grandmother, whose guest she was, and the grandmother not daring to interfere, for the reason that it was at her suggestion, implied rather than direct, that the mother had relaxed her somewhat rigid discipline. It was natural, under the circumstances, that the little fellow should become somewhat wilful and obstinate, and he bade fair to develop that spirit of disobedience that will make the brightest child ugly and discontented.

Uncle Remus, as has been said, observed all these symptoms, and while he had been the first to deplore the system that seemed to take all the individuality out of the little fellow, he soon became painfully aware that something would have to be done to renew the discipline that had been so efficacious when the mother was where she felt free to exercise her whole influence.

"You ain't sick, is you, honey?" the old man inquired one day in an insinuating tone. "Kaze ef you is, you better run back ter de house an' let de white folks dose you up. Yo' mammy knows des zackly de kinder physic you need, an' how much, an' ef I ain't mighty much mistooken, 'twon't be so mighty long 'fo' she'll take you in han'." The child looked up quickly to see whether Uncle Remus was in earnest, but he could find nothing in that solemn countenance that at all resembled playfulness. "You may be well," the old man went on, "but dey's one thing certain an' sho — you don't look like you did when you come ter we-all's house, an' you don't do like you done. You may look at me ef you wanter, but I'm a-tellin' you de fatal trufe, kaze you ain't no mo' de same chil' what useter 'ten' ter his own business all day an' night — you ain't no mo' de same chil' dan I'm dat ol' hen out dar. I 'low'd I mought be mistooken, but I hear yo' granny an' yo' mammy talkin' t'er night atter you done gone ter bed, an' de talk dat dey talked sho did open my eyes, kaze I never 'spected fer ter hear talk like dat."

For a long time the little boy said nothing, but finally he inquired what Uncle Remus had heard. "I ain't no eavesdrapper," the old man replied, "but I hear 'nuff fer ter last me whiles you stay wid us. I dunner how long dat'll be, but I don't speck it'll be long. Now des look at you! Dar you is fumblin' wid my shoe-knife, an' mos' 'fo' you know it one een' er yo' finger will be down dar on de flo', an' you'll be a-squallin' like somebody done kil't you. Put it right back whar you got it fum. Whyn't you put it down when I ax you? — an' don't scatter my pegs! Put down dat awl! You'll stob yo'se'f right in de vitals, an' den Miss Sally will blame me. Laws-a-massy! take yo' han' outer dat peg box! You'll git um all over de flo', an' dey'll drap thoo de cracks. I be boun' ef I take my foot in my han', an' go up yan' an' tell yo' mammy how good you is, she'll make you take off yo' cloze an' go ter bed — dat's des zackly what she'll do. An' dar you is foolin' wid my fillin's! — an', bless gracious, ef you ain't settin' right flat-footed on my shoemaker's wax, an' it right saft! I'll hatter ax yo' mammy ter please'm not let you come down here no mo' twel de day you start home!"

"I think you are very cross," complained the child. "I never heard you talk that way before. And grandmother is getting so she isn't as nice as she used to be."

"Ah-yi!" exclaimed Uncle Remus in a triumphant tone. "I know'd it! you done got so dat you won't do a blessed thing dat anybody ax you ter do. You done got a new name, an' 'tain't so new but what I can put bofe han's behime one, an' shet my eyes an' call it out. Eve'ybody on de place know what 'tis, an' I hear de ol' red rooster callin' it out de yuther day when you wuz chunkin' at 'im." At once the little boy manifested interest in what the old Negro was saying, and when he looked up, curiosity shone in his eyes. "What did the rooster say my name is, Uncle Remus?"

"Why, when you wuz atter him, he flew'd up on de lot fence, an' he 'low, 'Mr. Hardhead! Mr. Hardhead!' an' dat sho is yo' name. You kin squirm, an' frown, an' twis', but dat rooster is sho got yo' name down fine. Ef he'd a des named you once, maybe folks would 'a' fergot it off'n der min', but he call de name twice des ez plain ez he kin speak, an' dar you sets wid Mr. Hardhead writ on you des ez plain ez ef de rooster had a put it on you wid a paint-brush. You can't rub it off an' you can't walk 'roun' it."

"But what must I do, Uncle Remus?"

"Des set still a minnit, an' try ter be good. It may th'ow you in a high fever fer ter keep yo' han's outer my things, er it may gi' you a agur fer ter be like you use ter be, but it'll pay you in de long run; it mos' sholy will."

"Well, if you want me to be quiet," said the child, "you'll have to tell me a tale."

"Ef you sit still too long, honey, I'm afeard de creeturs on de plantation will git de idee dat sump'n' done happen. Dar's de ol' sow — you ain't run her 'roun' de place in de las' ten minnits er sech a matter; an' dar's de calf, an' de chickens, an' de Guinny hens, an' de ol' gray gooses — dey'll git de idee dat you done broke yo' leg er yo' arm; an' dey'll be fixin' up fer ter have a frolic if dey miss you fer longer dan fifteen minnits an' a half. How you gwine ter have any fun ef you set an' lissen ter a tale stidder chunkin' an' runnin' de creeturs? I mos' know you er ailin' an' by good rights de doctor oughter come an' look at you."

The little boy laughed uneasily. He was not the first that had been sobered by the irony of Uncle Remus, which, crude though it was, was much more effective than downright quarreling. "Yasser!" Uncle Remus repeated, "de doctor oughter come an' look at you — an' when I say doctor, I mean doctor, an' not one er deze yer kin' what goes 'roun' wid a whole passel er pills what ain't bigger dan a gnat's heart. What you want is a great big double-j'inted doctor wid a big black beard an' specks on, what'll fill you full er de rankest kin' er physic. Ez you look now, you put me in min' er de 'oman an' de dinner-pot; dey ain't no two ways 'bout dat."

"If it is a tale, please tell it, Uncle Remus," said the little boy.

"Oh, it sho is a tale all right!" exclaimed the old man, "but you ain't no mo' got time fer ter hear it dan de birds in de tree. You'd hatter set still an' lissen, an' dat 'ud put you out a whole lot, kaze dar's de chickens ter be chunked, an' de pigs ter be crippled an' a whole lot er yuther things fer ter be did, an' dey ain't nobody else in de roun' worl' dat kin do it ez good ez you kin. Well, you kin git up an' mosey long ef you wanter, but I'm gwine ter tell dish yer tale ef I hatter r'ar my head back an' shet my eye-balls an' tell it ter myse'f fer ter see ef I done fergit it off'n my min'.

"Well, once 'pon a time — it mought 'a' been in de year One fer all I know — dey wuz a 'oman dat live in a little cabin in de woods not so mighty fur fum water. Now, dis 'oman an' dis cabin mought a been in de Nunited State er Yallerbammer — you kin put um whar you please des like I does. But at one place er de yuther, an' at one time er nuther, dis 'oman live dar des like I'm a-tellin' you. She live dar, she did, an' fus' an' las' dey wuz a mighty heap er talk about her. Some say she wuz black, some say she wuz mighty nigh white, an' some say she wa'n't ez black ez she mought be; but dem what know'd, dey say she wuz nine parts Injun an' one part human, an' I speck dat's des ez close ter trufe ez we kin git in dis kinder wedder ef we gwine ter keep cool.

"Fum all I kin hear — an' I been keepin' bofe years wide open, she wuz a monstus busy 'oman, kaze it wuz de talk 'mongst de neighbors dat she done a heap er things what she ain't got no business ter do. She had a mighty bad temper, an' her tongue wuz a-runnin' fum mornin' twel night. Folks say dat 'twuz long an' loud an' mighty well hung. Dey lissen an' shake der head, an' atter while word went 'roun' dat de 'oman done kil't her daughter. Ez ter dat, I ain't never is hear de rights un it; she mought, an' den ag'in she moughtn't — dey ain't no tellin' — but dey wuz one thing certain an' sho, she done so quare dat folks say she cut up des like a Friday-born fool.

"Her ol' man, he done de best dat he could. He went 'long an' ten' ter his own business, an' when her tongue 'gun ter clack, he sot down an' made fish-baskets, an' axe-helves. But dat ain't make no diffunce ter de 'oman, kaze she wuz one deze yer kin' what could quoll all day whedder dey wuz anybody fer ter quoll at er not. She quolled an' she quolled. De man, he ain't say nothin' but dis des make her quoll de mo'. He split up kin'lin' an' chopped up wood, an' still she quoll'; he fotch home meal an' he fotch home meat, but still she quoll'. An' she 'fuse fer ter cook what he want her ter cook; she wuz hard-headed des like you, an' she'd have her own way ef she died fer it.

"Ef de man, he say, 'Please'm cook me some grits,' she'd whirl in an' bile greens; ef he ax fer fried meat, she'd bake him a hoe-cake er corn-bread. Ef he want roas' tater she'd bile him a mess er beans, an' all de time, she'd be givin' 'im de wuss kinder sass. Oh, she wuz a honey! An' when it come ter low-down meanness, she wuz rank an' ripe. She'd take de sparrer-grass what he fotch, an' kindle de fier wid it. She'd burn de spar'-ribs an' scorch de tripe, an' she'd do eve'y kind er way but de right way, an' dat she wouldn't do, not ter save yo' life.

"Well, dis went on an' went on, an' de man ain't make no complaints; he des watch an' wait an' pray. But atter so long a time, he see dat dat ain't gwine ter do no good, an' he tuck an' change his plans. He spit in de ashes, he did, an' he make a cross-mark, an' turn 'roun' twice so he kin face de sunrise. Den he shuck a gourd-vine flower over de pot, an' sump'n' tol' 'im fer ter take his res' an' wait twel de moon come up. All dis time de 'oman, she wuz a quollin', but bimeby, she went on 'bout her business, an' de man had some peace; but not fer long. He ain't no more dan had time fer ter put some thunderwood buds an' some calamus-root in de pot, dan here she come, an' she come a-quollin'. She come in she did, an' she slam things 'roun' des like you slams de gate.

"Atter kickin' up a rippit, an' makin' de place hot ez she kin, de 'oman made a big fier un' de pot, an' flew'd 'roun' dar des like she tryin' fer ter cook a sho nuff supper. She made some dumplin's an' flung um in de pot; den she put in some peas an' big pods er red pepper, an' on top er all she flung a sheep's head. De man, he sot dar, an' look straight at de cross-mark what he done made in de ashes. Atter while, he 'gun to smell de calamus-root a-cookin' an' he know'd by dat, dat sump'n' wuz gwine ter happen.

"De pot, it biled, an' biled, an' fus' news you know, de sheep's head

'gun ter butt de dumplin's out, an' de peas, dey flew'd out an' rattled on de flo' like a bag er bullets done busted. De 'oman, she run fer ter see what de matter is, an' when she got close ter de pot de steam fum de thunderwood hit her in de face an' eyes an' come mighty nigh takin' her breff away. Dis kinder stumped 'er fer a minnit, but she had a temper big nuff fer ter drag a bull down, an' all she had ter do when she lose her breff wuz ter fling her han's in de a'r an' fetch a snort, an' dar she wuz.

"She moughter been mad befo', but dis time she wuz mighty nigh plum' crazy. She look at de pot, an' she look at her ol' man; she shot her eye-balls an' clinched her han's; she yerked off her head-hankcher, an' pulled her ha'r loose fum de wroppin'-strings; she stomped her foot, an' smashed her toofies tergedder.

"She railed at de pot; she 'low, 'What ail you, you black Dickunce? I b'lieve you er de own brer ter de Ol' Boy! You been foolin' wid me fer de longest, an' I ain't gwine ter put up wid it! I'm gwine ter tame you down!'

Wid dat, she flung off de homespun sack what she been w'arin' an' run
outer de house an' got de axe.

"Her ol' man say, 'Whar you gwine, honey?' She 'low, 'I'm a gwine
whar I'm a gwine, dat's whar I'm a gwine!' De man, he ain't spon' ter dat
kinder talk, an' de 'oman, she went out in back yard fer ter hunt fer de
axe. Look like she gwine ter keep on gittin' in trouble, kaze de axe wuz
on top er de wood what de man done pile up out dar. It wuz layin' up dar,
de axe wuz, des ez slanchendicklar ez you please, but time it see her
comin' — "

"But, Uncle Remus!" the child exclaimed, "how could the axe see her?"

The old Negro looked at the little boy with an expression of amazed
pity on his face. He looked all around the room and then raised his eyes
to the rafters, where a long cobweb was swaying slowly in a breeze so
light that nothing else would respond to its invitation. Then he sighed
and closed his eyes. "I wish yo' pa wuz here right now, I mos' sholy
does — yo' pa, what useter set right whar you er settin'! You done been
raised in town whar dey can't tell a axe fum a wheelbarrer. Axe ain't got
no eye! Well, whoever is hear de beat er dat! Ef anybody else is got dat
idee, I'll be much erbleege ef you'll show um ter me. Here you is mighty
nigh big 'nuff fer eat raw tater widout havin' de doctor called in, an' a-
settin' dar sayin' dat axes ain't got no eyes. Well, you ax yo' gran'ma
when you go back ter de house an' see what she say.

"Now, le' me see; whar'bouts wuz I at? Oh, yes! De axe wuz on top er
woodpile, an' when it seed de 'oman comin', it des turned loose an' slip
down on de yuther side. It wa'n't tryin' fer ter show off, like I've seed
some folks 'fo' now; it des turned loose eve'ything an' fell down on de
yuther side er de woodpile. An' whiles de 'oman wuz gwine 'roun' atter
it, de axe, it clum back on top er de woodpile an' fell off on t'er side. Dem
what handed de tale down ter me ain't say how long de 'oman an' de axe
keep dis up, but ef a axe is got eyes, it ain't got but one leg, an' it must
not a bin so mighty long 'fo' de 'oman cotch up wid it — an' when she did
she wuz so mad dat she could a bit a railroad track in two, ef dey'd a
been one anywhar's 'roun' dar.

"Well, she got de axe, an' it look like she wuz madder dan ever. De
man, he say, 'Better let de pot 'lone, honey; ef you don't you'll sholy wish
you hadder.' De 'oman, she squall out, 'I'll let you 'lone ef you fool wid

me, an' ef I do you won't never pester nobody no mo'.' Man, he say, 'I'm a-tellin' you de trufe, honey, an' dis may be de las' chance you'll git ter hear it.'

"De 'oman raise de axe like she gwine ter hit de man, an' den it look like she tuck an'er notion, an' she start todes de pot. De man, he 'low, 'You better hear me, honey! You better drap de axe an' go outdoors an' cool yo'se'f off, honey! ' It seem like he wuz a mighty saf'-spoken man, wid nice feelin's fer all. De 'oman, she say, 'Don't you dast ter honey me — ef you does I'll brain you stidder de pot!' De man smole a long smile an' shuck his head; he say, 'All de same, honey, you better pay 'tention ter deze las' words I'm a-tellin' you!'

"But de 'oman, she des keep right on. She'd a gone faster dan what she did, but it look like de axe got heavier eve'y step she tuck — heavier an' heavier. An' it look like de house got bigger — bigger an' bigger; an' it seem like de do' got wider — wider an' wider! She moughter seed all dis, an' I speck she did, but she des keep right on, shakin' de axe, an' moufin' ter herse'f. De man, he holler once mo' an' fer de las' time, 'Don't let ol' Nick fool you, honey, ef you does, he sho will git you!'

"But she keep on an' keep on, an' de house got bigger an' de do' got wider. De pot see her comin', an' it got fum a-straddle er de fier, whar it had been settin' at, an' skipped out de do' an' out in de yard." Uncle Remus paused to see what effect this statement would have on the child, but save the shadow of a smile hovering around his mouth, the youngster gave no indication of unbelief. "De 'oman," said Uncle Remus, with a chuckle that was repressed before it developed into a laugh, "look like she 'stonish', but her temper kep' hot, an' she run out atter de pot wid de axe ez high ez she kin hol' it; but de pot keep on gwine, skippin' long on three legs faster dan de 'oman kin run on two; an' de axe kep' on gittin' heavier an' heavier, twel, bimeby, de 'oman hatter drap it. Den she lit out atter de pot like she wuz runnin' a foot-race, but fast ez she run, de pot run faster.

"De chase led right inter de woods an' down de spring branch, an' away over yander beyan' de creek. De pot went so fast an' it went so fur dat atter while de 'oman 'gun ter git weak. But de temper she had helt 'er up fer de longest, an' mo' dan dat, eve'y time she'd sorter slack up, de pot would dance an' caper roun' on its three legs, an' do like it's givin' her a dar' — an' she keep a-gwine twel she can't hardly go no furder.

"De man he stayed at de house, but de 'oman an' de pot ain't git so fur but what he kin hear um scufflin' an' scramblin' 'roun' in de bushes, an' he set dar, he did, an' look like he right sorry fer anybody what's ez hard-headed ez de 'oman. But she look like she bleeze ter ketch dat pot. She say ter herse'f dat folks will never git done talkin' 'bout her ef she let herse'f be outdone by a ol' dinner-pot what been in de fambly yever sence dey been any fambly.

"So she keep on, twel she tripped up on a vine er de bamboo brier, an' down she come! It seem like de pot seed her, an' stidder runnin' fum 'er, here it come a-runnin' right at 'er wid a chunk er red fier. Oh, you kin laugh, honey, an' look like you don't b'lieve me, but dat ain't make no diffunce, kaze de trufe ain't never been hurted yit by dem what ain't

b'lieve it. I dunner whar de chunk er fier come fum, an' I dunner how de dinner-pot come ter have motion, but dar 'tis in de tale — take it er leave it, des ez you please.

"Well, suh, when de 'oman fell, de pot made at her wid a chunk er red fier. De 'oman see it comin', an' she set up a squall dat moughter been heard a mile. She jump up, she did, but it seem like she wuz so weak an' tired dat she can't stan' on her foots, an' she start fer ter fall ag'in, but de dinner-pot wuz dar fer ter ketch 'er when she fell. An' dat wuz de last dat anybody yever is see er de hard-headed 'oman. Leas'ways, she ain't never come back ter de house whar de man wuz settin' at.

"De pot? Well, de way dey got it in de tale is dat de pot des laugh twel it hatter hol' its sides fer ter keep fum crackin' open. It come a-hoppin'

an' a-skippin' up de spring paff. It hopped along, it did, twel it come ter
de house, an' it made a runnin' jump in de do'. Den it wash its face, an'
scrape de mud off'n it foots, an' wiped off de grease what de 'oman been
too lazy fer ter clean off. Den it went ter de fierplace, an' kinder sprad-
dle out so it'll fit de bricks what been put dar fer it ter set on.

"De man watch all dis, but he ain't say nothin'. Atter while he hear a
mighty bilin' an' bubblin' an' when he went ter look fer ter see what de
matter, he see his supper cookin' an' atter so long a time, he fish it out
an' eat it. He eat in peace, an' atter dat he allers had peace. An' when
you wanter be hard-headed, an' have yo' own way, you better b'ar in min'
de 'oman an' de dinner-pot."

VI

The tales from

Uncle Remus
and Brer Rabbit

With illustrations by

J. M. CONDÉ

1
The Creeturs Go to the Barbecue

"ONCE 'PON A TIME," said Uncle Remus to the little boy — "But when was once upon a time?" the child interrupted to ask. The old man smiled. "I speck 'twuz one time er two times, er maybe a time an' a half. You know when Johnny Ashcake 'gun ter bake? Well, 'twuz 'long in dem days. Once 'pon a time," he resumed, "Mr. Man had a gyarden so fine dat all de neighbors come ter see it. Some 'ud look at it over de fence, some 'ud peep thoo de cracks, an' some 'ud come an' look at it by de light er de stars. An' one un um wuz ol' Brer Rabbit; starlight, moonlight, cloud-light, de nightlight wuz de light fer him. When de turn er de mornin' come, he 'uz allers up an' about, an' a-feelin' purty well I thank you, suh!

"Now, den you done hear what I say. Dar wuz Mr. Man, yander wuz de gyarden, an' here wuz ol' Brer Rabbit." Uncle Remus made a map of this part of the story by marking in the sand with his walking-cane. "Well, dis bein' de case, what you speck gwine ter happen? Nothin' in de roun' worl' but what been happenin' sence greens an' sparrer-grass wuz planted in de groun'. Dey look fine an' dey tas'e fine, an' long to'rds de

shank er de mornin', Brer Rabbit 'ud creep thoo de crack er de fence an' nibble at um. He'd take de greens, but leave his tracks, mo' speshually right atter a rain. Takin' an' leavin' — it's de way er de worl'.

"Well, one mornin', Mr. Man went out in his truck patch, an' he fin' sump'n' missin' — a cabbage here, a turnip dar, an' a mess er beans yander, an' he ax how come dis? He look 'roun', he did, an' he seed Brer Rabbit's tracks what he couldn't take wid 'im. Brer Rabbit had lef' his shoes at home an' come bar'footed.

"So Mr. Man, he call his dogs — 'Here, Buck! Here, Brinjer! Here, Blue!' an' he sikt um on de track, an' here dey went!

"You'd a thunk dey wuz runnin' atter forty-'lev'm rhinossyhosses fum de fuss dey made. Brer Rabbit he hear um comin' an' he put out fer home, kinder doublin' 'roun' des like he do deze days.

"When he got ter de p'int whar he kin set down fer ter rest his face an' han's, he tuck a poplar leaf an' 'gun ter fan hisse'f. Den Brer Fox come a-trottin' up. He say, 'Brer Rabbit, what's all dis fuss I hear in de woods? What de name er goodness do it mean?' Brer Rabbit kinder scratch his head an' 'low, 'Why, dey er tryin' fer drive me ter de big bob-bycue on de creek. Dey all ax me, an' when I 'fuse dey say dey er gwine ter make me go anyhow. Dey ain't no fun in bein' ez populous ez what I is, Brer Fox. Ef you wanter go, des git in ahead er de houn's an' go lick-ity-split down de big road!'

"Brer Fox roll his little eyes, an' lick his chops whar he dribble at de mouf, an put out ter de bobbycue, an' he ain't mo' dan made his disap-pearance, 'fo' here come Brer Wolf, an' when he got de news, off he put.

"An he ain't mo'n got out'n sight, 'fo' here come ol' Brer B'ar, an' when he hear talk er de bakin' meat an' de big pan er gravy, he sot up on his behime legs an' snored. Den off he put, an' he ain't got out'n hearin' 'fo' Brer Coon come rackin' up, an' when he got de news, he put out.

"So dar dey wuz an' what you gwine do 'bout it? It seem like dey all got in front er de dogs, er de dogs got behime um, an' Brer Rabbit sot by de creek-side laughin' an' hittin' at de snake doctors. An' dem po' cree-turs had ter go clean past de bobbycue — ef dey wuz any bobbycue, which I don't skacely speck dey wuz. Dat what make me say what I

does — when you git a invite ter a bobbycue, you better fin' out when an' whar it's at, an' who runnin' it."

2
Brer Rabbit's Frolic

THE LITTLE BOY, when he next saw Uncle Remus, after hearing how the animals went to the barbecue, wanted to know what happened to them: he was anxious to learn if any of them were hurt by the dogs that had

been chasing Brother Rabbit. The old darky closed his eyes and chuckled. "You sho is axin' sump'n' now, honey. Und' his hat, ef he had any,
Brer Rabbit had a mighty quick thinkin' apple-ratus, an' mos' inginer'lly, all de time, de pranks he played on de yuther creeturs pestered um
bofe ways — a-comin' an' a-gwine. De dogs done mighty well, 'long ez
dey had dealin's wid de small fry, like Brer Fox, an' Brer Coon, an' Brer
Wolf, but when dey run ag'in' ol' Brer B'ar, dey sho struck a snag. De
mos' servigrous wuz de identual one dat got de wust hurted. He got too
close ter Brer B'ar, an' when he look at hisse'f in runnin' water, he tuck
notice dat he wuz split wide open fum flank ter dewlap.

"Atter de ruckus wuz over, de creeturs hobbled off home de best dey
could, an' laid 'roun' in sun an' shade fer ter let der cuts an' gashes git good
an' well. When dey got so dey could segashuate, an' pay der party calls,
dey 'gree fer ter insemble somers, an' hit on some plan fer ter outdo Brer
Rabbit. Well, dey had der insembly, an' dey jower'd an' jower'd des like yo'
pa do when he ain't feelin' right well; but, bimeby, dey 'greed 'pon a plan
dat look like it mought work. Dey 'gree fer ter make out dat dey gwine ter
have a dance. Dey know'd dat ol' Brer Rabbit wuz allers keen fer dat, an'
dey say dey'll gi' him a invite, an' when he got dar, dey'd ax 'im fer ter play
de fiddle, an' ef he 'fuse, dey'll close in on 'im an' make way wid 'im.

"So fur, so good! But all de time dey wuz jowerin' an' confabbin', ol'
Brer Rabbit wuz settin' in a shady place in de grass, a-hearin' eve'y word
dey say. When de time come, he crope out, he did, an' 'roun', an' de fust
news dey know'd, here he come down de big road — bookity-bookity —
same ez a hoss dat's broke thoo de pastur' fence. He say, sezee, 'Why,
hello, frien's! an' howdy, too, kaze I ain't seed you-all sence de last time!
Whar de name er goodness is you been deze odd-come-shorts? an' how
did you far' at de bobbycue? Ef my two eye-balls ain't gone an' got
crooked, dar's ol' Brer B'ar, him er de short tail an' sharp tush — de ve'y
one I'm a-huntin' fer! An' dar's Brer Coon! I sho is in big luck. Dar's
gwine ter be a big frolic at Miss Meadows', an' her an' de gals want Brer
B'ar fer ter show um de roas'n'-year shuffle; an' dey put Brer Coon down
fer de jig dey calls rack-back-Davy.

"'I'm ter play de fiddle — sump'n' I ain't done sence my oldest gal
had de mumps an' de measles, bofe de same day an' hour! Well, dis
mornin' I tuck down de fiddle fum whar she wuz a-hangin' at, an' draw'd

de bow backerds an' forerds a time er two, an' den I shot my eyes an' hit some er de ol'-time chunes, an' when I come ter myse'f, dar wuz my whole blessed fambly skippin' an' sashayin' 'roun' de room, spite er de fack dat brekkus wuz ter be cooked!'

"Wid dat, Brer Rabbit bow'd, he did, an' went down de road like de dogs wuz atter 'im."

"But what happened then?" the little boy asked. "Nothin' 'tall," replied Uncle Remus, taking up the chuckle where he had left off. "De creeturs ain't had no dance, an' when dey went ter Miss Meadows', she put her head out de winder, an' say ef dey don't go off fum dar she'll have de law on um!"

3
Brother Bear's Big House

"Uv ALL DE CREETURS," said Uncle Remus, in response to a questioning look on the part of the little boy, "ol' Brer B'ar had de biggest an' de warmest house. I dunner why ner wharfo', but I'm a-tellin' you de plain fack, des ez dey tol' it unter me. Ef I kin he'p it I never will be deceivin' you, ner lead you inter no bad habits. Yo' pappy trotted wid me a mighty long time, an' ef you'll ax him he'll tell you dat de one thing I never did do wuz ter deceive him whiles he had his eyes open; not ef I knows myse'f. Well, ol' Brer B'ar had de big house I'm a-tellin' you about. Ef he yever is brag un it, it ain't never come down ter me. Yit dat's des what he had — a big house an' plenty er room fer him an' his fambly; an' he ain't had mo' dan he need, kaze all er his fambly wuz fat an' had what folks calls heft — de nachal plunkness.

"He had a son name Simmon, an' a gal name Sue, not countin' his ol' 'oman, an' dey all live wid one an'er day atter day, an' night atter night; an' when one un um went abroad, dey'd be 'spected home 'bout mealtime, ef not befo', an' dey segashuated right along fum day ter day, washin' der face an' han's in de same wash-pan in de back po'ch, an' wipin' on de same towel ez all happy famblies allers does.

"Well, time went on an' fotched de changes dat might be 'spected, an' one day dar come a mighty knockin' on Brer B'ar's do'. Brer B'ar, he holler out, he did, 'Who dat come a-knockin' dis time er de year, 'fo' de corn's done planted, er de cotton-crap's pitched?' De one at de do' make a big noise, an' rattle de hinges. Brer B'ar holler out, he did, 'Don't t'ar down my house! Who is you, anyhow, an' what you want?' An' de answer come, 'I'm one an' darfo' not two; ef you er mo' dan one, who is you an' what you doin' in dar?' Brer B'ar, he say, sezee, 'I'm all er one an' mighty nigh two, but I'd thank you fer ter tell me yo' full fambly name.' Den de answer come.

" 'I'm de knocker an' de mover bofe, an' ef I can't clim' over I'll crawl under ef you do but gi' me de word. Some calls me Brer Polecat, an' some a big word dat it ain't wuff while ter ermember, but I wanter move in. It's mighty col' out here, an' all I meets tells me it's mighty warm in dar whar you is.' Den ol' Brer B'ar say, sezee, 'It's warm nuff fer dem what stays in

here, but not nigh so warm fer dem on de outside. What does you reely want?' Brer Polecat 'spon', he did, 'I wants a heap er things dat I don't git. I'm a mighty good housekeeper, but I take notice dat dar's mighty few folks dat wants me ter keep house fer um.' Brer B'ar say, sezee, 'I ain't got no room fer no housekeeper; we ain't skacely got room fer ter go ter bed. Ef you kin keep my house on de outside, you er mighty welcome.'

"Brer Polecat say, 'You may think you ain't got no room, but I bet you got des ez much room ez anybody what I know. Ef you let me in dar one time, I boun' you I'll make all de room I want.'"

Uncle Remus paused to see what effect this statement would have on the little boy. He closed his eyes, as though he were tired, but when he opened them again, he saw the faint shadow of a smile on the child's face. "'Tain't gwine ter hurt you fer ter laugh a little bit, honey. Brer Polecat come in Brer B'ar's house, an' he had sech a bad breff dat dey all hatter git out — an' he stayed an' stayed twel time stopped runnin' ag'in' him."

4
Brer Rabbit Treats the Creeturs to a Race

ONE SULTRY SUMMER DAY, while the little boy was playing not far from Uncle Remus's cabin, a heavy black cloud made its appearance in the west, and quickly obscured the sky. It sent a brisk gale before it, as if to clear the path of leaves and dust. Presently there was a blinding flash of lightning, a snap and a crash, and, with that, the child took to his heels, and ran to Uncle Remus, who was standing in his door. "Dar now!" he exclaimed, before the echoes of the thunder had rolled away. "Dat dust an' win', an' rain, puts me in mind er de time when ol' Brer Rabbit got up a big race fer ter pleasure de yuther creeturs. It was de mos' funniest race you ever hear tell on. Brer Rabbit went 'way off in de woods twel he come ter de Rainmaker's house. He knocked an' went in, an' he ax de Rainmaker ef he can't fix it up so dey kin have a race 'tween Brer Dust an' Cousin Rain, fer ter see which kin run de fastes'. De Rainmaker growl'd an' jower'd, but bimeby he 'gree, but he say that ef 'twuz anybody but Brer Rabbit, he wouldn't gi' it but one thunk.

"Well, dey fix de day, dey did, an' den Brer Rabbit put out ter whar de creeturs wuz stayin' at, an' tol' um de news. Dey dunner how Brer Rabbit know, but dey all wanter see de race. Now, him an' de Rainmaker had fixt it up so dat de race would be right down de middle er de big road, an' when de day come, dar's whar he made de creeturs stan' — Brer B'ar at de bend er de road, Brer Wolf a leetle furder off, an' Brer Fox at a p'int whar de cross-roads wuz. Brer Coon an' Brer Possum an' de yuthers he scattered about up an' down de road.

"Ter dem what has ter wait, it seem like de sun stops an' all de clocks

wid 'im. Brer B'ar done some growlin'; Brer Wolf some howlin' an' Brer
Possum some laughin'; but atter while a cloud come up fum somers.
'Twa'n't sech a big cloud, but Brer Rabbit know'd dat Cousin Rain wuz
in dar' long wid Uncle Win'. De cloud crope up, it did, twel it got right
over de big road, an' den it kinder drapped down a leetle closer ter de
groun'. It look like it kinder stop, like a buggy, fer Cousin Rain ter git
out, so der'd be a fa'r start. Well, he got out, kaze de creeturs kin see 'im,
an' den Uncle Win', he got out.

"An den, gentermens! de race begun fer ter commence. Uncle Win'
hep'd um bofe; he had his bellows wid 'im, an' he blow'd it! Brer Dust got
up fum whar he wuz a-layin' at, an' come down de road des a-whirlin'.
He stricken ol' Brer B'ar fust, den Brer Wolf, an' den Brer Fox, an' atter
dat, all de yuther creeturs, an' it come mighty nigh smifflicatin' um! Not
never in all yo' born days is you yever hearn sech coughin' an' sneezin',
sech snortin' an' wheezin'! An' dey all look like dey wuz painted red.

Brer B'ar sneeze so hard dat he hatter lay down in de road, an' Brer Dust
come mighty nigh buryin' 'im, an' 'twuz de same wid de yuther
creeturs — dey got der years, der noses, an' der eyeses full.

"An den Cousin Rain come 'long, a-pursuin' Brer Dust, an' he come
mighty nigh drownin' um. He left um kivver'd wid mud, an' dey wuz wuss
off dan befo'. It wuz de longest 'fo' dey kin git de mud out'n der eyes an'

years, an' when dey git so dey kin see a leetle bit, dey tuck notice dat Brer Rabbit, stidder bein' fuller er mud, wuz ez dry ez a chip, ef not dryer.

"It make um so mad, dat dey all put out atter 'im, an' try der level best fer ter ketch 'im, but ef dey wuz anything in de roun' worl' dat Brer Rabbit's got, it's soople foots, an' 'twa'n't no time 'fo' de yuther creeturs can't see ha'r ner hide un 'im! All de same Brer Rabbit ain't bargain fer ter have two races de same day."

"But, Uncle Remus," said the little boy, "which beat, Brother Dust or Cousin Rain?" The old man stirred uneasily in his chair, and rubbed his chin with his hand. "Dey tells me," he responded cautiously, "dat when Cousin Rain can't see nothin' er Brother Dust, he thunk he am beat, but he holler out, 'Brer Dust, whar'bouts is you?' an' Brer Dust he holler back, 'You'll hatter scuzen me; I fell down in de mud an' can't run no mo'!'"

5
Brer Rabbit and the Gold Mine

THERE HAD BEEN SILENCE in the cabin for a long ten minutes, and Uncle Remus, looking up, saw a threat of sleep in the little boy's eyes. Whereupon he plunged headlong into a story without a word of explanation.

"Well, suh, one year it fell out dat de craps wuz burnt up. A dry drouth had done de work, an' ef you'd a struck a match anywhar in dat settlement, de whole county would a blazed up. Ol' man Hongriness des natchally tuck off his cloze an' went paradin' 'bout eve'ywhar, an' de creeturs got bony an' skinny. Ol' Brer B'ar done better dan any un um, kaze all he hatter do wuz go ter sleep an' live off'n his own fat; an' Brer Rabbit an' his ol' 'oman had put some calamus root by, an' saved up some sugar-cane dat dey fin' lyin' 'roun' loose, an' *dey* got 'long purty well. But de balance er de creeturs wuz dat ga'nt dat dey ain't got over it down ter dis day.

"De creeturs had der meetin'-place, whar dey could all set 'roun' an' talk de kind er politics dey had, des like folks does at de cross-roads grocery. One day, whiles dey wuz all settin' an' squattin' 'roun', jowerin' an' confabbin', Brer Rabbit he up'n say, sezee, dat ol' Mammy-Bammy-Big-Money tol' his great gran'daddy dat dar wuz a mighty big an' fat gol' mine in deze parts, an' he say dat he wouldn't be 'tall 'stonish' ef 'twa'n't somers close ter Brer B'ar's house. Brer B'ar, he growled, he did, an' say dat de gol' mine better not let him fin' it, kaze atter he got done wid it, dey won't be no gol' mine dar.

"Some laughed, some grinned an' some gapped, an' atter jowerin' some mo', day all put out ter whar der famblies wuz livin' at; but I boun' you dey ain't fergit 'bout dat gol' mine, kaze, fum dat time on, go whar you mought, you'd ketch some er de creeturs diggin' an' grabblin' in de groun', some in de fiel's, some in de woods, an' some in de big road; an' dey wuz so weak an' hongry dat dey kin skacely grabble fer fallin' down.

"Well, dis went on fer de longest, but bimeby, one day, dey all 'gree dat sump'n' bleeze ter be done, an' dey say dey'll all take one big hunt fer de gol' mine, an' den quit. Dey hunted in gangs, wid de gangs not fur fum one an' er, an' it so happen dat Brer Rabbit wuz in de gang wid Brer Wolf, an' he know'd dat he hatter keep his eyes wide open. All de creeturs hatter dig in diffunt places, an' whiles Brer Rabbit wa'n't much uv a grabbler, he had a way er makin' de yuthers b'lieve dat he wuz de best er de lot. So he made a heap er motion like he wuz t'arin' up de yeth. Dey ain't been gwine on dis away long 'fo' Brer Wolf holler out:

"'Run here, Brer Rabbit; I done foun' it!' Brer B'ar an' Brer Fox wuz bofe diggin' close by, an' Brer Rabbit kinder wunk one eye at de elements; he say, sezee, 'Glad I is fer yo' sake, Brer Wolf; git yo' gol' an' 'joy yo'se'f!' Brer Wolf say, 'Come git some, Brer Rabbit! Come git some!' Ol'

Brer Rabbit 'spon', 'I'll take de leavin's, Brer Wolf; you take what you want, an' den when you done got nuff I'll get de leetle bit I want.' Brer Wolf say, 'I wanter show you sump'n'.' Brer Rabbit 'low, 'My eyes ain't big fer nothin'.' Brer Wolf say, 'I got a secret I wanter tell you.' Brer Rabbit 'low, 'My years ain't long fer nothin'. Des stan' an' do yo' whisperin', Brer Wolf, an' I'll hear eve'y word you say.'

"Brer Wolf ain't say nothin', but make out he's grabblin', an' den, all of a sudden, he made a dash at Brer Rabbit, but when he git whar Brer Rabbit wuz at, Brer Rabbit ain't dar no mo'; he done gone. Weak an' hongry ez

he is,w Brer Wolf know dat he can't ketch Brer Rabbit, an' so he holler out, 'What's yo' hurry, Brer Rabbit? Whar you gwine?' Brer Rabbit holler back, 'I'm gwine home atter a bag fer ter tote de gol' you gwine leave me! So long, Brer Wolf; I wish you mighty well!' an' wid dat he put out fer home."

6
How Mr. Lion Lost His Wool

"'Twuz des sech a day ez dis dat Mr. Lion lost his wool," remarked Uncle Remus to the little boy. "Mr. Man tuck a notion dat de time done come fer him fer ter have a hog-killin', an' he got 'im a big barrel, an' fill it half full er water fum de big springs. Den he piled up 'bout a cord er wood, an' ez he piled, he put rocks 'twix' de logs, an' den he sot de wood afier at bofe een's an' in de middle. 'Twa'n't long 'fo' dey had de hogs kilt, an' eve'ything ready fer ter scrape de ha'r off. Den he tuck de red-hot rocks what he put in de fier, an' flung um in de barrel whar de water wuz, an' 'twa'n't long, mon, 'fo' dat water wuz ready fer ter bile. Den dey tuck de hogs, one at a time, an' soused um in de water an' time dey tuck um out, de ha'r wuz ready fer ter drap out by de roots. Den dey'd scrape um wid sticks an' chips, an' dey ain't leave a ha'r on um.

"Well, bimeby, dey had all de hogs kilt an' cleaned, an' hauled off, an' when eve'ything wuz still ez a settin' hen, ol' Brer Rabbit stuck his head out fum behine a bush whar he been settin' at. He stuck his head out, he did, an' look all 'roun', an' den he went whar de fier wuz an' try fer ter warm hisse'f. He ain't been dar long 'fo' here come Brer Wolf an' Brer Fox, an' den he got busy.

"He say, 'Hello, frien's! howdy an' welcome! I'm des fixin' fer ter take a warm baff like Mr. Man gi' his hogs; won't you j'ine me?' Dey say dey ain't in no hurry, but dey holp Brer Rabbit put de hot rocks in de barrel an' dey watch de water bubble, an' bimeby, when eve'ything wuz ready, who should walk up but ol' Mr. Lion.

"He had a mane fum his head plum' ter de een' er his tail, an' in some places it wuz so long it drug on de groun' — dat what make all de creeturs feard un 'im. He growl an' ax um what dey doin', an' when Brer Rab-

bit tell 'im, he say dat's what he long been needin'. 'How does you git in?'
'Des back right in,' sez ol' Brer Rabbit, sezee, an' wid dat, Mr. Lion
backed in, an' de water wuz so hot, he try fer ter git out, an' he slipped in

plum' ter his shoulder blades. You kin b'lieve me er not, but dat creetur
wuz scall'd so dat he holler'd an' skeer'd eve'ybody fer miles aroun'.

"An' when he come out, all de wool drapt out, 'cep' de bunch you see
on his neck, an' de leetle bit you'll fin' on de een' er his tail — an' dat'd
a come off ef de tail hadn't a slipped thoo de bung-hole er de barrel."

With that, Uncle Remus closed his eyes, but not so tightly that he couldn't watch the little boy. For a moment the child said nothing, and then, "I must tell that tale to mother before I forget it!" So saying, he ran out of the cabin as fast as his feet could carry him, leaving Uncle Remus shaking with laughter.

VII

The tales from

Uncle Remus
and the Little Boy

With illustrations by
J. M. CONDÉ

1
The Story of the Doodang

"I WISH," said the little boy, sitting in the doorway of Uncle Remus's cabin, and watching a vulture poised on motionless wing, almost as high as the clouds that sailed by — "I wish I could fly."

The old man regarded him curiously, and then a frown crept up and sat down on his forehead. "I'll tell you dis much, honey," he said, "ef eve'ybody wuz ter git all der wishes, de wide worl' 'ud be turned upside down, an' be rollin' over de wrong way. It sho would!" He continued to regard the little boy with such a solemn aspect that the child moved uneasily in his seat on the door-step. "You sho does put me in min' er de ol' Doodang dat useter live in de mud-flats down on de river. I ain't never see 'im myse'f, but I done seed dem what say dey hear tell er dem what is see 'im.

"None un um can't tell what kinder creetur de Doodang wuz. He had a long tail, like a yallergater, a great big body, four short legs, two short years, an' a head mo' funny lookin' dan de rhynossyhoss. His mouf retched fum de een' er his nose ter his shoulder-blades, an' his tushes wuz big 'nough, long 'nough, an' sharp 'nough fer ter bite off de behime leg uv a elephant. He could live in de water, er he could live on dry lan', but he mos'ly wallered in de mud-flats, whar he could retch down in de water an' ketch a fish, er retch up in de bushes an' ketch a bird. But all dis ain't suit 'im a 'tall; he got restless; he tuck ter wantin' things he ain't got; an' he worried an' worried, an' groaned an' growled. He kep' all de creeturs, fur and feather, wide awake fer miles aroun'.

"Bimeby, one day, Brer Rabbit come a-sa'nterin' by, an' he ax de Doodang what de name er goodness is de matter, an' de Doodang 'spon' an' say dat he wanter swim ez good ez de fishes does.

"Brer Rabbit say, 'Ouch! you make de col' chills run up an' down my back when you talk 'bout swimmin' in de water. Swim on dry lan' ol' frien' — swim on dry lan'!'

But some er de fishes done hear what de Doodang say, an' dey helt a big 'sembly. Dey vow dey can't stan' de racket dat he been makin' bofe day an' night. De upshot uv de 'sembly wuz dat all de fishes 'gree fer ter loan de Doodang one fin apiece. So said, so done, an' when dey tol' de Doodang 'bout it, he fetched one loud howl, an' rolled inter shaller water.

Once dar, de fishes loan't 'im eve'y one a fin, some big an' some little, an'
atter dey done dat, de Doodang 'skivver dat he kin swim des ez nimble
ez de rest.

"He skeeted about in de water, wavin' his tail fum side ter side, an'
swimmin' fur an' wide. Brer Rabbit wuz settin' off in de bushes watchin'.
Atter while de Doodang git tired, an' start ter go on dry lan', but de fishes
kick up sech a big fuss, an' make sech a cry, dat he say he better gi' um
back der fins, an' den he crawled out on de mud-flats fer ter take his nap.

"He ain't been dozin' so mighty long 'fo' he hear a mighty big fuss, an'
he look up an' see dat de blue sky wuz fa'rly black wid birds, big an' little. De trees on de islan' wuz der roostin' place, but dey wuz comin' home
soon so dey kin git some sleep 'fo' de Doodang set up his howlin' an'
growlin', an moanin' an' groanin'. Well, de birds ain't mo'n got settle' 'fo'
de Doodang start up his howlin' an' bellerin'. Den de King-Bird flew'd
down an' ax de Doodang what de name er goodness is de matter. Den de
Doodang turn over in de mud, an' howl an' beller. De King-Bird flew'd
aroun', an' den he come back, an' ax what de trouble is. Atter so long a

time, de Doodang say dat de trouble wid him wuz dat he wanted ter fly. He say all he want wuz some feathers, an' den he kin fly ez good ez anybody.

"Den de birds hol' a 'sembly, an' dey all 'gree fer ter loan de Doodang a feather apiece. So said, so done, an' in a minnit er mo' he had de feathers a-plenty. He shuck his wings, an' ax whar'bouts he mus' fly fer de fust try.

"Brer Buzzard say de best place wuz ter de islan' what ain't got nothin' but dead trees on it, an' wid dat, de Doodang tuck a runnin' start, an' headed fer de place. He wuz kinder clumsy, but he got dar all right. De birds went 'long fer ter see how de Doodang 'ud come out. He landed wid a tumble splash an' splutter, an' he ain't hardly hit de groun' 'fo' Brer Buzzard say he don't want his feather fer ter git wet, an' he grabbed it. Den all de birds grabbed der'n, an' dar he wuz.

"Days an' days come an' went, an' bimeby Brer Rabbit wanter know what done gone wid de Doodang. Brer Buzzard say, 'You see my fambly settin' in de dead trees? Well, dar's whar de Doodang is, an ef you'll git me a bag, I'll fetch you his bones!' An' den Brer Rabbit sot back an' laugh twel his sides ache!"

"Anyhow," said the little boy, "I should like to fly."

"Fly, den," replied Uncle Remus; "Fly right in de house dis minnit, ter yo' mammy!"

2
Brer Rabbit Has Trouble with the Moon

ONE DAY the little boy hurt his toe against a sharp rock, and he ran to Uncle Remus for both aid and consolation. The old man, in the course of his long life, had had considerable experience in such matters, and, after anointing the wound with a salve made of mutton suet and white resin, he bandaged it up as neatly as a woman could have done.

"Dar's a heap er up an' downs in dis worl'," he remarked, "mo' speshually downs. 'Tain't nigh like it wuz when Brer Rabbit an' all de yuther creeturs wuz nex' do' neighbors ter de Moon. Dar wa'n't no hard times in dat country. Dey had lots mo' frolickin' an' fiddlin', an' not nigh so much scufflin' 'roun' fer vittles."

"Where was that, Uncle Remus?" the little boy inquired.

"Up dar in dat country whar dey wuz nigh neighbors ter Unk' Moon," replied the old man, solemnly. "But dey had der troubles, kaze dar wuz one time when ol' Unk' Moon 'gun ter git puny, an' it look mighty like he gwine ter have a spell er sickness."

"But how could they live up there without falling off?" the child interrupted.

"Des like we does down here," Uncle Remus responded, "heads up an foots down. Now when de creeturs seed dat Unk' Moon wuz in a bad way, dey ax deyse'f what de matter. Dey call an' ax' 'im how he gittin' on an' he say he ain't feelin' so well. It got so, atter while, dat Unk' Moon 'ud set out in de back yard mighty nigh de whole time. It went on dis way, twel, bimeby, Brer Rabbit clum on de fence, an' 'tain't take him long fer ter see dat Unk' Moon wuz in a mighty bad way. It seem like he wuz swinkin' up.

"He hear de fuss Brer Rabbit make when he clum de fence, an' he look up an' say howdy. Brer Rabbit howdied wid 'im, an' den ax 'im what de name er goodness is de matter. He say, 'Ain't dar nothin' I kin do fer ter he'p you out?'

"Unk' Moon say, sezee, 'I'm feared not; you ain't soople 'nough.'

"'When it come ter soopleness,' sez Brer Rabbit, sezee, 'I takes it wid me wharsomever I goes.'

"Den Unk' Moon say, 'I'll tell you des how 'tis; I wanter sen' word ter

Mr. Man dat I ain't feelin' right well. I been shinin' fer 'im at night, an'
done cotch col' fum bein' out in de night a'r so much, en' ef I don't put
out my light, an take a recess, I'll be in a mighty bad way. I wanter take
a holiday, but ef I don't sen' Mr. Man word, he'll be skeer'd ter death.'

"'Des show me de way fer ter go,' sez ol' Brer Rabbit, sezee, 'kaze I
wanter see dis thing you call Mr. Man.'

"So Unk' Moon show'd 'im de way, an' tol' 'im what ter say: 'I'm gittin' weak fer ter be mo' strong; I'm gwine in de shade fer ter git mo' light!'

"Brer Rabbit say dis over an' over, an' den he tuck a runnin' start,
an' jump de long jump; an' it sho wuz a long un, mon! He tuck a notion
dat he wus fallin', stidder jumpin', an' dis make 'im open bofe eyes big an'

wide, an' dey been big an' wide sence dat time. He landed all right, an' den he got up an' kinder romp about fer ter see ef his j'ints wus soople. He look in Mr. Man's gyarden, an' dar he see green peas, an' cabbage an' collards, an' sparrer-grass, an' dey make 'im dribble at de mouf.

"He knock at de do', an' Mr. Man ax 'im what he want. He try ter say de words dat Unk' Moon had sont. He say 'Unk' Moon sont dis word: "I'm gittin' weak; I got no strenk; I'm gwine whar de shadders stay."'

"Mr. Man can't make dis out, so he sont word back: 'Seldom seed an' soon forgot; when Unk' Moon dies his foots gits col'!'

"Wid dat, Brer Rabbit tuck de long jump ag'in an' run an' tol' Unk' Moon what Mr. Man say, an' dis make 'im mighty mad; he up wid a shovel an' hit Brer Rabbit on de mouf an' split his lip. Brer Rabbit jump at Unk' Moon wid toof an' claw, an' dar dey had it up an' down. You kin see de marks down ter dis day — Brer Rabbit, wid his split lip, an' Unk' Moon wid de scratches on his face.

"Den, atter dat, Brer Rabbit tell de yuther creeturs 'bout de sheep an' de goats an' de fine fat pigs what Mr. Man raisin', an' bimeby, one day, dey all tuck de long jump, an' dey all been here sence dat time. An' mo' dan dat, you better not let yo' mammy see dat rag on yo' toe, kaze she won't let you go bar'-footed no mo'!"

3
Brer Rabbit Causes Brer Fox to Lose His Hide

ONE DAY when the sun was shining brightly, and everything appeared to be serene, the little boy seemed to be worried about something. Uncle Remus was putting the finishing touches to a fish-basket that had been taking up his time for several days, and, for a minute or two, he paid no attention to the youngster, who was sitting on the door-sill, gazing into far-off space.

"What de matter, honey? It look like ter me dat you got trouble on de min'. Dat kinder trouble is sorter like a baby's toof-ache: you dunner how ter git at it."

"I was just thinking," said the little boy, "how the lion could have any hair on his body if he was scalded.[1] Mother says he couldn't."

"What Miss Sally say?" Uncle Remus asked.

"Why, grandmother said she'd rather count the hairs on a tarrypin's back than to bother about the small things in a story that was worth listening to."

The grin on Uncle Remus's face was one of pure joy. "What I been telling you 'bout yo' gran'mammy. Miss Sally oughter be de gov'ner er de Nunited State er Georgy, kaze what she dunno, dey ain't nobody gwine ter tell you. You ain't hear all dat tale, an' by good rights, you oughter ax

---

[1] See *Uncle Remus and Brer Rabbit*, "How Mr. Lion Lost His Wool," p. 691. — R. C.

me de questions what you ax yo' mammy. She ain't tell you de tale." This was a rebuke, and the little boy received it as such, and he appeared to be very penitent, though he said nothing.

"What you gwine do when you fin' yo'se'f in scaldin' water?" Uncle Remus inquired. "Is you gwine ter set in it twel you done cooked? Well, Brer Lion, he scramble out des ez hard ez he kin, an' dat wa'n't quick 'nough fer ter save his wool. An' needer wuz it quick 'nough fer ter keep 'im fum bein' mighty so' in a 'bunnunce er places here an' dar on his hide. He went home, he did, an' tuck ter his bed, an' he stay dar twel he get so dat he kin move about widout squallin'.

"In dem times, he wuz de king er de creeturs, an' whiles he wuz layin' dar in bed dey all call on 'im fer ter see how he gittin' on. Dey all pay him visits 'ceppin' ol' Brer Rabbit; he ain't gone ter de house, but he went nigh 'nough ter fin' out dat Brer Fox been tellin' some mighty mean tales 'bout 'im.

"When de yuther creeturs hear Brer Fox runnin' Brer Rabbit down, an' see dat Brer Lion wuz willin' fer ter lissen at 'im, dey all jine in an' say de wuss dey kin; an what dey ain't know dey make up. Eve'y whar he go, Brer Rabbit hear 'bout de talk dey been havin', an' some un it wuz so bad dat it fa'rly make his years burn. Den one day he hear tell dat Brer Lion, bein' de King er de creetur's, had tol' Brer Fox fer ter ketch 'im an' fetch 'im dar whar Brer Lion live at.

"Dis make Brer Rabbit set down an' study. He know Brer Fox can't ketch 'im, but he study how he gwine ter git even wid 'im. He study, an' study, twel bimeby, one day, he put out fer ter see how Brer Lion gittin' on.

"De road he went tuck 'im right by Brer Fox house. Brer Fox wuz settin' on de front porch when Brer Rabbit went by, an' he look like he 'stonish'; but he ain't say nothin'. Brer Rabbit ain't turn his head, kaze he know'd dat Brer Fox 'ud foller 'long atter.

"He went on, he did, twel he git ter Brer Lion's house. He rap on de do', an' Brer Lion groan an' growl, an' say, 'Come in.' So said, so done. Brer Lion watch Brer Rabbit mighty hard, an' bimeby he say, 'What's all dis I hear?'

"'You'll hatter tell me,' sez ol' Brer Rabbit, 'kaze I been off on a long journey. Stidder callin' on you an' settin' 'roun' here, a-doin' uv no good whatsomever, I been tryin' fer ter fin' sump'n' dat'd kyo' you.'

"'Don't tell me 'bout it,' sez Brer Lion, sezee. 'Eve'ybody been tellin' me what'd kyo' me, an' I ain't kyo'd yit; I'm wuss off dan befo'!'

"Brer Rabbit say, 'I could a come des ez much ez de rest er de creeturs, an' 'twould a done des ez much good. But I know'd,' sezee, 'dat when anybody gits scald' wid milk-warm water, dey's sump'n' de matter wid um sho 'nough. So I tuck'n went off whar Mammy-Bammy-Big-Money live at, an' I ax her what de matter when some folks kin git scald' in milk-warm water. She tuck off her lef' slipper, shuck out de pebbles an' count 'em ez dey fell out, an' say de onliest way fer ter work a kyo' is ter poultice de burns wid de fresh hide er his best frien'. I ax who it is,'

sez ol' Brer Rabbit, sezee, an' she say he got sharp nose, short years, slim legs, an' a bushy tail.'

"Brer Lion ain't wait a minnit; he call ter some er de creeturs what hangin' 'roun', an' he say, 'Fetch me de hide er Brer Fox!'"

Uncle Remus paused and leaned his head on his hand.

"What then?" the little boy inquired.

"De creeturs, dey fotch it," replied the old man, with something like a sigh.

4

How Brer Rabbit Saved Brer B'ar's Life

JUST ABOVE the spring, on the home-place, there was a large over-hanging rock that was a source of great interest to the little boy. He wondered how it grew there, he wondered if it had anything to do with the water-supply that bubbled beneath it, and when he had forgotten to wonder about one thing, he speedily began to wonder about something else concerning the rock — whether there was a gold mine beneath it, or a cavern, and if this were so, whether a door would fly open if some particular word or phrase was said. It presented a problem to the youngster that he could not long escape from; and it was so interesting in all its parts and particulars that it would be well if some of our noisy modern scientists would leave their foolish speculations, go to the old plantation, and there contemplate the puzzle presented by the hanging rock. The little boy asked Uncle Remus about it more than once, and he was so persistent in recurring to the matter that the old man finally told him a story about it.

"Ef I ain't mighty much mistooken," he said, "dat ar rock is de ve'y one what Brer Rabbit fool some er de creeturs wid. I dunno ef 'twuz Brer B'ar er Brer Fox, but we'll say dat 'twuz ol' Brer B'ar, an' let it go at dat. In one way an' anudder, Brer Rabbit wuz all de time a-pesterin' de yuther creeturs, pullin' der tails an' runnin' off, er makin' jokes 'bout um, er playin' pranks on um.

"Ef you been follerin' me 'long dis fur, you know dat some er de pranks dat ol' Brer Rabbit played on de creeturs got um in deep trouble. Ol' Brer B'ar ain't got no tail fer ter be pulled, but he had feelin's fer ter be hurted. I dunner what Brer Rabbit done ter him at dis intickler time, but he done sump'n' an' I speck 'twuz a-plenty. Anyhow, Brer B'ar got right behime Brer Rabbit, an' he push't him so close, dat befo' Brer Rabbit kin git in a holler-tree, Brer B'ar ketched him by de behime leg an' helt 'im. He try fer ter pull 'im out, but Brer Rabbit kinder brace hisse'f ag'in' de inside, an' dar he wuz. He stick his head ez fur up de holler ez he kin an' den he laugh an' say, sezee:

"'You think you got me, don't you, Brer B'ar? Well, you ain't; dat what you er pullin' an' tuggin' at ain't nothin' but a last year's sprout growin' out'n de groun' in here. Ef you think it's my behime leg, des git a rock an' hit, an' hit, an' you'll see dat I won't flinch.'

"Brer B'ar looked aroun' fer ter fin' a rock, but dar wa'n't none right at han', an' so he went off fer ter git one. Time he come back, he say, sezee, 'Whar de sprout, Brer Rabbit?'

"Brer Rabbit, he 'spon', sezee, 'I thought you wa'n't comin' back, Brer

B'ar, an' I tuck'n broke it off so I kin take it ter my ol' 'oman fer ter make a toof-bresh out'n; she'll like it fine!'

"I speck," Uncle Remus went on, looking curiously at the child, "dat dat holler-tree must a been up dar in de pastur' whar de barn is, an' ef dat's so, we kin foller de tale wid bofe eyes an' min'. When Brer Rabbit come out'n de holler fer ter go home, he know'd in reason dat Brer B'ar wuz somers close about watchin' fer 'im He crope out, he did, an' look all 'roun', an' den he made a dash fer de open, but ol' Brer B'ar wuz right at han', an' when Brer Rabbit made his dash, Brer B'ar made one too, an' he wuz so servigrous dat Brer Rabbit hatter run un' dat hangin' rock dat's been a-pesterin' you. He run un' dar, he did, an' Brer B'ar retched fer 'im, an' he come so close ter gittin' 'im dat he 'uz skeer'd mighty nigh col'.

"He holler out, he did. 'Look out dar, Brer B'ar! I feel dis rock a-fallin'! It'll git me, but it'll git you, too, an' den what good is yo' temper gwine do you? Don't you feel it sinkin' down? Go git sump'n' fer ter prop it up wid! I don't min' gittin' ketched myse'f, but I don't wanter set here an' see you mashed ez flat ez a battercake!'

"An' so Brer B'ar, he run off fer ter get a pole fer ter prop up de rock wid, an' when he come back, Brer Rabbit wuz done gone, an' 'twuz many a long day 'fo' he seed 'im ag'in.''

The little boy sat reflecting, and finally he said:

"Well, I knew there was something curious about the rock."

Whereupon, Uncle Remus closed his eyes and held them so until the child slipped out of the house and went to play.

5

The Story of Teenchy-Tiny Duck

As USUAL Uncle Remus made his appearance just before dinner. When asked about it, he laughed heartily. "Well, suh," he said, "I never yit seed a dinner dat could skeer me. I don't keer how big it is, ner how fine, I kin look it right in de face an' eyes, an' never turn a ha'r. Ol' Miss use ter say dat I wuz a mighty bol' nigger when it come ter vittles, an' I speck dat's so, kaze de onliest skeer I have is dat de cook won't save me none."

"Where is the little boy?"

"Oh, he done come back. He went out dar ter Californy fer ter fix his lungs an' livers, an' he come wid me fer ter see how fur you live fum town. He's out dar in de yard fishin' fer jacks. He'll take a piece er grass an' run it down in a hole, an' de fust news you know, he done cotch one. I tol' him dat ef he wanted ter hear me tell a tale, he'd hatter come in here an' tell you howdy. I'm mighty glad yo' room is so close ter der kitchen; I kin set on dis trunk an' tell you what you gwine ter have fer dinner. Cabbage fer one thing, an' inguns fer an'er. De cook sho must a know'd I wuz comin'.'"

At this juncture, the little boy ran in, full of health and perspiration; he had been having a glorious time, and he wished that he lived somewhere where there were plenty of trees and grass. The jack-bugs that you caught in town were hardly worth fishing for, they were so small and poor. His trip to Southern California had evidently done him a world of good. His pallor had disappeared, and he was now as ruddy and rugged as you could wish. He was very polite, too, for he knew that Uncle Remus was regarding him with critical eyes. But when all the formalities were over, his mind reverted to the story that he had been promised, and he reminded Uncle Remus of it.

"You hear dat!" the old Negro exclaimed. "All you hear fum dat boy is tell me a tale, tell me a tale, an' when dat's done, it's tell me anudder, tell me anudder; it don't make no diffunce dat age is a-creepin' on de ol' nigger. An' I speck I'll hatter turn over an' do de best I kin. It puts me in mind er ol' Teenchy Duck dat foun' a money-purse in de river."

"How was that?" the little boy asked; "you never told me that story; you've been keeping it to yourself all this time."

"Name er goodness, honey! I'm bleeze ter have some secrets; look how ol' I is, an' how wobbly! You don't want me not to have no secrets, does you?"

"No," said the boy unblushingly; "not story secrets. How can a common everyday story be a secret!"

"Well ef de tales I tells is des eve'y-day tales, an' common too, you mought ez well not take de trouble fer ter lissen at um. Go out dar an' ketch you some mo' jack-bugs."

The little boy looked at the old Negro as though he didn't understand what had been said; he made no movement to go, but was evidently uneasy. "Well, tell me about Teenchy Duck," he said after a while.

"'Tain't no use," replied Uncle Remus; "she wa'n't nothin' but a common eve'y-day puddle duck; an' mo' dan dat she ain't got but two foots fer ter waddle about on. Ain't she too common fer you?"

The little boy made no answer whatever; he had grown wise to the old

Negro's methods, and so he simply waited. Uncle Remus, seated upon the low trunk, pulled a few ravelings from his sleeve, cleared his throat, and told the following story:

"One time — I dunner ef it wuz in Greene County, er in Bald'in — dar lived a man an' a 'oman dat wuz mighty poor. Dey ain't got no money, an' dey ain't had time fer ter save none; much ez dey kin do fer ter keep body an' soul tergedder. Dey ain't got no farm, an' dey ain't got no gyarden patch. All dey had in de roun' worl' wuz a little puddle duck dat walked 'roun' an' 'roun' all day singin' de hongry song — 'Quack! quack! gi' me a piece er bread!' Look like it wouldn't a took much ter feed her, kaze she wuz sech a little bit er duck dat folks called her Teenchy-Tiny Duck. Well, one day, whiles she wuz paddlin' in de river — I dunno ef it wuz de Oconee er de Ocmulgee — she up an' found a money-purse all full er shiny gold. No sooner did she see it dan she made a turrible racket: 'Somebody los' der purty money! Purty money! purty money! Who los' der purty money?'

"Brer Rabbit, on de bank, look out'n his hidin'-place, an' kinder grin, an' den he wunk one eye, but he ain't say a word. Bimeby a rich man come 'long; he had a walkin'-stick in his han', an' eve'y once an' awhile he'd stop an' make marks in de san', a-countin' up de money what he had, an' dat what he done lent out; he wuz one er de kind what you call big rich fer dem days. Well, whiles he wuz walkin' 'long, he hear de fuss dat Teenchy-Tiny Duck's a-makin', an' he look close fer ter see what de matter. Den an' dar his eye lit on de money-purse, an' he seed de gold a-shinin' thoo. He holler out: 'Dat's mine! dat's mine! I des now drapt it;' an' wid dat he tuck de gold an' slapped it in his kyarpet-sack.

"Atter he done gone, Teenchy-Tiny got so mad dat all she kin do is ter dance 'roun' on her two footsies. She say, 'De gran' rascal done took it all, an' ain't never gi' me nothin' fer findin' it!' Den she waddled off home an' tol' um what done happened. De man wuz so mad dat he wanter pull all his ha'r out; he say, he did, 'Git outer my house an' lot, sech as dey is, and don't never come back here twel you git dat money what de rich man tuck!' Teenchy-Tiny Duck ain't know what ter do. She went back ter de river bank, an' sot down an' cried. Brer Rabbit see her an' ax her what de matter mought be. She up an' tol' 'im all about it, an' he wiped one eye an' wunk de udder. Sezee, 'Well, whyn't you go atter de man an' git de

money?' She say, 'How I gwine ter git de money atter I find de man?' Brer
Rabbit say, sezee, 'Dey's allers a way, ef not two,'

"So off she put, a-waddlin' an' a-quackin', 'I want my purty money! I want my purty money!' She foller'd de man by de marks er de cane in de ground. She pass by ol' Brer Fox, an' he ax her what de matter. She up 'n tol' 'im. He ax her what she gwine ter do when she fin' de rich man, an' she say she gwine git de purty money an' take it back home. 'Shill I go wid you?' sez ol' Brer Fox, sezee, an' she say dat nothin'll suit her better. 'I'll hatter hide,' sez ol' Brer Fox; 'how I gwine do it?' 'Git in my satchel,' sez Teenchy-Tiny. Brer Fox say 'tain't nigh big 'nough, an' she make answer. 'My satchel is a stretchin' satchel.'

"She ain't gone fur befo' she met ol' Brer Wolf. He lissen at de talk 'bout de money, an' say, 'Whar you come fum an' whar you gwine, an' what you gwine atter?' She up an' tol' 'im. 'Maybe I kin he'p you,' sezee, 'but I'm tired, an' I can't go so fur.' She says, se' she, 'Git in my satchel.' He say, "Tain't nigh big 'nough.' She say, 'It's de stretchin' satchel; jump in.' Well, in he jumped, an' atter dat, Teenchy-Tiny can't go so mighty fast, kaze she got too big a load. But she waddled on, quackin' 'bout de purty money.

"Bimeby, whiles she wuz gwine on down de road, she come up wid Uncle Ladder, takin' his noon rest by de side of a tree. Uncle Ladder, he say, sezee, 'You must not feel so well fum de way you er gwine on.' Den Teenchy-Tiny up an' tol' him about de bad luck she done had; she shuck her head backerds an' forerds, an' quacked so loud, dat Uncle Ladder wuz sorry. He ax her ef he kin do anything fer ter he'p her out, an' she say she speck he kin do a heap to he'p her. Uncle Ladder says, sezee, dat he'd be glad ef he kin, but he can't walk, an' he dunner how he gwine wid her. Teenchy-Tiny say, 'Des git in my satchel, an' I'll tote you de best I know how.' So Uncle Ladder got in de satchel, an' off she started."

At this point Uncle Remus glanced suddenly at the little boy, who had an expression of unbelief on his face. He caught the eye of the old Negro, and remarked, "I was just thinking what mother would say to that."

"Is she here?" Uncle Remus inquired in a matter-of-fact way. "Well, den, honey, ef she ain't here, an' not likely ter be, dey ain't no reason why de tale ain't des ez good ez some yuther tales you've hearn me tell 'fo' now.

"Well, Uncle Ladder clomb in de satchel, an' he had plenty er room, an' Teenchy-Tiny Puddle Duck went wobblin' on, quackin' 'bout de purty money what done been tuck fum 'er. Now whiles she gwine on, follerin' de tracks er de rich man's walkin'-cane, she come right face wid de bes' frien' she'd yever had, an' dat wuz Gran'pappy River. He stop runnin', he did, an' say, sezee, 'Why, what de matter? When I seed you dis mornin', you look like you wuz happy, an' now, here you is in deep trouble. How kin I he'p you? Maybe I'd better go wid you; I sholy would ef I had legs.'"

Here Uncle Remus paused a moment to glance at the little boy out of the corner of his eye, but the youngster had ceased to be doubtful; he had become interested. Uncle Remus shook his head triumphantly, and went on: "Gran'pappy River got in de satchel widout drownin' anybody, an' Teenchy-Tiny Duck went on, still follerin' de tracks dat de rich man's

walkin'-cane had made in de groun', an' purty soon, ef not sooner, she
come ter a big Bee Hive. Ol' man Drone wuz a-sunnin' hisse'f, an' when
he seed her he got ter laughin' an' 'twa'n't long 'fo' all de Bees had come
out fer ter see what de trouble wuz all about. An' when dey seed her, dey
laugh an' laugh twel some on 'em fell down fum de bench. But Teenchy-
Tiny Puddle Duck look so sollum dat dey hushed up one an'er atter
while, an' say, 'We-all wuz des laughin' kaze you got sech a big fat
satchel. Tell us what de matter is.'

"She sot down an' tol' 'em all about her troubles, an' it look like dey git

bigger an' wusser de mo' she talk about um. De Bees said dey'd be mo' dan glad fer ter he'p out ef dey know'd how, an' dey ax ef dey can't go wid 'er. 'Git in my satchel,' se' she, an', sho 'nough, in dey swarmed. She went on, sometimes a-waddlin' an' sometimes a-toddlin', an' long about night, she come ter de place whar de rich man live at. She crope und' de gate, an' went up ter de big house hollerin' fer her purty money. De rich man he hear her, an' he know'd des zackly what she come fer. He laugh, he did, an' make some er de niggers put her in de hen-house 'long wid de geese an' de turkeys, an' tol' de cook fer ter have 'er fer dinner de nex' day. So said, so done. Inter de hen-house she went, an' time she git in dar de yuther fouls 'gun ter make a mighty racket; I speck dey must er ketch a whiff er Brer Fox. Anyhow, dey got atter her, dark ez 'twuz, dey got atter her, an' pecked on her an' beat her wid der wings, an' she hatter call on Brer Fox fer ter come outer de satchel an' see what he kin do ter settle de 'spute.

"Well, out he come, an' mighty glad er de chance. All de fowls quit der 'sputin' an' when de cook come out de nex' mornin' fer ter git Teenchy-Tiny, she sho did open her eyes. De groun' wuz strowed wid dead chickens, an' turkeys, an' gooses, kaze Brer Fox sho had done his work well. De cook was so 'stonish' dat she run ter de big house widout takin' time fer ter pull de hen-house door shet. Teenchy-Tiny Duck marched out wid her fat satchel an' went 'roun' ter de front, quackin' an' squallin', 'Gi' me back my purty money! Gi' me back my purty money!' De rich man's wife, when de cook got thoo tellin' her tale, up an' say, 'Dat ain't no Duck; it's a witch. Ef you don't gi' her her money back, we'll sho have bad luck!' But de man des laugh, an' he laughed eve'y time he hear Teenchy-Tiny Duck holler. An' she kep' it up all day long. Sometimes she'd set down an' rest, but de most er de time, she wuz totin' her big satchel about over de place, an' hollerin' ter de man fer ter gi' her back her purty money what she found.

"Night come ez night will, an' de rich man made de niggers take de Duck an' put her in de stable 'long wid de Mules an' hosses. He say, 'We'll see what she'll holler in de mornin'.' No sooner said dan done, an' Teenchy-Tiny Duck wuz so skeer'd dat she call ter Brer Wolf, dat ef he don't come an he'p 'er, she sholy will be trompled under de creeturs' foots. Well, Brer Wolf ain't need no second tellin'; he work so hard an' he work so fast, dat when de plough-hands an' de waggin drivers come fer ter git der teams de nex' mornin', dey fin' um all stretched out stiff. When dis word went out, de rich man's ol' 'oman beg an' beg 'im fer ter gi' de money back ter Teenchy-Tiny Duck. But de man wuz too mad ter lissen. So he went out in de yard, an' tell his niggers fer ter fling her in de well.

"All dis time, an' whiles dey wuz totin' her off, Teenchy-Tiny Duck keep on squallin' and quackin', 'Gi' me back my purty money!' Dey flung her in de well, an' ez she fell, she holler ter de Ladder fer come he'p her. De Ladder got out'n de satchel an' kinder stretched itse'f, kaze it had been might'ly cramped in dar. It stretched itse'f twel it got ter de top, an' Teenchy-Tiny Duck clomb it round by round, an' come out, an' she come

a-hollerin' fer her purty money. You may well b'lieve dat dem 'ar niggers an' all de balance wuz might'ly 'stonished. But de rich man got madder dan he wuz befo'. He stomped his foots an' pulled his ha'r, an' des vow dat he ain't gwine ter turn de money loose. He run out, he did, an' tol' um ter heat de bakin' oven red-hot an' put her in. An' all dat time Teenchy-Tiny wuz marchin' up an' down squallin' an' quackin' fer her purty money. Dey got de oven mighty hot, an' de rich man tol' um fer ter fling her in. De niggers wuz skeer'd but dey hatter do what der marster tol' um. Time dey done it, Teenchy-Tiny Duck call fer ol' frien', de River, an'

he bust outer de satchel an' squelched de fier, an' Teenchy-Tiny come marchin' out, hollerin' louder dan ever fer her purty money.

"An' still de rich man won't turn de money loose, no matter how much his wife beg him. He say he'll 'ten' ter de job hisse'f; an' dat night, when eve'ybody but him had done gone ter bed, he tuck his walkin'-cane, an' went out an' got Teenchy-Tiny Duck, an' wuz des in de ac' er beatin' her plum' ter death, when she called on de Bees fer ter come an' he'p her. Dey come swarmin' out, an' de way dey treat dat rich man wuz 'nough fer ter make you smile er cry, whichever way yo' mind mought lean. He couldn't run fast nuff fer ter git de money, an' when he got it he hand it ter Teenchy-Tiny Duck, an' tol' her ter go on 'bout her business, an' pester him no mo'. She waddled off down de road, an' she tuck all her frien's back whar dey jined her — de Bees ter de Hive, de Ladder ter de wall, an' de River ter its bed. Brer Wolf an' Brer Fox 'low dat dey kin walk faster dan she could tote um. Her marster an' mistiss got de money dat ain't b'long ter um, an' it look like dey oughter be happy, but dey wa'n't; dey know'd dey wuz spendin' dat dat wa'n't der'n. But dey feed Teenchy-Tiny Duck twel she got so fat an' sassy dat she won't 'sociate wid nobody but de fambly dat dey calls Muscovy; you know what I mean."

Of course the little boy knew, but he was thinking about it so hard that he forgot to laugh. Uncle Remus adjourned to the kitchen, where he soon had the cook talking in wrathful tones. As for the little boy, he found a big picture book in which he became so absorbed that it would have been difficult for a stranger to imagine that there was a little boy in the house.

6

The Story of Brer Fox and Little Mr. Cricket

THE LITTLE BOY had made no comments on the story of Teenchy-Tiny Duck after Uncle Remus told it, preferring to bury his talents in the new picture book, but he asked the old Negro about it when they were ready to go home. "How did the Duck get the Ladder in her satchel?" he inquired.

Uncle Remus sighed and looked around him. "We ain't in no court-house, is we, honey? Kaze ef we is, I'm gwine off somers whar dey ain't no court-houses an' lawyers; I done had my fill un um. Plain livin' suits me, an' de plainer it is de better I likes it. Now, maybe dat Ladder wuz one er de telescopius kind what kin fold up. I ain't never seed one un um myself, but I speck dey had um in dem days. We got mighty big idees, but we ain't no smarter dan folks dat's done come an' gone. Mo' dan dat, a tale's a tale, an' you can't make nothin' else out'n um. When de tale wuz tolden unto me, I ain't ax nothin' about no Ladder. 'Twuz in de satchel in de tale, an' 'twa'n't no business er mine fer ter take it out. It'd be dar yit, if I had my way. Furdermo', when you git so you can't b'lieve tales, it's time fer yo' pa fer ter put you in some sto' whar you kin l'arn all about swindlin' yo neighbors. Dat's de kind er folks dat wanter pick a tale ter pieces like dey wuz pickin' a chicken — an' goodness knows I wish I had one ter pick right now!"

"How deep was the well that the Ladder helped the Duck out of?" inquired the little boy.

"Ah! now you're tryin' fer ter talk hoss sense! I dunner how deep de well wuz; it mought a been a inch an' a quarter, er it mought er been sev'mty-five feet; ez de well wuz, so wuz de Ladder, an' I'll let you medjur um fer yo'se'f, kaze I ain't gwine roun' medjurin' yuther folks's wells an' ladders; I got sump'n' better ter do dan dat. I had a tale on my mind dat I wuz des gwine fer ter tell you, but, la! you done got me so mixt up dat I ain't got right good sense. Is terday yistiddy, er is it day 'fo' yistiddy? I wish you'd tell me dat, kaze somebody done tol' me dat my all-manac is got rain whar it oughter be shine."

"Can't you remember the story?" asked the little boy. "Can't you tie a string around your thumb and remember it? That's the way mamma does when she wants papa to bring her something from town."

"No, no, honey! Dey tells me dat when a man git in de inhabitants of tyin' strings on his fingers, he'll be sho ter die wid a rope 'roun' his neck. Dat may not be so, an' you nee'nter run an' tell yo' mammy 'bout it; you may tell Miss Sally, but nobody else, kaze ef you does you'll sho git me in trouble when I go atter you fer ter fetch you down. An' speakin' er town, dat ve'y word makes de tale pop back in my mind. Ain't I tell you a tale once 'bout little Mr. Cricket? Ef 'twa'n't you, den it wuz yo' pa.

"Well, you know Mr. Cricket ain't so mighty big, but he big 'nough fer ter make a heap er fuss in de worl'; some er de creeturs say dat he made mo' fuss dan he done good. I ain't 'sputin' dat, an' I ain't 'greein' wid it, kaze we er all here fer sump'n', good er bad, an' we bleedz fer ter foller our noses ef we git anywhar 'tall, an' ef we don't fall down an' git talked about, we may thank all de stars on de underside er de sky.

"Dis Mr. Cricket I'm tellin' you 'bout ain't never had no chance fer ter live in no chimbley-jam. He stayed out in de bushes an' de high grass, an' he didn't do nothin' in de roun' worl' but play on his fife an' his fiddle; when he got tired er one, he'd turn ter de udder.

"He done dis spite er de fack dat dey'd had a mighty bad year; not much rain, but a mighty sight er thunder. When you git ez ol' ez Noah you'll know what I mean. Little Mr. Cricket went on dis a-way twel de cool nights an' days 'gun ter come on, an' sometimes he hatter warm hisse'f by gittin' under a clump er grass. But he wuz cheerful; he ain't drapt no sobs, an' he ain't shed no sighs, an' he kep' on a-flutin' an' a-fiddlin'.

"One day when de sun wuz shinin' kinder thankful like, he clum on top er de tall grass, an' fiddled away like somebody wuz fryin' meat. He hear some un comin', an' he look right close, an', lo beholes! it wuz ol' Brer Fox. He 'low, 'Hello, Brer Fox! whar you gwine?'

"Brer Fox kinder pull hisse'f up, an' ax, 'Who dat?'

"Little Mr. Cricket say, 'It ain't nobody in de roun' worl' but me; I know I ain't much, but I'm mighty lively when de sun shines hot. Whar you gwine, Brer Fox?'

"Brer Fox, he say, 'I'm gwine whar I'm gwine, dat's whar I'm gwine, an'

I wouldn't be too much 'stonished ef I wuz ter land in town in time fer ter git my dinner. I useter be a rover in my young days, an' I'm still a-rovin'.'

" 'Well, well!' sez little Mr. Cricket, sezee, 'we all goes de way we're pushed by mind er hand, an' it takes a mighty little shove fer ter send us de way we're gwine. I useter belong ter de rover fambly myse'f, but now I done settle down, an' don't do a thing in de worl' but have my own fun in my own way an' time. But sence I seed you an' hear you talk so gaily, I done tuck a notion fer take dinner in town myse'f.'

"Brer Fox 'low, 'How will you git dar, little frien'?'

"Mr. Cricket say, 'Ain't you never watched my motions? I got legs an' feet, an' I done cotch de jumpin' habit fum ol' Cousin Brown Grasshopper — de kind what crawls a little, walks a little, flies a little, an' hops like two-forty on de shell road. What time you speck fer ter git ter town?'

"Brer Fox 'spon', 'Gi' me two good hours, an' I'll be right dar wid my appetite wid me.'

"Little Mr. Cricket seem like he wuz 'stonish'; he helt up all his hands an' mighty nigh all his footses. 'Two hours! Well, by de time you git dar, I'll done been had my dinner, an' ready fer ter take my nap.'

"Brer Fox grin at him, an' 'low, 'Ef you'll beat me so much ez ten

inches, I'll pervide yo' dinner, an' let you choosen yo' own provender. Ef I beat you, why, den you'll hatter pervide de dinner — a half-grown lam' an' a sucklin' shote.'"

"Little Mr. Cricket say he'll be mo' dan glad fer ter fill out dat p'o-grance. An' den Brer Fox, atter grinnin' ag'in, started off in a lope. But, des 'fo' Brer Fox make his start, little Mr. Cricket made his; he tuck a flyin' jump an' land on Brer Fox big bushy tail, an' dar he stayed.

"When Brer Fox had been gwine a little mo' dan a hour, he meet Brer Rabbit on de road, and' dey howdied. Brer Fox laugh an' up an' tell Brer Rabbit 'bout de race 'twix' him an' Mr. Cricket. Ol' Brer Rabbit, he smole a smile an' roll his eye-balls; he do so funny dat Brer Fox ax 'im what de nation is de matter wid 'im.

"Brer Rabbit say he wuz des thinkin' how Brer Fox'd feel fer ter find Mr. Cricket dar befo' him. Brer Rabbit 'low, 'De cute little creetur passed me on de road a quarter hour ago; ef you er gwine ter git dar ahead un um, you'll hatter whip up yo' hosses. What you been doin' all dis time? You must a fell asleep an' didn't know it.' Brer Fox pant an' 'low, 'No, suh, I been comin' full tilt all de time.'

"Brer Rabbit 'spon', 'Den all I got fer ter say is dat Mr. Cricket is got a mighty knack fer gittin' over groun'. I speck he done dar by dis time!'

"'Ef he ain't,' sez Brer Fox, sezee, 'I'll ketch him,' an' wid dat, he put out an' went des ez hard ez he kin; but fast ez he went Mr. Cricket wuz gwine des ez fast; I dunno but what he had gone fast asleep in de saft bed whar he wuz hidin' at.

"When Brer Rabbit see Brer Fox mend his gait, he des roll over an' waller in de san', an' laugh fit fer ter kill. He say ter hisse'f, 'I'm mighty glad I met my ol' friend, kaze now I know dat all de fools ain't dead — an' long may dey live fer ter gi' me sump'n' ter do. I dunner how in de wide worl' I'd git along widout um. Dey keeps me fat an' sassy, whedder craps is good er not.' Kaze when Brer Rabbit wuz lookin' Brer Fox over, his eyes fell on little Mr. Cricket, an' dis what make he roll it so; he seed Mr. Cricket settin' up dar des ez snug ez a bug in a rug, ef you know how snug dat is.

"Well, de upshot er de whole business wuz dat when Brer Fox got ter town an' come ter de gate — dey had towns walled in in dem days — Mr. Cricket tuck a flyin' jump an' landed on top whar he could watch Brer Fox, an' see what he gwine ter do.

"Brer Fox, he knock at de gate, an' den walk up an' down waitin' fer some un ter open it.

"Mr. Cricket, on top er de wall, holler out, 'Heyo, Brer Fox! whar you been all dis time? You must a stopped some'rs on de road fer ter git yo' dinner; an' I'm sorry, too. I done been had mine so long dat I'm e'en about ready an' willin' fer ter eat ag'in. I had de idee, fum what you said, dat you wuz gwine ter come on ez hard ez you could. You must a stopped on de way an' had a confab wid Brer Rabbit; I met him on de way, an' it look like ter me dat he wuz ready fer ter pass de time er day wid anybody dat come along.'

"Brer Fox look like he wuz 'stonished. He say, 'How in de wide worl' did you git here so quick, Mr. Cricket?' Mr. Cricket, he make answer, 'I kin hardly tell you, Brer Fox. You know how I travels — wid a hop, skip an' a jump — well, I hopped, an' skipped an' jumped a little quicker dis time, an' got here all safe an' soun'. When ol' 'quaintances holler at me on de road, I des kep' on a-gwine; I done foun' out long ago dat de way fer ter git anywhar is ter go on whar you gwine.'

"Brer Fox shuck his head, an' panted, an' when dey let him in de

gate, he run his han' in his pocket, an' paid fer Mr. Cricket's dinner; an'
den, atter dinner, Mr. Cricket sot back an' tuck a chaw terbacker, an'
warmed hisse'f in de sun.

"Now, den," remarked the old darkey, "ef you want ter know de rest
er de tale, you'll hatter git some un else fer ter tell you, kaze it ain't no
nigger tale, nohow."

But the little boy seemed to be satisfied with it all, and presently he
was lying flat on the floor gazing at the ceiling.

VIII

The tales from

Uncle Remus Returns

With illustrations by
ARTHUR BURDETTE FROST
and **J. M. CONDÉ**

1
Brother Rabbit's Bear Hunt

THE LITTLE BOY had, naturally, a good deal of the simple faith that is one of the most beautiful characteristics of childhood, but his training had been to some extent along the lines marked out in certain periodicals that contain departments in which mothers are instructed how to deal with children, and in which sage advice is given by young men and young women, under names not their own, as to the training of youngsters.

Young as he was, the little boy had been denied pretty much all the romance that belongs to childhood; for him the beautiful story of Santa Claus, with all the associations that belong thereto, had been shattered. The grandmother deplored it, and wept over it during the long watches of the night — but you know about these grandmothers, with their anti-quated ideas and their old-fashioned notions. The mother had been caught in the net laid for the ignorant, by so-called scientists, and she regarded her own views (which were far from being her own) as of the ut-most importance.

The youngster yearned to believe the tales told by Uncle Remus, but his mother managed to keep the wings of his imagination clipped as close as those of a chicken that we desire to keep from flying over the garden fence. One thing about the stories that he failed to understand was the remarkable success of Brother Rabbit in keeping out of trouble. He was obliged to identify Uncle Remus's Brother Rabbit with the rab-bits that he saw occasionally on the plantation, and they were not only weak, but seemed to be very stupid; they had neither claws nor tushes, nor strength of limb. He asked his mother about it, and she gave him an explanation that he had no desire to hear; he asked his grandmother, and she laughingly referred him to Uncle Remus. "He can tell you about it much better than I can," she said.

Thus it happened that the little boy was compelled to fall back on the most gifted fabulist that the plantation had ever known. He laid his puz-zle before Uncle Remus one afternoon when the old Negro had just fin-ished his dinner, and was therefore in a very good humor. Apparently the child had some difficulty in making clear to Uncle Remus the nature of his doubts, but after a while he seemed to understand what the youngster wanted to know. To make sure, however, Uncle Remus stated the case as he understood it in his own simple way.

"Ef I ain't mighty much mistooken, honey, you wanter know how come Brer Rabbit kin outdo de yuther creeturs when he ain't got no tushes ner claws, an' not much strenk." The old Negro's eyes twinkled as he looked at the little boy. "Well, dat's de ve'y idential thing dat de tales is all about. Look like he wuz born little so he kin cut up capers an' play pranks no matter whar'bouts you put 'im at. What he can't do wid his foots he kin do wid his head, an' when his head git 'im in trouble dat's deeper dan what he counted on, he puts his 'pen'ence in his foots, kaze dar's whar he keeps his lippity-clip an' his blickety-blick." The little boy brightened up, for it was the purely pictorial language that Uncle Remus sometimes used that appealed to his sense of the fitness of things.

"'Tain't been mo' dan a good half hour ago," Uncle Remus casually remarked, "dat I wuz laughin' fit ter kill 'bout de way Brer Rabbit done when he went b'ar-huntin'. He sho had his fun, no matter ef he went huntin' or fishin', but when he tuck a notion fer ter go a-huntin' ol' Brer B'ar, he had mo' fun dan you kin shake a stick at. Some folks mought not a liked dat kinder fun what you kin have when you go b'ar-huntin', but Brer Rabbit wuz monstus fond un it, kaze de kinder huntin' what he done wuz a mighty quare kind, an' de fun what he git out'n it wuz de kin' what make 'im laugh twel he can't stan' up no mo' dan a week-ol' baby. But la! I speck I done make yo' mammy mad by tellin' you deze ol' timey tales so much. She look mighty hard at me yistiddy when I went up dar an' ax Miss Sally fer ter gi' me a piece er poun' cake ef she had any lef' over fum las' Christmas."

"Why, Christmas has been gone so long that I had almost forgotten it," said the little boy.

"Dat's so," Uncle Remus assented, "but we'll hatter whirl in an' have an'er one 'fo' de year's out. By dat time you'll be gone back home, an' me an' Miss Sally will have sump'n' dat's got mo' claws an' mo' color dan plain silly-bug."

There was a long pause, during which Uncle Remus watched the youngster out of the corner of his eye. Presently the little fellow stirred uneasily, and then made this statement. "I don't see why Brother Rabbit wanted to go bear-hunting. He would be in a worse fix when he caught the bear than he was when he hit and kicked the tar-baby."

Uncle Remus laughed heartily. "I speck yo' pa done gone an' tol' you 'bout de tar-baby. Ol' Brer Rabbit sho wuz in a mighty close place dat time, but ef you take notice, he ain't stay dar long. No, suh! Not him!"

"But, Uncle Remus!" exclaimed the child, "why did he want to hunt the bear? I don't see how he showed his sense by doing such a thing as that. He ought to have known better."

"Well, honey, you ain't got no needs fer ter pester yo'se'f wid de ups an' downs er ol' Brer Rabbit. Ef he got sense, er ef he ain't got none, it don't make no diffunce now, kaze de ol' times is done gone, an' ef 'twa'n't fer deze ol' tales nobody wouldn't know dat dey yever wuz any ol' times." Saying which, Uncle Remus filled his after-dinner pipe and turned to his unfinished task, whatever it was.

But the little boy was by no means satisfied to let the matter go at that. He wanted to know why Brother Rabbit hunted Brother Bear, and how the hunt ended; and he was so persistent about it that the old Negro was compelled to tell him the story in self-defense.

"Dey wuz one time," said Uncle Remus, "when de creeturs had laid by der craps, an' dey ain't got nothin' fer ter do but set down on a log an' chaw der terbacker an' tell all dey knows an' lots mo' besides. One day Brer Rabbit wuz gwine down de road, des ter be a-gwine, when who should he meet but Brer Fox an' Brer Wolf. Dey wuz amblin' an' a-ramblin' 'long tergedder, des ez chummy ez you please, laughin' an' talkin', an' ol' Brer Rabbit j'ined in wid um. Atter while dey sot down by de side er de road, an' got ter talkin' 'bout der neighbors an' 'bout de dull times in giner'l.

"Brer Fox say dey ain't nothin' 'tall gwine on, no parties, no picnics, an' no bobbycues. Brer Wolf say he's a ol' settle' man, an' he ain't keerin' much fer parties an' dem kinder doin's, but he like fer ter see young folks 'joy deyse'f whiles dey er young an' soople. Brer Rabbit he up an' 'low dat dey ain't no dull times wid him, kaze it look like he got sump'n' n'er fer ter do eve'y minnit er de day whedder he's at home or whedder he's abroad. Brer Wolf, he ax, 'What you doin' right now?' an' den he look at Brer Fox an' wunk one eye.

"He wunk mighty quick, but not quick 'nough fer ter keep Brer Rabbit fum ketchin' a glimp' un it. Brer Rabbit wipe his mouf sorter slow like, an' look up at de clouds floatin' by. He 'low, he did, 'Well, frien's, ef I hadn't a seed you-all, I'd a been well on my way fer ter look at my fishtraps, an', dat done, I'd a come 'roun' by my turkey blin'. I ain't got too much time, nohow you kin fix it, an' when I does set down, it's a thrip ter a gingercake dat I draps ter sleep 'fo' anybody kin head me off.'

"Brer Wolf say, 'Wid me it's diffunt. When I lay by my crap, I allers take a little recess, an' pass de time er day wid my neighbors.'

"Brer Rabbit 'low, 'Dat's what make me stop here a little minnit. When I gits home my ol' 'oman is sho ter ax me who I seed an' what dey say, an' how wuz der folks an' der famblies. You know how de wimmin is — dey'll tantalize de life out'n you twel you tells um who you seed an' what dey had on. But me! I ain't got time fer ter tarry. I'm fixin' up fer ter go on a big b'ar-hunt termorrer, an' it's a-gwine ter take up all my time fer ter git good an' ready. My ol' 'oman been beggin' me not ter go; she say she's all uv a trimble, she so skeered I'll git hurted somehow er somewhar. But dat's de way wid de wimmin; dey make out dey are monstus skeery, but when you fetch de game home, dey allers ready fer ter clean an' scal' it, an' fix it up fer de table.'

"When Brer Rabbit say dis, Brer Fox an' Brer Wolf flung back der heads an' laugh fit ter kill. Brer Rabbit, he 'low, 'Frien's, what's de joke? Be sociable an' le' me laugh wid you.' Sez Brer Wolf, sezee, 'We er laughin', Brer Rabbit, kaze you say you gwine b'ar-huntin'. You know mighty well dat you ain't big 'nough fer ter ketch no b'ar. Why, I'm lots bigger dan what you is, an' I'd think twice 'fo' I started out fer ter hunt Brer B'ar'. Brer Rabbit, he kinder smole one er his ol'-time smiles. He 'low, he did, 'Yes, Brer Wolf, you er lots bigger dan what I is; but will you an' Brer Fox head 'im off ef I git 'im on de run?' Brer Fox, he up an' 'spon', sezee, 'You git 'im on de run, Brer Rabbit, an' we'll head 'im off; I'll promise you dat much — we'll head 'im off ef you git 'im on de run.'

"Brer Rabbit 'low, 'It's a bargain, den, an' we'll shake han's on it.' It wuz a law 'mong de creeturs dat when dey make a bargain an' shuck han's on it, dey wa'n't no way er gittin' 'roun' it; an' so when Brer Rabbit made um shake han's wid 'im, Brer Wolf an' Brer Fox bofe know dat ef dey wuz any b'ar-hunt, dey'd hatter be on han' fer ter head 'im off when

Brer Rabbit got 'im on de run. Dey shuck han's, but dey ain't gi' Brer
Rabbit ez hard a grip ez dey mought, kaze dey ain't had no notion er gittin' in a sho 'nough b'ar-hunt. Dat 'uz one er de kinder things what dey
wa'n't in de habits er doin'. Dey kinder had de idee dat Brer Rabbit wuz
des a braggin', but when he make um shake han's, dey 'gun ter feel sorter
skittish, yit dey wa'n't no gittin' 'roun' a bargain what dey done shuck
han's on.

"Brer Rabbit ain't stay so mighty long atter dat; he say he gotter go
an' make all his 'rangements fer ter bag de game an' ter bobbycue it atterwuds. He flipped Brer Wolf an' Brer Fox his so-long, an' ax um fer ter
meet 'im at de same place de nex' day. 'Meet me right here, frien's,' sez
ol' Brer Rabbit, sezee, 'an' I'll show you sump'n' dat'll kinder stir you up
an' make you feel like dey's sump'n' gwine on 'roun' here same ez what
dey is in de j'inin' county, whar dey hunt b'ar eve'y day in de year 'cep'
Sunday.'

"Dey say dey'd be dar, ef nothin' don't happen, an' dey ax Brer Rabbit what must dey fetch fer ter he'p 'im out, an' he 'spon' dat all he want
um ter do is ter head Brer B'ar off when he git 'im on de run. 'I'll show
you whar ter take yo' stan',' sez ol' Brer Rabbit, sezee, 'an' all in de roun'
worl' you got ter do is ter stan' yo' groun' an' not git skeered when you see
'im comin', an' make a little fuss like you gwine ter ketch 'im. But you
don't hatter put yo' han' on 'im; I'll do all de ketchin' dat's gwine ter be
done. All I ax you is ter stan' whar I'll show you an' make out you gwine
ter he'p me. All you got ter do is zackly what you say you'll do — head
'im off when you see 'im comin'.'

"Brer Rabbit went on down de road, singin' one er de ol'-time chunes,
an' Brer Wolf an' Brer Fox sot whar he lef' um an' look at one an'er.
Atter while, ol' Brer Wolf say, sezee, 'What de name er goodness you
reckon he's up ter?' Brer Wolf grinned one dem ar grins what make col'
chills run up an' down yo' back. He 'low, he did, 'He des tryin' fer ter fool
us; he done got de idee dat we er skeer'd. Ef we go dar, he'll say he
mighty sorry dat he ain't fin' Brer B'ar an' ef we don't go dar, he'll laugh
an' tell it eve'ywhar dat we wuz fear'd fer ter stan' up ter our part er de
bargain.' Ol' Brer Fox grinned his kinder grin, an' say, sezee, 'We'll be
dar, sho!'"

At this point Uncle Remus paused to indulge in a hearty laugh, and it was some little time before he resumed. He laughed so long indeed, that the little boy was moved to ask him what he had found that was so funny. This inquiry seemed to have no effect on the old Negro. He continued to laugh, and when he could laugh no more, he chuckled, all the time watching the little boy, although he pretended to be looking in another direction. Finally, however, he became more serious, and settled himself in the attitude he always assumed when telling a story.

"Well, suh, Brer Rabbit went down de road a piece, an' got off in de bushes, an' lay down an' des roll'd over an' over wid laughin'. Bimeby he lay right still, an' a little bird, settin' up in de tree, holler out, 'Run here! Run here!' 'N'er bird say, 'What de matter? What de matter?' De fust bird make answer, 'Brer Rabbit dead! Brer Rabbit dead!' T'er bird say, 'Don't you b'lieve it! Don't you b'lieve it!' Brer Rabbit lay dar, he did, twel he got good an' rested, an' bimeby he jump up an' crack his heels tergedder, an' put out fer home like de booger-man wuz atter 'im.

"He went home, he did, an' split up some kin'lin' fer his ol' 'oman fer ter git supper wid, an' frail out four five er his chillun, an' den he sot in de shade an' smoke his seegyar. Atter he done e't supper, he comb his ha'r, an' tuck down his walkin'-cane, an' put out thoo de woods, fer ter go ter de place whar Brer B'ar live at. He got dar, atter so long a time, an' hello'd de house, an' ol' Brer B'ar come shufflin' out an' ax him in. Ole Miss B'ar sot out de cheers, atter dustin' um wid her apern, an' Brer B'ar an' ol' Brer Rabbit sot dar an' confabbed des like two ol' cronies.

"Atter while, Brer Rabbit ax Brer B'ar is he hear de lates' news, an' Brer B'ar say he don't speck he is, kaze he ain't went out much, he been so busy cleanin' de grass out'n his roas'n-year patch. Brer Rabbit pull his mustaches, an' look at Brer B'ar right hard. He 'low, he did, 'Well, suh, dey's big news floatin' 'roun'. Brer Wolf an' Brer Fox, dey say some un been gittin' in der roas'n-year patch, an' dey say dey done seed some tracks in dar what look mighty s'picious, mo' spechually when dey got on der fur-seein' specks.'

"Ol' Brer B'ar sorter shuffle his foots an' cross his legs. He say, 'What did dey do den? Whyn't dey foller up deze yer tracks what dey seed so plain?' Brer Rabbit 'low, sezee, 'It seem like dey know'd purty well whar de tracks wuz gwine ter lead um, an' dey wuz fear'd fer ter foller um, less'n dey had mo' comp'ny fer ter come wid um.' Ol' Brer B'ar lean

down, he did, an' knock de ashes out'n his pipe, an' den he look at Brer
Rabbit an' grin twel his mouf look red an' hot. He say, 'Feard fer ter foller
de tracks, wuz dey? Well, you can't blame um much, mo' speshually ef
dey know'd de tracks. What dey gwine do 'bout it? Dey ain't gwine ter
des set down an' let der roas'n-years walk off down de lane, is dey?'

"Brer Rabbit kinder helt his head on one side, an' look at Brer B'ar.
He 'low, sezee, 'I wuz des comin' ter dat, Brer B'ar, when you broke in on
me. De news what I hear is dat Brer Wolf an' Brer Fox is gwine ter have
a big b'ar-hunt. Dey done sont der invites ter some er de neighbors, an'
de neighbors will do de drivin', whiles dey does de ketchin'. Dey ax'd me
ef I wouldn't he'p do de drivin' an' I tol' um dat I'd be mo' dan glad.' Brer
B'ar look hard at Brer Rabbit an' Brer Rabbit look in de fierplace. 'You
said dat? You said you'd be mo' dan glad?' sez ol' Brer B'ar, sezee. Brer
Rabbit, he 'low, 'I mos' sholy did. I tol' um dat I'd git you started, an' den
dey kin do de ketchin'.'

"Ol' Brer B'ar laugh, an' when he do dat, it soun' like thunder
a-grumblin' way out in de hills. He say, sezee, 'How much uv a fambly is
dey got, Brer Rabbit?' An' Brer Rabbit, he 'spon', sezee, 'I can't tell you,
Brer B'ar, kaze I ain't neighbored wid um fer de longest. I don't like um,
an' dey don't like me — an' dat's de reason dat I come fer ter tell you de
news. I had de idee dat maybe you'd like fer ter take part in dis big b'ar-
hunt dat dey gwine ter have.' Brer B'ar kinder scratch his head an' lick
his paw fer ter slick over de place. He say, sezee, 'It seems like I'm
bleedz ter be dar, kaze ef I ain't, dey won't be no fun 'tall.'

"Well, dey sot dar, dey did, an' lay der plans, an' laugh fit ter kill at
de ol' jokes dat dey swapped wid one an'er, an' de ol' tales dey tol'. Dey
sot dar, dey did, twel ole Miss B'ar hatter come in an' tell um fer goodness' sakes ter go ter bed, kaze ef dey sot up an' went on dat away, dey
won't be no sleepin' fer her an' de chillun. Brer Rabbit jump up when he
hear dis, an' tell um all good night, an' put out fer home, an' when he git
dar he can't git ter bed fer laughin'. Ol' Miss Rabbit, she stuck her head
out fum under de kivver, an' 'low, 'What de name er goodness is de matter? You sholy must 'a' hearn sump'n' outdacious in yo' rambles, an' now
dat you done woke me up, you des ez well ter tell me 'bout it,' but ol' Brer
Rabbit, he's dat tickled dat he can't fish up words fer ter tell 'er; all he
kin do is ter laugh an' cough, an' wheeze an' sneeze, an' keep dis up twel

it look like he bleeze ter strankle er git smifflicated. But you better b'lieve dat ol' Miss Rabbit sot up wid 'im twel she fin' out all 'bout it. An' she ain't laugh when he tell 'er; she shuck 'er head an' 'low, 'You'll keep on wid yo' foolishness twel some er dem yuther creeturs will ketch you in yo' own trap — an' den what me an' de chilluns gwine do?' Ol' Brer Rabbit laugh an' say dat dey's been widders an' noffuns yever sence de worl' 'gun ter roll.

"Now, Brer Rabbit done tell Brer Wolf an' Brer Fox dat de b'ar-hunt wuz gwine ter come off bright an' early, an' dat dey mus' be dar whar he lef' um at, an', sho 'nough, when he went down de road, dar dey wuz. He know'd dat dey'd been talkin' 'bout 'im, kaze dey look right sheepish when he come up behime um. He ax um is dey ready, an' dey say dey is, an' he tell um fer ter come on, kaze dey ain't got no time fer ter lose ef dey gwine ter git any b'ar meat dat day.

"Dey went 'long, dey did, but when dey git ter whar de bushes wuz thick an' de shadders black, Brer Wolf an' Brer Fox kinder hung back. Brer Rabbit see dis, an' he say he hope dey ain't noways bashful, kaze ef dey gwine ter he'p him ketch de b'ar, dey got ter stan' up like dey er well an' not be droopy like dey er sick. Bimeby dey come ter de place whar dey wuz a blin' paff runnin' thoo de woods, an' Brer Rabbit, he say dat he want um ter stan' right dar, an' ef de b'ar come by dey wuz ter he'p 'im ketch 'im.

"Sez ol' Brer Rabbit, sezee, 'I'm a-hopin' dat I'll ketch 'im 'fo' he gits dis fur, an' ef I does, I'll holler; but ef he's too quick fer me — ef he gits de idee dat I'm atter 'im, an' starts ter run 'fo' I gits my han' on 'im, mo' dan likely he'll come dis way. Ef he do, des stan' yo' groun', kaze I'll be right behime 'im; des make out you gwine ter grab 'im an' hol' on ter 'im twel I kin git 'im, an' den our day's wu'k will be done.' Brer Wolf an' Brer Fox say dey'll do des like Brer Rabbit tell um, an' dey tuck der places. Wid dat, Brer Rabbit went lopin' thoo de woods des ez gaily ez a race-hoss.

"De place whar Brer Rabbit make um take der stan' wa'n't so mighty fur fum de place whar ol' Brer B'ar live at, an' 'twa'n't skacely no time 'fo' Brer B'ar wuz on de run, wid Brer Rabbit close behime 'im. Brer Fox an' Brer Wolf hear a mighty racket gwine on in de woods des like a har- rycane wuz a-churnin' up de leaves an' de trash, an', mos' 'fo' dey know it, here comes Brer B'ar, wid Brer Rabbit close behime 'im. Dey'd a got out'n de way, but dey hear Brer Rabbit holler, 'Head 'im off, dar! Head 'im off! Hol' 'im twel I git dar!' Ol' Brer B'ar wuz a-comin' like a pot abilin'. His mouf wuz wide open an' his tongue hangin' out, an' de blue smoke riz fum 'im eve'y time he fetched a pant.

"Brer Wolf an' Brer Fox stood der groun', kaze dey fear'd dat Brer Rabbit would have de laugh on um ef dey broke an' run. Dey stood dar, dey did, an' do like dey wuz gwine ter ketch Brer B'ar. He come on wid his head down, an' his breff comin', hot, an' ez he run, he fetched Brer Wolf a swipe wid one han' an' Brer Fox a wipe wid t'er han'.

"Well," said Uncle Remus, looking hard at the little boy, "dey ain't no use fer ter go on wid dis tale. De swipe dat Brer B'ar fetched um come mighty nigh takin' out der vitals, an' ef you never is hear hollerin' befo', you mought a hearn it den. But Brer B'ar, he kep' on a-runnin', wid Brer Rabbit atter him, an' ez dey run, dey laugh fit ter kill; an' fum dat day ter

dis, Brer Wolf an' Brer Fox been givin' ol' Brer B'ar all de elbow room dat he needs by day er by night."

"Did Brother Bear hurt them very much?" asked the little boy.

"Hurt um! Why, he ripped open der hides fum year-socket ter tail-holt. Fer de time bein' dey wuz mighty nigh ruint."

2
Impty-Umpty and the Blacksmith

LATE ONE AFTERNOON, when the little boy was trying his best to slip up behind Uncle Remus and frighten him with a big "Boo!" he heard noises that caused him to pause in his tracks and listen with all his ears. The sound he heard was the voice of the old man, and he seemed to be in deep distress. Apparently something had happened that the child had not heard of. It was something serious, too, for, although the old man was explaining something to someone in a low tone, he frequently paused to sigh and groan. The child's sympathy was aroused to such an extent that he forgot or forbore to put in execution the plan he had in mind when he started to the cabin. After listening a while in a futile effort to discover the nature of the trouble, he boldly entered the door, and looked around the room which, for the lack of windows, was not very well lighted. He was surprised to find that the old man was alone, and more surprised still to find that he was gazing at the rafters with a smile of satisfaction on his weather-beaten features.

"What is the matter, Uncle Remus?" asked the child.

"Matter!" exclaimed the old man. "Dey may be sump'n' de matter wid you, honey, but dey ain't nothin' 'tall de matter wid me."

"Why, I heard you talking to someone, and groaning; that's the way people do when they have trouble."

"Ef I wuz talkin' ter anybody, dey must a slipped out when you slipped in; ef dey ain't done dat dey er in here right now. Ez fer groanin', dat's 'bout all dat folks kin do when dey gits ez ol' ez what I is. By good rights dey oughter groan eve'y time dey draws der breff."

"But you were groaning just as though you had a terrible pain, and needed some of the medicine that mother gives to me when I have the stomach ache."

"De ailment what I had, honey, wuz somers on de right-han' side er my min'. When I got word fum a little bird dat you wuz comin' down here fer ter slip up on me an' skeer me, it put me in min' er de time when yo' pappy wuz 'bout yo' age; an' den I got ter ramblin' back twel my 'membunce hit me a whack dat come mighty nigh knockin' me flat. Sump'n' up'd an' said dat one er der tales what I tol' 'im in dem days wuz de wrong thing — yasser, de wrong thing! Dat 'uz when you hear me talkin' an' groanin'. I dunner how I'm gwine ter git ter feelin' much better less'n somebody up dar at de big house sen's me some er de truck what gi's you de stomach-ache — ressins, an' minch pies, an' appile dumperlin's. It makes me right hongry when I think 'bout tellin' yo' pappy de wrong thing when he wa'n't nothin' but a little bit er chap. But I done de best I know'd how."

"What tale was it, Uncle Remus?" the little boy inquired.

"'Twain't needer mo' ner less dan dat ol' time tale 'bout 'Impty-Umpty an' de Blacksmiff.' I gun it out des ez 'twuz gun ter me, but 'twuz de wrong thing — an' de wrong thing can't be made de right thing. Anybody'll tell you dat."

"Impty-Umpty!" exclaimed the child, "why, what is that?"

"It's des Somebody's name," said Uncle Remus, with a sigh. "Some folks call 'im one thing an' some an'er. Ain't you never hear yo' pappy talk 'bout 'im?"

"No, I never did," replied the little boy.

"Not when he drap his collar button on de flo', an' it roll way un' de buryo?" The child shook his head solemnly. "Is you right sho you ain't hear 'im call a name when he can't fin' de button?" persisted the old man, leaning back in his chair. He laughed heartily when he saw the light of comprehension dawning in the child's eyes. "Ol' Impty-Umpty is got mo' names dan yo' kin count on yo' fingers. Some calls 'im Satan, some calls 'im de Ol' Boy, some calls 'im Cloots, an' some calls 'im what yo' pappy do, an' he answers ter all un um; an' dey's times off an' on, when he'll come long 'fo' you call 'im. Fum all I hear, he's e'en 'bout de busiest creetur dat yever run 'bout wid two behime legs an' a tail ter boot.

"Well, de tale what I done gone an' tol' yo' pappy 'bout ol' Impty-Umpty an' de Blacksmiff wuz de wrong thing, an' I dunner whedder ter righten it wid him er wid you. It seem like you er de handiest, yit ef I righten it wid you, I'll hatter git yo' promise fer ter righten it wid him."

The little boy was enthusiastic in making the promise, so much so that Uncle Remus was compelled to wipe an untimely smile from his mouth, using the back of his hand for the purpose. He seemed to be in no hurry to "righten" things, however, for instead of beginning the story at once he leaned his head against the wall as though he were about to take a nap, this being his favorite attitude when he wanted to doze. The little boy was not as impatient as his father had been under the same circumstances. He sat perfectly quiet, awaiting the good pleasure of Uncle Remus. Peeping from under his eyelashes, the old Negro was again compelled to employ the back of his hand to smother a smile. This seemed to arouse him.

"I ain't been 'sleep, is I? How fur did I git wid de tale?"

"Why, you didn't even begin to tell it," said the child.

"Well, suh!" exclaimed Uncle Remus, with well-feigned surprise. "Now, ain't dat too much? One thing I notices, an' dat ain't two — I notices dat de mo' Anny Dominoes what crawls over me, de bigger my fergittance gits, an' I boun' it'll come ter dat pass dat de time'll come when I'll fergit ter eat; an' dey ain't nobody dat I knows un dat's gwine ter come 'long an' put vittles in my mouf. Dat's what!"

The little boy said not a word in response to this, nor did he smile. The trouble with him was that he was inclined to take Uncle Remus too seriously. This made the old man more solemn than he would have been otherwise, but he began very bravely, in spite of his fear that the simple tale he had to tell would fail to appeal to a youngster who had had nearly all his mischievousness trained away under the modern system of parental instruction.

"One time," said Uncle Remus, "not yisteddy, ner de day befo', but 'way back yander in de days when folks knowed lots mo' an' a heap less dan what dey knows now, der wuz a blacksmiff what had his shop at de big cross-roads. It seem like dat ef folks wuz gwine anywhar er comin' back dey bleeze ter pass dish yer blacksmiff shop. 'Tain't make no diffunce whar dey gwine, er whar dey comin' fum, de blacksmiff an' his shop wuz right spang on der road. Time an' time ag'in some un um'd set right flat on de groun' an' try fer ter figger out how an' why 'twuz dat dey'd hatter pass dis shop, no matter which way dey started ner which way dey come back. Dey figger'd an' figger'd, but 'tain't do um a grain er good. In de due time, dey'd hear a whangin' an' a clangin', an' when dey'd look up, dar wuz de shop, lookin' red inside on 'count de fier, an' dar wuz de bellus a-wheezin' an' a-snortin', an' de big sledge hammer a-bangin' on de anvil, twel it look like it'd bust it wide open. No diffunce what road dey tuck dey'd hatter pass de shop, an' ef dey pass de shop dey'd hatter see de red light a-shinin' an' hear de sledge hammer a-bangin'.

"De shop got so het up in de daytime dat it helt de heat all night, an' de blacksmiff ain't been workin' dar long 'fo' ol' Brer Rabbit fin' out dat ef he want ter git warm an' feel good all he had ter do wuz ter creep un' de do' an' set by de fier an' nod. In dem days folks had a better 'pinion er de creeturs dan what dey got now, an' dey wuz mo' familious wid um dan what dey is now. But de blacksmiff wuz so big an' strong dat he sot eve'ybody an'er kin' er pattern. He wa'n't skeer'd er de biggest creetur dat come 'long, let um be rhinossyhoss er hippytamypottymus.

"Ez fer Brer Rabbit, he wa'n't nowhar. He wuz lots bigger in dem days dan what he is now, but he wa'n't no match in muscle fer de man what been slingin' de sledge hammer — an' so dar 'twuz, de blacksmiff wid big arms an' strong legs, an' ol' Brer Rabbit, wid nothin' but a long head an' big years. Ol' Brer Rabbit had a mighty habit er settin' up late at night. He'd set up so late, a-playin' his pranks an' a-cuttin' up his capers, dat when he woke up de nex' mornin' he wuz e'en 'bout ez sleepy ez he had been de night befo'; an' dey wuz times when he ain't wake up twel he hear de blacksmiff fumblin' at de do'. An' mo' speshually dey wuz one time when de blacksmiff walk right in on 'im an' foun' 'im settin' up close ter de place whar de fier done been at.

"Stidder shooin' Brer Rabbit away like he oughter done ef he ain't want 'im dar, de blacksmiff flung a hammer at 'im, an' ef it had a hit 'im dey wouldn't a been 'nough un 'im lef' fer ter stop a hole in a chigger's house. But Brer Rabbit dodge de hammer, an' went scootin' ter de briar-patch whar he born an' bred at. He went out dar, he did, an' felt er hisse'f all over fer ter see ef he wuz all dar, an' den, when he fin' out dat he wuz, he jump up an' crack his heels tergedder an' wunk one eye like somebody done tell 'im a great secret.

"He sot out dar in de briar-patch an' study what he gwine do nex', an' 'long 'bout dat time who should come 'long dat way but ol' man Billy Rickerson-Dickerson. Knowin' Brer Rabbit long an' well he stopped ter pass de time er day an' ax de news, an' he ain't been dar long 'fo' Brer Rabbit tol' 'im many a long tale dat nobody ain't never hear befo'. By de time he wuz ready fer ter sing out his so-long Brer Rabbit ax 'im ef he'll do er favor fer one er his ol' time frien's, an' Mr. Rickerson-Dickerson 'low dat he will. 'Well, den,' sez ol' Brer Rabbit, sezee, 'when you er passin' de blacksmiff shop, des poke yo' head in de do', an' say, "Frien', you'll have comp'ny soon," an' de nex' passer-by you meet, tell um ter do de same.'

"Well, suh, de word went 'roun', an' 'twa'n't long 'fo' eve'ybody dat come by de blacksmiff shop had de same sayin' in der mouf — 'Frien', you'll have comp'ny soon,' — an' dis sot de blacksmiff ter studyin'. He ax hisse'f what dey all mean by dat, an' it got so atter while dat he'd put de hot i'on on de anvil an' let it git stone col' befo' he hit a lick wid de hammer. He wuz so worried dat he can't sleep at night, an' de nigh neighbors wondered when dey hear de bellus a-snortin' an' de hammer a-bangin'. Dey say ter deyse'f dat de blacksmiff bleeze ter have a mighty heap er work ter do, an' dey dunner whar it all come fum, ner who wuz havin' it done.

"Bimeby, atter so long a time, de neighbors got so dat dey'd drap in on 'im atter supper an' set an' talk an' dodge sparks whiles de blacksmiff run de bellus an' swung de hammer. One night, de talk turned on de Ol' Boy an' his b'longin's. De fier burnt so blue an' de sparks flew'd so fur, dat dey can't he'p but think 'bout de Bad Place, an' wid dat, dey bleeze ter think 'bout ol' Impty-Umpty, de one what runs it. De blacksmiff wuz monstus busy, but he ain't so busy but what he kin hear what dey talkin' 'bout. He blowed de bellus, an' he hammered de red-hot i'on, but he ain't los' none er der talk, speshually when dey 'gun ter talk 'bout ol' Impty-Umpty.

"He lissened, he did, but he keep on a-makin' what he started fer ter make when he fust got word dat he wuz gwine ter have comp'ny, an' 'fo' dey got thoo tellin' what dey know'd 'bout ol' Impty-Umpty, he done finish it. He sot it up on de anvil an' pushed it all 'roun' wid his tongs, an' dem what wuz settin' dar sees dat 'twuz a box — a big i'on box wid de sides all welted tergedder, an' de top fixt so dat he kin welt dat up tight de minnit he got good an' ready.

"He turn de box all 'roun' an' 'roun', an' den he wipe de sweat off'n his forrerd an' grin. He 'low, 'Dar's a box what is a box; ef anybody kin beat it, le' 'im do it. Eve'ybody been tellin' me I'm gwine ter have comp'ny soon, an' I speck it mus' be so. But dey can't come 'fo' I'm ready fer um.' Den he ax um all how come dey hatter talk 'bout ol' Impty-Umpty, an' what do dey know 'bout 'im anyhow. Dis start de talk ag'in, an' ef de Ol' Boy had a had any character dey'd a ruint it right den an' dar. Dey say dat dey ain't but three things dat he can't turn hisse'f inter whilst he roamin' 'roun' de worl' seekin' whomsoever he mought destroy; one wuz a hog, one wuz a monkey, an' one wuz a cat.

"De blacksmiff laugh an' say dat ef ol' Impty-Umpty is gwine ter be de comp'ny dey er talkin' 'bout, well an' good, kaze he des ez ready fer 'im ez what he is fer anybody else. He ain't no sooner say dis, dan a tall black man stepped inside de do' an' bowed, wid 'Howdy, marsters an' frien's!' Dey all looked at 'im up an' down, an' well dey mought, kaze never in all dey born days is dey see anybody like dat. He wuz black, but he ain't look like no nigger. His eyes shined like er piece er glass in de moonlight. He had on a stove-pipe hat an' a broadclof suit, he wuz slim an' slick an' soople, an' it seem like he wuz club-footed and double-j'inted.

"Well, honey, he stood dar smickin' an' smilin', an' it look like dat de mo' you look at 'im, de slicker he got. He 'low, 'Marsters an' frien's, you'll hatter skusen me fer comin' in so sudden like. I use ter be a blacksmiff myse'f, an' I never ketches a glimp' uv a forge an' a fier but what it seem like I'm a bleeze ter stop in a minnit ef only fer ter warm my han's like dis.' He helt out his han's to'rds de live charcoals, an' de fier sprung up des like it do when you er workin' de bellus for all she's wuff. De flame burnt white, an' den it burnt blue, an' bimeby it burnt right green, an' all de time it got bigger an' bigger, twel it 'gun ter wrop 'roun' de Black Man's han's des like snakes. Nobody ain't say a word; dey ain't had no needs ter; it took up all der time fer ter watch what de Black Man gwine ter do nex'.

"Bimeby, when he done warm his han's ez much ez he want ter, he turn ter de blacksmiff an' say, sezee, 'I hear you spectin' comp'ny soon.' De blacksmiff he up an' ax, 'Who been tellin' you?' De Black Man make answer, 'Why, I seen ol' man Rickerson-Dickerson dis mornin', an' he ain't mo' dan tol' me howdy 'fo' he 'low dat you 'spectin' comp'ny, an' soon's I hear dat I tol' 'im fer ter set down in de big rockin'-cheer an' make hisse'f at home, an' off I put fer ter see who dis comp'ny mought be dat wuz comin' ter see you.'

"Now, all dem neighbors what had come in ter set up wid de black-smiff know'd mighty well dat ol' man Rickerson-Dickerson had done been buried de day befo', an' it make um open der eyes when dey hear de Black Man say dat he had seed 'im dat mornin'; an' one ol' man, what had white ha'r, an' wuz kinder shaky in de legs, up an' ax, 'Whar'bouts is it you see 'im at?' De Black Man say, 'I seed 'im comin' down de road, an' he look like he wuz kinder col', an' I axed 'im in fer ter warm by my fier. We had a little chat, an' den it wuz dat he tol' me 'bout how dey wuz comp'ny 'spected at de cross-roads blacksmiff shop.'

"De ol' man 'low, 'An' did he warm hisse'f?' De Black Man flung back his head, an' laugh twel de smoke came out'n his mouf. He say, 'Mr. Rickerson-Dickerson sho did git warm, an' de reason I knows is kaze I hear 'im sesso hisse'f!' De ol' man shuck his head, and say, sezee, dat he reckon he better be polin' on to'rds home, on accounts er de lateness er de hour."

"Did you say that smoke came out of the Black Man's mouth, Uncle Remus?" the little boy asked. He was so much in earnest that a curious little pucker appeared between his eyebrows right over his nose.

"Dat what I said, honey. Smoke! an' 'twa'n't no nachal smoke needer, kaze it smell des like it do when you strike one er de ol'-timey, smifflicatin' matches. It kinder gi' de neighbors a turn, an' one by one dey sneaked off home, twel de fust news you know, dey wan't nobody lef' in de shop but de Black Man an' de blacksmiff, wid ol' Brer Rabbit peepin' thoo a crack. De Black Man he say, sezee, 'I done had my eye on you, an' I like de way you do mighty well. You been workin' too hard an' too much, but you'll git over dem kinder habits one er deze long-come-shorts. I use ter be a blacksmiff myse'f, an' I'm fear'd you go at it in a mighty roun' about way. What does you want wid a fier, an' what use is you got fer dat great big bellus, which you hatter work yo'se'f ter pieces fer ter blow?'

"De blacksmiff he 'low, he did, dat he bleeze ter have a fier, an' de on-liest way he kin have one is ter make de bellus blow its breff on it. De Black Man, he say, sezee, 'Dey mought been a time when I had de same

idee, but dat time is done past an' gone. Le' me show you how I does de business.' Wid dat, he tuck up a plow tongue, helt it close ter his mouf, an' blowed on it once er twice, an' it got red-hot, an' den tuck on a white heat, de kin' dey calls a weltin' heat. He put it on de anvil, an' hit a lick er two wid de hammer, an' it come out de purtiest shovel plow you ever is lay yo' eyes on.

"He helt it out, but de blacksmiff back off, he did, an' 'low, 'Who de name er goodness is you, anyhow?' De Black Man frown when he hear de word 'goodness' but he make answer, 'Folks got a heap er diffunt names fer me, but I ain't no ways proud, an' so I 'spon's ter all un um.'

"De blacksmiff say, sezee, 'I b'lieve you ain't nobody but ol' Impty-Umpty.'

"'An' yit,' sez de Black Man, sezee, 'some calls me de Ol' Boy, an' den, ag'in, dey calls me Satan, an' I got wuss soundin' names dan dat.'

"'Dey tells me,' sez de blacksmiff, sezee, 'dat dey's three things you can't do," sezee. Ol' Impty-Umpty 'low, 'Be pleased fer ter homnyname

um,' sezee. "Well, suh,' sez de blacksmiff, sezee, 'it' talked 'roun' in de
neighborhood dat you can't change yo'se'f inter a hog, ner a monkey, ner
needer into a cat.' Ol' Impty-Umpty grinned an' showed his sharp tushes,
an' den he lipped in de a'r wid a little twist, an' when he hit de groun'
ag'in, he wuz in de resemblance uv er hog, an' he look so much like er
hog dat he went gruntin' all over de shop, an' gobblin' up eve'y scrap er
vittles he kin fin'. Den he lay down an' waller'd like he wuz in a mud-
hole, an' got up a monkey. Well Mr. Monk wuz mo' livelier dan what de
hog wuz, an' he run up de wall, an' got on de rafters, an' sot dar chatterin'
an' whis'lin' des like a sho 'nough monkey.

"He drapped fum de rafters, an' when he hit de groun', de monkey
wuz a cat, not a great big un, but a little black un dat you'd a been sorry
fer ef you'd a seed it. By dat time de blacksmiff had his i'on box ready,
an' settin' on de groun', an' when de cat come close 'nough, he grabbed
it by de back er de neck an' soused it in de box, an' slammed down de
led an' fastened it. Den he laugh an' laugh, twel it look like he ain't never
gwine ter git done laughin'.

"But ol' Brer Rabbit, wid his eye ter de crack, 'gun ter git kinder un-
patient, an' he fetch de groun' a whack wid his behime foot. He hit so
hard an' so quick dat you'd a thunk somebody wuz beatin' on de muffle'
drum. Blacksmiff say, sezee, 'Who dat?' Brer Rabbit 'spon', 'I'm de man
what you had in de box' — des so. Blacksmiff say, sezee, 'Go 'way! You
can't fool me! Ol' Impty-Umpty in here whar I put 'im at, an' he'll be
impty-umptied 'fo' he's emptied. You hear me talkin'!' Brer Rabbit say,
sezee, 'Shake de box, man! Shake de box!' An' sho 'nough, when de
blacksmiff shake de box, he ain't hear nothin' in dar. He shake it ag'in,
an' he don't hear nothin' in dar.

"Well, dis kinder thing ain't what he been 'spectin' an' he kinder
scratch his head. He study an' he study what he gwine do, an' bimeby he
sot right flat on de groun' an' open de box fer ter see ef it's empty er
Impty-Umpty. He open it, he did, an' raise de led an' try ter peep in, but
he ain't see nothin'. He raise it a leetle higher, an' when he done dat, a
great big black bat flew'd outer de box an' hit 'im right spang in de face.
He done his level best fer ter ketch it; he struck at it wid his hat, an'
slapped at it wid his han', but de bat done gone out'n reach, an' when de
blacksmiff look up, it wuz sailin' 'roun' 'mongst de rafters, flufflin', an'

grittin' its toofies. De bat flew'd 'roun' much ez it wanter, an' den it made a dart fer de do' an' wuz gone — done gone!

"Well, time went on, an' de day come when de blacksmiff shop wuz shot up, an' de blacksmiff hisse'f wuz swopped fum de coolin'-board ter de graveyard." Uncle Remus paused, and looked hard at the little boy, who was listening with the composure and the complacency that were so puzzling to the old Negro. He paused, cleared his throat, and then went on: "Fum coolin'-board to the graveyard ain't sech a mighty fur ways, but I don't speck de blacksmiff keer'd ef 'twuz long er short. Dey tells me — I dunno ef it's so er no; it mought be des de hearsay — but dey tells me dat de blacksmiff had 'casion ter go down dar whar Impty-Umpty live at; he mought des been passin' by; leas'ways he went ter Impty-Umpty's house an' knock at de do'. He knock once an' he knock twice, an' den ol' Impty-Umpty holler an' ax, 'Who dat?' Blacksmiff say, sezee, "Tain't no-body but me.' Impty-Umpty 'low, he did, 'Ef you er dat blacksmiff what shet de cat up in a box, you can't come in dis place,' an' den he call one er his little Impties, an' say, 'Go git 'im a chunk er fier an' let 'im start a sinner fact'ry er his own. He can't come in here.' Dat," remarked Uncle Remus with something like relief, "wuz all de fur de tale could foller de blacksmiff."

The little boy sat as though lost in reflection. Finally, however, he stretched himself and spoke. "Oh, pshaw!" he exclaimed, and ran laughing toward the big house.

3
Taily-po

WHEN NEXT the little boy put in an appearance at Uncle Remus's cabin, the old man was engaged in making something that appeared to be very much like a hammock. Indeed, it was so very much like a hammock that the youngster took the fact for granted and at first asked no questions about it. He was really as inquisitive as most children, but he had been taught that this, the most natural way of improving his mind and adding to the small sum of his knowledge, was rude and countrified.

"What de matter, honey?" asked Uncle Remus, observing that the little fellow was more serious than usual. "I hope de ole Shanghai rooster ain't hauled off an' kicked you." The child blushed. The big rooster, which had been raised as a pet, and which had a habit of pecking and pulling viciously at the buttons on people's clothes, was the only thing on the plantation that the little boy was really afraid of. He didn't know why he was afraid of the rooster, but it seemed that the rooster himself had discovered this weakness, and whenever he saw the child he would come running with his feathers ruffled, and making queer noises that seemed to issue from the depths of his craw. The youngster always made it a point to get out of the rooster's way as promptly as his nimble little feet would carry him.

He blushed, therefore, when Uncle Remus placed a blunt finger on his weakness, but made no reply to the comment. Instead, he declared that his mother had said that Uncle Remus had no business to fill the little boy's head full of foolish notions, especially about Satan, and other topics almost equally as impolite. "What Miss Sally say ter dat?" inquired the old Negro with a smile of genuine amusement. Miss Sally was the child's grandmother.

"Why, grandmother said that if Satan ever got me, it wouldn't be at your cabin."

"Ah-yi! An' den what yo' mammy say?" the old Negro asked.

"She said it wasn't nice to talk about such things, and grandmother asked if the Bible was a nice book."

"Dar, now! What I been tellin' you? Honey, you better study yo' granny close an' look at 'er good, kaze some er deze odd-come-shorts, she gwine ter take wings an' flew'd away; an' once she gits outer yo' sight, you ain't gwine ter see no mo' like 'er. Lots er folks could git rich an' make deyse'f happy des by pickin' up what she done forgot. Ef she'd a been a man, she'd a been a preacher, an' ef not dat, den she'd a been one er deze kinder folks what leads all de rest. No matter what crowd she got in, she'd a headed de whole gang — dey ain't no two ways 'bout dat. Why, Miss Sally kin stan' on dat back porch up dar, an' gi' her orders, an' you kin hear eve'y word she say plum' ter de two-mile place — you sho kin."

The little boy disputed nothing that was said in regard to his grandmother, for he was very fond of her; but he was too small to appreciate the qualities that Uncle Remus was dimly endeavoring to indicate, and so his mind wandered from the old Negro's words to his work. "What are you doing, Uncle Remus?" he asked.

"Des a-knittin' an' a-knottin', honey — des a-knottin' an' a-knittin'. Ez you see me now, des so you mought a seed me fifty year ago, mo' speshually ef I wuz doin' den what I'm a-doin' now."

"Where will you hang the hammock when it is finished?" inquired the youngster, his curiosity temporarily getting the better of his training.

"Ef I kin git two men ter hol' de staffs, an' an'er one fer ter swing it, I'll hang it up in de middle er de creek, an' gi' de catfishes an' de suckers, an' de peerches a ride. I hope dey'll like it well 'nough not ter be disapp'inted. But you mos' never kin skacely tell; ef fishes is like folks, I know purty well dat dey don't like it. Der wuz Mr. Gristle — I most know you ain't never see 'im, kaze he been dead eve'y sence I wuz in my teens. Well, dey tuck Mr. Gristle ter de court-house, whar dey wuz a whole passel er lawyers, an' dey made great long speeches 'bout 'im, an' de jedge jedged 'im, an' de jury sot on 'im; but spite er all dis de man wa'n't satchified, an' he made a turrible racket when dey went ter hang 'im.

"It's purty much de same way wid de fishes. Spite er de fack dat I been settin' here workin' on dis seine off an' on mighty nigh two mont's, de fishes won't no mo' dan git in it good 'fo' dey'll make a turrible splut-teration, an' try fer ter break out."

"Well, I reckon so," the little boy exclaimed.

"Yasser, you can't please eve'ybody. Ef you er hangin' um, er makin' a seine, er tellin' a tale, somebody er sump'n' will say 'tain't de right thing. I had fresh in my min' a tale dat follers right 'long atter de one 'bout ol' Impty-Umpty, same ez de behime wheel uv a buggy follers de front un — but, bless gracious! dar's yo' mammy warnin' me not ter call names in vain, an' I dunner which way ter turn. Look like dey ain't nothin' lef' fer me ter do but ter keep my mouf shut, er tell my tales ter myse'f atter I go ter bed."

The little boy laughed, for Uncle Remus had, as it were, by chance, hit upon one of his own little tricks. In a moment he was serious again. "But grandmother says there is no harm in the stories," he declared.

"An' a mighty good thing!" exclaimed Uncle Remus; "kaze ef dey wuz any harm in um, all our folks would a gone ter rack an' ruin, an' 'lev'mty-'lev'm ginerations befo' an' atter. Dey may be de wrong thing, but dey ain't done nobody no harm, not sence I kin fust ermember white fum black — an' dat wuz a long time ago."

"But what was the story, Uncle Remus?" asked the little boy, whose interest was now whetted to a very keen edge.

"Inquirements like dat allers leads ter mo' talk," remarked the old man, with that air of wisdom that can only be assumed by those who are old in years and experience. "It's one er dem ar tales what I never is tell ter yo' pappy. Nothin' ain't suit 'im ceppin' dem tales 'bout Brer Rabbit, wid de creeturs persuin' on atter 'im, an' him a-persuin' on atter de cree-turs. But dey tells me dat in dem days — de times dat de tales tells 'bout — Mr. Man an' his kinnery wuz e'en about ez servigrous ez any er de creeturs what wuz persuin' on atter Brer Rabbit. Dat what de ol' folks say, an' ef anybody knows it sholy ought ter be dem.

"Well, dish yer tale, what I had fresh in my min', is got a song in it, an' dat's de reason I ain't been eetchin' fer ter tell it; kaze I ain't got de knack er singin' what I useter have. When I wuz young, de ol' folks wuz allers a-tellin' me dat ef I don't stop hollin' so loud, I'd break my puckerin' string, an' I 'speck dat what de matter wid me now. I done holler'd so much, callin' de hogs an' de sheep, an' one thing an' an'er, dat you can't 'speck me ter chune up an' sing des anywhar an' any time.

"When dis tale wuz handed down ter me — an' dat 'uz too long ago ter talk about — it seem like dat some kinder hard feelin's done sprung up 'twix' Mr. Man an' ol' Brer Rabbit, some kinder 'spute 'bout gyarden peas, an' goobers. Mr. Man say dat Brer Rabbit nipped off de tops time dey git out'n de groun' good. Mr. Rabbit, he 'low, dat dem what Mr. Man miss ain't never come out'n de groun'. Mr. Man say dat may be so, but he tell Brer Rabbit to des look at de cabbages, whar dey nibbled. Brer Rabbit 'low, he did, dat it mought be the calfies er de big green worms, an' he ax Mr. Man what needs do he have fer ter be nibblin' at spindlin' greens like dem, when he got a fine gyarden er his own. Mr. Man say he'd a heap rather see dat fine gyarden dan ter hear tell un it.

"An' so de 'spute run on; one word callin' fer an'er, an' dar dey had it twel bimeby bofe un um wuz tryin' fer ter say two words ter de yuther's one. De upshot un it wuz dat Mr. Man git so mad dat he wuz red in de face, an' he call his dogs, Ramboo, Bamboo, an' Lamboo, an' sikt um on Brer Rabbit; an' you know mighty well dat ef dey'd 'a' been any pardnership 'twix' um dis sickin' de dogs on would a bust it up.

"Now, de dogs ain't got no better sense dan ter do de best dey kin. Dey track ol' Brer Rabbit, dey trail 'im an' dey track 'im 'roun' an' 'roun' an' up an' down, twel bimeby he say ter hisse'f dat ef dey don't kinder let up he sho will drap in his tracks. Whiles he lopin' 'long, wid his tongue out an' his tail off, he come ter de big holler poplar by de cool spring. He went in, he did, an' run up sta'rs an' sot down in a cheer, an' panted like he'd been playin' hop-an'-go-fetch-it."

The old Negro paused at this point, as if to see what effect the last statement would have on the child. The youngster knew as well as any one that a hollow tree has no stairway and no place for chairs, but the matter-of-fact way in which Uncle Remus had made the announcement seemed to be sufficient evidence of its truth. Indeed, one of the queerest results of the old man's manner of telling his stories — the charm of which cannot be reproduced in cold type — was that all the animals, and all of the various characters that figured therein, were taken out of the reality which we know, and transported bodily into that realm of reality which we feel: the reality that lies far beyond the commonplace, everyday facts that constitute not the least of our worries. Fortunately for childhood, the little boy failed to discover that Uncle Remus had made any statement out of the ordinary.

Observing this, the old Negro's face seemed to be lighted up with enthusiasm, and he resumed the story with more cheerfulness than the child had ever seen him exhibit. "He went upsta'rs, he did," said Uncle Remus, insisting on renewing the statement, "an' sot down in de big rockin'-cheer, an' panted twel he got kinder rested. An' all dis time, Ramboo, Bamboo, an' Lamboo wuz a-runnin' 'roun' 'wid der nose ter de groun' tryin' fer ter pick up de trail where dey los' it at. Dey run here an' dey run dar, dey run hether an' dey run yan'; but dey can't fin' it, an' bimeby dey drapt der tails an' went on home."

"But, Uncle Remus," the little boy interrupted, "why didn't the dogs tree Brother Rabbit? Don't you remember how you told me that the dogs on the place here could tree 'possums?"

If the child had been older and wiser, he would have made sure that he had the old man in a tight corner, but he never even suspected that he had Uncle Remus "treed." He was simply seeking information. After a little pause, the venerable story-teller was himself again, and the little boy never knew how near he was to catching the old Negro as he never had been caught before. Uncle Remus closed his eyes when the little boy asked why the dogs didn't trail Brother Rabbit to the tree, and then tree him, and gave utterance to a heart-rending groan, as though he was suffering some fearful pang, physical or mental. He thought quick and hard, and wondered what reply he should make, when the youngster himself came to the rescue, "I reckon that was before dogs had been trained to tree things."

The old man opened wide his eyes, and grinned from ear to ear. "Honey, you sho hit de nail on de head dat time. I wuz des waitin' fer ter see ef you'd hatter be tol', an' here you come an' take de words right out'n my mouf. Dey ain't a day pass dat you don't git smarter, an' you'll soon be so dat nobody can't fool you. Yasser! dat's why de dogs ain't trail Brer Rabbit ter de tree an' den bay de tree. Dey ain't been l'arned how; der wa'n't no needs fer it, an' so when Brer Rabbit went in de holler tree an' run'd up sta'rs, he des mought ez well a took wings an' flew'd away, for all de dogs know'd.

"Well, de dogs went on back home, an' atter so long a time, atter Brer Rabbit done chaw on his cud much ez he wanter, he come down, an' went on 'bout his business. An' I tell you, hon, it 'uz big business, too, ef you'll b'lieve me. He put out, he did, an' he went, lippity-clippity, 'way off in de middle er de swamp, whar ol' Mammy-Bammy Big-Money live at. He wuz gwine 'long mighty gaily 'fo' he got in sight er de house, but time he see dat, he 'gun ter git droopy, twel, time he git ter de gate — ef dey wuz a gate — he look like he been sick a mont' er mo'.'"

As soon as Uncle Remus had mentioned the name of Mammy-Bammy Big-Money the child straightened himself on the bench which he was using as a chair, and gave unmistakable evidence that his interest in the story had been strengthened and renewed. He had heard his grandmother saying something about a witch named Mammy-Bammy Big-Money, and now he seemed to be on the point of hearing a good deal more about her.

"Weak ez he look, he kin' holler, an' he hailed an' hailed twel somebody hello'd, an' in he went. When he got in dar, he look mo' droopy an' puny dan ef he'd a had a spell er swamp fever. Mammy-Bammy Big-Money ax 'im what de matter, an' he say he in deep trouble, an' den he up an' erlate all de circumstance, 'bout how Mr. Man been treatin' 'im, an' Mammy-Bammy Big-Money shuck her head an' say dat it look like ter her dat dem kinder doin's ain't much less dan scandalious. Hangin' on de wall er de place wuz de hide er some kinder varmint — I dunner what. It had de head, de footsies, an' de tail on. She tuck it down, an' laid it on de flo', an' den got a han'ful er salt an' sprinkle it on de fier, a little at a time, singin':

> "'Rise, skin, rise,
>   Open yo' big red eyes —
>   Sharpen yo' long, black claws,
>   An' work yo' big strong jaws!'

"So said, so done, kaze whiles de salt wuz a-snappin' an' a-crackin' in de fier, de varmint hide 'gun ter move, an' stretch itse'f. Den it 'gun ter roll an' waller on de flo' an' time de salt done all burn up, dar 'twuz, big ez life an' twice ez nachal, walkin' 'roun' an' rubbin' 'g'in' ol' Mammy-Bammy Big-Money fer all de worl' like a great, big, double-j'inted wil'-cat. Brer Rabbit gi' de varmint plenty er room, whenever it come his way. Bimeby, de ol' witch up an' tell Brer Rabbit dat he kin go home now an' rest in peace, kaze 'tain't gwine ter be many long hours 'fo' Mr. Man will have all he kin 'ten' ter widout pesterin' wid anybody else.

"De hide had been hangin' up so long, an' wuz so hard an' stiff, dat de varmint had some trouble 'long at fust. Dey wuz big hard wrinkles here an' dar, but 'twa'n't so mighty long 'fo' it all limbered up, an' de creetur, whatsomever de name mought be, got so dat it kin rack 'roun' des ez soople ez any udder creetur.

"Brer Rabbit went off home an' went ter bed, so dat when night come he kin be up an' about, wid bofe eyes open, an' bofe years ready fer ter hear a bug flyin' a mile off. When 'twuz time fer Brer Rabbit ter git up an' be a-moseyin' 'roun' fer ter see what dey is fer ter be seed, Mr. Man wuz fixin' fer ter go ter bed. He got in dar, he did, an' de bed feel so satchi-fyin' dat he fetch a grunt an' a groan, an' den, 'fo' you kin say Billy Billups, wid yo' mouf open, he wuz done gone, an' eve'y time he drawed a breff it soun' like somebody wuz tryin' fer ter grin' coffee.

"Well, it went on dis away, twel some time endurin' de night, an' den, all at once, Mr. Man opened his eyes an' fin' hisse'f wide awake, des like folks do when dey git de idee dat dey's somebody in de room. He lissen, an' he lissen, an' bimeby he hear sump'n' stirrin' 'bout 'mongst de pots an' de pans in de little room whar he does his cookin' at. He hear it an' den he don't hear it; den he hear it, an' it soun' like dey's sump'n' in dar huntin' fer scraps er vittles. So, out er de bed he slips, an' slams de do' to, which it done come open. He slams it, but not befo' de creetur what's in dar done gone out, all 'ceppin' de tail. He cotch de tail when he slam de do', an' off it come right smick smack smoove. De tail wuz wigglin' so dat he can't hardly pick it up, an' when he do, he can't hardly hol' it in his han'. He look at it, an' he say ter hisse'f dat he ain't never is see no tail like dat.

"He tuck 'n tuck it in de room whar he sleep at, an' onkivver'd de fier, an' kindle it up, an' all dis time de tail what he had in his han' wuz givin' him 'bout ez much ez he kin do fer ter hol' it. Bimeby, he put it down on de h'a'th, an' put his foot on it, but it wuz a long tail an' a strong tail, an' it kep' up a mighty wigglin' an' squirmin', an' it worked itse'f out so dat it had some room, an' den it 'gun ter hit de man on de legs, an' it hit so hard dat it made 'im holler. Den he got mad, an' he grab up de tail an' flung it in de fier, spang in de middle er de red-hot embers. Ef you never see squirmin' you mought 'a' seed it den ef you'd 'a' been dar. You know how lizzud's tail'll jump, an' do like dey er 'live long atter dey been knocked off — well, dish yer tail wuz lots mo' liver dan what dey is. It 'uz a big strong tail, an' it jump 'bout so dat it knock de ashes an' de embers out on de h'a'th, an' de onliest way dat Mr. Man kin keep it in de fier, is ter hol' it down wid de tongs whiles he tuck de shovel an' kivvered it wid de live coals. It fried an' shook, an' shook an' fried, twel bimeby it look like dey wa'n't nothin' fer ter fry an' shake.

"Den Mr. Man went ter bed ag'in, atter lookin' at de sev'm stars fer ter see what time 'tis, an' he make up his min' he gwine ter ketch up de sleep what he done los', but time he git ter dozin' good, he hear a mighty scratchin' an' gnyawin' at de top er de do' whar dey wuz a crack at. He 'low, 'Who dat?' an' den he lay still an' lissen, an' atter while he hear sump'n' say an' sing:

> " 'Taily-po! You know an' I know
> Dat I wants my Taily-po!
> Over an' under an' thoo de do',
> I'm a-comin' fer ter git my Taily-po!' "

Uncle Remus gave to this nonsense a queer, whining intonation, and while he was singing, or intoning it, he pretended to be crying. Its effect on the little boy was peculiar. He frowned in sympathy, and caught his breath. "Wasn't Mr. Man scared?" he asked. "Why didn't he get his gun?"

"Shoo, honey! in dem times all de guns wuz pop-guns," the old man replied. "De fightin' dey had wuz fist an' skull; dey knocked down an' drug out, an' bit an' gouged. Gun's! why, ef a gun had a went off whar dey could hear it, dey'd er run spang ter de Jumpin'-Off Place, wharsomever dat may be. Mr. Man laid dar in bed, an' he ain't know what ter do. De scratchin' an' gnyawin' went on, twel Mr. Man fa'rly shuck an' shivered; but bimeby he thunk er his dogs, an' he made so bol' ez ter go ter de back do' an' call um." At this point, Uncle Remus raised his voice to a very high pitch, as people do in the country places when they call their dogs. " 'Here, Ramboo! here, Bamboo! here, Lamboo — here, here! Here, dogs, here!' Well, de dogs ain't got no better sense dan ter come when dey er called, an' dey come a-runnin'. Mr. Man sikt um 'roun' ter de front er de house, an' it seem like dat when dey got dar, dey tuck right atter sump'n', an' off dey went a-flyin' twel dey git plum' out'n hearin'.

" 'Fo' dey kin git back home ag'in, Mr. Man wuz des 'bout ter drap off ter sleep when he hear de same scratchin' fuss, an' dis time it wuz at de back do', whar dey wuz a bigger crack. He ax who de name er goodness is dat, an' what does dey want at dis time er night, when all honest folks oughter be in bed. An' no sooner is he ax dis, dan dere come de answer:

> "'Yo' name, I know, is Whaley-Joe,
> An' 'fo' I'm gwine ter r'a'ly go,
> I'm bleeze ter have my Taily-po;
> Gi' me dat an' I'll gaily go —
> Taily-po! my Taily-po!'

"Mr. Man went out ter de front an' call de dogs, but dey ain't dar, an' so dey can't 'spon'. Dar wuz Mr. Man, an' some'rs not fur off wuz de scratchin' an' gnyawin' creeture, cryin' out:

> "'I know you know, an' I know I know,
> Dat all I wants is my Taily-po!'

"Mr. Man shut an' barr'd de do', an' went back ter bed an' pull de kivver over his head, kaze he dunner what mo' ter do. He can't ketch de creetur in de dark, widout de he'p er de dogs, an' de dogs done gone 'way off yander. He got his head kivvered, but 'spite er dis he bleeze ter lissen at de scratchin', an' gnyawin', an' growlin', an' he shake an' shiver wuss'n he yever done.

"Somehow er 'nother, by toof er toenail, de creetur got in de house, an' no sooner is he git in dan he 'gun ter ramble 'roun' huntin' fer his tail. He rambled, he did, an' when anything got in his way, he'd hunch it over, an' root it out'n de way. Pans fell on de flo' — slam-bang-er-rang! — pots got turned over, an' when dey roll 'cross de flo' dey soun' like a young thunderstorm. De man, he lay dar, an' shuck an' shiver'd.

"Bimeby de varmint come ter de fierplace in de room where de man sleepin' at. In dem days, dey wa'n't no matches, not even deze here smif-flicatin' kin', an' folks hatter kivver up der fier ef dey 'speckted ter fin' any dar de nex' mornin'; 'twuz dat, er walkin' a mile er mo' fer ter borry a chunk. Well, Mr. Man had kivver'd his fier atter he put de creetur's tail in de embers; he had ashes on topper de embers, an' de embers on top er de chunks an' coals. De creetur come up ter de h'a'th, he did, an' nosed 'roun', an' it seem like he smell sump'n', kaze he growled, an' den he whined, an' wid dat, he start ter paw in de fier. De way he scratch an' claw it up wuz er sin. De red-hot embers flew'd out on de flo', de live coals foller'd um, an' den out come der chunks, an' wharsomever dey hit a blaze sprung up. Some flew'd on de bed, an' some flew'd clean over it.

When de creetur had claw'd all de fier out, dar wuz his tail all safe an' soun', an' he grabbed it up in his mouf, an' went outer de house like dey wuz sump'n' atter him.

"By dat time de house wuz in a blaze, an' not only de house, but de bed whar Mr. Man wuz layin' at. 'Twuz den gittin' close ter daybreak, an' when de yuther folks 'gun ter wake up an' stir 'roun', dey say, 'Heyo! some neighbor is burnin' off his new groun'.' Ol' Brer Rabbit, settin' in his rockin'-cheer, kinder wunk one eye, an' say, 'Humph! I 'clar' ter gracious ef I don't smell smoke!' Ol' Mammy-Bammy Big-Money, 'way off in de swamp, raise her head an' say, 'I smells meat a-fryin'!'"

The little boy waited a few minutes to see if Uncle Remus had finished the story, and then he ran off to tell it to his grandmother.

4
Brother Rabbit, Brother Fox, and Two Fat Pullets

THE LITTLE BOY to whom Uncle Remus told his later stories was not as persistent, not as insistent, as was his father before him, when he was a youngster. This fact was not as pleasing to the old man as might be expected. He liked to be asked for a story so that he might have an opportunity of indulging in a friendly dispute, a wrangle of words, and then suddenly end it all by telling the tale that happened to be in his mind at the moment. In short, he delighted to whet the expectations of the youngster, and arouse his enthusiasm.

This particular little boy never appeared to be very anxious for a story unless the old man led up to it by means of conversation and comment, or indicated it by some evasive allusion, and when the story was once under way, the child rarely interrupted to ask a question, so that Uncle Remus was frequently in great doubt as to whether the tale had been an enjoyable one. What the old man liked best of all things was to hear children laugh, and to feel that he had in some measure added to the sum of their enjoyment. Most of his quarrels were mock quarrels, and his severest frowns always had pretense for a basis.

Over and above the results of his training which the old man —
agreeing with the grandmother — thought had been of a severity out of
all proportion to the character of the child, the little boy was as much interested in Uncle Remus himself as he was in the stories he told, for the
old man had already developed into a tradition. His name was as much a
part of the family as that of any member thereof, and if the child had any
hero, such as dwell in the realm of mystery and romance, it was Uncle
Remus himself, with his gray head and his air of belonging to some other
place and some other time; and all this in spite of the fact that no other
person could take his place, or fit and fill the position which he occupied.

One day when the little boy came to see the old man, he seemed to be
somewhat disturbed about something. "Uncle Remus — Uncle Remus!"
he cried, and then, remembering some admonition that had to do with
conduct, he paused.

"Why, honey, what's de matter? Who been pesterin' you? Des tell me
der name, an' how big dey is, an' I'll see ef I can't put a flea in der
year — an' maybe two."

"There isn't anything the matter — much. After I was ready to go to
bed last night, I didn't feel very sleepy, and grandmother told me a story.
She said it was one you used to tell papa. But that wasn't all: she said that
all the animals were once meat-eaters. I don't see how that could be."

"Well, ef dat's all yo' trouble, honey, it sho ain't much. You kin put yo'
'pennunce in what Miss Sally say. Ef she tells you de creeturs wuz meat-
eaters, dey sho wuz, an' ef she tell you dat dey ain't never is eat no meat,
you kin put it down des dat away."

"Grandmother was telling how Brother Rabbit got some meat from
Mr. Man," said the little boy by way of explanation.

"Yasser!" exclaimed Uncle Remus, enthusiastically. "It seem des
like yistiddy I wuz tellin' dat tale ter yo' pappy. He wuz settin' right on
dat bench dar, foolin' wid my shoe-knife an' mixin' de big pegs wid de
little uns, an' I hatter holler at 'im mo'n once. He wuz some bigger dan
what you is, an' he had mo' life in him dan a quart er camphene. It seem
jus' like 'twuz yistiddy, but he done grow'd up, an' now here you is, not
much bigger dan a bunch er ripe chanyberries what de robins been tam-
perin' wid. Ez Miss Sally say, Time is got a heaper flewjus mixt up wid it.

You think it's a-standin' still, but all dat time it's des a-callyhootin', an' a-humpin', an' a-totin' de mail. You can't hear de ingine, but dey's one dar, an' a mighty big un at dat, an' it's gwine yander."

"Where is it going?" asked the little boy.

"It's gwine whar it's gwine, dat's whar it's gwine," replied Uncle Remus, in a tone and with an air that seemed to render further inquiry not only unnecessary, but altogether absurd. "It ain't doin' nothin' but des a-gwine, an' when it gits whar it's gwine, it keeps on a-gwine; an' ef you wanter go wid it, go you kin, ef you'll des le' me stay right whar I is."

The little boy said nothing more on that subject, which was quite beyond his comprehension. He sat quite still while Uncle Remus sharpened his pocket-knife, which was a large horn-handle affair, and bore the marks of long usage. "Grandmother said you were not the only person that said the animals ate meat, or something else besides vegetables. She told how Plutarch said something about the sheep eating fish."

"Did she say dat?" inquired Uncle Remus. When the little boy nodded his head in the affirmative, the old Negro closed his eyes and seemed to be reflecting. Presently he returned to the subject. "Plutarch! Is Miss Sally say what plantation he live on?" The child shook his head. "Well," responded Uncle Remus, with a sigh of relief, "he ain't never is live in deze parts, kaze ef he had I'd a know'd 'im. I 'speck Miss Sally hear talk un him de time she went ter Ferginny, kaze ef dey'd a been any Plutarch 'mongs' de niggers in deze diggin's I'd a know'd 'im.

"Le' 'im be whar he will er whar he kin, de creeturs all use ter eat meat stidder grass an' hay, an' it hatter be fresh. Dey wuz all so greedy dat bimeby fresh meat 'gun ter git skace, an' dey hatter study how an' whar dey gwine git it, an' how dey gwine keep it fum de balance un um atter dey got it. It got so, atter while dat dey hatter all gi' a sheer er what dey got ter King Lion, an' it seem like he had a yappetite bigger dan a th'ashin' machine. Den de time come when King Lion stuck a briar in his foot, an' de yuther creeturs hatter set up all night an' git up 'fo' day fer ter keep 'im wid 'nough fresh meat fer ter keep 'im fum starvin' ter deff.

"He'd lay dar an' groan, twel some un um come in wid a hunk er fresh meat, an' den he'd growl an' ax um ef dat 'uz all dey kin fetch. Long 'bout dat time his foot got so bad dat he hatter sen' fer de doctor — an' whom should de doctor be but ol' Brer Rabbit hisse'f! He ain't had no powders an' he ain't had no pills, but he know a mighty heap 'bout yarbs an' sech like green truck. He know how to make bergamot grease fer ter put on his ha'r when he go to see Miss Meadows an' de gals; he know dat peach-leaf poultice is good fer biles; he know dat sheep-sorrel salve is good fer ol' sores; an' he know dat white turkentime an' mutton-suet will heal up fresh hurts an' cuts. De creeturs hear 'im talkin' 'bout all er deze salves an' truck, an', des fer fun dey call 'im dock when dey ain't frettin' 'bout de way he been doin' um.

Well, ol' King Lion sont fer de doctor, an' Brer Rabbit looked in on 'im fer ter see what mought be done fer 'im. Now, ter look at de paw what de brier wuz stuck in, Brer Rabbit hatter go monstus close ter King Lion's mouf, which wuz spang full er blood-red tongue an' shiny tushes, an' he ain't like dat kinder business nohow. Eve'y time Brer Rabbit 'ud feel de hot breff er King Lion blowin' on 'im, he'd flinch an' swink up, an' when ol' King Lion gaped, Brer Rabbit like ter fainted dead away. But he fumble 'roun' an' stayed dar de best he kin, an' fix up de paw wid some kinder soothin' salve fer ter draw de infermation out, an' den he say his so-long.

"When he come out'n King Lion's house, he tuck notice dat uv all de creeturs waitin' der turn fer ter go in, Brer Fox wa'n't dar. He up an' ax, he did, 'Whar Brer Fox?' Nobody make answer. Den Brer Rabbit holler out, loud ez what he kin, 'Is anybody seed Brer Fox?' Dey shuck der heads, one an' all; nobody ain't seed 'im. Den Brer Rabbit he poled off down de big road. Soon ez he got out'n sight er de crowd, he sot down by de side er de road an' had a laughin' spell dat lasted fer de longest. Mo' dan once he made a motion like he gwine ter git up fum dar an' go on whar he gwine, but 'fo' he got on his feet good, de giggles'd git de better un 'im, an' he'd hatter set down ag'in.

"Atter so long a time he got so he kin walk, an' den he put out down de big road. He come ter whar de roads cross, when who should he meet but ol' Brer Fox! An' not only Brer Fox, but two fat pullets, an' de ol' pud-dle duck what been waddlin' 'roun' in dem neighborhoods fer mo' years dan I kin tell you. Brer Rabbit, he howdied, an' Brer Fox, he hello'd, an' den Brer Rabbit he up an' ax him whar he been all dis long time, mo' speshually sence he wa'n't up dar whar King Lion live at. 'Dey wuz a mighty inquirement fer you, Brer Fox,' sez ol' Brer Rabbit, sezee, 'an I tol' um all dat you wuz kinder feeble, here lately, an' dat you wuz tryin' fer ter pick up some flesh. An', sho 'nough, you wuz.' Wid dat, Brer Rabbit flick a thistle seed off'n his nose wid his behime foot.

"Brer Fox look kinder sheepish when he hear dat, an' he ax Brer Rabbit ef King Lion make any inquirements 'bout 'im. Brer Rabbit 'low, 'He call out yo' name mo' dan once, an' he put some langwidge 'roun' it dat 'ud burn a hole in my tongue ef I wuz ter say it. I hope he'll be feelin' better when nex' you see 'im.' Brer Fox, he say, sezee, 'Fer goodness' sake, Brer Rabbit! Did he up an' cuss?' Brer Rabbit 'low, he did, 'I ain't no toter er tales, Brer Fox, but ef you kin git out'n yo' min' anything wuss dan cussin' den dat des what King Lion say.' Brer Fox ax what he gwine ter do 'bout it, an' Brer Rabbit say he be bless' ef he know.

"Dey jower'd awhile, an' 'bout de time dat Brer Fox wuz gwine ter say his so-long, Brer Rabbit, atter feelin' in his pockets, an' lookin' skeered like he done los' sump'n', pull out a piece er paper an' hol' it up. He 'low, 'Atter ol' King Lion had his spell er warm talk, he han' me dis, an' say dat I wuz ter show it when I seed you. Now, ter make sho dat you seed it, des t'ar off one cornder, an' gi' it to King Lion when nex' you see 'im. 'Tain't nothin' 'tall but a soople-peeny.' Brer Fox, he look at it kinder sideways. He 'low, 'Is dey any writin' on it? Kaze ef dey is 'tain't gwine ter do me no good fer ter look at it; I kin read readin', but I can't read writin'.' Brer Rabbit say dat's de case wid him, 'ceppin' dat he kin read writin', but he can't read readin'. Brer Fox, he ax, he did, 'What do de writin' say?' Brer Rabbit, he kinder wrinkle up his forrerd, an' hol' out de paper like you've seed ol' folks do. He make like he readin', an' he 'low, 'All an' simely, whichever, an' whoever, an' wharsomever, speshually de howcome an' de whatshisname, de 'fo' said, flainter an' flender, le' 'im come headfo'most inter de court-house, whar de high she'ff an' de low kin lay 'im down an' flatten 'im out; all whomst she mought consarn. 'Nough said.'"

The little boy stared at Uncle Remus with wide eyes, as though the old man had lost his senses. "What did all that mean?" he asked.

"It mean dat King Lion want Brer Fox fer ter come up dar whar he kin git bofe paws on 'im, dat what it mean!" When he began to answer the little boy's query, Uncle Remus had pretended to be somewhat indignant, but it suddenly dawned on him that Brother Rabbit was only pretending that he had a paper from King Lion, and his own frown spread itself out into a smile that was pleasing to see. "'Twould a meant dat, honey, ef dey'd a been any writin' on de paper, but Brer Rabbit wuz des playin' one er his pranks. He had one eye on dem fat pullets an' dat ol' Widdle-Waddle Puddle Duck, dat's what he had, an' time he see Brer Fox totin' um, he 'gun ter worry how he gwine ter git one er bofe, or all un um.

"Brer Rabbit ain't let on 'bout de pullets an' ol' Widdle-Waddle, but he had um in his eye an' likewise in his min'. So he say, 'Now you done hear what de paper say, Brer Fox, you better foller de sesso. Here de piece what's tor'd off; take dat an' put it in yo' pocket, an' when ol' King Lion ax you is you seed me, des show it — an' don't be all day 'bout it, nudder.' Brer Fox ax is he got time fer ter take his meat home, an' Brer Rabbit 'low dat he is. Wid dat, he put out down de road, an' Brer Rabbit sot right flat on de groun' an' laugh, twel, ef you'd a seed 'im, you'd a said he done fin' a new gigglin' place.

"He foller'd long atter Brer Fox, but tuck keer fer ter keep out'n sight. He seed Brer Fox run in his house, fer ter put ol' Widdle-Waddle an' de pullets 'way. Den he run out ag'in, foller'd by his ol' 'oman, an' he hear her holler out, 'You better come on back here an' he'p me wid deze

chillun er yone, kaze it's a mighty fine sitiwation when a 'oman, an' her not well at dat, has ter do eve'y blessed thing dey is ter be done — split up de wood ter make a fier, pick up de chips fer ter kin'le it wid, do all de cookin', all de pullin' an' haulin', an' take keer er all yo' good-for-nothin' chillun! You better come on back here, I tell you!' But by dat time, Brer Fox wuz done gone.

"Brer Rabbit stay'd whar he wuz a right smart whet, long 'nough fer Brer Fox ter mos' git whar he gwine, an' den he sa'nter'd out in de big road an' make his way ter Brer Fox' house. He went up, he did, monstus perlite — it look like butter won't melt in mouf. He open de gate slow, an' he make sho it wuz shet behime 'im. He went ter de do' an' rap on it, an' stan' dar wid his hat in his han', an' look mighty 'umble-come-tumble.

"Ol' Miss Fox, she open de do', she did, an' Brer Rabbit pass de time er day wid 'er, an' den say he got a message fer her somers in his pocket, ef he kin yever fin' it. Atter so long a time, he fin' de paper what Brer Rabbit say come fum ol' King Lion. He han' her dis, an' Miss Fox say she ain't a good han' at readin', not sence de chillun broke her fur-seein' specks, an' she dunner what de name er goodness she gwine do, speshually when her ol' man ain't skacely got time fer ter stay at home, an' when he does run in it look like de flo'll burn blisters in his feet, an' she say ef she'd a know'd at fust what she know at last, she'd take two long thinks and a mighty big thunk 'fo' she'd marry anybody in de roun' worl'. Brer Rabbit, he 'low, 'Yassum!' an' den he up an' tell 'er dat he met Brer Fox, which King Lion done sont 'im a soople-peeny. Brer Fox ax 'im how he gittin' on, an' Brer Rabbit say he'd be gittin' on purty well ef he had anything ter eat at his house. (All dis is de tale dat Brer Rabbit wuz po'in' in ol' Miss Fox' year.) Den Brer Fox wipe his eye an' say 'tain't gwine do fer Brer Rabbit ter go widout eatin'. Ol' Miss Fox break inter de tale wid, 'I wish he'd wipe his eye 'bout some er my troubles; his eye is dry 'nough when he's 'roun' here.'

"Brer Rabbit 'low, 'Yassum!' an' den he say dat Brer Fox 'low ez how no longer'n dat ve'y mornin' he fotch home two fat pullets an' ol' Widdle-Waddle Puddle Duck, an' he say Brer Rabbit kin have his choosenment er de pullets er der puddle duck. Mo' dan dat, Brer Rabbit say, Brer Fox sot right flat in de road an' writ Miss Fox a note, so dat she'll know his will an' desirements.

"Ol' Miss Fox look at Brer Rabbit mighty hard. She done tell 'im 'bout her fur-seein' specks, an' she say dat ef de letter ain't read twel she reads it, she mighty sorry fer de letter. She tuck it an' turn it upperside down an' 'roun' an' 'roun', an' den han' it back ter Brer Rabbit, wid, 'What do she say?' Brer Rabbit, he cle'r'd his th'oat, an' make out he readin'; he say, 'Ter all whomst it mought contrive er consarn, bofe now an' presently: Be so pleased ez ter let Brer Rabbit have de pullets er de puddle duck. I'm well at dis writin' an' a hopin' you er enjoyin' de same shower er blessin's.'

" 'Whatsomever it mought er been, 'tain't no love-letter,' sez ol' Miss Fox, sez she, an' den she fotch out de two fat pullets, an' Brer Rabbit, he moseyed off home, singin' de song dat tells 'bout how Mr. Fox done lef' towny-o."

Uncle Remus paused, leaned his head back, and groaned. "Is that all?" asked the little boy. "It mought be, an' den ag'in it moughtn't," the old man responded. "It 'pen's on who's a-tellin' de tale. Some folks would cut it right short off an' let it go at dat, but not me. When I starts fer ter tell a tale, I pursues it right ter de een' des like de creeturs wuz pursuin' one an'er — des like de big men is pursuin' de little men, wid de little men gittin' ter kivver, an' a-hittin' back ez dey run.

"One thing Brer Rabbit know mighty nigh ez well ez he know dat he's hongry. He know 'twon't never do in de roun' worl' fer Brer Fox fer ter go back home, an' fin' out how de pullets went. So when he git out'n sight er Brer Fox' house, he whipped up an' went a-runnin' home des ez hard ez he kin, an' he tell his ol' lady fer ter take de pullets an' fix um fine wid de kinder doin's dey has wid chickens, kaze he mought have comp'ny. He say he got ter go back an' see how ol' King Lion's paw gittin' on, an' he put out fer ter be dar 'fo' Brer Fox come 'way.

"He lit out, he did, an' fa'rly burnt up de big road wid his footsies — *bookity-bookity* — an' when he git dar, sho 'nough, Brer Fox wuz dar, lookin' like de really-truly goodness wuz des drippin' fum his mouf, an' oozin' fum his hide. You may a seed folks dat look 'umble-come-tumble, but you ain't never is see nobody dat got 'umble-come-tumbleness down ez fine ez what Mr. Fox had it. An' a mighty good reason, kaze he wuz skeered dat King Lion wuz gwine ter haul 'im over de coals fer not fetchin' de meat dat he ought er fotch 'im. When Brer Fox got ter whar King Lion do de kingin', dey wuz a whole passel er creeturs ahead un 'im, an' mighty nigh all un um had some meat, an' dem what ain't had it come wid some tale fer ter skusen deyse'f. Dey went in, one by one, an' had der confab, an' den come out ag'in, some lookin' glad an' some lookin' mad; an' all dat time dar sot Brer Fox waitin' his turn.

"He wuz might'ly holp up when he see Brer Rabbit, kaze he know'd dat Brer Rabbit, bein' de doctor, kin git in dar 'fo' anybody. He hail Brer Rabbit, an' say he mighty glad fer ter see 'im once mo', live an' well, an' Brer Rabbit 'spon' dat he monstus glad fer ter see Brer Fox. He 'low, 'I'm mo' dan glad fer ter see you ain't been in dar whar de King's doin' his kingin' at,' sez ol' Brer Rabbit, sezee. 'I wuz fear'd you'd take a notion an' go in dar 'fo' I kin git back, an' dat 'ud a been mighty bad fer you — it sho would.' Den Brer Rabbit look like he studyin', an' bimeby, he up an' say, sezee, 'Brer Fox, you stay right whar you is, an' don't try ter go in dar whar de King at twel I gi' you de word; I dunner what he mought do ter you.' Brer Fox say he mighty glad Brer Rabbit got dar in time fer ter save his hide.

"Now, Brer Rabbit bein' de doctor, he had de right fer ter go in dar whar de King at widout any stan'in' 'roun' an' waitin', an' he elbow'd his way thoo de waitin' creeturs, spite or der spittin' an' growlin', an' went right on in whar King Lion at. His paw wuz all wropped up, an' he wuz des drappin' off ter sleep, an' whiles Brer Rabbit wuz lookin' at 'im, he turned loose, he did, an' 'gun ter sno' like he done swaller'd a hoss, mane an' huff. Seein' dat, Brer Rabbit make a bow, an' go right out whar Brer Fox an' de yuther creeturs wuz waitin' at.

"Soon ez Brer Fox see dis, he ax Brer Rabbit what de news. Brer Rabbit tuck 'im off one side, an' tell 'im he better go on home, kaze King Lion wuz tur'bly put out by de way Brer Fox been gwine on. 'I begged off fer you, Brer Fox,' sez ol' Brer Rabbit, sezee, 'an' he say dat he'll skuzen you dis time, but de nex' time — ' Brer Rabbit make a motion like he takin' off his head. 'You better go on home, Brer Fox,' sezee, ' 'fo' yo' ol' 'oman gives 'way dem fine fat pullets what I seed you wid dis mornin'.' Brer Fox laugh; he say he'd like fer ter see somebody git dem pullets 'way fum his ol' 'oman. 'Ef you kin git um, Brer Rabbit,' sezee, 'you er mo' dan welcome.' 'Desso!' Brer Rabbit 'low, 'Thanky, Brer Fox, thanky!' an' he went lippity-clippitin' down de road, laughin' so loud dat Brer Fox stop an' look at 'im, wid 'I'd like ter know what's de joke' kinder 'spression on his coun'nance."

5
How Brother Rabbit Brought Family Trouble on Brother Fox

THE LITTLE BOY sat in a thoughtful attitude after Uncle Remus had told him how Brother Rabbit had fraudulently secured Brother Fox's pullets. He had been taught never to ignore the difference between right and wrong — justice and injustice — and in his mind the line between the two was sharply and deeply drawn. He sat reflecting, while Uncle Remus busied himself about his work-bench, on one end of which was his favorite seat. He arranged and rearranged his tools, and then folded his hands in his lap with an air of satisfaction. He evidently expected the youngster to make come comment or observation, and when he had waited a little while, he made a remark calculated to draw the child out.

"I'm fear'd you ain't feelin' well, honey. Sump'n' in dat tale must a made you feel bad." The little boy looked at him, but made no response. "Whar'bouts in de tale wuz you tooken sick at?" Uncle Remus inquired, with a great display of solicitude.

"Why, I'm not sick, Uncle Remus," replied the lad.

"Well, I'm monstus glad ter hear it," the old man responded, "kaze you sho had me skeer'd. A little mo', an' I'd a tol' you fer ter run an' let yo' granny look at yo' tongue an' feel er yo' pulsh." The child laughed at this, and then became serious again. "Dey's sump'n' de matter wid you," Uncle Remus insisted, "kaze eve' sence I tol' you dat tale, you been lookin' like you got mo' on yo' min' dan you kin tote."

"I was just thinking," said the child, somewhat shyly — he was always embarrassed when commenting on Uncle Remus's stories — "I was just thinking that when Brother Rabbit got the chickens from Brother Fox, he was really stealing them."

"Dey ain't no two ways 'bout dat," said Uncle Remus complacently. "But what wuz Brer Fox doin' when *he* got um? Pullets an' puddle ducks don't grow on trees, an' it's been a mighty long time since dey been runnin' wil'. No, honey! Dey's a heap er idees dat you got ter shake off ef you gwine ter put de creeturs 'longside er folks; you'll hatter shake um, an' shuck um. Creeturs could talk like folks in dat day an' time, an' dey kin do a heap er things what folks do; but you kin see de diffunce fer yo'se'f. Folks got der laws, an' de creeturs got der'n, an' it bleeze ter be dat away.

"Brer Rabbit took de pullets when by good rights he oughter lef' um whar he fin' um, but you'll l'arn fer yo'se'f dat dey's a heap er folks lots wuss dan Brer Rabbit, when it comes ter takin' what ain't der'n, an' when you l'arn it you'll look back on deze times an' feel so sorry dat you ain't got um wid you dat you'll hatter wipe yo' eyes an' blow yo' nose — an' I'm a-hopin' mighty strong dat you won't be tryin' fer ter show off in no gal comp'ny when you does it, kaze dat'd make Miss Sally turn in her grave."

These remarks were way beyond the little boy, but he accepted them as an explanation, though it was not altogether satisfactory. He seemed to imagine that if the animals could talk and reason in the way that Uncle Remus represented them, they should have some idea of the difference between right and wrong. The old Negro had no difficulty whatever in perceiving the nature of the child's trouble, and he dealt with it as seriously and as solemnly as he knew how.

"It seem like," he said, glancing at the little boy, "dat folks is got one way er lookin' at things, an' it's all bleeze ter be des de way dey think it oughter be. Ef dey had diffunt eyes, an' ef deze eyes wuz on a diffunt level, dey wouldn't see de way dey does now; what dey see would be a little mo' slonchways, an' den eve'ybody would git diffunt idees. Well, de diffunt eyes an' de diffunt idees dat folks mought a had, dat des zackly what de creeturs got. What dey see dey see slonchways, stidder upendickler. Folks got der ways, an' de creeturs is got der'n, an' deze yer ways wuz proned in um fum de fust.

"Creetur law ain't folks' law, nohow you kin fix it," Uncle Remus went on, with the unction of a country preacher. "Dar wuz ol' Brer Fox, wid his pullets an' his puddle duck; an' you done got de idee dat Brer Rabbit done wrong when he work his head an' han's fer ter git holt un um. But le' me ax you dis: Whar did Brer Fox git um? He ain't git um at home, kaze he wuz totin' um dar when he fust run across 'im; he ain't git um in de wods, kaze pullets an' puddle ducks ain't grow on trees — an' ef dey is, Brer Fox can't clim' no higher dan he kin jump. Now, you kin put it down an' carry four, dat wharsomever Brer Fox lay han's on um, he ain't buy'd um, an' needer wuz dey gun ter 'im. Dat much you don't hatter guess at; you des knows it by yo' nose an' yo' two big toes.

"Let 'lone dat, de pullets an' de puddle duck mought not a b'long'd ter de one what Brer Fox tuck um fum, an' I boun' you dat 'twould take a mighty long time fer ter hunt up an' s'arch out de nick-names an' de pet-tygrees er all dem what had um 'fo' Brer Rabbit drapped um in his rasher-bag." Uncle Remus paused to take note of the direction of the wind and the appearance of the sky; then he sighed and closed his eyes. After a while, the spirit seemed to move him, and he straightened himself on the work-bench, and exchanged the somewhat uncomfortable seat for a chair.

"I'm mighty glad you spoken'd up an' say what you did, honey," he remarked, "kaze a leetle mo', an' I'd a up an' a whirled in, an a tol' you de t'er part er dat tale 'bout Brer Rabbit an' de pullets an' de puddle duck; I sho would, an' den you'd a felt so mighty sorry 'bout de way de creeturs look at things, dat you'd a went behime de smoke-'ouse an' a boo-hoo'd des like yo' gizzard wuz gwine ter break in two."

The little boy gave the old Negro a quick glance of reproach. "Why, Uncle Remus!" he exclaimed, "I thought you always finished a story when you began it; you said so yourself."

In spite of a desire to treat the child seriously, Uncle Remus grinned broadly. "De way I look at it, honey, you hatter harness two hosses one at a time, less'n you got a man fer ter he'p you; an' when you er tellin' a two-hoss tale, you hatter tell um one at a time. Ef I wuz ter try fer ter tell um bofe at once, you'd run ter de house an' tell yo' granny dat ol' man Remus had done gone an' got rid er his sev'm senses, an' wuz tryin' fer ter gi' you a good strong dose er Chinee; an' when you done dat, Miss Sally sho would preach my funer'l march. I wa'n't born'd yistiddy, an' I take notice dat yo' daddy ain't got de double-bairl gun, an' dat Miss Sally don't have but one hoss fer ter haul her ter church Sundays. Dat ar double-buggy dat yo' daddy use ter drive up dar in Atlanty would look mighty funny ef it had mo' dan one hoss hitched ter it. Lawsy, yes! Eve'ything is mo' samer now dan what it use ter be; an' I bet you right now dat ef de trufe wuz know'd we er stan'in' on our heads."

The little boy was obliged to laugh at this whimsical explanation, and this gave Uncle Remus as much pleasure as the stories gave the child. "Ef you'll wet yo' thum', an' turn back in yo' min' 'twon't be hard fer you ter reckermember dat Brer Fox tol' Brer Rabbit dat ef he kin git dem two fine, fat pullets fum his ol' 'oman, he's mo' dan welcome fer ter git um.

But when Brer Fox say dat, de pullets wuz hangin' up at Brer Rabbit
house; he done got um wid dat piece er paper what he tuck an' show ol'
Miss Fox. Dat what make him laugh so loud an' so long.

"Well, suh, atter Brer Rabbit git done laughin', he moseyed off home
whar his wife and chillun live at, an' Brer Fox, he went on to'rds his
house whar his ol' 'oman live at. Ef he'd a had his eyes shet, he'd a
know'd when he got dar, kaze ol' Miss Fox wuz stan'in' in de do' waitin'
fer 'im. She 'gun ter jaw at 'im, long 'fo' he got in lis'nen' distance, an'
you mought a hear her a mile er mo'. When he got whar he know'd what
she wuz sayin', he ain't say nothin'; he des amble 'long twel he come ter
de do'. By dat time ol' Miss Fox wuz so mad dat she can't say nothin' an'
do jestice ter herse'f, so she des stan' dar an' make motions wid de broom
what she had in her han'.

"Brer Fox, he wipe de persweat off'n his face an' eyes, an' say, 'It
seem like ter me dat I hear you talkin' ter some un des now; what wuz
you sayin', sugar-honey?' Soon ez she kin ketch her breff, she 'low, 'I'll
sugar you! I'll honey you! What make you fetch vittles home ef you gwine
ter sen' it off ag'in? What you wanter put yo'se'f ter de trouble er totin' it
ter dis house, when you know you gwine ter gi' it 'way des ez soon ez you
turn yo' back on de place? An' what business you got sen'in' ol' Miss
Rabbit de two fine, fat pullets what you brung home, which dey made me
dribble at de mouf de fust time I seed um? An' I ain't mo' dan seed um
'fo' here come ol' Brer Rabbit, a-bowin' an' a-scrapin', an' a-simperin'
an' a-sniggerin', an' he 'low dat you done sont 'im fer de pullets. Ef it had
a des a been his own 'lone sesso, he'd a never got dem pullets in de roun'
worl' — I'd a gouged out his goozle fust — but here he come wid a letter
what you writ, dough you know'd good an' well dat when it comes ter
writin' I dunno B from Bull's-Foot.'

"Brer Fox shuck his head; he say he ain't never writ no letter, kaze he
dunner how, an' it seem mighty funny ter him dat his sugar-honey an'
dumplin'-pie don't know dat much. Ol' Miss Fox, she 'low, she did, dat
dumplin'-pie ain't chicken-pie, an' den she rail at Brer Fox. 'How come
you givin' pullets ter ol' Brer Rabbit an' his fambly, when yo' own chillun,
'twix' yo' laziness an' de hard times, is gwine 'roun' here so ga'nt dat dey
can't make a shadder in de moonshine? You know mighty well — none
better — dat we ain't never is neighbor'd wid dat kinder trash, an' I

dunner what done come over you dat you er takin' vittles out'n yo' own chillun's mouf an' feedin' dat Rabbit brood.'

"Brer Fox vow an' declar' he ain't done no sech uv a thing, an' his ol' 'oman vow an' declar' dat he is, an' she shake de broom so close und' his nose dat he hatter sneeze. Den he 'low, 'Does you mean fer ter stan' dar, flat-footed, an' right 'fo' my face an' eyes, an' whar yo' own chillun kin hear you, an' tell me dat you tuck an' gi' Brer Rabbit dem ar fine, fat pullets what I brung home? Does you mean fer ter tell me dat?' She say, 'Ef I done it, I done it kaze you writ me a 'pistle an' tell me fer ter do it.' Brer Fox 'low, 'Is you got de imperdence ter tell me dat des kaze Brer Rabbit han' you a piece er paper, wid sump'n' n'er marked on it, you ain't got nothin' better ter do dan ter up an' gi' 'im de fine, fat pullets what I brung fer ter make some chicken-pie?'

"Dis make ol' Miss Fox so mad dat she can't see straight, an' when she git so she kin talk plain, she vow she gwine ter hurt Brer Rabbit ef it tuck a lifetime fer ter do it. An' dar wuz Brer Fox des ez mad, ef not madder. Dey bofe sot down an' grit der tushes, an' mumble an' growl like dey talkin' ter deyse'f. Brer Rabbit wa'n't so mighty fur off, an' he laugh an' laugh twel he can't laugh no mo'.

"But whiles he laughin', he laugh too loud, an' Brer Fox hear him. He say ter his ol' 'oman, I'm gwine ter git some rabbit meat fer ter make up fer de chickens what you done give 'way. You be sweepin' here in front er de do', an' I'll slip 'roun' de back way, an' come up on him when he ain't thinkin' 'bout it; an' whiles you sweepin' make out you talkin' ter me like I'm in de house.' So said, so done. Miss Fox she sweep an' sweep, an' whiles she sweepin' she make out she talkin' ter Brer Fox whiles he in de house. She say, 'You better come on out'n dar an' go on 'bout yo' business ef you got any. Here I'm constant a-gwine, fum mornin' twel night, an' dar you is a-loungin' 'roun', waitin' fer Brer Rabbit fer ter play tricks on you. You better come on out'n dar an' go fin' sump'n' n'er ter eat fer yo' fambly.'

"Dat's de way she talk, whiles she wuz pertendin' ter sweep, an' des 'bout dat time, up come ol' Brer Rabbit wid a mighty perlite bow. He tuck off his hat, he did, 'Good evenin' dis evenin', Miss Fox. I hope I see you well, ma'am.' Miss Fox 'low dat she ain't ez peart ez she look ter be, an' mo' dan dat, her ol' man layin' in de house right now wid a mighty bad case er de influendways. Brer Rabbit say he mighty sorry, but it's what we all got ter look out fer, kaze 'zease an' trouble, an' one thing an' an'er, is all de time makin' de roun's er de places whar folks live at. Den ol' Brer Rabbit kinder hol' his head on one side an' sorter smile; he up an' ax, he did, 'Miss Fox, how you like dat cut er caliker what King Lion sont you fer ter make a frock out'n? Reason I ax, I'm a-gwine ter see 'im dis evenin', an' I 'most know dat he'll ax me ef you like de pattern.'

"Miss Fox lean her broom ag'in' de house, an put her han's on her hips, an' make Brer Rabbit say over what he done tol' 'er. 'Well, well, well!' sez ol' Miss Fox, se' she; 'de King sont me a caliker frock, an' I ain't never lay eyes on it! Ef dat don't beat my time!' Brer Rabbit, he put his han' over his mouf an' cough sorter sof'; he 'low, he did, 'You'll hatter skuzen me, ma'am,' sezee. 'I'm afear'd I done gone an' said sump'n' dat I oughtn'ter say. When I knows what I'm a-doin', I never likes fer ter come 'twix' man an' wife, ef I kin he'p myse'f — no, ma'am, not me! Yit Brer Fox is right dar in de house an' you kin ax 'im, ef you don't b'lieve me.'

"Fer one long minnit, Miss Fox wuz so mad dat she hatter wait twel she cotch her breff 'fo' she kin say a word. Lots er wimmen would a stood up dar an' squealed, but Miss Fox, she helt her breff. Quick ez she kin, she holler out, 'No, he ain't in de house; he's out yan' tryin' fer ter slip up on you 'bout dem pullets.' 'I'm glad you got dat idee,' sez Brer Rabbit, sezee, 'kaze it's liable fer ter keep down trouble. Ef you wuz a man, Miss Fox,' sezee, 'you mought git de idee dat he seed me comin' an' wuz hidin' out kaze he fear'd I'd ax you 'bout dat frock what de King sont you. It sho wuz a mighty purty piece er caliker, an' ef I'd a know'd den what I know now, I'd a got it fum Brer Fox an' gi' it ter my ol' 'oman — I sho would!'

"Wid dat, Brer Rabbit make his bow an' light out fum dar; an' he wa'n't none too soon, nudder, kaze he ain't mo' dan got in de bushes whar he kin hide hisse'f, 'fo' here come ol' Brer Fox. He look all 'roun', but he ain't see nobody but his ol' 'oman, kaze Brer Rabbit done gone along. Brer Fox say, sezee, 'Whar is de triflin' scoundul? I seed 'im stan'in' right here — whar is he? Whar he gone?' Ol' Miss Fox, she up wid de broom an' hit him a biff side de head dat come mighty nigh knockin' 'im inter one er de j'inin' counties. 'Dat's whar he is,' se' she, an' she fetch her ol' man a whack 'cross de backbone, dat soun' like ol' Miss Jenkins a-beatin' dat ole rug kyarpit by hittin' it ag'in' de fence.

"Ole Brer Fox tuck a notion dat he been struck by lightnin'; he fell down an' roll over, an' by de time dat ol' Miss Fox had mighty nigh wo' de broom out, he fin' out what 'uz happenin'. He holler out, 'Why, laws-a-massy, honey! What de matter wid you? What you biffin' me fer? I ain't Brer Rabbit! Ow! Please, honey, don't bang me so hard; I ain't gwine do it no mo'.' Ol' Miss Fox says, se' she, 'Ah-yi! you owns up, does you? You ain't gwine do it no mo', ain't you? Now, whar my fine caliker frock what de King sont me?' An' all de time she wuz talkin' she wuz wipin' 'im up wid de broom. Mon, de way she beat dat creetur wuz a start-natchul scandal.

"Well, when Brer Fox got out'n reach, an' she'd kinder cooled down, she up an' tol' 'im 'bout de caliker frock what King Lion had sont 'er, an' she ax 'im what de name er goodness is he done wid it, an' ef he ain't brung it home onbeknownst ter her, who in de dashes an' de dickunses is he gi' it to? He vow he ain't seed no caliker frock, an' she 'low dat he done say, whiles she wuz a-biffin' 'im, dat he ain't gwine do it no mo'. Brer Fox say he ain't know what she wuz beatin' 'im fer, an' he was mos' bleeze ter promise not ter do it no mo', kaze she wuz hurtin' 'im so bad.

"Dey put der heads tergedder, dey did, an' collogue an' confab 'bout how dey gwine ter git even wid Brer Rabbit, kaze de King ain't sont no fine caliker frock, an' needer is dey got der two fat pullets. Dar dey wuz, no frock, no pullets, an' Brer Rabbit still cuttin' up his capers an' playin' his pranks on eve'ything an' eve'ybody. Dey say dey wuz gwine ter ketch 'im ef it kilt eve'y cow in de island, wid a couple er steers thow'd in fer good medjur. Dey wuz gwine ter hide close ter de places whar he hatter pass by; dey wuz gwine ter do dis an' dey wuz gwine ter do dat, but whatsomever dey done, dey wuz gwine ter ketch up wid Brer Rabbit.

"Now, den, it takes two ter make a bargain, an' one mo' fer ter see dat it's done all right. Brer Rabbit, he know mighty well — none better — all de gwines-on in dat part er de country, an' he make his 'rangerments 'cordin'. He been use ter keepin' his eye-ball skunt when all 'uz peace, but when dey wuz any trouble ahead, he wuz so nervous dat he'd kick out wid his behime foot ef a weed tickled 'im. When it come down ter plain nerviousness, he can't be beat.

"Brer Fox can't make a move but what Brer Rabbit would know 'bout it; he know'd when he went out an' when he went in, an' he keep sech a close watch on um dat 'twuz e'en about all he kin do fer ter keep Brer Fox fum ketchin' 'im. Atter so long a time Brer Rabbit got tired er leadin' dis kinder life. He could a put up wid it maybe a fortnight, but when it run over dat, he got plum' tired, Brer Rabbit did. Yit it look like dat luck wuz constant a-runnin' his way, kaze he ain't been dodgin' 'roun' in de bushes, tryin' fer ter keep out'n Brer Fox's way — he ain't been doin' dis mo' dan a week, when dere come word fum ol' King Lion fer go an' see 'im. It seem like de place whar he stuck de brier in his han' wuz kyo'd up too quick, an' had done turn inter a bile — a great big un — an' got so dat de King had ter walk de flo' all night des like yo' pappy useter do when he had de toofache.

"Well, Brer Rabbit ain't no sooner git de word dan he run right straight ter de place whar dey done der kingin' at, an' 'tain't take 'im long, needer, kaze I let you know, honey, when Brer Rabbit take a notion fer ter go anywhar right quick, he des picks up de miles wid his feet an' draps um off ag'in, des like a dog sheds fleas. He got dar, he did, an' when he see how bad de bile wuz, he kinder shuck his year an' rub his nose des like de sho nuff doctors does. He ax um whyn't dey tell 'im 'bout dis when de bile 'gun ter show, an' dey say dey been huntin' fer 'im high an' low, an' dey can't fin' 'im nowhar an' nohow.

"Brer Rabbit put on his specks an' 'low, 'Tut, tut, tut! Ef dis ain't too bad! I'm fear' dey ain't but one kyo' fer a place like dis. I hate might'ly ter be de 'casion er any trouble, but it look like I'm des a-bleeze ter.' King Lion kinder flinch an' frown when he hear dis, but Brer Rabbit say dat de trouble ain't for him, but fer one er his ol'-time 'quaintance. 'Ef you wa'n't de King,' he say ter de Lion, 'I'd des let you go on an' suffer, but bein' what you is, I'm bleeze ter pull ol' frien'ship up by de roots. Ef you wanter git well, you'll des hatter wrop yo' han' up in a fox-hide. Not only dat, but de hide mus' be so fresh dat it's warm.'

"Den Brer Rabbit make out he 'bout ter cry. He 'low, 'I can't b'ar ter tell my ol' frien' good-by, kaze we done had many a night tergedder, up an' down an' 'roun' de worl'. De sooner you gits Brer Fox here de better — but I'll hatter ax you fer ter le' me out de back way, an' I'll go off somers in de woods an' wonder at de flight er time an' de changes dat de years is brung.' Den he bow ter King Lion; he say, 'De nex' time I see you yo' han' will be well, but whar will Brer Fox be? De King he say, 'Why, I'll sen' you de kyarcass,' but Brer Rabbit say, 'No, please don't, kaze I couldn't b'ar ter look at it. Des sen' it ter Miss Fox; it mought be some sort er comfort ter dat po' creetur.'"

6

The Most Beautiful Bird in the World

UNCLE REMUS and the little boy were returning from a long and leisurely walk in the woods. They had had a pretty good time, all things considered, and the old man was in high good humor. The little boy had an idea that the walk had been undertaken solely for his pleasure, and Uncle Remus allowed him to think so; but the truth was that it had a purpose behind it. The old Negro wanted to locate some wild hogs that had long been devastating the growing stuff on the plantation. The wild hogs gave him no trouble until they began to destroy stuff that he himself had planted — watermelons and sugarcane — and he argued from this that they were growing bolder, and that they would have to be captured. So, on this particular day, he had set out to find where they had their headquarters, and he was successful.

The next thing would be to take the dogs and capture them one by one, taking care not to disturb the hogs that came up to be fed every evening, when the hog-feeder began to call. The two companions — the old man and the little lad — had started out immediately after dinner, and dusk was falling when they returned. But neither one was weary; they had gone leisurely along, stopping occasionally to talk about the interesting things they saw, and resuming their walk whenever Uncle Remus thought the child had rested long enough.

The squirrels ran noisily over the leaves that winter had flung on the ground, and went home by jumping from tree to tree; birds that the city-raised child had never seen before, flitted in the bushes, or went hopping, or running on the ground. The little boy was interested in all of them, but the joree seemed especially to attract his attention, and he was for stopping whenever he heard a scratching in the dead leaves and trash. The joree is a very lonely bird, and you would judge that it was mortally afraid of man; but it is not so shy as its habits would lead you to believe. It is not for flying away every time it hears a noise, but will continue scratching for its food in the fence corners and under the bushes, until the observer ventures too close, and then, with a cheery little trill, it will fly away.

In its coat of black and brown and white, it is a very pretty bird. Its markings are peculiar, but nature has laid them on so that they may harmonize effectively with its surroundings in wood and swamp. The enthusiasm of the little boy was such that Uncle Remus felt obliged to clip its wings. This he endeavored to do, not by arguing or disputing, but in a way quite characteristic.

The little boy had said over and over again that the joree, with its comical hop, back and forth, as it stirred up the leaves and trash, and its peculiar coloring, was the funniest as well as the most beautiful bird he had ever seen.

"Dat bein' de case," remarked Uncle Remus with a judicial air, "you ain't never is see de Baltimer bird."

"Oh, yes!" said the child; "don't you know you showed me the hanging nest, and told me it was the Baltimore bird? Grandmother says it is the oriole."

"She do, do she? Well, ef she sesso, I speck it's so, but you ain't gwine ketch me twis'in' my tongue 'roun' fer ter talk dat kinder outlandish talk — not me! An' I knows dis, dat ef anybody don't wanter call dat bird de Baltimer bird, dey don't hatter. I been callin' it dat a mighty long time, ef you take one year wid an'er, an' ef it's yever fotch de bird any bad luck, I ain't never hear tell un it. I ain't gwine ter 'spute wid you, honey, 'bout de joree; in his place an' whar he b'longs at, dey ain't no better ner no purtier bird; but when it comes ter sayin' dat he's de puniest er all de birds, why, dat's de way de lawyers talk when dey er jowerin' in de court-house. When it comes ter de purtiest bird er all de birds, she's done gone away too long ago ter talk about, an' nobody can't fin' her. She wa'n't de purtiest bird des kaze some un sesso; not her — no, suh! She wuz purty kaze all de yuther birds sesso. Dey done 'cide it — dey done 'gree ter it — an' you can't rub it out. Dey ain't wanter sesso, but dey bleeze ter do it; dey wa'n't no gittin' 'roun' it. One bird ain't like de idee er sayin' dat any udder bird is purtier dan what she is, but dey bleeze ter do it, at-ter dey seen what dey seed.

"I ain't never is seed dis purty bird myse'f," the old man went on, "an' de nex' man you ax will tell you de same; but I done hear tell un 'im — ef he wuz a him. Time an' time ag'in I hear folks tell de tale — some one way an' some an'er, but it all come ter de same thing in de een' — dar wuz de tale."

"But what about the bird?" the little boy asked.

"Shucks, honey! ain't I des a-tellin' yo' dat 'twa'n't des a plain bird; you kin say dat 'bout all un um but dis un, which she wuz de purtiest bird on de face er de yeth. I'm kinder rattled 'bout de entitlements er dis yer bird, kaze it seem like dat dem what fust 'gun ter tell de tale kinder got de name mixed up wid der own foolishness. Some call 'im de Coogly Bird, some call 'im de Cow-Cow Bird, an' some call 'im de Coo-Coo Bird — some say 'twuz a lady bird, an' den ag'in some say 'twuz a gem-man bird. By good rights, she oughter been a lady bird, fum de fuss she kicked up, an I boun' she wuz. It's des like I tell you 'bout de name, yit, call 'er what you please an' when you please, she ain't gwine ter come fer yo' callin'. She'd a come long ago ef callin' would a fotch 'er, kaze, fum dat time ter dis, some er de yuther birds been hollin' an' callin' 'er. Dey been callin' 'er sence de day dat all de birds had der semblement des like white folks, an' niggers, too, fer dat matter, when dey wanter up an' out a man what ain't been doin' nothin' in de roun' worl' but gittin' pay fer settin' 'roun' doin' nothin'.' "

"Don't you mean a convention, Uncle Remus?" inquired the lad. "Papa's gone to Atlanta to attend a convention."

"Dat zactly what I mean, honey, 'ceppin' dat yo' daddy oughter be right here now wid his ma. But dat's needer here ner dar, ez de man sez 'bout de flea what he ain't cotch. 'Way back yander, when de clouds wuz thicker dan what dey is now, an' when de sun ain't had ter go to bed at night ter keep fum bein' tired de nex' day, de time come when de cree-turs, fur an' feather, ain't had much ter do, mo' speshually de birds. Dey flew'd 'roun', dey did, an' fed tergedder widout fightin', an' made der houses in de trees an' on the groun', an' dey wuz all des ez sociable ez you please. But atter while dey ain't had much ter do, an' when dat time come dey got ter wranglin' an' 'sputin', des like folks does now. One 'ud sail up an' say 'Howdy?' an' de yuther'd 'fuse ter 'spon', an' dar dey had it. While de gemman birds wuz gwine on dis away, de lady birds wuz des ez busy. Dey 'sputed 'bout der feathers an' bout der looks twel it seem like dey wuz gwine ter be sho 'nough war, kaze de most un um had bills an' claws.

"Atter while, dey fin' dat dis kinder doin's ain't gwine ter pay, an' so dey bowed ter one an'er, mighty perlite, an' make out dey gwine on 'bout der business. Well, dey played like dey wuz mighty busy, but dey soon git tired er dis, an' dey say ter deyse'f dat dey'd die dead ef dey didn't run 'roun' an' have a chat wid de neighbors; an' here dey went, axin' de news, an' tellin' dat what ain't news. One say she hear dat Miss Red Bird up an' 'low dat she de purtiest er all de birds, an' dar dey had it, squallin', chattin', an' squealin'. De word went 'roun' an' when it come back ter whar it started, it ain't look like itse'f. 'Twuz Miss Blue Bird, 'twuz Miss Jay Bird, 'twuz Miss Dat an' Miss T'other. It seem like dat eve'y one un um think dat she de purtiest.

"Well, suh, de 'spute got so hot dat dey had ter be sump'n' done — dey wa'n't no two ways 'bout dat. Miss Wren an' Miss Blue Bird an' Miss Robin put der heads tergedder, an' ax how dey gwine ter stop de 'spute. Na'er one un um 'pended on der good looks, but der havishness wuz er de best, an' dey wanted ter stop de jowerin'. Dey study an' dey study, dey talk an' dey talk, but dey ain't hit on nothin'. Little Miss Wren wuz de spryest, an' she had a slice er temper wid salt an' pepper on it. Dey talked so fast an' dey talked so long dat she wuz skeer'd she might git sorter sassy, an' she up'n say, 'Ladies, le' me make a move an' motion. Le's p'oc'astinate dis session uv our confab, kaze some un us mought say sump'n' dat de yuthers won't like. De sun gittin' mighty low anyhow; le's put off our colloguin' twel termorrer. We'll go home an' ax our ol' men what dey think, an' dey'll tell us what dey kin — you know how men folks does: dey knows eve'ything 'ceppin' dat dey does know, an' dat dey done fergot. Dey'll tell us, an' when we go ter bed we kin dream on it.'

"Miss Blue Bird an' Miss Robin 'low dat dis de smartest thing dey yever is hear, an' dey 'gree ter what little Miss Wren say. Dey put on der things an' marched off home fer ter feed de chillun an' put um ter bed. Bright an' yearly de nex' mornin' dey met at de same place, an', atter dey got over der gigglin' an' der howdy-doin', dey start up de confab whar dey lef' off. Miss Robin say she can't think uv a blessed thing. She say dat when he ax'd her ol' man 'bout it, he up an' 'low'd dat she better j'ine 'im in huntin' bugs fer de chillun fer ter play wid, stidder gaddin' fum post ter pillar. An' de yuthers raise der wings, an' say, 'Well, well!' an' 'Who'd a thunk it?'

"Miss Blue Bird 'low dat when she ax her ol' man 'bout it, he say she better stay at home stidder gwine 'roun' spreadin' scandaliousness thoo de neighborhood. Miss Wren kinder hunged her head like she 'shame fer ter tell 'bout her speunce. She say dat her ol' man wuz monstrus sassy twel she tol' 'im dat ef he wanter change his boardin'-house he wuz mo' dan welcome. Wid dat, he whirled an' ax her why in de name er goodness don't she 'swade um fer ter have a big 'sembly er all de lady birds at some place er 'nother whar dey'll have plenty er room, whar dey kin all march 'roun' an' let somebody pick out de purtiest in de whole crowd, an' den when dat's done all de balance un um must be put under de needcessity er 'greein' ter what de picker picks. Ef he say de owl is de purtiest, den all de yuther birds got ter sesso too; ef he say de buzzard is de purtiest, dat's de way it gotter be.

"'La, me!' sez Miss Robin, 'did you yever hear de beat?' Miss Blue Bird 'low, 'Now, ain't dat des like a man!' You may not b'lieve it, but de three tuck up wid de idee, an' when dey talked it over wid de balance er de lady birds, all un um say it's des fine, an' dey tuck up wid it quicker dan a cat kin smell a mackerel layin' on de shelf. De funny thing 'bout de whole business wuz dat dey had ter have two 'semblements.'"

"That certainly was funny," said the little boy, so seriously that Uncle Remus closed his eyes and sighed. He never could reconcile himself to the fact that a little child could be almost as old-fashioned as a grown person.

"Yasser!" the old man continued, "dey had two semblements. De 'greement wuz dat all de lady birds, er all kin's an' color, wuz ter be dar, an' all wuz ter march by de place whar de one dey had chosen fer ter pick out de purtiest wuz ter be settin' at. De one dey choosen wuz ol' Brer Rabbit, so dat de sayin' mought come true:

> "'When you choosen a creetur,
> Des shun de bird-eater.'

In dem days, de doctor done tol' Brer Rabbit dat de best eatin' fer him wuz honey-an'-clover an' sweet barley, an' he wuz stickin' to dat kinder doin's. When de time come fer de fust 'semblement, Brer Rabbit wuz right on de spot, wid a fresh plug er terbacker, an' a pocketful er honey-bee clover. De birds all come, des like dey say dey would, an' when some un motioned ter Brer Rabbit fer ter say de word, dey 'gun ter march 'roun' an' 'roun', one by one, an' two by two. Dey ain't been marchin' long 'fo' Brer Rabbit shuck his head an' sot down ag'in.

" 'La, Brer Rabbit!' dey say, 'what de matter? We er all here; whyn't you pick out de purtiest? We ain't gwine ter peck yo' eyes out.' 'I dunno so well 'bout dat,' sez ol' Brer Rabbit, sezee. 'You say you er all here. No, ladies! You'll hatter skusen me!' an', wid dat, he riz up, he did, an' make sech a nice bow dat ol' Miss Swamp Owl's mouf 'gun ter water. Dey say, 'Lawsy mussy! Who's missin'?'

"Brer Rabbit he 'low, 'Whar Miss Coo-Coo Bird? I put on my specks, but I can't see 'er. Is she 'roun' here anywhar's?' Dey looked all 'roun', in de cornders, an' under de bushes whar anybody mought hide, but dey ain't fin' de Coo-Coo Bird. An' a mighty good reason, kaze she wa'n't dar, le' um hunt whar dey would an' s'arch whar dey might. Den Brer Rabbit up an' 'low, 'Ladies, all, we bleeze ter p'oc'astinate dish yer 'semblement, an' put it off twel you kin sen' word ter de Coo-Coo Bird, kaze you can't do nothin' 'tall widout 'er. She got ter be in, er she won't bide by de choosement. You des bleeze ter git her in ef you gwine ter stop de 'sputin'. Dey ain't no two ways 'bout dat.'

"Den dey all 'gun ter look at one an'er, an' giggle, an' make a great 'miration 'bout how sharp Brer Rabbit wuz. Some say dat dey don't think dat de Coo-Coo Bird is wuff foolin' wid, kaze she ain't no great shakes, nohow, but dey bleeze ter have her in de crowd when de 'semblement 'sembles, kaze dey ain't no yuther way fer ter stop de jowerin'. All de birds wuz bleeze ter be dar.

"Well, time went on just like it do now; ef dey wuz any diffunce, meal-time came a right smart sooner den dan it do now. Endurin' de time 'twix de 'semblement what hatter be called off, an' de nex' un dat wuz ter come, de lady birds had a scrumptious time. Dey went callin' on der neighbors, an' dem dat dey ain't fin' at home dey'd hunt up. Dey wuz mo' backbitin' dan you could shake a stick at, an' de chatter went on so long an' so loud, dat you couldn't hear yo' own years. Miss Peafowl called on Brer Rabbit, an' axed him how she wuz gwine ter come out in de parade, an' Brer Rabbit say dat she'd have a mighty good chance ef 'twa'n't fer her footses an' her scaly legs. He 'low dat ef she come dar wid dem, she won't have no show a tall, an' dar dey had it, up an' down. An' 'twuz de same way wid all un um; dey tried fer ter make ol' Brer Rabbit, which he wuz gwine fer ter be de judge, look at um thoo dey own eyes.

"While all dis wuz goin' on, dey wuz huntin' up de Coo-Coo Bird, an' atter so long a time dey foun' her right whar dey moughter foun' her at fust, stayin' at home an' lookin' atter de housekeepin'. But 'twuz a mighty quare thing 'bout de Coo-Coo Bird: she ain't got a rag er cloze ter 'er back. Whar de feathers oughter been dey wa'n't nothin' but a little bit er downy fuzz. When dey fin' 'er, dey say, 'Why'n't you come ter de 'semble-ment, whar dey gwine ter choosen de purtiest er all de bird tribe?' She 'low, 'La, I got sump'n' else ter do 'sides tryin' ter fin' out who de purtiest; an', mo' dan dat, how I gwine ter come when I ain't got no cloze ter w'ar? No, ma'am! You'll hatter skusen me! Go on an' parade on yo' Bullyfard, an' I'll parade at home.'

"Dey try ter tell 'er dat dey bleeze ter have her dar, so dey'll all be satchified, but she shuck her head, and went on cleanin' her house. Dey 'swaded, an' dey 'swaded, an' bimeby she say dat ef dey'll loan her some cloze among um, she'll go; ef dey don't, well an' good — she won't budge a step. An' so dar 'twuz. Well, all de yuther birds kinder collogued tergedder, an' dey say dey better loan her some cloze. Dey went 'roun' an' got a feather fum eve'y bird, an' fum some un um two. Ol' Miss Os-t'ich know'd she ain't stan' no chance in de parade wid her bony neck an' long legs, an' she sont de Coo-Coo Bird a bunch er de purtiest feathers you ever is lay eyes on.

"When de time come fer de 'semblement, Miss Coo-Coo wuz dar, an' dressed up fit ter kill; an' when dey all 'gun ter march, she wuz at de head er de crowd, an' stepped along ez gaily ez you please. Well, dey wa'n't no two ways 'bout it, Miss Coo-Coo wuz way yander de purtiest er de whole gang. De way she look, de way she walk, de way she hol' 'erse'f, de way she bow an' s'lute um all — eve'ything put 'er in de front place. Brer Rabbit stood up, he did, an' wave his han', an' dey all stop still. Den he say dat dey ain't no doubt an' no s'picions but what Miss Coo-Coo Bird wuz de purtiest er all de birds, an' dey all 'gree wid 'im. Den dey wuz ter have a dance, but 'fo' de music struck up, Miss Coo-Coo say dey must please excusin' her, an' wid dat, she slip inter de bushes an' wuz gone — done gone! Gone fer good, an' dey ain't nobody seed her fum dat day ter dis, less'n maybe ol' Brer Rabbit, an' he ain't tellin' nobody 'bout it.

"De yuther birds hunt fer 'er, but dey can't fin' 'er, an' dey er huntin' plum' twel yit, huntin' eve'ywhar, an' a-callin' ez dey hunt. Dey do say dat when de big owl holler, he ain't axin' 'Who cooks fer you-all?' He's sayin', 'Coo-coo, Coo-coo! whar you at?' an' de turtle-dove hollers, 'Coo-Coo, Coo-Coo, Coo-Coo, Coo-Coo! Coo-Coo-oo!' an' e'en down ter de rooster callin' out 'fo' day, an' all thoo de night, 'Please fetch my feather back!' An' so dar you is! Coo-Coo Bird done flew'd away, an' all de yuther birds huntin' fer 'er. An' dey tells me," remarked Uncle Remus, after a pause, "dat when folks think de birds is pickin' deyse'f an' straightenin' out der feathers, dey ain't doin' nothin' in de roun' worl' but seein' ef de one what dey loaned de Coo-Coo Bird is done growed back."

The little boy made no comment, but seemed to be waiting for the story to end. The old Negro threw his head back, and in a sing-song tone made this announcement:

> "Jig-a-ma-rig, an' a jig-a-ma-ree!
> Dat's all de tale dat 'uz tol' ter me!'"

IX

The tales from

Seven Tales of Uncle Remus

Edited by

THOMAS H. ENGLISH

Introduction[1]

As a part of Emory University's contribution to the observance of the centennial (1848–1948) of the birth of Joel Chandler Harris, Litt.D. '02, the *Emory Sources & Reprints* present seven hitherto uncollected tales of Uncle Remus. The first five appeared in special Christmas and Easter issues from 1889 to 1892 of an Atlanta publication entitled *"Dixie": A Monthly Record of Southern Industrial Possibility and Development,* for which they were "written expressly." The last two were found among the manuscripts placed by Mr. Harris's family in the Joel Chandler Harris Memorial Collection of the Emory University Library, a description of which is also included in this number.

Although the contributions to *"Dixie"* were never printed in a collection of Uncle Remus tales, it appears that it was the author's original intention that they should be. Among the papers in the Memorial Collection are five leaves containing the stories torn from copies of the magazine. The tales are numbered XXV to XXVIII, and bear many proof corrections and emendations in Mr. Harris's hand, though the revision is not thoroughgoing. Eventually four of the tales were taken out of the Negro dialect and retold in *Little Mr. Thimblefinger* (1894). The fifth, "How Brother Bear Exposed Brother Rabbit at the Barbecue," never reappeared.

Of the two stories that remained in manuscript, one was taken out of the Negro dialect and retold as "Why the Bear is a Wrestler" in *Mr. Rabbit at Home* (1895), the second of the Thimblefinger series. The other has not been found to have been printed in any form.

The preface of *Little Mr. Thimblefinger,* "A Little Note to a Little Book," may furnish grounds for conjecture as to why the tales failed of final conclusion in the Uncle Remus canon: "The stories that follow belong to three categories. Some of them were gathered from the negroes, but were not embodied in the tales of Uncle Remus, because I was not sure they were negro stories. . . ." Although he disavowed a special competence in the science of folklore, Mr. Harris was severely conscientious to insure the genuineness of his legends of the old plantation. There can be little doubt that the five stories here printed finally failed to survive his rigid tests.

If there were no other reason than the pleasure which is to be found in the racy idiom of Uncle Remus, it would be worth while to rescue these tales from

[1] Reprinted with permission. Excerpt from Introduction to *Seven Tales of Uncle Remus,* by Joel Chandler Harris, edited by Thomas H. English, curator Joel Chandler Harris Memorial Collection, the Library, Emory University, Atlanta, Georgia, 1948.

more than a half-century of oblivion. But there is more. Readers will never weary of the plantation background sketched in with few but deft strokes; here is something rescued from time past that can never return. A special feature of this group is the evidence presented for Mr. Harris's discovery of the Jamaica Negro and his characteristic folklore. The "Two Little Tales" are attributed by Uncle Remus to a slave brought from Jamaica called Jimps whom he had known in his boyhood. There is nothing particularly exotic about either of them. But the second of the sketches left in manuscript is notable in that it introduces a character called Aunt Nancy, identified as "de granny er Mammy-Bammy-Big-Money," "de ole Witch Rabbit," who is readily recognizable as Annancy, the spider hero of Jamaican folk tales. Here is a new element to be reckoned with in the complete study of the sources of the legends.

If the tales had appeared in a volume of the Uncle Remus series, it is certain that they would have received further revision. The first five stories were rather badly printed in *"Dixie"* and the author did not complete their correction on the tear sheets. It was necessary, therefore, that the editor undertake to complete the task. Changes were introduced sparingly, however, for the most part on the authority of corrections already made. The tales in typescript exhibit Mr. Harris's characteristically clean copy and they presented no problem.

T. H. E.

December, 1948

1
Mr. Crow and Brother Buzzard[1]

"NOW, DEN," said Uncle Remus, smacking his lips over a piece of light-bread which the little boy had brought him — "now, den, ef you got any notion in yo' head dat I ain't thankful fer my vittles, mo' speshually dish yer kind er vittles, you er mighty much mistaken. Yasser! you is dat; kaze w'en I des smell vittles, let 'lone eat it, hit puts me in min' er de time w'en ole Brer Turkey Buzzard en Mr. Crow tried fer ter see which one un um kin starve deyse'f out fust. 'Bout dat time," the old man went on, "I lay dish yer bread would er tas'e like poun' cake."

"When was that, Uncle Remus?" the little boy asked with some eagerness.

"Lord, honey!" responded the old man, "'taint fer no nigger like me, ole ez I is, fer ter gi' you de year en de day. What I knows, I knows des ez good ez de nex' man, but I ain't gwine no furder dan dat."

"Well, what did they starve themselves for?"

"Now you er talkin', honey!" exclaimed the old man, brightening up — "now you er comin' at me! You ain't got nary nuther hunk er dis bread in yo' pocket, is you?"

The little boy produced another "hunk," and Uncle Remus proceeded.

"Well, den, one time ole Brer Buzzard en Mr. Crow struck up wid one er n'er in a big pine tree. Dey howdied, dey did, but der wuz a sorter coldness betwix um, kaze ole Brer Buzzard had been gwine 'bout de neighborhood makin' his brags how he kin out-fly Mr. Crow. Dey ain't bin up in de tree long 'fo' dey got ter 'sputin'. Brer Buzzard, he can't talk loud, but Mr. Crow, he kin squall mo' samer dan a Philadelphy lawyer. So dar dey had it, up en down en all aroun' en back ag'in."

"What were they quarreling about, Uncle Remus?" the little boy asked.

"Lord, honey! you know how folks is. Well, Brer Buzzard en Mr. Crow wuz des like folks; dey wuz 'sputin' 'bout who wuz de outdoin'est man, en

[1] Originally published in *"Dixie,"* Vol. VI, No. 12 (December 1889), pp. 1009–1010. The text has been revised on the basis of Mr. Harris's own corrections on tear-sheets in the Joel Chandler Harris Memorial Collection. This story is retold without dialect in *Little Mr. Thimblefinger*, Chap. XII, "A Singing Match." — T. H. E.

little mo' en dey'd er had a pitched battle right den en dar. But, bimeby, Mr. Crow up en say:

"'Maybe you kin out-fly me, Brer Buzzard, but I boun' you can't out-sing me.'

"'I ain't never tried,' sez Brer Buzzard, sezee.

"'Well, 'spoz'n you try it now,' sez Mr. Crow, sezee. 'I'll go you a fine suit er cloze en a hat to boot, dat I kin set yer en sing longer dan what you kin,' sezee.

"'Hit's a go, Brer Crow,' sez Mr. Buzzard, sezee.

"''Tain't no fa'r bet,' sez Mr. Crow, sezee, 'kaze you er lots bigger man dan me, en it stan' ter reason dat you got mo' win', but I'm a-gwine ter try you one time ef I split my gizzard,' sezee.

"Dey shuck han's, dey did, en den Mr. Crow, he raise de chune, he did —

"'Susu! susu! gangook!
Muther, muther, lalho!'

"Den Brer Buzzard, he lay he head back en chime in —

"'Susu! susu! gangook!
Muther, muther, lalho!'

en sech another racket ez dem creeturs kep' up you ain't never hear befo' ner sence."

"What sort of a song is that?" the little boy inquired.

"Well," said Uncle Remus, "you kin make yo' inquirements, en I'll make my argyments. Dar's de song. Dat's de way hit wuz gun out ter me. Ef you kin git at de innards un it, well and good; ef not, don't fling none er de blame on me. Young ez you is, you knows des ez much 'bout dat song ez what I does — en lots mo', I speck, kaze you ain't bin pesterin' 'long wid it like I is."

"What did they do then?" asked the little boy by way of a compromise.

"Well," said Uncle Remus, resuming the thread of the story, "dey sot dar en dey sung des like I bin tellin' you. Brer Buzzard would stop en ketch his win', en den break out —

"'Susu! susu! gangook!
Muther, muther, lalho!'"

"Den Mr. Crow would ketch his win' en squall out —

"'Susu! susu! gangook!
Muther, muther, lalho!'

"Hit went on dis away twel bimeby bofe un um gun ter git sorter hongry; but Brer Buzzard bein' de biggest man, hit look like he gwine ter hol' out de longest. Yit Mr. Crow wuz right dar, en he sung right in spite er de gnyawin' at his stomach. He ain't squall so loud, but every time Brer Buzzard would sing Mr. Crow would up en sing too. But dey bofe got mighty weak. Bimeby, Mr. Crow see Miss Crow flyin' over, en he holler out:

"'*Susu!* go tell my chillun — *susu!* — fer ter bring my dinner — *gangook!* en tell um — *muther, muther* — fer ter bring it quick — *lalho!*'

"Now," said Uncle Remus, laying the bread crust away for future reference, "dat kinder singin' is what I calls sho nuff singin'. Mr. Crow wuz singin' fer his dinner, en I let you know he got it.

"'Twan't long 'fo' all de fambly er Crows come a flyin' up en w'en dey fin' out how de lan' lay, dey whirled in, dey did, en dey brung Mr. Crow mo' vittles dan what he kin eat. Co'se dey wa'n't nobody fer ter bring old Brer Buzzard no vittles, en he des sot dar en sung twel he was plum famished, en bimeby he got so weak dat he drapped out'n de tree.

"Yasser!" Uncle Remus continued, "he drapped right out'n de tree, en fum dat day to dis dey ain't bin no mo' singin' in de Buzzard fambly. You may listen at um all day, but you ain't gwine ter hear none un um sing. Yit Mr. Crow, he bin flyin' 'roun' singin' ever sence."

"Pshaw!" exclaimed the little boy, "I don't call that singing."

"Well, honey," said the old man, looking curiously at the youngster, "What else you gwine call it? W'en a man sing de bes' he know how, what mo' kin you ax?"

Two Little Tales As Told by Old Uncle Remus[1]
2
Mr. Goat's Short Tail

"NOW, DEN," said Uncle Remus, as the little boy settled himself in a chair, "I'm gwine ter flip you some little tales what ain't run inter my membunce deze many long year. En dey wouldn't a run'd inter it now ef I hadn't er been a-huntin' in my chist atter a brad awl. I wuz a-huntin' in dar en a-turnin' de scraps over, w'en all on er sudden I run'd across dish yer."

The old man was smoothing out a piece of dingy red cloth on his knee, and as he spoke he held it up for the little boy's inspection. It seemed to be a red-velvet skull cap, and it was surmounted by a small yellow tassel.

"What is it, Uncle Remus?" the youngster asked.

"Hit look like it mought be a skull cap," replied the old Negro, cautiously, "en den ag'in hit look like it mought be some er deze yer milintery fixin's. Den w'en you tu'n it roun' hit look like hit mought belong ter some er dem ar circus doin's. Yit 'tain't none er dem. I bin had it now gwine on fifty year er mo', en it use ter belong ter er ole nigger man what cum fum 'cross de water."

"Did he come from Savannah?" asked the little boy.

"Uh-uh!" exclaimed Uncle Remus, solemnly: "wuss'n dat — lots wuss. You dun been see Daddy Jack? Well, suh, de ole nigger man what dish yer cap b'long ter wuz mo' drieder up dan what Daddy Jack is. Ole man Jack, he talk Affikin talk, but de ole nigger man what I'm a-tellin' you 'bout, he talk wuss'n dat. Look like he head mo' addled en he tongue mo' twisted. Now, wharbouts is he come fum?" said Uncle Remus, changing the tone of his voice as if addressing some third person in the room. "Wharbouts wuz it — wharbouts wuz it?" Then changing his tone and addressing the little boy, he went on: "Hit sump'n ne'r what got ginger in it. Ah, Lord! some er deze days my min' gwinter git away fum me,

[1] Originally published in *"Dixie,"* Vol. VII, No. 12 (December 1890), pp. 1002–1004. The text has been revised on the basis of Mr. Harris's own corrections on tear sheets in the Joel Chandler Harris Memorial Collection. These stories are retold without dialect in *Little Mr. Thimblefinger,* Chap. IV, "Two Queer Stories." — T. H. E.

en I ain't gwine git it no mo'. Now den, honey, how many kinds er ginger is dey?"

"Well," said the little boy, trying to think, "there's — there's ground ginger."

"'Tain't dat!" exclaimed Uncle Remus, shaking his head emphatically.

"And there's root ginger."

"'Tain't dat!"

"And then there's — Oh yes! I know now! There's Jamaica ginger."

"Ah-yi!" cried the old man in a tone of triumph, his face broadening into a smile. "Ah-yi! den you hit me. Dat de place what he cum fum."

"Now, Uncle Remus," said the little boy, "you know he couldn't have come from Jamaica ginger."

"Tooby sho not, honey," responded Uncle Remus. "Dish yer old nigger man come fum whar de ginger come fum. What you call it?"

"Jamaica" —

"Now, den," said the old man, lifting up a warning hand, "stop right dar. Kaze dar whar he come fum. Dat sholy is the name. Now, when I say ginger," he went on, "you holler out de udder. Well, dis old nigger mun, he come fum — ginger" —

"Jamaica!" cried the little boy, laughing.

"He come fum dar 'long time ago, when dey wuz a kind er flar' up out dar. He lan' at Charlestin, he did, wid his marster, en den his marster died; en yo' Unk Jeems got 'im en sont 'im up yer. He say he name Zeemzy, but we all, we des tuckin tuck dat name en trim it off en plane it down, en call 'im Jimps. Well, suh, you oughter seed dat ole nigger Jimps. He wuz wil' ez a buck, en he can't no mo' talk like folks den a th'ashin machine. He des stan' up en make motions wid his head en han's, en jabber wuss'n drappin' shot on a rawhide. Marse John 'low he talkin' furrin talk like dey talk yander in — ginger!"

"Jamaica!" exclaimed the little boy.

"But ef dat de way dey talk, I hope de Lord spar' me fum ever gwine dar. Atter while, ole Jimps got so he kin talk ef you shet one eye en listen at 'im right close. I wuz a young chap den, en I useter go set up wid de ole nigger, en fetch 'im water en run er'ns fer 'im, en sorter he'p 'im 'long de best way I kin. Well, suh, dat ole nigger man useter set up agin de chimbly jam en jabber at me half de night, en I'd lean back en make out I wuz a-takin' it all in. Den w'en he got so he kin talk sorter like folks, he'd shet bofe eyes en tell me tales, en he had dish yer red night-cap on his head, en de way he'd stick it fust on one side en den on de udder wuz a plum sight.

"What was the tale, Uncle Remus?" asked the little boy, growing somewhat weary of these reminiscences.

"Wait now, honey! Des lem me tell you — deze yer tales ain't my tales, en I ain't axin you fer to put no 'pen'ence in um. Ole man Jimpsy tole me, en dat all I know 'bout um. De tales what I tell you myse'f, dem I'll stan' by, but deze yer dey wuz gun ter me. Ef you wanter 'spute um, you kin 'spute um; dey ain't mine, en I ain't gwine ter stan' by um.

"Well, den, one time (now, min' yo' eye, honey, 'tain't none er my tale) — one time Mr. Billy Goat en Mr. Dog wuz a santerin' 'long en a promenadin' roun', a-makin' deyse'f sociable, when a big rain come up. Mr. Billy Goat say he mighty sorry he lef' his parasol at home, kaze rain make his horns rust. Mr. Dog say he ain't got no parasol en don't need none, kaze he use ter water, but Mr. Goat, he run'd along en bimeby dey come ter Mr. Wolf house. De door done shet fas', but Mr. Goat, he stomp he foot on de door-step, en say, 'Ba-a! ba-a!' en Mr. Dog, he wag his tail en say, 'Bow-wow-wow!' Den Mr. Wolf onlatch de door en look out. He see Mr. Goat and Mr. Dog stan'in' in de rain, en he 'low, he did:

"'Heyo, folks! what kinder day is dis fer ter come visitin'? But sence you done come, you best come in out 'de wet.'

"But Mr. Dog, he shuck he head, en flirt up gravel wid his behime legs. He done smell blood. Mr. Goat, see how Mr, Dog do, en he 'fraid ter go in. Mr. Wolf 'low:

"'You best come en set by my fire,' but dey skeered.

"Den Mr. Wolf tuck down his fiddle, en chuned her up, en start in ter play. Man, suh! he fairly made her talk, kaze he know ef he kin make Mr. Goat dance, he sholy have 'im fer dinner. De rain it come down on Mr. Goat horn en drip off'n his beard, en Mr. Wolf keep on playin' de fiddle. Den he low:

"'How you-all git meat?'

"Mr. Dog say he 'pen' on his toofies, en Mr. Goat say he 'pen' on his toofies too. Den Mr. Wolf put down his fiddle, en 'low:

"'I 'pen' on my four foots,' en wid dat he tuck atter um.

"Dey run'd en dey come whar dey wuz a big creek. Mr. Goat ax Mr.

Dog what he gwine do. Mr. Dog say he gwine swim. Mr. Goat 'gun ter cry, kaze he can't swim a lick, en den Mr. Dog pull out de rabbit foot what he tote in his pocket, en totch Mr. Goat wid it; en time he done it, Mr. Goat turned inter a white rock. Den Mr. Dog lipt inter de creek en swum 'cross. Mr. Wolf come up on de bank, but he skeer'd er water. Mr. Dog stan' on t'er side en 'low:

"'Oh, yes! you skeerd! You done make Mr. Goat drown, but you skeerd er me. I dar' you ter fling dat white rock at me!'

"Dis make Mr. Wolf mighty mad, so he pick up de white rock en flung it at Mr. Dog. Time de rock hit de t'er side it tu'n back inter Mr. Goat, en he holler out:

"'What you tryin' ter do, you obstropolous vilyun? Is you tryin' ter break my neck?'

"Den Mr. Wolf holler out: 'Nummine! I'll git you w'en de creek run dry!'

"Ole Jimpsy say," remarked Uncle Remus, incidentally, "dat w'en Mr. Goat struck on t'er side de creek, his tail got broke off. Whedder or no dat de case, you kin see fer yo'se'f dat goat tail mighty stumpy."

"Is that all of the tale?" asked the little boy.

"Dat's all er de goat tail," replied Uncle Remus, with a chuckle. The little boy laughed, but not as heartily as the old man thought he ought to; so there was a long pause.

3

The Baby and the Punkins

"I DON'T LIKE ter be tellin' tales what dat ole nigger man done tole," said Uncle Remus, finally. "Dey don't soun' right ter me, en fer all I know he mought er made um all up hisse'f. He wun't none too good. He had n'er tale 'bout de punkins — but maybe some er deze udder niggers done tell you 'bout dat."

The little boy, however, protested that they had not, and after the usual preliminaries the old man began:

"One time dey wuz a 'oman livin' by de side er de road, en dish yer 'oman had lots er chilluns. De reason er dat wuz kaze she wuz mighty poor. When folks git so poor dat dey er mighty nigh famish fer sump'n nice ter eat, den you kin des put it down dat dey gwine ter have lots er chilluns. Look at dem Faverses. Deyer pine-blank on de p'int er starvation, en yit dey got mighty nigh ez many chilluns ez what dey got shingles on der roof, ef you kin call um shingles.

"Well, dish yer 'oman, she wuz poor ez de Faverses, en she had mighty nigh ez many chilluns. One day she went down by de creek fer ter wash her cloze en her chillun cloze, en w'en she got dar she fine a old man settin' on de bank. De old man he say 'Howdy,' en she 'spon ter his howdy. Den he ax de 'oman ef she'll wash his coat an' his wes'cut. De 'oman low she be glad fer ter do so, en de man say he much 'blige. Wid dat de 'oman wash um, and w'en she git em done, de ole man run his han' in his pocket en gun her a string er black beads, en den he tole her ter go down behime her house w'en she git home en dar she'd fine a punkin tree full er punkins. He say, de ole man did, dat she mus' take de beads en bury um at de root er de tree, en den ax fer many punkins ez she want. So say, so do. De 'oman went home, en done des like de ole man tole 'er. She fine de punkin tree en bury de beads dar, en den she call fer many punkins ez she want.

"Hit kep' on dis away twel de 'oman en de chilluns git fat, kaze dey have des ez much ter eat ez dey want. But one mornin' w'en de 'oman woke up, she foun' a baby on her door-sill. So she tuck de baby in en put it wid her chilluns, en dar dey wuz, des ez sociable as you please. But dish yer baby wuz a witch-baby, en when de 'oman 'ud fetch in de punkins en go off, de baby'd whirl in en eat um all up, en de 'oman's chillun 'ud hatter go hongry. Den w'en de 'oman come back en fine all de punkins gone, she'd quar'l at de chilluns, en say she gwine frail um ef dey don't stop bein so greedy.

"But de chilluns 'low dat 'twa'n't dem what eat de punkin, but de baby, en dey whimple en say dey so hongry dey dunno what ter do. Tooby sho, de 'oman don't b'lieve um, kaze it don't look like a little bit er teenchy baby, what can't walk, kin git about en gobble up all dem punkins, so she tuck en tell her chilluns dat ef dey don't quit der hogishness en stop talkin dat away 'bout dat baby she gwine gi' um a good spankin' en sen' um ter bed widout any supper. But it kep' on dis away twel bimeby de 'oman tuck en sot a trap fer de baby, en baited it wid punkins.

Atter she done gone, up jump de baby fer ter eat de punkins, en 'twa'n't long 'fo' hit got his head cotch in de trap.

"Den w'en de 'oman come back home dar de baby wuz. She tuck it out, she did, en 'low dat de baby what kin git up en mosey 'roun', en eat up all de vittles, is lierbul fer ter take keer un itself. Wid dat, she tuck en gin it a larrupin en tu'n it out'n de house.

"Atter de 'oman tu'n de baby loose out doors, it took'n change inter a great big man, en dish yer great big man walk down by de creek, en dar he fine de ole man a-settin' on de bank. De ole man ax him will he please comb his head, but de t'er man 'fuse, en den de ole man ax him ef he will have a punkin, en he 'low he be mighty glad. De ole man tell 'im wharbouts de tree is, en tole 'im dat w'en he git dar he must ax for one. He fine de tree, he did, en dey wuz so many punkins growin' up dar, en dey look so nice, dat he holler out en ax for twenty punkins."

"What then, Uncle Remus?" asked the little boy, as the old negro paused.

"Down dey come 'pon top er his head," responded Uncle Remus, puffing away at his pipe, "en smashed 'im. En knocked 'im flatter'n a pancake. En broke 'im inter jiblets. En pounded 'im inter jelly. En kilt 'im!"

4
Two Plantation Stories[1]
Brother Rabbit's Barbecue

"MISS SALLY," said Uncle Remus, one afternoon, as his mistress sat sewing in the veranda, "Whar dat chile?"

"I don't know, I'm sure," the lady replied, with affected indifference. She knew by the tone of the old man's voice that he had some complaint to make or some criticism to offer.

---

[1] Originally published in *"Dixie,"* Vol. VIII, No. 4 (April 1892), pp. 236–238. The text has been revised on the basis of Mr. Harris's own corrections on tear sheets in the Joel Chandler Harris Memorial Collection. The first of these stories has never previously been collected; the second is retold without dialect in *Little Mr. Thimblefinger*, Chap. XI, "How Brother Bear's Head Was Combed." — T. H. E.

"Ah, Lord!" exclaimed Uncle Remus, with a tremendous sigh, as he placed his hat on his head.

"He was playing around here awhile ago," the lady went on. "Do you expect me to trot around after him all day?"

"I wisht ole Miss wuz 'live!" sighed the old man.

"So do I!" exclaimed the lady. "You'd be in the cotton-patch instead of lazying around here doing children's work."

"I lay ef she wuz here," Uncle Remus continued, tranquilly, "she wouldn't have none er her gran'chillun playin' out in de big road yander wid dat Stallins brood, rastlin' en wallerin' in de mud. Dat what she wouldn't do. She mought sen' me furder dan de cotton-patch, but when I got dar, I'd know dat chile wa'n't a-honeyin' up wid dem Stallinses — dat what I'd know."

"Go and bring him here this minute!" exclaimed the lady, rising angrily, "and bring a hickory with you."

Uncle Remus had raised a bigger storm than he bargained for, and it was not with a cheerful air that he went to do the bidding of his mistress. After he had gone a little way, he paused and looked back, but his "Miss Sally" had gone into the house, leaving her sewing piled upon the porch. This was an ominous sign, and the old man shook his head and mumbled to himself as he went along. Where the big road crosses the spring-branch, he found the little boy playing with the Stallings, children, and he was having a hilarious time, running, jumping, wrestling, laughing as only a healthy youngster can.

"Honey," said Uncle Remus, leaning on the fence and smiling benignly, "whar Clary?" Clary was the Negro girl who was supposed to look after the little boy.

"She's yonder in the fence corner asleep," responded the child. "Look at me jump, Uncle Remus! — can you beat that?"

"You'll jump wuss'n dat when yo' mammy git you," the old man remarked. "She done sont me atter you. Mun, sir! she sholy is mad! Look at de san' in yo' head! Look at de mud on yo' cloze! Wharbouts dat nigger gal? You Clary! Git up fum dar, you low-life huzzy! What you doin' settin' dar noddin' in de sun whiles dish yer chile runnin' wil'? Git up fum dar, you owdacious piece! Miss Sally gwine sen' you ter de overseer! I lay he'll wake you up!"

"Please, sir, Unc' Remus, don't talk dat away! Dat chile worry my ve'y soul-case out'n me tell I come wid 'im down yer. Please, sir, Unc' Remus, tell Mistiss not ter sen' me ter no overseer! Tell 'er you done whip me yo'se'f." Clary whimpered in the most distressful way.

"Go up dar ter de house," said the old man savagely, "en slip in dar en git dish yer chile some clean cloze, en bring a towel en some er dat ar smellin' soap. Pick up yo' foots, now! don't I'll frail you out 'fo' de overseer git you."

Uncle Remus saw that the little boy's pleasure had been spoiled, and so, to humor him, the old man told a story, while Clary "fixed" him up.

"When I see dat nigger roachin' yo' ha'r, en slickin' you up dis way, it puts me in min' er de time when Brer Rabbit larned ole Brer B'ar how ter comb his ha'r. Ef I ain't never been tell you 'bout it," Uncle Remus went on, "it's mighty quare ter me, kaze hit des ez plain in my min' ez ef it happen yistiddy. Look like I kin set yer and see um movin' and year um talkin'." Uncle Remus paused a moment as if reflecting. Then he proceeded to tell the story of

How Brother Bear Exposed Brother Rabbit at the Barbecue

"ONE SAT'DAY, when de creeturs wuz done thoo wid de week's work, en whiles dey wuz a-settin' 'roun' in de sun whittlin' sticks en talkin' politics, dey got ter 'sputin' 'bout which un um kin eat de mos'. Ef you ax me how de 'spute riz, I'm never is ter tell you. Dey wuz gwine on talkin' en fus news dey know'd dey wuz 'sputin' 'bout der appetite. Brag breeds brag, en 'twa'n't long 'fo' dey wuz a-jawin en a-contendin' des like you year de wite folks do. Brer Wolf say he never is see de day when he had nuff ter eat. Brer B'ar 'low he b'lieve he kin eat a hoss ef he had salt fer ter go wid it. Brer Fox say he kin eat des ez much ez de nex man. All had der sesso, en den dey look at Brer Rabbit. Brer Rabbit he sot back, he did, en chawed his tubbacker, crosst his legs, en shot his eyes slow, like he done sont his min' off some'rs. Den he sorter laugh. Dis kinder fret de t'er creeturs, en dey gun ter make game un 'im. Den Brer Rabbit 'low, sezee, dat ef de t'er creeturs will des come ter time, he'll show um what eatin' is.

"'Des gimme a show,' sezee, 'en I'll eat mo' dan all put tergedder, let 'lone one un you. Ef I don't do it, you kin have my hat,' sezee.

"So dey all had a confab, en dey give it out dat dey wuz gwine ter have a bobbycue at de Nine Mile branch."

"Why, Uncle Remus," said the little boy, "that is right out here."

"Tooby sho 'tis, honey!" responded the old man. "Wharbouts did you speck it wuz? Way off yander in some outlandish country? Bless yo' soul! de creeturs wuz right 'roun' dis plantation, same ez some un um is dis ve'y minnit, ceppin' dey ain't nigh ez mannish ez dey wuz in dem days.

"So den! Dey got up de bobbycue, dey did, en I hear tell it wuz a mighty nice un. Dey had shote, en dey had sheep, en gravy — " Uncle Remus closed his eyes dreamily, and smacked his lips. "Dey got it good en ready, en put it on de long table, en den dey ax, where wuz Brer Rabbit? Dey bin so busy dey ain't miss 'im. Dey look fer 'im, en dey call 'im, but dey ain't fin' 'im. De bobbycue smell so good dat de creeturs fairly dribble at de mouf, en des 'bout time dey wuz gwine ter whirl in en wipe it up, dey see Brer Rabbit comin' cross de hill. He had on a long cloak, en he walk wid a cane — slow, like you see ole folks do.

"When Brer Rabbit come up de creeturs ax 'im what de matter.

"'Sick, mighty sick," sezee. 'A leetle mo' en I'd a never got dis fur in de roun' worl'.'

"Den all un um ax, 'What de matter, Brer Rabbit? What de matter?'

"Brer Rabbit 'low, sezee, 'Don't holler so — I got de headache; don't you run up agin me — I got de backache. I went down in de swamp atter some calamus root, en got my foots wet,' sezee. 'Dat gimme a bad col' en de col' flewed ter my head, en spread out on my back, en drapt down in my legs, en ef I don't be laid up wid de pleu'sy I'd like ter know de reason.'

"Oh, Uncle Remus!" suddenly exclaimed the little boy, "mamma says the right name of calamus is sweet flag."

The old man drew a long breath; the ardor of the story-teller deserted him.

"Well," he remarked in a subdued tone, "Miss Sally mighty smart 'oman — dey ain't no two ways 'bout dat — but I been hear it call calamus root long 'fo' she wuz born'd." Then there was a long pause.

"What was the rest of the tale, Uncle Remus?" the little boy asked somewhat timidly. He saw that his interruption was not relished.

"What tale, honey?" inquired the old man. "De tale 'bout de calamus root? Shoo! I done tole you all I know 'bout de calamus root. Miss Sally kin tell you de balance."

"Please, Uncle Remus," persisted the little boy; "please tell me the story."

The old Negro looked at the child out of the corner of his eye. Then he laughed foolishly, and exclaimed: "I be bless ef you ain't got mo' winnin' ways dan a gal!" Then he went on:

"Whurbouts wuz I, when you choked me off wid dat hunk er calamus root? Brer Rabbit wuz tellin' de t'er creeturs how his coporosity come ter be segashuatin' dat away. Well, den, dar dey wuz — Brer Rabbit wid his long cloak on, en his neck all tied up, en feelin' mighty weak en bad, en all de t'er creeturs feelin' mighty hongry. When a man git sho nuff hongry," Uncle Remus went on, rubbing his chin thoughtfully, "he mighty apt ter be mad. Same way wid de creeturs. Dey wuz mad. Mo' dan dat dey all had der 'spicions er Brer Rabbit. Fust en last dey wa'n't none un um but what he'd played his pranks on, en when dey seed 'im walkin' 'roun' wid a cane en all wrapped up, dey gun ter jower at 'im. Dey ax 'im what he make um git up all dis great ter-do if he gwine git sick, en ef he sick how he beat um all a-eatin'?

"Brer Rabbit 'low, sezee, dat he sholy is feelin' mighty bad, his pulse runnin' high, en he ain't got no appetite, but druther dan be outdone he come spite er his sickness. Ef he can't beat um eatin', well en good; ef he kin so much de better. Dis make de creeturs feel some better, en 'twa'n't long 'fo' dey tuck der stan' at de table en made ready fer de trial. De vittles wuz put in piles, en de pile at de place whar dey made Brer Rabbit stan' wuz de biggest er all. De meat in dat pile wuz in hunks. Dey fix it dat way so Brer Rabbit can't chaw it fast. He look at it, he did, en 'low, sezee:

"'De bet is bones en all.'

"De creeturs looked at one ernudder like dey wuz tuck down, but dey bleedz ter 'gree. Brer Rabbit 'low, sezee:

"'Bones en all! Give de word!'

"So dey gun de word, en den dey wuz a scramble en a scuffle. Mos' 'fo' you kin tu'n 'roun', Brer Rabbit holler out, sezee:

"'Fetch on yo' vittles! Gimme a showin'!'

"De creeturs look at 'im, en dey seed dat Brer Rabbit is done wallop up his pile er vittles, en wuz a-reachin' out fer mo'. Dey fotch 'im some mo', en he wiped dat up, but whiles Brer B'ar wuz gnawin' on a bone he kep' one eye on Brer Rabbit, en he seed 'im drap de meat down in his cloak.

"Brer B'ar ain't say nothin'; he des wait, en when dey wa'n't no mo' vittles in sight, he say he speck dey'll hatter 'gree dat Brer Rabbit had outdone um all. Den Brer B'ar make out he want ter shake Brer Rabbit by he han', but he cotch holt er de cloak, he did, en jerked it off, en dar dey saw a great big bag what had been hid behime it. Brer Rabbit gin hisse'f a flirt en shuck loose fum de bag en made fer de bushes wid all de creeturs in full cry atter 'im.

"Dey mought out-eat 'im," said Uncle Remus, after a pause, "but I be bless ef dey kin ketch 'im."

5

Brother Bear Learns to Comb His Head

THE LITTLE BOY was disappointed. He had come to regard Brother Rabbit as a sort of hero, and it wasn't pleasant to fancy that the nimble-witted creature had been brought to grief by such a clumsy animal as Brother Bear.

"Why, Uncle Remus," the youngster said after a while in a disconsolate tone, "I thought Brother Rabbit was smarter than all of the animals."

"Who said he wa'n't?" the old man asked, eyeing the child curiously.

"Well, Brother Bear found out his trick, and he lost his bet."

The old man closed his eyes and chuckled for some moments. Then he suddenly straightened his face and said:

"Dey ain't nobody so smart dey ain't cotch up wid. Old Brer Rabbit wuz des havin' his fun. He wa'n't gwine ter hurt nothin' ner nobody by puttin' all dat vittles in de sack what he had 'neat' de cloak. He wuz des playin' one er his pranks, but when he see how servigous ole Brer B'ar wuz, he laid off fer ter pay 'im back, en, bless yo' soul, honey, dat what he done.

"What did he do, Uncle Remus?" the little boy asked.

"Wait, honey! Des gimme time for ter ransack my 'membunce. So, den! Brer Rabbit tuck ter primpin' up. He put bergamot grease on his ha'r en reached it up scan'lous. Eve'y day he'd slick hisse'f up, en den he'd make a convenience er promenadin' down de road front er Brer B'ar's house. Miss Rabbit she got sorter jubous 'bout dis kinder gwines on, en dey had a fambly spat er two, but eve'y day Brer Rabbit ud slick up en go promenadin'. Sometimes ole Miss B'ar ud be hangin' out cloze, en den agin she'd be a workin' in de gyardin, but eve'y time Brer Rabbit laid eyes on her he'd bow des ez perlite ez you please.

"It went on disaway twel bimeby ole Miss B'ar 'gun ter ax her ole man how come he ain't look nice like Brer Rabbit. Brer B'ar say he don't want ter look like no sech a gran' rascal ez what Brer Rabbit is. Ole Miss B'ar 'low, se' she, dat, gran' rascal er no, Brer Rabbit allers got his head combed, en he look lots better dat away dan dem what go 'roun' wid rat nesses in de ha'r.

"Dat de way 'oman folks does," Uncle Remus continued, frowning significantly at Clary. "Dey'll jower, jower, fum mornin' tell night. Brer B'ar can't git no sleep en he can't have no peace, all on de 'count 'er Brer Rabbit gwine 'bout wid his head combed. Bimeby, one day, Brer B'ar meet Brer Rabbit in de big road, en atter dey passed de time er day. Brer B'ar 'low, sezee:

"'Brer Rabbit, how you keep yo' ha'r combed so slick all de time? My ole 'oman been pesterin' me kaze I don't keep my head comb like you.'

"Brer Rabbit 'low, sezee, 'You look like she been touzlin' you 'bout it.' Den he up'n laugh.

"Brer B'ar, say sezee, 'I want ter ax you plump en plain, how you comb it so nice.'

"Brer Rabbit twist his mustache en make answer — 'I don't comb my ha'r, Brer B'ar.'

"Brer B'ar look 'stonished. He 'low, sezee: 'How you do, den Brer Rabbit? I bleedz ter know, kaze my ole 'oman done worry my life outer me.'

"Brer Rabbit say, sezee: 'My ole 'oman combs my head eve'y mornin'. She des takes de ax en chops it off so she kin git at it good, en den when she git it fixed she des slaps it back on de place, en dar 'tis all combed.'

"Brer B'ar say: 'Don't it hurt, Brer Rabbit?'

"Brer Rabbit 'low: 'Hurt who? I ain't no chicken!'

"Brer B'ar say: 'Don't it bleed?'

"Brer Rabbit 'low: 'No mo' dan nuff fer ter keep my appetite good.'

"Well," Uncle Remus went on, "de upshot uv it wuz dat Brer B'ar went home en tole his ole 'oman how Brer Rabbit got his ha'r combed. 'Oman like, she 'uz keen fer ter try it, en den Brer B'ar put his head down on a log of wood en old Miss B'ar got de ax en raise it up high. Brer B'ar shot his eyes en holler out, sezee:

"'Cut it off easy, ole 'oman!'

"En bless yo' soul, he ain't mo'n got de words out'n his mouf 'fo' *wop!* she tuck 'im, en dar he wuz!"

"Uncle Remus," said the little boy, after awhile, "did it kill Brother Bear sure enough?"

"Hit sorter look dat away," the old man answered. Then he took the child and carried him to "Miss Sally." But the threatened storm had blown over. The lady was sitting on the veranda sewing and singing.

6

Why the Bear Is a Wrestler[1]

WHILE THE LITTLE NEGROES on the place were waiting for their daily allowance of buttermilk, two of them engaged in a wrestling match. Both Uncle Remus and the little boy were interested spectators of the contest, and both laughed and applauded when one of them succeeded in putting the other to the ground. Uncle Remus settled himself back in his chair and regarded the little boy with a broad smile. "I ain't never tell you 'bout de time when ol' Brer B'ar start out fer hisse'f, is I? No, I mos' know I ain't, kaze it's been e'en about forty-lev'm year sence de tale come in my min', an' I don't speck it'd a crope in dar den ef dem ar chillun hadn't 'a' hatched up a rastle betwix' an' betweenst um. Well, when Brer B'ar got grow'd up, de time come when he hatter kinder scratch aroun' an' scuffle fer hisse'f. He l'arned how ter shet his eyes an' rob a bee-tree, an' how ter grabble taters an' how ter tote a big turn er roas'n y'ears, an' his daddy gun 'im a hint dat 'twuz 'bout time fer 'im ter shuffle 'roun fer his

1 Printed from the untitled typescript in the Joel Chandler Harris Memorial Collection. Typewritten on one sheet of newspaper copy paper, $10^6/_8 \times 8^9/_{16}$ in. This story is an earlier version, in dialect, of that printed in Chap. XVIII of *Mr. Rabbit at Home* under the above title. — T. H. E.

own livin. Brer B'ar say he 'gree'ble, an' when de time come fer ter tell um all good-bye, his daddy gun 'im sev'm pieces er honey-in-de-com', an' he say, sezee, 'Dis all I got ter gi' you, but it's mo' dan a plenty, kaze whosomever eats a piece er dat honey, will hatter rastle wid you sev'm year, er gi' you all he got.' Wid dat, Brer B'ar put de sev'm pieces er honey-in-de-com' in a bag an' slung de bag on his back, an' went down de big road. He shuffled along all day, an' dat night, he camped out in de woods. Nex' mornin', des ez he wuz 'bout ter eat brekkus, he hear a rus'lin' in de bushes, an' dar wuz ol' Brer Tiger, a-huntin' fer whatsomever he mought gobble up. Dey howdied ter one an'er, an' den Brer Tiger sot an' watch Brer B'ar take out a piece er his honey-in-de-com', an' it look so good it fa'r make 'im dribble at de mouf. Brer B'ar say he'd like mighty well fer ter ax Brer Tiger ter j'ine 'im, but he say dat whosomever partooken er dat honey would hatter rastle wid 'im fer sev'm long year, er gi' 'im all his b'longin's. Brer Tiger say, sezee, dat he's a mighty good rastler hisse'f, an' he'd like mighty well fer ter tas'e dat honey-in-de-com'. Brer B'ar done so funny dat Brer Tiger got de idee dat he wuz stingy, an' he say ez much. Wid dat, Brer B'ar tol' 'im ter come get des ez much er de honey ez he want, but he tol' 'im ag'in dat he'd hatter rastle sev'm year er gi' up all his b'longin's. Brer Tiger grinned, an' tuck some er de honey-in-de-com', an' it tas'e so good dat he say he be mo' dan glad fer ter rastle 'lev'm year stidder sev'm. Atter Brer Tiger got much honey-in-de-com' ez he want, he say he b'lieve he'll go home an' see how his ol' 'oman gittin' on. Brer B'ar slap at a honey-bee flyin' 'roun his head an' grin. Brer Tiger start home, but he ain't git fur 'fo' he feel a zoonin' in his head, an' a crawly feelin' on his hide. An' it got so bad dat present'y it seem like he bleeze ter t'un 'roun' an' go back ter whar he lef' Brer B'ar. When he git dar, Brer B'ar wuz quil' up takin' a nap. Brer Tiger tell 'im fer ter wake up, kaze he feel so good dat he wanter rastle an' be done wid it. Brer B'ar, he put his grin on, an' it look like it fit 'im. Dey tuck off der coats, an' got ready. Brer B'ar say he'll gi' Brer Tiger de all-under-holt, an' promise not to fling wid de in-turn, de ham-twist, er de knee-lock. Den he grab 'im an' kinder swing 'im 'roun', an' snort in his face an' eyes, an' hugged him close ter his beheavin' bosom, an' cuffed 'im a time er two, an den fell sprawlin' all over him. When Brer Tiger got so he know'd what he wuz doin' he say, sezee, 'Ef dat what's you call rastlin', I'm fear'd I'll never git in de habits.' His britches wuz split, an his head got big ez a milk-pail. He went home, but soon de nex' mornin', Brer B'ar knocked at his do', an' he hatter come out an' rastle, an' when dey got thoo, nobody ain't know Brer Tiger but his ol' 'oman an' ol' Brer Rabbit; an' he say, ol' Brer Rabbit did, 'Brer Tiger, what you need is a change.' An' 'twa'n't so mighty long 'fo' he move out an' Brer B'ar move in."

7
Brother Rabbit Doesn't Go to See Aunt Nancy[1]

UNCLE REMUS, one day, was doing his best to patch an old waistcoat. The little boy was interested in this work mainly because it became neces-sary once and again for the old man to thread the large needle with which he was doing the work. Sometimes he tried to place the thread in the sharp end, where there was no eye, and even when he held it correctly, it required several attempts before he succeeded. He watched the little boy closely at each effort, expecting him to laugh at his failures, but the youngster was as solemn as could be desired. "I wuz des a-wonderin'," Uncle Remus declared in the midst of his mending, "ef you had de strenk fer ter go on a long journey." "On the wagon, or in the train?" in-quired the little boy. Uncle Remus chuckled. "No, honey; ef we go we'll hatter set right whar we is an' let time take us. You know how de birds does — de peckerwoods, an' de swallers, an' de bee-martins; dey'll ketch bugs roun' here de whole blessed summer, an' den, 'fo' fros' comes, dey'll h'ist up an' fly off some'rs, I dunner whar. Dey has der sea-sons an' der reason fer comin' an' gwine. Well, des ez de birds does now, des dat-a-way de creeturs done twel Brer Rabbit tuck an' broke it up. It seem like dat when de time come, dey 'gun ter feel ticklish; dey had dat creepy feelin' runnin' up an' down der backbones like folks does when a possum runs cross der grave." Uncle Remus looked hard at the little boy to observe what effect this last statement would have, but beyond mov-

---

[1] Printed from the untitled typescript in the Joel Chandler Harris Memorial Collection. Typewritten on one sheet of newspaper copy paper $10^{11}/_{16} \times 8^{1}/_{2}$ in. Placed with the typescript is an earlier draft of the story on one sheet, marked "Copied." — T. H. E.

ing uneasily in his seat, the lad gave no sign of mental disturbance. "It seem like," Uncle Remus went on, "dat all de creeturs, big an' little, long-tail, bob-tail, an' no-tail, hatter go once a year fer ter make der peace wid ol' Aunt Nancy." "But who was Aunt Nancy?" the child asked. "It seem like," the old man responded, "dat she was de granny er Mammy-Bammy-Big-Money — dat's de way dey han' it out ter me. Her rule went furder dan whar she live at, an' when she went ter call de creeturs, all she hatter do wuz ter fling her head back an' kinder suck in her bref an' all de creeturs would have a little chill, an' know dat she wuz a-callin' un um. But ol' Brer Rabbit, he got over havin' de chill, an' he say he wa'n't gwine trapesin' way off ter de fur country fer ter see no Aunt Nancy. De creeturs all tell 'im dat he better come on an' go, but he say he done been an' seed, an' he wa'n't gwine no mo'. He 'low, 'when you-all git whar you gwine des ax Aunt Nancy fer ter shake han's wid you, an' den you'll see what I done seed.' De yuther creeturs shuck der heads, but went on an' lef' Brer Rabbit smokin' his corn-cob pipe an' chawin' his cud. Dey went on, an' bimeby dey come ter Aunt Nancy's house. Ef you'd 'a' seed it, honey, you'd 'a' said it look des like a big chunk er fog. I speck 'twuz ez big ez dis house, but it kinder wavied in de win' des like de fog you see on de two-mile branch. Ol' Brer B'ar, he hailed de house, an' den ol' Aunt Nancy, she come out wid a big long cloak on her an' sot down on a pine stump. She look roun', she did, an' her eyeballs sparkle red des like dey wuz afire. 'I hope all un you is here,' se' she, 'an' I speck you is, but I'm agwine ter count you an' call de roll.' Eve'y count she made, she'd nod her head, an' de creetur dat she nodded at an' had her red eye on, would dodge and duck his head. Well, she count an' count, an' when she git thoo, she say, 'I done counted, an' ef dey ain't one un you missin', I'm mighty much mistooken.' She helt Brer Fox wid her red eye, an' he up an' say, 'I speck 'tain't nobody in de roun' worl' but Brer Rabbit.' Aunt Nancy say, se' she, 'I'll Brer him! Is he sont any skuse?' An' Brer Wolf, he tuck up de tale, an' say, 'No, ma'am, not ez I knows un.' Den ol' Brer B'ar, he say, 'Brer Rabbit sont word fer ter tell you howdy, an' he ax us fer ter tell you ter shake han's wid us, an' 'member him in yo' dreams.' Aunt Nancy roll her red eye an' work her jaws like she chawin' sump'n' good. She say, se' she, 'Is dat what he tell you? Well you des tell 'im, dat ef he'll come ter dis place I'll shake han's wid 'im, an' ef he don't come ez hard ez his legs'll fetch 'im, I'll go an' shake han's wid 'im whar he lives at.' Ol' Brer B'ar, he up an' say, 'How come you don't shake han's wid we-all, when we come so fur fer ter see you?' Aunt Nancy roll her red eyes an' work her jaws. She got up fum whar she wuz settin' at, an' try fer ter pull de cloak close 'roun' her, but it slipped off a little way, an' de creeturs what wuz watchin' un her, seed wid der own eyes dat she wuz half 'oman an' half spider. She had sev'm arms an' no han's. When dey see all dis, de creeturs tuck ter de woods, an' got away fum dar des ez hard ez dey kin. An' dat de reason de house look like it 'uz made out'n fog. It 'uz wovened out'n web; 'twuz web fum top ter bottom. De creeturs went back an' tol' Brer Rabbit what dey done seed, an' he jump up an' crack his heels tergedder, an' holler 'Ah-yi!' an' den he went on chawin' his cud like nothin' ain't happen."

GLOSSARY

In order that the reader might have one accessible reference for the meaning of words we have assembled in this glossary all of the footnotes by Joel Chandler Harris which concerned word definitions. They are reprinted exactly as they originally appeared in the text and are designated by the initials J.C.H.

Richard Chase has added a number of his definitions which are designated by the initials R.C.

A-bait er	a helping of — R.C.
A-gone gump	crazy or silly — R.C.
A-rackin'	pacing — R.C.
Ager, agur	ague — R.C.
Ah-yi	A corruption of aye-aye. It is used as an expression of triumph and its employment in this connection is both droll and picturesque — J.C.H.
All-night-Isom	the jig is up — R.C.
Ally	alley, n. (Contraction of *alabaster*, of which it was originally made.) A choice playing marble — R.C.
Ant'ny over	A game played by throwing a ball over the schoolhouse roof. The side throwing the ball called out "Ant'ny over" — R.C.
Badoon bit	bit of a bridoon, or double bridle — R.C.
Bang my times	beat all — R.C.
Battlin'-stick	a heavy stick or paddle used to beat the dirt out of clothes being laundered — usually at the creek, against a big boulder — R.C.
Bauk	balk — R.C.
Be dog his cats	be darned, be blowed, be blessed — R.C.
Beau-ketchers	spit curls, at the ears, to catch a beau — R.C.
Bee-gum	a beehive made from a section of a hollow gum tree, hence a beehive of any kind — R.C.
Bee-martin	the king-bird — J.C.H.
Bellust	wheezing and puffing like bellows — R.C.
Bergamot grease	essential oil from the bergamot — R.C.

Bittle	victuals — J.C.H.
Bodaciously	bodily, completely, all over — R.C.
Brinjer, binjer	brimstone and ginger in the general sense of hell. Used of a hot day, "It's going to be a brinjer." Severe punishment — R.C.
Bubby-blossoms	a species of sweet shrub growing wild in the South — J.C.H.
Bullaces	a muscadine grape or a wild plum — R.C.
Calaboose	jail — R.C.
Calamus root	sweet flag root, used as seasoning — R.C.
Calomy	calomel — R.C.
Chanybenies	chinaberries — R.C.
Chigger	red bug, a tiny spider that gets under the skin, usually on ankles and wrists, and causes an itching bump — R.C.
Chimbley-jamb	the side of the fireplace opening — R.C.
Chinkapin	a dwarf chestnut — R.C.
Chunkin'	pelting, or chucking stones at — R.C.
Claw-hammer coat	swallowtail coat — R.C.
Clay galls	misshapen swellings on limbs or twigs — R.C.
Compelerments	compliments — J.C.H.
Complassy	a mixture of complacent and placid — J.C.H.
Coolin' board	board on which a corpse is laid out in preparation for burial — R.C.
Cross 'en piles	probably the throwing of a handful of sticks in some way, to determine lots or turns by how the sticks cross each other or pile up — R.C.
Dram	a small drink often of distilled alcoholic liquor — R.C.
Endurin' er	during the — R.C.
Enfloons	influence — R.C.
Fibble	feeble — J.C.H.
Fices (fiest, feist)	small dogs — R.C.
Flat	flatboat — R.C.
Freezlin' hen	moulting hen — R.C.
Fresh'	freshet — R.C.

Freshen himself	to exercise himself — J.C.H.
Friday-born fool	unlucky person — R.C.
Fum who lay de rail	from the foundation or beginning — J.C.H.
Gallin'	galloping — J.C.H.
Gawm	grease, from the verb to gaum or smear, with grease, "boots all gawmed up with mud" — R.C.
Gits my Affikin up	gets my dander up (my *African* wildness) — R.C.
Goober-patch	peanut patch — R.C.
Goozle	gozzle, throat — R.C.
Graveyard rabbit	a sickly rabbit — R.C.
Han'-roomance	terms used by Negroes in playing marbles, — a favorite game on the plantations Sunday afternoons. These terms were curt and expressive enough to gain currency among the whites — J.C.H.
Haslett — haslet	The edible viscera of a beast, as heart, liver, or lights (lungs) — R.C.
Hether en yan	Hither and yon — J.C.H.
Hone	to pine or long for anything. This is a good old English word, which has been retained in the plantation vocabulary — J.C.H.
Hope, holp	helped — J.C.H.
Infa'r	in fare, housewarming party for a newly wed couple — R.C.
Ingun	onion — R.C.
Intruss	interest — J.C.H.
Jacks	must be the same as doodle bugs. This is the ant lion, an insect that burrows in the sand making a small funnel-shaped depression. It will catch hold on a straw thrust down — R.C.
Jimber-jaw'd	with lower jaw projecting — R.C.
Jollup	jalap, a bitter medicine — R.C.
Joon 'roun'	to hurry about — to sail around like a June bug — R.C.
Joree	the towhee or chewink — R.C.

Jubously	dubiously — R.C.
Killdees	killdeers, a species of plover — J.C.H.
Kuse	curious — R.C.
Less	let us, let's — J.C.H.
Level	levy — J.C.H.
Maul	stomach lining — R.C.
Medjun	measuring — J.C.H.
Moggin hoss	Morgan (after Justin Morgan, an American horse breeder). One of a celebrated American breed of light horses which originated in Vermont — R.C.
Mo' samer	just as well as, or better than — R.C.
Muched her up	to make much of; to soothe, as to "much" a hurt child or a timid dog — R.C.
Muster	a gathering or crowd — R.C.
Nummine	never mind — R.C.
Odd-come-shorts	some one of these days, also odds and ends — R.C.
Ole Scratch	the devil — R.C.
Patter-rollers	patrols. In the country districts, order was kept on the plantations at night by the knowledge that they were liable to be visited at any moment by the patrols. Hence a song current among the Negroes, the chorus of which was: "Run, nigger run; patter-roller ketch you — Run, nigger, run; hit's almos' day." — J.C.H.
Piggin	a small wooden pail with an upright stave as a handle — R.C.
Pine-blank	point-blank — J.C.H.
Pleezy-plozzy	pleasant and plausible — J.C.H.
Pot-rack	a bar of iron across the fireplace with hooks to hold the pots and kettles. The original form of the crane — J.C.H.
Projickin' son	prodigal son — R.C.
Projickin' wid	fooling with — R.C.
Proned inter	ingrained into — R.C.

Prop-en-tickler	proper and particular — J.C.H.
Puckerin' string	a string to tighten a bag or money purse — R.C.
Put on de block	to put on the block and sell — J.C.H.
Puzzuv	preserves — J.C.H.
Quills	the veritable Pan's pipes. A simple but very effective musical instrument made of reeds — J.C.H.
Quolled	quarreled — R.C.
Reckembembunce	remembrance, recollection — R.C.
Rig	trick or joke — R.C.
Rippit	a fight or ruckus — R.C.
Roach	topknot or forelock — J.C.H. Also to comb or brush the hair — R.C.
Scaly-bark	a species of hickory nut. The tree sheds its bark every year, hence the name which is applied to both tree and fruit — J.C.H.
Scantlin's	small pieces of lumber — R.C.
Scrouge	crowd, squeeze, or scrounge — R.C.
Season	in the South, a rain is called a "season," not only by the Negroes but by many white farmers — J.C.H.
Segashuate	How duz yo' sym'tums seem ter segashuate? How do you do? — R.C.
Servigous, servigrous	see suvvigus — R.C.
Sesso	say so — J.C.H.
Shoot yo' shekels	lay down your money — R.C.
Shorance	assurance — J.C.H.
Shucks	corn husks — R.C.
Shut	shirt — R.C.
Sic, sick, sik't (past tense)	sick, v.t. (dial. var of *seek,* v.) to incite, as a dog; chiefly with *on* — R.C.
Silly-bug	sillabub, a dish made by mixing wine or cider with milk, forming a soft curd; also sweetened cream, flavored with wine and beaten to a stiff froth — R.C.

Skaddle	It may be interesting to note here that in all probability the word "skedaddle," about which there was some controversy during the war, came from the Virginia Negro's use of "skaddle," which is a corruption of "scatter." The matter, however, is hardly worth referring to — J.C.H.
Slanchendicklar, slonchindickler, slonchways	slantways oblique — R.C.
Slorate	to destroy, slaughter — R.C.
Soon	quick, or fast, speedy — R.C.
Soople-peeny	subpoena — R.C.
Soopless	supplest — R.C.
Snake doctors	dragonflies, hellgrammites — R.C.
Speckerlater	speculator — J.C.H.
Speeshy	money — R.C.
'Speunce	experience — R.C.
Splimmy-splammy	feeling fine — R.C.
'Swaje	assuage — J.C.H.
Stribbit	distribute — J.C.H.
Suvvigus, servigous, servigrous	wild; fierce, dangerous; courageous. The accent is on the second syllable, ser-*vi*-gous; or ser-*vi*-gus, and the *g* is hard. Aunt Tempy would have said "vigrous." — J.C.H.
	This may be another of Uncle Remus' combination words like "prop-en-tickler" (proper and particular J.C.H.). I have heard *severe* used to describe a dangerous dog, and *vigrous* (long *i*) in the same sense, or a "vigrous woman," i.e., a "virago" — Webster: 2. "A turbulent, quarrelsome woman." Dr. Thomas H. English says "savage and vigorous." John Powell: "That's what a dog is when you feed him raw meat and gunpowder!" — R.C.
'Swade	persuade — J.C.H.
Swinge	singe or curl — R.C.

Swinkin', swink	here used to mean shrinking, shrunk instead of the usual meaning to toil or labor — R.C.
Tacky	dowdy in appearance; of a party, made up of guests in ridiculous costume — R.C.
Thrip	a threepenny piece (e.g., thrupenny-bit) — R.C.
Tollin'	alluring, enticing, leading, or dragging. I have heard "toll" used in connection with driving a pig with a rope attached to its hind leg — R.C.
Trangle	triangle — J.C.H.
Tushes, toofies, toofs	teeth — R.C.
Two-forty **on de shell road**	like a horse that can do a mile in two minutes and forty seconds on a good road — R.C.
Uppance	*see* han'-roomance — R.C.
Varmint, varment	according to Webster, "a dialect variation of vermin." I have heard the word used by Negroes in North Alabama in connection with a large supernatural beast "seen" on various occasions. Aunt Julie, our cook for thirty years, refused to walk home alone because "Dey done seen a varment. Hit come down out the mountain and chewed the ears off John Hereford's dog. I seen de po' dog! And some of you-all got to car' me home!" — R.C.
Wahoo bark	any of various American trees or shrubs. In the South frequently wild magnolia — R.C.
Whimzies	a man with the whimzies is known simply as a crank — J.C.H.
Whully-win's	whirlwinds — R.C.
Wiggletail	the embryo mosquito — J.C.H.
Willis-whistler	a variation of will-o'-the-wisp — R.C.
Wool	to get the better of, beat, or handle roughly — R.C.
Wull-er-de-wust	probably a fantastic corruption of will-o'-the-wisp," though this is not by any means certain — J.C.H.
'Zeeze	disease — J.C.H.
'Zef	as if — J.C.H.